BARBARA DELINSKY

THREE COMPLETE NOVELS

BARBARA DELINSKY

THREE COMPLETE NOVELS

A WOMAN BETRAYED
WITHIN REACH
FINGER PRINTS

WINGS BOOKS

NEW YORK ❧ AVENEL, NEW JERSEY

This omnibus was originally published in separate volumes under the titles:

A *Woman Betrayed*, copyright©1991 by Barbara Delinsky.
Within Reach, copyright©1986 by Barbara Delinsky.
Finger Prints, copyright©1984 by Barbara Delinsky.

This edition contains the complete and unabridged texts of the original editions. They have been completely reset for this volume.

This 1993 edition is published by Wings Books, distributed by Outlet Book Company, Inc., a Random House Company, 40 Engelhard Avenue, Avenel, New Jersey 07001, by arrangement with HarperCollins*Publishers*.

Random House
New York • Toronto • London • Sydney • Auckland

Printed and bound in the United States of America

Library of Congress Cataloging-in-Publication Data

Delinsky, Barbara.
  [Novels. Selections]
  Three complete novels / Barbara Delinsky.
    p. cm.
  Contents: A woman betrayed—Within reach—Finger prints.
  ISBN 0-517-09383-9
  1. Love stories, American. Title.
PS3554.E4427A6 1993
813'.54—dc20

8 7 6 5 4 3 2 1

93-10982
CIP

CONTENTS

A WOMAN BETRAYED

As always, to Eric, Andrew, Jeremy, and their dad

ONE

T

HE SILENCE WAS DEAFENING. Laura Frye sat in a corner of the leather sofa in the den, hugged her knees, and listened to it, minute after minute after minute. The wheeze of the heat through the vents couldn't pierce it. Nor could the slap of the rain on the windows, or the rhythmic tick of the small ship's clock on the shelf behind the desk.

It was five in the morning, and her husband still wasn't home. He hadn't called. He hadn't sent a message. His toothbrush was in the bathroom along with his razor, his after-shave, and the sterling comb and brush set Laura had given him for their twentieth anniversary the summer before. The contents of his closet were intact, right down to the small duffel he took with him to the sports club every Monday, Wednesday, and Friday. If he had slept somewhere else, he was totally ill equipped, which wasn't like Jeffrey at all, Laura knew. He was a precise man, a creature of habit. He never traveled, not for so much as a single night, without fresh underwear, a clean shirt, and a bar of deodorant soap.

More than that, he never went anywhere without telling Laura, and that was what frightened her most. She had no idea where he was or what had happened.

Not that she hadn't imagined. Laura wasn't usually prone to wild wanderings of the mind, but ten hours of waiting had taken its toll. She imagined that he'd had a stroke and lay unconscious across his desk in the deserted offices of Farro and Frye. She imagined that he'd been in an accident on the way home, that the car and everything in it had been burned beyond recognition or, alternately, that he had hit the windshield, climbed out, and begun wandering through the cold December rain not knowing who or where he was. She had gone so far as to imagine that he'd stopped for gas and been taken hostage by a junkie holding up the nearby 7-Eleven.

More rational explanations for his absence had worn thin as night had waned. By no stretch of the imagination could she envision him holed up with a client at five in the morning. Maybe in April, with a new client whose tax records were in chaos. But not the first week in December. And not without telling her. He always called if he was going to be late. Always.

Last night, they had been expected at an opening at the museum. Cherries had catered the affair. Though one of Laura's crews had handled the evening, she had spent the afternoon in Cherries' kitchen stuffing mushrooms, skewering smoked turkey and cherries, and cleaving baby lamb chops apart. She had wanted not only the food but the tables, the trays, and the bar to be perfect, which was why she had followed the truck to the museum to oversee the setting up.

Everything had been flawless. She had come home to change and get Jeff. But Jeff hadn't shown up.

Hugging her knees tighter in an attempt to fill the emptiness inside her, she stared at the phone. It had rung twice during the night. The first call had been from Elise, who was at the museum with her husband and wondered why Laura and Jeff weren't there. The second call had been from Donny for Debra, part of their nightly ritual. Sixteen-year-old sweethearts did that, Laura knew, just as surely as she knew that forty-something husbands who always called their wives if they were going to be late wouldn't *not* call unless something was wrong. So she had made several searching calls herself, but to no avail. The only thing she had learned was that the phone worked fine.

She willed it to ring now, willed Jeff to call and say he had had a late meeting with a client and had nearly fallen asleep at the wheel on the way home, so he'd pulled over to the side of the road to sleep off his fatigue. Of course, that wouldn't explain why the police hadn't spotted his car. Hampshire County wasn't so remote as to be without regular patrols or so seasoned as to take a shiny new Porsche for granted, particularly if that Porsche belonged to one half of a prominent Northampton couple.

The Frye name made the papers often, Jeff's with regard to the tax seminars he gave, Laura's with regard to Cherries. The local press was a tough one, seeming to resist anything upscale, which the restaurant definitely was, but Laura fed enough luminaries on a regular basis to earn frequent mentions. *State Senator DiMento and his entourage were seen debating ways to trim fat from the budget over steamed vegetables and salads at Cherries this week*, wrote Duggan O'Neil of the *Hampshire County Sun*. Duggan O'Neil could cut people to shreds, and he had done his share of cutting where Laura was concerned, but publicity was publicity, Jeff said. Name recognition was important.

Indeed, the police officer with whom Laura had talked earlier on the phone had known just who she was. He even remembered Jeff's car as the one often parked outside the restaurant. But nothing in his records suggested that anyone in the department had seen or heard of the black Porsche that night.

"Tell you what, Miz Frye," he had told her. "Since it's you, I'll make a few calls. Throw in a piece of cherry cheesecake, and I'll even call the state police." But his calls had turned up nothing, and, to her dismay, he had refused to let her file a missing persons report. "Not until he's been gone twenty-four hours."

"But awful things can happen in twenty-four hours!"

"Good things, too, like lost husbands coming home."

Lost husbands coming home. She resented those words with a passion. They suggested she was inept as a wife, inept as a woman, that Jeff had been bored and gone looking for fun and would wander back home when the fun was over. Maybe the cop lived that way, but not Jeff and Laura Frye. They had been together for twenty good years. They loved each other.

So where was he? The question gnawed at her. She imagined him slain by a hitchhiker, accosted by Satanists, sucked up, Porsche and all, by an alien starship. The possibilities were endless, each one more bizarre than the next. Bizarre things did happen, she knew, but to other people. Not to her. And not to Jeff. He was the most steadfast, the most predictable, the most uncorruptible man she'd ever known, which was why his absence made no sense at all.

Unfolding her legs, she rose from the sofa and padded barefoot through the dark living room to the front window. Drawing back the sheers that hung beneath full-length silk swags, she looked out. The wind was up, ruffling the branches of the pines, driving the rain against the flagstone walk and the tall lamp at its head.

At least it wasn't snowing. She remembered times, early in her marriage, when she had been home with the children during storms, waiting for Jeff to return from work. He had been a new CPA then, a struggling one, and they had lived in a rented duplex. Laura used to stand at the window, playing games with the children, drawing pictures on the glass in the fog their breath made. Like clockwork, Jeff had always come through the snow, barely giving her time to worry.

He worked in a new building in the center of town now, and they weren't living in the duplex, or even in that first weathered Victorian, but in a gracious brick Tudor on a tree-lined street, less than a ten-minute drive from his office. It was a fast drive, an easy drive. But for some unknown and frightening reason he hadn't made it.

"Mom?"

Laura whirled around at the sudden sound to find Debra beneath the living room arch. Her eyes were sleepy, her dark hair disheveled. She wore a nightshirt with UMASS COED NAKED LACROSSE splashed on the front over breasts that had taken a turn for the buxom in the past year.

Aware of her racing heart, Laura tried to smile. "Hi, Deb."

Debra sounded cross. "It's barely five. That's still the middle of the night, Mom. Why are you up?"

Unsure of what to say, just as she'd been unsure the night before when Debra had come home and Jeff hadn't been there, Laura threw back a gentle, "Why are *you?*"

"Because I woke up and remembered last night and started to worry. I mean, Dad's never late like that. I had a dream something awful happened, so I was going to check the garage and make sure the Porsche was—" Her voice stopped short. Her eyes probed Laura's in the dark. "It's there, isn't it?"

Laura shook her head.

"Where is he?"

She shrugged.

"Are you sure he didn't call and tell you something, and then you forgot? You're so busy, sometimes things slip your mind. Or maybe he left a message on the machine, but it got erased. Maybe he spent the night at Nana Lydia's."

Laura had considered that possibility, which was why she had driven past her mother-in-law's house when she had gone out looking for Jeff. In theory, Lydia might have taken ill and called her son, though in all likelihood she would have called Laura first. Laura was her primary caretaker. She was the one who stocked the house with food, took her to the doctor, arranged for the cleaning girl or the exterminator or the plumber.

"He's not there. I checked."

"How about the office?"

"I went there too." To the dismay of the guard, who had looked far more sleepy than Debra, she had insisted on checking the garage for the Porsche, but Jeff's space—the entire garage under his building—had been empty.

"Is he with David?"

"No. I called." David Farro was Jeff's partner, but he hadn't known of any late meetings Jeff might have had. Nor had Jeff's secretary, who had left at five with Jeff still in his office.

"Maybe with a client?"

"Maybe."

"But you were supposed to go to the museum. Wouldn't he have called if he couldn't make it?"

"I would have thought so."

"Maybe something's wrong with the phone."

"No."

"Maybe he had car trouble."

But he would have called, Laura knew. Or had someone call for him. Or the police would have seen him and called.

"So where *is* he?" Debra cried.

Laura was terrified by her own helplessness. "I don't know!"

"He has to be *somewhere!*"

She wrapped her arms around her middle. "Do you have any suggestions?"

"Me?" Debra shot back. "What do I know? You're the adult around here. Besides, you're his wife. You're the one who knows him inside and out. *You're* supposed to know where he is."

Turning back to the window, Laura drew the sheer aside and looked out again.

"Mom?"

"I don't know where he is, babe."

"Great. That's just great."

"No, it's not," Laura acknowledged, nervously scanning the street, "but there isn't an awful lot I can do right now. He'll show up, and I'm sure he'll have a perfectly good explanation for where he's been and why he hasn't called."

"If *I* ever stayed out all night without calling, you'd kill me."

"I may well kill your father," Laura said in a moment's burst of anger.

Given what she'd been through, Jeff's explanation was going to have to be inspired if he hoped to be spared her fury. Then the fury died and fear returned. The possibilities flashed through her mind, one worse than the next. "He'll be home," she insisted, as much for her own sake as for Debra's.

"When?"

"Soon."

"How do you know?"

"I just know."

"What if he's sick, or hurt, or dying somewhere? What if he needs our help, but we're just standing here in a nice warm dry house waiting for him to show up? What if we're losing all this time when we should be out looking for him?"

Debra's questions weren't new. Laura had hit on all of them, more than once. Now she reasoned, "I looked for him last night. I drove around half the city and didn't see the Porsche. I called the police, and they hadn't seen it either. If there was an accident, the police would call me."

"So you're just going to stand here looking out the window? Aren't you upset?"

Debra was a sixteen-year-old asking a frightened sixteen-year-old's questions. Laura was a frightened thirty-eight-year-old with no answers, which made her frustration all the greater. Keeping her voice as steady as possible, given the tremulous feeling she had inside, she turned to Debra and said, "Yes, I'm upset. Believe me, I'm upset. I've been upset since seven o'clock last night, when your father was an hour late."

"He never does this, Mom, never."

"I know that, Debra. I went to his office. I drove around looking for his car. I called his partner, his secretary, and the police, but they won't do anything until he's been gone a day, and he hasn't been gone half that. What would you have me do? Walk the streets in the rain, calling his name?"

Debra's glare cut through the darkness. "You don't have to be sarcastic."

With a sigh, Laura crossed the floor and caught her daughter's hand. "I'm not being sarcastic. But I'm worried, and your criticism doesn't help."

"I didn't criticize."

"You did." Debra said what was on her mind and always had. Disapproval coming from a little squirt of a child hadn't been so bad. Disapproval coming from someone who was Laura's own five-six and weighed the same one-fifteen, who regularly borrowed Laura's clothes, makeup, and perfume, who drove a car, professed to know how to French-kiss, and was physically capable of having a child of her own was something else. "You think I should be doing more than I am," Laura argued, "but I'm hamstrung, don't you see? I don't know if anything's really wrong. There could be a logical reason for your father's absence. I don't want to blow things out of proportion before I have good cause."

"Twelve hours isn't good cause?" Debra cried and whirled around to leave, only to be held back by Laura's grip.

"Eleven hours," she said with quiet control. "And, yes, it's good cause, babe. But I can't do anything right now but wait. I can't do anything else." The silence that followed was heavy with an unspoken plea for understanding.

Debra lowered her chin. Her hair fell forward, shielding her from Laura's gaze. "What about me? What am I supposed to do?"

Scooping the hair back from Debra's face, Laura tucked it behind an ear. For an instant she caught a glimpse of her daughter's worry, but it was gone by the time Debra raised her head. In its place was defiance. Taking that as part and parcel of the spunk that made Debra special, Laura said, "What you're supposed to do is go back to bed. It's too early to be up."

"Sure. Great idea. Like I'd really be able to sleep." She shot a glance at Laura's sweater and jeans. "Like you really slept yourself." She turned her head a fraction and gave a twitch of her nose. "You've been cooking, haven't you. What's that smell?"

"Borscht."

"Oh, gross."

"It's not so bad." Jeff loved it with sour cream on top. Maybe, deep inside, Laura had been hoping the smell would lure him home.

"I can't believe you were cooking."

"I always cook."

"At work. Not at home. Most of the time you stick us with Chunky Chicken Soup, Frozen French Bread Pizza, or Microwave Meatballs and Spaghetti. You must feel guilty that Dad's missing."

Laura ignored the suggestion, which could have come straight from her own mother's analytical mouth. "He isn't missing, just late."

"So you cooked all night."

"Not all night. Just part of it." In addition to the borscht, she'd done a coq au vin she would probably freeze, since no one planned to be home for dinner for the next two nights. She had also baked a Black Forest cake and two batches of pillow cookies, one of which she would send to Scott.

"Did you sleep at all?" Debra asked.

"A little."

"Aren't you tired?"

"Nah. I'm fine." She was too anxious to sleep, which was why she had cooked. Normally, cooking relaxed her. It hadn't done that last night, but at least it had kept her hands busy.

"Well, I'm fine too," Debra declared. "I'll shower and dress and sit down here with you."

Laura knew what was coming. Debra was social to the core. Rarely did a weekend pass when she wasn't out, if not with Donny, then with Jenna or Kim or Whitney or all three and more. But as drawn as she was to her friends, she was allergic to anything academic. At the slightest excuse, she would stay home for the day. "You'll go to school when it's time," Laura insisted, "just like always."

"I can't go to school. I want to be here."

"There's nothing for you to do here. When your father comes home, he'll want to sleep."

"Assuming he hasn't already slept."

Laura felt a flare of indignance. "Where would he have slept?"

Debra's eyes went wide in innocence. "I don't know. Where do *you* think?"

"I don't know! If I did, we wouldn't be standing here at this hour discussing it!" Hearing the high pitch of her voice, Laura realized just how short-tempered she was—and how uncharacteristic that was. "Look," she said more calmly, "we're going in circles. I know nothing, you know nothing. All we can do for the time being is wait for your father to call. If I haven't heard from him by eight or nine, I can start making calls myself." Framing Debra's face with her hands, she said, "Let's not fight about this. I hate fighting. You know that."

Debra looked to be on the verge of saying something before she caught herself and reconsidered. With a merciful nod, she turned and left the room. Laura listened to her footfall on the stair runner, the occasional creak of a tread, movement along the upstairs hall, then the closing of the bathroom door. Only when she heard the sound of the shower did she turn back toward the den.

"Damn it, Jeff," she whispered, "where *are* you?" It was one thing to put her through hell for a night, another to involve the children. Scott was at school, sleeping in blissful ignorance in his dorm room at Penn. But Debra was home, awake now and aware that her father was missing.

Laura couldn't believe he had willfully stayed out all night. He was a devoted husband and father. *Something was wrong.*

At the door to the den, she stopped. This was Jeff's room, his retreat. Technically it was a library, lined top to bottom with books. The books were still there, but so were a new television and a VCR for fun. He also worked there, which was why the gleaming mahogany desk—which had originally sported a gold-edged blotter, several leather-bound volumes braced by brass bookends, and some scrimshaw—now bore a more functional pad, a computer linked to the one in his office, and a Rolodex filled with the names and addresses of anyone and everyone with whom Jeff had professional dealings.

Should it come down to a search, Laura wouldn't know which names to call first. Jeff didn't discuss clients with her unless they bumped into one at a party. He put a high value on confidentiality, and she respected that. He was a decent person.

Drawn into the room by the musty scent of Jeff's collection of old books, Laura let the atmosphere take the edge off her tension. Gently lit, as it had been all night, by the green clerk's lamp on the desk, the room had a feeling of history, and with good cause. On those shelves were an assortment of books, pictures, and mementos that documented their life together.

Neatly arranged, as was Jeff's style, were books from their college days, Jeff's on such subjects as Financial Reporting, Advanced Federal Taxation, and Auditing, hers on American Literature, Beginning Anthropology, and French. Jeff's shelves progressed to books on advanced accounting issues that he had read for graduate courses, as well as ever-growing collections of the *Journal of Accountancy* and the *Massachusetts CPA Review.* Laura's shelves, reflecting the fact that she had dropped out of college after a year, branched out into photography books, years of *National Geographic,* and diverse fiction. Those books bought used or in paperback early in their marriage were more weathered. The shelves filled more recently held handsomely packaged hardcover books. And, of course, there were the antique volumes, first editions that Laura had given Jeff over the years.

Interspersed with the books were mementos from trips: a Mayan bowl they had bought in the Yucatán the first time they had left the children and flown off for vacation eight years before; a conch shell they had found on a St. Martin beach the year after that; an ironwood sculpture they had bought in Arizona two years later.

The Arizona trip had been special. All four of them had gone. It had been the first time any of them had seen the desert, and Laura, for one, had adored it. She loved the barren beauty of the landscape, the clear sun, the dryness of the air, the hotel, the food. Lifting a photograph taken on that trip, Laura let her finger glide over the glass. Scott had been fourteen, Debra eleven, both healthy, happy, and handsome, both looking markedly like their parents. With their dark hair, lean athletic builds, easy tans, and bright smiles, they were the picture-perfect American family.

Laura's finger lingered on Jeff's face. Where was he? The house was quiet, empty without him. *Where was he?*

Feeling the same itch to do something that she'd felt on and off all night, she returned the picture to the shelf and went out into the kitchen. The sink was clean. So was the counter and the granite island. Other than the pot on the stove, the plastic-wrapped platter of cookies by the refrigerator, and the footed cake dish in the center of the island, there was no evidence that she'd been cooking. She had scrubbed everything clean with the same energy with which she normally worked. She didn't do well with idle time, didn't do well with it at all.

She glanced at her watch. It was five-forty-five. She glanced at the digital readout on the microwave, but it was the same. After letting out a frantic whimper, she dragged in a slow, deep breath and forced herself to relax.

Jeff had to be somewhere. He was alive and well and intact. There was an explanation for what had happened—a misunderstanding, crossed signals. Surely someday they'd laugh over the folly of the night.

Clinging to that thought, Laura headed for the stairs. If Jeff would be coming home soon, she didn't want to look tired and washed out. A bath would help. She felt wound tight.

The master bathroom was her pride and joy. High-ceilinged, skylit, and spacious, it was of variegated marble, deep green and lush. The towels and small area rugs were white, the wallpaper a broad floral sweep of green and white. Though there were several groupings of botanical prints, the main decorative force came from the plants that sprouted in every imaginable spot. They gave the room the feel of a forest glen.

By the time Laura had run the water, undressed, and climbed in, the heat lamp had made the room comfortably warm. She sank down, stretched out, closed her eyes. Had the Jacuzzi not hummed she might have turned it on. But she didn't want to miss a sound. So she took a deep breath and let it out, then repeated the procedure when the jitters in her stomach didn't let up. She concentrated on relaxing her hands, then her thighs, then her knees and feet. Each floated. Each moved with the water as she breathed.

At a creaking from the bedroom, her eyes flew open. "Jeff?" she called excitedly and held her breath.

"It's me, Mom. Are you okay?"

The jitters resumed. Trying not to sound too disappointed, she said, "I'm fine, babe. Just taking a bath."

"Nothing happened while I was in the shower?"

"Nope."

"Want me to listen for the phone?"

Laura knew if the phone rang she'd be out of the tub like a shot. "That'd be great," she said. "I think I'll just soak for a while. Then I'll fix us some breakfast."

"Isn't it a little early for that?"

"I thought I'd do some waffles."

"I'm not hungry."

"And maybe some eggs."

"I'll be downstairs, Mom."

"Okay. I'll be there soon."

Pleased that she'd managed to sound relatively normal, Laura took a hand from the water and studied her nails. She'd done a job on them during the night, destroying the pale polish she wore in ways that her work, for all its manual labor, rarely did. Tonight she and Jeff had a dinner party to go to, tomorrow night a political fund raiser. She'd have to redo them. Before the dinner party. Or the fund raiser.

Where was Jeff?

Feeling panic, she sat up in the tub. She glanced at the door, peered at the watch she'd left on the closed commode. It was five past six. "Come on, Jeff," she cried in an urgent whisper and climbed out. "Come on, come on!"

After slipping into a pair of gabardine slacks and a loose cashmere sweater, she put on a smattering of makeup, pushed a brush through her shoulder-length auburn waves, swallowed two aspirin, and headed down the stairs.

Debra was perched on a stool in the kitchen, wearing her school uniform of lace-edged leggings under a short denim skirt and a high-necked blouse under a large wool sweater. She gave Laura a strange look. "Why are you dressed like that?"

"I have meetings all morning."

"You're going to meetings? Dad's been gone all night, we have no idea where he is, and you're going to *meetings*?"

"He'll show up." Laura looked at her watch. It was nearly six-thirty. "Soon, now. You'll see." She plugged in the waffle iron and pulled a carton of orange juice from the refrigerator. "Want some?"

"How can you think of food at a time like this?"

Laura doubted she'd have anything herself, but she was hoping Debra would, so she poured her a glass of juice. "We have to keep things in perspective. Panicking won't help. We have to stay cool."

"I'm not going to school."

"Yes, you are. And while you're there, if your father hasn't come home, I'll be making calls."

"What if there was an accident, like he skidded off the road into a tree, and the police suddenly see it when the sun comes up?"

"Then they'll come get me."

"Will you come get *me?*"

Seeing the fear in Debra's eyes, Laura reached over and gave her a hug. The contact felt good. "Of course I will. If I hear anything either way, I'll let you know. Fair?"

"Not really. I don't see why I can't stay here. I won't get anything out of school with this on my mind."

She had a point. Not even in the best of times was Debra a student. But Laura wanted her out of the house. No matter how distracted she'd be at school, she would be better off there than waiting at home for the phone to ring. Besides, if Jeff didn't show up, if the morning wore on without any sign of him, if Laura had to call in help, there would be a reality to the situation that didn't quite exist yet. The thought of that made her tremble.

"Do me a favor and get the newspapers?"

Debra's eyes grew wide. "Would there be something in the *Sun?*"

"No, but it's nice to see what's happening in the world." There was an absurd normalcy in headlines of economic recession or strife in the Persian Gulf.

"It's raining."

"It's stopped. Get them, babe? Please?" Without waiting for an answer, Laura opened a deep drawer under the island and pulled out the mixing bowl. By the time Debra returned with the *Wall Street Journal* folded under an arm and the *Hampshire County Sun* open in her hand, Laura was vigorously stirring waffle batter with a wooden spoon. She poured some on the hot iron. Its sizzle overlapped the rustle of newsprint. The waffles were done just as Debra thrust the paper aside.

"Nothing," she announced in disgust. "Where is he?"

Laura forked the waffles onto a plate. "Don't know."

"What happened to him?"

"Should I whip some cream for that?"

"No! Mom, I'm not eating."

"You have to. You love waffles."

"I told you before I wasn't hungry."

"You have to eat."

"I can't!" Pushing away from the island, Debra disappeared into the hall.

Laura felt abruptly deserted. "Where are you going?" One part of her did want to keep Debra home from school, she realized, for the company and the noise if nothing else. The more rational part, the practical part, the protective part would send her on.

"Getting my books," came the distant call.

Blankly Laura looked at the plate of waffles in her hand. She looked at the waffle iron and at the batter remaining in the bowl, and put on a second batch. It was done, and a third was on the way, when Debra returned.

"I really want to stay home."

"I know," Laura said as she whipped cream into a froth, "but you can't."

"What am I supposed to say to my friends?"

"You can say what you want. But there's no need to get them all in a stir. I'm sure everything is fine. There must be a perfectly good explanation for last night. Your father will be home, Debra. I know he will."

"I'm glad one of us is so sure."

Laura wasn't sure at all, and the pretending was growing harder. The longer Jeff was missing, the more ominous the possibilities and the less sure Laura was of anything. But she was a mother, and she was an optimist. She had to be positive for Debra. "I'm sure." She looked at her watch. "It's ten after seven." The bus came at seven-twenty. "Why don't you run on now? Jenna will be there." Jenna was Debra's best friend, and had been since nursery school. The fact that she lived on the very next street from the Fryes had been an added selling point for the house.

"Will you get a message to me if you learn anything?" Debra asked, looking young and frightened as Laura walked her to the door.

"Uh-huh."

"Promise?"

"I promise."

Seemingly satisfied, Debra pulled up the collar of her leather jacket, hitched her backpack to one shoulder, and left. The instant she turned onto the sidewalk and was lost from sight beyond the neighbors' hemlock hedge, Laura made for the phone.

TWO

❀ ❀ ❀

D APHNE PHILLIPS WAS, in Laura's view, one of the classiest women in Hampshire County. Tall and chic, with thick honey-colored hair that she habitually wore sleekly knotted, a fine hand at makeup, and impeccable taste in clothes, she presented a striking figure. Beyond that, she had brains. She had graduated from law school at the top of her class and remained, Laura was sure, better versed in the field of criminal law than any of the ten men in her firm. Beyond *that*, she had tact. She knew when to talk and when not to, when to argue and when to be still. In a town like Northampton, that was important.

Laura and Daphne had been best friends since junior high school. They had studied together, dated together, summered together. Daphne had been the first to know that Laura was dropping out of college to marry Jeff; Laura had been the first to know that Daphne was accepted at Yale. Laura experienced law school through Daphne; Daphne experienced motherhood through Laura. They went to the same hairdresser, the same seamstress, the same gynecologist. They were closer than sisters often were.

Laura needed someone that close to help her now, which was why, when Daphne swept through the door thirty minutes after Laura called, she felt a wave of relief.

"Tell me again," Daphne ordered. "He didn't come home at all last night?"

"Not once. I've been racking my brain, trying to remember something he may have told me, but there isn't anything, and anyway, if he had plans to go somewhere overnight, he'd have packed a bag. I went through the bathroom, the bedroom, the cedar closet. Nothing's gone." She told Daphne about the calls she had made to David, to Jeff's secretary, to the police.

"Maybe he's with friends," Daphne suggested.

"All night? Jeff wouldn't do that."

"Maybe with an *old* friend?"

Laura shrugged. "Who?" Jeff didn't have many friends from the past. He wasn't the sentimental type.

"Could he have gotten drunk somewhere and passed out?"

"He doesn't drink."

Daphne arched a brow. "He drinks."

"Only one or two," Laura insisted. "He's never even been high. It couldn't be that. And if it were, some bartender would have kicked him out or called the police or called *me*."

"Could he have been with a group from the office?" Daphne asked.

"There is no group. His tennis foursome is the closest he comes to doing things with a group. Jeff doesn't have buddies. His family is his life." She pushed her fingers through her hair in total bewilderment. Her voice fell to a drone. "This isn't like him, Daph. If he says he'll be home by six, he's home by six. If he says he's going to be an hour late, he's an hour late. He is ve-ry organized, ve-ry predictable, ve-ry punctual." With Debra, she'd had to be brave. With Daphne, it wasn't necessary. "It's been light for nearly an hour. Even if the police were blind, if there'd been an accident off to the side of the road some commuter would have seen it by now." Aware that her knees were starting to shake, she drew out a stool and sat down.

"Did you sleep?"

"I couldn't. I feel off balance. This is so unlike Jeff." She looked at Daphne. Daphne was good at solving things. "You know him. You were the maid of honor at my wedding, and you've been in and out of wherever we've lived ever since. Second to me, you probably know him best. Where could he be?"

Daphne drew a stool close so they could sit thigh to thigh, facing each other. "He didn't show up at the museum?"

She shook her head.

"Was he looking forward to going?"

"Uh-huh. He likes things like that. Being seen is an important part of his business."

"Maybe he was feeling overshadowed by the fact that Cherries catered the show."

Laura couldn't believe that. "He's been at other affairs we've catered, and it never bothered him. He's proud of what I do."

"I know, but some men—"

"Not Jeff. He was a CPA long before I was a caterer."

"But the restaurant—"

"He loves the restaurant. It enhances his name. It brings him business. Believe me, Daph, he isn't threatened that way, and even if he were, he wouldn't just disappear." At the sound of the phone, she flew off the stool and snatched it up. "Hello?"

"Hi, Laura, it's David. I'm assuming Jeff finally showed up. Is everything okay?"

Laura's hand shook as she held the receiver to her ear. "He didn't come home, David. He's not here."

"Not there? Didn't go home at all?"

"That's right."

"That's not like Jeff."

Her laugh had an hysterical edge. "Do tell."

"Are you all right?"

"No, I'm not all right. I'm worried sick."

"Have you called the police?"

"For what it was worth." She related the contents of that particular phone call. "The police won't do anything. But he must be out there somewhere. Maybe we should hire a private investigator."

Daphne waved a hand and shook her head.

"No?" Laura asked her.

"Not yet. Not yet."

"I take it someone's with you," David remarked.

"Daphne Phillips."

"Should I come over too?"

Laura wasn't wild about the idea. David was a fine accountant and a good friend, but his company could be cloying. "I'd rather you went to the office and checked out Jeff's desk. Maybe he left a note or jotted something down."

"Good thought. I'll be there in half an hour. I'll call you once I've looked."

Replacing the phone, Laura braced a shoulder against the wall and turned tired eyes on Daphne. "Where could he be?" Her voice was a weak echo of all the other times she'd said the words.

Calm, cool Daphne was looking disconcertingly concerned. "I haven't the foggiest."

"So what should I do? Should I start making calls? I would have last night, except it seemed ridiculous. I was sure Jeff would be home, I was *sure* of it, and I didn't want to start bugging our friends and then have him walk in at eleven or twelve with some perfectly good explanation for where he'd been." Pushing off from the wall, she put the plate of waffles into the microwave. "But it's eight in the morning and he isn't home yet. Am I supposed to sit here or go out looking or call people? What?"

"Have you called Lydia?"

"I can't. Jeff's her pride and joy. I can't tell her he's missing. She's seventy-three and not well."

"What about Jeff's brother?"

Laura took a breath that went down the wrong way. She coughed, and pressed a hand to her heart. "What about him?"

"Maybe he's in some kind of trouble."

"No doubt he's in some kind of trouble." Christian Frye created an uproar wherever he went, often with little more than a look.

"Maybe Jeff took off to help him."

The microwave sounded. Laura removed the plate. "They don't get along."

"But they're brothers."

"They're as different as night and day."

"Still," Daphne argued with quiet persistence, "family is family. It's not inconceivable that if Christian needed help he'd call."

"He might call, but Jeff wouldn't go." Laura opened the refrigerator and took out the whipped cream and the juice that Debra hadn't touched. "You know Christian, Daph. You've seen him at work. He came to our wedding stoned, came to Lydia's sixty-fifth birthday party drunk, has been abrasive at every Thanksgiving he's come to."

"I never thought he was so bad."

"I did—do."

"But you keep inviting him."

"Because he's family!" Laura cried, setting the egg tray and a stick of butter on the counter. "And because I feel bad that he's alone." But every time she saw him, she was on edge, and though she tried not to let it show, Jeff had sensed it. "No, Jeff wouldn't have gone to help Christian."

"Maybe you should call him anyway, just to check."

"I think he's away."

"Try him. It wouldn't hurt."

But it would. Laura knew that, as surely as she knew why Christian had come to her wedding stoned. She couldn't call him. Not about something like this.

She took a spatula from the utensil drawer. "Something awful has happened. Nothing else makes sense."

Daphne came up off the stool. "I have a friend in the police department. I'll give him a call."

"They told me they wouldn't do anything yet."

"He owes me." She was already punching out the number. Into the phone, seconds later, she said, "Detective Melrose, please."

Laura pulled out a skillet.

"Laura, what are you cooking?" Daphne murmured above the receiver.

"Breakfast."

"For you?"

"For you. I have waffles, and I'm making eggs."

Taking her arm, Daphne pushed her down onto a stool. "Stop. Sit. Relax."

"I can't relax," Laura cried. "I don't know what's happening, and I don't give a damn if my mother *does* say I have an unhealthy fixation on control. I want to know where Jeff is, and I want to know now!"

Daphne held up a hand to still the outburst. "Dennis, it's Daphne Phillips." She started to speak, then paused. "Fine, thanks." She started again, paused again. "No, I didn't know he'd been released, but that isn't why I'm calling." Briefly, she outlined the situation. "I know you can't do anything formal until tonight, but given who and what Jeff Frye is, I thought you might do a little snooping." She paused, listened, came back with an indignant, "No, he's not involved in anything dirty. But he's well known in the area, and if it should happen that he's been hurt, it wouldn't look great that the police took their time getting on the stick, *capiche?*"

Unable to sit still, Laura went to the oak table that nestled in the kitchen's windowed bay, opened the large leather purse that sat there, and pulled out her notebook.

"He'll make some calls and look around," Daphne said, joining her a minute later. "And he'll be subtle about it. We don't want the papers thinking there's a story in the air."

The papers. Good God, that would be a nightmare. "Jeffrey Frye, well-known Pioneer Valley CPA, disappears as mysteriously as the cherry crescents at his wife's restaurant," Duggan O'Neil might write.

Loath to deal with that potential twist, Laura looked at her calendar. "I'm supposed to have meetings all morning, but I want to be here when Jeff calls." Her gaze drifted toward the window. Under an overcast sky, the back yard was gray and barren. "*If* Jeff calls. What if he doesn't?"

"He will."

"I sent Debra to school. If Jeff isn't here by the time she gets home, it'll be awful." She sent a frightened glance Daphne's way. "If we don't know anything by then, I'll have to call Scott." Her breath came shorter. "This is unreal."

The silence that followed was proof. Normally, at eight-thirty in the morning, Jeff would be in the kitchen having breakfast. By eight-forty-five, he would leave the house. By nine, he would be at his desk opening the mail.

The phone rang. Laura jumped for it.

"There's nothing here," David announced without preface. "I've gone over his desk, the credenza, the bookshelves. The place is immaculate," which was typical Jeff, Laura knew. He was a neat man. He turned his socks right-side-out before putting them into the hamper, hung his trousers with the creases knife-edge to knife-edge, stacked books on his nightstand three at a time, in the order in which they were to be read. When other women complained that their husbands were slobs, Laura counted her blessings. Jeff was the ideal husband for a woman with kids and a job.

Fighting a numbing disappointment, she forced herself to think clearly. "What's his schedule today? When's his first appointment?"

"Nine-thirty," David said, adding in a more solicitous tone, "I'm sure there's some answer here. Jeff wouldn't just up and leave you."

Leave you. For an instant her blood ran so fast she couldn't hear past its rush. Then she swallowed. "Of course he wouldn't. Something's happened to him. I have to find out what."

"I think I should come over."

"No. Stay there. Maybe you could make a few calls." She raised questioning eyes to Daphne, who held out her hand for the phone. "Hold on, David. Here's Daphne."

"David? Be nonchalant. As your people come in, ask if they've seen him. Say you need him for something." She paused, heard David out, then said, "We don't want to embarrass him if he turns up with a perfectly good explanation for where he's been. Mostly, we don't want one person to smell something wrong and call another and then another. It's important to keep things under control."

Laura agreed with that, though she wished she felt more in control herself. Her mind was skipping back and forth, from the immediate present to the night that had passed, from hope to bewilderment to fear. Her eyes were dry and tired, but her heart didn't seem to sense the fatigue. It was pounding against her ribs without respite.

Leaving Daphne, she wandered into the dining room. Her fingertips skimmed the sculpted top of a Chippendale chair, slid down its side, and came to an unsteady rest on the edge of the table. On Thanksgiving Day, less than two weeks before, the table had been covered with food and the room filled with people. Twenty-six, they'd had in all, from immediate family to extended family to friends and friends' families and even a few employees. Laura loved doing things that way, and everyone present liked it too. Even Maddie was mellow—no doubt on her good behavior, with Gretchen in from Sacramento—and what a coup that had been on Laura's part, getting her mother and younger sister together for a whole weekend. The two were like fire and water, which was why Gretchen had fled the East Coast in the first place. But somewhere in the course of the past few years, Maddie had accepted that if she wanted to see Gretchen she would have to behave. She couldn't constantly badger, constantly scrutinize, constantly analyze. She had to keep her big mouth shut.

Laura, who hadn't broken off with her mother the way Gretchen had and therefore still felt the brunt of her hounding, shuddered at the thought of what Maddie would have to say about Jeff's disappearance. She prayed he would materialize and the mystery be solved before Maddie knew about it.

"We're set with David," Daphne said from the doorway. "Are you okay?"

Laura gave a shaky smile. "I'm okay." She took an uneven breath. "What do I do now?"

"Want to call a few friends?"

She went to the window. "He'd have come here before going to any friend. I mean, who does he have? There's us, and the people in the office. And his tennis group. They played on Monday. They're due to play again later today," she realized.

"Call one of them," Daphne suggested in a low, gently coaxing voice. "Maybe he canceled. That'd be a start."

"Only if he planned to be gone. Are you thinking he did?"

"No. I'm just trying to get a general fix on him."

Laura barely heard. She was feeling a vast loneliness. "How could he plan to be gone without telling me, without taking his things, without saying good-bye to Debra?"

Coming close to wrap an arm around her, Daphne said, "I shouldn't have mentioned it. There's no need to think about it now."

"It couldn't have been deliberate. We've been happily married for twenty years. He loves me, loves the kids, loves the house."

"You're right. It couldn't have been deliberate."

The phone rang. Laura broke away to get it. "Hello?"

"Thank goodness I caught you," came Madeline McVey's strident voice. "I was worried you'd already left. Do you have a minute?"

Laura's eyes went wild. "Uh, this is a bad time, Mom."

"But I have to leave soon. I won't be free again until after dinner tonight, and we really should settle this now."

The knot in her stomach was familiar. For a split second Laura was eight years old again, being called into the parlor that was Maddie's home office to explain why she hadn't volunteered to do a project for the Science Fair. Needing to know what her offense was this time, she asked, "Settle what?"

"There's a problem here regarding the department Christmas party. We have you booked for the nineteenth at the Dean's house, but there's been some grumbling from people who want to hold it off-campus. Not that it matters to me—"

"Can you hold on a second?" Laura interrupted loudly. Without waiting for permission, she put Maddie on hold. Pressing the receiver to her chest, she looked frantically around at Daphne. "I can't take this now."

"Tell her you'll call later."

"What if later's worse?"

"Tell her you're waiting for another call."

"She knows I have two lines."

"Tell her you feel ill."

"She'll say it's morning sickness and go off on a diatribe about women having children at my age."

Daphne paled. "*Are* you pregnant?"

"God, no! I don't have the time or strength to be pregnant! I'm thirty-eight years old!"

"And scared of your mother."

"No more. No more. Not for a long time."

"Then talk with her now and get it done."

Laura stared hard at Daphne before turning back to the phone and punching in the call. "Sorry about that, Mom. What were you saying about the party?"

"There is a contingent in my department," Maddie began again, injecting faint censure in her tone to chide Laura for the delay, "who want to hold it off-campus. They say we owe it to our graduate students to make the party as festive as possible." She snorted. "As if they'll be better psychologists for it. The Dean's house is festive, don't you think?"

"Definitely," Laura said.

"Well, you and I are in the minority. I could make an issue of it, but then they'll say I'm afraid to let go of the past. Now, I ask you, have I ever been afraid to move forward? Not once! I am the most enlightened member of that department!"

Laura didn't doubt it for a minute. Nor did she doubt, given that at sixty-seven her mother was the oldest active member of the department and its chairman, that some of the younger members would like to see her replaced. The rest were thrilled to have her fight their battles. She was a formidable opponent.

Placatingly, Laura said, "I'm sure they appreciate all you do. And they want the best."

"They want the restaurant," Maddie informed her. "Can you handle us?"

Forcing herself to think business when every other instinct protested, Laura pictured the schedule on her office wall, where PARTY QUOTA FILLED was written in bold red print beside DECEMBER. She had been thrilled to write it there for the success it marked, and she should have been thrilled to brag about that success to Maddie. But she didn't have it in her to brag just then, so she simply said, "It's a little late to be making changes."

"Three weeks' notice? We're not canceling, just switching from a catered affair at the school to one at the restaurant." Maddie's voice grew softer, in the dangerous way it had of doing. "Laura, will this present a problem for you?"

The challenge was there, as old and familiar as Laura's earliest memories. Maddie McVey was a woman of singular drive and power. A lifelong academician, she was not only the head of her department but a high-muck-a-muck in professional organizations, all of which made her a hard act to follow. Laura often wondered if that was why she herself had dropped out of college. Maddie had been appalled when she did and only slightly less appalled when Debra had finally gone off to school and Laura had started selling cherry cheesecake out of her home. That had been ten years ago. When that small business evolved into a catering service, Maddie was hardly impressed. As a career, gastronomy wasn't on her acceptable list. Then, two years ago, the restaurant had opened. Its success meant Laura could finally deal with her mother from a position of strength.

Given the mystery of Jeff's absence and the anxiety Laura was feeling, she clung to what little strength she had. "There's no problem. I can shift things around. But I'll have to get back to you on the exact time."

"We booked for cocktails at six and dinner at seven."

"You booked for the Dean's house. If you want to hold the party at the restaurant, you may have to make it a little earlier or a little later. The schedule is full. I'll fit you in, but you'll have to be flexible."

There was a pause at the other end of the line. Laura knew those pauses. They were designed to intimidate. But she was in the right in this case, even powerful, and while she had never aspired to power per se, holding a bit of it over her mother for a change felt good.

Lord knew little else in the last twelve hours had felt good.

"I don't have much choice, I suppose," Maddie finally conceded. Then, as though she simply couldn't resist, she issued another challenge. "I trust the cost won't be greater."

"For you, Mother? Same price."

"Very good," Maddie decided. "Call me as soon as you know the time. We'll talk more then."

Laura hung up the phone. She had barely savored the fact that she'd held her ground when worry about Jeff returned in full. Her eye caught on the answering machine. "Maybe I did miss it somehow."

"What?" Daphne asked.

"A message from Jeff." She pressed the button to rerun the last batch of messages.

The machine beeped. "Laura, it's Sue. We have a problem here. The guys loaded the wrong filet mignon onto our truck. We got the stuffed one, but our client ordered it plain. The plain one must have gone with Dave. I'm calling Dee right now, in case you're at the shop. If you're not, she'll have to handle it." The message beeped off.

"Sue Hirshorn," Laura explained. "She heads one of my crews. She reached me at Cherries."

The machine beeped again. "This is Dr. Larimer's office calling to confirm that Jeffrey Frye has an appointment with the dentist at noon on Wednesday."

Laura's eyes shot to Daphne's as the message beeped off, but before she could tell her about Jeff's toothache, the next message came on.

"Hi, Mom." It was Scott's voice, rising above a background clatter. At its happy-go-lucky sound, Laura pressed her fingertips to her mouth. "Guess I missed you again. I just wanted to tell you that I got a B-plus on that Ec test I thought I fleegled. The art paper's coming along okay. And I'm working out. The whole team is. Uh, what else? Oh. We had a wild party here last weekend." There was raucous laughter, then a muted, "Shut up, you guys." Then, "My friends ate all the food you sent back. They loved it." Hoots and applause supported that. "So thanks. I guess that's all. Talk with you soon. 'Bye."

"What happened to the shy little guy who used to collect seashells with me on the beach at St. Croix?" Daphne asked.

Laura's eyes were glued to the machine. "He's grown up." She stared, waited, finally let out a discouraged breath when the machine said that was her last message.

Daphne touched her arm. "He'll show up. We'll find him."

Laura's thoughts barreled ahead. "What about Christmas? What about the reservations I made for Saba after New Year's? What about the surprise birthday party that invitations are being printed for even as we speak?"

"He'll be here."

"What if he isn't?" The phone rang. Grabbing it, she gasped out a high-pitched "Hello?"

"It's me. You sound strange. Is everything okay?"

"Oh, God, Elise."

"He isn't home?"

"Not yet. Not all night. Something's wrong."

"I'm coming over."

The phone went dead before Laura could argue, not that she would have. Elise Schuler was, besides Daphne, one of her closest friends. They had been roommates at Smith before Laura dropped out; she swore that Elise was the only thing she had liked about the school. They had grown even closer in the years that followed. Indeed, it was at a party at Laura's that Elise had met one of Jeff's clients, the man she had been married to for six years now. The marriage wasn't quite made in heaven. Peter Schuler was older than Elise and conventional in ways that doubled that difference. But Elise had wanted children, and Peter was accommodating. So she had two little girls under the age of five, plus the maid and the au pair that Peter insisted upon, which left her time for Cherries and Laura. Laura thanked heaven for that. Offbeat to the point of being mistaken as daffy, Elise was a bundle of energy with a heart of gold. Daphne might be the one to tell Laura what to do next, but Elise would keep her spirits up.

Given that it was nearly nine, that David hadn't called with news from the office or Daphne's detective with news from the police station, Laura had the awful feeling her spirits would need all the uplifting they could get.

THREE

❀ ❀ ❀

JEFFREY FRYE CAME AWAKE to a fierce throbbing in his head. He put up a hand to still it, but it was pervasive, radiating through his scalp in a way that one clammy palm, no matter how large, couldn't possibly touch. Hangovers were like that, he'd been told, and now he knew. Not that he regretted drinking himself into a stupor. It had been the only thing to do. Like a rite of passage long overdue. As if, six weeks before his forty-second birthday, he had finally become a man.

That thought echoed in his head, ricocheting between the pain there and a world of deeper meaning. He tried to open his eyes, to determine whether what he'd done was real or still a dream, but his lids resisted. So, leaving his fingers splayed on the top of his head, he lay still, very still, and let the unfamiliarity of his surroundings tell him what he needed to know.

His bed was narrow, a simple wood frame that accommodated his length with little room to spare. The sheets were stiff and smelled of the plastic packaging he had taken them from the night before. They were askew now in a commentary on his bed-making skills, the upshot of which was that with each shallow breath he felt the scratch of wool blankets against his skin. The blankets had a smell too, a newness that was at odds with the rest of the place.

Lying on that bed with his eyes closed and his head aching, he was aware of mustiness and the odor of age. A fisherman had once lived here, he could smell that, and the fisherman had a dog. If the fisherman had a wife, she hadn't washed her hair with apple shampoo, or scented her drawers with sachets, or sprayed her pulse points with Joy like Jeff's woman did. There was nothing soft or sweet about the odor of the place, or about its sound. A winter rain that should have been snow beat a harsh tattoo on the roof, while beyond the scrub pines and the dried sea grass and the broad stairwell of cliffs and boulders, the sea hurled itself against the rocks, over and over again, in a song of defeat.

He had chosen the shore because he loved the sea. When he was little, when his family had vacationed at the beach, he had sat for hours watching the waves. They hypnotized him. He felt their power.

Now, listening, he heard that power and, in a split second's insight, guessed that the song of defeat was his own. But the second was gone as quickly as it had come, and he let it go. He didn't want to think of defeat. Didn't want to think of what he'd left behind. *Couldn't* think of it. So he pressed a hand more tightly to his head, gingerly eased his legs over the side of the bed, and, with painstaking respect for the nausea snaking around his insides, pushed himself to a sitting position.

Determinedly he held himself in place until the world behind his lids stopped spinning. Very slowly, he opened his eyes. He didn't have to move them to take in the entirety of the cottage, it was that small, but he didn't mind small. Small was cozy. It was also practical. Everything he needed was in sight, albeit myopic sight at that moment. He made out the blur of a kitchen sink and cabinets against one wall, a blur of bookshelves and a desk against a second wall, a blur of living room furniture sprouting from a third. In the center of the room was a wood stove, radiating remnants of warmth from the logs he'd lit there the night before. Between the stove and the kitchen was a small round table and two ladder-back chairs.

Everything was made of wood. Everything was scarred from use. Everything needed work. But Jeff wasn't complaining. He needed a place to hide, and there was none better. No one would find him here. The town was too far north, too remote for anyone from civilization to think to look.

No. No one would find him. He had planned things too well. When he had come in search of the cottage the summer before, he had disguised himself, used a false name, and paid in cash. During the fall he had gathered supplies— not only the sheets and blankets but cooking utensils, dishes, and warm winter clothing. He had been infinitely careful about that too, purchasing things in cash, one or two at a time, in stores as far from Northampton as his client base allowed. Within two weeks he would have a beard, within four weeks his hair would grow out, and during that time he could subsist on the food he had been stashing, along with his other supplies, in the back of the Porsche.

The Porsche, the only luxury he'd taken with him, was safely stowed beneath a dark gray tarp in the old boat shed behind the house. The town had been shrouded in thick fog when he had driven down the deserted main street in the morning's wee hours. No one would ever know it was there.

He hadn't taken anything else, other than the clothes on his back, his briefcase, and fifty thousand dollars in small bills. That would last him awhile.

His expenses here would be small. The cottage came with its own generator, but he rather liked the hurricane lamps that were suspended from hooks at random spots around the room. Using those, plus wood for heat and the supplies of food he had brought, he wouldn't have to venture out for days. He had even brought books, which meant he wouldn't die of boredom, but even without the books he doubted that would happen. There was work to do on the cottage. For years, after that fisherman of yore, a writer had lived in the place. An eccentric sort, according to the realtor, he had died two years before, which meant that the dirt on the windows was probably older than that. Jeff had brought cleaning supplies. He had even brought a hammer and nails for emergency repairs. When those were done, when he was suitably hairy and grungy, he might just wander into town and hire on as a carpenter's assistant. That was how Christian had started out—no, Christian had started out building a bridge in a remote West African village, but doing odd jobs in a remote New England one would be just as good. No matter that he didn't know much about carpentry. If Christian had learned, so could he. They had the same genes, didn't they? He could build up calluses if he wanted.

Hard to believe, above the throbbing of his head, but for the very first time in his life he could do whatever he wanted. He was free, totally free. Without a name. Without a past. Without the kind of responsibility that tied a man to a desk for eight hours a day, five days a week, fifty weeks a year. He was free.

But he felt like shit.

It could be the cold, he reasoned. The wood stove worked fine, but the place was drafty—something he hadn't noticed the summer before, when the air had been warm. There was a dampness now that was seeping into his bones, making him shake.

But no, the problem was his hangover. With an effort, he maneuvered himself to his feet and crossed the planked floor to the scarred table and the smooth leather briefcase that looked so out of place on it. He shook two aspirins from a bottle and, in a gesture that was suitably macho for a free-as-a-bird man with a stinking hangover, tossed back his head and swallowed them dry.

The gesture was sadly misconceived. His head exploded in pain at the sharp backward movement. His stomach reacted to all that had soured it the night before. Turning blindly, without a thought of being cold or macho or free, he stumbled to the bathroom and threw up.

With the breaking of dawn on the other side of the world, Christian Frye came awake to a heat that, not even in those first semiconscious seconds, let him forget where he was and why. He had been to Australia before. It wasn't one of his favorite places. But he'd been asked to do a job that appealed to him, the timing was right, and with a stretch of the imagination, Australia was in the same neighborhood as Tahiti, where he was heading later that day. Tahiti would be fun. He had been there before, too, and was looking forward to seeing old friends. He was also looking forward to living in luxury for a while, which was something he hadn't done much of here.

His bungalow was little more than a tropical lean-to, a plank floor raised off the ground, with a center post that shared support of the thatched roof with the single wall that stood on the forest side. The ocean side was open to let in what little breeze might push through the trees, though Christian didn't feel any breeze now. The air was warm, humid, and still, draining him of energy before he'd moved an inch. Just then, he would have traded his Nikon for a ceiling fan without a second thought.

Cairns, with its modern waterfront hotels, hadn't been so bad. Nor, a bit farther north, had Port Douglas, where he had stayed on a yacht that was state-of-the-art in everything from hot tubs to women. North of Port Douglas, though, fancies of the flesh had taken a back seat to the lushness of the land, specifically the dense, wild growth of the Daintree.

Rainforests were like that—dense and wild—and the Daintree was the greatest Christian had ever seen. As tropical vegetation went, the Daintree's was richer, larger, more vibrant. In the sunlight that dappled down through a towering canopy of leaves, his camera had captured vivid flares of reds, oranges, and pinks, deep and fertile greens, darker blues and magentas. He had photographed not only plant life but birds, butterflies, rodents, and reptiles. Many of them were found in no other place on earth but this one. The expression "endangered species" was so overused as to be taken for granted. A person couldn't truly understand its meaning until he saw at first hand the beauty to be lost.

Christian had seen that beauty. It wasn't the beauty of a perfectly set diamond, or a Georgian mansion built on a knoll, or a well-dressed woman. Rather, it was raw, primitive, untouched by humans. It was hot and moist, smelling of new growth, old growth, rotting growth, crowded high overhead and closely packed underfoot, stifling at times but alive, always alive.

The goal was to keep it that way, which was why Christian had been asked to photograph it. He had gone through dozens and dozens of rolls of film, now safely stored in his cooler. If even a small number of those pictures helped the cause, the sweat that had poured from him over the last week would be well worth it.

Even now, at dawn, when day was at its coolest, he was sweating. At least he wasn't dressed. Being dressed was the worst. There had been times in the forest when the heat was so oppressive that every stitch he'd worn had been soaked through with sweat. Other times, rain had done the deed. He had been warned that December wasn't the best time to visit, but December fit into his schedule. He liked being away for the holidays, and if that meant the rainforest in the rainy season, so be it. It didn't matter whether it was sweat or pelting downpours that soaked his clothes so that they had to be peeled off, so that they never quite dried, so that they grew increasingly rank. The clothes would be disposed of when he returned to Cairns, and in Tahiti he wouldn't wear much of anything at all.

At that thought, he smiled and stretched, extending an arm over his head to the top of a mercifully long hammock and a leg to its foot. When he relaxed again, he ran a hand through the hair on his chest and middle to his belly. He'd lost weight, no doubt sweated off seven or eight pounds, which was fine. It wouldn't hurt to have a few to play with. He liked being in shape—not that he usually gave much thought to diet or formal exercise, given what he did for a living—but vacations were something else. Good food, less exercise than usual, a minimum of nervous energy; he could put on weight during vacation.

For that reason he was glad he had left for Australia before Thanksgiving. When Laura made a dinner, there were no holds barred. She went all the way, soup to nuts, with a different kind of soup, a different kind of nuts, a different kind of everything else each year, except for the turkey. That big bird—huge bird, given the number of people she usually invited—was the one constant in the meal. Everything else changed according to her whim. Thanksgiving was a time for showing off all she had and did and was. Christmas was more of the same. And though Christian had to hand it to Laura for building a life out of nothing and building it well, he just couldn't be there to watch. It was too painful, too stark a reminder of all he didn't have himself.

So he kept busy over the holidays. That way he didn't have to see things. He didn't have to remember what it had been like once upon a time. And he didn't have to behave like an asshole, tossing around mockery and innuendo in a show of disdain for what Laura and Jeff had made of their lives.

He was getting too old for that anyway. It was growing tiresome—and the irony of that admission was something else. For years, Gaby had said the same thing.

"Why do you do it, Christian?" she used to ask. "You hurt your family and you hurt yourself. You're too old for that kind of thing. Why do you do it?"

He had never had an answer, at least not one he'd been willing to share, and what he wasn't willing to share with Gaby, he wasn't about to share with anyone else. They had been together, on and off, for nearly sixteen years. Best friends, on and off. Lovers, on and off. She had been the closest he had ever come to having a wife. But she was busy producing talk shows in New York, and he was busy building homes in Vermont. And something was missing, some force that told them to grab it while they had it, some incentive for one or the other of them to compromise. Something was missing.

Then Gaby had gotten sick. He had wanted to marry her, but they both knew the gesture was misplaced, a useless weapon against a disease that wouldn't be stopped. So he had stayed with her, held her hand when she was lucid enough to be frightened, dealt with the doctors, and helped make her last days as comfortable as possible. When there was nothing else to be done, he had buried her.

A slow trickle of sweat inched its way down his face as tears might have done if Christian had been the crying type. He missed Gaby. She had been a good friend, a point of reference in his life. For three years, now, she'd been gone, and though he didn't think about her constantly, there were many times when he would have liked to talk with her, take her out, see her smile.

She wouldn't have smiled in the Daintree, Christian realized with a chuckle. Gaby liked her luxuries. She would have hated the heat, hated the humidity, hated the congestion of the forest. She needed space. And silence. Waking up to the cacophonous chatter of starlings nesting nearby wouldn't have thrilled her. Nor, as the day wore on, would the buzz of the insects or the shrill of the cicadas or the screeches and squawks of the other birds of the rainforest. No,

Gaby was one for luxury and privacy. She wouldn't have slept as he had, bare save for a thin pair of boxers, in a hut with one wall. She wouldn't have bathed naked in the stream. And she wouldn't have liked walking through the jungle, where one was always watched by creatures one couldn't see.

Even Christian had found that disconcerting at first, though he'd been. warned it was so. Every sound he made was heard, every move he made was seen. No doubt he had spotted only a small number of the creatures that spotted him. But he couldn't really blame them for their watchfulness. After all, the forest was their home. He was the trespasser.

But then, wasn't he always?

Four in the afternoon, Boston time, found Taylor Jones wide awake in bed. The bed wasn't his own, but he knew it well. He knew the feel of fresh white percale, the feel of ruffled pillows, the feel of the thick white quilt. He also knew the feel of the woman whose body, even now, fit his with precision. Her skin was warm and smooth, her curves sweet, her desire everything a man could want.

Unfortunately, she was leaving town. Within one short week, the fresh white percale sheets would be stripped from the bed, packed up, and shipped to San Francisco, where a job as the assistant manager of a four-star hotel was waiting. The job was a plum, an honor for a twenty-seven-year-old, a big step up for a woman who planned one day to run the show. But there were hotels all over the country, and four-star ones at that. She wouldn't have chosen this one if leaving the East Coast would have broken her heart.

They had something good going, she and Taylor did, but it was purely physical. He knew that; so did she. They came from different places, liked different people, wanted different things down the road. But the sex was good, so they kept at it. Her moving clear across the country was probably the only way to stop.

"Tack?"

He moved his face against the back of her head, where the hair lay thick and warm. "Mmmm?"

"What are you thinking?"

Inhaling deeply, he held her scent in his lungs like pot, for the maximum effect, before letting it out. "I'm thinking I'm gonna miss you."

"Don't lie."

"I'm not." He raised his head over her cheek. "What did you expect I'd say?"

"That you had to get back to work. That's what you usually say."

She was right. He wasn't the kind to linger or get hung up with sweet nothings when the loving was done. But today was different. He wasn't such a total heel that he couldn't acknowledge in some small way the end of a relationship. "I thought maybe we could go out for dinner. It'd be appropriate, don't you think?"

"Only if we won't be seeing each other again before I leave."

He smoothed a strand of blond hair off her cheek.

In the absence of a response, she raised questioning eyes to his.

"It might be better if we didn't," he finally said. "It won't get any easier."

"It won't be so hard. We don't love each other."

"No." He ran a hand around her breast, feeling the lure of her warmth, even though she'd drained him less than ten minutes before. "But we share this." It was like an addiction. He needed a fix every few days or he was climbing the walls.

She stilled his hand, holding it there, and returned her cheek to the pillow. "It's not enough. I need more. And you need a sweet little homebody for a wife. But you pick the wrong women, Tack. Over and over again you do it. You go for women who have active and visible careers, but that's not the kind who's going to give you the home and hearth and the five kids. Me, I'd only give you heartache, because I have dreams of my own and I can't give them up."

"If you loved me, you would."

She sent him a challenging look. "You don't love *me*. Or if you do, you have a funny way of showing it. Quick sex three or four times a week with one call to set each date and even then you're late. No gifts, no flowers, no wining and dining—"

"You have all the wining and dining you can take with your friends."

"Friends, I might point out, whom you never made any attempt to get to know." Her annoyance mellowed into the indulgence of a friend who knew some things would never change. "You're a bastard, Taylor Jones. God only knows why I've put up with you this long."

"I know why." He grinned. "Great sex."

She nodded. "Great sex. As long as you have me, you take me, and as long as I want you, I let you. The chemistry is there. It's perfect. I'll want you forever, and that's a fact." She put her fingertip to the groove in his chin. "But I've worked my butt off for this career, and now that it's finally getting off the ground I can't let anything stop it. I may marry and have kids someday, but only after I've nailed down a place for myself. I need that place. Can you understand why?"

He could. God knows she'd explained it enough. Hotels were in her blood. Both her grandfathers had owned them. One still did, and that was the hotel chain she wanted. The stipulation was that she earn it. She was determined to do that.

"I understand," he said, but with indifference. Yes, he admired her determination, but he had contempt for the games she and her family played. He had come from nothing, himself. The only games his family had played were ones of survival.

"So my staying here is pointless. It keeps you from looking for other women." She brushed one of his eyebrows with the pad of her thumb. "One of those women will be right for you. One of them will inspire you to be thoughtful and doting."

"Thoughtful and doting? Me?"

"Why not? You make love that way. But it ends the minute we get out of bed, because I'm the wrong woman. Maybe if we were closer in age—"

He cut her off with a shake of his head. "An eight-year difference isn't a hell of a lot. But that's not the problem. We could have been born on the same day, and still we'd have been wrong for each other. You're gloss, and I'm not." She had furs, jewelry, and a Jaguar. Her insurance bill alone probably equaled what he spent on food for a year. He worked for Uncle Sam. No one got rich working for Uncle Sam. In his next life, he decided, he'd be a mega-mogul, but for now he liked his work, particularly when a meaty case came along. "You're going up and up and up. I'm not, and that's okay, because I wouldn't be caught dead in a tux three times a week."

She smiled. "More's the pity. You look great in a tux."

He smiled back. "So. How about dinner?"

"I'd rather see you again before I leave."

But he shook his head. She was the one who was moving. He had to take the upper hand in this, at least.

She slid a hand up his thigh. "You'll want me."

"Damn right." It had been that way from the start. Seeing her fully dressed was tempting enough. Seeing her naked, he didn't stand a chance. And when her hand left his thigh and did wonders between his legs, he was lost.

Covering her, he settled into the slip of her thighs and entered her. His movements were slow and steady, in time more steady than his heart, but he was determined to watch her, to see one last time the look of pleasure on her face when she came. He brought her close, then slowed, brought her closer still, then slowed again. He prolonged her final release as long as he could, until she cried out with its force, until he did with his own.

When it was over and she dozed off, he slipped from the bed. He dressed, watching her all the while, then watched her a little longer before letting himself out. Leaving the waterfront, he walked up State Street to Tremont, across the Commons and the Public Garden, all the way down Commonwealth to Massachusetts Avenue, and over the river to Cambridge. By the time he climbed the three flights to his Central Square apartment, he was half frozen, but he wasn't numb, and if cold turkey was the way to go, numb was what he wanted. So, ignoring the files on his desk that were waiting to be read, he changed out of his suit and went to the gym, where he punished his body with the kind of workout he hadn't done in months. Then, feeling vaguely back in control, he stopped for a pizza with the works to go, went back home, thumbed open a cold Sam Adams, and turned on the Celtics.

FOUR

"I'M SORRY, MRS. FRYE. I know this is difficult for you, but if I repeat myself, it's only to make sure I know the facts." Dennis Melrose, Daphne's police detective, studied his notes. "Your husband was due home at six o'clock last night, but he never arrived. You haven't seen him or heard from him. He hasn't sent a message through a third party."

"That's right," Laura said. She was feeling dazed, trying her best to focus on everything the man was saying but having trouble. It wasn't the detective's fault. He was pleasant enough, in his mid-fifties, with a slight paunch and a more than slightly receding hairline. But she hadn't slept in a day and a half, and she was wrung dry with worry.

"He hasn't called his mother," the detective continued. "He hasn't called his friends. He hasn't called anyone from the office."

David confirmed the last. Standing close behind Laura in a proprietory way, he said, "Total silence. He's had no contact with anyone there. Or with the clients he was supposed to see."

"Did he have many appointments?"

"A full day's worth. Jeff is a successful accountant. Clients like him because he knows what he's doing, and because he's dependable. If he sets up a meeting, he's on time and prepared."

"That's how he is in everything," Laura put in, "which is why this is so bizarre."

"Jeff is a family man," Elise said, coming forward in her chair. Between her rhinestone-studded chartreuse sweat suit and the blond hair that stuck out at odd angles from a ponytail at the top of her head, she would have looked ditsy had it not been for her earnest expression and the somber tone of her voice. "In all the time I've known him, he hasn't once given Laura reason to doubt that he'd be home with her and the kids exactly when he was supposed to."

"Something's happened to him," Laura insisted.

The detective studied her with disconcerting innocence. "Do you think there's been foul play?"

"Clearly."

"It isn't possible that he just needed a break?"

"A break from what?" Laura knew the man was doing his job; still, she resented his suggestion. "We're his family. We love him, and he loves us. And he loves his work. Besides, he's already planning a break. We're going to the Caribbean in January."

"What Detective Melrose is asking," Daphne said in a dry tone as she turned away from the window to approach the group, "is whether Jeff might have cracked."

"No way!" Debra cried. She was sitting close beside Laura and hadn't budged from the house since she'd come home from school at two—after skipping history, she had told Laura, with a defiance that Laura didn't have the strength to fight.

"My husband is totally sane," Laura informed the detective. "He's happy and healthy, at least he was when he left here yesterday morning. If anything was bothering him, I would have known."

The detective made a note in his book. "Okay. Can you give me a description? How tall is he?"

She swallowed. Statistics were so stark. But necessary, she told herself. "Six feet."

"Weight?"

"One-sixty."

"He plays tennis," Debra reminded the detective.

David added, "A mean game. He beat the pants off me when we played last summer."

"Okay, he's athletic. And competitive. Eye color?"

"Not competitive," Laura corrected. "He really isn't."

"Sure he is," Daphne said.

"Not intensely. He doesn't get hung up on being first. He's easygoing that way."

When no one challenged her, the detective said, "Eye color?"

"Brown," she answered.

"Hair?"

She put a hand to her throat. Taking Jeff apart, feature by feature, was gruesome in the same way that some of her imaginings had been.

Daphne came to her aid. "Brown, side-parted, trim cut, neatly combed. And he wears glasses. Wire-rimmed ones."

"Is there a picture I can see?"

Laura sent Debra to get one.

"What was he wearing when last seen?"

"Uh, a suit." She tried to think back thirty-six hours, but she'd been busy getting herself and her thoughts organized for the day, while Jeff had been dressing. "A dark suit." All his suits were dark. Dark and sedate, which was the image he chose. "Blue, I think."

"Three-piece?"

"No. Jacket and trousers. White shirt. Striped tie." It was a fair guess. Most of his shirts were white, most of his ties striped.

Debra returned with the picture and handed it to Laura, who held it for a minute, studying Jeff's face. It was a kind face and a dependable one, two qualities that had drawn her to him from the first and hadn't changed. He was a good-looking man, well-kept, in his prime. She was sure he would have been able to defend himself against a mugger—unless a gun or a knife had been involved. With a shudder, she passed the picture to the detective.

"Can I hang on to this for now?" he asked.

She nodded.

He reached for his topcoat. "I'll go back to the station and type all this up. Once the report is filed, we may be able to come up with something."

Laura stood. "How soon?"

"I'll have men at work on it tonight."

"How soon do you think you'll come up with something?"

He slipped the picture from its frame. "As soon as we can."

But Laura needed specifics. Jeff was her husband. She was terrified for him. "In general, what is your experience in cases like this?"

He shrugged. "If there's been foul play, we should be able to pick up on it pretty quick. If not, it may be awhile."

"If not? What do you mean, if not?"

"If he's split on his own."

"He hasn't," Laura said, looking him straight in the eye. One policeman was as bad as the next. But she needed them. They had access to resources she didn't have and experience in locating missing persons. So she would use them.

She walked him to the door and managed a gracious goodbye, but the instant he was gone she set off for the kitchen. She was putting the coq au vin on to heat when the others joined her.

"There," David said with satisfaction. "Now that that's done, we can expect some results." He threw an arm around her shoulder. He was a bear of a man, dark and bearded, as unlikely-looking an accountant as Jeff was a likely-looking one. "Don't worry, hon. The police know what they're doing. This is their business. They'll find him. And in the meanwhile, we have everything under control at the office. Jeff's accounts won't fall behind."

"Did you cancel for tonight?" Elise asked her.

Sliding out from under David's arm, Laura opened a cabinet and rummaged inside. "Uh-huh. It's okay. There were twelve couples invited. One less won't hurt." She had had a worse time explaining to Georgina Babcock why she and Jeff hadn't shown up at the museum, but she'd done it without falling to pieces. Likewise calling the dentist to cancel Jeff's appointment. Likewise calling Lydia. That had been the hardest, trying to learn if Lydia had heard from Jeff without tipping her off about his disappearance.

No, she decided, the call to Scott had been worse. He had been stunned, then frightened. One part of her wished she had spared him that and waited. Selfishly, though, she wanted him home. He was a comfort to her. "Scott is flying in after his classes tomorrow—assuming we haven't found Jeff by then." She set a box of rice on the counter. "He doesn't have classes on Friday."

"Should you have called him so soon?" David asked.

"I was worried he might hear it from someone else."

"But he and Jeff were so close—"

"Are." Laura put a saucepan under the faucet. "He and Jeff *are* so close."

"Scott's nineteen," Debra told David. "He can be here worrying with us. He doesn't have to be pampered all the time."

Laura looked at her. "He isn't pampered."

"He is," she argued, then mimicked, " 'Scott can't do this, he's at school. Scott can't do that, he's at school. Let Scott sleep late, he works so hard. Give Scott a little money, he's earned a little fun.' " The voice became her own again. "What do you think Scott's doing at Penn?"

"Studying," Laura said.

"He's playing. Didn't you hear the message on the machine? He's having the time of his life with his fraternity brothers." Her voice fell. "What a bunch of geeks!"

Laura set the water on to boil. "Scott's friends aren't geeks."

"Didn't you hear the stupid noises they were making?"

"Look who's talking about making stupid noises." Nudging David out of the way, she removed the cutting board from its slot. "What would happen if I were to record every sound you and your friends make at the Stones' concert next week?"

At mention of the concert, Debra went very still. In a vulnerable voice, she said, "I'll be able to go, won't I?"

Laura felt a twinge in the pit of her stomach. She knew just what Debra was thinking. For so long, Jeff had been by her side. Suddenly he wasn't, and she felt disabled. She didn't know how to picture the future, didn't know what would be the same and what wouldn't.

But the confusion wasn't fair to Debra. She was so young. "Of course you'll be able to go to the concert."

"What if Dad's not back?"

"You'll go anyway."

"How can I do that? How can I go and have a fantastic time while he's out there somewhere, missing?"

Laura removed a collander of washed green beans from the refrigerator. "Debra, life isn't going to stop."

"Not for you. Surely not for you. You don't stop for anything. Look at you now. You're fixing a dinner no one is going to eat."

"I'll eat it," David said.

"Do that, and Beth will never forgive me," Laura told him in a subtle hint she followed up not so subtly. "You should run along. You've been a big help, but there's not much more to do."

"I want to be here for you."

"I need some quiet time, I think." David had always liked her a bit more than he should, which was fine as long as Jeff was around. But Jeff wasn't there now, and she felt uncomfortable. "It's okay. I'll be fine."

"There ought to be a man around here."

"Uh, David," Daphne said, predictably annoyed with the comment but in control, "Laura's right. She needs time and space. It's been a tough day. I'm going to try to get her to sleep as soon as she eats, but I can't do that if she has a house full of guests."

"I'm not guests. I'm family. Or almost."

"Then be a dear and understand." Taking him by the arm, she led him from the kitchen. "We'll give you a call if anything happens. If not, Laura will talk with you tomorrow."

More than happy to leave David to Daphne, Laura pulled a long knife from the butcherboard block and began to cut the green beans into small diagonal slices. She hadn't gone through more than a handful when the phone rang.

Debra jumped for it with an expectant "Hello?" After a pause, she said, "Oh. Sure, Gram. Hold on." With a look that said Laura was getting her due, she held out the receiver.

Laura grimaced. She hadn't given a thought to her mother's party. Frantically, she whispered to Elise, "She wants to switch the department Christmas party to the restaurant. It's on the nineteenth. Can we do it?"

Elise held up a let-me-check finger and headed for her purse.

Laura took the phone. "Can I call you back in five minutes, Mom? I'm in the middle of something."

"What's going on over there, Laura?"

Laura swallowed. "What do you mean?"

"Has something happened to Jeff?"

Closing her eyes, she leaned a shoulder against the wall. She should have figured Maddie would find out. It wasn't that the woman was a busybody. Being in a prominent position at the university in a region dominated by academia, she was well known. She was also an authoritative figure, the proverbial horse's mouth, the first one a person would contact to check out something bizarre.

"Who called you?"

"Amanda DeLong. She gave me an earful about Jeffrey just climbing into that car of his and driving away."

Laura felt a flash of anger. "Amanda DeLong is about as reliable now as she was thirty years ago when she left Janie and me in Boston because she finished lunch with her friend, forgot she was supposed to pick us up after the ballet, and drove two hours back home alone. Jeffrey did *not* just climb into his car and drive away!"

"My goodness, you're overreacting."

"Given the day I've had, I can react any way I please!"

"So where's Jeffrey?"

"I don't know! He didn't come home last night. I'm assuming he was hurt or abducted. The police are working on it right now."

"Well," Maddie said with a flourish, "I'm pleased to find out. It's always nice to know about family crises."

Laura sighed. "I'm sorry, Mother, but I've been hoping all day that Jeff would show up so there wouldn't be anything to call you about. We called people—"

" 'We'?"

"David, Daphne, Elise, and me. We called people we thought might have contact with Jeff. Amanda must have talked with Janie. Janie's husband is one of Jeff's tennis partners. They were supposed to play today. We called to let him know Jeff wouldn't be there."

"Does Scott know?"

"I talked with him a little while ago."

"How did he take it?"

"He's upset."

"How do you feel about that?"

"How do you think I feel? I'm upset too."

"I can hear that, Laura, but I'd be careful about letting the children know. With Jeff gone, they'll be looking to you for strength even more than usual, and you'll have to provide it. A trauma like this can wreak havoc with the adolescent self-image—"

"Please, Mom," Laura cut in. She could feel instant analysis coming on. The thought of it made her sweat. "I'm doing all I can. Debra's here, and Scott will be home tomorrow. Until I know more about Jeff, I don't want to get into discussions of psychological ramifications. When it comes to the kids, I'm trusting my instincts as a mother."

"And your instincts as a wife? What do they tell you?"

"That Jeff is out there somewhere needing help."

"Interesting. That can be taken different ways, you know."

Anything could be taken different ways by Maddie when she started in with double meanings, hidden agendas, and Freudian slips. "I have to run, Mom."

"So do I. I have a dinner meeting at seven that will probably run until ten or so, or I'd drop over. Will you be all right?"

Laura wasn't sure, but she knew she'd be better off without Maddie around. "I'll be fine."

"I'd appreciate your keeping me posted, Laura. I don't like hearing family news from other people."

"I'll call you."

"You said you would do that about my party, and you didn't."

Laura sought out Elise, who arrived at her side with the restaurant's December party schedule in her hand. "It's been an impossible day," she said, following Elise's finger. "We've been trying to leave the phone lines open. But I did check. You can have your party at the restaurant as long as you're willing to move it from six to six-thirty. We'll need the extra time to get a four o'clock cocktail party out."

"I suppose that's all right."

"Good. I'm hanging up now, Mom. Have a nice meeting tonight." Before Maddie could say anything more, Laura broke the connection. With barely a breath, she returned to the beans. Her knife blade flew. Heads and tails were discarded, a new handful grabbed, and the slicing repeated, and all the while Laura felt like her competent self. Then the phone rang again, and the knife clattered from her hand. "Hello?"

"Mrs. Frye, this is Donny. Is Deb around?"

With an involuntary moan, Laura looked at Debra, who took off for the other room. Laura put the call on hold, but before she could get back to work the other line rang. "Yes?"

"Laura Frye, please."

The voice was businesslike, not coarse or disguised like a kidnapper's would be, but her heart beat faster. She sent Daphne a frightened look. "Speaking."

"Duggan O'Neil here, from the *Hampshire County Sun*."

Duggan O'Neil. She saw him in her mind, a man in his mid-forties, rumpled about everything except the pen and paper in his hand. He was nearly as bad as a kidnapper. That pen and paper had power.

The panic she felt showed in her eyes, but she kept her voice commendably steady. "Yes, Mr. O'Neil. How are you?"

"I'm fine, thank you. Actually, I'm wondering how you are. I heard your husband disappeared."

She moistened her lips. "Who told you that?"

"It's a matter of public record. I believe a missing persons report has been filed. Is it true?"

She made a frantic gesture toward Daphne, who made a bewildered gesture back. "Uh, can you hold a second, Mr. O'Neil? My other line is ringing." She put him on hold and crushed the phone to her chest. "He knows about the report, Daph. So much for police discretion. Now it'll be splashed all over tomorrow's *Sun*!"

Daphne came close and spoke softly. "It was inevitable."

"But broadcast from here to kingdom come? That makes it so *real*."

"It *is* real, Laura. We don't want it to be, but it is."

"Oh, God." She hugged her stomach. If only Jeff were there! Things were getting out of hand, more so, it seemed, with each hour that passed. She wanted to turn back the clock, to rewind things and make life the way it had been. But she couldn't. If Dennis Melrose didn't make sure of that, Duggan O'Neil would. "What should I tell him?" she asked in a nervous whisper.

"As little as possible. Do you want me to talk?"

One part of Laura wanted that more than anything. The other part sensed that if she didn't give Duggan O'Neil a show of composure, she'd suffer for it. "No." She cleared her throat. "I'll do it." Drawing herself straight, she put the phone to her ear and punched in the call. "I'm sorry. How can I help you?"

O'Neil sounded no worse for the wait. "You can confirm that your husband is missing."

"As you said, a report has been filed with the police."

"Then he has disappeared?"

"Yes."

"Do you have any idea where he might be?"

She answered slowly, as though she were talking to a child. "No. That's why I filed a report with the police."

"When was the last time you saw him?"

"When he left for work yesterday morning."

"Did you talk with him during the day?"

"No. I was working all day myself."

"What time was he due home?"

Laura sighed. Bowing her head, she put a hand to the tense muscles at the back of her neck. "That information is all in the police report, Mr. O'Neil. I don't believe I need repeat it again."

"Then tell me about you. How are you feeling about all this?"

She held the phone away, staring at it as though the man at the other end of the line were insane. "How do you think I'm feeling?" she finally asked in disbelief.

"Upset, maybe. Worried."

"Very perceptive, Mr. O'Neil."

If he was bothered by her sarcasm, he didn't let on. "Do you think your husband may have been kidnapped?"

"Anything is possible."

"Would you pay a ransom if one was demanded?"

"Of course. What kind of question is that?"

"Then there's money in the bank?"

Daphne had told her to say as little as possible, but she couldn't let certain questions and their implications pass. "If you're asking whether my husband and I are so wealthy as to provide grounds for a kidnapping, the answer is no. But if a ransom was asked, I'd do anything I could to raise the money."

"Will this hurt business?"

"Excuse me?"

"Your husband is a successful accountant."

"If he's not here," she snapped, "he can't do any accounting, so yes, business will be hurt."

"Easy, Laura," Daphne warned softly, but Duggan O'Neil was speaking again, capturing Laura's full attention.

"I was thinking of you. Cherries is young and still growing. Part of its appeal is that it's upbeat. Something like this can be a real downer. Are you worried?"

Laura could feel her heart pounding, harder and faster, in equal parts anger and distress. Aware that every word she said was being noted for possible publication, she answered, "Mr. O'Neil, my husband is missing. No one knows where he is. The police have been brought in, but they're not rushing back to me with quick discoveries. Right now, I'm doing whatever I can to find Jeff. But Cherries is operating as usual. I have an excellent support staff to carry on when I can't be there."

"That wasn't what I asked."

"If people choose to boycott the restaurant because they feel my husband's disappearance is a threat to them," Laura declared, "that's their choice. Personally, I have more faith in the residents of Hampshire County. They're smart. They're strong. And they appreciate good food, which is what I give them." She took a fast breath. "Now, if you don't mind, Mr. O'Neil—"

"One last question," he said, and she could sense a subtle change in his tone. It should have warned her, but he spoke again before she could hand the receiver to Daphne. "How about the possibility that your husband skipped town on his own?"

Her hand tightened on the phone. "That's not a possibility."

"A mid-life crisis—"

"Not Jeff."

"Perhaps a secret life—"

"No. I'm sorry, Mr. O'Neil, but your wild speculation is not welcome." With a resounding *thwack*, she hung up the phone. "The gall of that man!" She took a wooden spoon to the chicken and began to stir with a vengeance. "Mid-life crisis! Jeff did not—*would* not—willingly leave here." A chicken leg hit the spoon, sending a spatter of sauce up and out. Swearing, she grabbed a dishtowel and began to blot sauce from her sweater.

In the next instant, Elise took over the stove while Daphne put an arm around Laura's waist. "I think you've had enough of this, Laura. You're ready to drop. Come on upstairs."

"My sweater's a mess."

Taking the towel from her hand, Daphne steered her toward the hall. "The dry cleaner will fix it."

Laura didn't fight her. She didn't have the strength. She was suddenly so tired that the thought of standing on her feet for another minute was torture. Once upstairs in the master bedroom, she sank down on top of the paisley comforter that covered the bed, curled up her legs, and closed her eyes.

"I'm sorry," she whispered.

"For what?"

"Caving in. It was just something about that call. Why did he ask that? Why did the police? Is everyone so cynical they have to look for evil motives behind innocent events?"

"A man's disappearance isn't exactly innocent."

"It is if it's Jeff." Laura paused. In a smaller voice, she asked, "Isn't it?" She opened her eyes to look at Daphne, who had come to sit on the edge of the bed. Daphne was smart. She was worldly and realistic. Laura trusted her. "Jeff wouldn't deliberately leave, would he?"

Daphne looked troubled. "Who knows what another person would do? Do any of us really know each other?"

"Yes," Laura insisted, but weakly. "I know Jeff. I know Debra and Scott and my mother and you and Elise."

"But deep inside another person's mind—can anyone else really be there?"

The words weren't spoken lightly. But then, they never were. Daphne was a serious, straightforward woman and a good friend. Laura could count on her for an honest opinion. "Do you think he might have done it, Daph?"

"Gone on his own?" She gave the possibility more consideration than Laura liked, before shaking her head. "And it doesn't make any sense to dwell on it. The police will do everything they can."

"In the meantime, what do I do? Debra thinks we ought to sit here waiting for something to happen, but what if nothing does? What if Jeff's gone for days? There's a big void here where he should be. What do I do with it?"

"You work. You said it to O'Neil. Business goes on as usual."

"But I don't have to be there. I'm with the production team, not the cast. With Elise handling bookings and PR, and DeeAnn hostessing and managing the restaurant, and people like Sue and Dave and Jasper running the catering crews, I don't have to *be* there."

A bit dryly, Daphne said, "Would you rather be here waiting by the phone every day?"

"You know I wouldn't. I'd go mad."

"Then keep busy."

"People will think I'm awful."

"Since when do you care what people think?"

"Since I got into a business where it mattered. Since Duggan O'Neil pointed it out."

"Duggan O'Neil is a whore," Daphne said with a look of disdain. "He'd suggest anything, just to get a rise out of you. That's his business, Laura." With barely a pause, she said, "What else would you expect from someone who works for Gary Holmes?"

Laura grunted. Garrison Holmes III was the publisher of the *Sun* and as right-wing as they came. His editorials were notorious. The man himself was notorious. In his late seventies and more handsome than any man that age had a right to be, he was on his fourth wife, was rumored to have illegitimate children scattered around the globe, yet raged on against the poor and oppressed for doing the same. That was only one of his pet peeves. Another was the welfare system, which he considered a hand out for lazy good-for-nothings. Another was the criminal court system, which he felt pandered to thugs.

"Duggan needs headlines," Daphne went on, "and when they don't pop up on their own, he helps them along."

Laura thought back wearily to the things she'd said. "I gave him a few, I guess."

"Not too bad. If he quotes you, he'll be indicting himself for putting asinine questions to a woman under stress."

"If he quotes me. But you know he won't. He'll pick and choose words and phrases and put them into whatever context he wants. God," she said, "I wish he hadn't called. We could have used a little more time. Come morning, every one of Jeff's clients will know something's wrong."

"They would have found out anyway."

"What will I tell Lydia?"

"That you're doing everything you can to find Jeff."

"And Debra? Everyone at school will know. She has trouble concentrating on work as it is. Now it'll be a whole lot harder. She won't even be able to pretend nothing's wrong."

"Debra will do fine," Daphne insisted and gave an affectionate smile. "She's a hot sketch."

"Mmmm. Mouthy. She can complain that I'm running around doing things with Jeff missing, but she'll be at that Stones concert. Even if Jeff's not back, she'll go. She'll also go to New York with you. She's been asking if the trip was on this year."

"Of course it's on," Daphne said. "I wouldn't miss spending a few days on the town with my favorite sixteen-year-old."

"She adores you, Daph."

"The feeling's mutual." Her voice grew nostalgic. "I remember when she was born. Seems like yesterday."

Laura's voice, too, was soft, but from exhaustion. "It wasn't. I have the gray hairs to prove it."

"Where?"

"Under the color Julian puts on." She let her eyes drift shut. "Same auburn as when I was little."

"Don't talk. Go to sleep."

"Where do you think Jeff is?"

"I don't know."

"Do you think he's okay?"

There was a pause. "Yes, I think he's okay."

"Will he be back?"

"Uh-huh."

Laura took a breath that would have been a yawn if she'd had the strength to open her mouth wide. "I should take this sweater off," she mumbled.

"Later."

She felt the mattress shift when Daphne stood. Moments later, she was covered by the afghan that normally lay on the end of the chaise lounge. "Thanks, Daph," she whispered.

"My pleasure," Daphne whispered back and gave her shoulder a squeeze. "Get some sleep. I'll be downstairs."

Laura wanted to tell Daphne to go home and sleep. She wanted to remind Daphne that she couldn't miss another day of work. Law practices were serious things. Clients depended on Daphne. So did her partners.

But Laura was too tired to say anything more and too eager to escape into oblivion to risk anything that might delay it. So she simply pulled the afghan up to her chin and let go.

FIVE

MOVEMENT ON THE BED woke her. Feeling as though she were forcing her way from a sleep miles deep, she shifted, then drifted.

"Mom? Wake up, Mom. There's something you have to see."

It was Debra's voice. A maternal sixth sense nudged Laura further awake. "Hmm?" she whispered.

"Wake up."

With an effort, Laura opened her eyes. Debra was sitting on the edge of the bed in a pool of early morning light that made Laura squint. "What is it,

babe?" she murmured, but the words were no sooner out when reality re-
turned in a rush. She pushed herself up, pushed a handful of hair off her face.
Wide-eyed, she looked from Debra's pale face to the newspaper she held.
Reluctantly, she reached for it.

LOCAL CPA VANISHES WITHOUT A TRACE, the headline read, jumping out at
her from the bottom-left column of page one. Beside it was Jeff's picture, but
Laura's eyes went to the words that followed.

> Jeffrey Frye, prominent Northampton accountant, was officially identified as
> a missing person by the Northampton Police Department last night after his
> wife, Laura Frye, filed a report. According to that report, Frye failed to
> return home after work Tuesday night and hasn't been heard from since. In
> an interview with the *Sun*, a distraught Mrs. Frye confirmed her husband's
> disappearance and admitted that she had been busy with her own work on
> Tuesday and hadn't spoken with him since that morning.
>
> A lifelong resident of Hampshire County, Frye graduated from
> Northampton High in 1967. In 1971, he received a business degree from the
> University of Massachusetts, where he was known to be a loner but a hard
> worker. That image carried over into his work and translated into significant
> earning potential. In addition to bankrolling his wife's restaurant, Cherries,
> which opened on Main Street two years ago, Frye owns a brick Tudor in the
> exclusive Child's Park area of Northampton. He also purchased a condomin-
> ium in Holyoke last summer and a Porsche, which sources say he had always
> wanted.
>
> His wife insists that Frye's disappearance will have no impact on her
> business, which sources say is having a record season. According to those
> sources, Mrs. Frye is capable of carrying on without her husband.
>
> Detective Dennis Melrose of the Northampton Police Department has
> announced that a search is already under way. So far, there has been no sign
> of Frye in the area, but the police intend to broaden their search today. A
> crew is ready to dredge the lake, and the canine corps will comb the sur-
> rounding woods.
>
> Melrose did not rule out the possibility that Frye masterminded his own
> disappearance. "Men have been known to vanish for personal reasons. If we
> come up with any in this case, we'll certainly check them out."
>
> Mrs. Frye has vehemently denied any possibility that her husband walked
> out of his own accord.

Laura dropped the paper on the bed. Her jaw was clenched, her lips thin.
Fighting fury, she wrapped her arms around Debra and held on tight.

"He didn't leave on his own," Debra asked, "did he?"

"No."

"And he isn't a money grubber."

"No."

"Why does the article sound that way?"

"Because that's how newspapers work. When there isn't much of a story,
they try to spice things up."

"I thought journalists were supposed to be accurate."

"Not Duggan O'Neil. We don't own a condo in Holyoke. I don't know where he got that idea."

"Aren't you upset?"

"About the article? I'm livid."

"You don't sound it."

"Because I'm tired." Despite the night's sleep, she felt emotionally drained, which in itself was discouraging. "And confused. And worried. This article is annoying, but it's just an article. Daddy's still missing."

"All the kids in school will know now."

"It'll be okay."

"Fine for you to say. You're not the one who has to walk by them in the halls after your dad was accused, on the front page of the local rag, of masterminding his own disappearance."

"Duggan O'Neil doesn't know what he's talking about."

"Tell that to the kids at school."

"You tell them. They'll listen."

Debra sighed. "You sound so sure. You're *always* so sure."

Laura drew back. She used her thumb to erase the tiny crease between Debra's eyes. "Is there any other way to be?"

"Yeah. Scared."

"I'm that, too. But I can't let it paralyze me."

"So you're going to work today, huh?"

"First I'll have to go over to Nana Lydia's. If she doesn't see the paper herself, someone else will call her."

"Poor Nana Lydia."

Laura smiled. Debra had always loved Jeff's mother. She felt the same kind of compassion for her that Laura did, but then, Lydia inspired it. She was a soft, sweet, gentle lady. "I wish I could spare her the torment. But she'll have to know."

"Maybe I could come with you when you tell her?"

"Uh-uh. You're going to school."

Pulling a face, Debra said, "And you'll go to the restaurant?"

Laura hesitated. "Maybe."

"Just like nothing's wrong?"

"No. Something's wrong. I won't forget it for a minute. But the police are out looking for your dad, and there's work to be done. Like I told you last night, life goes on."

Twisting away, Debra stood and scowled. "When you say things like that, you sound like the coldest person on earth."

"But you know better," Laura said, in an attempt to tease the scowl away.

"I don't." She took a fast breath, hesitated, then went on. "Y'know, it's not so hard to believe that Dad deliberately skipped that art opening Tuesday night. He hates art. He only goes to those things because you drag him."

Laura was stung by the accusation. "He goes to cultivate clients. It's important to his career."

"So he can bankroll Cherries and buy the brick Tudor and the Porsche?"

"Which, sources say, he always wanted," Laura put in. If Debra could quote Duggan O'Neil, so could she. "What are you suggesting, Debra?"

"Nothing." She headed for the door.

"Should I remind you that your father also pays for your clothes, which aren't cheap, and your vacations, and your braces, and the tutoring that will hopefully keep your grades high enough to get you into a decent college?"

At the door, Debra turned. "I'm not going to college. I've told you that."

"College costs a whole lot, but your father will pay without blinking an eye."

"I'm not going."

Laura saw the stubbornness on Debra's face, just as she'd seen it over and over again in the course of sixteen years. Debra was willful. Sweet and spunky, but willful. But Laura wasn't in the mood to lock horns with her. "We'll discuss that later."

"Yeah," Debra drawled and turned again to leave.

"What does *that* mean?"

"You'll be at Cherries later."

"If I go. But I'll be home after that."

"You'll be busy with other things," Debra called from the hall.

"Then we'll discuss it another time." Laura left the bed and went to the door. "Debra, you're a junior in high school. It's not like a decision has to be made today."

"That's not the point," Debra said, going into her room.

"Then what is?"

"Never mind."

"Debra?" There was no answer. "Debra!"

"I'm getting dressed. Donny is picking me up soon."

"I thought we agreed you'd take the bus to school."

"Given the shit I'll have to take when I *get* to school today, I think a ride might be nice."

Laura opened her mouth to argue, then closed it again. She didn't trust Donny McKenzie. But she did trust Debra, and Debra had a point. School was going to be tough.

Turning back into her own bedroom, Laura remembered when Debra was little, when she could protect her—and Scott—from the outside world. She wished she could do that now, wished it desperately. But she couldn't.

Raising her eyes, she moved them slowly around the room, from the bed that had never been pulled back that night, to the closets that hadn't been opened, the alarm clock that hadn't been set, the bench that hadn't been sat on, the books that hadn't been read.

She thought of Jeff, whose absence was growing more ominous by the minute, and though Laura had never wanted protection over the years, she felt strangely in need of it now.

Lydia Frye lived in a modest white-frame house off Elm Street. It was the house her husband, William, had owned, the one in which Christian and Jeff had grown up. For twenty years, the house had been in a state of decline. For the last ten of those twenty, Laura had been urging Lydia to sell it and move.

"A garden apartment would be perfect. You wouldn't have the responsibility of upkeep, and there would be people around. I worry about you sometimes."

But Lydia wouldn't hear of moving. She was attached to the house, she argued back. It was hers; she owned it outright. She had lived there too long to abandon it just because the roof needed reshingling or the water heater had gone. So Laura had hired a roofer to do the reshingling and a plumber to replace the water heater. And an electrician to rewire the kitchen. And a tile layer to retile the bathrooms. And she'd been happy to do it, because Lydia was so pleased with the results, and when Lydia was pleased, so was Laura.

Laura adored her mother-in-law. She had felt drawn to her from the first time they'd met, when she and Jeff had announced their engagement. Laura was still seventeen, Jeff was still in college, and they had been dating for only three weeks. Everyone had been stunned except Lydia. She had looked at Laura with approval, then had turned her sparkling eyes on her son and given him her blessing.

Many times over the years, Laura had wondered about that approval. She liked to think that Lydia saw in her many of the same qualities she possessed herself—a keen nesting instinct, natural curiosity, resourcefulness—and though those qualities had taken different twists in Laura over the years, Lydia had supported her all the way. For that reason and others, Laura felt closer to Lydia than to her own mother. Lydia was approachable. Laura could talk to her. She was quiet and nonjudgmental, and though she had definite opinions on most any subject, she didn't foist those opinions on others. She was a liberal in the broadest sense of the word, which was why, Laura assumed, she could let Christian go his own way. Then again, maybe she could do that because she had Jeff.

That thought filled Laura with dread as she drove her Wagoneer up to the small white house on Thursday morning. Fearing that the paper would do damage before Lydia could be properly prepared, Laura had left the house shortly after Debra and driven directly over. The newspaper was on the walk. Tucking it under an arm along with the wedge of Black Forest cake and half a dozen pillow cookies she'd wrapped in a bag, she rang the doorbell—her usual signal: two short, one long, one short—and unlocked the door with her key.

"Lydia?"

"I'll be right there," Lydia called from the room they had converted into a bedroom five years before, when crippling arthritis had made climbing the stairs an ordeal. The room was on the first floor not far from the kitchen, which facilitated things on those bad days when Lydia used a wheelchair.

"Do you need any help?" Laura called.

"No, Laura, I'm fine. I have water on for tea. Why don't you help yourself?"

Any other woman might have wondered what Laura was doing there so early in the morning, but in this, too, Laura and Lydia saw eye to eye. They were both morning people. Laura often stopped at Lydia's before eight.

Going into the kitchen, she had two cups of tea steeping by the time Lydia appeared at the door, and a heartrending picture she made. A small woman, with snow-white hair and the fine features that age like porcelain, she had a fragile look, so much so that Laura had often marveled that she had given birth to such strapping men as Jeff and, even more so, Christian. She was leaning heavily on a cane as she made her way forward.

Meeting her halfway, Laura gave her a hug, then helped her to a chair. "How are you?" she asked softly.

Lydia gave her a sad smile. "Stiff." After the briefest pause, she added, "Worried."

Laura caught her breath. Her eye flew to the paper, which was still in a roll on the table.

"MaryJean Wolsey called," Lydia explained. Her voice creaked as her swollen joints might have had she been on her feet and moving. "When I put what she said together with your very careful phone call yesterday, I knew I didn't need the paper for verification."

"Lord, Lydia, I'm sorry. I was hoping he'd be back before I had to tell you."

"I figured as much. Is there anything new?"

Laura shook her head.

"How are things at the house?"

"Quiet. Strange. Tense."

"Is my favorite granddaughter giving you trouble?"

"Not really. She's just upset." Laura looked at her mother-in-law, looked at the gentle blue eyes—Christian's eyes—that had seen their share of heartache over the years. Lydia had lost one child in infancy, a girl who had come between Christian and Jeff. She had lived through her husband's stroke and early death. She had seen Christian come and go, come and go, and now Jeff, her baby, was missing. "How are you, Lydia?"

"Oh, I'll be all right."

"They'll find him. We have to believe that."

"I know."

Laura could have sworn she heard resignation, which was odd. She would have expected fear or doubt instead. Puzzled, she took Lydia's gnarled hand. "The police are doing everything they can."

"I'm sure they are."

"And there hasn't been any sign of violence, so we can be hopeful that Jeff is well."

Lydia nodded. Her eyes grew moist.

"What is it?" Laura asked in a whisper.

Lydia's mouth turned down at the corners. She frowned, then shrugged.

"What?"

"I don't know. Something in his eyes when he stopped over here the other day."

"The other day?" He hadn't told Laura.

"Monday afternoon." She smiled and cocked her head toward the vase at the center of the table. "He brought me tulips."

Laura was stunned. She had assumed the flowers to be from one of the friends who periodically stopped in. But from Jeff? Jeff was great at calling the flower shop and having bouquets sent. He did that often. Laura couldn't remember the last time he'd delivered flowers himself.

Feeling a yawing in the pit of her stomach, she forced herself to ask, "Did he say anything unusual?"

"No. Nothing unusual."

"Did he say *anything?*"

"Just that work was going well. And you and Debra were fine, but I already knew that, because I'd talked with you that morning."

Laura took a sip of tea, but it dribbled down a chip on the rim of the cup. She wiped her chin with her hand, then wiped her hand with a paper napkin. "He didn't—uh, say anything about needing to get away?"

"No."

"But there was something in his eyes?" She looked up at Lydia. "What was it? I have to know."

Lydia took awhile to gather her thoughts. She was still frowning when she said, "A look. Sadness. Discouragement. I knew that look. I used to see it when he was little, when something disappointed him in school, when he didn't do well in a test, or he wasn't elected to the student council, or he asked a girl to the prom and she turned him down." Her wrinkles shifted around the saddest of smiles. "Boys suffer, too, about things like that. And mothers of boys. Your Scott is more like Christian that way; things come easily. Not for Jeffrey, though. He used to try his best, then come in second." She stopped talking. After a minute, more softly, she said, "That was the way he looked, as though he'd tried his best but failed. I'm worried."

So was Laura, more than ever. "Did you ask him about it?"

"Oh, yes. He assured me nothing was wrong. But when he left he didn't say he'd talk with me soon."

The significance of that wasn't lost on Laura. *Talk with you soon, Mom.* It was Jeff's trademark, the way he ended every visit, every phone call to Lydia. He wouldn't tell her he loved her, he was too reserved for that, and he wouldn't tell her he'd see her soon, because if things were busy, he might not. But if he couldn't visit, he did call.

"Was something bothering him, Laura?"

Laura was asking herself the same question. "I don't know," she said. "I didn't see anything. He didn't say anything."

"Was he more quiet than usual?"

"I don't think so, but things have been so busy lately that he hasn't had much of a chance to *be* more quiet than usual. At least, not with the two of us alone." Horrible thoughts were chasing one another around in her mind, making her feel empty and alone. "He wasn't unhappy. He didn't *look* unhappy. If he'd been unhappy, he would have told me."

"He should have."

"Even if he hadn't, I would have *sensed* it. You don't live with a man for twenty years and not be tuned in to his moods," she said with conviction, then added, less sure, "Do you?"

"Only if you don't care for him. But you do, Laura. You've been good to Jeffrey."

Laura wondered how "good" was defined. If it meant looking pretty and acting poised, raising beautiful children, keeping a perfect house, and having a successful career at the same time that she made sure that there were always clean shirts in his drawer, she had been good to Jeff. If it meant spending hours over dinner or an evening or a weekend with him, she hadn't been so good. But he'd never complained. Hadn't he been the one to urge her expansion of Cherries into a large rented kitchen and then a restaurant?

Clinging to those thoughts, she searched Lydia's eyes. "We'll find him."

"Yes."

"Will you come stay at the house until we do?"

"No. I'm comfortable here. I have everything I need. I can get around. And besides, if Jeffrey were to call . . ." her voice trailed off, but the point was made. If Jeff were to call, she wanted to be there for him.

Laura nodded. She wished she could have said she had been thinking solely of Lydia, but her motives were partly selfish. Lydia had a quiet strength that Laura and Debra could have used. "Lydia?"

"Hmmm?"

Laura frowned. She was thinking of what Daphne had suggested. "Is there any chance that Jeff might have contacted Christian?"

Taking a spoon to her tea, Lydia considered that. After several stirrings, she tapped the spoon on the rim of the cup and set it gently in the saucer. "I honestly don't know. For a short time, when they were small, they were close. But that changed. As you know. Things came between them."

Though the words were offered innocently enough, Laura looked away. Of all the things she and Lydia had discussed over the years, the rift between Christian and Jeff wasn't one.

If Lydia was thinking the same thing, she didn't let on. "Christian came to symbolize everything Jeffrey wasn't, which isn't to say that Jeffrey didn't want to be like him a little. But he couldn't. It wasn't in his nature. The times when he was most upset with himself were times when he tried to compare himself to Christian, so I taught him not to make those comparisons. I taught him that he was a very different person from Christian." She sighed. "I don't know if I succeeded, but no, I doubt if Jeffrey would have taken his failures to Christian."

"Failures?" Laura cried. "What failures? Look at Jeff's life. He's been a total success."

"Success is relative. Each person defines it differently."

"But look what he *has.* Look at Scott and Debra and the house and his firm. How can a life with those things be considered anything *but* a success?"

"Success is relative," Lydia repeated.

Laura let out a breath. She supposed that there, too, Lydia was right, though it boggled her mind to think of the kind of life Jeff wanted if he didn't call this one a success.

She had never sensed he was unhappy. Never sensed he wanted anything more. Or anything different.

Maybe he hadn't. Maybe what Lydia had seen in Jeffrey's eyes on Monday afternoon had been nothing more than fatigue or a mother's imaginings. When a woman had as much time on her hands as Lydia did, she might easily dwell on a look or read into an expression something that wasn't really there. Laura didn't do that. She didn't have the time.

At the reminder, she glanced at her watch. "I have to get back to the house." She looked at Lydia. "Will you be okay?"

Lydia smiled. "I'll be fine."

"You won't reconsider and come home with me?"

Lydia shook her head. "MaryJean will be stopping by, and Theresa from next door. But I'll be near the phone. If you hear anything, you call."

With a promise that she would, Laura gave her a gentle hug and left.

SIX

❀ ❀ ❀

RESTAURANTS WERE A DIME a dozen in New England college towns, particularly upscale restaurants with cute names and clever menus that included Buffalo chicken wings, Cobb salads, stir-fry anything, and Häagen-Dazs. Cherries' menu included all those, but Laura had a hook. Her specialty was the fruit, used equally as garnish and ingredient. On a given day, a diner could start with cold cherry soup, move on to cherried duck, and end with cherries jubilee. Not that Laura recommended that particular menu. Cherries were her stock-in-trade, but variety was the spice of life.

That was what she told her staff, whose exacting preparation, artful presentation, and gracious delivery of an ever-evolving array of dishes was what brought patrons back to the restaurant time and again. As for Laura, surrounded continually by food, she rarely ate. Still, when she walked into the restaurant, when she stood in the front foyer and took it all in or worked her way between the tables, greeting people she knew, she felt a sense of pride.

The decor enhanced that pride. Though the restaurant was located in an old stone building that stood shoulder to shoulder with others of its kind and might well have been dark and confining, she had gutted the inside and opened things up, enlarged windows, put in recessed lighting, and painted everything white. Then she had decorated with plants—lush, green, live ones that required a great deal of care but were worth it. So were the trellised archways dividing one eating area from the next, and the natural-oak bar, with its high stools, its suspended stemmed glasses of every size and shape, and the imported porcelain that stood as art. The tables were of wicker, the same light oak shade, with glass inserts, but the chairs—the chairs were Laura's pièce de résistance. Interspersed with traditional wicker ones, all with seats cushioned in rich green and burgundy, were graceful chairs with high fan backs.

Laura's idea of luxury was sharing brunch with friends at an alcove table, each of them perched on a peacock throne, shielded from the rest of the world by lavish cascades of Swedish ivy.

Tuesday mornings were like that. Those were the times, before the restaurant opened to the public, when she met with Daphne, Elise, and DeeAnn to talk business. At least, that was what they were supposed to talk about, but they usually touched on things like DeeAnn's French manicure, Elise's daughter's birthday party, and Daphne's assault-and-battery-with-intent-to-murder case, while they ate. Jonah would come in early to cook for them, sometimes testing out a new recipe, other times preparing tried-and-true goodies such as Brie-baked eggs, bacon-and-bran muffins, and Bellinis. Eventually the discussion would turn to the new linen place mats Laura wanted to order, or the holiday copy Elise was giving the newspapers, or the parking lot permit Daphne was trying to prize from the city, or DeeAnn's approach to drunken patrons, and when the four of them parted ways, Laura was always left with a warm, secure feeling.

She would have given anything for a little of that warm, secure feeling when she arrived at Cherries on Thursday morning. She felt chilled to the bone and shaken. There was still no news about Jeff.

After returning from Lydia's, she had spent two hours on the phone, first with the police, then with Daphne, then with David, then with a reporter for a local cable station, then with all those friends who called to say they'd seen the article in the paper and would do anything to help. But none had seen or heard from Jeff.

By ten-thirty, she'd had it with answering the phone and feeling helpless, so she had put on a mint green sweatshirt and leggings set, brightened her pale cheeks with blusher, run a vigorous brush through her hair, and gone to Cherries. She didn't know whether her mind was functioning well enough to accomplish much, but, if nothing else, her appearance would bolster her staff, which had to be wondering what effect Jeff's disappearance would have both on the business and on Laura herself.

She came through the back door and went directly into the kitchen, where, amid gleaming stainless steel counters and the scent of warm fresh-baked bread, four people plus her chef, Jonah, were working. "Hi, guys," she said brightly, but the face she made—half smile, half grimace—was a dead giveaway that business as usual wouldn't be easy.

She was immediately surrounded by concerned employees.

"Hi, Laura."

"How *are* you?"

"We can't *believe* what's happened!"

"If there's anything we can do—"

She raised a hand to stop the barrage. Offering a more genuine if tired smile, she said softly, "Thanks. I'm doin' okay."

"Has there been any word?"

"Not yet."

"No leads?"

"Not yet."

"They'll find him."

"I'm sure they will."

"Have you eaten?"

When she shook her head, the one who had asked, Annie, the baker of the bunch, reached into a nearby bin and handed her a warm croissant. "On the house," she said, grinning.

Laura took the croissant, bit off an end, and rolled her eyes.

"Not that you feel like eating," Annie said with a knowing look.

Annie was in her mid-twenties, as were most of Laura's kitchen staff. Like the others, she hoped to move on one day to bigger and better kitchens, in Boston, New York, or even Paris. In the meantime, she learned her trade under Jonah, who, at twenty-eight, had not only a degree from the Culinary Institute but three years' experience as a sous-chef in Quebec. He was a tough master, but the results were worth it. Working at Cherries held a certain status. Laura knew that if Annie were to leave, it wouldn't be out of discontent or boredom.

"I'll eat," Laura assured her. Catching sight of Jonah separating himself from the others and moving toward the door that led into the restaurant, she joined him out of earshot of the rest.

"Are you okay?" he asked, in a voice so gentle that if it had been anyone but Jonah she would have leaned into him for a hug. But Jonah wasn't a toucher. He was macho and aloof. Of average height with a tapering body, pale gray eyes, and thick blond hair, he was a low-key operator who, with a minimum of words and motion, did wonders in the kitchen. Laura was glad to have him as her chef.

"I'm fine."

"You look tired."

"I am."

"How's things at home?"

"Tough." She pulled at the croissant. "It's the same, but so different. Scottie's coming in later today. He'll stay for the weekend, then go back if nothing's happened by Monday."

"Is Debra behaving?"

Laura smiled. Debra had a crush on Jonah, which meant that, in an attempt to sound mature and independent, she mouthed off whenever she saw him, usually at Laura's expense. "Debra's being Debra. She's upset. She doesn't understand what's happening any more than I do." She took a small bite of the swatch of croissant she'd torn from the whole.

"That was an interesting article in the paper. O'Neil sure got his little digs in. What'd ya do to annoy him?"

"I didn't like some of his questions, and I let him know it." She glanced toward the seating area of the restaurant, where DeeAnn was checking the table settings—stunning, sexy DeeAnn, whose appreciation of men came second only to her appreciation for the finer things in life, like Chanel scarves and Dom Perignon.

"Did you mean what you said about the business?"

Laura looked right back at him. If maintaining morale was the issue, convincing Jonah that all was well was critical. "I did. Everything goes on as usual. Jeff's absence won't affect things here. He wasn't active in the everyday workings of the restaurant."

"He wasn't active in *any* part of the restaurant," Jonah said with an archness that took Laura aback.

A bit defensively, she said, "He was the money behind it."

"Maybe, but it must be showing a profit by now."

"There's still a mortgage on the building and loans for the renovation. But we're breaking even." She put the swatch of croissant in her mouth.

"Take credit where credit is due," Jonah advised. "You're the brains behind this operation. You built the catering service from nothing and you conceived of the restaurant. You were the one who found the building, chose the furnishings, hired the staff. It's been your baby all the way."

"I couldn't have done it without Jeff."

"Sure you could have. You're one strong lady. You can carry on just fine." He winked and drawled, "That's a vote of confidence, Mama." Then he flashed her a brilliant grin.

"Look out for those grins," DeeAnn shouted from across the restaurant. Seconds later, she was headed their way. "Those are killer grins. They blind you; then, when you can't see the forest through the trees, they zap you dead."

"Zap you dead?" Laura echoed. She looked at Jonah, whose grin grew lazy.

"But it's okay," DeeAnn said, coming up between them. "Anyone with buns like these—" she gave the backside in question a pat, "—can zap me dead any day." When Jonah spared her a bored look and calmly sauntered away, she slipped an arm around Laura. "How're you doin'?"

"Hangin' in there, Dee."

"They'll find him."

"God, I hope so."

"I know so. Jeff is too much of a homebody to be gone for long. He'll miss you. He'll come back. You'll see."

Laura eased back to look at DeeAnn. In a controlled voice, she said, "If he didn't leave of his own free will, he may not be able to return that way. Missing me may have nothing to do with it. I don't know why people assume that he just up and took off."

"I'm not assuming that. But Jeff *is* a homebody. He likes this place because it's familiar. He sits there at the bar, getting pleasure watching you come and go, and when he orders it's always one of the same few favorites. You can be sure he'll fight to get back here." She frowned. "What do you think, Laura? He's been gone a day and a half. Where do you think he is?"

Laura had spent nearly every wakeful minute of that day and a half wondering and worrying. Now, croissant in hand as she walked aimlessly into the restaurant, she wondered and worried some more. "I don't know. I don't think it was a car accident. We'd have known. The police have checked all the roads and the hospitals, and there's nothing."

DeeAnn walked beside her. "Are they still planning to dredge the lake?"

Laura shot her a sidelong glance. "You read Duggan O'Neil too?"

"Everyone reads Duggan O'Neil."

"Well, he was wrong about that. Or misleading. The police are not planning to dredge the lake. He asked whether they'd do it if there was cause, and they said they would. But there isn't any cause. As of nine-thirty this morning, they've been around every inch of that lake, and there isn't a single tire track remotely like one the Porsche would leave." Reaching one of the alcoves, she mounted the step and slipped into a peacock chair. "There's still a chance that he blacked out, came to with amnesia, and is off driving God only knows where. But at some point he'd stop for gas and get a look at his credit card, or the name and address on his license."

DeeAnn slipped into the adjacent chair. "What if he was robbed? If his ID was taken and he had amnesia, he wouldn't know where to go. He could have been tied up and stuck in the back seat, then driven out of the county, out of the state, and into the Midwest. He could have been dumped on a deserted road between cornfields in Wisconsin."

"In the middle of winter," Laura added dryly. "Thanks a heap, Dee." She tugged off a piece of croissant, then dropped both that piece and what was left of the whole on a dish.

"But winter or not, if he's on a road, he'll be found. He'll be *found*, Laura."

Laura nodded. She had to believe that. Even if he *did* leave on his own, which she refused to consider seriously despite Lydia's comment about the look in his eye, he would be found. Fingering the stem of a spoon, where CHERRIES was engraved in tiny block letters, she said, "In the meanwhile, we operate as usual."

"Will you be here or at home?"

"I don't know." She prodded the croissant with the spoon. "Some of each, I guess." One part of her was itching to go to the lower kitchen and pitch in, preparing food for the day's catered events. The other part was already wondering whether anyone had come to the house or called—and she hadn't been gone half an hour. "Scott's coming home. I want to spend time with him. But I want everyone here to know that the business is fine." Setting the spoon aside, she began shredding the croissant.

"People will talk," DeeAnn said softly.

"I know." She pulled one piece off, then another.

"They'll sit here, have a glass or two of wine, and speculate about Jeff over their salads."

"Uh-huh." She pulled off a third piece, then a fourth.

"If they ask me what I know, what should I say?"

Laura gave a crooked grin and pulled some more. "You could hit 'em with that story about the cornfield."

DeeAnn put her hand over Laura's to stop the shredding. "Seriously."

Taking an unsteady breath, Laura said, "Use your judgment. I trust you." And she did. They had met eight years before, when DeeAnn had answered an ad in the paper and come to work for Laura's catering business. She hadn't known much about food, but early on it had become clear that she was a whiz with people. Shapely, with a stylish mane of sandy waves and skin that looked more twenty-six than thirty-six, she was an eye-catching woman and a natural now as the restaurant's hostess. She was friendly and upbeat, good with names, faces, and favorite drinks—and not only with men. Women liked her too. Besides, she was tactful. She knew not to seat the head of the Amherst History Department anywhere near the head of the Smith History Department in the days immediately following the awarding of a hotly contested grant to one or the other. Politics was alive and well in western Massachusetts, and DeeAnn Kirkham was very much tuned in.

Yes, Laura trusted her. DeeAnn was perfectly capable of managing the restaurant in her absence.

Feeling an abrupt need to move, she said, "I think I'll run downstairs." She studied the mangled croissant. "What a mess."

"Not to worry," DeeAnn said and handed her a burgundy napkin that had been folded into a fan nearby. "Wipe up. It's buttery."

Laura wiped. Then she glanced at her watch. It was eleven-fifteen. The restaurant would open at eleven-thirty. "Are you set for lunch?" Even as they talked, two of her waiters had arrived.

"I'm set. You go on. I'll handle things here."

Laura smiled her thanks. The fact was that, aside from the need to be up and active, she wasn't in the mood to face patrons. She knew too many of them, and DeeAnn was right; they would ask questions. Well, she didn't feel like answering. Not until she had something to say.

So she went back through the kitchen and down the stairs. At the bottom, she was greeted by those of the catering crews whose job it was to prepare food. They too had seen the newspaper article. Each offered words of encouragement before returning to work.

Taking an apron from the shelf, Laura joined them, and for a short time she was able to immerse herself in cutting, slicing, stuffing, and skewering. Soft rock wafted from a radio high on the wall, blending in with occasional conversation to create a pleasant environment. As long as Laura concentrated on that environment, she was fine. Inevitably, though, her thoughts turned to Jeff. When twice running she found herself slicing air rather than mushroom, she dropped the knife and mopped her damp upper lip with the back of her hand. She took a breath, picked up the knife again, and resumed slicing, only to stop again several minutes later when her hand began to tremble.

Leaving the slicing to someone else, she turned to packing plastic containers with prepared hors d'oeuvres. After half an hour of that, with her stomach clenching and unclenching in much the way her hands would have done had they been free, she removed the apron, said her goodbyes, and returned home. Holding her breath, she opened the garage door to put the Wagoneer inside— but the Porsche wasn't there, and, once inside the house, she found it as empty as when she had left.

There were three messages on the answering machine, though. With a rush of hope, she pushed PLAY. After a beep, the first message came on. "This is Grandy Pest Control. We'll be at your house between eight and ten next Monday morning for your quarterly spraying. If the time is bad, call us back." The man gave the number. Laura made a notation on her calendar, then bit her lip and waited.

The machine beeped again. "Hi, Mrs. Frye," a bright female voice said. "This is Diana from the boutique. The sweater you special-ordered just arrived from Wales. We'll have it here whenever you want to pick it up." Three months it had taken, just as they'd said. Laura jotted down the reminder, then held her breath for the last of the messages to replay. She let it out in a rush of frustration when Maddie's voice came on the line.

"You know how I hate these machines, Laura, but this is important. My phone has been ringing off the hook with calls about the article in the *Sun*. Was it absolutely necessary to speak with that man? The suggestion that you are distraught about your husband but perfectly capable of carrying on at work makes you sound heartless, for God's sake. Jeffrey comes across as being shamelessly materialistic, between the house and the restaurant and the car. And what's this about a condominium in Holyoke? You never told me about any condominium. Are there other things you haven't told me? I would like to know what is happening, so I can answer people in an intelligent manner. I'll be in my office between eleven-thirty and twelve-fifteen. Call me there." The machine beeped off.

Slipping onto a stool by the island, Laura put her head in her hands. Yes, the exterminator could come. Yes, she would pick up the sweater she'd ordered. No, she would not call Maddie back. She was a nervous wreck. She needed comfort. It was a sure bet Maddie wouldn't give it.

Scott arrived at six. He had flown into Bradley Field and been picked up by a girl Laura didn't know, someone named Kelly whom he said he'd dated the summer before. Clearly he had kept in touch with her, and though in other circumstances Laura would have invited her in, she was just as happy to see her little red Chevy drive off. She wanted time alone with Scott, wanted to fill him in on all that had happened, wanted to talk about Jeff.

But if she thought that Scott, by virtue of a closeness with his father, might have some idea of what had happened to him, she was wrong. Scott hadn't a clue.

"All those times you two drove into Boston to go to games at Fenway, what did you talk about?"

"Baseball," Scott answered. He was sprawled on his bed, just as he always was within minutes of arriving home from school. His excuse was that he had to put his duffel in his room, but Laura knew he never felt quite at home until he had reclaimed his turf. Banners covered the walls and trophies lined the shelves, along with other memorabilia of the high school days that had been so happy for him. He was happy in college too, Laura knew, but he wasn't the hero he had been. It didn't matter that he was six-two with broad shoulders and a day's stubble, all of which made him gorgeous in her eyes. In the eyes of the thousands of other students at Penn he was a small fish in a big pond. It had taken him most of freshman year to adjust to that, but by the time he returned home in May with his fraternity pin and a healthy grade point average, his ego had been restored.

Laura had been sure that, with Scott so grown up, Jeff would have had heart-to-heart talks with him. "Didn't your father ever talk about work?"

"No. He wanted to get away from it. That was one of the reasons he liked baseball so much. It was a nine-inning escape. When Dad dreams, I think he sees himself as a professional baseball player."

"Do you really?" Laura asked, surprised.

"Sure."

She remembered what Lydia had said about Jeff always coming in second. Christian hadn't gone into professional baseball, but he'd played varsity in college. Five years later and at a different school, Jeff hadn't made the team. He had married her instead.

"Did he ever say that?" she asked.

"No. But the way he followed the game and shouted tips to the players and criticized the manager, you could tell. But hell, Mom, we're only talkin' dreams. Everyone has dreams."

Laura knew that. Still, she wondered. Sitting sideways in the desk chair, she propped her elbows back on the desk. "Do you think he was unhappy with his work?"

"He liked it just fine."

"Enough to want you to do it?" she teased.

Scott made a face. "He knew not to ask. I was never good at math. I could never do what he does. Besides, he knows I want to be a lawyer."

That had been the plan since the summer, when he'd done an internship with the Legal Aid Society, but before that he had alternately debated being an architect, a psychiatrist, and an investment banker. "You still do?"

He nodded. "A prosecutor. Wouldn't it be wild if I tried a case against Daphne some day?"

"I don't wish that on you. She's tough."

"So they say. Then again, maybe when I'm done working for the prosecution, I'll switch over to the defense side, open my own firm, and take Daphne in when the men in her firm think she's getting too old."

"Daphne too old? Don't hold your breath. She'll outlive her partners."

"But she works too hard. She should be having more fun." When Laura eyed him warily, he said, "You're the one who's always trying to fix her up. If she was willing to look at a younger man, I'd have just the one."

"Who?"

"Alex."

"The friend you had home over Thanksgiving?"

"He thought Daphne was cool."

"Scott, Alex isn't twenty-one yet. Daphne is nearly forty."

"So are you, but the guys think you're a looker. If I were Dad, I'd get back here real quick before someone else makes a move."

Any lightness Laura may have felt in the repartee with her son faded fast. "That was inappropriate, Scott."

"I was just kidding."

"But why would you say it? Or even think it? We believe in fidelity. I don't look at other men; your father doesn't look at other women."

"He looks."

"He does not."

"Mom, I've been *with* him when he's looked. He's not blind. He sees a knockout on the street, and he looks. Do you honestly think I'm the only one waiting for the swimsuit edition every year? He's human. He's a man."

"A *faithful* man."

"But no Don Juan."

"What does *that* mean?"

"It means that he isn't what you'd call romantic."

Laura didn't take the criticism to heart. Scott was stretching, courting adulthood. Putting his father down was one way of boosting himself up. But she couldn't be still. "Sure he is."

Folding his arms behind his head, Scott asked, "What has he done in the last six months that you'd call romantic?"

"He sent me flowers last July, on my birthday."

"He made a phone call and charged it," Scott argued, "which couldn't have taken more than three minutes of his time. I don't call that romantic."

Laura remembered the tulips on Lydia's kitchen table, remembered the surprise she had felt knowing Jeff had brought them. "It's the thought that counts. And what about the ring he gave me for our anniversary?"

"You saw it first, when you and Dad were in Northeast Harbor, and you fell in love with it. Dad thought it was too expensive."

"Unusual," Laura corrected. "He thought it was too unusual." But it was a beautiful ring, hammered gold crisscrossed by silver bands, with a pear-shaped sapphire mounted off-center. "He's used to more traditional things, but he bought it. He phoned the store after we got home and arranged for it to be sent. If that's not romantic, I don't know what is."

"It's a *thing*, Mom. What about something that involves real time and effort and ingenuity?"

"Like what?" Laura asked. She was curious to know what her nineteen-year-old son had in mind.

"Like surprising you with a trip to Paris. Or putting a single rose in a vase and bringing you breakfast in bed. Or hiring a limo and having the guy drive through the Berkshires while Dad makes love to you on the back seat."

Laura arched a brow. "I'm impressed. Where do you get your ideas, Scott?"

He had the good grace to blush, but he wasn't backing down. "Women like romantic gestures. The girls at school are as modern as they come; still, they like it when you give them a book of poems and write something sweet on the flyleaf."

"You do that?"

"Sure."

"I'm really impressed."

"Sure you are, because you're that kind of person. You were always the one who made a big thing out of Valentine's Day or birthdays or Christmas. Dad just went along."

Laura's fingernail caught on a nubby spot on the back of the chair. "Does that have anything to do with what's happening now?" she asked softly.

Scott shrugged. "No. But you idealize him, Mom, and he wasn't perfect."

"Isn't perfect. Your father isn't gone. He'll be back." She tried to sound sure of it, but the conviction wasn't there the way it had been at first. Jeff had been missing for two days. If he'd been in an accident, or suffered from amnesia, he'd already have been found. He didn't have enemies who would want him hurt, and if he had been abducted by a stranger for reasons unknown, surely the Porsche would have been seen.

So, much as she didn't want to, much as she rejected the idea when other people mentioned it, much as the thought of it hurt badly, she had to consider the very remote possibility that Jeff had knowingly driven himself out of town on Tuesday night.

"Scott?"

"Mmmm?"

"Do you think—" she paused, then forced herself on, to get the words out before she lost her nerve, "do you think that it's at all possible your father did want to leave? Do you think maybe he needed a change?"

"If he did, he was crazy."

Laura's smile was a sad one. "You're sweet."

"I mean it," Scott said earnestly.

"And I appreciate that, but I want to know what you think about your father. You're a man—maybe a young one, but still a man. You can vote. You can, God forbid, go to war. You can make love to a woman." When Scott opened his mouth to say something, she held up her hand and said gently, "It's okay. I'd be worried if you couldn't. You're old enough. If you didn't want me to know you were sexually active, you wouldn't have left that box of condoms in your underwear drawer when you went back to school last fall. You knew I'd be putting the clean things back after they were washed. But that's getting off the subject, which is your father. As a man, looking at another man, I want to know if you think he could have left here on his own."

Scott struggled with the question for a moment. "How can I look at him as just another man? He's my father, and you're my mother. Plenty of my friends' parents got divorced while I was growing up, but I never had to worry about that. You and Dad always got along. Our house was always peaceful. Nobody seemed unhappy. When I was saying those things about Dad before, it was more to make the point that, of the two of you, you're the one who's given more. You worked while Dad finished school, then you went back to work when we were little. Dad never changed diapers. You did that, and you fed us and drove us around, and at the same time you were building a career. All Dad did was go to work and come home."

Laura had never looked at their lives that way. "He was always the head of the family."

"In theory. In practice, you're the mover around here. So if you're asking me whether I think Dad walked out, the answer is no. I don't think he'd toss away this life." He paused. "You want my honest opinion?" He sent her a look of scorn far older than his years. "I don't think he has the guts."

Laura didn't get into another discussion with Scott quite like that one. His scorn had stunned her. She had no idea where it had come from, had never seen evidence of it before. But she couldn't deal with it yet. Finding Jeff was her first priority.

The waiting was abominable. She didn't go to the fund raiser for Tom

Connolly, who was a gubernatorial candidate from the home district. Even if it had been appropriate, which it wasn't, she was too shaken to stand around with a drink in her hand and a smile on her face, answering questions. Everyone had seen the paper. The phone hadn't stopped ringing. Though the people who called expressed concern for her, beneath each expression of concern was curiosity. People wanted to know the whole scoop. Laura wished she had it.

Friday morning dawned without Jeff, just as Wednesday and Thursday had. Laura sent Debra to school, left Scott to handle things at home, stopped by to see how Lydia was doing, then went to the restaurant. She had always worked alongside her staff, in part for morale, in part because she liked the people, in part simply because she enjoyed the work. Looking on it as therapy, she went down and up, from one kitchen to the other, until, as had happened on Thursday, she needed to go home.

Nothing had happened there. Scott had fielded calls from Maddie, David, and Elise, a local radio talk-show host, and a handful of friends who were disturbed that the small follow-up article in the newspaper held no news of Jeff. Though Laura would have welcomed news of Jeff from any source, she was relieved that the paper's story had been so bland. Every respite was a blessing, particularly since she was beginning to fear, with each passing day, that Jeff would be gone awhile.

That fear increased as the weekend passed. There was no call from a kidnapper demanding a ransom. There was no call from a neighboring state that Jeff had been found wandering in a daze. There was no call from anywhere that a black Porsche had been abandoned, with or without a body in the trunk.

Left with so little by way of alternatives to cling to, she was beginning, more often, to think that maybe Jeff *had* left on his own. She didn't know why he would do it, or how—just disappearing into thin air that way. But it seemed the one possibility that the police kept coming back to, the one possibility that everyone else kept coming back to. She had begun to feel she was rowing against the tide.

On Monday morning, the current picked up.

SEVEN

TAYLOR JONES LEFT the Northampton Police Station after spending an hour with Dennis Melrose. The detective had cooperated fully; in Tack's experience, local police usually did. When the federal government entered a case, it meant serious business.

The timing couldn't have been better for Tack. The case had been handed to him two weeks before, after civil agents suspected fraud and suspended their own investigation. As soon as the tax forms and bank records that had been gathered were transferred to his office, he began to pore through them.

When it came right down to it, the case was pretty small-time. He had worked on ones like it before and knew just how it would go. He would conduct his investigation, present his evidence to a grand jury, and get an indictment. The accused would stand trial and be found guilty. Run-of-the-mill. Interesting, given the gall of the guy; still, run-of-the-mill.

Until the guy took off.

Tack had gotten the call early Saturday morning, when one of his men caught an item in the *Globe* and made the connection—which was one hell of a lousy way to find out, in Tack's book. He should have known sooner, while the trail was still hot. But as computerized as the IRS was—it scared him sometimes to know how much—the agency wasn't hooked into local police computers. So four days had passed since the disappearance. Tack knew if the guy had wanted to clear out his bank account, he would have already done it. He sure couldn't do it on Saturday, any more than Tack could put a freeze on the accounts before Monday. But Tack could work. He could milk his own computers of information over the weekend, so he'd be ready to move on Monday.

The diversion was welcome. He had been feeling upended since he'd walked away from Gwen, kind of empty, without direction. Once or twice he had debated going back on his word and calling her. Or hitting a singles bar. But he hated those places like hell. He hated the crowds and the phoniness. Mostly, he hated the desperation. He wasn't desperate. Just horny. And only because he'd been spoiled.

So he'd have to unspoil himself a little, he had decided, which was the whole purpose of cutting it off with her cold turkey. He would put her behind him, give his glands a breather, get busy with other things.

He considered shooting hoop. The guys were still after him to join the winter league, but he hadn't wanted to be tied down. Better still, he could call Freddy Maroni and get tickets for the real thing at the Garden. Freddy had them, right behind the bench. When Freddy had come under investigation by the IRS the year before, Tack had been assigned to the case. So Freddy had put all the tax money he had evaded paying toward buying the slickest lawyer in town, and he'd beaten the rap. But he knew Tack was watching. All Tack had to do was give him a call and Freddy would sell him—at box office price, nothing more, nothing less, as a show of how straight he was—the same tickets that he sold at a monumental markup to any schnook off the street.

Then again, Tack considered taking a leave from the office, driving north to the Laurentians, and playing ski bum for a while. He'd done it before. The resort there knew him. He had been a popular instructor with the ladies. But he'd been younger then. Thinking of ski bunnies gave him the same hollow feeling that thinking of singles bars did. He wasn't looking for a pickup. He wanted more.

The question was how to find it. In the good old days, he could have put an ad in the paper. *Government agent looking for wife. Wants five kids. Needs a brave woman. Will pay passage.* But those days were gone, and thought of putting an ad in the personals made him sick. The kind of woman he wanted wouldn't read the personals. She wouldn't trust them. And even if trust weren't an issue, she would be too proud. She would rather stay home alone reading Robert Parker, or listening to the Eagles, or stripping an old rolltop desk that she'd picked up at a flea market, than date just anyone. She was a resourceful woman.

But he was resourceful himself, which was why he was where he was. The Criminal Investigation Division was small, as was the number of cases it handled each year, but it had a glamour the other IRS divisions lacked. A position in Criminal Investigation was highly coveted. Tack had it and made the most of it. Agents worked under him and were glad to do it.

So he'd been given the Frye case, and the disappearance of its lead player couldn't have suited his needs better. The investigation would take awhile, with most of that time spent in and around Hampshire County. Coming off the highway, he'd seen a Hilton. That wouldn't be a bad place to stay. Melrose had already offered him an office to use. He could keep in touch with Boston by phone, could go back there one day a week, maybe two, but for the rest of the time he would be out of sight and sound of anything that would remind him of Gwen.

He didn't love her. They had never had much to say to each other of a substantial nature. He was trying to enforce the law while she took advantage of every tax loophole around, and though that was legal, it stuck in his craw. So they couldn't talk about his work, and they couldn't talk about her money, and they didn't like each other's friends or movie preferences or favorite restaurants. But they did have good sex. He acknowledged that, again, as he followed Melrose's unmarked car through the center of Northampton.

When Melrose pulled over, he did the same, then rolled down his window when the detective walked back and hitched his chin toward a nearby building. "Frye's office is in there. His firm takes up the whole second floor." He peered in at Tack. "You say you don't have anything on anyone but Frye?"

"Not yet. But we're looking."

While Melrose returned to his car, Tack studied the building. It was another of the old buff-colored stone ones that lined the main drag. This one stood alone and had arches over the windows. It might have looked like a church if it had had a steeple, but there were just those arches. Tack liked the style.

Driving on, he decided he liked the town. Even in December, when the trees were bare and things should have felt barren, there was a depth to the place. Where there were shops and restaurants, there were posters advertising drama productions or concerts. There was a theater and an art center, then street after street of houses that looked quaint and cozy and academic.

He had a thing for academia. In his next life, he planned to be an economics professor, well published and revered, pursued by presidents at home and abroad. Until then, he was satisfied to live in an apartment halfway between Harvard and MIT, in the no-man's-land that was still vaguely affordable, but he wasn't so far from the Square that he couldn't take advantage of street shows, bookstores, and the ivory tower ambiance that spoke of intellectual superiority.

Northampton, he decided, was a cleaned-up, spread-out version of Cambridge—but with Smithies instead of Cliffies. He'd passed a few cute girls. If any of their professors were in their early thirties, pretty and classy and looking for a tall, suave, handsome kind of guy, he'd be in luck.

He drove on, past side streets that branched less frequently from the main. He saw an elementary school, a modern church, a park that still had a few scattered patches of snow. He saw lots of trees, some stark skeletons of winter, others evergreen. Melrose made a right, and he followed. They drove straight for a while, then Melrose made a left. Before long, they turned onto a street that was more elegant than the rest. When Melrose pulled up in front of a large brick Tudor, Tack did the same, parked the car, and climbed out.

Not bad, he thought, looking at the house. Not bad at all. Actually in good taste, for someone who had probably bilked the government of half a million bucks. He had expected something more showy.

Side by side with the detective, he went up the walk and rang the bell. "Think she'll be home?"

Melrose shrugged. "She goes to the restaurant a lot, but the restaurant's closed on Mondays. She's been staying pretty close to the phone. She should be around."

"You really don't think she knows where he is?"

"I'd put money on it. She's a together lady who's coming apart a little because she's worried sick he's been killed."

"And you don't think she knows of any fraud?"

Melrose shook his head. "Nope."

Rocking back on his heels, Tack blew out a breath, looked at the door, and muttered, "She ain't gonna like what I gotta say."

"Nope," Melrose said.

Then the door opened, and Tack immediately understood why Melrose had been so sure. Assuming that the woman before him was Laura, she was as unnerved, as vulnerable, as innocent-looking as could be—which didn't mean Tack wasn't wary. To the contrary. He was from the big city. He knew looks could deceive, particularly where stolen money was concerned.

"Yes, Detective Melrose?" Sounding frightened and expec tant at the same time, she flicked an unsure glance at Tack.

"Uh, Mrs. Frye, this is Taylor Jones. He's an agent with the government. He'd like to talk with you. Can we come in?"

"A government agent?"

Tack held his ID for her to see. "I'm with the IRS, Criminal Investigation Division, out of the Boston District Office. I'd like to ask you some questions about your husband."

"My husband—uh, my husband isn't here. The IRS? *Criminal* Investigation Division?"

"That's right, ma'am."

She looked at Melrose, then back at Tack, either truly bewildered or putting on one hell of an act. Tack had seen that before too. In ten years with the service, he had seen most everything. Bewilderment, confusion, shock— they could come as easily from being caught as from being startled by something new.

"What is this about?" she asked, then turned to Melrose. "Have you learned something about Jeffrey?"

"Not about where he is," Melrose answered. "Just about why he might have gone."

That seemed to frighten Laura more. Her eyes were wider when she looked back at Tack. He could see her mind working, though he could only guess at its direction. "Why did he go?" she asked point-blank.

He glanced beyond her. He wanted to get a look inside the house. "May we come in? It's pretty cold out here."

As though she hadn't realized, she moved quickly aside. "Of course. I'm sorry. Please do."

Tack let Melrose go first, since he'd been there before. Leaving their coats in the foyer, they followed her into the living room. She gestured toward the sofa. "Sit down, please, and tell me what this is about." Rather than sitting, herself, she stood behind an upholstered chair, holding its back hard enough for her fingers to turn white. "Detective Melrose?" she prompted, but Melrose deferred to Tack.

He watched her closely. First reactions could say a lot. "For the past few months, your husband has been the subject of an investigation by the IRS—"

"An investigation?" she cut in. "For what?"

"Tax fraud."

She stared at him, blinked, then moved her head forward, as though she hadn't heard him right. "Excuse me?"

"Tax fraud," he repeated, but he was beginning to think she was legitimately shocked, so he explained. "The investigation started with a random check on a 1040 filed from a post office box here in town. The taxpayer didn't match the profile we have for the income bracket he claimed to be in, so the computer spit out the form for us to take a look. Even though W-2s were submitted to the IRS for that taxpayer, he's been dead for three years."

She frowned. "But what does a tax form from a post office box have to do with my husband?"

"We ran that particular post office box through the computer and found ten other forms listing the same box. Those ten other taxpayers are also dead."

"But what does this have to do with Jeffrey?"

"The post office box was rented in his name."

She flinched. Composing herself, she patted the air with a shaky hand. "Fine. Okay. But that doesn't mean he had anything to do with fraud. Someone else could have rented the box in his name. Or someone else could have fed him information to file. He doesn't run a check on every client who walks into his office. If someone came in claiming to be someone else, he wouldn't have any way of knowing if that someone else was dead."

"Eleven times? Maybe more, if our suspicions pan out. We think he may have used more than one post office box. I have a team working on it now."

"More than one box? What makes you think that?" She sounded more indulgent than disbelieving now, as though she found the whole theory too bizarre to give credence to it.

But Tack wasn't a madman. He had the makings of a solid case. "The refund checks. Running anywhere from eight hundred to twelve hundred, deposited into your account during the months of February, March, April, and May. And that was only for this year. We have no idea what was done in the years before that."

"My account." Not a question but a statement. "You've been examining my account."

"We have that right."

"Without telling me?"

"Without telling you or obtaining a warrant. It's perfectly legal, well within our power. My guess is that the bank notified your husband that we were looking around, and he got real nervous and—" he gestured, "—took off."

Laura stared at him in utter disbelief. Then she looked down and pressed her fingers to her forehead, looked up again, and pressed her fingers to her mouth. Tack noticed she wasn't wearing lipstick, though otherwise she was lightly made up. She had on jeans and a sweater and looked younger than the thirty-eight his file told him she was. She certainly didn't look old enough to have a son in college.

In the next minute, she didn't look old enough to own a restaurant or a catering service or be married to a guy who had committed multiple counts of tax fraud. She looked little more than twenty, totally confused and helpless, and though Tack told himself that could be part of the act too, he was having trouble believing it.

She swallowed. She looked quickly from him to Melrose and back, as if she hoped to see one of them smile and say it was all a gag. Fingers splayed, she rubbed her hands together. "Uh, I think I should call someone," she said in an unsteady voice. Her eyes sought Melrose's. "I can do that, can't I?"

"Sure thing," Melrose said in the kind of gentle voice Tack might have used if he hadn't been in the position he was. Melrose was the good guy, he was the bad guy. That was fine for now.

Tack watched her leave the room, only then realizing that she was barefooted, but even barefooted she had style. So did her home. Pushing up from the sofa, he wandered around. Furniture, art, oriental rugs—nothing was cheap, but nothing was lavish or gaudy either. The government should have decorated *his* office so nicely.

He turned a small crystal swan in his hand. "Think she'll take off through the back door?"

"No," Melrose said from the sofa.

"You're so sure."

"You're so cynical."

Tack sniffed in a breath. "That's my job. Where I work, a person is guilty until proven innocent."

"Not where I work," Melrose shot back without losing a beat. "We get to know people around here. Maybe not all of them, and maybe not well, especially since so many of the academics are just passing through. But people like Laura Frye give this town a good name."

"Her husband sure as hell won't."

"He's an exception. We don't get many like him."

Tack put the swan down. "But you don't think she's involved."

"No."

"Gut instinct?"

"That, and lack of any evidence to the contrary."

"Guilty until proven innocent," Tack reminded him, then caught sight of Laura. She was walking steadily, holding her head up, but she looked pale. "Was that a lawyer you called?" he asked.

"Yes. She's on her way over. She suggested I not say anything more until she arrives." She went to the chair she'd been standing behind and sat this time, folding her legs under her.

Tack returned to the sofa. "Do you think you'll need a lawyer?"

"She's also a friend."

Melrose sat forward, dangling his hands between his knees. "I'm surprised you're alone here now, Mrs. Frye. The driveway was pretty crowded all weekend."

"People dropped in. Friends. Business associates. My mother."

Tack heard the faint pause before the last, but before he could ask its cause, she went on.

"My son was in from college. He went back this morning. My daughter's in school, the restaurant's closed, and everyone else has gone back to work. Jeff's been gone for six days, six long days, without any sign he'll be back. At some point life has to return to normal." She shot a stricken look at the floor before raising her eyes to Tack's. "With or without my lawyer, I want you to know that I find what you're saying really hard to swallow. Jeff worked hard. He built his way up from nothing and earned everything he had. There's no reason why he would do what you suggest."

Tack sent a meaningful glance around the room.

Laura was fast to argue. "We bought this house with money that he earned."

"Did you buy the building your restaurant is in that way?"

"Both this house and that building are mortgaged."

Tack knew all about that. Even before Frye's disappearance, the bank had provided all sorts of nifty information. "So there are mortgage payments, rent for your husband's firm's office and salary to secretaries and associates, loan payments for the restaurant's remodeling, tuition to an Ivy League school, plus living expenses. That's a pretty big nut to crack every month, Mrs. Frye. And that's not counting the Porsche. Or your Wagoneer. Or the operating expenses for your restaurant."

"The restaurant pays for itself."

"With enough profit to help pay for the rest?"

"No. Not yet. In another two or three years, maybe. For now my husband's income pays for the rest."

Tack had dealt with lots of accountants. Those working out of big firms in Boston, with clients who were high-powered people and corporations, could rake it in. Compared to them, Jeffrey Frye was small potatoes. "How much do you think he earns?"

She seemed surprised by the question. "Jeffrey?" She thought about it. "One fifty, maybe two hundred thousand a year. I don't know for sure."

It was Tack's turn to be surprised. "You don't know?"

"Should I?"

"He's your husband."

"But he takes care of everything financial."

"Even to do with your business?"

"No, I do that, but he does the rest. It's always been that way."

Tack knew that many women deferred to their husbands on money matters. But Laura Frye was successful herself, and to be that she had to be bright. Right then, she didn't sound it. "For the record," he drawled, "on your husband's last 1040 he reported an income of ninety thousand dollars."

"Ninety," she echoed. After thinking about that for a minute, she withdrew deeper into her chair. She looked at the floor, frowned, looked at the knotted hands in her lap. She took a breath to speak and changed her mind, then changed it again. "It can't be, this business of tax fraud. It just can't be."

Tack almost felt sorry for her. "The investigation is just starting. We have a whole lot more to wade through before we know the extent of it."

She made a small sound and put a hand to her mouth in a belated attempt to hold it in.

"Are you all right, Mrs. Frye?" Melrose asked.

She held up a hand, but it shook. "Fine. I'm fine, detective. This just doesn't—it can't be—I don't understand." The hand went back to her mouth. In the next instant, the doorbell rang. Before its peal had died, she was on her feet. "That'll be Daphne." She half ran into the hall.

"Who's Daphne?" Tack asked Melrose.

"Daphne Phillips. She's a local lawyer and one tough broad. She's been here a lot since Frye disappeared. She's a close friend."

"Of Frye or his wife?"

"Both."

"But tough?"

"You bet."

"Hell, I hate that type," Tack muttered, but before he could add something choice about ball-busters, Laura returned with her friend in tow. Actually, Daphne Phillips wasn't in tow. She was walking beside Laura, looking like her in so many ways that Tack could imagine they were either related or had been friends forever. The details were different—Daphne was taller, her hair was lighter and pulled into a knot, she wore a silk dress and heels, she had lighter eyes and lighter skin—but they held themselves with the same kind of quiet pride, and they were both looking disturbed.

"Daph, this is—" Laura stopped, drawing a blank on his name.

"Taylor Jones," he filled in, rising, and offered his hand. Her clasp was strong, not strangling but firm. "I'm with the Criminal Investigation Division of the IRS."

"So Laura told me," Daphne said. Retrieving her hand, she turned on Melrose. "How long have you known about this, Dennis?"

"About two hours," he said and sat back on the sofa. Tack had the distinct feeling he wasn't saying another word, which put the burden of explanation smack on his own shoulders. That was fine. He wasn't intimidated by a lady lawyer. He had total faith in who he was and what he was doing.

"I drove out from Boston this morning," he said. "Detective Melrose didn't know I was coming until I showed up at his office. We didn't find out Mr. Frye was missing until Saturday morning."

Daphne looked torn, as though she wanted to say something but couldn't. Disbelief seemed to get the best of her. "Tax fraud?"

"That's what the computer says."

"Computers are machines. What do you say?"

"Tax fraud."

She made a face. "Jeff Frye?"

"That's right."

Laura touched her arm. "There has to be some mistake. Jeff wouldn't do anything like that. He doesn't have a mean bone in his body—or a dishonest one."

"I take it this is still speculation," Daphne said to Tack. "You haven't been to a grand jury yet."

"No. It'll be awhile until I have all the evidence together. Normally I'd have done that from Boston, but Frye's disappearance changes things. If I can speed things up by working here, I can get an indictment, and once I do that I can get the FBI in on the search for him. As far as I'm concerned, though, as of right now he's a fugitive from the law."

Laura began to tremble visibly. Without a word, she moved back to the chair and sat down. Daphne shot her a worried look.

"I'm okay," Laura assured her, but her voice was small.

Daphne turned to Tack. "What is it you want from Mrs. Frye?"

"Information on her husband. Where he might be. What he might be doing. I'm not asking for incriminating evidence, just something to help us find him."

"He's innocent of what you say," Laura put in.

"If we find him, he can tell us that."

Daphne went to Laura, knelt by her chair with her back to the men and said softly, "You don't have to talk with him. This isn't a deposition. If his questions will be upsetting—"

"This whole *mess* is upsetting," Laura cried. "What's a little more?"

"You could wait for another time."

"But maybe he can help find Jeff."

"I can," Tack said. Seeing the look of helpless desperation on Laura's face, he knew she wasn't covering anything up. She was an innocent victim whose neat little life had been turned upside down. Finding her husband was in her best interest. Tack didn't want her lawyer friend to make things worse by prolonging the ordeal. "If we can locate your husband, we'll be able to straighten things out. But we can't do that as long as he's on the run."

"Maybe he's not on the run," Laura pleaded. "Maybe whoever committed your fraud did something to him so he'd *look* guilty."

"Did something?"

"Had him kidnapped. Or killed."

"Maybe," Tack said. She was desperate for an explanation that would find her husband innocent, and while he didn't think for a minute that Jeff Frye was innocent, if dangling that bit of hope before her would clinch her cooperation, he'd do the dangling. He could be accommodating that way, just as long as he got his conviction in the end.

"Uh, excuse me, could you fellows wait up a minute?"

From halfway down the walk, Tack turned to see Daphne trotting up. Other than one or two wisps of hair that blew in the light breeze, she looked as neat as she had throughout the interview with Laura. That interview had ended several minutes earlier, with Tack nearly as much in the dark about Jeffrey Frye's whereabouts as when he arrived. But Daphne had been okay. Aside from the occasional warning when she felt his questions were coming too fast or too strong, she had kept out of the way. He wondered what she wanted now.

"I have a favor to ask," she said and went on without pause. "When the story of Jeff's disappearance hit the papers last week, it was devastating for Laura. The media are already hounding her. If word of what you've told us leaks out, it'll be worse. Is there any way to keep a lid on things?"

Keeping a lid on things was the last thing Tack wanted. In his experience, breaks in cases came about through tips, anonymous or otherwise. The more publicity there was about Jeffrey Frye, the greater the chance of someone coming forward. But Tack couldn't say that in as many words to Daphne. He didn't want to antagonize her. He might need her help.

So, scratching his head, he said, "I won't be making any public announcements, but I don't really know how things work in this town. Detective Melrose would know more about that."

She caught something in his tone. He could tell by the look she gave him, a look that wasn't exactly dirty but wasn't appreciative, either. Turning to Melrose, she said, "Could you try, Dennis? If Duggan O'Neil gets wind of this, we won't hear the end of it. Jeff will be tried and convicted on page one. You can forget about his getting any kind of a fair trial after that."

"The trial would be in Springfield," Tack couldn't resist pointing out. "That's where the nearest federal courthouse is."

"I know that," Daphne said patiently, and again turned to Melrose. "Word spreads like wildfire. You know how awful it can be."

"Your friend should have thought of that when he was doing the dirty deed," Tack said, then added, "Deeds, plural."

"Alleged deeds," Daphne corrected. "Let's not forget the assumption of innocence here."

Tack shook his head. "Doesn't fly in my department. When it comes to tax fraud, a person's guilty until proven innocent."

"That's unconstitutional," she argued.

He shrugged.

Starting to shake from the cold, she folded her arms under her breasts and said, "Do what you can, Dennis, okay?" Without sparing a glance at Tack, she turned and trotted back to the house.

"Great pair of legs," Tack remarked. Her skirt barely hit her knees, and the legs in question were long and lithe.

"Cool it, bud. She's older than you."

"Really?" He wouldn't have guessed it. "How old?"

"Forty."

That surprised him. He would have given her thirty-four, maybe thirty-five. But forty? That ruled out five kids. Forget Daphne Phillips.

Not that he'd been considering her anyway. With her hair pulled back and her dress just so, she was too cool. Which was a shame. Whispers of her perfume caught in the air, as enticing as they were fleeting. And she really did have a great pair of legs.

Tuesday morning dawned clear and cold, the kind of December day when people take deep, bracing breaths, think about the holiday season, and smile. Laura took a deep, bracing breath when she went out for the paper, but the last thing on her mind when she opened it was the holiday season, and when she saw what was on the front page under Duggan O'Neil's byline, she couldn't possibly have smiled.

MISSING CPA UNDER INVESTIGATION FOR TAX FRAUD, the headline stated. Heart pounding, she read on.

Jeffrey Frye, whose disappearance last week mystified family and friends, has been named as the subject of an intense investigation into tax fraud currently being conducted by the Internal Revenue Service. The investigation is being led by Taylor Jones, Special Agent with the Criminal Investigation Division of the IRS. Jones arrived in Northampton Monday morning to coordinate his efforts with the Northampton Police Department.

When questioned by the *Sun*, Jones acknowledged that the investigation has been going on for some time but that Frye's disappearance throws a new light on things. "We certainly have to consider the possibility that Mr. Frye left town to escape apprehension by the authorities."

To date, Frye has eluded the police. His wife, Laura Frye, owner of Cherries, claims to have no knowledge of his whereabouts. She was equally mum when questioned about the charges being leveled against her husband by the government. Though Jones refused to elaborate on those charges, the *Sun* has learned that many hundreds of thousands of dollars may be involved, over a period of up to ten years.

A Northampton native, Frye has been living in the exclusive Child's Park area for the last seven years. He is one of the founding partners of Farro and Frye, a local accounting firm. Originally located on Route 9 near the Hadley line, Farro and Frye moved into spacious new quarters on Pleasant Street in 1985. In 1987, Frye bought the old Wentworth Building on Main Street. It was gutted and outfitted to house the kitchen for his wife's catering service, Cherries. Her restaurant opened there after an elaborate renovation in 1988.

According to sources, Frye prided himself on being invited to important social, political, and cultural events in the area. He contributed heavily to Stanton Ferry's unsuccessful bid for a seat in the U.S. House of Representatives last year, and was known to be a supporter of gubernatorial candidate Tom Connolly. Friends report Frye moving into the fast lane in recent years. He reportedly took regular vacations to the Caribbean, was in tight with the yachting crowd out of Newport, and hosted gala parties at his wife's restaurant. He is best known to some for driving around town in his shiny black Porsche.

The Porsche has disappeared, along with Frye. Law enforcement agencies across the country have been put on the alert for both the car and the man. Agent Jones has asked that anyone with information on Frye's whereabouts contact him through the Northampton Police Department.

EIGHT

L AURA WAS AT THE ISLAND, staring in horror at the newspaper, when Debra entered the kitchen that morning. She knew she probably looked a sight—pale, after a night with only sporadic sleep, and stricken—but she couldn't help it. She was appalled by the article before her.

"Mom?"

She didn't answer; she didn't know what to say, how to break the news. Debra had gone to the Stones' concert the night before, but Laura knew whatever euphoria remained was about to die an instant death. Within seconds Debra was by her side, looking down at the headline that, even on the fifth reading, cut Laura to the quick. MISSING CPA UNDER INVESTIGATION FOR TAX FRAUD. And there, below the headline, the very first words of the very first paragraph, clear as day and impossible to miss, was Jeff's name.

Debra's jaw dropped. "Tax fraud? *Tax* fraud? What are they talking about?" She leaned closer to Laura.

"The paper says that your father is under investigation for tax fraud."

"Dad?"

Laura nodded.

"That's the most absurd thing I've ever heard. Dad wouldn't do anything like that." Pulling the paper close, she read past the headline. Laura could feel the anger vibrating from her, growing with each paragraph until she finally exploded. "That's bullshit!" She slapped the paper with her hand. "Total bullshit! They make it sound like Dad is a jet-setter or something, but he isn't at all. We go to the Caribbean once a year, and that's the only vacation we take. He went to *one* yacht race in Newport, and only because he was invited by a client whose cousin was racing. And the gala party at the restaurant was a benefit for AIDS research."

"I couldn't have put it better," Laura remarked.

Debra was too angry to appreciate the compliment. "What they're saying is totally untrue. How can they *do* that, Mom?"

"It's called freedom of speech," Laura said, in a voice that shook with her own anger. "The same words put in different contexts can have different meanings, depending on what the writer wants to convey."

"But that's not fair! Can't you stop him?"

Laura shook her head. "He can print whatever he wants."

"But Dad *didn't* commit tax fraud."

"That was what I told the IRS agent."

"What IRS agent?"

"The one who stopped by yesterday."

"Mom!" Debra cried, and Laura knew that the complaint was aimed at her this time. "Why didn't you tell me?"

"I didn't want to upset you. I keep thinking, expecting, *hoping* that this will all be straightened out. We thought—Daphne and I—that we could keep this latest thing out of the paper. Apparently Duggan O'Neil couldn't resist."

"I'm not a child. You should have told me."

"Maybe," Laura conceded.

The concession seemed to take the wind from Debra's sails. Less angrily, she asked, "What did the IRS agent say when you talked?"

Laura folded the paper to put the offending article out of sight. It was like a wound, less hurtful when covered. "He said the government has incriminating documents. Until your father is found, he can't defend himself."

"Why isn't he here?" Debra cried, angry now at Jeff. "If he was here, he'd tell them how wrong they are. What's tax fraud, anyway? What do they say he did?"

"They say he filed tax forms in the names of dead people and pocketed the refund checks himself."

"That's impossible."

"No. It can be done."

"I mean, it's impossible to think that Dad did it. He's so straight. Remember the big deal he made about your filing W-2s for me when I worked for Cherries last summer? God forbid someone should think we weren't going to pay taxes on what I earned. So they think he stole tax refunds from dead people? Why on earth would he do that? We have plenty of money."

Laura shot her a dry look. "That's a switch. You're the one who's always saying we don't have enough."

"Because *you* keep saying I can't have a car. Scott got a car when he turned sixteen."

"Scott was on the school newspaper and in the drama club and the debating society. He had something going on at school nearly every night."

"So do I."

"At school?"

Debra didn't answer, but before Laura could wonder about her silence, it ended on a pleading note. "I can't go to school, Mom. Not today. Not after this. Last week was bad enough. The kids were talking behind my back."

"How do you know?"

"I know. Kids always talk behind other kids' backs. When Sara Kaine's parents split, they talked about the man Sara's father found in bed with her mother. When Matt Remson's brother died, they talked about the beer he and his friend drank before they drove off in their car. *This* will keep them talking for weeks. It's all so absurd! My family is the most normal of any of the families I know. None of this makes any sense." As though she had exhausted her supply of indignation, she said, more timidly, "What are we supposed to do?"

Laura pushed a hand through her hair. "First we call Daphne to see what she can do about getting a retraction."

"Do you think she can?"

"She's persuasive. She'll try."

"And if nothing comes of it?"

"We'll have to weather the storm as best we can."

"Are you going to call Scott?"

"Later. He'll be just as angry as you are."

"What about Nana Lydia? She'll be sick."

Laura knew she would be. "I'll go there in a little while." She paused. "Want to come?" She almost smiled at the way Debra's eyes lit up.

"And skip school?"

"Just for today. She loves having you around. If you wouldn't mind going."

"Mind? I *love* Nana Lydia. She's the kindest, gentlest person on earth. She loves it when I call, and listens when I talk, and she remembers every word I say."

"You'd be a comfort to her," Laura said. "If I could leave you with her while I go talk with Gram, that would be one load off my mind."

"Go talk with Gram?" Debra echoed in a pitying way.

"I'd better. If she hasn't seen the paper yet, she will soon, and if she doesn't, someone is sure to call her. She'll be furious."

"Furious at you, Dad, or the paper?"

"Either, both, all three. I'm not sure she'll distinguish between them."

"Gram can be such a pill."

Laura grunted her agreement.

Debra frowned. In a small voice, she said, "How much longer do you think Dad will be gone?"

Laura tried to sound optimistic. "I don't know."

"What if he's gone awhile? What if this not knowing goes on for weeks and months and years? We were talking about MIAs in school last week. Do you know that some families are still waiting for word twenty years after the fact? Do you know the *agony* they must go through day after day after day?"

Laura nodded slowly. "I can begin to imagine it."

But Debra shook her head. "Not me. I can't, and I don't want to. This is not Vietnam. This is the United States, and someone out there has to know what happened to Dad. People don't just vanish. He has to be somewhere."

"I'm sure he is," Laura told herself aloud, "I'm sure he is."

"Tax fraud?" Lydia asked. She was still in bed, which boded ill. Laura knew it wouldn't be one of Lydia's better days—and that was before she had broken the news. "Jeffrey?"

Laura sat on the side of the bed, feeling her share of the heartache. "That's what they say."

Lydia was quiet, frowning at the chenille spread that lay folded over her feet.

"They haven't proved anything," Laura offered. "It's still not much more than speculation."

Lydia regarded her sadly. "We have to consider the source of the speculation. Special agents of the government are usually pretty accurate."

"Not always," Debra put in from the other side of the bed. "They can be wrong."

Lydia tried to smile for Debra, but Laura could see that the smile came hard. She wished she could cheer both grandmother and granddaughter, but the situation was discouraging. "The article in the paper wasn't very generous. Duggan O'Neil has jumped in with both feet, and I'm sure Gary Holmes is loving it. I think we have to be prepared for more of the same."

Lydia sighed. "Ah, yes. From Gary Holmes, definitely."

"Do you know him?" Debra asked.

"A long time ago I did. He was a hard man then. A leopard doesn't change its spots."

"The key," Laura went on, "is finding Jeff. He can't defend himself until then. They keep asking me where he might be, and I've racked my brain, but I can't come up with one place more than any other for them to look. Can you?"

Lydia lifted a frail shoulder in a helpless little gesture. "I've racked my own brain, but I'm at a loss. If Jeffrey had dreams when he was little, he didn't share them. Did he ever talk to you about retiring somewhere?"

Laura shook her head. "We've been so busy reaching our prime we haven't begun to think of retirement. I told them about the islands. He loved those when we went."

"No, he didn't," Debra said. "He complained about the heat. And the food. And the pace. Everything was so *slow*. He got antsy. Don't you remember?"

"I'm sure it won't do the government any harm to check them out," Lydia said. "Debra, sweetheart, would you be an angel and fix me a cup of tea? You make it just the way I like it."

Debra jumped up. "With a muffin. Mom brought some cherry-raisin ones, and if you don't eat them, she'll force them back on me. She hasn't stopped cooking since Dad left. There's so much food at home!"

"With a muffin," Lydia agreed affectionately. The minute Debra was through the door, though, she sobered and reached for Laura's hand. "Does any of this make sense to you?"

Laura gave way to bewilderment. "None at all."

"Did you have any inkling that he was unhappy?"

"None. Jeff never got philosophical about things. He didn't talk about vague feelings and thoughts. He just wasn't like that."

"No," Lydia mused. "He wasn't with me, either. There was always a part of him he kept to himself, and because he was so good I never pushed him. I figured the proof of the pudding was in the eating, and Jeffrey was a dream to raise. Christian caused havoc, but Jeffrey never gave me a moment's trouble. Still, I never quite knew what he was thinking." She frowned. "Maybe I should have asked more. Maybe I should have been more insistent. Maybe I should have *taught* him to share his thoughts.''

Sensing an engulfing grief in the woman, Laura gave her hand a gentle shake. ''You're letting yourself believe that he's done something wrong. Don't do that, Lydia.''

But Lydia focused her blue eyes on Laura and said, ''I have to be realistic. Maybe it's time you were too. You have a wonderfully rosy view of the world, and it's worked perfectly well until now. But you have to take off those rose-colored glasses. The fact is that Jeffrey has disappeared at the very same time that he's under investigation for a crime. Doesn't that seem suspicious to you?''

Laura wanted to argue. For a minute she said nothing. Then, with a frustrated frown, she nodded. ''But it doesn't mean he's guilty. It could be that he simply got scared and didn't know what else to do but run. And it could still be that someone else, someone responsible for the crime, is also responsible for his disappearance.''

Lydia shivered. ''An even more frightening thought. If only we knew more about what went through his mind. Did he like the islands or didn't he? Was he happy with his work or wasn't he? I did ask him those things, and he always said yes, but he never elaborated, so I let it go. I should have pushed.''

This time Laura squeezed her hand. ''I didn't push either, but how can you push a person Jeff's age? He's not twelve or thirteen or fifteen. Scott's just nineteen, and already there are things I can't push with him any more. You can't force a person to pour out his heart to you.''

''No. Jeffrey wasn't the pouring-out kind.''

''No.''

''And if he didn't pour his heart out to either of *us*, he wouldn't have poured his heart out to anyone else.''

''My mother would call his inability to communicate an inborn personality trait.''

''Personality traits can be modified. I let him down.''

''You didn't,'' Laura insisted. In the kitchen, the teakettle whistled. Her voice cut through it, steering the conversation in a slightly different direction. ''They keep asking me about Christian. They keep suggesting that, as Jeff's only sibling, he might know something.''

Lydia looked doubtful.

''When we invited him for Thanksgiving,'' Laura went on, ''he said he was going to be in Australia. The IRS man thought that would be a great place for Jeff to hide.''

''Have they found evidence that he flew there?''

''No. But they're still looking.''

''Fine,'' Lydia said. ''Let them look. It wouldn't bother me to know he was with Christian. Christian has his faults, but he's strong. Jeffrey could do worse.''

Laura wasn't so sure. There were hard feelings between the two men, some of which, she feared, had to do with her. But if Lydia took comfort from the thought, that was fine. Lord knew the poor woman had little else to take comfort from.

An hour later, Laura was at the restaurant nursing a cup of coffee when her mother swept through the door. At sixty-seven, Maddy McVey was still an attractive woman. Taller than Laura by an inch, she was trimly built. Her skirt, blouse, and single strand of pearls were tasteful, if conservative, and her short silver hair was brushed neatly back from her face. She might have caught more eyes if her expression weren't always so stern. It seemed to Laura that a half-scowl had settled permanently over her features.

She was still winding through the tables toward Laura's alcove when, in a booming voice, she said, "I know why you dragged me down here, rather than meeting me at the house, Laura. This is your turf, your pride and joy, and that peacock chair is your fortress. But if you think I'll be intimidated, you think wrong. I'd like some explanations, and I'd like them now."

No matter how conscientiously Laura steeled herself against Maddie, it was never enough. With a sigh, she said, "Actually, I thought the restaurant would be cheerier than the house. Don't you think so?"

Having reached the table, Maddie stood with her purse in her right hand and her left on a chair. "Compared to some of the other restaurants in this town, this one is cheery enough. Those others are old and dark, which isn't to say they don't have charm and a certain ambiance. They remind me of the coffeehouses of my day, where we used to sit talking for hours. But my peer group is gone now, scattered here and abroad, some even dead, and the only thing the darkness does for me is make it harder to read the menu."

"It's plenty light here," Laura coaxed. "You won't have any trouble reading my menu. Would you like something to eat?"

"Do you honestly think I can eat at a time like this?" Maddie demanded. Laura was about tell her that was fine, she didn't have to eat, it would save Jonah some work, when Maddie said, "I will have some of that coffee, though. You have an interesting hazelnut blend."

It was as close to a compliment as she would come, Laura knew. Rather than push for anything else, Laura reached for the silver coffeepot and poured her a cup. By the time she set the pot down again, Maddie had put her coat aside and taken a seat.

"That was a fascinating article in the paper," she declared. She took a sip of the coffee. "Quite an allegation against a man who, according to the people closest to him, is totally honest and uncorruptible."

Laura was quiet. She studied her coffee cup, slowly raised it, took a sip.

"What happened?" Maddie asked.

Without looking up, Laura said, "I don't know."

"Do you believe what the paper is saying?"

"I don't want to."

"But *do* you?"

At Lydia's, optimism was the prime objective. Laura didn't want Lydia's spirits to fall. That wasn't a consideration where Maddie was concerned. Pride was. As disillusioned as Laura might be with Jeff, she wanted to defend him against Maddie's attack. "I don't know."

"You either believe it or you don't, Laura."

"No," Laura said, slowly raising her eyes, "there's a middle ground. I don't believe Jeff did what they say, but I do believe they have some sort of evidence against him."

"Then he's guilty."

"I don't know."

"If they have proof—"

"They need more. Before we condemn him, let's give him the benefit of the doubt."

Maddie's eyes bore into hers, suggesting the indignation that her controlled voice downplayed. "That's a difficult thing to do, given the turmoil he's caused in our lives. You do know the whole town is talking about this."

"Yes. I supposed they would."

"Doesn't that bother you?"

"Of course it does. But I can't control it. If people want to talk, they'll talk."

"If your husband was home where he should be, they wouldn't have anything to talk about—unless what the paper says is true, in which case if he were here he'd be under arrest."

"Mother, there hasn't been any indictment. The only reason all this has come out now is because he disappeared. He hasn't been charged with a thing."

"Yet."

"Do *you* believe it's true?" Laura shot back.

"Frankly, I don't know Jeff well enough to begin to answer that question," Maddie said with an arrogant flourish. "He may have been my son-in-law for twenty years, but we've never been close. We never had a thing in common. We never discussed anything of significance. He didn't understand my work any more than I understood his. He was there at your house, he was cordial, he seemed devoted to you and the children. Beyond that . . ." Her voice trailed off as she gave an eloquent shrug. "But you're his wife, Laura. You're the one who's lived with him all these years. You're the one who's shared a bed with him and borne his children. If anyone knows what he's done, you should."

Laura scowled. "Well, I don't."

"Don't you two talk?"

"Of course we talk."

"About substantial things?"

"Yes, about substantial things."

Maddie sat back in her chair and gave Laura a look. "My, you're defensive. That's just the way you sounded when you told me you were doing well at Smith. It wasn't until later that I learned you were doing well indeed—in the one and only class you bothered to attend. So, fine. You and Jeff didn't deal with some of the deeper issues you should have. Still, I wouldn't have taken you for a fool. Didn't you see any of this coming?"

"I saw nothing."

"Where were you? What were you doing?"

"I was working, raising the kids, starting a business."

"In hindsight, was that wise?"

"It was what Jeff and I both wanted."

"Apparently he didn't."

Laura bristled. "Mother, you have no evidence—"

"Did he *never* say anything to suggest that he was into something like this?"

"If he'd done that," Laura cried, able to hold her temper only so long, "I wouldn't be so mystified!"

"Keep your voice down," Maddie scolded. "Your whole kitchen staff doesn't have to hear you."

"My whole kitchen staff knows what's going on. I've been honest with them."

"The question is whether your husband has been honest with you. If he lied about this, God only knows what other things he lied about."

Laura put a hand to her head. "This was a mistake," she said quietly. "It's always a mistake. You have a way of making things worse, not better."

"Did you really expect me to make things better?" Maddie asked with blatant sarcasm. "How could I do that, when your husband is the one who's messed everything up? Good grief, this is being talked about all over campus. It was bad enough when Jeff first disappeared. People could speculate that he experienced a breakdown and had to get away. But now he's been accused of fraud, which throws a sinister light over the whole disappearance. A man who suffers a breakdown is innocent. A man who commits a crime is not. Do you know what that does to me, Laura? I've worked hard to build a reputation—"

Laura interrupted her with a sharp look. "Mother, what my husband has or has not done will in no way affect your professional standing."

"I'm not so sure of that. In the years I've been at the university, politics has come to play an increasingly powerful role. There are people who want me to retire, and if these charges prove true, that may just give the powers-that-be the excuse they need. For the sake of the department, they'll say. For the sake of the *university*, they'll say. I say hogwash, but what I say won't count."

Laura couldn't believe what she was hearing. Dumbfounded, she shook her head. "I can't deal with this, Mother."

"What can't you deal with?"

"This. You. Your position." Her voice started to shake. "Jeff is God-only-knows where, having done or not done God-only-knows what. How it will affect *me*, I don't know, let alone how it will affect my children. You're worried about your job. Well, I'm worried about our *lives*. You're my mother. If you can't give me a little encouragement for a change, maybe you'd best go on back to school."

Maddie looked startled. "I can give you encouragement. What makes you say I can't?"

"Because you never do!" Straightening in the peacock chair, she gave a resigned sigh. "But that's nothing new, is it?"

Maddie stared at her. "Is there something you'd like to say to me?"

"Not now. Now's not the time."

"That's where you're wrong. It *is* the time. If there's something on your mind, by all means get it out. The last thing you should be doing in the middle of all this other turmoil is harboring a deep-seated grudge. Now," she said calmly, "apparently you feel that I haven't been sufficiently encouraging to you over the years. Is that correct?"

"That's correct," Laura said.

"Go on."

"You've criticized most everything I've done."

"Only when I felt criticism was warranted."

"Which is nearly all the time." Laura leaned forward, desperate to make her point. "But don't you see, your standards are impossible to meet! I don't know what you wanted me to do with my life, whether you wanted me to be a miniature version of you or what, but I'm different." She jabbed her chest with a finger. "I'm *me*. I've built the kind of life *I* wanted, and up until a week ago it was a *good* life. A *great* life. I had a husband, two super kids, a house, a successful career. I had everything I wanted, and that should have made you happy, but it didn't, because what I wanted wasn't what you wanted. You're a dictator, Mother. You want things done your way."

"Things *work* when they're done my way," Maddie stated. "Look at my life with your father. He had his doctorate in English literature to match mine in psychology. Then he settled in to writing esoteric books on obscure literary figures, and we nearly starved. It was only when I took over as the breadwinner that we were comfortable again."

"You took over *everything*." Laura remembered the quiet, almost timid man her father had become in the wake of Maddie's domination. "But why did that have to be? And why does it have to be now? Why must you have the upper hand in everything? Why can't you ever accept that a decision I make, even though it's not necessarily one you'd make, may be the right one for me?"

Maddie pushed her chair from the table and stood. "You're right. This isn't the time to discuss this. You're too upset. Most of what you're saying is nonsense."

"See?" Laura cried. "There you go. You don't like what I say, so you criticize it."

Maddie looked down at her. "You're not making sense, Laura. I am not a dictator. You wanted to drop out of college, so you dropped out of college. You wanted to marry Jeffrey Frye, so you married Jeffrey Frye. You wanted to sell cheese cake, so you sold cheesecake. I have let you go ahead and make your own mistakes."

Laura dropped her chin to her chest in a gesture of defeat. She couldn't win, just couldn't win. When she looked up again, her voice was weary. "And now? What mistake am I making now? Maintaining my husband's innocence until he's proven guilty? Trying to hold my family together? Keeping my business going?"

"The mistake you're making now," Maddie said, "is alienating me. I won't stand around under attack. I don't need that at this stage in my life."

Laura gave a sad smile. "No, I guess you don't. It isn't much fun to be attacked, is it, Mother?"

Maddie gathered her coat. "I'll call you later, Laura. Hopefully you'll be in a more receptive mood." Holding her head high, she left Laura alone in the alcove once more.

NINE

T ACK WASN'T SURPRISED when Daphne Phillips showed up at the police station midmorning on Tuesday. He figured if she was any kind of a lawyer she'd be annoyed by the article in the *Sun*, and if she was tough, like Melrose said, she'd be more than annoyed. So when he saw her at the door to the office he was using, he rocked back in his chair, linked his fingers behind his head, and waited to see what she'd do.

"I'd like to talk with you, Mr. Jones," she said. She had one hand on the doorjamb, the other resting with surprising ease around the straps of the briefcase that hung from her shoulder.

"Sure." He hitched his chin toward a chair. "Come on in."

She moved into the room, but rather than sitting she came right up to the table he was using as a desk. Regarding him steadily across it, she said, "We weren't at all pleased with the article in the *Sun*."

"No. I didn't think you would be."

"It was unfairly damaging to my client."

"Are you representing Mr. Frye?"

"If you folks ever find him, I will. In the meantime I'm representing his wife, whose interests certainly aren't served by misleading articles like this one."

"Misleading?" Tack shot a glance at the paper, which lay on the side of his desk. "I thought it was pretty accurate, actually."

"Perhaps word for word, but put all together, it has Jeffrey Frye more or less tried and convicted."

Tack shrugged. "I can't be responsible for the way the press presents its material. You'd better take that up with them."

"I have. I just came from Duggan O'Neil's office. He refuses to back off or print any kind of retraction."

"So sue him."

Daphne pursed her lips and shook her head. "He's Gary Holmes's puppet, and Gary Holmes is a powerful man in these parts. One doesn't go up against powerful men without a powerful case. I haven't got a case for libel, and you know it."

Tack did but was surprised that she admitted it. It was a classy thing to do. Actually, that was how she struck him overall: classy. Her suit was that way: wool, with a loose jacket, a short skirt, and a silk blouse, clearly a set, clearly from Saks or Neiman Marcus. Same thing with the perfume she wore, which came to him in sweet bits and snatches. Her behavior was classy, too. Her voice was firm but pleasant. She wasn't the harridan he might have wanted her to be so that he could goad her on. He had a feeling her cool was inbred.

In his next life, he decided, he'd be a classy guy with inbred cool. Back in this life, though, he let his arms drop to his sides. "So what do you want from me?"

"A little restraint. There may be nothing illegal about your saying that Jeffrey left town to avoid being caught, or that hundreds of thousands of dollars, collected over a ten-year period, may be involved, but things like that are incendiary. They spread like wildfire, and I don't care if the federal court-house is in Springfield, articles like the one that appeared today will make it harder to get an unbiased jury if the case ever comes to trial. Not to mention," she added, and her cool seemed to slip for a minute, "the effect this kind of publicity has on the Frye family. You must know, after talking with her, that Laura Frye is totally in the dark about where her husband is or, if your charges prove true, what he did. This is a woman who up until one week ago thought she had the perfect life. Jeffrey's disappearance alone was enough to turn that life upside down. This latest twist makes the pain and confusion ten times worse. And that's only for Laura. She has a daughter who is sixteen and in school here. Do you know how difficult this is for her? Do you know how cruel other kids can be? Laura let her stay home from school today, but she can't stay home forever. Laura's son, Scott, is out of state, but he'll be back soon for the holidays. Imagine what the holidays are going to be like for these kids."

"Don't tell me they still believe in Santa Claus," Tack said and waited for her to blast him for being a cynical old man. Cynical *young* man. He couldn't forget that she was five years older than he was. She didn't look forty. But forty-year-olds never did, these days. The experts said it had to do with diet and exercise. Tack guessed it had to do with being in his mid-thirties himself. Everything was relative. When he'd been ten, forty had looked old. The closer he got, the less old it looked.

Daphne didn't blast him. Rather, she stayed quiet and calm, but that didn't mean she didn't get her point across. In her calm, quiet way, she was an impassioned speaker. "If they did believe in Santa Claus, they sure as hell won't any more. What's happened is nearly as shocking to them as to Laura. All their lives, they've been the epitome of the average, normal, healthy, happy family. Suddenly that family is torn apart, and no one understands why. They don't know where Jeffrey is or why he left. They can't believe he is guilty of the things you people say, and if he is, that shakes the foundation of their lives even more. Put yourself in their shoes, Mr. Jones. What would *you* be feeling in a situation like that?"

Tack wasn't one for putting himself in other people's shoes. He had a job to do, and compassion only got in the way. Besides, he hadn't been born into any average, normal, healthy, happy family. "You're barking up the wrong tree, counselor. My daddy was a rummy, my mama wiped down tables at the Hayes-Bickford, and my big brother was killed in 'Nam. I can't dig up too much sympathy for people who have it all and then bring disaster on themselves."

"Laura and the kids haven't done a thing. They're good people. So was Jeffrey, we all thought. If any of what you say is true, we were all taken in."

Tack could have sworn he saw a haunting look in those pretty brown eyes. Brown? No, hazel. Pretty, even though haunted. With a sigh, he crossed his arms over his chest. "That surprises me. Being a tough lawyer and all, I would have thought you'd see through him even if the others didn't."

"I didn't see a thing," she said, frowning. "Not a thing."

"And you knew him well?"

She pursed her lips again, thoughtful for a minute. "Very well. But I wasn't looking for evil. Laura can be confronted with evil and not see it, because she doesn't want to. That's the way she is, a starry-eyed optimist. I like to think I'm more realistic. Still, I had no inkling that Jeffrey could or would have done anything like what you say."

"Life does have its little surprises, I guess."

"True." She took a breath that brought her head up a notch, and those pretty hazel eyes had a sudden edge. "But they don't have to be made worse by public crucifixions. If and when Jeff Frye is brought to trial, the public will see and hear all it wants. In the meantime, let's not cater to the lowest of the low curiosity seekers, huh?"

The way she said it made Tack feel like a cad—which he was, only it bothered him coming from her. "Did you tell that to the press too?"

"You bet." Without blinking, she said, "What I want to know from you is exactly what you're doing to find Jeff. I take it the FBI is on the hunt."

He unfolded his arms, took up a pen, and began to doodle. "The FBI can't officially enter a case until a person is declared a fugitive, which won't happen until he's indicted."

"Unofficially?"

"They're in on the hunt. We've been going through airline records, but so far there's nothing. Same with trains and buses."

"Of course there's nothing. He took his car."

"He couldn't very well drive his car across the ocean."

"You think he went abroad?"

"If he wanted to escape the long arm of the law, he'd go as far as he could. He could have stashed the car in an airline lot or stored it somewhere. We're checking out those possibilities."

More softly and with affection, Tack thought, Daphne said, "He really loved that car. It was something he'd always wanted. He took such good care of it. It's hard to believe he would have left it behind."

"He may not have. He may be holed up somewhere not far from here, but we're looking into that too. We're looking into most everything we can. Even the brother."

"Christian?"

"He was in Australia at the time of Frye's disappearance. He's in Tahiti now. If Frye wanted to get away from things here and have a little fun in the process, Tahiti would sound mighty appealing." Tack slanted a grin her way. "There's nothing like a bare-breasted girl to take a man's mind off his problems."

Daphne's mouth turned down. "You've watched *Mutiny on the Bounty* one time too many."

"Right you are, which is why I may just make that trip to Tahiti to check out old Christian myself. Funny, his name being Christian and all. You know, like Fletcher Christian?"

"Yes, I know," she said, sounding annoyed. "But you're barking up the wrong tree if you think you'll find Jeffrey in Tahiti. In the first place he hates hot weather, and in the second place he wouldn't be looking for fun like that."

"Something wrong with him?"

"Of course not, he's just not the type."

"Faithful to his wife all these years?"

"He's not promiscuous. Believe me, he's not promiscuous."

That didn't really answer the question, but he let it go for the time being. "According to you, he's not a thief either, but all the evidence is against him. Why should I believe you about his sex life?"

"Because I've known him for twenty years, and I've known his wife a lot longer." She looked more upset than she'd been since she had arrived. "I know this. Believe me. I *know* this."

Tack was inordinately pleased to get a rise out of her. Rocking back in his chair again, he said, "Okay. I hear you. We'll check it out anyway, of course. That's what Uncle Sam's payin' us to do. If your Jeff has a honey stashed away somewhere, his phone records will be interesting. Bank records, too. Did you know he has a bank card for a little account in his name—not in both their names, like the rest, but in his name alone?"

Daphne shook her head.

" —'Course, he won't be able to use it now, any more than he'll be able to take money from any of the other accounts. The whole kit and caboodle's been seized."

For a long minute, she stared dumbly at him. Then her face drained of all color. "Seized?"

"Frozen. Your man is suspected of stealing a whole lot of money from the government, and now he's run from the scene of the crime—"

"But he hasn't been indicted!" she cried.

The look on her face was one of such genuine dismay that the sound of her raised voice didn't give Tack the satisfaction it should have. Putting all four chair legs to the ground, he said, "We don't need an indictment to do what we did. All we need is suspicion that he's contemplating flight. We have more than that. He's already gone. So we have to make sure he can't take any more money with him than he already has."

"He's taken money?"

"Bits and snatches from different accounts for a total of somewhere in the neighborhood of fifty grand. Now, unless that money was taken to pay for legitimate expenses, it looks like that's his spending money."

Daphne closed her eyes for a split second too long to make it a blink. She took a breath. "You didn't tell that to the paper."

"There's a lot I didn't tell the paper."

"Like this business with the bank accounts. You can't do that. You can't freeze things without proving probable cause."

"I sure can. It's called making a 'jeopardy assessment,' and I don't need the say-so of a judge. It's one of the special powers the IRS has."

"Special powers?" She looked appalled. "Those bank accounts are crucial. This isn't a family that plays with the stock market."

"I know. We checked it out. If Frye owned stocks, those would have been seized too. We've frozen every one of his assets."

"But his assets are the family's assets. Laura doesn't have a stash of her own, and the kids certainly don't. What are they supposed to live on?"

"She has a business."

"Right, and she deposits every cent of its take into one of those bank accounts you've frozen. What in the hell is she supposed to do when she goes to do the payroll for the month and finds she can't touch a cent of that money?"

"She should have had her own business account."

"But she doesn't. So what's she supposed to do?"

"Better tell her to open an account of her own and put the take there from here on."

"Okay," Daphne said, eyes flashing. She was back to holding the strap of her briefcase, but so tightly now that her knuckles were white. "I'll tell her that, and maybe, just maybe, her employees will stick with her when she tells them she can only pay half of what she owes them for December and they can forget Christmas bonuses. But what about the money she'll owe the bank for the loan and mortgage on the restaurant building? And the house? And Scott's tuition? First her husband disappears, so she loses his income, then you come along and take control of her savings. That's a double whammy."

Tack did feel sorry for the woman, but there wasn't much he could do. People brought things on themselves. Laura Frye should have paid more attention to what her husband was doing. She shouldn't have been so damn naïve. She should have been tougher, like her lawyer friend here, who was eyeing him like he was the devil himself.

Wanting the advantage of height, he stood. Then, because that advantage felt good, he decided to push it by walking around the table to face Daphne at close range. With a compassion that surprised even himself, he said, "Look. I hear everything you're saying, and it's a shame for your friend and her kids. But I don't make the laws."

"You enforce them. It was your 'assessment' that froze her assets. It could just as easily be your 'assessment' that unfreezes them."

Her face was tipped up to compensate for his height. It was as composed as ever, save for the pleading in her eyes. Standing there, Tack felt a tug. "If I could, I would," he said quietly, "but it's gone too far for that. I've filed records with the agency. A dozen financial institutions have already been notified. It's out of my hands."

Daphne didn't move. Not once did her eyes leave his face, nor did the pleading leave her eyes. Tack sensed this was a woman who cared deeply for her friends. Given the cavalier way he often treated his, he felt vaguely humbled.

"Doesn't it bother you," she asked, seeming almost confused, "to see a woman ruined?"

He tried to come up with a clever answer but found none. In a low, serious voice he said, "If she's innocent, yes, it does."

"Still, you'll put Laura through this?"

"I have no choice. It's the way things work. I'm only doing my job."

"Your job sucks."

He had to smile at her choice of words, but it was a sad smile. "Sometimes. Like now."

For another minute, Daphne continued to look at him. He didn't know what she saw, but he worried that whatever it was didn't overly impress her. That bothered him. He didn't know why, but it did.

"Listen," he said, "we'll do everything we can to find her husband and, after that, to resolve this thing as quickly as possible. That's why I'm working here. To get things done with haste." He drawled the "with haste," since the words weren't exactly his style.

Daphne didn't smile. After another minute, she nodded, tore her eyes from his, and turned to leave.

Tack watched her go, watched those spectacular legs move her body forward. "Counselor?"

She stopped and looked back.

"Like I said, to get things done fast I'm working here instead of operating from Boston. I stayed at the Hilton last night, but I don't think Uncle Sam's going to approve that expense for long. Any suggestions for some clean, cheap digs?" He could have asked Melrose, he knew. He could have asked any one of a dozen others in the Northampton Police Department. But he wanted to asked Daphne. She might know of a cheap place with a little class. And she'd know he was around.

"Try the Valley Inn, on Route Nine heading out of town."

"Thanks," he said and started to raise a hand in a wave, but she had already turned and left.

Laura stood in the front hall, staring at Daphne in utter disbelief. "Come again?"

"Jeff's assets have been frozen," Daphne repeated. Her voice held a chill that spread to Laura, though the words made no sense. "It's something called 'jeopardy assessment.' If a person is under suspicion for something and the agents investigating him have reason to believe he may try to flee, they can make a 'jeopardy assessment' and seize bank accounts, stocks, bonds, homes, cars, whatever."

"They actually come and take these things?"

"No. They just make it so that no one else can."

"You mean Jeff."

"And you."

"But I haven't done anything wrong."

"Your assets are Jeff's. Everything is either held jointly or in his name. The IRS has put a freeze on all of it. You can't touch a thing."

"Daphne, that's absurd," Laura said, but the look on Daphne's face deepened the chill. "Are you saying I can't cash a check?"

"That's right."

"I can't withdraw money from my own bank account?"

"That's right."

"You must be kidding." She gave a scornful laugh that even sounded strange to her own ears. She wasn't normally a scornful person. She wasn't normally sarcastic or bitter. But little in her life had been normal in the last week, and she was still hurting from her meeting with Maddie. "Tell me you're kidding, Daph."

"I can't," Daphne murmured. "Much as I want to, I can't."

"I have no money?"

"You have money. You just can't use it."

Laura couldn't believe what she was hearing. On top of everything else, it was too much. Sagging back against the wall, she ran a shaky hand through her hair. "There has to be some mistake."

Daphne didn't say a word.

"Come on, Daph."

Daphne shrugged.

Laura scrambled to gather her thoughts. It seemed she'd been doing that a lot lately. Too often she found herself feeling overwhelmed by some of the simplest things in life, like deciding what to wear or whether to make dinner. This was far from one of those simple things. "Are you saying," she said very slowly, "that I have no access whatsoever to the money I've put in the bank?"

Daphne sighed.

"What am I supposed to live on?"

"Cherries."

"But my daily take goes right back into overhead — buying supplies, paying staff, mortgage and loan payments. What's left isn't enough for us to live on." With dawning horror, she added, "Jeff's income covered our living expenses, but if Jeff isn't here, there won't be any income, and if I can't touch the money in the bank, I can't pay those bills. My God!" she cried, and felt dizzy. Too many things were happening, none of them fair, none of them under her control. The helplessness was making her sick. Unsteadily, she went to the stairway and lowered herself to the carpet runner. "This is unreal."

Daphne joined her on the step. "I know."

"Things keep getting more and more complicated. Where will it end?"

"I don't know."

Laura fought off her dizziness with a flare of red anger. "They can't *do* this. The government can't *do* this to me."

"They can. It's legal. I just came from checking, and they can do it. The IRS can seize assets without so much as winking at a judge."

"But that's not right!" Laura shouted. She and Daphne were the only ones in the house, the doors and windows were shut, and she didn't care if her voice carried clear to the attic. She was so filled with fury that if she didn't let some of it out—her mother was right—she'd explode. "My husband may be under suspicion, but I'm not, and half of our money is mine. What am I supposed to live on? Tell me that! How am I supposed to survive while Jeff is off twiddling his thumbs somewhere and the IRS diddles around looking for him? I have a business, a house, and two children to support. How does this government, to which I pay huge taxes every year, expect me to live? Those are my own *after-tax dollars* they're preventing me from touching. How am I supposed to make ends meet?"

"For starters," Daphne said in a voice that sounded doubly low in comparison to Laura's, "you'll open an account in your own name. From here on, everything you take in goes there."

Laura could feel panic rising. She tried her best to tamp it down, but it kept coming. "Fine, but that won't cover everything. From the start we knew that with a financial investment like the one we made in the restaurant, we wouldn't see a significant profit for several years. What about the mortgage for this house? Or food for the kids, for God's sake?"

Daphne touched her arm. "Calm. Keep calm."

"I'm trying, but it's getting harder and harder." She hugged her knees. "When Jeff first disappeared, I felt like I'd been dunked in icewater and stretched on a rack. For every day he's been gone, I've been stretched tighter. Now it's like the rack is starting to twist."

She pressed her mouth to her knees, hard enough to feel her teeth through the leggings she wore. She closed her eyes tight, but even that didn't help, so she opened them wide on Daphne.

"How could Jeff *do* this to me? What was he thinking when he left—that if he wasn't here, everything would be fine? He must have known the IRS was on to him, so he just ran away."

"Hold on, Laura. You're starting to talk like he's guilty."

"I don't want to think it, I honestly don't, but after a while, after the questions keep coming with no answers and the coincidences start mounting, I'm beginning to wonder."

"Don't. You're his wife. If you don't believe in his innocence, who will?"

"You're right, I'm his wife, and that means I'm the one left holding the bag," Laura cried. "My name is being smeared in the papers. My daughter doesn't want to go to school. I have no idea how I'm going to manage to pay for basics that I've always taken for granted." Her voice grew beseechful. "Okay. Debra can live without New York. We can live without Saba. But what about sending Scott back to Penn? What about the dentist and the doctor? What about insurance and gas for the car? My God—" she wiped cold beads of sweat from her forehead with the back of her hand, "—the ramifications are mind-boggling. I mean, talk about pulling out the rug!"

Daphne clutched her hands. "Come on, Laura. It's not like you to be pessimistic."

"But my world is falling apart!"

"No, it's not. You have your business, your kids and your health. You also have Maddie—"

"— Who makes everything worse!"

"She's still your mother. She won't let you starve."

Laura shook her head. "I will *not* take money from Maddie. I won't ask her for a red cent."

"Well, that's something to think about another time. The point is that we do have other options."

Laura eyed her warily. "What options?"

"We can appeal this 'jeopardy assessment' through the courts."

"What does that entail?"

"It entails my going through your records and proving that much of what you have in the bank is your money, proceeds from your business."

"But I'm entitled to half of what's in the bank anyway," Laura cried. "If I were divorcing Jeff, that's what I'd get. *At least* that. Or I should. I was the one who supported him while he finished college, and it was money in my own personal account that helped us live when he started working. So now he takes off after stealing hundreds of thousands of dollars. What was going through his mind? Twenty years, we've been married twenty years, yet he could do this to me! And what about Debra and Scott? They're his own flesh and blood. Didn't he wonder what would happen to them when he vanished? What in the world did he *do* with that money?"

She hadn't given that question much thought, since up until then she hadn't allowed herself to think of Jeff being guilty. Now, in her fury, she wondered. Hundreds of thousands of dollars was a lot of money. What had he done with it all?

An awful thought hit her. Several, actually. She looked at Daphne, whose expression was telling, and it was as if the rack she was on took another twist. This one stole her breath. "My God," she whispered. "My God. This house? The Porsche? The restaurant?" It was bad enough to think that her husband was a thief, but to think that she had been enjoying the fruits of the thievery was crushing. She didn't care one way or another about the Porsche, that was Jeff's baby, but she'd been so proud of the house. And the restaurant. If the down payments on those buildings had been made with stolen money, the whole thing was tainted. "So help me," she said in a venomous voice, "if he used that money to make my dreams come true—"

"Don't say it," Daphne interrupted. "Don't say anything you may regret."

Laura looked her in the eye. "You're my best friend. If I can't say it to you, I can't say it to anyone. If these charges against Jeffrey prove true, if he stole money to help build the life I've been so proud of, I'll divorce him."

"You're angry."

"Very, but I mean what I say. I've been in hell for a week now. If that hell goes on much longer, all because Jeffrey wanted to be a big man and buy big things, I'll divorce him."

"You don't know the facts, Laura. If it's true, *if* it's true, there may have been reasons you know nothing about."

"No reason could be that good. Why are you sticking up for him?"

"I'm trying to be reasonable. You're upset. I'm trying to be calm. We don't know the facts."

"Until Jeff gets back, we won't."

"Not true. Jones's investigation will tell us things. Between the bank records and the records at Farro and Frye, he'll be able to piece together how much of Jeff's own income went for what."

Laura could hope that Jeff's income had covered the important things, but she kept remembering what Taylor Jones had said. Jeff had barely earned half of what Laura thought he earned. Either he made up the difference with money obtained through fraud, or he had lied on his income tax form. Neither possibility thrilled her.

But Daphne was right. Until they knew the facts, she had to be calm. That was easier, now that she'd blown off the worst of her steam. She was still livid, but tired. Very tired. "Tell me again about appealing the freeze on our funds. What are our chances of success?"

"They're good. The only problem is time. I'll work as fast as I can. Still, it may be awhile before a judge will hear the case."

"Awhile? Two weeks, four weeks, eight weeks?"

"It could be three to six months. We can make a case for hardship, but you're not exactly on welfare."

Three to six months. Laura thought of the cash flow she would be needing in that time and how she might get it. Jeff would know the answers—but of course she couldn't ask Jeff. "I'll sell the house. I don't need it. The market isn't great, but I could get enough to keep us going."

"You can't sell the house. That's what a freeze on assets is about. You can't sell the house, because the government has taken a lien on it, which means that at this moment it isn't yours to sell."

Irritably, Laura filed that fact. "Then I'll take out a loan. But that would be taking out a loan to make payments on another loan," she argued against herself. "I'd be going round and round in circles."

"In one sense, yes. But a loan would help tide you over until we unfreeze some of those assets."

"Then you think I should do it?"

"I think you should talk to David. Find out what the situation is at the firm. There may be money owed you from there."

"Won't the government take it?"

"Maybe not, if it's put directly into your own private account."

"Won't the government freeze the firm?"

"Not unless there's evidence that David and the others were involved in what Jeff did. Jones will be looking for that."

Laura put her elbows on her knees and her hands on either side of her head. "I'm so confused. So frightened. So tired."

"Still not sleeping?"

"Not well. I wake up and start asking the same questions over and over again, and I never have answers. Jeff's the one with the answers. Wherever he is." Thinking about that, wondering, she was angry all over again. "My God, if he's really done all this to me and the kids, I hope he burns in hell!"

TEN

JEFF NORMALLY HATED hot weather, but he would have gladly burned in hell just then, he was so cold. The wind cut through him sideways as he made his way down the hill into town. Feet, legs, hands, nose, even his eyeballs were cold, and it seemed they'd been that way forever. No matter how valiantly it worked, the wood stove in his cottage couldn't counter the insidious gusts of frigid air that found their way through invisible cracks in the walls.

Going into town was a risk. He had only been in hiding for a week, which was nowhere near long enough for him to look different. The beard on his face itched like hell and looked scruffy enough, but it wasn't yet the mask he wanted, and even though he wore a wool cap on his head, if there had been pictures of him in the papers or on television, he might well be recognized. But he was willing to take that chance. If he didn't go somewhere to warm up for an hour or two, he would go mad.

He would also go mad without human companionship. He had never been without people for so long in his life. His transistor radio offered noise, but it wasn't human. He needed to know that he wasn't at the end of the world. Walking into town would tell him that. It would also give him exercise. He had always climbed stairs in his building, walked around downtown during lunch, shoveled snow or raked leaves or packaged up garbage to take to the dump, and that was aside from his tennis games, which were fierce. In the cottage, there was nothing to do but jog in place and do push-ups and jumping jacks and deep knee bends. He did all those faithfully, morning and night on a regular schedule, and he wandered out on the rocks of his bluff. But he couldn't walk there, couldn't stretch his legs and really *move*.

There was another reason for going into town. He was in desperate need of the diversion. In between reading his books, listening to his radio, and cleaning up the cottage, he inevitably thought about those he had left behind, thought about Laura and David and Daphne and Lydia and how he had let them all down. He wondered how messy things were, whether the IRS had come out in the open, whether they were making life hard for Laura. She would survive, he knew she would, she always had. She would make the most of the situation and carry on. But he wondered about Debra and Scott. They were the toughest part of all this. He worried about them—not about their daily well-being, because Laura would ensure that, but about their feelings for him. He knew they would come to hate him, and he supposed he deserved it; still, the more he dwelt on it, the more pain it caused. With no one to look at, no one to divert his thoughts, no one to ease the isolation he felt, he was becoming an emotional wreck. Living in solitude meant living with a man he didn't particularly like. That was a punishment in and of itself.

So he was risking discovery by taking a walk into town. Not having dealt with any locals except the Bangor realtor from whom he'd bought the cottage, he wasn't sure what brand of humanity he would find. But he wasn't picky. Human contact was human contact. He wasn't any prize himself, after what he'd done.

The town consisted of one main street, down which he had driven the first night, plus several side streets he would have guessed were footpaths if he hadn't seen pickups parked along the way. There were pickups in the main street, too, just a handful drawn up to a string of buildings that housed, in order, a general store with a post office, a laundromat, an auto supply store, and a diner.

He made a mental note about the laundromat, which he figured would be a good place to visit twice a week. Since he hadn't had the foresight to bring clothes this time, he made for the diner. He walked casually, as though he were out for nothing more than a late-afternoon stroll in a place where he'd been living all his life.

The diner was in a low cement building with a flat roof. Between a large Santa face, an arch of flying reindeer, and snowflakes of various shapes and sizes were hand-printed signs advertising breakfast, lunch, and dinner specials. The heat within had steamed up the windows, preventing him from seeing much of what was inside, but the lights were on and the place looked warm and inviting, which was all the temptation he needed.

He pulled open the slatted wood door, setting off some jingle bells that were tacked inside. They were real jingle bells, not the little kind sewn onto a piece of ribbon but big ones attached to a strip of worn leather that had once been a horse's bridle. Seeing that gave Jeff a nice feeling, as did, incredibly, the smell of burgers on the griddle, but the nicest feeling of all came from the immediate warmth he felt. He would have sighed with pleasure had he not been afraid of drawing attention to himself.

His glasses fogged, so he took them off. As had happened more than once in the last week, he was surprised at how much he could see without them. There were two men at the counter, and a man and woman in one of the booths. All four were older than he was and more burly. All four were looking at him by the time he closed the door. Leaving his gloves on lest the smoothness of his hands brand him a foreigner, he nodded and headed for the empty booth at the end of the row. He slid in, keeping his back to the others. Once he felt shielded by the tall wood of the booth, he set his glasses on the table, removed his gloves, and unzipped his parka.

The warmth was heavenly. For a week it seemed he'd been huddled up against the chill. Now, slowly, he opened his hands, relaxed his arms at the elbows, lowered his shoulders, stretched out his legs.

"Hello," a small voice said.

He looked up to see the waitress. She was a young woman, in her late twenties, he guessed. Slim, almost fragile looking with dark hair and pale skin, she wore a white blouse, a loose denim jumper, wool tights, and sneakers. On the collar of her blouse was a plastic Rudolph with a short string hanging from the bottom. It was the kind of pin Debra wouldn't have been caught dead wearing, which went to show how different people were in the sticks. Jeff thought the pin was sweet. And the young woman looked harmless.

"Hi," he murmured.

She gave him a shy smile and said in a careful kind of way, "Do you know what you want?"

He had been so hungry for warmth he hadn't given a thought to food. "Uh, no, I haven't—looked." As he said it, he searched for a menu, but it wasn't between the salt and pepper, and it wasn't on a chalkboard above the counter.

The waitress extended an arm and touched the tabletop with the tip of her pencil, then quickly drew back again. Sure enough, under the sheet of glass that covered the table were signs like those in the window, plus others, each with bits and snatches of a menu.

"Ahhh," he said. Putting his glasses on, he began to read. When he realized that the waitress was still there, he gave her an apologetic look. "Sorry. I'll just be a minute."

"It's okay. There isn't any rush." As though to prove her point, she didn't move.

Fearful that the longer she stood there looking at him the greater the chances would be that something about him would ring a bell, he said, "I'll start with a large bowl of corn chowder and a cup of hot coffee. While you're getting that, I'll decide on the rest." He glanced up to see that she was writing down the order, then looked down again. Though his focus was on the papers under the glass, she was in the corner of his eye. He waited for her to leave, but she didn't. Daring another glance, he saw that she was still writing. She seemed to be concentrating deeply.

For an instant, he wondered if she was making notes on his features to report to the police or, worse, drawing a pencil sketch of him, and he had a momentary urge to up and run. But that would be a dead giveaway that he had something to hide. Besides, she looked so innocent he couldn't imagine her doing either. Seconds after he tempered that fear, she put the tip of the pencil to the paper and said in that same careful voice, as though she were making a deliberate effort to do everything right, "That's one large bowl of corn chowder and one cup of hot coffee. And you'll decide on the rest while I'm getting them."

"That's right."

She shot him another shy smile, then disappeared from his line of sight. He could hear the gentle slap of her sneakers on the cracked linoleum as she moved along the length of the counter toward the kitchen. The men at the counter were talking quietly. The couple in the other booth were eating with a click of forks and knives. From the kitchen came sizzling sounds.

Jeff took a deep breath, flexed more of the chill from his hands, pushed the parka off his shoulders to better enjoy the heat, and sat back in the booth. Within seconds, it seemed, the waitress was back, carrying a white mug in one hand and a coffeepot in the other. She set the mug down near the edge of the table, carefully filled it with coffee, set the coffeepot down, slid the mug closer to him, then picked up the coffeepot.

"The sugar is next to the salt," she said. "Would you like cream?"

He was about to say no—he always drank his coffee black—but there was something rich-sounding about cream, and he felt in need of something rich, so he nodded. "Please."

Again he heard the pit-pat of her sneakers, and before he could do more than empty two sugar packets into the coffee, she was back with a small pitcher of cream, a spoon, and a napkin.

"There are napkins there"—she pointed to the metal container behind the salt and pepper—"but this one's nicer."

"Thank you," Jeff said.

"You're welcome." She lingered for a minute, watching him pour cream into his coffee. Then she moved off again.

He sipped the coffee. The brew was muddy, had probably been sitting for most of the afternoon, but it was good. Since he had neither the pot nor the know-how to brew coffee, he had been making do with instant all week, but he didn't care what the label said, instant just wasn't the same.

"Here you go," the waitress said. Her voice reached him first. He glanced around to see her approaching from behind him, walking slowly, gingerly balancing a large bowl of chowder on an even larger plate. She was working so hard at delivering it without a spill that he almost reached out to help her. But something stopped him. He sensed she wanted to do it herself. There was an element of pride involved. So he waited, his eyes widening a fraction each time the chowder came perilously close to the rim of the bowl, and when the plate finally rested flat on the table, he felt nearly as victorious as she did.

"That looks just fine," he said with enthusiasm, then added an even more enthusiastic, "Delicious, actually," because it did. He had been opening cans all week and either heating the contents in a small pot on the stove, or, as in the case of sardines, tuna, and even hash, eating the food cold. He didn't know how to cook. There had never been any reason to learn. His mother had ruled the kitchen of his childhood, and then he had met Laura. From the beginning she had loved to cook, and she did it so efficiently it wasn't worth his while even to try. In the same amount of time that he would have spent deciding whether to use butter or margerine, she could put a whole meal together. She was so competent it made him sick.

"Is something wrong?" he heard the waitress ask and, looking up, found worried eyes on his face. "You look angry."

He quickly erased his scowl. "No. I'm not. I was just thinking about the

soups I usually make for myself, and they look awful, compared to this one."
Using the large spoon that lay on the bottom plate, he sampled the chowder.
"They taste awful too, compared to this one. This is good." He took another
spoonful, then another, enjoying the chowder. It was thick and hot, mildly
flavored, faintly sweet. Not only did it taste good, it warmed him all the way
down. He gave her a smile and spooned up more.

"Do you always cook for yourself?" she asked.

He swallowed his mouthful. "Um-hmm."

"Don't you have anyone ever to do it for you?"

"No."

"Then you live alone?"

"Yes."

"Where?"

He had been concentrating on the chowder, keeping his eyes downcast, but
when one question came after another, albeit slowly, he grew uneasy. So he
looked up but, again, saw only innocence on her face, and though he reminded
himself how innocent he had looked at home at the same time that he'd been
hiding so much, he gave the waitress the benefit of the doubt. After all, he
reasoned, he had answers to her questions. He had thought them all out, just
for situations like this.

"At the top of the hill," he said with the slight toss of his head in the
direction from which he'd come.

Her eyes widened. "Are you the one who's living in the bluff house?"

Jeff wouldn't have called the cottage a house, but there was only one
structure at the top of the hill. "I guess so," he said. Then, because he didn't
want to make anything big of it, he returned to the soup. The spoon was
halfway to his mouth when she disappeared from the corner of his eye. He had
taken several more mouthfuls when a different form appeared. This one was
larger, far larger, and had on a greasy white apron over an undershirt and jeans.
He also had on a mean expression, which Jeff took in at a glance. So he pointed
to the bowl with his spoon.

"This is wonderful chowder. Really good."

"You livin' up in the bluff house?" the man asked. His voice was a hoarse
smoker's voice, but it was less ominous than his looks.

Jeff figured he had no choice but to answer. "If that's the one up on the hill,
I am."

"We heeyad it was bought."

Jeff nodded. He ate another spoonful of chowder.

"Must be cold."

"Um-hmm."

"S'how come ya theya?"

Jeff was prepared for directness. He knew backwoods folk didn't beat
around the bush. "I wanted a place of my own, and it was cheap."

"It's fallin' ta pieces."

"Um-hmm. But it's mine."

"Wheya ya from?"

"Pennsylvania."

"Wheya theya?"

"Western part of the state."

"Why'd ya leave?"

"My mother died, so there was no reason to stay."

"Whatcha do theya?"

"Teach."

"Whatcha gonna do heeya?"

"Read and think. Maybe write." Jeff figured that if the previous owner of the cottage had been a writer, he could be too.

"Write what?"

"I don't know. I haven't decided yet."

The man snorted. "Ya ma musta left y'a load a money."

Before Jeff could respond, the waitress was back, eagerly asking, "Can I take his order now, Poppy?"

The large man's face gentled the instant it turned to her. "Do that, Glorie. I gutta cook." He sent Jeff a look that said he'd have more questions another time. Then he sauntered off.

Jeff looked at the waitress, who was waiting expectantly with her pencil poised over her pad. "Poppy? Is that his name?"

She blushed. "That's what I call him. I've been calling him that all my life. He's my daddy. His real name's Gordon."

Jeff had to smile at the way she drawled the name, but aside from the drawl, she had said it well. Given the way her father spoke, her pronunciation was remarkable. She seemed to take the same care with it that she took with her manners. She sounded educated, but not really. It was odd.

Aware that he was staring, Jeff took a quick breath. "Does he own this place?"

She nodded. "And my name isn't really Glorie, it's Gloria, only everyone calls me Glorie. You can too, if you want."

Jeff wasn't in town to make friends; still, he found himself nodding. "Okay." Then, because there was something about her that was very sweet, he said, "You can call me Evan."

"Is that your name?"

He nodded.

"Evan what?"

"Walker. Evan Walker." That was the name he had bought the house under. It was also the name on the birth certificate, the Social Security card, and the driver's license he had in his briefcase. Evan Walker—at least, the one who had been born in South Connellsville, Pennsylvania in 1948—had died two years before, but no one had to know that.

"That's a nice name. And I'm glad you're here. People grow up and move away, but no one moves in very often." She lowered her voice until it was just above a whisper. "It's nice talking with new people. Some of the old ones just keep saying the same things over and over and over—"

"Glorie!" came a call from the kitchen. "Gut that odda?"

Glorie was quickly the waitress again. Looking apologetic, almost fearful, she poised her pencil over the pad. "Have you decided what you'd like to eat?"

Jeff glanced down at the scattered pieces of menu. There was a T-bone steak that sounded good, but it was more expensive than the other things, so he didn't want to get it. Gordon had already decided that he was a do-nothing with lots of money. Loath to foster that image, he looked around for something in the middle price range. "How's your beef stew?"

"Oh, it's delicious. Poppy makes it fresh every morning. It has carrots and potatoes and onions in with the meat, and it comes with cornbread; or if you'd rather have plain rolls, I can bring those instead."

"Cornbread will be fine. How are the portions? Pretty good size?" Her description alone had set his mouth to watering. He felt like he could eat a horse.

"Oh, very good size," she said in an earnest tone. "And if it's not enough, I can bring you seconds. Poppy lets me do that, especially at this time of day. Our biggest rush is at lunch. Poppy doesn't like to throw food away at the end of the day, and he always makes fresh stew the next morning."

"The stew will be wonderful," Jeff decided. He set to finishing the last of his chowder.

By the time it was gone, Glorie delivered the stew, and it was every bit as good as she'd led him to believe. The cornbread was good too, as were seconds on both, and he finished with apple upside-down cake and another cup of coffee. Thinking back to some of the elaborate meals Laura had made, he couldn't remember one he had enjoyed as much as this.

Of course, part of that was because he'd been alone for a week, and because he felt human for the first time in that week, and because Glorie was the most gentle person he'd seen in a long time. He drank the last of his coffee slowly, feeling reluctant to be done and leave. The thought of returning to the cottage on the bluff didn't thrill him.

But it had to be done. That cottage was his hideout until he decided where to go and what to do. So he paid his bill at the diner with some of the wrinkled singles he had stuffed into his pocket, left a healthy tip for Glorie, and said goodbye. Then he walked down the street to the general store.

There were half a dozen people inside. Keeping to himself, he bought a wedge of cheese, a dozen eggs, several cartons of orange juice, and a handful of Hershey bars.

"Pretty cold up theya on the hill," the man at the cash register said. Jeff recognized him as one of the men at the counter in the diner.

"Yup," he said, digging into his pockets. He used tens this time—wrinkled, also by design. "Say, you wouldn't know anyone who wants to sell a truck cheap, would you? I need something to get me around."

"How'd'ya get heeya?"

"A friend dropped me. But I'm stranded now, and I'll be needing some supplies pretty soon." He figured he could venture a little farther in a week or two.

"I can getcha supplies."

"I'll be needing some papers and books and things."

"They's books right theya." He aimed a finger at the single rotating rack of paperback novels. Most of them were dog-eared. Jeff suspected that the fine art of browsing had evolved, here, into the fine art of reading the book in the store.

"Ah," he said and nodded. He didn't want to offend the man. "Good." Walking over to the rack, he found that he had already read some of the books in hardcover. Several others caught his eye, though, and while he probably wouldn't have bought them in Northampton, where Adventure Fiction was tucked way behind Tibetan Culture, Modern Astrological Thinking, and Introspective Therapy, they might just be diverting.

So he picked out a few, nonchalantly took a newspaper from the top of the pile, and went to the cash register to pay for the extra things. "I'd appreciate it if you'd keep an ear out about a truck, though. I'll stop back in a few days."

"Evan Walkah, is it?"

"That's right."

Jeff fastened up his parka, pulled the wool hat lower on his head and the gloves on his hands, lifted the bag holding his purchases, and set out for the bluff.

ELEVEN

I F CHRISTIAN EVER RETIRED, he would retire to Tahiti. He had decided that long ago, after he had returned to the island for three years running and found it more beautiful each time. He loved the tropical breeze, the towering cliffs, the warmth and honesty of the people. He also loved the glossy black hair of the women. And their deep golden skin. And their grace. And the smiles that sprang so readily to their full Tahitian lips, and the way those lips formed French words to compensate for his primitive grasp of Tahitian.

He stayed on the side of the island far from the dirt, noise, and crowds of Papeete, in a resort owned by an old college friend, a Minnesotan who had come to visit soon after graduation, fallen in love with a Tahitian woman, and stayed. The resort had grown more luxurious over the years to accommodate the cream of the island's visitors.

Whenever he came he took pictures, not only in Papeete and the interior but on other islands in the French Polynesian chain. They were very different from the pictures he had taken in the Daintree, but there was always a travel magazine that would buy them.

Aside from that, he did nothing of an industrious nature. With its lush landscape and its tropical climate, Tahiti was for vegetating. He either lounged on a cushioned chaise on his own private deck overlooking the lagoon, or sat in his favorite restaurant and watched the people go by, or enjoyed sunsets from the beach. He also visited with friends. Over the years he had come to know not only other transplanted Americans but many of the natives, the *taata Tahiti.* At any given time, if he wanted company, it was his for the asking.

On this particular afternoon he hadn't done any asking, so when a loud knock came at his door that carried out onto the deck, he was puzzled. Setting his drink on the railing, he went back through the bungalow to the front.

The man on the other side was a stranger. He was new to the island, if his pale skin and weary look meant anything. He was also dressed wrong. He had on a white business shirt that was open at the neck and rolled to the elbows, dark suit trousers, and loafers. He was about Christian's height, maybe ten years younger, and not a bad-looking guy, Christian decided, though his hair was too short. But he looked too formal, far too formal, particularly next to Christian, who wore nothing but shorts.

"Just get off the plane?" Christian remarked, propping a hand on the doorjamb.

"After two goddam days in and out of airports, with missed connections at every stop," the man grumbled. More clearly, he said, "Are you Christian Frye?"

"That depends. What do you want?"

"To talk." Pulling a leather folder from the back pocket of his trousers, he flipped it open. "Taylor Jones. Special Agent, Internal Revenue Service."

Christian studied the ID. "You look better in the picture."

With a thanks-a-lot-buddy look, Jones flipped it closed. "Mind if I come in?"

"Yeah, I do. If you're here about those deductions I took for expenses last year, you're wasting your time. My accountant warned me you guys wouldn't like it, but my client lived in Connecticut, four hours from me, and the only way I was going to get my usual crew down there was to put them all up, and the only way I could do that without going broke was to rent a house and a cook. So it cost a bundle, but it was a legitimate business expense." He went suddenly quiet. Something didn't make sense. "The IRS sent you all the way out here just to check on me?"

"Not in that way. Can I come in?"

"Then in what way?"

Jones stared at him hard. "If you let me in, I'll tell you. I'm hot and tired, and I don't give a damn if it's against regulations; I could use a drink. Got anything strong?"

Christian had just the thing, and though he didn't normally fraternize with establishment types like Taylor Jones, if the man was asking to buck regulations, Christian would be the first one to oblige. Gesturing him in with the jerk of a thumb, he closed the door, then went to the bar and fixed one of his specials. He found Jones on the deck looking out over the clear blue lagoon.

"Not bad," the agent remarked.

Christian retrieved his own drink and leaned back against the rail with his legs crossed at the ankles. "It's as close to Eden as I've ever come, which means that I resent anything that threatens to spoil it. So. You're in, and you've got a drink. Now tell me why you're here."

Jones took a healthy swallow of that drink. Once it was down, he flexed his neck. "Better."

"Business, Jones."

The agent lifted a hibiscus blossom from the deck rail, one of the many the hotel staff scattered around fresh each day. "For starters, I wanted to see if you were alone."

Christian took immediate offense. "Hey, the IRS may have a say in how much of my hard-earned money I get to keep, but it doesn't have any say in my love life."

Jones took another drink before he turned to face Christian. "When was the last time you saw your brother?"

"My brother." That didn't make any sense either, but for a different reason. Most people he knew didn't know he had a brother, much less a sister-in-law, a niece and nephew, and a mother. Family had never been Christian's strong suit. "Jeff?"

"Do you have another?" Jones asked with a look.

"Obviously, you know I don't. You didn't come all the way out here looking for me without trying to nab someone closer. What happened to Jeff?"

"I don't know. No one seems to."

"What's that supposed to mean? Where is he?"

"I thought maybe he'd be here in Eden with you."

"Jeff hates hot weather."

"So why does he go to the Caribbean once a year?"

"Because his wife plans the vacation," Christian said, growing impatient. "Jones, what's going on?"

"When was the last time you saw Jeff?"

"Last June. Laura threw a birthday party for my mother, so I went."

"And you haven't seen him since?"

"No." He waited. "Jones?"

Jones took another drink. Lowering the glass to the railing, he said, "Two weeks ago, your brother failed to come home from work. No one's seen or heard from him since." He looked skeptical. "No one called to tell you?"

"I've been away. Incommunicado. No phones most of the time." But that wasn't the whole story. After taking a drink of his own, Christian said, "We're not close."

"You and Jeff? Or you and the whole family?"

"Him. Them. Same difference." He frowned. "'Failed to come home from work.' Just disappeared?"

"Just disappeared."

That didn't sound like Jeff at all. "Of his own free will?"

"That's what we think."

"But why?"

"Because he's on the verge of being indicted for tax fraud."

Christian laughed. "Tax fraud? Jeff? You're putting me on."

"No," Jones said, "I'm not."

Christian could see that, but it didn't make the allegation any less preposterous. "Jeffrey Frye breaking the law? You obviously don't know my brother."

"Straight as an arrow, huh?"

"Yeah, straight as an arrow, but not dumb or naïve. He'd know exactly how to break the law if he wanted to do it. When we were kids, he used to give me elaborate plans for sneaking out of the house at night without being caught. Or snitching a five from the old man's wallet. Or dialing long distance without having to pay."

"He sounds pretty crafty."

"Yeah, except he wouldn't ever do any of those things himself. He might tell me to do them, but he kept his own hands clean. He didn't have the nerve." Christian swished a finger through his drink. "And you want me to believe Jeff would commit tax fraud? No way, José." He brought the glass to his mouth and took a drink. Then, because the prospect was so intriguing, he asked, "Out of curiosity, how is he supposed to have committed this tax fraud?"

"By filing bogus forms and collecting returns."

"How much?"

"One fifty and counting."

"One hundred and fifty *grand* and counting?" Christian whistled.

"It could total half a million, when all the figures are in."

"Without you guys knowing?" If Jeff had pulled that off, Christian had to hand it to him. The little shit had balls. "How's he supposed to have done it?"

Jones raised a finger from his glass and pointed to the chaise. "Mind if I sit?"

"Be my guest. This is fascinating."

Jones stretched out on the chaise, wiped the sweat from his forehead with an equally sweaty arm, and took a drink. Then he said, "The way we figure it, he chose people from the obituary pages of the paper, waited until they'd been dead a year, submitted W-2s in their names, then 1099s, then 1040s."

"Clever," Christian said. "Sounds like the kind of thinking my brother could have done, but carry it out? Nah. I'm telling you, he wouldn't have the nerve." Even when he was taunted, Jeff had been a coward, and God only knew Christian had taunted him enough. From the time Jeff had been four and Christian nine, they had been arch rivals. Jeff was the angel, Christian the devil, and no amount of goading on Christian's part had led the angel astray. Granted Jeff had never achieved what Christian had on the playing fields or with women—until Laura, which was something else entirely. Still, Jeff was good, with a capital G. "He wouldn't even steal a cookie from the cookie jar, for Christ's sake!"

"Maybe he should have," Jones remarked. "The punishment would have been a helluva lot easier to take than the one he'll get now, if we ever catch him, which brings me back to the reason I'm here, which is fuckin' hard to remember with this drink in my hand." He peered into the glass, where the liquor came barely a third of the way up, with most of that third being ice. "What's in this, anyway?"

"Island stuff."

"Is it the same as you're drinking?"

Christian was drinking iced tea, which was pretty much the same color. "Sure. I live on it."

"Whew, it's potent."

"Throw in jet lag and exhaustion, and you're in a pickle. When was the last time you ate?"

"Real food? Two days ago."

"You'd better eat."

"Yeah, well, I thought of that, but by the time I finally found the damn hotel, the first thing I wanted was a bed, and then the damn room wasn't ready because someone else loves paradise so much he's refusing to leave, so they're trying to find me another place to stay. While they were doing that, I figured I'd check you out."

"Well, you have," Christian said and drained his drink, "and unless you want to check under the bed and in the closet, you can see I'm not harboring any fugitives from justice. But I want to know more about all this, so before you pass out, I suggest we eat. There's a great restaurant next door." He eyed the white shirt and dark trousers with distaste. "Only thing is, you can't go looking like that. Don't you have anything decent?"

With an effort, Jones sat up and put his feet on the floor. "Sure, I do. I didn't come all this way just to talk with you for five minutes. I brought shorts and bathing suits, the works. As far as the agency is concerned, I'll need at least three days here to find you and then interrogate you about anything and everything to do with your brother."

"That won't take any goddamned three days." Christian had a whole lot he could say about his brother as a kid, but he barely knew the man now. They were very different people who had taken very different roads in life.

Jones pushed himself to his feet and regarded Christian with surprising clarity, given what Christian had put in his drink. "Tell you what. If you don't tell on me, I won't tell on you."

"What'd I do?"

"Deducted something suspicious."

"It was a legitimate deduction."

Jones shrugged. "Could be. But audits are a pain in the butt. Don't you agree?"

"You're threatening me with an audit?"

"They're done all the time for pettier reasons than this."

"Like what?" Christian had heard stories—none of which surprised him, since he didn't think highly of government workings—but he'd always assumed some exaggeration in the stories. So he was curious about what an authority would say.

"Like tips from an ex-spouse or a business competitor. Like the personal grudge of a legislator, or a friend of the tax agent, or the agent himself."

"That's lousy."

"That's how it is. So. Do we have a deal?"

"Of course we do. I don't give a damn if you stay here three days or five or ten. You can stay here a goddamned month, for all I care. Besides, who in the hell would I sing to? I steer clear of the IRS. Bureaucracies aren't my style."

"So I gather," Jones said and started back into the room.

Christian followed, curious now about Jones's source. "Who's been talking?"

"Frye's wife."

"Ah. Interesting."

"Why's that?"

"Laura and I have our differences."

"She didn't volunteer information. I asked, she answered."

That made more sense. Laura was uncomfortable with anything to do with Christian and had been that way for better than twenty years. Yes, she invited him to her home—and the invitation always came from her, rather than Jeff, simply because she was the one in the house who did that sort of thing—but she wasn't thrilled when he accepted. Granted, when he came, she was cordial. She gave him the guest room and fed him, but she avoided being alone with him and never allowed him to draw her into a personal discussion. As far as the rest of the world was concerned, she didn't trust him. He suspected she didn't trust herself.

At the door, Jones said, "That restaurant's right next door?"

"Ask in the lobby. They'll direct you."

"Give me fifteen minutes." He paused. "You'll be there, won't you?"

Christian grinned crookedly. "You mean, will I take the time to collect my brother from the shower stall, pack my bags, and skip town?" The glance he shot toward the lagoon took in every bit of opulence along the way. "Would I leave all this for a guy who never once even remembered my goddamned birthday?" Without waiting for an answer, he shut the door.

Twenty minutes later, he and Jones were drinking again, Christian for real this time. But they were also eating, which made things safer. Despite his family's image of him, Christian wasn't a big drinker. The beers with the guys after work didn't count. He drank socially, but that was about it. He liked to be able to control just how drunk he was.

Besides, on Tahiti, he was plenty loose without booze, which was probably why he had said what he had about Jeff back at the bungalow. Normally he kept his gripes to himself—not that a birthday was any big thing, but it was one more little memory of his brother that irked him. He didn't want to get into the big things. They were no one's business, least of all a government agent's. So he stayed fully sober by alternating swallows of Scotch with forkfuls of *poisson cru*.

He wanted to know more about what was happening back in good old Hampshire County. "So Jeff is gone and no one has any idea where he is. Laura must have had some suggestions. She's a wellspring of information." He rather liked those words. They happened to fit.

"No. She didn't have any suggestions."

"Laura, without suggestions?"

"She's pretty much in a state of shock."

"Shock? Laura?" That was nearly as preposterous as the idea of Jeff committing fraud, as far as Christian was concerned. The Laura he had known adapted to whatever situation she was in. When she found herself face to face with adversity, rather than fight it, she would simply turn and go off in another direction. She was like Lydia. So like Lydia.

And there he did feel a twinge. He didn't see eye to eye with his mother, and on some pretty major issues at that. But she was still his mother, the only one he'd ever had. "What about Lydia?" he asked, looking nonchalantly around the restaurant. The vivid clothing rivaled that of the flowers, both totally different from the eminently practical woman back home. "How did she take all this?"

"She's pretty calm. Disturbed about it, but resigned. No help with suggestions about where Jeff could be, though. How about you? Have any ideas?"

Christian wasn't sure he'd hand any over if he had them, but since he didn't, the point was moot. "I can't picture the guy committing a crime, let alone running off. He's led a sheltered life. He's been coddled by controlling women."

"Laura didn't strike me as being controlling."

"No, she doesn't, does she, and that's the kicker. She slides in on the blind side. In her own quiet way, she gets things done just how she wants."

"Is she manipulative?"

"No," Christian said. He scratched his head. "Manipulation implies something negative, and she doesn't have a mean bone in her body. But she has a very specific idea of how things should be done in life, and she knows how to get people to do them in such a way that they think it's their idea."

"Give me an example."

Christian grabbed at the most obvious one. "Marriage. She decided she wanted to drop out of college, get married, and have a family. Jeff was still in school. I doubt he had any intention of getting married until she came along — and made it worth his while," he hastened to add, because it was only fair. "That's the whole point. She does give. She made him a nice home, gave him two nice kids, and then, when he wasn't earning enough money, she started a business of her own to supplement his income."

"Sounds like any guy's dream."

"Not mine," Christian said with feeling. "I don't take to being led around by the nose."

"Were you ever?"

"No."

"Not even by your mother? If she was controlling of Jeff, why wasn't she the same with you?"

"Because the circumstances were different," Christian said. "And because I'm a different person from my brother."

"That's what they kept saying. You don't look much like his picture. Same coloring, but that's about all. Guess he got the looks in the family."

"Guess so," Christian agreed, because he figured he had it coming after his comment about Jones's mug shot. In point of fact, while he didn't have Jeff's cultured looks, he stood out in a crowd. His height helped — he was six four to Jeff's six even — but there was also a rugged look to him that turned women on, or so they said. He looked exciting, they said. He looked daring and dangerous, they said. He had to take their word for it, because he didn't spend hours looking at himself in the mirror. He wore his hair on the long side because he hated getting it cut. He always had color because so much of his work was outside. And when a man spent his life tossing two-by-fours around, his shoulders were bound to be broad. No, he wasn't at all sensitive about his looks.

"They told me," Jones went on, "that it was a waste of my time to come looking for you, because you would never help Jeff out if he was in trouble."

Christian shouldn't have been sensitive about that either, but he was. "That's not necessarily true."

"You would help him out?"

"If he'd come to me, I might have." He ripped off the tail end of a loaf of French bread. "But the point is he wouldn't have come. Certainly not all the way to Tahiti, all by himself, without Laura to make sure he made his connections, and you know she isn't here." Then Christian thought of something. "I take it you checked out my place in Vermont?"

Jones nodded. "He's not there."

"Are the plants dead?"

"Close to it."

"Jeez, I can't win. I can build a terrific house where nothing was there before, but I can't keep a goddamned plant alive. Did you water them?"

"Hell, no. That's not *my* job."

"It's not your job to be breaking and entering either. Did you have a warrant?"

"Didn't need one. I was looking for a fugitive."

Christian figured he wouldn't have much of an argument there. "Did you at least lock up when you left?"

Jones nodded, but he was looking at Christian like he had something else on his mind. "Those were incredible photographs on the walls. Did you do them all?"

"Most of them," Christian said, because there seemed no point in denying it. "I travel a lot. I like visible reminders of where I've been."

"They're impressive. So's your darkroom."

Christian didn't much like the idea of strangers combing through his things. "So you took the Cook's tour."

"Like I said, I was looking for a fugitive. What better place to hide than in a darkroom?"

"I can think of better places. Apparently, so can Jeff." He was pleased to see a moment's discomfort on the agent's face. Jones might be adept at studying tax forms and financial records, at interviewing women and tracking potential witnesses halfway around the world, even at breaking and entering. But he couldn't find Jeffrey Frye.

In all fairness, Christian knew, Jones wasn't as bad as he might have been, particularly when it came to his taste in art. That was probably the reason why, when Jones asked where he learned to take pictures like that, he shared information he usually kept to himself.

"The Peace Corps."

Incredulity. "The Peace Corps? You were in the Peace Corps?"

That was precisely the response Christian usually got, which was why he'd learned not to talk about it. "Something wrong with that?" he asked in annoyance.

"Wrong? No, not wrong. Just surprising."

"If you'd done your homework, you'd have already known it."

"You're not the suspect. Just a potential witness."

"Or accomplice," Christian reminded him, just to keep things interesting. But Jones was more interested in the other.

"The Peace Corps," he said, looking bemused. "I had the impression you were a troublemaker when you were a kid. How did you ever make it into the Peace Corps?"

"People see what they want and believe what they want. I was a wretch at home, but that didn't mean I didn't do anything well. I happen to be smart and athletic."

"And modest."

"Modesty has its place. But you want to know how I got into the Peace Corps, I'll tell you." And he was proud to do it. It wasn't often that he talked about himself, and in his younger days he might as easily have perpetuated a misconception as tell the truth. But his younger days were gone, and at that moment it mattered that the government agent have the facts. "I played four years of varsity sports at Amherst and graduated magna cum laude. I had great recommendations, and I made it through three months of training in Montana, which is more than some of the people who showed up there can say. So I went overseas."

He remembered those days so clearly. They had been good.

"Some people will say I did it to avoid the draft, and given a choice between Africa and Vietnam I'd have chosen Africa any day, but with the lottery number I pulled, I wouldn't have been drafted anyway. Other people said I was a revolutionary with a missionary urge, but I have never in my life been political. The truth of it is that I joined the Peace Corps to get away from home. I wanted to go somewhere where I wouldn't be prejudged." He smiled at the irony of that. "Little did I know how prejudged I'd be in Africa. I was an American. I was there to upset the natural order of things. I was not a friend."

"So how did you get anything done?" Jones asked.

Therein lay the challenge, and if nothing else, Christian loved a challenge. "First I had to scrounge around and find a job that needed doing—initially, for example, a bridge that needed building. Then I had to scrounge around for materials, then scrounge around for people to help. And all the while I was scrounging, I was getting better at speaking the language and understanding the local customs, so that by the time we got around to actually building the bridge, I was able to convince the people that they would benefit from it."

"That sounds worthwhile. Wasn't your family impressed?"

"If they were, they never told me. We never talked about my experience in Africa."

"Why not?"

Christian knew the answer to that. He had come home from the Peace Corps, after re-upping and serving nearly four years, in March of 1970. He had barely been home for two days, both of which he'd slept through, when he'd gone off in search of women and seen Laura. She had been seventeen, young for a freshman, but intrigued by his beard and his worldliness and his age. In turn, he had been intrigued by her enthusiasm. She seemed to have boundless energy, which she had no intention of expending over books. So he accommodated her. They spring-skied Tuckerman's Ravine, went to photography exhibits in Cambridge, spent hours listening to Simon and Garfunkel. And they made love. She had boundless energy for that too. They made love for hours and hours in the attic apartment he was borrowing.

He had only planned to stay around for a week but he ended up staying for four, because she could be so persuasive. Then she asked him to marry her. She wanted a home, a husband and kids, and the kind of rosy family life she hadn't grown up with. But he wasn't ready to settle down. He didn't know what he wanted to do with his life, but the last place he wanted to be was Northampton.

So he left. Several weeks later, having no idea where he was, she stopped by his house to find out on the pretense of returning a book of poetry he'd lent her. Jeff was the one who opened the door.

Christian hadn't told his family about the Peace Corps because all the time he had spent in Northampton had been with Laura. Sure, he had told her about his experiences, but afterward she wouldn't have let on to that. The depth and intensity of their relationship was a secret.

And he had no intention of telling Taylor Jones. So he simply said, "We didn't communicate much, my family and me. Once I hit college, I wasn't home a lot. It worked out better that way."

Jones seemed to accept that. "So you started taking pictures in the Peace Corps. Have you ever worked at it professionally?"

"I sell pictures, but that's never been my occupation. I'm a builder."

"But you graduated magna from Amherst. I wouldn't have put the two together."

"Then you're as narrow-minded as the rest. Why in hell can't a smart guy be a builder?"

"He can. It's just unusual. Most smart guys take high-paying jobs where they can call the shots from behind a desk."

Christian raised a cautioning hand. "I went to college—and did well—because I had a point to prove. I wasn't the total misfit they thought, and I didn't get my grades just by charming the teachers. That might have worked in high school, but it didn't in college. I earned those honors so I could thumb my nose at the doubters. But there was no way they were goading me into wearing any three-piece suit for the rest of my life."

"So you wore a dashiki in Africa."

"And oilskins when I was working my way around the Horn on a tramp steamer, then a wet suit when I dove with a salvaging crew off the coast of Florida, and a tool belt when I signed on to frame houses in Nantucket."

"And that's how you got started?"

Christian sat back. "That's how." He crossed his arms over his chest. "And that's all I have to say. Anyone listening would think you're writing a fucking biography. Have I given you any clues about Jeff?"

"No."

"I didn't think so."

"What about women?"

Christian shook his head. "Forget it. Jeff's a one-woman man."

"Not him, you. Didn't you ever want to get married?"

Wanting to get married wasn't the issue. Wanting a family of his own was. There were times he'd wanted it so badly he could taste the need. But the timing had been wrong with Laura, and Gaby hadn't been the family type.

He shrugged. "It just never happened."

"But there were women."

"Damn right, there were." He caught sight of one approaching and opened an arm to her. "Hey, pretty lady." She was the daughter of the restaurant's owner. Once she was safely in the crook of his elbow, he made the introductions. "Taylor Jones, She'laya Malone."

Looking instantly enthralled by the island's natural beauty, Jones stood and offered a hand. "Tack. Please."

"How are you, Tack?" She'laya asked with a pretty white smile and just a hint of a delicate accent.

"I'm fine," Tack replied.

"Have you just arrived?"

"This afternoon."

"Are you a friend of Christian's?"

"He is," Christian supplied to avoid explanations. "Busy night?"

She'laya sent a look around the crowded room. "As you can see. But if business is good, I cannot complain." She ruffled his hair. "Enjoy your dinner." Nodding to Tack, she left.

Tack slipped back into his seat. "Are they all like that around here?"

"No. She's special." When Tack looked disappointed, he said, "But I know some others who come pretty close. Two sisters, just a little younger than you. They run a dress shop in town. If you want, I'll give them a call."

"Two, as in kinky?"

"No. One as in mine, the other as in yours."

"A double date."

"Only until things get hot, and if they don't, no sweat. Think you can stay awake long enough to give it a try?"

"Sure."

Christian stood. "I'll make the call."

"That's sounds great," Tack warned, "but if you think it's going to stop me from going after your brother, you're wrong."

"You can go after my brother. You can go after him all you want. But that's not why I'm calling the girls."

"Why are you?"

Christian straightened his shoulders. "Because you look like a decent guy.

And because you've had a rough day. And because you like my pictures. But mostly,'' he added with a twist of his lips, ''because you can't come to Eden and not taste the fruit.''

TWELVE

❀❀❀

MONEY MATTERED. For the first time in her life, Laura realized how much. She needed it to buy food for her children. She needed it to keep a roof over their heads. She needed it to pay the people who worked for her, or they would go elsewhere to satisfy their own needs for food and housing. If they left her, she would either have to take on replacements at lower pay or make do with a skeleton staff. In either case, the business would suffer, and if the business suffered there would be less money coming in, which meant she would be even less able to meet the obligations of feeding her children, keeping a roof over their heads, and paying her staff. It was an endless circle, a crisis that would be self-perpetuating unless she did something to stop it.

Jeff had been gone for two weeks. No one knew where he was or what he was doing. He had the Porsche and enough cash to live on for a while—Laura knew that now, but that was the extent of her knowledge. There were times of intense anger when she actually wished they'd find him dead. At least then something would be resolved and she could go on with her life. Not that she was sitting around waiting for the phone to ring the way she had at first. She was determined to be a visible presence at work, so she was busier than ever. Duggan O'Neil was right, she knew. Her personal situation was a downer, and if any of that feeling settled into the restaurant, people wouldn't go there. The atmosphere had to be as upbeat as ever. She had to look and act perfectly normal.

Unfortunately, there was nothing normal about pulling in and out of an empty garage, climbing in and out of an empty bed, or, when Debra was out, cooking for herself. Jeff had always been there. Now he wasn't. And she couldn't forget it for a minute.

The media wouldn't leave her alone. Rarely did a day pass without a call from a reporter. The *Sun* was the worst. Several times a week there were articles to the effect that Jeff was still missing, the FBI was in on the case, the IRS investigation was going ahead full tilt. Wherever she went—grocery store, post office, dry cleaner—people knew what had happened. Some asked outright if there was any word of Jeff, others asked how she was in a you-poor-thing tone, still others carefully avoided her eyes. And just when things began to stabilize, another article would appear. So even if Laura wanted to set aside the whole thing for the sake of sanity, Duggan O'Neil wouldn't let her.

Nor would the IRS. She received near-daily calls from Taylor Jones or one of his cohorts with questions relating to Jeff. Often the calls were follow-ups to calls the agency received. Since Jeff's picture had appeared in the papers, particularly in the *Boston Globe*, dozens of people thought they had seen him. So the IRS wanted to know whether Jeff knew anyone in Andover or Grafton or Barnstable. Each time Laura was asked, her hopes rose, but none of the reported sightings panned out.

And then, in addition to the *Hampshire County Sun* and the IRS, there was the U.S. Mail to contend with. Bills began to arrive. To his credit—if she should credit him with anything, which Laura doubted she should—Jeff had paid the December bills. Come the first of January, though, a new batch was due. Some of the smaller ones, even those for gas, electricity, and the telephone, could be put off for one month without fear of shut-offs, but two months would be chancy. And then there were the big things, like the mortgage payment for the house and Scott's tuition. They had to be paid.

Doing her best to keep a clear head when what she wanted most at times was to burst into tears and crumble, Laura saw that she had two options. The first, which she did the day after she learned of the IRS seizure, was to follow Daphne's suggestion and open a bank account in her own name, into which Cherries' proceeds would be deposited daily. The second, which she hated to do but saw as a necessity, was to take out a loan to cover her expenses until Daphne was able to convince a federal judge that half of what was in the Frye accounts belonged to her.

Going shopping for a loan took preparation. She spent time at Cherries' computer itemizing and totaling the money she would need to keep the business running smoothly, then setting that total against what she estimated the business would make by the week. After she had those figures, she spent time in Jeff's den fumbling her way through his records in an attempt to determine what she would need at home. After those figures were compiled, she spent another several days holding her breath with the hope that maybe, just maybe, Jeff would show up and spare her from begging for money. In the end, she realized that even if he showed up, thanks to the IRS freeze she would come up short. So she swallowed her pride and embarrassment and went.

First she approached the bank where she'd opened her account, but that bank was a small one, the loan officer explained, and simply couldn't offer the loan she wanted.

She could accept that. She didn't like it—it was bad enough asking for money under her present circumstances, which were slightly humiliating— but she could accept it. There were other banks in town. She promptly went to a larger one, but the loan officer there was equally apologetic.

"I'm sorry, Mrs. Frye," he said, studying the application she had filled out, "but a loan would be out of the question. You don't have a credit rating."

"Excuse me?"

"Loans, mortgages, charge cards—your husband has always been the principal signer. Therefore, you don't have a credit rating, and without one I can't grant you a loan."

"But I have my own business," Laura said with what she thought was perfect logic. "You've seen it. You've probably eaten there. Cherries brings in steady money."

"Yes. But you don't have a credit rating."

She felt a surge of frustration. Being denied the money she deperately needed on a technicality seemed almost as wrong as the government freezing her funds to begin with. "I would think that your bank would go out of its way to help a local businesswoman."

"We would if we could. But there are certain rules. The best I can suggest is that you apply for a credit card in your own name. Then, after a time, you can come back and we'll talk."

But "after a time" was no good. Laura needed money by the end of the month. Refusing to be discouraged, she put his obstinacy down to small-town thinking and tried another bank. This one had branches statewide. She hoped its employees would think more broadly.

As fate would have it, the loan officer was a woman. Sure that a woman would better understand what she was going through and the bind she was in, Laura filled out the loan application and presented it along with the figures she had gone to such pains to prepare. But the woman wasn't any more help than the men before her.

"I'm sorry, Mrs. Frye," she said, looking regretfully at Laura's papers, "but given the circumstances I simply cannot justify a loan of this size. You have no collateral. The government has taken a lien on every asset you might have used."

That was a new twist. Being a novice at borrowing, Laura hadn't considered it. Now she did, and it seemed unfair in the same way that the argument about her credit rating was. "But I have a successful business."

"Yes, you do, but there's absolutely nothing behind it. You have a mortgage on the building and loans outstanding on work that was done in it."

"But the business itself is worth something."

"Actually, no," the woman told her, still politely but firmly. "The business is you and your staff. If you were to close up and disappear one day, there would be no way this bank could recoup its loan."

Laura could see her point, but it didn't apply in her case. "That business is the only livelihood I have. It's the only means for me to provide for my children. Believe me, I'm not about to close up and disappear."

But Jeff had done just that, as the woman's awkward look reminded her. Laura was Jeff's wife. Hence, Laura was a risk.

"Guilt by association?" she asked, incredulous. "Is that the problem? I'm a bad risk because of allegations that have been made against my husband? But that's unfair! I'm not my husband, I'm me. I have my own business, and a great reputation in this county. Ask anyone."

"I know that, Mrs. Frye," the woman said. She was about Laura's age, wore a wedding band, and had a photo of two teenagers on the corner of the desk. Laura had thought for sure she'd be on her side, but she wasn't. She was a team player—for the opposing team. "I know your business and your reputation, and you're right, it is a fine one. But you have to understand the precarious position banks have been in lately. What with the downturn in the economy, we've lost large amounts of money on loans. Businesses have folded. Developers have gone bankrupt. We have to be doubly careful."

Laura struggled to stay reasonable and calm. "I'm not asking for a construction loan. I'm asking for a loan to keep my business going until I can free up some of my own money, and I'll pay whatever the going interest rate is. I'm not asking for any favors."

But the woman shook her head. "You're not a good candidate. We simply can't do it at this time. I'm sorry."

Three more banks came up with variations on the same theme. Fighting panic by the end of the day, Laura stopped in at the offices of Farro and Frye to talk with David.

It was a bold move. She hadn't been at the firm since she'd gone looking for Jeff on the night he had disappeared, and given her druthers she wouldn't have come now. The firm was Jeff's minus Jeff. She felt uncomfortable seeing the people he had worked with, people she had entertained at her home many times, people who had respected Jeff once. But that was before Jeff had run off with fifty thousand dollars in cash, before the IRS had begun bandying about criminal charges to the tune of ten times that amount, before the *Sun* had done its thing. She didn't know what they felt about him now—or what they felt about her.

But she was desperate. The thought of returning home without promise of relief was worse than the thought of suffering the censorious stares of the colleagues Jeff had betrayed. Besides, David had been either at the house or calling her on the phone once a day, solicitous to the hilt. *If there's anything I can do, just yell. If you need anything, give a call.* Rather than yelling or calling, she decided to appear in the flesh. She needed a savior, and she needed one fast.

David was poring over a deskful of papers when she appeared at his door, and at first glance he didn't look thrilled to see her. By the time he had jumped up, drawn her into the room, and closed the door, though, the displeasure was gone.

"I didn't expect you here." He put an arm around her shoulder and pulled her close. Bending his dark head over hers, he said, "How are you doing?"

Laura wasn't any happier about the arm around her shoulder than about that fleeting look of displeasure or about having to be there in the first place, but she didn't have much choice. As far as she was concerned, the faster she said her piece and left, the better. "Not great. I've spent the day hitting every bank in Hampshire County, and not one will loan me a cent. I know the firm can't give me a loan per se"—she had asked about that several days before—"and I understand. There are cash-flow problems here, and the IRS watches everything you do. But there has to be money coming in from Jeff's clients. That's money he earned. It'd be a huge help to me if I could have access to it."

"You're discouraged," David said and dropped a kiss on her forehead. "That's normal, hon. Going from bank to bank looking for loans has to be the pits."

She leaned back so she could look up at him without being as close as he wanted. "That's not the point. I'll head into Boston on Thursday to try the banks there, and I'll keep at it until someone gives me a break, but in the meantime I need money."

"What you need," he said, flexing a large hand along her arm, "is to relax. You're tense as a wire."

His touch grated on her skin. She would have shrunk from it if she hadn't been loath to offend him. "I'll relax when I find a way to see us through these next few months. I mean, relatively speaking, I don't need all that much to buy a little time. There's three thousand due on the mortgage for the house, two to pay other bills, eight for Scott's tuition—the tuition payment will carry him through the rest of the year. By the time we have to put down a deposit for next year, I should have my money again." She had to believe that. "So it's really five thousand for the month, plus the tuition. That's not so much, given the amount of money you guys deal with all the time."

David looked pained. "But I don't have access to that money. It's the cash-flow problem I was talking about. There are associates to be paid here, and secretaries and rent."

"The money from Jeff's clients—"

"Goes toward overhead."

"But what about his monthly draw? Isn't it possible for me to get an advance on that?"

"Jeff isn't here. He isn't working."

Studying the benign expression on David's bearded face, Laura felt a twinge of annoyance. "Jeff's a partner here, and the definition of a partnership is that one covers for another if times are bad. What I'm asking is no different from what I'd be asking if Jeff had a heart attack and couldn't work for a month."

David arched a brow. "But he hasn't had a heart attack. He ran off of his own free will, after committing a crime that is an embarrassment to every person in this firm. Now it's left to us to salvage our reputation. It won't be easy. We'll all have to work our butts off to repair the damage."

Laura was suddenly desperate for breathing room. Along with his look and his tone, David's size had become intimidating. Breaking from his hold, she crossed the office to stand facing the window. "You're telling me that even if you were to go for it, the others wouldn't."

"Some of them are feeling pretty angry."

She turned to confront him. "Do you stick up for Jeff?"

"It's hard to stick up for a guy who's done what he has."

"But he's your friend."

"And because of that, my whole business is suddenly on the line."

"Nothing's been proven. Taylor Jones doesn't have his indictment."

"Only because he's off chasing after Christian in the hope of learning something more. But the indictment will be coming."

"That doesn't mean Jeff is guilty."

David started slowly toward her. In a quiet voice, he asked, "Do you think he's innocent?"

Part of her wanted to. The rest wanted to distance herself from Jeff and what he'd done. Her own reputation had suffered just as much as the firm's, but in different ways. She had wholeheartedly placed her faith and trust in the man. If he was guilty, she'd been a fool. "Someone has to think he's innocent."

"But do you?" David asked again. He stood directly in front of her. When she didn't answer, he touched her cheek. "The worst thing about all this is what he did to you. Sure, he's screwed things up here, but we'll survive. But you—what he did to you is inexcusable."

"He loved me," Laura argued. "We've had a good life."

"But no more. Now you're living through hell."

She tipped up her chin, as much to dislodge his hand from her face as to express the determination she felt. "I'll survive too."

"Let me help." He leaned closer. "Let me make it easier."

She felt the heat of his body and was chilled through and through. "Fine. Lend me money."

If he heard the frost in her voice, he chose to either ignore it or misinterpret it. His own voice was seductively low. "I can't do that. But I can help you. It has to be lonely, all by yourself in that house night after night. And depressing. You need someone to divert your mind."

"I have plenty to divert my mind. What I need is money."

"Come away for the weekend with me, Laura."

"David!" Slipping from him, she went straight to the door. With her hand on the knob, she turned. "You've been saying you'd help me. That's all I've been hearing for the past two weeks. But what you're offering isn't the kind of help I need."

"Sure it is," David replied. He stood straight and tall, without the least bit of remorse. "Every woman needs that kind of comfort."

"What era are you from?"

"Beth needs it. You need it. Every woman I've ever known needs it. Don't look so surprised."

"This isn't surprise," she said, pointing to her face. "This is dismay." She nearly said disgust, which was closer to what she felt, but a germ of wisdom warned her against being so blunt. It was enough that she was rejecting David; men didn't take kindly to rejection, and she might yet need his help. "I can't believe you're suggesting what you are."

He held her gaze. "It's no more than dozens of other men in this town have been thinking since Jeff disappeared." When she shook her head in denial, he said, "It is. I know. I've heard talk. You're a sexy lady, Laura."

"I'm a *married* lady."

"Whose husband has deserted her."

The word cut deep, eroding what little self-confidence she had left. In an attempt to save it, she argued, "Desertion is the wrong word. We don't know what Jeff was feeling when he left. He may have been torn apart inside but thought he had no other choice. Even as we talk, he may be sitting somewhere thinking about me, and if that's true I wouldn't call what he did desertion."

"He didn't leave you a note."

"Maybe he felt it was better that way."

"If he really cared, he would have left a note."

"He *did* really care. We were married for twenty years."

"That doesn't mean a thing," David mused in a lofty tone. "Believe me."

But Laura refused to do that. In the past two weeks, she'd had her own doubts about the strength of her relationship with Jeff, but she wasn't ready to air those doubts to anyone, least of all someone who was proving to be as traitorous—and lecherous—as David. "Jeff cared. I know he did. But that's not the issue here. The issue is that my husband is missing and you're looking to crawl into my bed. That's *awful*, David. You were supposed to be his friend."

"But you're alone."

"Not quite," she said, drawing an angry breath. "I have Debra and Scott and Lydia and my mother. I have lots of friends and a business to run, and the last thing I want is sexual involvement—and even if I did, you'd be out of the running. You happen to be married too, and your wife is my friend!"

"Not really," David argued. Laura caught defiance in his look. "Beth would have had an affair with Jeff if he'd asked her."

"David!" she cried again. "Why are you saying these things?"

"Because they're true. Beth hasn't been faithful to me. Why should I be faithful to her?"

"Maybe because it's the right thing to do?" Laura asked, though she had the feeling David wouldn't get that message at all. He seemed perfectly comfortable with what he was doing, which apparently already included cheating on Beth. "I have to get home," she murmured and opened the door.

Suddenly he was there, closing it again. With one hand flattened on the wood, serving both to hold the door shut and to curve his body around Laura's, he said in a deep voice by her ear, "I've wanted you for a long time. You know that, don't you?"

She kept her eyes on the door, concentrating more on staying composed than on anything else. Her stomach churned. Her voice shook. "I shouldn't have come here. It was a mistake."

"No. It's good you know how I feel. Okay, maybe this weekend isn't the right one. But another time—"

"Not another time."

"You just tell people you need to get away for a day or two, then I'll manufacture a business trip for me. Or if you don't want to be away overnight, we can go somewhere private for an afternoon. I know some discreet places."

"I'd like to leave now, David."

"Will you think about it?"

Laura had always prided herself on being honest, and the honest thing would have been to tell David to screw himself and leave her the hell alone. But she was still a pragmatist. She knew she might need him for something someday. And while she would never in a million years sleep with him, she was as hesitant to alienate him now as she'd been earlier.

"I don't want sex," she said in a fragmented breath, which was all her revulsion allowed her. "I have to leave."

He didn't move. "I'll call you later."

"If you're calling to ask about this, don't." Bile rose in her throat. She swallowed it down. "I have to leave," she whispered, and something of her frantic feeling must have made it through to David, because he finally stepped back.

"I'll call," he promised.

She fled without looking back.

Laura didn't take David's calls. Under the guise of not being in the mood to talk, she had Debra take messages, and when Debra wasn't home she let the machine do it. Actually, there weren't many calls—not from David or from the others who had been so solicitous when Jeff had first disappeared. People seemed to have lost interest. Either that, or they thought Jeff was guilty.

So Laura reasoned, and she grew more depressed. It didn't help that the search for a loan in Boston proved as futile as the local one had been. But the harshest blow of the week came Saturday morning, when Elise stopped by, clearly worried.

"I think we may have a problem," she said, so meekly that Laura slid closer along the kitchen counter to hear. "We've had a couple of cancellations."

"Everyone has cancellations. We always manage to fill them back up."

"These are for parties."

"For this week?" Laura asked and held her breath. She was desperate for every cent Cherries brought in. That money was the only income she had.

"For after the holidays."

Grateful for small favors, Laura let out a sigh. She found herself holding her breath again, though, when Elise went on.

"For late January and February. Three bookings."

"Which ones?"

"For catering, the Macon Company luncheon and the Kramer anniversary dinner. For the restaurant, the Hickenwright Sweet Sixteen." Elise looked to be in an agony of regret. "I didn't want to say anything, Laura. God knows you have enough on your mind. I was hoping I'd fill in with others before now, but the calls aren't coming in."

They'll come. Just wait. Once the holidays are done, people will start making plans for January and February and March, and they'll call.

Laura thought the words. A month ago, she would have spoken them. She'd been optimistic about the business right from the first, even when small setbacks had hit, and her optimism had always proven out. Now, though, things were different. The cancellations could have been coincidence. Then again, they could be related to the charges against Jeff.

Thinking aloud, Laura said, "Those bookings were made in October and November, if I remember right, which means that we've long since received deposits. Do they know they're forfeiting the deposits?"

Elise nodded. "I asked, and they do. I also asked if there was any particular reason for the cancellation. The Macon Company decided to move its conference from the corporate headquarters to a hotel, and the hotel will do the luncheon. That's logical."

Assuming it was the whole story. "Why did they decide to move the conference?"

"I didn't ask. It didn't seem like my business."

It wasn't, Laura knew; still, she'd have liked to know. If the conference had been moved because there were suddenly more people than could be handled in corporate headquarters, that was fair. If the conference had been moved because Jacob Macon, who knew Laura and Jeff socially and had personally made the initial call to Laura about the luncheon, wanted to dissociate himself from Cherries without causing a stir, that was more disturbing.

"What was Diane Kramer's excuse?"

Elise answered softly. "She said that too many of their guests knew of the connection between Cherries and Jeff, and she didn't want anything to mar the party."

Laura swallowed. "And the Hickenwrights?"

"They were worried we might fold, and they didn't want to be left in the cold. I told them Cherries wasn't closing. I assured them we were booked solid. I warned them that if they gave up the date and then changed their minds and wanted it back, the slot would be taken." Her voice dropped even more. "They said they'd already made other arrangements for their party."

Laura nodded. "I see." She took a long, loud breath and tried to still the frightened knock of her heart. But the fear was pervasive and real. "Oh, God," she whispered on the exhalation.

Elise immediately had a hand on her arm. "Maybe I shouldn't have said anything yet. We're smack in the middle of the holiday season. People won't be thinking about after the holidays until after the holidays. Bookings will pick up."

Laura gave a wistful thought back to the first of the month. "They were so good for December."

"And they're okay for January and February. Really they are."

"As good as last year?"

"Almost."

"They should be better. We're a year older. We're more established. They should be better."

Elise squeezed her arm and said with greater enthusiasm, "They will be. Just wait, Laura. We'll have ads going in the paper after the first of the year. That'll help."

Hearing near desperation in her enthusiasm, Laura forced a smile. "You're right. I can't help but worry sometimes, but you're right. It's the time of year and the economy. If there'd be any months when things weren't booming, it'd be January, February, and March." She paused, frowned. "Let me know if you get any more calls, though. Either way, cancellations or bookings. I have to know what we're facing."

THIRTEEN

❋❋❋

"PEACE ON EARTH, GOODWILL toward men." If you've heard the words once, you've heard them a dozen times. They are being preached from pulpits all around town this week; they appear on greeting cards that fill the mailman's bag; they are written on store windows up and down Main Street.

Another year, another Christmas. The message is the same, yet as much of a dream as ever. War continues to rage in the Middle East, perpetuated by the cowardice of our leaders who, in the name of diplomacy, stand back, shake hands, and smile. Likewise, poison continues to flow from the drug lords of South America into the veins of our children, while government bureaucrats sit at their desks, scratching their heads and mulling over possible courses of action. Infuriated by their impotence, we are driven to action ourselves, only to be arrested in front of abortion clinics where our voices may well save the lives of human beings too tiny to speak for themselves.

How can there be peace on earth when muggers walk the streets, when convicts are parolled long before their sentences have been served, when rapists are freed on technicalities of law? How can there be goodwill toward men without pride and trust, and how can there be pride and trust when intelligent men scheme to steal money that belongs to others?

Before the streets of the world can be cleaned up, the streets of the country must be cleaned up, and before that, the streets of the state, and before that, the city, which brings up the case of Jeffrey Frye. His situation is particularly disheartening because of his local ties. He was born and raised in Northampton, and he established a successful business here. Yet the government claims he willfully defrauded it of hundreds of thousands of dollars, and that is a major blot on our community and on us. He must be apprehended. Until then, we share his guilt.

Bringing Jeffrey Frye to justice will be a beginning. Indeed, it may take many such beginnings before we make serious headway in the quest for peace on earth, but the goal is worth it.

As a child, Laura had hated Christmas. Her parents cared far more for intellectual endeavors than for holidays, which meant that while the rest of the world decorated trees, sang carols, and opened presents, the senior McVeys spent the holiday season reading or writing or comparing notes with colleagues. Santa Claus was someone Laura visited with her little friends, though she knew from the start that he wasn't for real. Her parents told her so. Yes, they bought her gifts so that she wouldn't feel left out, but those gifts were practical, never frivolous, and by the time she and her sister were teenagers, the gift-giving was done.

As early as she could remember, Laura had vowed that when she was an adult in her own home, Christmases would be different. And so they were. Starting the very first year of her marriage, though she and Jeffrey couldn't afford much of anything, she had cooked and decorated and generally dedicated herself to making the holiday a lighthearted and festive affair. It was all the more so after the children were born. For months, Laura would stash small fun gifts in a sack in the back of the closet. She made a ceremony of decorating the tree, with the children inviting friends to join in the fun. She helped them make long strings of popcorn and baked Christmas cookies and lit scented candles. She planned Christmas dinner, much as she did Thanksgiving, with an eye toward brightness, excitement, and pleasure.

Christmas this year was different. Oh, she tried. She bought a tree and had Scott set it up the night he came home from school, then dragged the decorations from the attic and trimmed it well. She had gifts, though nothing that had been bought since Jeff had disappeared, not so much because of the money but because she'd been distracted. But she wanted—needed—a semblance of holiday cheer, so she went through the motions of planning an elegant Christmas dinner.

Then Gary Holmes's editorial appeared in the *Sun* on Monday, Christmas Eve, and it became harder to pretend the holiday was a happy one. Debra was furious at the paper, Scott was furious at Jeff, Maddie was furious at Laura, and Laura didn't know *what* to do.

"You're just as bad as those bureaucrats he mentions," Maddie said across the kitchen island. Classes were out, and though it would have been nice if she'd come over to tell Laura what a success the department party at the restaurant had been, she was far more concerned with the Holmes editorial. "Here you sit on your neat little stool, mulling over your options. Isn't it time to do something, Laura? Don't you think you ought to take the offensive for a change?"

Laura was chopping roasted chestnuts for a turkey stuffing. "What would you have me do?"

"Sue Gary Holmes. He's slandering your family."

"He's only repeating charges the IRS made against Jeff. What he's doing may be irresponsible, but there's nothing illegal about it. I don't have a case." As frustrating as that was, she had already checked with Daphne and knew it was true.

But Maddie was in her bulldog mode. "Sue him anyway. You need a forum to present your side of the case."

"I can't afford the forum, Mother. Lawsuits cost money, and I don't have a whole lot to spare right now." Shoving the chestnuts to the side of the cutting board, she went to work on a bunch of scallions.

"There are times, Laura, when certain things have to be done on principle alone. This is one of those times. We are being scapegoated by that man and his paper for all the ills of the world. I think you ought to fight back."

But Laura wasn't in the mood to fight anyone, so she let her mother talk while she finished the stuffing, then she dashed off to oversee Christmas Eve at the restaurant. In the past, Jeff would have come along with her. Together, they might have returned home for the kids and gone to midnight mass. Laura didn't feel the least bit inspired this year, and she didn't want to force the kids into anything, so she had let them do as they wanted and go out with friends. As a result, the house was grotesquely silent when she returned. She put on a CD of Christmas carols, with the volume turned high to fill the silence, and went back to the kitchen to cook.

Unfortunately, the music couldn't drown out her thoughts, which wouldn't stay put in the harmless spaces she wanted them. They kept darting from Jeff to the kids to the business to the future. Several times her hands began to shake and she had to take a breath and steady herself. Other times she found her eyes filling with tears and had to stop again and wipe them away.

Debra and Scott came home within fifteen minutes of each other, lingering in the kitchen to talk with Laura while she cleaned up. Debra reported on what she claimed was a totally uneventful night watching videos at Jenna's. Scott told of taking Kelly to the local sports bar to watch reruns of the World Series on a five-by-five screen.

He was no sooner done when Debra came out with, "Dad didn't call, did he?"

Laura shook her head.

"Why would he call tonight?" Scott asked Debra.

"Because it's Christmas Eve."

"You think that matters to him, if he's been gone this long?"

"It might," Debra said, scowling. "Don't you think so, Mom?"

Laura would have thought it, if for no other reason than that he knew how much the holiday meant to the kids. But he hadn't called, which she supposed was in keeping with everything else he'd failed to do in the last month. "Maybe we'll hear from him tomorrow."

"Don't hold your breath," Scott said, and Laura felt a pervasive sadness. Scott had always been happy-go-lucky, easy to please and upbeat. Jeff's disappearance had changed him. He'd grown cynical. Innocence had been lost, and she mourned it.

"I know you're angry," she said gently. "So am I, and we have a right to be, in some respects."

"*Some* respects? Try *lots* of respects. He walked out on us. He just took off and left us to deal with a really ugly situation. I saw half a dozen guys in that bar tonight who were in my graduating class, and every one of them saw me, but they weren't coming near. No way. You'da thought I was a leper."

"Maybe it's that shirt," Debra said. "It's puke green."

Scott ignored her. "They read the paper, and if they don't, someone reads it and tells them. They know what he did. The whole town knows what he did, and the stink's rubbing off on us."

"Come on, Scottie," Laura said. "You're the one who wants to be a lawyer, but you're breaking the basic rule. You're making judgments when we don't know the facts."

"We know enough."

"No, we don't," Debra argued. "You two may think he's guilty, but not me. If Dad left here, he had a reason."

"Yeah. He tried to rip off the government and got caught."

"But he may have an explanation for what he did."

"How do you explain grand theft?"

"I don't know," she cried, "but that doesn't mean you can't." She turned to Laura with a trembling voice. "It's Christmas, and I know the restaurant's closed tomorrow and you're planning a big dinner and all, but are we really supposed to celebrate with Dad missing?"

"We have to," Laura insisted softly. Seeing tears in Debra's eyes, she felt her own throat knot. Dropping the dishtowel, she put an arm around her shoulder. Her voice was very low, her head bowed beside Debra's. "It's Christmas, and Christmas is supposed to be a happy time." When Debra opened her mouth to argue, she hurried on. "I know you're not feeling happy. Neither am I. Neither is Scott. But we'll only feel worse if we sit around and mope. We have things to be grateful for. You can think about them tomorrow."

"Name one," Debra muttered.

"Nana Lydia. She'll be here and she loves you, which is more than some of your friends can say about their grandmothers."

Debra relented, but only to the extent that her jaw wasn't thrust out so far. "Won't it be awful for her with Dad not here?"

"It might be. So it's up to us to keep her cheery. Same thing with Gram." Laura looked at Scott. "She's feeling as angry as you are about all this. To her way of thinking, the negative publicity we're getting will drive her career right down the drain."

"Gram McVey's career down the drain?" Scott snorted. "The only way that'll happen is if the American Psychology Association holds its annual conference in the sewer. I mean, she's got it made for life."

Laura tried to see things from her mother's point of view. "She's getting older. For a while now she's been worried that they'll want someone younger to head the department. She thinks this might be the lever they need. So it's a tough holiday for her too. We can't just let her sit alone and brood."

"But to smile and laugh and run around like everything's hunky-dory?" Debra asked. "What if Dad's dead? The police haven't ruled that out."

"If Dad's dead, the laugh's on us," Scott said. "The government can't bring charges against a dead man, so we'll have gone through all this shit for nothing."

"Scott," Laura said in a pleading tone, "don't say things like that. It doesn't do any good."

"Mom's right."

"But it's the truth," Scott insisted.

"It may be," Laura conceded, "but saying it doesn't help. We don't know where Dad is. We don't know what he's doing. I don't accept that he's dead. All we can do for now is to keep on going the way we are, which means having a regular Christmas dinner tomorrow with all the fixings and trying to have a little fun."

"It won't be the same without Dad," was Debra's shaky response. "I want things back the way they were."

Laura hugged her tighter, and not just because Debra sounded young and upset. Laura was frightened herself. The future was full of unknowns. She hadn't been as unsure of what was going to be since she had decided to drop out of Smith, and she'd been young then, without children or a business or employees who depended on her. Now she had a world of responsibility on her shoulders, and Jeff wasn't there to help her. Okay, so he hadn't really done all that much before; still, he'd *been* there. Now he wasn't. And on Christmas Eve, she was frightened and lonely.

Feeling Debra's warmth, knowing that Scott was close by, she drew on remnants of strength to say, "Life doesn't always stay the same. With the passage of time, things change. It's inevitable. But that doesn't mean they have to be worse."

"Do you think life will be better without Dad?" Debra asked.

"It'll be *different*. We have to keep an open mind about things. Like tomorrow. If we sit down to dinner thinking about nothing but the fact that Dad isn't here, it'll be dismal. If we sit down with the idea that the rest of us are together and we're healthy and we have the hope of good things happening in the next few weeks or months—" her voice broke "—we'll be okay." She would have said more, but she didn't trust her voice. She didn't trust her eyes, either. They had filled with tears again. So she closed them to keep the children from seeing the extent of her fear.

Seeming to sense that silence had merit, Debra didn't speak. Neither did Scott, but after a minute, Laura felt his hand on her shoulder. Freeing one of her own, she linked her fingers with his.

Those few silent moments were the highlights of Laura's holiday.

Two days after Christmas, Daphne took Debra to New York. Laura had been hesitant, given the money situation, but Daphne insisted.

"I have money, Laura. I earn plenty, and I have no kids. If I can't spend it on Debra, who can I spend it on?"

"You're already spending it on me," Laura reminded her. Daphne had been dividing her evenings between Jeff's home files and Laura's business records in search of the information she needed to put together a motion to lift the IRS freeze. "You're doing all this work for me, and I can't pay you a cent."

"I don't want a cent. I don't *need* a cent."

"But this is your *time*."

"And you're my friend," Daphne informed her, with a look that brooked no argument. "I don't want to hear another word about it."

Laura didn't say another word. Debra was thrilled to be going off with Daphne, which made Laura happy, and Scott had taken it upon himself to work at Cherries. Laura appreciated his help, enough so that she didn't dwell on the fact that he should be sleeping late and having fun before returning to Penn.

Besides, she had enough else to dwell on. Bills continued to arrive with the mail each day, and no matter how much Laura deposited in her new bank account, no amount of fiddling could get that amount to equal the amount at the bottom of her bills-to-be-paid list.

So she continued to cut back. She spoke to Emmie, who had been coming in twice weekly to do cleaning and laundry, which Laura could do herself, and that included the armloads of clothes she would otherwise have taken to the dry cleaner without thinking twice. Now Laura thought twice. She had already put off the carpet cleaner, put off the painter who was to do the downstairs bathroom, put off buying new linen place mats for the restaurant. She had called Diana at the boutique and asked her to try to sell the Welsh sweater she had special-ordered. She had canceled the trip to Saba, with just enough time to get a refund on her tickets.

But those were all small things in the overall scheme. They barely made a dent in the discrepancy between what she had and what she owed. She had nightmares about having to close Cherries and take a job waiting tables at Timothy's, her chief competitor, and even aside from the nightmares she didn't sleep well. Night after night she woke up in a cold sweat, shaking, afraid she wouldn't be able to hold things together. There were times when she woke up in the morning wanting nothing more than to stay in bed all day and hide from the world. If no one could see her, no one could hurt her, she reasoned. But the reasoning was faulty, she knew. The bills would arrive, whether she opened them or not, and if she didn't pay them, she'd be in worse trouble than ever.

If the government could freeze her assets so that no one could buy or sell her house, could a bank foreclose on it?

Half facetious, half frantic, she put the question to Daphne soon after she returned from New York, and Daphne took it seriously. She asked around in the legal community. She went to the lawbooks for precedents. She learned that Laura could file for a stay of foreclosure if that particular point was reached.

That point was a long way off, Daphne assured her.

But Laura wasn't easily assured. Too much had been knocked out from under her. The rosy world she'd known, where things went her way if she wished it and worked hard enough, didn't exist any more. Her whole future was shaky. There was too much she didn't know.

That was why, rather than arguing with Daphne about stays of foreclosure, she broached another idea. "It's time we hired a private investigator. That's one of the things I think about when I wake up in the middle of the night. I keep asking myself whether we'd have already found Jeff if we'd hired one from the start, and just the wondering is driving me crazy."

It was a minute of silence before Daphne warned, "Sleuths cost."

Laura could see that she wasn't any crazier about the idea of a private investigator than she'd been at the start, but Daphne wasn't the one living with the dregs of Jeff's folly. "True, and I certainly can't walk into someone's office and set down a retainer. But I'd think a private investigator would welcome this case. There's the challenge. And the publicity. And there's the promise of money. Once I get into those bank accounts, I can pay."

Daphne pushed a hand through her hair. She was wearing it loose, in keeping with her weekend outfit of a blazer and jeans, and she looked as classy as ever. She also looked bothered. "Laura, those accounts aren't loaded. There's money in them, but if you're thinking you'll be on Easy Street once you get your half, you're wrong."

"They'd be something. They'd tide me over. They'd give me a *little* to fall back on, at least." She didn't know why Daphne had a problem with private investigators, but she was desperate to make her point. "It'll be four weeks on New Year's Day that he's gone, and I don't know anything more now about where he is than I did then. The police follow up on the phone calls they get, but other than that they're not doing much. Neither is the IRS. And if the FBI is on the case, I know why so many of the Ten Most Wanted are still walking the streets. Jeff has to be somewhere. I want to know where. If I had the time and energy and know-how, I'd go out looking for him myself, but I don't have any of those things, so I'm stuck here waiting for other people to find him. Well, they're not doing it, and I'm tired of waiting. I want to *do* something."

Daphne studied her for a minute. "Let me talk with Taylor Jones."

"Why not a private investigator?"

"Because we shouldn't have to spend our own money to do the government's job."

"But the government isn't doing the job, and I want it done."

"We owe Jones a final shot."

"Do you know any good PIs?"

Daphne nodded. "I've worked with some."

"Call one."

"First, Taylor Jones."

FOURTEEN

TACK HADN'T SEEN DAPHNE since the morning she had shown up at the police station to blast him for opening his mouth to the press. He had thought about her, though, enough to mystify him. Sure, she had great legs, but he knew lots of women with great legs, so that didn't explain why she kept coming to mind. He figured it had something to do with her style—the way she moved, the way she talked, the way she defended her friends. She intrigued him.

For that reason, he felt distinct pleasure when she appeared at his door.

Actually, there was another reason too. It was after four on the last day of the year. Little more than a skeletal staff remained at the police station, with most everyone else off getting ready for New Year's Eve. But Tack didn't have plans for New Year's Eve—or New Year's Day, for that matter. So he was hanging around the station, shuffling papers on his desk, pretending to be on the verge of a breakthrough in the Frye case, when what he was really doing was feeling sorry for himself.

The smile he gave Daphne was broad and natural and seemed to startle her. She stook stockstill for a long moment. Then, with care, he thought, she ventured a tentative smile of her own. "That's nice," she said, almost curiously. "People in this building usually freeze up when I set foot inside the door."

"Not me. Not today. I need company. Wanna sit?"

The last time she'd come, she had stalked up to his desk and stood the whole time. He half expected her to do the same thing now, especially when she gathered herself in a businesslike way. But then, with a puzzled look, she seemed to pause, and in the next second what he saw in her eyes wasn't businesslike at all.

In the second after that, though, she blinked, and he figured he must have imagined whatever he thought he'd seen. Just when he was beginning to feel sorry for himself again, she came forward and slid into the chair across the desk from him. She lowered her briefcase to the floor. She crossed her legs. And though she deftly smoothed her skirt over her thighs so that little by way of enticement showed, he couldn't help but look. When he finally raised his eyes to hers, her expression was reproachful.

"Sorry," he murmured. He glanced at the side wall to get his bearings, then cleared his throat and looked back at her. "Actually, I'm not sorry. You look great. But then, you always do. You must be used to men staring at you. I'll bet it happens all the time."

She shook her head.

"No?" He couldn't believe that.

"I'm a lawyer. They don't dare."

"Oh." He guessed that said something about the men in Hampshire County and wondered if she meant it as a warning to him. If so, he figured he'd better set her straight. "Well, I dare. You really do look great. Best thing I've seen all day." He grinned and seconds later could have sworn she blushed. When the color remained, he decided it was her makeup, which made more sense, given the image he had of Daphne. He didn't think she was the blushing type. "So how are you doin', counselor?"

"Not bad." Her eyes were still on his face. "That's a nice tan you've got."

"Thanks. There's something about the sun in Tahiti that does it. Hey, you spend all that time running from from one end of the island to the other trying to track down a witness, and you're bound to catch a few rays, right?"

"Did you snorkel?"

"Sure did—when I needed a break from tracking down the witness."

"And wind-surf?"

"When I needed another break. Tracking down witnesses is hard work."

Either her lips were pursed in a prissy way or she was holding back a smile. "I know Christian, Agent Jones. My guess is that once you found him, he did his best to corrupt you."

Tack scratched his head. "I guess you do know him, at that." Remembering the Mahanoa'ee sisters, he had a disconcerting thought. "How *well* do you know him?"

"He's my best friend's brother-in-law. He was at their wedding, and so was I. He was at the kids' christenings, and so was I. He was at Lydia's sixty-fifth birthday bash, and so was I. And that's not to mention the occasional Thanksgiving, Christmas, and Easter dinner."

"That's a lot. He's a lucky guy. It must be real convenient to come visiting and find you waiting."

It was the wrong thing to say. He knew it the instant the words were out of his mouth, when the pleasant look she'd been wearing turned cold as ice and she started to rise.

"Hey," he said, half out of his chair himself, with a hand out to halt her escape. "I'm sorry. That was uncalled-for."

"It was also *wrong*," she informed him. Her eyes flashed, that pretty hazel color he remembered. He wasn't sorry he'd asked after all, particularly when she went on. "There's never been anything between Christian and me. Why you'd think there was is beyond me."

"He's single, you're single—"

"We haven't a blessed thing in common. He's as anti-establishment as I'm establishment, and that's just for starters. I could go on ad infinitum about our differences, but it would be a waste of time for both of us."

"That's okay. I'm in no rush." To prove his point, he sat back in his seat and linked his fingers over his middle.

Daphne didn't quite sit back, but at least her bottom was touching the seat again. "It's New Year's Eve. Everyone's clearing out. Shouldn't you be heading back to Boston or somewhere?"

"There's nothing for me in Boston."

"Uh-huh."

"You don't believe me?"

"Of course, I believe you—" she caught herself "—no, you're right, I don't. You look like the kind of guy who has a girl in every port."

"That sexy, huh?" He rushed on before she could deny it. "Actually, I broke up with someone a few weeks ago, and I've been alone ever since. So there's no one in Boston, and there's no one here, which means I have all the time in the world to sit and talk." He rocked farther back in his chair, folded his hands behind his head, and grinned.

The grin got to her. Again. It seemed to surprise her, make her forget what she was going to say. Then again, Tack mused, maybe that was wishful thinking on his part. But he kept on grinning on the chance it was true, and because he was feeling better than he had for a while.

After staring at him longer than she should have, Daphne shot a glance at the ceiling that reminded him of the one he'd sent toward the wall. When she looked down again, she was in control. "I came here for a reason."

"I figured."

She took a deep breath. "Laura wants to hire a private investigator. Before we go to the expense, I want to know what you've learned. Dennis tells me Christian wasn't any help."

"Not in locating Jeff," Tack confirmed. He had no problem sharing information, particularly if it would win her confidence. "Christian hasn't seen him or heard from him. We've checked out airlines, bus lines, train lines. We've checked out rental car companies—yes, I know he took the Porsche, but there's always the chance he ditched it somewhere and rented something less conspicuous. We've checked hotels and motels and police in this state and in every contiguous state, then every state contiguous to those contiguous states, and no one's seen hide nor hair of the bastard."

"Has he used any credit cards?"

"No."

"Has he tried to use his bank card?"

"No. He's clever. Hasn't left a single crumb for us to follow."

"So what are you going to do?" Daphne's voice held a challenge that Tack was only too happy to meet.

"We're shifting our focus to his life here. We're talking with friends, clients, business associates." He thought about what he'd found out. "It's interesting."

"How so?"

"No one seems to know him real well. When he was around, they liked him. They even respected him for his know-how or his manner. But when you ask if they thought he was capable of committing a crime like this, they don't immediately say no."

"What do they say?"

"That they didn't know what he was thinking. That there were times when he went through the motions but he just wasn't there." Tack paused again, this time to study her face. She was close to the family. She was close to Jeff. Of all the people he'd spoken with, she was in a position to give him the most. "Did you ever get that feeling?"

"No."

"He seemed attentive?"

"Yes."

"Was he happy?"

She opened her mouth to answer, then closed it again, which surprised Tack. He would have assumed she'd say yes. That had been the family story, that Jeff was happy and content and honest and kind. The guy sounded boring as hell to Tack, which was one of the reasons why he loved it when people paused and thought twice, then gave him answers he didn't expect. The surprises were what made his job interesting, and this case had a few.

"He was as happy as most people," Daphne finally said.

"Is that happy or not?"

"Happy, I guess."

But she seemed to be having trouble with the word, and he wanted to know why. "Either he was happy, or he wasn't. It's a black-and-white issue."

"No, it's not. A person can be wildly happy, meaning that he loves absolutely everything in his life, or he can be relatively happy, meaning that if things were different he would be happier, but since they're not—and can't be—he can live with what he's got."

"Jeff was the relatively happy kind?"

She frowned at her hand, which lay quietly in her lap. "I think so."

"What would have made him happier in life?"

She continued to frown, looking torn now.

Softly, and in earnest, he said, "This is between you and me, Daphne. Totally off the record. I'm trying to get some insight into the man. That's all."

Her eyes rose. A crease came and went between them. In a voice that was as soft as his had been, she said, "I think he'd have been happier if he were married to someone other than Laura."

"But Laura's your best friend."

"I know, and I adore her for her strengths, but those strengths kept Jeff down. I mean, he loved her. But he had to live in her shadow, and that can be hard for a man to do year after year. If he'd married someone not quite so overpowering, he'd have been able to shine more than he did."

Tack scratched his head. "Laura overpowering?" Christian had said something similar, and he'd been doubtful then too. "She didn't strike me that way."

"Of course not. You're seeing her at her worst. She doesn't have any control over what's happening now, and, believe me, it's driving her nuts. But if you look at the way she and Jeff lived, you'll see it. She shaped their lives. When something needed doing, she did it. When something needed arranging, she arranged it. The trip to Saba is a perfect example." She sat back. "You heard about that, didn't you?"

"Just that they were planning to go."

"Let me tell you about those plans. A while back, Laura decided that once every winter the whole family should go someplace warm. In the past, it's been St. Martin or St. John or Nevis. This year it was supposed to be Saba. She rented a villa with seven bedrooms, a maid, and a cook. She booked airline tickets not only for Jeff and the kids and her, but for her mother-in-law, one of Scott's roommates, and me. She arranged for a surrey to meet us at the airport. She arranged for a sloop with a full crew and a scuba instructor to take us island-hopping. She arranged for the cook to do a Caribbean feast on the beach one night. She even found a calypso trio to serenade. And the thing of it is that she arranged all this thinking we'd all be as ecstatic as she was, when in fact Jeff hates hot weather, Scott would rather be with girls, Lydia is terrified of flying, and I can't take the time off from work."

"I'd take time off from work. The trip sounds great."

"The trip is now canceled, but that's not the point. The point is that Laura gets things done. She's a very competent woman. That's tough for a guy who may not be so competent."

"And Jeff wasn't?"

"He could have been, given the chance."

"But he wasn't given the chance. So why didn't he leave her?"

"Because there were lots of things he liked about his life. It gets back to that issue of happiness. He wasn't giving up the good for the unknown."

"Looks like he did," Tack said.

Daphne grew guarded. "We don't know that for sure. Until somebody finds him, we don't know *anything* for sure, which is why we're thinking of hiring a private investigator. If you can't make any headway—"

Tack interrupted her. He heard criticism coming on, and he wasn't in the mood. There was more he wanted to know. "You say Jeff loved his wife."

After a pause, she said, "Yes."

"But her competence frustrated him."

"That was my opinion. Just mine. I don't know whether he identified competence as the problem or not."

"Could he have been physically dissatisfied?"

Daphne was silent. "Physically?"

"Sex. Was it good between them?"

"Since we weren't into a *ménage à trois*, I wouldn't know, Agent Jones."

"The name's Tack, and I realize that," he said. Thought of a *ménage à trois* involving Daphne gave him a jolt somewhere low, but he ignored it. "But did Laura ever hint that things weren't so hot in bed?"

"No. I've told you before. She thought her marriage was great."

"Did *he* ever drop any hints?"

"Why would he do that?"

"Maybe because he had someone on the side and wanted reassurance that what he was doing wasn't so horrible."

Daphne sat still as stone. Her lips—thin lips, Tack saw, but gentle and covered with a stylish buff-colored gloss—were pressed together. Finally they parted. "I've been forthright with you, Agent Jones, more so than I should have been, since the Fryes are my clients. But in the sense that we both want to find Jeff, we're temporarily on the same side. If you know something I don't, why don't you come right out and say 'it."

Tack took her up on the invitation. "He was having an affair."

Her face drained of color, and though she didn't move an inch, he could see she was shaken. "What?"

"He was having an affair. We have a witness who places him at his condo in Holyoke with a woman who wasn't his wife."

Daphne looked so dismayed that any pleasure he might have gotten from hitting her with a fast one was lost. "You have a witness?" she asked in a low voice.

He nodded. "A neighbor. She didn't know Jeff's name. But I was wandering around out there last week, talking with people, showing his picture. She recognized it right away."

"She was sure it was Jeff?"

"Very."

"Did she know who the woman with him was?"

"No. She mentioned long, loose, sand-colored hair, so we knew it wasn't Laura, and she confirmed it when we showed her Laura's picture."

Daphne stared at him. "Jeff loved Laura. There must be a mistake."

"The witness was certain. She saw him with this other woman more than once."

"How does she know they were lovers? How does she know they weren't just friends or business associates?"

"She saw them kissing in a way that friends wouldn't do."

Daphne compressed her lips. Hesitantly, she asked, "Was there only one woman? Was that all your witness saw?"

"Just one."

"No others brought to the condo at other times?"

"No. She said she rarely saw him there, which was why she always noticed when he came. On the times he was with someone, it was always the woman with the super hair."

Daphne took a slow breath, then swallowed. "Has your witness been down to the station?"

Tack nodded. "This morning."

"Then this is formally entered in your records?" Her voice retained a still quality, as though she were holding her breath.

He nodded.

"Is it common knowledge around here yet?"

"Not unless Melrose talked. He was the only one with me when the witness came in."

"Have you called the *Sun?*"

Tack took offense. The front legs of his chair hit the floor. "Why would I do that? You may find this hard to believe, but my goal in this job is not publicity. It's to find Jeffrey Frye and see that he's brought to trial. I don't get any great kicks out of providing the paper with copy."

She was wary. "You've talked before."

"Because O'Neil called and asked. Mostly I gave yeses and nos in response to his questions. If he tosses out scenarios and I give him yeses and nos, and then he writes his piece like I was the one doing the tossing, it's not *my* fault."

Her wariness faded, but she didn't look away. After a minute, she swallowed again. Then, before Tack's eyes, it was as though the tension left her and she was suddenly, overwhelmingly tired. "Don't tell him about this," she pleaded. "He'll plaster headlines on page one, and it'll be one more humiliation for Laura to endure. This will be the worst. It'll hurt her so much." Her voice caught. She put a shaky finger to her mouth.

Tack remembered the times he'd thought of Daphne Phillips losing her cool and the pleasure he'd found in the thought. She hadn't exactly lost it now. She was still a lady, sitting there with her hair pulled back in a shiny knot, her skirt smooth, and her ankles crossed, but she was clearly upset, and there wasn't any pleasure in it for him.

"Hey," he murmured gently, "I'm not gonna tell." Leaving his chair, he rounded the desk and hunkered down by her side. "I'm not a total bastard, Daphne. I know this isn't easy for Laura, and I won't do anything to make it any worse than it has to be. Obviously I'll be doing my damnedest to identify the woman, but I won't be running to the papers. If I did that, whoever it is will take off, and I'd look like a *real* fool."

Her eyes stayed on his face, searching his eyes, then moving down to his mouth for a second before she dropped her hand to her lap and looked off at the wall. "This case is a nightmare."

"And you're living through it with Laura."

"Oh, I have it easy. I can push it aside to work on other cases, then go home and not notice the silence, because silence is par for the course."

"You live alone?"

"Yeah." She took a fast breath and stood. "And I'd better be going."

He stood too. "Have any hot plans for tonight?"

She threaded the straps of her briefcase over her shoulder and pulled her coat tighter. Then she tipped up her chin. "Actually, I'm planning to read a good book."

"All by yourself?"

"That's the best way to do it."

"What about food?"

"If I get hungry, I'll get something from the freezer."

"I have a better idea," Tack said. He hadn't given it a whole lot of thought, mainly because he hadn't expected Daphne Phillips to fall into his lap this way, but he wasn't blowing what could be a once-in-a-lifetime chance. "Let's get something together."

She blinked. "Uh, I don't think that would be smart."

"Why not? It's New Year's Eve. I'm alone, you're alone, and being alone on New Year's Eve sucks. I'm still new here. I don't know where the hell to go. So you choose. We could eat Italian, Chinese, French. We even could go to Cherries."

She chided him with a look. "Not smart at all. Laura will be there. What do you think she'll think if she sees us together?"

"Let her think you're sweet-talking me into dropping the case against her husband."

"But I'm not doing that," Daphne said with an instructional half smile.

He wanted a full smile. He wanted more of the little curls in his stomach each time he got a whiff of something faint and sweet. He wanted someone to talk with. He wanted a decent meal for a change, not the fast-food stuff he'd been living on. Mostly he didn't want to be alone.

"I won't drop the case against her husband," he told her without a bit of smartness. "I can't. It's not mine to drop. It's the government's. All I am is an agent—"

"Not a good idea," she repeated and started for the door.

"No one has to see us," he argued. "And so what if they do? It's not like there's anything fishy going on. We'd just be discussing business."

At the door, she turned and asked quietly, "Would we?"

"If that was what you wanted."

"What if we got tired of discussing business?"

"Then we could discuss something else."

"Like what?"

"Like whatever book it is you're planning to read, or what kind of job you think the President's doing, or why you ought to plan a trip to Tahiti. Hell, Daphne, we can talk about whatever we want. Isn't that what people do when they go out together?"

He hadn't meant to say it that way, mainly because he knew it would scare her off. God, was she prickly! Prickly, and pretty, and smart, and challenging. Maybe the prickly part came with old age. Maybe prickly was really picky, and she really didn't like him.

He stuck his hands in his slacks pockets. "You're right. I'd probably bore you to tears."

"I didn't say that."

"I'll bet you love that silence of yours."

"Not always."

"Restaurants are awful on New Year's Eve. People drink, and they're loud, and the prices are higher and the service slower. I don't blame you for not wanting to go out."

She tucked her chin to her chest for a long, pensive minute. Then, reaching a decision, she looked up. "Maybe a drink. It's too early for dinner, but we could go somewhere for a drink. Just one. Just for an hour."

"You're on," he said with a grin. Without waiting to see what effect the grin had, he quickly collected papers from the desk and shoved them into a briefcase, grabbed his topcoat from the hook behind the door, and escorted her out.

* * *

Daphne chose a bar on the lower end of Main Street that she claimed was a favorite of the town's legal eagles. Tack didn't see any legal eagles around, but that could have been because of the holiday, or because the place was so dark he wouldn't have been able to see them if they had been there. He was sure that was why she had chosen the place. She wanted privacy for professional reasons. He wanted privacy for other reasons.

She ordered a glass of wine to his Sam Adams, and as soon as the bartender served them up, they slid into a booth near the back of the bar. "So," Tack said, after he'd taken a hefty swallow of his beer, "tell me what a nice girl like you is doing in a small town like this."

Her mouth twitched. "I like small towns. I was born here. I'll probably die here."

"Is that resignation I hear?"

"No. I went to law school in New Haven and could have gone anywhere from there, but I chose to come back. It was what I wanted to do."

"Why?"

She considered that. "My family's here, or was. My parents are dead now, and my brother's long gone. Still, this is where I grew up. I've lived in the same house all my life."

"No kidding," he said. "That's neat."

She smiled. "Yeah. I suppose. I like the place, at any rate, and since the mortgage was paid off a long time ago, it comes dirt cheap."

"How about Hampshire County? Is it a good place to practice law?"

"Yes and no. I have a good practice. It's a criminal one, but the crime here isn't as gruesome as it is in the big city, and that pleases me. I'm not big on blood and guts."

Melrose had called her tough, and on the surface she was. But Tack was beginning to think the toughness ended there. "So things are tamer here. That's the yes. What's the no?"

"People are less liberal." She narrowed it down. "Lawyers are less liberal." And again. "Male lawyers are less liberal."

He understood. "You've had to do the women's lib thing from scratch."

"Uh-huh. When I started practicing, I was the first female lawyer some of these guys had ever met. It's the old story—I had to work twice as hard and be twice as good. It's been an experience."

"But the worst must be over."

"I guess."

"Does that mean the challenge is gone?"

"Not at all. Every case is new and different. Each one is a challenge."

He sat back in the booth and sighed. "In my next life, I think I'll be a lawyer. You guys have exciting lives. Me? I may get an exciting case once a year, but you get 'em all the time, and then there's the glamour of the courtroom, with everyone watching you, and the jurors hanging on your every word, and the press quoting you. By the time my cases end up in court, I'm back in the office with my nose stuck in spread sheets until one in the morning, and by then everyone else has had their fun and is sound asleep, so there isn't a damn thing to do but go home to a cold, empty apartment."

From the dimness across the booth came a quiet reply. "After a long day in court, my house is just as cold and empty. If there's glamour trying a case in front of a jury, it ends on the courthouse steps. Believe me, being a lawyer isn't the answer to a cold, empty house."

It was hard to feel sorry for himself when she sounded sad like that. "You don't strike me as the type to want glamour."

"I'm not."

"What do you want?"

She finished her wine and set down the glass. "I'm not sure."

"Tell me."

"I would if I could."

He wagged two fingers at the bartender to order seconds for them both. "You want to be a judge someday?"

"Maybe."

"That'd be a nice way to grow old. Lots of adulation."

"But still a big empty house at the end of the day."

"Maybe you'll go into politics. Could you see yourself running for the House of Representatives?"

"No."

"Why not?"

Her mouth twitched again. "I smoked pot in college. Voters around here don't like that."

"I'll smoke pot with you any time you want," Tack said.

"Shhh."

"I mean it."

"I'm sure you do. You'd love to blow my career."

"I'd blow mine too. But then I'd *have* to start over. Don't you ever wonder what you'd do, if you had to do that?" He freed his hands from his empty beer bottle when the bartender took it, then settled in around the new one. "Guys down at the police station wonder about it a lot. I hear them joking, y'know? 'Jeffrey Frye is one lucky sonofabitch,' they say. 'Jeffrey Frye is one *smart* sonafabitch,' they say. 'Wish I could pick up and leave. Wish I had the balls.' " Tack caught her startled gaze and shrugged. "That's what they say."

"They're crude."

"Maybe some of them. But not all. Some of those guys are locked into jobs and debts and obligations they can't stand, and it isn't their fault. They got swept up into it straight from high school, and before they knew it they were in too deep to turn around or bend over or get out. So they think what Frye did was real neat."

"Do you?" Daphne asked.

"Hell, no. He broke the law, and besides that, he deserted his family. There's nothing heroic about that. If I had a family—"

"Why don't you?"

He took a swig of his beer. "Because I go for the wrong women. Gwen told me that, and she's right. I go for smart, sophisticated career types like you, but types like that don't want what I do."

"What do you want?"

"Meat loaf and mashed potatoes waiting, fresh and hot, when I get home from work, a house with a white picket fence, and five kids." He stared at his beer and flexed his jaw. "Pretty backward, huh?"

"Actually," Daphne surprised him by saying, "it's sweet. Impractical, especially if you like smart, sophisticated career types, but sweet."

"Why can't a smart, sophisticated career type want all that?"

"Because she doesn't have the time. She can't be managing a career at the same time that she's cooking meat loaf and mashed potatoes and raising five kids. Much as she might like it."

He fancied he heard wistfulness. "Would you?"

She raised her eyes from her wineglass and gave a quick shake of her head. "I missed the boat. I'm too old."

"No you're not."

"I'm forty." She said it looking him straight in the eye, like she was daring him to be shocked.

"So?" he said calmly.

"So I can't be having five kids at my age."

"You could have one or two."

"If I started right now. But then my career would go down the drain. And, besides, I'm a lousy cook. I've never made meat loaf and mashed potatoes in my life."

"All you have to do is follow a recipe."

She snorted. "That can be easier said than done."

"Hell, it's easy." He suddenly had a brainstorm. "Hey, let's do it now."

"Do what?"

"Make meat loaf and mashed potatoes."

"Are you kidding?"

"I'm dead serious." More so with each passing second, he thought. "You don't want to be seen going out to dinner with me—"

"That's not—"

"But we both have to eat—" he glanced at his watch," —and if we left here now, we'd have just enough time to pick up stuff at the market before it closed. You must have a cookbook lying around the house."

She looked like she wanted to deny it. Then again, she looked interested. One second to the next, she wavered.

"Come on, Daphne," he said in his most urgent boy scout voice. "It'd be fun. Y'know how long it's been since I've done something just for fun with a woman? I mean, sex is just for fun, but I'm not talking about sex. I'm talking about doing something different and creative and practical. Just dinner. We can make dinner, then eat, then I'll leave so you can read your book. What are we talking about—one more hour, maybe two? I mean, the alternative is going back to that damn motel with a Whopper and fries. Nothing we put together can be as bad as that."

"Don't be so sure," she murmured, but he could see she was leaning in his favor.

"I am sure," he said, and dug in his pocket for bills to pay for their drinks. "Trust me."

* * *

On Daphne's recommendation, they walked. Her house wasn't more than fifteen minutes from the center of town, she explained, and there was a market right on the way. Tack was feeling a little high, not from the beer—hell, he could drink a six-pack without feeling a thing—but from the unexpected anticipation of having something to do on New Year's Eve. As he walked, though, he realized that the anticipation wasn't just of doing something, but of doing something with Daphne.

He didn't tell her that, lest she run off into the night and leave him lost on the streets of Northampton. But he was thinking it. He was thinking he couldn't have arranged a nicer date if he'd planned it all out beforehand. Then again, if he'd planned it all out beforehand, he'd never have planned this. He'd have planned something sophisticated to impress her, like a theater date, or something lavish, like dinner and dancing in Boston. He wouldn't have planned something as down-home ordinary as cooking meat loaf and mashed potatoes. But she wasn't complaining, which made him think. He liked her. He really liked her.

The cold air felt good at first, crisp and bracing. Then they cleared the downtown buildings and the wind began to bite. He ducked his head to shield his ears as best he could in the collar of his coat. "Geez, it's cold," he muttered.

"Awful," she agreed, and he thought he heard teeth clicking in the single word.

Shifting the grocery bag to his outside arm, he wrapped his inside one around Daphne and pulled her close. She gave a tiny laugh—a nervous one, he thought—when it took a minute for their strides to coordinate, but she didn't pull away. It felt good having her tucked against him that way. He didn't feel as cold as he had before. Even his ears, which were as exposed as ever, felt warmer. He guessed it had something to do with the rising fire in his blood.

Leaning into the wind, they walked on and on. Daphne directed, pointing with a gloved finger when they had to turn, then putting the hand back in her pocket. When they reached her street, she said, "Almost there," as though that would make him happy. But he could have walked more. Holding Daphne made him feel part of a couple. It was an illusion, he knew; still, he liked it.

The houses on her street were old and set equidistant from one another on neat little lots. Tack couldn't see much, since the streetlights had long since been swallowed in thick mazes of tree branches that, even bare of leaves, restricted their scope, but he got the impression of vintage New England. Most of the houses had lights by their doors. Some had Christmas lights in front windows.

Daphne's house was dark, making Tack doubly grateful he was with her. Coming home to an empty house on New Year's Eve was bad enough, but coming home to a *dark* empty house was worse. So, though the wind wasn't anywhere near as bad here as before, he kept her anchored to his side as they went up the walk. They took the three steps without faltering. She fished in her bag for her keys, opened the door, and reached in to flip on the outside lights—all without moving from under his arm. If anything, she turned into him more.

He knew he should let her go, but for several seconds longer he waited, giving her a chance to make the move herself. Her head was lowered, like she had something to say but couldn't find the right words. He was beginning to wonder what that something was when she looked up at him, and in the new light the look of silent longing he saw on her face made his heart thud.

Swearing softly, he hurried her into the house and closed the door. Letting the groceries slide unheeded to the floor, he bent his head to hers. He kissed her once, tentatively, and when she didn't protest, a second time. When he felt her respond, he deepened the kiss, and when she responded to that, he was lost.

He hadn't planned it. Christ, he hadn't planned it. But kissing Daphne was the most natural thing in the world. It was also the most exciting, and before he knew it, kissing wasn't enough. His body was heating at an alarming rate, so he shed his coat and let Daphne touch him while his own hands were busy on her ribs, her waist, her breasts. Buttons came undone, flesh met flesh, and breathing grew harder, but there was no stopping the hot and heavy need that flared between them.

He bunched her skirt high on her thighs and reached underneath. "Okay?" he whispered against her mouth. She gave her tongue in answer, and when he felt her hands on the fastening of his trousers, then his zipper, he didn't ask any more. He was so full, he was ready to burst. With only one goal in mind, he crowded his fingers at the notch of her pantyhouse and pulled, making a hole that his thumb widened, and while that thumb stayed to bask in her heat, he braced his legs between hers, knees against the door, and entered her.

The cry she gave was soft, throaty, and one of such pure female pleasure that he nearly came then and there. But he wanted to wait, wanted Daphne's release to come before his, so he held himself still for a minute, and even that was wild. With her arms high around his neck and her back arched in a way that kept her breasts touching his chest, and her mouth mirroring his, she stirred him up, and that was before he allowed himself to concentrate on how hot and tight she was around him. Realizing he couldn't last long, he began to stroke her inside. Within minutes, she cried out, clutched him even tighter, and held her breath. The rhythmic spasms of her body were his undoing. They hadn't yet begun to abate when he threw his head back, gritted his teeth, and gave her everything he had.

That was the start of what proved to be the most satisfying New Year's Eve Tack had ever spent. As soon as he regained breath and enough strength to move, he discarded the clothes that were hanging half on and half off him and did the same for Daphne. Then, there, just inside the front door in the dark, he learned her body with his hands and tongue until the heat rose again. When it was extinguished, he lifted her like the chivalrous knight he must have been in another life and carried her to the bedroom, where he made love to her again, long and hard.

They did make meat loaf and mashed potatoes. Stark naked, using two candles on the kitchen table for light, they followed the recipe in one of Daphne's mother's cookbooks, and the meat loaf might have been delicious if they hadn't left it in so long. The way Tack figured it, though, a slightly crispy crust was a small price to pay for what they'd been doing that had made it that way, and the potatoes were perfect. Most importantly, once they'd eaten, they had renewed strength, and renewed strength is an important thing to have when two people have the hots for each other. So they went back to bed and made love again, and then again, after they'd slept for a bit.

By the time morning came, even Tack had to admit that he wasn't as young as he used to be. For a guy who worked out all the time, his shoulders and upper arms, even his thighs, were suspiciously sore. But there was working out, and there was working out. What he'd done with Daphne was in a class by itself.

In the light of dawn, she was subdued, and after they'd showered she sent him home. "I need time," she said.

"Can I see you later?"

She shook her head. The movement fascinated him. He drew his fingers through her hair, which, unbound, was wildly light. Putting his nose to her neck, he breathed in the sweet scent that lay there.

"Can I call you later?"

She nodded.

So he got dressed, put on his coat with the collar up, and headed out into the cold. As he walked, he thought about where he had been twenty-four hours before and where he would be right now if he had his way. But life was a compromise. He and Gwen hadn't been able to do it, but things were different with Daphne. He wanted to stay, she wanted him to leave. So he'd left. But he had incredible memories, plus permission to call, plus a small scented sachet he'd pinched from her drawer.

All in all, he figured he'd come out ahead.

FIFTEEN

T HE WAVES HIT THE SHORE with stunning force, sending a plume of spray high, nearly to the spot where Jeff Frye sat. He didn't budge, though, not when he felt the mist touch his face, not when a new, even larger wave exploded against the rocks below.

It was New Year's Day, and if anything could make him believe that life did go on, it was this. The surf shimmered in, gained speed and strength and size, rolled, crashed, and receded, only to shimmer on the horizon again. So life went through phases, he told himself. Right now he was down. Soon he'd begin to shimmer, then slowly, gradually, eventually gain in speed and strength and size. It would help if he knew where he was headed, but he wasn't any clearer on that than when he left Northampton four weeks before.

Four weeks. It was a long time. He looked different now; his hair was longer, he had the solid beginnings of a beard, and hours sitting here on his rock had given ruddiness to his skin. Thanks to that, and to the laundromat's unforgiving machines, he looked decidedly broken in. The townsfolk no longer stared when he walked down the street, which he did every day. A trip in for the paper and a stop at the diner had become part of his ritual, a necessary part of his life.

Still, he felt empty. He missed home, missed it with a deep, dark ache, so he tried to keep his mind occupied with other things. But it was hard. He read every book he bought, then bought more and read them too; still he had time on his hands. The man at the general store—Horace Stubble was his name—came through with a used pickup, which helped some. Jeff arranged to pay for it in installments, so no one would know how much money he had, and though his first impulse was to clean it and polish it and make it look present-able, he resisted. The last thing he needed was to display the instincts of a Yuppie. Besides, the truck was fully functional without a cleanup, so when he needed supplies, or when he thought he'd go mad if he didn't get out, he drove to one of the local strip malls and wandered around. He never went far and was never gone for long. As lonesome as he was in his cottage on the bluff, he felt a certain security there.

He wondered how Scott was doing at school and whether he understood anything of what Jeff had done. He wondered whether Debra was the butt of school gossip and, if so, how she was taking it. He wondered how badly he'd hurt Lydia, and whether Laura was burying herself in Cherries, and whether Daphne had everything legal under control.

"Ev-an!"

Lost in his thoughts, he didn't hear the voice at first, and then it was a minute more before he identified with the name. But the call came again, closer this time, and he was quickly on his feet, on his guard. The only people who knew that name were from town, but no one from town had ever come to see him before.

"Hi, Ev-an!"

It was Glorie, waving and picking her way through the rocks, nearly unrec-ognizable with her dark hair hidden under a thick wool hat and her slim body swallowed up in her coat. But her pale skin stood out against the grayness of the day, and her smile stood out against that. Both cried of innocence, identify-ing her in an instant.

Had it been anyone else, Jeff would have been nervous. But in her own sweet, ploddingly slow way, Glorie had become a friend.

Fearful she might slip on the rocks, he hurried to where she was. "What in the world are you doing all the way up here, Glorie?"

She looked suddenly unsure. "I came to see you."

"But it's so cold."

Seeing that he was concerned, not angry, she smiled. "I don't mind."

"Does Poppy know you're here?"

She nodded. "He made me wear this." She tugged at a bright wool scarf that was wound twice around her neck, immobilizing her much as a surgical collar would have done. "And he said not to stay long. But it's a special day, and I knew you were alone, and I wanted to bring you this."

She was wearing a backpack. She tried to grab it, tried to push one of the straps from her shoulder, but between her mittens and the bulk of her coat and scarf, she couldn't grasp a thing. He quickly helped her with it. When it was off, he gave it an experimental heft.

"What's inside?"

"Dinner. I figured you wouldn't cook much up here all by yourself, and we're closed all day. So here's some ham and potatoes and cabbage and rolls that Poppy made. I wrapped it all up in lots of foil. It was hot when I left. Maybe if you take it inside it'll still be warm."

Jeff's mouth was watering. "Let's go see," he said. Holding the backpack in one hand, he took Glorie's hand in the other and led her over the rocks. They were nearly at the cottage when he questioned what he was doing. If his goal was to keep as low a profile as possible, showing Glorie into his home wasn't the wisest thing to do.

But Glorie was Glorie. She was naïve, harmless. He didn't see how she could betray him. With the Porsche under its tarp in the boat shed and his briefcase stashed along with his business clothes far back under the bed, there was nothing of a revealing nature in the shack. Besides, he certainly couldn't turn her away, not after she had made such a kind gesture, not after she had climbed all this way in the cold.

So he pushed the door open and let her inside, and, for the look on her face, Jeff would have thought she was a child in a crystal castle. She was all eyes and an excited smile that turned shy when she looked at him.

"This is nice," she breathed. She tugged her mittens off and stuffed them in her pockets. "It's cozy." She walked around the perimeter of the room, running her hand along the back of the sofa, then along the desk and shelves that Jeff had sanded and polished. She fingered the books. "Have you read *all* these?"

"Most."

"Wow."

Setting the backpack on the table, he began to unload it. Package after package emerged, most warm to the touch. Jeff hadn't eaten since breakfast, which had consisted of two muffins and a dish of cold cereal and milk. Mindful of the New Year's Day dinner Laura had always made and would no doubt be making again, he had opted for nothing. But Poppy's ham smelled incredible, and he was suddenly ravenously hungry.

"Will you share this with me?" he asked.

Glorie was still looking at the books, touching one spine after the next. She shook her head. "I already ate." As though recalling something, she looked around. "If you have some plates, I'll set it out for you." Spotting the cabinets flanking the sink, she headed that way.

Jeff stopped her. "You don't have to wait on me here. It's enough that you brought the food." He steered her toward the table and drew out a chair. "It would make me very happy if you would sit with me while I eat." He realized that he meant it. With Glorie there, he wouldn't be so lonely. "Will you take off your coat?" He had already hung his own on a hook by the door.

She shook her head. "I told Poppy I wouldn't."

He felt a moment's disappointment. The cottage was comfortably warm, now that he'd filled in the cracks in the walls, and with the cleaning and sprucing up he'd done, the place had grown more homelike. He would have liked Glorie to stay awhile. But Poppy was protective. He respected that.

Satisfied that at least she was sitting, he went back to opening foil packages. In an instant, she was on her feet, helping him.

"I don't want you working," he reminded her.

"I'm supposed to work."

"Not here. Here you're my guest."

"I don't think I'd be very good at that. I'd rather help."

She said it in such an earnest way that Jeff gave in. Within minutes, he had a plate of food before him the likes of which he had never expected to see on his bluff. "Whoa," he drawled with a smiling glance around the room, "this is the crowning touch."

"Crowning touch?"

"Pièce de résistance."

"Pee-ess?"

His smile gentled. "It's terrific, Glorie. Thank you."

Pleased, she sat back down in the chair. With the exception of her mittens, she was bundled as tightly as before.

"Are you sure you won't have some?" he asked.

She nodded. Since she seemed perfectly happy—and looked adorable—sitting there enveloped by her coat and hat, Jeff didn't argue. Besides, he was starved. The smells coming from his plate were nearly as incredible as the food looked, and he was familiar enough with Poppy's cooking to know that it would taste every bit as good.

Catching the expectant look on Glorie's face, he took a bite of ham. He followed that up with potatoes, then cabbage. Unable to help himself, he closed his eyes and smiled. "This is so good."

As though she'd been waiting to hear just that, Glorie allowed herself a relieved grin. "Lots of people don't like cabbage. They tell me that at the diner. But Poppy said it goes nice with ham. Nicely."

Jeff could take or leave cabbage, or he could have in the past. But he wasn't leaving any of what Glorie had brought. Everything tasted wonderful.

"Did you have a nice New Year's Eve?" he asked between bites.

She bobbed her head. "Uh-huh."

"What did you do?"

"Poppy took me to visit with the Schmidts. They live a little ways down the coast."

"Are they friends of yours?"

"Uh-huh. They're nice. I really wanted to go to a movie, but Poppy doesn't like the movies. He says they're not good for me."

"Some of them aren't," Jeff said. He thought of Debra, who, at sixteen, could walk into any R-rated movie she liked, which didn't thrill him. But Laura was convinced she was mature enough to handle what she saw, so Jeff had never made an issue of it. He guessed Poppy had more power in his home than Jeff had had.

For a minute he wondered about that home. "Where's your mom?"

"Dead," Glorie said lightly.

"I'm sorry."

"It's okay. I have Poppy." She seemed perfectly happy with that.

Jeff ate more, while Glorie watched. Whenever he looked up, she smiled, but she didn't initiate conversation—which was a new experience for Jeff. Laura had never been at a loss for things to say, and Debra, not to be outdone, had always come in a close second.

The irony of it was that Glorie was being quiet at a time when he really did want to hear the sound of another person's voice. So he asked, "Have you always helped him at the diner?"

She nodded. "When I was going to school I couldn't be there until the end of the day, but I don't have to go to school any more now, so I'm there all the time."

"You must have done well at school. You speak well."

Her eyes lit up and she smiled, then took a breath and looked off toward the books. "It was a special school."

"What kind?"

"For people who need extra help, Poppy says. I wouldn't do well in the school here. I did when I was little, but then there was the accident, and now I have trouble reading, and I can't do math. So Poppy sent me to Longfellow." She got up from the chair and went to the bookshelf. "You've read all these books. You must be very smart."

"No. But I like to read."

"So do I. But it's hard."

Jeff wished he knew something about learning disabilities. In the next instant, he wished he knew more about Glorie, because if she had had an accident, the problem possibly went beyond that of a learning disability.

"Reading is like most anything else," he said. "It takes practice."

"That's what Poppy says. And I do practice, but it's hard."

"What do you read?"

"*National Geographic*," she told him. "Poppy got it for me for my last birthday, and it comes every month. The pictures are so, so pretty." Her voice fell. "Sometimes I just look at the pictures. Poppy would be upset if he knew, but the stories have so many words I don't know that it's easier just to look at the pictures." As though realizing what she'd said, she looked suddenly stricken. "I'm not dumb. I just have . . . trouble sometimes."

Jeff's heart went out to her. "Of course you're not dumb. You're smart and hard-working. You also happen to be the nicest person I've ever had in my home. So I want you to come and sit down and talk with me some more."

She looked relieved, even pleased, but shy. Stuffing her hands in her pockets on top of her mittens, she said softly, "I should be getting back home. Poppy will worry. He wanted to come with me, but he wasn't feeling well, so

I told him I'd go alone and come right back. I have to leave."

Jeff stood. He looked down at the meal she'd brought and was touched all over again. He would have liked her to stay. But he understood her father's concern. Reluctantly, he gathered up the empty backpack. He was just about to pass it to her when a jarring thud came at the door. The sound was so loud and unexpected that he jumped. He looked quickly at Glorie, who was looking horrified, and for a heart-stopping instant he wondered if she'd betrayed him after all.

Then she said, "That's Poppy, I know it's Poppy," and while he stood in a state of near paralysis, she went to the door and opened it. "I'm *fine*, Poppy. I *told* you I'd be fine. I brought Evan his food and was just sitting with him for a minute, but I was already getting ready to leave, so there wasn't any need for you to come after me. I thought you said you wanted to stay inside in the warm all day."

Gordon regarded her carefully, then looked past her to Jeff. "I gut worried," he said in a hoarse voice.

"She's fine," Jeff assured him.

"I gut worried," he repeated, looking steadily at Jeff. "She's special, Glorie is. Ya bettuh know it."

"I certainly do."

"Poppy—"

"She isn't like othuh girls," Gordon warned. "She's good an' sweet, an' she may be thirty, but she was sleepin' fuh three a those yee-ahs, an' when she woke up she was younguh than bufoah." He broke into a thick cough.

"Poppy—"

"So ya best know I look out fuh Glorie. She's simple. I won't have ya hurtin' huh."

"I wouldn't hurt her for the world," Jeff said.

"I'll hold ya ta that." Pulling his coat more tightly around him, Gordon held out an arm to Glorie and said in a gentler way, "I'm ready ta lie down some more. Ya bettuh let me take ya home."

Glorie turned to Jeff with a look that was apologetic and, in that, surprisingly astute. "I'm sorry. Poppy worries too much. Will you come to the diner tomorrow?"

"Yes, and please, don't apologize." He glanced back at the table. "You brought me a wonderful New Year's Day dinner. I thank you. Both of you."

With a final shy smile, she and Gordon left. Jeff watched their pickup head down the dirt road. When it disappeared from sight, he closed the door and returned to the table to finish the dinner she'd brought.

All the time he was eating, he thought of Glorie, then of Gordon and the others whose faces he was coming to recognize. He couldn't say he knew them in the way Laura defined "knew," which involved sharing thoughts and backgrounds and interests. But he didn't think that was necessary. He didn't see why friends had to bare their souls to each other, or, for that matter, why they had to share anything more than the simplest of thoughts. Who he was deep inside, what he was thinking—it wasn't anyone's business but his own, and it didn't matter, in the everyday run of things.

That, he decided, was one of the differences between where he'd come from and where he was. Back in Northampton, life was complex. Competition was a big part of it, and when people weren't obsessed with job advancement or social climbing, they turned to reasons and feelings and analyses. Here, life was simpler. The name of the game was living, and that meant earning enough money to buy food and clothes, braving the elements, and maybe—just maybe—going visiting on New Year's Eve.

Part of him believed he could live the simpler life just fine, once he settled into a rhythm. He had started to do that. But he needed more. He needed something to get him up and out in the morning and back home at night. He needed structure in his life.

He couldn't be an accountant. He couldn't be anything noticeable. And while he was proud of the job he'd done fixing up the cottage, he didn't think he had a future as a handyman. His hands were a mess of blisters and cuts, one or two of which probably should have been stitched. But he had survived without getting lockjaw or whatever the hell else people always got shots to avoid, and he supposed the scars added character.

Any help in *that* department was welcome. He was still feeling like a snake when he thought of the way he'd left Northampton. Granted, he hadn't had any choice. Granted, they were better off without him. Still, he felt lousy— all the more so, he supposed, because it was New Year's Day, which had traditionally been for family. So, long after Glorie and Gordon had left, long after he had finished eating their food, long after the time when he should have been reading or doing push-ups or wrestling with the pipes he had bought that, when properly assembled, would provide him with a shower, he thought of Northampton.

By late in the afternoon, he'd had his fill of thinking, so he climbed into the truck and coasted down the hill into town. A phone booth stood at the far side of the gas station. He idled beside it for a minute or two, jiggling the change in his pocket while he tried to decide whether his call could be traced. If he kept it short, it wouldn't be, he figured, but he didn't want to take any chances.

So he drove on. He passed the first strip mall, where he usually did his shopping, passed the second one, where he ventured when he was feeling either brave or bored. Driving farther than he had in four weeks, he finally pulled up at a restaurant that stood closed and lonely at the side of the road. The phone booth looked to be in better repair than the restaurant, which wasn't saying much. The door was off its lower hinge, and the phone book was torn in half. But he didn't need the book, and since there was no one around, he didn't need the door for privacy. He didn't even need it for warmth, since he was bundled up. If his hands shook slightly as he pumped change into the machine, it wasn't from the cold.

The phone rang once, then a second time, and his heart beat louder with each one. Then, just before the third, it was picked up and he heard her.

"Hello?"

"Hi," he said in a quiet, tentative voice.

There was a long pause, then, "Jeff?" His failure to correct her was confirmation enough. "Jeff! My God, we've been so worried! How *are* you? *Where* are you? Are you all right?"

"I'm all right."

"Are you sure? We imagined all kinds of things—that you were hurt or sick or kidnapped. How could you leave without a word that way?"

"I had to. I couldn't tell anyone."

"Not even me?"

"Not even you."

"Not after everything?"

"Especially not then. Think about it."

"That's all I've been doing." Her voice trembled. "I feel so guilty."

"Think how you'd have felt if you'd known I was leaving and no one else did. I couldn't do that to you."

Her voice grew harder, though he wasn't sure whether it was from anger or hurt. "Apparently there were lots of things you couldn't do. Tax fraud, Jeff? You never breathed a word of that to me. I thought we were best friends. I thought we shared secrets. What else couldn't you tell me about?"

"Nothing."

"Were there other women?"

"No," he said in an angry tone that quickly grew tentative again. "Is everyone okay?"

It was a minute before she said, begrudgingly, "As okay as they can be in the circumstances."

"Hurt? Angry? Disillusioned?"

"All those things. The IRS came out pretty fast with its charges, and the *Sun* loves it." She paused for the briefest minute before crying, "Why, Jeff? Why did you *do* it?"

Jeff didn't want to go into explanations. That wasn't why he had called. "How's my mother doing?"

"You didn't *need* the money. You were doing so *well*."

"How's my mother?"

There was another long pause, then a sigh. "She's a trouper."

"Has Christian been around?"

"Christian's in Tahiti."

"Does Scott hate me?"

"Scott is angry. He feels you let everyone down. Debra misses you, and Laura's trying to carry on. Things are a mess for her, Jeff. She didn't deserve this."

But Jeff didn't want to go into that either. "Has David taken my name off the door?"

"Not yet. When are you coming back?"

"I'm not."

"You have to."

"I can't."

"You have to. Until you do, nothing will be settled, and that would be the cruelest, *cruelest* thing to do to Laura and the kids."

"I'm not coming back."

"Then why did you call?"

He didn't answer.

"Where are you, Jeff? At least tell me that. I won't tell a soul, God knows I won't."

He trusted her. The problem was he didn't trust himself. If he told her where he was and she came looking, he wasn't sure he wouldn't give in if she begged him to return. He had never been strong when it came to women, which was part of the problem. If he'd been able to stand up to Laura once in a while, he might have felt more like a man.

Well, he was a man now. He'd done his thing, and he was determined to stick with it. Let them call him a coward for leaving Northampton when the fire got hot. They were wrong. Leaving Northampton was the bravest thing he had ever done in his life.

"Jeff? Talk to me, Jeff. Are you still there? Jeff!"

Quietly, he replaced the receiver, returned to the truck, and headed back to the bluff.

SIXTEEN

❋ ❋ ❋

LAURA CONTINUED TO STRIKE out on the loan scene. The banks in Hartford were as reluctant to give her money as those in Boston had been. David, who was still holding out for an affair, suggested she speak with her life insurance agent about borrowing against Jeff's policy, but the government had reached him first and frozen those funds too. Privately — humbly — she talked with friends who had the resources to loan her money, but none came through. One claimed he'd had a bad year, another mentioned the big wedding his daughter was planning, still another vowed that what money he might have lent her was tied up in investments. A fourth suggested a business arrangement whereby he would buy into Cherries, but Laura wasn't ready for that. She was sure that if her take remained stable, and if the court ruled in her favor, she could survive as an independent restaurateur, which was what she wanted. The business was all she had. Even aside from the pride involved, she couldn't afford to siphon profits off to a silent partner.

On the second of January, Daphne petitioned the court to release to Laura that portion of Jeffrey's assets which by rights were hers. The petition was accompanied by voluminous documents supporting the claim. Daphne had spent long hours compiling them, and Laura was impressed. She was also optimistic. For the first time since she'd learned of the freeze, something concrete and positive was in the works. Hope was in sight.

When Daphne reminded her not to expect a response to the motion for up to six months, which, she said, was typical of the backlog in the court system, Laura's optimism wavered. "But this isn't a typical case," she argued.

"Not to you," Daphne explained. "To the court it is. Everyone filing petitions feels his case is unique. I've argued for expedience, but I'm sure those others have too. How long it takes will depend on the judge, and I have no control over who's given the case. What I'm saying is that you shouldn't count on immediate relief."

But the bills were still due. Having no other recourse, Laura finally took Daphne and Elise up on their offers, borrowing money from them to pay the most pressing of those bills. She felt bad doing it, but Lydia had no money to spare and Laura refused to ask Maddie, so she was over a barrel.

Her one best hope, she realized over the course of many long middle-of-the-night hours, was to maximize the profit she took from the business. To that extent, once the holidays were past, she pared down the restaurant's staff to the exact number she and Jonah figured they could get by with. They had already lost one waitress, a part-time student who was transferring out of state to study full-time, and they didn't replace her. Likewise, on the catering end, two of her staff were leaving to make a stab at their own service in upstate New York. Rather than having three separate catering crews on the payroll, Laura regrouped into two. Even with Scott and Debra pitching in at odd hours, that meant each of her employees had to work a little harder. She talked with them individually, making a personal plea. That, along with the loyalty she had already accrued, paid off.

So she dared be optimistic again. The business was more efficiently run than ever. Service was remaining at the high level she wanted. She felt she just might be able to make it.

She would have, had business been good in those early January days. But the cancellations Elise had received in December went unfilled, and fewer than normal new bookings came in. Time and again, Laura reminded everyone around her that January was the slowest month of the year. In the wee hours of the night, though, she worried.

Her worry increased when, one week into the new year, a grand jury returned indictments against Jeff. The media started in again with phone calls and visits. Duggan O'Neil carried the story as though it were the most important thing to happen in Hampshire County since Noah Webster published his dictionary in 1828. Gary Holmes wrote not one but two editorials in as many days, decrying modern morality, middle-class greed, and the challenge to law enforcement officials that the Frye case presented.

Laura was beside herself with frustration. The *Sun's* attention did nothing to improve business, which seemed, to her terrified eye, to be slackening by the day. Both Elise and DeeAnn assured her that this wasn't happening to any significant degree, but she suspected they were just trying to make her feel better. In her darkest, most private moments, she doubted anything could help. Her life had gone from perfect to perfectly horrid with terrifying speed. All its discouraging threads seemed to be spinning around on themselves, growing more tangled by the minute.

When Taylor Jones stopped in at the restaurant the day after the indict-ments came down, she wasn't alarmed. Things were already so bad she was sure nothing he said or did could make them worse. And she was right, at first. He updated her on the leads the government was following in its search for Jeff and questioned her on whether she'd seen him, heard from him, or had the slightest contact with him, no matter how indirect. He told her he'd learned that the fraud went back eight years, that Jeff had apparently worked alone, and that Farro and Frye had been uninvolved in the scheme.

Then he told her what else he'd learned.

They were sitting in her office, with the door closed, when he announced that he had a witness placing Jeff on more than one occasion with a woman at the condo in Holyoke. Actually, "announced" was the wrong word, since he sounded almost apologetic, but the message hit Laura as though he had screamed it at the top of his lungs.

She instantly denied it. "That can't be. Jeff wouldn't have had an affair." Of all the indignities she'd suffered in the last month, that one would be the worst. She couldn't conceive of its being true.

But Tack was confident. "The witness consistently identified Jeff's picture. She picked it out of a large group we gave her and then gave us his height and build, neither of which was apparent from the photo."

Laura's head began to buzz. Like pieces of an ugly puzzle, one element of Jeff's treachery fit into another. Still, publicly, she had to maintain his inno-cence. There was loyalty involved, and self-defense.

"It couldn't have been Jeff," she insisted.

"The witness is certain."

"She's wrong. Jeff couldn't have had an affair."

"How do you know?"

"I'm his wife. I know."

"The wife is usually the last to know when it comes to affairs."

Her heart was pounding. "Jeff wouldn't betray me that way."

Taylor Jones's voice dropped. "You didn't believe he would willingly van-ish, or commit tax fraud, but the evidence says he did both those things."

"You haven't proven either."

"No, but the evidence is strong."

A sharp rap came at the door, followed immediately by Daphne, who regarded Laura with concern. "DeeAnn let me know he was here." Her gaze sharpened when it flipped to the agent. "As the Fryes' attorney, I'd like to be notified before meetings like this."

Though he had risen at her entrance, he appeared otherwise undaunted. "Mrs. Frye isn't being charged with anything."

"She has the right to representation." To Laura, Daphne said, "Is every-thing all right?"

Laura fought hysteria. "Not really. He says Jeff was having an affair."

Daphne froze for an instant; then, in the next instant, boiled. Her anger was a visible thing. Knowing that she had an impassioned defender in Daphne was vague solace for the devastation Laura was feeling.

Swinging the door shut with more force than was necessary, Daphne said slowly and with barely contained fury, "I thought you were going to hold off telling her about this."

It was a minute before the implication registered, and then Laura was appalled. "You knew?"

"I knew," Daphne admitted. "He told me last week."

"But you didn't say anything to me!" Laura cried, feeling betrayed. She knew it was irrational, given all Daphne was doing for her, and it was probable that the betrayal she felt was really related to Jeff. But Daphne was the one who was there.

Daphne defended her inaction. "It was right after the holidays, which had been hard enough on you. I didn't see the point in making things worse."

"But this *affects* me."

"It's an unsubstantiated claim."

"He has a *witness*, Daphne."

"But no warm body. If Jeff was having an affair, he had to have it *with* someone. Agent Jones doesn't have any idea who that was."

"Yes, I do," Tack said. Both pairs of eyes flew his way.

"Who?" Laura asked, but the agent was looking at Daphne.

"When I first told you about this, I had no leads on the woman, and as long as that was so, I agreed with you that there was no need to further upset Mrs. Frye."

"What's a little more?" Laura cried, but Tack didn't take his eyes off Daphne.

"My witness is certain that the woman in question is the hostess here at the restaurant." At Laura's gasp, he turned to her. "We had to identify the woman in case your husband was in contact with her. We figured she may have been someone local, so we took our witness around to the places your husband frequented. One look at DeeAnn Kirkham, and she made a positive identification."

"DeeAnn," Laura breathed and clutched at the pain cutting through her chest. "DeeAnn." Tears came to her eyes. She *adored* DeeAnn. She *depended* on DeeAnn. It was bad enough to think Jeff had had an affair; it was much worse to think he'd had one with DeeAnn. "It can't be."

Still standing, Tack said, "We didn't leave it there. We took the witness all over town, but she kept coming back to your hostess. She said that the hair was the thing, that sandy color, the thickness, and the length. The woman she saw with your husband had great hair. She said that over and over again: great hair."

"Lots of woman in this town have great hair," Laura argued. She was desperate to discredit the witness's claim. *Jeff couldn't have had an affair.* "Lots of woman in this town have sandy hair. Look at Daphne. Hers is that color, but I wouldn't accuse her of having an affair with Jeff. DeeAnn isn't only my hostess, she's my *friend*."

"She's very attractive," Tack remarked.

Daphne bristled. "What does that have to do with anything?"

"Attractive women attract men," he answered, then asked Laura, "What do you know about her personal life?"

Laura could barely think. The accusation—even the idea—that Jeff had gone looking for sex was devastating. Putting her fingers to her temples, she tried to slow the wild whirl inside. "I—uh, I know she dates."

"Lots of men, or is there someone special?"

She wanted to say there was someone special with whom DeeAnn was head over heels in love, but there wasn't. Dee dated a lot. Her taste ran toward men who were mature enough to appreciate the fine points of feminine allure and wealthy enough to reward those points accordingly. Laura wouldn't have put Jeff into either of those categories.

"Laura?" Daphne prompted. "Was there anyone special?"

"Uh, no. No one special."

"Does she pick up men here?" Tack asked.

"No!" Laura cried, because the implication of that turned her stomach. "This isn't a singles bar."

He reworded the question. "Does she meet men here?"

Laura wanted to answer as definitively as before, but she couldn't. "I suppose she might. Men are in and out all the time." And DeeAnn was an inveterate flirt, which, irony of ironies, was one of the things Laura had always loved about her. She did things Laura might have wanted to do but couldn't. Watching her was great fun. Or had been. The idea was fast turning sour. Laura took a shallow breath. "What do I do, Daph?"

Daphne deferred to Tack. "What do you suggest?"

"Let me talk with her," he said. "I don't think she had anything to do with the tax fraud scheme, but if she's heard from him and hasn't come forward, she'll be considered an accessory after the fact. She ought to know that."

"What do I do, Daph?" Laura asked. She was feeling battered again, as though she'd taken another hit and was on her knees, needing help to get up but not sure what to do once she got there. "Do I assume it's true and confront her? Do I scream and yell? Do I fire her on the spot?"

Daphne pulled up a chair and sat close. "What do you want to do?"

"I want to beg her to tell me it isn't true. I like DeeAnn. I've always liked DeeAnn. If it turns out she was having an affair with Jeff, I'll be crushed."

"I doubt she'll confess to it. Unless she does, you won't know for sure."

There was so much lately that Laura didn't know for sure that she wanted to scream. But screaming wouldn't accomplish a thing. Nor, she realized, would shooting questions at Daphne. In the end, the decision was hers. She had to regain control. "Let's call her in. I need to hear what she has to say." Clinging to the idea of control, she left Daphne with Taylor Jones while she went into the heart of the restaurant.

DeeAnn's eye was easily caught. The smallest movement of Laura's head brought her over. As she approached, Laura watched her face for signs of a guilty conscience. All she saw was concern.

"You're not upset that I called Daphne, are you? That guy may be big and gorgeous, but he's trouble with a capital T. Is everything okay?"

"I'm not sure," Laura said. She was quivering inside, trying not to let it show. "Do me a favor? Get Kammie to cover and come talk with us for a minute."

"Sure, hon," DeeAnn said and set off to find the waitress.

Laura had always known DeeAnn was a knockout, but that fact took on added significance as she watched her walk off. The features were right—the casually styled hair, the bright clothing, the slender legs, slightly flared hips, full breasts. But there was something else, something sensual in her walk, in the way she cocked her head, the set of her eyes, her smile. Laura had never before had cause to compare herself to DeeAnn. Now she did. And she came up short. Next to DeeAnn, she was efficient and bland. If, somewhere beneath that placid exterior of his in a place Laura hadn't known existed, Jeff had wanted a temptress, Laura wouldn't have been it. DeeAnn might have.

Shrinking back into the shadows of the hall, Laura waited with her arms crossed hard over her breasts until DeeAnn appeared. Without a word, she led the way back to her office.

Inside, DeeAnn looked from one face to the next. "Uh-oh," she said in a singsong voice that in other circumstances might have been amusing. "Something's up."

Laura stood back against the wall and focused expectantly on Tack, who took her cue and, in a straightforward, no- nonsense way, filled DeeAnn in on what they'd been discussing. By the time he was done, Laura was feeling more raw than ever and DeeAnn was looking stunned. Her eyes flew to Daphne and, after a minute, to Laura, but she didn't say a word.

"Is it true?" Laura forced herself to ask.

DeeAnn gave a quick, jerky shake of her head—too quick and too jerky for Laura, who had had optimism thrown in her face once too often. This time she was being smart. She was believing the worst.

Tack seemed skeptical of DeeAnn's denial too, because he said, "As far as the law goes, whether you were his mistress or not doesn't matter. All I want to know is whether you've been in contact with him since he disappeared."

Eyes wide, DeeAnn shook her head.

Turning sideways to the wall, Laura huddled into herself. Behind her, the conversation went on. She was aware of its hum, but none of the words registered over the clamor of her thoughts. *Jeff had had an affair. He'd slept with another woman.* She tried to grasp the idea, but it was too repulsive to hold. In the next breath there were other ideas to repulse her. *Where were you? Why didn't you see? How could you not have known?*

The disillusionment that had come before was nothing compared to this. Fidelity had been a given in her relationship with Jeff, or so she'd thought. Apparently Jeff hadn't thought so. While she'd been raising the kids, keeping the house, and building a business to supplement Jeff's income, he had been having affairs in a condo he'd bought on the sly.

Feeling suddenly nauseated, she pressed a hand to her mouth, but instantly knew that wouldn't be enough. Wordlessly, she ran down the hall to the bathroom, where she was violently sick.

A soft knock came at the door, then Daphne's gentle plea. "Let me in, Laura."

Still hanging over the toilet bowl, she took a deep breath. Helplessly, she retched once, then again. She was taking another breath when the doorknob jiggled.

"I want to help, Laura. Open up."

Laura flushed the toilet and straightened, holding the edge of the sink for support. She ran the cold water and rinsed out her mouth.

"Please, Laura."

Reaching back, Laura turned the doorknob enough to unlock the door, then sank down on the toilet seat and put her head in her hands.

Daphne went right to the sink. "It'll be okay," she soothed. "Everything's going to be okay." She moved Laura's hands out of the way and pressed a cool cloth to her forehead. Moving her hair aside, she pressed a second one to the back of her neck. "He's a bastard. He never should have broken it to you like that."

Laura assumed the bastard to be Jeff. It was a minute before she realized Daphne was referring to Taylor Jones. "He was just doing his job," she reasoned in a paper-thin voice.

"If he wanted to do *that*, he could find Jeff, for God's sake. I don't know why they're having so much trouble finding one man."

Laura knew. "Jeff is clever. Apparently, much more so than any of us ever thought." Her voice broke as the reality of what she'd been told slammed into her again.

Daphne rubbed her back. "You're a survivor, Laura. You'll do fine."

"How could he *do* that to me?" she cried. "How could he be off sleeping with other women—how could he be digging up the names of dead people—how could he be plotting his disappearance—and still get up in the morning and look me in the eye like everything was fine and dandy? I had no idea, Daph, no idea at all. Was I so preoccupied with my own life that I didn't see? Or am I just stupid?"

Daphne kept on rubbing. "You're being too hard on yourself."

"I *should* be hard on myself. I was married to that man for twenty years, but I didn't know him. I thought I did. I honestly thought I did. But I guess I thought wrong, which doesn't say a whole lot for my insight or intelligence or sensitivity. Or sex appeal," she added morosely.

"You have sex appeal."

"Yeah. That's why my husband felt the need to sneak off with other women."

The hand on her back grew gruffer. "You don't know that there were other women. You don't even know that there was *one* other woman."

"It was Dee."

"She said no."

"What else could she say?" Laura squeezed her eyes shut for a minute. "Dee. Of all people. Right under my nose!" She made an anguished sound, then slowly straightened. Taking the cloth from her forehead, she pressed it against first one cheek, then the other. "Oh, God," she breathed, feeling weak and discouraged, "what do I do? I could fire her, but that'd be like cutting off my nose to spite my face. She's a real plus here. If she left, I'd have to look for someone else, and I'm not sure I have the strength for that."

"Then keep her. It might be better to have her nearby where you can watch what she's doing. If she understands that you're giving her the benefit of the doubt and trusting her, she may tell us if Jeff gets in touch with her."

Laura's mind drifted. Her life used to be so simple — busy, but simple. All that had changed. "What a nightmare," she whispered.

"You'll come out all right."

"But when? How long will this go on?"

"Until they find Jeff, I guess."

"No. Longer than that. Because if they find Jeff, he'll be arrested and charged and booked, and then we'll be stuck with the horror of a trial." Her mind drifted again. She found herself wondering whether she'd be able to stand behind Jeff through a trial, after what he'd done to her. If everything Taylor Jones said was true, Jeff didn't deserve her support. When she looked past the hurt of his betrayal, there was anger enough to choke a horse.

"I need some air," she muttered and pushed herself to her feet. Tossing the cloths into the sink, she left the bathroom. DeeAnn was still with Taylor Jones, waiting for Laura's verdict. But Laura avoided her eyes, grabbed her coat, and left. She was too wrapped up in her own unhappiness to care that DeeAnn was in limbo. If the woman had been with Jeff, she deserved the worst. Letting her stay on the job was about as compassionate as Laura could be.

The January cold hit her face with welcome force. She breathed it in and fought a wave of dizziness as she walked quickly down the street. She pulled up the collar of her coat against the wind, then pulled it higher for privacy. She didn't want to be seen. She didn't want to be recognized. She didn't want to be talked about or laughed at or pitied.

Doing an abrupt about-face, she headed for the parking lot behind Cherries, climbed into the Wagoneer, and drove off. There was better protection from knowing eyes in the car, particularly once she left the streets of Northampton behind. She headed south simply because that was one way to go. She wondered if Jeff had gone that way too. But she wasn't Jeff; she'd be back. She would be home by the end of the day, because she had Debra and Scott to care for, and Lydia, and the house, and the business. She wouldn't shirk her responsibility like Jeff had. She wasn't a coward, or a cheat.

But that didn't mean one part of her didn't want to keep driving and driving until she reached a place where no one knew her, and no one knew what a fool she'd been. She had trusted Jeff. She had built her life around him. She had worried when he disappeared, had even defended him when the first charges came up.

These new charges were something else. *Jeff . . . DeeAnn . . . an affair.* People had affairs all the time. Men wandered, marriages fell apart. But not Laura's. She didn't understand how things had gone awry.

With the blare of a horn on her immediate right, she slammed on her brakes, then, heart pounding, glided through the intersection that she had distractedly entered too soon. Driving on, she gradually stopped shaking, but her distraction persisted. She kept wondering what she'd done wrong, but the only thing she could come up with was that she had wanted everything to be right. Was that her crime? If so, it seemed totally unfair. She hadn't hurt a soul in her life. The people around her were happy.

Or were they? Had she chosen to think that, just as she'd chosen to think

Jeff was honest, hard-working, and faithful? Had she been wrong about *all* those things?

Not sure what to think and what not to, she turned the Wagoneer around and headed home to cook dinner. With a recipe card telling her exactly how much of what ingredients to use, she was safe. She supposed it was only fair that if her children had to be stuck with a mother who couldn't keep their father happy and in his own bed, at least they should be well fed.

Patiently Tack stood by while Daphne told DeeAnn that Laura wanted her to stay on as Cherries' hostess. Personally, he didn't understand why Laura would want that. He would have thought Laura would kick her out in two seconds flat. Apparently she was more forgiving than most women — either that, or more practical, which was probably the case. She had a business to run, and DeeAnn did her part well.

Daphne must have agreed with the decision, because, if anything, when she talked to DeeAnn, she sounded solicitous. Her voice was quiet, even gentle, making him wonder exactly where Daphne's loyalties lay. As soon as DeeAnn left the office, he asked her about it.

"Considering that she's been fingered as the mistress of your best friend's husband, you were very kind."

Daphne closed the door and turned on him with startling speed. Her voice was hushed but harsh. "She denied it. For God's sake, Tack, did you have to tell Laura?"

He should have known she'd still be ticked off. She wasn't one to let things go, though he thought he'd explained himself perfectly well. "Yes, I did," he said, coming to his feet. "It was time."

"Did you see how upset she was?"

He had. He wasn't *that* unfeeling, and he didn't like Daphne thinking he was. So he gentled his voice. "Do you think she'd be any less upset if she found out a month or two from now?"

"Yes. She's barely gotten over the shock of Jeff's leaving. A month or two from now, it wouldn't have been so raw."

"It'd be raw. A woman like Laura would be hurt whenever she learned something like that." He scratched his head. "It absolutely amazes me that she didn't see any of this coming."

"She wanted to see a perfect life, so that was what she saw."

"But she isn't dumb. She isn't blind. How could all this have been happening without her sensing *anything?*"

"You tell me," Daphne said, daring him with a straight-in-the-eye look. "You're a man. You tell me whether it's possible for a man to tell his wife one thing and do something else. You tell me if it's possible for a man to let his closest friends believe one thing and do something else. You tell me if it's possible for a man to lead a double life."

Tack came close. His voice was only as loud as it had to be to cross the few inches between them. "It's possible. I feel like I'm doing it now. I'm on your side at night and on the opposite side during the day." He looked at her mouth, at the mutinous set of those thin, strangely delicate lips, and the sides blurred. "Don't look at me like I'm the enemy, Daph."

"You are," Daphne complained and flattened herself against the door. "You upset my friend and sent her running off."

"Me? I wasn't the one who lied to her. I wasn't the one who deserted her. I wasn't the one who two-timed her. Hell, I've got more than enough to keep me busy with you." Unable to resist her closeness, he ducked his head for a kiss. She evaded his mouth.

"Not here, Tack. Someone could come in."

"Not with you standing against the door," he said. Taking her chin in his hand, he forced her face around and held it still while he covered her mouth.

She protested the kiss by keeping her mouth closed, and though she pushed against his chest, he had no intention of budging. When she discovered that, she tried to say his name in complaint. He took advantage of the opening to deepen the kiss.

He guessed she'd take thirty seconds to give in. She actually did it in fifteen. Not that it took great brains to figure out why. They had been together five nights of the last eight, crafting a history that positively smoked. When he had been with Gwen, he thought no one could drive him hotter or higher, but Daphne had proved him wrong. She was dynamite undressed. She was also dynamite dressed, and he meant that in terms of her mind. Gwen hadn't held great appeal for him that way, but Daphne and he had interests in common. Law enforcement was one of them. The fact that they came at it from different sides was appealing. They challenged each other. Being adversaries in the Frye case and being lovers at the same time was naughty and very exciting.

Could a man live a double life? Damn straight.

"Tack," she murmured against his mouth when he allowed her a breath. "Oh, Tack."

"What, sweetheart?"

She looped her arms around his neck. "I'm worried. This is all such a mess."

"Give Laura time, and she'll do okay. Cream always rises to the top."

She smiled against his jaw. "That's a nice thing to say."

"She's a nice woman."

"Does that mean you'll forget about this business with DeeAnn?"

"I can't do that."

"Sure you can. It has nothing to do with the charges you brought against Jeff."

Tack liked Daphne a lot, but he wasn't about to compromise himself or his job. "Come on," he chided, "you know as well as I do that when it comes to a trial, there are issues of motive to consider. And character. The government will try to show that Jeff Frye was devious. What better way than to come up with a mistress? And that's totally aside from the fact that, in terms of finding the man, DeeAnn may be our strongest link."

"She isn't in touch with him."

"How do you know?"

"She said so."

"And you believe her?"

"Yes."

The conviction in her voice reminded him of the gentle way she'd dealt with DeeAnn earlier and the questions he'd had about that. Drawing back his head, he looked at her. "How close are you to DeeAnn?"

"Not as close as Laura. I only know her through Cherries. We have brunch every Tuesday—Laura, Elise, DeeAnn, and me. I like the woman."

"Did she have an affair with Jeff?"

"I didn't see her do it."

"Do you think she did?"

Daphne considered that for a minute, then shrugged.

"My witness is solid," he warned. "You can plead on DeeAnn's behalf all you want, but you're not changing my mind." He had a thought and smiled. "Go ahead. Plead."

Some of the thought must have come out in the smile, because Daphne smiled back at him. "Not here."

"Then where? Can we go for a quickie in the men's room?"

"I can't go into the men's room."

"Then the ladies' room."

"You can't go into the ladies' room."

"Then my motel room. It's not far."

But she shook her head.

"Tell you what," he said. "I'll meet you after work and take you to dinner. That's a damn good offer, coming from me." She should only know. Gwen would be green with envy. "You pick the place. If you'll be more comfortable, we'll drive a distance."

At his final words, she sobered. Slowly, she drew her hands down from his neck. "I want to make sure Laura's okay, first. Call me later?"

Though disappointed, he respected the compassion Daphne felt for her friend. With a last sweet, sucking kiss, he let her go.

SEVENTEEN

J EFF'S BETRAYAL CUT to the quick. It was a nagging ache in the back of Laura's mind, held in abeyance if she kept busy, but hovering, always hovering. Of all the injustices Jeff had done her, this was the most personal and the most humiliating. For that reason, she didn't say anything to Lydia or, God forbid, to Maddie. For other reasons as well, she didn't say anything to Debra or Scott.

Debra, who missed Jeff badly, still held out the hope that he would return. She staunchly maintained his innocence to her friends at school and was quick to defend him at home when she felt either Laura or Scott said something of a derogatory nature. Laura had been increasingly careful not to do that as the weeks had worn on, and she was particularly careful now. After all, she reasoned, Jeff was still Debra's father. It was natural that he hold a special place in her heart.

He held a special place in Scott's heart, too, though that place was far less positive. Scott was angry. He was angry for Laura, in a protective way that touched her deeply, and angry for himself. Even without Maddie's analysis, Laura could understand that. Being male, Scott identified with Jeff. He took Jeff's behavior more personally than Debra would, almost as a reflection of his own, and he was affronted. Laura knew that telling him about Jeff's infidelity would only add fuel to his anger.

So she was quiet. She knew that if the *Sun* got wind of this twist in the case, the whole world would quickly know, and that prospect was so humiliating as to be nearly unthinkable. But if she spent her days worrying about the *Sun*, she wouldn't be able to function, and if she couldn't function, what little that still worked in her life would unravel. She couldn't have that. She had to carry on. She had to hold things together.

To that end, she left the house early the next morning. After visiting with Lydia, she went on to Cherries to work. She was in the kitchen alongside her staff, chopping and listening to their chatter, almost forgetting that her world was so crazy, when DeeAnn came in. "Can I have a minute out front?" she asked softly.

Laura kept her composure. She nodded. She set down the knife she was using, wiped her hands on a nearby towel, hooked her apron at the back of the door, and followed DeeAnn into the restaurant.

As soon as they'd come far enough to allow for privacy, DeeAnn stopped. Looking worlds away from her usual confident self, she faced Laura and, in a nervous voice, said, "You don't believe me, do you?"

Furious at DeeAnn and Jeff and the entire situation, Laura said tightly, "I don't know what to believe any more." She had been wrong about so many things.

"I didn't have an affair with Jeff."

"Why did that witness identify you?"

"I don't know." She waited for Laura to say something, but Laura had nothing to say. "Are you sure you want me to stay?"

"I'm sure."

"If my being here will upset you, it may not be the wisest thing."

Of course, your being here will upset me, Laura wanted to scream. *Every time I look at you, I think of what Jeff did. I feel ugly and unappealing. I feel betrayed.* But she refused to say any of that. She wasn't giving DeeAnn the satisfaction. So she pressed her fingertips to her mouth and, after a minute, took a calming breath. "Since the beginning of December, it's been one upset after another. If I let each one get to me, I'd be an absolute wreck. I want you to stay because, quite frankly, I don't have the time or strength to find and train someone new. You're very good at what you do."

Still DeeAnn persisted. "Another person would have fired me on the spot. I can understand if that's what you want."

"What do *you* want?" Laura asked in frustration.

"To stay. To help keep the restaurant going. To help see you through this mess."

"Then stay. I've already said you should." Maddie would have called her a masochist for that, but what did Maddie know about business? "But let's pray that the papers don't pick up this part of the story, because if that happens and you're named, I'll have no choice but to let you go. Business is shaky enough, and you're the first thing people see when they walk in here. It would be suicide."

That talk with DeeAnn was on Wednesday. When there was no article in the *Sun* that day or the next, Laura began to think that Taylor Jones might be keeping his promise to Daphne, and when Friday came and went without a word, she let herself relax just a bit. She didn't know where Jeff was, what he was doing, when he'd be back, or what would happen then, but she was holding her own. Each day she did that was a victory.

Then Saturday morning's paper arrived with a front-page article about the "mystery woman" with whom Jeffrey Frye had been seen in the months before his disappearance.

"Why are they doing this to us?" Debra cried the instant she saw the paper. "Why do they make up stories like this?"

Laura was more upset than Debra. Just when she had begun to believe that the downhill spiral was ending, that things were leveling off, that life might actually go uphill from there, she'd been knocked down again.

"They didn't make up the story," she said defeatedly. "The police have a witness who claims to have seen your father with a woman."

Scott, who had been brooding over the article before Debra had come down, felt called upon to add, "At his condo. More than once."

"I know that, Scottie," Laura said. She didn't need the reminder. The mechanics of Jeff's infidelity haunted her.

"It's a lie, isn't it?" Debra asked.

Laura wanted to deny it, but how could she? "We won't know until we ask your father."

"Or find the woman," Scott put in, then hit the counter with the full force of his rower's fist. "Damn it, what's *with* him? A man is supposed to love his family. He's supposed to want to be with them. He's supposed to want to take *care* of them. So why didn't he feel all that? What's so awful about us? We're not good enough for him? This house isn't good enough for him? *You're* not good enough for him? What the fuck did he want?"

Laura put shaky fingers to her forehead. "Maybe he didn't know. Maybe it was a mid-life crisis. I don't know, Scottie. I just don't know."

"I do," Debra said, looking straight at Laura. "He wanted someone to be with and talk with and do things with. You weren't ever around, so he went looking for someone else."

"Shut up, Debra," Scott warned, but Laura clutched his arm hard to keep him from saying more. She didn't want them going at each other. She couldn't bear the thought of internal warfare, when it seemed the rest of the world was against them.

"You may be right," she told Debra. "But, if so, he never told me he wanted something I wasn't giving. He never complained. He never nagged. He never commented. He never hinted. So how was I to know?"

"You should have seen he was unhappy."

"Did *you?*" Laura asked. "Did he look unhappy to you?" When Debra didn't answer, she said, "People are supposed to speak up if things are bothering them. I'm not a mind reader. I don't stand around here monitoring tiny little changes in facial expression. I don't have time for that. If you want to criticize me for being too busy with my business, go ahead. That's your right. I've tried to do my best juggling family and career. Obviously, you don't think I've done a very good job. Fine. Learn from my mistakes and do better when you're grown and have a family of your own." The phone rang. Rolling on a wave of anger, she snatched it up. "Hello!"

"Did you know about this, Laura?"

Laura sank back against the wall, only then realizing that she was trembling. And Maddie's call wouldn't help, that was for sure. "Oh, hi, Mom," she said in a breezy voice. "Yeah, I'm okay. How are you?"

"Did you know he was having an affair?"

"Sure." The voice stayed breezy. "That was why I was so puzzled when he left. That was why I was terrified he'd been in an accident. That was why I told the IRS agent he couldn't possibly have committed tax fraud. My husband *never* does anything I don't know about."

Maddie was silent for a time before coaxing softly, "Go on."

Laura sighed. "I'm done."

"Do you feel better now?"

"I'll feel better when you stop asking insulting questions. If I'd known Jeff was having an affair, do you honestly think I would have stuck up for him all this time? Give me credit for *something*, Mother."

"You're upset."

"That's a brilliant deduction."

"Sarcasm doesn't become you, Laura."

The anger Laura felt spilled out. "If you're going to complain that my husband's having an affair with a mystery woman may hurt your career, don't. I only have a certain amount of sympathy, and right now I'm saving it for Debra and Scott. And myself. I'm saving it for myself. God only knows I've earned it." There were tears in her eyes. She handed the phone to Scott. "Talk with Gram," she whispered brokenly. "I can't do it now."

Too upset to care what Scott said to his grandmother, she turned away and went to the semicircle of windows overlooking the yard. She stared out, hugging herself against the emptiness she felt, so lost in her private unhappiness that she jumped when Debra slipped an arm around her waist.

"Don't cry, Mom. If you do, I will, and if I do, my eyes will be puffy for the rest of the day, and I'm going out with Jace."

Laura blotted an eye with the heel of her hand. "Jace?"

"You know Jace."

For the life of her, she couldn't remember the name, let alone put a face to it, and though it was the least appropriate time to be discussing Debra's love life, there was a lightness to it that Laura grabbed at. "Have I met him?"

"No, but I've mentioned him lots of times. He's this swell guy from school."

"What's his last name?"

"Holzworth."

Still nothing clicked, but that didn't mean anything. If Laura had been half as inattentive as Debra seemed to think, she might have heard the name dozens of times without taking it in. "What about Donny?"

"Donny's going out with Julie."

"But you were with Donny on New Year's Eve."

"I went to the party with him, but he spent more time with Julie than with me. But that's okay. Jace was there, and we've been wanting to go out for a while. Mom, do you think this thing in the paper will turn him off?"

"Did the other stuff turn him off?"

"No. He doesn't blame me for what my father is accused of doing. Some of the kids do, but not Jace. He's mature that way."

"Mmm," Laura said. "It *is* a mature thing to do, not to blame one person for another person's misdeeds." She gave Debra a pointed look.

Debra got the message, but she wasn't entirely ceding the point. "I'm not saying you *made* Dad go out and do all those things. I'm just saying that maybe if you had paid more attention to him, either he wouldn't have done them or you would have known."

"He always encouraged me in my career."

"Because it was what you wanted. He knew you loved to cook. You've always loved to cook." She smiled in a young, innocent way that instantly lifted Laura's heart. "Remember the chocolate-covered heart-shaped waffles you used to make for Valentine's Day?"

"I remember," Laura said with a smile of her own, but hers was sad. Those days seemed so simple, and so far off. "You always loved them."

"So did my friends. They loved coming here for Valentine's Day—and St. Patrick's Day, and Patriot's Day, and the Fourth of July. You always made holidays fun."

"Then I did something right?" Laura asked, needing all the encouragement she could get.

"Sure you did. You were more of a supermom than any of my friends' moms, but it wasn't just for us, it was for you too. You liked being that way. You liked having the kids ooh and aah and race over here thinking you were terrific, even though all you were doing was what you liked doing best. You liked doing stuff in the kitchen. We knew that, and Dad knew that, so when you started Cherries, *of course* he was behind you. But that didn't mean he liked it when you were out all the time."

"Did he tell you that?"

"No, but he was thinking it."

"Was he, or were you?"

Debra looked for a minute like she was caught. Then she gave Laura a disgruntled look. "You're as bad as Gram, with the questions that always have a message. Yes, I was thinking it. You were always busy, always doing something."

"I was home."

"*Doing* something. If you weren't cooking, you were doing business on the phone or making lists for yourself or sorting through the mail. You never do one thing at a time. It's always two or three. There were times when I wanted to be the *only* thing you were doing."

You're a selfish twerp," Scott announced, coming up from behind. "Y'know, Debra, you've had a hell of a lot more than most kids, and you never complained."

Debra separated herself from Laura. "I was too young to appreciate it."

"Sounds like you still are."

She tipped up her chin. "I can appreciate money. And you're a fine one to talk. You're the one whose school costs a bundle. You're the one who had to join a fraternity. You're the one who had to get a whole new wardrobe this year because you said your clothes weren't right. You're the one with the car."

"Don't mention clothes to me. You spend ten times as much on clothes as me any day."

"Only because I'm still growing."

"Yeah, *out*. Get any bigger and you'll need hoists to hold 'em up."

Debra made a face. "You're dis-gus-ting."

"She's right, Scottie," Laura put in. Her head had started to pound. "That was unnecessary."

"Well, so's her criticism of me. At least I *worked* in high school. All she does is sashay down the halls, waving her butt at the guys."

"Scott!"

"So I'm normal," Debra shot back. "When you were in high school, the most important thing in your life was the football team. You *loved* those guys. If that isn't perverted—"

"Debra!"

Scott was livid. "Let her talk. She's just proving how stupid she is. Mention male bonding to her, and she'll think it's a service offered by the post office. Stupid and juvenile."

"Better that than gay, dork."

"Debra!"

Scott barked with laughter. "Gay? Uh-huh. Why don't you ask Christina Lakeley about that. Or Megan Tucker. Or Jenny Spitz. Gay?" He leaned close. "Don't let Kelly hear you say that, or she'll *know* how dumb you are. Remember, Kelly's a senior."

"So what?"

"So she knows the guy you have your eyes on—"

"Debra doesn't date seniors," Laura tried to tell him, but he went right on.

"—and she won't hesitate to tip him off about you."

"Let her," Debra challenged. "She might also be interested in hearing about Christina Lakeley, Megan Tucker, and Jenny Spitz."

"Enough," Laura cried, holding up her hands, which she promptly put on either side of her head. "I can't take this. Not on top of everything else."

"You twerp," Scott said to Debra, who wasn't giving an inch.

"I'll talk if you do."

Laura kicked the leg of the chair. "Enough! *Stop it!*"

"I can't stand being in the same room as him," Debra announced and ran from the kitchen.

"If she opens her big mouth to Kelly, I'll kill her," were Scott's parting words before he, too, was gone.

Laura was left in the sudden silence with a foot that hurt, a heart that ached, and the terrifying vision of things falling apart.

The vision kept coming back to her. Repeatedly over the weekend she had panic attacks, times when she broke into a cold sweat, when her heart throbbed and her hands shook. No amount of positive thinking helped. Not even Cherries was the escape it had once been, since DeeAnn was there to remind her of all that was wrong.

Things were falling apart. The cohesive family unit she had worked so hard for had been shattered by Jeff's disappearance. Scott and Debra weren't talking to each other. Lydia was weak. Maddie was carping. Money was scarce. Business stunk.

And Monday was Jeff's birthday. There was a bittersweetness to that which occupied Laura's mind as she lay in bed in the day's predawn hours. Jeff had cheated on her. He had lied and stolen and bought her dreams with dirty money—and all the while she'd been planning a surprise birthday party for him.

The day should have been a happy one. They should have just returned from Saba, all rested and brown, anticipating the party that night. Instead, Laura dragged herself from bed feeling numb, taking comfort from the knowledge that with all that had gone wrong nothing else could faze her.

Debra didn't want to go to school. She was tired of being the butt of school gossip and was sure things would be even worse after the weekend's article in the *Sun*. It took ten minutes of arguing before Laura finally got her off to the bus.

Scott, who was organizing himself to return to school that Wednesday, ended a flurry of phone calls with the decision to move out of the dorm and into the fraternity house. Laura was hesitant. She wanted him to have fun, but not so much fun that his grades fell, which she was afraid might happen if he lived in the house. His enthusiasm was so welcome, though, after the bleakness of the vacation, that she gave in with little more than token argument.

Then Lydia decided she was too stiff to go to the doctor and wanted to postpone her morning appointment. Laura was worried about her pallor and didn't want to wait another week to check it out, so she insisted they go. The doctor detected a slight heart murmur that he wanted to watch, which meant twice-weekly appointments and more worry.

Returning home shortly before noon, Laura found Scott staring at a widening pool of moisture on the ceiling of the front hall. "I don't know what happened," he said. "I showered an hour ago, and when I came downstairs, this was here." His bathroom was directly over the hall, and the spot was spreading smack in the middle like a drawn-on chandelier.

"I don't believe it," Laura cried in dismay, and went to call the plumber. Repairing the ceiling would have to wait until she had more money, but the leak itself had to be stopped.

She was hanging up the phone when she saw that there were two messages on the machine. They had come fifteen minutes apart—which said something about the length of time Scott had dallied in the shower. Both were hang-ups.

She listened, saved them, listened again. They were from the same person, she knew. The static was the same.

Convinced that it was Jeff, she sat by the phone for the next two hours waiting for him to call back, and all the while she thought of what she would say. She imagined her way, line by line, through one dialogue after another, and though each one played up a different emotion, anger was always a factor. Whether blistering, scornful, or leashed, it was there, all the more so as the hours passed. More than anything, she realized, she wanted to yell at him. She wanted to tell him what he'd done to her life. She wanted to tell him he was a snake. But he didn't call, and by the time she acknowledged that he wasn't going to, she was suffering acute frustration.

That was when the doorbell rang. Dennis Melrose stood there, looking somber. Beside him were two uniformed officers. Laura didn't like the way they looked either.

"May we come in, Mrs. Frye?" the detective asked.

She stepped back, then closed the door when the three were inside. Warily she looked from one face to the next before settling on Melrose as the spokesperson. "Is something wrong?" She would have laughed at her own words if the detective hadn't looked so grim.

"Is your son here?"

"Scott?" Her heart beat a little faster. "Uh, no. He's out visiting a friend."

"Do you expect him home soon?"

"In an hour, maybe. Why?"

Melrose pulled a piece of paper from his pocket. "I have a warrant for his arrest."

She stared at the paper. Her heart beat much faster. "Scott? For what?"

"Rape."

"Rape? Are you crazy?"

"I wish I were," he said. "Charges were filed by a young woman named Megan Tucker."

Laura recognized the name. "Megan? Scott *dated* Megan Tucker. He wouldn't rape her." The idea of it was absurd. "This is a joke, isn't it, detective? On top of everything else, this really is a joke." But the piece of paper was still in his hand, the look of regret still in his eye.

"I'm sorry, Mrs. Frye. We spent a good part of yesterday with the young woman and a good part of today investigating her story. I may not like it, but there was probable cause to go for an arrest warrant. It's signed by the court."

With an effort, Laura remained calm. She tucked her hands in her jeans to keep them from shaking. "When was this supposed to have happened?"

"Last August the twenty-sixth."

Scott had dated Megan in August but had broken off with her to go back to school. He had left for Penn on the twenty-eighth. Laura remembered that well. Scott's leaving was always hard for her.

"Why did it take her so long to come forward?"

"Rape is an emotional crime. Victims are often silent for years."

"And the timing of this doesn't strike you as strange?" Laura asked. Her voice was higher than normal, but she couldn't help it. Trying to stay calm was just fine, except that her son, her first-born, the absolute apple of her eye, was being accused of rape. "It seems pretty obvious to me, detective, that Megan Tucker has been following the Frye case in the papers, and either she or her family decided to cash in on a good thing. Is she pregnant?" If the girl needed money, that would explain it.

"She lost the baby last fall. It was a spontaneous abortion."

"I'll bet," Laura said. "I'll also bet that if she was ever carrying a baby, it wasn't Scott's. He uses condoms. My son is responsible that way." She had a sudden intense need to have Melrose and his men gone. "Whatever the girl said isn't true. You'd best take that piece of paper back to the station and rip it up."

"I can't do that," Melrose told her. "It's a warrant for Scott's arrest. I'm bound to serve it and take him in."

Take him in. Oh, God. Her heart skipped a beat this time. "What do you mean?"

"He'll have to be booked."

She knew what that entailed and couldn't imagine her son going through it. "But he hasn't done anything wrong!"

"He's been accused," Melrose explained patiently. "At the arraignment, he can plead not guilty. But I do have to bring him in. Do you know where he is?"

"No." Laura wouldn't tell him even if she did. Scott couldn't be *booked*. He was an innocent kid!

"Then do you mind if we wait here until he gets back?"

She did mind it. She didn't want them anywhere near her house, and she didn't want them touching her son. "You can't wait here. You can't arrest Scott. He hasn't done anything."

With a glance at his sidekicks, Melrose turned and started for the door. "We'll be outside in the car." He was about to open the door when Laura heard the muted sound of the garage door rising. Melrose heard it too and paused. "Is that him?"

Since Jeff was gone, Scott had been parking in his space. "No, it's my daughter coming home from school," Laura lied. Knowing that Debra was going downtown with her friends after school, she ran back through the kitchen. She didn't know what to say to Scott, but she couldn't let the police get him. She had no faith in the legal system, not after the last month, when she'd lost so much without committing a single crime. Scott was her son. She wasn't having him booked and fingerprinted and photographed. She wasn't having him dirtied in any stinking jail while the arbitrators of justice played their games. She didn't care *what* Megan Tucker said. Scott hadn't raped her.

But it wasn't Scott who came through the kitchen door. It was Christian, wearing corduroy jeans, a sweater, and a shearling jacket. He looked large and tanned, stunning in a rugged way. But the sight of him was one trauma too many, shattering Laura's fragile composure.

EIGHTEEN

❧❧❧

"N O," LAURA SAID and backed up to the wall. "No! No-ooo!" Screaming the last, she flattened her hands over her ears, then moved them up until her arms covered her head. She slid down the wall on her spine and hit the floor, where she curled into a ball.

Christian's voice was suddenly inches away. "Laura? Jesus, what's wrong?"

She spoke in muffled bursts. "Not you. Not on top of everything else. Go, Christian. Leave. I can't handle you too."

"What's *wrong* with you?"

"Everything! My life is in pieces!"

He paused. "Is this pessimism I hear coming from Mary Sunshine?"

"Leave, Christian!" she screamed. "*Get out of here!*"

"I'm not leaving until I know what's going on."

In a high-pitched voice, she reeled off the problems. "Jeff left, then they froze my money so I can't pay my bills, then the IRS indicted him for tax fraud. The *Sun* is tearing us to shreds, and Cherries' business is off. They say Jeff was having an affair with my friend, and now"—she raised her head, uncaring that Christian saw her tears—"now they want to arrest Scott for rape." The tears welled. "Scott. My Scott!"

Christian shot a glance toward the door. "What the hell is she talking about?"

Laura realized that Melrose and his men were there. Not wanting to see them, she returned her face to her knees.

Close by her ear, and with a hand on her neck, Christian murmured, "I'll be right back."

Then the hand was gone, and Laura had her wish. Christian disappeared into the hall with Melrose, leaving her alone in the kitchen. She couldn't deal with Christian, simply couldn't deal with him. For twenty years he had tormented her. She had only to look at him to feel his pull, and he knew it. So he had taunted her with a goading look, a suggestive word, a scornful smile. Ever fearful that Jeff would learn the truth, she was nervous and uneasy when Christian was near — and that was when she felt strong. She didn't feel strong now. Christian would have to turn around his RV or pickup truck or jeep, or whatever he was driving this time, and go away. She had too much else to handle.

Christian! Of all times to show up! Jeff had been gone for six weeks, and Christian hadn't so much as called his mother to see how she was. He hadn't called Laura to see if she'd heard from Jeff. He hadn't even sent a postcard telling them how great it was in Tahiti. No doubt he'd been too busy having fun, which, she knew, was vintage Christian. Put kindly, he was a free spirit. Put less kindly, he was a self-centered hedonist.

Christian was more likely to commit tax fraud than Jeff. Christian was more likely to commit rape than Scott.

Scott. Innocent Scott. Booked, fingerprinted, photographed in that hideous way the police photographed the dregs of society. She couldn't let that happen.

"Laura?"

She jumped when Christian's voice came at her again. "Please leave," she begged.

"These men want to arrest Scott," he said in a gentle but firm voice. "Whether the charge is justified or not, they have a warrant, and there's nothing we can do about it. I don't want Scott talking to the police unless he has an attorney with him. Can your friend Daphne handle this, or should I call someone else?"

She wanted to tell him that he had to get out of her house, that he would only make things worse, that she didn't need his help. But there was an assuredness in his voice that reached out to the part of her that felt sheer panic. If she was selling her soul to the devil, so be it. She'd do that to help her son.

"Daphne," she whispered.

"I'll call her now. Where's Scott and when will he be home?"

"He was with Kelly before. By now he's probably working out at the health club. He said he'd be home by five."

"That gives us an hour and a half. The detective and his men will wait."

Her head came up fast. "Don't tell them where Scott is!" She had nightmar-ish visions of the police storming the health club and leading a handcuffed Scott off in front of everyone he knew.

"I won't. They're in the other room. Let me get Daphne over here. What's her number?"

Laura said it wrong the first time, confusing Daphne's work number with Jeff's. When she finally got it right, she turned her head away with her cheek on her knee, wound her arms tightly around her legs, and listened while Christian made the call. His voice was low, level, commanding. He seemed to be in control of the situation.

She was glad someone was, since she sure as hell wasn't.

Seconds later, he had hunkered down on her blind side. "Daphne's in court. She's supposed to finish up at four and go back to the office. I told her secretary to get a message to her at the courthouse. I said it was urgent."

Laura hugged her knees tighter. "It is. It's Scott they're waiting for. They want to take him away. For rape!" She felt a hand on her hair. It was soothing, like his voice.

"The cop says Scott knows the girl."

"They dated last summer."

"Do you know her?"

"I met her once. She's a senior. She's pretty, like all the girls Scott dates. He's such a good-looking guy." She cried out at the injustice of it. "He doesn't deserve this. Not Scott. If Megan Tucker had a thing for him and was angry that he ended it to go back to school, that's *her* problem."

"She charged him with rape, so it's Scott's problem too."

Laura raised her face to his. "Whose side are you on? I meant what I said a little while ago, Christian. I can't cope with you along with everything else. Since Jeff left, nothing's gone right. I'm trying to hang on, but it isn't easy, and if you think you can come along and start taunting me, you can think again. I don't want you here. Not like that." His face blurred before her eyes. She swiveled sideways, away from him, and put her cheek to the wall.

After a silence, he said, "I'd like to help."

"I'm not sure anyone can. Things are so awful."

After another silence, he said, "They must be, or you wouldn't be down this way. You were always the most optimistic person I knew."

"It's hard to be optimistic when you get whipped at every turn. I've had six weeks of traumas, one after another." She covered her face with a hand. "This thing with Scott is the worst. The police are waiting out there to arrest my son the minute he steps foot in this house." Her fingers went rigid, and her voice slowed. "I don't know why this is happening to me."

Christian smoothed strands of hair, one by one, back from her face. "We'll get it straightened out, Laura. We will."

Dropping her hand to her knee, she closed her eyes and went limp against the wall. "I feel so tired. At the beginning, I could bounce back. I could find excuses for why things were happening, and even when those excuses fell apart I could count my blessings. But it's like they keep taking those blessings away from me one by one, and now I'm so drained I don't know what to do. I could handle Jeff's disappearance. I could deal with the bank accounts being frozen. I could survive the articles in the paper, and business slowing down, and even Jeff having an affair."

"Did they really say that?"

"Would I make it up? It's devastating." So much so that pride was forgotten. "It makes me feel like a worthless, empty shell parading as a woman, and that's okay, because you're right, it's not the end of the world. But if they do anything to Scott, I'll die."

"They won't do anything to Scott."

She gave a bitter bark of a laugh. "Two months ago, I would have agreed. I mean, he's not guilty, right? Some girl's gone a little nuts, right? Justice will prevail, right?" She sighed. "After a while, when one unfair thing after another happens, you lose faith."

"Don't do that, Laura. It's no way to live."

"And this is? I don't sleep because my mind keeps churning things around. I don't eat because my stomach keeps churning things around. I can't walk down the street without someone turning to stare, because the *newspaper* keeps churning things around." She squeezed her eyes shut. "The paper will crucify Scott."

"Not if I can help it," Christian vowed. He took her by the arms. "Come on, Laura. I want you up at the table. You can have some tea while I make my calls."

"Who are you calling?"

"For starters, Tack Jones. I want to find out what's going on."

Laura let herself be settled into a chair. "He's the enemy. He won't help."

"He'll help." Christian spoke with such conviction that she simply watched while he put on a teakettle, then pulled out his wallet and took a business card from it. Within minutes, he was talking with Tack.

Laura didn't move. She wasn't sure whether she was so exhausted that she didn't have the energy, or whether she was saving up what little energy she did have for the moment when Scott would be home, or whether it was Christian's presence that kept her still. Years ago, she had gone weak in the knees every time she'd set eyes on him.

He still looked good.

More than that, he sounded strong. She didn't have to follow his conversation to know he was asking pointed questions. And he'd get his answers. Christian was that way. When he dedicated himself to something—be it taking photographs, disrupting a family gathering, or making a seventeen-year-old girl fall in love—he succeeded.

The teakettle whistled. Pure reflex had Laura on her feet, but a motion from Christian sent her back to her seat. She watched him take out the mugs, then the tea bags, then the sugar. Seven months had passed since he'd been in her house; still, he remembered where things were. But that was Christian too. He had an incredible memory. He was one of the few people she knew who, like her, could do two things at once—which he proceeded to demonstrate by fixing her tea with two sugars, like she always drank it, without missing a beat in his talk with Tack.

He stretched the phone cord to bring her the tea. Laura wrapped her hands around the warm mug. She was so tired. Every time she thought of the ordeal that was sure to come before the day was done, she started to shake. But the shaking was more distant now than it had been, as though she didn't have enough energy for that either, another frightening thought. She had to be there for Scott. She had to be strong for him. She was his mother. With Jeff gone, she was all he had.

She sipped her tea, then took another sip when the sweetness went down the right way. Her gaze drifted to the window. She wished it were summer, with the crabapple trees full, the grass a rich green, and birds swooping about. If she could have had warmth and sunshine just then, she wouldn't have begrudged the squirrels her birdseed, she was that desperate for something cheery and light.

Christian slid into a chair with his own mug of tea. Looking at it, Laura realized she didn't know many male tea drinkers. She imagined men were drawn to coffee because it had a more macho image. Jeff was a coffee drinker. But not Christian. Twenty-one years ago he'd been drinking tea, and he still was.

Her eyes rose to his face, but he was looking at his mug and seemed lost in thought. She wondered whether he was considering putting his coat back on and leaving, now that he knew how bad things were. He had left her once before, when things weren't bad at all. She wouldn't put it past him to do it again.

Still he sat brooding. She was starting to wonder if he would wait until after his tea to leave, when he raised his head and met her eyes. "Why didn't you tell me?"

"About what?" She thought she had blurted out most everything when she'd been crouched on the floor.

"The money. Tack says you're strapped."

"How does Tack know?"

"He knows. Is it true?"

There didn't seem any point in denying it. Christian knew so much already, he might as well know it all. She was too tired to play games. "When you find yourself one day suddenly cut off from every cent you have to your name so that you're basically starting from scratch, you're strapped."

"You should have told me."

"How? You were in Tahiti."

"Tack knew where I was. You knew he had seen me. You could have gotten a phone number from him."

Laura looked off toward the yard. She supposed she had known that. But she hadn't wanted to call Christian. She hadn't wanted him to know how badly she'd failed.

He tapped the side of his mug. "Tack said Daphne and Elise are helping you out."

She frowned. "How does *he* know?"

The tapping stopped. "I'll help too. I've got money sitting in the bank doing nothing. I'll get a draft tomorrow and deposit it in your account."

She took a deep breath. "That's not necessary. I think I have things under control. I borrowed enough from Daphne and Elise to get me through the worst of this month, and if business is good—"

"It isn't. You said that before."

She let out the rest of the breath and turned back to the window, only to freeze moments later when the garage door went up. "Oh, God," she whispered. The pounding in her chest started again. "Oh, God, Christian, they'll take him to jail."

Christian looked at the door to the hall, where the detective had materialized, then swung around in time to see Debra breeze in from the garage. She began talking the instant she saw Laura.

"What is that *police* car doing outside? And the Miata. Whose is that?" She caught sight of Christian and her eyes went wide. In a hushed voice that reflected the mix of awe and amusement that Debra and Scott both held for their uncle, she said, "Oh, wow, we knew you'd get in trouble one day. What did you do, Christian?"

"Nothing yet," Laura said.

"The police cars aren't for him?" The wide eyes went from Laura to the detective. "Why are they here?"

Laura tried to say it, but the words wouldn't come. With wide eyes of her own, she stared at Debra for a minute before looking frantically at Christian.

"They want to ask your brother a few questions," Christian explained.

"Questions about what?"

"A girl he used to date."

"Which one?"

"Megan Tucker," Dennis Melrose said from the door.

"What's she done now?" Debra asked, in a way that suggested she fully expected Megan to be in trouble.

Laura pulled out of her silence to grab onto that. "Do you know her?"

"I know who she is. Most everyone does."

"Why?" Christian asked.

"She's popular. She's pretty."

"Does she go out a lot?"

"Sure. She gives boys what they want. What'd she do?" Debra asked the detective, who promptly looked at Laura, but she couldn't get the words past her throat any more than before. Again she sought Christian's help.

"She filed criminal charges against Scott," he said.

"For what?"

The room was silent. Debra's eyes went from one face to the next. "What's going on?"

"Rape," Laura blurted out. "She says Scott raped her."

Debra's jaw dropped. "Are you kidding?"

The disbelief on her face was so genuine Laura wanted to hug her. For the time being, though, she only shook her head.

Debra stared at the detective. "Megan's lying. If she says Scott raped her, she's lying. I know my brother, and he may be obnoxious—"

"Debra—"

"Babe—"

"—but that's to me, because I'm his sister," Debra finished in defiance of Christian and Laura's simultaneous attempts to warn her into silence. "Scott's a nice guy. He treats his dates well. He gives them little gifts and does these romantic things that any girl would be crazy not to like. If he wanted sex, he wouldn't have to rape a girl to get it." She deposited her backpack on the island with a thud. "He sure wouldn't have to rape Megan. She practically gives it out on the street corner, and I'm not the only one who'd say that. Ask anyone. She's known for it."

Christian grinned at her. He winked at Laura, then turned his grin on the detective. "There you have it, Detective Melrose. Your first character witness. She won't help your case."

"Neither will I," Daphne said from the hall, having let herself in through the front door. She looked livid. "I'll fight you tooth and nail, and if either of you guys—" her eyes touched briefly on the uniformed officers, "—think that's a typically feminine response, you'd better believe it. It's feminine and hard and can be very unpleasant if you're on the other end. I've known Scott Frye since he was born, and if there's one kid who is incapable of rape, he's it. Dennis, what *gives*? You know as well as I do that girl's lying. I won't know why until I look into the case, but my guess is she's jumping on the bandwagon. She sees what the paper is doing to this family, she hears the scuttlebutt around town, and hell, date rape is a hot topic, so why not? She figures she'll get a little sympathy, a little attention, maybe even some money. Is she suing for damages?"

"I don't know," Melrose said. "The only thing that concerns me is the criminal complaint."

"Well, it *should* concern you. It's a trumped-up charge."

The detective looked uncomfortable. "You know how the system works, Daphne. If the girl comes in, swears she's been raped, and wants to file charges, we have to investigate. You may be able to get the charges dismissed at the probable-cause hearing, but in the meantime I have to book the boy."

A small, involuntary sound came from Laura's throat. Resting her elbow on the table, she put her forehead in her palm. Daphne continued to spar with the detective, though it was an exercise in futility, Laura knew. After a minute, Christian touched her arm.

"Hangin' in there?" he asked.

She nodded.

A minute later, the detective retreated from the kitchen. Fishing in her bag for a notebook, Daphne turned to Debra. She spoke quietly but with purpose. "While we're waiting for Scott, I want you to tell me everything you know about Megan Tucker—who her friends are, who she dates, whether she belongs to any clubs or has any school extracurricular activities."

Debra told her what she knew. When Laura didn't hear anything to significantly change her impression of the girl's motive, she tuned out of the discussion and turned her thoughts to Scott.

"He'll be okay," Christian leaned close again to say.

Laura's sigh came out as a moan against her wrist. "He has to be. He's such a good kid. *Such* a good kid. He works hard, he does well, and he has promise. His whole future is ahead of him. The thought of it being spoiled by some spiteful little bitch makes me sick." She curled her fingers into a fist. "Damn Jeff. Damn his greed and his cowardice." Lowering her hand, she looked at Christian. "I keep wondering if he knows what's going on. For all we know, he's hiding out somewhere ten miles away, following the stories in the paper."

"If that were so, they'd have found the Porsche. Boy, I'll bet he loved that car. It had the flash he never did. When did he get it? He didn't have it when I was here in June."

"He bought it in July."

"Did he pay in cash?"

Laura pressed her lips together for a minute. She'd asked herself that question over and over, and each time she felt greater self-reproach. "I don't know. I didn't ask. Pretty dumb of me, huh? An expensive car like that, and

I didn't ask if we could afford it. But if I'd done that," she defended herself as she'd done so many times in her mind, "it would have been like I doubted him, and that would have been an insult. It was my job to build him up, not knock him down. Or so I thought." In a dry murmur, she added, "Looks like I thought wrong on a whole lot of things. I thought he cared for me. I thought he cared for the kids. Let's see if he comes forward when he learns about *this.*"

Christian shook his head. "He's probably long gone. He's probably somewhere where he couldn't possibly get either the *Globe* or the *Sun* without tipping his hand. Jeff's crafty. More than any of us thought. He pulled off that scam for eight years before anyone caught on, and now he's eluding the FBI. He's being careful. I doubt he'd go looking for news, and that's even if he wanted it, which I doubt he does. If he made the decision to cut loose, he won't want to know about the mess he left behind."

"Which is something I'll never understand as long as I live," Laura said in defeat. "I'll never understand *any* of this." Elbows on the table, she linked her fingers and pressed them to her mouth, which was propitious. They were able to stifle her cry when the garage door opened for the third time.

NINETEEN

I T TOOK SCOTT LONGER to enter the kitchen. He had to pull into the garage and turn off the car. Pressing those fingers harder to her mouth, Laura listened to the car door opening, then slamming shut. She heard his footsteps on the landing. His entrance was on a burst of energy, much the way Debra's had been, but he came to an abrupt halt when he saw the faces turned his way—including those of Melrose and his men.

"Yo, Christian! You throwing a party?" he asked curiously. He was wearing an open parka over sweatpants and a sweatshirt, and his hair fell in spikes on his forehead.

Laura went to him and slipped an arm through his. Her voice shook. "We have a problem here."

Scott looked suddenly frightened. "They found Dad?"

"No."

"But it has to do with Dad."

"No."

He looked at Christian. "Are you in trouble?"

Christian shook his head. "Not me. You."

"Me?"

Daphne came up. "Megan Tucker is accusing you of rape."

"She's what?"

"Accusing you of rape."

Scott looked dumbfounded. "*Megan Tucker?*"

"That's right." Daphne glanced at the detective. "Back off, Dennis. We'd like a few minutes alone."

"We'll be waiting outside," Melrose told her.

Scott stared after him until he was gone, then turned back to Daphne. "Rape?"

Laura held his arm tightly. She could feel the tension there, even through the layers of his clothes. "She says it happened last August."

His eyes flashed. "She lies."

"That's what *I* said," Debra put in.

"Why would I rape her?" Scott cried. "She gives it out like there's no tomorrow."

Debra bobbed her head. "That's what *I* said."

"It doesn't matter what either of you says right now," Daphne explained. "What matters, Scott, is what the girl said and the fact that those men out there hold a warrant for your arrest."

Laura saw his color drain, felt the tremor that shot through his arm, and it nearly tore her apart. She opened her mouth to reassure him, but her throat was thick and tight and no words came out.

"My arrest? For what? I didn't rape Megan Tucker. I didn't do anything but date her for a few weeks."

"Did you sleep with her?" Daphne asked.

Scott looked at Debra, then at Laura. "Yeah, I slept with her. I'd have been a fool not to. She's pretty and she's sexy and she's willing. *More* than willing. I did not rape her."

"I know," Laura managed through the knot in her throat. Her knees had started to shake, and she felt perilously close to tears, but she ignored both. "She's a sick girl."

"So where does that leave me?"

"You'll have to go down to the station—" Daphne began.

"The *police* station? I'm not going to the police station! I haven't done anything wrong!"

"You'll tell them that," Laura urged, but that was as much as she got out before her lower lip began to tremble.

Daphne took over. "I'll be with you. We'll go down to the station. They'll go through the formalities of charging you. We'll get bail set, then you'll be home. Tomorrow morning you'll be arraigned—ten minutes in court—and then you'll go back to school like you planned."

"With a rape charge hanging over my head."

"Yes," Daphne conceded. "But while you're gone, I'll be working to get the charges dismissed."

Laura had bleak visions of the agony lasting for months, even years. "Can't you get them dismissed now?"

"Not now. Maybe soon. I have to learn more about the case. Once Scott's back here, we can talk about his relationship with Megan Tucker. By then we'll have a copy of the statement she gave the police." To Scott, she said, "Let's go on down now and get this over with. The sooner we're back here, the better."

Laura released Scott's arm and looked frantically around the floor. "I just—uh, I need some shoes."

Christian materialized beside her. "Stay here, Laura. I'll go with Daphne. It'll be better that way." He went for his jacket.

Laura swallowed back her tears. "Oh, God, no. I wouldn't think of not being there. I *have* to be there."

"Christian's right," Daphne said. "It's a routine thing. No one's making any kind of statement. Stay here."

"But I want to be with Scott." She looked up at him. "I've always been there for you. I couldn't not be there now."

"Stay here, Mom," he said in a voice that was tense but very grown up. "Stay here with Debra. It'll be awful enough for me there. It'll be worse if you have to see it all."

"I don't mind," she argued. She felt more frightened than she had ever been in her life. "I never minded when you were a little boy and threw up, or bashed your lip playing and bled all over the place."

"I'm not a little boy anymore, and this isn't play."

Her breath caught. Of all the things he might have said, that stopped her cold. Because he was right. On both counts. And she didn't want either to be true. "But what'll I do here?"

"Fix dinner," Christian said. Taking Scott by the shoulder, he moved him toward the garage. "We'll all be hungry when we get back. I haven't had a decent home-cooked meal since I was here last June. Do something special, Laura. And you help her, Debra," he called over his shoulder. "Stay here with her and help."

"I'm not leaving," Debra said in a frightened voice, but the only one who heard her was Laura, since the other three were gone.

The garage door rolled open, then rolled shut. Debra moved close to Laura, who was hugging herself against the pain.

"Whose car are they taking?" she whispered.

"Daphne's," Laura whispered back. She thought to run to the front window and watch, but her legs wouldn't work.

"Will Scott have to go with the police?"

"Maybe."

"They won't handcuff him, will they?"

Laura was asking herself the same thing. "I don't think so. He's going in with his lawyer. They know he's not running away."

The whispering went on. "Will they fingerprint him and stuff?"

"I think so."

"That's *awful.*"

Laura turned to find Debra looking so distraught she immediately took her in her arms. What she wanted to say was, Don't worry, babe, it'll be all right,

Scott will be right back, this whole thing's a mistake, but she had no faith in the words. Words were empty. Reason didn't always prevail. The only thing with meaning was the warmth of another human being, the closeness and the comfort. Debra must have agreed, because they stood there holding each other, silent in a silent house, for a long time.

"You're shaking," Debra whispered at one point.

"It's getting better," Laura whispered back, and held her a bit longer. Finally, knowing that Christian's suggestion was good in ways that went well beyond food, she took a deep breath and said, "Okay. What should I make?"

Mercifully, Debra didn't ask how she could possibly cook. Instead, she said, "What do you have?"

Laura studied the refrigerator, then the freezer. She took a flank steak from the latter and put it in the microwave to defrost, then began piling fresh vegetables onto the counter. "I don't know how long they'll be. I can slice everything now, then put it in the wok when they get home." It made sense, she thought, and was pleased that *something* did. So she took out the cutting board and a knife and went to work.

She sliced scallions, celery, and spinach.

"Don't you usually leave the spinach leaves whole?" Debra asked. She stood at the counter watching.

"I need to cut," Laura told her, but she dropped the knife with a clatter when the phone rang.

Debra reached it before she could. "Hello?" After a silence, during which time Laura felt her life was on hold, she repeated the greeting. "Hello?"

"What do you hear?" Laura whispered.

"Nothing," Debra whispered back. "*Hello.*" After another second, she hung up the phone. "Must have been a wrong number."

Laura wanted to ask if there had been static, but then Debra would wonder why she'd asked, and to tell her would be like putting her on the alert that her father might be calling any time, which wasn't the truth.

So Laura said nothing and went back to her chopping. Between thoughts of Scott and thoughts of Jeff, she was nowhere near as efficient as usual. Her hands weren't steady. Her concentration was off.

"What do you think they're doing to Scott?" Debra asked nervously.

"Booking him."

"Do you think he's scared?"

"Uh-huh."

"Will Daphne be with him the whole time?"

"I hope so."

"And Christian. Funny his showing up today. I mean, on Dad's birthday and all."

Laura dropped the knife and wiped shaky hands on her jeans. Going back to the refrigerator, she took out several sweet potatoes and began to pare them.

"Can I do something?" Debra asked.

Laura shook her head. "I need to keep busy."

"Christian told me to help."

"You can set the table."

While Debra did that, Laura set about cutting the potatoes down to shoe-string size, but she had barely cut the first potato into quarters when the knife went too far and cut into the heel of her hand. Swearing, she grabbed the nearby dishtowel and pressed it to the cut.

Debra looked over her shoulder. "Is it bad?"

"Nah."

"Let me see."

"It's fine. Do me a favor and get a Band-Aid."

While Debra went to the bathroom, Laura took off the towel and put her hand under the faucet. The cut wasn't fine. It was deep. But it wouldn't kill her. Neither would the sight of the blood flowing from it, though it made her weak in ways the sight of blood never had before.

Debra brought the tin of Band-Aids. Laura put one on as tightly as she could, but she'd barely thrown away the tabs when blood began seeping through the pad.

"That's disgusting," Debra said. "It's really bleeding. Maybe it needs to be stitched."

Laura felt vaguely light-headed. "All it needs is to be wrapped tighter. Were there any gauze pads with the Band-Aids?" When Debra went to check, she stumbled to a chair, and while she put pressure on her hand, she hung her head between her knees. She hadn't fainted many times in her life, but she knew the signs.

"Mom? Are you okay?"

She raised her head and took a breath. "I'm fine, babe. Just a little woozy there for a minute."

"Maybe you should lie down."

"I'm okay." She opened two gauze pads, removed the bloodied Band-Aid, and pressed the pads in place, then taped them there with a new Band-Aid. "There." Tossing the papers in the basket, she pushed herself up, took some ice water from the refrigerator, and sipped it. It helped.

"You look pale," Debra told her. "Are you sure you're not going to pass out?"

"No. I'm okay now." To prove it, she went back to work. Before long, the potatoes were arranged in tiny slices beside the other vegetables on a plate. She gathered the ingredients for the sauce, then put white rice on to boil.

Then she looked at Debra. "What should I do for dessert?"

"There are a million things already in the refrigerator."

"Humor me, babe. I have to work. How about a hot fruit compote?" Scott loved that. She took out the ingredients, most of which were canned, and began to arrange them in a large baking dish. All too soon the dish was in the oven, and she was looking at Debra again. She pressed the heel of her hand, which was beginning to throb. She glanced worriedly at the clock.

"They've been gone an hour," Debra said. "Is that good or bad?"

"I don't know."

"Does your hand hurt?"

"A little. It'll be okay."

"Shouldn't they be back soon?"

Laura nodded.

"Y'know, Megan Tucker really is awful. She goes through a guy a month. No judge will take her word over Scott's."

"I hope it never comes to that," Laura said. "With any luck, we can get the charges dismissed." Needing to do something—and remembering the brief comfort she'd found earlier—she said, "Want some tea?"

"I hate tea. Tea is for when you're sick and your stomach is upset. When we were little, you used to make us drink it. I don't think I'll ever be able to look at it without thinking of dry toast and Kaopectate. No, thanks."

Laura put the light on under the kettle.

"Mom?"

"Mmm?"

"You've known for a while that Scott was sleeping with girls, haven't you?"

Unsure where the conversation was leading and, therefore, how much she should say, Laura shrugged. "Why do you ask?"

"Did you know when he first did it?"

"He didn't run right home and tell me, if that's what you're asking."

"Did you talk about it beforehand with him—I mean, about birth control and stuff?"

Laura nodded. "Like I talked with you."

"Did Dad give him condoms?"

Laura doubted that. She doubted if Jeff had even discussed the matter with Scott. He had been uncomfortable talking about intimate things. "I assume Scott went into a drugstore and bought them himself." She glanced at the clock and wondered what was happening and when they'd be home. She wished she'd gone with them. The waiting was awful.

"Boys are lucky. They can do that so easily. If a girl wants to go on the pill, she has to go to a doctor, and then her parents know beforehand what she's going to do."

"Maybe it's better that way," Laura said. "Girls are more vulnerable. They *should* think seriously about what they do." She wandered into the dining room.

Debra followed her. "That's a sexist thing to say."

"Maybe." She pulled back the sheer and looked out into the night, but the red Miata parked in the driveway was the only car in sight.

"What if I wanted to go on the pill? Would you let me?"

"You're only sixteen."

"Maybe Scott was sixteen when he did it."

"Scott wasn't sixteen. He was eighteen."

"He was not. He was dating Jenny Spitz when he was seventeen, and Jenny's hot stuff."

"Scott was over eighteen when he was first with a girl."

"Okay. But the girls were sixteen and seventeen. That's the way things work. Girls who are my age date guys who are seventeen and eighteen."

"Donny's your age."

"Jace isn't."

Laura looked at her, but the darkness hid her expression. "How old is Jace?"

"He's a senior."

"How old is he?"

"Eighteen."

"I didn't know that."

"I'm sure I said it at some point. You just didn't hear. But it's no big thing. He's the nicest guy in the world."

So was Scott, Laura mused, looking back at the window, and now he was being taken for a ride by a girl he had made love to and shouldn't have. Unless the Frye luck changed, the mistake could prove to be disastrous.

Headlights came from down the street. Laura held her breath, half expecting the car to go on by. When it turned into the driveway, she whispered, "Thank God." Whirling around, she ran back through the kitchen to the garage. She opened the door and, barefooted, waited at the edge of the cement for Scott to get out of the car.

Daphne got out, then Christian. Something about the way they looked at her, even before their doors slammed shut in the night, made Laura cold all over.

"Where is he?"

"They're keeping him overnight," Daphne said.

Christian put an arm around her shoulder and turned her back toward the kitchen. "Come on inside. It's cold."

Laura shrugged off his arm. "Why isn't he home?"

"There was a problem with bail," Daphne said.

Christian's arm returned to propel her forward, but she didn't take her eyes off Daphne. "What kind of problem?"

"Since it was after four, there wasn't a judge around, so they had to call a bail commissioner. He didn't want to set bail."

"Why not?" Debra asked from the door, then stepped aside as they came through.

"He felt that, given the seriousness of the charge, it was better to wait until morning."

Laura began to shiver. "Scott's spending the night in jail?"

Christian's arm tightened around her. "The arraignment will be first thing tomorrow morning. The judge will set bail then."

Laura looked up at him and swallowed hard. "He's in jail?"

"He'll be okay, Laura. Trust me. He will."

The words seemed to come from farther and farther away. She felt light-headed again, and this time there was a buzzing in her ears. "I want . . . I think . . . I have to . . ." The world turned stark white. The next thing she knew, she was on the living room sofa, with no idea how she'd gotten there. Debra and Daphne were hovering in her periphery, but Christian was the one pressing a damp cloth to her forehead. "I must have . . ."

"You did," he said. "Very elegantly." He tugged at the Band-Aid on her hand, then whistled through his teeth when he got a look at what was beneath.

Laura glanced down, but the bloody gauze made her close her eyes and moan.

"I'm taking her to the hospital," Christian told the other two. Laura didn't have the strength to argue. "Debra, can you find me something warm for her feet, socks and sneakers or something?" When she went off, he looked back at the hand. "How did you do this?"

"I was holding the potato. I should have put it on the cutting board."

"That's great. Just great." To Daphne he said, "Think Julia Child cuts potatoes in her hand?"

Laura turned her face away. "What kind of jail is it? Is it filthy? Crowded?"

"Not in this town," Daphne leaned over to assure her. "He'll be in his own cell. They'll give him dinner. He'll have a cot to sleep on, and he'll be as warm as he wants."

"How early can he get out?"

"Court is at nine."

"Nine!"

"He'll be okay, Laura. Christian and I talked with him for a while before we left. He's a strong kid. He'll do just fine."

All that might be true, but he was still Laura's son, and each time she thought of where he was, she felt chilled to the bone. Shivering, she pushed herself up.

"Dizzy?" Christian asked.

She opened the cloth and pressed it over her face for a minute before setting it aside. "I'm okay."

Debra returned with sneakers and socks, which Christian promptly went to work putting on. When Laura bent over to do it herself, he pushed her hand away. "Any fresh gauze for that cut, Deb?" Debra ran off.

"I can do this," Laura insisted.

Christian shot her an annoyed look. "I'm sure you can, but why should you have to if I'm willing to do it for you?"

"Because I'm not helpless."

"No, but you're upset and dizzy, and that hand probably hurts like hell. So do me a favor?" He reached out and took the fresh gauze from a slightly breathless Debra. "Hold your hand higher than your heart, press this gauze to it, and let me do the rest, okay?"

Laura couldn't remember the last time someone had helped her dress. She wanted to protest, but it wasn't worth the effort. She wanted to feel embarrassed, but she didn't have the strength. So she concentrated on doing what Christian had said, holding her hand in the vicinity of her neck, pressing the gauze to the cut. When he finished tying her sneakers, he drew her to her feet and guided her into the hall. With his help, she put on her coat, and when he tucked her into the passenger's seat of the Miata, she sank down and closed her eyes.

The hospital was ten minutes away. Laura was silent during the drive. She felt Christian look her way from time to time. Twice he asked how she was, but all she did was nod. She kept thinking of Scott and wanting to cry.

Determinedly, she held it in. Christian did most of the talking at the hospital, and, having decided not to fight, it was a relief to let him. It was also a relief to have him by her side the whole time, where she could lean against him for comfort. She wasn't normally a coward, and she didn't shy from physical pain, but she wasn't herself. She was weak, battered, stripped down, and frightened, so frightened. So she took what he offered.

In no more than half an hour, the cut was sewn up and they were back in the car heading home. Again she was silent. Her throat kept tightening up, and if it wasn't her throat, it was the sting of tears in her eyes.

"Feeling okay?" Christian asked, sounding concerned in spite of the lightness he forced into his voice.

That concern made her throat even tighter, but she managed to push out an "Uh-huh."

Several minutes later, he asked, "Does it hurt much?"

"It's still numb," she answered, wishing she were as numb as the hand. But her mind seemed to be working with remarkable clarity, producing pictures she didn't want to see.

"Are you hungry?" he asked several minutes after that.

She shook her head. When, soon after, they pulled up at the house, went through the garage and into the kitchen, and the smell of sukiyaki hit her, she knew she couldn't eat a thing.

After assuring a frightened Debra that she was fine, she excused herself and went upstairs to her bedroom. Without so much as kicking off her sneakers, she pulled back a corner of the bedspread, climbed under it, pulled it to her ears, and gave in to the tears that had been wanting to come for such a long, long time.

That was how Christian found her. He had seen those tears threatening time and again at the hospital, and he knew they had to do not with her hand but with everything else happening in her life. He also knew she wouldn't let them fall in front of other people. She was too proud and independent for that.

Christian understood pride and independence. They were mainstays of his own personality. But so was determination. When he had first driven into Northampton that afternoon, he hadn't expected half of what he'd found. Seeing Laura vulnerable had shaken him. He wasn't sure he knew what had happened to her, but he wasn't leaving until he found out. And while he was there, he planned to help. That was in his nature too. He helped his friends. He would have helped his family if he hadn't been shut out from the time he'd been nine. And he had let them do that. He had played into their hands, given them reason to think the worst of him, given himself reason to walk away from the hurt. But he wasn't doing that now. Now he could do some good.

That was why, when Laura cried between sobs, "Leave me alone—please, Christian—just leave me alone!" he kicked off his shoes and climbed right into bed with her. Propping himself against the headboard, he took her in his arms and held her tightly until her resistance faded. Then he rubbed her back, smoothed her hair from her face, and held her gently until she cried herself to sleep.

TWENTY

SCOTT WAS ARRAIGNED the next morning. After entering a plea of not guilty, he was released on his own recognizance—though not without a fight from the assistant district attorney, who argued that the family history suggested Scott might flee before his trial. Daphne argued that given Scott's age, the total absence of a criminal record, his enrollment at Penn, and his mother's position in the community, the concept of flight was absurd, and the judge agreed.

That was the first time Laura felt that anything legal had gone her way, and it gave her an iota of encouragement. With Christian at the wheel of the Wagoneer, they drove Scott home. While Scott showered, Christian took the *Sun* out of the wastebasket, where Laura had thrown it that morning.

"This is quite an article," he commented dryly.

She stood against the counter with her arms crossed in distaste. "It's nothing more than Duggan O'Neil has been doing regularly since Jeff disappeared. He puts in every detail he can dig up, then speculates about others. Wait a day or two. Gary Holmes is sure to write an editorial about this."

"What's his problem? Did you put rotten cherries in his pie?"

"I don't serve rotten cherries, so I have no idea what his problem is. My mother thinks I should yell and scream and threaten lawsuits, but that would be a waste of time. The *Sun* isn't doing anything illegal, just cruel. Every time there's an article, we feel the fallout, and I'm not only talking about business. People stare. They talk. I'm getting used to it, I suppose, but it isn't so easy for Debra. Some of her friends—supposed friends—are ignoring her. She's being excluded from parties. Parties wouldn't matter to me, but they do to her. She's a social kid."

"She's a knockout."

Laura couldn't resist a small smile. "Yeah."

"She looks like you."

Her eyes met his. For a minute she thought she saw admiration, then she decided she was wrong. Christian had lost interest in her years ago. Apparently, so had Jeff, which didn't make her worthy of much admiration, at least not of the appealing-woman type.

"About last night." She lowered her eyes to her hand. It was neatly bandaged, and though it was sore, there was no blood in sight. "Thanks are due. I kind of fell apart. I'm glad you were here."

"I'm happy I was," Christian said quietly.

His tone brought her head right back up. The Christian who had visited over the last twenty years would have been more apt to throw out a smug "Yeah, I saved the day, you really were a mess." This one reminded her of the younger, gentler, totally mesmerizing man she had known before Jeff.

"Why are you here?" she asked. She kept wondering about that. Christian wasn't one to pop in. As far as she could recall, he had never come without an invitation before. "What made you come yesterday? What made you come at all?"

He folded the paper, then folded it again and returned it to the trash. Pensive, he straightened. "It had been awhile. I hadn't heard anything from Jones, and I wondered what was happening." He paused. "I was just in from Tahiti and didn't have much else to do." He paused again, looking hesitant. With an uncertain frown, he said, "Yesterday was Jeff's birthday. When he was a baby, it was always a fun day. He loved the party and the presents, and I loved seeing that."

Laura was instantly skeptical. "You resented Jeff from the day he was born."

"Not true," Christian insisted. "I loved him when he was little. He was so cute and so good and so serious. I worked as hard as everyone else to make him happy, and he was happy on his birthday." He thumbed the edge of the footed cake plate that held, under a glass dome, two thirds of an apple torte. "I guess I thought maybe he'd show up yesterday, or write, or call."

Laura heard the shower cut off. She figured she'd give Scott a few minutes to get dressed before she went up. "He may have called. There were some hang-ups."

"No sound?"

Laura shook her head. "Two on the machine had a little static. Debra answered a third, so I don't know."

"Is there a tap on the phone?"

"You mean, is the FBI monitoring my calls?" She listened for little beeps, and though she didn't hear any, she was conscious of everything she said on the phone. "I assume so. They don't trust me to tell them if he called. Isn't that a laugh? The man has torn apart everything I've wanted and worked for, and they think I'd protect him."

"You are his wife," Christian pointed out.

"Which is why I'm so angry." She had promised herself that she wouldn't ask the question again, still it slipped out. "How could he do this to me, Christian? How could a rational man who supposedly loved his family turn on them this way?"

"He didn't turn on you. He ran away."

"Same difference. I was his wife. If something was bothering him, he should have told me. I keep going over the last few years in my mind." She raised her good hand to her head, as though that might help her. "I keep trying to remember if he was unusually quiet, or sullen, or moody, or impatient. But he wasn't any of those things, or if he was I didn't see it. Maybe Debra's right. Maybe I was too busy to see it. But I've had hours to look back now, and I don't see a thing." Her hand fell. She looked at the injured one, ran her fingertips over the gauze. "Did he ever say anything to you?"

"He wouldn't have."

"You were his brother."

"Yeah. And he met *you* when you went to return *my* poetry book." He lowered his voice. "How much did he know about us, Laura?"

She felt a moment's pain that had nothing to do with her hand. "Not much. He knew we knew each other. That's all."

"Did he know we were together?"

"I don't know."

"He must have sensed something."

She shrugged.

"He must have known you weren't a virgin."

"He never said anything."

"Do you think he suspected it was me?"

"He never said anything," she repeated. She didn't want to talk about that. She didn't see the relevance. What had happened between Christian and her had been over for years. "He couldn't have been holding a grudge all that time. He loved me."

"But he left."

She let out a breath. "Yes." She shot a glance at the ceiling. "I want to talk with Scott." Without another look at Christian, she left the kitchen.

Scott was in his bedroom, scrubbed clean and looking forlorn as he sat on the edge of the bed with his elbows on his knees. Slipping down beside him, Laura touched his back. "I'm glad you're home."

"Me too."

"Was it awful?"

He nodded.

"Want to talk about it?"

He shook his head.

She extended her arm to rub his shoulder, and as she did, her mind drifted back to when he was little, when he used to come to her for comfort if something hurt. She had held him on her lap then, rocking him gently, cooing the way mothers do when the message is more love and closeness than anything else. In time, when he grew too big for her lap, she used to sit beside him and press him close. Now he was too big even for that. He was man-sized, just like the charges Megan Tucker had brought.

"Why do you think she did it?" Laura asked softly.

He shrugged. His eyes were glued to the shag carpet that had hidden a multitude of sins over the years. The sins were bigger now, Laura mused. There was no hiding them.

"She didn't want to break up," he said. "She wanted to visit me at school. I told her I didn't want that. She got angry."

"This was at the pizza house?" Laura had learned some of the details from Daphne. They were in the report the police had prepared.

Scott nodded. "I didn't want to argue with her, especially not there, with all her friends watching. And I didn't want to just end it like that, so I grabbed her hand and pulled her to the car." He looked back at Laura. "I wasn't rough. I didn't do anything more than I'd have done if I was annoyed with Debra."

"That isn't saying a whole lot, Scott. You and Debra can really go at it."

"I didn't hurt Megan. I got her to the car and drove her back to her house, and the bitch of it is that we didn't even make love. Not that night. I went inside for a while, and we rehashed the whole thing about my going back to school. I don't think she would have minded if it had been her idea to break up. She likes to call the shots. But it was me who did it, and that got her pissed."

"Where were her parents?"

"They're divorced. She lives with her mother."

"So where was she?"

"Out with her boyfriend."

Laura moaned. "Setting a good example."

"The thing is, Mrs. Tucker's a nice lady. The few times I met her, she was really nice. Maybe it was the boyfriend's idea to go for the money —" they had learned that Megan was suing for damages, "— and in order to do that they had to charge me with rape."

"Maybe." Laura wasn't even thinking about the civil suit. The criminal one was the more frightening of the two by far. "Did you know she was pregnant and miscarried?"

He paled, but an instant later there was anger in his eyes. "No, but if so, it wasn't mine. I never made love with her, ever, without using something."

Laura had told the police as much the day before, though she'd been walking on thin ice with the declaration. Just because she'd found a half-filled box of condoms in his drawer didn't mean he hadn't slipped up once or twice.

"Are you sure, Scott? Maybe in the heat of the moment —"

"Never. Hey, I may have been dumb to date her in the first place, but I wasn't so dumb as to be careless. And I'm not talkin' about a baby. I'm talking about *disease*. Megan's been around more than most girls. The guys joke about it. Nobody's lookin' to pick up anything from her." With a snort, he stared off at the wall. "So instead of VD, I pick up a rape charge. That's gonna do great things for my future."

"We'll get it dropped."

"And if we don't?" When he looked back at her, the fear on his face was clear as day, making him look young and vulnerable. "What if Daphne can't get me off? I mean, if Megan has friends who say they saw us argue, and I have friends who say she sleeps around, it'll boil down to her word against mine."

"Daphne says there aren't any medical records to support her claim."

"But there's still her word, and she can lie like a pro. I know three guys who were dating her at the same time, and she conned each into thinking he was the only one. It was her idea of a joke. She wanted to see if she could pull it off."

"Do you know the guys?"

"You bet."

"Think they'd testify?"

The frightened look eased a little. "Probably."

"Well, that's something." Laura took comfort from it herself, but the comfort was short-lived.

"What if it doesn't work? What if nothing works?"

"Don't think about that."

"What if I'm convicted and have to spend time in prison? *Prison*, Mom. Prison's different from jail. Last night was scary enough. I don't think I could *survive* prison."

"You are not going to prison."

"If I'm convicted, I will. And even if Daphne manages to make a deal so I don't have to, if I'm convicted I can forget about being a lawyer."

"That won't happen."

"A convicted felon would have one hell of a time getting into law school, and if he did make it, he'd have one hell of a time getting admitted to the bar." He kicked out at the leg of the desk. "I can't believe this is happening to me. *Shit*." He kicked again, harder.

Laura flinched with each kick. She knew how upset he was, and his upset magnified her own. Only an act of will kept her voice low and steady. "Daphne's going to get the charges dismissed."

"And if she doesn't?"

"She will."

"Come on, Mom. Daphne isn't the only one involved here. There's a prosecutor and a judge, and if we go to trial there's a jury. And there's Megan."

"But you're not guilty."

"I know that, and you know that, but do you think other people will believe it? I saw that piece in the paper today. The cop brought it along with my breakfast. He thought I'd get a kick out of seeing my name in type. Hell, maybe some kids would, but not me. I feel branded"—he stamped his forehead with a fist—"like I've got an R for rapist stuck right here. I mean, forget a relationship with Kelly. She won't want to be seen with me. And if word gets back to Penn—"

"Stop it, Scott!" Laura cut in. She couldn't bear to hear the things he was saying. More than that, she couldn't bear to see the glitter of tears in his eyes. "If Kelly can't handle this, she isn't the girl for you. Same with your fraternity. You've been hit with false charges. If the people you call friends—people who supposedly know you and know you wouldn't commit rape—don't stand by you, then that says something about *them*."

"But where does it leave *me*?" he cried. "My whole life will be screwed up, and I haven't done anything wrong!"

Laura didn't know what to say, so she just worked at relaxing the tense muscles in his back. After a bit, when his eyes weren't looking as wild or as moist, she slipped her arm around his waist. "We'll make it, Scott. We will make it."

He sighed. "I don't know. Things keep getting worse."

"But this is the turning point."

"How do you know?"

"Because nothing worse can *happen*," she said on a note of mild hysteria. "Look at it that way. Can you come up with anything worse than what we've already suffered?"

"Yeah. My being convicted."

"No. That can't happen. Try again."

"Dad being found and tried and convicted."

Laura thought about that. "Okay. That would be pretty bad. But would it be worse than this not knowing that we're living with now?"

Scott didn't answer at first. After a minute, he dug his heel into the rug. "Do you miss him?"

"I haven't had time to miss him. I've been too busy trying to hold things together."

"If they found him and brought him back, then put him on trial, would you stand by him?"

Laura had asked herself the same thing more than once. Anger was never far from the surface when she thought of Jeff, but that anger couldn't erase certain facts. "He was my husband for twenty years, and he's your father. That's worth something."

"Do you love him?"

She chose her words with care. Scott was Jeff's son and would continue to be, regardless of what happened between his parents. "I did."

"Do you now?"

"I don't know the man he is now. Obviously," she admitted dryly, "I didn't know the man he was then."

"Would you take him back?"

"He's not coming back."

"But if he did? If he came back and was arraigned and let out on bail like me, would you take him back?"

You ask tough questions, Laura wanted to say. Instead, she sighed. "I think that would depend on what he had to say for himself. Assuming he's guilty of what they say, he was wrong. He's hurt us dreadfully. I don't know if I can just pick up where we left off. I don't know if that's possible. Too much has happened." She focused on Scott. "What would you want to do? You feel a whole lot of anger toward your father. Would you want him back?"

"I suppose if he explained why he did what he did, if he could make it make sense, if he *wanted* to live with us." He frowned. "Assuming I'm here. I might be in jail."

"Don't say that."

"Anyway, I'm not the one who'd have to live with him. You are."

Tucking her hands in her lap, Laura leaned against his arm. Somewhere in the course of the discussion, she had ceased to be the comforter, which was incredible, given the mess of Megan Tucker's claim. But Scott was growing up fast. Talking with him was like talking with a friend.

"Well," she said, "I don't have to make a decision now. The best I can do is to take each day as it comes."

"I'm glad Christian's here for you."

"For me?"

"Sure. If Dad isn't, it's nice that Christian is. Boy, he really came through last night. He kept talking to me, and what he said made sense. He calmed me down a lot."

He had calmed Laura down a lot too, if she wanted to count holding her while she cried her heart out. "Funny," she confessed, "when he showed up here, I thought that was the end. I mean, *really* the end. I thought he was one more awful thing in a line of perfectly awful things, and I just couldn't take another one. But he was okay."

"Will he be sticking around?"

All Laura knew was that he had put his duffel bag in the guest room and his shaving kit in Scott's bathroom and made himself right at home in the kitchen, but that was no more than he'd done any other time he had come for a visit. "You know Christian. He's a free spirit. He comes and goes as he pleases."

"Is he gay?"

Laura sputtered out a startled laugh. "God, no! What makes you ask that?"

"He never got married. It's strange. He was with that pretty lady—Gaby—for a while, but he never married her. I wondered if she was a front."

Laura gave a vigorous shake of her head. "Gaby was for real. And I'm sure there were—are—plenty of other women in his life. Christian is as virile as they come."

"So why didn't he ever get married?"

"I guess he didn't want to. He likes his freedom."

Scott mulled over that possibility. "I think he misses having a family."

"Christian?" Laura shook her head. "If he wanted one, he'd have had one."

"Maybe." Scott looked at the rug again, then straightened and dropped his head back. "Shit, what am I gonna do?"

Laura didn't have to be told that his mind was back on the rape charge. She was surprised he'd been able to talk around it for so long, though she was glad he had. They both needed the break.

"You'll get packed," she told him, "and tomorrow you'll go back to school just like you planned."

"How am I supposed to concentrate on classes?"

"You will, somehow. What's the alternative, Scott? Are you going to sit for three weeks worrying about the hearing?"

"Maybe I should get drunk and stay drunk for three weeks."

"Don't you dare," she shot back, teasing, then realized it wasn't a teasing matter. Scott was a good kid. She had never had to lecture him before. But he had never been charged with a felony before. "It's important that you behave. I mean, really behave. It's not like anyone's watching every move you make, but if something happens at Penn—like a wild party with lots of drinking or, God forbid, some girl screaming that she was abused, or even hazing that gets out of hand—word could get back here. The prosecution would love it. You know that, don't you?"

"I know it," Scott said.

"So think twice about everything you do. And remember—" her voice softened, "—if you want to talk, I'm just a phone call away."

"You sound like an ad."

"I'm serious. Call me whenever you want. If you get the urge to come home, get on a plane and come home."

"That's not the kind of expense we need right now." He rolled his eyes. "This whole thing will cost a fortune."

"It's money well spent."

"It's money we don't have."

"We will. Business will pick up. The charges against you will be dropped. Daphne's petition will dazzle the judge, so he'll release my money. Things will get better. You'll see."

Scott gave her a look that said he thought she was either incredibly wonderful or totally insane. "It blows my mind that you can still be positive, with all that's happened."

Laura decided it blew her own mind a little. Granted, the positive feeling was coming and going in waves, but that was an improvement over the evening before. Those hours, first when she'd waited with Debra for Scott to come home, then when she'd learned he was being held in jail, had been the lowest of her life. She felt as though she'd hit rock bottom and had nowhere to go but up.

"You really think things will get better?" Scott asked.

"Yes."

"How can you be sure?"

"I can't. I just feel it."

"You were sure they'd find Dad, then you were sure he couldn't have committed a crime, but it looks like you were wrong on both counts."

"This is different."

"Why?"

"Why?" Laura didn't know why. All she knew was that she didn't feel as low as she had. "Maybe because Christian's here now," she said, and stood up. "Come down to the restaurant with me?"

He sat back, with his weight on his hands. "I don't want to be seen. I think I'll stay here."

"You have to be seen sometime. What better time and place than Cherries?"

"I'll hurt business."

"You couldn't do that. Come on, Scott. I could use your help."

"I have to pack."

"You'll pack later. I'll help. So will Debra."

"I ought to call Kelly."

"Do that, then come with me. Please? It'd make me very happy."

"That's blackmail."

"What's one more crime? Really."

Scott scowled at her, then looked away. By the time he looked back the corners of his mouth were turning up, and though the upturn was reluctant, Laura knew she'd won.

TWENTY-ONE

❦❦❦

C HRISTIAN SINGLED OUT the key from the others on his ring. He wasn't sure why he'd kept it there all these years; it only added to the bulk of the ring and wasn't worth the weight when he considered how seldom he used it. But over the years when he had changed key rings, this one had gone right along with the rest.

It was the first key he had ever owned. William Frye had given it to him on the morning Lydia went to the hospital to give birth to Jeff. Christian had been five at the time, and for the first few days, wearing that key on a string around his neck, he had felt very grown up. Then the novelty of coming home to an empty house and being alone for hours wore off. After a while it was scary. He remembered sitting on a wooden bench in the tiny breakfast nook, wondering what was happening to his mother, wondering what was happening to the baby coming out of her stomach, wondering what was happening to his father that he had to be gone from the house for so long.

After a week, his mother was home and the wondering ended, but by then life had changed. He was the big brother, which meant he went off to school with his key and had to be content to come home and watch his parents dote on the baby. He tried to understand when they explained that his little sister had died in her crib when she was just Jeff's age, so they had to watch Jeff all the time. But he didn't like it.

In his child's mind, the key was the culprit. He tried losing it, but his teacher found it in the wastebasket before the janitor could take it away. He tried flattening it under the tire of his father's Ford, but it wouldn't flatten. He tried flushing it down the toilet, but it stayed in the bowl like a dead weight until his mother fished it out.

The key had been all over the world with him, a good luck charm perhaps, since he had emerged from more than his share of adventures unscathed, but for years it was also the embodiment of his anger. It opened the door to the house from which he had been locked out for so long.

In time, the anger had faded. He built his own life, found his own pleasures. Still, there was something about that key.

He turned it in his hand once, then turned it back and slipped it into the lock. With an easy twist, the door opened. He pushed it wider, stepped inside, closed it behind him, and all the while he fought the scent of memory. Small things had changed, Laura's doing, he knew—the attractive wooden coat tree just inside the door, a throw rug on the floor, a pale floral print on the walls—but the shape of it all was the same as it had been in his mind for forty-seven years.

"Hello?" he called. His mother knew he was in town—Laura's doing also—though he hadn't spoken with her yet. He might have postponed this visit longer, if it hadn't been for two things. The first was that Laura wanted to be alone with Scott before he went back to school, which left Christian with time on his hands. The second was that someone had to tell Lydia about the arraignment, and though a tiny voice inside Christian said it wouldn't kill Lydia to brood over the morning paper for a while, a louder voice said that would be cruel.

When there was no response to his call, he called again, then stood listening in the tiny front hall, feeling very much a stranger. He didn't know his mother well and wasn't sure what to do next, which was the strangest thing of all. He wasn't an indecisive person. Nor was he bashful. Here, in his mother's house, he felt both.

Not hearing any sound at all, he started down the hall toward Lydia's room. "Mom?" he called tentatively. The name came uneasily, rusty from disuse, but he didn't want to frighten her, or embarrass her if she was getting dressed. Still getting no answer, he cautiously peered into her room. She was propped against two pillows in bed. Her eyes were closed, her head sagged on her shoulder, and for a minute he had the awful thought that she was dead. Then she jerked, and her hand came up to her ear before dropping gently back to the bed.

Christian was surprised by the tightening in his chest. He had never seen his mother this way. She was seventy-three. He had helped celebrate her birthday in June. But she hadn't looked old then, with her snow-white hair and pale, almost translucent skin. She had looked pretty, in a delicate way, which was how he always remembered her. Now she looked old, too old for seventy-three.

As though sensing his presence, she straightened her head and slowly opened her eyes. They focused on him for a minute before she seemed to realize who he was.

"Christian," she said softly. He imagined there was a thread of pleasure in the sound.

"Hi." He gave her a self-conscious smile. "I—uh, let myself in. If you want to sleep more, I can come back another time."

"No. Don't go. I can sleep later." She looked fully awake, though she had continued to speak slowly and softly.

He shifted against the doorjamb. "So. How've you been?"

She gave a sad smile. "Stiff and weak. Getting old isn't all it's cracked up to be. There are things I want to do, but I just don't have the strength. It's frustrating."

He nodded. She was watching him closely, taking in each of his features, one by one, in a ritual he knew well. Whenever he came home, she did the same thing, just looked at him for a long time with an unfathomable expression on her face. He always had the feeling that she was cataloging who he was for comparison with who she would like him to be.

"You're looking good, Christian. They tell me you were in Tahiti."

"I have friends there. They make me feel right at home." It sounded like a dig, though he hadn't meant it as one. He was glad when Lydia didn't seem to take offense.

"You've been missing out on all the excitement."

"So I hear. I got back right in time for this biggie. Laura wanted me to tell you that Scott's okay. He was arraigned this morning and released on his own recognizance. There'll be a probable-cause hearing in a few weeks. With a little luck, Daphne will get the charges dismissed then."

Lydia lay quietly for a minute. Though she continued to look at Christian, her concentration wasn't as intense. She seemed to drift. He could imagine where.

Finally, in a voice that was slow and thin, she said, "My heart is breaking over everything that's happened. On the one hand, I don't understand any of it. On the other, it's all crystal clear. I lie here asking myself what I did wrong."

"You didn't—"

"I did. I did lots of things wrong. You know that more than anyone else, Christian."

He hadn't expected a confession, and though years ago he might have welcomed one, it made him uncomfortable now. Lydia was a small, sad figure, sufficiently depleted without chipping away at the past. "We all make mistakes."

"True, but some are more far-ranging than others. A mother's mistakes, in particular, can be that way."

"More so than a father's?" he asked in a spurt of bitterness. "Seems to me my father made some pretty far-reaching mistakes. So did Jeff, as a father. Look at the havoc he's caused for his kids. Scott would never be facing this charge if Jeff's actions hadn't set the scene."

Lydia considered that. "Maybe not. But Jeffrey wouldn't have done what he did if it weren't for me. I took something valuable from him when I pampered him all those years." Her eyes clouded. "I thought I was doing the right thing. We were so afraid we'd lose him as a baby and then so grateful when we didn't, and he was such a good boy. Things didn't come easily for him.

"It starts when you're young, don't you see?" she went on. "People are who they are because of how they were raised. Lessons learned then are hard to shake. Look at you. I couldn't give you what you needed. I made you feel like a left shoe. So here you are in middle age without a wife and children of your own."

"That wasn't your doing. I chose not to have a wife."

"Man wasn't put on earth to be a solitary figure. He was put here to enrich his life by sharing it with a wife and having children."

"How do you know I haven't had children?" he asked. "How do you know there aren't a bunch of little Christian Fryes running around?" The bitterness was back. "Lots of men make women pregnant, then leave them." Pivoting from the door, he went into the kitchen. He was standing at the sink several minutes later, looking angrily out the window, when he heard the sound of Lydia's cane. The shuffle of her feet seemed almost an afterthought. "You didn't have to get up," he said without turning. "I'm not staying long."

Her voice came with surprising strength. "You can stay as long as you want. It's good to see you, Christian."

He wasn't sure whether to believe her or not. With one son gone, it would be natural for a mother to turn to the only other one she had, even if that son had been an unwelcome adjunct to the family for a good many years.

Very softly, she said, "I know what you're thinking. You're thinking the only reason I'm happy to see you is that Jeff's gone, but that isn't true. I love you, Christian. I've always loved you."

"Could've fooled me."

She was quiet for so long that he dared a look at her. The look was surprisingly downward. Lydia had always been a petite woman, but she seemed to have shrunk inches since he'd seen her last. That shook him a little.

The look on her face shook him too. He saw deep sorrow there, and unless it was wishful thinking on his part, the sorrow was genuine. "We all have to make decisions in life. Some are more crucial than others. The crucial ones are the ones we have to live with, and it isn't always easy, especially when there are other people involved. William Frye was good to me. He provided me with a stable home and security, and I needed those things. And he did love me. Whatever quarrel you had with him, you have to admit that. He did love me."

Begrudgingly, Christian agreed. The kind of love he had seen between Bill and Lydia wasn't the kind of love he had dreamed about for himself. It was too sedate, too studied, too deliberate and controlled. Apparently that was what his mother had wanted.

"I apologize to you," Lydia went on.

Christian was instantly unsettled. "Don't."

"I have to. It's been something I've been thinking about for a long time, only I never had the chance. Every time you were home there were either lots of people around or you were unapproachable."

"Diplomatically put."

She acknowledged that with a bob of her head. "You didn't have to act out in that way, you know. I was aware you were home. Everyone was. You're not the kind of man who could ever fade into the woodwork."

"I didn't do it for attention."

"Then why?"

He ran a hand along the lip of the porcelain sink. There was a crack in the lower left corner that had been there forever. He rubbed it with his thumb like he used to do when he was a child. "I was angry. Everything was so perfect around here. I wanted to spoil things a little."

"You certainly succeeded."

"Yeah," he said without pride.

"Are you planning to do it this time?"

Annoyed at the suggestion, he shot her a sharp glance, but she seemed truly worried, which made him think twice about saying something smart. She had reason to worry. He had been difficult for years.

"No, I'm not planning to do it this time," he said quietly. "Things are bad enough. No one needs me to make them worse."

"Then what are you planning to do?"

He shrugged. "Laura's in pretty bad shape. I thought I'd loan her some money."

"She wouldn't take any from me or from her mother."

"That's because neither of you have much to spare. I do."

"Will she take it?"

"She'd better."

"That's generous of you."

"Maybe it's selfish," he said. Leaving the sink, he went to the breakfast nook. Though sanded and freshly painted, the table was as small as he remembered, the bench seats as narrow. He had outgrown them when he was fourteen, which, in hindsight, was perfectly understandable given the size he'd grown to be. At the time it seemed one more way in which he didn't fit in. "Maybe I'm trying to buy forgiveness for years of giving her a hard time."

He heard Lydia moving behind him. The refrigerator door opened, then shut. He heard the rattle of plates, the clink of knives. When he looked back, he saw her arranging muffins.

"Don't put anything out on my behalf," he said.

"They're wonderful muffins. Laura made them."

He didn't have to be told that. Laura took good enough care of his mother to put Jeff and him to shame. "Yeah, and she made me a big breakfast. When she's nervous, she cooks."

Lydia smiled fondly at that, looking for a minute like the woman he remembered. The smile faded as she carried the plate of muffins to the table. "Will you have tea with it?"

"Only if you want some." When she turned back toward the stove, he said, "Why don't you sit and let me do it."

"No. You sit." She paused with her hand on the kettle. "I've been doing a lot of reminiscing since Jeffrey's been gone. Do you remember that his favorite meal growing up was meat pie with peas mixed in with the hamburger and mashed potatoes piled on top?"

"I remember." It would have been impossible for him not to. They had eaten it once every week or two, and a big deal was made about it each time.

Lydia turned to him with a stricken look on her face. "I don't know what yours was. I've been trying to remember, but I can't. Did you have one?"

He certainly did. "Lamb chops. With mint jelly. And those little rolls you used to make."

"Why didn't I know that?"

"Because you never asked and I never said. No one else was wild about lamb chops. You didn't make them often."

Silently, she turned back to the stove, and while she waited for the water to boil he looked around the kitchen. It was old, like the rest of the house, but clean and well kept, which was no more than he'd have expected of Lydia. He knew she had help. Still, he suspected she did more herself than either Laura or the cleaning girl imagined.

When the tea was done, he carried it to the table, then squeezed onto one of the benches. He had to sit sideways, half sprawling along the bench. It was a minute before Lydia was seated across from him and several minutes after that before either of them spoke, and then it was Lydia, sounding oddly shy.

"This is the first time we've been alone in a long, long time. I've missed you, Christian."

He couldn't believe that. "You didn't miss me. You had Jeff."

"Jeff wasn't you."

"But he was special to you. He was the one who didn't die."

"You didn't die."

"It wasn't the same." He studied his tea. Lydia was right. It had been a long time since they'd been alone. They had never had the kind of relationship Laura had with Scott. If they had, he might have asked certain things sooner—one of which refused to be repressed any longer. "If you hadn't been pregnant with me, would you have married Bill?"

Lydia let out a breath. It was another little while before she answered. "I'm not sure. I might have waited longer. I might have waited to see who else would come along."

He tried to imagine growing up under the wing of another man, but only one came to mind. Over the years, Christian had fashioned him into a more stately replica of himself. "Did you love him?"

Lydia began a subtle rocking. "Your father? Yes, I loved him."

"But you wouldn't marry him."

"No. I couldn't have been happy with him. He was—" she frowned, struggling to find the right words, which then came in a rush—"too flashy, too opinionated, too controversial, too public. He wanted to rock the boat. He frightened me."

"But you loved him." It was a puzzle Christian had been trying to figure out for years. "If you loved him, how could you turn away from him?"

"It was a decision of the mind, not the heart. Haven't you ever made decisions like that?"

He could remember one, though he hadn't identified it as such at the time. "Did you ever regret it?"

"Often," she said. She tipped her chin up just enough to give him another glimpse of the purposeful woman she had been in her prime. "I knew passion with him. Sons don't like to think of their mothers as being sexual creatures, but with him I was. With him, I forgot about everything else. With him, I was someone totally different from myself. Yes, there have been many times over the years when I regretted my decision, many times when I'd have given most anything for a few more minutes of what I had with him. But those times always passed, and not once did I think my decision was a mistake. I may have made mistakes in the way I treated you and Jeff, but in the choice I made regarding him, I know I was right."

Restless, Christian extricated himself from the bench and began to prowl the kitchen. "Is he still alive?"

"Yes."

"Do you ever see him?"

"No."

"Does he still live around here?"

"I never said he lived around here. You won't catch me that way."

He faced her with his hands low on his hips. "I can't catch you any way, but that's not fair. I'm forty-seven years old, for Christ's sake. I have a right to know who my father is."

Lydia gave him a pained look. "I made a vow that's even older than that. I promised him, Christian. When I found out I was pregnant, he wanted to marry me, but I knew the marriage wouldn't last—he was already involved with someone else—and I knew it would kill me when it didn't. So I refused him. He was furious. He gave me a choice. Either he could expose me for being a tramp—and in those days the ramifications of that were harsh—or I could go my way and find someone else, but if I did that, I was never to tell you who he was. He kept his part of the bargain. He never talked about me. So I have to keep mine and never talk about him."

Christian had heard the story before. If anything, it grew harder to take the older he was. "Did he plan to tell me himself?"

"Has he yet?"

"Will he?"

"Only he knows that."

Christian felt a little like a sitting duck, knowing that someone out in the world had information about him that he didn't have. "Do you think he watches me?"

"I doubt that. You move around a lot."

"But I'm headquartered in Vermont. I'm never gone from there for more than a month, maybe two at the most, without checking in, and during the building season I'm around much more. Do you think I know him?" It wasn't a thought he lived with every day, just one that came at times when a man of the right age took an interest in him.

"I don't know that."

"The bastard," Christian muttered, feeling an old, familiar frustration. "Isn't he *curious* about me? Doesn't he want to see who I am or what I've done with my life? What kind of man can turn off feelings that way?"

"Some can," Lydia whispered. "I thought you had. You've been so difficult all these years."

"I told you. I was angry."

"Maybe he is too."

"Angry because you wouldn't marry him? After all these years?" He tried again. "Has he married?"

She nodded. "More than once. Never happily."

"Is he successful?"

She bobbed a thin shoulder. "Success is relative."

"Is he rich?"

"He lives well."

"Then you've kept tabs on him?"

"I loved him once. The sound of his voice made my heart pound, the sight of him made me quiver. Of course I've kept tabs on him. What woman wouldn't?"

She was trying to be light about it; still, Christian saw sadness in her eyes, and he felt the frisson of a different anger. "Is it painful?"

The sadness spread to her smile. "It's growing old that's painful. That's when reality hits. You find yourself with special memories that have nowhere to go and dreams that will never be fulfilled, and it doesn't matter how whimsical or impossible those dreams were. While they were yours, they were lovely." She sighed. "At my age, there isn't much point left in dreaming. That's the painful part."

"Do you want to see him?"

Still smiling that sad smile, she tipped her head. "I already do. In you. You're a lot like him, Christian. Same size, same coloring, same build. Same dominant personality. Are you happy in life?"

"You've never asked me that before."

"Well, I'm asking you now. Are you happy?"

"If I weren't, I'd do something different."

"But are you happy?"

Something about the way she said it again made him stop to consider the question. Something about the way she was looking at him, as though she really *cared* if he was happy, made him answer honestly.

"I have a rewarding life. I do things I like, when I like, with people I like. If you're asking whether there are things I want that I don't have, the answer is yes."

"What is it you want?"

He looked straight into the same blue eyes he'd been seeing in the mirror for forty-seven years. "The name of my father."

"I can't tell you that. What else?"

"My own private island in the South Seas."

"I can't give you that. What else?"

"Laura."

Lydia sucked in a breath. "Be careful, Christian. That's a dangerous one. Laura is Jeffrey's wife."

"Jeffrey is gone."

"She's been his for twenty years."

"And she was mine before that."

"I know."

He had thought to shock her with his announcement, but he was the one to be shocked. "You do?"

She nodded. "That time you came home from the Peace Corps, when you took over your friend's attic apartment—did you think I imagined you were alone? You're your father's son, Christian. I knew you were with a woman. It wasn't until Laura came to return your book that I knew who she was."

"But you didn't tell Jeff?"

"Why should I? You were long gone, and anyway I figured you weren't ready to settle down. You were your father's son in that respect too. But you'd picked a fine woman. I liked Laura from the start. She had strength and spirit. I knew she'd take care of Jeffrey. Left to his own devices, he could have done worse."

"But she was with me before she was with him. Doesn't that bother you?"

"Should it? She was faithful to him. She was a good wife. What more could a mother ask for her son?" She glanced away and her eyes glazed. "Of course," she said in a distant voice, "maybe it wasn't the best thing for him after all. Maybe if he'd picked his own wife he would have been better off. Maybe he'd have been happier with someone less strong, someone who needed him more. Maybe I made a mistake in that too." Her eyes returned to Christian. "But be careful, Christian. She is still his wife, and he could well come back."

"And if he doesn't? If we never see hide nor hair of him again? You love Laura like a daughter. Would you be satisfied to see her with me," he goaded, "knowing that I'm my father's son?"

Lydia didn't bat an eyelash. "You're also your mother's son, and though children inherit some things, they learn about others by example. One of the reasons I married William Frye was because he was dedicated to me. I wanted to raise you in a stable home, just the kind your father couldn't give me. If nothing else, I like to think that from Bill and me you learned the sanctity of commitment." Her breath wavered like a feeble hand in the air. "If Jeffrey is truly gone, and if you are truly committed to Laura, I think I could go in peace."

She lowered her head. Wrapping both thin hands around her teacup, she raised it to her lips and slowly sipped from it. Watching her, Christian felt more warmth for his mother than he had felt in years.

TWENTY-TWO

DAPHNE SPENT HOURS interrogating Scott. She wanted to know every detail of his relationship with Megan Tucker: when they met, who their mutual friends were, when they started dating, what they did together, when they first made love, and how often after that. Scott squirmed at some of the questions, Laura squirmed at some of the answers, but both could appreciate their importance. Brutal honesty was the only thing that could help Daphne plan her case.

He left for school on Wednesday morning. Laura and Christian drove him to the airport, and though in other circumstances Laura might have wanted to be alone with him before he left, she was grateful for Christian's company. Sending Scott off was always difficult for her, now even more so. By the time they left the terminal to return to the car, she was teary-eyed. She was glad not to have to drive.

Christian handed her a tissue and let her collect herself. Finally, when the car was cruising north on Route 91, he said, "So. Are we going to work?"

"I am," Laura replied. Keeping busy was both therapeutic and practical. "But you don't have to hang around again today. Why don't you just drop me off? You must have other things to do."

"What other things?"

She shrugged. "People to visit."

"There aren't any people."

"Old flames."

"You're the only one."

"Oh, come on," she said. She turned to the window. "That was a long time ago. I was so young it frightens me sometimes."

"I thought you were twenty when I first met you."

She shot him a disbelieving look.

"I did," he insisted. "I thought you were a junior. I had no idea you were a freshman, let alone such a young one. You looked older. You acted older."

Laura didn't know whether that was a compliment or not. "My mother had me skip the third grade. She managed to convince the teachers that I was so brilliant my psyche would suffer if they didn't push me ahead."

"Did you mind?"

"Then? No. I minded in seventh and eighth grades when all the other girls were getting bras and I wasn't."

"You caught up," Christian said.

His words reminded her of the intimacy they had once shared. Christian had been her first lover. He had known her body in ways not even Jeff had. The memories were exciting, poignant, sweet. But she couldn't pursue them.

Looking at him, she said in a quiet voice, "I mean it, Christian. You don't have to hang around. You posted bail for Scott, then you insisted on putting money in my account. On top of that, you spent yesterday packing food and hauling crates. You even tended bar." She was still amazed at that. "Where'd you learn to mix drinks so well?"

"Charleston, South Carolina," he drawled, "during my thumb-around-the-country phase." Laura didn't know about that phase, which meant it had come after the Peace Corps. She knew about most of the adventures that had come before. Intrigued by them, she had questioned him mercilessly during the month they were together. There had been times when she suspected he made love to her simply to get her to stop talking. "I was passing through and ran out of money," he went on. "When you need money, you can learn things real fast."

"We didn't get any complaints from the customers."

"Of course not."

"But if you wanted to work, you'd be back in Vermont."

He shook his head. "Bad season. Can't do a thing till the ground thaws."

"So what would you normally be doing?"

"I don't know. Working in my darkroom. Drawing up house plans. Drinking beer with the guys. But none of those things is urgent. I can do them just as well in a couple of weeks."

"Is that how long you're staying?"

He took his eyes from the highway for a second. "That depends."

She wasn't sure what to make of his look. At this stage in her life, Christian was an enigma. "On what?"

"On how much there is to do here. Yesterday there was a lot."

"That's because my hand was sore, so I couldn't do anything for myself."

"You're understaffed."

"Just barely, but I can't hire anyone else until business picks up. My hand feels better today, and it'll feel better tomorrow, so I'll be able to do more."

She returned her attention to the window. They passed a semitrailer with license plates from five different states, a four-by-four from Alabama, a sedan from Delaware, a VW from Utah. Glimpsing their drivers, Laura wondered where they were headed and why. She let her eyes wander out over the landscape beyond the highway, and her mind wandered even farther, transporting her somewhere warm and carefree. The place didn't have a name. It didn't need one. It could have been any one of dozens of spots. In the impulse of the moment, she didn't care which.

"Ah, for a week away from it all," she whispered.

Christian's easy "You could do it" brought her back to reality.

"Uh-uh. Even aside from work, there's Debra. I couldn't leave her alone. And what would Scott think if I just up and took off?" She sighed. "But, boy, it's tempting. Maybe this is what Jeff was feeling. I haven't committed a crime and I'm not living with the threat of discovery, but there's a tiny part of me that would love to turn this car around and keep driving and driving. I mean, I wouldn't do it. I couldn't. But one part of me would love to."

"You'll get back on your feet."

"I know." She lapsed into silence, thinking about the day when things might return to normal, which wasn't to say they'd ever be the way they were before. That could never happen. Her life was irrevocably changed. "There's still Jeff. Where he's concerned, I'm in limbo. What if he never shows up? What if the FBI doesn't find him?"

Christian straightened his fingers before relaxing them around the steering wheel again. "You won't be in limbo long, Laura. Limbo isn't your style. You're a doer. Whether they find Jeff or not, you'll go on with your life."

He sounded so confident she believed him, but then, that was a weakness of hers. She always believed Christian. When he had first approached her so many years ago, after watching her cross the campus with her friends, and told her she had a captivating laugh, she believed him. When, later, over French bread and cheese and wine in his tiny attic room, he told her she had a captivating mind, she believed him. And when, later still, they lay on his rumpled sheets after making the newest, gentlest, sweetest kind of love, he told her she had a captivating body, she believed him. She had even believed him when, days later, in the sleepy afterglow of yet another coupling, he told her he would love her forever.

Clearly he hadn't, and that alone should have been reason enough to make her distrustful. But it didn't. Nor did it tarnish her view of him. For the first time in nearly twenty-one years, allowing herself to remember the fit of their bodies in bed, she felt a warm current spread through her. Even when she pulled herself back to the present, the warmth remained as long as she continued to look at him. She couldn't deny it. She found him as appealing as ever.

That thought unsettled her, but it wasn't so disturbing that she asked him to leave. He went along with her to Cherries that day, and the next and the next, and he made himself useful. When she dared suggest, only half in jest, that she put him on the payroll, he gave her such a dirty look she didn't mention it again.

Given the heartache he'd caused during her marriage to Jeff, he was a surprising comfort to her now. She kept waiting for him to do something to mock her—to get drunk while tending bar, or deliberately botch up drinks, or seduce DeeAnn—but he didn't.

And Laura watched, particularly on the matter of DeeAnn. With his broad shoulders and tapering body, the rangy way he had of walking, and an irresistible pair of blue eyes, Christian was far more appealing than Jeff, Laura thought. She wanted to see whether DeeAnn would make a play for him or vice versa.

Neither happened. They chatted every so often, but Laura couldn't detect serious interest in either of them. Besides, by his own choice, Christian was with Laura nearly all the time. They went to Lydia's together. They went to the supermarket together. They went to Cherries together, and when they were done there they came home. With Debra either at a friend's house or in her room on the phone, they took to retreating to the den to unwind with tea or hot chocolate or wine, whatever took their fancy on a given night. And they talked.

"How do you feel?" Christian asked one night, nearly a week after Scott had left.

"Right now, tired," she answered. Slipping off her shoes, she curled her legs under her and settled more comfortably at one end of the sofa. Christian was at the other end, with his feet up, not far from hers. "It was a long day."

"I mean, in general. You're looking better. Not as pinched."

She couldn't take offense. Christian had seen her at her absolute worst. "I'm only waking up one or two times a night. For a while there, it was three or four."

"What wakes you?"

"Thoughts. Fears. Nightmares."

"You're worried about the hearing."

It was two weeks off, and, yes, she was worried. Daphne had connected with some of Megan's friends but was hitting a wall of silence where helpful information was concerned. Still, she claimed to be undaunted. Laura couldn't make that claim. But there was more. "Other things, too. I start thinking about me, and about everything that's happened since December, and it scares me."

"In what sense?"

She dropped her eyes to the mug in her hand. They were drinking hot chocolate that night. Christian had made it, and though he had blobbed far more whipped cream on top than she would have, she didn't complain. It was a treat to have someone fix it for her, especially in her own home, especially when she was tired.

Absently brushing the foam at the top, she said, "I really messed up. I didn't see things I should have. I didn't see what Jeff was doing or what he was feeling. I didn't see that anything was wrong with my marriage, and that makes me wonder what other things I didn't see over the years. So I wake up and I think back, and I imagine everything else I missed."

"Like what?"

She didn't look at him. "Like vacations I planned that Jeff really didn't want to take, or presents I bought him that he didn't really want." She pointed around the mug. "See those books up there? The first editions? I thought they were the most incredible gifts. I used to drive all over the state looking for them and spend hours and hours picking each one out. One or two were falling apart, so I had them rebound; then I wrapped each one up in paper that matched either the subject or the binding. And you know what? After a while, Jeff knew the shape. I mean, you can't disguise the shape of a book very well. We'd joke about it—what could *this* be?—and he'd so-o-o carefully take off the wrapping and fold it up and put it aside, then open the book and nod and smile and say all the right things, then very carefully put it on the shelf next to the others. And that was that. I doubt if he ever gave any of them a second look. But I did. If I had a free minute, I'd come in here and read a few pages, or look at the faded script on the flyleaf, or just touch the binding. There's such a luxurious feel to old leather." She raised the cup to her lips, then lowered it without a sip and raised her eyes to Christian's. "So who wanted a collection of ancient books in the first place? Did he or did I?"

"Does it matter?" Christian asked. "You put time and thought into each purchase. That should have been present enough for Jeff."

Laura wasn't letting herself off the hook so easily. "But was I putting in the time for him or for me? I loved shopping for those things. Suppose he said he wanted to collect tin soldiers. Would I have loved shopping for those?"

"Probably, knowing you. Even if you didn't like tin soldiers, you would have made a game of it. Besides, if Jeff didn't like the books, he should have said something."

"And hurt my feelings? Do you honestly think he could have done that? This is a man who stole money from the government to underwrite the restaurant his wife wanted so badly."

Christian gave her a gentle nudge with his foot to soften his words. "But was that to please him or you? Take your argument and turn it around. Did he underwrite the restaurant to please you or to make himself feel good? Cherries was an asset for him. It was good for his business. It painted him as a successful businessman."

Laura knew all that was true, but she wasn't caught up in Jeff's faults. She was caught up in her own. Tucking her foot against Christian's for the warmth of it, she pointed to the shelf with the photograph. "He didn't want that picture taken. We were playing tennis when the photographer came around, and he didn't want to stop. He was worse than the kids. But he did stop. And he went on the jeep tour of the desert. And he went into every ticky-tacky cowboy store I dragged him to. And he ate everything Southwestern and Tex-Mex and *straight* Mex, but it's only now, looking back, that I realize he wasn't the one who was raving about the trip when we got home. He wasn't the one who wanted to go back. It was me and the kids." She sent Christian a beseechful look. "Why didn't I see that? Everyone's right. He hates hot weather. But I ignored that. All those years, I planned what I thought would be terrific trips and just assumed Jeff would agree, and all those years he just went along. It's no wonder he finally cracked."

Christian reached for her foot and drew it up under his thigh. "So you're gonna take full blame for what he did?"

"No. But some. I have to take some." She looked down again, frowning, and before she knew it, the words spilled out. "I messed up. I failed him. Husbands don't wander if they're satisfied at home."

"Sure they do. They can have perfectly wonderful wives but still have bizarre needs driving them on. Jeff's might have been as simple as needing to know he's still attractive to women. He saw himself moving into his forties and had a little mid-life crisis."

"Did you?" Laura asked, catching his gaze.

"I didn't need to. I'm a bachelor. It wasn't like I'd been with one woman for twenty years. Even with Gaby it was on and off, and during the off times there were others. They did for me what DeeAnn might have done for Jeff." For a minute, he looked puzzled. "She's a nice woman. Seems honest. I'd never have pegged her for an affair with a married man."

"Me neither," Laura murmured, "but that's my problem too."

He stroked her leg. "You're too hard on yourself."

"Maybe it's about time," she said with a sigh. Closing her eyes, she laid her head back on the sofa, but her thoughts drifed to gentler places. Sitting with Christian, hearing his voice, feeling his hand on her leg was so relaxing that she couldn't sustain anger against herself, Jeff, or anyone else for long. She couldn't even move when Debra burst in to ask if she could use the Wagoneer on the weekend. "You can use my car if I can use Christian's," she said and looked at him.

"Your mom can use mine," Christian told Debra, who vanished as quickly as she'd come, leaving Laura with her eyes closed again, thinking it was nice having Christian around.

She thought the same thing the next night, and the next. She kept bracing herself for the day when he would announce he was restless and had to move on, but that day didn't come. On the weekend, in and around work, he dragged her to a theater production in Springfield that she enjoyed, and on Monday, when the restaurant was closed, he took her to Boston.

"I shouldn't be doing this," she grumbled in the car on the way.

"Why not? You work six days out of seven. You need a break."

"I should be cleaning the house or doing the books at the restaurant or cooking. We need new recipes."

"Jonah has all the new recipes you need, the restaurant books will wait, and the house is spotless. You clean every morning, then you go to work, and you refuse to accept any of the invitations to dinners or parties that you get, so you have to do *something* for fun."

Laura thought of Scott's hearing, which was little more than a week off. "I'll have fun when this is over. I'll relax then."

Christian didn't argue, but he proceeded to take her to a show at the museum, lunch at Biba's, then shopping on Newbury Street. To her horror she spent money, but by that time she was feeling slightly reckless and very much removed from reality anyway, and when Christian insisted on traipsing across town to the North End for cannoli he claimed he'd been hankering for for twenty-one years, she went happily along.

They headed home with the intention of taking Debra out for dinner, only to find her in a panic about a chemistry test she was having the next day. She was mollified by the sweater Laura had bought her, but seconds after admiring it she was out the door, gone to Jenna's to study.

That left Laura and Christian alone. They considered taking Lydia out, until they realized she would have already eaten. They considered taking Daphne out, but they didn't want to talk law, and seeing Daphne would necessitate that. They didn't begin to consider taking Maddie out, since neither one of them wanted the aggravation, so they debated going out at all, since they'd been out all day.

In the end, they brought in Chinese and ate it with chopsticks straight from the carton. Laura couldn't remember the last time she'd done that—yes, she could. It was with Christian years ago. She and Jeff had brought in Chinese many times, but by then it had become a matter of pride that she make the table look pretty regardless of what they were eating. So she emptied each carton into a serving dish and set the table with forks and knives, since Jeff wasn't wild about chopsticks. She had probably even put a rose in a vase in the center. That was the kind of thing she used to do, not because it was romantic but because it was part of her image of the good wife.

With Christian, she would have done it because it was romantic, which was precisely why she didn't do it now. She was fully aware of him as a man without any help from a rose.

She did have roses in the house, though, fresh ones brought by David Farro that morning. It was the first time she'd seen or heard from him in weeks. The roses were white and could have been either a peace offering or a bribe. Either way, she wasn't interested. Though she invited him into the house, she made sure Christian was with them, standing beside her every minute. If David jumped to conclusions, so be it. She wanted him to know she had a protector, and if he chose to assume that the protection extended to long, lonely nights, fine. After the humiliation she had suffered, having a ruggedly handsome man by her side wouldn't hurt.

Loath to think of David, she left the white roses in the living room while she and Christian ate perched on stools at the granite island in the kitchen. Their talk was light and relaxed, moving from chopstick technique to travel in China to travel anywhere to Christian's recent trip. Having never seen a rainforest, Laura wanted to hear all about the Daintree. Having never been to Tahiti, she wanted to hear all about that too. Not only was Christian an adventurer, he was an eloquent speaker. Both had been true years before. Neither had changed.

When she had had enough Chow Gai Kew, Shrimp Mona Mona, and fried rice to keep her for weeks, Christian decided he wanted a piece of the coconut torte she'd made the day before. While he went for it, she cleared the cartons away, emptying what little remained of the food into the disposal. When she tried to turn it on, the water promptly backed up in the sink. She flipped the switch several times, rolled up her sleeve, stuck her hand down the disposal, and swished the food around. Then she tried the switch again. There was a noise and a funneling of the water, but nothing went down.

"Something's caught," Christian decided.

"Looks it." She worked a tool around inside the disposal to no avail.

"What'd ya put down here?" he asked. He whipped his sweater over his head and rolled up his sleeves.

"Food."

He hunkered down to study the underparts of the sink. "Food you're not supposed to put down?"

"Food I *always* put down," she said, squatting right beside him. "This is my field. I know what a disposal takes and what it doesn't."

He reached underneath to check the pipes. "Think Debra put something down here?"

"I don't know when. She was at school all day, and if she had dinner before we got home we would have seen the remains. She's not real good about cleaning up after herself."

Christian stood, turned the switch to watch the funneling action again, then headed for the garage. He returned with the large red toolbox Laura had bought Jeff—not for this house but for the Victorian before it, which had been old and in need of repairs. He may have opened the box five times over the years. It looked nearly as new now as when she'd bought it.

Wrench in hand, Christian returned to the floor, angled himself under the sink—no mean feat, given his size—and set about removing the elbow. "Got a pot to catch the water in?"

She pulled one from a cabinet and passed it in, then sat on her heels and watched him work. He was perfectly at ease with the wrench in his hand and knew just what he was doing. "God, it's amazing," she breathed.

"What?" he asked.

"How different you two are. I doubt if Jeff ever held that wrench in his hand. He probably wouldn't know what it's called, let alone how to use it."

"He never had to learn, that's all."

"No, it's more than that. You could show him what to do with it, and he'd still do it wrong. Some people, all they need is to be shown and an innate ability takes over. I mean, I can look at what you're doing and understand that the elbow is clogged and has to be removed and cleaned. Jeff wouldn't necessarily make the connection, but you do. And that's only the first of your differences. The list is endless: personality, manner, tastes. How can two brothers be so unlike?"

In a voice that reflected the strain of something he was trying to turn, Christian said, "Haven't figured that one out yet?"

Laura tried to see his face but couldn't. Figured what out? A bizarre thought came to mind, but she ruled it out. "Explain, Christian."

He pushed harder at whatever he was doing. The muscles of his forearm strained with the effort. His voice held that same distant, distracted quality when he said, "Bill Frye wasn't my father. Lydia had a lover before she married him."

"That's impossible," Laura said with calm confidence.

He chuckled. "Oh, it's possible. The little lady had a very passionate love affair that produced yours truly."

"How do you know that?"

"She told me."

Laura's calm confidence slipped a bit. "Told you? I can't even picture her saying it, let alone doing it."

"I'm the living proof," was all Christian said before his hand moved suddenly. "Here we go." There was the clatter of the wrench being set aside, then a rush of water into the pot. Seconds later, he emerged holding a curved piece of pipe. "Let's take a look." Standing at the sink, which had quickly drained, he worked his finger into the curve and began tugging out fibrous strands. "What's this?"

"Bear grass," Laura said. She should have known. Nothing David ever did came without strings. "It's the tall green stuff that was packed with David's roses. I cut it to go in the vase and threw the ends down the drain."

Christian looked vaguely amused. "This is your field, huh?"

"Food is. Flowers aren't." She put her hand on his arm. "Christian, are you serious about Bill Frye?"

He went back to pulling shreds of bear grass from the pipe. "Dead serious."

"If he wasn't your father, who was?"

"I don't know. She won't tell me."

"If she won't tell you that, why did she tell you anything?"

"Because I went through a hard time when Bill died. I was nineteen and into the self-analysis college kids used to do. I stood there at his funeral, and the only thing I felt was the same anger I'd been feeling for years. There was no grief. None at all. I thought there was something wrong with me. I guess she was afraid I'd be permanently damaged if she didn't clue me in."

"Did it help?"

"Oh, yeah. It explained lots of things." He shook the last of the bear grass from the pipe. "Might have been nice if she'd told me a little sooner, while all the other damage was being done."

"What other damage?"

"The pain."

He disappeared under the sink again, giving Laura time to digest what he'd said. It made sense, so much sense—Christian being so different, Christian being the renegade, Christian being the family outcast. He and Jeff shared a mother, which explained a certain familial resemblance, but Christian's size clearly came from his father. Whether his daring came from his father too or was simply a reaction to the passivity in his home was something else.

Sliding down against the cabinet to the floor, Laura said, "Tell me about the pain."

Christian didn't, at first. He finished what he was doing under the sink, took out the wrench and the pot, and closed the cabinet door before sitting back against it. Laura handed him a cloth to wipe his hands, then the piece of coconut torte he'd cut. He took a bite. "Good torte."

"Christian."

He spread his legs, knees bent, and set the plate on the floor between them. After taking another bite, he put his head back against the cabinet. "I adored Jeff when he was little. My life had changed drastically with his coming, but I just assumed that was what happened to all families with babies, and even though I hated that part, I didn't take it out on Jeff. I couldn't. He was so cute. He was so innocent, so totally dependent. I used to play with him for hours, and he'd smile for me more than he'd smile for anyone else. When I came home from school, he'd grin and kick his little arms and legs"—he smiled at the memory—"and then, when he could walk, he used to be waiting at the window for me. You know how good that made me feel? My parents were totally focused on this kid, but the kid was totally focused on me." His grin faded. "Then, right around the time Jeff turned four, the old man decided I wasn't such a good influence on him. It started with his birthday, I guess."

"What happened on his birthday?"

Christian picked at the torte for a minute. "They planned this birthday party for him, you know? They could barely afford it—they sure wouldn't have done anything like that for me—but they brought in a magician to entertain the neighborhood kids. I thought the magician was great, but the kids were pretty antsy by the time he was done, and there was still another hour before they were supposed to go home. So everyone bundled up and went outside to try out the sled Jeff got for his birthday. It was a Flexible Flyer, a real beauty, runners all waxed and ready to go. We went to the hill down the street, and the old man thought that since it was Jeff's birthday and his gift, he should be the first one on the sled. But Jeff didn't know how to use the damn thing. So I got on behind him and steered with my feet and we went down the hill like a whip—right into a tree. Jeff started bleeding all over the place, and I caught hell for being irresponsible."

His eyes were pleading. "I didn't want him hurt. I adored the kid. I've never felt so helpless in my life as when he was crying and bleeding." The plea seemed suspended in air for a minute, before he ended it by looking away.

"Anyway, from that day on, the old man had me pegged. I was the enemy. I was the one who would hurt Jeff if given the chance. If Jeff did anything wrong—I mean, we're not talking real trouble here, but stuff like writing his name backwards or calling someone a jerk or refusing to eat his dinner—it was my fault. And the worst of it was he turned Jeff against me. The kid who adored me grew to blame me for everything too."

Laura was appalled. "But where was Lydia through all this? I can't believe she'd just stand there and let him bully you."

He sighed. "Lydia had made a bargain. Bill Frye would marry her, give her his name and support, and provide a name for her bastard son, in exchange for her giving him the home and family he wanted. If she was bothered by the things he said and did to me, she never let on. She was determined to stick to her part of the bargain. Frankly. I think she bought into the business about my being a 'bad' kid. That way she could condone his attitude toward me."

Laura shook her head. "Lydia's too smart for that. If you acted out, she would have understood why."

"*Your* mother would understand why," Christian argued. "That's her profession. And you'd understand why too, because you're Maddie's daughter. But Lydia wasn't into that. For all practical purposes, she wore blinkers. She'd made a deal with Bill, and she wouldn't allow herself to see or think evil of him."

"Was he evil?" Laura asked. She couldn't begin to imagine what Christian had suffered, living all those years with a man who must have resented his presence.

"No. He loved my mother, and he loved Jeff. It was just me he had trouble with." He took a bite of the cake, chewed, swallowed. "So I gave him cause. God knows I gave him cause. He thought I was bad, so I *was* bad. He thought I was fresh, so I *was* fresh. He thought I was stupid, so I *was* stupid—until it occurred to me that my brains were my only revenge, so I started to study. He's probably responsible for my getting into a school like Amherst. I swear, I did it to spite him."

"You did not."

"I did," he insisted.

"Do you regret it?"

"I regret the anger I felt. No one should have to live with anger like that. Because of it, I probably missed out on a lot of what was happening around me."

"But you've done well."

"In some ways. I have a good business. I lead a comfortable life." He smiled. "Think old Bill's turning over in his grave? Think he's dying ten times over, seeing I'm not the total waste he thought I'd be? Shit, if he were alive now, he'd be blaming me for getting Jeff into trouble. He'd be telling the police I was the one behind it. Bill needed a scapegoat for anything that went wrong, and I was it." He rolled to his feet. "So that's why Jeff and I are so different. And that's why I was a hell of a kid to raise." He stuffed the remains of his torte down the disposal and muttered, "Let's test this fuckin' thing."

The disposal worked perfectly.

Aching for the little boy who'd been hurt, for the bigger one who'd been angry, and for the grown man who tried but couldn't hide the bitterness he felt, Laura slipped an arm around his waist. "I'm sorry."

"For what?" He stared at the sink. "It wasn't your fault."

"I'm sorry you had to go through that. I never knew."

"It's not the kind of thing you tell people. You're the only one who knows, besides Lydia."

"Jeff doesn't know?"

He shook his head.

She moved her hand on his back, over muscles that were hard and well toned. Nearly twenty-one years had passed since she'd touched him there, but little of his strength had been lost. Likewise, the years had been kind to his face. Crow's-feet at the corners of his eyes added character, tiny grooves on either side of his mouth added dash. His dark hair, now sprinkled with gray, was thick and vibrant and rakishly long.

Twenty-one years ago she had thought him compelling. He was even more so now.

"I wish Jeff had known," she said softly.

He looked down at her. "Why?"

"He might have been kinder."

"He was kind enough," Christian said with an odd smile on his mouth and his eyes on her lips. "He let me see you."

Laura's heart tripped. She was trying to decide whether he meant what she thought he meant when the back door opened and Debra burst in. She came to an abrupt halt when she saw them.

"Hi, babe," Laura said. She dropped her arm from Christian's back and turned to greet Debra, but before she could say another word, Debra was on her way to the hall. "Everything okay?" Laura called after her. When she didn't get an answer, she gave Christian a worried look. "I think I'd better check."

He touched her cheek lightly with the back of his hand and sent her off.

The instant she reached Debra's door, Debra turned on her. "What are you doing?" she asked furiously, sounding so incredibly like Maddie that Laura had to blink.

"Excuse me?"

"What are you doing with him?"

Laura drew back. "With Christian?"

"Is there any other man you've been with twenty-four hours a day for the last two weeks? Anyone walking in here without knowing would think *he* was your husband. Really, Mom, it's disgusting. Dad is somewhere out there in trouble, and you're here fooling around with his brother."

Laura was stunned. "I'm not fooling around with Christian."

"Sure looked that way to me. I'm not just talking about tonight. Most other nights the two of you are in the den playing footsie. It makes me wonder what's going on all the time I'm not here."

"Nothing's going on," Laura said defensively, then couldn't believe she'd said it. Debra was her daughter, not her mother. Laura wouldn't even have taken this kind of criticism from Maddie. Flaring with anger of her own, she said, "And if it were, it wouldn't be any of your business."

"It is so. You're married to *my father.*"

"And *your father* deserted me. He left me with no money, no resources, no inkling of what was going on. All he left was dirty laundry piled up from the life he was leading behind my back."

The argument didn't dent Debra's fury. "He's still your husband—" she jutted her chin toward the door, "—and *he's* your brother-in-law."

"That's right. My brother-in-law. He's family, and that's why he's here in this house. He's here out of concern for his brother and concern for his brother's family, and, whether you like it or not, that includes me."

"Oh, he's concerned all right. He's concerned about whether he's going to be able to pull it off."

"Pull what off?"

"Stealing his brother's wife." Her eyes sparked. "Are you having an affair with him?"

Laura was outraged. "Of course not."

"But you could. I can see it. You spend more time with him that you ever spent with Dad."

"That's because Christian is *here*. He isn't in an office with his head buried in piles of papers, he isn't having conferences with clients, and he isn't working at the computer in the den."

"Ah, so now you're saying Dad was wrong for working so hard?"

"I'm simply saying that Christian *isn't* working so hard, which is why he has time to hang around."

"You could tell him to go home."

"I don't want him to go home. He's the first relief I've had in almost two months of nonstop trauma. He'll stay here as long as he wants."

For the first time, Debra's fury seemed to waver. Her eyes grew larger and more frightened. "Do you honestly think Dad will come home while he's here? Dad hated it when Christian came to visit. If you keep Christian here, Dad will never come back."

Suddenly seeing the source of her fear, Laura felt her own anger break. "Oh, babe," she said softly and went to put her arms around Debra, but Debra stepped away and grew sullen.

"I don't like having him around."

"I'm sorry you feel that way," Laura said quietly.

"You're not. You're just thinking about yourself."

"I'm thinking about you and Scott, too. Christian is helping me through this, and when things are better for me, they're better for all of us. Whether you like it or not, your father has opted out of our lives. For all practical purposes, I'm the head of the house."

"You always were."

"Your father was."

"He wasn't. Can't you see that yet? Can't you *admit* it yet?"

Laura studied her fingernails, running the pad of her thumb over the polish. She had done a lot of thinking in the weeks past, with her eyes wide open in ways they had never been before. Debra was right. Laura hadn't wanted to admit it aloud, because she hadn't wanted to further belittle Jeff in his children's eyes. But Jeff was gone and Laura was here, and now her credibility was at stake.

Raising her eyes, she said, "Okay. I suppose I did run things. I gave your father credit where credit was due and then some, but in the final analysis he didn't take the lead."

If she had been hoping that the confession would calm Debra into a workable truce, she was wrong. Debra wasted no time in turning that confession against her. "He *couldn't* take the lead. You always did things your way. You wouldn't give him a chance."

"I gave him plenty of chances. He just wouldn't take them."

"Because he knew you'd be angry if things didn't go your way. Face it, Mom. You're a dictator."

"Careful, Debra—"

"That's what drove Dad away. He couldn't stand not being able to express himself, so he did it in a way that told you what he thought of you, then he took off."

"You've been talking to Gram." It was the only explanation Laura could find for Debra's attack.

"I didn't need to. Between you and her, I've heard enough about self-expression and repression and resentment and rebellion to get me college credits in psychology—if I wanted them, which I don't, because I'm not going to college; I'm not getting into that rat race. And don't say that you didn't finish college and you're still in the rat race, because that's just *you*. You're as ambitious as Gram is. It's no wonder Dad ran off!"

Laura was feeling a combination of hurt and indignance that threatened a short-circuit in her system. Stiffening, she said, "This discussion is going nowhere. You're angry—"

"I'm right!"

"—and because you're angry, you're saying things that are better left unsaid at this point. I'm going downstairs. We'll discuss this another time." She left the room.

"My feelings won't change," Debra yelled after her.

Laura kept walking down the stairs. She knew that Debra missed her father and feared he would never come back. She was blaming the one person who was the most accessible. But Laura was also the most vulnerable. For that reason, she would wait until Debra calmed down before tackling the discussion again.

TWENTY-THREE

❈❈❈

TACK CAME OUT OF A light doze to bring Daphne closer. It wasn't easy, given the tangle of sheets, and he had to do a little pulling and tugging—both of the sheets and of Daphne—to manage it, but when he finally had himself propped against the pillows with Daphne tucked against him, he knew the effort was worth it. With gentle fingers he combed her hair back from her face. Just as gently, he slipped a hand down her back to the warm curve of her hip.

"Mmmmm," she purred.

"You up?"

"When you touch me?" she murmured sleepily. "Always."

He smiled. Daphne was good for his ego. She didn't always say a whole lot, but the words were right when she did, and when she didn't, she knew all the right moves. She made him feel tall and handsome and important and smart. Mostly, she made him feel wanted.

"I thought we were supposed to work," he teased. The light was on, casting a dim glow over the papers on the floor by the side of the bed.

"So did I. But this happens every time. Why I listen to you when you suggest we work in bed is beyond me."

"You listen to me because you know exactly what's going to happen. Face it, Daph. You're insatiable."

"Pot calling the kettle black?" she asked and drew in a deep breath. On the way out it stirred the hair on his chest. "It's chemistry," she murmured and snuggled closer.

Chemistry was part of it, Tack knew, but there was more. Daphne intrigued him. She had from the first, and she still did, and it wasn't simply the slope of her back or the thrust of her breasts or the shapeliness of the lovely, long legs that could wind around his waist and make him explode. If it had only been those things, he would love her and leave her, like he'd done with Gwen.

But he stayed with Daphne. They made love, and he spent the night. He kept his room at the Inn more for show than anything else, since he was rarely there, and he returned to Boston only when absolutely necessary.

"It's your mind," he told her. "I've always been intrigued by legal minds."

"That's because you've always wanted to be a lawyer. Why wait for your next life? Why not go to law school now?"

"Because it costs money. And it takes time. And it means studying. I'd hate that, at my age."

"Old man." She ran a thumb over his nipple.

He tightened up and gave her a squeeze, but he didn't want to make love again. Not yet. First he wanted to talk. "Does my age bother you?"

"Should it?"

"Traditionally the man is older."

She flipped her head so that she could see him. "Traditionally the woman is younger. Does my age bother you?"

"Only the idea that at your age you don't want five kids."

She frowned. "Five. You always say five. Why five?"

"Because five means that one or two can be strange but the other three still have one another. Three's a good number."

"Try one. Maybe two."

"Are you considering it?" he asked.

"Of course not. But overpopulation is a problem. When you leave me behind and go on to that twenty-five-year-old who wants all the babies you do, you should remember that."

He took a handful of hair from her shoulder and brought it to his face. His voice was muffled behind it. "I'm not going on. You're my last stop. Mmmm, do I love the smell of this." She used apple shampoo. The faint tang of it, mingling with the scent of woman and sex, gave him a hard-on every time. He doubted he'd ever be able to walk through an apple orchard again without wearing an overcoat.

Ignoring his erection, she crawled up his body so that her face was inches from his. "Why do you say things like that, Tack?"

"Because I *do* love the smell."

"About us." The look on her face fell somewhere between frustration and longing. "You say things about us that are crazy."

"They're not. We're wild about each other. We can talk work or music or sports and never get bored. We both like pizza, we both sleep late on Sundays, and we're both slobs. Baby, it doesn't get much better than that. Trust me. In my infinite experience, I know."

"Your infinite experience," she echoed, and her expression eased.

"That's right."

After grinning that dry grin of hers, she ducked her head and put a wet kiss on his neck. "You're outrageous."

"Not gorgeous?"

"That too. And sexy." Somewhere between outrageous and gorgeous, she had extended a hand to his groin, and what that hand was doing to him would have made him hard even without the smells he loved. If there was more to talk about, he couldn't remember what. By the time she straddled him and took him inside, the only thing he was thinking about was coming so hard and high and long in her that she would be his slave forever.

This time when they were done, they showered. While Daphne went to fix a snack, Tack neatened the bed. It wasn't that he didn't like love wrinkles, but Daphne had to work, and unless the bed looked less bawdy, he'd never let her.

She returned with a plate of what she called lover's hors d'oeuvres, so named, she claimed, because no amount of lovemaking could overdo or underdo them. They consisted of cucumber slices on Ritz crackers, topped with a dollop of peanut butter.

Tack smacked his lips, as the peanut butter dissolved in his mouth, and came out with a slightly gummy "These're good."

She climbed into bed beside him. "You're easy to please." She punched at the pillow behind her and then, when it was arranged to her satisfaction, pulled the sheet to her waist.

"Are all your men this easy?"

"All my men," she drawled. "Sure."

He studied her expression, but it told nothing of her deeper thoughts or needs. He would have given anything to be inside her head. "You always make light of that."

"They don't matter. Not when I'm with you." She helped herself to a cracker.

"When you're not with me, do you think about them?"

He saw the same tiny would-have-missed-it-if-he-didn't-know-her-so-well look come and go from her eyes. "No. They're in the past." The cracker went into her mouth whole.

"Did one of them hurt you?"

Chewing, she eyed him curiously. When she had swallowed, she said, "Why do you ask that?"

"You have a look sometimes. It worries me."

She took his hand. "You're imagining things."

"I hope so. I keep wondering why none of them snatched you up."

"None of them snatched me up because I wasn't up for the snatching. I was too busy with my life. None of them barged into it like you have."

"Is it so awful, what I've done?"

"Would I be sitting here naked beside you if it were?" She held a hand across him and wiggled her fingers. "Hand me my stuff."

"I fit into your life."

"Uh-huh." She wiggled her fingers again.

"It's not like I'm screwing up your career."

"You will be, if you don't let me work."

"But I want to talk about us."

She sighed and dropped her head. When she brought it back up, the longing was there, all alone, on her face. "I know you do, but it frightens me. I've spent my whole life building a career, and no man's threatened that until you."

"I'm not threatening it."

"You're offering things that one part of me wants so badly I could choke on the wanting."

"Then *take*."

"I can't! Not so fast, at least. I have to get over the next few months with Laura before I can think of where to go from there."

"Laura means so much?"

"She's my oldest friend. I have a history with her, and with Jeff. I have to see her problems resolved."

There was something about the way she mentioned Jeff that always annoyed him. He was jealous of her loyalty. "You're worried we'll have a falling out when it comes to a disposition of the case, but let me tell you, a disposition's way off there in dreamland. We're no closer to finding Jeff than we were six weeks ago."

"No response from the dentists?"

On the premise that Jeff might have needed dental care, since he had had a toothache that was to have been tended the day he disappeared, Tack had put notices in dental publications all over the country. He had thought it a clever tactic at the time, but it hadn't produced. "No response. Zip from acquaintances and clients, and Zip from family. You'd think the guy would call *someone*."

Lips pursed, Daphne sank back against the headboard. After a minute, she said, "Laura gets hang-ups."

"I know. The tap picked up a couple and we checked them out, but they were wrong numbers—probably people expecting someone to pick up and say 'Pizza House' or 'Gas Company' or something." When Daphne's lips went back to being pursed, he said, "He may never show up."

"Where does that leave Laura?"

"Where does that leave *us*?"

She drew in a breath and closed her eyes, neither of which was the response Tack wanted. He wanted her to throw her arms around him, look him in the eye, and say she'd go off with him whether Jeff showed up or not. But she was cool, the old Daphne he'd first met, the one with walls around herself.

"Don't do that," he whispered and rolled to face her.

She opened her eyes. "What?"

"Shut me out. When we're making love, you don't. You're hot and open and almost as greedy as me, and that's the way you are with lots of the other things we do. But there are times, like just then, when you close your eyes and go off into another world. I don't like being left behind."

"I'm just tired. I'm worried about this hearing. I've known Scott since he was a baby. I have to get those charges dismissed."

He knew she had closed her eyes against the discussion of "us," not Scott. He let her get away with the change of subject because Scott did mean a lot to her. "If you can't do it, Daphne, no one can."

"I wonder. Maybe I shouldn't be representing him. Maybe I'm too close."

"But you're the best," he said with conviction. Several times he had stolen into the courtroom while Daphne was in action. She was forceful, in a low-key way, and quick. Nothing slipped past her. "Besides, Scott's case will be stronger with a woman presenting it—a woman claiming that the woman who cried rape is a fraud.''

"She is. Megan Tucker got a whiff of anti-Frye sentiment and jumped into the fray.''

He had enough of a feel for court proceedings to know that that wouldn't be the crux of Daphne's argument. "Are you going with lack of evidence?''

She nodded. "There's nothing of a physical nature, absolutely nothing. Sure, the doctors said Megan was a little hyper when they saw her at the time of the miscarriage, but she didn't say anything about rape then, or about not wanting the baby, or about who the father was. The timing is even iffy. She miscarried at the end of November, which doctors guessed was the end of her first trimester, but they only guessed. She could as easily have conceived in September as in August, and Scott was back at school then.''

"What about her claims of severe emotional strain?''

"They weren't severe enough to send her to a psychiatrist,'' Daphne said dryly. "So she was difficult at home; her friends tell me she's always difficult at home. So she's failing math and French; she nearly failed them last spring. If anything happened to that girl in August, it didn't affect her social life. She was active all fall, right up until the miscarriage. Her mother was furious with her after that. There were harsh words at the hospital; one of the doctors made a notation to that effect on her record. Then Jeff disappeared.''

"It couldn't have been that alone that got her going.''

"No. When he first disappeared and we thought he might have been sick or hurt, sympathy was in his favor. Then you guys showed up.''

"Daph—''

"I know.'' She curled a hand against his chest. "You did what you had to do. But then the paper took over and went above and beyond that, and Megan must have got to thinking. When the mystery woman business hit the stands, that was all she needed. The world reads that Jeff cheated on his wife, so the world will believe that Jeff's son raped his date. Megan has her answer. She becomes the good girl who was wronged.'' She sighed. "It's Megan's word against Scott's, but in the current political atmosphere that may give Megan the edge.''

For a minute she was lost in thought.

"I wish my case were stronger. The Rape Shield Law prevents me from talking about Megan's past sexual history, so the fact that she's loose does no good. I may be able to undermine her word if I catch inconsistencies in her testimony, but my guess is the prosecutor will have her well prepared. I was hoping to pick up something from her friends, and there's still one of them who looks like she has something to say. She was a friend of Scott's too, and I think she still likes him. But she's keeping quiet. I've given her my card twice, with both phone numbers on it, but I haven't heard a word.''

"Scott must be terrified.''

"Uh-huh. I talked with him yesterday. He's having trouble doing his school-work, and this is a kid who usually gets great grades, at an Ivy League college, no less.''

"Is Laura nervous?''

"Very. I'm glad Christian's there. He's a help."

"Nice guy, Christian."

Daphne studied him for a suspicious moment. "What did you two do in Tahiti?"

"Me and Christian?"

"Do you know anyone else there?"

Tack put on his choirboy look. "He showed me around. That's all."

"Are you sure? There are times when I wonder. Tahitian women are supposed to be spectacular-looking."

"They are."

"Tack."

"Well, if I said they weren't, you'd know I was lying. Tahitian women are gorgeous." He kissed the tip of her nose and lowered his voice. "But that doesn't mean I prefer them to American women. Not one of those women can hold a candle to you."

Daphne rolled her eyes.

"I'm serious." To prove it, he took her mouth in a sucking kiss that threatened to go on and on and might have, if she hadn't pulled sharply on his chest hair.

"I have to work," she said. Drawing back, she wiggled her fingers in the direction of the papers he'd taken from her earlier.

Reaching to the floor, he handed her the papers, along with the glasses she used for reading. The frames were large and round and made her look delightfully bookish from the neck up. From the neck down, with the sheet barely brushing her navel, she looked wanton.

"Come on, Tack. If you don't stop leering, I'll have to put on a nightgown."

"I'll stop leering," he said and looked quickly away.

He gave her half an hour, which he thought was generous indeed, given the size of his need. By then, she was willing to be distracted.

That willingness decreased the closer they came to the time of the hearing. She was preoccupied with the case, mentally running through every contingency, determined to push the parameters of a probable-cause hearing to its limits. It wasn't a trial to determine guilt or innocence, simply a hearing to determine whether there was cause to believe that a crime had been committed. If that determination was made, the case would be bound over to the grand jury for indictment.

Night after night, Tack watched her with those owl-eyed glasses on her nose, poring through her papers, making notes to herself, even mouthing responses. "The problem is twofold," she complained. "Not only do I have to convince the judge that there isn't probable cause to bring Scott to trial, I have to convince the prosecutor that there isn't even enough to take to a grand jury. If he wants to be stubborn, he could go ahead and do that anyway."

Tack knew about stubborn prosecutors. He'd seen plenty in his day. Usually they were on his side, though. It was odd rooting for the defense, but root for the defense he did. He wanted Daphne to get her dismissal so badly that if there were anything he could have done to help, even if it verged on the unethical, he'd have done it. She had lost cases before, she told him, and she was philosophical about it. She knew she couldn't win all the time. She also knew that a loss sometimes had to do with things totally unrelated to the lawyer's skill or performance. But she wanted this win so badly.

The day before the hearing, she got a break in the case. The girl Daphne had been pursuing with gentle insistence, the one who was Megan's friend but liked Scott, called her. Accompanied by her parents, she met with Daphne in her office. Several hours later, when Daphne arrived home, she was ebullient.

"This is it," she told Tack. "It's the first viable weapon I've found." But by the time she had spent hours plotting out exactly how she was going to use it, she was sober again.

The next morning she was so far away from him mentally that he was frightened. "You'll do fine, Daph," he said, as she put on her pantyhose.

"Mmmm."

She was buttoning up her silk blouse when he said, "Hearing's at eleven?"

"Mm-hm."

He waited until she had the blouse tucked into a matching skirt before asking, "How long do you think it'll last?"

She shrugged and reached for the blazer that went with the set.

He really wanted to know so he'd know when to call her. "Thirty minutes? An hour? Six hours?"

She adjusted her collar. "I don't know."

"Can you give me some idea?"

"I don't know," she repeated in a tone that was too harsh for his liking.

"Are you always a crab before trials?"

She shot him a look. "No one's asking you to stay here."

He knew that only too well. Not once had Daphne said "Come spend the night with me" or "Don't leave till next week" or "What would I do without you?" He stayed at her place because he wanted to, and because she didn't tell him to leave. In poetic moments, he imagined that Daphne said all those things to him with her body. But he wasn't, first and foremost, a poetic guy. He was a pragmatist who happened to be in love with her.

"I'm not complaining," he said, while she checked the knot of her hair for any loose strands. "I'm just trying to figure out whether it's me or the trial."

"It's the trial," she said and grabbed her purse.

He followed her from the bedroom downstairs to the kitchen, where the pot of coffee he'd made was waiting. While she poured a glass of juice, he fixed her a mug of the dark brew.

"Then it'll be better when it's over?"

"Depends on the outcome," she warned. "If I lose, I'll be in a blue funk for a week."

"That's lovely."

She shrugged. "It's always been that way."

"Charming."

"Maybe you'd like to avoid me for a while."

"I wouldn't like that at all," Tack said. Slipping his hands inside her blazer, he brought her against him. All he wore was a short terry robe, and though he was barefoot to her heels, he still had the height advantage. "Are you trying to get rid of me?"

"Of course not. I'm just warning you about my moods."

"Warning taken. Now, if you can give me some idea how long the fuckin' hearing will last, I can call you when it's done. I'll be sitting on pins and needles. You know that."

She had been leaning back to hold her juice glass between them. Now she rested it in the vee of his robe. "I know," she said more gently.

He tipped up her chin. "How long?"

"Two hours. Maybe three. I can't be more specific."

Tack could accept that. "I'll be thinking of you the whole time. You know that too, don't you?"

Almost shyly, she raised her eyes to his and whispered, "I know."

That shy look, her nearness, the sweet scent of her perfume—Joy, appropriately enough—all had an effect. Determinedly, Tack stepped back. "Here." He handed her the mug of coffee. "Drink up."

TWENTY-FOUR

❈❈❈

I F DAPHNE WAS TENSE on the morning of the hearing, Laura was nearly beside herself with worry. Scott had come home from Penn the day before, looking pale and far older than his years. He wouldn't talk much and spent most of his time in his room, where all that was old and familiar gave him comfort. Laura went regularly to his door, but either he feigned sleep or told her he was fine or refused whatever food she brought. Debra, too, tried to get him to talk, but he wouldn't.

Christian was the only one who made it over the threshold for any length of time, which made Laura infinitely grateful—again—that he was there. He was the male figure Scott needed. She didn't know what they talked about; she didn't feel she should ask. All she needed was the reassurance that Scott was all right, and Christian gave her that.

More than once it occurred to her that if Jeff had been around and Scott had been in the same mess, Jeff wouldn't have been the comfort Christian was. If the thought was disloyal, she didn't care. It was the truth. Christian was, always had been, the stronger of the two. She was grateful he was there for her son.

She was also grateful, in a roundabout way, that Scott opened only to him.

It was good for Christian. He hadn't ever had children of his own; he had hardly had family of his own. But he was genuinely fond of Scott, and clearly the feeling was returned. Each time he came down from Scott's room, his expression told Laura how much that meant to him.

Conversely, Debra treated him like a nonentity. One look at him when she entered the house, and her expression soured. She spoke to him only when he spoke to her and walked right past him whenever she could. When Laura would have scolded, though, Christian stopped her.

"She has a right to resent me. I'm here, and her father isn't."

"But she's being ugly."

"I can take it," Christian assured her.

So Laura let it go. She didn't have the heart for a confrontation with Debra. Not until the hearing was done.

The arrangement, by order of Daphne, who had been over for hours the afternoon before, was for the whole family to be in the courtroom for the judge and prosecutor to see. With Lydia too weak to attend, that meant Laura, Scott and Debra, Christian, and Maddie. Debra was thrilled to take a day off from school. Maddie wasn't.

"I don't see why my face is needed," she argued when Laura asked her to come.

"Daphne says it would help Scott's case if we presented a cohesive, supportive unit," Laura explained. Willing to do most anything for Scott, she poured it on thickly. "You're the matriarch of the family. Of all of us, you have the most highly regarded position. Just by being there, you'll add credibility both to Scott's character and to Daphne's arguments."

"This is not the kind of publicity I need."

"I know that, Mother, but I'm asking you — begging you — to be there for Scott. Do it if for no other reason than that he sends you Mother's Day cards every year."

"You send those for him."

"Only when he was little. He does it now." Granted, Laura had to remind him, and she did it more so Lydia would receive a card than Maddie, but Maddie didn't have to know that. "He's thinking of you at times when he doesn't have to. Can't you think of him now?"

"I've never bought into emotional blackmail, Laura."

"Will you come?"

Maddie paused, then sighed. "How long will it take?"

"Maybe an hour." Daphne had said it would probably go longer, but Laura hoped that, once there, Maddie would understand the importance of staying. "I don't ask you for much, Mom, but I'm asking for this. One hour of your time, for Scott."

Maddie finally agreed and showed up at the house at ten-thirty that morning. They all got into the Wagoneer, which was also part of the image of the wholesome American family that Daphne wanted to project — and wisely so. A group of photographers was waiting on the courthouse steps. Christian promptly went to talk with them, buying time for Laura, the kids, and Maddie to slip into the courthouse.

"They'll be there on the way out," Laura said worriedly when he joined them inside.

He grinned. "Yeah, but by then the charges will be dropped, so they can take all the pictures they want. It'll be the best publicity you've had."

Laura liked the sound of that. She also liked his grin, which was so bold and confident that she would have savored it like a charm, had not Daphne been waiting just inside the door to guide them to a small office to wait until the case was called.

They were a quiet group. Scott sat at the table with his legs sprawled, his head bowed, and his hands fisted in his lap. He looked pale, but so handsome in his shirt and tie, blazer, and slacks that Laura wanted to cry. Tears actually came to her eyes at one point, but before they could drop, Christian put a hand on her shoulder to give her strength.

On the surface, she was remarkably calm. Her suit looked good, her hair looked good, her makeup looked good. Inside, she was a mass of raw nerve ends. *What if the charges aren't dropped? What if he's put on trial and found guilty? What if he goes to jail?* The minutes ticked by too slowly, then again too quickly. She wasn't ready when a court officer appeared at the door and led them to the courtroom down the hall.

Scott sat within the bar at the defense table with Daphne. Laura sat between Debra and Christian in the first row of benches directly behind them. Since this wasn't a trial, there were no jurors. There were plenty of spectators, though. The courtroom was packed. There were even people standing at the back of the room, so Debra said.

Laura didn't look back. Nor did she look to the side, where Megan Tucker sat with her mother. Rather, she sat with her hands folded tightly in her lap and her face forward. She rose with the others when the judge entered, then sat down again and listened in a mother's silent agony while the charges against Scott were read into the record.

The Assistant District Attorney immediately called Megan Tucker to the stand and, question by question, led her in recounting her version of the events leading up to and through the night of August twenty-sixth. She told of being picked up by Scott, of going to the pizza place and arguing over their future. She claimed she wanted to end the relationship but Scott didn't; and when she demanded he drive her home, he argued; and when they reached her house, he pushed her inside and raped her.

"He did not," Debra whispered. Megan was the enemy, temporarily relieving Laura of that onus.

Laura squeezed her hand. She felt the same blazing fury she had heard in Debra's whisper. That Megan should sit there, looking demure in her high-necked sweater and skirt and her pitifully innocent expression while she was lying through her teeth, was a travesty of justice.

"Now, Miss Tucker," the prosecutor went on. "Would you tell the judge what you did when Mr. Frye left the house?"

"I stayed in my bedroom. I was afraid he'd come back."

"Did you call the police?"

"No."

"Did you call your mother?"

"No."

"Did you go to the hospital?"

"No."

"Why didn't you do any of those things?"

"I was scared. I thought no one would believe me. I had been dating Scott. We had already . . . done things together."

"You mean, you'd had sex?" the prosecutor asked.

"Yes," Megan admitted, looking embarrassed.

Debra choked out a disparaging sound.

Laura squeezed her hand again.

"Tell me, Miss Tucker," the prosecutor continued, "how did you feel in the weeks following this night?"

"Upset." She paused. "Used. Dirty."

"Still, you didn't seek help. Can you tell us why?"

"The same reasons as before. Also because I was afraid my mother would be angry. She hadn't wanted me to date Scott."

"Why not?"

"She thought he was arrogant."

Debra made another whispered sound.

"But you did date him," the prosecutor said. "You dated him for five weeks. When you decided you didn't want to see him any more, he raped you. And it's taken you five months to come forward. Why now, Miss Tucker?"

Laura was asking herself the same question.

Megan looked down at her lap. "I finally told my mother. I just couldn't keep it in any longer. It was messing up my whole life." She raised her eyes. "My mother understood. We talked it all out. I finally realized the only way I could get over what had happened was to go to the police."

"Thank you, Miss Tucker," the prosecutor said and turned to Daphne. "Your witness."

"He didn't ask her about the miscarriage," Debra whispered to Laura.

Laura whispered back, "Daphne said he wouldn't. It's not appropriate here."

"But her mother was angry about it. That's why Megan tried to pin something on Scott."

Daphne was conferring quietly with Scott.

"What's she saying?" Debra whispered again, but Laura could only shake her head. Debra added, "The IRS agent is here. He's standing in the back by the door."

Laura shot a worried look around. Then she leaned close to Christian and whispered, "Why is Taylor Jones here? He doesn't think Jeff will show up, does he?" The thought of that made Laura very nervous. Jeff was the last person she wanted to see just then.

"No. He likes Daphne."

Laura smiled feebly at the joke, but the smile vanished the instant Daphne rose to approach the witness stand. She took her time, moving smoothly and with confidence. Laura couldn't see her face but guessed she was looking straight at Megan.

"Before I begin, Miss Tucker, I'd like to remind you that a few minutes ago you swore to tell the whole truth and nothing but the truth. You understand what that means, don't you?"

"Yes."

"Do you understand that if you tell anything other than the truth you will have committed perjury?"

"Yes."

"Good." She straightened her shoulders and took a breath. "You have stated that you began dating Scott Frye on the twenty-third of July. Is that correct?"

"Yes."

"You have also stated that during the five weeks you dated Mr. Frye, you had sexual relations with him. Is that correct?"

In a quieter voice, Megan said, "Yes."

"Would you please tell the court when you first had sex with Mr. Frye?"

The prosecutor rose. "Objection. This is irrelevant to the issue of rape. Miss Tucker has already admitted that she had sex with the defendant. That should suffice."

But the judge looked curious. "I'd like to see where defense counsel is headed." He nodded to Daphne to proceed.

She rephrased the question for Megan. "How soon after you began dating Mr. Frye did you have sex with him?"

"I don't know. I didn't keep track."

"Eighteen years old, and you take something like this for granted?"

"Objection."

"Sustained."

Daphne put a hand on the dark wood bordering the witness stand. "Did you have sex with Mr. Frye the first time you went out with him? The truth, Miss Tucker, so help you God."

Megan hesitated for a minute before murmuring, "Yes."

"Was there any coercion involved on that occasion?"

"No."

"You dated Mr. Frye for five weeks. During those five weeks, how often did you see him?"

"Nearly every night."

"Did you have sex with him on each of those nights?"

"No," Megan said with mild indignance.

"Did you have sex with him, perhaps, every other night?"

"No."

"How about three times a week? Is that a fair guess?"

"Objection," the prosecutor said.

But the judge overruled the objection and instructed the witness to answer. Daphne repeated her question. "Three times a week?"

"Maybe."

"Is that a yes or a no?"

After another pause, Megan said, "Yes."

"And was that by mutual choice?"

"Yes."

"You had sex with Mr. Frye of your own volition?"

"Yes."

"If I understand correctly, then," Daphne summed up, "you had sex with my client somewhere in the vicinity of fifteen times without any show of force on my client's part. Is that right?"

"Yes," Megan said. Tossing her hair back from her shoulders, she tried to look composed.

Daphne nodded. She turned away from Megan, took several steps, turned back. "Just a few minutes ago, you testified, under oath, that the incident of which you accuse my client was—I believe your exact words were—'messing up my whole life.' Is that true?"

"Yes."

"Could you tell the court in what way?"

The prosecutor stood. "Objection, your honor. Defense counsel must know that the issue of Miss Tucker's emotional health is not relevant to this hearing. We are here simply to determine whether there is probable cause to find that a rape occurred, not to discuss the aftereffects."

Daphne approached the bench. "Your honor, given that the prosecution has no physical evidence whatsoever to show probable cause, the only thing left is the emotional. And if I may remind the Assistant District Attorney—" she looked at him, "he was the one to introduce this matter in direct examination, —which gives me the right to raise it now."

"I'll allow it," the judge stated.

Laura was grateful for every small victory. She took a deep breath, only then realizing how tense she was.

"Daphne's good," Christian whispered.

"Yes," Laura whispered back.

"So's the judge. We lucked out."

"God, I hope so."

Daphne returned to Megan. "Miss Tucker, would you please tell the court in what ways your whole life was messed up after the alleged incident with Mr. Frye?"

Megan shot an unsure glance at the prosecutor. The unsureness remained when she told Daphne, "I couldn't concentrate. My grades went down. I started flunking French and math."

Daphne nodded. "Would you tell the court what marks you received in those two subjects on your final report card last June?"

Megan swallowed. In a small voice, she said, "D."

In a loud voice, Daphne said, "D? In both courses?"

"Yes."

Laura heard several murmurs and a snicker or two from behind her, but she didn't turn. She wasn't amused. Nor did she feel a stitch of compassion for Megan Tucker.

Apparently Daphne didn't either, because she said, "Tell me something, Miss Tucker. You didn't start dating Mr. Frye until July. What happened last spring to mess you up then?"

"Objection!"

"Sustained. Counselor Phillips, you know that's not relevant to this case. Please limit yourself to questions that are."

Daphne nodded. Walking over to the jury box, she rested an arm on its mahogany rail. "You say that your whole life was messed up, Miss Tucker. Did that extend to your social life?"

Megan made a tiny movement with her head. "I don't know what you mean."

"Have you dated since the alleged incident with Mr. Frye?"

"Yes."

"One fellow? Two? Three?"

"Objection." The prosecutor rose. "Miss Tucker is protected by law from this line of questioning."

"I'm not talking about sex, your honor," Daphne argued, approaching the bench. "I'm talking about simple dating. I believe this is relevant to the issue of the messed-up life that Miss Tucker claims resulted from the alleged rape."

The judge nodded. "You may proceed."

Daphne faced Megan. "Yes or no—and I remind you that you are under oath—is it fair to say that you dated on a regular basis last fall?"

Megan tipped up her chin. "Yes, but it wasn't—"

Daphne cut her off. "Yes or no. Just answer the question, please."

"Yes," Megan said, looking bothered.

"Ah. Then you weren't so messed up that you couldn't date. Tell me," she asked, sounding genuinely curious, "how soon after the alleged rape occurred did you start dating again?" When Megan didn't answer, Daphne simplified the question. "Another yes or no, please. Is it true that you started dating a sophomore at U Mass named Jim Krupp on August the thirty-first, five days after the alleged incident with Mr. Frye?"

Megan pouted. "I don't remember the date."

"Do you remember the boy?" Daphne asked.

"Yes."

"Do you remember that you went to a fraternity party to kick off the Labor Day weekend?"

"Yes."

"Do you remember the party being on Friday night?"

"Yes."

"Do you remember leaving the fraternity house after the party with Jim Krupp?"

"I may have."

"Yes or no, please."

Reluctantly, Megan said, "Yes."

"Do you remember going out with the same young man on Saturday night and then again on Sunday night?"

"Yes," she snapped.

"So within five days of allegedly being raped, you were back to dating on a regular basis. Did you have sex with Jim Krupp on the first date too?"

"Objection!"

"Sustained. Please, counselor, you know the rules."

"Sorry, your honor," Daphne said and returned to the defense table to confer with Scott again.

The prosecutor ran a hand through his hair.

"He's getting nervous," Christian whispered.

"That's good," Laura whispered back. Clutching her hands tightly in her lap, she kept her eyes on Daphne, who was back before Megan.

"I just want to go over one or two things again, Miss Tucker. A bit earlier, you testified that you wanted to break up with Scott Frye, but that he wanted to keep dating you. Is that correct?"

"Yes."

"Did you hear from him after the night of the alleged rape?"

"No."

"You must have been pleased."

"I was relieved. I was afraid he'd try to see me again."

"And you didn't want that?"

"No, I did not."

Daphne nodded. "I wonder if you can tell me who Bethany Ludden is."

"Objection," the prosecutor said. "I don't see the relevance of this line of questioning."

"Please, your honor, the relevance will be obvious in just a moment."

"Go ahead," the judge said.

"Who is Bethany Ludden?" Daphne asked Megan.

Megan looked wary. "She's my friend."

"A good friend?"

"My best friend."

"Have you known each other long?"

"Since first grade."

"Is it the kind of relationship where you confide in each other?"

"Yes."

"You tell her things you don't tell anyone else?"

"Sometimes," Megan said. Her wariness remained, but Daphne looked unconcerned. Returning to the defense table, she removed a small piece of paper from among those by her briefcase, brought it back to the witness stand and handed it to Megan.

For the benefit of the judge, she said, "This is a note that was passed back and forth between two young women during class one day last January. Miss Tucker, I wonder if you could identify the handwriting on this note for the court?"

Megan had gone white. She didn't say a word.

"May I remind you that, if necessary, I can bring in a handwriting expert to make the identification. You can save us time and money, which is the least you can do under the circumstances. Whose handwriting do you see?"

Megan pressed her lips together. She didn't look up, not in the direction of the prosecutor, not toward her mother. "Mine," she said in a thin voice.

"Your handwriting. This is your handwriting. Is that correct?"

"Yes."

"And who else's?"

"Bethany's." She took a quick breath. "But I don't know how you got this, because Bethany would never—"

"This is a note," Daphne interrupted firmly, "passed back and forth between Bethany and yourself. If I may—" she swept the note from Megan's limp fingers, "—I'd like to read this for the record, your honor. It starts in Bethany's handwriting, with the question *What is going on?* Each word is underlined. Megan has written back, *Didn't you read the paper?* To which Bethany replied, *But it's absurd. He didn't rape you. Scott's the nicest guy you ever dated.*"

"She was jealous!" Megan cried.

But Daphne went on. "Megan wrote back, *He dumped me. He's been home for two vacations since the summer, and the rat hasn't called me once. He deserves this.* Bethany argued, *Not rape. That'll screw up his life.* Megan replied, *That's his problem.*"

A wave of low murmurs swept through the courtroom. With the same smooth, confident movements that had characterized her presentation, Daphne laid the note before the judge.

Debra clutched Laura's hand. Laura held her breath.

"Miss Tucker," Daphne said, pressing her advantage, "I would like you to tell us, under oath, that what you wrote in that letter is the truth."

Megan's eyes brimmed with tears. "The letter was supposed to be destroyed. She said she burned it."

"Was what you wrote in that letter the truth?"

The tears overflowed. "This wasn't my idea. I wouldn't have done anything, except everyone kept telling me—"

"The truth, Miss Tucker," Daphne prodded, emphasizing each word. "Is what you wrote in that letter the truth?"

"Yes!" she shouted, then put her head in her hands as the courtroom erupted.

With a dignity that held threads of triumph, Daphne returned to sit beside Scott. The Assistant District Attorney looked disgusted. Laura pressed her cheek to Christian's shoulder for a minute before taking Debra's hand.

The judge rapped his gavel. When the crowd quieted, he directed a solemn gaze at the prosecutor. "I find this case appalling. In a day and age where women are finally receiving protection against the perpetrators of legitimate brutality, this is an embarrassment. It is an embarrassment to the women's movement, which has worked long and hard for women's rights, and an embarrassment to the government, which should have known better. It is also an embarrassment to the taxpayers of this commonwealth, whose money has been wasted on a case that had no business seeing the light of day." He turned to Megan, who was crying silently on the stand. "Miss Tucker, I would suggest that you learn a lesson from this. Pettiness and a young woman's vanity have no place in a court of law." He hit the gavel hard against the desk. "The charges against the defendant are hereby dismissed." Rising, he left the bench for his chambers.

Scott hugged Daphne, then vaulted over the railing to give Laura a bone-crushing hug. Grinning through her tears, Laura hugged Daphne next, then

Debra, then even her mother. Then she threw her arms around Christian and clung to him as the courtroom slowly emptied. Her eyes were still damp when she finally drew back.

Thank you, she mouthed, hugged him again, then turned to the others. "This calls for a celebration." She rubbed her hands together. "There's a table waiting for us at the restaurant. Jonah's been cooking, just in case we're hungry. Are we?"

They were, of course. It took awhile to get there, since the press wanted statements. Christian was right. After all that had come before, positive publicity was welcome. Not even Maddie seemed to mind.

The height of the lunch hour had passed by the time they arrived at Cherries, which was just as well. Half of the staff celebrated along with them. Uncorking a bottle of the restaurant's best champagne, they toasted Daphne, then Scott, then the judge, then Daphne again. Laura smiled and laughed more than she had in two full months. For the first time since Jeff had vanished and life as she'd known it had fallen apart, she was optimistic not because she was trying to convince one of the kids or herself that things would be all right but because she truly believed it.

After a stop to celebrate the victory with Lydia, they arrived home shortly before four. Daphne left to check in at the office. Maddie left to check in at school. Debra left to check in with Jenna.

Scott, who hadn't stopped smiling, was sprawled in the kitchen chair, talking with Laura and Christian. Actually, his talk consisted of one effusive expression of relief after another. "Man, am I relieved," he said with one grand sigh. "Wow, do I feel better!" he said with another. With a third, he said, "I feel like a million bucks!"

"You aren't the only one," Laura told him. She also felt tired, incredibly tired. The strain of the past weeks was finally hitting her, she knew, but she had no intention of sleeping until Scott was headed back to school. Just a few hours; then he'd be gone and she could sleep to her heart's content.

So they sat in the kitchen talking about the trial, about Scott's school, about his fraternity. Much as she wanted to hear everything, Laura couldn't keep her head up. When Christian suggested he take Scott to say goodbye to Lydia, Laura wanted to protest but couldn't. She put her head down on her pillow, fell instantly asleep, and remained so until, much later, Scott shook her shoulder.

"Time to go," he whispered. It was nearly seven. His flight was at eight.

Fighting grogginess, Laura pulled herself up, put on jeans and a sweater, and went downstairs. Debra had been home but was back at Jenna's. Christian was waiting to drive them to the airport.

The parting was easier. Scott was happy, which made all the difference in the world. Laura made it to the terminal and back to the car without crying, but once there, the same pervasive fatigue hit her again. When Christian opened his arm, she curled up against him and quickly fell back to sleep.

This time when she woke up, she was many miles from Northampton.

TWENTY-FIVE

❀ ❀ ❀

W AKEFULNESS CAME SLOWLY. Christian was such an accommodating cushion that Laura was tempted to stay snuggled against him and go back to sleep. She might have done it if she hadn't caught a glimpse of the dashboard clock. It was nine-thirty. They should have been home long ago.

"Where are we?" She pushed herself up and peered out the window, but other than sparsely scattered headlights and taillights that reflected off snow on each side of the road, she saw nothing.

"About halfway between Brattleboro and St. Johnsbury."

She was groggy and hence slow on the uptake. It was a minute before she realized. "That's in Vermont."

"Right."

"What are we doing in Vermont?"

"I'm taking you home. I thought it was time you met my houseplants."

They were light words, offered in a tone that wasn't quite so light. Laura tried to make out his expression in the dark. "Are you serious?"

"Actually, most of the houseplants are dead, but I *am* taking you home."

She moved a little away from him. "To your place."

"That's right."

She moved a little farther away. "Uh, Christian, I hate to tell you this, but I have to be in Northampton for an early meeting tomorrow morning."

"No, you don't," Christian said. "Elise is going for you. She loves the linen people. She's also handling the meeting with the organic gardeners tomorrow afternoon, and the one Friday morning with the graphic designer. DeeAnn and Jonah are running the restaurant, and Maddie is staying with Debra. You're cleared through Monday. It's vacation time."

Backed against the passenger door, Laura stared at him. "I don't believe this."

"Believe it. Everything's arranged."

"But when did you do it?"

"Before, when you were sleeping. You're exhausted, Laura. You've been driving hard since Jeff disappeared. You need a rest."

It had been years since anyone had made a decision like that for her. "Don't I get any say in the matter?"

"No."

"Christian, that's not right!"

"Of course it is. You would have said you couldn't go. You would have said you had too much to do."

"I *do*."

He shook his head. "You have great friends and a great staff. You picked them and trained them, and everyone I spoke with was thrilled to take over so you could get away."

Laura was feeling confused, trying to take in what he'd done, while at the same time figure out how she felt about it. She wasn't really angry. The more she thought about it, she wasn't angry at all. She was actually feeling . . . well cared for. "My *mother* is staying with Debra?"

He nodded.

"She wouldn't do that out of the goodness of her heart. You must have had to promise her something."

"Not much."

"What?"

"A new roof."

"Christian, that's crazy! She won't forget. She'll hold you to it."

"I expect her to, but it's no sweat, Laura. I do roofs with my eyes closed. They're part of building houses, and building houses is my livelihood." He paused. "Aren't you curious to see the house I built for myself?"

She was, more and more so as the reality of her unplanned escape hit her. Not only was she curious to see his house, but where he worked and who he worked with. She knew nothing but the bare bones of Christian's life.

"Cleared till Monday?" she asked.

"*Through* Monday. I said we'd be back that night."

Five days of relaxation. Five days of doing nothing. Five days of sleeping. Five days of letting someone else run the show.

The idea was growing on her. She hadn't had five days off in over a year, and that had been a family vacation, and on family vacations she was nearly as busy making arrangements as she was at home. She liked things that way. Except that she'd never been as tired before.

Five days of rest. The idea was growing on her fast.

Relaxing against the door, she studied Christian. His profile was faintly outlined by the dashboard lights — *her* dashboard lights — which got her to thinking. "Did Debra agree to this?" Debra thought something was going on between Laura and Christian, and she was furious about it. Laura couldn't see her conceding anything to Christian unless there had been a bribe involved.

"Debra agreed. I left her the Miata."

"I had a feeling you were going to say that."

"She was thrilled."

"The car may never be the same."

He shrugged. "It's only a car."

Granted, there was a big difference between a Miata and a Porsche; still, Laura couldn't help but think of Jeff and his car. She hadn't ever seen him as excited as he was on the day he had driven it home. He used to wash it every weekend, more often if it got at all dirty. He spent hours polishing it, had it waxed before winter, even bought a car vacuum and regularly did the seats and the floor mats. Laura hadn't wanted to drive it. The kids did, but he never let them.

And here was Christian saying, It's only a car. He was incredible.

But that wasn't the only way he was incredible. He had materialized just when she needed him most and had helped her out immeasurably. He had loaned her the money she desperately needed, had guided Scott through a tough time, had stood beside them. And now he was surprising her with a vacation.

"No one's ever done anything like this for me before," she said, feeling deeply touched that Christian had.

"That's because you're too competent. You do everything for yourself. You beat other people to the punch. I succeeded because I caught you in a rare moment of weakness. If you hadn't been dead to the world back at the house, you would have heard me making phone calls, and if you'd done that, you would have nixed the idea. Am I right?"

"Probably." Her mind went back again, not to Jeff this time but farther, to the glory days she had spent with Christian twenty-one years before. She had been young and eager to do whatever he suggested, and he had been full of suggestions. More than once, he had picked her up after class and spirited her off toward an unknown destination.

"Just like old times?" he asked, darting her a quick look.

"That depends. Do I have a change of clothes?" Often, back then, she hadn't.

"Sure do. I packed for you while you were sleeping."

So it wasn't quite like old times. She had clean clothes of her own. She also had the body of a thirty-eight-year-old woman who had given birth to two children. And she had a wedding band on her left hand.

Just then, she wished the ring were gone. She wished she were eighteen again, with all the freedom in the world to run with her senses and all the freedom in the world to love Christian.

She did love him. She supposed, deep down, she always had. She had fallen in love with him twenty-one years before and had spent the intervening years wishing it weren't so. Now he was back, the same spontaneous and compelling man, but grown up, with new strengths and interests, plus a history to give him even greater depth.

Her pulse raced. Taking a measured breath to slow it, she looked out at the night. "How much longer?"

"Forty-five minutes."

She took another breath, put her temple to the glass, and closed her eyes.

"Want to put your head on my shoulder again?" he asked.

"No." She didn't dare. "This is fine."

They rode on in silence for a time. Once, when she opened her eyes, the headlights bounced off a highway sign that confirmed they were heading north through Vermont. She could make out trees rising from a thin layer of snow on either side of the highway, but beyond the beam of the headlights all was dark. "Are there towns out there?"

"Sure, but they're back from the highway. We'll be taking the next exit, and then you'll see. The center of town is fifteen minutes down the road."

He was as good as his word. Fifteen minutes after they left the highway, they encountered a patch of civilization. The post office was at one end, a white-spired church at the other. In between were an assortment of clothing, crafts, home supply, and food shops.

"Are they cute?" she asked. She couldn't quite tell.

"You can decide for yourself. We'll come in tomorrow. I have to warn you—the refrigerator's empty. I haven't been up here for more than a night since before Thanksgiving."

"Aren't you curious to see if it's still standing?"

"Oh, it's standing, all right. Friends check on it for me. If something happened, they'd call."

Laura wanted to ask what kind of house it was. She wanted to ask when he built it, how large it was, whether he designed it himself—but they were such basic questions she was embarrassed to ask them. He was her brother-in-law and, before that, her lover. She should have known the answers already. But she had never asked. In all the years Christian had been coming to visit, she had never asked a single personal question.

You were afraid of the answers, Maddie would have said if she had known anything of what had gone on years before. You were afraid of finding him more interesting than Jeff. And she would have been right.

Now Laura sat with her hands in the pockets of her wool topcoat, watching the road to see where Christian would turn off. They passed a pair of mail-boxes, though she didn't see any houses nearby. They rounded a curve, swung straight, rounded a curve that was the reverse of the first. The headlights reflected off a low fence, beyond which the landscape fell off to what Laura assumed was a brook or a gully. She searched the road ahead.

"What do you look for?"

"We go down a short incline—this is it now—then up again." The car crested the rise and leveled. "There's a mailbox coming up on the right—there." He turned onto a narrow plowed lane.

Laura kept her eyes peeled for a house and was still looking when Christian suddenly turned left, stopped the Wagoneer, and climbed out. They were a scant five feet from a garage. She leaned forward to see what the garage was attached to, but the darkness hid the details. All she could do was to wait for Christian to open the garage door and return to the car.

"There's a circular drive that curves around to the front of the house," he explained, driving into the garage. "If it were daylight, I would have shown you the view from there—both of the house and of the valley. That'll have to wait until morning."

Laura nodded. She didn't know whether she was more excited or nervous. There was an intimacy in being here that she wasn't quite sure how to handle.

After closing the garage, Christian unlocked a door that led into the lower level of the house. "It'll be cold. I'll have the heat up in a minute." He strode ahead to see to that, leaving her to follow more slowly.

The house was multilevel, presumably designed to fit into the hillside. The style was clearly modern. Everything she saw was sleek and clean, from structure to decor. The main living area was open, with a sweeping cathedral ceiling, a broad expanse of windows, and an integration of function that had sectional sofas and low coffee tables flowing into a dining area, which in turn flowed into a sleek kitchen, which flowed into a den.

What caught her breath were the photographs, huge black-and-white prints simply framed, that hung on the walls at intervals broad enough to give each one the attention it deserved. Laura moved closer. One photograph was of a lone sandpiper running at the edge of the surf. Another was of a cornstalk, its full husks set in relief against a bold autumn sky. Yet another was of a tall, textured Douglas fir, so intricate in detail she could almost feel its needles. In the lower right corner of each picture, in small penciled script, was the artist's signature.

She darted a glance back to where Christian stood in what would have been the hall had there been walls. "I had no idea," she said, and felt the same kind of embarrassment she had felt earlier in the car. Christian was a gifted photographer. She should have known.

Years before he had been interested in photography. In the month they had been together, he had taken her to half a dozen exhibits, and she had become hooked herself. In the years since then, she had seen every major photography exhibit in the area and gathered a sizable collection of books. Maddie would have said she had been making a subconscious effort to remember Christian. Maybe so.

He was good. She should have known.

Coming back to where he stood, she looked more humbly out over the room. The photographs got to her, but so did the flow of the room, the cream, tan, and brown colorings, and the surprisingly soft look of the modern furnishings. Aside from the occasional wilted fern, the overall effect was peaceful.

"Come on," he said with a toss of his head back toward the hall. "I'll show you around."

A spacious side wing held two sprawling upper levels, each with two bedrooms, and a lower level housed Christian's darkroom. More of his photographs were hung in the halls and the bedrooms. Laura stopped before one, a head-on shot of a stunning dark-skinned woman. The fact that the woman was bare-breasted was incidental to the arresting expression on her face. "Tahitian?"

"Very much so."

"Lover?"

"Not mine."

"She's beautiful."

They walked back through the house to the living area. Though the heat had begun to come up, taking the nip from the air, Laura hugged her coat around her. "Make yourself at home," Christian said. "I'll get the things from the car. I'm putting you in the top bedroom. Is that okay?"

"It's fine," she said and went off toward the kitchen in an attempt to look casual. She had wondered where she would sleep. Christian's bedroom was on the lower of the bedroom levels, which meant that there would be two spare bedrooms plus a handful of stairs between them. The arrangement was respectable enough.

She wished her thoughts were. She had been living in the same house as Christian for the past three weeks, but it wasn't the same. This was his house. There were no children around, no neighbors, no friends, no mothers. There was no work to do by way of sublimation. She couldn't even cook, since there was no food in the fridge.

Telling herself that the restlessness she felt was an aftershock from all she'd been through with Scott, she crossed through the kitchen to the den. One full wall was covered by a built-in unit in natural ash. A large television sat at its center, with a stereo system above it. Other than those and strategically placed speakers, the only things showing were two shelves of photography books. Other books, cassettes, and compact discs were stored behind cabinet doors.

Make yourself at home, Christian had said, so she put on a Boston Symphony Orchestra recording of Tchaikovsky's piano concertos. Still wearing her coat, she settled into a large Eames chair, kicked off her shoes, and tucked up her legs. She closed her eyes, took a slow deep breath and let it out in a *whoosh*, then repeated the procedure, and all the while she directed relaxing thoughts from one part of her body to the next.

She didn't hear Christian until he materialized with two glasses of wine. Taking one, she sipped it slowly.

"When you're done with that," he suggested from the sofa, "you may want to use the Jacuzzi. There's one in the bathroom by your room."

There was also one in the bathroom connected to *his* bedroom. She had spotted it during the tour. Resting her head against the leather, she smiled. "You live a cushy life, Christian."

"No more so than you."

"But I never claimed to be antiestablishment. Jacuzzis are as establishment as you get."

"In my line of work, they're a necessity. I'm damned sore when I get home some days."

She thought of his work and the questions she wanted to ask, then she thought of him in his Jacuzzi. The image lingered. Not quite ready to shake it off, she closed her eyes and let the music take her where it would. By the time the tape was done, she had finished her wine and was feeling mellow enough to be able to say, "I think I'll have that soak now," without feeling self-conscious. Softly, because she felt it was needed, she added, "Thanks, Christian. I'm glad you brought me here."

"My pleasure." His eyes followed her until she reached the stairs, warming her all the way.

The Jacuzzi took over from there. She lay in it until she was nearly asleep.

Feeling clean, soft, and drained of all but the last bit of energy, she climbed out, dried off, and put on a nightgown from her bag. It was long, white, and satiny and whispered against the sheets when she slipped into bed. Her head had barely hit the pillow when she was asleep.

She was disoriented when she awoke. It was a minute before she realized where she was and how she'd come to be there, a minute more before the events of the past day returned.

The digital clock by the bed read three-twenty. The room was pitch black, as was the world beyond the skylights. She closed her eyes with the intention of falling back to sleep, but fifteen minutes later she was still wide awake. Her mind seemed bent on rerunning Scott's hearing, lunch at Cherries, the farewell scene at the airport, the drive north.

It moved on to Christian and stayed. Memories came and went. Emotions came and went. Moral considerations came and went. But Christian remained.

Feeling as restless as she had when they'd first arrived, she climbed out of bed and slipped through the hall, stole down one set of stairs, past Christian's room, and down another set of stairs to the living room. Stopping before the tall windows, she folded her arms under her breasts and gazed out.

"Laura?"

The sound of his voice made her tremble. She willed herself not to turn. "Uh-huh."

"Is everything okay?"

"I woke up and couldn't go back to sleep."

"Strange beds can do that sometimes."

He hadn't moved. His voice told her that he was staying back by the hall. She tightened her arms.

"Want something to drink? Maybe more wine?"

"No."

"Milk?"

"There isn't any."

"Oh. Right."

"I'm fine. Really."

"Are you warm enough?"

She didn't think he could see her shaking. Most of it was inside, and what little showed should have been lost in the dark. "Plenty warm." The house itself was toasty.

She felt, more than heard, his footsteps sinking into the deep carpet, and before she could adequately brace herself, he was standing so close she could feel his large body's warmth. She kept her eyes on the glass.

"What you're looking out over," he said in a voice vibrant with softness and depth, "is a world of mountains and forests and small country villages so quaint and pure as to have escaped time. Deer run through the woods, foxes hunt in the fields, beavers dam up the streams. When there's snow, like there is now, the evergreens carry it on their limbs like epaulets, and when the snow melts and spring comes, the woodland comes alive."

The words were lovely. So was his closeness. She felt she was the one melting, then coming alive.

"Spring is my favorite season," he went on gently. "Everything is new and fresh. Buds show up on the trees, and grow and burst into blossomlike clusters, then open and spread into leaves of every imaginable shade of green. Beyond the greens are the purples and pinks and whites of the early wildflowers. Bird songs fill the air. The earth smells moist and full of promise."

The cadence of his voice was magnetic. Unable to resist, she raised her eyes to his gaze.

"Summer is something else," he told her, more hushed now as his eyes held hers. "Everything out there becomes lush. Walking through the woods is like having French vanilla ice cream with hot fudge, whipped cream, Heath Bar pieces, and a cherry on top. It's sinful. There are times when I sit on the deck and close my eyes and listen, just listen, to the wind in the trees, the bees in the wild azaleas, the rumble of thunder in a distant cloud. Summer is warm and lazy and—"

Her fingertips covered his mouth to silence him, then glided lightly over his lips. They were as lean and firm as the rest of him, and as blatantly masculine.

"Don't you want to hear about fall?"

She shook her head. Seconds later, she dropped her hand to his bare chest. The hair there was thicker than it had once been, but still soft. The skin beneath it was firm, the muscles beneath that as solid as the thud of his heart. Savoring every inch, she palmed him, from one side to the other. Her hand stuttered slightly over his nipple before following a tapering trail of dark hair to his navel.

He wore slim-cut boxer shorts, just as he had so many years before, and he filled them as provocatively as he had then. Her hand stopped at his waistband, and her eyes rose again.

"Are you sure?" he asked, his voice thicker this time.

She nodded. It wasn't right, she knew—she was married to Jeff—but she didn't care. She loved Christian. She wanted his gentleness, his protection, and his fire, all of which she knew he could give because he had before, and she'd never forgotten it. Memory was an aphrodisiac, but nowhere near as potent as the man in the flesh. She needed his loving more than she'd ever needed anything else in her life.

Slipping her arms around his waist, she buried her face in his chest. The warmth was there, as was the scent she remembered so well. It was a natural scent—Christian never used cologne—the scent of clean male flesh, and it was more heady than anything in a bottle could be. Then again, she realized, the headiness had help from that part of him pressing against her stomach. He was fully aroused, and when Christian was fully aroused, nothing halfhearted would do. She knew that from experience. One look at his face, eyes blazing in the dark, told her it hadn't changed.

"I have a fierce need," he warned in a gritty whisper.

In answer, she slipped her hand into his shorts, ran them from the tightness of his buttocks to the smooth skin at his sides to the hot, heavy swell of his erection. While she stroked him, she raised her mouth to his. He seized on it like a starving man, cupping her head in that gently protective way he had and taking charge in a heart-stopping instant.

By the time he lowered her to the carpet, the satiny gown lay in a pale pool by his shorts. He touched her everywhere, telling her in his inimitable way that he thought her feminine and exciting and appealing, and wherever he touched, she burned. She came once with his hand between her legs, and again when he thrust inside her. She was on the verge of doing it a third time when he erupted into an orgasm so powerful she was distracted. The look of rapturous agony etched on his face, the deep cry torn from his throat, the wire-tightness of his muscles, then their sudden tremor—not even when they'd been younger had she seen anything like that.

If Jeff's betrayal had made her feel less of a woman, Christian's pleasure more than repaired the damage. The minute he was able, he pulled back to his knees, lifted her, and carried her to his big bed, where he proceeded to show her that his desire for her wouldn't be sated by one coupling or even a second. He made love to her over and over again. He reacquainted himself with her body by inches, using his hands, his mouth, his body parts in ways that Jeff, for all the years he'd had with her, had never imagined doing. Christian made her feel worshiped, and she worshiped him in turn. Her passion ran without reserve, heightened by time and maturity and an awareness of the rarity of true love.

TWENTY-SIX

"**W**HY DID YOU MARRY Jeff?" Christian asked. The question had eaten at him for years. He needed an answer.

She rubbed her cheek against his chest. "Because you weren't there."

"I'm serious."

"So am I. I loved you."

"You were so young."

"I was devastated when you left."

"Devastated because I wouldn't marry you?"

"Devastated because you were gone. Devastated because I was sure I'd never see you again."

"Did you marry Jeff to make sure that you did?"

"No."

"Then why?"

"Because I liked Jeff. Because he was steady and dependable. Because I thought he could give me the kind of life I wanted."

Christian knew just what kind of life that was. She had spelled it out for him and scared him off, then proceeded to live it with his brother. "The house and the babies."

"Not a house, per se. I didn't want a building, I wanted a home." She looked up at him, and he could see it vivid on her face. "Family picnics in the park, bicycles with baby seats on the back, a Christmas tree with lots of lights and decorations and presents wrapped so gaily you hate to open them. Those were all the things I didn't have when I was a kid."

"But you were barely eighteen. If you'd finished school and waited for me, we might have done it together."

"I didn't want to finish school. Besides, you told me you didn't want all that."

"I was angry. We had such a good thing going, and suddenly you had this detailed plan to change it all."

"You said you didn't want any of it."

"I lied," he said. "I wanted a lot of it, but not then. I was still too angry and too hurt about Lydia and Bill and Jeff and whoever the hell fathered me. I didn't know what I wanted to do with my life—and if the clock was turned back with the situation the same, I'd probably walk out on you all over again. I just wasn't ready to make a commitment."

"If you'd loved me enough, you would have."

"That's starry-eyed talk," he said, feeling sadness, affection, and protectiveness all at once. Laura was a romantic in the broadest sense of the word. She dreamed things, then set out to make them true. He adored that in her. He also ached, because inevitably she was hurt. "It's unrealistic. What did we know of love back then? Sure, what we had was strong, but did we know what it meant or where it would go or if it would last? I had my own demons to tame, and I couldn't do it in Northampton. You were the only reason I stayed around as long as I did."

"Would you have come back to see me if I hadn't married Jeff?"

"Probably. It might have taken me a year or two. But I'd have been back. Wasn't I there for your wedding? Wasn't I there after Scott was born?"

"Quite," she said in a chiding tone.

He cupped her head, applying light pressure until she returned her cheek to his chest. "I was unhappy those times. I was angry at you and jealous of Jeff and feeling sorry for myself because the life you were making for yourselves had so much of what I wanted. I was also frustrated, because each time I looked at you I wanted you. There you were—my brother's wife. I swear, if you'd been married to anyone else, I might have tried to lure you away. But he was my brother. I had thumbed my nose at many conventions, but that one I couldn't break. And then you had Scott and Debra, and you seemed so happy." He touched her hair lightly. "You were happy, weren't you?"

He felt her nod. "I got the life I wanted. I worked to make it work." She paused. Less certainly, she said, "Looking back, it wasn't always easy."

"How not?"

"Jeff wasn't a leader. He wasn't a doer. I pushed him in subtle ways, and when that didn't work, I did things and gave him the credit. But I shouldn't have. I robbed him of pride. If he'd succeeded on his own, he would have felt better about himself. I keep agonizing about that."

"Don't agonize, Laura."

"How do I stop?"

"By telling yourself that what you did, you did with the best of intentions. You're not God. You can't shape people into the kind of individuals you want them to be."

"I sure tried," she said in self-reproach.

He gave her a squeeze. "With the best of intentions. We all make mistakes. But your heart was in the right place, and anyway, look at what you gave Jeff. You made things great for him. He had more with you than he would have had with any other woman."

"So where is he now?"

Christian didn't know where Jeff was, either physically or emotionally. He did care—he could admit that too. Feelings that he had when Jeff was a baby, with smiles and baby talk and arms up just for him, had never quite died. Jeff was his brother. He hoped that wherever he was he was happy.

He also hoped he would stay away. He wanted Laura to himself. He knew it was selfish, but it seemed time for him to have some of the love he'd been craving for so long.

"Do you miss him?" he asked.

Her answer was awhile in coming, and tentative at that, as though she was testing thoughts she hadn't dared voice before. "At the beginning, I did. He was a companion. He listened to me. He gave me encouragement. He was always there. Then suddenly he wasn't, and it was strange." She paused. "Do I miss the day-to-day things he did?" Her voice grew sad. "There weren't many of those. He went to work, he took me out at night, he paid the household bills. That was it. I took care of the kids and ran the house and my business. The kids said it early on—he made more of an impact on our lives being gone than being there. It took me awhile to see that." She raised her head. "Why did it take me so long?"

"You didn't want to see it."

"But why?"

"Loyalty. Respect. Habit. Maybe even love."

The idea hung in the air, seeming out of place amid the lingering scent of passion that rose from the bed.

"Did you love him?" Christian asked, needing to know that most of all.

She dropped her chin to his chest. "I thought I did."

"Did you love him when you married him?"

"I wanted to. I told myself I did."

"Did you?"

"Not the way I loved you," she said with sudden clarity. "What you and I had was hot and exciting and spontaneous. What I had with Jeff lacked that passion."

"And you were prepared to live without it?"

"I didn't know it was missing. I didn't make comparisons. I didn't allow myself to. Maybe I didn't dare. But Jeff was there, he loved me, and he wanted to get married, and that meant I could drop out of school and be free of my mother, and I wanted that above all else."

"That much?"

"That much. I was the older daughter. She wanted me to be brilliant. She wanted me to achieve. She wanted me to perform. She had visions of my walking in her footsteps. But I didn't want to go in that direction. Her life scared the hell out of me. It was cold and analytical. I didn't want any part of it."

"I'm surprised you enrolled in college at all."

"She made me."

"Will you make Debra?"

Laura was quiet for a long time. Finally, in a voice filled with self-doubt, she said, "I want the best for her. Is that wrong?"

"In theory, no. But you define the best from your perspective. Your perspective isn't necessarily Debra's."

"Am I like Maddie, then?"

"You take the best of her—the intelligence and the dedication—and add things she lacks, like warmth and compassion."

"I don't listen. Debra tells me that. Actually, I do listen, but I don't hear; that's what Maddie always did."

"You lead a busy life," Christian said. "I'd put money on the fact that you hear a whole lot more than Maddie ever did. Okay, so you may not hear everything. What mother does?"

"Debra's been angry since Jeff left."

"That's understandable."

"I haven't dealt with it the way I should."

"That's understandable too. You've had a few things on your own mind. Now that Scott's back at school free and clear, you can give Debra more time."

"I will," she vowed. "I definitely will."

He smiled at the determination in her voice, loving her for that on top of everything else.

"Do you think about your father much?" Laura asked. It was Friday night, and other than running out for groceries they had done little but sleep and make love for two whole days. On this night, they had finally dressed and gone out to dinner. They were back now, standing in the dark, looking out over the valley, which was moonlit and lovely. Christian's arms were around her. Resting back against him, she felt indecently happy.

"I think about him," he admitted.

"Often?"

"Often enough."

"Do you want to find out who he is?"

"Sure I do, but my mother won't tell, my birth certificate can't tell, and Bill is past the point of telling, which means that the only ones who know are Lydia and the man himself. If he hasn't come forward in forty-seven years, I doubt if he will now."

Laura hated to think that. Letting her imagination roam, she said, "He has to be at least as old as Lydia, if not older. Maybe he's sick. Maybe he's staring his own mortality in the face. People see things differently when that happens."

"There you go," Christian said with a smile in his voice, "painting pretty pictures again."

"But it could be, Christian. Maybe you should hire an investigator."

"I thought of that, but the only way an investigator would learn anything is through talking with people who knew my mother forty-seven years ago. I can't go behind her back that way."

"Since you told me about him, I've been looking at men who might be the right age and wondering."

"You think I don't? You think I don't get absolutely furious that some guy doesn't care to make contact with his own son? I mean, hell, I can keep a confidence. It's not like I'd run to the *Sun* with his identity. And I wouldn't be demanding money. I have plenty of my own. I'd like to know for me: nothing else, just for me."

Laura tried to imagine herself in his place and knew she would feel the same. "Are you still angry at Lydia?"

"Sometimes, when I'm alone. It's hard to sustain anger when I see her. She's old and frail. I feel sorry for her. Whoever he was, she loved him, but she gave up that love for something she felt was safer and more lasting. Bill wasn't an exciting man. He was reliable and constant."

"Like Jeff," Laura said and shivered. She layered her arms more snugly over his as they circled her waist. "History repeats itself, doesn't it? Only I have a second chance." Feeling sudden urgency, she turned and coiled her arms around his neck. "I'm divorcing Jeff. As soon as we get back, I'm filing papers. I'm not losing you again, Christian. I don't want to end up like Maddie, with a wonderful career and no companion, or like Lydia, with nothing but distant memories."

"You could end up alone anyway. I could die in five years."

"Don't say that."

"It's true."

"Your mother is seventy-three, and your father is probably older."

"I could still die."

"Or I could. But at least we'd have the time until then. I want that time, Christian. Don't you?"

His answer came in his kiss, which consumed her from the inside out, and in the arms that held her as though they would never let her go.

"What would you say if I told you I was thinking of closing the restaurant?" Laura asked.

Christian shot her a sidelong glance. "I'd say you were looking for me to argue you out of it, which is exactly what I'd do." It was Monday evening, and they were on their way back to Northampton. She was sitting as close to him as she could without actually being on his lap, which was pretty much an extension of how they'd spent the past five days. They hadn't been out of each other's reach for more than a few minutes at a stretch. He couldn't get enough of her, be it touching, talking, just looking, or making love. He was totally smitten, but not so much—never so much—that he wouldn't give her his honest opinion. "You've worked your butt off to get that place established. It's a good restaurant, and it has a loyal following."

"Business is lousy. We're struggling."

"Only in comparison to how it was before. I've seen your books, Laura, so I know. You've been growing since you opened. Now you've leveled off—but no worse, which is really remarkable. Give it a little time. The publicity will die down. People will forget about Jeff, but their stomachs will always rumble. You can give it a promotional push, and things will pick up. You love that restaurant."

Her fingers moved along the inseam of his jeans in a way that would have driven him wild if she'd known what she was doing. But he doubted she did. Her mind was elsewhere.

"It's all-consuming, the restaurant is," she complained. "It takes so much time and effort. I don't want to work evenings or weekends, not with you around."

"In another month, I'll be working myself."

"Not on weekends. That may be the only time we can see each other. If I closed the restaurant, I could concentrate on catering and be picky about when I work. I could drive up on weekends, or you could drive down, or we could meet somewhere. Southern Vermont has some adorable country inns—"

He squeezed her hand to cut her off. "You're frightened because we're heading back to Northampton and you don't know if things will be the same for us there, but they will, Laura. I won't spend the night in your bed, because Debra isn't ready for it, but we'll still be together."

She released a breath against his throat. "That's what I want."

"Then we'll do it. Without any elaborate arrangements. We'll just be together, and we'll take things day by day."

He thought about what she'd said about divorcing Jeff. One part of him wanted that more than anything. Another part felt the same guilt he had felt over the years, lusting after his brother's wife. Granted, his relationship with Laura had gone past the "lusting after" stage. Still, Jeff was a part of their lives.

"I want to talk to Tack Jones," he said. "There must be something more we can do about finding Jeff."

"I'm still filing for divorce," she insisted. "I couldn't ever live with him again. Not after what he did to me. Not after what he did to the kids. If he chooses to be lost, why not let him stay that way?"

"Because even if you divorce him, he's still the father of your children. He's still under indictment on multiple counts of tax fraud. There's still a cloud hanging over all our heads."

"If they find him, try him, and convict him, it'll be worse."

"But at least there'll be an end to it. Debra and Scott will know where their father is. They'll be able to see him. Maybe he'll even be able to give them an explanation for what he's done. Maybe he can give you one too."

"It won't change my mind."

"I know, but it'll give finality to this whole thing, and that's what we need. We need to put it behind us, Laura, and the only way we can do that is to find Jeff."

Jeff pulled up in front of Glorie's house and reached across the cab of the pickup to wake her gently. She was so tired that he hated to do it, but he knew tomorrow would be just as long as today had been, and she needed rest. "We're here, Glorie." He pushed the big wool hat higher on her forehead. "Come on, honey. Wake up."

She opened her eyes and looked at him with a total absence of recognition for a minute, before his face finally registered. A smile came. In the next instant, sadness returned to her eyes and the smile dissolved. She gathered herself, frowned, and reached for the door handle.

Jeff was out of the truck and around to help her before she could get more than one foot on the ground. Holding her hand as they walked to the house, he said, "Poppy will be okay, Glorie. He's getting very good care at the hospital."

"He doesn't look very good."

Jeff wouldn't have said it as gently. Poppy looked like hell. Most people with lung cancer did, especially when the cancer had spread to the brain. The prognosis wasn't good, though Glorie didn't know that. She was still trying to deal with Poppy's being sick.

"He'll look better tomorrow," Jeff assured her. "You'll see. He'll have a good night's sleep tonight." That was for sure. The pain medication they gave him was knocking him out cold.

"When is he coming home?" she asked in the same frightened voice she'd used to ask that question at regular intervals throughout the day.

"Only the doctors know that. Maybe they'll tell us tomorrow." He opened the front door and drew her inside. The door was barely closed behind them when a whale of a woman waddled into the hall. Hannah Mack lived next door. Jeff found her more laconic than most, but she was a worker. Her husband was a fisherman, and when she wasn't repairing his nets or traps, she was baking bread for the local pastor or anyone else in need. With Poppy in the hospital, Glorie was in need. Hannah had been staying at night with her, so that she wouldn't be frightened and alone.

"Hello, Mrs. Mack," Jeff said, then sniffed the air. "You've been cooking. Something smells wonderful." Turning to Glorie, he began to unwind the scarf from her neck. "What do you think it is?" he asked softly.

Glorie's eyes were woeful, but she went along with the game. "Stew?"

He weighed that possibility as he pulled the hat from her head. "I think it has tomato sauce in it."

"Spaghetti?" she guessed.

He unbuttoned her coat. "Wider than spaghetti. Is that cheese I smell too?"

A drop of enthusiasm joined the sadness in her eyes. "Lasagna?"

He grinned. "That'd be my guess." He was a pretty good guesser when it came to food. He'd had lots of practice. "Should we ask her?"

"Is it lasagna, Mrs. Mack?" Glorie asked.

On his way to hang Glorie's things on a peg by the door, Jeff saw the woman nod. "She likes that," he said. "Thank you."

Glorie was suddenly by his side again, whispering. "I'm not very hungry."

"But you haven't eaten all day. You have to have something, Glorie. You have to stay strong for Poppy."

Her eyes filled with tears. "I'm so scared."

He put an arm around her and said by her ear, "There's nothing to be scared of. Mrs. Mack is staying the night, and I'll be right here in the morning to take you back to Poppy."

"Will you stay now? Please? You have to eat too."

She looked so forlorn, and so eager, that he glanced at Mrs. Mack. "Is there enough?"

"More'n."

So he stayed. He ate lasagna with them in the kitchen, making sure that Glorie had a fair amount. When she seemed reluctant to have him leave even then, he sat in the living room and read her an article from one of her *National Geographics*. He had done that before when he'd been at the house. She loved being read to, and he loved doing the reading. It was peaceful and rewarding— so much so that he kept several books just for her in a pile by his own books. When she came to his place, which Poppy allowed her to do on weekends, he read to her there. She listened with rapt attention, understanding most everything, though when he coaxed her into reading an occasional paragraph herself, it was a struggle. So he pampered her and was rewarded by her bright smiles of appreciation.

On this particular night, she was so sleepy when he finished reading that she went right to bed. Driving back to his place, he thought about her. The doctors had given Poppy no more than a few months to live. Jeff didn't know what Glorie would do without him. Neither did Poppy.

"I'm worried," he rasped each time Glorie stepped out of the hospital room. He didn't have to elaborate. Glorie depended on him to direct her life. She could take care of herself when it came to dressing and grooming and she could even cook, as long as the food was in the house. Small, carefully defined tasks, such as waitressing at the diner, were no problem for her. More creative tasks that involved organizational skills were harder.

Poppy had been failing for a while. After developing a chronic cough the year before, he had stopped smoking, but the doctors suspected that his cancer had been well entrenched by then. They also suspected that he had tried to will himself well by ignoring the symptoms, to no avail. He was increasingly tired and weak, and his cough worsened. On Sundays, when the diner was closed, he didn't move from the house. His motor skills had grown sluggish shortly after New Year's, and then, the Wednesday before, he had collapsed at the diner.

Jeff had been there at the time. While two of the men had taken Poppy to the hospital, he and a third stayed to keep the diner open. Between them, they managed to serve up the food Poppy had already prepared. They also managed to grill burgers, hot dogs, and bacon and fry up potatoes—all of which Jeff still found incredible. He had never cooked in his life. But someone had to do the work or the diner would close, making things ten times worse for Poppy than they already were and a hundred times worse for Glorie.

Jeff had worked at the diner every day that week. Falling into a pattern, he took Glorie to the hospital for a morning visit, then again for one late in the day, and in between she waitressed and he cooked. There was usually someone with him who knew more about cooking than he did, but he paid attention and learned quickly, so that by Monday he had made the stew all on his own. More so even than fixing up the cottage, that was an accomplishment.

If Laura could see him, she'd die, he decided, as he pulled up on the bluff. Her jaw would drop. She would stare in utter amazement. In no time, she'd be thinking about ways to spruce up the diner, make the menu more sophisticated, and bring in new customers, all of which would be inappropriate and unrealistic, and he'd tell her so. He'd tell her that he liked the simplicity of the menu because it reflected the simplicity of the people, and he didn't want new customers, because that would mean more work, and he rather liked the slower pace of this life, compared to the old one. He also liked the fact that he could handle it all on his own. Glorie and Poppy were depending on him, and he was coming through for them, which felt good. The people in town accepted him, particularly since Poppy had been sick. He was defining his days in ways that weren't so bad, for a man on the run.

He missed Scott and Debra. There were times when he thought of them and felt wretched. No doubt they thought the worst of him now, and he supposed he deserved it. He wished he could explain why he'd done what he had. He wished he could tell them what he'd found.

But they wouldn't understand. They were Laura's children. Scott had the same spirit of adventure Laura did, and Debra, for all her vows to the contrary, would grow up to do something constructive whether she went to college or not. They didn't need him. They never had.

Still, he thought about them.

Putting the truck in reverse, he backed out, drove down the hill again, and eastward for a bit until he came to a deserted phone booth. He hadn't used this one before. He was careful that way. After dialing the number and pumping coins into the slot, he waited. It was nearly nine-thirty. She was bound to be home.

After the second ring, she answered. She sounded different — either breathless or sleepy, he didn't know which — not quite the composed woman he'd always known.

"Hi," he said.

She was quiet for a minute. Then, in a voice that was definitely breathless and unusually high, she said, "Oh, hi. Listen, this is a really bad time. Can I call you back another day?"

She recognized his voice. He was sure of it. He had the feeling she was with someone, which was different too. He wondered who.

"Great," she said when he didn't respond. "Talk with you then."

She hung up before he could this time. Slowly he returned to the truck and drove off.

TWENTY-SEVEN

❧ ❧ ❧

L AURA AND CHRISTIAN arrived in Northampton shortly before ten. On the kitchen island was a note from Maddie saying that Debra was with friends and Maddie had gone home.

Holding the note with its familiar handwriting brought back memories for Laura. "When I was growing up, Maddie always had somewhere to go. Sometimes my father was around, sometimes he wasn't, but in any case, she left a note. I guess she felt that as long as she left that note, she was excused." Laura leaned against Christian, who was by her shoulder. "I should call and thank her for staying with Debra, but her voice grates on me. I hate to spoil a nice evening."

"Call her now," Christian said in a deep, slow voice. "I'll make the evening nice again."

Feeling feminine and warm, she smiled. Then she looked up at him. "How do you plan to do that with Debra due in any minute?"

His eyes were full of mischief. "We could do some laundry down in the cellar."

Laura shook her head.

"Photograph cobwebs in the attic?"

She had been the one to insist he return with his camera. Still, she shook her head.

"Okay," he allowed, "no making love. How about I follow you around and feel y'up a little each time we turn a corner?"

She laughed. It was such a light sound, so refreshing in that room after so many weeks of unhappiness there, that she nearly laughed again. "You're incorrigible."

"Just a kiss then. That'd make the evening nice." He gave her a sneak preview, something that was whisper-light and tormenting. "Go on, Laura. Call her and get it over with."

Purely for the sake of the "get it over with" part, Laura called. "Hi, Mom, it's me. We just walked in. I want to thank you—"

"You're later than I thought you'd be," Maddie interrupted in a strident voice. "It's a good thing I didn't wait around. Honestly, Laura, you surprise me. You know it's a school night. Didn't you think I'd want to get home?"

Having relinquished responsibility for the weekend, Laura hadn't thought of it at all. Now that she did, she didn't see a problem. "You did the right thing. There was no need for you to hang around. Was Debra much trouble?"

"How could she be trouble when I rarely saw her? She got up in the morning in time to race out to school, and she was with her friends most every afternoon and evening. We had dinner together twice. She claims that's about all she eats with you in an average week." More softly, though no less stridently, she said, "Is that true, Laura?"

"It's more like three or four times a week, Mother, which is par for the course when it comes to teenagers. That's more often than Gretchen and I had dinner with you."

"I was working. I wasn't running around with my brother-in-law. Laura, what is going on? According to Debra, you've been cozying up to Christian ever since he walked in that door."

"Big mistake," Laura whispered to Christian. "I shouldn't have called."

Christian hooked an elbow around her neck and drew her close.

Maddie went on. "Debra may not have gone through quite the trauma Scott did in court, but she's at a vulnerable age. First, her father deserts her. Then her mother does."

"I didn't desert her," Laura argued, in part to clue Christian in to the conversation. "I simply went away for the weekend."

"With a man who has been an annoyance at every family gathering he ever deigned to attend. Even apart from the dubious merits of Christian Frye as a father figure, there's still the matter of your behavior. It's inappropriate, Laura. You're a married woman."

"Jeff and I are separated. I'll be filing for divorce this week."

"Because of Christian?"

"Because of Jeff. Whatever I had with him is gone. He ran out on me, and before he did that, he was leading a whole other life from the one I saw. Obviously, what he and I had wasn't real."

"You thought it was."

"That's right, but we all live and learn."

"Are you learning? It looks to me as though you're acting on the rebound, trying to compensate for the hurt Jeff caused you by taking up with his brother."

"Not quite," Laura said in a confident tone.

"Are you hoping Jeff will find out and be hurt right back?"

"That's the last thing on my mind."

"Feelings of anger and the desire for revenge are perfectly normal, Laura. You don't have to be ashamed of them."

"I'm not." Laura looked at Christian and grinned.

"Then you do admit to feeling them?"

"Anger, yes. Revenge, no. Any other questions?"

Maddie let one fly with barely a pause. "Are you so desperate for a man that you grab the first one that comes along? Honestly, Laura, I knew you were a nurturer. You proved that when you dropped out of school so young to bury yourself in wifedom and motherhood—"

"That's called throwing oneself into the job and doing it well."

"—but it never occurred to me that you did it for security reasons. Are you *afraid* to be without a man?"

"Of course not."

"Yet you insist on defining yourself in terms of a man. Why do you do that? You're a strong woman. Jeff could never quite rise to your level. So now he's gone, and you're free. Why do you feel a compulsion instantly to tie yourself to someone else? I'll tell you something, Laura. Your father's death was the best thing that ever happened to me."

The indulgence Laura had been feeling faded. She had loved her soft-spoken, instrospective father. "That's an awful thing to say."

"It's the truth. He slowed me down, just like Jeff did you. They were alike, your father and Jeff."

"No," Laura said carefully. "My father was honest and faithful. In that sense, he was totally different from Jeff."

"They were both weak men. Is Christian any different?"

"Christian is very different." Laura met his gaze. "He's strong. He has his own life and knows his own mind. No one tells him where to go and what to do."

"And you like that kind of man?"

"I *love* that kind of man."

There was a brief silence. "Don't you think you're getting a little carried away?"

"I think I'm getting a lot carried away," Laura replied with a smug grin for Christian.

"Get hold of yourself, Laura. Think of your children. Think of your future."

"That's exactly what I'm doing."

After another brief silence, Maddie said, "Are you seriously contemplating a future with Christian Frye?"

"Finally, yes."

"What is that supposed to mean?"

Laura took a breath. Slipping an arm around Christian's neck, she sank her fingers into the hair that lay thick against the collar of his turtleneck sweater. "Did you know that I knew Christian before I ever knew Jeff? Did you know that I was in love with Christian before I ever knew Jeff? Did you know that I begged Christian to marry me, but he wouldn't?"

Maddie sounded appalled. "You *begged* him? How old were you at this time?" she demanded.

"Eighteen, and I wanted to get married. Christian wasn't ready but Jeff was, so I married *him*. You can analyze that all you want, Mother, but the fact is I was happy with the decision. I raised two terrific kids and had a rewarding life, and I didn't let myself dwell on what might have been wrong in my relationship with Jeff."

"All along, I told you—"

"What was wrong, yes, you did, and I didn't listen, because you've *always* told me what was wrong. All my life I've heard about what I do wrong. It gets tiresome, Mom. When you never hear the good and always hear the bad, you begin to tune out, because the constant criticism is destructive. So I didn't hear what you were saying about my relationship with Jeff, and even if I'd heard it I probably wouldn't have believed it. I was too busy living my life to pick it apart piece by piece." She might have left it there, but she was on a roll. "I've done that now. All those hours waiting for Jeff to come back, wondering where he was and why he was gone—I had time to think. Little by little, things became clear, things that had nothing whatsoever to do with Christian. The fundamental problem with my marriage was that I did overshadow Jeff, and he allowed it. Christian will never do that." She clutched a fistful of his hair to keep from drowning in his blue-eyed gaze. "I love him."

"You're making another mistake, Laura. You'll be compromising yourself if you marry a man like that."

"I'll be enriching myself," Laura corrected.

"You don't need him. You and I are cut of the same cloth. We're strong women."

"Yes, and I'm even stronger when I'm with Christian."

"All right. Look at it this way. If he was the man for you, you would have waited for him, instead of rushing off to marry Jeff."

"I might have waited if I'd had a little advice from you." She slid her hand to Christian's shoulder and lowered her eyes to focus on the discussion with Maddie. "But even if you and I had had that kind of relationship—which we didn't—you were nowhere to be seen. When I finally got to college, you were thrilled. One down, one to go. You wanted your freedom."

"I never said that."

"You didn't have to." Many years had passed, yet the hurt remained. "Everything else you did made it clear that your own interests came first. There was never any question about it. You weren't around to know what I was thinking or feeling. You didn't have the time to care."

"I cared," Maddie contended. "And who are you to criticize me? It doesn't look like you're doing things terribly differently with your own daughter. You have a business that keeps you busy and a lover who takes you away. A paragon of motherhood you are not."

Laura scowled. "Anything I know about mothering, I learned from you."

"You certainly didn't learn this lack of respect from me."

"No? I'm an adult, Mother. I've been one for a long time. When did you ever respect *me*?"

"I'll respect you when you start acting like a responsible human being. Running off with your brother-in-law for the weekend was not responsible. Do you think people haven't seen you around town with him? Do you think they aren't talking?"

"Christian is my brother-in-law. He's family. He's here to help me. If people don't understand that, screw them."

"Now, that's an adult response."

"It's an honest one," Laura said. "I don't really give a damn about what people are saying. They've already thought the worst of us, and we were vindicated in one instance, at least. We'll be vindicated in others, and in the meantime I have no intention of playing either the grieving widow or the martyr. Christian is here, and I love him. When I was eighteen, I couldn't appreciate what that meant. I'm older now, and believe me, I'm not passing it up."

"You're hopeless," Maddie said in disgust.

"Thank you," Laura said, as though she'd just received the compliment of a lifetime.

"I won't talk with you when you're this way. When you feel you can relate with me in a productive way, call."

"Fine. But answer me one question now. If you feel so strongly that what I'm doing with Christian is wrong, why did you ever agree to stay with Debra?"

"Because I need a new roof. Remind Christian of that, please," Maddie said and hung up the phone.

Christian did his best to salvage the evening after the phone call to Maddie, but his efforts ran into a snag. By the time Laura had vented the worst of her anger, it was eleven and Debra still wasn't home. Concerned, particularly since it was a school night, Laura called Jenna.

"She's not here, Mrs. Frye."

"Do you know where she is?"

"No, I don't."

That did nothing for Laura's peace of mind, since Jenna was Debra's best friend. She phoned several lesser friends, but the answer was the same. When eleven-fifteen came and went, then eleven-thirty, Laura was nervous enough to risk Debra's wrath by calling Jace Holzworth.

He sounded more nervous than she felt, which only heightened her worry. "Oh, hi, Mrs. Frye. Yeah, I did see her earlier tonight."

"What time was that?"

"Uh, around eight. I was—uh, getting off work."

"How long were you with her?"

"Maybe half an hour, I guess. Then she—uh, took off in the Miata. I thought she went home."

"Did she call you after that?"

"No. No phone calls. Gee, I'm sorry I can't help you. Hey, if I hear from her, I'll tell her you're looking."

"Please do," Laura said and hung up the phone with a stricken look at Christian. "It's happening all over again. This is unreal. First Jeff, now Debra. What's going on?"

Christian glanced out the dining room window. "There she is." The words were immediately followed by the rumble of the garage door.

No longer one to trust that sound, Laura raced to the kitchen door and flung it open. The Miata was in one piece, which meant that Debra hadn't been hurt. When she stepped out of the car, though, she didn't look well at all. Totally aside from the defiance that Laura had half expected, she was frighteningly pale. More subtle, but no less recognizable to a mother, was the haunted look in her eyes.

Laura went right to her and gave her a tight hug. "It's so late, babe. I've been worried."

Debra tolerated the hug, neither returning nor rejecting it. "Worried about the car?"

"No." Laura held her back and studied her face. "About you. What's wrong?"

"Nothing." Freeing herself from Laura's hold, she went into the house. She passed Christian with only the briefest of glances. "The car's okay."

"I don't care about the car," he said. "We were afraid something had happened to you."

"Sure you were," Debra muttered, continuing on through the kitchen.

"Your mother's been calling all your friends."

Debra turned to Laura in dismay. "You didn't!"

"I did. None of them knew where you were."

"Why did you do that? They're *my* friends. What right do you have to call my friends?"

"I'm your mother. When eleven-thirty on a school night comes and goes and you're nowhere in sight, I have a right to be worried."

"You never have been before."

"You never stayed out like this before."

"How do you know?" Debra challenged. "How do you know what I'm doing when you stay late at the restaurant or go to a party?"

"You've always been home when I expected you to be."

"You ran off to Vermont with him"—she pushed her chin toward Christian—"and left me to fend for myself. So I was fending for myself."

"I left you with your grandmother."

"Same difference. She's just like you. She wasn't here half the time."

"She said *you* weren't."

"Because I didn't want to be here alone!" Whirling around, she strode toward the hall. "I'm going to bed."

"I think you should," Laura called after her, but her own words brought her up short. The argument was old and familiar, a replay of the one she'd had earlier with Maddie, which was a replay of dozens of others over the years. Maddie always grew indignant and either hung up or walked out. It struck Laura, in a moment of grand dismay, that she had done her share of that with Debra. Though Debra had done the walking this time, Laura's voice had certainly held the indignation.

Laura didn't want it to be that way.

Christian came to her side. "I'm a part of the problem. The Vermont trip was my idea. Let me talk with her."

Laura touched the back of her fingers to his neck, where his pulse was steady and strong. "I'll go," she whispered. "It's time."

Debra's door was shut. Laura knocked lightly, opened it, and went in. She closed the door behind her and leaned on the knob. Debra was on the floor with her back against the bed and her arms around her knees. At Laura's entrance, she turned away.

"Let's talk, Deb."

"It's late."

"So it'll be a little later when we're done. But this is important." When Debra didn't say anything, she tried a gentle question. "Where were you so late?"

"Driving around."

"Alone?"

"Yes."

"For two hours?"

"Three." Sullenly, Debra added, "Don't worry. I filled the car with gas."

"I wasn't worried about that. You're the one I care about, not the car. Why were you driving around alone for three hours?"

"Because I wanted to."

Laura couldn't see much beyond the defeated slope of her shoulders. "Did something happen in school?"

"No."

"With the kids after school?"

"No."

"With Jace."

"No!"

Laura didn't believe her. The no's had come too readily. Something was wrong, and it went beyond the anger Debra felt toward Christian and her. Anger would have made her belligerent, not defensive or defeated, as she seemed to be.

It used to be Debra came to her with her problems. It used to be she couldn't shut Debra up. She wished that were the case now. Getting her talking again was the first priority.

Coming to sit on the bed, not far from where Debra was slouched, she asked softly, "What's happened to us?"

"You tell me," Debra snapped. "You're the expert. If you need a second opinion, you can call Gram."

"I don't want to call Gram. I don't get along with her. We had a royal argument tonight, and we'll probably have another one next time we talk. We see things differently, which would be okay if we didn't let our emotions get in the way of common sense and compassion and understanding. It's sad, Deb. What's even more sad is that you and I could end up the same way. I don't want that. I want us to be close." Tentatively, she touched Debra's hair. "We have to talk, not argue. Things have been tough since your father left. We've been under intense pressure, and because of that, all the weaknesses in our relationship have come out. I haven't been a perfect mother. But it wasn't that I didn't want to be. I honestly thought I was doing things well. Now I see I wasn't."

She paused, waiting for a response. Debra was curled in a ball, with her knees drawn up, her hands buried in her lap, and her head in a slant against the side of the bed. Laura knew she wasn't asleep. Her body was too tense. She chose to believe she was listening.

Keeping her voice low and gentle in its urgency, she said, "I can change, Debra. If you tell me the things that bother you, I can change. I never realized you didn't like my working. I always thought you complained because all kids complain. But I can plan to be home more now, if that's what you want. You and I can do more together. If I'm doing something else, I'll stop and listen when you want to talk. I'll listen now. I'm not doing anything else. I'm not going anywhere."

Debra's voice was subdued. "Not to him?"

"Not to him. You're my daughter. Right now, you're my first obligation in this world. I'll sit here with you all night if you want. I'll stay here with you all day tomorrow if you want. Tell me what's bothering you, Deb. Let's talk it out."

Debra didn't say anything. One minute passed, then another and another. Laura stroked her long, dark hair with a touch that was light and slow, wordlessly telling her that she had all the time in the world. And it was true. By stealing her away for the weekend, Christian had broken the rhythm of the life she had been leading for so many months. She hadn't cooked, hadn't run from one place to the next accomplishing all the things an efficient person accomplished. He had slowed her down. He had shown her the pleasure of quiet times. She remembered that pleasure from when the children were little, when she had read them stories or held them close to talk, or rock, or sing. With the passage of the years, those times had been lost—not so much with Scott, but with Debra—and Laura missed them. She wanted them back.

Continuing that light, slow stroking, she said, "You can talk to me, babe. I won't criticize. I won't get up and walk away. I'm here for you now. You can tell me anything."

Still Debra didn't speak. When she hunched her shoulders and curled into an even tighter ball, Laura felt more helpless than ever. By the time the first of the soft sounds of crying came, she was through staying at a distance. Sliding to her knees on the floor, she wrapped her arms around Debra and drew her close. She encountered no resistance, either then or when she began to rock her, just as she had years before, holding her tightly while she cried.

"What is it, babe?" Laura whispered. "You can tell me."

"It's awful," Debra sobbed.

"Nothing is that awful."

"This is. I did the stupidest thing."

"We all do stupid things sometimes."

"But this was so dumb! I hated it, and it hurt, but it's done now and I can't ever go back."

Frightening things ran through Laura's mind. She kept up the rocking, rubbing an arm, then a shoulder, putting her cheek to Debra's temple and whispering, "It'll be okay. It'll be okay."

"But I feel so awful!" Debra whispered back between sobs.

Laura held her tighter. "You'll feel better. Give it time, and you will. Nothing stays that awful for long."

"I'll never be the same again."

"You'll be better. Older and wiser. Whatever it is, babe, we'll work it out." When Debra made a sound that was more moan than sigh, Laura wondered if she were in physical pain. "What can I do for you, Deb? I feel so helpless."

"You can't do anything. No one can."

"Talk to me. Tell me more."

All she heard for the next several minutes was the sound of soft weeping. Then, nearly as softly, came a muffled "You'll hate me. You'll be so disappointed."

"I'll love you anyway, regardless of what happened. That's what love's about, babe. It's about accepting weaknesses along with the strengths. It's about forgiving mistakes."

"You stopped loving Daddy when he did what he did."

Laura stopped rocking. "What I felt for him was very different from what I feel for you."

"Didn't you love him?"

"I thought I did."

Debra was the one who started to rock this time. "I thought I loved Jace," she said in a pitifully broken voice, but once she started, the words kept coming. "I thought he was the coolest, nicest, best-looking guy in school, and I thought he thought I was cool too. I could tell him anything. I mean, I told him about what was happening here, and he understood, he really did. Then you went away, and Gram was here, and she's so hard to be with that I went down to the yogurt shop every night to be with Jace. Whenever he got a break, he sat with me, and when he was done with work, we'd drive somewhere and park."

She hiccuped. Laura reached for a tissue from the nightstand and pressed it into her hand.

"I'd get in his car, 'cause the Miata has bucket seats, and we'd talk and kiss, and it was nice. Then, on Saturday night, we went to a movie, and afterward he took me back to his house. His parents were away, and he wanted to do more than kiss."

Laura felt a hollowness in the pit of her stomach. She tucked Debra's hair behind her ear, just like she used to do when she was little. Those were such innocent times. The children were small, the problems were small. Such innocent times.

"I didn't want to go all the way," Debra went on, "and I told him that. So he said we wouldn't, that we'd just touch and all." She stopped abruptly. "It's gross, telling you this."

"Why is it gross?" Laura asked gently. "Do you think I don't know what touching's about?"

"How old were you when you did it?"

"Touched? About your age, I guess."

"How old were you when you went all the way?"

"A little older." Holding Debra as tightly as ever, she rocked her again. One part of her didn't want to ask, didn't want to know, but it was the cowardly part. "Is that what happened at Jace's?"

Debra started crying again.

"It's okay, honey. It's not the end of the world."

"Nothing happened on Saturday night," Debra managed between gulping sobs. "I told him I didn't want to. I just didn't want to. He said I didn't love him enough. I tried to explain what I was feeling, but he wouldn't listen. He wouldn't see me last night, and then I got to school today and heard that he'd been out with Kara Hutchinson."

"Oh, babe."

The tears started flowing again, but the words wouldn't stop. "Kara Hutchinson is a total space shot. Jace is too good for her. I went to see him tonight when he got off work, and I told him that. And he said he didn't care, that if I didn't love him he'd find someone who would. I said I *did* love him, and he told me to prove it, and I didn't know what to do."

Laura remembered the phone conversation she'd had with Jace not so long before. He had sounded nervous, and no wonder. She hoped he was scared to death.

In a smaller voice, Debra said, "I didn't know what to do. All I could think about was that Scott did it all the time, and you were probably doing it with Christian, and lots of girls I know do it, so it couldn't be all that bad. Jace had a condom. So I let him." The crying was quieter, almost internal and, in that, more disturbing.

Laura closed her eyes and rested her head on Debra's. She might have cried herself if it would have done any good. But the damage had been done. The loss of innocence was far more than physical. "Oh, babe," she whispered again.

"See? You are disappointed."

"Not the way you think. I'm disappointed because what should have been wonderful wasn't. Lovemaking should be a very beautiful experience. I'm sorry it wasn't that way for you."

"Jace said there's something wrong with me."

Taking Debra's face in her hands, Laura forced it up. Looking her straight in the eye, she said, "Jace Holzworth knows about as much about you as he does about making love. He's a boy, Debra, just a boy. He blackmailed you into doing something you didn't want, then he didn't even know how to make it good. That's *his* problem. There's nothing wrong with you. You're a normal young woman who simply made the mistake of jumping the gun and doing something she wasn't ready for."

"When will I be ready for it?"

"When you're older. When the right man comes along."

"I thought Jace was the right man."

"You wanted him to be," Laura said, brushing at Debra's tears with her thumbs, "and I suppose that's part of being sixteen. Then again, maybe it's my fault. I do love you, Debra. I may not have shown it the way you wanted me to, but I do love you."

"Dad doesn't. If he did, he would have written or called."

"That's not necessarily true. He may be afraid that if he calls or writes, someone will find out where he is, and he doesn't want that to happen."

"I miss him."

"I know you do."

"Do you miss him?"

"I miss what we all had together."

"But you don't miss him, because you have Christian."

Laura searched her eyes for resentment. Her voice held it, though it was nowhere near as strong as it had been before. Laura was grateful for the improvement, but she knew it wouldn't continue unless she could be honest. "What I have with Christian is completely different from what I had with your father."

"Is it better?"

"It's healthier, I think. Christian is his own man. He's successful and confident. I can give him things, but I can't take over; he's too strong for that."

"Do you love him?"

There was no doubt about that in Laura's mind, but she was uncomfortable saying it to Debra, just as she was uncomfortable telling her about her relationship with Christian twenty-one years before. Debra's emotions were too raw. She needed time to adjust. Then again, maybe they would *never* be able to discuss those early days without impugning Laura's relationship with Jeff, and Jeff would always be Debra's father. Some things were better left unsaid, Laura knew. Still, she couldn't lie outright. "I think I could love him, once we get things straightened out."

"Are you going to marry him?"

"I'm not free to do that."

"You could be. You could divorce Dad."

Laura searched her tear-streaked face. "Do you think I should?"

"No. I want Dad back here with us. But you don't."

"It's not that I don't want him to come back," Laura tried to explain, "it's that I don't think it will happen. Even if it does, I don't think it would work. Too much has happened since your father left. I've learned a lot about him and a lot about myself. I'm not the person I was before. Neither is your father." She paused. "I'm not rushing into anything, Deb. I want us to get back on track." She kissed Debra's forehead, then brought her against her again. "I feel so bad about tonight."

Debra didn't answer, but for the first time, she slipped her arms around Laura's waist.

"Are you hurting?" Laura whispered.

"Not much."

"A little?"

Debra nodded.

"Want to use my Jacuzzi?"

After a pause, she nodded again.

As Laura continued stroking her daughter's hair, she couldn't ignore the irony of the situation. Scott had been charged with rape for doing nothing and had been put through hell because of it. Debra, who had come far closer to being raped than Megan Tucker ever had, couldn't even raise the charge. The unfairness infuriated Laura, but she knew that fury wasn't what Debra needed.

"It'll be better one day," she said softly. "When the time is right and the man is right, you'll know what it means to make love. Believe me, you will."

Debra was silent, but she made no move to free herself from Laura's hold. Laura saw that as a good sign and clung to it.

TWENTY-EIGHT

❀❀❀

C HRISTIAN HAD NEVER felt the responsibility for another person that he felt for Laura. His relationship with Gaby had been one of two people leading very different lives, coming together for pleasure, then parting. Even when Gaby had been so sick, what he felt had been more compassion than responsibility, and what he had felt for other women over the years had fallen short of both.

With Laura it was different. She was a strong woman, but vulnerable in ways Gaby had never been. He liked it when she smiled at him, when she leaned against him for the pleasure of the closeness or raised her face for his kiss. He felt more of a man with her than he had ever felt, and that made him want to smooth over the rough edges Jeff had left in her life, to make things better than ever.

He could do that for her in Vermont. She had told him as much during the intimate hours they had spent there. Whether he could do it for her in Northampton remained to be seen. Debra kept him at a cautious distance. He had done what he could for Scott, but Scott was back at school. He could help out at Cherries, but the truth was that Laura ran it well. He had no wish to be a major player there and take anything away from the pride that she felt.

That left him two major objectives. The first, and most critical in the long run, was to find Jeff. To that end, first thing Tuesday morning he paid Tack a visit.

"You think we aren't trying?" Tack said when Christian dared suggest the government wasn't doing enough.

"I think maybe the investigation's gone stale. It's been ten weeks of nothing. We need a fresh approach. I'm hiring a private investigator."

"If the FBI couldn't come up with anything, a private investigator won't."

"Is that you talking or Daphne?" Christian knew something was going on between Tack and Daphne, though he wasn't sure just what. He did know that every time he mentioned hiring an investigator, Daphne vetoed the idea.

"It's me talking, you asshole, and only because I want to save you some money. The guy working with me is good. So's his team. If they couldn't find your brother, maybe he doesn't want to be found."

Christian studied the calluses on his right hand. "Jeff broke a window once when he was a kid, couldn't have been more than six or seven at the time. It was an accident. We were having a snowball fight, and his aim wasn't so hot. One look at that broken window, and he panicked. Took off like a shot, ran halfway across town to an old gardening shed, and nearly froze to death. I looked all over for him, but I couldn't find him, and then I got the blame for the window *and* for his being lost. They finally found him late that night. He was scared shitless."

"What's your point?"

Christian dropped his hand to his side. "Maybe Jeff wants to be found but doesn't have the courage to turn himself in. Maybe he's miserable wherever he is. Maybe he's crying for help somewhere, only there's no one around to hear." All those things had been true that time when they'd been kids. Sucker that he was, even in spite of the beating Christian had taken on his account, he had felt sorry for Jeff. Some of that same feeling remained.

Tack drew a bow across an imaginary violin.

"Damn it, Jones, it's possible."

"Possible but not probable. He's a big boy now. If he's miserable enough, he can go to the nearest phone booth and call home. Since he's not doing that, we have to assume he's not so miserable."

"How long are we supposed to go on wondering where he is?" Finality was the operative word. Divorce or no divorce, if he and Laura were ever to build a life together, they had to close the book on her time with Jeff.

"You may wonder forever," Tack warned. "If a clever man wants to stay hidden, he stays hidden. Any dick will tell you that."

"Maybe. But I have to try."

Tack shrugged. "It's your money."

Christian was aware of that, but he didn't care. He had the money. And the cause was worth it. Still, there was a reason why he had sought Tack out. "You could save me some money and a whole lot of time by sharing your information with the person I hire."

"The Agency may not be wild about that idea."

"There are lots of ideas the Agency may not be wild about, including the one that you were out in Tahiti playin' around with my friends. Can't you do this for me, Tack?" Christian pushed.

Tack looked torn. For a minute, Christian thought he would raise the issue of questionable tax deductions, but he didn't. "What the hell," he finally said. "I'll get you what I can. It's in my best interest too, I suppose. I'm getting flack from the Boston office."

"They don't think you're doing enough?"

"They don't think what I'm doing merits my hanging around here."

"Does it?"

"Technically, no." Tack leveled him a challenging stare. "But I like it here."

Christian rose to the challenge. "It or her?"

After a minute, Tack said, "Same difference."

"She's a great lawyer."

"She's a great lady."

"She knows how to drive. She'll visit you in Boston."

"I want more," Tack said, again with a challenging look. "Think she'd consider moving there?"

"How would I know?"

"You've known her for years."

"Barely. Have you asked her?"

"Not yet."

"Maybe you should."

"Yeah."

"Wondering is the pits, isn't it? It's lousy not to know what's going through a woman's mind—or a brother's."

Tack regarded him for a minute longer before his expression turned droll. Reaching for a pen, he scrawled something on a pad of paper near the phone, ripped off the top piece, and passed it over. "If you're bent on doing it, do it right. This guy is the best in the business. If he can't find your fuckin' brother, no one can."

Christian arranged a meeting with the man, and while that meeting was pending, he looked to his second objective. Showing up unannounced late Tuesday morning at the offices of the *Hampshire County Sun*, he demanded an audience with Gary Holmes. When word came back that Holmes was out of town, he settled for Duggan O'Neil.

"I'd like an explanation for this," Christian said, tossing a copy of the weekend paper onto O'Neil's cluttered desk. In clear sight was an article O'Neil had written as a follow-up to those that had covered the dismissal of charges against Scott. Tucked inside was Gary Holmes's editorial. Both suggested that Scott had gotten away with murder. "Is there a personal vendetta going on here that we don't know about?"

Duggan O'Neil was of medium height and wire thin. His clothes hung loosely on him, giving him a rumpled look in keeping with the mess on his desk. Only the computer screen and keyboard looked well tuned, which was deceptive, Christian knew. He had no doubt that Duggan O'Neil's mind was razor sharp.

"Personal vendetta?" O'Neil repeated in an innocent way.

"Against the Frye family. Since Jeffrey disappeared, you people have been on his case. Scott Frye never would have been accused of rape if it hadn't been for the articles you've written. My God, man—" he tossed a hand toward the paper, "—you barely report that the charges against the kid were dropped before you take off on the difficulty of proving rape." Laura had been furious when she'd read it, which made Christian all the more angry. "Is there some method behind this madness?"

"I'm simply reporting the news," the man said without remorse.

"As you see it, O'Neil—which is *not* the way the court sees it, and not the way the government sees it. The Attorney General decided against going to a grand jury, so the case is dead, but you didn't report that, did you? You didn't report the fact that the supposed victim admitted she was pressured into bringing charges. You didn't report the fact that she admitted, on the stand and under oath, that no rape had taken place. You didn't report the fact that the civil charges were dropped. Two and three weeks ago, you were free enough in reporting about what Scott had allegedly done. Don't you think you owe him equal time now that he's been cleared?"

O'Neil shrugged, but he wasn't looking as casual as the gesture suggested. He was watching Christian intently. "Innocent people don't make for interesting news."

Christian felt utter contempt for the man. "Then why have you been after Laura Frye? She's an innocent party in all this. Whether or not her husband committed a crime has yet to be proved, but nobody's come after her with indictments, and she's sitting right here where they could easily nab her. But they haven't, because she knew nothing whatsoever about any alleged tax fraud scheme. All she wants is to run her restaurant and carry on with her life, and she'd do it if you people didn't slam her at every turn. Every time you run an article, she loses business."

"You give us too much credit."

"That's blame, O'Neil, and you deserve it. Why can't you leave her the hell alone? Get on someone else's case, for Christ's sake."

"Are you her champion?"

"I'm her brother-in-law."

"I know that, but what else are you?"

"I'm the guy who's in a position to make a whole lot of noise about the shoddy stuff that's been passed off as journalism in this town for too many years."

"You should be talking to my boss."

"He's conveniently out of town, so I'm talking to you," Christian said. Planting his fists on the desk, he let distaste eclipse anger in his eyes. "You slander my brother, you slander his wife, you slander his family, you slander me. They're struggling to survive, so they won't challenge you, but I will. Keep up what you've been doing, and I'll push the law to the limit."

"You'll never win."

"Maybe not, but I'll dirty you good in the process. The *Hampshire County Sun* isn't the only paper around. There are others that will jump at the chance to one-up the *Sun*. Gary Holmes may be a powerful sonofabitch, but he isn't exactly beloved. I'll take him down, and you right along with him."

O'Neil seemed distracted. "Have we met before?"

"No way," Christian declared and straightened.

"You look familiar."

"Must be from those victory shots your photographer took on the courthouse steps, the shots you decided not to run lest they attract too much attention." He started for the door. "Have your boss call me when he gets back. Meanwhile, watch what you do, O'Neil. Keep up the one-sided reporting, and I'll see the second side gets an airing—maybe at your own expense."

"Is that a threat?"

"You bet," Christian said and stalked out.

At the end of February, Tack got his orders to return to Boston. He had seen them coming, but that didn't make it any easier. Telling Daphne would be tough. Surviving the telling would be even tougher, if she took it all in comfortable stride.

He arranged to pick her up from work, with the intention of taking her for a drive. Knowing that she was stuck in the car with him until he decided to stop gave him a measure of control. He wanted time to convince her to come with him.

She was beaming when she slipped into the car, her mind clearly on something else. "Laura's getting her money released," she said excitedly. "The judge ruled in her favor."

"I heard," Tack said, with what he thought was enthusiasm. He knew how much each victory meant to Daphne, particularly where the Frye case was concerned. "She must be pleased."

"She will be once I reach her. She wasn't at home or at Cherries. DeeAnn said she was with Debra. So I left a message on her machine that I had exciting news and she should give me a call."

Tack nodded. He drove on, heading away from the center of town, with no specific destination in mind.

"Are you annoyed?" Daphne asked cautiously.

"Why would I be annoyed?"

"You were the one to put on the freeze. By ruling for Laura, the judge ruled against you."

"Come on, Daph. You know I don't think that way. I do what I have to by law, but that doesn't mean I always enjoy it. I agreed with you that the freeze was a hardship for Laura. Things will be easier for her now, and I'm glad."

He stared through the windshield and drove on. After several minutes of silence, Daphne asked quietly, "Is something wrong?"

He shook his head. "I'm really pleased for you too. You did a great job."

"It wasn't all that hard." She paused. He could feel her eyes on him. "You're looking very serious."

He took a deep breath. "I have to go back, Daph."

"Again? You were back for three days last week."

"For good. I got the call this morning. They want me in the district office full time by Monday." It was Thursday, the twenty-eighth of the month. He had Friday to clean up his desk and be gone.

She was silent for a minute. Then, in a logical tone, she said, "But the case is still open. Nothing's been resolved."

"I doubt if anything will for a good long time, which is why they want me back. I've done everything I can here. I've done *more* than everything." It was really funny when he thought about it. "Let me tell you: never in my life have I researched a case as thoroughly as I have this one. I have facts and figures to prove every one of my claims. If Jeff Frye ever shows up, he hasn't got a chance in hell of getting off."

"That depends on who his lawyer is," Daphne teased, but so lightly that the teasing lost its punch. Tack imagined there was a warning beneath it.

"You wouldn't really defend him, would you?"

"Laura would be counting on me to do it."

"Laura would understand. It'd be a conflict of interest."

"If you and I were still together."

Not liking the sound of that "if" at all, he drove on. "Come back to Boston with me, Daph." When she didn't say anything, he reworded the plea. "What we have together is good. I want to keep it." He dared a glance at her. She was looking out the side window. "Daph?"

"Why can't you stay here?"

"Because my job is there."

"You were doing fine traveling back and forth."

"Maybe at the beginning, when most of my assignment had to do with this case. But now there's other work to do, and doing it long distance just isn't the same. Things take twice, three times as long. I spend half my time either on the phone or at the fax machine, and that's not to mention the people I'm supposed to be supervising. I have to be in Boston, running things firsthand. Besides, there's nothing more I can do on the Frye case. I can't justify staying here any longer." He turned down one street, drove on a ways, then turned down another. "I want you to come back with me."

"I know you do," she said quietly, "but I don't know what that means."

"I want you to live with me."

"In Cambridge?"

"Cambridge, Boston, Belmont—we could live wherever the hell you wanted."

"How about Northampton?" Again there was a light teasing, just as ineffective this time as the first.

"I can't commute from here."

"And I can't commute from there."

"But I'm asking you to marry me."

She sucked in a breath, then let it out in a frighteningly soft "Oh."

" 'Oh'? Is that a yes or a no?" He couldn't gauge her reaction in the dark. One minute she was looking down at her hands, the next she was looking out the window again. "I'm dying here, Daph. Say something."

It was another minute before she did, and then it wasn't quite what he wanted. "No one's ever proposed to me before."

"It's no wonder, given your enthusiasm for the idea. I guess I'm a little dense when it comes to matters of the heart. Is it marriage you're against or me?"

"Neither. It's me who's the problem."

"Do you love me?"

"Yes."

"So what's the problem?"

"Oh, Tack," she said in that same frighteningly soft voice. This time she reached for his hand. "You want me to say I'll drop everything and go with you, but I can't. I have commitments here."

He closed his fingers around hers. "What commitments?"

"My law firm. My practice."

"Your partners will forgive you. They're human. And they're married."

"But I've worked so hard to make a place for myself. My practice is a good one."

"A criminal practice is portable. Your client pool is constantly changing. You can start drawing on a pool from the eastern part of the state."

"It's not so easy. Out here I'm known, there I'm not. The competition is greater, the pace faster. Boston is saturated with lawyers. The last thing the city needs is another one."

"You could open a practice in one of the suburbs. I know lots of lawyers. One of them would take you in."

"I don't want to be taken in. I have my own practice. I want to keep it."

"You're being stubborn."

"Me? You change jobs, Tack. You have a degree in accounting, and you have great experience. You'd find a job in a minute."

"I like the job I have now."

"And I like mine. So where does that leave us?"

Tack drove on. He had no idea where he was, no idea where he was going, but getting lost in Northampton was the least of his worries. After a while, he said, "Supposing I was to look for a new job. Would you marry me?"

"A job out here?"

"Well, I wouldn't be looking for another one in Boston."

"What kind of job were you thinking of?"

Her tone was too casual for comfort. He wasn't letting her change the subject. "Forget the specifics. If I agreed to move here, would you marry me?"

She hesitated a little too long.

"It's marriage that you don't want, isn't it?" he asked.

"It's not that I don't want it."

"Then what?"

"It's a big step."

He nodded vigorously. "Yup. A major commitment."

"Not something to rush into."

Tack pulled over to the side of the road, set the emergency brake, and faced her in the dark. "If we were twenty or twenty-five, I could agree with you, but we're all grown up, Daphne. It's not a question of rushing into something. It's a question of seeing something right and grabbing it while we still have the chance."

"But what if it's wrong?"

He took her face in his hands. "Does it feel wrong? In all the time we've spent together in the past two months, has it ever felt wrong?"

"No," she admitted.

"Thank you," he said and gave her a hard kiss by way of punctuation.

His mouth had barely parted from hers when he heard a catch in her breath. He knew the sound. She liked his kiss and wanted more, but as flattering as that was, he wasn't giving in to sex. There was too much he wanted to tell her first.

He continued to hold her face, wanting her undivided attention. "I knew this was coming. I knew I couldn't stay here forever, and I knew there would be some kind of confrontation when it came time to leave. I've agonized over it, Daph, because the thought of going back to Boston and seeing you only on weekends stinks. I like spending time with you. I like coming home from work and spending the night with you. It's more than the sex."

"I know," she whispered.

"I've had lovers, God knows I've had lovers, but they never gave me anything more than physical gratification. You give me more, Daph. You fill up my mind. Hell, I don't want to go back to being alone. I'm tired of it—and you are too, if you dare admit it. I see it in your eyes sometimes, a longing for things you thought you'd never have. Well, you *can* have them. I can give them to you. But you have to commit. That's the way it works."

She curved a hand around his thigh. "Why can't we just live together?"

"Because I don't want to. I want to know you're mine. I want to be married. I want babies."

"God, Tack, I can't," she cried.

"Sure you can. You can do anything you want."

"But I'm scared."

"Of what? Of me? Of marriage? Of having babies? What?"

"Of failing. I'm a great lawyer. I've trained at it and worked hard at it. But a wife? A mother? I don't even know if I can hack it as a live-in lover. I'm a lousy friend. I have a selfish side you've never seen. I've done some awful things—"

He kissed her silent. By the time he raised his head, her hand was moving on his thigh. "I don't give a damn what you've done," he told her. "I've done some pretty shitty things myself. But the past is done. We're talking about the future now."

She leaned forward and kissed him again, more deeply this time. He had wanted to talk, but it was hard to think when she demanded so much of his mouth and tongue, and when she cupped him and began to caress him through his trousers he abandoned his resolve.

"Daph—"

"I want you," she whispered, with an urgency that sent heat pouring through him.

"Oh, God." He tried to control it. "Not here." The bucket seats were ungiving, and the back seat was worse.

"Take me home, then. I need you."

"I'm lost."

She continued to stroke him. "Take me home. We'll find you together."

With a hoarse laugh that was part humor, part incredible frustration, he cried, "I don't know where the hell we are! I don't know *how* to get home!"

It was a minute before his meaning sank in, a minute before Daphne began to direct him through the streets she'd grown up in, and all the while she touched him, driving him wild while he drove her home. They left a trail of clothes from the front hall up the stairs to the bedroom, where they made love with a fierceness that made his argument for their staying together all the stronger.

"I don't want to be without you," he whispered into the damp riot of her hair when they finally lay still. "Not ever."

She mouthed his name and kissed his lips and was about to say something meaningful, he was sure, when the doorbell rang.

Neither of them moved.

When it rang again, more insistently this time, he swore.

"I'll go," she whispered. "It's probably the little boy from down the street begging money for the Boosters Club. It's cold out. He shouldn't have to come back another time." Slipping out of his arms, she put on a robe and, combing through her hair with her hands, headed for the stairs.

Laura rang the bell a third time. The downstairs lights were on, and a strange car was in the driveway. She assumed that Daphne was meeting with a client and felt bad about interrupting, but DeeAnn had mentioned exciting news. Laura had an idea what it was. The timing was right. She wasn't waiting to get home to give Daphne a call.

The Daphne who opened the door, though, wasn't the one she had expected to see—the lawyer at work, with her hair in a knot, her makeup immaculate, her silk skirt and blouse neatly arranged. This Daphne wore nothing but a long wrap robe. Her makeup was gone. Her hair was loose and messed.

Laura had seen Daphne disheveled before. They had grown up together, sleeping at each other's houses. They had spent weekends together as teenagers, had shared Saturday morning coffee together as adults. Laura had seen Daphne when she'd been sick, looking awful, and when she'd been vacationing, looking loose and light-hearted. But Laura had never seen her with the blush of lovemaking on her cheeks.

"Ooops," she murmured, feeling her own cheeks go red. "Looks like I've come at a bad time. God, Daph, I'm sorry. Dee said you'd called, and since Debra was staying at Cherries to wait tables, I thought I'd drop by to hear your news. When I saw the car outside, I figured you were with a client." Daphne was the driven professional. She was the cool, classy lady, far too preoccupied with her career to indulge in affairs of the heart. She indulged in sex sometimes. Laura knew that. But it was an infrequent event. "I'm really sorry. I'll come back another time." She started to turn away, but Daphne stopped her.

"Wait." She held her robe closed at the throat, looking embarrassed but eager to give Laura the news. "We won. The judge ruled in our favor. You'll have a healthy portion of those frozen assets back at your own disposal."

Laura broke into a smile. "Thank God! Thank *you.*" She sighed. "That's so good to hear."

"I'll pick up a formal copy of the decision in the morning. I was told that we got nearly everything we asked for. The government will hold whatever is left in the event that Jeff is found and brought to trial."

"That's fine," Laura said. "As long as we can live again. I want to pay you back, and Elise. And Christian." She felt giddy with relief and would have hugged Daphne if the circumstances had been different. But Daphne had been hugging someone else when Laura had shown up at her door. It seemed only fair to thank her quickly and let her return to whoever it was.

Whoever it was. However fleetingly, Laura's curiosity was piqued. Daphne was her best friend, and there was a man in her bed.

"I'm really grateful, Daph. You put in a lot of work for me. I want you to send me a bill."

"No bill. You're my friend."

"Between me and Scott, you've put in hours and hours. Now that I have money again, I want to pay you."

But Daphne shook her head. "You may have more money tomorrow than you did today, but things won't be back to where they were before Jeff left. Even with what we calculated was your fair share of joint assets, you'll come up short. Jeff isn't here to work. You're functioning on one income, not two. We figured that his interest in Farro and Frye was worth something, but you can bet the government will keep its freeze on that."

"The government can't find Jeff. How long can they keep his money?"

"The way the government sees it, it's the government's money."

The proprietary way she said it made Laura want to argue. She actually opened her mouth, only to close it again when a movement on the stairs caught her eye. She stared, sure she was mistaken. But Daphne had looked around and grown suddenly pale, and the man had stopped mid-step, wearing only half fastened trousers and a look of dismay.

Laura didn't want to believe what she was seeing. "Daph?"

Daphne gestured for Tack to go back upstairs.

Laura was mortified. "No, no. It's okay. I'm leaving." But Daphne caught her arm before she could do more than turn away.

"Let me explain."

"No need. You can see whoever you want."

"But you're angry."

"No." Laura swallowed. "I'm surprised. I'm confused. I thought he was on the other side."

"Legally. Not personally."

"He's the one who put me in this mess."

"Jeff put you in this mess." Daphne pulled at her arm, but Laura didn't budge. "We have to talk. Please, Laura?"

"Another time. This is too awkward."

"It's more awkward for me. Please?"

Laura wanted to leave. She wanted to go home and pretend that the man in Daphne's house was no one she knew. But Daphne was her oldest friend, and there was a pleading look in her eye. So she stepped inside and let Daphne shut the door. But she didn't move toward the living room. She couldn't make herself comfortable, knowing Taylor Jones was upstairs in Daphne's bedroom.

"He's a nice man," Daphne said in a beseeching half whisper. "He was all in favor of your getting your share of those assets. He froze them because that was his job, it was what he had to do, but he didn't like it. Even at the beginning, when he wasn't sure whether you were involved in Jeff's scheme, he was uncomfortable with the freeze, because he knew it would hurt. He doesn't like hurting innocent people."

Laura had always trusted Daphne. It wasn't that Daphne was the stronger of the two of them, or the leader, if their relationship came down to that. But Laura had always seen Daphne as an intelligent, level-headed, honest person. If Daphne said Taylor Jones was a nice man, it was probably true. But that didn't rid Laura of the feeling that she'd been betrayed.

"Have you been seeing him right from the start?" she asked, not sure how foolish to feel. She hadn't known Jeff was into tax fraud, hadn't known he was into other women. She wanted to know how much she'd missed when it came to Daphne.

"We went out for drinks on New Year's Eve. It wasn't anything formal—I showed up at his office to ask about our case, and he was alone with no plans, and I was alone with no plans, so we went for a drink."

"You could have spent New Year's Eve with me."

"You were at Cherries, and I didn't want to go out. I hate New Year's Eve. I've always hated New Year's Eve. All I wanted was to go home and read a good book."

"So you met him instead." Laura tried not to make it an accusation, but it came out that way. She wasn't sure what bothered her more—that her best friend was sleeping with the enemy, or that she hadn't known a thing about it. "Why didn't you tell me?"

"I couldn't. You were going through too much. I didn't think you'd understand."

"You could have tried me."

But Daphne shook her head. "The trouble with Scott started soon after. If you'd known about Tack, you wouldn't have been so eager for me to defend Scott, and I wanted to do that. I didn't trust anyone else to get him off."

"You were with Tack through all that?"

Daphne nodded.

"From New Year's to now?"

Daphne nodded again.

Laura tried to think of the last time Daphne had been with a man for more than an occasional date and couldn't. "Is it serious?"

Daphne didn't answer, but she looked torn.

"I thought we were so close," Laura cried. "I've shared things with you that I've never shared with another person, and I thought you did the same. I guess I was wrong. You've been seeing someone for two months without saying a word—someone with the capacity to injure me. That hurts, Daph."

Daphne pushed her hands into her pockets and pressed her palms to her thighs. "I didn't want to hurt you. I've never wanted that, but things haven't been as easy for me as they sometimes seem. I grew up wanting to be a lawyer, so I went to law school and busted my tail to do well, and I did, and then I had to bust my tail to make a name for myself, and I have." She hesitated. "But I've been lonely, damn it. It doesn't matter how busy my days are, my nights are empty. All I wanted was to be with someone who cared, someone who would hold me and maybe talk a little." She sent Laura a plaintive look. "You've always had people around you. First you had your mother and Gretchen, then you married Jeff and had Lydia too, then Scott and Debra came along. But my family's gone. I don't have anyone."

"You have us."

"It's not the same."

"We always thought of you as family."

"It's not the *same*. Being with a man—really *being* with him—fills a need that no career, no friend, no friend's family can fill."

Laura couldn't take her eyes from Daphne. With her hair tousled, her features soft, and her robe falling sleekly over her shapeliness, she seemed a stranger—and that was before she spoke. Her words were as foreign as her look. "I didn't know," Laura whispered.

"I'm human. I'm a woman."

"But you never talked about loneliness."

"It's not something you talk about, or dwell on, if you have other things you want in life."

"All those times I wanted to fix you up, you fought me."

"I didn't want to be fixed up. I didn't want a steady date. I had my own agenda, and that agenda didn't include getting married and having babies, which was the route you took. You were so convinced I was missing something that I probably went overboard in my own mind convincing myself that I wasn't. And for a while it worked."

She took a step away, then turned back to Laura with tears in her eyes.

"I told myself that the law was enough. I told myself that I really didn't have time to give to a husband and kids, and I was a lousy cook because I didn't have time for that either. So I had my career, and the success of it reinforced the image I'd created. I was the crackerjack lawyer. I was every bit as cool and commanding and ballsy as any man in the county. My partners saw me as one of the guys, which was just what I wanted." She wiped the corner of her eye with a sleeve. "But then there were those times—they didn't come often at the beginning—when I wanted something else. I looked around and saw that everyone else had it. The world was paired up, and I was alone." She pulled the lapels of her robe together again and hung on tightly. "The problem was that the life I'd made for myself really didn't have room for a husband or kids, but I wanted *something*. You don't know what it's like to be lonely like that, to have attacks of it, when you feel an awful ache and you can't do much but sit it out."

Looking as though her heart were breaking, she covered the short distance to where Laura stood.

"I didn't want to hurt you," she cried. "So help me God, I never wanted to hurt you. But he was lonely, and I was lonely, and it just seemed like a way to make both of us feel better."

Laura barely breathed. There was something about the glazed look in Daphne's eyes, something about the anguish on her face and the desperation in her voice, that caused a prickling at the back of Laura's neck.

"It's all right," she said guardedly. "Your being with Tack isn't the end of the world."

With a tiny, almost imperceptible snap of her head, Daphne blinked. She swallowed, then moistened her lips. In a thin voice, she said, "He's a nice man."

"Is it serious, then?"

"I like him a lot."

"Does he like you as much?"

"More. He has to go back to Boston. He wants me to come."

Pushing guardedness aside, Laura smiled in delight. This was her best friend, sharing exciting news. "Daph, that's great!"

Daphne seemed buoyed enough by the smile to relax a little. "I'm not sure I can go. My life is here."

"Do you love him?"

Daphne nodded.

"Then you can go."

"Good God, you're still a romantic. After everything that's happened, that's remarkable."

"Why can't you be one too?"

"I don't know, but I can't. Love doesn't conquer all. It just doesn't. I have my practice here. I have my house, my friends." Her eyes clouded in a way that made Laura uncomfortable again. "I have unfinished business to see to."

"So see to it." Daphne didn't respond, but the expression on her face was so sad that Laura wanted to turn and run. "I have to go," she said. "Can we talk more tomorrow?"

Daphne nodded.

Laura reached for the door and let herself out. She didn't look back. She didn't want to see that sad look again, didn't want to wonder about its cause. But not wanting to wonder didn't prevent it from happening. At odd times during the week that followed, her mind flashed through memories, looking for things she might have missed, clues she might have overlooked, messages she might have innocently misconstrued. She wanted to ask people— DeeAnn, Elise, even Christian—but she didn't want them to tell her what she didn't want to hear, so she kept still. And then Lydia took sick.

TWENTY-NINE

❀ ❀ ❀

CHRISTIAN WAS THE ONE who found her. He had been in Vermont for the day and, on impulse, decided to drop by Lydia's house before going on to Laura's. Assuming she was up and about, probably fixing dinner for herself, he rang the bell before fitting his key to the lock and opening the door.

"Hello?" he called and started through the house. "Mom?" He was on the kitchen threshold when he saw her in a small pile on the floor. "Jesus," he breathed and quickened his pace. He knelt by her side and touched her cheek. Her skin was gray, though still warm. She was breathing, but shallowly.

"Mom? It's Christian. Can you hear me?" He took her hand. "Mom? Come on. Open your eyes for me."

She didn't respond.

Heart pounding, he scooped her limp, pitifully light body into his arms and strode toward the bedroom. He didn't stop to think that maybe she'd hurt herself in the fall and should be immobilized. He only knew that she was too fragile to be left lying on the floor.

Easing her gently onto the spread, he grabbed the phone and dialed 911. Without taking his eyes from Lydia's face, he gave the dispatcher the information he needed to get an ambulance to the house. Then he sat by her side, holding her hand, and waited. After a minute, he covered her with a blanket, thinking she might be cold. After another minute, he began rubbing her hand. "They're on their way," he said evenly. "We'll get you to the hospital. You'll be fine." After another minute, his helplessness hit him. He would have taken her to the hospital himself if he didn't feel she had a better chance with the paramedics. They had oxygen and intravenous solutions, knowledge of CPR techniques, and communication with the hospital. In his own car he'd have nothing.

Freeing one hand to grab for the phone again, he dialed Laura's number. As soon as he heard the recorded message click on, he disconnected, then dialed Cherries' number.

"DeeAnn, it's Christian. Is Laura there?"

"Sure. She's out back."

"Can you get her quick? It's an emergency."

An agonizingly long ten seconds later, Laura picked up the phone. "Christian? What's wrong?"

"I'm at my mother's. She's unconscious." He heard Laura gasp, but his eyes didn't stray from Lydia's face. "I think it's either a heart attack or a stroke, but she's breathing. I'm waiting for an ambulance to get here. Meet us at the hospital?"

"I'll leave right now."

He was hanging up the phone when he heard the distant siren. It drew closer, then was suddenly still, and he had the awful fear that it was on another mission entirely, until he realized that once off the main streets there was no need for the noise. Leaving Lydia's side, he reached the front of the house just as the ambulance pulled up. He showed the paramedics to her room and watched while they ministered to her, bundled her onto a stretcher, and carried her from the house. Then he rode in the ambulance, holding her hand again.

When they arrived at the hospital, Laura and Debra were waiting. They looked positively stricken when a silent Lydia, with her eyes closed, her coloring poor, and an oxygen mask covering her mouth and nose, was whisked past them.

There were forms to fill out. Christian knew the answers to some questions but not all and was grateful Laura was there to help with the rest. He was grateful Laura was there, period. He was feeling unhinged, which was surprising given the length of time he had been estranged from his mother. He wasn't dependent on her, hadn't been for years; still, the blood tie was there. She was his mother, after all. Seeing her lying so still, lifeless in everything but the tiny breaths her body continued to take, was a chilling experience. Laura's nearness helped temper the chill.

"What's taking them so long?" Debra asked in a frightened voice.

"They're examining her," Laura explained. "They want to find out what's wrong and get her stabilized."

Legs sprawled, eyes glued to the door through which they'd taken Lydia, Christian wondered if stabilization would be possible. She hadn't regained consciousness in the ambulance, and as if the ashen tinge of her skin hadn't been ominous enough, he had the negligible weight of her in his arms to remember. Something inside told him the prognosis wouldn't be good.

After what seemed an eternity of waiting, the doctor came out to confirm that Lydia had had a heart attack and was being placed in the Coronary Intensive Care Unit. "The next seventy-two hours will be critical," he said. "If she makes it through those, she has a chance."

"A chance to live normally?" Christian asked.

"A chance to live. We won't know about normally until we do more tests."

"Then she isn't awake yet."

"No."

"Why not?" Debra asked.

The doctor explained. "My guess is that she suffered the attack several hours before she was found. Between oxygen deprivation and the weakness of her system, she doesn't have the strength to rouse herself."

"Will she ever wake up?"

"I can't answer that yet."

Christian stirred. "Can we see her?" He kept picturing her in that heap on the floor, alone in her house with no help, perhaps even conscious at first and unable to get help. He didn't want her waking up alone, too, and was fully prepared to fight the doctor if he limited their visits. That wasn't necessary.

"She may be aware of what's happening without being able to show it," the doctor said and looked from one face to the next. "Assuming none of you intends to upset her, having someone with her will be good. Give us fifteen minutes to get her settled. I'll send someone down for you then."

They returned to the waiting room and took seats close together. No more than ten minutes passed when Maddie unexpectedly breezed in.

"I tried to reach you at the restaurant," she told Laura. "DeeAnn told me what happened. How is she?"

Christian had seen Laura tense the instant she'd spotted her mother. He was quiet now, knowing that Maddie would probably ignore him, but ready to come to Laura's aid. He knew how worried she was about Lydia and didn't want Maddie making things worse.

For Maddie's benefit, Laura repeated what the doctor had told them, ending with, "We're just waiting to go up."

Maddie sat down, looking for all the world as though she were joining the vigil. After several minutes of silence, she said to Debra, "Are you all right?"

"I'm scared."

Maddie patted her hand. "She'll do just fine."

After several more minutes of silence, she turned to Laura. "Was there any hint of this coming?"

"There was an irregularity in her heartbeat. Her doctor's been watching her closely."

"Apparently not closely enough. Is he handling her case here?"

"No. The hospital has its own cardiac man."

"Does he know what he's doing?"

"I'm sure he does."

"You may want to consider having her transferred to Boston. The doctors there see so many more cases."

Laura shook her head. "She's too weak to move. They'll do everything they can for her here."

"Still, it might be worthwhile—"

"Or pointless," Christian interrupted to say. "If she has a massive coronary within the seventy-two-hour time frame the doctor gave us, it won't matter much where she is. If she makes it past that, and there's a discussion about possible surgery, we may think about getting a second opinion. I know a fine man at Dartmouth."

Maddie gave him a where-did-you-come-from? look, which he ignored. His eyes went to the clock.

"Well," she said after another minute, "since I'm not directly related and therefore won't be allowed to visit, I'll run along. Let me know what's happening, Laura." Tucking her purse under her arm, she left as abruptly as she'd come.

When she was safely through the door and out of earshot, Debra said to Laura, "What was that about?"

"I don't know, babe."

"She looked odd."

"I know."

"Think she's sick?"

"Gram doesn't get sick."

"At some point she may. She's not much younger than Nana Lydia."

"Maybe that's what has her worried."

"Do you think she really cares about Nana Lydia?"

"I suppose we could give her the benefit of the doubt."

Christian had to admire Laura for that. Maddie had done plenty to make her life miserable over the years. Laura had good reason to despise her mother. Yet she had kept the lines of communication open, which was more than he could say for himself and his relationship with Lydia. He was the one who had stayed away. He was the one who had never written. He was the one who had assigned blame, though as an adult he had no right to do that.

In a quiet voice, he said, "I should have come home sooner. She's had stress in her life. I never realized how much."

Laura reached for his hand. "Maybe none of us did. She internalized so many things. I don't remember a time when she wasn't soft-spoken and calm. She couldn't have been feeling calm all the time, but that doesn't mean one upset or another caused the heart attack. She's not strong, Christian. It could have been a purely physical thing."

Christian nodded. One part of him wanted to believe Laura; the other part refused to. He was feeling confused about lots of things to do with his mother, not the least of which being why he cared so much.

He was momentarily spared these thoughts when the hospital aide came to take them upstairs. Once there, though, the confusion, the helplessness, the guilt returned in force. Lydia was as white as the hospital sheets. Tubes ran from her arm to bottles hanging on a pole, wires anchored to her chest escaped through the loose sleeves of her gown, oxygen entered her nose directly, and her eyes were still closed. Without the padding of her clothes, she looked sunken.

"Hi, Nana Lydia," Debra said, with such brave enthusiasm that Christian instantly forgave her her resentment of him. She stood close by Lydia's shoulder, holding tightly to the rails of the bed. "The doctor says you'll be fine. Really. You just need some rest and a little medicine. Then you'll be home again, and we can have tea and cookies and talk." Her voice faltered. "Can you hear me?"

Lydia gave no sign of awareness.

Debra whispered to Laura, who was standing close beside her, "I don't think she hears."

"Lydia?" Laura asked, leaning closer. "We're right here with you. Are you in any pain?" She paused. "If you are, the doctors can give you something. They're good doctors, Lydia. They're going to fight to get you better. You fight right along with them, and we've got it made."

On the opposite side of the bed, Christian lifted Lydia's lifeless hand from the sheet. It felt shadowy in his palm, small and feather-light. He cradled it as though with the slightest mistreatment it would break. "I came by the house to show you the plans for the house I'm building this spring," he told her. "I mentioned it to you the other day, remember?" He always would. It was the first time that Lydia had shown genuine interest in his work, the first time he had felt comfortable opening up to her about what he did. "I was back in Vermont today and picked them up. I thought you'd like to see them." Damn it, he wanted to show them to her!

"Christian was the one who found you," Laura added. "If it hadn't been for him, you might be lying there still. Once you get home, we'll have to arrange a way for you to call for help when you're not feeling well."

But Christian knew that heart attacks often gave little or no warning. He also knew that if Lydia recovered, she couldn't go back to living alone. And that wouldn't please her at all. Given the way she had spent the past twenty years of her life, it was clear that she valued self-sufficiency.

He was that way too. Maybe he got it from her. Then again, maybe his father possessed the same trait. "Mom?" he called, trying to sound casual but failing miserably. She couldn't die without talking to him. Despite all she'd said, he couldn't believe she really intended to take her secret to the grave. "Is there anyone you want me to call? Anyone you want me to tell that you're here?" His real father might want to know she was ill. He might want to see her. For all Christian knew, he might have been pining for her for years. "All I need is a name. I can get the number myself."

Debra leaned closer to Laura. "Her neighbors will be terrified. Shouldn't we call them?"

Laura nodded and reached for her purse, but before she could remove her wallet Christian passed over a handful of change. "I'll stay here," he said.

To his surprise, Debra stayed too. It wasn't often that they'd been in the same room together without Laura as a buffer. In a sense, lying unconscious between them, Lydia served that role now.

For a time they stood in silence. Christian held Lydia's hand, willing her to survive. Debra stood opposite him, clutching the bed rail. Finally, sounding small and vulnerable, she whispered, "I hate hospitals. They're so depressing."

Christian knew just what she meant. The smells, the sounds, and the sterility all seemed props for death. "I guess we have to think about the babies who are born here. And the sick people who are cured."

"Will Nana Lydia be cured?"

He wanted to be as positive as Laura would have been, but he was too much a realist for that. "I don't know."

"I hope so. She's one of my best friends."

He figured that was about the nicest compliment a grandmother could get from her granddaughter. "She'd probably say the same about you. She loves you, Debra. I'm glad you're here."

"I love her, too. She's so giving. And understanding. I can tell her absolutely anything."

Giving and understanding—two of the things Christian had missed most in Lydia when he'd been Debra's age. Circumstances had a lot to do with that, he knew. So did personalities. So did relationships. Parents expected different things from their children than from their grandchildren. Lydia had been disappointed in Christian over the years. He wondered how she would have taken to a child of his. It saddened him to realize that he would never know.

"Do you think my father is dead?" Debra asked, bringing him back from that might-have-been world with a start. She sounded begrudging, as though she hadn't wanted to ask but couldn't help herself. He shot her a look, but her eyes were on Lydia.

"No. I think he's in hiding."

"Do you think he'll ever come out?"

"Not unless someone makes him."

"What if he knew Nana Lydia was sick? Do you think he would come then?"

Christian had been too preoccupied with Lydia's condition to consider that before. "Possibly." He thought about it more. "The problem is letting him know. We can get it into the papers and on television, but unless he's reading or watching, it won't do any good." Still, the idea had merit. The press would jump at an opportunity to revive the Frye case, particularly with such a melodramatic twist. The investigator would know exactly who to call. It was worth a shot.

"You don't want him back, do you?" Debra asked. She was looking straight at him this time.

He looked straight back. "Would I have hired a private investigator if I didn't?"

"You did that to please my mother."

"I did it to please myself."

"He's not very good," she challenged. "Really. He hasn't come up with much."

"The FBI had two months and couldn't come up with a thing. My guy's had two weeks. He's working on it, but all the leads are cold. It may take him awhile to hit a hot one." He continued to stare at her until finally she looked away. He felt instantly petty. "Hey," he called softly. "How about a truce? I don't want to stir up hard feelings between us. Not now. I'm having enough trouble trying to deal with what's happening to Lydia."

Debra was skeptical. "You are?"

"She's my mother."

"That never seemed to matter before."

He could understand her bitterness. She had been watching him for most of her sixteen years. "There are things you don't know, Debra, two sides to every story," he cautioned her. "Another time, we can sit down and talk, but not now. Now's a time for us to concentrate on helping your grandmother through this."

Seeming startled by the reminder, Debra looked quickly down at Lydia's inert form. She glanced at the pole holding the IV solutions, then at the machine monitoring Lydia's heart. "I hate these things," she whispered.

Christian circled the bed to put an arm around her shoulder, undaunted when she kept her body rigid. "So do I. But if they can help her, who are we to complain?"

Debra didn't have an answer to that, but she didn't relax against him either. After several minutes, he gave her a squeeze and dropped his arm, but he didn't move far. He had meant to offer comfort to Debra, but he was in need of some too. Lydia looked weaker than ever, and the machine gave weird bleeps every so often that gave his own heart pause. She was sinking. He knew that, just as he'd known when Gaby's life was nearing its end. Her skin had grown waxy, like Lydia's was doing. He wondered if she'd last the night.

She lingered through Thursday night, then Friday and Friday night, with no change. Aside from a quick trip to Laura's to shower and shave, Christian was at her side the entire time. Sometimes he stood, sometimes he dozed in the chair. When they were alone, he talked softly, telling her all the things he might have told her over the years if they'd been closer. He wanted to believe she heard, though he had no way of knowing. She didn't acknowledge him, didn't open her eyes once or make a single sound.

By the time Saturday morning rolled around, he was drained.

"Go home and sleep," Laura begged. "I'm here; I'll spell you."

"I'll stay."

She held his head and looked into his eyes with the kind of compassion he still couldn't believe was his to have. "She won't know you're gone."

"I'll know it." He wrapped her in his arms, feeling less bereft when he did. "If she wakes up I want to be here."

"And if she doesn't?" Laura whispered.

"I want to be here then, too. She was with me when I came into the world. We missed each other most of the way through, but I want to be with her when she leaves. It's only right."

Lydia died on Saturday afternoon, slipping peacefully away without ever having regained consciousness. Christian was with her, as were Laura, Debra, and Scott. He held them as they cried, gave them what comfort he could. He didn't shed a tear himself, but the sorrow he felt was soul-deep.

That sorrow ate at him over the next few days. He saw to the funeral arrangements, and though a steady stream of people trickled in and out of the house paying their respects, he felt removed from it all. He hadn't been part of Lydia's everyday life for so long. He knew that, as did all those people who came and went.

Laura sensed the depth of his grief and stayed close. Each night, after Debra was asleep, she stole into his room to lie with him. They didn't make love, but he held her. And in the dark, he talked of his frustration.

"I didn't come back with reconciliation in mind," he said in an anguished voice. "I came back because of Jeff and because of you. Lydia was just part of the package. Then something happened. I felt she was looking at me, at *me*, for the first time. After all these years. It felt so good."

Laura touched his jaw. "She was pleased that you came when we needed you."

"Pleased? I don't know. More likely just surprised. But that was enough to open her eyes."

"She loved you, Christian."

"Mmmm. Maybe."

Laura's head came up. "You doubt it?"

"No. All mothers love their children on some level. That doesn't mean they respect them or like them. What bothers me most is that Lydia and I barely knew each other. Remember the time I spent with Scott when the rape case was pending? I didn't do it because he was your son or my nephew, but because I liked him. He's a nice person. Well, I think I'm a nice person too, only my mother never knew that."

"She knew it."

"With the stunts I pulled over the years?"

"She knew it."

"She might have if we'd had more time. We were just starting to break the ice." He felt the clenching sensation in his middle that he'd been feeling since finding Lydia on the floor. "It shouldn't have happened so soon, damn it, not so soon."

Laura ran a soothing hand over his back. He held her tighter against the irrational fear that he might lose her too.

"It's unfair, Laura."

"All death is unfair."

"Not always. Some people know it's coming and can tie up all the pieces, but she left so many undone. There's Jeff, and me, and the bastard who fathered me. I'll never know who he is, now that Lydia's gone." And now that she was gone, with her part of the bargain upheld to the end, he knew it would haunt him forever.

Lydia was buried on Tuesday morning, lowered into the ground beside William Frye in the simple carved box that Christian had chosen. The day was cold and blustery, March at its leonine best, and although robust pines and firs were scattered over the knoll, the bare bones of birches and maples gave an air of desolation.

Christian felt that desolation deep inside as he stood in the front row of mourners. Laura was on his right, holding his arm in defiance of local gossip. Debra, surprisingly, had positioned herself on his left, and though Scott was on her other side, Christian was the one she leaned against, all the more so when he put an arm around her.

The minister who conducted the short graveside service had known Lydia for years. The genuine affection and respect with which he spoke of her humbled Christian. So too did the sheer number of mourners who had cared enough for his mother to brave the wind and pay her their final respects. He had seen some of them at the house, but there were others who dabbed at their eyes or took his hand at the conclusion of the service and said kind, often touching words about her. Laura was at his elbow, accepting condolences as well, but also giving him the names of people and their relationship with Lydia.

The crowd thinned and then became a trickle making its way back down the hill. Christian sent Scott and Debra down with Maddie. He thanked the minister and watched him go, then turned back to the grave with Laura for a final goodbye. That was when he spotted a man standing by the wide trunk of one of the maples, well apart from the others. Every bit as tall and trim as Christian, though far more advanced in years, he wore a dark topcoat, creased trousers, and polished shoes. His hair was thick and silver, in marked contrast to the darkness of his clothing, and his skin was tanned and weathered.

Laura gasped.

"Who is that?" Christian asked. Handsome in an aristocratic way, the man made such a striking figure that Christian would have known if he'd seen him before. There had been strangers at the service—curiosity seekers and a smattering of reporters—but instinct told him this man wasn't either.

"That's Gary Holmes. What's *he* doing here?"

Garrison Holmes III. Publisher of the *Hampshire County Sun*. Power broker for the whole of the Pioneer Valley. The man who had spent the last three months making the Frye family woes worse.

"Good question," Christian said and turned to her. "You go on down. I want to find out."

Laura looked fearful, and rightfully so. Holmes had shown he had the power to hurt her. "Maybe you should ignore him."

But Christian couldn't do that. He had spent the last two days dealing with grief and frustration over Lydia's death. He was primed for a confrontation. Unless Gary Holmes had good reason for desecrating his mother's grave by his presence, Christian had his outlet.

Hugging Laura closely, he said, "Go on. I'll be down in a minute." He released her. Laura looked dubious, but she went.

Tugging up the collar of his overcoat, Christian buried his hands in his pockets. Holmes was regarding him intently, almost expectantly. Christian started toward him. The closer he came, the more aware he was of the man's age. While he didn't look anywhere near eighty, there were loose folds at the corners of his eyes and deep wrinkles beneath that shocking silver hair on his brow. The squareness of his jaw was marked, exaggerated by the years.

When they stood on an eye level with each other, Christian said, "After all you've done to my family, you have one hell of a nerve showing up here."

Holmes didn't flinch. In a voice that was gritty with age, he said, "I didn't cause your family's problems."

"You made them worse. Did your lackey tell you I was looking for you?"

"He told me."

"A decent man would have called me back."

"I'm not a decent man. Never have been, never will be."

Christian took an angry breath. "My mother was decent. Now she's gone. I don't want you here."

Undaunted by his hostility, Holmes looked at Lydia's grave. "She was a fine woman. An honorable woman."

"So fine and honorable that you saw fit to smear her family."

"A fine woman," Holmes repeated, as though he hadn't heard Christian. The distant look in his eyes aged him. It also gave Christian a moment's pause.

"Did you know my mother?" he asked uncertainly.

"I knew her," Holmes answered, distant still.

"When?"

"Years ago."

Christian's stomach grew unsettled. "In what context?"

Holmes's eyes shifted to his. "You're a bright man. Take a guess."

Christian swallowed hard. With the power of suggestion, he suddenly saw certain things, subtle things—the texture of the hair, the shape of the eyes, the tightness of the ears to the head—things a man might have missed if he hadn't seen them in the mirror morning after morning. Other people wouldn't necessarily notice, though Duggan O'Neil had, Christian realized. He had seen something familiar in Christian. But even then, Christian might have been able to attribute the physical resemblance to coincidence, if it hadn't been for other things. Gary Holmes's age was right. So was his reputation as a philanderer. *Too opinionated,* Lydia had said. *Too controversial, too public. He wanted to rock the boat. He frightened me.* All those things could easily have applied to Gary Holmes.

"You?" Christian asked in disbelief. Gary Holmes had been a legend in

Hampshire County from the time Christian had been young. He wasn't photographed often—by design, Christian was sure. He was a backstage player. His name and his pen were the source of his power. "*You?*"

Holmes held his chin at an arrogant angle. "That's right."

For a split second, Christian was a child again, feeling excluded and punished and alone. He was a teenager, looking at his changing body and wondering whose genes he carried. He was an adult, wading through the emotional aloneness of holidays, birthdays, and graduations. He was a professional, wanting to make someone proud that he'd built a beautiful house or taken a breathtaking picture. Gary Holmes could have been there for him. "You bastard."

"Me?" the other man said innocently. "Why so? I asked her to marry me, but she wouldn't."

"So you abandoned her."

"She turned around and married someone else, my friend," he said with confidence. "She didn't suffer. He gave her a stable life, and that was what she wanted far more than she wanted me."

"She loved you," Christian argued. "She would have married you in a minute if she felt you could have been faithful to her, but you'd already moved on. She knew you wouldn't give up your playthings, and she couldn't live with them."

Holmes shrugged. "We all have to make decisions in life. She made hers."

"And she lived with them, regardless of the pain they brought."

A fleeting frown touched Holmes's brows. "What pain?"

"Me. My relationship with her. My relationship with William Frye."

"None of those things had anything to do with me."

"If you honestly believe that," Christian said, taking pleasure in the rebuke, "you're either pigheaded, egocentric to the point of blindness, or downright ignorant. How could my being another man's child not affect our family? Do you think Bill Frye could treat me on a par with his own son? Do you think Lydia could feel good about the fact that he didn't? Do you think I could be close to her when you'd forbidden her to tell me the truth about something as fundamental as the name of my own father? Didn't you think I'd wonder? Didn't you think I'd be hurt that my father never took the slightest interest in me?"

"I took an interest. I followed your career."

Christian was too angry to give Holmes credit for anything. "A fat lot of good it did if I didn't know it. And what about my mother? She's been a widow for nearly thirty years. The last five of those years she was confined to her house with crippling arthritis. Did you know that? Did you do anything to help?"

"Did you?" Holmes shot back.

"No," Christian said, baring his soul, "and I'm suffering for it now. I've faced regrets in the last few days that I'll be living with for the rest of my life. I like to think that makes me human—more so than you, at least."

"You're quick to make judgments, my friend."

"Like father, like son."

A gust of wind swept over the knoll, blowing Holmes's hair in the same way that Christian knew it was blowing his own. The cold hitting his face didn't have a chance against the hot anger he felt. That anger poured from him, fed by confusion and hurt that had been collecting for years.

"Why did you go after Jeff? Did you resent that he was Lydia's son too? Were you still resenting her marriage, still angry that she had turned you down?"

Holmes didn't answer. His lower lip came out to half cover its mate, but his gaze didn't waver.

"From the day Jeff disappeared," Christian went on, "your paper crucified him."

"We never printed anything untrue."

"But you suggested plenty, and you knew damn well that people would pick up on the suggestions and bandy them about. Rumor is a powerful thing. Once it gets going, it snowballs. Let me tell you, those rumors hurt my mother. They hurt Lydia and Debra, and they hurt Scott most of all. Do you think he would have ever been accused of raping that girl if you hadn't set the scene for it? No way. He's a damn good kid. He didn't deserve that, any more than Debra deserved the kids snickering behind her back in school, or Laura deserved the decline in her business, or Lydia deserved the heartache. If wielding that kind of power gives you a thrill, you can have it." He paused, wanting nothing more than to turn his back and walk away, but something kept him rooted to the spot. "Why? Why did you do it?"

"You're a businessman, Christian. You should know the answer to that."

Incredulous, Christian asked, "You did it to sell papers? Given the relationship you once had with my mother, you could be that cruel?"

"Business is business."

"Hell, I hope not. I hope I never do anything like that."

Holmes gave him a twisted smile. "You haven't been any angel. I followed your shenanigans when you were in school. You were your father's son then, and you've been my son other times since. Face it, Christian. You can call me whatever names you want, but if you're angry it's because you see in me the same traits you criticize in yourself. The apple doesn't fall far from the tree."

Staring at the man who was his father, Christian thought about that. Yes, he was a free-thinker. He was independent and could be irreverent, even thoughtless when he chose—all of which were traits Gary Holmes possessed. But he had never in his life used power to inflict pain. "In the things that matter," he said in a smooth voice as he drew himself straighter, "I'm not like you. I have my mother to thank for that. I may have inherited aspects of your character, but she gave me compassion. She gave me the ability to love."

Seeming threatened by Christian's conviction, Holmes spoke more sharply. "And where has it gotten you? You sowed wild oats aplenty when you were younger, and you've had women as an adult, but you've never married. Forty-seven years old, and you've never married. Couldn't ever get a woman to commit, eh?"

"Didn't ever *ask* a woman to commit," Christian said more smoothly than ever. "I'm not like you, getting married and divorced, married and divorced.

I place more value on the institution than that. Maybe that's another thing I got from my mother. She loved you, but she made a bargain. In keeping that bargain, she married another man, and she made the best of it. She was faithful to him. She made him happy, and she was happy herself.''

Holmes snorted. "Frye was a Milquetoast. She made a mistake when she turned me down."

"She never saw it that way."

"I'd have made her ten times happier than he did."

"And ten times more miserable. Now that I've met you, I think she made the right decision."

Christian guessed that not many people stood up to Gary Holmes, and he felt a certain satisfaction in doing it. Holmes looked angry, which pleased him no end. In the next breath, though, the anger faded. In a deliberate attempt to regain control of the interaction, the older man said with studied calm, "You're my son, all right. Just as glib. Just as hateful."

But Christian shook his head. "Not hateful. When I think of who you are and what you've done, I feel intense dislike. But if you think it'll motivate me to lash back the way you have, you're wrong. I've got too many things going for me to stoop to that."

Holmes shot a look over Christian's shoulder. "Is she one of the things?"

Christian looked back to where Laura stood. She looked so cold, so concerned, so hesitant that he immediately beckoned her forward. When she reached him, he drew her close to his side. "Meet my father, Laura. Years ago, Lydia jilted him. I do believe that's why he's been tearing us to shreds."

"Jeffrey Frye is as crooked as they come," Holmes said in a defensive tone. "He deserves to be tracked down and made a spectacle of, which is exactly what I intend to say in my editorials at regular intervals until it happens."

"I wouldn't do that if I were you," Christian warned. "My mother is dead. Perhaps you ought to keep that in mind."

"Oh? And what relevance does her passing have to my work?"

"None, unless you write about my family again. If Jeffrey is ever found and tried, you can report the facts. But if I see anything in your publication that even hints at libel, you'll have me to answer to."

"Is that a threat, my friend?" Holmes asked, smug to the end.

"Damn right," Christian told him. "I have the goods on you, *my friend*. You either leave us the hell alone, or you'll be seeing the true story of your life plastered in the headlines of every blessed publication I can reach. In large part thanks to you, Jeff's disappearance has received broad coverage. Lydia's death is another part of the story. Her love affair with you will be the next, if you're not careful."

"Why would I care? People know what I am. No one's ever called me a saint."

"No one's ever had quite the story to tell that I have. You were jilted, *my friend*. Do you want people to know that? Do you want them to know that you watched you son grow up without giving him a cent, even though you're loaded?"

"You want money?"

"From you?" Christian asked, gaining momentum. "Never. Write me a check to buy me off, and I'll tear it up in your face. What I want from you is respect for my family. I want fairness. I want clean play. I want objectivity. You pride yourself on the quality of the *Sun*? What do you think it will do to that image if the public learns that you took out personal grievances in your stories? It won't be great for credibility, *my friend*."

"No one will believe you. You haven't even any proof that I'm your father."

"Not yet. But I already have a good private investigator on my payroll. It'd be no sweat off his back to start talking with people who knew my mother then."

"You think they'll remember back forty-seven years?"

"Where you're involved, yes."

Holmes raised his chin. "No one saw anything. You won't be able to prove a thing."

"No," Christian said, savoring the victory, "but I'll be able to make a whole lot of noise that will be mighty embarrassing for an old man. You won't look very pretty when I'm done. There's one pertinent fact that you ought to keep in mind, *my friend*. My mother's gone. She made a bargain to hide your identity, and she kept it. I didn't make any such bargain. I wouldn't have interviewed her friends if she'd been alive. I wouldn't have put her through the indignity. But she's gone." Turning, he started down the hill with Laura.

"Smear me," Holmes called, "and you're just as bad as you say I am."

"Smear my family," Christian called back, "and I'll fight fire with fire. I'm your son. I can do it." In that instant, he felt that he could. Whether Lydia would have approved of his threat was questionable; she had loved the man once. But Christian had his family to defend, and that was just what he intended to do. He felt every bit as ruthless, where Gary Holmes was concerned, as Gary Holmes himself had ever been.

THIRTY

L YDIA'S DEATH WAS reported as a human interest story in nearly every major newspaper in the Northeast. Tack thought it was a smart move and made many of the calls himself. He figured that if anything would smoke Jeff out, his mother's death would. Besides, by reviving activity in the case, he had an excuse to return to Northampton.

This time, he didn't even make a pretense of taking a room at the Inn. Daphne's bed was waiting, and he wasn't wasting a minute. She had spent the weekend before with him in Boston, but that had left something to be desired. When he was with her, he thought about having to leave. When he wasn't with her, he thought about what she was doing and whom she was with. He also thought a lot about the conversation she'd had with Laura, nearly every word of which he had heard from the top of the stairs. Parts of it haunted him. Daphne said she loved him, yet she wouldn't leave Northampton. She talked of aching with loneliness, of realizing that she needed more than her career; still, she wouldn't commit herself to him. She talked of unfinished business; he wanted to know what the hell she meant by that. He phoned her every night, but he was sure of her feelings for him only when they were together.

The FBI staked out Laura's house, Lydia's house, and the cemetery. Tack took Daphne to the funeral and looked for anyone lurking on the fringes of the crowd of mourners who might fit Jeff's general description. Weeks before, a police artist had make sketches of ways Jeff might look if he disguised himself. Tack kept those sketches in mind, but he saw no one remotely resembling any of them.

The stakeouts continued for two days following the burial. At that point the FBI called off its men, claiming that the crime didn't warrant the continued expenditure. Tack was furious—not because he didn't see their point, but because he wanted Jeff found. Daphne was hung up on the case. He wanted it solved.

With a little fast talking, he managed to convince his boss to let him stay in Northampton through the end of the week. During that time, when he wasn't with Daphne, he traced and retraced a large circle from Laura's house to Lydia's to the cemetery. Christian's private investigator was doing nearly the same thing, but Tack didn't mind. The investigator was his friend, hired on his recommendation, and though there was a rivalry between them, it was a healthy one. Tack didn't care who nabbed Jeff, as long as the man was nabbed. With two of them making the rounds—three, if he counted Dennis Melrose, who took an occasional turn—they stood a better chance of success.

Jeff didn't show. By Sunday afternoon, Tack had decided to be a psychic in his next life. Mere human skills were getting him nowhere, and he was discouraged. He was expected in Boston on Monday morning. Not only did he have nothing to show for the time he'd spent in Northampton, but he had to face saying goodbye to Daphne again. He wasn't sure how many more times he could do it. Each time was harder than the one before, which was consistent with the way his love was growing. He adored her. He thought she was sexy and smart, and he was sure she adored him back. He wanted to marry her. To hell with five kids; if she'd only have one or two, he'd be happy. He would even be their primary caretaker, if that was what she wanted. It would mean a change of jobs—but if she refused to move to Boston, he'd be changing jobs anyway. He could use his business degree and his experience with the IRS to get a job he could do from home. He could be the perfect house husband, which went to show how the mighty were humbled. From macho male to house husband—it boggled the mind.

He was thinking about that late Sunday afternoon, dozing on and off after making love with Daphne, when the phone rang. Too sated to move, he didn't even open his eyes when she answered it.

"Hello?" she said softly, thinking him asleep. He let her go on thinking it, just to hear that soft, soothing sound. But the next sound was a gasp, then an even softer, "Hold on. Let me move to my office phone."

He opened an eye to see her grab up her robe and go quietly out of the room. Uneasy, he sat up. He wondered why she had gasped if the call was business, why the urgency in her voice, why she was picking up downstairs.

He looked at the phone. He listened to Daphne's footsteps reaching the bottom of the stairs, then the hall. Just after she picked up the receiver in the den, he picked up the one by the bed, keeping his hand over the mouthpiece.

"Are you there?" she asked, still softly.

A male voice, low and defeated, said, "I'm here. I read about it in the paper on Monday. I wanted to call sooner but I didn't know—wasn't sure— couldn't. How did she die, Daph?"

"She had a heart attack. Christian found her, but by then it was too late."

"Did she die instantly?"

"No, but she never regained consciousness. She didn't suffer, Jeff. She died in her sleep."

Tack closed his eyes.

Jeff was silent for so long that Daphne said, "Are you still there?"

"Yes." His breath shuddered. "I take it she was buried beside my father."

"Yes. The minister gave a beautiful eulogy. It was a lovely service."

"I'm sure it was. Laura does a great job arranging things."

"Laura didn't arrange it. Christian did."

Jeff choked. "Ah, the irony of that."

"He's been a godsend—not only to Laura, but to Scott and Debra. They've needed someone. Come back, Jeff. You have to come back."

"They don't need me."

"Come back," she begged.

"You know I can't. We've been through this before."

"But the not knowing isn't fair. We have to go on with our lives, and we can't do that now. There has to be an end to the whole thing. You have to come back."

"I'd only wind up in prison. That would be worse for my family than the not knowing."

"I'd defend you," she argued. She sounded desperate to Tack. "I could make a deal. I could get you off with a fine and probation."

"No, you couldn't," Jeff told her, while Tack nodded in agreement. "There's too much against me."

"You have no record."

"I can't come back."

"Jeff—"

"Are Debra and Scott okay?"

Daphne paused. Tack heard her take a resigned breath. "They're fine, but you owe them an explanation. You owe Laura an explanation. You owe *me* one. You have to come back."

"I can't."

"Please, Jeff."

" 'Bye, Daph."

"Jeff? Don't hang up! Oh, please, Jeff."

But Tack knew, well before the dial tone returned, that Jeff was gone. He hung up the phone himself and sat for a long time on the edge of the bed with his hands clenched on the sheets and his head bowed. Daphne didn't return. He assumed she was in the kitchen recovering from the call, maybe fixing coffee to bring to him as though nothing at all were wrong.

Suddenly furious, he rose, threw on his clothes, then went through the bedroom and the bathroom, stuffing the rest of his things into his bag. When he was done, he went down to the kitchen.

Daphne was standing at the counter, cupping a steaming mug, staring out the window. At the sound of his footsteps, she turned and smiled. "Tack. I was just coming up." His thunderous expression wiped out her smile. "Is something wrong?"

"I'm going home."

"But you said you'd stay for supper."

"I changed my mind. I'm going now."

"Why?" she asked.

He was so angry he couldn't answer at first.

"Tack?" She looked uneasy. "What's wrong?"

"I have been one hell of a Class A fool."

She stared at him for another minute, then wrapped her arms around her middle. In a quiet voice, she said, "You heard me talking."

He nodded. "Every word. I picked up the phone. How long has he been calling you?"

She tightened her arms around herself. "Since New Year's Day. He hasn't called much, no more than three or four times."

"And you didn't tell me."

"There was no point. He won't tell me where he is. He won't tell me what he's doing. He just wants to check in."

"Why with you? Why not with Laura?"

"Laura intimidates him. He doesn't want to get into an argument with her."

"Have you told her that he calls?"

"No. She'd be hurt worse than she already is."

"At least she'd know he was alive. She doesn't even know that for sure now."

"It doesn't matter. He's not coming back."

Tack had heard Jeff say it more than once. But that wasn't what was bothering him most. "Why does he call *you*?"

"Because I'm a friend. He trusts me. He knows I won't tell on him."

She might have said that she was Jeff's lawyer and that lawyer-client privilege was what gave Jeff the assurance he needed. It would have been the simplest argument, the one Tack couldn't have fought. The fact she hadn't made it shook him up and drove him on.

"How does he know? How does he know you won't tell Laura? She's your childhood friend. She's your *best* friend."

"He knows, because he and I talked before he left."

Tack's heart hammered against his ribs. "You knew he was leaving?"

"No."

"Did you know he'd been ripping us off?"

"No. I didn't know any of that. I was as much in the dark as Laura was. But I knew he was unhappy about some things. He confided in me."

"What else did he do?" Tack asked tightly. His body was a drawn wire, every muscle clenched.

"What do you mean?"

"Did he make love to you?"

She swallowed. Her head went back and forth, but not in the definitive headshake Tack wanted. "Tack—"

"Forget it," he said, holding up a hand. "Forget I asked." Curling that hand into a fist, he slammed it against the doorjamb. The pain felt good. "Dammit, Daph, *why?* Why couldn't you have been honest with me? Why couldn't you have told me about Jeff?"

Daphne pressed her fingertips to her lips. Her eyes filled with tears.

He wanted to shut his own against them, but he couldn't. "I love you, goddammit. Why does that have to be so hard? I want to fill the loneliness. Why can't you see that?" He thrust a hand through his hair, leaving it standing on end. "Jesus, I don't believe this. You and Jeff. But I should have seen it coming." All the pieces were suddenly falling into place. "You said there wasn't any *ménage à trois*, but every time you mentioned him there was affection in your voice, and there were times when you knew more about him than Laura did. You didn't want a private investigator getting in on the case." He snorted. "I thought that was because you were impressed by the job I was doing. Wrong, Jones, dead wrong. She thought you were doing such a lousy job you'd never find out it was her."

"No! That's not—"

He cut her off, needing to say it all, to compensate somehow for having been so dense. "It makes sense now—the shock on your face when I told you we knew he was having an affair, then the shock when I said I knew who the woman was. My witness kept saying the woman had great hair, great hair, and Christ, you've got it, just about the same color as DeeAnn Kirkham's." He paused to get hold of his emotions, but that was impossible. His voice shook. "Do you love him?"

She shook her head.

"Then what's his hold?"

"He's a sad person," she managed in a broken voice. "My heart aches for him."

"So much that you'd sacrifice your friendship with Laura, your career, your relationship with *me?* God, I can't take this." He started to turn away. In the next breath he faced her again, uncaring that his feelings were totally exposed. "I sat upstairs holding that phone in my hand, listening to what you were saying, and finally figuring out the puzzle. I felt betrayed and hurt and stupid and sad, and I knew you were the one who'd done all those things to me." He pushed his hand through his hair again. "So I tell myself I don't need that shit.

I don't have to take it. And I pack my things and come down here to tell you that it's over, that I'm out of here for good. Then I take one look at you and my insides melt. After everything, I'm still melting." He was disgusted with himself, but it didn't seem to matter. "It's been that way from the first. It'll probably always be that way. I want to spend the rest of my life with you, Daphne, want it so bad that I was actually ready to give up what I have in Boston and move out here. But I won't do that now. I won't live with you here. Not with the specter of Jeff Frye around."

Again he turned to leave. This time he stopped with a hand on the door and his eyes on the floor. His voice was low and more controlled than before. "I'm going back to Boston now. I don't want you to come, or even call, until you've made a decision. It's either him or me. You can stay here and wait for him to phone and be prepared to defend him if he comes back, or you can give that up and come to Boston and marry me. You have to choose."

"I don't love him!" Daphne cried. "There was never any love."

He kept his eyes down, afraid that if he looked at her he'd lose his resolve. "For the record, I'll forget he called you today. I'll forget he called you other days. No one will ever know. That's putting my job in jeopardy, but I'm willing to do it because I love you." Pushing off from the door, he grabbed his bag and his coat. He walked quickly, trotting down the front steps, half running across the lawn to his car. He backed out of the driveway and drove down the street, and he didn't stop once until he was back in his apartment in Cambridge, when it was too late to take back the words.

You owe them an explanation.

Jeff thought about Daphne's words long and hard. The idea wasn't new to him. From the day he left Northampton, he had known he was being unfair. But life was unfair. People were often locked into circumstances that they neither wanted nor could control. He had broken free of what he felt was a stifling life, and he had done it the only way he could. He regretted that the break hadn't been cleaner.

You owe them an explanation.

For weeks he had been wondering how he could provide one. He had considered writing letters, but there was no way to mail them without disclosing his location, and he couldn't do that. He liked the little niche he had cut out for himself. His cottage was livable, the townspeople accepted him, he was running the diner as Poppy got progressively sicker. And then there was Glorie. Glorie needed him. They weren't lovers. Some day they might be, but for now she was too innocent. With Poppy sick, she needed someone to take care of her, and Jeff was glad to do it. No one had ever depended on him quite the way she did. It was both a responsibility and a treasure.

You owe them an explanation.

His mother's death had hit him hard, perhaps harder than anything else since he left. Lydia had loved him. She had devoted herself to him in ways she hadn't done for anyone else, and if at times he wished that hadn't been so, she had always meant well. It occurred to him that, with her death, one loose end had been tied up. It also occurred to him, after too many sleepless nights, that he had to tie up a few more. The threat of prosecution would always hang over his head, but he could live with that. What he couldn't live with was the knowledge that his children would suffer forever for what he'd done. Daphne was right. There had to be an end to it somewhere.

Christian sat in the den watching the last of the late news. Laura was curled against him, asleep, and he was nearly asleep himself. He was tired. Lydia's death had deeply affected him, and on top of that he had Gary Holmes's revelation to deal with. He was slowly coming to terms with both, one day better than the last, and the progress was welcome. April was coming fast. He had to be ready to get back to work. He had put off returning to Vermont too long, but he had commitments there that had to be met.

The problem was that he had commitments here too, unspoken ones that meant more to him than the others. He was losing his share of sleep agonizing over how he could reconcile the two.

His first thought when the phone rang was that Laura would be upset with Debra if one of her friends called so late. His second thought, coming fast on the first, was that he could spare both of them that upset. His third thought, coming even faster, was that he didn't want Laura waked by another ring. Slipping out from under her, he caught the receiver up just in time.

"Hello?" he said softly.

The greeting was met by silence. Assuming his hunch had been right about the call being for Debra, he said, still softly, "It's a little late. Can she see you in school tomorrow?"

When there was still no response, he nearly hung up. Something stopped him. He had an odd feeling. "Hello?" The feeling persisted, even grew stronger. "Jeff?"

"I didn't know you'd be staying at the house." The voice was just as Christian remembered it—quiet, even vaguely defensive—but it pleased Christian as it never had before.

"Jeff, my God, we've been worried. Are you all right?"

"I'm fine. I want to visit Mom's grave. Are they watching for me there?"

"Not any more."

"Are you sure?"

"They told us they canceled the surveillance."

"Will you meet me there?"

"Name the time."

"Twenty minutes."

"From now?" Christian was stunned. "Are you that close to us?"

"Not usually. I just got here. Don't bring anyone, Christian."

"I'm bringing Laura. You owe her this."

"She won't be able to convince me to come back."

"She won't try. But she has a right to talk to you." For purely selfish reasons, Christian wanted Laura to have that chance. He didn't know what Jeff would say, didn't know if Laura would feel better or worse afterward, but it was worth a shot. His own future was at stake.

"Twenty minutes," Jeff repeated, and hung up the phone.

* * *

Exactly twenty minutes later, Christian parked the Wagoneer at the bottom of the knoll. Laura's heart was beating wildly and had been since Christian had waked her and told her about the call. She opened the door and climbed out, then waited for Christian to join her before starting up the hill.

"Thank God there's a moon," she whispered and hugged her coat tightly to her. "I've never been to a cemetery at night." But there was no question why Jeff had chosen this spot. He wanted to be near Lydia. She had always been his champion.

Taking Laura's hand, Christian led her up the hill. They were nearing the spot where the Frye headstone stood when a dark figure emerged from behind a tree. Laura stopped. When Jeff slowly approached, she stared.

He looked so different, so dark. The overcoat he wore was the only thing she recognized. His jeans were slim and worn, not the designer variety he had always favored, and his work boots were scuffed in ways he never would have let work boots be—if he'd ever had cause to own them before, which he hadn't. Mostly, though, what was different about him was his face. His hair had grown full, looking darker than she remembered, and that darkness extended to his jaw and upper lip in a close-cropped beard.

He looked strikingly like the Christian of years before, which was remarkable, since Laura had never seen much resemblance between the brothers. It was as though Jeff had become the renegade that Christian had always been. But where Christian's nonconformity excited her, Jeff's didn't. He was a stranger to her. They had been married for twenty years; he had been gone for almost four months; she had imagined him dead more than once and was relieved that he wasn't. Still, she didn't make a move toward him. She wasn't driven to touch him. She didn't know the man he had become.

"Jeff," Christian said with a nod of greeting.

"Thanks for coming," Jeff said. Moonlight glinted off his glasses when he turned to Laura.

"You're looking good, Jeff."

"So are you. How have you been?"

She thought of a dozen answers, any of which might express her anger and the sense of betrayal she still felt. But he had called, and come, and she was grateful for that. So she said simply, "I've been okay."

He nodded, then looked down at Lydia's grave. "I'm sorry about this. I'm sure I contributed to it."

Laura remained silent. She wasn't about to absolve him of the guilt he was feeling.

"How did you find out?" Christian asked.

"There was an article in the paper."

"What paper?"

Jeff met his gaze. "If I told you that, the game would be over."

"It's not a game," Laura said before she could stop herself, and then suddenly she didn't want to. The agony of the past months spilled out. "You've put us through hell. We were frantic when you first disappeared. We thought you'd been hurt or killed. Then the government came forward with its charges, our money was frozen, the papers started in—did you read about Scott? Do you know what he went through?"

"Yes."

"Do you realize that the only reason that happened was because of the accusations against you?"

"Yes."

Laura had never been a violent person, but at that moment she wanted to hit him, and hit him again and again, for all the pain he had caused them. "Why, Jeff?" she cried. "Why did you do all those things? What was so wrong that you had to tear our life apart that way?"

He was slow in answering. In the March moonlight, his features were sad. "I wanted . . . needed . . . to do something. I was tired of following. I wanted to lead."

"By stealing?"

He flinched, but the movement was over and done in an instant. "It was a challenge. When it worked, I felt a rush. There was another rush when I found out all the things I could do with the money. When you have money, people see you. They pay attention to you. You matter. I felt good about the house and the restaurant and the car."

"What about the condo?" Laura asked.

Jeff glanced at Lydia's grave again, looking for a minute like a guilty little boy.

"Of all of it," Laura told him, "that hurt the most. I tried to be a good wife. I tried to be an *appealing* wife. Was it me? Or was it you?"

Without looking up, Jeff said, "There was nothing wrong with you. You just weren't right for me. You were too good. You had too many answers. Next to you, I felt diminished."

"I tried not to let that happen."

"I know, and that made it worse. You thought you were fooling everyone, but you weren't. People knew the truth. I knew the truth. It was humiliating."

"So you wanted to humiliate me back?"

"No, that wasn't it. All I wanted was to feel more like a man."

"And did you?"

He hesitated for only a minute. "Yes."

The admission hurt more than Laura had thought it would. "You should have asked for a divorce. I would rather you had done that than have an affair behind my back."

"You wouldn't have given me a divorce," he argued. "You thought our marriage was great. You thought our *lives* were great. If I had told you I was unhappy, you would have set out to make me happy. You would have been determined to fix things. You would have been sure you could make things right. No problem's too great for you, Laura. No hurdle's too high. You're a supremely competent woman. That's tough on us mere mortals."

"I'm a mere mortal too," Laura said, feeling very much so just then. "I have my faults. One of them happens to be blindness. I know that now. I didn't see that you were bothered. But if you'd told me, I might have changed."

He was shaking his head before she finished. "You are who you are. If you had changed to accommodate me, you would have been the one diminished, and that wouldn't have been right either. The truth is, we were a bad match."

"We had a solid marriage for twenty years," Laura argued. She had worked hard to make that so and wasn't ready to call her efforts a waste.

"Solid doesn't mean healthy. I wasn't any better for you than you were for me. You needed someone stronger, someone like Christian." He looked at his brother. "You knew her before me. You should have grabbed her."

"I know," Christian said.

"Why didn't you?"

"I wasn't ready to settle down."

"Are you now?"

"Yes. It's about time, don't you think?"

"Do you want her?"

Laura raised a hand. "Uh, excuse me, Jeff, but whether or not he wants me is none of your affair."

"It is. I'll feel better about disappearing again if I know you're with him."

"You won't consider staying?" Christian asked.

Jeff shook his head.

Christian tried again. "Where will you go?"

"I have a place."

"What will you do?"

"You wouldn't believe me if I told you."

"Try me."

But Jeff simply shook his head.

"What about the charges against you?" Laura asked.

"They'll stay pending for a while. Nothing will happen if I'm never found."

"They'll keep your money frozen."

"But you have your share. That should help."

Laura wondered how he'd known about the court decision. To her knowledge, it hadn't been in the papers. "What about Debra and Scott?"

"I miss them."

"But you won't come back."

"I can't."

She pointed an angry finger back in the direction of the house, where Debra was sound asleep, unaware that Laura had left. "Is that what I tell them—just that you can't? Scott's angry and Debra's hurt. They don't understand how a father who supposedly loves his children can abandon them the way you did."

Jeff took a deep breath. He blew it out in a puff of white and looked off into the distance. He pursed his lips and thought for a minute, then said, "If I'd known what was going to happen, I might have made different choices. But I now have to live with what is. The way I see it, coming back will only make things worse."

"Where will you be?"

He smiled sadly and shook his head.

"What if one of the kids gets sick? How will I contact you?"

"You won't."

"Not at all?" It was difficult to think of never seeing him again, even after spending four months apart, even after all he'd done. She didn't love him now. Still, he was the father of her children. She didn't see how one could be so close to a person for so long and not feel twinges at parting.

"Come on, Laura," he chided, "don't sound so unhappy. You don't need me. You never did."

"But I loved you." It had never been the wildly passionate kind of love that she felt for Christian, the kind of love that neither time, distance, nor adversity had been able to kill. It had been a sedate, conscious affection. Distance and adversity had quickly done it in.

"You never needed me," he repeated. "You'll do fine."

"Jeff—"

"I'm going now." But he had barely taken a step when Christian came forward and put a hand on his arm.

"If you ever need anything, if you're ever in trouble, wherever you are, you know where I'll be."

Jeff stared at him for a minute, then nodded. His eyes shot past them, down the knoll. "Shit, I told you to come alone."

Laura turned to see a pair of headlights on the road near the Wagoneer.

Christian, too, was looking down the hill. "We did come alone. If that's a cop car, it's here by coincidence." He gave Jeff a shove. "Get going. We'll cover for you."

Jeff ran.

Laura called his name once, then pressed a hand to her mouth when his dark figure disappeared into the night.

Christian drew her close. "He'll be fine. He'll make it."

Instinctively she knew that she would never see him again, knew that the door was finally closing on that part of her life. In the emotion of the moment, the four months of pain he had caused slipped to the back of her mind. She remembered the good times of the months and years before, and she worried. She couldn't imagine where Jeff was going or what he would do. He had never lived alone before. She feared for him.

Maddie would have said that she feared for herself, feared that something would be missing from her life without Jeff leaning heavily on her. She didn't think that was so. She much preferred Christian's strength. It was nice to lean on someone once in a while. It was nice to *have* someone to lean on, someone as able as Christian.

Still, where Jeff was concerned, old habits died hard. "Maybe he should have stayed," she whispered against Christian's jacket.

"He couldn't."

"But he's totally alone now."

"He's been alone for four months, and he's survived. It's about time he took care of himself, don't you think?"

Before she could answer, the beam of a flashlight hit them. Seconds later, a policeman approached. Squinting into the light, Laura recognized the man as one who occasionally stopped by Cherries for a break when he was on patrol. "Kind of late to be here, folks. Everything okay?"

"Fine, officer," Christian said in a purposefully slow voice. He still had his arms around Laura. "Mrs. Frye was missing my mother and got an urge to take a ride up here."

"Tough, losing someone like that. I didn't know her myself, but from what I hear she was a nice person."

Christian gave a leisurely shrug. He spoke as though it were high noon and he had all the time in the world. "Death isn't picky. It takes everyone sooner or later."

"Guess so," the officer said. Laura held her breath when he swung the beam of the flashlight in a wide, searching arc. But he seemed satisfied that no one else was about. "Well, I won't intrude on you any longer. Mourning's a private thing."

"We won't be long."

"Take your time. I just wanted to be sure there wasn't a problem." After touching the flashlight to the tip of his cap, he lowered the beam and started back down the hill.

Holding very still against Christian's chest, Laura whispered, "Do you think he had enough time to get away?"

"I think so."

"Will he think we betrayed him?"

"Does it matter?"

"Yes. I wouldn't betray him."

"He betrayed you."

Laura lifted her head and met his gaze. "Just because Jeff hurt me doesn't mean I have to hurt him back."

"Do you love him?"

"No."

"What did you feel when you saw him?"

"Awkwardness. Concern. Pity."

"You kept asking him to come back. Was that for your sake?"

"No. For Scott and Debra. I've already filed for divorce, Christian. You know that." She was working through a local lawyer who specialized in quickies. Daphne had given her the name, but even if Daphne had done that kind of work herself, Laura wouldn't have used her. Something had changed in their relationship. Laura knew it had to do with Jeff. "Even if he came back, I wouldn't live with him. I couldn't. The love is gone."

She hadn't been aware of the tension in Christian until it faded away. In the moonlight, he smiled, then kissed her gently. "It's spooky up here," he whispered. "Wanna go home?"

She nodded. Home sounded just right.

THIRTY-ONE

I T RAINED FOR THREE DAYS after the meeting at the cemetery, and during that time Laura thought a lot about Jeff. She had said goodbye to him that night. Now, in remembering all they had shared in the course of twenty years, she was saying goodbye to their marriage. Maddie would have called it a period of mourning, and Laura saw it as that and more. So did Christian, who returned to Vermont for several days to give her the room she needed.

She remembered the good times, just as she was supposed to. But she also remembered the bad. She hadn't identified them as such at the time, because she had refused to admit negatives into her life, but they were there—times when she and Jeff had argued, times when he had been angry at the children or frustrated with his work. Looking back, she didn't know how she could have missed them. It scared her that she had, because Christian was waiting for her on the horizon, and she wanted to be good for him. She wasn't sure she trusted her ability to do that.

She was still feeling unsure of herself on Friday morning when the police showed up at her door to tell her that Jeff's Porsche had been found in a gorge off Route 91 in Vermont. The car had been half submerged in the Connecticut River, which was running high because of the rain, and because of the rain it hadn't been spotted for what the Vermont police estimated to have been at least two days.

Aside from his wallet, which contained his license, credit cards, and a smattering of small bills, there was no sign of Jeff. The car had been badly battered in its long tumble against the rocks, but the driver's door was ajar. On the assumption that Jeff had managed to climb out, the police were searching the river and the nearby woods.

Laura was stunned. She had done much of her own grieving, but the children hadn't. And there were suddenly new issues to consider. She wondered whether the crash had been an accident or a suicide attempt. She wondered whether it had occurred the same night as their meeting or another. She wondered whether she might have prevented it somehow.

Haunted by that thought, she quickly called Christian, who returned in time to meet Scott at the airport. She broke the news to Debra the minute she came home from school. She called Maddie at work, to alert her before the evening news went on, and called Gretchen, to alert her before Maddie did. She called Elise, who promised to call DeeAnn. And she called Daphne, who was over in a flash looking pale as could be.

The vigil that began then was different from the one in December. That one had been wide open, a vigil that wasn't really a vigil, since Laura didn't know whether anything had happened to Jeff at all. This vigil was more pointed. Jeff had been in an accident. Those who gathered waited to hear if he—or his body—had been found.

This vigil was different, too, in that friends began stopping by as they hadn't done in months. The media carried the story—the *Sun* with a total absence of editorial comment—and after the negative publicity that had preceded it, the news seemed welcome to many. Death was universally tragic, more acceptable than crime. Laura understood that, as people who had kept their distance now came around to express their support. Had she been a vengeful sort, she would have turned them away. After all, if they hadn't stood by her when things were tough, what good were they? But she wasn't vengeful—which wasn't to say that she forgave. She knew who her real friends were now. She wasn't forgetting it quickly.

For four full days, search teams scoured the area. By the start of the fifth, they abandoned the effort. All signs pointed to the probability that Jeff had escaped the car with some degree of injury and then either drowned in the rushing water or died in the woods. Laura was bluntly told that a body might never be found.

For another week after the search was called off, she waited. While Elise and DeeAnn saw to Cherries, she stayed close to the house. It wasn't so much that she expected a call to come—she suspected that the new Jeff would crawl to the road and hitch a ride to the Canadian border before he would turn himself in—but she wanted to spend time with Debra and Scott and with Christian. She was feeling shaken. She wanted to be with the people who meant the most to her.

Finally, for Debra and Scott's sakes more than her own, Laura acknowledged that Jeff was dead. The police had already done so. So had Maddie. So had everyone at the restaurant. Daphne hadn't said anything, but she had been quiet of late. Something was bothering her, Laura knew, and though she had an idea what it was, she refused to bring up the subject herself.

With no body to be had, there could be no burial. After talking with Christian, Laura decided on a memorial service—again for Debra and Scott's sakes. They had a right to know that their father was remembered in a positive way now that he was gone.

The service was held in a small chapel, conducted by the same minister who had been so kind in his words about Lydia. Every bench was filled, and this time Laura didn't care in the least whether those present were true friends or not. She wanted Debra and Scott to see the crowds of people their father had touched in some way during his life.

Many of those people dropped by the house after the service to express their condolences to Laura. Daphne stayed until most of the others had left. Then she approached Laura and, looking timid in a way Laura had never seen her before, said in a nearly inaudible voice, "Can we talk for a minute?"

Laura sensed what was coming. She didn't know if she was up for it, but she supposed there wouldn't be a better time. Daphne was clearly suffering, and regardless of the wrongs she'd done, Laura felt badly. So she led the way up the stairs to the master bedroom, where in the past the two had had many a heart-to-heart talk.

The instant the door was closed, Daphne turned to her. "I'm leaving Northampton, Laura. I'm resigning my partnership and putting the house on the market."

Unprepared for quite those words, Laura felt an immediate sadness. She and Daphne had lived close to each other for years. The thought that she was leaving, even in spite of everything, unsettled Laura. "Where are you going?"

"Boston."

Laura was puzzled. "I haven't seen Tack around much. I thought it had ended between you two. He wasn't at the service today. Christian was surprised."

Daphne looked away and frowned. "It's my fault he wasn't here. He was furious about something that happened shortly after Lydia's death. He left town then and swore he wouldn't be back. I guess he meant it."

Laura knew Daphne was hurting. She knew how much Tack meant to her. Daphne wasn't one to fall in and out of love with ease. "Christian likes him a lot."

"So do I."

"Will you marry him?"

"If he still wants me."

"You don't know if he does? You'd give up everything here, without knowing it?"

Daphne studied the window, where the sun had broken through the April clouds. "I have to," she whispered. "I need a fresh start, whether it's with Tack or without him. There are ghosts that haunt me here. I have to get away."

She looked so miserable that Laura started toward her. "Oh, Daph—"

But Daphne skirted her and went to the window. The sun cast a frail halo around her sleekly knotted hair. With her back to Laura, she started to speak. "I haven't always been the best friend to you. I did something horrible."

Laura's heart sank. From the first time she had begun suspecting this, she had desperately wanted to be wrong. Realizing that she wasn't was heartbreaking. "I know."

Daphne bowed her head. "I figured you did. That day when you came over and found me with Tack, I felt so awful, so guilty. I knew what I'd done, and it had nothing to do with Tack. Your mother would have said it was my subconscious talking. I guess it was. I had bottled everything up for a long time and it all kind of spilled out."

"Not all," Laura said. There were things she had wondered about often in the past few weeks. "I never suspected anything. I never *saw* anything. How did it happen? When?"

Daphne raised her head and braced a hand on the window. She was a somber figure in her slim black dress, and the glint of sun off her hair turned eerie. In a voice that was low and filled with regret, she said, "He used to wait for you at the restaurant. You'd be out in the kitchen, or in your office going over the receipts, and he'd be at the bar. He could drink more than you thought, Laura. I never saw him drunk, but there were times when he was loose enough to say more than he should have. He was lonely. So was I. We had a lot else in common, too—people we knew, places we'd been. I started looking forward to seeing him there, and I guess he felt the same. Then he said he wanted me to see the condo he'd bought, and I was flattered." Her voice fell, as though weighed down by shame. "I didn't plan on anything happening. I went because it was something to do with someone I liked at a time when my only other alternative was being home all alone. It hadn't occurred to me that he had bought it with me in mind."

Laura sank down on the bench that Jeff had used morning and night to lace and unlace his shoes. She ran a hand along the polished wood. "He never did tell me about the condo."

"I kept asking him to. I kept telling him it was an investment, that he could rent it out and get tax benefits from it. I was bothered about going there."

Laura clutched the wood. "But you did it, you did it." Her head came up. "Didn't you think of me? Didn't you think I'd be hurt?"

"All the time," Daphne cried, turning to her. "I felt guilty as sin, but once it started, it was hard to stop. I didn't love him, but he cared about me."

"So did I!"

"Differently, Laura, differently."

"And that excuses it?"

"No. Nothing excuses it. That's why I'm giving up everything I have here, and I'm doing it whether Tack wants me or not. I don't deserve to stay around any longer."

Laura wanted to argue with that. After all, Daphne had loaned her money when she had been in dire need, and though she had been repaid there was the matter of Scott's defense, for which she refused to submit so much as a bill. She had been a good friend in both of those instances, and in many others over the years. Still, there was Jeff. Laura knew that whenever she saw Daphne she would remember that betrayal. It was already happening. Since that night at Daphne's house, when Laura had begun to suspect the truth, she had been feeling the pain.

That pain spilled out. "What you did to me was cruel. If I'd found out about it at the time, I would have been devastated. I can almost accept it now, because even before Jeff died I knew that our relationship had been flawed, but what about DeeAnn? You let her take the rap for you. How could you do that, Daph?" Laura had a horrid thought. "Or was it planned that way?"

Daphne was quick to shake her head. "It just happened. Tack had promised me he wouldn't tell you that Jeff had been seen with a woman. Then his witness made an identification, and before I knew it he was in your office fingering DeeAnn. She had the reputation and the looks."

"Did she know what was going on between you and Jeff?"

"I didn't tell her, but she knew that Jeff and I spent hours talking at the bar. She'd seen us there a lot. When Tack broke the news in your office that day, she must have made the connection."

"But she didn't speak up." Laura had to admire the woman. "She was a good friend to you, Daphne."

"And to you. She knew how close you and I were. She felt you would be less hurt by thinking she was the one than by learning it was me."

"What if I'd fired her?"

"I would have spoken up. I think." Daphne averted her eyes. "Tack was there. I was already involved with him. I didn't want him to know."

"But he knows now," Laura said, suddenly understanding what their fight must have been about. "Can he live with it?"

"He said he could. Anyway, Jeff's gone."

Laura nodded. Straightening her arms on the edge of the bench, she sagged between her raised shoulders. "Oh, Daph," she whispered. "I wish I understood. Not the part with Jeff. The part with me. Do I invite betrayal? Is it because I see the good before the bad? Should I be doing it the other way around? Should I be assuming that everyone I know will stab me in the back, given the chance?"

"No," Daphne said quickly and came to sit beside her. "No, no, no." She looked like she wanted to touch her but didn't dare. "Don't assume that. It'll ruin who you are."

"But I'm being ruined anyway."

Daphne shook her head. "Just awakened. You've been naïve, but that's not so bad, because you've been happy. You've been *happy*, Laura. Now you have Christian and you'll be happier. He's so good for you." She faltered. "I think he knew about me. There was always something about the way he approached me, a wariness. For years, we were the two singles at your family events, but we were never attracted to each other in the least. I think he distrusted the kind of woman I am." She seemed to wilt. "He's a good judge of character."

"Oh, Daph," Laura whispered again. "None of this should have happened. You were always my best friend. I'll miss you."

Tears came to Daphne's eyes. "You'll miss who I was," she whispered back, "not who I am. I'm sorry, Laura. You're such a special person. I didn't set out to hurt you. I want you to know that."

Laura knew it. She may have been a fool for not seeing what was right in front of her nose, but there had been too many good things that had come before that to label her friendship with Daphne a fraud. She would remember the good things, she knew.

There was a light knock on the door, followed by the appearance of Christian's head. "Sorry, I'll come back."

"Don't go," Daphne said and rose from the bench. "I'm leaving now." She looked down at Laura, reached out to touch her shoulder, but withdrew the hand before it made contact.

Laura caught it. Using it as a lever, she stood and gave Daphne a quick, tight hug. Then she stepped back. "Be happy, Daph," she said, her throat tight. "I wish you only the best."

Daphne dashed a trickle of tears from her cheek and smiled. "You would." Her voice softened. "But I do love you for it." Her eyes filled again, but before the tears could overflow, she left the room.

Laura lowered herself to the bench once again, straightened her arms, and began to rock back and forth. When Christian hunkered down before her, she raised her eyes to his.

"It hurts."

He tucked an auburn wave behind her ear. "I know."

"She was such a good friend once."

"She still is. She loves you. She was desperate and made a mistake, but she'll suffer for it for the rest of her life."

"I hope not. No one should have to suffer that way."

"People do. It can't be helped."

"She's moving to Boston."

"I figured she would. Tack is crazy about her. He'll keep her human—"

"Christian."

"Soften her up, I mean," he said. "Sensitize her. Maybe even keep her barefoot and pregnant."

Unable to resist despite the aching inside her, Laura smiled. "You're bad."

"You're right. Wanna keep *me* human?" Slipping onto the bench, he curved an arm around her and pulled her close. "Marry me, Laura."

It was the first time he'd asked. With no warning at all, Laura burst into tears.

"Hey," he said, holding her tight to his side, "I know it's a lousy request. I'm kinda time-worn and not much of a bargain, but I'd promise to love, honor, and obey."

"Oh, Christian," she sobbed.

"That bad, eh?" He looked around and scowled. "Where's a goddam tissue?"

She pulled one from her pocket and pressed it to her nose. Gradually her tears slowed. She wiped her eyes, took a shaky breath, let it out in a tremulous sigh.

"Well?" Christian asked.

"Oh, God," she whispered.

"What does that mean?"

"I feel so inadequate."

"Inadequate how?"

"I've made so many mistakes."

"Join the club."

"I mean it. I was a lousy wife, and I didn't even know it."

"You were a good wife, too good a one. If that's the worst of your crimes—"

"I can't get along with my mother, I'm blind to my friends' problems, and I don't listen to my kids."

"No sweat. I can live with all that."

She drew away from him. "You're not taking me seriously, Christian."

"Should I? Should I be disappointed that you're not perfect? Well, I'm not disappointed, Laura. I don't want a goddess for a wife. I want a woman who's fallible, just like me."

"I'll let you down."

"You couldn't do that."

"I'll get so involved with my business that I won't see your needs until you'd been driven to someone else."

"Would you do that? Honestly? Think about it. Would you be so preoccupied that you didn't notice I was there?" He put a finger to her mouth. "Don't speak. Think about it first."

She hadn't done that for more than a few seconds when she realized the absurdity of what she had said. Christian wasn't a man to be forgotten. He wasn't a man to be overlooked. He was a strong presence, a decisive one. He wasn't afraid to disagree with her, or to drive her off to Vermont without her permission, or to take command of a situation, as he had when he'd first shown up in Northampton. He wasn't Jeff. He wouldn't be walked over. He would protect her from herself.

A wave of peacefulness swept through her. Wrapping her arms around Christian, she laid her head on his shoulder and closed her eyes. She could take care of herself and everyone around her. She had spent years proving that. But it was nice to be taken care of once in a while. Very nice.

The waves lapped the shore with unusual calm. Even the boulders seemed less formidable, a cushion for the occasional breaker that hit them. At the horizon, the sky was the deepest of blues, a perfect foil for the glitter of the late-afternoon sun on the surf.

High on the bluff, Evan closed the book of poems from which he'd been reading. "Feel better?" he asked Glorie, who sat beside him. They had buried Poppy that morning, and her limitations weren't so great that she didn't understand what death meant. Evan doubted she had understood much of Robert Frost, but if the gentleness of the words and their soft cadence had soothed her, that was enough.

"I'll miss him," she whimpered.

He rubbed her back. "So will I." He had liked the man, if for no other reason than his devotion to Glorie.

"He took good care of me."

"I'll do that now. You don't have to worry about a thing."

"What if you leave?"

"I won't leave."

"Promise?"

"I promise." He was content with the life he had here. It was modest but meaningful. Glorie needed him. She would always need him. It was a responsibility he welcomed.

Filling his lungs with the fresh ocean air, he savored the freedom he felt. The Porsche was gone, along with Jeffrey Frye, and, yes, there was sadness in that. He had irrevocably separated himself from his past, would never see his children again, and the sadness of that would linger. But there was also pride. He had tied up loose ends, had given Laura and the children the means to forget him and move on. It had been the only decent thing to do.

"Want to go to a movie?" he asked. Some people would have thought that an inappropriate thing to do on the day of a burial. But he and Glorie weren't some people.

Glorie's face lit up. "Can we?"

"If we want to, we can."

"I do," she said and scrambled to her feet. With the innocence of a child blotting out the past, she led Evan over the rocks and between the scrub pines to where his pickup waited to take them off the bluff.

WITHIN REACH

ONE

ONE MINUTE THERE WAS NOTHING but a cloud of fog before him; the next she was there, materialized from the mist. Stunned, Michael Buchanan came to an abrupt halt. He hadn't expected to encounter anyone on the beach at such an inhospitable time of year, much less as striking a figure as the one before him.

She was a vision of loneliness standing there, with the March wind tucking her long skirt around her legs, whipping strands of hair across her cheeks. As he watched, she pressed her pocketed hands closer to her body, enveloping herself more snugly within the oversized jacket she wore.

He took several steps forward and, still unnoticed, stared. She was lovely. Smooth of skin and with a delicately sculpted profile, she was young enough, old enough, just right. And she was slender. Even the protective folds of her clothing, whose mist-softened hues of hunter green and plum contrasted smartly with her fair skin and the sandy hair that escaped the confines of her stylish wool cloche, couldn't hide that fact.

In her solitariness she was regal; at least that was what he fantasized as he stood, spellbound, studying her. She bore the weight of the world on her shoulders, while at the same time she remained apart, isolated from the masses. Even the fog kept its distance, as though in awe.

Regal . . . stoic . . . brave . . . each thought came to him through the mist, then another. Vulnerable. Body braced against the cold, she shivered from time to time, but she didn't move either to seek warmth or to escape the threat of the pounding surf. She'd fallen victim to the sea, he knew, and he felt an even greater affinity for her. He wondered who she was, this woman who stood alone, tall yet humbled, seeking strength from within. Bidden by a curiosity that went beyond the purely male, he tugged his collar higher and started slowly forward.

Eyes downcast, she didn't see him at first. He paused, hesitant to intrude on whatever thoughts possessed her, but moved on again when his own need nagged. When he came to a halt several feet from her, her head snapped up. With a quick step back, she pressed a hand to her heart.

"You startled me!" Her voice was little more than a ragged whisper above the thunder of the tide.

Michael drew in a sharp breath when he found himself looking into the most stunning violet eyes he had ever seen. It took him a minute to find his tongue.

"I'm sorry. I didn't mean to frighten you. It's just that you looked so alone."

For an instant he thought she was going to cry. Her eyes widened and tears gathered on her lower lids. He saw it then, the haunted cast that fear had momentarily overshadowed, and he wondered what dark thoughts had upset her so. Then they were gone—the torment, the tears—replaced by a composure that suggested he had simply imagined the cracks.

"My fault," she said in a voice whose tremor might well have been caused by wind. "I was miles away." She gave him a sheepish half-smile by way of apology, and he felt something new and special curl up and glow inside him.

"I hope it was somewhere exotic."

"Exotic? No. Not exactly."

"Exciting, at least?"

She searched his face, then shook her head quickly, almost as if in guilt at her admission.

"Your secret's safe with me," he teased on a note of conspiracy that ended in a smile, "as long as you're back here now."

"I am." Her whisper was carried away by the wind, but she continued to stare at him. When she finally spoke again, she sounded confused. "I'm not even sure what happened. One minute I was here, and then . . ."

"The ocean has a way of doing that. Of transporting you from one place to another." Tucking his hands in his pockets, he tore his eyes from hers and gazed toward the waves. "It's very sneaky, actually. First you're lured by the sense of freedom of the open beach and the fresh salt air. Before long—you barely know it's happened—your pulse has adjusted to the rhythm of the surf." He looked down at her and was so taken with her rapt expression that his voice thickened. "Some people call it hypnotic, like staring into a flickering fire." He cleared his throat. "I think it's something more. In no time you're caught, laid open, exposed. Nature here is raw and utterly truthful and commands no less from those of us who dare intrude." His voice lowered as he studied the delicate features before him. "Falling victim to the sea means baring one's soul. It can be painful."

For a minute they simply looked at one another. "I'd never thought of it that way," she said at last.

"Neither had I, until it had happened too many times to ignore."

"You've felt the pain?" she asked in a small, surprised voice.

"Many times. Shouldn't I?"

"I don't know. You look so strong."

Dropping his head back, he took a deep breath. "I like to think I am, but that doesn't mean I never suffer. I think strength comes from facing pain, from dealing with it. It's either that or crumble. Pain is part and parcel of being human.''

Her expression grew all the more solemn, her voice soft in a wistful way. "I sometimes wonder. It seems . . . it seems . . .'' When her gaze flicked to his then darted away, he coaxed her gently.

"Go on.''

She hesitated for a moment longer, and there was a note of despair in her voice when she spoke. "It seems that some people are immune to it.''

"Immune to pain? No,'' he mused, "I doubt that. There are those who choose to deny it. They're the ones who'd never be caught dead alone with themselves in a room, much less on a deserted expanse of beach.'' He winked. "It takes a pretty brave person to expose himself this way.''

She gave a lopsided smile. "Either that or a dumb one.'' Then she eyed him cautiously. "Tell me. After this . . . this baring of the soul takes place, what happens?''

"You go home and cry.''

"I'm serious. Does the sea provide answers?''

"Sometimes. Once I stood here in my agony and this little bottle floated ashore with a message inside—'' He was interrupted by the audible breath she took. When she simply held it without speaking, though, he prodded. "What's wrong?''

She exhaled slowly. "Your name. I want to scold, but I don't know your name.'' Then she murmured more to herself than to him, "Isn't that odd?''

Michael understood. There was a warm familiarity about this woman. If he believed in reincarnation, he might have suspected he had known her in another life. Grateful, if that had indeed been the case, that he'd been given a second chance, he held out his hand. "Michael Buchanan.'' Without breaking eye contact, he tossed his head back in the direction from which he'd come. "I live down the beach.'' He raised a brow. "And you?''

She hesitated for just a minute before carefully putting her hand in his. "Danica. Danica Lindsay.'' As he'd done, she flicked her head, but in the opposite direction. "That's my house.''

Instinctively he raised his free hand to seal hers between his palms. When her downward glance drew his attention to the move, he was as surprised as she.

"Your fingers are cold,'' he explained. Though his answer had been an impromptu one, it was apt. He rubbed her hand between his, back and forth, stimulating her circulation and his own. Her fingers were slender, pliant, fitting.

She actually blushed. "I didn't expect it'd still be winter here. It's much milder at home.''

"Home?''

"Boston.''

"Ah, Boston,'' he drawled, "the birthplace of liberty.''

"So they say.''

"You don't sound convinced.''

She merely shrugged and looked out at the water as she slid her hand from his grasp and tucked it back into her pocket. He'd been right about the ocean, she decided. It had seen through her facade, making her look at things she would rather have ignored. And, yes, he had been right about something else; some people simply refused to acknowledge the presence of pain, which was why she was here, alone, today. Was she free? Only in the most literal of senses.

"Liberty is relative, I suppose," she commented. But before Michael had a chance to pursue the matter, she tipped up her chin and put on a pert smile. "So. You're a neighbor. Mrs. Sylvester warned me there were some pretty important people up here."

She studied the man before her. He wore a sheepskin jacket, well-worn cords and hiking boots whose laces were undone. He was tall—she guessed him to be a good six-three to her own respectable five-eight—and sported the faint shadow of a beard, which might have given him a roguish look had it not been for the extreme gentleness of his features. Then, too, there was the healthy rumple of his hair, which was a shade of blond not unlike her own. Dirty blond, they always called it, which had never failed to annoy her as a child, since she washed her hair every night.

"You don't look important," she teased.

His lips twitched. "How is an important man supposed to look?"

"Oh, he wears a three-piece suit and wing-tipped shoes—"

"On the beach?"

"No. Okay. Make that flannel slacks, a designer sweater and loafers, perhaps with a cashmere topcoat in this kind of weather. He's fresh-shaven all the time—" she drew out her words in mockery "—and his hair is perfectly groomed."

"In this wind? He must use hair spray."

She smiled. "He's been known to."

"Sorry, I don't fit that mold, but, then," he chided, "you knew that all along. Does that mean I'm a nobody?"

"Oh, no. It means you're very refreshing and, in that sense, very definitely a somebody." She had never spoken truer words. At the moment she'd had it with three-piece suits, wing-tipped shoes, flannel, cashmere and hair spray.

"Ahhhh. That's a relief." Then he thought. "Were you talking about Mrs. Sylvester, as in Judy, the realtor?" When Danica nodded, his pleasure grew. "I assumed you were visiting the Duncans. You mean to say they've sold?" Again she nodded. "And you've bought their house?" Another nod. "That's great!"

"I'm not so sure right about now," she grumbled. "There've been workmen all over the place for a month. I'm beginning to think they'll never finish."

"Tell me about it," Michael mused, remembering all too well the work he had done over the years. "New roof, new heating system, thermapanes—"

"Not to mention a total overhaul of the plumbing system." She sighed, but there was a whimsical expression on her face. She had enjoyed seeing each piece of work done. It had given her something to think on, something to wish on. "And that was before we even discussed decorating. But I do adore the house. It'll be fantastic when it's done." Her eyes scanned the oceanscape as it grew more visible with the slow lifting of the fog. "With a view like this, how can you miss?"

"It's addictive, isn't it?"

"Mmmm." She tugged her jacket closer, aware of being cold but having no desire to return just yet to the house. Strange, the last thing she would have thought she wanted a little while ago was company, but Michael Buchanan was nice. "How long have you owned your house?"

"Nearly ten years."

She arched a brow. "Not bad."

"More the rule than the exception. Kennebunkport has a loyal following. Even the summer swell is largely made up of people making return visits."

Danica thought about that for a minute. It was in keeping with what the realtor had said about the population being stable. "Judy told me this was a quiet area, that people keep to themselves pretty much. That must be why you didn't know about the Duncans moving."

"Actually, I've been away."

She grimaced. "That was stupid of me. You probably have another place."

"No. This is my one and only. But I've been gone since November and just got back last week. I was never that close to the Duncans. We moved in different circles." The fact was that the Duncans barely tolerated the presence of a Buchanan nearby, but Michael wasn't about to tell that to Danica. He didn't yet know who she was. Her name hadn't rung a bell, but she obviously came from class, and he knew how much she had to have paid for her house. He prayed that her family had somehow managed to steer clear of his. Powerful people—important, to use her word—were natural media targets, and his family was very definitely the media. "I knew they'd sell sooner or later. I guess I thought it would be later."

"Fortunately not." Danica had considered it a stroke of luck that there had been a house such as this on the market for her to see. She'd also thought it to be a harbinger of good things to come. Once the house was done, it would be a "gem," to quote her decorator. The word she preferred to use was *savior*, but that remained to be seen.

She jumped when warm fingers brushed a strand of hair from her mouth, and her eyes flew to Michael's.

"Your cheeks are getting windburned," he explained, wishing he'd had an excuse to linger at her lips. He tried to decide what he saw in her eyes, but he wasn't sure if what he wanted to think was yearning was in fact nothing but surprise. Her eyes were rounded, her lashes long and dark. They were the only tip-off he had that she wore makeup, so skillfully and subtly was it applied.

His attention was drawn again to her mouth. Almost simultaneously she looked away, and he grew anxious. She was withdrawing. But he couldn't let her go so quickly, not when he'd finally found her. He tucked his hands in his pockets for safekeeping. "It's pretty cold out here. How about a warm drink at my place?"

Hot chocolate, like his eyes, she thought to herself. He was a very attractive man.

She shook her head a little too quickly. "Thanks, but I'd better not. I'm heading home in a couple of hours and I have to check on a few more things before I leave."

"When will you be back?"

"Next month."

"Not till then?" he asked with such boyish dismay that she laughed. It was lovely to feel wanted. Lovely and new.

" 'Fraid not."

"What's so important for you to do in Boston?"

"Oh—" she rolled her eyes "—this and that."

"Do you work?"

"Not in the traditional sense."

"Then, in what sense?"

Danica thought for a minute, wondering exactly what it *was* she did or, more precisely, how to explain it to a man she wanted to impress. It struck her as incredible that she had never faced such a task before, but she had always lived and breathed in exclusive circles. Anonymity was something she had never known. She was rather enjoying it now, even in spite of the urge she had to lie and say that she was a pediatrician or something equally as impressive.

But Michael was expecting the truth. He seemed like that kind of person, different from so many of the people she knew. He made eye contact; that said a lot.

"What do I do?" she finally repeated, then echoed herself, with one strategic change. "What do *you* do?"

He indulged her with a gentle smile. "I'm a writer."

"Oh, God."

"Uh-uh. Nothing threatening. I write about the past. They call me a historian."

" 'They'? What do you call yourself?"

He shrugged, eyes twinkling mischievously. "A writer."

"Why not a historian?"

"It sounds too pretentious and I'm not that way."

She could see that. She could also see that he looked nearly as cold as she felt.

"What are you staring at?" he asked.

"Your ears. They're turning red." Though his hair was on the long side and his ears hugged his head nicely, the wind was having a field day.

"That's okay. Between my red ears and your blue lips, I'd say we liven up the scenery. Come on. How about that drink?"

She was smiling now, too. "I can't. Really."

"I've got a fire going. It'd warm you up. Your place is probably like a barn."

"Mmmm, close." With workmen running in and out, there seemed to be a steady draft. "But the heater of my car works fine, and I have to be back in Boston before dark."

"Your car turns into a pumpkin then, does it?"

"Something like that."

"Then, I guess you'd better go. I wouldn't want you stranded on the highway or anything." He shifted from one foot to another, then cleared his throat. "Well, I guess I'll see you when you come back up next month."

"You'll be here?"

"Should be."

She nodded and took a step back. "Maybe it'll be warmer then."

He nodded but didn't move. "The beach is nice in April."

She took another step. "I'll bet it is. Well, take care, Michael."

"You, too, Danica." He raised a hand in mock salute as she took a third step. "May the good fairy be with you."

She laughed and shook her head as though to chastise him for his silliness, then realized that she loved it. When he winked, she loved it even more. But she had to leave. She had to.

Michael watched her turn and take several plodding steps through the sand toward her house. She turned back to give him a broad smile and a wave, and he wondered if there was in fact such a thing as love at first sight. Then a gust of wind whipped across the sand and she drew her free hand from her pocket to hold the cloche on her head.

The last thing he saw as she disappeared into the fog was the wide gold wedding band on the ring finger of her left hand.

TWO

$\boxed{S}$ EVERAL DAYS LATER, Danica sat on the edge of the kingsized bed she shared with her husband and watched him pack.

"Is there anything I can do?" she asked, but she already knew the answer. It was the same every time. Blake had been a bachelor for better than thirty-five years. He would either pack for himself or have Mrs. Hannah, their maid, do it. Danica knew she should be grateful; Blake coddled her, asking of her only the social amenities required of the wife of a man of his position. Any number of women would die to be in her shoes. Yet, rather than privileged or pampered, she felt superfluous.

"All set, I think." He didn't look up, but concentrated on setting his dress shoes at just the right angle in the bottom of the bag.

"Are you going with Harlan?" Harlan Magnuson was the head of the computer division of Eastbridge Electronics, Blake's corporation. He was young, brilliant and aggressive, and often accompanied Blake on business trips. From what Danica could gather, the combination of Harlan's daring and Blake's solid business sense was a potent one.

"Uh-huh."

"How long will you be?"

"No more than three days. I'll be back in time for the cocktail party Friday night."

"That's good. The Donaldsons would never forgive us if we missed it." She absently rubbed the edge of the suitcase. They had bought it as part of a matching set four years ago when they'd been headed for Italy. She recalled that trip with a smile. Blake had business in Florence, but from there on they simply relaxed, spending several days in Milan en route to the villa they had rented on Lake Como. It seemed so long since they'd taken a vacation like that. Or rather, she amended, it seemed so long since they'd had *fun* like that. Sighing, she looked at the bag. For all its use—and Blake used it often—it appeared to be wearing better than her marriage. "I wish you didn't have to go."

Taking underwear and socks from the drawer, Blake returned to the bed. "You know I do," he said. She wished she could have said that she heard regret in his tone, but she just wasn't sure, which seemed to be a recurrent problem lately. She couldn't read Blake; perhaps she'd never been able to but had simply deluded herself.

"You do so much traveling. I tell myself that you've got to, but it doesn't help sometimes. You won't reconsider and let me come along?"

He straightened and spoke quietly. "I really have to be free this time, Danica. With the exception of a dinner tomorrow night, it'll be business all the way."

"I know. But it's so quiet here when you're away." Saying the words, she realized that it wasn't the quiet that bothered her but the fact that she felt widowed. Twenty-eight years old and widowed.

Stifling the thought, she watched him carefully coil and pack two leather belts. Her gaze slowly climbed to his face and she was struck, once again and for the umpteenth time, by how handsome a man he was. The very first time she had been so struck she'd been nineteen and attending a fund-raiser for her father. Blake Lindsay had been impressive then, tall and dark and immaculately groomed. Now, nine years later, he was no less attractive. The years had barely touched him, it seemed. His forty-three-year-old body was firm and well toned, but then, he believed in exercise, jogged regularly, played squash several times a week and watched his weight. That he prided himself on his appearance had been obvious to Danica from the start. Unfortunately, between exercise and work, he seemed to have little time for much else, let alone her.

"You have plenty to keep you busy, haven't you?" Pivoting, he went to the closet, selected several ties from the rack, then moved toward the window to scrutinize the possibilities in daylight.

"Oh, yes. There's a board meeting at the hospital tomorrow and I have an appointment with the printer on Thursday to order our invitations."

"Plans are going well for the party?" He sounded distracted, which was no wonder, Danica decided, since he faced the monumental task of choosing between two blue and gray silk ties, the stripes of which varied infinitesimally in width. She could no more understand how he could choose one over the other than she could why he owned two such similar ties in the first place, but then, perhaps he felt the same way about her blouses or panty hose or belts.

"The caterer's all set. So's the florist, and I've booked the chamber music ensemble from the conservatory. That pretty much does it until after the invitations are printed. Have you decided whether or not to invite the group from SpanTech?"

Having somehow decided between the two ties, Blake put the loser back in the closet and returned to lay the others carefully in his suitcase. "SpanTech? Mmmm . . . not sure yet." He rubbed his upper lip, then set off for the bathroom. When he returned, he carried a case containing his grooming needs. After fitting it into the space he had purposely left, he returned to the dresser for shirts.

"It'd be easy enough, Blake. Another ten or twelve people won't make much difference as long as we notify the caterer in time. It certainly won't mean any more work for me, if you think it'd be worthwhile to invite them." She knew that Blake had been negotiating to bring in SpanTech, outstanding for its research in microelectronics, as a division of Eastbridge.

He sent her a brilliant smile, which flared, then was gone. "Let me think about it a little more, okay?"

She nodded. When a silence fell between them, she searched for something else to say. "Did I tell you Reggie Nichols called?"

"She's in town?"

"Mmmm. She's seeing some guy, I guess."

"Isn't she playing the circuit?"

Reggie Nichols had been top-rated in women's tennis for more than a decade. She and Danica had been friends since Danica's own tennis-playing days when the two had trained under the same coach.

"Sure. But I guess she needs the break. From what she said on the phone, things have been rough. Every year there are younger faces. I think it's getting her down. . . . My Lord, Blake, you've got six shirts there." She had been watching him place them one by one, starched and cardboard-backed, in the suitcases, and couldn't resist teasing him. "Are you sure that's enough?"

"I'd rather have extras, just in case," he answered in dead earnest, which Danica found to be all the more amusing, since Blake Lindsay never spilled, rarely sweated, barely wrinkled.

"Anyway—" she was smiling "—Reggie and I are having lunch on Saturday, unless you want to do something, in which case I'll cancel."

He had finished packing the shirts and was reaching for his suit bag. "No, no. Don't do that. I'll be at the club."

It was either that or at work, so Danica had known she would be safe making the lunch date with Reggie. Until recently she had spent her own Saturdays waiting for him to come home. Perhaps in her old age she was wising up. Then again, perhaps not. More than once it had occurred to her that though she had convinced Blake to buy the house in Kennebunkport as a hideaway for the two of them, it was going to be something else getting him there. Last week was a perfect example. He had promised he would take the day off to drive up with her, then had been besieged by a handful of last-minute emergencies, that demanded his attention. She didn't quite understand why a man who headed his own company couldn't get subordinates to do the work.

"Is something wrong, Pook?" he asked gently.

Her head came up. "Hmmm?"

He sent her that same ephemeral flash of a smile as he threaded hangers through the slot at the top of the suit bag. "You look angry."

She realized that she felt it, but the last thing she wanted was to sound like a shrewish wife, so she forced herself to relax and spoke with measured calm. "Nothing's wrong. I was just thinking of Maine."

"Any more word from the decorator?"

"She called yesterday afternoon to say that the cabinets are set to go in." They had been special-ordered in a white oak that Danica had fallen in love with, but she had debated the decision for days, since using the white oak had sent a number of other dominoes toppling—namely countertops, ceiling fixtures and flooring, all of which were now in the process of being changed. But Blake had said to go ahead, so she had. "When I was there last week, the kitchen was barren."

Blake laid the suit bag on the bed, straightened the lapel of the tuxedo he had put in last and drew up the zipper to close the bag.

Taking a breath, she forged cautiously on. "Once the cabinets are in, the refrigerator and stove will be hooked up. At least then we'll be able to have something to eat or drink. I mean, the place won't really be livable until May or June, but it's getting there. I was hoping to go back up next month to check on things. You'll come with me, won't you?"

"If I can."

"You haven't been there since we first looked at it. I'd really like you to see what's been done. If there's anything you don't like—"

He was doubling up the suit bag and fastening the straps. "You have wonderful taste." His smile was on. "I'll like it."

"But I want you to *see* it, Blake. This was supposed to be a joint venture, a place where we could be alone together."

Blake made a final scan of the room. "All in good time. When it's finished, we'll spend the time you want there. Things must be pretty primitive now. Did the decorator say anything about those kitchen cabinets you wanted?"

Danica opened her mouth in reproach, then shut it tight. He hadn't been listening. That was all. His mind was on other things.

"Next week. They'll be in next week," she murmured, rising from the bed and heading for the door. "I'll send Marcus up for the bags," she called over her shoulder as she started down the stairs. But Blake was soon beside her, putting his hand lightly on her waist. It bobbed as they descended; their steps never quite matched.

"You won't forget to RSVP to the Hagendorfs, will you?" he asked. Danica could almost see his mind's eye going down the list headed Remind Danica. It came right after What to Pack and right before Names (and Wives' Names) of Business Associates in Kansas City, which was where he was headed this week.

"I've already done it," she said evenly. Patience was a virtue; so read the tag on her tea bag that morning.

"And the charity ball at the Institute?"

"They're expecting us."

"Good. You could give Feeno a call and see if my new tux is ready. If it is, have Marcus pick it up." They rounded the second-floor landing and made their way toward the first. Blake dropped his hand from her waist. Danica slid hers along the lustrous mahogany banister. "Oh, and Bert Hammer mentioned something about your serving on the nominating committee."

"For the Institute?"

"They need younger faces. Are you interested?"

"Sure. You know I love art."

Blake chuckled, more the indulgent parent than the amused mate. "This would have very little to do with art, I'm afraid. It'd mean sitting at a table, tossing around names of the most popular and up-and-coming Bostonians. They know you're in the social mainstream. They'd be picking your brain."

Danica gave a small smile. "I don't mind. It's nice to feel useful. And besides, I know three women who would each give her right arm for an entree to the board; two of them would be fantastic."

"Not the third?"

"Uh . . . Marion White?"

"Oh." He cleared his throat and tried not to grin. "Yes, I think you're right." They'd reached the street floor, where Marcus Hannah stood waiting. "The bags are by the bed," Blake instructed in a voice of quiet command. "I'll be in the library when you're ready."

Marcus nodded and headed up the stairs while Blake disappeared, leaving Danica standing alone by the front door. She walked slowly back toward the library, but when she heard Blake talking on the phone, she reconsidered and took refuge in the den.

It hurt that he should be calling the office, which he'd left no more than ninety minutes before, when he might be talking with her. After all, he was going to be away for three days, and though she knew he would call her at least once or twice during that time, she also knew that he would call the office much more often. She wished she could say that he worked too hard, but he looked wonderfully healthy and seemed perfectly happy with his life. If he was busy, it was by choice. Perhaps that was what hurt most. He did choose.

At a sound in the hall she looked up to see Marcus, bags in hand, heading back through the lower pantry toward the courtyard where the car was parked. On cue Blake emerged from the library, set his briefcase on the floor by the closet and reached for his topcoat. By the time he retrieved the briefcase, Danica was by his side.

"Behave while I'm gone," he said with a bright grin, then leaned forward and kissed her cheek. For an instant she was tempted to throw her arms around his neck and hold him there, but she knew she would be grasping at straws. Blake would no more be swayed by an emotional appeal than her father would have been. They were so alike, those two, so alike. Disturbed by the thought, she slid her hands into the pockets of her skirt and put on a smile. Her father would have approved.

"I'll behave." She followed Blake to the back door, watched him cross the cobblestone courtyard and climb into the Mercedes's rear seat. It was a scenario that had grown all too familiar to her, as had the accompanying sadness. But the sadness had altered in nature over the years, she realized. It wasn't so much Blake's departure that affected her now, for she saw little enough of him when he was home. Rather, the sadness she felt was a more general one dealing with love and happiness and promise.

Blake looked up once to smile when Marcus backed the car around. She waved, but his head was already lowering. He was opening his briefcase, she knew. She suspected his mind was miles away by the time the car disappeared from her view.

"Ahhh, Mrs. Lindsay. Mrs. Marshall is already seated. If you'll come this way . . ."

Breathless, Danica smiled. "Thank you, Jules." She was a graceful figure breezing after the maître d', her blond hair looking stunningly windblown, her calf-length silver-fox fur undulating gently as she let herself be led to the corner table the Ritz always held for her when she called.

"Mother!" She leaned down to press her cheek to the woman whose eyes lit up at her approach. "I'm sorry! Have I kept you waiting long?"

"Not more than a minute or two, darling. How are you? You look wonderful! Your cheeks are so pink." Eleanor Marshall frowned at her only child. "You didn't *walk* here, did you?"

"Sure. I cut through the Public Garden. It'd have been silly to drive, and besides, I love the fresh air."

Eleanor eyed her daughter reprovingly. "Danica, Marcus is *paid* to drive you, silly or not. The Public Garden isn't the safest place in the world." She paused to place her order for a vermouth cassis to Danica's kir.

"I'm all right, Mother. Here, safe and sound. And you look pretty fine yourself! New earrings?"

"They were a gift from the family we stayed with in Brazil last year. They're topaz, a little too much for some occasions, but I thought you'd appreciate them."

"I do. You wear them well." Which was one thing Eleanor did do. Though far from being beautiful, she dressed to play up the best of her features. At fifty-two, she was a stylishly attractive woman, though she rarely turned heads unless she was with her husband. "Is it ethical for Daddy to accept gifts like that?"

"Your father says it is," Eleanor answered with quiet assurance. "He usually knows."

Danica wondered, but she said nothing. It wasn't often her mother came in alone for lunch—it wasn't often she *ever* had her mother to herself—and she didn't want anything to mar their time together. Shuttling between Connecticut and Washington, not to mention flying off on numerous trips each year, her parents weren't easily accessible.

"I'm so glad you called. This is a treat. Somehow talking on the phone just isn't the same." It never was, though she wondered if her mother agreed. "How's Daddy? You said he was going to Vancouver?"

"He left yesterday morning, just before I called you. It was a last-minute trip; he's filling in for a committee member who took sick. He sends his love, by the way. I told him I was seeing you when he called last night."

"Didn't you want to go with him?"

"I felt—" Eleanor took a breath and let it out with a sheepish grin "—like staying home. It must be the years creeping up. When your father's away, things are quieter. I find I need that from time to time."

Strange, Danica thought, how her mother enjoyed that quiet, while she found it terrifying. It wasn't that she craved her parents' political whirl of a life; that was the *last* thing she wanted, and besides, she was busy enough socially. No, what she wanted . . . what she wanted was the noise of a happy home. What frightened her was the thought of a lifetime filled with the silence that too often entombed the Beacon Hill town house she shared with Blake.

She refocused her thoughts on her mother with a hint of concern and good cause. "You're feeling all right, aren't you?"

"Oh, yes. Fine. The doctors' reports are wonderful." Four years earlier Eleanor had had a hysterectomy when a uterine tumor had been detected. Between the surgery and subsequent radiation treatments, it appeared she was cured. "It's just that I get tired of living out of a suitcase. And since your father's going to be at meetings most of the time . . ."

Danica thought of Blake and wondered how her mother managed to avoid the frustration she felt. It was difficult when a man's work was his mistress, as Blake's seemed to be. "Daddy doesn't mind the meetings, does he?"

"What do *you* think?" Eleanor smiled. "He thrives on it. In fact, he's that much more relaxed. He doesn't have to run for another four years." William Marshall was the senior senator from Connecticut, a twenty-one-year veteran of the United States Congress. "He's as active as ever, but the pressure isn't as intense. When he's up for reelection himself, it's a matter of life or death."

She spoke matter-of-factly and Danica understood, knowing that to her father winning *was* a matter of life and death. What she didn't understand was how her mother could stand it, but Eleanor seemed fully acclimated to that way of thinking.

Not so Danica. More than once over the years she had wanted to rebel. First she hadn't had the courage; later she'd seen the futility of it. It would have been a losing battle, and very simply, she couldn't afford another loss. More than anything, she wanted her father's approval, and to win that, she had to follow his rules.

"Campaigning for someone else," Eleanor continued, oblivious to Danica's thoughts, "well, it's easier. By the way, he's come out for Claveling. You know that, don't you?"

Danica knew that her father had been torn between two men, both announced candidates for his party's presidential nomination. With the first of the primaries over, it appeared that Claveling was the one more likely to succeed. "So I read. It's been all over the papers."

Eleanor made a sound that Danica might have called a snort if it had been anyone else making it in any other place. But her mother was impeccably controlled, and the Ritz was exquisitely proper. Therefore there had been no snort. It had been a nasal moan, Danica decided, and reflected the same tempered displeasure that Eleanor proceeded to express.

"Don't mention the papers to me."

"Has something happened?"

"Oh, just a small article in the local paper criticizing your father for a speech he gave last week. It didn't bother him, but *I* got annoyed. The newspapers are always looking for something to attack. If they can't cry income tax evasion or conflict of interest, they pick on petty little things. The powerful are always targets. If the powerful are well-to-do, so much the worse. You should remember that, Danica."

"Me? I'm not in the limelight like you and Daddy."

"You may be. After all, Blake is standing right beside your father in support of Claveling."

It was the first Danica had heard about it, and she wasn't sure whether to be shocked, angry or downright depressed. The minute it took for the waiter to set their drinks before them gave her a chance to compose herself.

"I hadn't realized it was definite," she finally managed. When push came to shove, she was embarrassed to admit to her mother that her husband hadn't communicated with her on so important a matter. Blake had to know she wouldn't be thrilled. He had to know that she craved something in life other than parties and rallies and press conferences.

"It's definite. They've spent hours discussing it on the phone."

"Daddy and Blake?" Again Danica hadn't known, though she knew how close the two men were. They had been friends since long before Danica and Blake had married. Their relationship had always been one of contemporaries, rather than father and son-in-law.

"Your husband has influential contacts in the business world, my dear," Eleanor announced quite unnecessarily, with a hint of excitement that only increased Danica's dismay. "He's the kind of man who inspires confidence, the kind who can coax people to contribute to a worthy cause. Jason Claveling is a worthy cause. If he wins the nomination, he'll be elected."

"Are you sure?"

"I'm sure. And it never hurts to be on the good side of the president of the United States."

Ethical issues aside, Danica couldn't argue with that. Political pull did wonders, particularly when it came from the top. "I'm surprised Daddy's never gone for it."

"For the presidency?" Eleanor laughed softly and grew more pensive. "No. The risk is too great, I think. Over the years your father has made his share of enemies. Any strong figure is bound to, and William has been known to be unbending at times. But he plays to win. He needs to be in full control, and that's not possible in a national election. Besides—" she perked up "—he's enjoying seniority in the Senate."

Danica nodded, still trying to assimilate the fact of Blake's impending political involvement. She should have seen it coming, but she hadn't. And, for whatever his reasons, Blake hadn't seen fit to enlighten her.

"So," she sighed after having ordered a bowl of summer squash soup and a crabmeat salad, "when does the hoopla begin?"

"Soon, I'd imagine. You don't look wild about the idea."

Danica made a wavering gesture. "We have plenty of evenings planned as it is. This means there'll be that many more."

"Are there other things you'd rather be doing?" Eleanor asked in surprise. When she was Danica's age, she was entranced by every aspect of her husband's nascent political career.

"There might be." She was thinking of whimsical things like going to a movie, driving with Blake down to Provincetown for the day or up to Kennebunkport, for that matter. Unfortunately, her mother reached another conclusion.

"Darling," she began, eyes widening in excitement, "are you—"

Danica smiled. "No, Mom. Not yet."

"But you'd like to be."

"We've discussed this before. You *know* I'd like to be."

"Is there a problem?"

"Of course not!"

"Don't get defensive, darling," Eleanor said softly. "I was just asking. After all, you've been married for eight years—"

"Which is nothing, when you stop to think how young I was way back then. I don't think I would have made a particularly good mother at twenty or twenty-one or twenty-two. Goodness, you make it sound as though I'm running out of time. I'm only twenty-eight. Nowadays women have babies when they're forty."

"True, but when you're forty, Blake will be fifty-five, which is exactly the age your father is now, and look at *you*."

"Daddy was young when he married. There's a difference. If Blake's first concern had been a family, he'd probably have married a lot earlier."

"Still, I'd think he wouldn't want to wait too long. And besides, think of your father. He's ready to have a grandchild."

"So you've told me before," Danica managed in a dry tone. She didn't like this discussion, never had, never would. She wanted to have a baby very badly. She wanted to make Blake a father, to make William a grandfather, to be a mother herself. Unfortunately, it was easier said than done.

"Will you oblige him?"

"I hope so."

"Are you sure there's no problem?"

If there was a problem, it was that Blake was either out of town or tired, and there was *no way* Danica was going to discuss that with her mother. Sad as it was, she didn't feel close enough.

"I'm sure," she said, intent on changing the subject. "And as to what I'd rather be doing than going to political fundraisers, I'd rather be in Maine with Blake. You should see the house. It's exciting."

As they ate, Danica filled her mother in on the details of the remodeling work. It was a fairly safe topic until Eleanor raised the issue of physically getting to Maine and back.

"I don't like your driving there alone."

"Blake will be with me from now on. At least," she thought aloud, "he said he would be, but if the Claveling campaign takes much of his time—"

"It may. You know that. Which means you'll be making the trip by yourself."

Danica wasn't thrilled with that idea, but her discouragement had nothing to do with the drive. "It's not much of a trip . . . an hour and a half, give or take for traffic."

"That's an hour and a half in a small car that could easily be mashed between two trucks on the highway. If Blake isn't there, Marcus should drive you."

"What in the world would Marcus do up there while I'm checking over all those little details?"

"He can wait. That's his job. Better still, he can familiarize himself with the area so he'll be comfortable when he and his wife go up."

"They won't be going." When her mother stopped midbite to stare at her, Danica explained. "The house is for Blake and me. An escape from the city. A place where we can be alone together. I don't see the need for having one in help there, let alone two. We can drive ourselves wherever we want to go, and there shouldn't be any massive cleaning to do, since we won't be entertaining there."

"What about food?"

"I can cook, Mother."

"I know you *can*, but wouldn't it be easier if Mrs. Hannah did it?"

Danica's mind was set. She had yielded on many things in her life. This was one on which she was determined to hold fast. "No. The Hannahs will watch things in Boston while Blake and I are in Maine." She slanted her mother a grin. "You never can tell. With a little practice, I might just emerge as a competitor to Julia Child. Daddy would love that. You'll both come up when the house is done, won't you?"

Before Eleanor had a chance to answer, a friend of Danica's approached to say a fast hello. Danica graciously made the introductions, then sat back and marveled at the skillful way her mother made conversation. It was as though Eleanor truly cared about this new acquaintance.

"Well?" Danica said softly when they were alone once more.

"She's lovely, darling. You serve on the hospital board with her?"

"Yes. But I wasn't asking about that. You and Daddy will come up to Maine to visit, won't you?" It meant a lot to her; she was hoping to impress her parents with the house, its location and her own abilities to play hostess.

"I thought you weren't entertaining there."

"Family's different."

Eleanor sighed. "Of course we'll come. But I wish you wouldn't be so difficult about things. I still don't like the idea of your driving up there yourself."

"Listen to you, Mother," Danica chided. "You'd think I was sixteen."

"I know you're not. But I do worry. At least you could take the Mercedes. It's bigger and heavier than the coupe."

"But I love the Audi, and I get so little chance to drive around here. Boston drivers are awful. By comparison, Kennebunkport is a dream." She took a deep breath and gazed down at the people walking briskly along Arlington Street. "There's a sense of freedom you get when you drive by yourself on the open road."

"You *sound* about sixteen. But you never craved freedom then."

Danica grew pensive. "Didn't you ever wonder whether I did things behind your back?"

"What kinds of things?"

"Smoke. Drink. Go places I shouldn't."

"You were always well supervised."

"Not every minute. The housemother at the dorm didn't know everything that happened."

"At college I wouldn't expect—"

"I'm not talking about college. I'm talking about boarding school. Even before I left to live at Armand's, there was plenty going on."

"Danica, you were thirteen years old then!"

"Still, I knew what was happening. Some of the girls smuggled stuff into the dorm. Either that or they'd sneak out, and they made it—and back—without being caught. Come on, Mother," she chided at the look of dismay on Eleanor's face, "you had to know that kind of thing happened."

"I suppose, but—" she was slowly shaking her head "—you didn't do any of that." She had effectively answered Danica's question.

Danica smiled. "No. I was too much of a coward."

"A coward? No, no, darling. You simply set higher standards for yourself."

"Daddy set higher standards for me, you mean." She rolled her eyes. "I was so innocent that if I'd tried the smallest thing, I'd surely have been caught, and if I'd ever been caught, Daddy never would have forgiven me." Her smile faded. "It was bad enough giving up tennis. He doesn't ever mention that now, does he?"

"He goes to matches whenever he can. You know he's always loved the game. But, no, he doesn't sit there fantasizing that it's you on the court. He accepts things when he has no choice."

Danica idly pushed a forkful of crabmeat around her plate. "I'm sorry that it didn't work out. He would have been proud if I'd been able to make it."

"Are *you* sorry it didn't work out?"

"In terms of the game, no. I just didn't possess that all-fire determination it took to be number one, at least not in that field. And besides," she sighed, "it's over and done. Maybe I'm like Daddy in that respect. I've accepted the fact that I'll never make it to center court at Wimbledon. . . . Strange to be talking this way ten years after the fact."

Not at all strange, she realized, though sad. There were many things she had never discussed with her mother, because Eleanor Marshall was first and foremost William Marshall's wife. That Eleanor had a daughter—that *William* had a daughter—had always seemed incidental.

"By the way," Eleanor went on, "I understand that your friend Reggie was given a run for her money at the Virginia Slims tournament in New York."

"How did you know that?"

"Your father was reading an article about young Aaron, uh, Aaron—"

"Krickstein."

"Thank you, darling. Anyway, he was reading that article and the other headline caught my eye. Have you heard from her lately?"

"We had lunch together last Saturday."

"You did! But I thought she was going on to Florida with the rest of the tour."

"They do have time between tournaments, Mom. Reggie was visiting someone here. Actually, she was thinking of skipping Florida altogether."

"Can she do that? Doesn't she have a commitment to the sponsors?"

"Commitments only go so far. If a player is injured, she doesn't play. In Reggie's case, she's mentally exhausted. One season finished and the next began on its heels, and she needs a break."

"From what I read I can understand it. She won by the skin of her teeth. That kind of thing has to be exhausting, both physically *and* mentally." Eleanor arched a brow. "Maybe while she's here she'll get you to play."

"She has other things on her mind."

"But I'm sure she'd love to play with you."

"I'm not playing. You know that."

"Mmmm, and I feel badly. You were *good*, darling. There was no reason why you had to give it up completely just because you couldn't be number one."

"You make me sound juvenile."

"Well, aren't you carrying it a little too far?"

"No."

"Darling, you were the fourth ranked player in this country—in this *country*—when you were sixteen. That was a feat that took quite some doing. And now nothing. How long has it been since you held a racket in your hand?"

Danica met her mother's gaze. "The last time I held a racket was on Saturday, June 2nd, three days before my eighteenth birthday."

"You see?" Eleanor exclaimed. "It's been ten years! Isn't that a little silly?"

"Not to me. I'd had it with tennis."

"Your shoulder was injured."

"It was much more than that," Danica argued softly. "We discussed it at the time, Mother—Armand and I, you and Daddy and Armand. I wasn't happy. I didn't want to play. My shoulder would have healed enough to continue, but I just wasn't interested." She counted to five. She was sure that if she and her mother were to get into a similar discussion in a week or a month, Eleanor would once again blame the demise of her career on that shoulder injury. To be forced out of competition by a physical injury was somehow all right; after all, one couldn't help that. To willingly withdraw—because of lack of drive, no less—was unacceptable. "Why the talk of tennis all of a sudden?"

Eleanor sighed. "No special reason. It just came up along with talk of

Reggie. And I do think about it from time to time. I'm sorry, but I can't help it. I still believe that if you'd wanted, you could have been right up there *with* Reggie." When Danica opened her mouth to argue, Eleanor went right on. "Tennis has come into its own in the past decade. Women are doing much better."

"My Lord, I don't need the money."

"Of course you don't. All right. Forget competing. What about playing for fun? It's wonderful exercise."

Danica smirked. "Are you trying to tell me something?"

"Don't be silly, darling. You're as thin as ever. I'm merely suggesting that exercise is good for you."

"I get exercise. I walk wherever I can."

"I'm talking about *organized* exercise."

"I have ballet class three times a week."

"That's not a particularly social activity."

Finally Danica understood. "You're wrong there too, Mom," she offered gently. "I've met some wonderful people dancing. Granted, they may not be the same type I'd be playing tennis with at the club, but they're every bit as stimulating, if not more so. They're refreshing. I like them."

If she had been trying to make a statement, it went right over her mother's head. Eleanor had evidently written off that particular subject. "Well, I hope so. By the way, did you know that Hiram Manley's brother died?"

Later, walking back across the Public Garden, more slowly this time, Danica thought about the two hours she had just spent with her mother. She had looked forward to them as she always did. As always, though, anticipation exceeded reality. She wished Eleanor was the type of mother with whom she could share her heart and soul, but she wasn't. Eleanor wouldn't understand. As a result, Danica felt the same frustration, the same loneliness she always felt where her parents were concerned.

All her life she had hoped it would change. When she was a young child in the care of hired help, she had dreamed of the day when she would be old enough to travel with her parents. But when she had been old enough, she'd been sent to boarding school, then to live and train at Armand Arroah's tennis academy, then to college. Even now, a grown woman married to a good friend of her father's, she found family warmth to be elusive.

Pausing at the apex of the footbridge over the pond, she was staring into the dark water when a movement at its edge caught her eye. A young child, his mother kneeling beside him, was offering torn bits of bread in jerky thrusts to the congregating pigeons. From time to time he stole a bite himself, then fed one to his mother. Both were bundled against the wind, which ruffled the water in random gusts. Neither seemed to mind the chill.

Danica guessed the little boy to be three and tried to remember what she had been doing when she was three. She couldn't. But she'd been in nursery school when she was four, and she had vague memories of that. By the time she was five she was enrolled in an exclusive private school in the suburbs of Hartford and was spending her summers at a select day camp. Her memory made little differentiation between the two. There were loud groups of children at each and a certain amount of regimentation. She played at friends' houses, had friends home to play at hers. There was a jumble of birthday parties and clowns and magic shows, frilly dresses and Mary Janes.

When it came to memories of specific events, she had very few. She did remember going to Elizabeth Park to feed popcorn to the fish, though. Now she wondered what kind of fish ate popcorn; then she had simply been overjoyed by the fact. But it hadn't been her mother who had braved the cold to share her excitement, who had set aside an afternoon to spend in unrushed play with her child. It had been the housekeeper.

Danica watched the little boy throw the last of his bread to the birds, then bat his mitten against his snowsuit. Moments later, when his mother swept him up into her arms and hugged him tightly before starting off down the path, she felt a pang of envy—envy of the child who had such a loving mother, envy of the mother who had such a warm, cuddly child.

Starting off toward Charles Street, she vowed that if she had a child, things would be very different from when she had been young. Money didn't buy happiness. Neither did power. She didn't care what obligations she had to cancel. She would spend time with her child.

Just thinking about it brought a lump to her throat. She had so much love to give, so much love to give that she sometimes thought she'd burst.

Chilled by the time she let herself into the town house, she settled into the leather couch in the den, tucked her legs under an afghan and watched while Marcus built a fire. When Mrs. Hannah brought her a cup of tea, she let it steep while she held it and absorbed its warmth. Only when she removed the tea bag and propped it on the saucer did she examine its tag.

"Happiness is a way station between too much and too little," she read and smiled her sad agreement.

THREE

DANICA MADE THE TRIP to Kennebunkport in record time. It wasn't that there was no traffic, for there had been. It wasn't that she'd been in a hurry, for she hadn't been. But she had been angry. And much as her better sense told her to slow down, she had found perverse satisfaction in stepping on the gas.

Even now, having left the highway at Kittery for the shore route, she burned when she thought of Blake. Over and over she replayed the conversations they'd had regarding the trip they were to have made together.

"Blake?"

"Mmmm?" He had been looking in the mirror readjusting the knot of his necktie.

"How does next Wednesday sound for taking a drive to Maine?"

He had stuck his chin up and tugged some more. "Next Wednesday, uh, next Wednesday's fine."

"It's still a week off. We could make it Tuesday or Thursday if you'd rather."

"Nope." He had smiled at his image. "Wednesday's okay."

That weekend she had asked him again. "Blake?"

"Hmmm?" This time he had been engrossed in the Sunday paper.

"Is Wednesday still okay?"

"Wednesday?"

"Maine?"

"Oh." He had noisily turned the page. "As far as I know it's fine."

On Tuesday morning, unable to help herself, she had raised it a third time. "Blake?" He had been in the library making a fast phone call before leaving for work.

"Yes, Danica."

His slight impatience hadn't deterred her. It wasn't often she asked things of him, but their driving together to Maine meant a lot. "I'm counting on you for tomorrow."

"I know," he had said evenly and had been out the door soon after.

Late that afternoon, though, he had called from the office, announcing that he had to fly to Atlanta in the morning instead. She hadn't argued then or later when he came home to pick her up for a dinner party. She had been the patient, understanding wife right through the moment when she had kissed him goodbye and waved him off to the airport.

Inside she was seething.

Now, approaching the house she had set such stock in, she felt the anger finally sweeping away. In its place was an overwhelming hurt, an abject loneliness, a sense of loss. She'd had a dream—for years and years, it seemed—but it didn't look like it was going to come true.

Pulling from the main road onto the curving driveway, she brought the Audi to a halt before the front door of the house. Either her timing was particularly good, or having turned off the car, she simply relinquished the taut hold she'd had on herself. Her eyes suddenly filled with tears, and unable to do anything else, she draped both hands over the steering wheel, dropped her head forward and cried.

Michael Buchanan had quietly kept an eye on the Lindsay house since the day he had last seen Danica. Oh, yes, he knew who she was now. A quick call to the realtor had given him the identities not only of Danica's husband but also of her father. A more lengthy call to his sister, Cilla, who lived and worked in Washington, had told him more. Anything else he learned had come from a study of newspaper microfilms on file at the public library.

Danica Lindsay was very definitely off-limits. Not only was she married, but she was the daughter of a man his father had never seen eye to eye with.

Still, he hadn't been able to put from mind the image of her standing so alone on the sand. He hadn't been able to forget the haunted look he had caught on her face before she composed herself. The realtor, his sister, the papers, had given him biographical facts. What they hadn't touched on was whether she was happy.

And he cared. Something had happened that morning on the beach, and he couldn't turn his back on it.

Okay, fine. So he couldn't court her as he would have liked. But she was going to be his neighbor for whatever period of time she chose to spend in Maine. And he intended to be her friend.

For a while all he had seen when he passed her house had been pick-up trucks and vans in the driveway. Lately, though, they had been there less often. Today there were none.

But there was a car, and on sheer instinct he knew it was hers. It fit her . . . a silver Audi coupe . . . classy, sporty but dignified. He saw the red brake lights go off and he knew she was in the car. At the end of her driveway he pulled up and watched, unable to see much more than a shadow in the driver's seat. When the shadow seemed to wither into itself, he frowned. Then, driven as much by confusion as by concern, he climbed from his Blazer and walked up the drive.

The morning's brightness was his ally. With each step he took, the shadow in the front seat of the Audi took on greater color and form. Danica. Wrists dangling over the top of the steering wheel. Blond head fallen against her arms. Shoulders quaking.

He picked up his step, trotting the last few yards, then, as softly as his thudding heart would allow, tapped two fingers against her window.

She looked up with a start and he saw her tears.

He felt a tightening inside. He tried to open the car door, but it was locked from the inside and Danica had put her head back down on her arms. She was frightened. No, embarrassed. But he didn't want her to hide. Not from him.

Again he rapped softly on the window. "Danica? Are you all right?" Her shoulders lifted. She seemed to be trying to get control of herself. Either that or she was crying all the harder. He didn't know which and spoke with a hint of panic. "Open the door, Danica."

Blotting her eyes with one hand, she opened the door with the other. Taking a shuddering breath, she laid her head back against the headrest and closed her eyes.

Michael pulled the door open all the way and hunkered down. "What's wrong?"

She squeezed her eyes shut and furrowed her brow as if she were in pain. "Are you sick?"

She shook her head and held up a hand. "Give me a minute."

On instinct he lifted his hand and closed it around hers. Her fingers curled around his thumb and held tight.

He spoke very softly. "Right about now I think I'm supposed to whip a neatly folded handkerchief out of my pocket to give you. At least that's what a real gentleman would do." He stuck his hand in his jacket pocket and, even as he drew out a crumpled supermarket check-out slip, knew there was no point in looking further. He had never been one for neatly folded handkerchiefs. "Guess I'd strike out as a real gentleman. Have you got any Kleenex?"

She released his hand and turned in the seat to fumble in her pocketbook. Moments later she was pressing a tissue under first one eye, then the other.

"I'm sorry," she whispered.

"Don't be silly. We all have our moments. Something upset you, that's all." He glanced around. Hers was the only car in sight and the house looked deserted. "Is there anyone I can call?" She shook her head. "You're alone." Fresh tears welled in her eyes. "Ahhhh. And that's the problem, or part of it, at least?"

Chin tucked to her chest, eyes closed again, she pressed a finger to the spot between her eyes and nodded. When once more she was composed, she sniffled and looked up. "I was really hoping my husband would come. At the last minute he rushed off to Atlanta on business."

"I'm sure he had to," Michael offered gently. "From what I understand, he's an important man." When Danica looked up in surprise, he smiled. "I know who your husband is. And your father. You weren't planning on keeping them a secret forever, were you?"

She responded to his gentle teasing. "It was kind of nice to be a nobody for that little while we talked."

Michael wondered if she remembered "that little while we talked" as clearly as he did. He had spent many an hour thinking about it. "You would never be a nobody."

"You know what I mean. Not Blake Lindsay's wife. Not William Marshall's daughter. It isn't often that I get to be with people who see me for *me*."

"I will."

Somehow she knew it. Looking into Michael Buchanan's eyes now, she felt the same warmth, the same lightness she had felt that first day on the beach. "I'd really like that," she said, breaking out into a slow smile, then sniffling and looking down self-consciously. "I must look awful."

"You look wonderful." Very gently he brushed a tear from her cheek with his thumb, then pushed himself up and held out his hand. "Come. Time to go in. That is why you've come—to see the house—isn't it?"

She gave him a sheepish grin. "Right." Putting her hand in his, she let herself be helped from the car. "My decorator's been checking. She says things are nearly done." For the first time she looked around, tipped her head back, took a deep breath—slightly uneven from her recent tears—of the ocean air. "Mmmm. Nice. An improvement over the last time."

"It's warmer. And sunny. No fog." Michael remembered that fog and the way it had given a mystical quality to his meeting Danica. He still felt it—a kismet of sorts. Much as he told himself he was crazy, he couldn't shake the feeling.

As they walked up the flagstone path to the door, Danica admired the landscape around the house. White pines dotted the yard, standing guard over clusters of bayberry and staghorn sumac. Though it was still too early for any of the flowering shrubs to blossom, the scrubby junipers looked fresher, in the first stages of rejuvenation.

Unlocking the door, she stepped inside, then walked slowly from one room to another in silent appraisal of the work that had been done. Michael followed her, standing in the doorway of each room she entered.

The house was almost identical to his own, which wasn't surprising given that the same architect had designed and the same contractor built them some twenty years before. Both were of a modified Cape style, sprawling and open, fashioned to take advantage of the spectacular view of the sea. The structural changes Danica had made—breaking through walls between kitchen and living room and foyer—only served to enhance the sense of freedom and space.

"What do you think?" he asked when they returned to the living room.

"Not bad," she said, but her smile was spreading. "Not bad at all. In fact, I think it looks great. Of course, it'll look that much better once the furniture's in, but I'll appreciate that all the more for having seen it as it is now."

Michael agreed. "Looks to me like the furniture is the only thing left to come."

"That and a few area rugs. I thought I'd buy artwork and pottery, ashtrays and things, up here. The walls look wonderful. When we decided to strip the paper off, I was worried about what we'd find underneath. But we did okay." The walls were painted a soft cream color to blend not only with the woodwork accenting doors and windows but also with the refinished planks on the floor. Excited now, she returned to the kitchen. "I love it." When she heard Michael behind her, she tossed him a quick grin. "I agonized over these cabinets, but I'm thrilled with the way they look." She studied in turn the ceramic tile underfoot, the Formica countertops—all in off-white shades—and the newly recessed ceiling fixtures that gave a more contemporary look to the room. "Perfect." She was beaming. "I love it!"

Daring to hope, she opened the refrigerator. The light went on; cool air wafted out. Leaving the door to swing shut on its own, she turned to test a burner on the stove. It worked.

In triumph she turned back to Michael. "I think I'm in business!" Rubbing her hands together, she backtracked to the hall to adjust the thermostat and bring up some heat.

He followed. "Whoa! What are you in business for?"

"Now that I have a livable home, I think I'll live in it for a while."

"For a while. How long are you up for?"

"The day." When he chuckled, she grew thoughtful. "Come to think of it, there's no reason for me to rush back to Boston tonight. Blake's away. Mrs. Hannah can cancel—"

"You're not planning to spend the night here."

"Why not?"

"My God, Danica, the place is little more than a shell!"

She shrugged, liking the idea more and more. "I can buy what I need for the night. There are stores up here, aren't there?"

"Sure, but—"

"I was going to have to buy pots and pans sooner or later. I can pick up soup and tea, maybe butter and eggs at the supermarket. I don't need much."

Michael remained silent, watching her as she walked to the window, ran her hand along the newly painted sill, knelt to touch the sanded and polished floor. Her pleasure was contagious—or was it simply the pleasure he felt in seeing her again? Her excitement was pure, refreshing, innocent in its way. "Uh, Danica?"

She turned to him with the brightest of smiles. "Uh-huh?"

"Where are you going to sleep?"

For an instant she frowned, but only for an instant. "Mmmm. I hadn't thought about that."

"You can't curl up on the bare floor."

Somehow curling up on the floor did seem to be above and beyond the call of duty. On the other hand, with a little ingenuity . . . "How about an air mattress and some blankets, maybe even a down sleeping bag . . . , that's a nice idea." She looked up to find Michael slowly shaking his head. "You think I'm crazy."

"No, no. I'm just . . . amazed. I wouldn't have imagined you'd want to camp out."

"You mean you wouldn't have imagined I'd be the *type* to camp out," she quipped, but there was no censure in her voice, because Michael's gentle manner precluded it. Besides, he was right. "There's always a first time for everything," she said, her voice soft, her gaze suddenly bound to his. He had such remarkable brown eyes, she thought. They were clear, warm, genuine, and made her feel very special. She needed that right now, when she felt incidental to so much of the rest of her life. She needed to be valued, and Michael did that. Basking in his approval, she glowed.

"Danica?" he whispered, then swallowed hard. When she looked at him that way, it was all he could do not to take her in his arms.

Her voice was scarcely louder than his whisper. "You shaved today." His jaw was square, strong, smooth now where she recalled it had been rough. "Last time you hadn't."

"I hadn't expected to see anyone last time."

"But you couldn't have been expecting—"

"No. I didn't know you were coming today. I was passing by on my way into town and I saw the car. But I always look to see who's here. I was wondering when you'd be back." He had been speaking very quietly. Now he swallowed again. "Does that bother you?"

How could it bother her when she felt better than she had in weeks? "It's kind of nice to know there's someone here."

"We can be friends, then?"

She burst into a smile. "I thought we already were."

"Do you want that?"

"Very much."

"I'm glad." He couldn't seem to tear his gaze from hers but realized that he had better do something if he hoped to behave himself. And he had to. She was off-limits . . . off-limits . . . off-limits. "Wanna go shopping?"

"Shopping?"

"For pots and pans and a sleeping bag and—"

"Ah. Shopping. Sure. But you don't have to—"

"I'm your friend, aren't I? What kind of a friend would let you wander around a strange town alone?"

"I've been here before," she chided, but she felt very pleased.

"Being here has little to do with *shopping* here. Come." His hand swallowed hers before she could refuse, and he was heading for the front door. "There are stores and there are stores. I know exactly where to find what you need. It'll save time for both of us."

"Both of us?"

At the door he turned. "If you refuse my offer, I'll only spend the day worrying that you've been ripped off."

"Michael, I can't take your time this way."

"Why not? I'm not complaining."

"What about your work? You said you were a writer."

"I am. But one of the nice things about being a writer is that my time is my own. I was going into town anyway. Now I'll have company."

She held more tightly to his hand when he would have tugged her forward. "Are you sure?"

He grinned. "I'm sure. Let's go." He had started to turn when she drew him back a final time.

"Michael?" He was looking down at her, one brow arched as though prepared to do further battle if she resisted his offer. "Thank you."

The brow lowered and he seemed to melt. "For what?"

"For stopping." She tossed her head toward where her car sat, but the motion came out like a half-shrug and she lowered her eyes. She couldn't forget that not an hour before she had been slumped over her steering wheel, crying her heart out. It still hurt when she thought of Blake, but she didn't feel quite so alone. "For helping me over that."

"I didn't do anything."

"You were here."

He cleared his throat and studied the slow movement of his thumb over her fingers. "Well, let's just say we're even then."

"Even?"

"I was feeling pretty lonely myself." The smile he produced was boyishly honest. "It's nice to have a friend to play hooky with."

On impulse Danica threaded her arm through his and squeezed tight. She was in a new place with a new home and a new friend. If Blake had chosen not to come, that was *his* problem. *She* was going to enjoy herself!

Taking Michael's Blazer, which would more easily hold Danica's purchases, they spent the next hours shopping for the things she would need if she intended to spend the night at her house.

"Are you sure you want to go through with this?" he said out of the side of his mouth as she stood debating between two particularly beautiful hand-made quilts they had found at a small shop in the Union Square group. He had set one arm straight against the counter she faced and had the other tucked in his pocket. His body was angled toward hers in a way that reflected the protectiveness she inspired. "It seems sacrilegious to be throwing one of these on the floor." In truth, he didn't like the idea of *her* spending the night on the floor—or spending the night alone, for that matter. Taking it one step further, what he really wanted was for her to stay with him, but he knew that was impossible.

"No, no. It'll be fine. This is something I'll be able to use in the spare room once the beds are in. Much better than wasting money now on a sleeping bag or a bunch of blankets. In fact," she thought aloud, "I think I'll buy matching quilts while I'm at it. And throw pillows. Since we're here now . . ." Her words trailed off as she sent him an apologetic glance. "Are you bored?"

"Are you kidding? It's a joy to watch you shop. You're so enthusiastic about it."

"But still . . ."

"Listen," he said softly, putting an arm around her shoulder, "I've shopped with women before and I swore I'd never do it again. They pick things up, put them down, pick up something else, go back to the first, leave the store, return two minutes later, having changed their minds again, but this is different. You're having fun and it's catching. Do I look like I'm suffering?"

He looked positively gorgeous. Suffering? "No. But I feel guilty."

"That's *your* problem." He flashed her a grin, gave her shoulder a squeeze and crooked a finger toward the saleswoman, who had been timidly hovering in the background, trying to busy herself by working on a new quilt while at the same time remaining accessible. "Have you got matching quilts to either of these two?"

It happened that only one of the quilts had a mate, but it was the one Danica favored, so she was thrilled. After purchasing six coordinating throw pillows—three for each bed when the guest room was furnished, plenty for Danica to choose from tonight—they moved on.

True to his word, Michael knew where to find what. Though he preferred to patronize local shops wherever possible—as had been the case with the quilts—he also knew of more practical places to shop for less esoteric things such as pots and pans. And he knew of the best place to stop for lunch, which happened to be an intimate chowder-and-salad house at the edge of Dock Square.

"This is a sight more than I expected when I left Boston this morning," Danica commented, knowing it was an understatement. When she had left Boston, her spirits had just about hit rock bottom. Now she felt distinctly renewed.

Michael reveled in her pleasure. "Me, too. I had expected just another ho-hum day."

"I can't believe your days are ho-hum. You can write. You can pick up and play hooky. You can come and go as you please."

He saw her frown. "What's wrong?"

"I was just envying you your lack of commitments but I'm just assuming that. I never asked whether you're married or anything." Her voice dropped to a self-deprecating whisper. "That was dumb of me."

"No. You never asked because you didn't have to. You know the answer."

She looked at him for a long time, then slowly nodded. "Why no wife?"

He shrugged. "There was never any need to get married. I've had intense relationships, but thanks to the women's movement, none of them ended in marriage."

"What do you mean?"

His cheeks reddened for a minute, a sensitivity that took the edge off what might otherwise have sounded chauvinistic. "The liberated woman is less apt to require a commitment."

"You sound relieved."

He thought about that for a while, finally choosing his words with care. "I haven't been ready for marriage. I travel—doing research and all—and I enjoy that. When I'm home, there's my writing to do and God knows writing is a solitary profession. I do have friends, so when I get lonely, I pick up the phone." His voice lowered on a sadder vein. "There are times though, times when I wish . . ."

"Wish what?"

He fiddled with the saltshaker, turning it clockwise, then counterclockwise. "There are times when I wish I did have a wife and children, times when my house is too quiet, when I'd give just about everything to have a family materialize and be there with me. My family. A wife who would sit talking softly with me late at night. Children who would look a little like each of us, who'd be half angel and half devil but thoroughly lovable." He paused for breath, then gathered the courage to look up.

Danica sat staring at him, her eyes large and moist. She blinked once and tried to smile, but it took her a minute to garner that control. It frightened her that he should share her dreams. "I can understand why you're a writer," she finally managed. "You express yourself well."

"Yeah, well, I'm not sure I like what I express sometimes."

"Your thoughts are beautiful."

"I don't know about that. They're pretty selfish. I'm not sure I deserve a family. It'd be like having my cake and eating it too. If I'd wanted children now, I should have made a commitment before."

Danica thought of Blake and of a similar conversation she had had with her mother. But Michael seemed so much younger than Blake, both in years and behavior. He was spontaneous where Blake was disciplined, casual where Blake was formal. She couldn't ever remember Blake's hair falling across his brow as Michael's did now. "Things aren't that simple sometimes. You said it yourself. You've wanted to travel. And write." She paused. "We all make choices at certain points in our lives. That doesn't mean we never have second thoughts."

Michael knew she was speaking personally. Her voice held sadness and there was the same haunted cast to her eyes that he had seen when she'd been on the beach a month before. "Do you?"

"Do I what?"

"Ever have second thoughts about the choices you've made."

She crinkled up her nose and forced a smile. "I'm like anyone else. I have moments when everything seems wrong." They were both remembering the moments she had spent that morning sitting in her car in tears. "But," she went on in a tone that reminded Michael of the stoicism he had detected in her on the beach that first day, "I have an awful lot that most people don't have."

He wanted to go back, to talk about what had seemed wrong to her before, but the waitress chose that moment to bring their lunch, and needing to see Danica smile, he redirected the conversation to more chatty topics involving Kennebunkport. Later, though, in the supermarket, he sought to appease his curiosity.

"Tell me what you have, Danica."

"I have tea bags, half a dozen eggs, a quart of orange—"

"Not that," he chided. "I can *see* what's in the cart." They were leisurely strolling down the aisle with paper supplies, Michael wheeling, Danica ambling beside. "When we were in the restaurant, you mentioned that you have more in life than most people. Tell me. I want to know."

She reached out to remove a roll of paper towels from the shelf and set it in the cart. "I have the usual, just more of it."

He sensed a modesty in her. "Nice home?"

"You've seen it."

"Not here." Again he was scolding, again, though, in the most gentle of tones. "Tell me about Boston."

She took a deep breath and grasped the edge of the cart as they walked. "We live on Beacon Hill."

"A town house?"

"Uh-huh. It's three stories high, with a charming front walk and a courtyard in back. We share the courtyard with our neighbors."

"The only town house I was ever in on the Hill was weird. It had the kitchen and living room—"

"On the second floor, with the bedrooms above and the family rooms below?" She laughed at his expression, which clearly said he thought the arrangement was awful. "That's how ours is. It's really the most practical setup. We have good space front to back and top to bottom, with next to none side to side. The stairs are steep and long. It makes sense to have the kitchen and living room in the middle."

"I guess." They had stopped at the end of the aisle, moving on only when the approach of another shopper necessitated it. "Still, it must be hard to get used to."

"Not really. The rooms may be narrow, but they're big. We entertain on the first and second floors. Anyway, my dad's place in Washington isn't that much different."

"You lived in Washington rather than Connecticut?"

She shook her head but had no desire to elaborate. "Do you have a dog?"

"Excuse me?"

"A dog. Do you have one?" She pointed to the shelf lined with dog food, but she was eyeing Michael speculatively. "I can picture you running along the beach with an Irish setter at your heels."

"I had one," he said, stunned. "It died last year. You had to know." But she shook her head. "That's uncanny." After a minute he took a breath. "One part of me wants to get another. I look in the papers every week. The other part still mourns Hunter. He was a beauty."

"How long did you have him?"

"Nine years. I bought him when I moved up here. It seemed a great place to have a dog."

"Get another," she urged, suddenly animated.

"I think *you* want one."

The animation waned. "I do, but it's out of the question."

"I'm sure lots of people on Beacon Hill own dogs, for protection if nothing else."

"I often see them out walking. But it's cruel. A dog needs room to run."

"You could have one up here."

"Blake hates dogs," she stated quietly.

"But if the dog is here and he's there . . ."

"The house up here is for the two of us." She gave a rueful laugh. "If he ever makes it. And anyway, the dog would still have to live in the city. It's not like we'll be here fulltime."

They moved on toward the check-out counter then, with Danica wishing she could live here full-time and Michael wishing she had the dog and no Blake. Both knew they were dreaming, but dreams were fun from time to time. And Danica knew for a fact that she was having fun.

Later, after they stowed her purchases in her house, they headed for the beach. It was breezy but comfortable, as it hadn't been that day a month before. Though she wore the same stylish jacket she had worn then, now it lay open over her soft, moss-green sweater and winter-white slacks. Michael, too, was more at ease with the elements than he had been then. They walked slowly, pausing occasionally to look at a cluster of seaweed that had washed up, moving on by mutual and unspoken consent.

"What are you writing now?" Danica asked, pushing her hair behind one ear so that it wouldn't blow in her face when she looked up at him. He was tall and sturdy. She liked that.

"Now? A short history of professional sports in America. It's something light, something I was in the mood to do."

"Doesn't sound all that light to me," she said. She wondered if he knew she had played tennis, wondered if he would say anything about it. She hoped not. She didn't want her past to intrude. Not just now. "There must be a whole lot of research to do."

"Yeah, but it's fun research, especially the interviews. I've talked with some of the old-time greats. Hockey, baseball, boxing—you name it. I needed a change of pace after last year."

"Last year?"

"Then it was an analysis of religious and racial bigotry as a function of economic depressions and recessions."

"A mouthful. But fascinating." And a wonderful diversion. "Is the book out yet?"

"Next month."

She grinned. "Congratulations."

He grinned back. "Thanks."

It took her a minute to catch her breath. "What was your theory?"

"That bigotry is heightened by economic crises. It's nothing people haven't known for years, but few have taken the time to document it."

"You were able to?"

"Easily. History speaks bluntly. In times of economic stress people look out for themselves. They blame their woes on the next guy, particularly if he's weaker or less able to defend himself."

"Even if he's stronger, I'd think. There's many an ethnic or religious group that's been *superior* in one field or another and because of that has become the bigot's target."

Michael beamed. He had known she would be politically astute. "I discussed that at length in the book. I'll give you a copy as soon as I get mine."

"I can buy one."

"Don't be silly. It'll be my pleasure."

They had come to an outcropping of rocks. Michael jumped up on the first, held out his hand to Danica, who readily followed him. When they reached the top, they perched on adjacent boulders.

"How many books have you written?"

"Four."

"All published?" He nodded. "Then it must be old hat to you, having another book appear on the shelves."

"It's never old hat. There's always the excitement and the pride. And the fear."

"Of how it'll do?"

"You bet. As it is, the books I write aren't blockbuster material."

"They're nonfiction. You can't compare apples and oranges."

"Still, we're talking another ball game." He laughed softly and added an aside. "Sorry about that. This new thing is in my blood."

"How *did* it get in your blood—writing, that is? Did you specialize in school? Did you always know you wanted to write?"

Michael gazed out across the sand and shifted one long leg to the side. "For a while I thought it was the last thing I wanted to do. Writing runs in my family. I wanted to be different."

"I can buy that," she said. "Did you try?"

"Oh, yeah." He looked down at his hands. "When I was in high school, I worked afternoons for a landscape architect. I was a lousy gardener, but I prepared a terrific PR brochure for my boss. During the year I took off after high school to bike across country, I did everything from short-order cooking to computer repairs to support myself; the real money came months later when my father had the letters I had sent home serialized in a magazine." Propping his elbows on his knees, he looked seaward again. "By the time I got to college I thought I was headed for law school and the diplomatic corps; I spent most of my senior year collaborating with one of my professors on a book about the Russian Revolution. Even my stint in Vietnam backfired; the things that kept me going were the editorials I was sending back home."

When he looked back at her, the frustration she had seen on his face had vanished. "Everything seemed to be pointing toward a writing career. I could only fight it so far."

"Is your family overbearing?"

"Overbearing?" He chuckled. "That's one way of putting it. But wait. I'm being unfair. My father is the only real villain there," he decreed, but he was grinning. "Everyone else is okay."

"How many are there?"

"Four of us kids, plus Mom and Dad."

Danica's eyes lit up. "Four kids? You must have had fun growing up."

"We did, thanks to Mom. She's a free spirit, as easygoing as Dad is demanding. She kept a handle on him as much as she could, at least until we were old enough to speak up to him. Poor woman," he mused fondly, "after all her struggles to offer us the world, we've *all* ended up doing one sort of writing or another."

"Really?"

"The oldest, Brice, works with my father in New York. The youngest, Corey, edits his own magazine in Phillie. Cilla writes feature articles for one of the papers in D.C."

"Cilla?"

"Priscilla. My sister."

"Is she older or younger?"

"Older by six minutes."

"Twins! I don't believe it! Are there *two* people like you in the world?"

He laughed. "She's a she, which means we're fraternal twins, which means we're no more alike than any brother and sister. She's very different from me—more outgoing, aggressive. She loves the rough and tumble of newspaper reporting; I'd be a basket case in a matter of months."

"Everyone has his strengths. And since you do what you do so well—"

"Now, you don't know that," he teased with a lopsided grin.

"I know," she vowed, guided by instinct. "And I think it's great that you're doing what you enjoy. And that you're so successful at it. The other Buchanans must be proud."

Michael hesitated for a moment, but not because he had doubts about his family's pride. Rather, he was wondering when Danica would begin to put two and two together. The mention of the name Buchanan, the talk round and about newspapers and magazines . . .

"Michael?"

"Hmmm?"

Her face was a study in dawning awareness, a showcase for dismay and apprehension. "You haven't said exactly what it is your father does." Her voice was suddenly quiet.

"I think you just guessed."

She closed her eyes and dropped her chin to her chest, then suddenly threw her head back and laughed. "I don't believe it." Her gaze met Michael's. "I don't believe it! Do you know how much my father hates yours?" But she was grinning. It had suddenly occurred to her that it wasn't her war.

Michael agreed. "I can imagine. I'm not sure if the two of them have ever actually met, but I'd hate to be around when that happened. Our papers haven't been kind to your father over the years."

"My father hasn't inspired kindness." She shook her head in amazement, trying to assimilate what she had learned. "The Buchanan Corporation. Unbelievable." Then a thought struck and her knuckles grew white on the rock by her hip. She had come to trust Michael completely; it would be a blow to find she had misplaced that trust. "You've known all along?"

But he was already shaking his head. He had anticipated her apprehension and prepared his defense. "I had no idea who you were that first day. It wasn't until I spoke with Judy that I learned you were the senator's daughter, and since then I've been wishing I belonged to any other family but my own." He swiveled on his rock to face her. "You could hate me for some of the things our papers have said about your father, but please believe me when I say that I never condoned that kind of attack. That's one of the reasons I'd never have made it with the Corporation. I meant what I said on the beach last time about my writing not being threatening. I would never do anything to hurt you, Danica. You know that, don't you?"

She searched his face then, seeing the things she had seen all day and more. It was a handsome face, with its melting brown eyes and its windblown cap of sandy hair, and it held warmth and strength and affection. It also held desperation, and that she understood.

Slowly she nodded, thinking how very lucky she was to have found a friend who wanted her friendship every bit as badly as she wanted his.

Danica took her time driving back to Boston the following day. She felt relaxed and refreshed, free of the anger she had felt the morning before. She knew that Blake would be home that night, that she would tell him about the house, what she had bought, how she had slept on the living-room floor.

She wouldn't tell him about Michael, though. Not yet. Michael was her own friend, neither a businessman nor a politician. Perhaps it was defiance she felt: after all, Blake had been too busy to make the trip; therefore he had no claim to what he had missed. Besides, she reasoned, she had a right to a friend, particularly one who was as easy to talk with and be with as Michael Buchanan. If there was something naughty about her associating with a Buchanan, so be it. She admired Michael. She enjoyed him. And she was thoroughly looking forward to seeing him again when she returned to Maine.

FOUR

BLAKE WAS WITH DANICA the next time she drove north.

"I still don't believe it," she teased in the car, hoping to cajole her husband into a better mood. She knew that he'd had second thoughts about making the trip but had yielded for her sake, and she was grateful. She firmly believed that given time alone in a place far removed from the maelstrom of the city, she and Blake could recapture the spark their marriage had had once upon a time.

"I shouldn't be here," he stated with the same quiet conviction that characterized his every move. "My desk will be piled high by the time I get back."

"We'll only be away for three days," she scolded gently. "Besides, you owe it to yourself. You're always working. It's been so long since you took time off just to relax."

"A weekend would have been better."

"But it's impossible to get away on a weekend, Blake. We've been busy every one of the past six, with more to come in June. It's the pre-summer rush of dinner parties, I guess, not to mention the fundraising you're doing."

"You aren't still bothered by that, are you?"

"No, no." Slowly, very slowly, she had acclimated herself to Blake's active support of Jason Claveling. There had been no argument. She and Blake never argued. They discussed. And with Blake his usual eloquent self when he wanted to make a point, she never really had a chance. So, in time, the hurt had simply faded, then disappeared, as it always did. After all, she did want to be a good wife to him. "I can stand it as long as you can. Doesn't it ever get to you, the backslapping and handshaking?"

He shot her a fast glance. "It's business. You should know that. What does Bill say when you ask him?"

"I never ask. With him, it's a way of life. From the earliest I can remember, he was going to political functions of one sort or another, and Mom accepts them, trouper that she is. You, well, I guess I didn't expect you'd become so involved."

"I was involved when you met me. Then I was raising money for Bill."

"For the longest time I wondered about that. After all, you were a resident of Massachusetts while Dad was the senator from Connecticut."

"Bill was a friend. I also happened to approve of his stands in the Senate, especially those affecting big business."

"You were buying an insurance policy."

His lips twitched at her subtle sarcasm. "It's done every day of the week. In Bill's case, it was easy. I liked him personally. And I liked you. With Claveling, it's business all the way."

They drove on for a while in silence before Danica spoke again. "If Claveling is elected, what will it mean to you?"

Blake's answer was on the tip of his tongue, suggesting where his own thoughts had been. "Import quotas. Favorable trade agreements. Tax benefits. Who knows, maybe a cabinet appointment."

She saw his grin when she darted a look his way. "Fun-ny," she murmured, and relaxed back in her seat as the Mercedes crossed the Piscataqua River and entered Maine.

In her very biased opinion, the house was stupendous. Since Blake had insisted she let the decorator supervise all the furniture deliveries—and since she had been unable to get away to do so herself—she was seeing the finished product for the first time alongside Blake.

He seemed to approve, though whether he was simply indulging her she wasn't sure. He walked from room to room, hands buried deep in the pockets of his slacks, and nodded from time to time.

"Well?" she finally asked. Her own excitement was tempered only by the suspense of not knowing what he thought.

"It's very nice."

He said the words without passion. Her shoulders sagged. "You don't like it," she murmured.

"I do. It's perfect. You've done a wonderful job, Pook." He gave her a broad smile, then turned. "I'll get the bags."

Very diligently, given the fact that they had only brought clothes for two days, and strictly casual ones at that, Blake unpacked while Danica went through the house a second, then a third time. Determinedly overlooking her husband's apparent indifference, she enthusiastically examined every piece of furniture that had been delivered. It was the antithesis of the Beacon Hill town house, which, in keeping with its structure, had been decorated in a more classical style. Here, newly installed skylights illumined modular sofa clusters, low swirling coffee tables, custom-made wall units. The feeling was one of openness and lack of clutter and was precisely what Danica had wanted.

Blake returned from the bedroom to wander around the living room. He didn't touch anything, simply wandered.

She rubbed her hands together. "What would you like to do?"

He shrugged and looked toward the deck. "Walk out there."

He stood on the deck for no less than ten minutes, staring in the direction of the waves. When Danica had grown tired of waiting, she came to stand several feet from him. "Pretty, isn't it," she offered with a smile, hoping to get him talking. She hated the lengthy silences that so often existed between them, because she could never tell what he was thinking. His face was always composed, his manner as unruffled as his hair. But she knew that he *felt*, that he *thought*. What she didn't know was why he couldn't share those thoughts and feelings with her.

This day, this setting, apparently was going to make no difference. He simply nodded.

"It's been interesting watching the changes since I've been here," she went on, trying to sound as nonchalant as possible when in fact she was forcing conversation. Normally she would have been perfectly happy just to quietly appreciate the scene. Somehow now, beside Blake, she felt impelled to chatter. "When I came up in March, it was really cold. The ocean was a mass of whitecaps. You couldn't smell much of anything because your nose was frozen. Then last month it was warmer. The air was moist and the wind didn't bowl you over." She inhaled deeply. "This is nice, though. May. You can smell the beach grass, feel the sun." Tipping her head back, she closed her eyes and basked, momentarily forgetting Blake's presence until he made it known.

"You said something about wanting to pick up paintings?"

Righting her head, she looked at him. "By local artists. Maybe a sculpture or two, also."

"Why don't we go now? I want to explore the streets and plot out a route to run."

"You're going to run up here? I kind of thought you'd take a break from all that." When he shook his head, she felt another tiny bit of hope die. "I suppose it would be nice for you to run along the shore," she rationalized, then sighed and forced a smile. "I'll get my purse."

They spent the next few hours idling through shops, looking unsuccessfully for artwork, then lunching at Cape Porpoise, buying groceries at the market, driving round and about the local streets while Blake calculated the best eight-mile route for him to run. In theory, it was an easygoing afternoon, just the two of them doing things together as Danica had dreamed.

In fact, it was a letdown.

To Danica, who was ever watchful, Blake seemed uncomfortable. It was as though he felt out of place, which she couldn't understand since Kennebunkport was sophisticated, certainly enough to satisfy his tastes. But he kept looking around, restless, as if waiting for someone to talk to. Evidently Danica wasn't that someone, for he seemed disinclined to carry on more than the most superficial conversation with her.

Between her watchfulness and those attempts at conversation, she felt drained by the time they returned to the house. Once there, things were no better. Blake wandered around like a lost soul, looking more frustrated than pensive, more awkward than unsure. She was half relieved when he disappeared into the den with the briefcase he had smuggled into the house. When she peeked in on him an hour later, he was talking on the phone and looking happy for the first time all day.

Busying herself in the kitchen, Danica studied the cookbooks she had brought, then painstakingly prepared a meal she felt sure would impress him. Indeed, he complimented her when he finally emerged for dinner, but no sooner had she brewed his coffee than he escaped back into the den, leaving her alone with her tea and her thoughts.

She lifted the tea bag tag. "Love is the magic that makes one and one far more than two," she read silently, dropped the tag and wondered what had gone wrong. She and Blake were very definitely two. No more, no less. Two individuals, wanting, it appeared, increasingly different things in life.

She went to sleep thinking about that, awoke early the next morning thinking of it. Blake lay on his side of the large bed, his back to her, distant even in sleep. She wondered what time it had been when he'd come to bed, wondering if it had even occurred to him that she might be waiting. Not that she had been; by now she was used to being alone. Still, he was a man. Surely he thought of sex *once* in a while.

Studying his sleeping form, she reflected on the early days of their marriage. She had been attracted to Blake for his sureness, his social grace, his maturity. Sex had never held a high priority in their relationship, and she had never minded it. She had never seen herself as being a highly passionate person. In that, she and Blake seemed well matched. Still, she couldn't help wondering whether he found her attractive. He rarely reached out for her, and even then she felt he did so more out of obligation than real need. Even now he looked untouchable.

The sound of a buzz jolted her from her thoughts. Blake stirred, pushed himself up on an elbow, reached over to turn off the travel alarm Danica hadn't known he had brought. She had assumed they would sleep late, awaken leisurely, break the pattern that dominated their everyday lives.

Clearly, she had assumed too much, a point the events of that day drove home. Bounding from the bed, Blake put on his fashionable navy running suit and left the house. She had a big breakfast ready by the time he returned and showered, but he ate only the amount he apportioned himself every other morning of the week, so the bulk of her efforts went down the drain.

At her gentle request, they drove up the coast toward Boothbay Harbor, stopping along the way to browse in craft shops and galleries, purchasing a ceramic sculpture and several planters for the deck. Blake was agreeable, if otherwise passive. Again she felt he was merely indulging her whim rather than finding enjoyment in the day himself. Again he disappeared into the den when they returned, and again she felt vaguely relieved. She also felt discouraged, though, and, with a quick word to him, headed for the beach.

Feeling suddenly freer than she had since she arrived, she wandered over sand and pebbles, around fingers of rocks, heading almost by instinct for the boulders she and Michael had shared a month before.

Michael. His name sparked thoughts of relaxation and fun and excitement. Just thinking about him, she felt better. He was different, so different. And he was her friend.

"Yeo!"

She looked up and started to smile, then, without thinking, broke into a jog, coming to a halt not six feet from him. "Michael!"

He looked as roguish, as bold, as welcoming as ever. He wore an open-necked plaid shirt with the sleeves rolled to the elbow, a pair of jeans that had seen better days, sneakers in a like state, and he was smiling from ear to ear. With his hair lightly mussed and his jaw faintly shadowed, he had to be the most stimulating sight she had seen in days.

When he opened his arms, she ran forward, tightly clasping his neck while he swung her gently from side to side. He smelled clean and felt strong, and she reveled in his affection.

Finally, he set her back to study each of her features in turn. "You look great!" he said at last, then swooped down to give her another fast hug. "It's good to see you, Danica."

"And you," she managed, breathless and flushed. "How are you?"

"Better now. I saw the car in the driveway last night and was wondering if I'd get a chance to see you." It had been the Mercedes rather than the Audi. Her next words confirmed his suspicion.

"Blake's up with me, but he's doing some work, so I thought I'd come out for a walk." She couldn't seem to stop smiling.

Neither could Michael. "I noticed that your furniture arrived."

She laughed. "Lots of trucks lately?"

"Lots of trucks lately. How does it all look?"

"Great."

"No more sleeping on the floor?"

"Nope."

Michael was about to express his satisfaction until he realized that the arrival of beds meant she would have slept with Blake last night, and he didn't care for that idea at all. Pushing it from mind, he reached for her hand. "Can you stay and talk for a while?"

She nodded and let herself be led to the same granite seat she had occupied last time, thinking that though there was many a higher spot, she felt on top of the world.

"I read your book," she ventured shyly when they were perched on the rocks facing each other.

"You *did?*"

"Uh-huh. It was wonderful."

"You must have gotten one of the first copies out."

She laughed. "I pestered the manager of the bookstore so often that he called me the minute it came in. It was really good, Michael. Interesting and informative. Your writing style makes the reading fun."

"You really think so?"

She could see that he was pleased because he was grinning and his voice was higher than usual. In response to his question she nodded, then asked several questions about the things she had read. Michael answered them enthusiastically, though, as quickly and comfortably as possible, he changed the subject.

"How have you been?" he asked more soberly.

His tone suggested that he knew there were things that bothered her, things that had been bothering her for a long time. She accepted his perceptivity without question. "All right."

When she didn't elaborate, he took the gentler course. "Tell me what you've been up to."

She gave a shy smile and hesitated until his gentle prodding coaxed from her a cursory account of what she had done since she'd seen him last. When she finished, she looked off toward the waves.

"What is it?"

"Oh—" she darted him a glance and smiled self-consciously "—I feel silly telling you all this. Nothing I do is earth-shattering. I mean, it's not as if I have a real profession."

"I wouldn't say that. You may not get paid for what you do, but you're certainly performing a service that needs to be performed."

She gave a dry laugh. "By going to luncheons?"

"By going to luncheon *meetings*, at which you plot out the futures of some very worthwhile institutions."

"I'm one of many."

"That doesn't matter. Every voice counts. If no one took the time to do what you do, many a charitable institution would fall apart. Besides, you care, and that makes your voice all the more valuable."

"Still, there are times when I wish I had a regular job."

"Is it a matter of your own self-image?"

"Maybe, in part. Also because I'd like to be busy."

"You're bored."

"Mmmm." She threw up her hands. "It's ridiculous. My days are filled with one thing or another and it's not like I have time on my hands, but . . . but . . ."

"Your mind's not occupied."

She gave him a helpless look that confirmed what he'd said. "Maybe that's why you can read it so easily. You do, you know." Playfully she narrowed her gaze. "What am I thinking right now?"

He grinned. "You're thinking that I'm a handsome devil who should have caught you before Blake Lindsay did."

"Well, you are a handsome devil, that's for sure." Her gaze fell to his arm, propped straight on the rock. Golden hair dusted his skin, which in turn was stretched taut over the twist of firm muscle. "You are . . ." she began, but her words trailed off.

With that very same arm Michael collared her and tugged her close. The gentle gesture brought her temple to his jaw. When he spoke, his breath warmed her brow. "I wish I had caught you first, y' know."

Danica melted against him, feeling very, very good. She'd never been a physically demonstrative person, but Michael was, and she found that she loved it. In hindsight, the way she had earlier run into his arms startled her, yet it had seemed the most natural, most desirable thing to do. She felt wanted, protected, valued. But more, she felt stronger, as if this long-denied human touch had renewed a certain faith in herself.

"You're special," she murmured, luxuriating in his touch for a moment longer. In the end, it was he who set her back.

"Not special. Just concerned." His voice was husky. He cleared his throat. "And we were talking about what you can do to keep your mind occupied."

"We were?" She felt slightly dazed. It took her a minute to get her bearings.

Michael's recovery was that much faster, but then, he had the advantage of knowing precisely how and what he felt. Not that knowing made things easier; to be wild about a woman who was married to another man was insanity, sheer insanity.

"If you want a job, why not get one?"

She took a long, unsteady breath. "I'm not exactly trained for anything."

"You have a degree, don't you?"

She was finally focusing. "In English. Not very practical in this day and age. But I never expected to do anything with it."

"What did you expect?" he asked without censure.

"Much of what I got. A husband. A home—two, now. A life similar in many ways to my mother's."

"But that's not what you want."

She looked down at her hand and nervously twisted her wedding band around. "I feel frustrated."

"What is it you do want from life?"

"Love," she blurted out, then realized what she'd said and colored. "I want children, but they haven't come. Maybe that's why I feel at loose ends. Maybe that's why I feel I have to work." Her laugh was brittle. "I mean, I don't *have* to work. I just—" she widened her eyes in emphasis "—*have* to work."

"I hear you." He had heard every word, including that one she regretted saying but which had told him a great deal, not the least of which accounted for the sadness he had seen in her from time to time. He wanted to ask about her marriage but didn't quite dare yet. "I think you should look for a job if that's what you want."

She was torn. "Yes, it's what I want. But there are so many factors involved. A job is a commitment. I'd have to shift everything else around. And then there's Blake. I'm not sure how he'd feel about my working. I've always been there when he's needed me."

"He's a big boy."

"I know, and I didn't mean 'need' in that sense. When push comes to shove, Blake doesn't *need* me at all. It's just that he expects me to be there when he gets home. I always have been . . . looking just right, dressed to go out if he wants. But if I work all day, I'll be tired at night . . ."

"He works all day. Doesn't he tire of the game?"

"He loves it."

Some guys did. Michael knew the type. They were driven by forces from without and were not, first and foremost, family men. "Okay. But wouldn't he be able to understand why you want to work?"

"I don't know. He's of a different generation in many ways. He's so like my father, and I *know* my father would resist the idea of my working."

"Would that bother you?"

A lone herring gull screeched overhead, drawing her attention. She watched it career along an air wave and envied it its smooth ride. "Yes," she said at last in a tone filled with resignation, "it would bother me. I've always wanted to please him."

"Wouldn't it please him to know that you're happy? Wouldn't it please him to know that you'd seen something wrong in your life and tried to fix it? If nothing else, Senator Marshall is a doer. When he sees something he thinks is wrong, he works to change it. I may not have always agreed with his stands, but I'm convinced that he truly believes in each and every one of them."

Danica chuckled dryly. "You must be the only Buchanan who has that faith, at least where it concerns either defense spending or foreign policy. The papers have alternately claimed that he was being bought, that he was carrying out a vendetta or that he was parrying for votes in an election year."

"Well," Michael sighed, "I'm not my family, and my argument is that your father might well be sympathetic to your cause."

"You don't know him, Michael," she murmured. "Oh, yes, he'd be sympathetic to my cause if he believed in it. But he doesn't."

"You believe in your cause. Wouldn't that be enough for him?"

"If only. Don't you see? It's not that in theory he'd have any objection to his daughter working. It's that he sees his daughter as already employed, and he's not particularly open to another view. He sees things one way and is terribly narrow-minded when it comes to those who think differently. I guess that's it. But isn't your father the same way?" From what she had heard, from what Michael had himself intimated, John Buchanan was a dictator in his own right.

"Sure. I was lucky, though. My mother goes to the other extreme." He thought for a minute. "Have you discussed all this with your mother?"

"God, no. She's an extension of my father. Not that I'm criticizing, mind you. She's been the perfect politician's wife. She enjoys the pomp and circumstance. Apparently, it's all she needs."

"Then, she'd agree with your father."

"Mmmm. And as far as he's concerned, my place is by Blake's side. In his mind, everything I do should have some bearing on Blake and his career and, therein, my future security."

"Do you believe that?"

"No. I've just never had cause to fight it."

"Before."

She nodded.

"Why the change now?"

She pondered his question. "I guess I'm getting older. I'm twenty-eight. I've been married for eight years. I'm beginning to sit back and take stock of things."

"And you want more."

Again she nodded, but her attention had focused on Michael's lips as he spoke. They were firm lips, with a hint of softness in the lower one that took masculinity into the modern age. He was a man to talk with, to understand. She wondered if he was that much less critical and more open-minded than the other men she had known or if it was simply that he shared her views.

When those lips moved to speak again, she dragged her gaze back to his eyes. They were more heated now, filled with a passion she had never seen directed toward her. If only Blake looked at her that way from time to time, things might be different.

"Would a job solve your problems?" he asked softly.

No, she knew. The problem went far deeper than a simple filling of time. Taking a job would be a stopgap measure. What she needed was love and the warm home she had always craved but never had. Financial security, social position—they weren't enough. What she needed was to be needed, to be respected as an individual in her own right.

She looked down "It would be a start, I suppose."

"Then go for it."

"Which brings us back to square one. If only things weren't so complicated. If only there weren't these other expectations."

"They're other people's expectations, not your own."

"That's what's so muddled. They've been my own for a long, long time—"

"Even though, deep down inside, you've probably always wanted something else?"

"Yes," she confirmed in a small voice. "Even then. I'm just not that courageous a person, I guess. I'm afraid of upsetting the applecart."

Michael reached for her hand. His thumb brushed her knuckles, gently caressed her fingers. "You're very hard on yourself, your own worst enemy, I think. Do you remember once we talked of choices?" When she nodded, he went on. "Life is filled with them, and they keep on coming. So many of the choices you've made in the past have been dictated by your desire to please. Now you're discovering that while you may be pleasing others, you're not pleasing yourself." He pressed her hand between both of his and searched her features. She looked so very vulnerable that he ached.

"There'll be other choices, Dani, other choices to be made. At some point you'll venture down a different road, and when that happens, you'll feel comfortable with the decision."

She brushed her free fingers over the soft sprinkling of hair on the back of his hand, then spread her palm there. His warmth seeped into her. His strength was contagious. "You sound so sure that I almost believe it."

"Come 'ere," he growled and hugged her to him again. *I know it*, he thought. *I have faith in you.*

I wish I could package you up, she mused, *and keep you in my pocket all the time. You make me feel so good. You give me such confidence.*

You've never been given a chance. There's so much inside you, so much just begging to be freed.

Why aren't the others like you? Why don't they understand?

They all take you for granted. I never could. But then, you're not mine, are you?

"Oh, Michael . . ." she whispered.

Reluctantly he set her back, but his gaze continued to embrace her a moment longer. "You're apt to be missed," he murmured thickly. "Maybe you'd better head back." *Before I do something that will complicate your life all the more.*

She nodded and, holding his steadying hand, climbed down from the rocks. When once again she stood on the sand, she focused on the horizon. "We'll be leaving tomorrow. The next few weeks will be busy. Then I'll be back. Will you be here?"

"I'll be here."

She looked at him. "Writing?"

"That, and relaxing. The summer's beautiful here. There's lots to do."

She smiled, but tears had gathered on her lower lids. On impulse she stretched to lightly kiss his cheek. Then, before she made an utter fool of herself, she quickly set off down the beach.

She didn't look back. She didn't have to. Michael's image was firmly planted in her mind, where it remained for the rest of the day. Much as she tried, given the fact that she was back in her own house with her husband, she couldn't forget those lips, so warm and firm, that arm, corded and strong, the masculine set of that body, which had hugged her, held her, made her feel special. And feminine. She had never felt so feminine before. She tingled in secret places when she thought of the curling hairs that had edged through the open neck of Michael's shirt, when she thought of the roughness of his cheek when she had pressed her lips there. She grew warm all over again when she thought of the clean, fresh smell of his skin.

And she was terrified.

That night, Danica Lindsay seduced her husband. It was a deliberate act, born of desperation. And it was a first.

The woman who had always waited for her husband to reach out now did the reaching. She who had been shy undressed openly. She who had been silent whispered an urgent "Make love to me, Blake." She who had always been in control of herself was now controlled by a greater force.

Aroused as never before, she demanded a fierce pace. Selfish as never before, she concentrated solely on the fire that raged in her straining body. When she reached a heart-stopping climax, she kept her eyes shut and bit her lip to keep from crying out. And when it was over, she curled in a ball and yielded to silent tears of anguish.

For in her heart she knew she had made love to another man. And she wasn't sure how she was going to handle that fact.

"You're awfully quiet." Hand on the banister post, Greta McCabe stopped at the bottom of the stairs to study Michael, who sat sprawled in the shabby armchair he had occupied since dinner. His eyes had been glued to the rug, but when she spoke, he glanced up and smiled.

"Pat ran out to get more beer. You ran up to put Meggie to bed. There was no one to talk with."

"All night, Mike. You've been quiet all night." She perched on the arm of his chair. "Is something bothering you?"

Michael took a weary breath and leaned his head against the back of the chair. Pat and Greta were two of his closest friends; he had known them for years and years. It didn't surprise him that he had sought out their company tonight, any more than that Greta had sensed something on his mind.

"I think," he began, emphasizing each word in a way that would have been comical if Greta hadn't known better, "that I'm in trouble."

"Work problems?"

He shook his head.

"Family problems?"

Again he shook his head.

"Uh-oh. Michael Buchanan, what have you done this time?"

He knew precisely what that tone of voice suggested and suppressed a groan. "Nothing. I swear to God—"

"You haven't taken up with Monica again, have you?" She was trouble from the start."

"No, I haven't seen or heard—"

"Then, you left another one waiting for you at La Guardia."

"Of course not. That happened four years ago and if I hadn't been so damned preoccupied trying to straighten out the manuscript that got screwed up—"

"You didn't get a girl pregnant, did you?" Greta said with such stoical calm that he could only grab her hand and squeeze it tight.

"No, Greta. I did not get a girl pregnant. Give me a little credit, will ya?"

"Then what is it?"

"I'm in love."

The back door slammed coincidentally with Greta's going perfectly still. "I've known you for a long time, Michael, but I don't believe I've ever heard you say that."

"Say what?" Pat asked, sauntering in with a six-pack under his arm.

"Michael's in love."

"Ahhhh. New book idea?"

Michael smirked. "Not exactly."

"No? Gee, it would be interesting. Taking participatory research to its limits."

"Pat," Greta scolded, "he's serious."

"He can't be serious. He told me once that he'd *never* fall in love."

"I was ten years old at the time," Michael muttered, more for Greta's information than in self-defense.

"And one hell of a ladies' man even then. But cool. Real cool. Babe, you shoulda seen him."

Michael dropped his chin to his chest in an exaggerated gesture of defeat, but he was grinning. "I taught you everything you know, didn't I, pal?"

"Welllll, I don't know if that's an accurate—"

"Okay, you two. Pat, give Michael his beer and go sit down. Michael, tell me. Who is she?"

"She's a super lady."

"No name?"

"Not yet." He looked from one to the other of his friends. "I trust you guys completely, but it's just that, well, she's very special and very vulnerable and the situation is really awful."

Greta could only imagine one really awful situation. "She's married."

"You got it."

"Oh, Mike, I'm sorry."

Michael snorted. "Not half as sorry as I am."

Pat was leaning forward, rolling his beer can between his hands. "How'd you meet her?"

"Innocently. On the beach. She was just standing there and I went up to her. She looked sad and alone. We started talking. She's beautiful. I mean, not in the physical sense—well, she is that, too—but from the inside out. She's gentle and bright. She looks at you and you want to melt because there's something there that's afraid and shy but so generous and in need of a friend." He wore a look of despair. "I swear I was half in love with her even before I saw the damn ring."

The room was filled with silence in the aftermath of Michael's confession. Finally Pat sat back in his seat. "It sounds like you've got it bad."

"Do you see her often?" Greta asked.

"No. But every time I do it's worse."

"What's the state of her marriage?"

"I think it's got problems, but I'm really only guessing. Once in a while she lets something slip."

"Does she know how you feel?"

"She knows that I like her, but I doubt she knows the extent of it. At least she hasn't put a name to it. She's down on herself right about now and I think the last thing she'd dare guess was that a man she'd just met was in love with her."

"How does she feel about you?"

"Right about now I think she feels confused. She's so innocent; that's one of the incredible things, Greta. We've just kind of fallen into this thing and she's so unsuspecting that it goes on and on and we fall deeper and deeper. The excitement is there for both of us when we see each other after being apart. She holds my hand. She lets me hug her. Very innocently. She trusts me as a friend. But I'm afraid, because lately. . ." He grew quiet, absently rubbing the moisture that had collected on the side of the beer can.

"Geez, don't stop now."

"Pat, pleeeze. What, Mike? What's happened?"

He took a swig of beer. "Well, I think she's beginning to feel physical things that she doesn't expect or want. It probably frightens her. Hell, it frightens me. And I'm not sure just where it's going to end."

"She's married. You'd never do anything. . ." Greta began, only to be silenced by Michael's pained expression.

"You both know me as well as anyone does. You know where I've come from. You know how I feel about homewreckers. I saw what happened to my mother when Dad took up with Deborah; I'd never want to cause that kind of hurt. But, God, I've never seen it from this side before. I mean, if the woman is unhappy and we can give something to each other . . ."

"You're right," Greta declared, "you are in trouble."

"I feel—" he threw a hand in the air, continuing his outpouring of thoughts as though Greta had never spoken "—torn by the whole thing. Oh, not when I'm with her. When we're together I can't think of anything but the pleasure

I feel, the pleasure *she* seems to feel. But when she's gone and I stand back and see the whole situation, it scares the hell out of me. I don't want to come between her husband and her, but I'm not sure that there's that much of substance between them. It seems more like a marriage of convenience, which, good soul that she is, she's trying to make work."

"How long has she been married?" Pat asked.

"Eight years."

"Any kids?"

"No."

"Statistically speaking, if there are problems, she'd be ripe for divorce."

"Perhaps statistically, but there are other factors at work here. Her family is strong and prominent."

Greta groaned.

Michael shot her a knowing glance. "To make matters worse, her father and mine aren't exactly admirers."

Pat grimaced. "You do pick 'em."

"No, Pat. She's different from any woman I've ever known." He gave a sheepish grin. "I could elaborate, but I've already said enough. I'll be boring you pretty soon."

"You won't bore us," Greta soothed. "I just wish there were something we could do to help."

"There is," he responded, realizing that the idea was coming only as he spoke but instantly liking it. "You can be her friend."

"Will we meet her?"

"She'll be here on and off through the summer. I'd like to bring her over one day. She'd enjoy it here."

Pat scanned the room. "This place isn't exactly the natural habitat for people from prominent families."

Michael didn't need to look around. He knew that the two-bedroom house was small, that the furniture was worn, the decor plain. He also knew that neither Greta nor Pat came from prominence, that Pat worked his tail off as a tuna fisherman, that the McCabes would never be wealthy, nor did they want to be. "She's had the other, and something's missing. I'm not sure she's ever been in a home. A real home. That's what you've got here."

Greta took a deep breath. "So you want to make a point. Isn't that playing a little dirty?"

They were too close friends for Michael to be offended. "I'm not out for points. I just want to see her smile. I want to share something with her. I want her to relax and have fun."

"What about her husband?" Pat injected. "Won't he question where she's going and why?"

"He's a busy man in the city. If his past behavior is any clue, I have a feeling she may be up here alone more often than not."

"I feel a little like a conspirator in crime," Greta moaned.

"Is it a crime to make someone happy?" Michael asked with such poignancy that neither McCabe could hold out against him.

"Of course not. And of course you can bring her here."

Pat agreed. "Hell, I'm curious to see the woman who's finally brought you to your knees."

"She has done that." Michael mused, "The question is whether I'll ever be able to stand again."

FIVE

❀❀❀

D ANICA CHOSE HER TIME WELL, waiting for a moment when Blake was relaxed and in as good a mood as possible. It came when Marcus was driving them home from a cocktail reception in Concord. The reception, a gathering to honor one of Blake's prominent friends in the business community, had been successful. Blake was seated beside her in the back of the Mercedes. He had no briefcase with him, no papers to read, and the drive home was going to take a good thirty minutes.

"Blake?"

"Hmmm?"

She knew his mind was elsewhere, but then, she couldn't ask for miracles. "I've been thinking." He said nothing, so she went on, schooling her tone to one of quiet conviction. "I've decided to spend the summer in Maine."

She looked over at him, but his expression was hidden by the night. So much the better, she mused. She wanted nothing to rob her of her confidence. And she did feel confident on this matter. She had given it much thought, *much* thought since their return from Kennebunkport three weeks before.

"The entire summer?"

"It makes sense. July and August are always quieter around here. Everyone is away."

"*I* can't spend the entire summer in Maine. July and August will be hectic for me. The convention's coming up."

If it hadn't been the convention, she felt sure it would be something else. She had been through summers in Boston before. Blake kept himself occupied, leaving her to wither, to suffer the heat or to frequent the country club. Neither option appealed to her. She would have loved to go to the beach, but Blake disliked public crowds. The same applied to a stroll through the Marketplace, a cruise in the harbor or an evening on the Esplanade.

When she had pushed for the house in Maine, she had hoped she and Blake would *both* escape there. His initial reaction to the place, though, hadn't been promising. And then there'd been this political campaign, which would complicate things all the more. "I haven't forgotten the convention. And it's another reason why it'd be silly for me to stay around. You'll be busy, but what will I do?"

"There are certain times when I'll want you with me."

She knew about those and had allowed for them. "I'll drive back whenever you want. And you can come up when you're free."

She held her breath, half expecting him to object. After all, it would mean that they would be separated for the bulk of two months. Deep down inside, she half *hoped* he'd object. It would be nice to know that he would miss her.

"Is that what you want?" he asked evenly.

"It's not what I want," she returned, unable to hide her frustration. "What I want is for the two of us to spend the summer there together. But you can't do that, can you?"

"You know I can't."

It occurred to her that he did that a lot—said "you know" this or "you know" that—and it annoyed her. It was a way of shifting blame, of evoking guilt, of putting her down. Too often that you-should-know-better tone of his made her feel like a child being chastised, and she resented it.

"You know, Blake," she began, purposely copying his tone, "if you really wanted to, you could. Many a man does, particularly one in as secure a position as you."

"This summer's different."

"Is it?" She listened to herself and realized that it wasn't often she spoke up to him. Once started, she couldn't help herself, though she kept her voice low. "You don't like it up there, do you?"

"Of course I do. It's a lovely place."

She knew he was patronizing her. "You were bored the whole time we were there. You were happiest when you were in the den going through papers or talking on the phone."

He didn't deny it and she wondered, as she had so often since their return, what he had thought of their lovemaking that night. He hadn't touched her since, which wasn't unusual for him. Nor had he said anything immediately after. He had rolled onto his side of the bed and gone to sleep.

"I love my work. You should be grateful. If I was bored and frustrated, I'd be impossible to live with."

"I sometimes wish that would happen. Maybe then we'd fight at least. It's so hard to get a rise from you, Blake. Does *anything* upset you?"

He gave a dry laugh. "If I let every little thing upset me, I'd never have gotten to where I am today."

"Not every little thing. How about one *big* thing?"

He seemed to hesitate longer than usual. "Yes, there have been *big* things that have upset me, but not for long. Nothing's accomplished by getting upset. You have to think clearly. You have to analyze the facts and your options. You have to make decisions and see them through."

"Spoken like the successful businessman you are," she murmured. In truth, she had been thinking about their relationship when she had asked if anything ever upset him. He had chosen to respond in terms of work. It was typical.

"Danica," he sighed, "is something bothering you?"

"Why would you think that?" Her sarcasm sailed over his head.

"You sound as though you resent my work." Still he didn't raise his voice. She wished she could have attributed that fact to Marcus's silent presence in the front seat, but she knew better. Marcus was the perfect chauffeur, trained to be blind and deaf as the situation demanded. Besides, it was raining, and the steady patter on the roof served as static to diffuse their low-spoken words. "I've worked hard to get where I am. You, of all people, should understand that."

There it was again. She gritted her teeth. "Why me, of all people?"

"You come from a family where achievement is highly prized. Your father has worked hard for years to cement his position."

"That's right. And in doing so, he sacrificed a good many of the finer things in life."

"I don't know about that. It seems to me he has pretty much everything he wants."

That, in a nutshell, was what was wrong, Danica realized. It had less to do with William Marshall being satisfied than with Blake Lindsay identifying with the components of that satisfaction. She seemed to be the one marching out of step in the parade.

"Power," she sighed in defeat. "He has power."

"Isn't that what it's all about?"

Staring at her husband's smug profile in the darkness, she knew there was no point in continuing the discussion. He didn't see the way she did; it was as simple as that. Perhaps it was her own fault, she mused. She had married a man so like her father that she was *bound* to suffer the same frustrations she had known growing up. A psychiatrist would have a field day. On the other hand, it didn't take a psychiatrist to explain why she'd done it. All her life she had wanted her father's approval. Marrying Blake and being the perfect corporate wife had fallen within that realm.

How to cope. That was the issue she faced. In actuality, she followed Blake's formula to the letter. "You have to think clearly. You have to analyze the facts and your options. You have to make decisions and see them through."

The fact was very simply that she was involved in a marriage that gave her little reward or pleasure. The options were also simple, since she couldn't quite abide by the concept of divorce. The decisions, ah, those were harder to reach.

She rose to the occasion. First, she realized that she had to accept Blake for both his strengths and his weaknesses. What he lacked on the human side of the scale he made up for as a provider, as a man well-known and respected among his peers.

Second, she realized that she was, at some point, going to have to look for work. It might take time, both to secure a job that would conform to her life-style and then to garner the courage to confront Blake with her decision, but she was increasingly convinced as each day passed that it was the wisest course open to her.

Third and finally, she *was* going to Maine. She had thought it all out. She wanted to be away from the city, away from the emptiness that seemed to characterize her life there. She wanted fresh air, open space, time to herself in a less prescribed environment.

She had also thought a great deal about Michael, and specifically, her attraction to him. In the weeks since she had seen him, she had put into perspective what she'd felt that day on the beach. She liked him very, very much. He stirred her in ways that might have been wrong if she hadn't been so committed to her marriage. True, she fantasized about him, but that was okay. The reading she had done—and she'd done a great deal of it on the subject since that last trip north—had said that fantasizing was normal and, in its way, healthy. Put in its proper place, it could do her no harm.

Michael knew the facts of her life, that she was married, that she could never offer him more than a friendly hug or companionable hand-holding. God only knew she needed both of those things. Should she deprive herself of a very lovely, very warm, close relationship?

Her real source of protection, though, came from something that was as yet only the merest suspicion, the faintest hope. She was overdue for her period, and she had always been punctual to the day. If she was pregnant, her problems might be solved. Not that she set great stock in Blake's attentiveness as a father—nothing he had done in recent years as a husband had warranted such faith. But she would be a mother, and a whole new world would open to her.

Thus fortified, she headed for Maine on the twenty-third of June. It was a Friday morning. Blake, surprisingly enough, was accompanying her, taking the Mercedes while she drove the Audi so that he could return to Boston the following day. He had said that he wanted to see her settled, and indeed, she had brought along several cartons of things—clothes, a stereo, records, books—so his help was appreciated. He hadn't even suggested that Marcus do the dirty work; perhaps he had known she would have insisted on doing it herself given that particular choice. Then again, perhaps he felt guilty.

He was a fine caretaker; she had to say that much. And though she sensed his accompanying her was more a conciliatory gesture than anything else, she couldn't look a gift horse in the mouth.

Ironically, Blake was more satisfied than she had ever seen him in Maine. He patiently helped her unload what she had brought, spent several hours out on the deck with her explaining all he would be doing back home that would keep him from joining her for several weeks at least, took her into Ogunquit for dinner, and was perfectly amiable the whole time. He made no attempt to touch her that night, and she felt no urge for him to do so, but he did kiss her sweetly before he set off the next day, and he did promise to call every few days.

For the first time his departure didn't bother her. He was going home. She felt she *was* home. This place was hers as no other house she had ever lived in had been. In part it was because the responsibility of its care rested on her shoulders, in part because here she was fully responsible for herself. There was no maid to cook or clean or make the bed, no handyman/chauffeur to open and close windows, to bring deck chairs in from the rain, to lock up at night.

She did everything herself, when and how she wanted, and she loved it. She felt confident and capable and thoroughly self-satisfied. She felt free.

The first thing she did after Blake left was to drive into town to buy food, then to stop at a local shop and pick up several pairs of jeans and some T-shirts. There was a certain perverse pleasure in wearing Kennebunkport plastered across her chest; she had never done anything as . . . as plebeian before, but then, she'd never wanted to be a part of the crowd before. The chic shops she patronized in Boston and New York would never have dreamed of carrying either the knockabout sandals or no-name sneakers she bought, a fact that made these items all the more valuable to her. Moreover, she totally enjoyed the salespeople who helped her and spent a startling amount of time talking with them, such that it was nearly dark when she finally returned to the house.

Too dark to seek Michael out. And on a Saturday night, not right. After all, the man might not be married or otherwise attached, but he still had to date. He was human. Very male. Certainly sought after by women.

Hence, it was midday Sunday when she finally felt it fair to intrude upon his weekend. Donning one of her new T-shirts, the sneakers and a pair of the jeans she had spent the previous night washing and drying three times, she set out across the beach. She had never seen his house. It was time she did.

Set at the end of a winding road in a way hers was not, the house was perched above the rocks and was sheltered by numerous clumps of pitch pines that kept it hidden from view until well after she passed the familiar boulders. A stairway of stone, guarded by a weathered handrail, had been etched from the rocks and led to the deck. There wasn't a back door, only a screen where the glass slider had been opened. Given the brightness of the day, she couldn't see inside.

She started across the deck, then, unsure for the first time, moistened her lips and wondered if she was being too forward. Previously Michael had done the approaching and it had been on the beach, a casual enough place for an encounter with a friend.

Then she caught herself. He *was* a friend, and had *he* been a *she*, Danica doubted she would feel any of the hesitancy she did now. It was just going to take some getting used to — this close friendship with a man — she told herself.

Bolstered by that understanding and by the sheer excitement of seeing him again, she approached the screen, shaded her eyes from the outside glare with one hand and peered inside.

"Michael?" she called softly. She heard voices, but it was too late to turn back. "Michael?" Slightly louder. She still couldn't see a thing.

Then she did. The man himself. Approaching the screen, sliding it back, surprise and pleasure lighting his face.

"Danica!"

She smiled, feeling as pleased as he looked. "I just, uh, just wanted to say hello."

He took a caressive hold of her shoulder. "You're back."

She couldn't help but laugh. "Looks that way."

"That's great," he said softly, taking in her features before slowly lowering his gaze and arching a brow in amusement. "You've been shopping."

"Uh-huh." She glanced down. "What do you think? Will I fit in?"

"You would fit in anywhere. God, you look great!" The sound came from deep in his throat, a near growl that made her believe every word contained therein.

"So do you."

He was wearing a velour robe that reached mid-thigh, and nothing else. Danica couldn't seem to drag her eyes from his legs, which were long and lean and spattered with the same tawny hair that escaped the robe at his chest.

Her appraisal was enough to startle him into realization of his disheveled state, and he swore under his breath. "Hell, I'm a mess!" Before she could argue, he held up a hand and commanded, "Wait here." He was halfway through the living room before he turned and hurried back to grab her hand and draw her into the house. When at his urging she slid into a chair, he popped a kiss on the top of her head. "I'll be right back." Then he was gone, leaving her grinning, which seemed to be a common affliction when she was with him, she mused.

His brief absence gave Danica time to look around, which she did with interest. The armchair she sat on, its mate and a matching sofa were of soft, aged leather that looked rich and well-worn, and wore the haphazardly strewn Sunday paper with flair. In the center of the room stood a low table of slate that matched both the fireplace and the floor. The latter was softened by a large and handsome area rug of Scandinavian design.

Very clearly, there had been a method to the basic decor, but basic was where the method stopped. For on every table, every wall, every shelf and the mantel were diverse assortments of plaques, masks, pieces of art and other memorabilia she guessed to have come from his travels.

Those that were within her reach she studied closely—a limestone burial jar, an ancient elephant tusk, a copper fish she guessed to be of Mayan design. Then she sat back and scanned the room again, marveling that one man could have amassed such an exotic collection.

By contrast, the small television, which rested atop the counter separating living room from kitchen, seemed mundane. It was, she realized, the source of the voices she'd heard when she first crossed the deck. But there was nothing mundane—or so the indoctrination went—about the program that was on.

Just then Michael reappeared wearing jeans and a short-sleeved shirt. He looked freshly showered and shaven, and his hair was damp but combed. He looked wonderful.

"That was fast," she breathed. "I always thought it took at least fifteen minutes for a man to shave, but I haven't been here more than five."

"I'm sorry to have kept you waiting even that long. If I'd known you were coming . . ." He grew hesitant. "I saw both cars in the driveway and thought you'd be busy at least till tonight."

"Blake had to be back in Boston last night. I would have come by sooner, but I wasn't sure if you'd be free."

Her suggestion was subtle but too obvious to ignore. "I did go out last night, but it was an early evening." He'd tried; oh, yes, he'd tried. But no other woman seemed to measure up to the one before him now.

Danica cast a glance at the television, which was still on. "It looks like I've disturbed you anyway."

"Are you kidding?" Padding barefoot across the stone floor, he flipped off the set. "I turn this on more out of habit than anything."

"*Face the Nation?* Shame on you. No Sunday is complete without it."

At her lightly mocking tone, he felt instant sympathy. "That's how it is?"

"You bet. Nothing, and I do mean *nothing*, comes between my men and *Face the Nation.*"

"We're not all like that," Michael said, pushing aside the business section to sit on the sofa not far from her. Then he looked back down at the paper, gathered it and several nearby sections and tossed them onto another pile on the table. "Sorry about this. Living alone, I get carried away."

"Don't apologize. I love the way things look."

"Now you *are* kidding."

"Uh-uh. It's refreshing." How often she used that word to describe things to do with Michael! "In my house the paper never gets a chance to be scattered. Blake keeps everything in neat piles, and if something by chance does get out of order, Mrs. Hannah is right there to straighten it." Another dig at Blake, and she felt quickly contrite. Yet she could neither apologize nor take the words back. Michael inspired an honesty in her, an impulsiveness she couldn't deny. She was just going to have to be more careful. After all, she really didn't want to malign Blake. He was her husband.

"Anyway," she sighed, looking around her, "I love your house. I've never seen it before."

"It's not much different in design from yours."

"No, but it looks lived in."

"It looks messy, is what it does."

She shook her head. There was so much to see here; by comparison, her own house seemed stark. "Lived in, and very happily so. These are all souvenirs of your escapades?"

"Yup." When she rose from the chair and crossed the room to gently finger one of a pair of unusually shaped iron candlesticks that stood on the mantel, he explained that they were from Portugal and that he had been studying emigration patterns when he found them. When she moved on to examine a hand-carved Mexican lava ball, then a pair of Majorcan grinding rollers, he told of their acquisitions, as well.

What he really wanted was to learn more about her home life, her husband, the frustrations she felt. But she was so enthused about the collection of hats on the wall, the cluster of baskets in the corner, the bronze Japanese vase on the table, that he found himself wrapped up in telling her one story, then another and another.

"You lead such an exciting life," she breathed, returning to sink down into the chair at last. Her face was glowing, as though for that little bit of time she had lived the excitement with him.

He knew then that that was what he wanted her to do, though he knew that life with her would be exciting in very different kinds of ways.

"It looks like you've been all around the world!" she exclaimed.

"Almost. There are still some places I'd like to see." He paused. "You must have done your own share of traveling."

She shrugged. "Some, but to none of the out-of-the-way places you've been."

"You didn't travel with your parents?"

"Only to vacation spots—the Caribbean, Hawaii, Hilton Head." Once a year, the mandatory family jaunt. "When it came to the truly exotic places, they went alone."

"Why? Surely it would have been educational for you."

"You'd think so," she mused, "but they kept me involved in other activities and assumed I wouldn't mind."

"What other activities?"

"School." She didn't yet want to go into her tennis years, when every free minute had been spent on the court. She had failed her parents' expectations there, and to a certain extent, she believed in that failure herself.

Her answer had been pat and was theoretically without argument, yet Michael wasn't ready to let the subject of her past drop. "Do you travel much with your husband?"

Her eyes clouded then. "I used to. He'd take me on business trips—in this country and abroad—and we'd have a few days to ourselves when the business was done. Lately, though, he's been so busy that it's just as well he goes alone."

"He doesn't have time for you," Michael stated quietly.

Danica opened her mouth to disagree, then closed it. "You have a way of hitting home, Michael Buchanan," she murmured.

He reached over to lightly stroke her cheek. "I don't mean to hurt, but something's not right." They both knew they were dealing with the present now. "What man in his right mind would leave his wife on a Saturday night."

"It was another political thing, and I'm very much in overload when it comes to those. So it was my fault as much as his. If I'd been agreeable, I'd have waited for Monday to drive up."

"Then he wouldn't have come at all."

She didn't deny that possibility. "He really was helpful. I wanted to bring lots of things with me. He helped carry them in and put them away."

Michael swallowed the sarcastic remark that was on the tip of his tongue. He knew that to openly criticize Blake at this point might endanger his relationship with Danica. As it was, Blake was the major obstacle standing between them. If that was ever to change, Danica had to be the instigator, not Michael.

Besides, something else interested him, something written between the lines. "How long are you up for this time?" he asked with studied nonchalance. He had dreams, and in those dreams he had made plans. He was tired of being alone. There was lots to do during a summer in Maine. He would settle, albeit regretfully, for a platonic friendship if it meant he might spend more time with Danica.

Her smile sent his hopes soaring. "The summer. The whole summer."

"The *whole* summer?"

"Uh-huh. I promised Blake that I'd go back for a day or two now and again, but otherwise I'm here to stay."

"Will he be up much?"

"He's very involved with the convention—he and my father, both. It's important that he be around. He said he'd make it whenever he could, but I'm not sure how often that will be."

"Was he upset with your coming?"

She crinkled her nose in a gesture that might have answered his question either way. "I think it'll be easier for him with me up here. He knows that I'm not as enamored with politics as he is."

"Strange, given who you are." He thought. "Then again, not strange at all. Rebelling at last?"

She grinned. "It's about time, don't you think?"

"I think," he stated with care, "that it's good you're beginning to think of yourself. I also think that I couldn't be happier." He paused. "Will Blake mind if I draft his wife to go to the flea market with me today?"

Danica answered his roundabout invitation by beaming. "The flea market! Fun! Are you looking for something special?"

"Just a few hours of relaxation, and it wouldn't be the same alone."

"You may not believe this, but I've never been to a flea market."

She was right; he didn't believe it. *"Never?"*

"Well, maybe an open-air market in London or Venice. But those were different, and they were very much souvenir-hunting excursions. I've never been to a real country flea market, and certainly never just for the sake of enjoyment."

"Well, pretty lady," Michael drawled, rolling to his feet and drawing her up with him, "you're in for an afternoon to remember." He was holding her hand, looking down at her, and suddenly he paused, all amusement gone. Her cheeks were flushed, her violet eyes filled with excitement and softness and warmth. He swallowed hard and squeezed her hand. "Danica, *will* Blake mind?"

"Blake doesn't know."

"You haven't told him about me?" Unable to resist the lure of flaxen silk, he stroked her hair. It was soft and shimmering beneath his fingers.

Giving a nearly imperceptible head shake, she held her breath. She was totally aware of the man before her and knew she should turn and run but was rooted to the spot.

"Why not?" he asked softly.

"You're *my* friend," she whispered. "Blake rules the rest of my life. You're *mine.*

Michael closed his eyes. His hand fell to her neck. He lightly kneaded the soft skin there. "Oh, God—" his deep voice trembled, as did his arm "—I'm not sure if I can do this."

"Do what?" she breathed, though she knew. She felt; she needed; she wanted. And she feared. She feared because what she craved was wrong, forbidden. Still, one part of her had to hear the words. She had to hear that she was wanted, needed in return.

Framing her face with both hands, he looked at her then. She felt the touch of his gaze flow through her like sweet honey, momentarily healing all those bruised and lonely spots left by a lifetime of need. "I'm not sure I can be just your friend, Dani. You mean too much to me."

She was thrilled; she was scared. Her eyes told of her dilemma, but before she could speak, Michael did.

"I need more. I want to hold you, to touch you. Right now, I want to kiss you."

She wanted it, too, more than she would ever have believed possible. Blake had never stirred her this way, and she felt a sudden anger at what she had missed. But the anger was fleeting because Michael was here with her now, making her forget . . . almost.

"We can't," she gasped, feeling torn apart inside.

"I know. Which is what makes it so unbearable." Swearing softly, he strode away from her, pausing before the slider, propping his hands low on his hips and dropping his head forward. He was the image of dejection, and Danica felt a new kind of pain.

She started to approach, "Michael . . ."

He held up a hand, though he didn't turn. "I have to ask you something." The hand that had held her off now rubbed the back of his neck. "Why did you come here today?"

"I wanted to see you."

"Did you know how I felt?"

"I thought . . . I thought. . ."

He whirled around, jaw tight. "Didn't you know after last time that I wanted more? Didn't you feel it yourself?" Her eyes held the guilt that was answer in itself. "What did you think was going to happen?"

Insides churning, she tried to gather her thoughts. "I was looking forward to seeing you. I thought we could talk like we did before, maybe . . . see each other from time to time." She wrapped her arms around her waist in a gesture of self-defense. It hurt when Michael spoke to her this way, even though she knew he was justified in doing so.

He persisted, his ultimate need at the moment being to air all that had been festering in his mind for weeks. "But what did you think would come of it all? Didn't you wonder how long I'd be able to take being with you without . . . without . . ." He didn't need to finish. He had said it before, and the words only made the wanting that much greater.

"No," she whispered, frowning in faint surprise. "I never wondered that. I guess I assumed that the fact of my marriage to Blake would be enough to keep us both in line." She paused, then heard herself go on. She needed to air things, too. "I guess I was thinking of myself. You're something new to me, Michael. With you I act differently, feel differently." She lowered her gaze. "I felt something last time. I think I've felt things from the beginning." She looked up and went on with more urgency. "But there's so much more. I can talk to you. I can relax, be myself. You don't expect; you simply accept. And I need that." Her eyes filled with tears. "I've never had it, and I want it so badly. I suppose, after last time, one part of me knew I was playing with fire by coming up here for the summer, by coming over here today. But I couldn't help myself! I swear I couldn't! You have to believe that! I couldn't help . . . myself . . . "

He was before her in two strides, brushing away the tears that trickled slowly down her cheeks. "Shhhh. Don't cry. Oh, sweetheart, don't cry."

Somehow she was in his arms then, and he was holding her tightly, rocking her gently from side to side while she clung to his neck. Her silent sobs cut through him, paining him nearly as much as her closeness did, but differently.

"Shhhh. I believe you. I believe you, and I feel the same. If I was smart, I'd stay away from you, but I can't. Do you understand that?" He held her back only enough so that he could see her face. "I can't, Dani. As God is my witness, I need you." He hauled her back against him, pressing her face to his throat. His own was tight. It was a minute before he could speak. "I don't want to do anything to destroy your marriage, but I can't leave you alone. I guess that puts us back where we started. Except—" he pressed his lips to her hair "—now you know how I feel. Does that scare you?"

She nodded, but all the while she was savoring the clean male scent of his skin. "It also makes me feel very good," she confessed in a tiny voice. "I'm being selfish again."

"Not selfish," he murmured against her hair, "just realistic. And honest. I want you to be that with me. Always. And I may be condemning myself to a hell of sorts, but I'm glad you feel the way you do. At least you'll understand when I need to touch you from time to time." His voice grew gruff with determination. "I'll be damned if I'm going to deny either of us the other's company. Not when that son of a bitch could care less."

Danica was the one to draw back then. "That's unfair. He doesn't know."

"*Would* he care?"

She took a quick breath to respond with what would have been an easy lie, then held it. Michael had asked for honesty. This she could give him, when there was so much she couldn't. Slowly she released her breath. "I . . . I'm really not sure. There are a lot of things about Blake that I'm not sure of anymore. But I married him willingly, and he has many strong points. He's never been the jealous type—"

"Has he ever had reason before?"

"No, but—"

"I think you should tell him about us."

"About *us?* You make it sound like we're having an affair, when—"

"That could be the case if we're not careful. Knowing that Blake knows we're friends, knowing that he knows we spend time together, might just help us be careful. Hell, Dani, we have to do *something.*"

His look of helplessness was so endearing that it gave her a measure of strength. She couldn't help but smile. "Self-control. That's all it takes. Self-control. As the tea bag says, self-control is the magic carpet to salvation."

"I drink coffee," he grumped, then tossed his head toward the door. "Come on. If we don't leave now, we'll miss the best buys."

As it happened, they bought nothing but ice-cream cones and time, the former to satisfy one appetite, the latter to put others on hold. It was evening by the time they returned, and they were both pleasantly tired.

Danica, for one, felt more at peace with herself than she had in a while. "Michael?" She'd just opened her front door. "There was a reason why I decided to spend the whole summer here."

"You mean aside from wanting me to distraction?" he teased over her shoulder.

She elbowed his ribs, then turned to face him. "I need to think. The last few years have been frustrating for me in many ways, and I'm not sure it all has to do with Blake." She was giving Blake the benefit of the doubt. After all, it took two to make a marriage work. Avoiding Michael's gaze, she continued softly. "I need a break from my life as it's been. I have to think about where I'm going. There's always the possibility of my getting a job; we talked about that before. But—" she hesitated for just a minute, then knew she had to go on "—there's also the possibility that I might be pregnant."

Almost timidly she raised her eyes, but Michael's face was shadowed, his expression hidden by the night.

"Pregnant." He breathed the word in near awe and reached out to touch her, then stilled his hands in midair and gave a short laugh.

"Michael?"

He shook his head. "Absurd. I swear I'm losing my marbles. My first reaction was pure joy, until I realized it's not even my kid."

"You can still be excited."

The hurt in her voice brought him to his senses. He did touch her then, taking both of her shoulders, smoothing his hands over her back. "I am, Dani, I am." Dipping his head, he kissed her softly on the mouth. "It's what you want, isn't it?"

"Very much."

"Then I'm happy, no, thrilled for you. But jealous. I have to say that. . . . You don't know for sure?"

"It's too early. I'll see a doctor in another couple of weeks."

"Are you feeling all right?"

"Fine. I mean, it's too early to feel sick or anything. The calendar is the only thing that says it might be so."

"Blake must be pleased."

"Blake doesn't know." It was the second time she had said those words that day, and she felt slightly sheepish. "I didn't want to get his hopes up. We've waited too long." From sheepish to guilty. She implied that Blake *would* be pleased, when, in truth, she wasn't sure. No, she amended, he would be pleased, but in his own inimitably dispassionate way.

"Then, I'm really pleased, on his behalf and my own. And I'm glad you told me, Dani." *Before* Blake. It was the little boy in him being perverse. "Now I'll know to be careful with you. No wrestling, no tackle football . . ."

She gave a soft laugh. "Thank you. I'd appreciate that." What she appreciated was the sentiment behind his teasing. Though she knew she was healthy and strong, and that nothing could dislodge a healthy baby, if indeed one grew within her, Michael made her feel special. But then, he always did. It was one of the reasons she was so drawn to him. "Well," she sighed, "on that note I'd better get in. It's been a wonderful day, Michael. Thank you."

"Thank *you*. I'll see you later in the week?"

She smiled. They had already talked about the work he had to do, as well as about the reading and sunning and relaxing she intended to do. "I'd like that." She stepped into the house. "Get a lot of writing done, you hear?"

"I hear. Lock that door good, you hear?"

"I hear. Good night, Michael."

" 'Night, Dani." He was halfway down the path when he couldn't resist a final note. "Sweet dreams!" he called, wishing the same for himself but somehow fearing it would be a different kind of dream he would have.

Oblivious to his lascivious thoughts, Danica watched him back from the drive, then closed the door softly and locked it tight.

Blake called on Wednesday night. "Danica?"

"Blake! Hi!"

"Did I get you from somewhere? The phone rang eight times before you picked it up."

"I was on the deck. The surf is wilder than usual and I didn't hear the ring at first."

"Bad weather?"

"Not yet. But it looks like it's going to pour. How is everything?"

"Just fine."

". . . Anything new at the office?"

"Not that I can think of."

". . . I assume the party went well on Saturday."

"Uh-huh. They were asking for you."

"Oh?"

"You sound surprised."

"A little. I never thought I was noticed at those things."

"Come on. There are always women there for you to talk with."

"Right. Well, I'm sure they had each other."

There was a brief silence from the other end of the line. Then: "So, how are you doing?"

"Really well. I finished Vidal's *Lincoln*. It was interesting." She paused to give Blake an opportunity to ask her about it. When he didn't, she went on. "And I've started Ludlum's latest. I'm not sure I like it as well as some of his others, but it may just be that I'm having trouble getting into it."

"So, you've been spending your time reading."

"Not all of it. I drive into town every morning. I'm thinking of getting a bike."

"Isn't it awfully hilly there for a bike?"

"Nah. It'd be great exercise."

"I suppose. And since you're not dancing—"

"But I am! I put music on and go through the routine from my class once a day. That was one of the reasons I wanted a stereo up here. Regarding the bike, though, it'd be fun as well as practical. With the summer crowds here, it's sometimes hard to find a parking space in town. I feel guilty taking the car when it's so close. It can't be more than five miles into town and back.''

"What do you do in town? The shops don't change that much from day to day, do they?"

"No. But the people are lovely. I got to talking with a woman who owns the sportswear shop. She's fascinating. She has a Ph.D. in biology and worked in research for six years before deciding to chuck it all and move up here. Her husband is an artist and has a gallery down the block from her shop. I bought one of his paintings. It's a seascape, but very modern. It looks great in the bedroom."

"Sounds good."

". . . Sara and I had lunch together today. It was nice. Oh, and I'm working up the beginnings of a tan."

"Be careful with that. Too much sun is bad for the skin."

"I use lotion."

"Make sure it's Factor 15. I wouldn't want you to be all wrinkled and leathery by the end of the summer."

"I won't be all wrinkled and leathery. I just may look healthy."

"Good. Listen, Pook, I have to run. We're meeting tonight with a new account. Harlan's giving me the high sign."

"You're still at the office?" It was seven o'clock. She assumed he would be calling from home.

"Not for long. I'm on my way." His words were directed as much to the man standing in the room, Danica guessed, as to her.

"Go ahead. Good luck with your meeting. And give Harlan my best." She couldn't stand Harlan Magnusson, with his French-cut suits, dark curly hair and wire-rimmed glasses. He was always moving. He made her nervous. Still, he was her husband's right-hand man.

"Will do. We'll talk more another time. Bye-bye."

It wasn't until the following Tuesday that he called again, and the conversation opened along similar lines. Yes, he was fine. No, there was nothing new at the office. Yes, she was fine. No, she wasn't bored.

"The Fourth of July was fun up here, Blake. I'm sorry you couldn't make it."

"You know that I had to be in Philadelphia. We discussed it when I drove you up there."

"Yes. Did everything go well?"

"Just fine."

"I'm glad. There was a fireworks display here. I went with one of our neighbors." She broached the subject with a nonchalance she didn't feel, but she realized that Michael had been right that she tell Blake of their friendship. It wasn't so much that she saw it as a deterrent to physical involvement; since she and Michael had aired their feelings, they seemed able to keep things under control. It was more a matter of accounting for her time, a good deal of which was spent with him. It was also a matter of being covered should she run into someone she knew when she was with Michael. It seemed only fair that if Blake was to get a report back that his wife was seen with another man, he would be able to say with confidence, "Oh, yes. I know. He's a good friend."

"You've met the neighbors?" Blake asked now.

"Several." It was the truth. She had taken walks by herself on the roads near the house and had encountered various of the homeowners nearby. "There's a retired banker and his wife—Kilsythe?"

"City Trust. I've heard of him."

"And an anesthesiologist and his family. The one I went to the fireworks display with is a writer."

"Oh?"

"A historian. You'll know his family. Buchanan."

There was a moment's silence. "Watch out for him."

"Oh, he's safe. He doesn't have anything to do with his family's papers."

"You can never be too careful."

She paused, about to argue more until she realized the futility of it. "I'll be careful. . . . Blake? We're still on for Saturday night, aren't we?" They had a long-standing commitment to attend a movie premiere, a benefit for the Heart Association.

"Of course. When can I expect you?"

"I thought I'd come in on Friday." She had made a doctor's appointment for that afternoon, though as yet she didn't want to say anything to Blake. "I'll drive back Sunday. Is that okay?"

"Sounds fine. I'll see you then."

"Okay. Bye-bye."

Friday afternoon Danica learned that she was indeed pregnant.

SIX

❀ ❀ ❀

D ANICA GAVE BLAKE the good word shortly after he arrived home from work on Friday evening. He was surprised, then pleased, and insisted on calling her parents immediately. It was easier said than done, though Danica might have predicted that. It seemed the Marshalls had left their Connecticut home, where Blake had expected they would be, to spend the weekend with a congressman friend of William's at a horse farm in Kentucky. After a series of forwarding calls, which Blake endured with characteristic patience, he eventually got through and passed on the news with a pride suggesting that he had accomplished the deed on his own.

For the most part, Danica let him do the talking. She couldn't help but feel that he was more pleased with the enhancement of his own image than with the fact itself. But she was loathe to criticize, when she, too, felt a little of the same. Her father was gratified; in his eyes, her status soared, and that mattered to her. Still, deep down inside, her greatest joy was in the prospect of holding a baby in her arms, of being needed by a helpless infant, of loving it and having it love her in return.

On the drive back to Maine on Sunday afternoon, that joy emerged full force. She couldn't keep from smiling. The prospect of her future had, with the doctor's pronouncement, taken a turn for the better. For the first time in months she felt optimistic. And she couldn't wait to tell Michael.

Unfortunately, he wasn't home. She let the phone ring for a while, dialed right back on the chance that she might have misdialed the first time, then tried again five minutes later, thinking that he might have been in the shower.

Undaunted, she changed from her city sundress into a tank top and shorts and walked the beach for a while, grinning, sighing happily, edging closer and closer to Michael's house in the hope that he would return and saunter out on the deck. In time she stationed herself on the boulder she'd come to think of as theirs, with the confidence that Michael would find her.

Sure enough, not long after, as the sun dipped low behind her, she heard his call and saw him trotting toward her down the beach. He came to a halt on the sand beneath her.

"You look like the cat that swallowed the canary," he said, eyes narrowed in speculation.

Beaming from ear to ear, she nodded. "I saw the doctor on Friday." She didn't have to explain.

"And it's true?"

She could only grin and nod again.

"Hey, Dani, that's great!" He made his way up the rocks to where she sat and hugged her soundly. "That's great!" Fortunately, he'd had time to get used to the idea. While on the one hand he regretted that a child would be another tie binding Danica to Blake Lindsay, on the other he was thrilled for her. He knew how much she wanted a baby. "When's it due?"

"In February. I'm just six weeks pregnant."

"And the doctor gave you a clean bill of health?"

"Yup. I've got vitamins to take, but that's it."

"How about Blake?"

She grinned. "No vitamins. His job is done."

"Not a very modern view, but that wasn't what I meant anyway. How did he take the news?"

"Happily. He called my folks, then his." He'd done the latter only reluctantly, and then, not until Sunday morning. Danica had never been able to understand his relationship with his family. His parents and only sibling, a brother, were of solid middle-class stock living and working in Detroit. Though Blake sent them money from time to time, he seemed to want little else to do with them. Danica was the one to send birthday and anniversary cards, not to mention keeping after Blake to call them. She felt badly; she had only seen them four times in the eight years of her marriage.

"I assume they were all duly excited," Michael speculated.

"Uh-huh. It was amazing. My mother grew really concerned. She went on and on about what I should and shouldn't do and how to take care of myself. She never did that when I was a child."

"You knew all the answers back then?" he teased.

"Not quite. I had to find them for myself, though. Mom was never there."

"Of course she was. You're exaggerating."

"Don't I wish. In fact, as I remember, I did an awful *lot* of wishing back then on this very topic. Mom was always in and out as my father's schedule demanded. She never seemed to be there when I needed her." She grew more pensive. "I remember when I had the chicken pox. I was seven at the time and my father was running for his first term. Was I ever sick. The only thing I wanted was for her to hold me. She was campaigning with him, of course. So I just burrowed under the covers and . . . and itched."

Michael ached for her. "There must have been someone with you."

"Oh, yes. We had a housekeeper. She was very efficient, a good cook, and she cleaned beautifully. Unfortunately, at the time I couldn't bear the thought of food and I could have cared less about a clean house. What I wanted was my mother."

He could understand it. He remembered being sick himself, having his mother sit with him, read to him, dote on him. There had been times when he had actually welcomed a cold, just to have that time alone with her. It had been very special, something he would always remember.

Thinking of the very different experience Danica had had, he had to struggle to curb his anger. "I'm sorry," he said at last.

She flashed him a sad smile. "It wasn't your fault."

"I know, but you're right. A mother should be there. I'm sorry you had to weather the storm alone."

"Well, I suppose it was good training. I got used to it, even though I always wished things were different. They will be for my child, that's for sure." She sighed. "Which brings us back to what I was saying. Among other things, my mother told me to stay put in Boston. She thinks I'm crazy to be coming up here."

"How did you answer that?"

"I *wanted* to say that it was none of her business, that she had no right to tell me what to do at this late date."

"But you didn't."

"No. In her own rather bizarre way, she does love me. I'm sure she's legitimately concerned, and I suppose I should be grateful after so many years of going without. I told her that the doctor recommended fresh air and exercise. I also told her that I wanted the baby very badly and that she'd have to trust that I wouldn't do anything to endanger its health."

"How about Blake? Does he have any second thoughts about your being alone up here now?"

"Blake echoed Mom's sentiments after I'd hung up, but I don't think he's really worried. I'm not an invalid, for heaven's sake."

"I can understand his concern. You are alone here."

"I have you," she said with a teasing glint in her eye.

He returned the look, though his own teasing was strictly on the surface. "True. . . . Is this new?" He fingered the gold necklace at her neck; it was a delicate serpentine chain with a diamond embedded at its center. Of course, her skin fascinated him even more, warm and soft where his fingers brushed it.

"Blake gave it to me on Saturday. He felt the occasion called for something." Blake was very good at that, very proper. As forgetful as he was when it came to his family in Detroit, he had a set image in his mind of how he should treat his wife. There was jewelry on each anniversary, a fur or other piece of expensive clothing on each birthday, a bouquet of flowers on Valentine's Day. Of course, Danica would have been just as happy with a quiet dinner for the two of them on any of those occasions, but she was never consulted.

"Not bad," Michael mused.

"Not necessary," she argued.

He accepted her curtness as a statement in itself, and leaned back. "Funny, you don't look pregnant." Given good excuse, he raked her length, admiring the firm thrust of her small breasts, the slimness of her waist and hips, the shapeliness of her legs.

"Thank goodness. If I looked pregnant at this early stage, just imagine how I'll look six months down the road."

"You'll look wonderful." He met her gaze without hesitation. "You'll be a beautiful mother."

She smiled, feeling self-conscious but pleased that Michael had thought to say such words. "Thank you. You're good for my ego."

"Blake doesn't say things like that?"

"Oh, he does. But he's big on physical fitness and I'm going to be pretty fat in a while." It had occurred to her that Blake might not be terribly attracted to a whale, but then he didn't seem to be terribly attracted to her now. She sensed he would use her pregnancy to keep his distance, sensed he would probably be relieved to have the excuse. When she had not so subtly informed him that the doctor hadn't ruled out any activity, he had simply nodded.

"Pregnant women have an aura about them," Michael said softly. "They glow from within. My sister-in-law says that she loves being pregnant, that she feels she's doing what God intended, that she's always proud as punch of her belly."

Danica grinned. "No wonder she and Brice have five kids."

"They should. They're wonderful parents. Brice may work with my father, but before he agreed to do it, he set down certain rules. He wants to be home most nights and weekends, and he is."

"Your father accepted that?"

"He had no choice. The options were either that or have none of his children there to take over when he decides to retire. He may be a tyrant, but he does love us. I guess he's finally accepted that we're adults."

"I wish my parents could do that," she mused.

"It took a while, Dani, and lots of fights. In Brice's case, he knew what he wanted and he stood firm. Some day you'll be able to do that."

Michael's words echoed in Danica's mind long after she and Michael had gone their separate ways that night. She wondered if the day would come when she would have the courage she sought. She was proud that she had stuck to her guns about spending the summer in Maine; it was a step in the right direction. Then again, perhaps it had been a matter of options after all. The alternative to being in Maine had simply become unacceptable to her; hence she'd held her ground. Perhaps in the future other choices would be as clear-cut. Now that she was expecting a child, the issue of working was temporarily on hold. She prayed that once she was a mother herself, she would find the strength to stand up for other things, to put her father's approval in perspective, to make the best decisions for herself and her child.

Her child. Not Blake's. Strange that she should think of it that way. Strange, and sad, but realistic. If Blake was going to prove to be the same kind of father her own had been, she would just have to be that much more attentive a mother. That was something to which she was fully committed.

"Danica, maybe this isn't such a good idea."

"Why ever not?"

"Well, you could fall or be hit by a passing car. The roads around here are pretty rutted at spots."

"Come on, Michael. You were so excited last week. You agreed yourself that it'd be good exercise."

"That was before your pregnancy was confirmed."

"And the doctor wants me to exercise."

"So dance." He had dropped by her house unannounced one day and had caught her in leotard and tights. Shyly she explained what she was doing, and though she had staunchly refused to give him a demonstration, he knew that in action she would be as graceful as a prima ballerina. As it was, he couldn't shake the image of how gorgeous she looked with her hair stuck behind her ears and the finest sheen of moisture on her skin.

"I do dance, but I want to be outside. You bike all the time. Are the roads too rutted for you?"

"I'm a man."

"You're a chauvinist." Strangely, though, she wasn't angry. Similar words coming from Blake would have riled her. She would have felt he was being condescending. There was none of that feeling with Michael. Rather, he seemed to be genuinely concerned for her well-being.

She waved toward the young man who worked at the bike store, then turned a bright smile on Michael. "I've made up my mind. Now, is this the right one, or do you think the blue one would be better?"

"Red. By all means. You'll be more visible."

"That's not what I—"

"For safety's sake, Dani. Please. And you have to get a helmet and a reflective vest."

"I hadn't planned on riding at night."

"Indulge me," he pleaded with a sigh.

It did the trick. She bought the best helmet the store carried, a reflective vest that she doubted she would ever wear, and a T-shirt with the name of the bicycle she had bought emblazoned on its front. The last she purchased with glee, finding as much pleasure in Michael's heavenward glance as in the prospect of wearing the shirt itself. In truth, Michael savored her glee nearly as much as he looked forward to biking with her.

Little did he know what the sight of her riding directly ahead of him would do. Her lithe body, bowed against the wind, hands propped low on the handlebars, firm bottom rocking gently from side to side as she pedaled, shook him. More than once he missed a rut in the road himself and nearly fell. It was sweet, sweet torture.

He had no way of knowing that the torture wasn't one-sided. Danica was as aware of him when they rode together, of the way his shoulders bunched when he leaned forward, of the way the veins in his forearms stood out, of the way his skin-tight pants molded his muscled thighs to perfection. She was grateful that she most often rode ahead where she didn't have to be constantly tempted. And she was grateful, in wholly new ways as the week passed, that she was pregnant.

It was too easy to pretend that she and Michael were together in every sense of the word. The fetus within her was a reminder of the man who had sired it. And Lord knew she needed reminders. In the six days since she had left Boston, Blake hadn't called once.

On Sunday evening she phoned home only to learn from Mrs. Hannah that Blake was in Toronto and was expected back the following day. She was hurt to learn this from the housekeeper and embarrassed when Mrs. Hannah had seemed surprised that she hadn't known. Covering as best she could, she hung up the phone and stewed.

Fortunately, Michael was working all day Monday; otherwise she feared he would sense her mood and that, with little coaxing, she would spill her marital woes in his lap. Instinct told her not to do that. Instinct and loyalty to Blake.

When Blake did call on Monday night, she couldn't hide her frustration. "I didn't know you were going to Toronto."

"I thought I mentioned it."

"No. And I felt like a fool learning it from Mrs. Hannah. She must have some great idea of how close we are."

"She's the housekeeper. It's not her place to pass judgment. Besides, she and Marcus have been with me for more than ten years. She knows that I travel a lot."

He had deftly avoided the issue, Danica mused. "Still, I'm your wife," she argued quietly. "I should have known."

"At the time I found out, I wasn't sure you'd be in."

"You could have had your secretary call and give me the message. Would that have been so difficult?"

"Honestly, Danica, you're making too much of this. It was a last-minute trip."

"It's always a last-minute trip."

"You know that it's business."

"It's always business," she murmured, but she was beginning to feel like a shrew. Determinedly she gentled her voice. "When will it be pleasure, Blake? I'd really like you to come up. In another two weeks you'll be off to St. Louis for the convention. Won't I see you before then?"

There was a pause and a shuffling of papers in the background. "I could try to make it this weekend."

She had the strangest feeling that she was being shuffled along with the papers, categorized, slotted, finally and reluctantly squeezed into her husband's tight schedule. It wasn't the nicest of feelings. For that matter, though, it wasn't totally new.

"I'd like that," she said in an even tone.

"I'll have to do some work while I'm there," he cautioned.

"Of course. I understand."

"Okay. Then I'll plan on it. Saturday and Sunday."

Friday through Sunday was too much to ask. "Great. I'll see you then?"

He confirmed it once more and neatly wound up the conversation. Only after she hung up the phone did Danica realize that he hadn't even asked if she felt well.

Michael was exactly what she needed when he breezed in excitedly the next morning. "Are you busy?"

She cast a glance back at the kitchen table where she'd been seated before the doorbell had rung. "Just writing a letter." To Reggie at the hotel where her itinerary said she would be staying.

"Can it wait?"

"Sure. What's— Michael, I'm not dressed!" He had her arm and was propelling her through the door.

"What do you mean, you're not dressed?" He darted a look—darting was all he dared allow himself—at her T-shirt and cutoffs. "You look great!"

"But these shorts are too tight."

He did take a look then and grinned. "They're fantastic. You're as slim as ever."

She blushed. "I washed them so many times to make them look faded that they shrank more than I expected they would." He couldn't see that the snap was undone since it was hidden beneath her shirt, but she felt uncomfortable. "Give me a second." Dashing back into the house before he could object, she quickly changed into a more comfortable pair of pleated shorts and a stylish jersey. "Where are we going, anyway?" she asked with a smile as she rejoined him on the front walk.

He was smiling, too. "You'll see."

Throughout the fifteen-minute drive she tried repeatedly to wheedle their destination from him, but he was clearly enjoying his secret. He was excited about something, and she sensed it went beyond the mere fact of the mystery.

When he pulled into the drive of an old Victorian house in Wells, she was no closer to an answer. When a large Labrador retriever bounded out to greet them, she was still stumped. Moments later, though, after they shook hands with a gentle-faced woman who led them to the rear of the house, she understood. There in the backyard, toddling round and about two towheaded children, were four of the sweetest strawberry-blond puppies she had ever seen.

"Michael," Danica breathed, "*look* at them."

"I am. I am. Are they wonderful?"

"Oh, yes." Slipping to her knees beside the children, she reached out to touch the small, trembling body of one of the puppies. "Are these yours?" she asked the child nearest her, a little girl, who, though shy, managed to nod. "How old are they?"

"Six weeks," her brother answered, clearly the older and bolder of the two. "My mom says it's time to find homes for them. We're keeping one, though."

"Jasper," the little girl murmured.

Danica leaned closer to her. "Jasper?"

"That one." The child pointed to one of the puppies, amazing Danica with her ability to differentiate one tawny bundle from the next.

"He's a sweetheart," Danica said. "You've made a good choice."

"What about *you?*" Michael asked with soft excitement, coming to squat by Danica's side. "Any preference?"

"They're all precious, Michael. I couldn't possibly choose between them, much less tell them apart." The last was muttered out of the corner of her mouth, lest she offend the children.

"Well, I can." Leaning forward, Michael scooped up one of the puppies and held him at eye level. "This is the one I want."

"How do you know?"

He shrugged. "Instinct. Something tells me he'll love to run along the beach when he gets bigger." He winked at Danica, then turned to the children. "Does this one have a name?"

"Magpie," the little girl announced in a wispy voice that trembled. Large, sad eyes darted from the puppy to Michael and back.

Michael knelt again, shifting the puppy to lie snugly on his arm. "Magpie," he repeated in a gentle tone. "That's an unusual name for a dog."

The little girl thrust out her chin. It trembled, too. "I have a doll named Magpie."

"You do?"

"And a duck," her brother injected with a hint of disgust.

"He's stuffed," the little girl added, ignoring her brother.

"Ahhhhh. So you like the name Magpie."

The child nodded with such solemnity that Michael had to force himself not to grin. He sensed she wasn't looking forward to parting with any one of the dogs.

Settling down on the lawn cross-legged before her, he rested his elbows on his knees and spoke softly, confidentially. "I have a favorite name, too. Y' see, when I was a little boy, I had this monkey." When the child's eyes widened, he quickly explained. "Not a real one. I don't think my mother would have cared for that. This one was like your duck. I called him Rusty because of his color."

The little girl thought about that for a minute. "Rusty's a nice name," she said at last. "What happened to him?"

"He was my best friend for years. After a while he got so worn-looking that my mom started patching him up."

"Then what happened."

"After a while you couldn't really tell he was a monkey anymore. Y' know what he looked like?" The child shook her head. Michael lowered his voice even more. "He looked like a puppy. At least that's what I thought, but maybe that was because I wanted a puppy so badly."

"Did you ever get one?"

"Yup. I loved him to pieces, too. But now I'm grown up and I live by myself, and I could really use a dog to keep me company." He gently scratched the warm ears of the puppy on his arm. "Do you think this little fellow would do that?"

The little girl gave a one-shouldered shrug. Her lip began to quiver.

"What if I promised to bring him back to see you from time to time?"

Again the child gave his question thought, finally whispering with the most tentative of hopes, "Would you do that?"

"If you'd like. That way you'd know he's happy and well."

Danica felt her throat grow tight. She had never seen Michael with a child before, but he was wonderful. He was attuned to the little girl's sadness and, without patronizing her in any way, had managed to ease it somewhat. It was but another thing to add to the list of qualities she admired in the man.

An hour later, with the back of the Blazer loaded with puppy supplies and the object of their use lying asleep in Danica's lap, she mentioned it. "You were terrific with that little girl, Michael."

"It was easy. She was sweet."

"Still, you handled her well. . . . Did you really have a monkey named Rusty?"

Michael's neck grew pink. "Ummm."

"And it got worn out?"

"Ummm."

"What did finally happen to it?"

There was a pause, then: "My mother threw him out." When Danica made a sympathetic sound, he rushed on. "It was only a toy. I'd outgrown it."

"I sometimes wonder if we ever outgrow toys like that. They represent an important part of our childhood. It's sad, the parting."

He shot her a curious glance. "You sound like you've had the experience."

"Mine wasn't the same as yours, but yes. I had a doll. I was probably closer to her than to my mother. I had to leave her when I went off to boarding school."

"Wasn't she waiting for you when you got home?"

Danica shook her head and gently stroked the puppy's soft fur. "My room had been done over into a teenager's room. Mom discarded her along with the canopy bed, the candycane wallpaper and the lollipop mirror. She had wanted to surprise me with what had been done to the room. Fortunately, she wasn't there when I saw it. I cried for hours." She laughed. "Maybe it's best that way.

You know, zip, gone. Brief period of mourning. Done.''

"Will you do it that way for your child?''

"No!" Her response had been instant. Now she softened her voice. "No. I think I'd like decisions like that to be joint ones. In any event, I hope I'll be a little more sensitive to my child's needs. Childhood is short. Often it's rushed all the more. I don't want to do that.''

Looking over at her, Michael felt a sudden swell of sadness, and love. Sadness for all she had missed in life, love for what she was in spite of it. She was going to make a wonderful mother. He only wished it was his child she would be mothering.

As promised, Blake came on Saturday morning. As warned, he brought work with him. By Sunday afternoon when he pulled out of the drive, Danica wondered why he had bothered making the trip. They had had little to say to each other beyond the mandatory surface conversation and had spent most of their time at the house, each on his own.

That the silence, the lack of communication, bothered Danica much more than usual was no surprise. For the first time in her life she had a source of comparison. *Don't do it. It's not fair. Blake's your husband. Michael's your friend.* But she couldn't help herself. The differences were glaring. The more she fought them, the more pronounced they became, and in consequence, the sadder she felt.

As always, though, Michael came through. She was feeling particularly low when he called on Wednesday afternoon. They had been out biking together the day before, but she had expected he'd be working.

"Can you come over, Dani?''

"Sure. Is everything okay?''

"Great! I want you to meet someone.''

"Someone? Who?''

"Come on over and see.''

He was the mysterious Michael again, and she could hear his smile. But why not? She was in the mood for another mystery. Lord knew she needed *something* to pick her up.

Forewarned was forearmed. Dressing in a pair of casual linen slacks and a matching short-sleeved sweater, Danica dabbed blusher on her cheeks, stroked a touch of mascara on her lashes and brushed her hair to a high sheen. Strapping on a pair of sandals, she set out across the sand.

Michael was waiting for her on the deck with a woman by his side. She wore a calf-length skirt of a soft cotton fabric that swirled about her legs in the gentle breeze, a loose shirt and a vest. A soft scarf was wrapped around the top of her head and knotted above one ear; its ends flowed into the dark hair that curled gently about her shoulders. Her stance was feminine, but somehow familiar. She was as slender as Michael was lean.

Michael met Danica halfway up the steps and took her hand to draw her the rest of the way. Danica smiled at him, but her curious gaze quickly returned to the woman who waited.

"Dani, I'd like you to meet—''

"Priscilla,'' Danica finished, her smile widening as she held out her hand to

Michael's sister. "You may not look like twins, but the family resemblance is marked." It was there in the strong line of the jaw, the firm lips, the open smile.

Cilla Buchanan offered a confident handshake. "You're more observant than most. I usually try to pass myself off as his date. He looks more gorgeous every time I see him."

Unable to argue, Danica simply arched a mischievous brow Michael's way. Michael, who was enjoying himself, completed the introductions. "Cilla, this is my neighbor, Danica Lindsay."

"Obviously," Cilla drawled, "since she came in across the sand. Well, Danica, I'm glad to meet you. Michael's been grinning in anticipation of something from the minute I arrived this morning. I was beginning to think he was going to keep his secret to himself all day."

"It's that element of mystery," Danica said softly. "He leans toward it, I've noticed."

"He should have been a mystery writer, not a historian."

"There's mystery in history," Michael argued. "That's the whole point in writing about it. It's the unraveling that's a—"

"Challenge," Cilla cut in to finish. "So you've told me many times. I still think you should work for the paper. There's nothing like smelling a story, sniffing out its details one by one and solving a true puzzle."

"You sound like a bloodhound," Michael retorted, but without malice. "Come on. Let's sit down. Lemonade, Dani?"

She shook her head.

"I'll have one, Mike," Cilla said, sinking down into one of the deck chairs and crossing her legs. "Make it tart."

Michael gave her a tart look before disappearing.

"He's a nice brother. I really wish he did work for the paper. Then we'd be able to see each other more often."

Danica drew over a nearby chair. "He didn't mention you were coming."

"He didn't know." She flipped the ends of her scarf back over her shoulder and shot Danica a buoyant smile. "I didn't know until last night. The city room's been a madhouse with the convention going on. Now that we're between the two, there was a sudden lull. I figured that I'd better grab the chance while I had it. Once I get back, it'll be off to St. Louis and pandemonium all over again."

"I didn't realize you did political reporting," Danica remarked with caution.

"Mostly I do investigative journalism, special assignments for the paper. When it comes to national elections, though, just about everyone gets involved in one way or another. I don't mind it; the excitement is contagious."

"Was there all that much excitement in San Francisco? I got the impression that Picard's renomination came off without a fuss."

"To an extent, but then, he's the incumbent. Still, there were some interesting floor battles waged. A vocal contingent of delegates wanted modifications in the platform. They're more moderate than the President and have been uncomfortable with his stands on the economy and foreign trade."

Danica could understand that. Blake and her father were supporting Jason Claveling for, among other reason, those very differences with the President. "They didn't get very far, did they?"

"Nope. Ahh, my lemonade." She reached for the tall glass Michael handed her. He offered a second to Danica on the chance she had changed her mind. When she shook her head again, he kept the glass for himself and sat down facing the two women.

"You're not talking politics, are you?"

"As a matter of fact," Cilla began without remorse, only to be interrupted by her brother.

"I'd better warn you that Danica's no innocent on that score." He was also warning her to be careful. He knew Cilla to be quick-tongued and opinionated in a way that had never bothered him but might bother another. He wouldn't have put it past her to inadvertently blurt out something that would offend Danica. "Her father is William Marshall."

Cilla's lemonade took a wrong turn in her throat. She coughed, pressing a hand to her chest. "William Marshall? Are you serious?" She was looking at Danica, who smiled apologetically and nodded. "Michael, you're courting the enemy!" she exclaimed, but the thread of humor in her voice echoed Danica's own upon first learning of Michael's family connections.

"I'm not courting her. In case you hadn't noticed, she's married. We're friends. Dani's keeping me sane."

"Fat chance," Cilla murmured with affection. Then she grew thoughtful. "Danica Lindsay. Danica Marshall. Why does that last sound familiar?"

"Probably because you've written so much over the years about Danica's father," Michael suggested. He was closely enough attuned to everything about Danica to sense the faint unease she was feeling at that moment, despite the perfect outer calm she projected. "Maybe you'd better quit while you're ahead, Cilla."

But Cilla would have no part of it. As her brother loved his little surprises, so she loved intrigue. She was smelling a story, and as always when that happened, her inquisitive nature took command. "What does *he* think about your living next to a Buchanan?" she asked Danica.

"I'm not sure he knows. Blake and I just bought the house a few months ago and my parents haven't been up yet."

The gears in Cilla's mind were turning. "Blake Lindsay . . . uh, Eastbridge Electronics out of . . . Boston?"

"Cilla has a photographic memory, Dani. She's probably seen some caption along the way."

"He's supporting Claveling, isn't he?" Cilla went on, recalling more and more.

"That's right," Danica answered. It was public knowledge. And besides, she wasn't ashamed of it. If Jason Claveling won the nomination, she would vote for him herself. No, the only thing that bothered her about the man was the fact that he commanded so much of Blake's time and effort.

"Your father's a big Claveling man." She frowned, struggling to organize fragments of memory. "I'm trying to . . . there's been so much written about

William Marshall . . . but . . . I hadn't realize he had a daughter."

"My parents kept me well-protected," Danica murmured.

Michael, who was growing uneasy himself, promptly made a move to shift the conversation. "Slightly different from our situation, but I don't think *anyone* could have kept *you* well protected, Cilla. You were an aggressive twerp, speaking of which, how's work going, aside from the conventions?"

Cilla accepted the diversion with grace, Danica with relief. In truth, Danica found herself fascinated with the ensuing talk, which centered on the daily rigor of the newspaper journalist. She had always viewed the papers from the outside; glimpsing them from the inside now was enlightening.

"You really do all that checking?" she asked when Cilla was describing the work she had recently done on a bribery report.

"Of our sources? If we didn't, we'd be risking lawsuits every day. Some papers take more chances than others, and of course, public figures are usually fair game. But sources of information can sometimes be pretty sleazy characters. It's in our interest to check them out before we make fools of ourselves. The headline that's slapped on a story can be misleading enough, but then—" she held up a hand "—I don't have any part in that." She glanced toward the sliding screen. "I think your baby wants out, Mike."

Michael twisted around to see the puppy standing forlornly at the screen. In an instant he had freed it from its cage and was gently placing it into Danica's outstretched arms. Quite appropriately, the talk turned to dogs, then, comfortably, to fond childhood remembrances, then old friends, then, as the minutes turned into hours, the novel written by one of Michael's old friends, which he and Danica had been reading simultaneously, then back to the puppy, who, having been romping by their feet after taking a nap in Danica's lap, had proceeded to pee on Michael's sneaker.

"That's it," Michael exclaimed in clipped words, "the final straw!" Scooping up the little dog, he stared it in the eye. "I've been up every damn night this week with you, you fool pooch. I've spoon-fed you, cleaned you, toted you to the vet, held your paw when you cried for your mama. And what do I get for all this love?" He glared at his sneaker and muttered a brief obscenity, which Danica was fast to contradict through her laughter.

"Not that, Michael. At least not yet. Maybe you'd better take him in." When Michael moved to do so, she looked at Cilla, who had shared her appreciation of the puppy's unique, if misplaced, demonstration of love. "How about you and Michael coming to my place for dinner?" She had already learned that Cilla was up for several days. Cilla, in turn, had already learned that Blake had returned to Boston the Sunday before.

"No way." Cilla stood alongside Danica. "I'm taking you both *out*."

"That's silly, Cilla. You probably eat out five or six nights a week."

"Now, how did you know that?"

"You're a working woman. You've got a hectic schedule."

Cilla lowered her voice as the two women entered the house. "The truth of it is I'm a lousy cook. Either I burn the butter or curdle the sauce or cut my finger instead of the tomato. I have this wonderful guy, though—"

"That you're seeing?"

"No, no. This guy cooks. When I'm planning to have a *guy* guy in for dinner, I give Fred the key to my apartment. He comes in during the afternoon and prepares everything, then leaves simplified instructions on what I have to do to make sure things are hot. My dates rarely know the difference."

"Pretty tricky."

"Tell me you think I'm awful. Are you a gourmet cook?"

Danica laughed. "Not quite. I've never had much of a chance to cook. The kitchen's always been occupied. What it boils down to is that I'm learning how to cook up here. I'm not too bad."

"Two women after my own heart," Michael hummed, catching talk of food as he passed them on his way from kitchen to bedroom. "Let's go, ladies. I'll just change my shoes and then I'm taking you both out to dinner."

"I'm taking us out to dinner!" Cilla called.

"No, you're not," Michael bellowed back from what Danica guessed to be the bottom of his closet. "I've never been a kept man and I don't intend to start now. Be gracious in defeat, Cilla. A docile woman is a thing to behold."

Cilla wasn't about to be either gracious or docile. "Try writing *that* in a book, Michael, and they'll boo you off the shelves. 'A docile woman is a thing to behold,' my foot. Modern men don't say things like that. They don't even *think* things like that." She lowered her voice so that only Danica could hear. "At least, if we keep telling them they don't, maybe they won't. I sometimes wonder if it isn't a losing battle." A frown creased her brow, as though mirroring the passage of a brief pain through her mind.

Danica was intrigued. Until that moment she hadn't seen a single dent in Cilla Buchanan. She seemed confident, optimistic, indeed a tiny bit intimidating to Danica. But with that fleeting frown something had emerged. Vulnerability? Sadness? Danica couldn't quite pin it down because it was already gone, but she sensed that Cilla's pain was very personal.

Over dinner she kept an ear out for anything that might lend credence to her suspicion. Once, in passing, Cilla spoke of her ex-husband, Jeffrey, but her tone remained even. Danica wondered whether she was well controlled, legitimately neutral or simply preoccupied. She kept giving Danica pensive looks from time to time.

The three were enjoying dessert when Cilla abruptly put down her fork. "I remember now," she said in a tone of dawning recognition. "Danica Marshall. Of *course* I've heard that name. Didn't you play tennis at one point?"

Danica knew that it would be foolish to feign innocence. "Yes. A long time ago." She dared glance at Michael and caught the discomfort in his eyes. It was enough to tell her that he'd known all along, that he had been waiting for her to raise the subject herself, that he hadn't wanted to dredge up something she would rather not have mentioned. Ironically, this knowledge gave her strength.

"You were good, as I recall. You made it to the top."

"I was ranked fourth in the country."

"But—" again Cilla tugged at her memory bank"—you stopped. Very suddenly."

"Cilla, I'm not sure Dani wants to discuss—"

"It's okay, Michael," Danica said softly, giving his hand a reassuring squeeze. "I don't mind talking about it." Maybe it was that, given the success of Cilla's career, she wanted to share her own, albeit defunct one. Maybe it was that she liked Cilla. Maybe it was that she needed Michael to hear. Then again, maybe it was the wine she had drunk.

"I was eight when I first started playing at our club. Our pro believed I had talent, and my parents jumped at the thought. They gave me lessons, twice a week during winters, every day during summers. When I began entering tournaments and winning, they were thrilled." She paused and looked down, momentarily unsure as to how much to say, then, with the sudden confidence that she was in the right, raised her eyes and went on.

"My father has always been a competitor. He imposed that drive on me. He was convinced that I could be the country's top-ranked female player. He was proud of what I was doing and that motivated me to work harder. I was twelve when I went off to boarding school. I had a private coach there." She arched a brow. "I had a special schedule and was excused from classes whenever there was a tournament. Not great for winning friends in school. Anyway, by the time I was fifteen, my parents decided to enroll me in a full-time tennis academy in Florida."

"Arroah's," Cilla prompted, recalling the association of the two names.

Danica nodded. "Armand was wonderful. He was just starting the academy. I lived in his house, along with several other players." She looked at Michael. "Reggie Nichols was one of them. We had met before, but that was where we became close friends. Eventually the school expanded enough to warrant a dorm, but Reggie and I stayed close."

"That's understandable," Cilla remarked. "You were well matched in skill."

"We liked each other. Reggie could usually beat me on the court, but I never felt myself in competition with her. That was where the trouble began, I guess."

"Trouble?" Michael asked.

"I just wasn't that competitive, at least not enough to take me to the top."

"You had an injury," he argued, revealing exactly how much he had known about her career before she had ever said a word.

Danica eyed him sadly. "The papers don't tell everything, and what they don't know they can't report. I'd been agonizing for months. I reached a point where I just didn't enjoy what I was doing. I mean, I had been living and breathing tennis for so long, and suddenly I just didn't see the point. It was supposed to be fun, but it wasn't. Winning didn't mean enough to me. I didn't have the drive it took to get to the top. And I couldn't stand the pressure."

"From home?"

She hesitated, then nodded. "Hurting my shoulder was the best thing that could have happened. It brought things to a head. If I'd wanted, I'm sure I could have played once the shoulder healed. I chose not to."

"Your father must have loved that," Cilla speculated dryly.

"Don't you know it. He tried to blame things on Armand, then on the doctor who was treating my shoulder, then, inevitably, on me."

Michael felt her hurt. "But you held your ground."

"For what it was worth. I'd become convinced I didn't have it in me to hit that top spot, and being second or third or fourth just wasn't acceptable where I came from. I was relieved when I bowed out, but I was also more than a little disappointed in myself. When you fail to come up to standards that have been solidly ingrained in you, it's hard."

"As if you don't have enough going for you without having to be a superstar. You were fourth in the country! Wasn't that good enough for him?"

"I wasn't number one," Danica pointed out.

Cilla, who had been momentarily taken aback by Michael's vehemence, grew thoughtful. "There's a fantastic story here."

Michael pinned his sister with a glare that went far beyond vehemence. "You wouldn't," he warned.

"Of course I wouldn't," Cilla said without a flurry. "I just think that one day Danica might want to write it all down. Hell, there are books galore on the shelves by one career athlete or another. It'd be refreshing to have the other side told."

"It's . . . too personal," Danica argued. She suddenly feared she had said too much and wondered why she had done it. Cilla was media, *real* media. If she ever pursued the story she smelled, Danica would be appalled. And embarrassed. And hurt. For once, she wished she had listened to her mother's advice, and Blake's. They said to be careful. She had blown it again!

SEVEN

DANICA'S FEARS LURKED strongly in her mind. Later that night, as he walked her back to her house, Michael addressed them head-on.

"She won't say a thing, Dani. I know her as well as anyone does. She won't betray your trust."

Danica held his arm more tightly. "I keep asking myself why I said all that. It's a part of my life I don't usually talk about."

"It's good to talk about it. You have nothing to be ashamed of."

"That's debatable but beside the point. I barely know Cilla. If I hadn't told *you* about it before, why did it all come out tonight?"

"Maybe because Cilla had the courage I lacked. I thought I was being thoughtful by not raising it. Maybe I was just frightened."

"Frightened? Of what?"

"Of crossing that little line between what's my business and what isn't."

"Anything's your business. You should know that by now." She had been with Blake too long, she realized. She was using his words. But she had barely begun to admonish herself when Michael disagreed.

"Not anything, Dani. There are some things I can't ask."

"Like what?"

"Like what goes on between you and Blake."

She gave a harsh laugh. "Practically nothing, if you want to know."

"I don't. Oh, God, that makes it harder." He closed his eyes for a minute, then went on, desperately needing to steer away from what she implied. "Why didn't you tell me about your tennis before?"

"Because I didn't want you to see me as a quitter."

"A quitter? Come on. You reached a point in your life where a decision was called for. You made it."

"I could have kept playing. I could have worked harder. I could have pushed myself on and on."

"And you would have been a basket case before you were twenty." They had reached her door. He put an arm around her waist. "You made the right decision, Danica. You did what was best for *you*."

"That was what I told myself at the time, but I've had my doubts since. I took the easy way out. That's all there is to it."

"That's what he thinks, isn't it?" They both knew Michael referred to her father.

"Sometimes there's not much difference between what he thinks and what I think."

Michael turned to firmly grip her shoulders. "There you're wrong. You think very differently from him. You *are* very different from him. You can't lead your life in his footsteps. You're your own person!"

Danica smiled softly. "You always say the right things."

"I believe them, sweetheart. I believe in you. I just wish you did yourself."

Touched in the most beautiful of ways by his words, his look, his faith, she stood on tiptoe and wrapped her arms around his neck. "Oh, Michael," she whispered, holding tighter when he enclosed her in a hug.

With a soft moan, he began to caress her back, and she could only close her eyes and enjoy his warmth. It was a physical thing, but emotional, too. She needed it. Lord, how she needed it.

She felt his lips on her hair, pressing small kisses against its silk, but she needed that, too. He prized her. She had nothing to offer him, still he prized her. With him she was herself and more of a person than ever before.

His lips moved lower, whispering her name with each small kiss he planted on her forehead, her eyes, her nose. Entranced by a new and unfamiliar joy, she tipped her head to ease his access. When his lips touched hers, she caught her breath. His was sweet, warm, wafting over her as his mouth hovered, close, so close, so tempting, so ready.

She couldn't think, could only feel and enjoy and live a dream. Her lips were open when his finally closed over them, and she gave him everything that the pent-up woman in her demanded. She had never kissed a man this way, with this hunger, this force. But sweet. It was so, so sweet. Their lips caressed and explored. Their tongues met and mated.

Then there was a quivering, from his legs to hers, her stomach to his, his chest to her breasts. And suddenly, as each realized that their bodies were taking command in a way that was forbidden, they parted.

Forehead to forehead, they breathed shallowly.

"Ahh, Dani. I've wanted to do that for so long."

She had wanted it, too, but she couldn't admit it. She couldn't admit anything, because her throat was a tight knot preventing sound.

"Don't be angry," he pleaded in a whisper. "I couldn't help myself. I love you, Dani, and I don't know what in the hell to do about it."

She swallowed hard, then whispered his name and buried her face against the warm column of his throat. *I love you, too,* she wanted to say, but she couldn't. It wasn't fair to either of them. And it wasn't fair to Blake.

"Maybe," she breathed unsteadily, "maybe we shouldn't see each other."

"Don't say that! Please don't say that. I need you too much. And you need me. We'll just . . . just have to keep things under control."

"Seems to me we said the same thing once before."

"We'll just have to say it again and louder." His tone echoed that determination, but when he held her back and took her face in his hands, his expression was exquisitely gentle. "There are times when I hate Blake, when I wish you could . . . you would leave him. . . . Do you love him, Dani?"

"I'm married to him," she whispered even as her body was yearning for closer contact with this man to whom she wasn't married.

"But do you love him?"

"There are . . . different kinds of love."

"Do you *love* him?

She closed her eyes and took a pained breath. *Not as I love you, Michael Buchanan.*

"I want you to love him, Dani. I want you to say that what we have together is just an aberration. Maybe if I know that, I'll be able to keep my distance. Say it. Say it!"

"I can't!" she cried, opening her eyes and returning the same look of helplessness Michael wore. She couldn't lie. Either to him *or* herself. She didn't know if she loved Blake. Certainly what she felt for him was far different from what she felt for Michael. Maybe what she felt for Michael was an aberration, but it had been building for far too long and there was no end in sight. "I can't. And there's really no point." Her voice held defeat. "I'm married to Blake; I bear his name, wear his wedding band, and . . . and . . ."

"You have his child in your belly." Michael let out the breath he was holding. His hands dropped to her elbows, then her hands. He released one to lightly touch her stomach. "I wish it was mine," he whispered, his voice cracking at the end. Then he turned and started down the path, knowing that he would only make things worse the longer he stayed. By the time he reached his house, though, he was regretting having left her so abruptly. She had been upset, too. And she was alone.

Bypassing Cilla's watchful presence in the living room, he went into his den and called her. "Dani?"

"Yes?"

He kept his voice low, very low. "I'm sorry. I shouldn't have pushed you."

"You didn't say anything I . . . haven't said to myself." Her words were broken.

"Are you all right?"

"Yes."

He shut his eyes tight. "You've been crying."

"I'm okay now."

"Oh, Dani," he whispered, "I'm so sorry."

"Damn it, Michael, stop saying that!" Frustrated and angered by the entire situation, she found a sudden strength. "If you're sorry you kissed me, remember that I kissed you back. So it's just as much my fault as yours. More so, even. I'm the one who should be thinking about Blake. I'm the one who's betrayed him. And I'm *not* sorry!"

There was a lengthy pause on both ends of the line.

"You're not?" Michael asked at last.

"No," she answered very softly.

"Why not?"

"Because I enjoyed your kiss. I'd been wondering what it would be like. Now I know. But we can't let it happen again. It's too tempting."

Relieved that she hadn't tried to deny what she had so clearly felt, Michael smiled. "Damn right about that. Listen, Dani, don't be too hard on yourself. If I know you, you'll sit there feeling guilty. It happened. Now we *both* know how careful we have to be. Okay?"

"Okay. . . . Michael?"

"Mmmm?"

"I like Cilla."

"I'm glad. So do I."

"Will I see her again before I leave?"

"I'll send her over to visit. How's that?"

"Great, as long as she promises to forget everything she's heard."

"I'll make sure of it. 'Night, Dani."

"Good night, Michael."

He replaced the receiver with a smile on his face and a fullness in the region of his heart. His momentary serenity was shattered, though, when a quiet voice came from the door.

"What are you doing, Michael?"

He whirled around, stared at his sister, then scowled. "How long have you been standing there?"

Arms comfortably crossed over her chest, Cilla was lounging against the doorjamb. "Long enough. Not that I really needed to hear anything. The vibes passing between you two were obvious."

"Funny, I thought we were pretty subtle."

"What's going on?"

"I'm not sure that's any of your business."

"Come on, Mike. This is Cilla. Your sister. Your twin. Your better half?"

"Good thing you made that last a question. It's always been up for grabs."

"You're avoiding my first question. What in the devil are you doing with her?"

"Don't you like her?"

"You know I do. She's lovely. She's poised and intelligent and pretty—"

"Beautiful. She's beautiful. Inside and out."

"She's also married."

He glared. "I know that."

"You seem to forget it from time to time. Michael, *what are you doing?*"

He gave her another long, hard stare, then turned and propped himself against the edge of his desk. "I'm trying to survive."

"What are you talking about? You've been surviving very well all these years."

"That's the whole point. All these years passing and where am I? Sure, I have a career and financial security. Sure, I have friends. But I want something else."

"I hadn't realized you felt something was missing." She came to perch by his side against the desk. "You've been with lots of women. How long have you wanted this 'something else'?"

"Since I met Danica. I hadn't realized it was there. No one's ever inspired the feelings she does."

"You're not talking survival. You're talking suicide. Mike, she's out of reach. You can't have her."

"Maybe not all of her. But I can have some of it." He turned to his sister in earnest. "Look, things aren't right with her marriage. That was one of the reasons she bought the house up here. She thought she and Blake would be able to patch things up if they got away from the city. But he doesn't come. Not often, at least. And I have a feeling that things aren't great when he's there. After he left last Sunday, she was in a blue funk. She tried to hide it, but I saw."

"Maybe you wanted to see."

"I *saw.*"

"So what are you saying? That you're going to sit around and hope that her marriage falls through?"

"Damn it, Cilla, you make me sound like a monster." He raked a hand through his hair, ruffling it more than the night breeze already had. "I'd give anything to see Danica happy, even if that means the recovery of her marriage. But regardless of what happens, we're friends. We were from the first, when we saw each other on the beach last March. It's something I can't change, something that's as much a part of me as a hand or a leg—"

"Or a heart?"

"Or a heart." He sighed. "Which is why I tell you that I'm only trying to survive. I can't live with her. I can't live without her. So I guess I'll have to take whatever I can get."

"Oh, Mike," Cilla said sadly, "it hurts me to hear you say that. You deserve so much more. Maybe you should be out there looking. Maybe now that you've realized what you want . . ." She let the thought lapse when Michael's expression grew hard. "Okay, I know. *She's* what you want. But there may never be a future for the two of you. Have you thought of that?"

"I try not to."

"Then you're a fool." She threw a hand in the air. "Hell, we're *all* fools. Love is a bitch. Do you know that?"

For the first time since he had found Cilla in his den, Michael smiled. "What's doing with you? Still seeing that guy . . . what was his name . . . Waldo?"

"Wally, please. And no, I'm not seeing him."

"What happened?"

"He started getting serious, so I called it off."

"I thought you liked him."

"I did. Just not enough to consider marriage."

"Would you ever consider it again?"

"If the right guy came along."

"But you're still bumping into Jeff?"

"It's inevitable, isn't it? Washington's not *that* big. He asked for you, by the way. He was wondering when you'd be getting down. He misses the talks you two used to have."

"I miss them, too," Michael mused. "We go way back, Jeff and I. Talking shop with him is fun."

"Whose shop . . . yours or his?"

"Either. Both. We pick each other's brains. He's one hell of a bright guy."

"I think the Defense Department's finally realized that. They've given him a promotion. From what he inferred, he's working on some pretty sensitive investigations."

"Really? Who's he investigating?"

Cilla gave a rueful frown. "If he'd been able to tell me that—if he'd been able to tell me *anything*—maybe we'd still be married. I doubt he trusts me any more now than he did then. I'm the *press*. Never forget that."

"Cilla, speaking of that, you won't blab about anything Dani said, will you?"

"Blab? Of course not. I wouldn't do that to her or to you."

"Good. Because I don't want her hurt. I'd never forgive you if—"

"Trust me, Michael. Please? Trust me." She wouldn't write about Danica; she wouldn't gossip. What she *would* do, she vowed, was to keep her eyes and ears open. There was a better than even chance that at one point or another she would run into Blake Lindsay. And she had every intention of finding out why a guy as good-looking and as successful as he was would all but abandon his lovely, lonely, pregnant wife.

During the next few weeks, Michael and Danica were very careful. While neither could not not see the other, they kept just enough distance between them to preclude a repeat of what had happened on her doorstep that night. They biked together, ate out from time to time, sat on the beach at sunset talking about a book, a TV documentary or some aspect of Michael's work that troubled him. For his part, he enjoyed running things past Danica. Often she was able to summarize a thought or a theory more succinctly than he could, given his closeness to the subject matter. For her part, she was intrigued by his work, by the intense research he had done, by the different slant he was trying to convey. Now that he knew about her tennis involvement, she felt comfortable discussing sports, though when he popped over one day suggesting that they play a game or two on the local court, she refused. He tried to talk her into it, and to her surprise, she nearly yielded. But she needed more time; thoughts of tennis still evoked vivid memories of drudgery, and exhaustion, and failure. In the end, they agreed to put it off for another time. Michael was determined to get her playing one day, though. He felt that it would be good for her, that she had to face the past in order to finally accept it. Moreover, he knew she had loved tennis once, and he desperately wanted her to share that love with him.

During the second week of August Danica drove back to Boston to see the doctor as ordered on a monthly basis. His report was good, and that pleased her. What didn't please her was the fact that Blake wasn't there. He had left several days earlier to spend time in Washington before going on to the convention in St. Louis. It hurt her that he hadn't wanted to meet her doctor, much less ask him questions that most prospective fathers would have. While Danica had read any number of books on the subject of pregnancy and childbirth since her pregnancy had been confirmed, Blake, to her knowledge, had read nothing. When she asked him if he wasn't even the slightest bit curious about what his child looked like at that moment or would look like a month, two, three months hence, he simply smiled that winning smile of his and said that nature would take its course whether he knew its intimate details or not. She realized then that it was her baby, literally and figuratively.

What bothered Danica most, though, was that during the two days she spent in the Beacon Hill town house, she missed Michael more than she did Blake. It was with relief that she finally returned to Maine and to the man whose excitement at seeing her again warmed her heart.

The convention began, and since she hadn't wanted a television in her own house, she spent every evening watching the proceedings with Michael. She sensed a part of her future lay in the outcome, and she was tense. Though Michael did what he could to alleviate that tension, it was never more apparent than at the moment that Jason Claveling mustered enough votes to secure the nomination.

When the floor erupted with sign-waving and cheering, she closed her eyes and let out a long sigh.

"Well, that's it," Michael announced. "Looks like your men are going to be a happy lot tonight."

"Are *you* pleased?" she returned. She would certainly classify him as one of "her men."

"We could have done worse. Claveling's the one who stands a good chance of unseating Picard, and I'm all for that."

"*You* won't be running around during the next three months trying to get the deed done." She moaned. "And I thought the past three months were bad."

Michael understood. He knew how much she resented the time Blake spent on the campaign. "Maybe it won't be as bad as it's been. The nomination was the hardest part, given four contenders. In a two-man race, things are simplified."

"I know you're trying to make me feel better, but you're talking through your hat, Michael Buchanan. I've seen my father in situations like these. More accurately, I've read about him in the papers, which was about as close as I was able to get. If he's busy under normal circumstances, during a campaign—be it his own or that of someone he's supporting—he's *doubly* busy. And this time around, Blake will be busy right with him."

"Then that's all the more time you'll have for me," Michael teased, eyes glinting in response to the scowl Danica threw him. "Come on, sweetheart, it won't be so bad. I'll keep you busy."

They both knew she would be returning to Boston in September, but Michael was determined to make good on his word at least until then. When she remained mildly depressed over the next few days—in some part due to the blatantly hurried phone call she received from Blake upon his return from St. Louis—he set a date with the McCabes.

The Sunday they all spent together was a smashing success. Without any of the initial trepidation Danica had felt upon meeting the media-minded Cilla, she found Greta and Pat to be equally as likable. They were fun, unpretentious, and took great joy in relating stories of Michael in his younger days. The baby stole her heart. By the time she and Michael left with promises of a return engagement, Danica was looking forward all the more to having a child of her own.

Four days later, though, she wasn't feeling quite as well. She had had an uncomfortable night and was dozing on the sofa when Michael rang the doorbell. Groggy, she pushed herself to a sitting position, then up to her feet. When she opened the door, Michael was quickly alarmed.

"What is it, Dani? Aren't you feeling well?" She was wearing her long robe and looked frighteningly pale.

She grasped the doorknob and leaned against the door. "I didn't sleep well. I'm sorry, Michael. Do you think we could drive to Freeport another time?"

"Of course. L.L. Bean isn't going anywhere." He took her arm and guided her back to the sofa. When she was seated, he propped a hip beside her. "Morning sickness?"

She shook her head. "I haven't had any of that. I've really felt terrific until now."

He put a hand on her forehead. "Maybe you have the flu. You feel warm."

"I'll be okay." Slipping her legs behind him, she curled into the corner of the sofa. When she closed her eyes, Michael worried all the more.

"You didn't get a call from Blake, did you?" That seemed a sure thing to upset her. But she shook her head. "From your parents?" Again she shook her head.

"I'll be okay. I think I'll just rest."

It wasn't like her, he knew. There was something she wasn't saying. He gently rubbed her thigh. "Can I get you anything?"

"No. I'll just lie here for a while."

Michael studied her for a long time, then finally got up and wandered through the house. The sheets on her bed were in a tangle. He made the bed, then returned to living room to find her lying with her arms crossed over her stomach and her knees drawn up close. Sitting down by her side, he smoothed the hair from her cheeks. She opened her eyes, but she didn't smile.

"What is it?" he pleaded. "I want to do *something*."

"Just stay around," she said. Her voice was as weak as the rest of her looked, he decided, and the knowledge added to his concern.

He spent the morning with a book in his lap, though he hardly read a word. His eyes wouldn't focus on the open page but kept going to Danica's face. By noontime she was looking more pale than ever.

"Maybe I should call a doctor," he suggested quietly. He knew she wasn't sleeping. She shifted from time to time, gingerly, he thought, and when her eyes weren't closed they focused blindly on the rug, the coffee table, the glass slider.

"Wait a little longer," she murmured. "I'm sure I'll pick up pretty soon."

She didn't. Rather she grew more uncomfortable. Michael reached his limit when she opened her eyes once again and they were filled with tears. He was up like a bolt and on his haunches before her.

"Damn it, Dani, tell me. Is it the baby? Do you think something's wrong?"

The tears hovered on her lids and she swallowed hard. "I don't know. I've felt weird since last night. I woke up with a backache."

"I have a heating pad at my place. Should I get it?"

"I feel cramps every so often. They were mild at first and I hoped they'd just go away, but they're not doing that."

Michael forced himself to remain calm. "Are they getting worse?" She nodded and met his gaze. He realized that she was terrified. "It's okay, sweetheart." He pressed a warm kiss to her forehead. "You stay put. I'm going to call the doctor."

"He's in Boston. I can't drive—"

"I have one here."

"Not an obstetrician."

"He'll give me the name of one. The best in the area." Squeezing her arm, he headed for the phone. When he returned, he squatted down. "A Dr. Masconi is waiting for us in Portland. Do you want to put on some clothes?"

Nodding, Danica tried to push herself up, but Michael was quickly lifting her and carrying her into the bedroom, where he set her gently on her feet. He turned toward the dresser. "Tell me what you want."

"I can do it," she breathed shakily. "You go wait for me. I'll be right out."

"Are you sure? Will you yell if you need me?" When she nodded, he left, but he was right outside her door waiting when she appeared moments later. She had thrown on a pair of jeans and a long-sleeved summer sweater. But she was crying. When he reached for her, she grabbed his arm. "I'm bleeding, Michael. I think I'm losing it. Dear God, I don't want that!"

Trying to contain the fear he felt, he lifted her up and made for the door. "I don't want it, either, sweetheart. Neither does the doctor. He's an expert. He'll do everything he can." Her arms were around his neck and she was holding him tightly, as if that might help save her baby. He felt more helpless than he ever had before. All he could do was to try to keep her calm and get her to the hospital as soon as possible.

The drive was an agony for them both. Danica sat curled beside Michael, holding his hand, wondering if she was being punished for feeling so much for him but needing his strength nonetheless. Michael tried to soothe her fears with gentle words of encouragement, praying that the baby would be all right, praying that she would be all right, that she wouldn't blame herself if something did happen.

The hospital wasn't the most efficient of places. The doctor had to be paged from somewhere in its labyrinthine midst, and in the meantime Danica was left on an examining table in one of the emergency room's small cubicles. Once she had undressed, Michael stayed with her for all but those moments when he angrily stalked to the nurse's station to demand to know what was keeping the doctor.

When the doctor finally arrived, Michael was relegated to pacing the emergency-room floor. He was allowed to see Danica for a brief minute as they were wheeling her upstairs. She had been sedated, but she saw him clearly. He had to be content with that until the time, much later that evening, when she was wheeled back to a private room.

He rose quickly from the chair in which he'd been seated, it seemed for days, and waited until she was settled in bed. She was still pale, but she was awake. He took her hand and smiled gently.

"Hi. How're you doin'?"

"Okay, I guess," she whispered. Her lower lip quivered. She bit down on it.

Settling beside her, he brought her hand to his mouth and kissed it. Her fingers were limp, her skin chilled. He lowered her hand to his chest and pressed it there in an offer of warmth.

"I feel so tired," she murmured.

"It's the anesthesia. It'll take a while to wear off. Why don't you try to sleep. I'll be right here when you wake up."

Without argument, she closed her eyes. He watched her until he was sure she was asleep, then carefully left the bed and stood staring out the window until he heard her stir. He was back at her side by the time she opened her eyes.

"What time is it?" she whispered.

"Nearly midnight."

She nodded and closed her eyes again, but he knew she wasn't sleeping. He took her hand and held it gently between both of his, sensing that she was mourning, wishing there was something he could do. If that small part of him had once upon a time regretted she was pregnant, it now felt her sorrow with the rest of him.

"Michael?" She didn't open her eyes. "It hurts up here." She raised her free hand to her head and he knew just what she meant.

"I know, Dani. I know."

"I wanted the baby so badly. It was going to open up new doors for me." A single tear, then another, trickled down her cheeks.

Unable to keep any distance when he felt her pain so intimately, Michael gently lifted her into his arms, holding her while she cried quietly, knowing she needed the outlet.

"I wanted . . . the baby . . ."

"I know. It'll be all right."

"But I don't . . . know what went . . . wrong," she sobbed. "The doctor couldn't . . . say."

"He doesn't know. Nobody knows. The only thing we can guess is that the baby wasn't well. Something may have been wrong right from the start."

"But why? Why me? Everyone . . . else has healthy babies."

"Shhhh. It's okay, sweetheart. Shhhh. There'll be other ones coming along."

"I don't think . . . so. Oh, Michael, I don't think so."

"Don't say that. The doctor saw nothing at all wrong that would prevent you from conceiving again and carrying the baby to term."

"That's not the point! Oh, God . . ."

She was crying again. He held her until the tears slowly eased, thinking all the while about what she'd said, wondering exactly how bad things were between Blake and her.

"Dani, I called Blake when the doctor gave me the news."

Her body went very still. "You called him?" she whispered against his chest.

"I had to." It had taken three calls, one to the town house, one to Blake's office, finally one to the men's club where he had met with success.

"What did he . . . did he say anything?"

"He was upset." He was actually relatively calm, perhaps stoic, or simply well controlled, but Michael saw no need in telling Danica that. "He wanted to know how you were. When I told him that the doctor said you'd be fine, he was relieved. He said to tell you that he'd be up tomorrow . . . uh, today."

If he had hoped the news would cheer her, he had miscalculated. She started to cry again, making soft, grieving sounds that tore at his gut, and he could only hold her, rock her gently, smooth back her hair. Eventually, inevitably, exhaustion crept up. She quieted but made no move to free herself from his arms.

"I wanted . . . our baby," she murmured as she drifted off. "Oh, Michael, I wanted our baby . . ."

Perhaps because he had wanted the baby to be his from the start, Michael could have sworn from her words that she agreed. But she was doped up and had spoken ambiguously, he reasoned; of course, the "our" she spoke of referred to her and Blake.

He had no way of knowing that she hadn't been that far gone. He had no way of knowing that, in her way, Danica had thought of the baby as hers and Michael's. He had no way of knowing that on the night the baby had been conceived, she had been loving him—not Blake, but him.

Blake arrived from Boston late that afternoon. Danica, who had been discharged from the hospital in the morning and had slept most of the time since then, was sitting on the sofa in her robe, covered by the light shawl Michael had insisted on, drinking the tea Michael had steeped. She was pondering the tag in her hand which read, "The human spirit is stronger than anything that can happen to it," when the sound of a key in the lock caught her ear.

Her gaze flew to Michael, who was already headed for the door. Heart thudding, she held her breath. The meeting of these two men was something she had assumed would happen eventually. She had never anticipated it taking place quite this way.

She watched them shake hands and exchange brief words, Blake's in appreciation of Michael's help, Michael's in praise of Danica. As unobtrusively as possible, Michael excused himself then, leaving Danica alone with Blake.

He approached and pressed a light kiss on her head before taking a seat across from her. Having come straight from the office, he was wearing a suit. It added to the formality that seemed to yawn glaringly between them.

"How are you feeling?" he asked quietly.

"Pretty good."

"I spoke with your doctor this morning." He proceeded to outline the conversation, which told Danica nothing more than the doctor had already told her himself, nothing more than she and Michael had already discussed. "He says that you shouldn't be worried."

"I'm not."

"He wants you to get lots of rest over the next few days."

"I haven't been able to do much else. Michael wouldn't let me move."

"He seems like a nice fellow."

"He is. I'm grateful he was here yesterday. I wasn't sure what to do."

"I knew you shouldn't have been alone here," Blake charged. "If Mrs. Hannah had been with you—"

"It's all right, Blake. I've survived." *Not my baby, though. Are you sorry?*

"The doctor said that the problem started the night before. What took you so long to get to the hospital?"

She closed her eyes, then opened them with a sigh. "It wouldn't have helped. Even if I'd gotten there sooner. I didn't do anything here that they wouldn't have had me do there. According to the doctor, it was just destined."

"I know. And I didn't mean that as criticism."

Then why did you say it? she argued silently. "I'm sorry. I guess I'm sensitive."

"That's to be expected. You've been through an ordeal."

Not you, though, she thought. Still not a single word of regret that she had miscarried. It was obviously her loss, not his.

"Well," she sighed, bunching the crocheted shawl beneath her fingers, "it's over." She looked up again. "Thank you for coming. I know how busy you must be."

In an apparent attempt to cheer her up, Blake proceeded to tell her exactly how busy he had been in the nearly four weeks since he'd seen her last. He spoke of work and his stay in Washington. He elaborated on the excitement of the convention, of the jubilation of the victory parties afterward, of the Claveling campaign's strategy for the weeks ahead.

Danica listened quietly. Blake had to have said more to her in that hour than in the past thousand. Yet not a word had been of a personal nature, at least none that directly concerned Danica. She recalled similar monologues she had heard on those rare occasions when her family had gathered together for dinner. Her father would ask her about school, then after hearing her initial response, would nod and launch into a dissertation on a subject not remotely related either to Danica or to school. She wondered if Blake enjoyed hearing himself speak as much as her father did, and was appalled at how much more alike the two men were than ever.

She was more appalled, though, when out of the blue Blake announced that her mother would be arriving in Maine the next day.

"Mom's coming *here?*"

"You don't expect her to be going to a hotel when you could clearly use her help."

"Her help." Danica carefully swallowed the bitter words that threatened to spill, but evidently she was less successful at concealing the cynical look in her eye.

"Look, Danica, I have to get back to Boston tomorrow. Eleanor felt that you shouldn't be alone at this time, and I agree. She's concerned about you. She and your father were both very upset when I called."

Strange, Danica hadn't given a thought to notifying her parents of what had happened. She must have simply blocked out that particularly odious chore from her mind. Of course they would be upset. They had wanted a grandchild, as though it were their God-given right. Well, what about *her* rights? What about the child *she'd* wanted? What about the warm, close family life she had dreamed about having for years and years?

"I wish you'd told her not to come," Danica murmured.

"She's your mother. It's her place to be here."

Danica's laugh held a touch of hysteria. "Her conscience must be coming to life after all these years. She never worried about 'her place' before. At least, she never worried about it with regard to me. She and Dad were always out doing something that was more important."

"You're being ungenerous, Danica. What she and your father did they had to do."

"That's a matter of opinion. Mine differs from theirs."

Blake's nostrils flared. His handsome features suddenly took on a harder cast, one she had never seen before. She wondered if she was getting to him . . . finally.

"Your mother loves you." He spaced his words as though he were talking to a child. "She wants to be here. I had no idea you objected to her company."

"It's hard to object to something you've had so little exposure to. I wonder what's come over her all of a sudden. Belated maternal instincts. Maybe she's going through menopause and—"

"That's enough, Danica." He got to his feet, automatically smoothing the crease in his trousers. "You're upset. You need some rest. I'll go get my bag from the car and change. Maybe you'll be in a better mood when I'm done."

He never saw the who-in-the-devil-do-you-think-*you*-are glance that hit his back as he headed for the door, and it crumbled as soon as he was gone. By the time he returned and changed his clothes, Danica's anger had given way to fatigue. She was tired. Tired of wanting and not having. Tired of needing and going without. Of course, things seemed worse right now, she told herself. The doctor had warned her that she might be depressed for a time but that it would pass. She could only take one day at a time. One day at a time. One day at a time. Four days later she breathed a sigh of relief when Eleanor Marshall kissed her goodbye and started back for Connecticut. Within minutes, she was out the glass slider, across the deck, down the stairs and running along the beach.

"Michael!" she bellowed from the sand beneath his house. "Michael!"

Mercifully soon, he was out on the deck, stunned at the sight of Danica standing with her bare feet planted firmly in the sand.

"I thought she'd never leave, Michael! I nearly went out of my mind!" Her call was fraught with pent-up frustration. The tension in her body was marked.

"Take it easy." He trotted down the stone steps. "Take it easy. We'll talk it out."

"Oh, God, Michael. I don't know what's gotten into me. For years I wanted her attention; then suddenly I had it and I felt stifled!"

He was beside her, taking in her look of wide-eyed exasperation. Unable to help himself, he grinned.

"What's so funny?"

"You. You look beautiful and independent and impulsive. Do you realize that I've never seen you quite this way?"

"Laugh, then, if you want. But I have the worst case of cabin fever and if I don't *do* something, I think I'm going to scream."

"You already did. Twice. Wanna do it again?"

About to argue, she looked at him, then squeezed her eyes shut, balled her fists and let out the loudest, most satisfying scream in the world. When the sound rose beyond the rocks and the pines and died, she dropped her chin to her chest, took a deep breath, then let it out very, very slowly. "Ahhh." She raised her head. "That felt good."

Grinning still, Michael wrapped her in his arms and whirled her around. He had missed her. He had stopped by twice, as a neighbor and friend, to say hello and offer his services to her mother, but he hadn't had a chance to visit with Danica. He hadn't wanted to push his luck that far.

"You're looking better," he said when he set her back on the sand. "I take it you got lots of rest."

"She wouldn't let me do a thing. Not that she's great around the house, mind you. I should be grateful we had a cook all those years. Then again, maybe if we hadn't, she'd have learned to make something other than baked chicken and hamburg."

"That's all you ate?"

"We alternated. Chicken on Sunday, hamburg on Monday, chicken last night. She left a hamburg patty in the refrigerator for me to broil tonight."

"What about lunches?"

"Tuna salad. Egg salad."

Michael winced. "And breakfast?"

"Oatmeal . . . every . . . morning."

He threw back his head and laughed.

"It's not funny, Michael. Between meals she doted like a mother hen. I didn't know how to act. One thing's for sure, my mind was so occupied trying to figure her out that I didn't have time to dwell on the baby."

Her expression sobered at the last. Draping an arm around her shoulder, Michael drew her into step beside him as he began to walk slowly along the beach. They talked of her mother and of her father, who had called and spoken to her twice. She told him of the visit she had from a flower-bearing Sara, of a sweet call from Greta McCabe and more dutiful ones from city friends. He told her of the progress he had made in his writing, of the discussion he'd had with his editor and the plans they had for publicizing his book.

And they talked about the baby, Danica's feelings, her discouragement but resignation.

In the end, though, the one thought that played most heavily in Danica's mind was the realization that in another two weeks she would be returning to Boston.

EIGHT

❦ ❦ ❦

THE NEXT FEW MONTHS were difficult ones for Danica. By the time she returned to Boston she was still trying to acclimate herself to the fact that there would be no baby come spring. She rationalized that her miscarriage was perhaps a blessing, that as the doctor had suggested, the baby hadn't been healthy from the start. She reminded herself that having a child was the worst thing she could have done if, by doing so, she hoped to save a floundering marriage. But she hadn't been hoping that. Not really.

The fact was that though her marriage was far from ideal, there were bonds holding it together, albeit ones that had less to do with any true love between Blake and her than with external factors such as social convenience and appearance and, of course, expectation.

True, a baby might have added a more personal link to the marriage, but the major reason she had wanted one had been to give meaning to her own life. She wanted to be a mother. She wanted to be able to create a little world with her child, a world that would welcome the love she had to give.

Many, many times she imagined that her miscarriage had been a form of divine punishment. She was married to Blake, but she loved Michael, and that was wrong, so the theory went. But it wasn't, she inevitably argued. Could something that was so beautiful, something that felt so right, be wrong? Could something that made her feel whole, that made her feel treasured, be wrong? Could something that drew from her warmth and caring and concern for another human being be wrong?

There were no answers to her questions. And as if accepting the loss of her baby wasn't enough, the return to Boston, itself, was something akin to drug withdrawal. She missed Michael terribly. The contrast between her life in the city—meetings, luncheons, cocktail receptions, charity benefits—and that she led all summer—biking the streets, walking the beach, reading, thinking, spending time with newfound friends—was harsh.

Blake was Blake, and more distant than ever. She told herself that he was simply up to his ears in commitments. But the fact remained that they made no use of what little time they did have together to discuss anything, much less their relationship. Blake never spoke of her miscarriage. He never spoke of Maine. She wondered for a time if he resented her love of the place, but as the weeks passed and she dutifully remained on Beacon Hill, she felt his resentment was unwarranted.

He arrived home at night talked out and tired. When he traveled, he rarely called. In desperation, Danica once again began to think of working. She took to reading the help-wanted ads in the paper each morning, but somehow seeing job demands in print made her acutely aware of both the scope of such a commitment and of her own very vague qualifications. She began to discreetly send out feelers among the people with whom she came into contact—the development director at the hospital, the curator of the museum, the university president with whom she often talked at dinner parties.

September became October. The leaves turned, then fell. She was thoroughly discouraged and on the verge of escaping to Maine, which she knew would be wrong because she couldn't expect that Michael would have solutions that she couldn't find herself. Moreover, she told herself, she couldn't always run to him when things were rough. It wasn't fair to either of them. He would allow her to use him, she feared, but she had to learn to be independent. If she was dissatisfied with her life, she had to take it in her own two hands and remold it.

The opening came when she least expected it, while she was attending a benefit lecture given at the Women's City Club by a renowned economist. Blake was out of town, so Danica had gone alone, not because she was a fan of the speaker or because she was deeply involved in economics, but because she had helped plan the affair, the proceeds of which were being put toward a scholarship fund at one of the smaller local colleges.

She knew many of the people there and spent much of her time at the subsequent reception talking with them. When the conversation waned or, rather, when her interest in the conversation waned, as it always did, she excused herself and graciously approached a group that included the young woman who had taken charge of publicity for the event.

"You did a wonderful job, Sharon. The crowd is more than we'd dared hope for."

Sharon Tyler smiled and sent her eyes in an encompassing sweep of the room. "It's more than I'd hoped for, either, and I couldn't be happier. Sometimes you can plug and plug an event and then have it fall through. It's gratifying when the reverse happens."

They talked for a bit about Sharon's other work; then Sharon introduced Danica to the three people with her. The Hancocks were a couple Danica had met in passing once before. The third member of the group was an older gentleman, a man in his late seventies, whom she had never met but whose name rang an instant bell. James Hardmore Bryant. Former Governor of the Commonwealth.

"Governor Bryant, it's a pleasure to meet you." She had had a moment's pause when an instinctive wariness reared its head, but the man before her was so gentle-looking that she was easily able to smile as she offered her hand. When he proceeded to speak, his voice echoed that gentleness.

"It's *my* pleasure, Mrs. Lindsay. I understand that you played a large role in organizing this affair, and I'd like to thank you. The cause is a good one." His smile was sweet in its wrinkled way, and it was genuine, as was the concern he went on to express. "It's hard for young people nowadays. At one time college was thought to be a luxury of the privileged. If you had the money, you went, and you went wherever you wanted to go. Today, the competition for college admittance is frightening, and the financial commitment is even worse. Yet a college education is a necessity if one hopes to rise in the world. There, too, things were different in my day. Whether or not you had a degree tucked under your belt, you could go out there, and if you had a few brains and a little ambition, you could make something of yourself.

"Take the case of Frankie Cohn. He had nothing. Dirt poor, his family was, but he needed a job, so they borrowed the money to buy him a paper route." He lowered his voice. "In those days you didn't just volunteer for the job. You had to put down hard cash for the rights to the list of customers." He paused only for a breath. Danica sensed that he loved to talk, but she was enjoying listening, as were the others, so she smiled her encouragement when he went on.

"He took on that first route when he was twelve, and it was hard work. He was a skinny kid and he used to keep the papers together with a strap and hoist the whole load—sometimes it was nearly as big as he was—onto his shoulder. There weren't bicycles as you and I know them in those days, and a little red wagon wouldn't have gotten him far. In order to get the papers in the first place, he had to take the streetcar—he wore a badge on his left arm that allowed him to ride for free—and he pick the papers up at one station, ride back to the station nearest his route, then start to deliver. The route, by the way, was four miles from his own house. On Sundays he would be up at four in the morning to take the streetcar to pick up the papers, come back to the basement of a nearby hotel, where he had to put them together, then deliver the lot. He would walk the four miles home for breakfast, then the four miles back to collect money from each of his customers. In wet weather he would wear big hip boots. On cold, snowy days his mother sometimes cried when he left. But he did it."

Danica was shaking her head. "That's amazing."

The Governor raised both brows. "You haven't heard the best. He kept that morning route for two years, then took on the afternoon and evening routes and hired seven kids to do it for him. He used to handle all the money, keeping track of everything in his little book. By the time he was seventeen he was in charge of delivering papers in all parts of the city." He made a gesture with his hand. "Of course, the city was different in those days. Safer." He chuckled. "Once he was accosted by a drunken prostitute. He pushed her away and ran like hell." The smile faded. "But he could've found that anywhere. Frankie Cohn loved Boston, and he got to know it by heart. Also made a neat profit for himself. Five thousand in one year, and five thousand was a lot of money then. He's a millionaire today."

"Cityside Distributors," Alan Hancock injected, supplying the key that had instant meaning for Danica, who had seen the name dozens of times on bills that had come in the mail for Blake. Alan smiled. "James is wonderful when it comes to stories like this. He's been on the scene for so many years that he's a treasure trove of information." He turned to the older man. "James, you have to write them down. You're missing your calling, keeping everything to yourself."

The Governor's ruddy complexion grew all the more so. "Ach, I haven't got the patience for that. Never did. Never will. No one wants to read about an old man's ramblings. I think I'll just save them up for times like these." He glanced at his watch. "But it's past my bedtime, ladies and gentleman. I'd better be running. It's a long way home."

Sharon chuckled. "Governor Bryant lives just a little ways down on Beacon Street."

"At my age, young lady," James admonished with a grin, "that's a long way." Nodding once, he made a graceful exit.

The talk within the group lingered for a bit on James Bryant's days in the State House, then turned to the college he supported, the same one that would offer the scholarship being established by the evening's proceeds, then to the Hancocks' daughter, who was a sophomore at a college out of state.

Danica's thoughts moved less quickly. An earlier part of the conversation stuck in her mind. It was there when she arrived home that night. It was still there two days later when, in a moment of impulsive bravery, she picked up the phone and called James Hardmore Bryant.

"Governor Bryant?" she began, sounding far more confident than she felt, "this is Danica Lindsay. Perhaps you remember. We met at the Women's City Club the other night?"

"Of course, I remember you, Mrs. Lindsay," came the gentle voice. "I'm not so old that I can't appreciate a pretty face when I see one. Did I tell you that you look very much like my late wife, DeeDee, God rest her soul? A wonderful woman she was. Oh, we fought like cats and dogs and she never did like me running around like I owned the city, but we did have forty-two good years together. . . . But there I go again. You didn't call to hear me reminisce about my marriage, now, did you?"

Danica smiled. "No, though it sounds like a lovely story. I'd like to hear it another time, which is in a way the reason I'm calling." She took a steadying breath. "I wonder if I could come see you. There's something I'd like to discuss."

"Something you'd like to discuss. Sounds serious."

"It could be. Well, that is . . . it's just something I've been thinking about. I don't live far from you. I could come over at your convenience."

The Governor cleared his throat. "Now, let me see. I've got my appointment book right in front of me. Ahhhh. Today's free. And tomorrow. And the next day." He chuckled. "I'm not in demand the way I used to be. You name a time. What's best for you?"

She was already feeling better. The research she had done in the library the day before had told her that James Bryant had been a powerful chief executive. The image of the spirited Irishman had clashed with the more mellow impression she received the other night. Other things she'd read had, in part, explained the mellowing, and she assumed much of it had simply come with age. Still, she hadn't been sure how he would react to her request.

"I could make it tomorrow morning at ten, if that's all right with you."

"Couldn't be better. It'll give me something to look forward to. I'll see you then, Mrs. Lindsay."

"Thank you, Governor."

She set down the phone with a sense of satisfaction, but by the time the morning rolled around she was feeling anxious. But she reasoned she had nothing to lose. So she set out on foot, heading down the hill to Charles Street, then over to Beacon. At ten sharp she was at James Bryant's door. Five minutes later she was seated in his high-ceilinged drawing room, pouring the tea that the Governor's maid had dutifully provided.

"I'd do that myself," the Governor explained, "but my hands have a nasty habit of shaking." He raised one in demonstration. "Some women today are offended by the thought of doing such menial work, so, my dear, please accept my apologies."

"No apology necessary, Governor—"

"James, please." He scratched the top of his head, which was bald except for the thin fringe of gray that ringed it. In Danica's mind, the gesture was an awkward one. When it was immediately followed by the slight lowering of his head, she realized that he felt self-conscious. Again, not quite the image of the elder statesman, but entirely endearing. "They insist on calling me Governor, when I haven't been that for some twenty-odd years. It's a form of respect, they say, but I've had plenty of respect in my day, and I no longer need to intimidate anyone. So, please, make it James. Now, what is it that's brought you to my humble abode?"

It wasn't quite humble, with its stately furniture, its tall windows, its original oils on the walls, but Danica wasn't about to argue. "I've been thinking about your stories and about Alan Hancock's suggestion that you write them down. I agree with him."

"That's because you haven't heard but one. They'd bore you to tears. At least, that's what they always did to my son. He told me so. He'd yawn and fidget. Still does."

"That's because he's your son, and perhaps because he's too close to you to appreciate them." The insight had been a spontaneous one, though her own case was different. Early on she'd come to resent the life that kept her father at such a distance.

But James was holding firm. "He's just not interested. Can't stand politics. Many people are that way, you know." He reached for a tea cake and belatedly offered one to Danica, who shook her head. "Funny," he said, turning the cake around in his hand, "when you're in the middle of it all, it's like that's all there is in the world. It's addictive, politics is. It completely takes you over."

"There are many people who agree with you, many people who love it as much as you do," Danica reasoned, knowing well of what she spoke. "But Frank Cohn's story isn't a political one. It's a charming anecdote that carries the flavor of another era. I'll bet you have many more like that just waiting to be told. What I'm suggesting is that you put together . . . not exactly your memoirs, though your own story would make a wonderful frame for the others . . . but a collection of profiles, anecdotes, if you will, about the Boston of forty, fifty, sixty years ago."

He was frowning. "You're serious." She nodded. "It's always been something of a joke when people have mentioned it, but you are serious."

"Very much so," she said.

He closed one eye. "Why?"

She was prepared for the question. "Let me tell you a little about myself. I have a degree in English from Simmons, but I've never really done anything with it because I married early—actually the year before I graduated—and I've lived the role of the wife ever since. I have no children and therefore more time on my hands than I want. I've been looking for something constructive to fill that time. It occurred to me while you were talking the other night that we might be able to work together to get your stories into print."

There was a long silence, during which James Hardmore Bryant ate his tea cake start to finish. Only after he dusted the last of the crumbs from his tweed trousers did he speak.

"An interesting proposition. But what makes you think you'd be qualified for the position of my, er, my collaborator? You said yourself that you have a degree and no experience."

For the first time she had a glimpse of the James Bryant who had once been on top of the heap. Though he hadn't spoken harshly, there had been a command to his words that must have stood him in good stead in his heyday.

Setting her teacup on the tray, Danica folded her hands in her lap as though to conceal the fluttering in her stomach, which, of course, she told herself, he couldn't see, but they had reached the hard part and she wanted to project conviction.

"I believe I do have experience in things that might help if we should decide to work together. My husband and I are both active in the community. Over the years I've dealt with many prominent people. I'm comfortable with them. I'm attuned to their thoughts. I've interviewed them, if you will. In some cases I've helped put together brochures and fundraising material incorporating personal material much as I might do for you. I think the key word is *organization*. I'm very good at that."

She paused. When James sat rubbing his lower lip and gave no indication that he wished to speak, she went on. "But my experience goes beyond that. I grew up in a household that revolved around politics. My father is William Marshall. He's been a member of the Senate since I was a child."

James dropped his hand and raised his head. "Well, why didn't you say that from the start?"

Something inside her snapped and impulse took over. "Because I wished I hadn't had to say it at all. I don't want anyone looking at me with greater interest because of who my father is. I'm my own person—" she dropped her voice "—or at least I'm trying to be."

As soon as the last words were out, she realized that they had been unnecessary. She was trying to secure a job, not an analyst. Determined to repair whatever damage she might have done, she resumed speaking in a calm and confident tone.

"The fact is that being William Marshall's daughter, I'm not ignorant of the political milieu. My parents sheltered me where the limelight was concerned, but through osmosis, if nothing else, I've learned a lot. I've heard most of my father's stories at least once, not to mention those of the guests he's entertained." She smiled. "You're not the only one who likes to tell stories. You're just different in that you have the time now to do something with them. Am I wrong?"

"I wish you were, but you're not. I have more time than I know what to do with."

"Then, why not try what I'm suggesting? You have nothing to lose. Neither do I."

He thought about that for a minute, then gave her a side-long glance. "What makes you think any publisher will buy my, er, our book?"

"You've had years of experience in circles of power. Yours is a well-known and respected name, and it carries clout. Given the dubious quality of some of the books out there, I think that a publisher, especially a local one, will jump at the opportunity to print something as interesting as this." It was a calculated guess, but it was all she had at the moment.

James knew it, too. But he was intrigued both by Danica's faith and her determination. "Well, then. Exactly what is it you propose?"

She took a deep breath. "I propose that we talk a bit, then that you let me approach several publishing houses. If and when we get a show of interest, better still an offer, we can begin the real work."

"And how do you suggest we do that? I haven't the patience to sit and write things down."

She remembered that from her first meeting with this man and had thought it all out. "You can talk to me. I can ask you questions. We can tape our conversations and have them transcribed. From there on it would really be a matter of organizing and editing."

He arched both brows. "I think you may be simplifying things, but I'll be damned if you don't make it sound tempting. You'd want to be paid, of course."

This, too, she had thought out. She certainly didn't need the money, though there was a legitimacy to being paid. If James Bryant was to respect her, he would have to see her in a professional light. "When and if we hear something positive from a publisher, we can draw up an agreement with regard to advances and royalties. There wouldn't have to be any monetary output on your part. The overhead will be negligible." She moistened her upper lip. "From what I gather, neither of us needs this money to survive."

He gave her a crooked grin. "You gather correctly."

She held her breath. "Then . . . ?"

He tugged at one ear. "They really are boring stories after a while."

"That's because you've heard them so many times yourself. All we're asking is that people read them once."

"And you really think some publisher will go for the idea?"

At that moment Danica knew she'd won. "As I said before, we have nothing to lose."

"You have *nothing to lose?* Danica, do you have any idea how much *time* a project like this could take?" her father bellowed.

Danica held the phone away from her ear, then returned it to speak calmly. "I have time, Dad. So does Governor Bryant. There isn't any rush. Spread out over a year or two, it won't be bad. It's not as if the material is timely. If it's waited this long to see the light, it can wait another while longer."

"It can wait forever. I don't see the necessity of it."

She bit her lip in a bid for strength. She was determined not to be cowed by her father, had been steeling herself for his call since she had told Blake about her plans the evening before. She knew Blake, knew that he would call William. A tiny part of her had hoped that, given the nature of the work she proposed, her father would be sympathetic. After all, it could be he who was proposing a similar book based on his own experiences. Unfortunately, sympathy was too much too ask. What she was getting was pure dismay.

"There isn't a necessity," she replied quietly, "and there doesn't have to be. Few published books are necessary. They may be interesting or educational or entertaining, but they're not necessary."

"Then why are you doing this?"

She took a breath. "Because I want to."

"You've never thought of working before."

"You've never been aware of my thoughts. I've toyed with the idea for a while now. This is the first time something that I felt was feasible has come up. My schedule will be flexible and I can work at home."

"I thought you said you'd be going to Bryant's place."

"Yes, but only for several hours at a stretch and at our mutual convenience. He lives five minutes from here. It'll be easy. It's not as if I'm taking a job in an office, working nine to five and commuting each way."

"I don't like the idea of your working at all. Neither does Blake."

"Blake didn't tell me he had any objections." In fact, beyond an initial surprise, he had taken the news with relative calm, when she had expected far worse. It still puzzled her that he hadn't put up a fight, particularly when he had apparently expressed some hesitation to William. She wondered if he had done so purely for William's benefit; he had to have known what the other's reaction would be.

"Then Blake was being diplomatic," William stated. "I don't have to be. It was bad enough that you barricaded yourself in that house in Maine for the summer when you should have been with Blake. You're his wife, for God's sake. Blake Lindsay's wife doesn't have to work. William Marshall's daughter doesn't have to work."

"Of course I don't *have* to. I *want* to."

"I say you're making a big mistake. Why in the devil do you feel you have to jump into something you don't know the first thing about?"

Danica bristled. "Are you saying that you think I can't do it? That you think I might make a fool out of myself?"

"There's always that chance."

"I'm glad you have so much faith in me."

"Sarcasm doesn't suit you, Danica. I'm only trying to think of what's best for you."

"Are you, Dad? Are you really? But what about me? Don't *I* have a say as to what's best for me? I'm not a little girl anymore. I've lived with myself for twenty-eight years and I think I have some idea of what I want."

"And what you want is to work with that old coot? How many copies of his book do you think will be bought? How many best-seller lists do you think it's going to make?"

"That's not the point. The point is that I want something to do and the prospect of doing this appeals to me."

William was silent for a moment. "Are you feeling all right, Danica?"

"Of course. What does that have to do with anything?"

"This work idea. Maybe you're still depressed about the baby. It's understandable. In time you'll come to your senses."

"I have come to my senses," she said under her breath.

"Speak up. You're mumbling."

"Nothing. It was nothing." She felt suddenly tired.

"Look. Why don't you put off making any decision for a while. Things are busy now. Just go on doing what you've always done. Be there for Blake. Relax. Who knows? Maybe you'll get pregnant again. You'll certainly have your work cut out for you then."

She had had enough. "Uh, Dad, I have to run. Blake will be home any minute and I'm not dressed. Give my love to Mom, will you?"

"But she wants to speak with you."

"Another time. Really. I have to go. I'll talk with you soon. Bye-bye."

Blake wasn't due home for another two hours, and though Danica had been fully dressed when her father had called, when Blake finally breezed in an hour after expected, she was in her robe and ready for bed. The only reason she had waited up was to tell him that she was driving to Maine the next morning and that if she wasn't back by eight he should have dinner without her.

Michael was ecstatic to open his door and find her there. He held her for a long time, enjoying the softness of her body, the sweet, fresh scent of her skin. "Ahhh, I've missed you," he growled against her hair.

"I've missed you, too." Neither had called the other on the phone. In unspoken agreement they had known that it would be difficult. Michael would have felt awkward if he had called and Blake had answered. Danica would have felt awkward if Blake found a slew of calls to Maine on his monthly bill. More critically, each sensed that it would be too difficult to hear the other's voice and then have to say goodbye.

Fitting a firm arm to her shoulders, Michael led her into the house. She freed herself only to kneel and greet a fast-growing and exuberant Rusty, but she quickly returned to Michael's side, unwilling to stay away for long. They had one day. She needed all the sustenance she could get.

She also needed encouragement, and she got it. Michael burst into a smile the instant she told him about her decision to work with James Bryant.

"Danica Lindsay, that's fantastic news! Tell me everything."

She did just that, detailing her initial introduction to James and the germination of her idea, the reading she had done on his life, the calculations she had made concerning the possibility of the project and the subsequent meeting at which she had put it all forward to James. She told of Blake's reaction and of her father's. And she told of her excitement, and her fear.

"Maybe I'm crazy, Michael. I don't know the first thing about putting together a book. I've been operating on sheer guts up to now, but it's time to put words into action. Where do I go from here? What do I do? Whom do I see?"

"First you sit back, take a deep breath and relax." He spoke slowly, reassuringly. "Then you tell yourself that everything you've said to Bryant, and to Blake and your father, for that matter, was correct. Because it is, Dani. You have the time and the desire. Regardless of how widespread the audience for a book like this will be, there is a market for it. And that's where you start. What you told Bryant was right on the button. The two of you have to talk; then you have to write up a proposal to send to various houses."

He elaborated on the contents of such a proposal, making suggestions and giving hints that had worked for him. She asked him questions galore, jotting notes for herself as he made their lunch. Later he mentioned the names of several publishers whom he thought might be interested, and she noted those, too, but when he offered to make calls on her behalf, she gently refused. Likewise, she was resistant to his suggestion that he call his agent.

"I'd like to try it myself first. It's not that I'm not grateful—"

His hand on her lips cut her off. "Say no more. I know you need to be independent. It's hard for me. If I had my way I'd probably be smothering you just the way you've been smothered in the past."

"You'd never do that."

"It's a temptation at times. I want to help you, to make things easier for you. I'll have to keep reminding myself that you need to do this yourself."

She took his hand and held it tight. "Thank you for understanding. Nobody else does. It helps just knowing that you're here." She felt suddenly guilty. Their time together was passing, focusing entirely on her. "How's your book coming, Michael?"

"Nearly done. Another few weeks should do it."

"That's great! Are you pleased with it?"

"Very. So's my editor, from what he said after reading the first half. I don't think I'll have any major problems."

"You look tired." She brushed the hair from his forehead. It was a joy to touch him, to care for him. "Late nights?"

"Yeah. When things roll, they roll. And since I don't have anything else to do with my time . . ." The last was said on a note of gentle accusation which Danica felt to her core.

She looked down. "I wish I could be here more. It's lonesome in Boston."

"With all those people around?"

"It's lonesome."

He touched his finger to her chin and tipped it up. "I know. I bury myself in work so that I won't have to think about how quiet it is here."

"You're not raising Rusty right. He's supposed to be your best friend."

"*You're* my best friend."

She wanted to scold him for tormenting her, but she realized that she had been the one to start it all by materializing on his doorstep that morning. Instead, she leaned forward against him, sliding her arms around his waist, pressing her cheek to his chest.

"Just hold me, just for a minute," she whispered.

He swallowed hard. "You're playing with fire."

"I know. But I need . . . just hold me, Michael."

He didn't argue further, because he needed so badly to do what she asked. His arms closed around her, strong and protecting. "Dear God, I love you," he whispered, unable to stem the words he'd been aching to say all day. She wouldn't return them, he knew, but the way she was holding him in return was enough.

Minutes passed and neither of them moved away. Danica rubbed her cheek over the wool of his turtleneck, imagining she felt the soft sprinkle of his chest hair, wanting desperately to touch it. Michael concentrated on the sleekness of her back beneath his hands, the press of her breasts against him, her soft curves waiting to be explored.

When his body grew tight, he tried to think of baseball or basketball or hockey, but it didn't work. "I need you, Dani," he warned hoarsely, "and it's only getting worse. I thought once you'd gone back to Boston, I'd be able to regain control of myself, but I lie awake at night thinking about you and I get hard and sore and . . ." He drew her head back so he could see her face. She looked as stricken as he felt.

"Let me make love to you, sweetheart. Let me—"

"We can't."

"Why not? The feeling's there. It's inevitable."

"But I'm married. I can't be unfaithful—"

"You're already being unfaithful," he argued, then half wished he hadn't when her eyes filled with tears. But it needed to be said, he realized. "Dani, you *already* feel things for me that you shouldn't feel." Taking her face in his hands, he brushed his thumbs back and forth along her cheekbones. "You don't have to say the words, but I know that you love me. If we were to make love, it'd only be an expression of what we both already feel."

"I can't," she pleaded, "I can't."

"I'm not quite sure what it is you have with Blake, but it can't come close to what we feel for each other."

"I'm bound to him."

"You're not in love with him, not the way you're in love with me. Do you have any idea how beautiful it would be for us?" He ignored the tiny sound of desperation that came from her throat. "I want to touch you, to kiss you all over. I want to see you, all of you. I want you to be naked, naked and warm and wet. You would be, Dani. I can feel you trembling right now."

"You're scaring me, Michael!"

"I'm only putting into words what you've thought about yourself. Am I wrong?" When she didn't answer, he pressed. "Am I?"

"No! But I can't make love to you. I'm not free!"

"With me you're free." His low voice quivered. "You'd touch me, Dani. You'd undress me and kiss me and move over me—"

Jerking from his hold, she bolted up from the sofa. Her body was hot and cold and tingling and taut and felt utterly foreign to her. "Stop it, Michael. Please? I can't do what you want. I just can't."

Her crushed expression gave him the control over his body that neither baseball nor basketball nor hockey had been able to do. Closing his eyes for a minute, he took several deep breaths, then slowly pushed himself to his feet. "Okay, sweetheart. I'll stop. But I want you to think about something for me. I want you to think about what *you* want. You know what I want. You know what Blake wants. You know what your father wants." When she swayed, he drew her against him and she didn't resist. "I want you to think about what you could have." He pressed her hips lightly to his, just enough to alert her to his still aroused state. "I won't force anything. I couldn't do that. When you come to me, I want it to be because *you* want it. I want you to need me to be inside you as much as I need to be there."

She moaned softly and began to shake. "Don't say things like that," she whispered. "I can't take it."

"But you're not moving away." If anything, she had arched her hips closer.

"It feels so good . . ."

He was the one to put inches between them. "Then, remember it. Remember how good it feels now, when you're back in Boston." His eyes fell to her breasts, then lower. "Think about how much better it'll feel without clothes and inhibitions and regrets. Think about it, Dani, because I'll be doing the same. Somehow we're going to have to come to terms with all this." He gave a tired sigh and rubbed the back of his neck. "Somehow. Someday."

There was a thick silence, then Danica's broken "And in the meantime?"

He took a breath. "In the meantime, I guess we'll have to go along as we have."

"Would you rather I didn't come?"

"That'd be the smartest thing. But it's not possible. We both know that. You don't come up much now, anyway."

She lowered her chin. "No. Blake can't, and now that I have this project . . . What will you be doing once your book's done?"

"I thought I'd take a few weeks off. Maybe go to Vail and do some skiing."
She met his gaze. "That'd be fun."

"Do you ski?"

"No. My parents wouldn't let me. It was a risk when I was playing tennis, and Blake never wanted to . . . Damn, I'd better be going. This isn't getting any easier."

There was another silence, then, "Will you let me know what's happening?"
She brushed at her tears. "I will."

"And you'll call me if there's anything I can do to help you with your work?"

"Uh-huh."

He cupped her chin in his hand and spoke more quietly. "Will you think about what I've said?"

He was looking at her with such love that it took Danica a minute to catch her breath. "I don't have much choice, do I?"

He smiled. "No."

"Then I guess I'll be thinking about what you've said." She forced a smile. "Wanna know what my tea bag said this morning?"

"What did your tea bag say this morning?"

"It said, 'Often it takes as much courage to resist as it does to go ahead.' "

"Smart tea bag. Who writes those things, anyway?"

"Smart men."

"If they were really smart, they would have written something like 'True love awaits you by the sea in Maine.' "

"That'd be a fortune cookie."

"Cookie . . . tea . . . same difference." Before she could respond, he swept her up for a quick hug, then all but shoved her out the door. "Better leave now or I'm apt to throw you over my shoulder, shackle you to my bed and make love to you until you beg for mercy."

"Brute," she teased, but she was running down the path toward her car. She still had the house to check, then the drive back to Boston. She knew she had better keep moving because to one increasingly large part of her the thought of being shackled to Michael's bed was very, very sweet.

Two and a half weeks later, Michael threw caution to the winds and called her on the phone. He reasoned that as a friend he had every right to do so.

"Lindsay residence."

"Mrs. Lindsay, please."

"Who may I say is calling?"

He grasped the phone tighter. "Michael Buchanan."

"One minute, please."

In less than that, Danica picked up the library extension. "Michael?"

"Hi, Dani."

"Michael," she breathed, feeling the abundance of tension with which she had lived for the past few days begin to ease at last. "Oh, Michael."

"How are you, Dani?"

"Better, now."

"It's been that bad?"

"Only in my mind. You know he won."

"Yup."

"Blake is ecstatic. So's my dad. You'd think Jason Claveling's election was the Second Coming."

"After all their work, they have a right to be pleased."

"Mmmm. Well, at least that's over. Somehow, though, I keep waiting for the other shoe to fall."

"Do you think Blake is expecting an appointment?"

"He joked about it a while back, but I'm beginning to wonder. God, Michael, can you imagine what would happen then? If Blake accepts a position in the Claveling administration, we'd have to move to Washington. That's the *last* place I want to be."

"I don't know. There are many people who'd find it exciting."

"Would you?"

"Not particularly, but then, I'm antisocial."

"You are not antisocial. You're anti-insanity. It's mad down there. Power and politics. Politics and power." She made a sound deep in her throat. "Sheer madness."

"There's no point in worrying about it now," he pointed out soothingly. "The election was just yesterday. Claveling will be taking time off to rest before he begins to think about any appointments."

"I suppose. Did you finish your book?"

"Yup. It's off. I'm heading for the Rockies tomorrow. What's doing with you and Bryant?"

"The proposal's all done. I'm ready to mail it out. Maybe I'll have heard something by the time you get back. When will that be?"

"Sometime before Christmas. Any chance you'll be up at the house?"

"I'm not sure. We always spend the holiday with my parents. Afterward, though, I might . . . I could, but . . . maybe it's not such a good idea."

"You mean, I'm scaring you away—" he began, then caught himself and lowered his voice. "There isn't any chance your phone is tapped, is there?"

The thought hadn't occurred to her, though it should have. "I don't know," she replied, shaken.

"Mmmm. Well, if you can come up," Michael went on with deliberate nonchalance, "it'd be great. Sara races out to ask about you every time I pass the store. And Greta and Pat call all the time."

"How's Meghan?"

"Adorable."

"And Rusty?"

"Resisting my every attempt to house-train him. I think I'm going to confine him to the beach."

"You wouldn't do that. It's cold now, and he's just a puppy."

"He's getting huge, which makes it all the worse."

Danica laughed in spite of herself. "Poor baby."

"Him or me?"

"Both. Michael?" Her voice grew soft, but mindful of his warning, she guarded her words. "It's good to hear from you."

"Can I call again?"

"I'd like that."

"Well then, take care."

"You, too, Michael. Don't break a leg."

He chuckled. "I won't. Bye-bye."

"Bye."

A week before Christmas Danica was upset enough not to care if Blake did see the call on the bill. She tried to call Michael, then tried again the next day, but he wasn't home. When he called to her on the third day, she was instantly relieved.

"Thank God, you're back" were her first soft-breathed words upon hearing his voice.

"I'm not back. I took a detour in Phillie to spend time with Corey. I wasn't sure if I should call." He dropped his voice. "Are you okay?"

"No. I'm torn to bits inside. Blake is in seventh heaven. So are my parents and his parents and our friends, and they all expect me to be, too. Secretary of Commerce. Can you believe it? I swear he had this in mind from the start. Never once did he stop to consider what I might have wanted."

"It won't be that bad."

She spoke brokenly. "I can't make it to Maine, Michael. Blake wants to go to Washington to look at places to live."

"I understand. Maybe it's just as well. You and Blake have a new life ahead of you."

"Maybe Blake. Not me. At least, not *that* life."

"What do you mean?"

"I've already told him that I won't live in Washington. I'll commute for weekends if I have to, but I'm staying here."

"How did he take that?"

"Well. Actually, complacently."

"And you're hurt."

"You'd think he'd have been upset. You'd think he would *want* me there. After all, I am his wife. It's strange."

"What is?"

"I've begun to wonder . . . I mean, he accepted my going to Maine last summer with literally no fight. He didn't argue when I told him I'd be working with James Bryant. Now he seems perfectly agreeable to the idea of a long-distance marriage. It's almost as though he's glad to have me occupied and out of his hair. I wonder if he has a mistress."

"Oh, Dani, I doubt—"

"It's not impossible. After all, we could easily be—"

He cut her off with an "Uuuuh! I don't think you should say things like that." It was a subtle reminder that something spoken might be irretrievable. "Besides, Blake has his image to consider. I doubt he'd do anything to jeopardize a position he's worked so hard to get."

"I suppose."

"Give him the benefit of the doubt."

Michael had no idea why he was standing up for Blake Lindsay when he wanted to scream at the man for the way he treated his wife, but he had to do it. The alternative was to give encouragement to something that might be totally false, and given his own less than impartial involvement in the situation, that would be wrong. He never wanted to be accused of actively encouraging Danica's alienation from Blake; if there was to be alienation that would lead to a breakup, it had to be the sole doing of husband or wife.

Danica sighed. "I guess I _have_ to give him the benefit of the doubt since the outcome suits me. It would have been worse if Blake had insisted I live full-time in Washington. . . . Michael, I haven't heard anything on the book yet."

"It's too soon. Don't be discouraged. Sometimes it takes two or three months for an editor to get a chance to read a proposal."

"Are you sure?"

"I'm sure."

They talked for a while longer, and when Danica hung up the phone, she felt better.

She felt even better when, in the first week of January, she received a summons from one of the most prestigious publishing houses in Boston.

NINE

T HE DAY AFTER JASON CLAVELING was inaugurated Blake was sworn in as his Secretary of Commerce. Danica stayed through the festivities, feeling pride in her husband in spite of herself. A stunning complement to him, she received her share of praise. None, however, came directly from Blake, who was more emotionally wrapped up in himself than ever. When she returned to Boston several days later, he didn't blink an eye.

Having signed a contract with the publishing house that had been their first choice, Danica and James spent every afternoon together, talking, discussing, recording their words for transcription by one of Danica's ballet friends who needed the money.

Danica enjoyed her time with James. He was interesting, sharp even in spite of his age, and lacked the arrogance that so turned her off to politics. Often he would turn around and ask her a question about herself and one of her own experiences. He seemed to accept her as an equal in their enterprise, and that enhanced her enjoyment of it. At last she felt she was _doing_ something. Between mornings spent at occasional meetings and ballet, afternoons spent at

James's town house and evenings spent reading what had been transcribed, she was busy.

She commuted to Washington several times a month to attend receptions and parties with Blake, and though she found the air of social climbing, ambition, competition and power hunger to be oppressive, she was satisfied to discharge her responsibility to Blake—and to her father, whom she saw more often than ever.

William accepted her presence with a this-is-your-rightful-place attitude and proceeded to pay her not much more heed than Blake did. Neither man asked about the work she was doing in Boston, as though ignoring it would make it go away. Eleanor, strangely, was the one who expressed interest, and though Danica did talk with her, she felt wary. She couldn't understand her mother's interest now, any more than she had been able to understand Eleanor's coddling the August before. As had been the case then, Danica didn't quite know how to react. More than once she wondered if Eleanor was doing William's bidding. *Snooping* was an unkind word, but given the woman's distance through Danica's childhood, Danica couldn't help but imagine that there might be some ulterior motive for her attentiveness.

Michael called Danica in Boston from time to time. He was traveling, doing research for a book on the roots of the environmental movement, spending time reading and interviewing in many of the nation's large cities. He purposely avoided the Northeast, fearing that the temptation to see Danica would be too great, particularly now that he knew how many of her nights were spent alone. He didn't want to take advantage of the situation. Moreover, he knew that she needed to be alone, to think. Her days were filled and she enjoyed her work; he gleaned that from the detailed phone conversations they held. And her tone of voice, sometimes growing exquisitely soft, sometimes broken, hinted that she missed him as she would never have expressed in words. He had to have faith that in time, when she felt comfortable with herself as an entity independent of both Blake and her father, she'd be more able to take a stand with regard to her future and to him.

By late May, having finished most of what he needed to do on the road, Michael headed for a few days' R and R visiting friends and his sister in Washington.

"Hey, Mike!" Jeffrey Winston half rose from his seat in the crowded restaurant to catch his friend's attention.

Michael quickly made his way to the table, shaking hands, then embracing the man he had been close to for years. They had met in college and had served together in Vietnam. For a time they had been brothers-in-law. The two were remarkably alike—both tall and rakishly good-looking, both intelligent, introspective and dedicated to their work.

"How's it going, Jeff? God, it's good to see you!"

"You, too, stranger. It's been too long," Jeff snagged a passing waitress around the waist and motioned for two more beers before turning back to Michael. "Cilla tells me you've been on the run."

Michael teasingly held up a hand. "Nothing clandestine. Just doing research for my next masterpiece."

"The last one was great, Mike. Religious and racial bigotry—whew! Remember the talks we used to have on that topic?"

Michael grinned. "Where do you think I got the idea for the book?"

"Yeah, but you carried it off, while I couldn't have written the first chapter. How's it doing?"

"Not bad. We're into a second printing, which isn't saying all that much given the size of the first one, but at least the book's sales have exceeded my publisher's expectations. It always helps to do well in their eyes. But tell me about you, pal. What's this I hear about a promotion?"

"Cilla's been talking."

"Why shouldn't she? It's exciting. He-e-ey, I'm her brother and your friend. She knew I'd want to know. That doesn't mean she printed it on page one. Besides, she's proud of you."

"She is? Funny, she always hated what I did when we were married."

"It wasn't what you did that she hated. It was what you *didn't* do, i.e., tell her all the little details."

"I couldn't. She's the press, for Christ's sake. I couldn't tell her what I was working on when it was confidential."

"You didn't trust her to keep it that way and she knew it. But, hey, I'm not blaming anything on you. It takes two to make a marriage work or not work. Cilla's constantly curious, about anything and everything. She can be pretty intense when she wants to be. She's like Dad in that way. I'm sure she was no joy to live with."

"I don't know," Jeffrey mused, "we had some good times. If it hadn't been for her occupation . . . okay, okay, *and* mine, we might have made it. I don't think she trusted me any more than I trusted her. She was constantly worried that I'd pry her sources out of her and then turn around and launch an investigation." He snorted. "As if I had the power . . ."

"Do you now? Come on, give. What's the story on the promotion?"

Jeffrey took a breath and sat back in his seat. Talk of Cilla always got to him. He had so many misgivings, so many lingering feelings for her. Lately, he seemed obsessed with the good times they'd had. In the six years since their divorce, he hadn't met another woman who came close to her in fun or challenge or sheer sexual abandon.

"The promotion. I'm in charge of DOD's investigative unit. It's not that I can go out looking for things to investigate, but when we get a referral, even a tip, I decide who's going to do the work and then keep tabs on things."

"So it's mainly administrative?"

"More so than before. I still do the nitty-gritty—you know I love that part—and I can assign myself to work on some of the plums, which is nice. It's a challenge."

"What are some of the things you're doing?"

Over roast beef sandwiches, Jeffrey talked. He kept his voice low and leaned forward from time to time, but he trusted Michael with his life, literally and figuratively. It occurred to him that if he had trusted Cilla a fraction as much, they might not have split. When he asked himself why he *hadn't* trusted her, he didn't like the only reason he could find, so he stopped pondering it.

"Is that the current project?" Michael asked after Jeffrey had told of an investigation into leaks of classified information within the State Department.

"No. Something else has just come up." He frowned. "It's a tricky thing."

It was Michael's turn to lean forward, which he did with both brows raised in invitation.

Jeffrey wavered. "I don't know. It's still pretty vague."

"Come on, Jeff. It's me. Michael."

"This is a little different from the counterinsurgency work we did in Nam. . . . Ah, hell. You'll keep quiet. Besides, there's not really much that's classified yet." Putting both elbows on the table, he spoke quietly. "You've heard of Operation Exodus."

"U.S. Customs Service, isn't it?"

"Mmmm. It's a program that was set up a few years back to halt the illegal export of high-tech products to the Soviet bloc. From the beginning it had plenty of opposition, congressmen and exporters who felt that it hindered the flow of trade abroad. The government's theory is that since the Soviet Union is years behind us in research and technology that can vastly improve its military systems, it will beg, borrow or steal what it can. One vital acquisition can advance them ten years. The same semiconductors and integrated circuits that are used in video games also go into guided-missile systems. Small computers, which businesses here use every day of the week, also can be used by the military to efficiently plot and track movements of troops. Laser technology used by our doctors can be used to disable enemy communication satellites."

"Dual-use technologies."

"Right. Like I say, it's a sensitive issue. There are constant battles being waged on what items should or should not be on the restricted list. Any number of advanced technology items could possibly be used for defense by a hostile country. Whether they *would* be is another story. The Pentagon takes the hard line, wanting to clamp down on every possibility. The Commerce Department is obviously more attuned to the country's commercial interests. It maintains that by stringently controlling what Americans are allowed to export, we yield a lucrative market to European concerns."

"What about the Coordinating Committee for Export Controls? Doesn't it have a say as to what's sold to Eastern Europe?"

"To some extent. Any one of its delegates can veto an American company's request. Mmmm, CoCom makes it easier, that's for sure, especially now that Germany and Japan are members. But the organization is voluntary. Member countries may agree on what is and is not sensitive material, but they have no obligation to enforce CoCom's bans."

"Which means that the Commerce Department could, by rights, go ahead and issue a license to a company for export of goods that CoCom has vetoed."

"Right. Not that that's happened often. Our government is firmer than others. But there have been slips, situations where licenses have been granted to companies they shouldn't have been granted to—companies headed by shady characters, companies with suspicious business contacts in other countries. Over the past few years Operation Exodus has managed to thwart smuggling of some pretty important stuff to the East."

"So I've read," Michael said pensively. "So where do you come in?"

"The Department of Defense has begun to suspect that certain super-minicomputers are finding their way to places they shouldn't be. Our intelligence agencies are seeing restricted items with very definite American stamps on them in use in countries which shouldn't have them. So we're investigating."

"Hey, exciting!"

"That's the spy in you speaking, Mike. Got a lot of mileage out of that book, didn't you?"

"It sold well. Hmph, it did more than that. Somebody saw it and liked it and because of it asked me to teach a course on intelligence work and counterespionage at Harvard next fall."

"No kidding? The JFK School?"

Michael nodded. He had just gotten word of his appointment. He was looking forward to being in Boston once a week for more reasons than one.

"You've never taught before, have you?"

"Only one-time seminars. This'll be an experience. From what I hear, the students are sharp. By rights I should have a Ph.D. to teach at a place like that, but I guess they felt my book—and the others I've written—were credential enough."

"I'd think so. What are you working on now?"

They talked for a while about Michael's latest project, then about mutual friends that one or another had seen, then, inevitably, about the legs of their waitress.

"Why does it always come down to this?" Michael asked, laughing. "You'd think we were still in college, sitting around the frat house rating the coeds on a score of one to ten."

"Some of them were dogs, weren't they?"

"Hmph. The same dogs are probably gorgeous today. Gorgeous and successful and married. And here we sit, the two of us, with no one."

"Is that a note of wistfulness I hear? A change of heart in the confirmed bachelor?"

"We ain't gettin' younger, pal."

"But wiser. Maybe we're getting wiser."

"I sometimes wonder," Michael mused and happened to glance at the opposite side of the restaurant. "I don't believe it. She's here."

Jeffrey twisted to follow his gaze. "Cilla! When did *she* come in? I didn't see her before."

"We weren't exactly looking around." Michael kept his eyes glued to his sister. She looked up once, met his gaze but quickly returned to her discussion with a well-dressed man of the diplomat type. "I spent yesterday with her. She knew I was meeting you here, but she didn't say anything about her own plans."

"Maybe she wanted to surprise you."

"Maybe she wanted to surprise *you*."

Jeffrey gave a half-laugh. "She's done that. Look at the guy. He's not her type. No flair. No excitement."

"She's probably interviewing him for a piece she's writing."

"I hope so. Jeez, I'd hate to think she's gotten desperate." He paused, still staring at Cilla. "She looks good, doesn't she?"

"Uh-huh."

"Wonder if she does date much."

Michael was grateful that Jeffrey wasn't looking his way. It was hard to keep his lips from twitching. "No one special. I think she's pretty fed up with it all. Face it, pal. You spoiled her for other men."

"Y' think so?" Jeffrey asked, then jerked his gaze back to Michael. "Don't shit me. *You* guys spoiled her. Made her too independent for her own good. I couldn't tame her, that's for sure."

"You've both mellowed. Maybe you should give it another try."

Jeffrey was shaking his head a little too quickly. "We have a basic conflict of interest. Her work and mine."

"It's only a matter of trust. . . . Don't you ever wish you had a family?" Michael asked hesitantly, wondering if he was the only one with the sudden affliction.

"All the time. But Cilla's not the type to slow down. Can you imagine her nine months pregnant and racing around the city after one story or another?"

Michael chuckled. "I almost can. She'd give birth on a street corner, stick the kid in her purse and keep going."

"A kangaroo. Just like a kangaroo, hoppin' all over the place with a kid in her pouch."

"Or an Indian squaw with a papoose on her back. Still, they loved their babies, the Indians did."

"Why do I hear a message in this?"

"Do you? Hey, look. Here she comes."

Sure enough, Cilla was approaching their table, having left her companion behind to pay the bill. "Look who's here." She leaned down to kiss Michael, then nonchalantly put a hand on Jeffrey's shoulder. "Hi, Jeff. How's it goin'?"

"Great, Cilla. Just great. Mike and I were having a fascinating talk."

"About what?"

"Kangaroos."

Cilla shot Michael a strange look before returning to Jeff. "Are you thinking of adopting one?"

"I had one once."

"You never told me that."

"It was strictly confidential. Classified information."

Cilla gave an exaggerated nod and diplomatically went along with the gag. "I hope you had more luck house-training it than Mike had with his pup."

"I had no luck at all. Finally had to let her go . . . for her sake *and* mine. I do miss her, though. She had her moments."

"We all do," Cilla said with a sad sigh. She rubbed her hand across Jeff's broad back. "Well, I'd better run." Leaning down, she pressed her cheek to his, waved to Michael and was off.

"Fool kangaroo," Jeffrey muttered.

Michael studied his friend but said nothing. He had seen the light in Jeff's

eyes when Cilla had been near, had seen the flush on his sister's cheeks when
she had been talking to Jeff. He was sure that strong feelings still existed
between these two people who meant so much to him. Nothing would make
him happier than to see them get back together, though it was out of his hands,
as it should be. After all, he mused, who was he to be matchmaking when his
own love life was at loose ends.

"Hi, Dani."

"Michael! Where are you?"

"Back home at last. Boy, does it feel good. It's beautiful up here now.
Everything's blooming."

"I saw. I was up several weeks ago and it was pretty then. It wasn't the same
though without you there. Did you get everything done that you wanted to?"

"Yup. I'm all set to spend the summer writing."

"Me, too."

"You're kidding! You finished all the taping?"

"Uh-huh. James is heading to Newport for the summer, so it's just as well.
Everything is transcribed. Now the fun part starts."

"You can do it, Dani. I've told you that before."

"I know. Still, it's a little awesome holding all this stuff in my lap and
knowing that I have to put it into some intelligible form."

"Jump in. That's what I do. The worst part is the anticipation. It's not so
bad once you get going."

"I'm counting on that. How's Rusty?"

"He's a monster. You won't believe it when you see him."

"He didn't give Greta and Pat any problems while you were away?"

"Are you kidding? Their house is full of crap anyway."

"Michael," Danica scolded, but she was laughing, "that's not fair. Greta
and Pat's house is wonderful."

He smiled. It was so good to hear her voice, so much better to hear her
laugh. "I know it and I know you know it, so it's okay for me to say what I
did."

"How are they, anyway?"

"Terrific. They're wondering when you're coming up. *I*'m wondering when
you're coming up."

She beamed. She didn't care how dangerous it was, but she had gone more
than eight months without seeing Michael and she was starved. "I'll be there
in a few weeks."

"For how long?"

It was her surprise and she savored it. "Till Labor Day."

"Till Labor Day?" He had assumed, given Blake's new status, that she
would have to spend time in D.C. "Sweetheart, that's great!"

"I think so. I need the time there badly."

He hesitated for just a minute. "Things have been rough?"

Her voice grew more quiet. "I guess you'd say that. There's not much for
me in Washington."

"Blake's busy?"

"Blake's busy. It's worse than it was here. He loves everything about the place—the glitz, the pomp, the power—everything I hate."

"Have you told him so?"

"Yes. He says that it's only for four years, but he's not kidding me. If Claveling is reelected it could easily be for eight, and even if it isn't, Blake's hooked. If it's not a Cabinet position, it'll be something else. Not very promising for the warm, close family I wanted."

There was nothing Michael could say to that. He wanted to say that *he*'d give her the warm, close family she wanted, but she already knew it. The ball was in her court.

"Well," he said with a sigh, "at least coming up here will be a break."

"Don't you know it," she said with feeling, and he laughed. "Unfortunately, my mother may be spending some time there with me."

"Uh-oh. She's still feeling maternal?"

"I don't understand it, Michael. I *still* don't understand it. All of a sudden she wants a close mother-daughter relationship. When I'm in Washington, we see each other. When I'm here, she calls at least twice a week. That's more than Blake does."

"Maybe she knows that and feels badly."

"No," Danica replied thoughtfully. "There's something more. I think she's feeling her own mortality."

"She's been sick again?"

"Oh, no. She's fine. It's just that, well, it's almost as if she's looking back on her life, looking for something now that she didn't have then."

"Have you discussed it with her?"

"We don't get into talks like that."

"You could."

"I know. But I feel awkward."

"Maybe it'll be good if she comes up, then. Maybe you'll be able to work through that awkwardness."

"I don't know. I still feel so much resentment. You remember how awful it was when she was up last summer."

He remembered very well. "You weren't at your best then, Dani. This time you can do things with her, take her out, maybe introduce her to some of the people you've met here."

"She's already met you. You're the one who matters most. And if she's around . . . it's so hard to pretend."

"Shhh. Let's face that when it comes. In the meantime, just concentrate on getting away."

"I will. Michael? I'm glad you're back. It makes me feel better knowing you're there."

"I'll always be here for you. You know that, don't you?"

"Yes," she whispered. She did know it. Regardless of where he was, she knew he would come running if she needed him, and she loved him all the more for it.

"Take care, sweetheart."

"You, too, Michael."

* * *

Michael sat brooding for a long time after he hung up the phone. On the one hand, he was ecstatic. Danica would be his for the summer. On the other hand, he was stymied. Danica wasn't really his, not in the way he wanted.

He had spent much time talking with Cilla on the subject of Danica and Blake, but it had taken him nowhere. Cilla had seen Blake several times since he had arrived in Washington. She had watched him in action at various functions and could only report that he was the epitome of propriety. On none of the occasions when she had seen him — and several were evening affairs — had Danica been present, yet he had neither been with another woman nor shown the slightest interest in flirting with one. The only thing Michael could conclude was that the man was a stiff. Unfortunately, he was the stiff to whom Danica was tied, and for the life of him, Michael didn't know what to do about it.

Several days before she was to leave for Maine, Danica received a surprise call from Reggie Nichols.

"Danica Lindsay, how would you like company for a day or two?"

"You can come? Reggie, I'd love it! I've been trying to get you here for months. Just tell me when and I'll pick you up at the airport."

Reggie affected a lazy drawl. "Oh, any time would be fine. I'll just browse through the newsstands until you get here."

"You're there *now?*" Danica asked excitedly.

" 'Fraid so."

"I'll be right over. Give me fifteen minutes?"

"Terrific! I'm at the Delta terminal. I'll be waiting outside."

"This is great! I can't wait to see you!"

Reggie laughed. "Hurry up then."

"Right! See you in a minute!" Slamming down the phone, Danica jumped up from Blake's desk and ran for her coat and keys. It had been a year since she'd seen Reggie, and she was very much in the mood to talk. Reggie Nichols fit the bill as only one other person could, and *he* would be there for her in another three days. It was her lucky week, she told herself, feeling absurdly lighthearted as she headed for the airport.

She had barely pulled up at the terminal when she spotted Reggie. She honked and waved, then slid from behind the wheel to run around the car and hug her friend. "You've made my day, Reggie Nichols!"

"Shhhh. I'm traveling incognito. See the shades?"

The sunglasses were oversized and dark but did little to disguise the Reggie Danica knew so well. "You look great!"

"I don't know. Same bumpy nose." She scrunched it up, then ruffled her layered hair. "Same mousy mess."

"You look great," Danica repeated firmly. "Come on. Let's put your bag in and get going. I don't like sharing you with the airport."

During the drive back to Beacon Hill Reggie explained that she had the French Open behind her and the All England Championships ahead of her, that she had come back for a rest in between and on pure impulse had flown to Boston. "I'm not coming at a terrible time, am I?" she asked. There was a quiet urgency in her voice that alerted Danica to something. Reggie looked tired. And older.

"You couldn't have picked a better time," Danica assured her gently. "Blake is in Washington, and I'm getting ready to go up to Maine. If you'd called a week later, I'd have been gone."

"How is Blake?"

"Fine."

"You're really jet-setting it now, I guess."

"Nah. You know how much I hate Washington. I only go there when I have to. But tell me about you. How's the tour going?"

As they neared the town house, Reggie told Danica about the tournaments she had played. An hour later, after they had dropped off her suitcase and the car and had walked across the Common to Locke-Ober's for lunch, she was still talking.

"It's getting worse all the time," she moaned, refilling her wine from the bottle the steward had left chilling in a stand by their table. "I'm not getting younger, and everyone else is."

"But you're a fantastic player, Reggie. What you have in experience makes up for what they have in energy."

"That's what I've been telling myself for the past few years, but you know something? It's not true anymore. They're good, Danica. They've got good legs, good arms and good court sense. Me, well, my knee kicks up and my back aches and I'm just plain tired."

Danica studied her friend. "You had the big one this year, didn't you?"

"Thirty? Yup. And it shows."

"Not from where I'm sitting," Danica began in denial, then softened her words. "What I see is a woman who is tanned and healthy-looking and in remarkable shape. But neither of us is eighteen anymore." She nudged a piece of brook trout with her fork. "Are you thinking of stopping?"

"Yup."

Danice looked up. "Are you really?"

"I'm not sure I have any choice. I'm not winning the way I used to, and the effort is killing me." Reggie paused. "Do you remember when we first went to Armand's? We were on our way up then. Each year we won a few more tournaments. Each year we moved up in rank. It was slow, but it was steady and exciting."

"Steady for you, slightly shaky for me."

"That was something else, Danica. You had reasons for not wanting to play."

"Yeah. I wasn't winning the big ones."

"Okay. Well, that's where I am now." She took a healthy gulp of wine, then set the glass down. "Only it's harder on the backward slide. I was on top for a long time, maybe too long for my own good."

"Success can't be bad."

"When it gets into your blood and then you lose it, it can." She looked at Danica. "I ask myself where I am, *who* I am, and I don't have the answers. Sure, I can retire now and rest on my laurels, but they'll fade pretty fast when the new superstars take over. I really don't know where I'm going anymore, and it's mind-boggling."

Danica didn't know what to say. Her heart went out to Reggie. "Have you discussed things with Monica?" Monica Crayton had been Reggie's coach for the past seven years, ever since she had split with Armand in a technical squabble.

"Monica." She sighed. "Monica is looking around. She won't admit it, but I've seen the way she sidles up to some of the younger players. Hell, she's not blind. She sees what's happening. She knows that it's only a matter of time before I retire, and she's looking out for her own future. I can't blame her, really. I suppose I'd do the same if I were in her shoes."

"Do you ever talk to her about what you should do . . . after?"

"If I don't know, how would she? God, it's awful. I mean, I've had a tennis racket in my hands since I was six. For as long as I can remember I knew where I was headed. There was never any question. Tennis was my future. Suddenly now I don't know anymore."

"Just because you won't be competing doesn't mean you have to leave the game. You could coach."

Reggie took a deep breath. "I've thought of that. And I could. But it wouldn't be the same, sitting on the sidelines watching someone else make it."

"There would be pride in it."

"Maybe. Then again, maybe I'd be a lousy coach. It's like starting all over again. It's scary."

"How about teaching at a tennis academy? You could easily do that. I'll bet Armand—"

"I couldn't ask Armand, not after the way we parted."

"Then, what about another school? There are hundreds of them out there now. With your name alone you'd be able to get a position."

"Maybe. Then again, maybe I'd be bored. It seems forever that I've been thinking of my year in terms of the pro tour. Without that tension, without that—" she made a subtle jab with one fist "—that adrenaline flow—"

"From what you say, that adrenaline flow isn't doing the trick anymore. Really, Reggie, you have choices."

Reggie looked her in the eye. "I think *you* made the right one way back then. I'd give anything to be in your shoes. Look at you: you have a husband in the President's Cabinet—the *President's* Cabinet—you have *three* homes, and you're financially set for life."

Danica smiled sadly. "The grass is always greener, isn't it?"

"Uh-oh. Things with Blake are still rocky?"

Danica rolled her eyes and motioned for the check. As she and Reggie walked slowly back, arm in arm through the Common, she brought Reggie up to date on exactly how rocky things were.

"He doesn't see me at all, Reg. I'm there, but he doesn't see me. It's like I'm a piece of furniture."

"The bastard. What's wrong with him that he can't see something good when he has it?"

"You're prejudiced, but that's beside the point. The point is that Blake sees a million good things he has, only I'm not one of them. It's really an ego trip for him down there. Maybe it was here, too, but I never saw it."

"Maybe you didn't want to see it."

"No. I guess I didn't. I've always tried to rationalize — you know, he's busy and important and he appreciates me even if he doesn't say it. But I look at myself and my life and I know that something has to give. I don't want to be an angry, bitter old lady forty years down the road. I don't want to look back and think of everything I've missed."

"Your work with James Bryant must help some." Danica had written her about it.

"It does. I really enjoy it. But . . ."

"But what?"

Danica looked at Reggie, then away. She motioned toward an empty bench and they sat down. June was in its glory, and its glory was epitomized in the vibrant canopy of trees, the sweet smell of grass, the sounds of emerging humanity that filled the Common.

"There's a man, Reg."

For a full minute Reggie didn't say a word. "A man. As in *other* man?"

"Uh-huh."

"You never mentioned anyone in your letters."

"I'm sure I mentioned him, just not in the proper light."

Reggie frowned, trying to recall. Then her eyes widened. "The fellow from Maine?"

Danica nodded. "No one knows. You're the first person I've breathed a word to. You won't say anything, will you?"

"Have I ever said anything?" Reggie retaliated in teasing reminder of the adolescent fantasies the two had shared when they'd been younger.

"No." Danica smiled, remembering those days. "No, you haven't."

"And I won't now. Michael . . . was that his name?"

"Yes. Michael. He is the most wonderful person you'd ever want to meet."

"Back up a bit. You first met him when you bought the house?"

Reliving it as she spoke, Danica told Reggie about those earliest days, about the slow development of her relationship with Michael, about biking and Rusty and her miscarriage. She told about the winter that had been, about the calls, about how Michael had been her touchstone when she had had no other.

"You're in love with him. It's written all over your face."

"Now, yes. I usually keep it well hidden."

"Does Blake know anything?"

"Blake's met him. He knows that Michael and I are friends. He doesn't really seem to care, but that's the way everything's been between Blake and me lately."

"How far has it gone with Michael? Have you slept with him?"

"God, you're blunt."

"Would you want me to be any other way?"

"No." Danica inhaled sharply and shook her head. "No, I haven't slept with him. I can't."

"Why not? If you love him —"

"I'm married, Reg, remember?"

"Hell, Danica, married people do it all the time. I know. Some of the best men I've dated have been married."

"You haven't."

"I have, and I did it with my eyes open. Not that I went looking for them. They came to me, willing and ready. I need a high from time to time. A good man, a nice, strong sexy one, can give you that, even if it's only for a night."

"But there's more to it with Michael and me. It's not just sex, and it wouldn't be a one-night stand if it started."

"Will it start? You're heading up there for the summer. Is Blake going to be there at all?"

"I doubt it. He gives me the same line that he'll make it whenever he can, but I doubt he will."

"Which means you'll be alone with Michael. What are you going to do?"

"I don't know."

"What do you *want* to do? Dream for a minute. If you had your way, what would you do?"

Danica didn't have to take a minute to dream because she had been doing it for months and months. "I'd divorce Blake, move permanently to Maine, marry Michael and have six kids."

"Then *do* it!"

"I can't! It's just a dream. I can't divorce Blake. Do you have any idea how hurt he'd be? Do you have any idea how hurt my parents would be?"

"To hell with them. What about *you?*"

Danica gave a clipped laugh. "You sound like Michael."

"You've talked to him about divorcing Blake?"

"No. He knows that I feel an obligation to my family, though."

"What good are obligations if you're miserable?"

"But I'm not. Not really. I mean, I do have a lot to be grateful for. And now that I'm working with James, there's some satisfaction."

"But you're missing so much," Reggie said more gently, then thought. "Is there any way you can work things out with Blake?"

"Resurrect our marriage? I don't know, Reg. I was trying to do that when I bought the house in Maine and look what happened. Blake and I are growing further apart. He has his own life. He's always had his own life. Because of that, I've begun to build one for myself. We're heading in different directions. I'm not sure if either of us can turn around and find the other."

"Then you have your answer."

"No, I don't. There's still that ugly little word, *divorce*. I don't want it. It scares me."

"It's just a word with a little paper work involved. People do it all the time, precisely because they realize that their marriages have failed. And it's easier than it used to be. You could fly to Haiti—"

"Please, Reggie. I don't want to talk about it."

"Okay. We don't have to. Not now, at least. But at some point you may have to face it."

"Not now. Not now."

"Okay."

Reggie fondly squeezed her arm, then gaily informed her that she wanted to go shopping in the Marketplace. By the time they returned to the town house much later Danica had managed to shove that ugly little word to the back of her mind. Reggie kept her mind occupied with tales of off-court escapades, both her own and those of other players Danica knew. Mrs. Hannah made their dinner, then they settled on the bed in the guest room to reminisce about the days at Armand Arroah's house. Danica felt like a teenager again, and was grateful that Blake wasn't around to look down his nose at the snickering and laughter that echoed through the halls.

No more was said about either of their futures until much later, when they had stolen down to the kitchen for tea and cake and Reggie raised her hand for attention. "Listen to this." She read from her tea bag. " 'We often discover what will do by finding out what will not do.' Is that apt or is that apt?"

"Listen to mine. 'The best kind of wrinkles indicate where smiles have been.' Neither of us has wrinkles. Is that good or bad?"

Neither one of them knew the answer. While Reggie distracted herself by marveling that the sun hadn't weatherbeaten her face into a thorough mass of wrinkles, Danica pondered switching to another brand of tea.

TEN

S INCE SHE WAS TRANSPORTING a word processor and its bulky accessories, not to mention dictionaries and reference books, in addition to her personal things, Danica allowed Marcus to follow her to Maine in the Mercedes. While she opened the windows and aired out the house, he emptied both cars, then helped her set up the word processor in the den. He was anxious to please, offering to run into town for food, but she gently refused. She breathed a grand sigh of relief when he finally pulled the Mercedes from the drive and headed back to Boston.

Dashing into the bedroom, she threw off her skirt and blouse and was in the process of tugging on jeans when she heard Michael's voice.

"Dani? Dani, it's me!"

Heart pounding as she shimmied into a T-shirt, she raced back into the living room just as Michael was opening the screen.

"Michael!" She was in his arms then, being swung off her feet and around. "Michael, oh, Michael, it's good to see you!" Her arms were around his neck, his around her waist. "I thought Marcus would never leave."

"So did I. I've been hiding behind the rocks, waiting."

"You haven't."

"I have."

He set her back then. "Let me look at you." He did, head to toe. "You look wonderful. Your hair's longer. I like it."

"So do I." She combed her fingers through his own clean hair. "Yours is shorter. I like it, too."

He colored. "The barber got carried away. It'll grow."

"No, I like it." What she liked was the way the front still fell over his brow but not low enough to hide the faint creases that made him look distinguished. She liked the way his sideburns were trimmed, making his jaw look all the stronger. She liked the way the back was layered, feeling feathery and soft to her touch. "It's so good to see you," she breathed, not caring if she repeated herself, because the words bore repeating.

He hugged her again, then kissed her softly, gently on her lips. "I thought you'd never get here," he murmured, reluctantly dragging his mouth from hers. "It's been so long."

"I know." She moved her hands over his chest, savoring his warmth, as though in proof of the living man before her. For so long he had been in her dreams. It was hard to believe she was here with him at last.

Taking her hand in his, he led her to the deck, asking her about what she had done since he had spoken with her last, then, as she talked, guiding her toward the beach and their favorite rocks. She wanted to know more about his travels than he had told her on the phone, and asked question after question, all of which he answered eagerly.

"I have some news," he said when they reached a comfortable breaking point. He had debated waiting to tell her but knew she would be hurt if she felt he hadn't been forthright. "I have a teaching position for the fall."

Her eyes lit up. "That's great! Where?"

He hesitated for only a minute. "Harvard."

Her eyes widened all the more. "That's so close!"

"I know. I wasn't sure if it would upset you."

"Upset me? I think it's *wonderful!*"

"It'll only be one afternoon a week and just for the fall semester; I've never done anything like this before so I'll have to spend a lot of time this summer getting ready, but I think it's kind of exciting."

" 'Kind of'?" she mocked, then wrapped an arm around his waist and squeezed. It amazed her that she had come to be so physical, but then, Michael inspired no less. "You'll be in Boston one afternoon a week. Now, that's exciting."

He grinned, unable to take his eyes from her face. "I think so. I was hoping . . . I mean, I thought . . . well, maybe we could have dinner together every so often."

She knew what he was saying, or not saying, as the case truly was. If they saw each other in Boston, it would be on her turf. They would be breaking an unspoken agreement, paving new ground, perhaps making things more difficult. But she had little choice. "I'd really like that."

"You would?"

She grew serious. "Yes, I would. This past winter was very long. I'm not particularly looking forward to a repeat of it." She tore her gaze from his and sought the solace of the sea. "But I keep asking myself the same questions, and I don't have any answers yet." She glanced back at him. "Maybe I'm being unfair to you."

"Am I complaining?"

"I can't promise anything," she warned softly.

"I know, sweetheart, I know. I also know how much I missed *you* all winter, and I'm not looking forward to a repeat of it, either." He took a breath. "Please take this in the right light, because I don't want you to feel guilty about anything. I didn't go looking for a position in Boston. It came to me, and the opportunity was too good to pass up. Being able to see you will be frosting on the cake. If it happens, it'll be wonderful. If not, then I'll just concentrate on the pleasure of teaching. . . . But this is crazy. Here we are with the whole summer to look forward to and we're worrying about the fall. I have another surprise. Wanna see it?"

"Is it as nice as the last one?"

He wiggled his brows. "Depends on your preference . . . man or beast." Turning away, he set his lips and whistled loudly. He repeated it seconds later, then waited.

"Rusty?" Danica whispered, looking down the beach as Michael was doing. Moments later a large and handsome Labrador retriever loped into view. "Rusty! My Lord, look at him!"

With Michael right behind her, she scrambled down the rocks, falling to her knees to give Rusty a sound hug. "You're beautiful!" she exclaimed, clutching his thick pelt while his entire rear end wagged.

"He's been waiting for you."

"He has not. He couldn't possibly remember me."

"Sure he does. And even if he didn't, he has a good eye for women."

"You're training him."

"Yup."

She stood. "He's magnificent, Michael. I'm so glad you got him."

"So am I. We've had some good runs together on the beach. You'd be pleased watching."

"I can't wait. He's a special dog made for a special man." She couldn't hide the adoration in her eyes when she gazed up at Michael.

"I'm gonna be swellheaded pretty soon. Come on. I want to see your word processor."

He saw that, and the piles of papers and tapes she had brought. When they returned to his house, he showed her the galleys for his book on sports and the reams of notes and outlines for his newest baby. They discussed it for a while, then drove into town together. Michael took pride in showing her off there, not only to Sara but to Sara's husband and the druggist and the librarian and the kitchen shop proprietor, all of whom Danica had come to know well the summer before.

They stopped at the market for food, then returned to Danica's house, where she cooked Michael what he swore was the best dinner he had had in weeks. After an evening of quiet talk and smiles, though, he wisely said good night.

It was a pattern of closeness that was to repeat itself as the weeks passed. They biked together each morning before going their separate ways to work. As often as possible they had dinner together, sometimes at her house, sometimes at his, sometimes out. They shopped together, walked the beach together, talked about everything from Dutch elm disease to the plight of the miners in Appalachia. They spent a Sunday with the McCabes on their boat, which was perfectly wonderful since Danica and Michael had eyes only for each other and Greta and Pat indulged them their pleasure.

In mid-July, Eleanor Marshall came for a visit. Danica was indeed in better shape than she had been the summer before, but she still found her mother's presence to be limiting, particularly when she wanted to be with Michael. At Danica's insistence, he joined them for dinner on several occasions. Not only was she desperate to see him, but she wanted her mother to get to know him.

Unfortunately, she underestimated her mother's perceptivity.

"Darling?" Eleanor had been home for three days, waiting for a moment when she and William were alone. They were having cocktails in the den prior to a rare quiet dinner. "There's something I want to discuss with you. It's about Danica."

William settled deeper into his high-backed chair. "I'm glad you went up there. I just can't get away."

"I'm sure she understands. But that's not what I wanted to discuss. I'm worried about Blake and her."

"What about them?"

"It's not right the way they never see each other."

"I've told her that. She doesn't listen to me."

"What does Blake say?"

"Blake can't do anything about it," William said gruffly. "He can't be traipsing north all the time when he's busy in Washington, and he can't force her to stay there. What in the hell does she have against the place, anyway?"

"She never did like it. You know that."

"But I don't know why. Okay, so she doesn't like going out every night. You'd think she could force herself for Blake's sake."

"She doesn't want to. That's what worries me."

Ice cubes clinked as William rapped his glass against the arm of his chair. "She has more than most women could ever dream of having. I don't know what's wrong with her. She should be grateful. Instead, what does she do? She buries herself with that old fart Bryant—"

"She says he's nice."

"This whole working thing is ridiculous. She's no bra-burner; at least, *I* never brought her up to be one. What possessed her to want to work? I still can't figure that one out."

"She says she loves it."

"Stubborn fool, she probably wouldn't admit it even if she didn't." He brooded for a minute. "Someone's influencing her. That's the only explanation. You say she's met people up there?"

Eleanor smoothed her dress over her knee, pressing the silk with her palm. "She introduced me to quite a few. They seem nice enough. I'm worried though."

When she didn't go on, William scowled. "What is it, Eleanor? Spit it out."

"Maybe I shouldn't."

"Eleanor," he warned, lowering his brows in command.

"The one . . . her neighbor . . . Michael Buchanan . . ."

"He's trouble. I could have bet on it."

"No, no. He's very nice. *Very* nice."

William sighed. "What are you suggesting, Eleanor?"

Eleanor's expression was pained. She didn't know if she was doing the right thing. On the one hand, she felt she was betraying Danica. On the other, she knew her ultimate loyalty had to rest with William, who would surely be furious if something did happen after she had kept mum.

"I'm wondering," she sighed, "if it's possible that Danica could be involved with another man."

William pulled in his chin. "With Buchanan?"

"They seem very fond of each other."

"Did they *do* anything?"

"In front of me, of course not. They were very proper. Danica went out of her way to be nonchalant when he was around, but I saw. A woman sees things like that."

"Things like *what?*" William demanded impatiently.

"Expression. Tone of voice. Little things. She's not that way with Blake."

"Blake is a man. Buchanan is . . . is . . ."

"A man, too," Eleanor provided softly. "A man who's just as good-looking in his way as Blake. A man who's just as successful in his way as Blake. A man who is *there*, while Blake isn't."

But William was shaking his head. "Danica wouldn't do something like that. She wouldn't dare."

"Danica isn't a child anymore. We both seem to have missed that somewhere along the line."

"She wouldn't dare. That's all there is to it."

Eleanor pressed her lips together, then nodded. "Well, I just wanted to mention it to you."

William finished his drink. "Why?"

"I thought maybe you might want to speak to her. Or to Blake. You know, not to make any accusations, just to suggest that they should try to be together more. I wouldn't want anything to happen, Bill. Blake's in a position of great visibility. If Danica does something foolish, you and Blake could both be embarrassed."

"Hmm. Maybe." He inhaled deeply. "By the way, Henry and Ruth were asking for you today. I saw them at the club."

For the moment, the discussion of their daughter was over. Feeling that she had discharged her duty, Eleanor gratefully seized on the subject of her friends. William, though, thought about the matter of Danica and Blake for a long time. He didn't want to confront Blake and risk being closed off by a man he considered to be an important friend and ally. He didn't want to confront Danica, who would surely deny everything.

No, he decided, there was a safer way to handle the matter. Determinedly, he put in a call the next morning to Morgan Emery.

On a Saturday morning in late July, Michael suggested they drive north along the coast to Camden. Danica, who didn't care where they went as long as they were together, readily agreed. For comfort's sake, and because she was feeling particularly feminine, she wore a new blue sundress she had bought in Boston that spring, and strappy sandals.

Michael was more quiet than usual. From time to time, when she glanced at him, he smiled and squeezed her hand, but he said little.

"You seem preoccupied," she ventured softly. "Is something wrong?"

"No, no. Well, not really wrong. I, uh, there was a special reason I wanted to bring you up here." They were no more than ten minutes from their destination.

"Another surprise?" she teased.

"In a way. There's someone I want you to meet."

"Last time I heard that, I found Cilla on your deck. Who is it, Michael?"

"Her name's Gena. Gena Bradley."

Danica thought, then shook her head. "I don't recognize the name. Who is she?"

"Bradley is her maiden name. She reverted to it after her divorce. When I was a kid, it was Gena Bradley Buchanan. She's my mother."

"Your *mother*? But I thought she lived in New York. I hadn't even realized your parents were divorced." Michael rarely talked of his father for reasons he had already explained, and though he had spoken fondly of his mother, Danica had just assumed their relationship had suffered some from the rift.

"It happened after we all left the roost. My memories are of the family together."

"What happened?" Danica breathed, stunned. "I thought . . . I mean, the picture was always so pretty."

"It was pretty, at least for us kids. We always knew that Gena had an independent streak. She was our greatest champion when Dad was trying to steamroll us. And I don't think she was all that unhappy then. She loved us, and she and Dad had struck what seemed to be a fair compromise."

"Then . . . why?"

"When we all left and there was just Dad and her, she realized something was more wrong than she'd thought. She discovered that Dad was seeing someone else, a younger woman."

"Oh, Michael."

"Gena was really hurt, mostly because she felt she'd been so loyal all those years. He didn't fight the divorce. And she moved up here."

"It must be a comfort having you so close."

"I don't see her as often as I'd like." He shook his head in admiration. "She's a remarkable woman. More independent than ever. She's not the type who expects her children to hold her hand. She's made a new life for herself and stays so busy that we all but have to make an appointment to see her."

Danica couldn't help but contrast Michael's mother and her own. The situations seem to have been reversed. She was glad, for Michael's sake, that he had gotten the better end of the deal. "What does she do?"

"What *doesn't* she do. She owns a small real estate concern in Camden. She teaches Russian at an adult ed program. She pots."

"Pots?"

"Works with clay. She's really pretty good. Do you know that big slate-colored lamp in my bedroom?"

Danica cleared her throat. His bedroom had been off-limits. "No, uh, I don't happen to know that big slate-colored lamp in your bedroom."

Michael shot her an embarrassed glance. "Right. Well, anyway, she made the base and had it wired up for me. She sells her things to some of the local shops." He paused. "You have one of them."

"I do?"

"The ashtray in the den."

Danica heard the quiet pride in his voice. "Your mother made that? Why didn't you tell me?"

"It was pleasure enough for me to know."

"I love it!" She lowered her voice. "I keep paper clips in it, though. Do you think she'll mind?"

He laughed and shook his head. "I keep telling her that she should try to sell in New York, but she claims she doesn't have the time. She says she doesn't want the pressure and that if she enjoys what she's doing, that's all that matters. I wish I could be as content. It's not that I need adulation, but I'm not sure my work would mean much to me if people never read my books."

"The situations are different, Michael. Your mother—"

"Call her Gena. She'll want that."

". . . Gena is at a different stage in life, and in a sense she already has public exposure. Her four greatest works are out on the streets of the world—Brice, Corey, Cilla, and you."

Michael grinned. "You two will get along fine. Just fine."

But Danica was suffering momentary cold feet. "Does she know about me?"

"I've spoken of you as a friend." He grew solemn. "I haven't told her everything. Given her own experience in life, I'm not sure she'd appreciate the fact that I'm in love with a married woman."

If Gena suspected anything, she kept it to herself. To Danica, she was warm and welcoming, to Michael openly adoring. Danica easily understood where Michael's physicality came from. Gena, too, was a toucher.

She was slender, more petite than Cilla, and had an attractive crop of short silver hair. Michael had her brown eyes—or maybe it was the warmth in them which was familiar—but there the physical similarity ended.

As with Cilla, Danica found herself quickly drawn to this other woman in

Michael's life. Gena was interesting and nonconforming in a way Danica found thoroughly refreshing. Though Michael claimed that Cilla was like their father in terms of agressiveness, Danica could see where she got her impulsiveness. In the course of the day Gena excitedly dragged them to see the house she had just sold to a painter, corraled them into the local movie house to view a short foreign film she had heard was superb, scrambled on Michael's shoulders to hang a bird feeder she thought was too low, and cooked the most delicious vegetarian dinner Danica had ever imagined could be made.

"Tired?" Michael asked as they drove back to Kennebunkport much later that night.

"Mmmm. But pleasantly so. She's wonderful. How lucky you are to have a mother like that."

Her tone held appreciation, perhaps a little envy, but no bitterness, and for that Michael was grateful. He hadn't wanted to underscore Danica's own problems by introducing her to Gena. Indeed he had spent hours worrying that that might happen. In the end, though, he had simply wanted these two women to meet. Danica's reaction to the day had convinced him he'd been right. Moreover, he was thrilled with the genuine affection Gena had shown Danica. It pleased him to know that his mother saw the beauty in the woman he loved.

Cilla was surprised to look up from the jumble of notes on her desk to see Jeffrey approaching. She wasn't sure what had alerted her to his arrival, certainly not his footsteps when the city room was filled with the steady click of computer keyboards. She broke into a smile, but waited for him to speak first.

"Hi," he said quietly.

"Hi, yourself."

"I was passing by and just thought I'd drop in. I wasn't sure you'd be here. You're usually out running around."

There had been no censure in his voice to discourage her. "I don't get any writing done when I'm out running around. For that matter, I don't get much writing done here." She gestured toward her cluttered desktop. "Look at this mess. I'm not terribly organized."

"You manage to get the job done." He slid into the chair adjacent to her desk. No one in the large room appeared to be paying him much heed. He was grateful to go unrecognized. "I read your piece on political corruption. It was good."

"It said nothing you didn't know before."

"But it was well researched and presented several new angles. Have you gotten any response?"

"You mean, from official-type people, as in we-want-to-look-into-this? Not exactly. But then, I didn't expect to. Official-type people work in strange ways. They keep things confidential until all of a sudden they're knocking down your door screaming for your sources."

"Come on, Cilla. I never did that."

"You didn't have to knock down my door. You were already inside," she argued, then softened her tone and looked down. "But you're right, Jeff. You never did that. Even though I was afraid you would."

"You shouldn't have been. I was the first one to realize that you couldn't divulge a source."

"Still, you always asked."

"I was curious." He leaned closer for privacy's sake, as well as for the simple pleasure of being nearer Cilla. "*Personally* curious. Not professionally. Personally. One part of me wanted to know everything you were doing." He lowered his voice all the more. "I suppose it was a kind of possessiveness, a male need."

"Possessiveness isn't limited to men. We feel it, too."

"That's the feminist in you talking, the woman who wants the upper hand."

"It is not! I don't need to have the upper hand all the time. Don't impose your insecurities on me, Jeffrey Winston. It's not fair."

He was about to soundly refute her claim when he caught his breath, then slowly let it out. "You may be right."

"I . . . what?"

His lips thinned. "Don't make me say it again. It was hard enough the first time."

"You acknowledge that you have insecurities?"

"I always did acknowledge it. Just not to you."

"Well," she sighed, "that's something. I guess we both have them."

Jeffrey wanted to talk more, but he knew there was a better time and place. He had come here to see if Cilla was truly as receptive as Michael suggested she might be. "So," he began more casually, "anything juicy on the fire?" He had been trying to lighten things up but realized instantly that he had only opened another old wound. To his amazement, Cilla didn't see it that way. She was frowning, studying the telephone that sat on the desk.

"I got the weirdest call this morning."

"From whom?" He winced. "Chalk that. Is it anything you can talk about?"

She shot him a helpless glance, one he'd never seen before. "Sure. There's nothing to it, really. Except that . . . instinct tells me . . . I can feel there's something there, but he wouldn't say much."

Jeffrey waited patiently, telling himself that he would have to trust Cilla to speak if she wished. He was rewarded when she met his gaze. "It was a man. He wouldn't identify himself. He mumbled something about sexual favors and power and lust. I don't know. He may have been drunk, or stoned. But it was like he had second thoughts the minute he called. I can't help but feel that he had something legitimate to say." She paused. "He hung up before I could get anything concrete from him."

"He'll call back if he wants. He knows where to reach you."

"Still, it's frustrating. I keep thinking that he's somewhere out there and that I can't begin to imagine who or where he is."

Jeffrey admired her dedication, which was as whole-hearted as ever. But there was something else, something that took the edge off. She seemed less confident, more vulnerable. He wondered if she was indeed mellowing as Michael had said.

"Uh, listen, Cilla. The reason I came by . . . well, I thought maybe we could have dinner together. I know you're often out with the gang—" he tossed his head toward the others in the room "—and I realize that it's important for you—"

"When?"

"Excuse me?"

Cilla had never been a shrinking pansy. She smiled. "When would you like to have dinner? I could make it Thursday night if you're free."

"Thursday night?" He somehow managed to master his surprise. He had fully expected she would make things challenging. But he was too old to play games; maybe she had outgrown them, too. Thursday was just two days off. He grinned, leaned forward and quickly kissed her cheek before he stood. "Thursday's great. Should I pick you up?"

"You know where I'll be," she said in that same soft tone that had emerged from time to time.

Again he was surprised. He had half expected her to suggest they meet at a restaurant. Mellowing? Very definitely, and becomingly. With an unsteady breath, he grinned. "Right. See you around eight?"

"That'd be great."

He nodded, then was off. Cilla stared after him, thinking that he had to be the most handsome man in the room. She felt satisfied, and excited. It occurred to her that she hadn't felt that way in a long, long time.

Morgan Emery shifted to a more comfortable position in his place of concealment just beneath the deck of the elegant cabin cruiser he had rented. It had been four weeks since William Marshall had hired him, and he was beginning to wonder whether the money was worth it after all. He had hidden behind boulders, skulked in rural doorways, walked in and out of restaurants, seen more of the southern Maine coast than he had ever wanted to see, and he was getting nothing, at least nothing worth anything.

Oh, he had pictures, but not a one was truly compromising. He had shots of the two on the beach, shots of them in the car, shots of them riding bicycles, shots of them coming out of the local library, shots of them at one or the other's front door. There would be a hand on a shoulder and he would hold his breath waiting to photograph a kiss, then nothing. There would be an arm around a waist, so close to a caress, then it would fall away. There would be a face before a face, a smile, then a backing off. Even now, as he trained the telescopic lens of his camera on Michael Buchanan's deck, all he could see was two people, sitting in separate chairs, eating the steaks they had just grilled.

Emery's mouth watered, but when he groped for the last ham and cheese sandwich he had brought, his appetite waned.

Surveillance. He hated it. Long hours sitting, waiting. What he loved was the action of the big city, where a private investigator could sink his teeth into something meaty. This? Hell, this was baby-sitting. High-paying, sure, but with little challenge.

Unfortunately, when a member of the United States Senate offered you a job, you didn't turn it down. Personal pull was worth a mint, and William Marshall had pull. A good word from him might, just might, get Emery

another stint working undercover with the Feds. Now, *that* had been a challenge, playing the part of a fence in a sting. He had had a good time. Maybe
he should have been an actor. Hell, he had the looks . . .

At movement on the distant deck Emery grew alert, but it was another false
alarm. They were carrying plates into the house. And there was the damned
dog again. Oh, he had fantastic pictures of the dog. It was a beautiful beast, he
had to admit. But Marshall didn't want to see the dog.

What in the hell was the matter with them? Was Buchanan a eunuch? A
beautiful woman . . . hours with her each day . . . and zilch.

With a snap, Morgan Emery tugged his equipment into the boat, then
swiveled around and hoisted himself into the pilot's seat. It was a magnificent
craft, he mused, sliding his hands around the gleaming brass steering wheel.
Marshall had given him carte blanche on expenses, and he had reasoned that
he had to look properly posh on the water. Someday maybe he would own a
boat like this himself. He deserved it. Hell, what he deserved was a pretty
young thing from town and a night of hot sex. He would be impressive. And
since he had the boat till morning . . .

With due care he resisted the urge to push the throttle all the way forward
and take off in a wild spray of sea water. But the automatic pilot kept him
cruising slowly, and he couldn't accelerate without risk of drawing attention
to himself.

One thing was for sure. He would be damned if he was going to sit around
any longer. Marshall wanted pictures. He would give him pictures. If they were
innocent, that was Marshall's problem. His own job was done. Over. Fini.

Danica had just returned to the deck and was looking out to sea when Michael
came from behind to slip his arms around her waist. She leaned back against
him and covered his hands with her own.

"Pretty, isn't it?" she breathed.

"The sunset or the boat?"

"Both. So very peaceful." She tipped her head against his chest. "It must
be even more so out there."

"On the boat?"

"Mmmm. The waves aren't too high. The breeze is light." She took a slow
breath. "It'd be nice to have a boat like that. I wonder whose it is."

Michael squinted at the sleek cabin cruiser that was moving steadily away.
"I can't see the name. It may be out of Bar Harbor or Newport, or somewhere
on Long Island."

"Mmmm, dream material. I didn't see anyone on deck. What do you think
they're doing? Maybe drinking champagne below or eating by candlelight?"

"Maybe bailing bilge water."

She elbowed him and he chuckled. "You're awful, Michael. Here I was,
creating a beautifully romantic picture and you shatter it in one fell swoop."

"I'm sorry. Go ahead. Create."

She couldn't resist the temptation, though her thoughts turned inward. "If
I had a boat like that, I'd be free. Oh, not in the most real sense, but then, being
on a boat like that would be a fantasy anyway. I'd just . . . take off. Cruise

away. Separate myself from the land and its restraints." She lowered her chin and gave a self-conscious laugh. "You must think I'm crazy."

"Not at all." He realized that Blake could buy her a boat like that in a minute. She could probably buy it for herself. *He* could buy it for her. So it wasn't the dream of having the boat that was beyond reach, but rather the dream of freedom. Freedom. What he'd give for her to have it! "I hear what you're saying. One summer, when I was in college, I crewed on a windjammer up here. It was hard work, but was it ever fun. We had passengers on for a week at a time, but the joy came on the days we were alone, when we could put up the sails, catch the wind and fly. We'd just lie out on the deck and relax. I felt like I owned the world then. All my worries were back on shore. I was free, for a little while at least."

"Sounds heavenly." Turning, she slid her arms around his neck. Darkness was quickly falling, cloaking the real world, though not enough. "But too short. I can't believe where the summer's gone. It's been wonderful."

"It has, hasn't it?" he asked. His fingers moved along the base of her spine, itching to climb higher. "When do you have to be back?"

"I told Blake I'd be in Boston a week after Labor Day." Religiously she talked to him on the phone every Sunday, but they had little to say of import. She wasn't interested in his doings in Washington any more than he was interested in what she was doing in Maine. He made no mention of flying up, and she was grateful. She felt estranged from him, physically and emotionally, and if he felt it, too, he didn't seem to care. "Thirteen days and counting. Reluctantly. When do you start in Cambridge?"

"The middle of the month. I'll be going down for orientation before classes actually start."

"You'll be staying overnight?"

"Only at the start. I've taken a room at the Hyatt. It's on—"

"Memorial Drive. I know where it is. It's not far from me." Hearing her own words, she was stunned. He was going to be so close, so *close*. She tried to picture the room he would have overlooking the Charles, but all she could see was a large, empty bed. When her knees grew weak, she wrapped her arms tighter around his neck and pressed her face to his throat. She felt so torn, so torn.

Michael crushed her even closer. His arms crisscrossed her back, fingers reaching the soft side swells of her breasts. "I don't know if I should tell you to think it or not to think it," he moaned. "We have to do something, Dani. We have to do *something*." The torment had been getting worse, the agony of wanting her, needing her, and not having her in every sense.

"I know," she murmured brokenly. "I wish I knew what to do."

"Just kiss me, then," he rasped, lowering his head and taking her mouth with the hunger that boiled from inside. Her hunger matched it, and she held nothing back, offering her lips, her tongue, her breath in the fevered exchange. Her body arched toward him, and when he unwrapped his arms and inched his hands to her breasts, a small, catlike purr slipped from her throat.

He had never touched her there, but she had imagined it many, many times. His hands caressed her and she grew fuller beneath his nurturing.

"So beautiful," he murmured hoarsely, his forehead against hers. When he brushed his thumbs over her nipples, they grew even more taut. She whimpered softly, unable to draw away because she loved what he was doing, but knowing that he had to stop.

"Thirteen days, Dani. That's all we have."

"I know, I know."

"I want you, sweetheart."

I want you, too, she thought. But she also thought of Boston and Blake and all else she would be returning to when those thirteen short days were done.

Michael spread his palms over her breasts, memorizing their very feminine shape for a final moment before slowly lowering his hands to her waist. He was breathing heavily. He knew that his shorts did little to hide his hardness, knew that she had to feel him with their hips pressed together that way. He could feel her warmth, could imagine her moistness. He also knew that she still wasn't ready in the emotional sense that would make it all okay the morning after.

"I had better get you home," he whispered. She nodded, though she was loath to move. "I don't know how much control I'll have if we stay here much longer. I've ached to touch you this way, but it only makes me want more."

Again she nodded, but this time she moved back. Chin tucked to her chest, hands clasped tightly before her, she was the image of misery. "I don't know what to do," she breathed so softly that he wouldn't have heard it had he not been so close.

He felt her misery, her confusion, tenfold because he wanted answers but had none. "We have time, sweetheart," he said at last.

Her head flew up, eyes wide. "Thirteen days. That's all. Thirteen days."

But he was shaking his head. "We have more. We have weeks, months. The situation isn't simple. We can't put a time limit on it."

"But it could go on forever!" she cried, hugging herself in place of him.

Again he was shaking his head. "It won't. When the time is right, something will give. You'll know it when it happens. Either way."

Later, long after Michael had walked Danica home, he was thinking of what he had said. The summer had brought them even closer. She was so totally a part of his life that he couldn't bear the thought of it otherwise. Yet, she could, indeed, go either way. She could go back to Boston and realize what he already had, that they were made for each other, that their life together would be unimaginably sweet. She could also go back to Boston and, for reasons beyond his control, decide that she had to stay with Blake.

He couldn't force the issue mainly because he was afraid of the outcome. He knew that she loved him, knew that she had little left with Blake. He also knew that though the bonds tying her to Blake were fraying, they remained strong.

In the final analysis, he wanted her to be happy. If that meant a reconciliation between Blake and her, he would have to accept it. In the meanwhile, all he could do was to wait and hope and do everything he could to make the time they had together very special.

Wandering out onto the deck late that night, he thought about the last. His eye caught on the horizon, which was dark and without the lights that would mark the passing of a boat. He recalled the handsome cruiser they had seen earlier, recalled her dreams, her wistfulness.

It was then that inspiration hit.

ELEVEN

❊❊❊

E ARLY THE NEXT MORNING Michael raced into town, where he found that the fates were very definitely on his side. Not only could he rent a cabin cruiser like the one Danica had dreamed on the night before, but the very *one* was a rental, being returned that same morning. Paying the full price in advance, he made the arrangements, then dashed back to Danica's house.

"Guess what!" he exclaimed, beaming proudly as he presented himself at her door.

She smiled, adoring the boyish way he looked when he couldn't contain his excitement. There was always something new with him. She knew he would make life exhilarating to say the least. "What?"

"It's ours."

"What is?"

"The boat."

"*What* boat?"

"The one we saw last night."

Her eyes grew round. "*That* boat? What do you mean, 'it's ours'?"

"I've just rented it for the weekend."

"You're kidding. No, you're not. Michael, I don't believe it!"

"Are you pleased?"

"You know I am! For the weekend? It's *ours*?"

He shrugged, but he was grinning. "Unless you'd rather just go to a movie or something."

"No way!" She pressed her hands together. "Oh, Lord, this is wild. I'll have to . . . have I got . . . what do I wear on a boat?"

"You've never *been* on one before?"

"Different. Very different. High heels and cocktail dress type thing." She glowed. "This will be so much better!"

Her excitement alone made it all worthwhile. "You can wear whatever you want. The more comfortable, the better." He paused. "I could have taken it for today and tomorrow, but it was just coming in this morning and the owner wanted to clean it up. Besides, these being weekdays and all, I figured you'd want to work."

Danica shook her head in continued amazement, both that he had actually rented the boat and that he respected her work enough to plan around it. Not that she wouldn't have dropped everything to go on that boat with Michael. . . .

"I can't wait," she breathed, then threw her arms around him. "Thank you."

Not trusting himself, he quickly set her back. "My pleasure. Now . . . work."

"No bike ride?"

He shook his head. "I have to take Rusty to the vet, then spend the morning on the phone. Some notes I took in San Francisco aren't right. I want to straighten them out before I make a mess of this whole book. After that I'd better get to finishing the plan for my class." He teased her. "You're not the only one around here who has to work, y'know."

She smiled and took the hand he offered, squeezed it, then watched him head back down the drive. Quickly, though, her thoughts turned to the weekend, and she sensed that working her way through the next two days was going to be easier said than done.

By seven o'clock Saturday morning she was up and dressed and packed and waiting. After much deliberation she had chosen to wear jeans and a shirt, putting varied changes of clothing in the small overnight bag that now sat by the door.

Michael had rented the boat from ten that morning to the same time on Monday. He had said he would be by at nine so that they might stop for food before heading for the Yacht Club. He would have been furious had he known she'd spent the entire afternoon before in the kitchen, but she hadn't been able to concentrate on her work, and she rather fancied the idea of sitting on deck with wine and homemade pâté, stuffed mushrooms and pea pods, and ramaki. She had baked a Black Forest cake, too, dashing out to the store for the freshest of heavy cream, the finest of semisweet chocolate, the richest of kirsch. All of her goodies were packaged and waiting in the refrigerator.

She wandered from room to room, looking out a window here, straightening a throw pillow there. She glanced at her watch, then began to wander again. She was on the deck with her face turned to the late August sun when a thought struck.

Blake would be calling on Sunday and she wouldn't be here. If he was worried—and she wasn't sure he would be, though she couldn't take that chance—he might call Mrs. Hannah, or worse, her father. She didn't want that.

Running back into the den, she picked up the phone, then hesitated. She had no idea what his Saturday schedule was in Washington. In Boston, he would have been up early and headed for the office, then the club. Deciding to take the course that would prove least embarrassing should she be wrong, she dialed his condominium.

The phone rang five times. She was about to hang up when he answered. Groggily. He'd been sleeping. Unusual.

"Hi, Blake."

"Danica?"

She could see him peering at the clock that sat so prominently on his nightstand. "I'm sorry. Did I wake you?"

"No. Uh, yes. I overslept. I should have been up an hour ago."

"I thought I'd call you now because I'm going out on a boat with some friends and I won't be here tomorrow." It was only a tiny half-lie, she reasoned, and if Rusty was coming, no lie at all. She prayed Blake wouldn't ask more.

He didn't. "That should be nice for you. How long will you be gone?" His tone was conversational, as if he didn't deeply care but felt some show of interest was called for.

"Just for the weekend. I'll be back on Monday."

"Well, have a good time."

"How are things there?"

"Very well, thank you."

"Is anything new?"

"Not that I can think of."

"All's well at the Department?"

"Very well."

She didn't know what else to say. "Okay. I guess I'll be going then. Talk with you next week?"

"That sounds fine. Bye-bye."

Only after she hung up the receiver did Danica realize she was gritting her teeth, but then, it wasn't the first time. Lately, when she talked to Blake, she was tense. He was always perfectly calm, properly composed—even today, after she'd woken him up. She pictured him lying in bed, with his hair barely mussed and his pajamas just so. For the life of her, she couldn't picture herself beside him. The thought held no appeal whatsoever.

It was a travesty, the stale ritual they were living. She wondered if it bothered him, wondered if he was even aware of anything amiss. He always seemed too complacent. She knew that they couldn't keep on this way, yet the alternative . . .

Unable, no, un*willing* to start her weekend by brooding, she left the den in a rush. For lack of anything better to do, she carried her overnight bag to the driveway, then returned to the kitchen to transfer things from the refrigerator to a large box.

Michael was early. "What in the devil have you done?" he exclaimed when she lifted the box from the kitchen table.

"I made a few things to eat."

He quickly took the box from her. "You didn't have to do that, Dani. I didn't mean for this weekend to cause you work."

The contrast struck her again. Blake would have objected on principle to his wife cooking, while Michael was simply and genuinely concerned that she had put herself out.

"It was fun. And don't tell me you won't be hungry all weekend."

He lowered his chin. "Now, I didn't say that. But we could have easily made do with store-bought things."

"We'll still need plenty. Are we all set?" She glanced toward the Blazer. "Rusty's coming!"

"We're dropping him at the Greta and Pat's. They miss him."

Danica made a face that said she wondered, but she didn't argue. She didn't want to share Michael with anyone, not even man's best friend.

After making the appropriate stops, they arrived at the Yacht Club shortly before ten, loaded the boat and were off. Michael knew exactly how to handle the craft, and he patiently pointed out levers and buttons and switches for Danica's benefit. She was content to stay close by his elbow, watching, listening, enjoying his nearness and the sense of release that increased with each nautical mile they put behind them.

Heading north, they cruised slowly and comfortably. At midday, Danica brought sandwiches up and they ate side by side, enjoying the food nearly as much as they did the tangy air and the salty sea. By midafternoon, they had passed seaward of Biddeford and Saco and were well into Bigelow Bight, approaching Casco Bay.

Changing into shorts, Danica stretched out on the forward deck, spreading her arms wide, delighting in the way the wind whipped across her skin.

"Like it?" Michael asked, sliding up beside her. He, too, had changed from his shirt and jeans into a tank top and shorts.

"Ahhh, yes." Aside from an initial peek, she kept her eyes closed. "It's won-der-ful."

He slipped his hand between the open tails of her shirt and rubbed the warm flesh of her middle. "You'd better be careful. The wind is deceptive. You can get sunburned."

"Nah. It's too late in the season for much of anything to happen. Besides, my skin's conditioned to the sun. I'll be fine." Her heart was pounding. She chose to attribute it to the exhilaration of the ride, but it slowed as soon as Michael withdrew his hand and stretched out nearby. "Michael? Who's steering?"

"My good friend, Auto. I must have forgotten to point him out. He's a gem."

With a smile, she flipped over onto her stomach and looked across at the shoreline. "Those poor people stuck on land. If they only knew what they were missing."

"Many of them do. They're just not as lucky as we are."

"We are lucky, you know that?" It occurred to her then that even if her relationship with Michael went no further than it had already, she would be forever grateful that he was her friend. He made her life so much easier to take. He inspired her to do so much.

"Why the sad face?"

She glanced down to find him squinting at her, shading his eyes with his hand. "Sad? I hadn't realized."

"What were you thinking about?"

She hesitated for just a minute. "You."

"Good thoughts or bad ones?"

"Good ones, of course."

"Why 'of course'?"

"Why not?"

"Because I may be complicating your life a helluva lot."

"Complicating?" She shimmied closer and propped her chin on her arms on his chest. "You're the best thing that's ever happened to me."

"You shouldn't say things like that. They'll go right to my head." They were going right to other parts as well, but he forced those to the back of his mind.

"I mean it, Michael. Since I met you, my life has had so much more meaning. I keep thinking what it would have been like—things between me and Blake, his appointment—if I hadn't had you. Even when I'm in Boston, I feel better just knowing . . . I've said all this before, I think."

"I like to hear it," he responded quietly. "It helps me cope with everything I'm feeling." When her expression grew pained and she opened her mouth to apologize for causing him what had to be terrible frustration, he put his hand against her lips. "Don't say it. I don't mind what I feel. In some ways my life wasn't much better than yours was before we met. I always tried to tell myself that it was full, that I was doing everything I wanted to be doing, but deep down inside I knew something was missing. Maybe if you'd never come along, I wouldn't have put a finger on it. Maybe I'd have settled for second best without realizing it." He moved his fingers only to lift his head and kiss her softly. "I have to be grateful for what we've had, for what we have right now. It means more to me than you can imagine."

"You're getting maudlin in your old age, Michael Buchanan," she whispered, but there were tears in her eyes and her heart was dangerously full.

He rolled over until she was pinned to the deck beneath him. "No worse than you, pretty lady." With a final smack to her lips, he was up and headed back toward the steering wheel. "I need a swim," he muttered under his breath.

"What?" she called.

"Nothing, sweetheart. Nothing." He didn't want to swim, because the water was like ice, but he had to do something or he would attack Danica before long. She was so beautiful. He cursed softly.

"Michael, what are you saying?" She began to get up.

"You stay there," he growled, pointing to the deck, then he held his open hand up and spoke more gently. "I'm just talking to myself. An old habit. I forget sometimes."

Though Danica stayed put, she wrapped her arms around her knees and sat looking back at Michael. He was so beautiful. Tanned just enough. Muscled just enough. Windblown just enough. And he was beautiful inside, too. She hadn't imagined that a man could be so sensitive to a woman's thoughts and wishes and needs, but he was. He put Blake and her father to shame, because he had success and so much more.

Looking at him, catching his gaze when he looked at her from time to time, she felt a familiar tingling deep inside. She knew what it was, where it was headed. *Don't think it. It's forbidden.* Could anything that promised to be so beautiful be wrong? she asked herself. *There's Blake to consider. He's your husband.* Blake doesn't want me, and I don't want him. *You're married to Blake. You're legally bound.* Can a piece of paper mean more than the feeling two people hold for each other? *What about your parents? They raised you to abide by commitments.* I'm a grown woman now. I have to make my own commitments. *But there's no future in it. You aren't free.* I'm . . . no, I'm not free, am I . . .

She swiveled on her bottom and faced the front of the boat so Michael wouldn't see the agony she felt. She concentrated on the waves, the shore, the horizon, anything to distract her. After a while, when she felt under control, she returned to sit by his side. From time to time they talked about what they saw — a sailboat, the gulls that soared overhead, points of land they passed. Often they simply shared the silence, though it wasn't really silent with the steady hum of the motor and the intermittent slap of waves against the hull, but those were hypnotic in their way and very peaceful.

Unfortunately, Danica couldn't settle the war within herself. It was like indigestion of the mind, she mused, and it gnawed relentlessly. Her thorough awareness of Michael's nearness made things simultaneously better and worse. She saw the way his shoulders flexed as he handled the steering wheel, saw the play of bronzed skin over muscle, sensed the strength, which was virility at its best. She saw the fine mat of tawny hair that edged above his tank top, the finer sprinkling on his forearms, even finer on the backs of his hands. She remembered the way his lips had felt earlier, the way his long, hard body had felt when he had pinned her down for that too brief moment.

She was toying with the fires in hell, but she was freezing and she needed the warmth to survive.

"There." Michael pointed. "That's the island I want."

She tore her gaze from his body and followed the line of his finger. "How do you know? We've passed so many."

"That's the one. I know. These are my old stomping grounds, remember? The big island to the left is Vinalhaven Island. Several of the other smaller ones are privately owned. So is this one, I think, but it's uninhabited. We'll drop anchor near its shore."

The island, a broad hump in the sea speckled with low-growing pines, was indeed uninhabited. They circled it once and saw sign of neither house nor humanity. Choosing the east side of the island for its relative calm, Michael killed the engine and, with Danica scrambling to assist him, dropped anchor.

"Now—" he turned to her and spoke with the satisfaction of the skipper who had done his day's work "—I would like some wine." With comical suddenness he grimaced. "Shit, do we have a corkscrew?"

She laughed. "I saw one down below. Don't ask me to use it, though. It doesn't have ears, so it'll take brute strength."

"Brute strength I've got, but I may need replenishment pretty quick. Can any of the stuff you made be eaten cold? I'm famished."

Smiling, she nodded. "I think I can find something." She climbed down the few steps into the cabin, which looked golden in the late afternoon sunlight that was filtering through the windows. Michael followed, taking the cork-screw she handed him and deftly opening the wine. In turn, she set out pâté and crackers for him to start on while she cooked the ramaki on the small butane stove.

"Mmmm, is this good!" he managed to garble through a mouthful of pâté. "You really made it yourself?"

"Yup," she answered without turning around. Something about the small-ness of the cabin, the fact that they had dropped anchor, the knowledge that they would be spending the night here, was making her edgy. It wasn't that she was afraid Michael might force her into something she didn't want; she knew that he would simply spend the night beside her if need be. What frightened her was the "something she didn't want" part because she didn't know if it was true. Her insides were a taut rope, with Michael at one end and Blake at the other. Michael was stronger and looked to be winning one moment; the next Blake gave a persevering tug.

When the ramaki was done, she joined Michael, but she merely nibbled on a cracker, the most her stomach could take. Even the wine, which might have settled her, held little appeal.

"Did I ever tell you about my friends who have a houseboat on the Missis-sippi?" Michael sat back against the dinette cushion, his wineglass in his hand.

She forced a smile, knowing he was trying to relax her. "No. Tell me about your friends who have a houseboat on the Mississippi."

"It's this big box of a thing. Ugly as sin. But fun? It's fantastic. A little home, really. I was down in Natchez once and they picked me up."

Danica struggled to concentrate on what he was saying, but she barely heard a word through the bedlam in her mind. Michael was so close, so dear, so willing. *There are other factors to be considered.* Those factors aren't here! *They should be.* But they're not and if they were, really were, I wouldn't be agonizing like this now. *You're making a mistake.* Maybe I'm only correcting mistakes of the past. *The past isn't over.* It is! There's nothing there! *But you can't divorce Blake, can you?* Oh, God, I can't think. *Are you being fair to Blake? Are you being fair to Michael?* What about me? What about what I want?

She squeezed her eyes shut and covered her face with her hands.

Michael put his arm around her. "What is it, sweetheart?"

Bolting from her seat, she pressed her trembling hands, then forehead to the cool paneled door of the forward cabin.

He was behind her in an instant, turning her to see her tears. "Don't cry, sweetheart," he begged. "Please, don't cry."

"I'm so tired, Michael."

He was breathing as hard as she was. "Maybe you—"

"I'm so tired of fighting it," she sobbed and sagged against him. "My mind goes i-in circles and my insides churn and the only thing that makes any sense is that I love you."

He was very still for a full second, then fiercely closed his arms about her. "You've never said the words before," he breathed unevenly. "You've looked them and acted them, but you've never said them before."

"I've thought them for such a long time and I've fought it because one part of me says that I shouldn't, but I c-can't help the way I feel! It's draining, the war is, and it makes me weak." She lifted her tear-streaked face to his and whispered, "Make me whole, Michael. I need you so badly."

He swallowed hard. "Do you know what you're asking?"

She nodded slowly. "I'm tired of fighting ghosts that shouldn't be there. I'm tired of letting something meaningless take away from me the one thing that has the most meaning in my life. I'm tired of feeling stifled, of feeling that there's so much love inside that if I don't do something with it I'm going to burst. I love you so much."

"Oh, God," he murmured, smoothing her hair back with hands that shook. "Are you sure? I want you to be sure. I don't think I can bear it if you're sorry afterward."

Lifting her hands to his face, she gently traced the features she so adored. "I won't be sorry. This has to be the best thing I've ever done."

Michael's body was already alive and when he saw the love in her eyes his control snapped. His mouth captured hers and ravaged it, but the ravaging was two-sided because Danica's control was gone as well. Having made the decision, she felt an urgency she had never known.

The door to the forward cabin was open then and, barely severing their kiss, they stumbled in and fell onto the V-berth. She was tugging at his tank top, greedily running her hands over his chest, his back, his chest again, while he tore at the buttons of her shirt. When they were both bare from the waist up, he hugged her to him. Her breasts flared against his chest and he wanted to touch them, to kiss them, but she was already tugging at his shorts and he knew that he had as little patience as she did. They had lived over a year of foreplay; there wouldn't be any teasing now.

Their hands tangled as each fought with the other's fastenings. Zippers were tugged, fabric was pulled, and then they were naked and straining for fulfillment.

"I love you, Dani," Michael gasped as he spread her thighs. With a groan he entered her. She cried out at the beauty of the union. But there was no time for more than repeated murmurings of love as they thrust violently toward each other, away, then back again, deeper, harder. And then there was no breath even for that because everything they felt for each other was gathering toward an explosive climax that went on and on in seemingly endless spasms until, at last, they fell back on the bed in a state of utter exhaustion. The sound of harsh panting filled the small cabin, slowing gradually as the minutes passed.

Danica couldn't move, but it wasn't that Michael's weight was too much, because she loved that, too. She loved the way his chest, his belly, his thighs pressed hers. She loved the way his entire being filled her senses. She was spent but exhilarated, tired but happy. When he slowly slid to her side, she turned with him, reluctant to let him go far.

"I love you, Dani," he whispered, folding her in his arms and pressing his face to her hair. "I love you so much."

She ran her hand along his damp skin to his hip. Her pulse was still racing, but at a breathable pace now. "You're so wonderful. And I love you, too."

"I never imagined it'd be that way. I mean, I knew it would be fantastic. Everything else between us always has been. But in my dreams I imagined undressing you slowly, looking at you, touching and kissing every part until you couldn't take it anymore."

"I couldn't. I thought I'd die when I couldn't get your shorts off."

He chuckled and shifted position so that he could see her face. It was flushed and damp. He gently kissed dots of moisture from her nose. "Are you happy?"

"Very."

"No second thoughts?"

"None. How could what we did be wrong? You said it once yourself, that it was only a deeper expression of what we already felt."

"That it was, but there was nothing 'only' about it. It was un-be-lievable!"

She smiled, knowing she felt more feminine and better loved at that moment than in all of the moments of her life combined. She smoothed her hand up from his hip to his chest, delighting in the firmness of his skin, in the rock-hard strength beneath. She closed her eyes and took a deep breath, imprinting the scent of his love-warmed body on her senses.

They lay like that, enjoying the quiet closeness as their bodies fully recovered from what had hit each with such force. Then Michael gently pressed her back to the bed.

"I want to look at you," he explained in a voice that shook with emotion. The light in the cabin was waning, but it was enough to cast a glow on her skin, and propped on an elbow, he took in every inch. His eyes touched her breasts, slid down to her navel, then lower.

Had it been anyone but Michael looking so openly at her naked body, Danica might have tried to cover herself. She wasn't used to such exposure, but the adoration in his eyes made mockery of her modesty. Tiny ripples of excitement surged through her as his gaze explored one spot, then another. When his hand slid around and over her breast, she bit her lip. Her nipple responded with an instant tightening, which its mate mirrored when his fingers spread the joy. She was trying not to arch off the bed when his hand fell to caress her hips, then her stomach, then the fair curls at the apex of her thighs.

A small whimper slipped through her lips. She closed her eyes and turned her head to the side even as she strained closer to the fingers that were opening her, stroking her. "Michael!" she gasped.

Without removing his hand, he leaned forward to lick the corner of her mouth. "You're lovely." His voice was thick.

"I'm awful. I mean, after that . . . I was so . . . I should be weak and tired . . . this couldn't be."

"It feels good?"

"Oh yes."

"That's how it should be."

She turned her head and looked up to find him grinning. "Not again. It's too soon . . ."

"You're not the only one who feels it." His voice was hoarse but held a definite satisfaction. Reaching for her hand, he drew it down his body. She resisted at first, but he was firm in the gentle way that was Michael, so she let him curl her fingers around him. When her eyes widened in surprise, he laughed. "When it's good, it's good."

"But I didn't think men could . . ."

"I believe," he teased gruffly, "that you have proof to the contrary in your hand." He was showing her the motion that most pleased him, and when she'd begun, timidly at first, to mimic the caress on her own, he returned his fingers to the warm, hidden spot that cried so silently for them.

He marveled at her innocence. From the very first he had known that she had been sheltered from many of the greatest joys of life, but he had never allowed himself to think of her innocence in sexual terms. She had been married for nine years. He had assumed that she was thoroughly aware of a man's body and her own. It seemed he had assumed wrong. In more ways than one he was pleased. He would be the one to teach her the fine art of love, to teach her the glory of her own body and the ways she could glory in his. She might not have come to him a virgin, but in many ways she was as pure, which made her every response that much more sweet, that much more stimulating. She wasn't acting on habit or fore-knowledge or training. She was acting on love.

This time he entered her only after he had done the kissing and touching he had so long dreamed of doing. He tasted every inch of her skin, nipping and sucking until she cried out his name, which encouraged him all the more. She was writhing and clutching his back by the time he reached his own limit. He watched her face as he slowly eased into her, delighting in the wonder she couldn't hide because it was too strong, too real, too heartfelt.

As much as his body would endure he prolonged the mating. He buried himself deep in her, then withdrew, slowly, nearly completely, before surging forward again. She sighed and moaned and sought his lips in a frenzy, but only when she caught her breath, held it, then burst into ragged gasps did he permit his own powerful release.

Arms and legs entwined, they slept then. When Danica awoke, the cabin was totally dark. Disoriented, it took her a minute to remember where she was and what was causing the weight that curved around her waist and over her legs.

"Hi, sleepyhead," came a familiar voice in the darkness.

"Michael! For a minute I didn't know . . ."

"Was it strange?"

"Yes. No. I mean, I've slept like this so often . . . no, that's not what I mean . . . I mean, I've dreamed of being with you so much that there's nothing strange about it, but it's so dark and at first I wasn't sure if I was still dreaming but your leg is very real and . . . and I'm . . . babbling."

He was laughing. "Don't stop on my account. I love it."

"I love you," she breathed, snuggling closer to his warmth as her heart resumed its normal beat. "What time is it?"

"Nearly ten."

"Have you been awake for long?"

"Long enough to get *my* bearings and to realize that I wasn't dreaming, either."

"Are you hungry?"

"Very."

"I can't move."

"I could always munch on cold ramaki."

"Yuk. Throw it overboard. Let the sharks have it."

"There are no sharks in this water, Dani."

"Oh." She took a breath. "Something else will eat it, then. As for me, I could go for one of those nice big juicy steaks we bought."

"That's supposed to be my line."

"Then we'll reverse roles all the way. You cook."

"Wh-whoa, wait a minute. I always cook. At least, whenever we're at my house I do. *You* cook. I can't move."

She pressed a kiss to his chest. "That was my line. I think we're going in circles. How 'bout if we both cook?"

"I guess I can live with that. Of course, there's still the problem of getting off this damned bed."

"I don't know. This bed is pretty nice."

"I am *not* going to serve you dinner here."

"You're serving dinner?" she asked sweetly.

He scrambled to his knees and picked her up, crawled to the edge of the bed, then promptly stumbled across the minuscule floor space and into the door. Danica yelped. Michael turned to brace his back against the wood.

"Shit, this place is too small."

"That's what you get for playing macho. Put me down. My funny bone kills."

He lowered her slowly, deliberately letting her body slide down his. "Good thinking. We'd never have gotten through the door that way." His hands were crossed over her bottom. "Wanna shower together."

"No way." She was arching back from him, rubbing her elbow. "I saw the shower. It was definitely not made for two."

"I think you're shy." He began to rotate his hips against hers.

"Mostly practical. And at the rate *you're* going, bud, you won't be able to fit in that shower even alone."

"Are you complaining?" he asked in a husky tone.

"Me? Complain about you?" Elbow forgotten, she put her arms around his neck as he hoisted her up and brought her legs around his hips. "I'd never complain."

"You don't sound sure," he murmured against her lips.

"It's not that I'm not sure, it's just that . . . I think the steak can . . . wait a little . . . longer . . . ." Her voice had grown steadily softer and the last of the sound disappeared into his mouth as it closed over hers. Drawn into his kiss, she waited for him to lay her back on the bed, but instead he simply raised her hips and lowered her onto his hardness. She gasped and clung more tightly to his neck, then muffled another cry against him when he began to do something with his finger that made the rhythmic thrust of his hips all the more electric. She was sizzling, burning, exploding into a million scattered pieces, and she wouldn't have cared if she had died just then because she knew she would have died happy.

* * *

Sometime around midnight, the steaks were delicious, as was their lovemaking when they returned to bed soon after, then again when they awoke at dawn. Danica had never known the physical pleasure Michael showed her, though she knew it would have been nothing without the love that surged uncontrollably between them. If she was stunned by her own abandon, which only increased each time, she was no less stunned by Michael's gentle skill, his patience, his fiercely tender passion. As she grew freer in touching his body, he grew bolder in touching hers. At one point, when he slid her to the edge of the bed and knelt between her knees, she demurred, only to be gentled by soft words, then sent to heaven by a velvet tongue, and that inhibition fell with the rest.

By the next morning she doubted she would ever walk again. "I feel about eighty years old," she told Michael over a breakfast of bacon and eggs.

"You don't look it. You're glowing."

She grinned. "Now that's a line if I've ever heard one. You're just making excuses for what your beard did."

He stared at her cheeks, then rubbed his jaw. "I think you're right. I should have shaved."

But she quickly reached out to stroke the light stubble. "I was just teasing. I didn't mind it. You look handsome with a shadow. Did anyone ever tell you that?" When he shook his head but still seemed unsure, she went on. "I remember it from the day I met you for the very first time. You looked so roguish then, but you were gentle, always gentle. I don't think you could be any other way."

"With you, no." He leaned forward to kiss her, sweetly and at length, before dragging himself off to shave.

Danica insisted on watching, which was not the easiest thing given the size of the head, but it was a small intimacy to go with the others and was a precursor of the day to come. They were beside each other constantly, holding hands, kissing, touching, making up for lost time and enjoying every minute.

They cruised leisurely through Penobscot Bay, then made their way slowly south, back down the coast, before dropping anchor for the night by an island just east of Port Clyde. They ate in style, by candlelight, with wine, and spent hours lying on the V-berth just talking, being close. Their lovemaking was different then, slower, more savoring, richer for the knowledge each had gained of the other, fuller for the confidence they shared.

Sated and content, they fell asleep. When Danica awoke the next morning, it was to the sound of the engine and the forward motion of the boat. Throwing on her clothes, she ran to the helm.

"Why didn't you wake me? I should have gotten up with you!"

Michael drew her close to his side. "It's only seven, and you were exhausted." He kissed her temple. "This thing's due back at ten, though. I figured I'd better get a move on."

The thought of returning to land put a damper on what was already a cloudy day. Danica tried to push it from her mind. "Have you eaten anything?"

"Nope."

"Would you like something?"

"Yup."

With a gentle smile and a promising pat to his stomach, she returned to the cabin and made breakfast. After they'd eaten, she cleaned up as best she could, then returned to his side. But the closer they came to Kennebunkport, the more uneasy she felt. Occasional glances at Michael told her that he too sensed the encroachment of reality. Though he maintained a constant physical contact with her—an arm around her waist or her shoulder, or her hand held tightly in his—he seemed somehow distant. They were thirty minutes from home when he abruptly killed the engine and turned to her.

"Divorce Blake, Dani. Divorce Blake and marry me."

For a minute she couldn't breathe. She wondered if she had known it was coming, if it was precisely this that she had feared might happen if their fantasy was given full reign.

"I know how you feel about divorce," he went on, his features tense, "and I know how you feel about your family. But we have something that most people spend a lifetime looking for and never find. We can't just let it go."

Danica stared up at him, wishing more than anything that he hadn't raised the issue but knowing that he wouldn't have been Michael if he hadn't, particularly given the weekend they had just spent. She was almost surprised he had waited this long. She took an unsteady breath, then moved to the far side of the boat and tucked her hands deep in her pockets.

"Talk to me, Dani. Say something."

She hesitated. When she finally spoke, her voice was soft and filled with a feminine version of the pain she had heard in his deeper voice. "What can I say?"

"Say 'yes.' Say 'no.' Say *something*."

She shook her head. "There's not much I *can* say. I've been through this so many times myself. I've asked the questions and made the arguments and gone back and forth with my mind saying one thing and my heart saying another, and I just don't know what the answer is. I don't think I can do anything, at least not yet."

Michael clenched a fist in frustration. "But what do you have with Blake that I can't give you?" When she simply shook her head and refused to look at him, he went on. "You hate Washington, which Blake loves. He hates Maine, which you love. Boston is the only ground you really share and do you really share it? From what you've said, the time you spend together is purely for the sake of social obligation. It's a marriage without feeling. Am I wrong?" She didn't answer. "Am I? When was the last time you laughed with him? When was the last time you enjoyed yourself, really enjoyed yourself, with him? When was the last time you made love with him the way you did this weekend with me?"

"Never!" Then she lowered her voice to a near whisper. "We haven't made love in over a year."

He had suspected as much, though he had felt guilty hoping it. "Have you missed it?"

She answered in the same small voice. "No. It's a mutual aversion at this point."

"Then what do you have with him?"

"Sex isn't everything."

"But it's something, one thing, and it's supposed to be a vital part of any marriage. The fact that it doesn't exist in yours, that neither of you seems to care, should tell you something."

She looked up then, her expression one of defeat. "Of course it tells me something. It tells me a whole lot. But there are so many other things to consider."

"Other things, or other people?"

"Whatever. Oh, Michael, don't you see? I know what you want, and in so many ways that it hurts, it's what I want, too. It's just that I've lived with certain other things for so long that I can't just turn around and ignore them as if they don't exist."

"Didn't this weekend mean anything to you?"

"God, yes! It's meant the world! In some ways I feel like a totally different person. I was never this way with Blake."

He had to hear her say the words. "What way?"

She faltered, feeling selfconscious but knowing that what she said was the truth. "Free with my body. Free to let go. Free to enjoy my partner's . . . your body."

"And why do you think that is?" he asked quietly.

"I *know* why, and so do you! It's because we love each other, because you're that kind of person and maybe because I always was but never knew it before. But it doesn't change things, Michael, at least not everything. I still have other responsibilities." She took a shaky breath. "This weekend puts a new light on things. When I said I had no second thoughts about our making love, I meant it, but that doesn't mean I can forget about everything else. I need time, Michael. I know that's asking a lot, but I need time." She looked away. "I have to consider what all of this will do to Blake. I have to consider what it will do to my father."

"To hell with your father! What about what it'll do to *you* if you stick with Blake? Have you stopped to consider that?"

"I don't have to. I'm the one who's been unhappy for years."

"So?"

She pressed her palm to the deck by her hip. "I'm also the one who has always wanted to do the right thing."

"The right thing as your father defines it, Dani."

"He is my father. I can't write that off."

Sensing he was pushing too hard, Michael softened. "I know. I know. It's just that I wish I could make you see that you've spent your life trying to please him and it hasn't worked. Because of his ambition, what should have been wonderfully carefree years for you were years of sweating and struggling on one tennis court or another, and for what? Something you once enjoyed lost all meaning. Same thing with your marriage. You had dreams of what you wanted, and where have they gone? You've tried to please your father, and that's noble and good and it shows that despite everything you love him. But maybe you *can't* please him. Maybe it's not worth it, if the price you have to pay is too high. It was with tennis; you realized that yourself. Isn't it time you analyze your marriage to Blake the same way?"

"It is, and I have. It's just that things are complicated."

"They don't have to be, Dani. You have a life of your own now. You're not dependent on Blake. You have your own interests, your own friends, even the means to support yourself."

"It's not a matter of money."

"I know that. But at some point you have to stand back and see yourself as the strong, independent woman you are. You don't need your father's approval. And besides, your father won't be around forever."

"Michael!"

He held up a hand and spoke very softly as he approached her. "He's mortal, Dani. Just like the rest of us. Someday something's going to happen, and when it does, are you going to find yourself looking back resenting all you didn't have, all you didn't do?"

"Michael, please."

He had his hands on her shoulders and was gently kneading the tension he found. "You don't need *anyone*'s approval if you decide to do what you believe is right. I wish you could see that."

"I'm trying, but it takes time." She crumbled against him. "Don't make me make promises now, Michael. I can't. I just can't."

Feeling her agony, he folded her in his arms and held her tightly. "I love you so much, Dani. I want us to be together, but if I can't have that, at least I want to know that you're happy. I think that's what bothers me most. I hate the idea of your suffering through this charade with Blake, because that's all it is, a charade."

Danica had no argument. So much of what Michael said was right, but when she thought of going back to Boston or Washington and announcing she was going to divorce Blake, she felt something akin to terror prickle her skin. Blake would be hurt, her mother would be disappointed, her father would be livid and the press would be in seventh heaven.

And then there was Michael, whom she loved more than she had ever loved another soul. For a long time she didn't speak, but simply drank in his nearness and the strength that was always there. When she looked up, his tender expression touched her. With a melancholy smile, she whispered her fingers across the crow's feet at the corners of his eyes, then the grooves by his mouth. "You have creases."

"I've earned them."

"But they're the best kind." She thought of the tea tag she had read to Reggie that night in Boston. "You've been happy. Regardless of what you say about feeling something was missing, you've been happy."

"Happiness is relative. I'm happier now."

"But your life has been good. I hope I don't do anything to spoil that," she said more quietly.

"How could you? You bring me joy."

"I also bring you pain, and I wish it didn't have to be. You love me and want to marry me, and I love you but I can't marry you. At least, not now. Not yet.

There's too much I have to work out. Will you give me time, Michael? Will you wait?"

He took a deep breath and released it slowly, willing the knot in his throat to ease. "I don't have any choice, do I?"

"You do," she said fearfully.

"No, Dani. I don't have any choice at all. I'll wait because you're worth it. I want you to remember that. You're worth it."

TWELVE

THE WEEKEND AFTER DANICA returned to Boston, she flew to Washington to see Blake. He had requested that she accompany him to a dinner party on Saturday night given in honor of a visiting dignitary, but even if he hadn't asked her down, she would have gone. She had to talk with him. One of them had to broach the topic of their deteriorating relationship, and it appeared that he wasn't going to be the one.

As it happened, he was at the office when she arrived on Saturday morning, and he returned only in time to change into a tuxedo and take her out. When she awoke on Sunday morning, he was playing squash. The first opportunity she had to talk with him was that afternoon, a short time before she was due to fly back to Boston.

His houseboy had fixed them an early dinner, then had left, and they were alone. Blake was about to vanish into his den when she stopped him.

"Blake? Have you got a minute?"

He glanced at his watch. "I need to make several calls before we leave for the airport."

"Can't it wait? There's something I'd like to talk to you about."

Though he seemed vaguely discomfited, he returned to his seat. "Yes?"

"I think that we ought to discuss what's happening?"

He hesitated for only an instant. "All right. What's happening?"

She resented his deliberate blandness, and that gave her the courage to blurt, "Our relationship is going nowhere." She saw a flicker of something in his eyes, but it was gone before she could identify it.

"Where did you expect it to go?" he asked in a pleasant tone, flashing her a patronizing smile.

"I'm not sure, but I didn't expect it would stagnate."

"Is that what you think it's doing? Danica, we've been married for nine years."

"And by rights we should be closer than ever. But we're not. We lead very separate lives."

"Whose fault is that?" he asked calmly.

"I won't take the full blame. Marriage is a two-way street. Each partner has to give."

"Danica, what do you want of me? I have a critical job with the government. I give as much as I can."

"To the government, yes."

"And not to you?" His laugh was short, his handsome features hard and belying humor. "What would you have me do?"

"You make no attempt to come see me in Boston. You didn't make it up to Maine once this summer." She wasn't sorry about either fact, but she felt they had to be said.

"My life is here now, and I'm very busy. I'm grateful that you're willing to make the trip down from time to time."

She felt she was dealing with a piece of wood. "Don't you want anything more? Don't you think that a marriage should be something more than an occasional weekend together?"

Blake pondered that for only a minute. "There are many kinds of marriages. In some the partners are inseparable. In others, such as ours, they lead independent lives. Commuting marriages are common. And as I recall, it was your idea. You were the one who didn't care to live here."

"You know why, but you don't want to accept it."

"I accept it perfectly well, which is why I don't know what's upsetting you. As I see it, we've reached a satisfactory compromise. What's the problem?"

Danica took a deep breath. "Blake, do you see other women here?"

"Of course I do. There are women everywhere I go."

"Do you *date* other women?"

He lowered his brows in his first show of impatience. "Of course not. I'm married to you. I wouldn't date other women."

"But don't you want to *be* with a woman?"

"What are you getting at?" he grumbled.

She couldn't believe he was so thick. "You're a man. I'd think you'd want female companionship far more than you're getting it."

"I'm busy. I don't have time to think about female companionship, much less seek it out." He gentled his voice. "Seeing you when you come down is enough."

She sighed. If he had intended his words to be flattering, they weren't. He was thinking solely of himself, as though by rights the parameters of their marriage should be defined by his needs. "Well, maybe it's not enough for me," she said quietly. "Maybe I need something more."

For an instant he was stunned, and she actually felt sorry for him. "I hadn't realized," he murmured at last. "I guess I've been so busy that I haven't thought about that."

"I have. A whole lot. There are times when I wonder if it wouldn't be better for both of us if we were free. You could find someone to satisfy your needs here. I could find someone to satisfy my needs in Boston."

"What are you suggesting?" he asked, his body deadly still.

"Maybe we should think about divorce."

"Divorce? I don't want a divorce! That's the craziest thing I've ever heard!"

Studying the utter horror on his face, she was humbled. But she had come too far to stop just yet. "Maybe it's the most practical," she offered softly. "You don't seem to take great joy in my company. I don't think you're particularly interested in what I'm doing."

"Of course I am! I ask you about your work, don't I?"

"Mostly I tell you about it. There are times when I feel you're hardly listening."

"I'm listening. I always listen. But it's your job. I would no more tell you how to go about doing it than I would expect you to tell me how to do mine."

She was shaking her head. "That's only a small point among many. We share so little in life, Blake. We have different interests, different friends. Do you remember when the last time we made love was?" He should have. She certainly did. It had been sixteen months ago, in Maine, when she had all but seduced him, when she had become pregnant.

He shrugged and frowned. "I don't keep a scorecard."

"Doesn't it occur to you that it's been a while?"

"Danica, I don't define my life in terms of sex. I'm forty-six years old. I think of other things now."

"Well, I'm twenty-nine, and I do think about the nonexistent love life I have with my husband."

Jumping from his chair, Blake paced to the far side of the dining room. He stood with his back to her, his hands on his hips. "Is that what you're missing most? Sex?"

"Of course it isn't. It's just one other thing that makes me wonder whether we have anything left at all."

"Christ, I don't believe this," he muttered. "I'm the one who should be going through a mid-life crisis, not you." He whirled around. "What is it you want?"

She crushed her linen napkin into a ball in her lap and spoke very quietly. "I want a family, Blake. I want a husband who's around, and children—"

"We tried for children and you lost it!"

Stung, she lashed back. "*We* weren't trying. I was."

He made a dismissing gesture with his hand. "The end result was the same. I thought I was being considerate giving your body a chance to recover."

"For sixteen months?"

He totally ignored that. "And as for a husband who's around, I *am* around. Around *here*. If you wanted, you could be with me more. It's been your choice to stay in Boston."

"But things weren't any different in Boston. You were always busy there, too."

"Damn it, I have a career. A very important one. I never promised you I'd sit around at home holding your hand, did I? *Did* I?"

He was angry. Danica felt her own rebellion wane. "No."

"I never gave you cause to believe that we'd have anything other than what we have now."

"When we were first married—"

"We were both a lot younger then. We had fewer responsibilities, and being married was a novelty. But the honeymoon's over, Danica. It has been for a long time. We've moved on, and I think you're being very shortsighted if you feel no pride in the direction we've gone. It's not every woman whose husband is named to the Cabinet."

"But what about me?" she asked in a small voice. "What about the direction I've taken?"

"It seems to me you've done pretty well," he retorted, gaining force as she lost it. "I give you the kind of freedom that some men would never give their wives because I'm self-confident enough to allow it. You have your work with Governor Bryant. You have your friends. You have your house in Maine. You even have that Buchanan fellow. Let me tell you, some husbands would never stand for *that*. Some husbands would be jealous. But I'm not. I realize you have to have your own friends, and I'm happy you do." His eyes grew steely. "But what I won't stand for is talk of divorce. I don't want one. You're my wife, and I like it that way. The arrangement we have is very comfortable for me. So I'd suggest you grow up a little and accept what's best for you."

She opened her mouth to protest when Blake stalked from the room, calling over his shoulder, "I'm going to make those calls you've kept me from, and after that I'll drive you to the airport. You can leave the things on the table. John will clean up when he gets back."

Danica stared after his retreating figure. Only when she heard the den door shut did she blink, then swallow. She hadn't known what she had expected, but it was certainly a little more tenderness than he had shown. Either that or that he would have agreed to a divorce. But he hadn't. He had rejected it in no uncertain terms. He had opted for the playing out of their prescribed roles, just as her father would have done in the same situation. She wondered if her mother had ever put her foot down, then decided not, because her mother was an accommodator. And Danica? What was she? She couldn't bear the thought of continuing with Blake, particularly after what she had found with Michael. But the battle lines were drawn. Blake would fight her. She knew her parents would fight her, too.

Discouraged, she allowed Blake to drive her to the airport. He made no reference to their talk, indeed said little during the drive. She made no attempt to break the silence because her thoughts were too raw. Their parting was as dispassionate as was everything else about Blake. When he leaned down to give her a dutiful kiss, it was on her cheek and she was grateful. Her lips ached for another man, and having known his kiss so thoroughly, one from her husband was a sacrilege.

Danica tried to settle back into routine, but her thoughts were never far from Michael. She worked diligently with James, going over what she had written during the summer, discussing the direction of the last few chapters of their book, but her concentration when she was home alone was often broken by brooding. She resumed her ballet classes, delighting in seeing all her friends again, but they didn't come home with her, either. On those mornings when she had board meetings at the Art Institute or the hospital, she found herself looking at the other women around the table, wondering if they were happy in their marriages, if they were loyal to their spouses and their spouses to them. She knew that several of them were on second, even third marriages, and she wished she were close enough to any of them to talk about it. But there was a formality among these people that she could never quite breach, so her questions went unanswered.

On the day that Michael was due to arrive in Boston, she stayed home, waiting. His call came at three in the afternoon.

"Lord, I'm sorry, Dani. I wanted to call you sooner, but they've had damned meetings scheduled since ten. How are you, sweetheart?"

"Missing you. When will you be done?"

"I should be free by six. Can you make it for dinner?"

She answered quickly and without pride. "I can make it for anything. You name the time and place."

He smiled at her urgency, which fed his own. "I love you."

"I love you, too. . . . Time and place?"

He named them, having decided that a small Greek restaurant on the outskirts of the Square would give them the privacy they sought. "Dani, maybe I should pick you up. I'm not sure I like the idea of your driving around at night."

"No, this is better. I'll lock all the doors. It'll be fine."

"You're sure?" He knew that what she said made sense. Though neither of them had spoken of proprieties, both knew that the more unnoticed their meeting went, the better.

"I'm sure . . . I can't wait, Michael," she whispered.

"Me, neither. I'm not sure how I'm going to make it through these meetings. It was bad . . . morning . . ." The connection broke momentarily.

"Ooops. There's your dime."

"That wasn't any three minutes," he yelled to an operator who wasn't listening.

"You'd better go, Michael. We'll have plenty of time to talk later. Okay?"

"Okay. Love you."

"Love you, too."

Danica hung up the phone feeling warmed as she hadn't since she had returned from Maine ten days before. She basked in the feeling for the rest of the afternoon, then dressed with special care. With just a momentary touch of guilt, she told Mrs. Hannah that she would be having dinner with a friend and that she wouldn't be back until late, but she was firm when the housekeeper suggested that Marcus could drive her wherever it was she was going.

"Thank Marcus for me, but I feel like driving myself," she said, taking the keys to the Audi and heading out to the courtyard. She hadn't lied. She felt strong, full of energy, very much on top of the world.

Her headiness didn't diminish even when it took her ten minutes and three trips around the block to find a parking space. She was running when she reached the restaurant, but it was a wise expenditure of energy in light of the self-control she had to then exercise to keep from flying into Michael's arms and telling the whole world she was in love.

With Michael in much the same state, they babbled steadily through dinner, not seeing what they ate and caring less. They skipped dessert. He couldn't get the check fast enough. Then they were out of the restaurant and he was walking her to her car, leaning low to kiss her in the opportune darkness of the quiet side street. Drawing back at last, he reached into his pocket and pressed his hotel key into her hand. "I'll follow you until we get there. Then you go on up. I'll join you in a minute."

She nodded, which was all she could do because she was shaking all over and not from fear of discovery. Being so near Michael yet unable to touch him, to say those things her heart needed to say, had been sheer torture. Only with the greatest of control did she manage to start her car, then wait until Michael had pulled up beside her. The ten-minute drive seemed endless. Her excitement grew such that her body was high-pitched and taut by the time she finally pulled into the parking lot. Michael pulled in beside her, then sat.

Taking a deep breath to steady her movements, she slid from the car and entered the lobby of the hotel, took the elevator to the eighth floor, found the room and let herself in. Once there, she leaned back against the door and waited, heart thudding, body trembling, juices flowing in anticipation of Michael, his body, his love.

His knock came so softly that she mightn't have heard it, given the hammering of her pulse, had she not been braced against the door. She peered out. He slid in. Then they were in each other's arms, hugging, kissing, laughing and sighing until even that wasn't enough.

"You look beautiful," Michael rasped, sliding her thin wool sheath up over her hips. "I love your dress." The item was over her head and discarded in a heap that would have made lie of his praise had Danica not understood, and shared, his impatience. She was tugging at his tie.

"You look gorgeous all dressed up," she said in hurried breaths. She left his tie draped loosely around his neck while she attacked the buttons of his shirt. "I've never seen you this way. You'll drive female students wild."

"I won't even see them," he managed, sending her slip the way of her dress. He fumbled with his belt, jerked down his zipper and shucked his pants while she threw her stockings aside.

Within minutes they were naked and falling on the bed, each touching the other with a greed born of a deprivation that seemed to have stretched for longer than ten days.

"I love you. Oh, baby, I love you," he panted, making a place for himself between her legs and thrusting upward.

Danica cried out and held him tightly, wrapping her legs around his waist, rising from the bed to meet his deep thrusts. It was only minutes before they climaxed, then an eternity of bliss and a slower, more reluctant return to earth.

"I've missed you," she breathed against his damp chest. "It's seemed like forever."

He held her snugly against him, an arm around her shoulders, a thigh over hers anchoring her to his hip. As physically sated as they were at that moment, neither would allow sleep to steal even a second of the time they had together. When they recovered enough to talk, they did. When talking gave way to revived physical needs, they made love again. Then there was more to say, more to share. All too soon, and with great reluctance, Danica pushed herself from the bed and reached for her clothes.

"I wish you didn't have to leave," he said.

She stepped into her panties, and sat to pull on her stockings. "So do I. But I have to get home or Mrs. Hannah will wonder." Even as she spoke, she hated the words. She didn't want to have to hide when what she was hiding was so wonderful. She knew that Michael felt the same because his jaw was tight, his expression grim.

She fastened her bra and pulled on her slip. Unable to resist, she looked back at Michael's sprawled form. "You have a beautiful body," she murmured, running her hand through the hair on his chest. It was warm and looked more golden than tawny in the dim light that flowed from the nightstand. She felt she was touching a treasure. But the treasure didn't end at his chest. It descended over the lean plane of his stomach, over narrow hips and the limp but nonetheless impressive parts that made him man, over the sinewed strength of legs that stretched forever. She met his gaze and smiled. "A bronzed god with a heart of gold. I love you, Michael."

Grasping her elbows, he hauled her over him and kissed her in eloquent return of the vow. By the time he was done, he was no longer limp, and she had to force herself from the bed to keep from responding to his desire.

"You'll be here for another day?" she asked.

He pushed himself up against the headboard and dragged a sheet over himself in the hope that what was out of sight would be out of mind. "I finish up tomorrow afternoon. I could drive back tomorrow night—" when she gasped, he grinned "—but I won't. I'll stay over if you can think of good reason why I should."

Throwing caution to the winds, she returned to the bed. As she kissed him, she stroked him through the sheet, stopping only when he arched upward in greater need.

"Good reason," he rasped. "That's it. Of course, I'll be in agony until then. Dani, you're not playing fair."

Because she loved him so much and because what she'd started had affected her nearly as much as it had him, she kissed him again, this time sliding her hand under the sheet.

"Take off your panties," he whispered into her mouth. "Just your panties. I'll be quick."

"No. Let me."

"Dani . . ." But he moaned and said nothing more, because she knew what she was doing and he couldn't think with the pleasure she gave him. When she eased the sheet back and leaned lower, he tried again. "Dani . . . no . . . ahhhh, my God . . . Dani . . ."

She was using her tongue and lips as he had done to her, and the love she felt for him bridged whatever gaps remained in her education. Eyes closed tightly, head pressed to the side, he strained upward. The tendons of his arms stood out vividly. His outspread fingers dug into the sheet. He gasped her name once more, caught his breath, then felt his body explode.

She was kissing him sweetly on the mouth when he finally regained awareness. "That was wonderful," she said with a feline smile, and, though still dazed, he sensed the full extent of her love.

"That was wonderful," he echoed, but weakly, because every inch of his body felt drained. He took a long, shuddering breath. "And you've won because there's no way I can touch you any more tonight. I don't think I'm going to move till morning."

"No need," she said softly. "When do you have to get up?"

"Seven," he mumbled without opening his eyes.

Without another word, she picked up the phone and requested a wake-up call, then quietly finished dressing and kissed him softly. He was already asleep. For a final moment she gazed at him from the door, then, smiling, carefully shut it and headed home.

The next night was every bit as heavenly. They ate at a different restaurant this time but returned to his hotel in much the same manner and spent the next hours in bliss. Unfortunately, the bliss faded when Danica dressed to leave.

"I don't like this, Dani. I don't like having to sneak around with you as though what we're doing is wrong. I don't like having to starve for a week between feedings."

She laughed and gently stroked his cheek. "You've been with Rusty too much. He always did make a fuss about mealtimes."

"I'm not talking about food," he growled.

"I know." She grew more serious. "I know. But I don't know what to say."

"Say you'll divorce Blake. This is getting ridiculous."

"I need more time, Michael. I'm trying. I've put the bug in his ear and all I can do is twist it around until he gets the message."

"What if he never does? Maybe the guy needs a good swift kick in the ass."

"We knew it wouldn't be easy."

"If you're waiting for *him* to suggest the divorce, maybe you're going about it the wrong way. Maybe you should tell him about us. Maybe you should tell Mrs. Hannah you'll be out all night."

"I can't do that. Please? I need you to be supportive. I'm doing what I can in the only way I know how."

Seeing, hearing her agony, Michael pulled her head to his chest. "Okay, sweetheart. And I'm sorry if I push you, but there are times when I get so impatient."

"I get that way, too, and it's so much worse because I feel an awful responsibility on my shoulders."

He stroked her hair. "I wish I could take some of it for you. Maybe I should go to Washington. Maybe I should have a talk with Blake."

She brought her head up fast. "No! Don't do that. You'll only end up taking the blame for something that isn't your doing at all."

"Isn't my doing? Hell, I'm screwing the man's wife—" At Danica's stricken expression, he quickly amended the thought. "I'm in love with his wife, with every last intimate inch of her." He lowered his voice. "Better?"

She nodded. "There's nothing sordid about what we do."

"I know, and I apologize for using that word. It's just that I get frustrated and angry. I wish something would happen."

"It will. In time. It will."

It happened sooner than either of them thought. That night, when Danica returned to Beacon Hill, Mrs. Hannah was up waiting with the urgent message that Danica's mother had had a stroke.

The Hartford Hospital was no different from any other, with its long halls, its antiseptic smell and the ever-present sounds of bleeps, rustling uniforms and muted conversation. Danica came to know it all well over the next two weeks as she sat at her mother's bedside.

Eleanor had been fortunate. Only her right side had been paralyzed, and even then she was slowly beginning to regain a measure of movement. Danica helped her eat, pushed her wheelchair around the halls, waited patiently while she was in physical therapy, and, more than anything, filled the void left by William Marshall's absence.

Oh, he had come immediately after Eleanor had been admitted. He had shown up on each successive weekend. But he always had to return to Washington, where pressing business waited. Danica was reminded of when her mother had had her hysterectomy, when William had been about as doting. She was reminded of when she'd had her own miscarriage, when Blake had popped up for twenty-four hours, then had left. And she was reminded of Michael, who had been there, who had cared for her, who had told her without words that she was far more important than any work he might be doing.

Indeed, Michael had driven to Hartford several days before to see Eleanor. Though Danica hadn't had much time with him alone, she had been deeply touched by his thoughtfulness. As for Blake, his lavish floral bouquet sat wilting now on the windowsill; he hadn't made it north at all.

Ironically, the freest times for Danica were during visiting hours, when a steady stream of the Marshalls' friends filtered in and out of the room. Danica would excuse herself, promising her mother she would be back soon, and would wander around the hospital or the nearby downtown area wondering why she was being so attentive. In the end, she only knew that she couldn't be any other way. What had happened in the past didn't seem as important as that what she was doing now gave her satisfaction. Eleanor, for all her faults, was her mother, and it was obvious from the frightened glances she sent toward Danica when Danica was leaving, from the way she held Danica's hand with her own strong left one, from the way she seemed more relaxed when Danica was around, that Eleanor needed her.

More than once Danica wondered whether Eleanor's recent attentiveness hadn't been a forewarning that something wasn't right. The doctors had said she'd had high blood pressure for years, though Danica had never known it. Her father, on the other hand, had his own thoughts on Eleanor's stroke.

"She's been worried about you lately, Danica."

They were sitting in the coffee shop on the third Sunday. Eleanor was to be released from the hospital the following week.

"There's nothing for her to worry about," Danica commented as casually as she could, given the sudden premonition she felt.

"She doesn't think so. She came back from Maine last summer quite concerned about you and Blake."

"About me and Blake? I'm not sure I follow." She certainly did, but she wanted to know exactly what her father had to say.

"You're never together anymore. You live in different cities and you leave him to go about his business on his own. That's no way to run a marriage."

"It doesn't seem to be much different from the way you and Mom ran yours."

William grew stern. "It certainly *is* different. Your mother has always been with me, whether in Washington or Hartford. It's only lately that she's here more, and that's because she's tired."

"Then I guess Mom's a better person than I am. She's undemanding and self-sacrificing."

"She's been a good wife. I'd have expected you to follow her example."

"Times have changed. Commuting is simpler now."

"That's hogwash. Commuting was always simple if you wanted to do it. You, obviously, don't want to do it. What's the matter with you?"

Danica forced herself to speak in an even tone. "I have interests that Mom never had."

William Marshall had never been one to beat around the bush when he had something on his mind. "You have this Buchanan fellow. What in the hell are you doing with him? That's what has your mother so upset. She's worried sick that something's going on that you're going to regret one day." ₸

"Just a minute, Dad," Danica warned. "If you're trying to blame Mom's stroke on me, that's unfair. According to the doctor, she's had high blood pressure for years, and that could as easily be from trying to keep up with the life you want to lead as from worrying about me. Let's not throw accusations around because we'll never know what caused the stroke."

"You haven't answered my question, young lady. I asked what was going on between you and that fellow in Maine."

Danica stared at her father for a full minute. "He's a good friend, probably the best I've ever had. You should be grateful he gives me his time. God only knows, no one else does."

"What in the hell is that supposed to mean?"

She sighed. "Ach, this isn't the time or place."

In deference to her reminder, he lowered his voice, but that was the extent of his surrender. "No, girl, spit it out."

"It's not important. What *is* is that we try to get Mother out of here and back on her feet."

"That will happen anyway. She has the best of doctors and therapists, and I've already hired a full-time nurse to take care of her when she gets home."

"I'll stay on for a while. She needs someone who loves her."

If Danica was trying to get a message across, she failed. William was still thinking about the stack of photographs Morgan Emery had handed him. "You're avoiding me, Danica. I asked you what you were doing with Michael Buchanan."

"And I answered." It was all she could do not to wilt beneath William's cutting stare, but she managed. She loved him because he was her father, and she had always tried to please him, but short of outright lying, she would be damned now by whatever answer she gave.

"Then listen to me, and listen good. I want you to stay away from him. He and his family are trouble from the word *go*. He'd like nothing more than to embarrass us, and if you do something to compromise Blake, you'll be doing just that. Honestly, Danica, I never thought I'd have to have a discussion like this with you." When her mouth remained set, he went on. "Stay away from Buchanan. Your running all over Maine with him is indecent. Blake Lindsay is a good man, and he's your husband. For your mother's sake, if nothing else, behave yourself."

Danica felt like a chastised child. Her resentment nearly overpowered her recollection of where she was and why. She would have liked nothing more than to tell her father to mind his own business, to tell him to clean his own house before he worried about cleaning hers, but she said nothing. One part of her feared the repercussions of such an outburst, and for her mother's sake, if nothing else, she controlled herself.

Gathering her purse, she stood. "I think I'll go back up and see how Mom is doing."

William stood and took her elbow. "Do we have an understanding, Danica?"

"You've said what you wanted to say. Trust me to do what I feel is right."

"That's a nonanswer if I ever heard one," her father grumbled. "Maybe I steered you wrong after all. You should have been a politician."

"God forbid," Danica replied with a deliberate touch of humor.

Unfortunately, William wasn't deceived, or rather, he didn't particularly trust his daughter. He felt that he barely knew her, that any number of things could be going on in her life that he didn't know about. For the most part, he didn't care what she did. He certainly wasn't interested in getting a rundown on her charity work or even the work she was doing with James Bryant. The matter of Michael Buchanan, though, was something else. He was damned if he would have a scandal rock his family.

He had seen those pictures, had studied them time and again. Though there had been no evidence that Danica was having an affair, there was plenty of evidence that she might well do so in the future. He had warned her, but he couldn't be sure she would listen. What he needed was solid evidence one way or another, and the only way to get that would be to keep Emery on the case. It was only a matter of money, a small price to pay if by doing so he could prevent Danica from making fools of them all. With evidence, something compromising, he could confront her. Better still, he could confront Buchanan, even the senior Buchanan if need be.

But that was a ways off. First, he had to get Emery on the stick. Once he had done that and once he knew that Eleanor was safely installed at home, he would be able to return his full concentration to more important business in Washington.

November in the Capital tended toward the chilly, yet Cilla had always preferred it to spring, when hordes of sightseers flocked to see the cherry blossoms and the myriad of historical sights the city offered. But then, she had always been a rebellious sort. She liked to root for the underdog in a baseball game, eat spinach instead of peas, wear her skirts long when designers said hemlines were rising. She thrived on doing the unexpected, so it was no surprise to her when she found herself very happily in bed with her ex-husband.

"Ahhh, Cilla, we always were good together," Jeffrey breathed when his pulse finally began to slow.

She tipped her head on the pillow to look at him. "In bed, yes. Why is it, do you think?"

"Chemistry?"

"I think there's something more. We're both committed, intense. Making love with you is always fierce. It's a challenge because there's always some new little part of you that comes out."

"Like a puzzle. We're both puzzle freaks."

"Mmmm. Ironic, isn't it? The same thing that makes us dynamite in bed keeps us apart out of it."

Jeffrey took a deep breath and drew her head to the crook of his shoulder. "Let's not talk about that."

"We have to at some point. This has been going on for two months now. We've been together several nights a week, but there's still a barrier there."

"Just like the old days."

"Right. Doesn't it bother you?"

"Of course it bothers me. Why couldn't you have made your millions producing homemade chocolate chip cookies?"

"Why couldn't you have made yours inventing Trivial Pursuit?"

He tucked in his chin to look at her. "Have you played?"

She stuck hers out. "Sure. I'm unbeatable."

"That's because you've never played against me. I never miss a question on history or geography or science or sports."

"That still leaves entertainment and art. You forget, I have the memory of an elephant."

"Mmmm. I bet we could team up and win championships all over the place. Hey, that's an idea. Why don't we both resign from our jobs and go on the road as trivia experts?"

She snorted. "We'd probably fight over who was going to roll the dice."

"No, we never fought over petty things." He grew pensive. "Just over big things, like cases we're working on."

She rolled over and propped herself on his chest. "Okay. Let's see how far we've come. Tell me about what you're doing."

"Cilla . . ."

"See. You still don't trust me. You trust me to do all kinds of wicked things to your body, but you don't trust me with your thoughts."

"God, we've been over this so many times before."

"And we'll go over it many times more. Unless—" she made to rise from the bed "—you'd just as soon call it quits now."

He snagged her back. "I don't want that. You know how I feel about you."

"No. Tell me."

"You know."

"I . . . want . . . to . . . hear . . . the . . . words."

He gave her a crooked smile. "You like it when I'm vulnerable, don't you? It gives you the upper edge."

"There you're wrong. There's nothing 'upper edge' about it. We're talking equality. I know that I'm at my most vulnerable when I'm with you. I just need to know that I'm not the only one."

"You're not." He hesitated a minute longer. "I loved you when we were married, and I love you still. . . . Hell, I feel so naked when I say that."

"You are naked."

He looked down the creamy length of her back. "So are you."

She caught her breath at his near tangible caress. "Guess so. I do love you, Jeff. So help me, I've tried not to. I've dated plenty since the divorce, but I keep coming back. In my mind, at least."

"Not only your mind."

"Well . . ."

"Come on. Give a kiss."

Her eyes grew sly. "Where?"

"Here, for starters." He pointed to his mouth and opened it when she came. But it was only for starters because the combination of chemistry and challenge and love was a potent one with a will of its own, and before long they were sprawling over and around each other in a mutual search for satisfaction.

Some time later, when they were once again at rest in each other's arms, Jeff sighed. "And we're right back where we started, aren't we, with a roadblock smack in front of us."

Cilla rubbed her cheek against the matted hair on his chest. She closed her eyes and took a deep breath. "I'm doing a story on toxic waste seepage into the Chesapeake Bay. The problem is that the source of the seepage is a chemical plant, which is owned by a very prominent and politically active taxpayer."

Jeff went still for a minute, not because of what she had said but because of the fact that she had said it. She had offered him a part of her work that she would at one time have guarded religiously. He felt very good.

"Have there been reports of the seepage before?"

"Oh, yes. For years officials have known the Chesapeake had problems. It was once thought to be the nation's most productive body of water, but that's changing. Industrial wastes from Pennsylvania flow in through the Susquehanna. Toxic kepone spills in through the James from Richmond and Norfolk. Even treated sewage adds chlorine toxicity to the bay." She forced herself on. "The particular chemical plant I'm looking at is in Baltimore harbor. Its owner has passed around enough money to keep its spills under raps."

"Do you have evidence?"

"Of the seepage? The Army Corps of Engineers has documented it."

"What about the money? Any evidence?"

Cilla looked up at him because his questions were coming strong and fast. She felt a habitual wariness rear its head. Jeffrey read her instantly.

"I'm sorry. That's the interrogator in me at work. And I'm not this way because of my job. The reverse is more accurate. I'm good at my job because I am this way. But it's just me now, Cilla. Just me. It won't go any further. Please. Trust me."

She saw the sincerity in his expression and knew that if they were to have any hope for a future together, she had to do as he asked. She nodded. "We're getting evidence of the money, but it's slow. Things have been well hidden. We have to be careful because if word gets around that we're on to something, doors will suddenly close on us."

"Sounds familiar. I'm having the same problem." In general terms—and with an ingrained caution—he outlined the investigation he was undertaking into high-tech espionage. "We know that Bulgaria received the goods. We know that they came from Austria. We even identified the Austrian firm that did the shipping, then nothing. There has to be an originating American firm, but we can't find it. Records have been destroyed; storefronts have been physically demolished. It's frustrating as hell when you *know* what's been done is illegal but you can't clinch it with hard evidence."

Cilla considered his frustration, then spoke with reference to her own. "That's the worst part, I think. Time passes and you know that the public good is in danger, but you have a responsibility to do and say nothing until you can back your words up."

"But you can't give up because you *know*. You *know*. And there's a responsibility in that, too. Maybe it's a good guy complex and corny as hell, but damn, it gets into your blood."

She slanted him an understanding smile. "I know. And it's nice to know you know."

He returned the smile, surprised that the sharing had been relatively painless. "Any more word from your sex maniac?"

"Which one?"

He pinched her bottom. "The one who called you that day wanting to talk about power and lust?"

"Oh. That one." She sighed. "No. No more calls. I did meet this guy, though. It was at a diplomatic reception. He was kind of standing by the wall looking disgruntled, like he wasn't terribly happy to be there but he just couldn't stay away. When he started talking to me, I could have sworn the voice was the same."

"As the one on the phone?"

"Mmmm." She shrugged. "I'm probably wrong. I mean, the telephone usually mangles tones."

"Not that much. What did he have to say at the reception?"

"Oh, he railed on about the power of the wealthy and how you had to play their game if you wanted to survive in this town."

"He's right."

"But he sure was angry."

"People who have to play by others' rules usually are. What was his position?"

"He mumbled something about working in one of the departments. State or Labor, maybe Commerce . . . I'm not sure which, and when I started to ask him more, he turned the conversation around to me. He just loved the fact that I'm with the press. He started asking all kinds of questions about the glory in that. I couldn't get away fast enough."

Jeffrey chuckled and hugged her closer. How does it feel to be on the other end of the firing line?"

"Pret-ty annoying. I like to do the asking, not the telling."

"Seems to me you've done a little of each tonight."

She smiled then and stretched up to kiss him. "I have at that, haven't I?"

"Was it painful?"

"Was it for you?"

"There you go, asking the questions again. Cilla, Cilla, Cilla, what am I going to do with you?"

Sliding her mouth to his ear, she proceeded to make several very naughty suggestions, after which Jeffrey had neither time nor strength to ask another thing.

THIRTEEN

❀ ❀ ❀

ELEANOR RECOVERED SLOWLY but steadily. Danica visited her often, driving to Connecticut and back twice a week, always on days when she was sure that her father would be otherwise occupied. She told herself that her mother would appreciate the company more on those days, but deep inside she knew that she didn't want another confrontation with her father.

To her surprise, she found herself more relaxed with her mother on each successive visit. While the time she had spent with Eleanor at the hospital had been devoted to supporting her in a time of great physical insecurity, the days she spent with her at home were more ones of discovery that the woman she had always thought to be merely an appendage of William Marshall was a thinking, feeling being on her own. They talked of many things, and as Danica gained confidence, she began to ask about her mother's life.

"Didn't it ever get to you—the steady stream of political functions?"

They were relaxing in the solarium, though the sun was pale and the warmth primarily from baseboard heating units. Eleanor sat on a lounge chair with a blanket covering her legs. Her weak right hand lay quietly in her lap, but she gestured freely with her left, and with the feeling returning to her face, she spoke with only the barest hint of impediment. Mercifully, her mind had been unaffected by the stroke.

"I loved them. Right from the start, I found them exciting. You have to remember that I came from modest means. Things you were weaned on I never had. I suppose at the beginning it was a novelty. But then, I had lived through William's first campaign with him. You were too young to realize it, but he ran for Congress with a few strong backers, a whole lot of determination and not much else. So there was a certain triumph in going to Washington and taking a place we had earned."

"You say 'we.'"

"And I mean it. Oh, I'm sure William could have made it on his own, but I worked every bit as hard as he did. I was on the campaign trail with him. I spoke at women's luncheons while he spoke at men's. On the day of his election I was every bit as tired as he was."

"I hadn't realized," Danica said slowly. "All I knew was that you were never here. I guess I didn't know much about what, exactly, you were doing."

Eleanor brooded on that for a minute. "My fault, perhaps. I didn't think you'd want to know the details. You were so young, and we were so busy. I felt it would be better to keep you here where we knew you were safe. Then, in time, there were other things we wanted for you."

"Tennis."

"That, and school. There's no place for a young child in politics. We were constantly in and out, doing one thing or another."

"Not all politicians' wives are that way."

"True. And maybe I was wrong to leave you behind. I worried about that."

"You did?"

"Any mother would," Eleanor answered defensively. "But I had to make choices, just like everyone else. On the one hand, I was William's wife. On the other, I was your mother."

"You opted for the first."

Eleanor looked off toward the yard. "It wasn't as simple as that, Danica. There was a third party involved. Me. I had to think of what I wanted in life. I had to look down the road and ask myself where I'd be ten or twenty years hence. I knew that one day you'd be off on your own, just as you are now, and that you wouldn't need me. I realized that William always would. Your father's position is very secure now, but I like to think that I still complement it. Maybe what I've done over the years is to cement my position in a personal bureaucracy. But it hasn't been bad, because I like what I'm doing." When Danica still looked skeptical, she continued. "I know that you think I'm a hanger-on—"

"No—"

"Maybe not using that word, and you're not alone. To the outsider, it might look like I'm nothing more than an ornament hanging on William's arm. Only the insider knows that what I do, that what any dedicated political wife does is important. We offer the eye in the storm, the quiet presence at the end of every day. Sometimes we don't ask questions, but even then that's what our men need. In social situations we act as a buffer. We can be charming and diplomatic. We can ease a roughness that may exist between our men and others. I think," she said with a deep sigh, "that like many women, we're highly underestimated." Then she laughed, but her jaw sagged. "This is wearing me out. I think I'm overdoing it."

Feeling quickly contrite, Danica handed Eleanor the glass of water that stood on a nearby table. "I'm sorry. I should have stopped you, but I enjoyed listening. Why didn't you ever tell me these things before?"

Eleanor sipped through a straw, then rested her head back against the lounge and spoke very quietly. "I guess because you never asked, and because we've never spent much time together, and because it's taken a long time for us to see each other as equals. Maybe, too, it's because I realize that I won't be around forever and there are some things I want to share with you before I go."

Leaning forward, Danica gave her mother a hug. She couldn't speak because her throat was tight, and it wasn't only the thought of Eleanor's mortality that saddened her. It was also the fact that there were some things she wanted to share with her mother, too, but she didn't yet dare.

Danica saw Michael every Thursday night. They ate at different restaurants each week, made love at different hotels. She never stayed the night, though, and while Michael tried desperately not to pressure her, his frustration grew. For a time he sublimated, throwing himself that much more deeply into both his teaching and his writing. It worked, though the end result was self-defeating. He finished the book and sent it off to New York shortly before Christmas. At the same time, his classes ended. Since his appointment had been only for the half-year seminar, he had nothing left but to grade the term papers he had assigned in lieu of exams.

Exhausted by the pace he had kept, discouraged by the fact that his love for Danica was growing even as his hopes that she would divorce Blake were fading, he decided that he needed to get away. Not to do research for another book. Simply to get away.

He was in the process of studying travel literature one Monday morning in mid-January when his doorbell rang. Rusty reached the door before he did. "It's okay, boy." He scratched the dog's ears as he opened the door. Then, in a flash, he knew it wasn't okay. He had never formally met the man standing before him, but the face was familiar enough to even the most impartial of observers, of which group he was definitely not one.

"Michael Buchanan?"

"Senator Marshall."

"You've been expecting me?"

"No. I recognize your face from newspapers and television." He could see no resemblance to Danica, but perhaps he simply chose not to. "I think I assumed that one day we'd meet."

William Marshall stood sternly, with a small portfolio beneath his arm. "May I come in?"

Nodding, Michael stepped aside. A glance toward the drive revealed a rental car—it was too small and common a model to have actually belonged to this United States senator—and no other driver. He deduced that William had flown into Portland and driven down himself. It was not terribly promising if he had hoped for an amicable chitchat, but then, he hadn't. There could be only one reason for William Marshall's seeking him out, and William, it appeared, had no intention of mincing words.

"I have with me," he began, "some photographs I believe you would like to see." He had already unclasped the portfolio and was pulling out a handful of prints.

Michael took them, looked first at one, then the next and the next, all the while struggling to contain the nausea that had begun to churn in his stomach.

"Where did you get these?" he asked, though his voice was hoarse and clearly revealed his shock.

"They were taken by a private investigator."

Michael's words came slowly and were laden with disbelief and disdain. "You hired an investigator to follow your own daughter?"

"And you," William added remorselessly. "Aren't you going to ask why?"

"I don't think I need to do that," Michael answered. "The pictures speak for themselves. The fact that you had them taken says the rest."

"Then you're smarter than I thought. Not that I'd have expected less from John Buchanan's son—" he pointed to the pictures, which hung limply in Michael's hand "—though you really were pretty stupid pulling this stunt."

"My father has no place in this. You're talking to me."

"That's exactly right, and I want you to listen. You're to stay away from my daughter. You're not to see her ever again."

"I'm not a young boy, Senator, and your daughter isn't a child. Do you really think you can lay down laws and have people obey them just like that?"

"I'm not the one laying down the laws you've violated. You've been having an affair with another man's wife. That's adultery."

There was no point trying to deny it. The photos in his hand showed him kissing Danica in her car, showed him holding her hand under what he'd thought was cover of a dimly lit restaurant booth, showed Danica entering a hotel room, then himself passing through the same door. Short of capturing the two of them in bed, the photos were condemning.

"I know exactly what it is. I also know that your daughter is stuck in a miserable marriage and that I've been able to give her a love she's never had."

"You're talking out of turn, boy. You don't *know* what she's had and what she hasn't."

"We've talked about many things, Senator Marshall. And regardless of what you think to be the case, Danica's perception of it is what matters."

"This is all beside the point," William stated boldly. "The point is that I'm prepared to use those pictures. I'll show them to Danica's husband, who can easily use them in an alienation-of-affection suit. I'll show them to the press right at the time your newest book is being reviewed. I'll show them to your father, if need be. The point is that you're going to get out of my daughter's life and stay out."

A slow fury rose in Michael. "You're threatening me."

"Damned right I am!"

Michael's nostrils flared when he inhaled. The strain of not hauling back and punching the man in the nose was tremendous. His fingers clenched the photographs, bending them, though he didn't notice. "It won't work," he said in a deadly quiet tone. "I won't be intimidated like one of your underlings in Washington. You may have power there, Senator, but you're off your turf here. The fact is that you'll hurt yourself and your family far more by making these photographs public than you'll hurt me. I have little to lose. My readers will buy my books regardless of any dirt you sling, and my publishers will keep on buying them because they're good. As for my father, he relinquished control over me years ago. In fact, the one person, the *only* person, who will suffer badly from these things is Danica. If you love her at all, I'd think you'd want to spare her that."

William was shrewd. "I could say the same to you. If *you* love her at all, I think you'd want to spare her that."

He had hit home, and for a minute Michael had no answer. Only for a minute, though. Then sheer disgust for the man before him took over. "I love Danica more than you could ever imagine. She's warm and intelligent. She's loving and giving. The only thing I don't understand is how someone as beautiful as that could have been spawned by someone as ruthless as you. Go ahead, Senator Marshall. Do what you want with your pictures." He shoved them forward. "I can promise you that when both Danica's marriage and her relationship with her parents fall apart, I'll be there to pick up the pieces. In fact, that's not such a bad idea. I've been wanting to take care of her for a very long time. Go ahead, Senator. Sling your mud. But don't be surprised when it lands right back on your own face."

Not quite prepared for such a show of force, William stared silently at the cold-eyed man before him. He wasn't bullheaded enough to deny that part of what Michael said was true, but he *was* bullheaded enough not to give up.

"You say she'll come running to you," he ventured confidently. "I say she'll go in the opposite direction. So where does that leave us?"

"It leaves us with Danica right in the middle." Michael paused, then went on in what he hoped would be a conciliatory tone. "Look, Senator, I really don't wish any harm or unpleasantness on your family. I've never had any part in the differences you and our papers have had. When I first fell in love with your daughter, I didn't know who she was, and by the time I found out, it was too late. For both of us. We were already involved, if only in an innocent sense."

He took a weary breath. "If you think it's fun, or easy, being in love with a married woman, you're nuts. I'd give everything I own to have it any other way. As it is, I've decided to go abroad for a few months. Danica needs time. So do I . . . Does that make you feel any better?"

"What will make me feel better is your word that you won't try to see her when you come back."

"I can't give it. I'm sorry."

William pulled himself up to his full, stiff height. "Then, you're going to have to remember that I have these pictures. Think about them when you call her on the phone, when you plan your little trysts, when you sneak in and out of hotels with her. If you thought it was hard before, it'll be that much harder in the future. Because I know what's going on now. These prints will be hanging over your head, and you never will know when I'm going to use them.'' He turned to leave, then gestured over his shoulder. "You can keep those copies. I have others and the negatives locked safely away.''

Michael clamped his lips together. He had nothing further to say, other than *Bastard! No good son of a bitch! Filthy, lousy blackmailer!* With eyes hard as stone, he watched the man who called himself Danica's father climb into his car and back from the drive. Only when the car had disappeared from sight did Michael close the door. Then, with the force of disgust and anger and frustration, he slammed his fist against the wood, welcoming the pain as a diversion from the deeper, more searing pain within.

"Hi, sweetheart.''

Danica settled into his arms, uncaring who saw. "Michael, I'm so glad you came in.'' Then she drew back. "You look so tired.'' She slid her hands from his shoulders down his arms, only then encumbering what he had kept hidden. "What did you do to your hand?''

He glanced sheepishly at the bandages. "I had a little accident. It's nothing.''

"Michael, it's a cast. It couldn't be nothing. And it's your right hand. How are you able to do anything?''

"I manage. A little slowly, perhaps. But I manage.''

Cradling his injured hand to her breast, she met his gaze. "Something's wrong, isn't it? I can hear it in your voice. Something's wrong.''

"Dani, I can't stay tonight. I have to get back.''

"But I thought—''

"I just had to turn in the last of my grades, but I wanted to see you.'' He was taking a risk, he knew. Marshall had been right; the threats he made weighed heavily in Michael's mind. Not that they could keep him from her. He meant his part of it. But he was uneasy and had kept a form of surveillance outside the restaurant before Danica had arrived. More than once he thought of the photographer who had stalked them, and he castigated himself for not seeing anyone. If this had happened in Nam, he would have been reprimanded, if not removed from his assignment. But it wasn't Nam, and he hadn't been prepared. He hadn't been looking. He hadn't wanted to look. To look would have been paranoid and would have cast something ugly over what he and Danica had done.

"Michael, what is it?'' Danica knew there was something he wasn't saying and she was frightened.

He cupped her shoulder with his left hand, "I'm going away for a while.''

For a minute she couldn't speak. She swallowed, then took a breath. "What do you mean . . . away?''

"I'm flying to Lisbon. I'm going to visit friends and explore the continent for a while.''

"A while?''

"A few months.''

Her breath was unsteady. "But why?''

Even as his eyes voiced his apology and begged her forgiveness, he began to speak the words he had so painstakingly prepared. "I need to get away, sweetheart. You need me to get away.''

"I don't—''

He put a finger to her lips. "You need to be alone for a while. You have your book to finish and lots of other things to do."

"But I want to be with you. Those things don't matter."

"Between your mother and me, you've lost a lot of good time. But it's more than that. You need to think about Blake and about us. I need to think about how much longer I can wait."

"No . . . Michael . . . no ultimatums."

"It's not that, sweetheart. It's just a chance to breathe, to reassess, to plan. All fall I've been pulled in different directions. I'm tired. That's all. I need time to recoup."

"We could take the time. I'd come up to Maine and—"

"Would you take off and go to Europe with me?"

"I can't," she whispered. "You know that."

"I do. And that's my point. We have to find some other way, Dani. It's just no good, sneaking around like this. Maybe by the time I get back something will have changed. Maybe Blake will agree to a divorce. Maybe you'll decide to go ahead anyway and fight him. Maybe I'll feel renewed enough to pick up where we left off. But, God, I'm so tired. Aren't you?"

"Yes, but I can live with it because the alternative is worse. Being with you is the focal point in my life." Dazedly, she shook her head. "A few months. I don't know what I'll do if I can't see you in all that time."

"You'll do just fine. In fact, you'll do even better than that. You'll be forced to see what a strong woman you are. It's one thing when I say the words, another when you see them for yourself. And you need that. You need it if you're ever going to be able to fight the odds that are still against us."

In defeat, she dropped her forehead to his chest. "I'll miss you."

"And I'll miss you. More than you can imagine."

When she raised her face, her eyes were filled with tears. "Will you be careful?" she whispered.

He nodded. "Take care of yourself, love." He lowered his head and gave her a soft, sweet, lingering kiss. His eyes too were moist when he drew back. He swallowed once, then turned to her. "Go on, now. It'll be too difficult if you stay."

Knowing he was right, she began to walk in the direction of her car. She looked back once, but Michael's figure was a blur through her tears. Tucking her head lower, she began to run. Only when she reached the Audi and had locked herself inside did she give way to the gulping sobs that welled up. Still crying, she started the car and headed home. When her tears didn't abate after several turns around the block, she finally parked and went in. It was long hours into the night before her tears gave way to sheer exhaustion and she fell asleep.

For a week Danica was unable to do much of anything but idle through the motions of life. At times when she least expected it she started to cry again. The sense of desolation that filled her was worse than anything she had ever known—worse than the loneliness she had felt as a child, worse than the unhappiness she had felt before she'd met Michael, worse than the continuing frustration she felt with regard to Blake.

She told herself that Michael would be back, that several months wasn't all that long a time. She reminded herself of the women who, in times of war, sent their husbands off for indefinite periods and even then without knowing whether they would return alive. She told herself that Michael did need the trip, that he had been working too hard, that he deserved a vacation. No amount of rationalizing seemed to help, though. She felt cut off from him, and hence from a part of her own soul. She missed him terribly.

At long last she threw herself into her work, realizing that it held her only salvation. She visited James several times a week and wrote furiously when she was at home. She poured her physical energies into ballet until the teacher had to remind her that the point of the exercise was grace and control, after which she took her frustrations out on the pavement, walking for a furious hour through the Common each afternoon.

Once a month she flew to Washington to satisfy her obligation to Blake. He said nothing on the matter of divorce, indeed acted as if it had ever come up. Though he made some attempt to be more solicitous to her, she knew it was a strain on them both. She was always relieved to return to Boston.

For the most part, the people she saw from day to day were unaware of her torment. She managed to keep it in control when she was out. Eleanor, once again, was more perceptive.

"Something's bothering you, darling. Would you like to talk about it?"

Eleanor had recovered remarkably. Though her walk held a slight limp, there were no other visible signs of her stroke. Indeed, she had traveled to Washington the week before, though she felt more comfortable returning to the quieter Connecticut countryside.

At Danica's suggestion, they had driven to a small restaurant in Avon, where they were dawdling over the last of their lunch. Hearing her mother's question, and sensing that she simply had to talk about it and that the time had come to trust Eleanor as a friend, Danica began in a quiet voice.

"It's about Blake and me . . . and Michael."

Eleanor pressed her lips together. "I think I suspected that."

"How much do you know?"

"I know that you and Blake are growing apart, and that what you feel for Michael is very strong."

"I love him."

Eleanor was still for a long moment. Danica could see her disappointment and wondered if she should have said anything after all. But she needed to. She had come to respect her mother over the past few months. On the sheer chance that Eleanor might have comforting words to say, the risk was worth it.

"And Blake?" Eleanor asked quietly.

"I . . . no, what I feel for him isn't love."

"What happened? How did it die?"

"I'm not sure it did. I'm not sure it was ever really there. Oh, I wanted to marry him and I thought I was in love. Looking back, though, I think that what I saw in Blake was the perpetuation of the life-style we all wanted for me. When I compare what I feel for Michael with what I feel, or felt, for

Blake . . . well, there's no comparison. They're both men, but so very, very different."

"I see." Eleanor looked down, frowning. "What do you propose to do?"

"I don't know. I talked to Blake about the possibility of divorce." When her mother winced, she reached out and took her hand. "I don't like it either, Mom. The thought of it ties me in knots. But then I look at what Blake and I have left, and it's so little. I can't believe he's any happier with the arrangement than I am, though he says he is."

"Does he know about what you feel for Michael?"

Danica drew her hand back. "No. I haven't been able to tell him."

"Why not?"

"He'll be hurt. He'll feel betrayed."

"So you do still feel something for him."

"I respect him, and I do feel compassion."

"Two very basic requisites for a marriage."

"But I don't feel love! I love Michael! And it's tearing me apart, leading a dual life this way."

Again, Eleanor was silent for a time. "How long has this been going on?"

"It'll be two years this spring since I met Michael. But things have been deteriorating between Blake and me for much longer."

"Why are they coming to a head now?"

Danica studied the silver spoon by her plate. "Because Michael's away now. Because I realize that he's not going to wait forever and that if I don't do something I might lose him."

"Then divorce is what you want?"

She looked at her mother. "What I want is to be happy. I'm not happy with Blake. With Michael I feel as though every dream I've ever had can come true. He loves me as much as I love him. He encourages me to grow, to do things with my life. He's always there when I need him."

"He's not there now," Eleanor said softly. "Darling, maybe you haven't been fair to Blake. Maybe you haven't given your marriage a chance."

"It'll be ten years this June. If that isn't giving it a chance, I don't know what is."

"But Blake has grown, too. Maybe you haven't made enough of an effort to grow alongside him rather than away from him. He is your husband. You owe him a certain responsibility."

"What about *his* responsibility? He's given me very little encouragement."

"Men are that way sometimes, particularly men like your father and Blake. They get wrapped up in themselves. They need prodding from time to time."

Danica was shaking her head. "I've prodded, but I get nowhere. I tried even harder with Blake after I met Michael, because I was afraid of what I was feeling. I didn't want to feel it. You have to believe that, Mom. I didn't want to fall in love with Michael. It just . . . happened. And regardless of what anyone says, it's the most wonderful thing that's *ever* happened to me." She paused. "I was hoping that you'd feel a little of what I do, but maybe that's asking too much."

"I'm trying to understand, darling. It's just that I see things from a different angle. Do you remember the day we talked about how I view my role in your father's life?" Danica nodded. "I am happy, but that's not to say that there haven't been times when I've wished for some things to be different. There was the guilt I felt in leaving you so much. There's the guilt I feel now in leaving William in Washington and the selfish desire to have him here with me. We all have our crosses to bear in life. It's simply a question of accepting them."

"And when the cross gets too heavy? When bearing it exhausts you, when it becomes self-defeating?"

"It's all a matter of the mind. You can do anything you want in life if you set your mind to it."

Danica set her mind to finishing James Bryant's book. By the end of February it was in her publisher's hands. Then she set her mind to thinking of another project she might tackle. As it happened, James gave her the contact, and the recommendation she needed. At his bidding, she called a man named Arthur Brooke, who proceeded to express great pleasure that she had called and asked if they might meet to discuss a proposal he wanted to make.

Over lunch several days later at the Bay Tower Room, Arthur Brooke offered her the role of hostess for a weekly current affairs talk show that his radio station wanted to produce.

"I realize that you've never done anything like this before," he explained while she sat in a state of shock, "but James has raved about how well versed you are in current affairs, and I can see, myself, after talking with you for an hour, that you're poised and articulate. We want a fresh voice for our programs. I believe yours is it."

Pressing a hand to her thudding heart, she forced herself to speak. "I'm so surprised. I never expected anything like this when James suggested I call you."

"James is a rascal for not prewarning you. He's probably sitting at home right now chuckling to himself."

"He's a wonderful man."

"I agree. Well, what do you think?"

She sucked in a breath and let it out through her teeth. "I think that your proposal is . . . very exciting. I'm not as sure as you seem to be, though, that I can do the job."

"There's really nothing to it. For an hour every week, you'll sit in the studio and talk with one or another of the local public figures. At the beginning we'll set everything up. After a while, if you want, you can make your own decisions as to whom you'd like to interview. You'll need to prepare beforehand, bone up on a particular issue. We'd like to stick to timely issues, which means that some of the preparation may be last-minute. On occasion, if there's nothing pressing in the news, we might invite an author to be on the show, in which case you'd have to read his book. But with the awareness you already have of what's happening in the world, I think you'll do just fine."

Danica still had doubts, but she was smiling. "When did you hope to begin?"

"In another month. We have a Wednesday evening slot that will be perfect. Is it a go?"

While one small part of her wanted to beg time to think, the other, larger part was driven by sheer impulse. She nodded quickly. "It's a go."

She felt better that night than she had in weeks, and spent hours wandering around the town house with a smile on her face. She called her mother to tell her the news. She sat down and wrote a long letter to Reggie. But when she thought of calling Blake, her smile faded. It wasn't Blake she wanted to call. It was Michael. Only she didn't know where he was or when he'd be back.

That weekend as prearranged she flew down to Washington. Blake was pleased for her in that same detached way he had reacted to her work with James Bryant. She waited for her father's call, but it didn't come. Only the part of her that had hoped he might be proud was let down. The other part, the larger part, was relieved that he hadn't put a damper on what was to her a challenging prospect.

After her return to Boston she set about poring through the local papers with a thoroughness that managed to fill her time somewhat. Still, she couldn't help but think of Michael, wondering where he was and what he was doing, whether he was well, whether he was missing her as much as she missed him. She wanted desperately to tell him about the radio show, to share the excitement, to express her uncertainties and savor his encouragement.

The following weekend, feeling that she would burst if she didn't find an emotional outlet, she drove to Maine. But it wasn't the seaside house in Kennebunkport at which she stopped. She drove on to Camden.

Gena, who was thrilled to see her, proceeded to chastise her for not having come sooner.

"But you're so busy. I wasn't even sure if I should come today."

"Busy? Nonsense. I always have time for those I love."

At the words, which were so freely and sincerely offered, something inside Danica broke. She bit her lip, but her eyes filled with tears, and before she knew it, she was being held by a cooing Gena.

"Hush, Dani. Hush. It'll be all right," Gena whispered, stroking her hair.

"I miss him . . . so much," Danica breathed brokenly. "I thought it . . . would get better in time, but it hasn't. And now, with . . . this new thing, I miss him all the more."

"Whoa." Gena eased her back and gently brushed at the tears on her cheeks. "What new thing?"

Slowly, regaining her composure as she went, Danica explained about the radio show. Gena's excitement was every bit as genuine as her expression of love had been, but it was the last which stuck in Danica's mind most.

"Gena?"

"What is it, pet?"

Danica struggled for the words, but she didn't know which ones were right, so she simply started to talk. "We've only met once before and neither Michael nor I said anything, but you seemed to know."

Gena smiled. "I know my son. I could see very quickly that he loved you. He's never come right out and said anything, maybe because he was afraid of my reaction. He told you about my own marriage, didn't he?" Danica nodded. "Well, what he may not know is that his father is happy with his second wife.

More aptly, Michael may not want to see it. He feels a loyalty to me, which is fine, except that he doesn't realize that I've come to terms with what happened." She reached for Danica's hand. "The only thing that saddens me is that the two of you have such hurdles to cross. I know you love him. I felt that affinity with you from the first." She smiled. "The sight of the two of you talking together, your heads so close, your hair so similar in color, your eyes smiling into one another's . . . it was beautiful. I couldn't have wished for a better woman for my son than you. You'll make his life very full and rich."

"You sound so optimistic, as though we really will be together some day."

"I know it, Danica. I said that there were hurdles to cross, but I didn't say there were uncrossable. If you set your mind to it, you'll see yourself clear and happy."

Danica remembered what her mother had said about matters of the mind, and she thought of the irony that these two women should express such similar thoughts with such different meanings. Eleanor implied that Danica should set her mind to making her marriage work, Gena that she should focus on extricating herself from a marriage that was obviously a source of pain.

"Have you heard from him?" Danica asked hesitantly.

Gena grinned. "I certainly have." She patted Danica's knee. "Wait here." Within minutes she was handing over a series of letters.

"But these are for you," Danica argued. "I shouldn't be seeing them."

"Nonsense. You love him as much as I do. I think he intended them for you as much as for me."

"He hasn't written to me."

"I'm sure it wasn't for not wanting to. Go ahead. Read the letters. You'll see." When Danica still hesitated, Gena coaxed her with a short nod. "Read them."

Carefully, Danica unfolded the first letter and read about Michael's adventures in Portugal, then Spain. Though his script was uneven, she presumed because of his injured hand, his style was familiar and flowing, and she took pleasure in his description of the people, the cities, the countryside he had seen. What caught her breath, though, were occasional breaks in the compelling narrative. "I wish Dani could see this with me," he wrote of Barcelona. "The port is so different from the ones we've seen together." Then, again, in a second letter, when he had crossed up into the Loire Valley in France: "I've been biking from place to place. Dani would absolutely love it here. There are long stretches of level road with views to the far horizon. On the other hand, she'd probably think I'm crazy. It's cold as hell some days."

All told, there were five letters. After leaving France, he had traveled through Belgium and Holland, in both of which places he had friends, before moving on to Denmark. She lingered over the last letter, rereading its final lines many times. "I miss you, Mom. I was never one to be homesick, but it's different this time. Either I'm getting old or simply sentimental, but I keep comparing things I see to what I have at home. I wonder how Dani's doing. Have you heard from her? . . . See? My mind must really be going. You have no way of answering my question since you don't know where I'll be next. I'm reminded about something I read once, actually, on one of Danica's tea bags.

'If you don't know where you're going, any road will get you there,' it said. When I started out on this trip, I think I *wasn't* sure where I was going. But I sure as hell am now. I'll be home by the middle of April. Can't wait to see you. All my love, Michael.''

Lowering the letter at last, Danica blotted her eyes. "He's a wise and wonderful man," she whispered.

"I think so. Has he been any help?"

Danica knew Gena was referring to the messages that had been meant for her in the letters. She nodded. "He's always a help. Even when he's gone. I can see that now. He was right to go. I needed time to analyze my priorities."

"And have you?" Gena asked gently.

With growing confidence, Danica smiled. "Yes, I believe I have."

Two days later she flew to Washington and flat out asked Blake for a divorce.

FOURTEEN

❀ ❀ ❀

"H E WON'T DO IT, MICHAEL. I asked him point-blank, and he said no."

They were in Kennebunkport, at Michael's house, where Danica had flown the instant he had called her to say he was back. It had been a happy reunion on both sides, with Danica's tears flowing freely and Michael's contained only with great effort. They had talked about his trip with the excitement of two children, though both of them knew the excitement was primarily in being together again. He told her that his book on sports would be hitting the shelves any day, and she informed him that it already had, that she had read it and loved it. When she told him about her radio show, the first installment of which had come off with high praise the week before, he was beside himself with pride, hugging her, telling her that he had known all along she could handle anything she wanted, demanding to hear the tape she had brought with her. But Danica was anxious to tell him that she had definitely decided to divorce Blake.

"He refused, even when you bluntly said you didn't love him?" Above and beyond his own slightly biased feelings on the matter, Michael couldn't comprehend a man clinging to a dead cause.

"He refused. Absolutely refused. It was a repeat of last winter, when I mentioned divorce as a possible mutual option."

"Did he say why he was so against it?"

"At first he just stomped out of the room like he did last time. When I followed him and pressed, he informed me that he needed a wife and that I had signed papers nearly ten years ago and that that was the end of it. I kept arguing, but he didn't want to listen. It was really heated, I mean, not like me at all. I'm usually more docile. I think he was shocked. He kept asking what was wrong with me. When I told him about you, he didn't bat an eyelash."

"You told him about me?"

"I had nothing to lose. I said that I loved you. Strange, he wasn't even surprised. Or maybe he just covered it up. Do you want to know what he said?"

"You bet I do."

"He said that he didn't mind if I had a dozen lovers, as long as I was discreet about it and kept up the front of our marriage."

"He said *that?*"

"More. He said that he was glad I'd found someone and that if it made things easier for me, he was happy. What *kind* of a husband would say something like that?" There was no hurt in her voice, only confusion.

"Beats me," Michael said. "So where does that leave us?"

"Not much further than we were before. When I threatened to call a lawyer myself and file for divorce, he assured me that he'd fight it. He harped on how cruel I was to even think of hurting my parents this way, but I'm telling you, Michael, it's getting to a point where I really don't care."

"You're angry, sweetheart."

"Aren't you? It's not fair that he can manipulate us this way. What does he hope to gain? What could possibly be in it for him?"

Michael thought for a minute. "If he had a mistress he liked but didn't particularly want to marry, staying married to you would be a convenient excuse."

"I asked him about that once, and he said that there wasn't another woman. He seemed so repulsed by the idea that I believed him."

"Do you think that his refusal to consider divorce may have something to do with his ties to your father?"

"I don't see how. They were friends long before Blake met me. I'm sure my father pulled his weight when it came to getting Blake his appointment, but that's a fait accompli. Blake has plenty of power on his own now."

Michael blew out an exasperated breath. "So we *are* back to square one."

"No," she said. "Not really, because I've made up my mind." She smiled gently at Michael. "Being without you helped in the perverse way I'm sure you intended."

"Dani—"

"Shhh. I'm not criticizing. I'm admiring. You were right. I did function on my own. The publishing house is thrilled with James's and my book. The radio station is pleased with my show. I know now that I can manage on my own, but the point is that I don't want to simply 'manage.' There's so much more. Am I making any sense?"

He slid his fingers into her hair and stroked her cheeks with his thumbs.

"You're making lots of sense. I think I realized many of the same things when I was abroad. It wasn't the same without you." His eyes explored her features. "Being away made me bolder, or perhaps just more desperate. I don't care who in the hell fights us; we'll somehow find away." He kissed her once, then a second time when their lips didn't want to part. At last, they sat back holding hands.

"Blake might come to his senses when he's had time to think about what I said," she ventured hopefully.

"Maybe, but I doubt it. This wasn't the first time you mentioned divorce as a possibility, so he couldn't have been totally stunned."

"I just don't understand the man. You'd think he'd have more pride than to want me now."

"It can work the other way round, though. He may be too proud to admit that his marriage has failed."

"But if that were true, you'd think that he would have been furious when I told him about you. I can't figure him out! He's making this all so difficult."

"No one ever said life was easy."

"I suppose. Michael?"

"What, sweetheart?"

"Will you wait it out with me? If nothing happens by the end of the summer, I'll go ahead and see a lawyer, but I'd rather Blake could see his way to an amicable agreement."

"So would I. And of course I'll wait. That's what my coming back was all about."

She raised his hands to her lips. "You're so special, Michael. You know how much I love you, don't you?"

"I could use a reminder from time to time."

"Now's the time."

"Where's the place?"

She looked around. "That sofa looks about right."

"Okay. How?"

She grinned and slid to his lap. "I think you'll figure that out soon enough."

Cilla joined Jeffrey at the restaurant in Georgetown where they had been meeting for dinner every Friday. They settled at a table in a quiet corner and ordered drinks. She smiled at him; he smiled back.

"So," he breathed, "what's doin'?"

She shrugged. "Not much. How about with you?"

"The same."

"Nothing new at the Pentagon?"

"Nope. The city room's still humming?"

"Uh-huh." She took a long sip of her drink.

Jeffrey did the same, then set his glass down. "I bumped into Stefan Bryncek yesterday."

"How's he doing?"

"Great. Sheila had another baby. Their third. A boy this time."

"Stefan must be pleased by that."

"He sounded it. He's been waiting for a boy."

Cilla nodded. She spread some cheese on a cracker and handed it to Jeffrey, then made one for herself. "Did you read that Norman was promoted?"

"Mmmm. Managing editor to associate editor, isn't it?"

"Uh-huh. Jason Wile left to be editor-in-chief of a magazine in Minneapolis, so the space opened up. I'm pleased for Norman. He deserved it."

"Do you ever think of editing?"

"Me? I'd make an awful editor. I get too involved. Besides, I like the action of chasing stories down. I can't see myself in an editorial position." Her eyes narrowed. "And if you're thinking that I could have whatever position I want just because my father owns the paper, you're wrong. He's a chauvinist. In his mind, women are far too emotional. Many people think that."

"Come on."

"No, Jeff. Think about it for a minute. Don't you feel the same?"

"I never said that."

"No, but it has come across subtly at times. You feel women lack that certain . . . professionalism to be on top."

"You're putting words in my mouth."

"But aren't they true? Think back to when we were married. Wasn't so much of the hesitation you had about confiding in me due to the fact that I'm a woman."

"You're a *newspaper*woman."

"But if I was a newspaper*man*, wouldn't it have been different?"

"Sure. I wouldn't have been married to you."

"You're skirting the issue."

He lifted his glass and took a drink, thinking that Cilla was right on the money. "Okay. Okay. It is possible that your gender had something to do with it. But I'm trying to change. It's been six years since the divorce, and in that time women have popped up in some pretty responsible positions. I'd have to be blind not to see it, dumb not to try to accept it. But attitudes don't change overnight. I grew up in a male-dominated household. It may have been wrong, but that's the way it was. When I was in college, women were still looking first and foremost for that M.R.S. degree."

"That's because they were told that was where they'd have the best chance of advancement. It doesn't mean that they weren't intelligent or responsible."

"I *know*," Jeffrey stated quietly. "I *know*."

He opened his menu and studied it. Cilla followed suit. When each had made a choice, the menus were closed and set back on the table.

"What are you having?" Jeffrey asked.

"Lemon veal. It was good last time. How about you?"

"Steak."

She nodded, observing that he had chosen the most macho offering. She wondered what he would say next, whether he planned to share his work with her tonight.

Jeffrey took another drink and pressed his moistened lips together. He had no intention of saying something if she didn't. If she wanted to be the liberated woman, he vowed, *she* could take the first step.

Cilla stared at Jeffrey, seeing that same closed expression he had worn so often during their marriage. It was unfortunate. For both of them, their work was nine-tenths of their lives. When they couldn't share that, there was little left. But if he was disinclined to discuss things of substance, why should she?

Jeffrey stared at Cilla, willing her to open up. She was stubborn sometimes. Wonderfully so. Maddeningly so. He supposed he was no different, but, damn it, she should be more flexible. They were at an impasse again, sharing nothing but the same silence that had plagued their married life. He wanted more, though. He had already told her that. He wanted another try. There was so much to love in Cilla. Maybe if he bent a little . . .

Cilla began to waver when she realized what was happening. The same rut. The same brick wall. Neither of them giving in, therefore neither of them benefiting. One of them had to take the first step. One of them had to make a show of faith.

She opened her mouth and took a breath at the very same instant he did. They both smiled. He dipped his head in deference. "Ladies before gentlemen," he said, then rushed on when she scowled. "Okay, I'll tell you mine first, if you'd rather."

Determined not to appear the weaker, she held up a hand. "No, no. I'll go first." She set her chin. "I heard from him again, the power-and-lust guy."

Jeffrey's eyes widened. "Good deal!"

"Uh-huh. He called two days ago."

"What did he say?"

She hesitated for only as long as it took to remind herself that Jeffrey was interested, not prying. "It wasn't what he said so much as how he said it. He wasn't mumbling, and his speech wasn't slurred. He sounded sober as a stone and very angry."

Jeffrey reworded his question to sound less pointed. "He was coherent in what he said then?"

"Very. He said that he knew I was a responsible reporter and that he was sure I'd be interested in his story. Front page material, he said."

"That's all?"

She shook her head. "He said that there were compromises being made in high places. That sexual favors were being traded among some very powerful factions."

"So what else is new?"

"That's what *I* said, only not in so many words. But when I tried to push him for details, he got nervous. When I suggested we meet somewhere to talk, he didn't respond. Unfortunately, I let my eagerness get the best of me and I asked for his name. I told him that his call lacked credibility if he wouldn't identify himself."

"What did he say to that?"

She sighed. "He hung up."

"Oh. Y' know, Cilla, it really isn't a new story. Everyone's heard of Elizabeth Ray. Wheeling and dealing with sex isn't unusual."

"No." She grew defensive. "But what if we're talking about a spy plot? What if there is *real* compromising going on? You know, secrets being passed around that threaten this country's security?"

He arched a brow. "Did this fellow give you any hint that that was what was happening?"

"No, but he didn't say it wasn't. I'm telling you, Jeff, I feel something. Call it instinct or intuition, but there's something behind this. You're right, everyone does know of the Elizabeth Rays of the world, and I'm sure this fellow must too, but he still felt that what he had to offer was front page copy."

"He may just be a crackpot."

Cilla knew Jeff was playing devil's advocate, and she wasn't offended. He was saying nothing more than her editor had said. Of course, she didn't agree. "That's possible. But I do have this feeling. More than that, I still think the voice was the same as that of the man I spoke with at that reception a while back. I've been poring through stacks of file photos, trying to recognize a face, trying to think about who might have been at that reception."

"Did you call the embassy where it was held?"

"The attaché I spoke with wasn't much help. He had the list of official guests, but he wasn't eager to hand it out, and even then he said that each of the invited guests had been given *several* passes, so the possibilities were much broader. I explained that I desperately needed to locate a man I'd seen there, but the attaché wasn't terribly sympathetic. I think he thought I was on the make, trying to track down a gorgeous, nameless, would-be lover."

Jeffrey grinned. "I think I'd think that, too, if I'd gotten a call from you like that. You have a damned sexy voice, Cilla."

She was feeling light-headed and strong now that she had taken the first step in communicating with Jeff. "I think you have a one-track mind."

"Not really. I can appreciate your sexy voice even while I'm thinking about your call and my lead."

"Your lead?" she asked. "In the Maris case?" When he shook his head and put on a smug grin, she sat straighter. "Okay. Your turn. What lead?"

"Remember I told you about the high-tech theft that's been going on?"

"Sure."

"Well, I think we're finally onto something. A shipment of sensitive micro-chips—a restricted commodity—was stopped at the Swedish border before it made it into the Soviet Union. We've traced it through several mediating companies to one in South Africa that actually exists."

"No dummy storefront this time?"

"Nope. That's what's so promising. We have a team in Capetown working on it now. It may take a while because our guys are working undercover, but we suspect that this particular company may be the source for a whole batch of similar shipments."

"And you want it all."

"You bet. It's possible that only one American company has been repeatedly involved, though I can't believe any one company would be so stupid. More likely, the South African firm has multiple contacts here—scientists, business people, diplomats, students—each of whom has a shopping list of what the East wants. It's mind-boggling when you think of it."

"Frightening."

"Very. The problem is that if we rush and close in on the South African firm based simply on the one shipment we stopped, the contacts will only sell to someone else. Money talks, and there's a whole load of money in illegal export.''

"So the motives aren't political?"

"In some cases they are. In many, they're financial. A true patriot wouldn't be tempted regardless of the amount of money offered, but we're not dealing with true patriots here."

Cilla nodded her agreement. "It's disgusting when you think of it. There are so many legitimate ways to earn a living. I was talking with a fellow last week who used to be one of the biggest bookies around. He earned a bundle, then one day wiped his hands clean and got out. He's in real estate development now, and while I detest what he did, and the fact that he founded his business on dirty money, I have to respect him more than someone who would knowingly jeopardize the country's security. Bookmaking may be illegal, but at least its victims are willing ones. In the case of something like what you're talking about, *all* of us stand to lose."

Jeffrey sighed. "Well, that's what I'm hoping to prevent, at least to prevent from happening again. I wish Commerce was on top of this, but, damn it, I'm not sure it is. Lindsay may be effective, but his interests clearly lie with big business."

"That might explain it, then," Cilla observed wryly.

"Explain what?"

"The fact that he seems so narrow. I've been watching the guy, and he's always straight and proper. I don't think there's a flexible bone in his body, much less a warm or sensitive one."

"There has to be. He's married, and to a stunner, I'm told."

Cilla eyed him cautiously. She started to speak, stopped, then forced herself on. "You don't know anything about her?"

"Only that I hear she's beautiful and that she's Bill Marshall's daughter."

"Nothing else?"

It was Jeffrey's turn to grow cautious. "You know something that I don't."

"When was the last time you saw Mike?"

"Your brother? Last summer."

"But you've spoken to him since."

"A couple of times."

"And he didn't say anything about the woman he was seeing?"

Jeffrey frowned. "Come to think of it, I've asked him several times if there was anything new in the legs department and he deftly avoided the issue each time. Is there someone?"

Cilla wondered if she had put her foot in her mouth. But she really did trust Jeffrey. And she knew that Jeffrey trusted Michael and vice versa. "Maybe he was trying to protect her," she murmured.

"Protect who?"

Cilla puffed out her cheeks, then let the air seep through her lips. "He's in love, Jeff. My brother Michael is very thoroughly and sadly in love."

"Why 'sadly'?"

"Because the woman he loves is Danica Lindsay."

"The wife? You have to be kidding!"

She was shaking her head. "I wish I was. Not that Danica isn't every bit as wonderful as he thinks. I spent some time with her at Mike's place last summer. She's a fantastic person, just perfect for him."

"But she is married."

"Umm-hmmmmm, though not happily, from what Michael says. That's why I've been watching the husband. He seems totally, and I mean totally, devoted to his job. I keep trying to figure out if there's another woman, but he seems removed from anything like that. Unless he's being very sly about it."

"I'd think he would, given his position. Geez, Mike's in love with *his* wife? That takes a little getting used to. I never thought of Mike as the type to go for a married woman."

"Because of Dad, you mean."

"And because he's so straitlaced. Hell, when we were in college, he wouldn't even look at another guy's girl."

"Jeffrey . . ."

"Okay, so he'd look. We'd both look. But if I liked what I saw, I'd go up and talk with her. Mike wouldn't."

"Well, I think this situation is a little different. He fell for her before he knew she was married. She loves him, too."

"Jeeeeez. Will she divorce Lindsay?"

"Your guess is as good as mine. Blake Lindsay was a successful businessman before he came down here. He supports Danica in the style to which she's accustomed, and he happens to be in good with her father."

Jeffrey's thoughts were running further. "Lindsay was in microelectronics, wasn't he?"

"Mmmm. I'd think you'd want to talk with him about your own work."

"Ve-ry carefully. Commerce and Defense have had their differences. But if I could strike up a casual conversation with the man in some nonofficial context, maybe I could pick up something."

"For Michael or you?"

"Both," Jeffrey mused, liking the idea more and more. Then he grinned. "I'd also like to meet this woman. She must be something to have snagged Mike."

Cilla returned his grin. "I can arrange a meeting once summer comes. That's when she spends most of her time in Maine. Her house just happens to be down the beach from Michael's. Of course, you'd have to drive up with me for several days."

Jeffrey found he liked that idea nearly as much as the idea of slyly seeking Blake Lindsay out. But while he left the former for Cilla to arrange, he was on his own regarding the latter. For several weeks he looked for an opening, then finally found it when one of his superiors mentioned in passing that the Secretaries of Agriculture, Transportation and Commerce were going to be at a large dinner party and that it wouldn't hurt to have a representative from Defense present. Jeffrey promptly volunteered.

There were nearly three hundred people at the party, which was held on the lawn of a sprawling home in Virginia, but Jeffrey had no trouble locating the face he sought.

"Handsome bugger, isn't he?"

Cilla, who had come along for the ride partly because Jeff had invited her and partly because she was dying with curiosity to see what he would learn, nodded. "He does stand out in a crowd. Dark hair, classic features, a smile that dazzles, a tuxedo that—"

"I get the point, Cilla. You don't have to rub it in."

Her arm was already through his elbow, partly because she was having trouble standing on the lawn in high heels, but she held it tighter. "I didn't say I preferred his looks to yours. There's something untouchable about him. I like to touch."

Jeffrey grinned down at her. "So I've noticed. By the way, you look gorgeous."

She was wearing a strapless gown whose hem was ragged by design and vaguely wanton. "I was going to wear red, but pale pink seemed more sedate."

"Sedate?" he echoed hoarsely, then cleared his throat. "Okay. If you say so." He couldn't take his eyes from a taunting hint of cleavage.

Cilla leaned even closer, putting her mouth to his ear. "Do you remember that time we were at the Dittrichs', when we slipped into the gardener's shed and—"

"Christ, Cilla," he cut her off. "What are you trying to do to me? I have a mission here, or have you forgotten?"

"Not me. I just wanted to make sure *you* hadn't."

"I hadn't. I hadn't." He cleared his throat again and looked across the lawn. "Come on. Let's ease over this way." He saw Blake Lindsay in the distance; that was where he headed. Then, abruptly, he halted.

"What's wrong?"

"Damn it," he swore through his teeth.

"What is it, Jeff?"

"*You.* My God, I must be out of it. Either that or you've well and truly got me wrapped around your little finger."

Cilla screwed up her face. "What are you talking about? I haven't done a thing."

He patted the slender hand that clutched his arm. "No, hon. It's not your fault. *I'm* the one who should have realized." He lowered his voice even more. "It wasn't very bright, my bringing you here."

"Why ever not? Nearly all the men have dates."

"That's not the point. In my own mind I think of you as Cilla Winston. But you're not, are you? You're Cilla *Buchanan*. All we need is for Lindsay to hear that name, and if he knows anything about what his wife is doing, he'll be suspicious."

Cilla looked stricken. "I hadn't thought of that. Damn it, I should have."

"We *both* should have. But look, there's nothing we can do now except steer clear of each other for a while. There may be one or two people here who know we've been married, but if we put a little distance between us, others may not make the connection."

"Much as I hate the thought, I think you're right."

"Good girl." He gave her bottom a light pat, then moved off, confident that

Cilla could fend for herself. She was a strong woman, he mused, and while there were times when he wished she was a bit less so, at the moment he was grateful.

He continued on at an ambling pace, stopping from time to time to acknowledge a familiar face, but maintaining a steady direction. Luck was on his side. The man with Lindsay was someone he knew, giving him the perfect excuse to approach.

"Thomas, how are you?"

Thomas Fenton turned his head, then grinned. "Jeff Winston!" He offered one hand and slapped Jeffrey's shoulder with the other. "Good to see you. Where have you been?"

"Not playing tennis, unfortunately." The two men were members of the same tennis club. Occasionally, when they found themselves without other partners, they played each other. "Gotta get back to it." He patted his stomach. "Everything's going to pot." He cast a glance at Blake, prompting Thomas to make the introductions.

"Blake, this is Jeff Winston. A good man. Mean serve. Jeff, Secretary Lindsay."

Jeff offered his hand to Blake's cool, practiced shake. "I've been following your work, Mr. Secretary. It's impressive."

Blake thanked him, and for several minutes the two men talked of relatively general, harmless matters dealing with life in Washington and the Claveling presidency. When Thomas Fenton excused himself and moved away, Jeffrey began to close in. He was hoping to learn whatever he could about the decision-making hierarchy of a corporation such as the one Blake had headed before his appointment. "I understand you had experience as an administrator back in Boston."

"That's right. My firm grew to be larger than I had originally expected. It took a lot of watching over."

Jeffrey gave him a quizzical smile. "I've always been fascinated by bureaucratic hierarchies. I assume you had underlings to help."

"I had to. There were four different divisions, each with a chief. I held regular briefings with them, though they handled the details of day-to-day production themselves."

"You set policy, of course."

Blake shrugged with one brow, nearly imperceptibly, duly modest. "It was my company."

"Were you the contact for sales, or did you have a special sales force?"

"There was a sales force, but the contacts were mine."

Jeffrey sighed in appreciation. "Not bad. Plenty of responsibility on your shoulders, though. You must have had the final word on what of your products went where."

Blake only had time to nod before two other couples joined them, and Jeffrey knew his chance was gone. He had wanted to ask if there was ever occasion when something happened that Blake didn't know about, such as one of his division chiefs channeling a sale on his own. Jeffrey would have been interested in knowing whether, in his own investigation, he had to look further into the bureaucracy than simply the top. But it was lost for now. He was bemoaning his fate when his ear perked up. One of the women was asking about Blake's wife.

"I haven't seen Mrs. Lindsay here. Couldn't she make it?"

Blake smiled with just the right amount of regret and shook his head. "She's back in Boston. She does a radio show there now."

"How exciting!"

"Yes. It's a current affairs talk show. Unfortunately, she has to spend hours each week preparing for it, so she can't spend as much time here as she'd like."

"You must miss her," the second woman observed.

"I do. But she's a modern woman doing her thing. I'm proud of her."

One of the men slapped him on the back. "You should be. She's a feather in any man's cap. Speaking of feathers in one's cap, you must be very pleased with the import restrictions the White House announced this week . . ."

When the conversation took off along more political lines, Jeffrey stood by, observing Blake. After several minutes, when others approached, he excused himself from the group as unobtrusively as possible. He mingled, talking with whoever happened to be close, scanning the crowd to keep track of Cilla, all the while trying to crystallize in his mind the impression he'd gotten of Blake Lindsay based on those few short minutes with him. Much later, on the way home, he discussed his feelings.

"It's strange, Cilla. He eludes me. You were right in that he's straight and proper. He says all the right things, makes all the right gestures. When he was asked about his wife, he gave a perfectly plausible explanation for her absence, even set the scene for her continuing absence. He claimed to miss her, but he seemed happiest when he was talking shop."

"Did you pick up anything on that score?"

"Not as much as I'd hoped. But look, maybe it was a half-assed idea anyway. I'd probably do better consulting with some less conspicuous corporate head. I had to be careful with Lindsay; I didn't want to sound too inquisitive."

"You can do that, Mr. Winston."

"Mmmm, but I have been better on that score, haven't I?"

"You have." She snuggled closer to his side. "I think we both have."

"I have a proposition, Dani."

"Uh-oh. Another one."

"This one's really exciting."

"Okay. Shoot."

It was early June. Danica was spending several days in Maine before returning to Boston to wrap things up before the summer. She no longer talked with Blake every week, but only on those occasions when he called to say that he wanted her with him on a particular date. She had refused him several times, yielding only when he pointedly mentioned that her father would be at a particular affair.

It wasn't that her father still intimidated her; she meant what she'd told Michael, that she had reached a point where she was beyond that. Rather, her deference was well planned, her mind set. The matter of divorce was between her and Blake. When they came to an arrangement—and she was sure it would eventually happen, because she didn't believe that Blake would take her animosity forever—she would simply inform William of their decision. She didn't want to give him cause for involvement any earlier, and at that late point his arguments would be moot.

"It's about a treasure hunt," Michael said.

"Sounds interesting."

"There's this fellow I know—actually, he's an army buddy—who's into salvaging."

"Treasure hunting sounds better."

Michael grinned. "You are a romantic, d'you know that?"

"I guess I am. Funny, when I was first married, I thought the most romantic things were the cards and flowers and gifts Blake would give me."

"And now?"

"They seem drab. Programmed. He never forgets a formal occasion, but the gifts are a travesty, given the ill will between us. I don't know why he even bothers. The feeling isn't there. Actually, I think his secretary does the dirty work. She must have all the proper occasions marked on her calendar."

"So what does turn you on?"

"Romantically? The quiet times we have together, like now. The talking and sharing." She leaned forward and gave him a gentle kiss. "Now *that*'s a treasure."

"Speaking of which, let me finish with my proposal."

"Your proposal. Right. I'm listening."

"My friend—his name's Joe Camarillo—is convinced that he's located the wreckage of a small liner that sank in 1906 off the coast of Nantucket. He believes there could be up to a million in gold coins aboard."

"You're kidding!"

Michael shook his head. "He spent months studying government reports and underwater surveys in the National Archives, and he's convinced that he's found the SS Domini buried in twenty feet of sand. He and a crew will be diving this summer. We're welcome to join them if we want."

"Join them? What would we do?"

"Observe, more than anything. I think I can get an interesting piece out of it. We'll be following the everyday activity of the crew, interviewing them and, of course, reading anything and everything we can find on the *Domini*."

" 'We'?"

"You can be my assistant. If you're interested."

"You *know* I'm interested, Michael! I've never done anything like that!"

"Then you'll come?"

"I'd love to! But what about my show? I suppose we could tape it beforehand, but it has to be current. I don't think I can hibernate on a boat *all* summer."

"No sweat. We'll be free every weekend. I can drive you back to Boston. You can tape your show. If we're late getting back, we can take a small cruiser out to rendezvous with Joe's boat."

Danica grew more and more excited. "It might work. I'll have a legitimate reason for avoiding Washington. Not that Blake expects I'll come during the summer. But my father might ask questions. If I'm *working*, he can't raise too much of a fuss."

At Danica's mention of her father, Michael, who had been fully pleased with the prospect of both working and living with Danica, grew sober. "Has he been making things difficult for you?" All too well Michael recalled the visit he'd had from William Marshall. It had been months ago, and even after he returned from abroad and resumed seeing Danica, he had heard nothing. He often wondered what the senator had up his sleeve and had more than once opened his door expecting to find a pair of thugs waiting to break his legs. It was possible that the senator had backed off and thrown in the towel. Somehow, he doubted it, and that made him nervous—precisely as William Marshall had intended.

"He hasn't been overly warm," Danica said, "but then, he and I were never on the closest of terms. He abides my presence. I'm sure in his eyes, I'm a great disappointment."

Michael knew that William hadn't dragged out his photographs for Danica's benefit, and that was some relief. Still, perhaps more subtly, William was making his point. "How do you feel about that?"

"About disappointing him? Not the way I once did, that's for sure. You were right. I don't think I *can* please him. He and I function on totally different levels. I like to think that mine reaches higher, to things like personal satisfaction and happiness and love, but who knows. His is just so different."

"It always has been. What do you think he'll say when you finally do leave Blake?"

"I already have left Blake, at least for all practical purposes. When the formal break comes, I'm sure my father will be livid. That's why I'm waiting. When Blake comes to his senses . . .' "

Her words trailed off as, simultaneously, she and Michael thought about the word *if*. But neither of them wanted to consider that possibility, which was one of the reasons a summer working with a salvage crew sounded so good. For Danica, it would be another step away from Blake. For Michael, it would be another tie with Danica.

"Should I tell Joe we're on?"

"Yes."

"Are you sure?"

"Very."

Michael hugged her then, appreciating both the commitment she had made and the risk involved. He wouldn't have thought it possible, but his love for her was still growing.

FIFTEEN

"**H**E CALLS HIMSELF RED ROBIN and we have a meeting set for tomorrow!" Cilla exclaimed, beside herself with glee as she opened the door to Jeff. Any reservations she might have had about so freely blurting her news were swept away by her excitement.

Jeffrey stepped inside and closed the door behind him. "Red Robin?"

"As in power-and-lust?"

"Ahhhh, *Red Robin*. Very dramatic. Sees himself as another Deep Throat, does he?"

"I don't know, but I'm sure not going to dismiss that possibility. I keep thinking of what he has to say, and my mind starts to whirl. Can you imagine my getting an exclusive on something really big?"

"You've done it before. Maybe that's why he chose you."

She frowned. "I've wondered about that. From the start he asked for me directly. There must be some specific reason."

"You're responsible, like he said. Where are you meeting him?" When Cilla hesitated, he scowled. "I'm not looking for a piece of the action, Cilla. It's just that I have images of Deep Throat and a shadowy garage late at night, and the idea doesn't thrill me too much. Give me a little credit for feeling protective, and *don't* tell me I'm being chauvinistic."

"All right," she said quietly, realizing that one part of her, the softer, feminine part, liked feeling protected. "I'm meeting him at nine o'clock in a parking lot in Bethesda."

Jeff easily recognized the address she gave him. "It's open enough, but it'll probably be deserted at that hour."

"I'll be okay. He couldn't possibly want to hurt me."

"What if he's a sex maniac who's been leading you on all this time?"

"Oh, Jeff, I doubt it. And anyway, I can't not go. I can't risk losing an opportunity like this."

"You could if it meant you'd be hurt. No story is worth that."

"I won't be hurt. If it'll make you feel any better, I'll bring along a can of mace."

Jeffrey snorted. "That'll do a lot of good. He could grab it out of your hand and turn it on you, then rape you and do any number of other ugly things."

"He *won't*. Damn it, Jeff. I thought you'd be excited for me. Maybe I shouldn't have told you after all."

"No, no, hon. I'm sorry. It's just that I'm worried. Maybe I should go along with you."

"Yeah. One look at you and he'll run off without a word. You're big, Jeff, and you can be intimidating."

"That's the point."

"No, the point is that I want this story."

"What if I hide in the back seat of the car. You could leave the windows open and yell if there's trouble."

She folded her arms over her breasts. "I think you do want in. This is *my* case, Jeff. You have plenty of your own."

He sensed they were reaching an impasse and didn't want that. He liked to think they'd come further. Pushing his fingers through his hair, he sighed. "I do, which is precisely why I don't 'want in,' as you so bluntly put it. I simply want to make sure you're safe."

"I will be. Trust me."

"I trust you," he snarled. "It's the other guy I'm not so sure about."

On the one hand, Cilla was determined to go. On the other, she respected Jeffrey's fears because, indeed, the same ones lurked in a distant corner of her mind. She also—contrary to what she had said—respected Jeffrey's motives. She wanted to meet him halfway. "What if you were to follow me and park several blocks away. If I had a beeper in my pocket, I could press it if there's any real danger."

Jeffrey didn't have to think about it. "That would make me feel better."

"Can you get the beepers?"

"Easily. . . . Cilla? Thanks."

She suddenly felt totally comfortable with her decision. They had reached a compromise. It was another step in the right direction. Smiling, she nodded. "You're welcome."

The parking lot was dark when Cilla pulled into it at eight-fifty-five the following evening. Seeing no other car, she parked, then sat and waited. And waited. Nine o'clock came and went, then nine-fifteen and nine-thirty. By ten o'clock she had the distinct impression she'd been stood up. She waited until ten-thirty, then started her car and sat with it idling for another five minutes before finally leaving.

Jeffrey was sympathetic, though not surprised. He knew better than to remind her of the crackpot theory, and suggested that as a consolation prize she lead him back to her place and take her frustrations out on his body. She liked the idea, and not only because of the guilt she felt in having dragged him along on what had proved to be a washout. He was a wonderful diversion, for a time at least. The following morning, though, she was back at her desk in the city room, staring broodingly at her word processing screen. When Red Robin called her shortly before noon, she had to work at sounding pleasant.

"I waited for you last night," she said.

"I couldn't make it."

"You said your story was urgent."

"It is. I just couldn't make it."

He sounded very nervous. She wasn't sure how much of it related to his having to call her after he had stood her up. "It's okay," she lied. "I spent the time thinking through other stories. Listen, if you got cold feet, you shouldn't have. I respect my sources. I don't reveal their names. I don't even know yours."

"Red Robin is enough, and my story is better than your others."

"I want to believe you. That's why I was there last night."

His voice grew muffled. "Tonight. Same time. Same place."

"How do I know you'll—"

The line clicked and went dead. She quickly called Jeffrey and arranged to meet him at her apartment at seven. But four hours after that, they were back.

"Damn it! That man is incredible!" She savagely threw her purse on the sofa. "Twice in a row—who does he think he is?"

"He thinks he's a man who has a story no one else has and that you'll come running when he calls."

"Well, he's right. But maybe he doesn't have anything after all. I was so *sure*. My instincts haven't failed me like this since . . . since . . . since I agreed to divorce you."

Jeffrey put a comforting arm around her shoulder. "We both blew it that time. It was an emotional issue. This, on the other hand, is an intellectual one. I wouldn't do any different than you've done."

"You wouldn't?"

He shook his head. "There's a chance that it's a hoax. But if it isn't, if the guy really does have something big to tell you, he may just be very nervous."

"He's a coward, is what he is. Why is he coming to me, anyway? He could go to the authorities."

"He may feel they won't believe him, that they're corrupt themselves. He may be afraid that if he goes to the cops he'll lose his anonymity. He may believe that the people he's out to expose have enough power to have him silenced."

"He may just want headlines," she sneered.

"Don't you? I mean, isn't it *your* byline you want on this thing?"

"Low blow, Jeff. You know I want the byline, but there's the story, too. Give me credit for a little civic responsibility."

"I do, hon. I do." He took her shoulders gently. "Look, let's just relax. If he calls back, you can put him on the spot. Tell him that you think he's full of crap and that if he makes another date and stands you up, you won't accept his calls. Call his bluff. That might scare him more than anything."

"It might just drive him to a rival paper."

"No. He wants you. He specifically asked for you. If he's got something to tell, you're the one he'll tell it to. So cheer up. He'll call back. And if he doesn't, well, then you won't have to spend any more nights sitting in a dark parking lot."

As it happened, there was another night, early the following week, though she didn't have to sit for long. She barely had time to park her car, turn out the lights and grit her teeth when a dark form materialized on the pavement. Not a car, but a man. She stared, refusing to believe at first that he had actually come. Disbelief quickly changed to excitement when he headed right for her, then was promptly quelled when the professional in her took over. She realized that he was clever to have come on foot, thereby preventing her from catching his license plate, which of course she'd had every intention of doing.

He approached cautiously. She opened her door and stepped out, reassured by the weight of Jeffrey's beeper in the pocket of her skirt. She remained silent, waiting for Red Robin to speak first, *if* this man was in fact Red Robin.

He came to a halt several feet from her and ventured a hesitant "Miss Buchanan?"

She wanted to say that she didn't know of any *other* fool who would come here for the third time, but instead she said, "Yes?"

"You're right on time. Early, in fact."

The night couldn't hide Red Robin's wiry slimness, or his glasses, or the head of dark, curly hair that contrasted sharply with his pallor. Nor could it diffuse his features enough to prevent her realizing that he was, indeed, the man she had seen at the reception so many weeks before.

"I've been early each night. I didn't want to miss you."

"Look. I'm sorry about that. It's just that this is difficult."

"I'm sure it is, Mr. . . . ?"

"Red Robin's fine."

She'd had to try, but she wasn't surprised when she failed. At least the man didn't look dangerous, she decided. She could probably put up a good fight if he turned on her, unless he had a gun or a knife. But she had her beeper. It was very dark.

She forced her thoughts ahead. "You have something you want to tell me?"

"I think I've given you the vague outlines."

" 'Vague' is no good. My paper won't print it."

"Try diplomatic corps."

"Still too vague."

"Try the United States Senate or . . . or the Cabinet."

She shook her head. "I need specifics."

"Try differential hiring and firing."

Again she shook her head.

"Try sexual harrassment."

"Nothing new. Try again."

He took a deep breath. "Try *homo*sexual harrassment."

Cilla grew still. The data bank of her mind flipped through cases she knew of. They were few and far between and had only involved one, maybe two, recognizable names. But he had mentioned three powerful groups, and his implication was that he had many names to offer. Homosexuality was a new twist to an age-old scam.

"You have my attention," she said. "Go on."

He fiddled with the lapel of his jacket, then nervously thrust his hands in his pockets. "There are powerful men in this town who have certain other men on their payrolls for doing nothing."

"Every bureacracy has its deadweight," Cilla pointed out.

"Well, it shouldn't! There are others of us who are more than willing to work, yet we're shunted around to make room for the favorites."

Cilla noted his anger and wondered if he was hurling accusations purely out of revenge. "You feel you've been wronged?"

He started to answer, then stopped. When he did speak, his tone was carefully modulated. "The fact is that many people have been wronged. Not only are the taxpayers footing the bill for the sexual antics of some of its most prominent leaders, but these same leaders are being influenced by people who are using their . . . their sexual prowess for precisely that purpose."

"We're being compromised."

"Exactly."

"Can you give me an example?"

He looked away and pressed his hands to his sides.

Cilla prodded. "I'll need specifics, Red Robin. I've already told you that."

"I've given you specifics."

"You've given me the general nature of the offense." She paused. "What is it you want of me?"

"I want you to expose these people."

"You're the one who knows who they are. I can't conduct blind witch-hunts, particularly not if we're dealing with as important people as you suggest. I need specifics . . . names, dates, places, files." She studied his profile. His brows were lowered, his lips tight. "Look, this is done all the time. A source comes to us, tells us all he knows; we verify it, then print it. I can assure you that you'll remain anonymous." She was beginning to wonder if he fit into the scheme. If he had lost his job or been demoted, her theory of revenge might fit. But if there was something more, a personal vendetta, she had to know. "Why have you come to me? Why do you want all this exposed?"

His head came around. "Because it's wrong."

"But why do you feel so strongly about it? Have you lost your job?"

"No. I have one."

"Where?" She didn't want to mention that she remembered meeting him before lest he get more nervous.

"It's not important."

"It is if I'm supposed to get a fix on what you're saying."

"It's not important."

"Then I have to assume you're gay and that you've been jilted and are out for revenge." It was a variation on her earlier thought and came spontaneously, spawned in part by the frustration of having to pull teeth.

He drew more agitated. "Assume what you will. My personal situation is beside the point."

"It's not if it's the reason you've dragged me here." She knew she was goading him, but she remembered what Jeffrey had said about calling his bluff.

She did need specifics, damn it, and if she had to badger Red Robin for them, she'd do it.

He took a step back. "Don't you want the story?"

"Of course I want it, but you haven't *given* me anything yet. Come on, Red Robin. Tell me something solid."

He shook his head, turned to walk off, then stopped. He looked down at his feet unsurely, then whirled to face her. "Did you know that much of the inside information we get on the Middle East comes from gays who infiltrate the upper 'echelons of those embassies?"

"Which embassies?"

"Did you know that one of the deputy secretaries of Labor is having an affair with a man who is a union lobbyist?"

"Which secretary?"

But Red Robin only shook his head and started off. He didn't turn this time, and when Cilla called out to him, he ran faster. Within minutes she was standing alone in the parking lot, her hands hanging limply by her sides.

"I need more!" she yelled to the night. "I need evidence!"

But the night didn't have it. All she could do was to hope that Red Robin heard and would think about what she had said.

William Marshall walked boldly through the offices of the Department of Commerce and announced himself to Blake's secretary. "He's expecting me," he added curtly, then stood straight while Blake was buzzed. Given his choice, William would not have requested this meeting. He had spent weeks debating it, had seen Blake socially any number of times during that period but had been unable to speak frankly with others around.

"Bill!" Blake appeared at his door and gestured. "Come on in." The two shook hands, then sealed themselves in Blake's office. "I was surprised when you called. Is everything all right?"

William settled into an upholstered armchair and propped his briefcase against the desk. "I'm not sure. That's why I wanted to talk with you."

Sinking into a matching chair, Blake frowned. "About what?"

"Danica. When was the last time you saw her?"

Blake's features tensed, though he maintained an even smile. "She was down last month. You saw her with me at the Weigner reception."

"You haven't seen her since?"

"She's busy now that she has this radio show of hers. It's a wonderful opportunity for her, don't you think?"

William ignored the question. "Will you be seeing her much this summer?"

Blake hesitated, growing more wary. "I doubt it. She spends her summers in Maine."

"It might be a good idea if you tried to get up there."

That was the last thing Blake wanted to do. "Why?"

William pressed his lips together, wondering if he was making a mistake by confronting Blake but not sure where else to turn. He had threatened Michael, but Michael had threatened him back and even now continued to see Danica. As for Danica, she was totally guarded when William was around, and he hadn't even *shown* her his pictures. Somehow he doubted she would pay him any more heed than Michael had done. William didn't like feeling impotent, and that was precisely how he had begun to feel on this matter.

"Because," he began angrily, "I think that she's far too involved with this Buchanan fellow, and if you don't do something to stop it, she's apt to embarrass us all. You do know that she sees him, don't you?"

Blake kept his expression bland while he chose his words with care. He had no idea how much his father-in-law knew, but was sure that Danica wouldn't have told William what she had told him. "I know that they're good friends. They like each other. It's only natural that they spend time together, particularly as his house is so close in Maine."

"They're more than good friends. They're lovers."

For a minute Blake was taken aback, not because he was hearing something he didn't know but because William had said it. "How do you know that?" he said coldly.

"I have pictures!"

This did stun Blake. "Of their *making love?*"

"Not exactly. But only an imbecile would fail to read between the lines."

Blake sat back stiffly. "Have you got them here?"

William drew the packet from his briefcase and handed it to Blake, then waited while the other man studied the prints inside. "I'm sorry to have to be the one—"

"How did you get these?" Blake growled.

"I hired a private investigator."

"On what authority?"

William realized that Blake was angry at *him* and decided that it was a defense mechanism. Accordingly, he softened his tone. "I'm her father. I've been looking at her from a greater distance than you have, so it's understandable that I'd have suspected things sooner. I wanted to know if there was any cause for alarm, so I hired someone to follow her around for a while."

"You shouldn't have done that, Bill." He tossed the photos on the corner of his desk. "It's not your business."

"I think it is. She's my daughter. What she does reflects back on me. As far as I'm concerned, she betrayed us both."

"She's an adult, and I'm her husband. This is a matter between Danica and me."

"You don't see her often. You have no idea what she's been up to."

"I know more than you give me credit for."

The conversation was not going as William had expected. He had assumed he would be bringing Blake shocking news, even more, shocking evidence, yet Blake seemed barely surprised. He was more angry at William than at his own wife! "Do you mean to say that you've known about this all along?"

"I've known about it. Danica told me."

"She *told* you?" For someone who had always been able to gauge and regulate others, William wondered if he was slipping.

"She told me."

"So what are you going to do about it?" William roared.

Blake grew all the more composed. "Nothing."

"*Nothing?* Blake, what kind of insanity is *that?* Your wife's carrying on with another man, *with* your knowledge, and you're just going to sit back and let it go on?"

Blake found a certain satisfaction in seeing William so ruffled. It made him look all the more in control by comparison. "Danica is discreet. You would never have known about this yourself if you hadn't hired an investigator. She's with Buchanan mostly in Maine, where no one's going to see or care."

"Don't *you?*" William gasped, unable to believe what he was hearing.

Blake took a deep, even breath and let it out slowly. "Of course I care. Danica's my wife. But I try to understand her. She's going through a crisis of some sort, perhaps sowing the wild oats she never sowed before we were married. I have faith in her, though. She knows which side her bread is buttered on. She'll get tired of Buchanan soon enough. You'll see."

William scowled. "You sound so damned confident. If it was me, I'd be screaming down the walls, making her toe the line."

"And she'd only rebel more. Don't you see, Bill? The more upset I get, the longer she'll carry on. Danica knows what her responsibilities are. When I need her here, she comes."

"Do you know what she's doing this summer?" William peered at him through narrowed eyes.

"She's on a boat hunting for gold." He chuckled. "Pretty amusing, actually."

"I don't see any humor in it. You know who she's with, don't you?"

"Buchanan. He's hoping to get a book out of it. She's working as his research assistant."

William snorted. "Fat chance."

"I believe her. She did a good job for Bryant. I'm sure she'll do no less for Buchanan."

"My God, man, but you're innocent. Do you honestly believe she's working? Doesn't it strike you that a boat is a perfect place for an ongoing affair?"

"There are four other men on that boat. I doubt she'll have the privacy to do much of anything. In fact, my guess is that she'll come back from the summer never wanting to step foot on a boat again. It can't be luxurious living, and we both know Danica's used to that."

William sat forward. "If you were smart, you'd hit Buchanan with an alienation-of-affection suit."

"Why would I want to do that? There'd be publicity, for one thing. For another, if I brought suit, it would only serve to alienate Danica." He held up a hand, pleased with his show of self-assurance. "Trust me, Bill. I know what I'm doing."

"Could've fooled me," William mumbled as he rose from his seat. "Well, I've said what I came to say. It's in your hands now."

"That's right." Blake stood to see the other man out. "And Bill? No more investigators, please. Let me handle this my own way. We've been friends for a long time. Danica's antics I can take; your interference I can't. I appreciate everything you've done, but it's mine now. Okay?" It was the closest he had ever come to telling William Marshall off, and he rather enjoyed it. He was a force in his own right now. It was time Bill accepted that.

William held up both hands palm out. "You can have it. Just don't come crying to me when she makes fools of us all, because I'll remind you of what you've said today. If she hurts her mother, it won't be because I didn't try to stop her." Lowering his hands, he flung open the door and stalked out, determined to have the final word.

Blake let him go because he knew he had made his own point. The last thing he needed was for Bill to be sticking his nose in, trying to change a situation that suited Blake just fine.

Closing his door, he leaned back against it and raised two fingers to massage the tension from the bridge of his nose. Lord only knew, he had enough to worry about without having Danica on his neck, he mused, then pushed himself wearily from the door and headed back to his desk.

Danica was happier than she had ever been. Michael had rented a small cabin cruiser for the summer—one not quite as fancy as they had been on the summer before, but they hadn't wanted to look pretentious mooring a luxury craft alongside Joe Camarillo's modest salvage vessel.

Actually, the smaller cruiser suited them just fine, since most of their hours were spent with the crew aboard the salvage vessel. Though Michael dived with the men from time to time, Danica opted to remain on deck. Salvage vessel or not, it gave her the same sense of freedom she craved. Away from land she didn't think of Blake or her father, but concentrated on helping Michael in whatever way she could.

Once a week they cruised back to shore and drove to Boston, where Michael waited proudly while she taped her program. She was always happy to return to the sea, though, loving the small cabin where she and Michael talked for hours at night, made love more often than not, and were nearly inseparable.

Late in July they returned to Kennebunkport to entertain Cilla and Jeffrey for the weekend. Gena, who had been keeping Rusty, joined them, and the five had many hours of lively discussion. It was a happy time for Danica, the glimpse of a dream come true. She felt she was one of the family, and basked in the love and closeness enveloping her so snugly. To her delight, Cilla and Jeffrey relaxed with her, drawing her into discussions of their cases in a way that stimulated her mind as well as her heart.

"Red Robin." She grinned. "I love it!"

"He's a doozy," Cilla remarked, lips thinned. "I think I'd like to wring his neck. He's the worst kind of tease."

"You haven't seen him in a month?" Michael asked.

She shook her head. "We've met twice, and he calls from time to time wondering why I haven't printed his story. I keep telling him that I need more, but I can almost hear him shaking in his boots."

"What will you do if you don't get more?" Danica asked. "Can you go ahead with anything you've got?"

"I'm working to verify the few things he's told me, but it's hard. The kind of liaisons we're talking about are well hidden. I've gone to several gay bars, but someone high in government isn't about to frequent those places, and anyway, when I start asking questions, everyone clams up. I have to be so careful, so vague. I can't ask if so-and-so has ever been seen there because, given the power level involved, I'll be in real trouble if I start pointing fingers. Anyway, gays protect each other."

"Not Red Robin," Michael reminded her.

"Mmmm. He finally did admit that he was gay, which was some victory. I assume he's been spurned. He's angry, but he's also frightened. I'm hoping that at some point his anger will overcome his fear and he'll give me what I need. It's one thing if I have evidence to work with, but can you imagine how awful it would be to accuse an innocent man?"

"It always is," Gena remarked.

"Well, in this case, it'd be even worse. Homosexuality isn't something you can prove, and innuendo alone can wreck a marriage. I like to think I'm a responsible enough journalist to avoid that kind of thing."

"So where do you go from here?" Danica asked.

"I try to follow up any leads Red Robin gives me. If I'm lucky, I'll find other witnesses, people who will corroborate Red Robin's claim. If I wait long enough, I may come across other jilted lovers. As far as Red Robin's allegations of policy-setting favors go, I need dates of hirings and firings, evidence of suspicious decision-making, perhaps even a third party who will state that a questionable compromise was made."

"It's going to be tough," Jeffrey warned. "Capital Hill is a strange place. On the surface it's wonderfully exciting and fun-loving. Subcutaneously, it's a hotbed of jealousy and mistrust."

"Good phrase, Jeff," Michael quipped. " 'Hotbed of jealousy and mistrust' . . . good phrase." He dodged the paper cup Jeff threw his way. "The question is whether you can use it in your own work. How's it going, by the way?"

Jeffrey frowned. "Not bad. We're getting there."

Michael sensed that he had reached a point in the high-tech theft case where he couldn't discuss it openly, so rather than prodding he steered the conversation along another vein. He was surprised when Jeff raised the issue himself later.

Having left the women to talk at the house, the two were walking the beach, at Jeff's suggestion. Rusty, one of the men, was trotting along beside them.

"I think we may have a problem, Mike."

"What kind of problem?"

"The investigation I've been working on. We've been able to trace illegal shipments of restricted goods back to several American companies. We're waiting for more so we don't blow the whole thing by cashing in the chips too early."

"Sounds solid."

"It is." He looked clearly pained.

"Don't keep me in suspense."

Jeffrey sent him an apologetic look, which held far more meaning than Michael could appreciate at that moment. "We've traced one of the shipments back to Eastbridge Electronics."

Michael stopped in his tracks. "Eastbridge?" he echoed weakly.

Jeffrey nodded. "This particular shipment was made nearly two years ago. It contained computer equipment with high-speed integrated circuits that are heavily restricted for export by our government and, needless to say, highly coveted by Moscow."

Michael was trying to assimilate the information. He could only mutter a soft, "Shit."

Jeffrey went on quietly. "Lindsay approved the shipment, but the main contact was one of his henchmen, a guy named Harlan Magnusson, who headed his computer division. The stuff was sold to a firm in Capetown, then went on through two dummy firms until it finally reached the Soviet Union. We have solid evidence all the way."

"Shit!" Michael propped his hands on his hips, then altered his stance and raised a hand to the back of his neck. "Lindsay! Christ! Why would he *do* something like that? The guy didn't need the money. You say the shipment was made two years ago?"

"Several months before Claveling's election. There was only one shipment, but it's condemning as hell."

"At least the crime isn't compounded. If he had let his company get something through after he was named to the Cabinet, he'd be in double trouble. How did he get a license, anyway? He didn't have anything to do with Commerce at that point."

"No. The license application said nothing about high-speed integrated circuits."

"And Customs didn't catch it on its way out?"

"They can't catch everything. In this case, the computer housing was older and suggested a different kind of matter than what was actually inside. Operation Exodus notwithstanding, this was one that slipped through." He sighed. "As far as Lindsay's motive goes, your guess is as good as mine."

Michael swore a third time and raised his eyes to the clouds. "I don't believe it." He met Jeffrey's gaze. "What do you do now?"

"The Justice Department should be going before a grand jury any day. It'll take a while—maybe a couple of weeks—before indictments are returned. Like I said, Eastbridge is only one of what may total eight or nine. We're going after them all at the same time."

With a moan, Michael turned toward the sea. "Poor Danica. She may not have loved the guy, but she did respect him."

They walked on for a time in silence while Michael struggled to ingest what he'd learned. Finally Jeffrey stopped and faced him. "You stand to benefit from all this."

"Yeah. I'd have chosen any other way, though." He shook his head. "I still don't believe it."

"Well, I wanted to warn you. When things break, they won't be pretty. Danica's going to need support."

"She has mine. She's always had mine. I only wish I could spare her."

"There's no way you can, Mike. I only wish I wasn't the one who headed the investigation. I really like Danica. She's apt to hate me after all this."

"No. She'll understand that you've done what you had to do."

"I hope so, for many reasons. Things have been really good between Cilla and me. If she'll consider it, I want to talk remarriage."

"Hey, Jeff, that's great!" Michael said, meaning it even if he had to push to sound enthusiastic.

"I think so. And if you and Danica can ever get together, well, I wouldn't want anything to come between us."

"It won't. I'm telling you."

"I've thought it all out. There's no way anyone can accuse her of helping me." When Michael sent him a quizzical look, he explained. "You know the press better than anyone. I'm sure one of the scandal sheets will have a field day suggesting that Danica may be thrilled with her estranged husband's fate."

Michael couldn't even begin to ponder the scandal sheets when his mind was racing. "What do you think he'll get?"

"He could get up to twenty years, plus half a million in fines. He could also be acquitted. I don't know the exact nature of his relationship with Magnusson. I'm sure a defense attorney can make a case for Lindsay being unknowingly conned."

"That's a way off. There's so much we'll have to get through first. Will you give me warning before things break? I don't want to say anything to Dani now. She'll only be upset and there's nothing she can do."

"Lindsay may be called to testify before the grand jury. He's sure to have some forewarning."

"He may not say anything to her. From what she says of the guy's confidence, he may assume that he'll escape indictment, in which case he won't tell that he was even questioned. She hasn't spoken with him since June. Will you let me know, Jeff? As a friend?"

Jeffrey put his hand on Michael's shoulder. "Of course I will. I'll give you a call as soon as I know anything definite."

Michael let out a breath. "Thanks. I'd appreciate that."

"I still feel like the villain."

"Lindsay's the villain, damn his soul. I hope he gets what he deserves!"

"That's the 'other man' in you speaking. Personally, I agree with you. In the end, though, it'll be up to the courts to decide."

Michael kept reminding himself that it was a matter for the courts when, over the next few weeks, he found himself time and again seething inside that Blake should have betrayed Danica, not the other way around. He knew he was being unfair, that the man was innocent until proven guilty, that perhaps he had indeed been duped by his henchmen. But Michael was emotionally involved, and even without this latest twist of fate, he had enough cause to resent Blake Lindsay.

Michael's greatest challenge was in maintaining an easygoing front for Danica. Oh, he was happy when he was working with her, eating with her, making love to her. During those times he readily surrendered to her charm, letting the love they shared blot out all else. In the quiet times, though, when he would stare unseen at her across the boat, when he would hold her sleeping form in his arms in the wee hours of the night, he couldn't help but worry, but feel the pain she was sure to experience when that fateful call from Jeffrey came.

Two weeks passed, then a third. Michael and Danica drove to Boston every Monday, then returned. He kept Jeffrey informed of how to reach them at any given time, but there was no word, and Michael was growing tense. In his mind, time was running out. He wanted to stop it, to turn it around, to give Danica and him just that little more time, but he couldn't.

Inevitably, Danica sensed his preoccupation.

"Something's been bothering you," she said softly one night, coming to sit by his side in the kitchenette of their boat. She brushed the sandy hair from his brow. "I know you're trying to hide it from me, but it won't work. What is it, Michael?"

He looked at her, debating, debating, finally opting to preserve the happiness of the last few days they would have together on the boat. "Nothing, sweetheart. I'm just thinking how wonderful it's been this summer. I'm not looking forward to returning this tub on Friday."

She smiled and kissed the tip of his nose. "But Joe's giving up for now. He wants to clean up the things he's found, then get back to the Archives." The crew hadn't found a thing by way of gold on the bottom of the sea. True, the ship had proved to be the *SS Domini*, and it had yielded some very beautiful nautical artifacts, but no gold.

Michael put an arm around her shoulder and anchored her close. "Are you disappointed that we didn't hit the jackpot?"

"But we did." She grinned. "You and I, at least."

Closing his eyes, he brought her fully against him. "You're so wonderful. God, I love you." The words had been whispered with a desperation that Danica might have caught had she not been so enthralled with their quiet force.

"I love it when you say that." She raised her mouth and met his hungry kiss. When it ended, she drew her head back. "I'm going to see a lawyer right after Labor Day. I have the name of the best divorce attorney in Boston. I think it's time Blake and I stopped playing games."

"Let's not think about that now," Michael said. Cradling her face in his hands, he kissed her again, deep and long. His tongue swept through the inside of her mouth, parrying with hers until breathlessness tore them apart. "Make love to me, Dani," he gasped, needing to know the strength of her love because he was frightened, so frightened.

She needed no coaxing. While her lips continued to play with his, her hands went to the buttons of his shirt, releasing them all, spreading the shirt open. Then she lowered her head and moved her mouth over the firm flesh she had unclothed. She dampened his light hair with her tongue and laved his nipple until he moaned. Releasing him only long enough to lead him to the V-berth, she sat on its edge and went to work on his belt and fly. Slowly she pushed his jeans over his hips, leaning forward to kiss each new inch of skin as it was unsheathed.

By now she knew his body as well, no, more intimately, than her own. She knew what pleased him, what was sure to propel him to heights of pleasure.

Using that knowledge, she pushed him back to the blanket and drove him to near fulfillment. When she felt he had reached his limit, she stood and slowly removed each piece of her own clothing.

"You're tormenting me," Michael accused in a rasping voice.

"No." She sank down over his body, brushing her bare breasts against his chest. "I'm loving you, Michael, very much."

There was no part of him she didn't love, both in thought and act, and Michael wasn't so disciplined that he could lie back and idly endure the ecstasy. He twisted around to love her as well, worshiping all the private spots on her body that she had saved for him.

When at last she straddled him and impaled herself, the fire they shared leaped out of control. Though Danica held the position of dominance, Michael took her again and again. They had never loved with such abandon, with such fury. Later, when their sweat-slick bodies lay languorously entwined, Michael vowed that whatever happened in the days to come, Danica would be his.

SIXTEEN

A FTER BIDDING AN AFFECTIONATE farewell to Joe Camarillo and his crew on Friday morning, Michael and Danica turned in their boat and drove back to Kennebunkport. It was the third week in August. Since most of the local celebrities were away and the producers of her show had suggested she take two weeks off, she had decided to stay in Maine until after Labor Day, when she would return to Boston and file for a divorce from Blake.

Having given up all pretense of living apart, she and Michael had agreed that she would stay at his house. They slept late on Saturday morning, savoring the comfort of his bed after weeks on the smaller, harder V-berth. After awakening, they showered and dressed, then worked together in the kitchen, cooking brunch. They had just finished eating when the doorbell rang.

Michael eyed Danica. "Were you expecting someone?"

"Not me. It's your house. Were *you* expecting someone?"

"And share you for a minute? No way."

The bell rang again. Popping a parting kiss on her cheek, Michael headed for the door. Even before he opened it, he felt a chill. The chill became ice when he saw Cilla and Jeffrey, the latter carrying an ominous-looking folder under his arm. He looked from one to the other, seeing the strained looks on their faces.

"Hi, Mike," Jeff, said quietly. "Can we come in?"

Danica came from behind Michael and burst into a smile. "Cilla and Jeff! Perfect timing. We just got back."

Jeffrey looked from Michael to Danica, then back. "I know. I tried to contact you on the boat and found out you'd returned it."

"We did. Yesterday."

Danica was startled by Michael's hard tone. "Michael . . ."

He put a protective arm around her shoulder. "What are you doing here, Jeff?" His voice was low and filled with anger. "I thought I said I'd handle it."

"Handle what?" Danica asked, but again she was ignored.

Cilla and Jeffrey were both concentrating on Michael, with Jeff the logical spokesman. "I wanted to be here. It's part my doing. I wanted to be the one to take the blame."

"Michael, what's going on?" Danica's tone was no longer calm but had escalated to one of utter confusion.

"It's all right, sweetheart," he said, holding her closer. "Cilla, couldn't you have stopped him? All I needed was a phone call."

"I agree with him, Mike. His argument makes sense."

Knowing that he was outnumbered and that it was too late to remedy the situation anyway, Michael stepped back to let Cilla and Jeff come in.

"What's this *about*, Michael?" Danica asked fearfully.

He was leading her to the sofa. "Let's sit down."

She let herself be seated, because she didn't know what else to do. Cilla looked pale, Jeffrey pained. Michael, who was evidently more informed than she, looked more tense than she had ever seen him.

Jeffrey began very quietly, directing himself to her. "I want to tell you about the case I've been working on." He outlined it briefly, then faltered when he came to the hard part. From the moment he had decided that he had to break the news to Danica himself, he had been trying to think of an easy way to say what had to be said, but there was none. "Danica, Eastbridge Electronics is one of the firms we've traced illegal shipments to. Indictments will be returned on Monday. Your husband is going to be named on several counts."

Danica eyed him blankly. "Excuse me?"

Michael put a light arm around her waist. "Blake is in serious trouble, Dani. It may be that he's done nothing wrong, but Jeff—and I—felt you should be prepared."

"For what?" she asked, still unable to assimilate what Jeffrey had told her.

"He's going to be charged with selling restricted items to the Soviet Union," Jeffrey explained as gently, as calmly, as he could. He was also simplifying the charges, but he felt she didn't need to know the details. "Once the indictments are handed down, he'll be arraigned, then released on bail until the trial."

Her body was completely still, save the visible thumping of her heart. "You must be wrong," she whispered. "Blake would never do anything like that."

"We've been studying this problem for a long time," Jeffrey countered softly. "We have solid evidence. The question isn't whether Eastbridge made the shipment, because we know it did. We have papers from several sources to prove it. Rather, the question is whether your husband knew what the shipment contained and, if so, why he approved it."

She was shaking her head. "He wouldn't."

"Believe me, the Justice Department would never take on a man as prominent as your husband if it didn't have a good cause."

Danica turned to Michael. "There has to be some mistake," she pleaded.

"I wish there were, sweetheart. Blake may be exonerated, but he will have to stand trial."

For the first time in this group, Danica felt on the outside. She inched away from Michael. "You knew about this before."

"Jeff told me last time he was up."

"And you didn't tell me," she accused, needing a scapegoat for the horror she felt. When Michael tried to take her hand, she pulled it away.

"I didn't see the point. There was nothing you could have done but be miserable."

Jeff broke in. "Blake appeared before the grand jury more than a week ago. He didn't see fit to tell you, either."

But Danica was staring at Michael. "You should have told me! I had a right to know!" She jumped up from the sofa and headed for the bedroom.

He started after her, but Cilla caught his hand.

"Let her go, Mike. She needs a minute alone."

He knew that it was true. Despite everything they shared, there was still the past, which was what Danica had to come to terms with now. Sagging back into the sofa, he hung his head. "I wish you'd let me tell her, Jeff. It might have been easier without an audience."

"Come on," Cilla chided softly. "We care for her and she knows it. She'll be back in a minute. You'll see. And besides, there's no easy way to tell a woman something like this. Better Jeff should take the flack than you."

"I'm taking it anyway."

"She's upset. She's looking for a heavy, and you're here. She won't hold anything against you, not when she can think clearly. She knows how much you love her and that what you did was out of that love."

Michael took an unsteady breath and raised his gaze to Jeff's. "It'll hit the papers Monday?"

Jeff nodded.

"I won't be touching it, if that's any consolation," Cilla offered. "I'm far too emotionally involved with this one. Damn, how could he do this to her!"

"I doubt he was thinking of her," Michael said. "I doubt he's ever thought of her. That was one of the big problems with their marriage. He put his career before everything else. Unfortunately, Dani's going to suffer the fallout."

Jeff screwed up his face. "I still can't figure a motive. Several of the other companies we caught did it for the money; the records show they were floundering financially. A third company has known leanings toward the East; in hindsight, Commerce should have been wary of issuing it any license. But Eastbridge— I can't figure it out."

"Who will be named in the indictments?" Michael asked. "Lindsay and Magnusson?"

Jeffrey grew still. "Plus the corporation itself. At least, that was what we thought. Unfortunately, Magnusson showed up in an alley two days ago with a bullet in his head."

"He was *murdered?*" Michael asked, stunned.

"Looks that way." He dug through his folder and tossed a set of photographs on the coffee table. Cilla and Mike both leaned forward to study them. "Someone wanted him silenced. The cops haven't got a lead yet."

One of the pictures showed the body at the scene of the crime, a second the scene with the traditional white chalk markers, a third the body as it lay in the morgue. When Cilla leaned closer, Jeffrey took her arm.

"Maybe you shouldn't, hon. They're pretty gruesome."

But she was staring at the morgue shot and was ashen for reasons other than the gruesomeness of the print. "My God!" she breathed, "that's him!"

Jeffrey nodded. "Harlan Magnusson. The former head of Blake Lindsay's computer division. He came to Washington with his boss, but he's been shuffled from one position to another in Commerce."

"No, Jeff." She clutched his arm. "That's *him*. That's *Red Robin!*"

The air in the room went very still, only to be broken by a weak "Red Robin?"

Three heads swiveled around to see Danica approaching. Michael quickly gathered the photographs together and turned them over, but the harm was done.

Danica was staring at Cilla. "Harlan Magnusson is Red Robin?" she asked in a distant voice. "But Red Robin is . . ." Her eyes lowered to the photographs and grew glassy. "He was Blake's right-hand man," she murmured. "They went everywhere together . . . to meetings, on business trips . . ." She swallowed convulsively and seemed to gasp for air. Michael was by her side in an instant and she clung to his arm. "I never liked him. He was too nervous, too aggressive. He used to glare at me. I was jealous of the time Blake spent with him . . ." She swayed on her feet. Michael tightened his hold, but she was looking at Cilla again. "You said that Red Robin was . . . was . . ." She pressed a trembling hand to her throat and whispered, "I think . . . Michael, I think I'm going to be sick . . ."

Trembling nearly as badly as she, Michael helped her to the bathroom, where he supported her while she lost the contents of her stomach. When there was nothing left to lose, he bathed her forehead with a cool cloth and helped her rinse her mouth. Then he carried her to his bed and gently laid her down. She clutched his hand.

"It's all right, sweetheart," he soothed. "Everything's going to be all right."

For a time she said nothing, then, "I feel so sick. So . . . dirty and used. No wonder he never came near me." Michael knew she was talking of Blake. "It wasn't *me* after all. It was the fact that I'm a woman. He must have suffered through the few times we were together, when all along he wanted to be with . . . with . . ." She heaved again, but there was nothing left to vomit. Michael ran back to the bathroom for the cloth and placed it gently on her throat.

"Take it easy, Dani. It'll be all right."

The stillness with which she lay belied the roiling torment in her mind. "It all makes sense now—why he wasn't upset when I started coming up here, why he hated the place, why he seemed almost relieved when I told him about you."

"He may not have shown it, but he was probably under a great deal of stress."

"You're more compassionate than I am."

"I wasn't married to him. It's natural that you feel hurt, and I'm not trying to condone what he did." To the contrary. He felt a slow anger boiling within. "He did use you. You were his key to acceptance. No wonder he was so vehement against getting a divorce. You were his cover. As long as he had you, he didn't have to worry about anyone suspecting the truth."

Danica rolled onto her side and tucked her knees up tight. Her insides were trembling in the aftermath of shock. "I can't believe it," she whispered, squeezing her eyes shut as if doing so would erase the ugly images that dominated her thoughts. Then she laughed, but it was a harsh sound. "Wait until my father finds out. It's poetic justice."

"He'll be as shocked as you are. He had no way of knowing, Dani. No one did."

"*Will* he find out? Will it come out in court?"

"That depends on Blake's defense attorney. The formal charges won't mention it. There's nothing illegal about a homosexual relationship between two consenting adults. As far as I know, the four of us here may be the only ones who know of the relationship between Red Robin and Blake. Cilla certainly won't mention it, and she's the only one who can identify Red Robin. Now that he's dead, so is her lead. . . . It does make sense now. Cilla's always wondered why Red Robin went to her rather than another paper. He must have thought our papers would be that much more interested, given the relationship between Blake and your father and the history of animosity between your father and our papers."

But Danica wasn't thinking of either her father or the Buchanans at that moment. "Do you think Harlan specifically wanted to expose Blake?"

"If Blake had shunted him aside when they came to Washington, it's possible. But Red Robin never did give Cilla Blake's name. And there's still the chance that the relationship between the two men was innocent."

Danica's mind was working clearly enough to realize the odds against that. "No. There were too many signs."

Michael agreed, but he had to be realistic. "We'll never really know, now that Harlan's gone. As far as the trial goes, I doubt the issue of homosexuality will come up unless the defense attorney feels that it's Blake's best chance for proving that he was unknowingly duped."

"God, I hope it doesn't come out." This time her laugh held a touch of hysteria. "I can't believe the irony of all this. When my father warned me about being involved with you, he kept saying that he didn't want the family embarrassed. He's going to *die* if Blake's . . . Blake's . . . comes out." Her voice broke and she curled into an even tighter ball, covering her head with her hands as though she was embarrassed even with Michael.

He wouldn't have it. Easily overpowering her resistance, he cradled her in his arms and spoke softly. "What Blake did has no reflection on you. He may not have realized what he was when he first married you. Gays have come out of the closet in the past ten years. He may have suppressed those instincts for a very long time." When she burrowed deeper against him, he went on. "There are many men who lead dual lives for years, who are happily married even while they have lovers on the side."

"We didn't have a happy marriage. He used me."

"In the end, yes. But he may have truly loved you once. He may still love you in his way."

"His way makes me sick."

"I know, sweetheart."

"I feel soiled."

"I don't see you that way. Knowing what we do now, I respect you all the more. Over the years you've given him every benefit of the doubt. You have to be credited with sticking by him so long."

"I didn't know!" she cried, berating herself.

"How could you?"

"I should have seen, but it never occurred to me. I kept asking him about other *women*. No *wonder* he was repulsed by the idea." She moaned softly. "I was so stupid. I actually forced myself on him that last time."

"You what?"

She raised her head. "The last time we made love was two years ago last May. He hadn't come near me in months, and I'd met you and was frightened by the attraction I felt for you, so I went home to Blake and seduced him." Her eyes teared. "I was fantasizing about you the whole time, Michael. Who do you think *he* was fantasizing about?"

Michael pressed her head to his chest, unable to bear the pain in her eyes. "Don't torment yourself, sweetheart. It's not worth it."

Her voice came muffled from his chest. "It's not that I wanted him then any more than I do now. We never had much of a sex life. Now I can see why. It's just that I feel so angry! He should have been honest. When I told him about you, he should have let me go. He had no right to do that to me, to us."

"I feel angry, too. Believe me. But anger won't get us anywhere. We have to think of the future. *You* have to think of the future."

"I don't want to. You know why."

He did. He knew Danica. She would foresee the ordeal that Blake was facing and would feel it her duty to stand by his side, at least until the trial was done. Michael didn't like the idea; in his book, Danica had suffered enough at Blake Lindsay's hand. But he knew that she would view deserting Blake now as callous. He had to admire her for it.

They remained in the bedroom until Danica felt stronger, then rejoined Cilla and Jeff, who had cleaned up the remains of Michael and Danica's brunch and had perked a fresh pot of coffee. Cilla insisted on making Danica a cup of tea, then took her out to the deck while the men talked inside.

"What do you think?" Michael asked softly.

"I think we may have our motive. If Lindsay and Magnusson were sexually involved, Magnusson could easily have swung his weight to get that shipment out. We know that he was the contact. Lindsay may never have even known about it if. Because of their relationship, he gave Magnusson an inordinate amount of freedom." He paused, thinking. "I talked with Lindsay briefly at a party several months back. He said that the responsibility of the company had been his, that he knew of everything that happened. Of course, that may have been arrogance speaking."

"So you do think he was conned by Magnusson?"

Jeffrey shook his head. "I think the guy knew exactly what was going on. His signature's right there on incriminating documents. But I do think that'll be his defense. And we'll never know otherwise, will we?"

Michael had said similar words to Danica. The fact was that Harlan Magnusson, a key element in the case, was dead. Michael wasn't sure he liked the implication. "Do you think Lindsay could have had something to do with Magnusson's murder?"

"Nah. It doesn't fit. As far as I know, Lindsay's been strictly on the up and up as Secretary of Commerce. Sure, he already knew of the investigation when Magnusson was murdered, but I can't believe he'd be so stupid. He's in a powerful position. He's well respected. Even if he was worried that indictments would be returned, he had to have known that he'd easily have the upper hand if it came down to Magnusson's word against his. Murder is something else entirely. There's no logical reason he'd risk it."

"Who do you think did?"

"Probably someone representing the guy in Capetown, who just happens to be a paid operative of the KGB. I'm sure it was a professional job, which is another reason to rule Lindsay out. For something that professional, he'd have had to hire a hit man, which would have only given him someone *else* to worry about. No, Lindsay wouldn't buy into that."

"Do you think the cops will?"

"I'm sure they'll consider it once the shit hits the fan on Monday, but I doubt it'll go far."

Michael sighed and sat back in his seat. "Christ, I hope not. That's all Dani needs." He glanced toward the deck. The two women stood at the railing, Cilla with her arm around Danica's shoulder, talking softly to her. "Will the trial be held in Washington?"

"Uh-huh. That's were Lindsay personally filed for the export license. Falsifying the information on that application will be one of the charges." His voice grew even quieter. "You're not still angry at me, are you, pal?"

"No. It's done. Maybe it was for the best. I think Dani's going to need all the support she can get over the next few days."

Her emotions raged in an endless circle. She was angry, then hurt, then frightened, then self-abasing, then angry, again and again. Cilla and Jeff stayed until Sunday night. They bolstered her as best they could, talking openly, if gently, about every aspect of what had happened, agreeing with Michael that the more Danica got off her chest, the better. They talked about what she could expect when she joined Blake in Washington, as they all knew she would, and tried to prepare her for any ugliness she might find.

Cilla saw the ordeal through Danica's eyes, and as a reporter whose stories

had more than once prompted other ordeals, she found it a humbling experience. Jeffrey, an investigator who had seen many of his targets go to jail, had
a similar view of the other side and was enlightened. Michael, who loved
Danica, felt her pain as his own and wondered if things would ever be the same
again.

When Monday morning rolled around, Danica clung to him for a long, long
time.

"Are you sure you want to do this?" he asked softly.

"I have to. It's the only way."

"You could stay here."

"If I was a different sort of person, yes. But I'm not."

"Are you sorry we told you?"

"No. It's helped. If Blake were a man, he'd have told me himself. But you
all were wonderful this weekend. I can think clearly now. I'm going to need a
level head if I hope to make it through all this."

Michael felt utterly helpless. "What can I do?"

She put her arms around his neck and pressed her face to his throat. "I'll
call you. Knowing that you're here . . . that's the biggest help."

"Will you call? Will you let me know what's happening?"

She nodded, unable to speak.

"I love you, sweetheart."

She drew back her head, studied the features she knew and adored, kissed
him very lightly, then disengaged herself and ran toward the car. Michael was
reminded of the winter before, when she had done much the same after he had
told her he was going away. He hadn't wanted a repeat of that. Damn it, he
wanted her with him!

But the car was disappearing from the drive, its sound a low purr, then a
growl, that faded and faded. He walked slowly around her house and down to
the beach, knowing that all he could do was to wait and watch and hope that
Danica's strength would see her through.

Mrs. Hannah said nothing about Danica's early return from Maine. The
house, as always, was in order, but Danica could only look around and wonder
at the farce she and Blake had lived there. One part of her didn't want to touch
a table, a lamp, a stick of furniture. The other part very carefully took a seat
in the den and waited for the inevitable call to come.

It was nearly two in the afternoon when the phone rang. Clenching her fists
over her fluttering stomach, Danica willed herself to be calm. When Mrs.
Hannah came to the door to announce that Mr. Lindsay was on the phone, she
nodded politely, waited for the housekeeper to depart, then slowly, coolly
lifted the receiver.

"Hello?"

"Danica, thank God, I found you. I tried the house in Maine, then Buchanan's house. He told me where you were. Danica, something's happened.
I need you here with me."

Where she had thought herself emotionally played out, anger flared. She
diligently curbed it, aided by the perverse satisfaction she felt at hearing

Blake's ruffled tone. "This is sudden, Blake. What's happened?"

"I'd rather not talk about it now. There's been a terrible misunderstanding. Look, I've been in touch with Hal Fremont. He's going to pick you up and fly here with you."

Danica tensely twisted a button on the soft leather sofa. "Hal? Your lawyer? Is there a legal problem?"

"Later, Danica. Can you be packed and ready in an hour?"

"Yes."

"Good. I'll see you later."

He was about to hang up when Danica blurted out, "Don't you think you should tell me now?" She was thinking about the press, which, if it knew of the indictments, would be sure to meet her plane. It wasn't every day that a member of the Cabinet was indicted on charges not far afield from treason.

"I can't. Hal will fill you in on the plane. I'll see you soon."

He hung up then, and Danica could only seethe at the idea that he was leaving his dirty work to others. With great effort, she composed herself and marched upstairs to pack the suitcase that Mrs. Hannah had just finished unpacking. Of course, she mused cynically, the clothes she would need in Washington were a world away from those she had taken to Maine. *Washington* was a world away from Maine, where more than anything at that moment she wanted to be. But she had a mission, a final mission with regard to her husband, and that conviction gave her the strength to put her own wishes on hold.

Within the hour, Hal Fremont was at her door, looking as pale and somber as Cilla and Jeff had looked two days before. The only difference was that this time she knew its cause and she was able to maintain her poise through the short drive to the airport, then the flight aboard the Lear jet Hal had chartered.

Danica had no quarrel with Hal, who, as gently as he could, broke the news of Blake's indictment while the jet winged southward. "I don't know all the details myself," he explained, "but I think you should be prepared for the worst. Of course, Blake is innocent, but he will have to face the charges."

She listened to his monologue in utter silence, but her initial concern about having to act stunned proved to be groundless because, despite how fully Cilla and Jeff and Michael had prepared her, the whole business was shocking and that much more real coming from Blake's personal lawyer.

A car was waiting for them at National, and Danica had actually begun to hope that she had beaten out the press, when the car rounded the corner near Blake's townhouse and she saw a large media contingent on his front steps.

"Oh, God," she murmured. "What do we do?"

"I'll get you in. Just keep calm and don't say a word."

The car had barely come to a halt when the horde closed in. Hal stepped out first, shielding Danica with his back.

"Does Mrs. Lindsay have any comment about the charges being brought against her husband?"

Hal gave a curt "No," reached in for Danica and, when she climbed from the car, put a firm arm around her shoulders. He wasn't a large man, but he knew what he was doing. She followed his lead toward the steps.

"Did you know of your husband's dealings in Boston, Mrs. Lindsay?"

"How did you feel to learn of the indictments?"

"Will your husband be resigning from the Cabinet?"

Hal pushed his way through the crowd. "Mrs. Lindsay has no comment at this time."

They half ran up the steps, but the questions followed.

"How close was the Secretary to Harlan Magnusson?"

"Do you feel that there's a connection between Mr. Magnusson's death and the charges brought today?"

"Has there been any communication with Senator Marshall?"

The front door was opened, and Danica and Hal fled through. In the abrupt silence that followed its closing, Danica sank trembling into a nearby chair. "I don't believe them," she murmured shakily. " 'How did I feel to learn of the indictments?' How do they *think* I feel!"

Hal patted her on the shoulder, then stepped aside. When she raised her eyes, she saw Blake standing on the stairs.

"I'm sorry you had to go through that, Danica," he said evenly.

She hesitated for a minute, though her gaze didn't waver. "So am I."

"Thank you for coming."

Aware that she was being watched not only by Hal but by Blake's houseboy and two other men who had come to stand at the top of the stairs, she simply nodded.

Blake's voice seemed to lose some of its force then. "Why don't you and Hal come up to the den. You'd better hear what we've been discussing."

Given little choice, she followed Blake to the top of the stairs, where she was introduced to Jason Fitzgerald and Ray Pickering, the local lawyers Blake had chosen to lead his defense. Once in the den, she refused invitation of a seat and propped herself on the back windowsill in an effort to remove herself from the talk. When an hour later Blake's houseboy, John, told Danica that she was wanted on the phone, she was grateful for an excuse to leave the room.

More than anyone she wanted it to be Michael because she felt chilled to the bone and in need of his encouragement, but she knew that he wouldn't call her here.

"Hello?"

"Darling?"

Danica felt sudden tears in her eyes. "Mom," she sighed, "oh, Mom, thank you for calling." It hadn't even occurred to her to call Eleanor. She had been conditioned for so long not to depend on her help, but she suddenly realized that, in lieu of Michael, Eleanor might be a comfort. "Where are you?"

"I flew down as soon as your father called me. Darling, I'm so sorry about all this."

"It's not your fault, Mom. But things are pretty awful."

"When did you get there?"

"About an hour ago. I flew down with Hal Fremont. Reporters are swarming all over the place. We had to fight our way through."

"Oh, darling, I'm so, so sorry. How are you holding up?"

"Barely." She was about to say that it had been a draining three days when she caught herself. "I'll do it, though. I'll be good. You don't have to worry about that."

"I wasn't. I have faith in you. Darling, your father wants to talk."

"Mom?" Danica asked urgently. "Mom, I . . . I don't want to stay here tonight . . . with the press outside and all." It was as good an excuse as any, and the only one she felt she could offer Eleanor. "Can I stay with you?"

"Of course, darling. I'm sure Blake will be with his lawyers for hours anyway. Why don't you call me when you want to come and I'll send the car."

"I will. Thanks, Mom."

"Don't thank me. I'm glad I can finally do something to help you." She issued a muffled, surprisingly impatient "Just a minute, William," then returned to Danica. "You'll call when you're ready?"

"Yes." She managed a weak smile. "Why don't you put Daddy on before he throws a tantrum."

"I think I'd better—"

"Danica?" Her father's voice held near belligerence. "Thank God, you're there, girl. I was worried you'd sit on your can up in Maine."

Forcing herself to adapt to the sudden shift of gears, she gritted her teeth. "I was in Boston. I came as soon as Blake called."

"Maybe you're finally coming to your senses." His tone grew even more authoritative. "Now, I want you to know that there's nothing to worry about. We've got trumped-up charges here."

"Daddy, the government has evidence that Eastbridge made those shipments."

"Well, Blake didn't. Someone's out to get him, and I don't know who in the hell it is, but he won't get far. Blake's lawyers will make sure of that. He's with Fitzgerald and Pickering, isn't he?"

"He's with them now."

"What are they saying? He's not resigning, is he?"

"No. He spoke with the President earlier and they agreed that he'd take a leave of absence. Blake will give a press conference tomorrow explaining that he feels that he can't give his all to the Department while he's preparing for the trial and that the Deputy Secretary will be acting in his stead until the trial's over."

"Good. Sounds strong. No suggestion of guilt. What line of defense are Fitzgerald and Pickering planning?"

"I don't know. They're discussing that now. I think it will be a while before they can get the information they need from the Justice Department."

"Maybe I can speed that up."

"You'll have to discuss it with Blake. Should I get him on the phone?"

"No. Don't disturb him. He doesn't like my interfering."

"I'm sure he wouldn't mind your help."

"Well, he knows where I am if he wants me."

Danica detected a subtle anger underlying her father's words, and she wondered if he, too, was irked that Blake had put them all in this mess. "Have you been hounded by reporters?"

"A few. I handled them."

She nodded. "Well then, I guess I'd better get back to the den. I'll see you later."

"Be supportive, Danica. He needs you now."

"Don't worry, I know my place." She certainly did, and it wasn't here. Hanging up the phone, she stood for several minutes. She debated calling her mother to send the car right then. After all, she had made her appearance. Blake had seen her. The press had seen her. Her father, though, expected her to stay for a time, at least. And since this entire ordeal was going to be her swan song, she mused, she could easily swallow her pride and acquiesce.

Rather than return immediately to the den, she wandered to the kitchen to make herself some tea. When John offered to do it, she suggested he see if the others wanted drinks or food. The few minutes alone that she bought were what she needed. When she rejoined the brainstorming session, she felt stronger.

Unfortunately, being closed in a room with three lawyers and Blake was enervating. She tried to concentrate on the discussion, which jockeyed between handling the press and anticipating the government's case, but after a time she tuned out, mentally exhausted. When the group relocated to the dining room, she could do nothing more than pick at the Oriental chicken John had prepared. Her thoughts centered on Blake, on the disgust she felt for him, the anger, the resentment. She kept thinking that if he had been a decent man he would have given her a divorce months ago and she would have been spared all this. She kept asking herself why he had done it, *if* he had knowingly okayed that shipment and, if so, whether he had truly expected to avoid punishment.

When the men prepared to return to the den, she called Blake aside. "Do you need me here now?" she asked quietly.

He seemed taken aback. "Where were you planning on going?"

"I'll be sleeping at my parents' place."

He stared at her. His lips twisted when he turned his head aside. "It won't look very good if you march out of here for all the world to see. They'll grab on anything, including the fact that my wife isn't sleeping with me."

"We haven't slept together for months, Blake, but that's neither here nor there. You can inform the press that precisely *because* of them I don't feel I can stay here. Say they make me nervous, which is the truth. Say that I'm distraught over what's happened, which is also the truth. Say that my *mother's* distraught and that I'm going to comfort her while you work with your lawyers."

"That might work for a day. At some point, though, we're going to have to present a unified front."

"I'm in Washington. Isn't that enough?"

"No. I want you with me when I appear in court for the arraignment tomorrow morning. I want you by my side at the press conference after that. And of course I'll want you sitting in court during the trial."

She wanted to lash out in anger, but she bit her tongue and willed herself to be calm. Her day would come, she told herself. Right now he was putting a down payment on her freedom.

"All right, Blake," she said slowly. "I will be there on those occasions you mention. But I won't live with you in this small town house for the next four months. If you want me to stay in Washington, we'll have to find some alternative setup."

He rubbed his forehead. "Danica, I don't need this. I have enough on my mind right now without having to deal with your whims."

"Call them what you will," she countered, keeping her voice low and steady, a miracle given the fury she felt, "but you'll have to deal with them." She headed for the stairs. "I'm going to call for mother's car now. I'm exhausted. It's been a difficult day. You can pick me up tomorrow morning on your way to court. You know where I'll be." She was halfway down the stairs when Blake called after her.

"Danica?" She looked back. "I . . . can count on your support through this, can't I?"

She almost felt sorry for him because at that moment he seemed so unsure. She felt no sense of victory, though, only a great sadness that he had brought all of this on himself. "Yes, Blake. You can count on me. I assure you I'll do nothing to hurt your case."

He came several steps closer and dropped his voice. "What about Buchanan?"

She was surprised. "Michael? He'd never do anything—"

"Are you still seeing him?"

"Yes. I love him. I told you that last spring."

"But while you're here, you won't . . ."

He didn't have to finish. She knew that once again he was thinking of himself. "No. I won't see him while I'm here. He agrees with what I'm doing. He's a good man, Blake, a decent, honest, compassionate man. And he believes in me much more than you ever did."

"I always believed in you."

"Not the way he does. He wouldn't have to ask if he could count on my support. But then, he wouldn't ever need it, at least not in the way you do now."

Blake stood for a minute staring at her and she realized that he looked every one of his forty-six years. "Well, at any rate, I'm glad to know you'll be standing with me. I'll pick you up at nine."

She nodded once, then continued down the stairs to call her mother from the lower living room. A glance out the window told her that the press throng had thinned, though even then she wasn't looking forward to making her way through. But there was no other feasible exit. She spotted her father's driver pulling around the corner when Blake came down the stairs.

"I'll walk you to the car," he said.

She saw that he had his suit jacket on again and that he looked perfectly composed, and wondered if one of the lawyers had suggested that a show of husbandly care might impress the media. She would have objected had she not desperately feared the thought of warding off the microphones alone.

Glancing out the window, she saw that the car was waiting. Taking a deep breath, she let Blake open the door and lead her quickly down the steps.

"Mr. Secretary, what can you tell us about the charges made against you?"

"Mr. Secretary, have you spoken with the President?"

"Mr. Secretary, is there a resignation in the offing?"

Blake opened the car door for Danica and saw her inside before he turned, still with the car door open, and faced his inquisitors. "I'll be holding a press conference tomorrow. Your questions will be answered then. Now, if you'll excuse me, my wife is going to see her parents and I'd like to say goodbye." Before Danica could anticipate his move, he leaned into the car and kissed her. But the words he murmured against her lips weren't directed at her. "Thank you, George. I appreciate your coming for Mrs. Lindsay. Drive carefully."

Danica didn't look back when the car began to move. She simply pressed the back of her hand to her mouth and wondered if she would ever make it through this last charade.

SEVENTEEN

B LAKE WAS ARRAIGNED the following morning in the United States District Courthouse. Dressed in a sedate gray suit, Danica sat in the courtroom and listened while he pleaded innocent to each of the four counts against him. As had been the case when they entered the building, he took her hand in his when they left, and she didn't resist. She had been up long hours the night before talking with Eleanor, and realized that if she was going to go through with the show, she would have to do it right. Public appearances were all that mattered here. When she and Blake were alone and in private, that was something else.

From the courthouse they drove to the Department of Commerce, where Blake held the press conference he had promised. Danica sat to his right, his lawyers to his left. She smiled at Blake when he smiled at her, looked poised if appropriately somber the rest of the time; in short, she handled herself as would the devoted wife of a man who was facing a grave challenge.

Later that afternoon, when she and Blake were alone in his condominium for the first time since she had flown in from Boston, she raised the issues that were foremost in her mind.

"What happened, Blake?"

They were having drinks in the living room and had barely said two words to each other since returning from lunch with Fitzgerald and Pickering.

He stared at her. "What do you mean?"

"How did that shipment containing high-speed circuits make it to the Soviet Union?"

"You heard what I told Jason and Ray," he said indignantly. "I had no more idea that those computers contained restricted circuits than I had that they were headed for Russia."

"But you were the one who filed the application for an export license."

"I thought I was shipping a decontrolled commodity."

"You were always on top of the things like that."

"I thought I was. Evidently I was wrong."

His statement was arrogant, containing no hint of the humility that his words should have suggested. Danica pressed. "Then Harlan was the one responsible?"

"Exactly."

"How did he manage it?"

Blake took a healthy drink, then set his glass down on the arm of his chair. "Go ask him."

"I can't. He's dead."

"Exactly."

"That must make your case easier. A dead man can't fight back."

He stared at her. "What are you getting at, Danica?"

"He was murdered. Neatly eliminated. You didn't have any part in that, did you?"

Blake bolted from his seat and stalked across the room. She could see the fists at his sides, the tension radiating through his shoulders. When he turned at last, his features were rigid. "I'm going to pretend you didn't ask that."

"I had to ask it. Someone else is bound to, and I want to know the answer."

"The answer is no. Unequivocally, *no*. Look, Danica—" he held out a hand that shook "—I know we've had our differences and I know that this trial business can't be pleasant for you, and even if you can't find it in you to believe me on the matter of the shipment, this you *have* to believe. I didn't kill Harlan! I could *never* do something like that. Believe I'm a crook if you will, but not a murderer!"

She hesitated for only a minute. "I do believe you," she said quietly. "I just wanted to hear you say it. In the ten years we've been married, I've never thought you capable of violence." She had come to realize he was capable of other things she hadn't imagined, but she had to believe violence wasn't one of them.

"Thank God for that." He slowly simmered down and returned to his drink.

"I think we ought to discuss where we're going to live until the trial is over."

"There's nothing wrong with this place," he grumbled over the lip of his glass.

"It's too small. There's only one bedroom and the den for sleeping." She had no intention of sharing his bed. She knew she would get no argument there, and she didn't.

"I'll take the den, if that will make you happier."

That would leave her in his bed, where for all she knew he had had lovers more than once. The thought made her flesh creep. "I think we should rent a house in one of the suburbs. That would give us both plenty of room. Look at it realistically. It's going to be a long few months before the trial starts, and since you won't be working, you'll be around more than you ever were. You'll go stir-crazy here, and I, well, I just don't want to be here."

He eyed her cautiously. "Then you agree that you can't stay with Bill and Eleanor?"

"I *can*, but you were right. Mom helped me see that last night. It wouldn't look very good if we live apart."

"Bless Eleanor."

She bristled. "It was *my* decision, Blake. Now, will you go along with the idea of renting a house?"

He shrugged. "If you want to do the looking, be my guest. I'm sure you understand that I'm not of a mind to do it myself."

"I'll do the looking. I'm going to need *something* to fill my time." Setting down her drink, she reached for her purse. "I'll take a cab back to my parents' for now."

"I can drive you."

"No. Come to think of it, it might be a good idea for Marcus to drive the Audi down. I'd like some mobility."

"You can drive the Mercedes."

"You'll need it. Once we're out of the city, it'll be harder getting cabs."

"Another reason to stay here," he muttered.

But that was out of the question. "I'll call Marcus later," she said on her way out of the room. In truth her mind was on another call, one she proceeded to make from a pay phone on a street corner several blocks from Blake's condo.

"Michael?"

"Dani! Sweetheart, it's good to hear from you!"

"Same here." The sound of his voice was like a balm. "I wanted to call sooner but I was worried about the phones being tapped. I wanted privacy."

"How're you doin'?"

"I'm surviving."

"I saw it all on television at noon — the arraignment and the press conference. You looked beautiful."

"I was dying."

"It didn't show. Blake handled himself well, I thought. Very dignified, very professional."

"That's his way. He's furious inside, but no one would ever know it."

"How's he behaving toward you?"

"Not much differently than he always did. He did thank me for coming, but we had an audience at that particular point. He's big on appearances. Not that I mind if he ignores me most of the time. I don't want him touching me."

"Did he try?"

"Only for the sake of the press. He held my hand whenever there were cameras around. He kissed me once, for the cameras, but I doubt he'll try that often."

"Have you said anything to him about . . ."

Her stomach twisted, then settled. "No. I confronted him about everything but that. It's my ace in the hole, Michael. When I use it, it'll carry weight."

"What did he say about the rest?"

"He denied that he knew what was really in the shipment. He's blaming the whole thing on Harlan. He also denied that he had anything to do with Harlan's murder."

"You asked him *that?*"

She smiled sadly. "I've gotten bold, I guess. I wanted him to know that even though I'm here, I'm far from a blind supporter. I do believe him as far as Harlan's murder goes, though. I'm sure he had no part in that."

"I agree, but I still don't like the idea of your living with him in that condominium."

"I told him I wouldn't. I'm going to look for a house in the suburbs for us to rent. I want a yard with some trees and fresh air, plenty of bedrooms and a live-in housekeeper as a chaperone. Until then, I'm staying at my parents' place. That was where I slept last night. My mother was wonderful. We talked for a long time. I mean, she was really *there.*"

"I'm glad about that. If you get nothing else out of this ordeal, at least you'll cement your relationship with her. It's long overdue."

"I think you're right. . . . Michael?" She grew misty-eyed and her voice wavered. "I miss you so much. I think about you all the time."

"Me, too. I haven't known what to do with myself."

"Have you done anything with the stuff we gathered this summer?"

"No. Every time I look at it, I think of you and my mind starts to wander. I managed to go over the galleys for my book, though. They've been sitting here a while. My editor was getting pissed."

"What about your class?" He had been appointed to teach another fall semester course at the School of Government. "Do you have much to prepare differently from last year?"

"I'll have to update things, but there's nothing major now that I have the basic curriculum set. . . . How about you? Will you go up to Boston to do your radio show, or will you be staying in Washington the whole time?"

"I have to call Arthur. I'd like to continue to do the show. Being here the rest of the time is going to be bad enough. During the trial I'll have to skip the show anyway. It wouldn't be seemly." She drawled the word with blatant sarcasm and rolled her eyes, but in so doing she caught sight of the cab. "I'd better go. My cabbie looks like he's getting impatient."

"Your cabbie?"

"I'm at a pay phone on the way to my parents. I didn't want Blake to drive me, for obvious reasons. I'll give you a call in a few days?"

"I'll be waiting. I love you, Danica."

She smiled, but her voice was shaking again. "I love you, too. You're my strength, do you know that? Hold the fort for me, Michael."

"I will."

He threw her a kiss, which she answered with two, then she quietly replaced the receiver on its hook and ran back to her cab.

* * *

Several days later Danica found the house she wanted. It was in Chevy Chase and was far enough from the capital to provide the respite she needed yet close enough so that Blake would have no trouble driving in to see his lawyers. Not that time was of the essence, since both she and Blake had more of it on their hands than ever before, but she wanted to be considerate, since she had been the one to demand the house.

It was furnished and in move-in condition, with five bedrooms plus a suite for the help, and its yard was large, well guarded from the public by thick stands of trees. If the cost of the rental was exorbitant, Danica reasoned that it was money well spent. She chose for herself the bedroom farthest from Blake's, hired the woman she wanted, and made arrangements for Marcus to deliver the Audi.

Two weeks after Blake's arraignment, she flew back to Boston to pick up more things from the town house. While she was there, she made several calls, the last one of which was to Michael.

"I lost the radio show."

"_What?_"

"I met with Arthur today. He explained that my presence would detract from that of a guest."

"That's _absurd!_"

"I'm furious. Arthur claimed that the live call-ins we'd get would be asking questions of _me_ and that he wanted to protect me from that. I argued with him, but his mind was made up."

"Screw him, then. There'll be other opportunities for you, and when this is all over, you'll laugh in his face."

She smiled in appreciation of his championing. "I also talked with James. He was angry, too, which made me feel a little better. You wouldn't believe it, Michael. I've called several friends to see how things were going—you know, at the Institute and the hospital—and they were cool to say the least. Some friends."

Michael gritted his teeth. "A little experience often upsets a lot of theory."

"Excuse me?"

"I read that the other morning on one of your tea bags."

She grinned. "You're drinking tea now?"

"It settles my stomach."

She was instantly alarmed. "Aren't you feeling well?"

"Only when I think of you down there, which is most of the time."

"Oh, Michael."

"I wish I were in Boston right now." A bulb lit. "Hey, I could be there in an hour."

"You'd kill yourself on I-95 making time like that, and anyway," she mused ruefully, "I have to get to the airport, and . . ."

He anticipated her next words and spoke with feigned mockery. "And it will only be harder if we see each other. I know, I know. But it's so hard right now I sometimes think I'll die."

"Don't you dare. I need to know you're there."

"I think that's what keeps me going. Will you call again soon?"

"As soon as I can. Take care, Michael."

"You, too, sweetheart."

Talking with Michael was her salvation. She called him every few days— Blake, for reasons of his own, had the phones checked regularly for bugs, which eased her worry—and she lived the times between with the memory of Michael's words, his gentle tone, and the knowledge of his love. They were the only things that kept *her* going when her days settled into a routine of marking time.

The press no longer badgered; more immediate news had taken precedence. Danica wasn't a fool to think that the media wouldn't be out in force come time of the trial, but she was grateful for the temporary break.

She spent most of her time at the house in the first-floor garden room whose floor-to-ceiling windows let in whatever sunlight September had to offer. Blake had come to accept that this was her room and left her alone there to read, to knit—which she had never done before, but which desperation inspired—and to think.

She spent several days a week with her mother lunching, shopping, sometimes just talking. Eleanor made herself accessible, realizing that Danica had few friends in Washington and that those she might have had would avoid her now.

"You look tired, darling," she commented one afternoon as they strolled through the Smithsonian. "Maybe I shouldn't have suggested we come here. There's so much to see that it can be overwhelming."

Danica laughed softly. "I'm the one who should be worrying about you, but you seem to be holding up fine."

"I am fine, knock on wood. My leg gives me trouble from time to time, but it's nothing. Aren't you sleeping well?"

"Oh, I sleep, but I still feel tired. I think its the tedium of the waiting. Sitting around with nothing to do but to think about where I am and why, where I *want* to be and why, where I'll be *six months* from now and why. I look down and find my knuckles white and realize that I've been clenching my fists without knowing it. Between tension and boredom, I sometimes think I'll lose my mind."

Eleanor hooked her elbow through her daughter's. "You won't. You're strong. And you're doing the right thing. I know it's difficult for you, missing Michael the way you do."

Danica smiled and offered a soft "Thank you for understanding. It's a help to know that I can tell you things."

"Just don't tell me *too* much." Eleanor was only half joking. "Keeping things from your father is something new for me. I'm not sure I like it."

"I'm sorry you're in the middle. I didn't want that."

"You didn't want to be facing a criminal trial with Blake, either, darling. Life doesn't always work out the way we want."

Danica gave a soft grunt of agreement. "Life is what happens when you're making other plans." When her mother sent her a quizzical look, she explained, "The tea sage," and Eleanor nodded.

"How's Blake taking all this?"

"He's tense. Now that the hullabaloo has died down, he's focusing on the trial and what might, just might, happen to him if something goes wrong and he's convicted. The thought of prison, even of a minimum security one, doesn't thrill him."

"Can you blame him?"

"No. I wouldn't want to be in his shoes. He's a proud man. I think what he fears most is the humiliation."

"Does he discuss it with you?"

"We rarely talk. But then, we never did."

"He's not rude to you, is he?"

"Oh, no. I don't think he'd dare. He knows that I do have an alternative to staying here in Washington with him."

Eleanor nodded. The one thing she and Danica hadn't talked about was the future. She assumed Danica would be leaving Blake once the trial was over, but she didn't want to think of that eventuality. "How is Thelma working out?"

"Just fine. She's a wonderful cook."

"I wasn't sure. You look like you've lost weight."

"I haven't been very hungry. My stomach is in knots most of the time. Blake's sitting like a stone across the table doesn't help."

"It's a trying time. For both of you."

"You can say that again." She sighed. "Well, I am getting a beautiful sweater out of the deal. Do you remember that pretty cotton yarn I bought last week?"

"The nubby pink stuff? It was delicious."

Danica smiled. "It's working up deliciously, too, and God knows, I have enough time to work on it. For all I know, by the time this trial arrives, I'll have an entire wardrobe worth of sweaters."

"Is the trial still set for November?"

"The lawyers have requested that it be put off to December, ostensibly to give them more preparation time. Personally, I think it's more of a tactical move. I think they're hoping to cash in on the feeling of seasonal goodwill. It might just soften the jury."

"How long do they think the trial will last?"

Danica shrugged. "It could be a week. It could be a month." As she figured it, even allowing for the worst, she would be back in Maine sometime in January.

"Will you do one for me?"

"Do what?"

"Knit me a sweater. I'd like to wear something you've made."

Danica squeezed her arm. "Sure. I'll do yours next." And after that she would do the one she had begun to picture, one designed for warmth against the cold, Down East sea air. She fantasized knitting a matching one for Michael, but knew that she couldn't be so crude as to do that in front of Blake. Maybe for Gena . . . or Cilla . . . or even Rusty . . .

By the first week in October Danica began to suspect that something was wrong. Well, not *wrong*, but different. And hopeful. Very hopeful.

With the knowledge that Michael's class met on Wednesdays in the back

of her mind, she flew into Boston for an early afternoon doctor's appointment, then, nearly bursting with pride and pleasure and excitement, took a cab
into Cambridge.

Michael was wrapping up the day's discussion with his class when she
slipped into the back of the room. He paused midsentence to stare. She wore
oversized dark glasses and had pulled her sandy hair into a knot under a chic
fedora, but she hadn't fooled him. Not for a minute.

He cleared his throat and began to speak again, only to stammer dumbly
and end up asking the class what he had been saying. Several of his students
glanced toward the back of the room and were grinning when they faced
forward again. Michael failed to see their humor.

The woman he had dreamed about for the past six weeks was thirty feet
away and he still had to finish the session. Pushing away from the chair he'd
been straddling, he fumbled through the notes on the table behind him, but
his eyes couldn't seem to focus any more than his mind could. In the end, he
simply deferred to the syllabus he had given the students at their first meeting
and dismissed the class.

He stood still for several minutes until the room had cleared, then stalked
to the back of the room, pinned Danica to the wall and gave her the hardest,
longest, most melting kiss she had ever received. Then, having summarily
dispensed with her hat, he buried his face against her hair, wrapped her in his
arms and squeezed until she squealed for mercy.

"Why didn't you tell me you were coming? I would have called in sick,
canceled my class, done anything if I'd known you were in town."

"I just came in this morning." She was beaming, eyes aglow. "Michael, it's
so exciting . . . I tried to wait, really I did . . . I walked around the Square for
what had to be hours but I couldn't get here fast enough. The man downstairs
must think I'm deranged because I couldn't concentrate on the directions he
gave me to find this room. I made him repeat himself three times . . . I'm so
excited!" She clapped her hands to her lips, but her smile was as wide as ever.

Her effervescence was contagious. "What is it? My God, you're bubbling.
Tell me!"

She put her hands on his shoulders. "I'm pregnant, Michael! I'm pregnant
and it's *our* baby! Really *ours*, this time!"

It was the last thing Michael had expected. His eyes grew very round and
his gaze dropped to her stomach while his voice jumped an octave. "Pregnant?
Our baby?"

She nodded vigorously, wanting to scream and jump but controlling herself.

"Our baby?" There was wonder in his tone as he placed his palm where his
gaze had been. "You're going to have our baby." This time it was a statement,
and it was followed by a bone-crushing hug that lifted Danica clear off her feet.
"Oh, sweetheart, that's *wonderful* news!" He set her down again. "You're
sure?" When she nodded, he swept her up again.

Just then the nearby door opened and a young man entered. He stopped
when he saw Michael and Danica, and grew red. He was about to retreat when
Michael held him there.

"We're just leaving." Dragging Danica by the hand, he raced through the door, down the hall and into the office that had been loaned him for his afternoons at the school. When the door was firmly shut, he ushered her to a chair, then knelt by her knees. "When did you find out?"

She was clutching his hand and couldn't stop grinning. "This afternoon. I've been feeling lousy for a while. I assumed it was because of everything down there—" she gestured vaguely "—but when I missed my second period I knew. I flew in this morning to see my doctor here, and he confirmed it. I'm so excited! You have no idea!"

"I think I do. You'd be bouncing off the walls if I hadn't pushed you into this chair. Hell, I'd be bouncing off them myself if I didn't have to hold you here!"

She took his face in her hands and kissed him softly. "I love you so much, Michael. Our baby is going to be so precious and bright and fantastic."

He closed his eyes and wondered if he was dreaming. "I know it will. Oh, Dani, I've missed you so much!" His voice cracked and he pressed his forehead to hers. "This means you'll come back to me."

"I'd have come back to you, baby or no baby."

He looked at her and his expression was urgent. "But you can do it now. Blake can't expect you to suffer down there when you're carrying another man's child."

"But I'm going to," she said with no less urgency. "Don't you see, Michael? The fact that I'm pregnant will help his case all the more."

"You want to help *him?*"

"I want to be free of him! That's what this whole farce is about. By sticking with him through the trial, I'll be discharging the last of my responsibilities as his wife."

"You don't owe him anything."

"But you know me, Michael. You know how I feel and what I've been raised to believe. This is the perfect solution for me. When the trial's over and I leave Blake, no one can say that I didn't do right by him."

"Your father will."

"Not when he hears what I have to say. And if he still insists that my place is with Blake, well, that's his problem. I won't feel any guilt."

Michael sat back on his heels. "That's what this is all about, isn't it? Guilt."

She reached out to touch his cheek. "I don't want anything to mar our marriage or the happiness we'll have together and with our baby. If we do it my way, nothing will."

He stood then and walked slowly across the room. "I still don't like it. Maybe I don't trust Blake. Who *knows* how he'll react when you tell him about the baby."

"He'll be thrilled, particularly knowing that he is the way *he* is. He'll love the idea of my sitting in the courtroom wearing maternity clothes. His lawyers will love it, too. The jury will be sympathetic. So will the press."

"Hell, I don't want you going through all that! The strain could do any number of things to you . . . or to our child."

Danica wasn't about to be deterred from her goal. "You're thinking about my miscarriage, but I asked the doctor about that and he doesn't see any problem. In the first place, I'll be sitting at home doing practically nothing for the next two months, and by the time the trial comes, I'll be past the critical stage. In the second place, the doctor saw nothing to suggest that there was anything wrong."

"He didn't foresee any problems last time."

Danica left her chair and went to him. "Last time it wasn't meant to be. Look at what's happened since, and you'll know I'm right." Taking his hand, she placed it on her stomach. "This time's different. I know it. I can feel it. And the fact that I've been feeling so awful is a good sign."

"It is?"

She nodded. "The doctor said so. It's when a baby takes well that a woman more often has things like morning sickness."

"You've had that?"

"It was what tipped me off. But it's nothing, not when I know its cause." Her heart overflowed with love for both the man before her and the baby inside her. "I feel so good now. I feel so happy. You can't be with me through that trial, but at least I'll have your baby. Do you know what that means to me?"

He looked from one to another of her features, then traced each with fingers that trembled. "I know that you have to be the most wonderful woman in the world," he murmured hoarsely. "I also know that the next few months are going to be absolute torment for me. Now I have two of you to worry about."

Wide-eyed, she grinned. "Isn't it wonderful?"

He held his breath for a minute, then chuckled and shook his head. "You're amazing."

"Another variation on 'the most wonderful woman in the world.' Kiss me, bud. I have to get back to the airport."

He kissed her then, and again more than once as he drove her to Logan. She was high on happiness, and it pleased him to see her that way. The knowledge that he was both biologically and emotionally responsible for that happiness was some comfort, given the many misgivings he had about allowing her to return to Washington.

After landing at National, she drove directly to see her mother. She was still bubbling and knew she would have to settle down before she faced Blake.

The housekeeper answered the door. "Ruth, where's my mother?" she asked, sweeping past.

"Upstairs, Mrs. Lindsay. She and Senator Marshall were about to sit down for dinner."

Just then Eleanor appeared at the top of the stairs. "Darling! I didn't expect you!"

"And I didn't realize how late it was. But I had to see you." Danica paused, and for the first time in hours her smile wavered. "Where's Daddy?"

Eleanor started down the stairs. "On the phone in the den. What's happened? You look . . ." She gestured eloquently with her hands.

"I am." Taking her arm, Danica led her into the living room. "I'm pregnant, Mom. It was confirmed today."

Eleanor turned to face her, her eyes wide with the very excitement Danica needed. "Pregnant? Darling, that's wonderful!" She hugged her, then set her back. "What does Blake say?"

It hadn't occurred to Danica that her mother wouldn't immediately sense the truth. "Blake doesn't know yet. I'm going to tell him in a little while." The chill in her tone was a hint.

Eleanor stared at her daughter for a long minute, then let out a soft breath. "It's Michael's, isn't it?"

Danica nodded, smiling again. "You have no idea how happy he's made me. First loving me, then giving me his child. It's exactly what I need to see me through everything here."

"Have you told him?"

Again Danica nodded. "I flew to Boston this morning to see my doctor there."

"You said you were driving to Virginia for the day."

"I didn't want to say anything. Not until I knew for sure. And Michael teaches in Cambridge on Wednesdays, so I took a cab over after my appointment. We didn't have long to spend together, but I wanted him to be the first to know."

"How did he take the news?"

"He was thrilled but worried. He's concerned that the trial will be too much of a strain. He wanted me to go back to Maine with him, but I told him I wouldn't."

"You wouldn't?"

"No. I owe Blake this much, Mom. You and Daddy didn't raise me to be a stoic for nothing." She squeezed Eleanor's hand. "I'm so excited. Be happy for me."

Eleanor hugged her. "I am, darling. Truly."

"Is that Danica?" William's roar came from the upper floor. Moments later, he was trotting down the stairs and joining them in the living room.

"William, Danica has the best news we've heard in months. She's pregnant!"

"Well, it's about time . . . again." He leaned forward to kiss Danica's cheek. "Congratulations, honey. At least Blake will have something to keep him going now."

"Thanks, Daddy," Danica said quietly, sending her mother a warning glance. "I have to run."

"Blake doesn't know yet, William," Eleanor explained, realizing that her husband might well pick up the phone and unwittingly spill the beans. "Danica's going to tell him tonight."

"Special dinner, eh? Well, then, run along. He'll be waiting."

Danica kissed her mother, waved to her father, then was out the door feeling like a little girl going off to school. Of course, there had been only a handful of days when her parents had seen her off as a child. For the first time she realized that her resentment had passed, and she guessed that it had something to do with her improved relationship with her mother and the understanding that had come forthwith. At least Eleanor now saw her as an adult. She wondered when her father would, *if* he would.

But that, too, didn't seem to matter anymore. Her father would always be her father, but, come trial's end, she intended to live her own life.

Blake was at the door when she arrived home. "Where have you been? I was worried."

She stepped past him and set her purse on the table in the hall. "I told you I'd be gone for the day."

"You could have seen a doctor here. There was no need for you to traipse all the way to Boston."

"I wanted to see the doctor I know. This town is strange enough for me as it is." Looking in the mirror, she removed her hat and smoothed her hair.

"Well, what's the verdict? Will you be well enough to stand by me through the trial as you promised?"

"I don't see why not." She turned to face him. "I'm pregnant."

"You're *what?*"

She laughed aloud, partly because his expression held such disbelief, partly because she was feeling so very, very good. "I'm pregnant, Blake. The baby's due in May." When he continued to stare, she couldn't resist a barb. "Aren't you pleased? If I'm lucky, I'll be into maternity clothes by the time of the trial. Think of how good that'll look on your behalf."

"I don't need your sarcasm, Danica."

She felt duly chastised. Regardless of the disdain she felt for Blake, he was going through a difficult time. "I'm sorry," she said. "It's just that this is the best thing that's happened to me in the last seven weeks and I'm very happy about it."

He was scowling. "Is it Buchanan's?"

She tempered a sudden burst of anger. "I haven't been with anyone else."

"And you didn't bother to think about birth control?"

"Honestly? No. You and I were married for eight years before I conceived. I've never had to think about birth control."

"Maybe you wanted it. Maybe you wanted his baby."

"Subconsciously I assume I did. I certainly do now."

"Does he know about it?"

"Yes." She was prepared to tell him how delighted Michael was, but he didn't ask.

"Who else knows?"

"That I'm pregnant? Just my parents."

"That it's Buchanan's child," Blake specified.

"Only my mother."

"Are you planning to keep it that way?"

She couldn't believe what he was asking. "Do you mean, am I planning on telling the world that this child isn't yours? What kind of fool do you take me for, Blake? Why in the hell do you think I'm doing all this?"

He looked at her strangely. "I don't think I've ever heard you swear before."

"There are *lots* of things you've never heard me say or seen me do, because I spent the first twenty-eight years of my life in a padded cell and the past two working my way out of it. I'm growing up, Blake. You—and my father—had better realize that. I have thoughts and feelings. I get angry when someone insults my intelligence, which is what you did a second ago. The fact is that I'd *never* be here with you if it weren't for the trouble you've gotten yourself into."

"I didn't *get myself* into trouble."

"All right. The trouble *Harlan* got you into. . . . Did you think I came down here for the sake of some great love we share?"

His surprisingly meek "no" was more powerful than the most loudly shouted curse, because it reminded her once again that he was facing hard times, and she felt instantly contrite.

"Blake," she sighed, speaking softly, "I'm here because I felt that my presence would help your case. Call it 'for old times' sake' or whatever else you will, but I wanted to do it. For you, and for my father." She smiled sadly. "Old habits die hard, but they do eventually die. While this one still has a breath of life, I'm using it to help you. A public announcement that this child is Michael's is *not* going to help you." The discussion had drained her and she spoke slowly. "Please. Trust me to do what's right."

His words, too, came slowly and held an undercurrent of defeat. "I guess I have no other choice, do I?"

"No." She straightened her shoulders and moved toward the stairs. "I feel tired. I think I'll lie down for a while."

She was halfway up the stairs when he called after her. "Is everything well . . . with the baby and all?"

She smiled then, offered a confident "Yes. Yes, I think everything's just fine," and continued up the stairs.

EIGHTEEN

❀ ❀ ❀

"**W**HAT HAPPENED?"

"I told him last night."

"Was he angry?"

"A little, at first. He came around though."

"On his own?"

Danica sighed. "With a little help. I lost my temper. I reminded him in no uncertain terms exactly what I was doing in Washington. My bluntness helped. He couldn't argue with anything I said, and my saying it got it out in the open. I also think that he's finally accepted defeat where I'm concerned."

"It's about time."

"He even asked me if everything was all right with the baby."

Michael tightened his grip on the phone. "Is it? How are you feeling today?"

"Not bad. The nausea comes and goes. It's always worse on an empty stomach, so I try to eat a little something as often as I can. I slept late this morning, too. That helped."

"Good. How did Blake act today?"

"He's been surprisingly cordial. He came in to me in the middle of the morning to ask if there was anything I needed."

"What did you say to that?"

"I wanted to say that I needed *you*, but I restrained myself. No sense rubbing salt on the wound. Blake knows he's lost."

"Just make sure he remembers it," Michael growled.

A similar theme emerged in their conversation several days later. "It's like there's a truce in effect, Michael. I think it's much better for both of us. We talk more than we did before, and he's been solicitous when I've been sick."

"Not *too* solicitous, I hope."

She chuckled. "It could never be that, not with Blake. A leopard doesn't change its spots. They may fade in one season or another, but—"

"Is that true?"

"I don't know, but it sounds good for the purposes of my analogy, don't you think?"

"You're impossible," he said with affection.

"Well, I just don't want you to worry, but you do, don't you?"

"That Blake's going to try to win you back? Of course I do. I'm only human, and I feel particularly so, sitting up here all alone."

"You're not alone. You have Rusty."

"Umm, the Labrador philosopher. Let me tell you, he may be great for helping me run my aggression out on the beach, but as a confidant, he leaves something to be desired."

Danica laughed, then paused. "You shouldn't worry, at least not about that, Michael. There's no way Blake could possibly win me back. I'm yours. The time I spend here is obligatory. Blake doesn't do anything in the least suggestive. He certainly doesn't touch me. I think that his verbal show of concern is as close as he can come to an apology for all he's put me through."

"There's more to come. That's what really worries me. Did his lawyers get the December date they wanted?"

"Uh-huh."

"Does Blake talk about it?"

"He's starting to, but I sometimes think that he's oblivious to my presence when he does. It's almost as if he's talking to himself, as if what's going on in his mind simply needs airing. He could as well be in an empty room, though. He doesn't expect any response from me. Maybe he's too embarrassed to look me in the eye."

"Has he told anyone of your pregnancy?"

"His lawyers. They were pleased."

"Do they know the truth?"

"No. Blake and I agreed on that. For all practical purposes, at least until the trial's over, this baby is his."

"I don't like that."

"It's part of the scheme. If I don't follow my game plan, *all* of this will have been a waste."

"I suppose. I still don't like it."

She smiled softly. "That's because you love me."

"Smart lady."

The following week Danica called Michael with an interesting piece of news. "You will *never* guess what happened this morning."

"You felt the baby kick?"

She laughed. "Not yet. It's much too soon. It's still a teeny, teeny thing, Michael."

"Oh . . . You caught Blake talking to the wall?"

"Maybe in time that, too, but not yet."

"Okay. I give up. What happened this morning?"

"I got a call from *Boston* magazine. They want me to keep a journal of what I'm experiencing waiting for the trial, then of the trial itself. They think it would make a dynamite article."

Michael stiffened. "Will you do it?"

"Certainly not! I told the fellow that it was too personal, that I couldn't possibly think of writing my private feelings for a magazine. When he offered me good money, I told him that it would be immoral for me to even think of cashing in on my husband's ordeal. That didn't sink in; he had the gall to ask if he could send a reporter down at intervals to interview me. Can you believe that?"

"Oh, I can believe it all right. I *know* how reporters work."

"Not all of them are like that. By the way, I had lunch with Cilla yesterday."

"I know. She called me last night. She knew I was worried about you and wanted to tell me that you look wonderful."

"We had a nice time together. She said she and Jeff are looking for a place."

Cilla had told Michael that, too. "But she's fighting the idea of remarriage."

"I know. And I feel badly. I guess Jeff wants it very much. But Cilla feels that they have a good thing going now and that they ought to give it more time before they get 'tangled' in legal papers again. I think she'll give in after they've lived together for a while."

"How do you feel about Jeff?"

"I think he's great!"

"You don't hold anything against him, then?"

"Because his investigation exposed Eastbridge? Of course not. He was doing his job. But it was just as well that he wasn't there yesterday. I'm not sure Blake would have appreciated it. He's not quite as understanding."

"Then he doesn't know the connection between Cilla and Jeff?"

"Not yet."

"Did he give you any flack about seeing Cilla?"

"He was nervous at first. He knew Cilla was a reporter and he was worried she would sink her claws into me and that I'd inadvertently say something I shouldn't. I told him that our meeting was personal, not professional. I reminded him that Cilla was my friend and *your* sister."

"'He must have loved that," Michael quipped.

"It did shut him up. But I have to give him some credit. He's been understanding of my need to get out. I have the freedom to come and go as I please."

"Do you get out much?"

She sighed and shifted the phone on her shoulder. "Actually, no. Where would I go? It's not as if I have friends here. I see Mom, and now Cilla, but that's the extent of it."

Michael remembered how, when she'd been with him, they had gone out each day, how she had enjoyed meeting new friends and seeing old ones. "It must be lonely for you. What do you do with yourself?"

"I sleep." She smirked. "I've been doing that a lot. I've been knitting, too. You should see the baby blanket I'm making. It's almost done and it's adorable. I think I'll make several—I've felt so good working on it because I think about the baby and about you and how wonderful things will be next spring."

"I like it when you say that. Sometimes I get discouraged."

"You know that it's only a matter of time."

"It's always been a matter of time. I guess I'm just getting impatient. I keep thinking about how much I want to be with you. I want to see every change in your body as the baby grows."

"There's nothing much to see yet. My breasts are bigger. That's all."

"That's *all*," Michael squeezed his eyes shut against the images that filled them. "Oh, sweetheart, this is doing nothing for my peace of mind, much less my bodily state."

Her voice came very softly. "Then we're even. I lie in bed at night remembering all the ways you've touched me and wanting you to do it again. I love you so much, Michael."

He sucked in an unsteady breath. "I love you even more. And I will do all those things again. I promise."

"Guess what! Greta's pregnant too!"

Danica burst into a grin. "That's fantastic! Does she know about ours?"

"I told her. I told them both. I had to, Dani. We've been so close for so long and I was so excited when Greta told me their news that I just couldn't keep it in. She and Pat are pretty isolated, at least from the other people you know. They won't say a word—"

"It's okay! I'm glad you told them. It's not fair that you have to hide so much. I feel awful about that, Michael. I may be committed to letting the world think this is Blake's baby for now, but I don't like it any more than you do."

"I understand why you're doing what you are."

"But I'm proud that my baby's yours. It makes me sick to think of Blake taking the credit. . . . His lawyers did leak it to the press, by the way. There was a small notice on the society page two days ago."

"Any reaction from that?"

"Not that I know of." Danica hesitated for a minute, thinking about the argument she had had with Blake concerning concealing the true parentage of the baby. But there were times to bend, times when it was safe to bend, as in the case of Greta and Pat and the person she now considered. "Michael? I'd like you to tell Gena. She'll be so excited. I think she'll understand what I'm doing."

Michael smiled and let out a breath. "I know she will. Thanks, sweetheart. I've been wanting to tell her, but I didn't dare. Maybe I'll take a drive up tomorrow."

"She'd like that."

"I'd like that."

"How is . . . everyone in town?"

"Very well. They ask about you all the time."

"Do you sense any hostility?"

"Because of the case? None. These people are different, Dani. They were never snowed because of who you were. They never particularly made the connection between you and Blake."

"I was always with you. They probably know more of the truth than anyone."

"If they do, they're not gossiping. They adore you. To a person, they've been totally sympathetic. Their main concern is that you're stuck in Washington having to face Blake's trial. They want you back up here."

"So do I."

"And I. How are you feeling?"

"About the same."

"No cramps?"

"No, thank God. Just a constant queasiness. The doctor says it'll pass. I see him again at the beginning of the month." She gave him the exact day and time. It was, of course, on a Wednesday.

"Can I come with you?"

"That might be pretty risky."

"But what if I was just a friend, meeting you at the airport and chauffeuring you around."

"You're not just a friend. I don't think we can carry the charade that far. Don't tell me you'd be satisfied sitting meekly in the waiting room while I see the doctor. Knowing you, you'll want to be in there with me asking a million questions. It'd never work, Michael. The doctor, the nurse, the receptionist— they'd all be sure to know."

"Well, then, at least meet me for lunch before my class."

She grinned. "Now *that* I think I can arrange."

"Good. I found this terrific Indonesian place. It's dark and you can wear your disguise—you know, a hat and dark glasses—and no one will ever know it's you. Hell, I might even forget it myself and think that I'm with a movie star. . . ."

* * *

Danica was feeling lower when she called Michael next. She hesitated for a long time but had finally dialed his number in pure selfishness.

"I'm warning you ahead of time, Michael," she began instantly. "I know that you expect a sweet, intelligent being, but you're about to witness something very different."

"What's wrong?" he asked in alarm.

"I'm going out of my *mind*! Some days are worse than others, but today was the pits! I started by throwing up, but that's nothing new, so I won't even comment on it." She spoke slowly then, clearly struggling to contain her frustration. "I have been walking around this house all day bored to tears. I don't feel like knitting. I don't feel like reading. I don't feel like going out because there's nowhere to go and no one to go with. Blake's been sitting in the living room staring at the walls and I don't want to talk to him anyway. His tension is contagious. He's coiled like a spring, and I get that way being with him for more than a minute. I don't have anything to do, Michael, at least not something that will take my mind off all this." She let out a loud breath. "So I'm calling you . . . and feeling guilty about whining."

He was so relieved that there wasn't a physical problem that he actually smiled. "Whine all you want, sweetheart. That's what I'm here for."

"It's not. You don't deserve it. You weren't the one who asked for this. *I* was."

"You didn't ask for it."

"But I was the one who chose to play the martyr."

"True," he drawled in an attempt to humor her. He knew that pregnant women leaned toward pickles and tears, but he hadn't thought to consider mood swings until now. On the other hand, he reasoned, even beyond pregnancy she had plenty of justification for testiness. The best he could do was to try to talk it out of her. "Why was Blake so bad today? Has something happened with his case?"

"Not necessarily today, but the tension's mounting. His lawyers are beginning to get a look at the documents the government has. Blake's signature is right there on the license application filed with the Commerce Department, then again on a paper okaying the shipment. He still claims that he didn't know the integrated circuits were in the machines *or* that the machines were headed for Russia."

"Can he prove it?"

"No. But the lawyers feel there's a solid case for reasonable doubt. The prosecution has to prove his guilt beyond that if they want a conviction, but most of what they have is circumstantial evidence. It may be strong circumstantial evidence, but it is only circumstantial. . . . There are so many ifs. I think that's what's getting Blake down. I don't know, maybe it's just boredom for him, too. And he doesn't have *you* to talk to."

"Does he talk to anyone?"

"Oh, yes. He plays squash at the health club several times a week and he sees old friends. But he's been warned not to say anything relating to the case and since that's what's preoccupying his mind these days, he really has no outlet other than Jason and Ray. I'm getting tired of them, too. They say the same things over and over again."

Michael chuckled. "That's because you tune out and you don't hear the fine differences." He paused and grew more hesitant. "Dani, what if the jury finds Blake guilty? How will you feel?"

"I've thought about that a lot. I'll be sorry, I guess. I'd hate to see Blake go to prison. But it won't make any difference in my own plans. My job is to see him through the trial, to help him present the best image possible. If it doesn't work, well, it's out of my hands."

"I was wondering."

"Worrying, you mean. Don't, Michael. Is this or is this not the voice of a woman of conviction?"

"It certainly is, but that woman also has a hell of a lot of compassion."

"Which is why I'm praying that Blake will be acquitted. For *his* sake, not mine. My own course is set."

"Does he know what it is?"

"He has to have guessed. We don't talk about what's going to be after the trial, but he knows how I feel about you and the baby, and he's not dumb."

"Does he know that we talk?"

"The phone bill came in last week."

"Y' know, I've asked you more than once to call collect."

"It's not a matter of money, and I don't want to call collect. I'm beyond caring if Blake knows we talk, and he hasn't said a word. Maybe he knows I'd be off the walls if I didn't have you to talk with."

"I'm always here."

"Except on Wednesdays."

"Except on Wednesdays. Are you all set for next week?"

"You bet, and I can't wait. It's been so long. . . . Michael?"

"What, love?"

"Thank you."

"For what?"

"For letting me spout off like that."

"Do you feel better?"

She smiled. "Yes."

"Then it was worth every minute."

Early the following Wednesday Danica flew to Boston. She had made her doctor's appointment for midmorning so that she and Michael would have that much longer together. Though she had expected to take a cab to the restaurant Michael had named, she was thrilled to walk out of the medical building and find the Blazer parked in front.

Quickening her step, she climbed through the door Michael leaned to open, and slid onto the front seat and into his arms. He held her tightly for several moments, neither of them able to speak through the flood of emotions. Only when the driver of a slightly battered, if vintage, Mustang passed, honked and offered a thumb up did Michael set her back.

"Smart aleck kid," he murmured, but his eyes quickly returned to Danica's features. His fingers followed, then his lips, and by the time he drew back again she was floating.

"Ahhh, Michael, that felt so good."

"You can open your eyes now."

"But will you be here?" she murmured, cinching her arms around his neck. "I can feel you, but I'm still afraid it's a dream."

"No dream, love. Open up."

She raised her lids slowly, and to her chagrin her eyes were filled with tears. Burying her face against his neck, she let him soothe her until she was more composed.

"Nothing's wrong, is it?" he asked in concern.

She shook her head. "I'm just so happy to see you."

He let out a breath. "Everything went well with the doctor then?"

"Wonderfully. I'm back to my normal weight."

"Back to?"

"I lost a few pounds at the beginning when I couldn't eat."

"But you can now?"

"Oh, yes. And I'm not anemic or anything. I have a prescription for vitamins. He offered to give me something for the nausea, but I really don't want to take a thing. I don't trust drugs. Ten years down the road there's apt to be some horrible revelation that they cause mental block or something."

Michael chuckled. "I'm as glad you're not taking them . . . as long as you're not too sick."

"Only when I'm hungry, and I'm hungry now. Let's go get some lunch, uh, brunch, before I barf all over your car. I didn't have much more than a piece of toast before I left Washington. I was too excited to eat."

Tucking her close beside him, Michael headed off. When they were seated in the restaurant—he had changed his mind and opted for simple American food rather than Indonesian in deference to the sensitivity of Danica's stomach—he wrapped her arm through his.

"I've eaten here once before, but the company wasn't half as nice."

"Was she pretty?"

"Actually, there were three of them."

"Three *women?*"

"Three professors. One was fat and bald, the second was thin and bald, and the third was so myopic that he kept his face close to his plate the whole time and didn't say a word."

"Poor man."

"Don't waste your sympathy. I understand he comes to life in the classroom. His course is one of the most popular at the school." Michael glanced around at the other patrons of the restaurant, then reached down and tugged Danica's chair even closer.

"We're taking chances sitting like this," she teased, leaning into him.

"Nah. No one will recognize either of us. With that wedding band of yours, they'll assume we're a happily married couple. Hell, Blake's borrowing my kid; the least he can do is to loan me his ring for a little while." His eyes were glued to her smiling face. "Cilla was right. You do look wonderful. Still a little tired, maybe, but you have good color."

"You look wonderful, too, Michael. Tell me what you've been doing."

First he snagged a waitress to bring bread sticks for Danica. While she was munching, he explained that he had finally begun to organize the notes they had made the summer before. "There's still a load of research to be done, and I want to interview several other men who've been salvaging. They're all on the northeast coast, though, so it won't be a hassle. If I can get that out of the way before spring, everything else can be done at home."

She knew he was thinking of when she would be joining him, and she squeezed his arm in silent appreciation. "Does your editor like the idea?"

"Very much. The book won't be terribly philosophical, but it'll be a good read. Hey, have the publishers set a date for *your* book?"

She nodded and there was a wry twist to her lips. "January."

"That soon? I thought they were talking of March or April."

"They were. They've pushed it up. They feel that the publicity surrounding the trial in December will familiarize the public with my name. They want to take advantage of that."

"Just what you didn't want."

"Mmmm. They may have a point in terms of sales, but I was a little disappointed. Especially for James. This is his book. I hate to have it tainted—"

" 'Tainted' is *not* the case, Dani. There's nothing 'tainted' about you. You'll shine through that trial like the special lady you are. People will admire you. Wait and see. *Boston* won't be the only magazine after you."

She rolled her eyes. "Heaven help me then. I don't want to see *any* of them. When that trial's over, I'm leaving Washington, leaving Boston and taking up permanent residence in Maine. When I think of being with you every day for the rest of our lives, I realize that I'm very, very lucky." She stopped talking and a pensive expression crossed her face.

"What?"

"Reggie came to see me yesterday."

"Did she!" Though Michael had never met Reggie Nichols, he felt that he knew her, what with all Danica had told him. "How's she doing?"

"Not great. It's amazing, the twists and turns life can take. At one point I thought my future hinged on being the best female tennis player in the world. When I quit, I was relieved but I also felt that I'd lost my claim to immortality. Now I look at Reggie. She's been at the top, she's had it all, and she's miserable. She's decided to retire when the current tour ends next March, and she's going through a real career crisis."

"Still doesn't know what to do?"

"She says she'll probably coach, but she's not looking forward to it. When you've been in the limelight as long as she has, it's hard to step out. It'd be one thing if she had a family, a man or children to fulfill her, but she doesn't."

"Many women today don't need that."

"I know. But I don't think Reggie's one of them. I know I'm not." She leaned forward and kissed him softly on the mouth. "That's why I'm so lucky. I look at Reggie and then at myself and I realize that I'd rather have my life any day. My future looks so bright . . . well, after December at least."

They talked then about what was happening in Washington, and once their food had arrived, they talked between bites about all the other little things they hadn't spoken of on the phone. Michael suggested several good books she should read. Danica suggested a good movie he should see.

"When did you see it?" he asked.

"Blake took me last week."

"He's taking you out now?"

"Not often, and only in desperation. He doesn't know what to do with himself any more than I do."

"Does he worry about bumping into people?"

"He did at first, I think. But depression does wonders. When things get so that you know you'll go mad if you don't get out, the risk of seeing people becomes secondary." She looked down at her sweater and frowned. "Have I spilled something?"

"No. Why?"

"You keep looking at my breasts."

He colored. "I want to see if they're really getting bigger."

She laughed. "Michael Buchanan!"

"Don't 'Michael Buchanan' me!" He put his mouth to her ear. "If it's my baby that's doing it, I want to see."

She reached for the hem of the sweater. "If you'd like, I can take this off."

He stopped her hand with his, then moved lower to feel her belly. "I can't wait until this grows. I dream of you lying in the living room several months from now, wearing nothing but the firelight. It'll cast a beautiful glow over your skin. I'll warm my hands on your big, fat, beautiful belly."

She sucked in a breath, then moaned softly. "I knew this was going to be hard."

"It sure is." Before she realized what he was doing, he slid her hand to his fly and was pressing it close. Closing his eyes, he inhaled deeply; his exhalation was a throaty groan.

"Michael!" she whispered, looking furtively around. "We're in a restaurant!"

"I'd do it anywhere, I'm that horny."

"You are a sex fiend."

He opened one eye. "But it is good with us, isn't it?"

She was grinning. "It is."

When he felt her fingers cup him, he threw back her barb. "Danica! We're in a restaurant!"

"Mmmm . . ."

Michael had trouble teaching his class that afternoon, not so much because of his state of physical frustration as that of mental. He kept thinking about Danica returning to Washington, languishing in the house with nothing to do, and he realized that he had been very thick. He couldn't drive back to Maine fast enough to get to work.

The next night, when Danica called, he was full of mystery. "I'm sending something down for you."

"Something? What is it?"

"You'll see. Can you be at the Lincoln Memorial at noon tomorrow?"

"Will you be there?" she asked excitedly.

"Not me. A messenger."

"What kind of messenger?"

"One bearing my surprise."

"*What* surprise?"

"You'll see then. Can you be there?"

"Of course I can, but the suspense may kill me. Can't you even give me a hint?"

"Nope."

"How will I know who your messenger is?"

"You'll know."

"Michael . . ." she warned, but he wasn't about to be coaxed.

"Indulge me. Noon tomorrow. The Lincoln Memorial."

Danica was there early. She looked all around, but the faces she saw were both unfamiliar and in selfcontained groups focused on the large statue of a seated Lincoln. Taking their lead, she studied the statue. Its gentleness, the look of wisdom about it, had always appealed to her. Michael knew that of all the memorials in Washington this was her favorite. She sensed he had purposely chosen it as a rendezvous point.

Tucking her hands in the pockets of her coat, she surveyed the sightseers again, then slowly turned in time to see a cab pull up to the nearby curb. She glanced at her watch. It was still five minutes before the hour. She was about to turn back to the statue when a small, silver-haired woman emerged from the cab. After only a moment's pause, she started excitedly down the steps.

"Gena!" she called, then waved when the other woman looked up and grinned. Running the rest of the way, Danica hugged her soundly. "It is *so good* to see you!"

Gena was beaming when Danica finally held her back. "I'll have you know that this is the first time I've left Maine in three years."

"And you came just to deliver Michael's surprise?"

Nodding, Gena gestured back toward the cab. "It's inside. Come on. We'll find somewhere to eat and then we can talk."

Danica followed her back into the cab, then at Gena's suggestion gave the cabbie the name of a restaurant where she knew they would be able to sit quietly and visit. Only when she settled back on the seat did Gena pass her the parcel Michael had sent. It was a large, thickly stuffed mailing envelope with Danica's name written in his bold script on the front.

"What's *in* here?"

"Papers and notes and assignments."

"Assignments?"

"Michael felt you could use something to help pass the time. The papers and notes are some of those the two of you made last summer. The assignments are suggestions of things you can research at the National Archives. He reasoned that since you were here, you could help him out. He also said something about the Archives being a very peaceful, inspiring place to work."

Danica laughed in delight and hugged the bundle to her chest. "I've been complaining about how bored I am. It'll be wonderful to have something to do!"

Gena gently touched her cheek. "That may be part of why he sent it, but I'm sure that you'll be helping him, too. The work needs to be done and he's been so distracted."

"I know. This all must be nearly as hard on him as it is on me."

"He feels helpless. He was furious that he didn't think of this sooner. You only have a month before the trial begins, but if this helps pass the time, then you'll be doing *both* of you a favor. . . . You do look beautiful, Danica. How are you feeling?"

"Great! Well, better, at least." She glanced toward the plastic separating them from the cabbie and lowered her voice. "I'll be through the third month in another two weeks. I think things are settling down."

"I feel for you. I was so sick carrying Michael and Cilla." She paused. "Any chance it might be two?"

"I asked the doctor that, but he doubts it. Twins usually skip a generation. Our children may be the lucky ones. It's still too early to tell with me, but I'll be happy with a single healthy baby."

Gena squeezed her arm. "We *all* will." She shivered and grinned. "I think I'm nearly as excited as Michael and you. It won't be my first grandchild, but, well, Michael and I have always been like souls. And you'll be so *close!*"

Danica felt gratified, then grew hesitant. "You do understand why I'm doing what I am now?"

"I love you all the more for it. Loyalty is a very fine quality. I know that there are times when you've felt it was a thorn in your side——"

"Michael told you about that?"

"He's told me most everything now and I'm glad he has. The way I see it, the only problem in your life is that your allegiances have been thrust on you. Now that you've chosen the direction of your own future, loyalty and responsibility will be positive forces. I know I've said this before, but it stands repeating. I couldn't have wished for a better woman for my son."

Choking up, Danica hugged her again. "I'll be lucky having a mother-in-law like you," she whispered. "Thank you—for coming today, for being Michael's mother, for making him the kind of person he is."

"Don't thank me," Gena chided softly. "Loving is what makes life worthwhile."

Much later, after they had eaten, Danica thought of Gena's words again. Smiling, she pulled the tag from the tea bag that lay damp and drained on her saucer. " 'True love is the renaissance of life,' " she read. Then she slipped the tag into her purse while Gena smiled knowingly.

The work Michael had assigned her was a godsend and Danica told him that. "I don't know what I'd do if I didn't have something to divert my mind. It's been really bad here. Jason and Ray are over every night working with Blake. They want him to take the stand."

"It makes sense. He gives an impressive appearance and he's articulate. He'll come across looking and sounding like an honest, respectable businessman who was conned by one of his employees."

"That's what they're hoping, but they want to make sure he's prepared. They go over and over his testimony, coaching him on exactly what words to use. Then they turn around and play the prosecution, trying to put him on the spot or get him to contradict himself or somehow punch a hole in his credibility. I'm usually asleep by the time they leave, but Blake is always a zombie in the morning. I try to cheer him up, but there's really nothing I can say."

"He's still not thinking about the future?"

"Not about mine. He referred once to returning to the Department when all this is done, but he grew stony after that. I assume he was thinking about the alternative. Even if he *is* acquitted, the President may ask him to resign."

"That would be illegal. Given our system of justice, a man is innocent until proven guilty, and if Blake is acquitted by a jury . . ."

"But we both know that little phrase 'beyond a reasonable doubt,' and we both know that, realistically, Blake is probably washed up here. Even if he *is* acquitted, he'll always carry a certain stigma. It's not right, but I think it's one of the things that worries him."

"And politics is politics," Michael mused. "Suing the President of the United States would be tantamount to political suicide. Blake may seethe inside, but he'll have to step down graciously and pray that his expertise will be called on at some time in the future."

"You've got it." Her thoughts moved on. "Whether Blake will want to return to Eastbridge is questionable. He founded it and built it from scratch into a large corporation, but he pretty much divorced himself from it when he got his appointment. Even if Blake is acquitted, the company will probably be hit with a stiff penalty for making that shipment. I doubt they'd want him back, even if he *did* want to go. It's strange, Michael. Eastbridge was his heart and soul for so long, yet he was able to turn completely off when he left for Washington—just as he turned completely off his own family when he went away to college."

Michael already knew the bare outlines of that relationship. "Has he talked with any of them since all this happened?"

"The night the indictments were returned, he called to tell them that he was innocent and that they shouldn't pay any attention to what they hear on television. To my knowledge, he hasn't spoken with them since."

"Nice guy."

"Maybe it's mutual. I don't know them well enough to say. Things will be so different with us." Then she stopped. "Have you talked to your father at all?"

"Yes, but not about us. Once the trial's over and we're together again, I thought we could both go to see him. He's been surprisingly open-minded when it comes to Blake. Maybe because he heads a large corporation himself, he can see how easily things go amiss."

"Has he ever had a similar problem?"

"None that involved the law, at least not in a criminal sense. There have been libel suits when he's had to answer for something one of his newspapers said. He may just identify with Blake."

"And, of course, you do nothing to encourage that," she teased, knowing that in spite of everything Michael would never malign Blake in front of John Buchanan.

"I've put in a good word here and there. When Dad finally learns the truth, I don't want him to think that I knowingly kicked Blake when he was down."

"I'm surprised that he's not more hostile, given Blake's relationship to my father."

"Nah. Dad may be a tyrant at times, but only concerning things he believes in. The differences he's had with your father have been ideological. Well, maybe there is a little jealousy there. I think he resents the power your father wields, particularly when it's wielded on the side Dad opposes. He's never had much of a quarrel with Blake. And I'm *sure* that he'd never hold anything against you."

"I'm glad. I wouldn't want to think I'd be coming between you and your father."

"Sweetheart, *life* came between him and me. As long as we go our own ways, we're fine."

She sighed. "With a little luck, maybe my father and I can reach a similar understanding."

"And that's another thing for you to worry about. Don't, Dani. Please? There's nothing you can do about it now, and you have enough else to handle. Everything will work out. You'll see."

Danica wasn't so sure about whether her father would ever graciously accede, but Michael was right. She had enough to handle, coping with the day to day anticipation of the trial, without worrying about that.

Every morning she worked at the Archives studying old records and maps, homing in on ships that had sunk with suspected bonanzas on board. Some afternoons she stopped on her way home at the local branch of the public library to pore through books and newspapers and microfilms, reading everything she could about shipwrecks and recovery operations. The thrust of his book was going to be the romance of it all. This Danica could identify with. When she worked, she was for all practical purposes back on Joe Camarillo's boat in Maine, back on Michael's and hers in the nights. It was a blessed escape.

The trial drew nearer with each day, though, and she couldn't help but suffer from the anxiety that was palpable in the house in Chevy Chase. Her own fretfulness was mixed with a growing impatience. Phone calls to Michael were no substitute for the real thing.

On the second of December she flew to Boston for her scheduled doctor's appointment. Having entered her fourth month of pregnancy, she found that all sickness, even the pervasive fatigue that had plagued her so at first, had vanished. Her doctor declared her in excellent physical shape aside from a slight elevation in her blood pressure, but when he suggested she might take a mild sedative to help her through the trial, she refused. The worst was the waiting, she reasoned. The trial itself couldn't possibly be as bad.

As he had the month before, Michael met her outside the medical building. This time, though, he brought lunch with him and they ate in his borrowed office at Harvard.

"I wanted privacy," Michael explained when he'd finished his sandwich and set the papers aside. He drew her from her chair and propped her against the desk. "Real privacy."

She didn't need to hear his hoarseness to know what he was thinking because he had been looking at her for the past hour with the very same longing she felt. She slid her arms around his neck as he lowered his head, and ghosted her parted lips against his mouth. Their sighs blended with the exchange of breath, as though one was giving life to the other and it was all they would ever need . . . but it wasn't.

When he began to undo the buttons of her light wool dress, she grew cautious. "Michael . . . here?"

"The door's locked. No one will bother us." He had the dress opened to the waist and was reaching inside to release the front catch of her bra. "I want to see you, touch you."

While she held her breath, he did both of those things, peeling the bra aside first to stare at the fullness of her breasts, then to reverently trace his fingers over the pale blue veins that had newly appeared. She bit her lip and closed her eyes, delighting in the gentleness of his touch and its awe.

When he lowered his head and put his mouth against her, she threaded her fingers through his hair. She moaned again when he took her nipple in his mouth and began to suckle. His thumb rolled its mate, then he reversed the attention. She was instinctively arching her hips to his when he drew back. The moistness he left on her breasts felt cold to the air, making them pucker all the more.

When he reached for his belt, she clutched his arms. "No, Michael. We can't . . ."

"We can and we will," he said forcefully, then softened his tone. But his fingers had the belt undone and were negotiating his fly, which took some doing because he was fully erect. "We have a month's worth of hell ahead, sweetheart. This will be good."

He seized her mouth then and thrust his tongue deeply in prelude while he began to bunch up her dress. "Just slip your panties down," he whispered against her lips. "I need you so."

All thought of protest was gone because she needed him as badly. Her body was thrumming, her blood surging through heated veins. She stood only long enough to do as he'd asked. Then he had her dress to her hips and was urging her back to the desk. Releasing himself from his pants, he spread her knees, raised them, and pressed forward.

She sighed as he entered her deeply. "I've been so empty . . ." Then she couldn't say anything more because he began to move slowly in and out and she could hardly breathe, much less return his kiss. Her fingers dug into his shirtfront while he manipulated her hips. Time and place fell by the wayside, the only thing of import being their union, its heat and its glory. It was no time before she cried aloud and burst into a sharp series of gasps. His own cry was deeper. He held himself close as he pulsed into her.

Then they were panting on each other's shoulders, laughing and wondering what a passerby in the hall would think of the sound effects.

"This has been decadent, Michael, but so . . . so wonderful!"

He agreed completely. Holding her there, staying inside her as long as he could, he felt that there was a rightness in the world after all. It wasn't the sex in itself, but the love it expressed, that made what they did so precious. Separated as they'd been by so many miles for so long, he had had to assert his love in this most basic way. Lord knew, there was little else he could do under the circumstances.

Slowly, reluctantly, his thoughts turned toward the future. They dressed more somberly. Both faces were grim by the time Michael dropped her at the airport.

"Take care, sweetheart, and remember that I love you," he said, memorizing her features with soft, sad eyes.

"I will," she said through gathering tears. She knew that the joy of the afternoon would linger with her, but she was already missing him. She also knew that there was no escape from what lay ahead. Turning, head down, she walked stoically toward her plane.

NINETEEN

❀ ❀ ❀

T WO DAYS LATER the trial began. Michael followed the proceedings on television and in the papers, but the calls Danica made to him every night were what he waited for.

"How do you feel?" he asked on that first night.

"Tired. I hadn't realized jury selection would be so slow. Two jurors picked out of eighteen interviewed. It could take as much as a week to get the full jury." Which would make it one week longer before she was free.

"But it's critical, sweetheart. You don't want a juror who's already made up his mind as to Blake's guilt or innocence. More subtle biases, well, I'm sure Blake's lawyers are looking for those. They'll want to stack the jury with professionals, for one thing, people who'll be able to identify with him."

"Mmmm. The foreman of a factory would identify with Harlan. A person from a lower socioeconomic bracket may resent Blake's wealth. On the other hand, the same person may be more awed by Blake's status, so it could go either way. I don't envy Jason and Ray. It's hard."

"How about the press? Does it bother you?"

"It was bad when we got to the courthouse this morning. They were all waiting, like vultures, ready to dive in for the kill."

"This is the first trial of the lot," Michael reasoned, "and since Blake is in such a prominent position . . ."

"Jason says that it'll get better as time goes on, that they'll lose interest." She sighed. "I hope so. It's bad enough going through the trial itself, but to have to deal with media questions and those microphones being stuck in our faces . . ."

"Were they questioning *you?*"

"They tried. They didn't get any more from me than they got from Blake, though."

"I saw the television clip and there you were," Michael quipped on a lighter vein. "Your dress was perfect—just enough of a hint of your pregnancy." As for himself, he had simply to close his eyes to see the added weight of her breasts, the thickening of her waist and the faint, faint rounding of her stomach. "You were the prettiest thing on the screen all night."

She moaned. "I would have rather stayed in the background, but Blake insisted that I be right there by his side when we met the press. You can't believe how difficult it was to sit in court all day looking calm and composed, and this was only the *first* day of the trial."

"It'll be better once the actual trial begins. There'll be plenty to think about then."

"I'm not sure if that's good or bad."

It was bad. After five working days the jury was complete. Immediately after that the prosecution opened its case.

"Tell me you're discouraged," Michael offered.

"How did you know?"

"I heard reports on two of the networks. I know enough about trials to imagine what you're feeling right about now."

"It's so nerve-racking having to sit there quietly while the other guy stands up and says all kinds of condemning things. For whatever differences Blake and I have had, I've never known him to be a 'ruthless hustler.' Did you hear that opening statement?"

"Just excerpts of it."

"It was powerful, Michael."

"I'm sure it was. But that doesn't mean Fitzgerald's won't be as good. Things only sound bad now because you can't rebut them."

"I hope that's true. Blake is really down. He barely ate dinner."

"Did you?"

"Some. For the baby's sake. I'll be damned if I'll let this child suffer for things it has no part in."

"Shhh. You're a good mother already, Dani. That baby's a lucky kid."

Luck had little to do with the events of the succeeding days. Everything Danica did was carefully planned and as carefully executed. She maintained her poise in the courtroom, never once wavering while document after document was introduced into evidence and witness after witness took the stand.

The Assistant United States Attorney prosecuting the case painstakingly detailed Blake's involvement with Eastbridge Electronics, then the licensing procedure that preceded the shipment in question and the fact that the items being shipped were restricted by the government. He brought in witnesses to testify that the high-speed integrated circuits had indeed been packed at and shipped from Eastbridge, then other witnesses—mercifully not Jeffrey—to outline the investigation that had traced the shipments back from the Soviet Union to Eastbridge.

Listening each day, Danica grew more and more discouraged. Back at the house she forced the healthiest of foods into herself and made sure she got the proper amount of sleep—well, rest, at least, because there were nights when, even after talking with Michael, she remained tense and sleep eluded her. The only thing that seemed to help during those late night hours when she lay awake in bed was when she put her hand on her belly and projected her thoughts to the future. She pictured her baby, newly born, perfectly formed, and Michael by her side, smiling, holding her hand, telling her how much he loved her, how much he loved their child. She wondered if it was a boy and tried to think of masculine names, then switched and considered the feminine possibilities. She and Michael discussed it from time to time, but for the most part their conversations revolved around the trial.

With Christmas fast approaching, Danica grew more restless. "It'll be several more days before the prosecution rests," she told Michael on the twentieth of the month.

"It's taking longer than we thought." In the back of his mind, as in Danica's, there had been the vague possibility that they would be reunited for Christmas. That possibility was now dashed.

"Since the burden of proof rests with the prosecution, every little thing has to be spelled out. At least that's what Jason and Ray say. It seems to me that only a moron wouldn't be able to move faster, and as far as I know there are no morons on the jury."

"It's the system of justice, sweetheart. One step at a time."

"One quarter-step at a time."

"You're impatient. So am I. We'll get there, though. Slowly, but surely."

The final witness the prosecution brought in was a surprise, and a shock. He was a man who had been employed at Eastbridge at the time of the shipment, a man who claimed he had been present during a conversation in which Blake had specifically referred to the high-speed integrated circuits, hence proving that he knew of their existence. On cross-examination Jason was able to tarnish the man's credibility, pointing out that the witness may have confused the point of the conversation in question and, more importantly, that he had been dismissed from employment at Eastbridge for reasons of alleged incompetency shortly before Blake had left.

Still, the testimony hurt.

That Christmas was one Danica wanted to forget. Though she and Blake had agreed not to exchange gifts, he presented her with a gold watch—a "thank you," he called it, for her support. She felt cheap, and it wasn't because she hadn't bought anything for him.

They had dinner with her parents, but there was little to talk about that wasn't depressing, and because talk of the baby was embarrassing, given that

William didn't know the truth, Danica avoided it. More than anything, she had wanted to be with Michael, who, along with Cilla and Jeff and Corey, whom Danica hadn't yet met, had gone to Gena's for the day. Her only solace was in talking with him later that night.

"Merry Christmas, sweetheart."

"You, too." She knew she was about to cry and she didn't want to do that, so she savagely bit on her lower lip.

"How did it go?"

"Okay," she managed, but sniffled. "Cheer me up. Tell me about yours."

He did, in great detail, and she loved every minute of it because she was imagining how things would be the following year when she and the baby would be there.

"Gena sends her love. So do Cilla and Jeff, *and* Corey, even though he said that you'll probably think him that much more of a lecher than you already do."

She laughed. Corey was the publisher of his own magazine, which was about as far to conforming with the other Buchanans as he went, since the magazine was a sophisticated version of *Penthouse*. Danica had seen it at Michael's house and had thought it inspiring.

"I don't think he's a lecher. I can't wait to meet him."

"I don't know," Michael teased. "He's still a bachelor. Maybe I should put off this meeting till we're married. By the way, he swore that our secret was safe with him."

Thoughts of the present tumbled in on her. "I wasn't worried," she said softly. "It won't be long now anyway."

"Another two weeks?"

"At most. Then we'll be . . . together . . ." Her voice broke and the tears she had tried so hard to stem defied her.

"Don't cry, sweetheart." But he wanted to cry himself. As lovely as Christmas day had been with his family, a vital part of him was missing. "Soon, it'll all be over."

"It's just that I wanted to be with you t-today."

"There'll be other Christmases for us, Dani. The future is ours. Keep telling yourself that. I do."

"The future i-is ours. I know. The future is ours." It was to become a litany that she would repeat many times each day.

The trial resumed immediately after Christmas with the defense's opening statement, then the presentation of its case. Indeed, it was easier for Danica to listen because things now sounded good for Blake.

Jason went into a history of Eastbridge, tracing a record which had been spotless for twenty years. He produced an independent accountant to state that, by his study, Eastbridge was neither in financial trouble nor had it benefited monetarily from the alleged sale. To the contrary, he claimed, the computers had been sold at a price in keeping with the older units in which the circuits had been housed, and Eastbridge had actually taken a loss on the deal—all suggesting that Blake had not known of the presence of the higher priced circuits in the computers as the prosecution contended.

Numerous witnesses testified to Blake's good character. Others testified that a corporate head such as Blake might well not be in immediate touch with what was happening at the production and shipping levels.

On the third of January, Blake took the witness stand on his own behalf.

"He was excellent, Michael. I have to hand it to him. Even after three days on the stand he wasn't ruffled under cross-examination."

"So I heard in the news. Are his lawyers optimistic?"

"Yes, but guardedly so. It's hard to judge the jury's reaction. They looked sympathetic when Blake was being questioned, but then, they looked sympathetic during parts of the prosecution's presentation."

"Closing arguments begin tomorrow?"

"Mmmm. I'm not looking forward to that. The prosecution goes last. *That's* what's apt to stick in the jurors' minds."

"No. The judge's charge goes last. If he's worth his salt, and I think you lucked out with Bergeron, he'll give a fair charge. Once the jury is locked up, they'll be looking at the evidence. That's what they have to base their verdict on—the evidence, not the theatrics of the lawyers." He knew he was taking the simplistic approach, knew that jurors were indeed often swayed by the antics of one lawyer or the other, but he sensed that Danica needed all the bolstering she could get. "From where I sit, the media coverage has been relatively unbiased."

"But they're gathering round again. They can smell the moment of truth coming."

"It's news, sweetheart. You can't blame them for it. By the way, you called the doctor, didn't you?"

"Uh-huh. He was wonderful. He said he'd fit me in as soon as I could make it to Boston. I made a tentative appointment for next week. With luck, the trial will be over by then."

Michael's voice deepened. "How are you feeling, deep down inside?"

"Scared. I really want him to be acquitted, Michael. From a purely selfish standpoint, it'll make things so much easier for me."

"Less guilt?"

"Less guilt."

"Well, for what it's worth, though I don't think I'll ever forgive the bastard for what he's done to you, I'm rooting for an acquittal too. You'll call me as soon as it's over, won't you?"

"From the courthouse. I promise."

"Collect?" he teased.

She gave a soft laugh of surrender and nodded. "Collect."

The closing arguments were dramatic and heated on both sides. The prosecution portrayed Blake as an opportunist, a man so driven by power and greed that he felt himself outside the law. The defense portrayed him as a man who was human, a man whose authority had been circumvented by an employee whose overriding ambition had led to his involvement with the KGB and his subsequent murder by foreign factions.

As for the judge's charge, Danica wasn't sure what to make of it. Blake's lawyers felt that it leaned toward their side, but all she heard was the oft-repeated "beyond a reasonable doubt."

The jury was out for three full days. If Danica thought the earlier part of the trial had been difficult, it was nothing compared to the hell of waiting. Each morning, as they had done now for over a month, she and Blake drove to the courthouse, where they were met by their lawyers and then ushered into the courtroom to hear the judge send the jury off to deliberate. Late each afternoon they returned to the courthouse to hear the judge dismiss the jury for the night when no decision had been reached. In the hours between, Danica and Blake sat in the offices of Fitzgerald and Pickering, saying little to each other. From time to time either Jason or Ray joined them to offer encouragement, but as the days passed, their words were more of a rationalizing nature.

Ideally, the jury would have been so convinced of Blake's innocence that it would have returned a verdict to that extent within hours. Realistically, as Jason pointed out, there was no way the jury could have reviewed the mountain of evidence offered in four weeks of testimony so quickly. Yet, as the days passed, minute by minute, hour by hour, Danica and Blake both began to wonder about the serious doubts the jury apparently had.

It was late on the third day when the call finally came. Jason, his features tense, came into the conference room where Danica and Blake had been sitting alone.

"The jury reached a verdict," he announced quietly. "They're waiting for us."

Danica's heart thudded. Her gaze flew to Blake, who was pale and hollow-eyed.

"Do you know anything, Jason?" he asked, his voice a shadow of its former confident self.

Jason smiled sadly and shook his head. "No more than you do. We'll have to hear it together in court."

Blake nodded and stood. He straightened his suit, but the rest of him was as immaculately groomed as ever.

For a split second Danica swayed when she rose from her seat. Her knees felt rubbery, her arms and legs weak. But she steadied herself, and when she clutched Blake's arm, it wasn't for her own sake. Rather she was remembering the Blake she had first married and the better days they'd had together. Her facial expression said that in spite of all that had come later she didn't wish him ill.

Blake met her gaze, studied it for a moment and gave her a rueful smile of thanks. Then, taking her hand in his, he led her after Jason.

They entered the courthouse through the back door, having to work their way through the media crowd only for the short distance from the elevator to the courtroom. Once inside, they took their familiar places, Blake at the defense table flanked by Jason and Ray, Danica directly behind Blake in the first row of seats.

The courtroom was packed, its air rife with expectancy. Danica took slow, deep breaths to steady herself, but it seemed futile because she began to shake when the jury slowly filed into the room. As a group they looked grim, which could very well have been from fatigue, Danica reasoned, though she had hoped for a smile or two in the direction of the defense table.

Everyone in the courtroom rose for the judge's entrance. When he was seated, he nodded to the clerk, who faced the jury.

"Madame Forelady, has the jury reached a verdict?"

The woman who had served as forelady of the jury since the start of the trial stood. "We have." She handed him a piece of paper. He carried it to the judge, who read it, nodded and handed it back.

Clutching her hands in her lap, Danica wondered how such a small piece of paper could hold such weight. Years of work by Blake at Eastbridge, months of investigation by the government, weeks and weeks of trial preparation, then the trial itself, not to mention Blake's future—all hung in the balance of the words written on that paper.

The clerk's flat voice filled the courtroom. "Will the defendant please rise."

Blake stood, as did both Jason and Ray. Danica could do nothing more than press her fingers into the wool of her dress and hold her breath as the clerk slowly went on.

"On indictment number 85-2343, is the defendant guilty or not guilty?"

The forelady spoke clearly. "Not guilty."

A murmur went through the courtroom and Danica swallowed.

The clerk continued. "On indictment number 85-2344, is the defendant guilty or not guilty?"

"Not guilty."

Danica didn't hear the murmur this time because her pulse was pounding.

"On indictment number 85-2345, is the defendant guilty or not guilty?"

"Not guilty."

Danica's eyes were round when the clerk spoke a final time. "On indictment number 85-2346, is the defendant guilty or not guilty?"

The forelady raised her chin and took a last breath. "Not guilty."

For a moment there was total silence. Then the courtroom erupted into a cacophony of excitement. Blake, smiling broadly, vigorously shook hands with, then hugged, each of his lawyers. Then he turned to Danica and she was in his arms, holding him tightly.

"I'm so glad for you!" she cried, her voice broken as tears of relief and genuine happiness welled in her eyes.

"We did it, Pook. We really did it." There was something akin to wonder in his tone, but she was too emotionally keyed up to analyze its cause, and he was separating himself from her, at his lawyers' request, so that he might nod his thanks to the jurors as they filed out of the courtroom, then shake hands with the prosecutorial team.

Moments later Danica, Blake, Jason and Ray were facing the press outside the courtroom.

"How do you feel, Mr. Secretary?"

"Delighted," Blake answered. "Our system of justice has prevailed. I feel fully exonerated."

"Did you have any doubts about what the verdict would be?"

"I was confident that my attorneys could convey the truth to the jury."

"Will you be returning to the Department?"

"I hope so. I'll be talking with the President later."

"Mrs. Lindsay, this must be a great relief for you."

Danica smiled. "Very great."

"What are your immediate plans? Will you and your husband be taking some time off together before he returns to work?"

Blake answered for her, quickly but smoothly and flashing his brightest smile. "I believe we'll have to come down off this cloud before we can make any plans."

Jason cut in before the next question could come. "Ladies and gentlemen, the Lindsays are happy but tired. If you'll excuse us now, I think they'd like some privacy."

Danica felt herself being swept toward the elevator. She clutched Blake's arm and leaned close to his ear. "I have to get to a phone."

"We'll go back to Jason's office."

"No, here." She made no effort to hide her urgency. "Isn't there one I can use?"

Blake gave her a guarded look, then turned to Jason. "Danica has to call her parents. Can we go down the hall for a minute?"

With a nod, Jason reversed their direction and led them through the crowded corridor to the small room they had often used during recesses. He and Blake stood talking by the door while Danica picked up the phone and, fingers trembling, dialed Michael's number. When the operator came on, she said simply, "Collect from Danica Lindsay."

He picked up the phone after a single ring. "Yes?"

"I have a collect call from—"

"Yes. I'll take it. . . . Dani?"

She felt her insides melt, and sank into a chair. "It's over," she breathed, putting her hand up to cover tear-filled eyes. "Not guilty on all counts."

"Oh, sweetheart, that's great! I'm thrilled! Congratulations!"

Danica wanted to say so much, but her throat was tight and she knew it wasn't the time or place. She spoke slowly and with effort. "Blake and Jason are with me now."

"And you can't talk. I understand. I'm just so happy for you. For *us!*"

She smiled through her tears. "Me, too."

"What are the plans now? When will I see you?"

"I'll have to . . . let me call you later. I just wanted to tell you."

"Thanks, sweetheart. I'll be waiting. Everything's going to be so wonderful. I love you."

"Me, too," she whispered. "Talk with you later." Mouthing a kiss, since her back was to Blake and Jason, she quietly pressed the disconnect button, then dialed her mother's number.

When she finally hung up the phone and turned, she brushed the tears from her cheeks.

"Is everything okay?" Blake asked cautiously.

Danica nodded and smiled weakly. She knew Blake had to have heard that she had made two calls, but she felt no compulsion to discuss the first with him, and she knew that he would never bring it up himself in front of Jason. "Mom was ecstatic. She says to tell you how pleased she is and that she'll call Dad right away. She asked if we wanted to celebrate with them over dinner and I told her that we'd probably be with Jason and Ray." She sent an apologetic glance toward Jason, who promptly put her at ease with a broad smile.

"That's exactly where you will be." He rubbed his hands together. "This is a victory for all of us. Let's make it good!"

It was much later that night before Danica was able to call Michael back.

"I'm sorry it's so late—" she began, only to be interrupted.

"Don't be silly. . . . You sound beat."

"I am. It's like everything—all the tension and worry and excitement and relief—was suspended and now it's suddenly fallen in on me." She settled back on the bed and threw an arm across her eyes. "We went back to Jason's office after I spoke with you, then out to dinner. I have an awful headache. But I am pleased for Blake."

"I saw him on television. He looked properly victorious."

"Oh, yes. In hindsight he saw that the verdict couldn't have possibly gone any other way."

"Back to his old self, eh?"

"Very much so."

"Dani, when will you be up?"

On a burst of strength, she spoke more forcefully. "I'm leaving here tomorrow, as soon as I can get packed."

"Have you told Blake?"

"I'll tell him in the morning."

"Do you think he'll give you any trouble?"

"I don't think so. In spite of all his chest-puffing, he treated me with kid gloves today. He must have an inkling of what's coming. I'm sure he knew it was you I called this afternoon."

"Maybe I should fly down."

"No, Michael. I need to do this myself. And there's really nothing that can go wrong. Even if Blake gives me an argument, my mind is set. I've given him more than he deserves. And I do have that ace in the hole."

"Will you use it?"

"If he gives me the slightest problem, you bet I will. He'll agree to a divorce, Michael. It's over. Our future's beginning."

Michael let out a long sigh of relief. "I love you so much. That future's going to be stupendous."

She smiled. "I know."

"I'll drive down and meet you at Logan."

"No. I'm driving the Audi up."

"From *Washington*? Oh, sweetheart, that's not such a good idea. It's a long trip, and in your condition—"

"My condition will be wonderful once I get done what I need to do here.

Besides, I need the winding-down time. The drive will do me good."

"Let me fly down and drive up with you, then."

"No." Her voice softened. "Just be there waiting. That's all I need, Michael. I'll be there the day after tomorrow. Just be waiting."

"I will, love. I will."

The following morning Danica was up early, packing her bags, listening for Blake, who had left even earlier to play squash. She knew that he was meeting with the President later that morning, though she also knew that the outcome of the meeting was irrelevant to her own plans.

She had the Audi nearly packed and was bringing down her overnight bag and purse when Blake came in the front door. He took one look at her, at her bag and purse, then set his jaw and walked past her into the den.

She followed him, coming to a halt just inside the room. He had his back to her and was staring out the window.

"I'll be leaving now, Blake," she said quietly but with conviction. When he said nothing, she went on. "I'll be taking the Audi—"

"Don't, Danica." He turned. "Don't leave."

"You knew I was planning to."

"But I thought, after all this and, well, you seemed so happy with the acquittal . . ."

"I am happy with it, but it's over. All of it."

He didn't miss the deeper meaning of her words. "It doesn't have to be. We could try to make a go of it."

She was shaking her head, smiling sadly. "It's too late for that. There's no point."

"We had something once."

"But it's gone now. It's been gone for a long, long time." She was surprised by the soft, almost pleading nature of his tone, but it couldn't affect her. "I'll wait about a month until things calm down here before I see my lawyer. He'll be in touch with yours to discuss the divorce."

"I don't want a divorce."

She ignored him. "I'll probably fly somewhere where I can get it quickly. I'd like things taken care of before the baby's born."

"I don't _want_ a divorce."

"Blake, this isn't your baby."

"I can live with that. It's the divorce I can't live with."

"You don't have any choice."

"I certainly do. I'm your husband. Besides, what do you think it'll look like if you take off like this one day after the trial?"

"It'll look like I'm exhausted and need to recuperate at our house in Maine."

"And the divorce? What do I say about that?"

"You say that the strain of the trial was too much."

"Bull. It has nothing to do with the trial. You had your mind made up when you first came down here."

She tipped up her chin a fraction. "You're right. I was going to demand a divorce before all this happened. Now I don't have to demand it. You'll give it to me. Quickly and quietly."

He eyed her strangely. "How do you know that?"

Taking that proverbial ace from its hole, she very slowly turned it over. "Because I know about you and Harlan, Blake. I was fooled for a long time, but now I know." She found some satisfaction in his sudden loss of color but no joy in furthering her point. Yet she felt it was necessary. "I only wish you could have told me yourself. I might have understood if you'd done that. Instead, you used me, even though you knew I had a chance for happiness elsewhere. I won't be used again, Blake. It's as simple as that."

Though his jaw was clenched, there was little force to his words. "Harlan got to you."

"Indirectly, I suppose." She saw no point in elaborating.

His voice cracked faintly. "It's over, Danica. It was over long before he was killed."

"But there've been others, and there'll be others again. And I have a new life to lead, one that I want, one that's waiting for me."

Blake looked at the floor, then slowly raised his gaze. "And if I decide to fight?"

"It'll all come out in court. I don't think you'll want another trial, particularly once you've considered what the testimony will entail."

He stared at her, then leaned back against the desk, which was as close as he could come to sagging in defeat. Sensing that there was little left to be said, Danica shouldered her purse and lifted her bag.

"Thelma can pack the rest of my things and send them on later. I'll be seeing the doctor in Boston tomorrow. After that I'll be in Maine. I hope all goes well with your meeting today," she said softly. "I'm sure I'll hear one way or another."

For a final moment, she stood looking at the man who had been her husband for better than ten years. Strangely, she felt neither anger nor resentment, but rather a kind of melancholy. He was so very handsome, so very talented. And they had been so very wrong for each other.

Bowing her head, she turned and left the house, aware of the finality of it all, of the fact that she was putting a lengthy, if painful, part of her life behind her. Only after several moments' respite in the car did she feel composed enough to drive. She still had another stop to make, and thought of this one unsettled her more because, though it wouldn't immediately affect her future, its outcome did touch her heart.

In a twist of fate that Danica took to be promising, William Marshall was available. He was sitting at his large oak desk, studying position papers his aides had prepared when his secretary buzzed him to announce Danica's arrival. Rising, he met Danica at the door.

"Well, girl, you did it." He smiled broadly. "You and Blake both."

"We did at that," she said quietly.

He shut the door and motioned to a chair. "Sit down, Danica. You shouldn't be standing around in your condition." He eyed her belly. "You're really beginning to look it now."

She put a reassuring, perhaps protective, hand on her stomach, but she didn't sit. "I can't stay long. I want to get as much driving done as I can today."

He frowned. "Driving? Where are you going?"

"I'm going home."

"*Home?*" He was standing before her, his eyes darkening. "*This* is home. I thought you realized that by now."

"Home for me is in Maine. With Michael."

William came close to exploding. "With *Michael!* Have you lost your *senses?* Your place is with Blake. You've stood beside him through this whole ordeal, and now that it's over the two of you should be able to patch up whatever differences you may have had. Blake still has a solid future in this town. Besides, you can't leave him. You're carrying his child!"

She raked her teeth across her lower lip. "No, Daddy. I'm not."

He glanced at her belly again, then her face. "What in the hell are you saying?"

"You know. Think. How could this child possibly be Blake's when Michael's the one I've been with most, when Michael's the one I love?"

"It's *his* child?" When she nodded, he cursed. "I'll kill the bastard!"

"No, you won't. He loves me and he loves this child, and he's going to make both of us very, very happy. I'd think you'd be grateful to him for that. After all, I'm your daughter and this will be your grandchild."

"It was supposed to be Blake's!"

"No," she said sadly. "You *wanted* it to be Blake's, that's all."

"Does he know?"

"Blake? He's known all along."

"And he sat back and took it?"

"I was serving his purposes. That was all that mattered to him."

"Why wasn't *I* told?"

"It wasn't your business then. It is now only because I want you to understand why I'm leaving Blake. Don't you see? *I love Michael!* Blake and I have nothing left. Nothing!"

"He won't let you go. He needs you here."

"He's letting me go. We've already talked and it's settled."

William stalked to the far side of the room, then swiveled to face her. His eyes were hard, and her heart sank. She had hoped he would yield, that he would defer to her judgment for once. Obviously, he wasn't going to do that.

"You're being very stupid, Danica. Blake is in a position of power and prominence, both of which can rub off on you. He has it over Buchanan any day."

It was one thing for him to put her down, quite another for him to do so to Michael. "You're wrong," she said in a warning tone. "You don't know the facts."

"Well, enlighten me!" he roared as he threw his hands out and paced back from the side of the room. "If you think you're so wise, tell me. And don't give me that hogwash about love, because it's flighty and feminine and it won't get you *anywhere* in this world."

"That," Danica responded angrily, "depends on where you want to go."

"You're sure gonna go nowhere, girl. You could've been on top with your tennis, and you quit. Now you're doing the same thing all over again. *What's the matter with you?* Haven't you learned *anything* in thirty-odd years on this earth?''

"I've learned plenty," Danica retorted, her eyes blazing right back at William's. "I've learned that you and I have very different definitions of what 'being on top' means, and that while your definition may be just fine for you, it's not for me. I've learned that I have options in life, that I can take the road *I* want rather than the road someone else wants me to take."

Shaking, she paused only to gasp for air. "There's only one thing I've ever really wanted in life. A family. A warm, loving, close family. I never had it when I was growing up because you and Mom were too busy with your career to even stop and consider my needs. I never had it with Blake because he was so involved with Eastbridge and . . . and . . . well, it just never came. I was ready to give up on my dream because you all kept saying that things like duty and responsibility were more important. Then I met Michael, and I learned that I wasn't crazy to want the things I did. I learned that by taking a road of *my own* choosing, I can have it all."

William patted the air. "You're pregnant, Danica. You're being emotional. You're not thinking clearly —"

"*I* am. *You're* the one who's missing the boat." Her eyes narrowed. "Do you want to know what else I've learned? I've learned that you're fallible. You make mistakes just like the rest of us. Your judgment on some matters leaves much to be desired."

William stiffened. "I won't have you talking to me that way, Danica. I'm your father. I deserve respect."

"So do I, and I'm going to get it!" She had reached the point of fury where there were no holds barred. "Do you have any idea why my marriage failed? *Do you?*"

"You gave up on it."

"I did not. *Blake* did." She straightened. "You may have thought that you knew him when you chose him to be my husband, but you didn't. And for ten long years I didn't know him, either. At first I thought I was doing something wrong. He spent more and more time out of the house, less and less time with me. I rationalized and tried to compensate, but it didn't work. Toward the end we shared little more than the same last name. *And do you want to know why?*"

"Yes," William goaded indignantly.

"Because Blake prefers men to women! He was having an affair with Harlan Magnusson!"

William raised his hand and, for a minute, she thought he was going to hit her. Then the hand curled into a fist and lowered slowly. "I don't believe you," he stated very quietly.

"You don't have to believe me," she said, suddenly even more quiet than he. "Blake confirmed it. And it explains certain things — such as why Harlan was able to get that illegal shipment out of Eastbridge."

"Are you suggesting that Blake was sweet-talked into it, that he knew about it all along? You're skating on thin ice, girl. A jury acquitted him."

"And I'm not making accusations one way or the other. All I'm saying is that there always was a special relationship between Blake and Harlan. Now I understand its full nature."

William was not one to accept defeat graciously. Danica might be his daughter, but Blake had always been his man. "Maybe if you'd been a better wife Blake wouldn't have had to . . . to resort to something else."

It was the final straw. Danica was the one who wanted to hit now, and only by pressing her fists to her sides did she refrain from doing so. Every one of her muscles was rigid. She didn't so much as blink, though her voice was tremulous when she spoke. "I don't have to justify my actions if you're so blind that you can't see what I've done even during these past five months of hell. All my life I've tried to please you, but that hasn't been enough—not for you, because I never quite reached the top, and not for me, because I don't want to get to the top as you see it."

She shifted her purse on her shoulder and swallowed. "I'll be leaving now. I'm going to stop in to say goodbye to Mom. By the way, she doesn't know about Blake and I don't want you to tell her. Considering the fact that she's had one stroke, she can do without the added strain. Besides, she accepts me for what I am, and she knows that I'll be ten times happier with Michael than I ever was with Blake. Thank God, that means something to her."

Danica turned and headed for the door. She walked slowly, waiting, praying that her father would say something to heal the rift between them. When he said nothing, her shoulders slumped and she quietly let herself out.

Eleanor insisted on driving as far as Hartford with her, and Danica was grateful for her company. She told her of the conversation with her father, omitting that one part about Blake, and about her fervent hope that one day William might see things her way. She told of her plans for the divorce, of her desire to sell the Kennebunkport house and move in with Michael as soon as possible. She told about her hopes for the future, her excitement, the dreams that seemed finally within reach.

And Eleanor was happy for her, which was some consolation for the pain Danica felt at her father's rejection.

The following morning, feeling more rested and alive with anticipation, she climbed back in the car for the drive to Boston and, after that, the final leg of what had been a long, long journey.

TWENTY

ONE MINUTE THERE WAS nothing but a cloud of fog before him, the next she was there, materialized from the mist. Stunned, Michael came to an abrupt halt.

He wondered if he was dreaming because he knew he had lived through this once before. Then the weather had been as inhospitable, the figure before him as striking. Now, though, it was the January wind that whipped through the ends of her sandy hair, and rather than a long skirt she wore jeans. Her jacket was as chicly oversized as the other had been on that March day nearly three years before, but this time it covered a rounded belly, inside which lay his child.

She was his dream come true. When he opened his arms, she came running, throwing her own around his neck, burying her face in the collar of his sheepskin jacket as he crushed her to him.

"Dani . . . Dani . . ." he murmured, defying the thunder of the waves by pressing his lips to her ear.

She was crying when he held her back, but she was laughing too, and she was beautiful. Unable to speak, she simply grinned at him while she brushed the tears from her face. He saw it then, the ring finger on her left hand. Taking it in his, he stroked its slender length.

"It's gone," he whispered hoarsely. "Your wedding band's gone."

She nodded vigorously, then laughed when she still couldn't stem her tears.

"You've left him?" he asked cautiously, knowing she had been planning to but refusing to count on it until it was done. She nodded, and his voice rose. "For good?" She nodded again, and he spoke even louder. "And you're free?"

This time when she nodded, he bent his knees, threw back his head and let out a great whoop of joy. By the time he straightened, she was burrowing against him again. Wrapping her tightly in his arms, he held her until she raised her head and sought his gaze.

"I'm . . . so . . . happy!" she cried.

He gave her a crooked smile. "So am I. I was beginning to think you'd left your tongue in Washington!"

"Oh, no. I'm just happy! Kiss me, Michael. We've made it!"

He kissed her once, then again and again. She was laughing when he finally released her. Opening his jacket, he drew her inside, then turned them both and started walking slowly along the beach. When moments later Rusty loped in from the mist, Danica knelt to hug him, then returned to her man.

"Tell me, Dani. Tell me what happened."

She did, though she grew sober from time to time. "I really feel sorry for him, Michael. I read in today's paper that he'll be back as Secretary, but I don't envy him his future."

"You don't envy him because it's not the life you want. You've chosen your own, thank God."

She slanted him a cautious glance. "When I said I was free before . . . you know that it's only in the figurative sense just yet. I still have to file for the divorce. I told Blake I'd wait a couple of weeks until things die down, but I'm going to get a quick one. He won't give me a fight."

"That's all that matters. What about your father? Do you think he'll ever come around?"

Her expression grew more pained. "I don't know. Mom will work on him. I know she'll be coming up here to visit whether he chooses to or not. I want him to, but it's up to him. I can't dwell on it, Michael. I've earned the right to our happiness."

He tucked her closer. They were both silent for a while before he spoke again. "Do you remember that first day we met here on the beach?"

She had been thinking of the same. "How could I forget? It changed my life. You talked of pain then, of how sometimes strength comes from facing pain and dealing with it. You were right. I think that's what's happened to me. I feel so much stronger, so much more *whole*."

"You were always strong, Danica. You'd been dealing with pain for a long time before I came along. The only difference is that now you see it, now you see the strength in yourself."

"Perhaps." She looked toward the waves. "You also talked about the ocean. Do you remember? You said that everything here was raw and truthful and commanded the same from us. You said that falling victim to the sea meant baring one's soul."

"I remember."

She turned into him then, sliding her arms inside his jacket and around his waist. "It can be painful, as it was then, or it can be beautiful, as it is now." Her voice grew hushed. "I love you, Michael. With my heart, my soul, everything, I love you."

For the longest time he could only drink in the adoration she offered. "I think I'm the luckiest man on this earth," he murmured at last. Unaware of the bounty of love his own gaze returned, he grew concerned when she began to tremble. "You're cold. Come on. Let's go back to my place for a warm drink." When she chuckled, he tipped his head. "What's so funny?"

"You said the same thing that day. I remember thinking to myself that it'd be hot chocolate, just like your eyes."

"And I remember thinking that you had the most stunning violet ones I'd ever seen. I have to amend that. They're even more stunning now, all love and glow. . . . Well?"

"Well what?"

"How about that drink? You refused me that day."

"I was scared then. You were too attractive."

"Are you still scared?"

"Not on your life, bud." She broke away from him. "I'll race you there." With Rusty at her heels, she started to run, but the sand slowed her down and Michael caught up with her after she'd taken no more than three plodding strides.

"Ohhhhh, no, you don't." He firmly anchored her to his side. "A woman in your condition doesn't race."

She didn't argue because in her joy to be reunited with him she had completely forgotten about her condition, and there was so much she wanted to tell him about that. "Michael, guess what?" Her eyes widened. "I heard the baby's heartbeat!"

His voice jumped. "You did?"

She nodded. "I saw the doctor this morning and he put the stethoscope in my ears and there it was."

Michael's eyes were round, too. "How did it sound?"

"Thu-thump. Thu-thump. A good, healthy little heartbeat. You'll hear it next month when you take me to the doctor." He grinned even more widely, but she had more to say. "And I can feel it moving now. It just kind of turns from time to time and there's this ripple inside me."

"When will *I* be able to feel it?"

She laughed. "As soon as its little leg is strong enough to kick when you have your hands on me."

"Mmmm, that's where I want 'em, babe. That's where I want 'em." Hastening his pace, he headed home.

An hour later they were sitting on the floor before the fire having seconds of hot chocolate. They had been talking nonstop since coming in, but the spell of the flames had taken over and they had fallen into a warm and comfortable silence. Curving his body behind hers, Michael rested his chin on her shoulder.

"Hypnotic, isn't it?"

"Mmmm. Maybe it's the time, though, or the place, or you."

He pressed his lips to her neck and murmured against her skin, "I think all of those things. You smell so good."

She smiled and tipped her head against his. "This is what I've always, always wanted. A home, a fire, the man I love, our child . . ."

Michael slipped his hand under the hem of her sweater and caressed her belly. "You *feel* so good."

Closing her eyes, she basked in the warmth of his touch. When his hand moved higher to cover her breast, she pressed her own atop it. "*That* feels so good," she murmured. A different kind of spell was taking over, well, not truly taking over because the other was still too strong, but mixing with it to make her float. She was still thinking about the heavenly sensation when she felt herself being lowered to the cushions Michael had tugged from the nearby chair. Opening her eyes, she met his gaze.

"I've been waiting a long time for this," he whispered and reached for the hem of her sweater again. This time he drew it up and she arched her back, then raised her arms to help him. The sweater was tossed aside and his fingers went to the buttons of her blouse. "Tell me if you get cold," he warned huskily, but she knew she wouldn't get cold because, between the fire in the hearth, the one burning in her body and that in Michael's, she was melting.

He had her blouse open and eased it off, then reached behind her and unhooked her bra. It too was discarded and he sat back on his heels to look at her. His gaze traced fire along her profile, retracing it again and again over her swollen breasts and their pebbled tips, then again down over the curve of her belly. With hands that trembled, he drew the stretch band of her jeans down until the curve was bare; then, with awe in his touch, he inched his palm back up over everything his gaze had scaled.

"So . . . beautiful," he whispered as he continued to familiarize his fingers with every nuance of her altered shape.

Danica lay with hands by her head and her hazy eyes on his. A tiny sound came from her throat when he rubbed the tips of his fingers over her darkened nipples, and in the delight of the moment she lowered her lashes and let her head fall to the side. He touched her everywhere then, always slowly and with wonder, always with the same devastating effect on her senses.

She heard him move and felt him taking off her flats and the stylish patterned socks she had worn. Then he was slipping the jeans and her panties off and she was naked. She opened her eyes to see him before her bent knees, and would have murmured a protest when he gently eased her legs apart had it not been for the worshipful expression he wore.

He looked at what he had opened, then placed a hand there and stroked her. She did murmur, but not in protest, because she felt the heat and the tension that had begun to gather and she wanted him to relieve it as only he could. He had the key to her heart, and hence her body. She knew he was feeling joy in pleasuring her and that enhanced her pleasure ten-fold.

Her knees fell farther to the side and he inched closer. He caressed her slowly, looking up along the creamy lines of her body from time to time to meet her gaze and smile. She smiled back while she could, but she was breathing more heavily and clear thought was fading fast.

"I love you, Danica," he breathed, slipping a finger into her. She arched at the sensation, then closed her eyes and bit her lip when he introduced a second finger and began to move both.

She whispered his name in a tattered gasp and closed her fists on the edges of the cushion beneath her head.

"I love you," he murmured again, and she cried out because his words, his fingers, his very presence, conspired to drive her to higher and higher peaks.

Then she sucked in her breath, held it, and let it out at last in a series of fierce bursts.

Michael watched her, heard her, felt her spasmodically hugging his fingers. Only when the tension had seeped from her and she lay limp did he remove them and slide up alongside her body. He stroked her face until, smiling shyly, she opened her eyes.

He spoke softly. "I've always wanted to do that, to watch you when you climax, but I can't when I'm in you myself because I can't think straight then." He smiled. "You have so much passion in you and you let it out with the same grace, the same beauty, with which you do everything else in life."

Blushing, she managed to raise a hand to stroke his face and the light shadow of a beard on his jaw. "You unleash the passion," she whispered brokenly. "You unleash so much of what's good in me."

"Then we complement each other, which is how it should be."

She thought about that for a time, until her pulse had returned to normal. "I read a tea bag tag once—"

He rolled his eyes.

She lowered her hand to his chest. "No, I'm serious. It was soon after I met you, but I was thinking about Blake at the time. The tag said something about love being a magical bond, which makes one and one far more than two, and I remember thinking that Blake and I were so separate that there wasn't any possible way we could combine to produce something else, at least not emotionally. Maybe deep down inside I was fantasizing about you and about how I *knew* we could make something more." She began to stroke his chest, absently at first, then with more direction when the swell of his muscles titillated her fingers. "But it's strange. When we're together, when we make love, we're totally united, really only one, though there's no 'only' about it. It's when we pull apart, when it's over, that I feel like so much more because I've still got a part of you with me and I'm that much fuller a person for it. Take your sweater off. This is absurd."

Laughing aloud, he whipped the sweater over his head, then curved his arm along her back, supporting her while she moved her lips through the hair on his chest.

"*You* smell good. What have you got on?"

"It's either soap," he mocked in his deepest voice, "or eau de Michael. You'll have to be the judge."

"Not soap, but clean. I love the way you smell."

"Thank God for that," he murmured, sliding his hand down to cover her belly. "And one and one does make more than two, if we count baby here."

"That was the obvious part," she breathed, dabbing his nipple with the tip of her tongue. "I was trying to be more . . . more esoteric."

"Esoteric." He arched his back, then cleared his throat, but his voice still came out sounding hoarse. "Good word, *esoteric*. . . . Dani, you're driving me crazy." Her lips were moving in lazy circles over his ribs, her breath warming his flesh. She lowered a hand to his jeans and cupped the firmness there.

"Take off your pants, then," she whispered.

"You do it."

"I can't. I feel weak. You've made me that way." Leaning back, she grinned. "I'll watch."

With a low growl, he rolled to his knees, tore at the fastening of his jeans and pushed them, and his shoes and socks, off to the side. Then he lifted her up and against him, groaning when her breasts touched his chest. Sliding his hands down her back, he cupped her bottom and raised her hips against his. She had her arms around his neck, which was good, because moments later he was lowering them both to lie face to face before the fire.

He kissed her then, drinking deeply from her lips in long, lingering sips. She offered her tongue, which he took readily, pulling it deeper and deeper into his mouth. Her hands were on him again. She used her fingers and palms to extend what was already so fully extended. When he could take no more of her torture, he lifted her thigh and opened her to his probing.

It was Danica's turn to whisper soft words of love, which she did repeatedly as he sheathed himself in her warmth. She kissed him between breaths, stroked him where she knew he would be inflamed, and tightened herself around him as though to hold him there forever.

There was something more beautiful to their coupling than there had ever been before because there was no element of desperation this time, no fear of separation. Their love was unfettered and invincible, their future here, now and always.

EPILOGUE

✿ ✿ ✿

B LAKE LINDSAY SERVED as Secretary of Commerce for another year. He was never quite as much at ease in Washington after the trial, and when he submitted his resignation just prior to the start of the campaign for Jason Claveling's active reelection bid, it was graciously accepted. He left for Detroit to take over the reins of a troubled automobile manufacturing concern. In time, given his keen business sense and his organization expertise, he was able to turn the corporation around.

Though he lived in the same city as his family, he saw little of them. He never married again.

Cilla Buchanan never did write a story such as the one Harlan Magnusson had suggested. Though she believed that he had told her the truth, she had lost her taste for that subject. There were other stories to write, which she did with much enthusiasm, but she had more important things on her mind as time passed. After living together for a year and realizing that their lives were much richer when they had each other, she and Jeffrey Winston were married— again.

Jeffrey was gratified that, of the eight companies and seventeen individuals indicted as a result of his investigation, twenty-two all told were found guilty of the charges brought against them. He went on to carry out other critical work for the Department of Defense, though was very happy to share what he could with Cilla at the end of each day. Chauvinist that he had once been, he took an active role in caring for the child they subsequently had.

Gena Bradley proved to be as wonderful a mother-in-law as Danica had known she would be. The two women shared a special bond, one that grew stronger with each passing year.

Michael's father, John, accepted Danica with remarkable grace. He seemed to see it as a victory that a Buchanan had stolen away a Marshall. Michael saw no point in reminding him that, in some regards, it had been the other way around.

Eleanor Marshall made up, in the years that followed, for all she hadn't done when Danica had been younger. Her health held up, so she visited often and was always there when Danica called. She quickly grew to love Michael and became Danica's and his champion, such that William, albeit begrudgingly at first, accompanied her to Maine for the birth of Danica's child. In time he seemed to accept what Danica had done, and though he and Michael never fully warmed to each other, he showered genuine affection on their child.

Michael and Danica were married in March, three years to the day after they first met. It was a quiet ceremony, with only Greta and Pat McCabe present to serve as witnesses, but it was precisely what Michael and Danica wanted, and it was beautiful.

Two months later Danica gave birth to a daughter. Michael was by her side, holding her hand, telling her how much he loved her and their child, just as she had dreamed. From the start he was a doting father, even more so as their daughter grew. And when, two years later, they had a son, his capacity for love seemed simply to multiply.

Professionally, they became a team, collaborating on many books as the years passed, though writing was far from their only interest. Michael continued to teach at Harvard one afternoon a week each fall, staying the night in Cambridge only when Danica could be with him. Danica, filled with the self-confidence that came from being a champion wife and mother, approached a cable television station in Portland and sold it on letting her host a program similar to that she had done in Boston. Michael and the children were her biggest fans.

When she stopped to look back over those years, the times that were closest to her heart were those when she and Michael and the children were together before the fire on blustery winter days. The warmth, the closeness, they shared then epitomized everything she had always wanted in life. She loved and was loved. She felt peaceful, fulfilled, and very, very pleased with the path she had chosen.

FINGER PRINTS

To my husband, Steve, for his endless support and the brilliant career that inspired
Finger Prints, *and to my sons, Eric, Andrew and Jeremy, for their indulgence in repeating
things twice to catch my attention.*

ONE

THE NOVEMBER AFTERNOON was gray, with dusk lurking just around the corner, waiting to ensnare the hapless passerby in its chilling shroud. Carly Quinn tugged the collar of her trench coat closer around her neck, then shifted the bag of books to a more comfortable spot on her shoulder without missing a step. She walked quickly. These days in particular, she didn't feel safe until she was home and the last of the three bolts on her door were securely thrown.

The tap of her slender heels on the sidewalk reminded her that she'd forgotten to change shoes before she'd left school, and she silently cursed the haste behind the lapse. But she'd worked late grading themes. And it was Friday. When she left the library her only thought had been of home.

Home. She gave a wry smile as she turned onto Brattle Street, waited for a break in the rush-hour traffic, then trotted across to resume her march among the smattering of pedestrians on the opposite side. Home. Strange how the mind could adapt, she mused. How utterly, unbelievably different her life had been a year ago. Now, Cambridge was home and she was Carly Johnson Quinn. She looked like a Carly, dressed like a Carly, was even beginning to dream like a Carly. Perhaps they'd been right. Perhaps she would adjust after all.

Momentarily lulled into security by the humanity surrounding her, she became mesmerized by the taillights of the cars headed into Harvard Square. She wondered where their drivers were going, whether to dinner at Ahmed's or Grendel's Den, for a beer at the Wursthaus, or to a show in Boston.

A car honked in passing and, stiffening, Carly jerked her head sharply to the left. When her gaze met the grinning faces of several of her students, her relief was immediate. They had just returned from a triumphant basketball game against their arch rival. She had talked briefly with them as she'd left the school and now tipped her head up to offer a smile. Then they were gone, swallowed up in the inbound traffic, leaving her to control the runaway beat of her heart. Oh, yes, she reflected, she might well adjust to a new life, a new identity. But she seriously doubted that this would ever change—the constant nervousness, the perpetual guardedness, especially now that the days were shorter and darkness fell that much earlier.

Quickening her step, she covered two more blocks before turning right and heading toward the river. Her apartment was no more than five minutes ahead. Yet this was the strip that always bothered her most. The side street was narrower and less traveled than the main one. It was darker too, barely lit by the streetlights that seemed lost among the network of tree branches and telephone wires. And there were any number of front doors and side paths and back alleys from which an assailant might materialize. An occasional car approached from behind, headlights slinging tentative shadows across the pathways ahead. Carly swallowed hard once, anchored her lower lip beneath her teeth and pressed onward.

There was nothing to fear, nothing to fear. She repeated the silent litany as she had so often in the past months, speeding it up in time with her pace. Perhaps, she mused, she should follow Sam's suggestion and take her car. But then she would have a parking hassle at the end of the day. Besides, the exercise was good for her, as was the crisp fall air.

She took a deep, restorative breath, then held it convulsively when a figure suddenly approached from the opposite direction. Only when she recognized the research technician who worked at the hospital did she slowly exhale. He was right on schedule, she realized, mentally calculating the time. She passed him whenever she left school at five-thirty, which wasn't more than once or twice a week and then always on random days. It was one of the things Sam Loomis had taught her. The more varied her existence, the more elusive a target she'd be. Not that she was a creature of habit. She'd been far more impulsive in the past, when she was driven by the demons within to prove herself as a journalist. Now, though, as a highschool English teacher, she led a life more conducive to order. Strange, she mused again, how things had changed.

The research technician passed on the opposite sidewalk without a word. But then, he'd have no reason to recognize Carly. She, on the other hand, had Sam, who had carefully checked out not only her neighbors, but the people they'd passed in those first few weeks when he'd been by her side walking her to school in the morning, then home at night. He'd been a godsend, given the circumstances.

Now, though, she was on her own and free to imagine all kinds of villains in pursuit on a dark and deserted street. But it wasn't really deserted, she chided herself. There were close-set houses on one side, low apartment buildings on the other. And there were cars lining both curbs as evidence of people nearby. Surely if she were in danger, she would only have to scream and there would be any number of people to help. Or so she hoped. In less optimistic moments she wondered if these urban dwellers would come to the aid of a woman they didn't know. She wondered if, with their doors and windows shut tight, they would even hear her.

When, silhouetted against the lights on Memorial Drive, the rounded turret of her building came into view, she felt momentarily lightened. Then she heard the crescendoing thud of footsteps behind and her calm vanished. Without thought to her heels, the broken sidewalk or the heavy bag that pounded her side with each stride, she broke into as steady a run as she could manage. Looking neither to the right nor the left, she sprinted forward with single-minded intent. Her breath came in short, painful gasps, intermingled with soft moans of fear. Through the wisps of auburn hair that had blown across her face, she saw the sanctuary of home drawing closer, closer. Ignoring the stitch in her side, she ran on, nearly there now, all but tasting refuge.

It was only after she'd turned in at the stone courtyard that, without breaking pace, she dared a glance over her shoulder. The look was ill-timed. She'd barely spotted the jogger who had turned onto Memorial Drive when she collided headlong with a firm wall of muscle.

Terror-filled, she caught her breath in a loud gasp and would have fallen on the rebound had it not been for firm fingers gripping her arms. One part of her wanted to scream; the other part recalled what Sam had told her.

"You're Carly Quinn now," he'd said in that soothing voice of his. "Stay calm. Whatever you do, if someone approaches, don't make the mistake of assuming that Robyn Hart has been found out. You've got to act with confidence or you'll blow your own cover. Carly Quinn has absolutely nothing to hide, nothing to fear. Remember that."

It was easier said than done. Now, breathless from running and with the drum of her pulse reverberating in her ears, she raised panic-stricken eyes to those of her captor. He was large, tall and broad-shouldered, intimidating. In the relative light of the courtyard, she saw that he was dark—his full shock of casually mussed hair, the beard that stretched from ear to ear and parted only briefly at his lips, the worn sweat shirt he'd shoved up to the elbow. She knew she'd never seen him before; there was an intensity about him that she would not have quickly forgotten. Yet as a hit man he was questionable. His features were too gentle, as were, oddly, the fingers that seemed now to grasp her arms more in support of her shaking limbs than in any form of detention. And his voice, his voice, too, lacked the coarseness for which she'd steeled herself.

"Are you all right?" he asked, frowning at the pallor that the courtyard lights illumined.

Slowly, Carly came to her senses. His concern was as inconsistent with imminent attack as was the leisure with which he stood there holding her in the light, in view of any neighbor who cared to look. Panic yielded to caution, which was tinged with embarrassment when she forced herself to speak. She'd obviously made a foolish mistake.

"Yes . . . yes, I'm fine," she whispered falteringly. As unwarranted as her alarm had apparently been, it had nonetheless taken its toll. She was breathless from her dash, and felt weak and tired. And she wasn't yet home free. Scrounging odd fragments of strength, she tore her gaze from his and took a step back. The man's arms dropped to his sides. Then she turned her head and murmured a chagrined, "Excuse me," before sidestepping him and heading for the door, which was mercifully propped open with a carton, saving her the trial of having to fit her key into the lock. With the trembling of her fingers, she never would have made it.

Bent only on reaching total safety, she walked quickly through the lobby to the open stairs that wound broadly around the plant-filled atrium. She neither stopped nor looked back until she'd reached the third floor and her own apartment. Glancing around then to see that she hadn't been followed, she quickly punched out the combination to disengage her alarm, fumbled with her key for a minute and let herself in. Before she'd even crossed the threshold she flipped a switch to brightly light not only the small foyer in which she stood but also the sunken living room beyond. Everything looked fine. Wonderful, in fact. Stepping inside, she shut the door firmly, reactivated the alarm, drove home the bolts, then sagged back against the door with a long, shuddering breath. For the many times she'd felt herself a prisoner of circumstance, her cell had rarely been more appreciated than it was at that moment.

Home. She'd made it. Through the harrowing trek, her worst enemy had been her own imagination. Her lips thinned in self-reproach. Nightmares were one thing—those she couldn't help. Though they varied in specifics, their general content was the same. She was caught. Cornered. Doomed. Sometimes by fire, blazing hot and out of control. Sometimes by an obscured face, by a gruff, terrifying voice. Or by a hand with a small but deadly gun.

Suppressing a shudder, she silently scolded herself. No, she couldn't control the nightmares. But *this?* Running through the streets in a state of sheer panic? Shaking her head in dismay, she gazed around at the comforts of home and took long, purposeful breaths. With the gradual steadying of her pulse, she pushed away from the door, dropped her shoulder bag on the hall table, shrugged out of her coat and tossed it over the arm of the living-room sofa before sinking into the adjacent cushions. Their welcome was heaven. She eased off her heels to allow her feet play in the plush carpet and laid her head back, closing her eyes and breathing deeply. In the four months that she'd been on her own, she couldn't remember ever having panicked. Yet just now she'd totally, pathetically lost her cool, and it baffled her.

She opened her eyes, first looking down at the sophisticated sweater and skirt that so fitted the image of the modern English teacher, then letting her eyes wander over the apartment that similarly spoke of her new life. Given the bizarre circumstances that had brought her east, she had much to be grateful for. She had this beautiful home, a newly converted condominium with every convenience and then some. And she had a good job, one for which she was well trained, if a bit rusty. It had been more than five years since she'd taught, and she had been hesitant, to say the least. But it had seemed the perfect answer to her relocation dilemma and, once her teaching position had been secured, she'd spent the summer preparing her curriculum. It had taken hours upon hours, long days of reading and study and thought. As with everything she'd ever done, though, she had wanted to do this right.

Initially she'd been simply grateful for the diversion. With thoughts of Melville, Faulkner and Hemingway dominating her mind, there was little time to brood on Barber and Culbert. Gradually, she realized that she truly loved what she was doing, all the more when school began in September.

Stretching to further relax herself, she reached back to lift the weight of hair from her neck and expose lingering traces of dampness to the air. Yes, she did love her job. She loved dealing with literature itself, she enjoyed the give and take with her colleagues, and she particularly adored the kids. They were fresh and open, eager to learn. Many came from families who sacrificed to send them to private school. All were college-bound. Even given the free spirits, the nonconformists, the occasional troublesome ones of the lot, their dedication to learning was a teacher's dream. She felt challenged and rewarded, far more than she'd imagined she would ever be when she'd been forced to abandon Chicago, and some of the happiest years of her life.

Happiest, yet most tragic. First Matthew. Then Peter. Two people she'd loved, though in very different ways, now dead. And she had lived to begin anew in a way that most people wouldn't, most people couldn't, dream of doing.

She wandered restlessly around the living room, trailing her finger across a white lacquered cabinet to the television, then on to the bookshelf where she paused for a moment's thought before padding to the kitchen for a glass of orange juice. That firmly in hand, she returned to the sofa, settling back into the cushions to cope with an all-too-familiar sense of emptiness.

The view that met her eye was comforting, though. Her apartment was a vision of subdued elegance, from the white-textured cotton of the modular sofa, with its gay throw pillows of mauves and pale blues, and the low sculpted tables of white marble, to the original silk-screen prints on the walls and the recessed fixtures overhead. It was easily something a decorator might have put together, yet Carly had done it all. For the first time in her life she had splurged indecently. But then, she'd reasoned, she owed it to herself, both in compensation for the years she'd worked nonstop and in consolation for her more recent heartache.

Helplessly, her thoughts turned to Matthew. He'd never have lived this way, in a spotless apartment, with everything in its place. The apartments they'd shared through six years of marriage had been older, more cluttered, eminently casual. She'd loved it then because she had been with him. How she'd loved him. How she missed him!

Sighing, she absently swirled her orange juice, then nearly spilled it when the jangle of the phone made her jump. Muscles that had just begun to relax tensed quickly. The phone didn't ring often. That too was a change. There was a time when it had never seemed to stop.

The second ring brought her to her feet. Once in the kitchen, she hesitated for an instant with her hand on the receiver before lifting it with a studied calm. "Hello?" she asked cautiously.

"Carly?"

She didn't immediately recognize the voice, yet it sounded friendly enough. "Yes."

"Carly, it's Dennis." Dennis Sharpe. Of course. History teacher at the academy. Coach of the basketball team. Tall. Good-looking. Personable. "I'm sorry I missed you this afternoon. I had hoped to catch you before you left, but you must have escaped before we got back."

Escaped. A potent word. With a wary smile, she stretched the phone cord toward the kitchen table, settled into one of its canvas director's chairs and forced a note of buoyancy into her voice. "I waded through your boys on my way out. Congratulations! Sounds like quite a win."

"The guys played a great game. Particularly against Palmer. I was proud of them."

"Are we in first place now?"

He chuckled. "The season's barely begun. I suppose you could say we're somewhere up there, for what it's worth."

"Dennis," she chided lightly, "where's that school spirit?"

"That school spirit is back at school. It's the weekend. Which is why I'm calling. I know it's late, and I've got to be on the road before long, but I thought I'd give it another stab. How about dinner? Something quick and light in the Square? I've got to have something to eat before I get going, and I'd hate to do it alone."

With a sad smile, Carly propped her elbow on the arm of her chair and rested her head on her hand. Poor man. He'd been trying for dinner since September. Without success. "Oh, I don't know, Dennis. It's been a long week and I'm really exhausted."

"That's why you need to get out. To unwind and relax a little."

She *knew* that she needed to unwind and relax. But "getting out," after the scare she'd had earlier, would never do. It was far safer to stay home. "You're sweet to call, but . . . I don't think so. You see, I've got this date with a hot bath. We were planning to lose ourselves in lots of bubbles and a good book."

"How can you do this to me, Carly?" Dennis kidded, his voice the faintest bit hoarse. "You mean to say that I'm competing with a bathtub? What kind of rivalry is that?"

She laughed, but refrained from comment. It was always easier to change the subject. "You're headed for the Cape?"

He gave a magnanimous sigh. "Guess so. I've got some work to do on the house before winter sets in. It won't be long now, and I'm really behind."

"Your cottage isn't winterized?"

"Oh, it is. Or it will be once I've recaulked the windows and put on the storms, turned off the outdoor valves, oiled the furnace. That type of thing."

"You've got your weekend cut out for you," she commented, half in envy, despite the work involved. There was something to be said for physical labor as therapy.

"Want to come? You're welcome to, you know. In fact, I'd love it if you were along. It gets lonesome down there."

Carly grinned. "Come on, Dennis. Don't tell me that you aren't in touch with every neighbor for miles. You happen to be one of the most outgoing people I know." From the first, she'd been struck by his way with people, not only the kids at school, but the acquaintances he'd run into on the few occasions when they'd lunched off-campus. It would be easy to warm up to him, which was all the more reason for Carly to remain aloof.

"Yeah, but it'd be different if you were there. I really enjoy talking with you, Carly. You're one bright lady."

Her smile was gentle in its sad fashion. "Flattery will get you nowhere, my friend."

"Then what will?" he blurted out.

"Oh—" she rolled her eyes to the ceiling and offered a tongue-in-cheek quip "—maybe a yacht in the Caribbean or a villa in Majorca. I could use a little sun about now."

"First a bathtub. Now the sun. I can't win, can I?" When she remained silent, he sighed in resignation. "Well, I guess I'll be going. Sure you won't join me even for a pizza?"

Her eyes held a melancholy look. "Thanks, Dennis, but I'd better not. You have a good weekend, though. See you Monday?"

He paused, as if wanting to say more, then gave up. "Right. So long, Carly."

After a quiet "Bye-bye," she replaced her receiver on its hook, took a sip of juice, set the glass down on the counter again, then crossed through the foyer and short hall to her bedroom. When she returned to the living room, she was barefoot and wore a hip-length tunic and jeans. Turning the lights down low, she stood by the window. Traffic on Memorial Drive, and on Storrow Drive across the Charles, was at its peak, heavy in both directions, whipping commuters home to family and friends. How envious she was.

Slipping down onto the window sill, she drew the drapes around behind her, enclosing herself in a semicocoon of darkness to gaze out on the world unseen. These were the hardest times for her, these times of leisure when, alone and admittedly lonely, she inevitably looked back.

Warm images filled her head of the comfortable Lyons home on the outskirts of Omaha, of her parents standing arm in arm in the large front hall when her father returned from a day at the office, of her brothers' lusty squeals coming from odd corners of the house. The boys had been rowdy by nature. Three of them, all close in age and strapping. When she'd come along, far from being the demure little girl her parents had expected, they found themselves with a tomboy who matched the boys round for round. Her brothers were grown now, each married and with children of his own. Only she had failed to find that niche.

A tiny smile touched her lips as she thought back to the imp she'd once been. A child filled with laughter and joy. Until her mother had died. It had been hard on them all—on her father, on the boys. When a woman in her early forties died as suddenly as Charlene Lyons had, it was always hard on the survivors. But on Carly—then Robyn—it had been the hardest. She'd been twelve at the time, just entering adolescence. As suddenly as the mother she'd adored was gone, so was the mischievous child, leaving in her place a more serious teenager, industrious, responsible, ever pushing herself despite her father's and brothers' protests.

She hadn't been unhappy. Rather, she'd been busy, burying her private grief in a newfound existence. Much as she did now.

Against her will, her thoughts returned to the present. She struggled with them, fought them, suffered with them, then bolted from the window. With the quickest glance at her watch, she ran to the kitchen, picked up the phone and punched out her father's number. Her throat was tight, her gaze desperate. She needed him, needed to hear that familiar voice just now.

After five long rings, she was rewarded.

"Hello?"

To her ears, the sound of John Lyons's deep voice, seeming immune to both age and a fragile heart, was golden. "Dad! You *are* home!"

"Of course I'm home!" His words were shaped by an audible smile. "You know what my orders are."

Carly breathed deeply, savoring this contact that had the power to defer the darker thoughts that plagued her. "Oh, yes, I know what your orders are," she countered smartly. "I also know that you've been regularly resisting them." Her tone lightened as her own smile flowed across the miles. "How are you, dad?"

"I'm fine, sweetheart. Just sitting here relaxing with my feet up and my daily allotment of wine in hand. How are *you?*"

"Not bad." The last thing she wanted to do was to burden her father with her woes. It was enough to talk with him, to draw from his indomitable strength. "What did the doctor say? You saw him yesterday, didn't you?"

"I certainly did."

"And . . . ?"

"And he says that for a man who had a major heart attack six months ago, I'm a wonder."

Carly gave a teasing guffaw. "We all knew that, even *without* William Drummond's medical wizardry. So he says you're doing well?"

"Yes, ma'am. I've been given the go-ahead to play golf. The proof of the pudding."

"No kidding? That's great!"

"*I* think so." He gave a dry laugh. "Too bad the season's just about gone. It's been bad enough having to stop smoking cold turkey, and Chablis isn't quite the Scotch I'd like, but it's my golf that's been most sorely missed."

"By whom?" Carly teased. "You or Uncle Tim? I half suspect that *his* fun is in being able to trounce you on the course."

Her father came readily to his brother's defense. "He's damn good at it. I'm lucky he'll play with me. Besides, I've been that much more fortunate in business. It's the least I can do, letting him win once in a while." Carly's Uncle Timothy was as different from his fraternal twin as night was from day. He had shunned the business world in favor of a life of ease, and now his summers were spent as the golf pro at a suburban Omaha club, his winters in a similar role in Arizona.

"Will you go to Phoenix this year?" Carly asked.

"I'm planning to head there for several weeks after I see you in New York."

New York. Thanksgiving. Carly had been looking forward to it ever since she'd come east. Now it was barely three weeks away. She felt excited, and sad. More than anything, she would have liked to have gone home. But it wasn't to be, not for a while, at least. Swallowing the lump in her throat, she forced a brightness to her voice that told only half the story. "I'm really looking forward to it, dad. It seems so long." Gritting her teeth, she fought the tears in her eyes. She wasn't usually this sensitive, or rather, she was usually better able to hide her sensitivity. Whether this lapse had been caused by the afternoon's fright or simply the approach of the holidays, she wasn't sure.

"Are you all right, sweetheart?" her father asked quickly.

She squeezed her eyes shut. A small tear trickled from each corner. "Sure," she managed to reply. "I'm okay." She hadn't wanted to do this. Her father would know in a second that she was *not* okay. It was perhaps one of the reasons they'd always been close. He could read her well.

"You sound as though you're on the verge of tears."

Unfortunately she'd passed that point. Her eyes were brimming now, her cheeks growing wetter by the minute. She should have waited to call, she chided herself belatedly. But she'd needed him.

"I'm sorry," she whispered, muffling the receiver against her mouth. "I guess . . . it's just. . . ." What was it? Fear? Loneliness? A simple need to be held? Dissolving into silent weeping, she couldn't say a word.

Her father seemed to understand. "It's all right, sweetheart," he crooned, his voice, despite its undercurrent of pain, gently soothing her as his arms might have done had he been there. "You just let it out. We all need to do it sometimes."

"I'm sorry . . . I didn't mean . . . to burden you. . . ."

"Burden me?" he countered with such tenderness that the flow of her tears only increased. "You're my daughter. I love you. And you've never in your life been a burden to me."

"But . . . all this. . . ." She sniffled, waving her arm in a comprehensive arc her father could only imagine. "How did . . . I ever get myself . . . in such a mess?"

With a gentle, "Shh" every so often, her father waited until her quiet sobs subsided. "Don't berate yourself, sweetheart," he began. "I'm so very proud of you. We all are. You faced the worst of danger, yet you went out on a limb for something you believed in."

"I know," she whispered, extracting a tissue from its box on the kitchen counter. "But I sometimes . . . wonder what good it does. Sure, Barber and Culbert are serving time, but I feel as though *I'm* the one being . . . punished." Pausing, she dabbed her eyes. "If only I'd listened to the others. They told me not to push it."

"It *had* to be pushed, sweetheart. Arson is a crime. People died in those fires."

Oh, yes. People did die. She winced at the finality of it. "I know," she murmured, and she did. All too well. She also knew that, given the same circumstances, she would do it all again. Yet she couldn't contain the note of bitterness in her voice. Only with her father could she vent it. She could count on him to love her nonetheless. "It's just that there are times when I wish it had been someone else who'd been hellbent on righting the wrongs of the world. There are times when I don't like the consequences I'm stuck with, times when I feel so alone."

"You've got friends, haven't you?" her father asked. "I can't imagine you teaching at that school of yours without meeting people."

"Oh, yes, I've got friends. But it's different."

"You're still staying in a lot?" Now there was gentle accusation in his question. It was something they'd discussed before.

Carly dabbed at her nose and shrugged. "I get out. But I always feel as if I've got to be on my guard. It's so tiring sometimes." Her voice broke. Again, her father waited patiently until she'd regained her composure.

"It'll take time, sweetheart. They told you that from the start. You'll gain your confidence little by little. Look at me. When I first came home from the hospital, I was sure that each day would be my last, that any bit of exertion would bring on that next attack. Then I woke up the second day and the third day and the fourth. After a week, I'd begun to hope. After a month, I'd begun to believe. That's it, sweetheart. You've got to believe that you can forge a new life independent of the old." His voice softened even more. "You can't spend your days looking back. You've got to look ahead now."

This was what she loved about her father, understanding mixed with a gentle dose of reality. And he was right in everything he'd said. "You speak with such confidence," she quipped, retrieving her poise.

"I *am* confident. Look at your own life. Your mother died and you pulled yourself together to become someone she would have been proud of. When Matthew died, you did the same. You've got a strength that many people lack. Don't you see that? You'll survive this, too. Just wait. In a year or two you'll have found yourself. You'll feel confident. You'll be happy. You're that kind of person, sweetheart. It's in your nature."

Her lips grew tight. "Then why do I sit here feeling sorry for myself? Feeling sorry for myself! How does *that* jibe with the person you describe?"

"You're human. Like the rest of us. Self-pity is only natural once in a while. And it's fine as long as it doesn't become the major force in one's life. That will never happen to you. You're a doer. You'll move on. Just be patient with yourself. Give yourself time."

"Time." Sighing, she leaned back against the counter. "You're right, I'm sure. Besides, things aren't really all *that* bad." And her father deserved to hear a little of the good as well. She sniffled away the last of her tears. "You should see the themes those kids turned in this week. They're pretty exciting."

For a while longer, father and daughter talked on a lighter vein. When Carly hung up the phone at last, she felt better. Her father, on the other hand, had another call to make.

TWO

T AKING A WORN ADDRESS BOOK from his desk drawer, John
Lyons dialed the number he'd been given to use in case of emergency. It was
a Washington number. His call would be forwarded without his ever knowing
its destination. Glancing at his watch, he wondered if he might be too late. He
was in the process of reminding himself that he had twenty-four-hour access
when the switchboard operator's efficient voice came on the line.

"Witness Assistance."

"Control Number 718, please."

"One minute." There was a click, a lengthy silence, then another ring.

"Seven-eighteen."

"This is John Lyons calling."

After the briefest pause, Sam Loomis grew alert. It wasn't often that John
Lyons called, though they'd struck a rapport from the first. Man to man, they
had a common interest. "Mr. Lyons. What can I do for you?"

"I just spoke with my daughter. She sounded upset. Nothing's happened,
has it?"

Sam frowned. He'd spoken with Carly himself a few days earlier, and she'd
been fine. "No, nothing's happened. At least, not that I know of. Did she
mention anything specific?"

"No. But something's shaken her. I'm sure of that. She's usually so composed. There's been no word on a new trial, has there?"

"Uh-uh. Nothing. And Joliet's got our men safely on ice." He pushed aside
his papers and glanced at the clock on the wall. "Listen, I'm sure everything's
fine, but let me give her a call."

"I'd appreciate that."

"And you relax." Sam was aware of John Lyons's precarious health. "I'll
take care of things from this end."

"Thanks, 718."

Sam chuckled. "No problem." Pressing the button on his phone to sever the connection, he punched out Carly's number.

Carly hadn't moved from where she stood, deep in thought, against the kitchen counter. When the phone rang by her ear, she jumped. For a fleeting instant she wondered if her father had forgotten something, then she caught herself. He never called her. He didn't have the number. It was part of the scheme.

"Hello?" she answered slowly.

"It's Sam, Carly." He paused. "Are you all right?"

Instantly she knew what had happened. "Uh-oh. He called you, didn't he?"

"He was concerned. He said you were upset."

"I'm okay."

"Were you? Upset, that is?"

The deep breath she took, with its remnant of raggedness, bore confirmation of that fact. She twisted the telephone cord around her finger. "I guess I was. Something must have just hit me."

Sam Loomis was good at his job. He wasn't about to shrug off a vague "something." "What was it? Did something happen at school?"

"No, no. Everything's fine there. I . . . it was really nothing."

A fine-tuned feeler caught the sound of fear, very subtle but present. "Listen, Carly, I'd like to stop by. Maybe we can go out for a bite. Okay?"

"No, Sam. You don't have to do that. I'm really tired—"

"Then I'll bring something in."

"I'm not hungry. Sam—"

"Give me fifteen minutes in this traffic. See you then." He hung up the phone before she could renew her protest. Then, shuffling the papers he'd been reading into a semblance of order, he flipped the file folder shut and tossed it atop a similar pile.

"You're leaving?" came a voice from the opposite desk. Sam looked up. "Yeah."

"Problem?"

"I'm not sure."

"Carly Quinn?"

Sam's gaze sharpened. Greg Reilly had been with the service for less than a year and Sam's assistant for most of that time, yet there was still something about the younger man that made Sam uneasy. "Yeah," he said simply, unwilling to say more.

Greg shifted his trim frame in his seat and adopted a more idle pose. "I wouldn't mind it. She's a looker."

Stuffing a pen in the inner pocket of his blazer, Sam rethought his plans, picked up the file he'd just closed, put it in the lower right hand drawer of his desk and locked the drawer tight. "She's a case, Greg."

"A very sexy one. Man, you must be a saint to keep your distance. Either that—" his grin twisted "—or you're mad."

Sam headed for the door. "Not mad. Married. And respectful of Carly. *And* aware of the rules. *Capice?*" He was into the darkened hall before Greg's parting shot hit him.

"Anytime you need assistance. . . ."

"Thanks, pal," he muttered under his breath, "but no thanks. This one's mine."

Carly stared at the dead receiver for several minutes before putting it back on its hook. He'd had the final say. He was on his way. Not that she didn't want him to be. She was almost glad he hadn't let her argue him out of coming. Sam was always a comfort. Though she'd never have called him on her own for such a reason as this, she welcomed his company.

Fifteen minutes later the buzzer rang. Having sponged her face and freshened her makeup, she took a deep breath and pressed the button on the intercom panel beside the door. "Yes?"

"It's me, Carly. Buzz me in."

Recognizing his voice, she did as she was told, then opened the door and ventured into the hall to lean over the banister and follow his ascent. To this day, Carly believed Sam Loomis to be the least likely looking deputy U.S. marshal she'd ever seen. Not that she'd seen many. But there was a stereotype that Sam definitely didn't fit. A six-footer of medium build, he was dressed with a casual, style-conscious flair in navy slacks and a tan corduroy blazer with a white shirt and snappy striped tie. His hair was sandy hued and full, brushing his forehead as he trotted easily up the steps. There was nothing formal or stiff or somber about him. He easily passed as Carly's beau.

"You must just love this on a Friday evening," she began in subtle self-derision as he mounted the last flight. "Bet you didn't expect quite an albatross."

"Albatross?" Sam snickered. "You should only know." Putting a strong arm around her shoulders, he leaned low to whisper in her ear as he led her back into her apartment, "You should get a look at *some* of my charges. They're nowhere near as pretty as you are." To the onlooker, he might have been whispering sweet nothings. Her comely smile would have supported the suspicion.

Carly nudged him in the ribs. "That's the oldest line I've ever heard. Besides—" the door slammed behind them "—you've already told me that most of them are thugs. Compared to a guy who's had his nose broken twice, his cheek slashed, his forearm tattooed and his fists battered, I should hope I come out ahead."

Giving her shoulder an affectionate squeeze, he released her. The affection was genuine and mutual. In the four months since they'd met, Carly and Sam had found much to respect in each other.

" 'Ahead' is putting it mildly. It's sheer *relief* to get a call from you."

"From my father," she corrected him gently. "I wouldn't drag you out here just to hold my hand."

Sam was quick to respond to the apology in her eyes. "That's my job, Carly. It's what I'm here for. You don't call me half as often as most of my witnesses do." Gently grasping her shoulders with his hands, he was all too aware of her fragility. "And I'm sitting there in my office, trying to decide whether I should pester you or leave you alone. You've got to guide me. Besides, we're friends.

Something really got to you today. You should have called."

"I'm *okay*."

"But you've been crying."

She looked away. "My father shouldn't have told—"

"He didn't tell me. I can see for myself." Cupping her chin with his forefinger, he tipped up her face. She had no choice but to meet his gaze. When her eyes grew helplessly moist, she broke away and went to stand before the window. With one arm wrapped tight about her waist, she pressed a fist to her mouth. The reflection in the window told her of Sam's approach. "You don't want to talk about it?" he asked softly.

She held out a hand, her fingers spread, asking him to give her a moment. When she felt herself sufficiently composed, she took an unsteady breath. "I was walking home and I panicked. It was dark. I heard footsteps coming fast from behind." When she closed her eyes, the scene was vivid before her lids. "I just assumed they'd found me, so I started to run. And all the while I was waiting to hear a shot or feel a hand clamp over my mouth." Her eyes opened wide, bespeaking her fear. "It was a jogger, a stupid jogger. But I thought . . . I thought. . . ." She waved her hand suggestively as her voice cracked and her tenuous composure dissolved. Though the last thing she wanted to do was cry in front of Sam, she couldn't help herself. "What's the . . . matter with . . . me, Sam?" she sobbed, her voice muffled against the hand she'd put up to shield her face from him. "I never cry. And here I am. Twice in . . . in one day. It's disgusting."

Without a thought, Sam put his arm around her and drew her close. Of all the witnesses he'd dealt with in his ten years on the job, only she inspired this kind of protectiveness. Oh, yes, she was a woman. And a looker, as Greg had said. But she was different all around—her intelligence, her personality, the very nature of the case that had brought her to him. Holding her now, offering her a silent kind of comfort, he recalled the first time he met her, when she arrived four months before with the marshal from Chicago in that unmarked car. She had been frightened and vulnerable. He'd found it hard to believe her to be the journalist who had so systematically, so single-mindedly probed an arson conspiracy. *That* was before he'd gotten to know her. Through the months of July and August he'd witnessed her dedication firsthand, tracking her day after day to the library, aware of the other days she spent, holed up in her apartment preparing to teach in the fall. When she set her mind to something, she went after it determinedly. He respected her tremendously. He also respected the susceptibility that now reduced her to tears.

"It's only natural, Carly," he said soothingly, as he rubbed her back. The other nice thing about their relationship was that he *could* hold her, even dote on her, without misunderstanding. He was happily married and loved his wife. Carly knew this, seemed able to relax with him all the more for it. Never once had either of them felt threatened. Theirs was a rare friendship, one that went well beyond the rules of his trade. He knew that wherever she went, whatever she did in life, they'd keep in touch. They were truly friends.

"You've lived through something most people would only dream about if they tried to sleep on a stomach full of Guido's supersubs with fried onions, hot peppers, diced pickles and salami."

She answered with a groan. "It's not funny, Sam. I don't have to eat *anything* and I have nightmares."

"Still?" He drew back to look at her face. "You're not sleeping again? I thought that was better."

"Oh, it is usually. It's just . . . once in a while . . . I really shouldn't complain."

"Do you want something for it?"

"No! God, the last thing I need is something to knock me out. Then I might never know if someone had broken in until he was on top of me."

"Carly!" Sam gave her a punishing glower. "That's exactly the kind of thinking that'll get you into trouble. No one is going to come after you." He deliberately enunciated each word. "No one is going to break in."

"Then why am I in this program?" she countered, matching his glower with the fire of her own as she took a step back and blotted her cheeks with her hands. There was nothing like healthy debate to stem tears. "If there was no threat, I'd still be Robyn Hart living in Chicago working for the *Tribune*."

"Your reasoning only goes half way. As Robyn Hart, you *would* be in danger. That's why you were admitted to the program. On the other hand, now you're Carly Quinn. No one knows that, or where you live, or what you do. That's the whole point. You have a new identity, a new background, a new life. Take my word for it, Robyn Hart has vanished. We've taken care of that. And we know what we're doing."

Carly eyed him, feeling guilty even as she cornered him. "That wasn't what Michael Frank said."

Sam stared for a minute, then raised his eyes to the ceiling in frustration. When he looked back down, his expression was one of regret. He should have warned her. "You saw the program last Tuesday." No wonder she'd been upset. That garbage would have been enough to frighten even the most uninvolved of viewers.

"How could I help it? It was advertised for a week, blasted all over the evening news."

"You didn't have to watch."

"Come on, Sam. How could I *not*? It was an intensive study of the Witness Protection Program, of which *I* am a part. I was curious."

"And you believed all that crap?" he growled. "I can't fathom that. You're an intelligent woman, Carly. You're *media*, for God's sake! You should know how the facts can be twisted, how they can be selectively used to make one point or another. Television is a medium of exaggeration, and that show was nothing but a crude distortion of the truth." He paused long enough to hear his own anger, then looked down, shook his head and let out a long breath. "I'm hungry."

Carly stared at him. "You're *hungry*? What does hunger have to do with anything?"

He looked around, then headed for the sofa to lift the coat she'd dropped earlier. "I can't think straight on an empty stomach. Let's go get a snack."

"We can't do that, Sam. Ellen is sure to be sitting home waiting for you. She's probably spent the afternoon planning dinner."

For the first time since he arrived, Sam smiled broadly. "You've never met

Ellen or you wouldn't worry. Ellen is the perfect deputy marshal's wife. She knows *never* to expect me unless I call."

To Carly it sounded awful. She and Matt had prized their dinners precisely because their days were so busy and apart. "How does she stand it?"

He grinned then. "My charm. She's a sucker for my charm." He held the coat for her. "Come on, lady. We've got some talking to do." Had it been anyone else, Carly would have steadfastly refused. With Sam, though, she felt safe on every level.

Once in his car, they headed toward a deli on the fringe of the Square. There, over corned-beef sandwiches and beer, they very sanely discussed the program she'd watched. "It only spoke of the failures, Carly, and those are a ridiculously small percentage of the whole. Sure, there have been thugs who've been brought into the program, who theoretically then have a clean slate to launch a second lifetime of crime; there have been misjudgments here and there. In most cases though, it's been decided that the importance of the testimony outweighed the potential risk."

"I know, Sam, but that wasn't what—"

"Bothered you most?" When she nodded, he grimaced. "That's what I thought." He took a long swig of his beer.

"I mean, you have to admit that hearing about cases where the person supposedly under protection is discovered and—and killed—isn't terribly encouraging."

"But look at those cases, Carly. Those were situations where the witness was a crook himself, where he had a whole army of enemies. And the one most important thing that bastard Frank failed to point out was that in every one of those cases, the witness was himself responsible for his cover being blown. Think about it." He spoke softly, a gentle urgency in his voice. "Here you are. You've got an entire background fabricated for you—birth certificate, social security number, school and employment records, even a marriage certificate and phony newspaper clippings of your husband's death. We've given you a past that parallels the truth enough for you to feel comfortable with it. Names, dates, places may have been altered, but as Carly Quinn, you're a complete, believable individual. And there's no way, *no way* that anyone can connect Carly Quinn to Robyn Hart. In fact, wasn't that the main thrust of Frank's argument? In the few cases he chose to explore, when the local authorities would arrest our witnesses on suspicion of a crime, they were unable to get so much as a fingerprint ID from the FBI. These were *police officers*, unable to break through the cover." He straightened and offered a half smile of encouragement. "In some situations, where local police don't know and can't learn that they have a dangerous person in their midst, it may be counterproductive. In your situation, it should be comforting. No one can find out who you are. Not Nick Barber. Not Gary Culbert. *No one.*"

Carly winced at the mention of the names that had brought terror to her life, then reflected on Sam's argument as she idly rearranged the potato salad on her plate. Finally, setting down her fork, she looked up. "I suppose," she murmured, but her skepticism lingered. "It's just that I get so frightened at times."

"Is that what happened this afternoon?"

Puzzled and frustrated, she frowned. "I don't know *what* happened this afternoon. I must have been edgy for some reason."

"Do you think it was Frank's program?"

"Maybe." She shrugged. "I don't know. It could also be the holidays coming up. These will be the first. It's kind of hard not to look back." Though her eyes were averted, her pain was evident. "We used to all get together, my father and brothers and their families and me."

"None of your brothers can get to New York?"

"Naw." She made light of it, but she knew she'd miss them terribly. "It's an expensive trip with the kids and all. I think that we'll try to rotate visits. I'll see my father in New York at Thanksgiving, my brother Jim and his family down south at Christmas, Ted and Doreen and the kids sometime in the spring God knows where. Exciting, huh?"

She made it sound anything but. In total sympathy, Sam felt helpless to come up with a remedy. "You really want to go home, don't you?"

Looking as sad as he'd ever seen her, she nodded. "Yup."

"It wouldn't be smart, Carly."

"I know." She gave a rueful smile. "But that doesn't stop me from wanting it."

This time it was Sam who nodded. He'd feel the same way if, for some reason, *he* couldn't go home. The times he spent in Montpelier had become more and more special with the years. Beyond that, he had Ellen, not to mention Sara and another child on the way. Carly Quinn was alone.

After several quiet moments during which they were both lost in thought, Sam shifted in his seat. "Why don't we get going," he suggested, gesturing for the check. "You can make me a cup of coffee at your place before I hit the road."

It was back in Carly's kitchen, over a second cup, that he finally broached the topic that had been on his mind since dinner's end. "You still don't date, do you?" he asked, stretching back in his chair with studied nonchalance.

Her gaze narrowed in mock reproach. "You're not going to start in on that again, Sam Loomis, are you?"

"You have to admit it's been a while since I mentioned it last," he argued good-naturedly, feeling not at all guilty. "And I've been patient. I've given you time. But you *aren't* dating, are you?"

"You sound like an older brother," she teased.

But he was serious. "No, Carly. Just a friend expressing his concern. When you were in protective custody, you were isolated, in a kind of limbo. It would have been impossible for you to lead a normal life then. But that's over. The trial is over. It's time you returned to the real world. You're young and attractive. You've got so much to offer a man. And you *need* one."

In vain she fought the blush that stole to her cheeks. "I *need* one?" A single auburn brow ventured high beneath her bangs. "Do I look that desperate?"

"You know what I mean," he scolded. "You need companionship. For God's sake, you're afraid to go out at night! A man would be company, protection."

"Ahhh," she drawled. "A knight in shining armor."

"You're not taking me seriously, Carly."

"I am." And she was, suddenly as sober as he. "I've given it lots of thought, Sam. Believe me, I have. I'm busy. There are always things to do for school— reading papers, planning classes. I want to be a good teacher. Honestly, it's better this way for now."

"Better? To sit up here alone, night after night? Hell, you'd never have gone out tonight had I not come over and trundled you off!" He glowered. "Maybe I should turn you over to Greg, after all."

"Hmm?"

"Greg Reilly. My assistant."

She grinned. "That charming fellow with the hungry eyes?"

"You noticed?"

"How could I help but notice. Every time I walk into your office he all but strips me naked." She held up a hand against Sam's scowl. "Figuratively, of course. I certainly wouldn't have to worry about nightmares with Greg around, would I?" she quipped, tongue in cheek. Actually, had the circumstances surrounding her presence in the U.S. marshal's office been different, she might have found Greg Reilly's appreciation to be flattering. Not tempting—just flattering. He was young, perhaps a year or two younger than she was, certainly more appealing than Brozniak, the assistant state's attorney she'd had occasional dealings with in Chicago. "It must be something about law enforcement as a profession that does strange things to you guys," she kidded, then added whimsically, "Actually, I prefer older men."

Sam ignored her humor, picking up his thought where he'd himself broken it moments earlier. His gaze narrowed. "But it's not only the nights, is it? Your weekends must be gruesome. My guess is that in the four months you've been here you've seen just about as much of the area as *I've* shown you. Hmm?"

Carly fingered her spoon. "I've gotten around some."

"Where?" He wasn't about to let up. She wasn't doing much more than existing. It was a waste.

She met his gaze with hesitance. "I've driven down to Plymouth to see the rock, and out to Lexington and Concord. The area's chock full of history. And I've been to the Faneuil Marketplace. You'd never have the patience to let me idle through the shops."

"And you did it? Without getting nervous?"

"Of course." It was a wee stretch of the truth, followed by a regurgitation of the arguments he had given her repeatedly himself. "I'm not *that* bad. I mean, if nothing else, I do look different from Robyn Hart. She had blue eyes and superlong straight hair. There was something—" she searched for the word, recalling an erstwhile wardrobe of peasant shirts, flowing skirts, floppy blazers and faded-to-nearly-nothing jeans "—Bohemian about her. Carly Quinn, on the other hand, is more conventional. She wears her hair at shoulder-length and lets it curl the way God intended. She has gray eyes. She dresses out of the career shop at Saks. It's not a bad disguise."

"That's the problem, Carly. You've got to stop thinking of it as a disguise. You *are* Carly Quinn now. If you're called back to testify, the *other* will be the disguise."

Those gray eyes widened in alarm. "They haven't contacted you, have they?" Her heart pounded against her ribs. "Will there be another trial?"

He reached across to squeeze her hand. "No. No word of a trial. Not yet, at least. You do know that it's a possibility though?" Without dwelling on it, he wanted her to be prepared.

"Yes." Barber and Culbert had both launched appeals after they'd been convicted. Though the judge had refused them immediate stays of sentence, their appeals went on. She closed her eyes over images of pain. "God, I don't want that. The courtroom. The crowds. The press. Culbert and Barber staring daggers at me. Their lawyers shooting question after question, putting *me* on trial, trying to get me to say that I simply wanted to do someone, *anyone* in because my husband had died in a fire." Her lids flickered up and she focused pleading eyes on Sam. "Matthew died in a hotel half a continent away. We'll never know if it was arson." Her tone grew more agitated. "But we *do* know that Culbert raked in hundreds of thousands in insurance money when he had those buildings burned in Chicago. And people died!" For an instant, she was in that other time. Her expression bore the agony of remembrance. "The smell. God, it was awful. Acrid. Suffocating. Terrifying. . . ."

Sam held her hand tighter. "Take it easy, hon. You're right. We all know what those two did. So does the judge, the jury, the public. But legal processes take strange turns. Even if there *is* a new trial, it doesn't mean the outcome will be any different." He paused. "You know you'd be safe, constantly guarded."

Shuddering with apprehension, she nodded. "Yes."

"Good." He sat straighter. "So. Where were we?"

She saw no point in discussing the possibility of a trial, which was sure to depress her, or in discussing her social life, which was sure to depress Sam. Much as she had to force it, her only out seemed to be in humoring him. "You were telling me that this pregnancy's been tougher for Ellen and that you really ought to head home."

"I never told you that. How come you know so much?"

"I have three sisters-in-law and ten nieces and nephews. It was a safe guess."

"And a definite hint."

She apologized with a tremulous smile. "I really shouldn't keep you any longer. Besides, even if Ellen's not tired, I am." Emotionally, she was beat.

With a sigh of lighthearted defeat, Sam pushed back his chair and stood, taking her arm when she joined him. "Then I'll leave you to your sweet but lonely virgin dreams," he drawled in her ear.

"You're terrible," she chided. "No wonder Ellen's pregnant again, and Sara not yet two."

"Did I tell you that?" he asked, his eyes twinkling. But before she could answer, the doorbell rang. Both heads flew its way. Both smiles faded. "Were you expecting someone?" It was nearly nine o'clock.

"If I was, I'd never have let you razz me as you did," she murmured under her breath. "I have no idea who it could be."

The bell rang again. Sam spoke softly. "It's not the intercom. Perhaps one of your neighbors?" He put an eye to the tiny viewer he'd had installed in her door and stared for several long seconds. Then, reaching a tentative decision, he held up a finger for her to wait while he nonchalantly took a seat in the living room. Then he motioned for her to answer the door. When she hesitated, he repeated the gesture more forcefully. Turning, she put her own eye to the viewer, and froze. But when she looked back Sam was vehement. "Trust me," his eyes said. The palms with which he patted the air told her to be calm, to act as she normally would.

Cautiously she released the upper bolts, leaving only the chain in place as she opened the door those scant few inches. In an involuntary flash, she relived the terror she'd felt in the courtyard earlier that evening. Her knuckles grew white, her knees weak. She was helpless to stem the race of her pulse. For before her, seeming to dominate that narrow slice of hall, stood the tall, dark stranger into whom she'd so unceremoniously barreled in her farcical escape from an imaginary hunter.

THREE

❧❧❧

"Y ES?" SHE ASKED softly, unsurely.

His voice was deep and as strangely lulling as it had been in the courtyard. "Uh, I'm sorry to bother you, but I wonder if I might use your phone. I've just arrived with another load of things and—" he grimaced in chagrin "—it seems that I've locked my keys in the car."

Unhinged, Carly stood stock-still. She had assumed him to be a delivery man, though why, she wasn't sure. Her mind drew up the fleeting image of a carton propped against the door. But it was Friday night. Another load of things? In his car?

Reading her confusion, seeing lingering traces of the fear that had so gripped her earlier, the man smiled. She was lovely. "I'm Ryan Cornell. We'll be neighbors. I'm moving into the apartment just under yours."

"The Amidons's?" She was perplexed. She hadn't known they'd been seeking a buyer, much less sold their place.

"That's right. Actually, I'm renting until they decide whether to live in Sarasota year-round." When she still seemed wary, he elaborated. "They'd been toying with the idea of moving. A place came through unexpectedly, and they felt they had to grab it. It was furnished, so they left most of their things here. If they decide to buy down there, they'll send for the rest."

Carly nodded, wondering how he could possibly have fabricated such a tale. She wanted desperately to believe him, yet she was, by habit, guarded. Standing there, silently staring up at him through the slim opening of the door, she was struck again by his aura of gentleness. A large man. Exquisitely soft brown eyes.

In the background, Sam coughed. Having momentarily forgotten his presence, she looked quickly back. Ryan's gaze flew beyond, only to be thwarted by the meager span of the opening. Not so his perceptivity.

"Oh, I'm sorry. You're not alone." A faint crimson blush edged above his beard. With a contrite grin, he started to turn. "I'll try elsewhere." But the sound of the chain sliding across, then falling, halted his retreat.

The door slowly opened and Carly offered a smile. Sam was there to keep her safe. Besides, Ryan Cornell, awkward in such an appealing way, seemed no more of a threat now than he had to her downstairs in the heat of her panic. She stood back. "Come on in. The phone's in the kitchen." When he hesitated still, she urged him on with a cock of her head.

He took a step forward, looking down at her in gratitude, then stepped into the foyer and, sending an apologetic glance Sam's way, followed her pointing finger to the kitchen. Feeling himself a perfect ass, he lifted the phone and punched out the number of the place he'd called home for the past year. Then he waited, his head down, one hand on his hip, for the phone at the other end to ring.

From an unobtrusive post by the kitchen door, Carly studied him. Lit generously now, his hair proved to be more brown than black. Though full, it was well shaped and neatly trimmed, as was the close-cropped beard that covered his jaw. Both were rich and well groomed. Indeed, despite her initial, irrational fear when he'd caught her arms downstairs, there was nothing of the scraggly cur about him. Though his sweat shirt was dark and faded, she could now detect its legend. Stretched across the muscled wall of his chest and slightly battered from washing and drying, it read Harvard. Though his jeans were worn, they were clean and hugged the leanest of hips. His sneakers were on the newer side. Just as she paused to admire his height, he glanced over at her, softly, silently, and she sensed that same gentleness she had earlier. When he offered a self-conscious smile, she half returned it.

Then, with the abrupt shift of his expression, and after what must have been eight or nine rings, his call was answered. He tore his eyes away and focused on the floor.

"Yeah." The voice at the other end was hoarse and begrudging.

"It's me, pal. Sorry."

"Ryan? What the——"

"I need a favor." His jaw flexed. He spoke fast and low. "In the kitchen, the cabinet by the fridge. There's a slew of my keys still on the hooks. Find the spares for my car and bring them over?"

"But you've got the damned car, haven't you?"

"Not the keys." He didn't have to elaborate. His brother knew him too well.

"Geez! What did you do, lock 'em in again?"

Ryan tucked his head lower. "Spare me the speech, Tom. Can you run them over or not?"

"Damn it, Ryan." The phone was muffled, dropped, then grabbed up again. "I thought I was free of you for the night."

"You are. I just need the keys."

"It can't wait till morning?"

"The car's running." Ryan forced the words out under his breath in the hope that Carly wouldn't hear.

With a pithy oath, Thomas Cornell sat up to cast a rueful eye at the woman by his side. "And you can't break in? You know, jimmy the lock with a hanger or something?"

"I've tried. It's not working." Ryan's patience waned. "Come on, Tom. I'm imposing on one of my neighbors—"

"You're imposing on *me!* Do you have any idea what you're interrupting?"

Ryan hadn't been blind to the fair-haired attraction of his kid brother's date. Nor was he blind to the fact that Tom was a skilled playboy who'd easily be able to pick up an hour later where he left off now.

"I think so. Don't forget, I've got a few years on you." He took a deep breath. "I'm parked right out in front. I'll be waiting downstairs in twenty minutes."

Tom tried to argue, but the phone was dead. Muttering something mercifully unintelligible, he rammed the receiver home. Then he looked down at the warm body in his bed. "He's done it again, babe." He sighed, feeling the last of his own passion fade as he lay back to stare at the mirrored image overhead.

The young woman snuggled closer. "Who was that?"

"My brother. You know, the guy who moved out tonight?"

"What's his problem?"

"He needs me."

"So do I." She slid one leg over his thigh.

Yeah, Tom thought, arching a brow, *but you'll forget me tomorrow.* Tossing back the sheet, he rose.

"Hey, you're not leaving me like this, are you?" came the sulky voice from behind.

"I'll be back."

"But, Tom—"

"I'll be back." Heading for his clothes, he crossed the black shag carpet to an oversize leather chair. It too was black, as was fully half of the room's decor. The other half was white. He'd thought it sleek and masculine when he'd done it up three years before. Ryan had thought it tacky from the start. But then, what did Ryan know, he thought angrily as he thrust first one leg then the other into his jeans.

What did Ryan know? A hell of a lot. Though absentminded enough to lock his keys in his car on a regular basis, Ryan had always been the responsible one, the one with a solid career, the one with a wife and home . . . well, once. Tugging his sweater on over his head, Tom took his brother's side on that one. Alyssa had been a bitch, anyway. Spoiled and demanding. Not that she wasn't half right in her accusation that Ryan was wedded to his work. He was. He was dedicated. And a whiz when it came to the law. He'd certainly come through for *him* on that score.

"Tom . . . ?" This time it was a whining complaint.

He stuffed his feet into his boots, then knelt to rescue the denim from their clutches. "Yeah, babe?"

"Come on, Tom. He'll wait a few more minutes."

"You don't know my brother." *And I do owe him.* Running his fingers through his thick blond hair, he headed at a clip toward the door.

"And if I'm not here when you get back. . . ?" was the taunt.

Tom paused once on the threshold to cast an arrogant glance back. "Then it'll be your loss, babe."

Ryan turned back to Carly, who'd all the while stood silently by the kitchen door. "Sorry about that." He thrust his hands in the pockets of his jeans and looked decidedly sheepish. "I guess you're not the only one I've inconvenienced."

"Can your friend help?" she asked softly, her wariness now held in abeyance. The half of the conversation she'd heard had been utterly believable. Either he was a superb actor, or he had told the truth about his dilemma. Not to mention the fact that Sam remained where he was, sprawled casually on the sofa, apparently unconcerned.

"He'll help. Well—" he took a step toward the door, then cast another glance at Sam "—I'm sorry to have bothered you. With any luck my phone will be in on Monday." He reached the door when Sam finally came to life.

"Can I give you a hand with something?" he asked, rising from the living room to stand behind Carly.

Ryan raised an open palm. "Thanks, but no. I've disturbed you enough." His gaze dropped once more to Carly's face. "Have a good night."

As suddenly as he'd come, he was gone. Sam closed the door, then turned to lean back against it and stare pointedly at Carly. "You didn't know they were moving?" he asked in subtle accusation.

"The Amidons? How would I know a thing like that?"

"Don't you ever talk to your neighbors? You can't be *that* much of a hermit. For Pete's sake, we've checked them all out and they're safe."

She deftly reversed the argument. "Why weren't *you* on top of this? You're supposed to be the one keeping an eye on me. It's your job. Isn't that what you said earlier?"

Realizing he'd come on too strongly, Sam softened. "Of course it's my job, Carly. But I need your help. I can't possibly have people snooping around all the time. It's up to you to alert me to changes like this. Then I can take over and have things checked out."

Feeling duly chastised, she turned away and wandered to the living room to sink into the sofa. Eyes closed, she laid her head back. "You seemed to trust him."

"I know who he is."

Her head came forward, eyes open and wide once more. "You know him? It didn't look like he recognized you."

"I said that I know who *he* is." He came around to stand before her. "His name really is Ryan Cornell. He's a lawyer."

A moan slipped from Carly's lips. "Another one of those? I'm beginning to wonder if there isn't an epidemic. A new kind of plague. You know—" she illustrated the point with two walking fingers of one hand "—an onslaught of little men in their natty three-piece suits, all bent on finding the lowest common denominator of humanity."

Sam chuckled. "That's got to be the editorialist in you seeking release. Either that, or you've truly had your fill of the legal profession in the last year."

"A little of both, I'm afraid."

"Well—" he sighed, scratching the back of his head "—it seems that Ryan Cornell doesn't fit the mold. He's not a little man by any measure, and I find it hard to picture him in a natty three-piece suit after—" he tossed his head toward the door "—that."

If Carly didn't know better, she might suspect Sam Loomis to be jealous of the other's rugged good looks. But she did know better. Sam would simply be doing his job, sizing Ryan up in advance of the phone call he'd be certain to make shortly. Sure enough, before she could begin to ask him what else he knew about her new neighbor, he headed for the kitchen to put through the call.

Fishing a dog-eared piece of paper from his wallet, he ran his eye down the list to one of the newest of the numbers. Then he punched it out. The phone was picked up after a single ring.

"Reilly."

"Greg. Bad time?" Much as he was unsure about his assistant, Sam respected his privacy. It was, after all, Friday night, and it had been a busy week.

Greg Reilly let his feet fall to the floor of the sofa and sat up. "Don't I wish it," he murmured, casting a melancholy eye around his slightly messy, thoroughly lonely living room. "Just catching up on some reading." He set the magazine aside. "What's up?" He knew that Sam wouldn't be calling to shoot the breeze, though at times he wished he would. Sam was a brilliant detective, able to find solutions to problems *he* wouldn't know where to begin on. But then, having served as a detective with the state police before coming to the marshal's service, Sam had ten years on him. As chief deputy, Sam had responsibilities that reflected his talent. It'd be nice to be in his inner circle.

As for himself, he seemed to be forever blowing it. Like today. He'd really hit a raw nerve when it came to Carly Quinn.

"Listen, can you do me a favor?" Sam asked.

"Sure."

"I need information on Ryan Cornell."

"The lawyer?"

"Yeah. You know something?"

Greg took a deep breath and let it out in a hiss between his teeth. "He's one bright man. And a damned good counselor."

"Who says?"

"Fitzgerald says. Dray says. I say."

Fitzgerald was the state's attorney general, Dray a justice of the Superior Court. Greg Reilly had come to the U.S. marshal's service with a load of clout in his back pocket. "You've seen him in action?" Sam asked.

Greg nodded. "Very smooth. Very sharp. Brilliant defense."

"And his character?" Sam's voice spoke of his concern. Greg picked up the ball.

"I know who to call. Where can I reach you?" He'd been on the verge of asking if Sam was still at Carly's house, but had caught himself just in time. The innuendo might have ticked Sam off again. Hell, he'd only been kidding before. He knew Sam was in love with his wife. He had eyes and ears and was vividly aware of those soft calls every day at four.

"I'll reach you," Sam replied, then gave a short, "Thanks," before hanging up the phone. Returning to the living room, he sat down across from Carly.

"Well. . . ?" she asked, tempering a fine line of tension.

"We're working on it."

"Do you know anything, other than that he's a lawyer?"

Sam shrugged. "Not much. I know he's handling more and more criminal work. That's why he looked familiar. Several months back, he defended a member of the governor's cabinet on charges of embezzlement. His face was all over the evening news."

"Did he get an acquittal?"

Sam scowled. "Yes."

"But you think his client was guilty?"

"From where I sat," which was only at his desk reading the newspaper, "yes."

"Then how did he get off?" It was a question born more of indignation than innocence.

"Very simply. The prosecution didn't have solid enough evidence to convince a jury beyond the shadow of a doubt. There wasn't any witness like you to make its case."

The terse reminder of her predicament brought furrows to Carly's brow. "Is Ryan a danger to me? Do you think he might have some connection to Culbert?" More likely Culbert, a high-placed political blackguard, than a lowly thug like Barber. Perhaps both. She wanted to believe neither. "He wasn't terribly threatening just now, even if he did give me a scare downstairs."

"Downstairs?"

Only then did it occur to her that Sam knew nothing of the blockbuster end to her fiasco. "I, uh, ran into him in the courtyard," she began, feeling foolish all over again. "I mean, *literally* ran into him when I thought I was being chased. I'd looked over my shoulder and wasn't watching, and wham. He caught me and kept me from falling." Recalling the events, she gave an involuntary shudder. "My first thought was that he was part of a brilliant scheme, that he'd been waiting right there to catch me. You know, the lamb being, in this case, chased to the slaughter? But he let me go as soon as I'd regained my balance. He was as harmless then as he seemed just now. Wasn't he?"

Pondering her vulnerability, Sam felt the full weight of his responsibility. How in the hell could *he* know about Cornell? If the guy were a faceless shoe salesman or the obscure manufacturer of computer parts, he might feel more confident. But a fairly visible criminal attorney might easily be the target of

Gary Culbert's maneuvering. Culbert had been a state legislator before greed had taken over. Though none would admit it now, Sam was sure that he still had friends in high places. And friends in Illinois high places had friends in other high places who could feasibly make calls and pull strings and find weaknesses in a man as the grounds for blackmail. What were Ryan Cornell's weaknesses? He was human. Surely he had some, aside from a knack for locking his keys in his car.

Perhaps it was wishful thinking, but in his gut Sam agreed with Carly. On the surface, Cornell seemed innocent enough.

"I'm sure he is," he said, forcing a smile. Carly was already on edge. There seemed no point in feeding her dark imaginings. He would, however, stop at the office before heading home. With Cornell apparently already installed in the apartment just below hers, Sam wanted fast answers on this one. "We'll check things out. I don't want you to worry." He glanced at his watch. "I should be going."

Pushing herself up from the sofa, Carly walked him to the door. "Thanks for coming, Sam. I guess I did need someone to talk with."

He threw an arm around her shoulder and gave her a parting squeeze. "You get some rest, you hear?"

"I will. See ya."

With a final smile and a thumbs up sign, he was gone. Carly very deliberately bolted herself in and activated the alarm, then turned to clear the cups from the kitchen table.

In that most innocent of ways, Sam was good for her, she mused. He exuded the kind of confidence she needed, yet it wasn't a blind, macho thing. He was thorough. Ryan Cornell would be carefully scrutinized. If there were any possible connection between him and either Gary Culbert or Nick Barber, it would be found. *And what then*, she asked herself as she had so many times before. What if it was learned that her cover *had* been breached? She sighed, laying the cups and saucers in the dishwasher and closing its door. Another name? Another place? It could go on forever. She didn't think she could bear that.

It was like chicken pox, she mused, flipping off the kitchen light, doing the same to all but one of those in the living room, the one she'd leave burning all night, then seeking the haven of her bedroom. As a child she'd been exposed year after year, waiting to get ill, and by the time she'd reached her teens she'd begun to pray for the inevitable if only to eliminate the fear. Now, at times, she felt the same, half wishing Culbert would come after her as he'd threatened. At times, she simply wanted it over! But then, she'd never caught the chicken pox.

Lifting the bell-shaped lid of a round rattan basket, she retrieved her needlepoint, took refuge in the fortress of her corner chair with the phone in arm's reach, and began to carefully weave a silk-tailed needle through the network of ultrafine mesh. It was to be a Christmas gift for her father, a hand-painted canvas of wheat fields at sunset that, when covered with silk and framed in bronze, would capture the vibrant reds and the golden tones that so spoke to her of home. From the time she'd first spotted the piece in a shop on Newbury

Street, she'd felt drawn to it. Even now, as she pulled the thread from front to back with slow, even strokes, she felt more peaceful than she had all day.

From the start, she'd found needlepoint to be therapeutic. She recalled vividly her introduction to it. She'd been sixteen at the time, a high-school senior living through the tension of college boards, applications and admissions. When she'd noticed the small eyeglass case in the window of the store in downtown Omaha that Saturday afternoon, it had appealed to her instantly. Not only was it practical, with her three pairs of glasses floating around the house at any given time, but the design had been too right to resist. A robin perched on a tiny branch—she'd loved it. How clearly she remembered the saleswoman's reaction.

"You've done needlepoint before, have you?"

"No."

"No? Then perhaps you ought to consider another design. This particular piece is quite delicate. It takes a lot of skill."

"I know how to sew. And knit. I can do it," she'd responded without hesitation. The thought of learning a new craft excited her. It would be something to divert her mind from the unsureness of the future.

The saleswoman had been far from convinced. "Did you look at the pillow kits on that shelf? They're perfect for a beginner."

But Robyn Lyons had known what she wanted. "I'll take the robin," she'd said gently but firmly. "If you have a good instruction book, I'll take that too. If you don't, I can get something from the library."

She'd left the shop that day with not only the eyeglass case, a supply of Persian yarn and needles and a how-to-book on basic stitchery, but a full stock of determination. In her wake she'd left one saleswoman smug in the conviction that the piece would be a disaster. When her young customer returned a week later, needing nothing more than instructions for blocking her skillfully completed work, the saleswoman had been duly put in her place. And when Robyn had proceeded to purchase a second piece, this time an Aran Isle pillow requiring no less than six different stitches, the saleswoman became the eager teacher. It was the start not only of a hobby that had carried Robyn Lyons through light times and dark, but of a close friendship as well. Sylvia Framisch saw her protégé only during college vacations after that first year, though the two kept faithfully in touch. Long after Robyn had married, she continued to return to the shop during visits home. In turn, Sylvia knew just which canvases to order with Robyn in mind.

Shifting to tuck her legs snug beneath her, Carly wondered how Sylvia fared. She missed her warmth, the friendly talk. It wasn't the same—the elegant Newbury Street shop she now visited once a month or so for supplies. Or perhaps it was she—Carly—who had changed. Robyn had been more outgoing, making friends easily. Carly was, of necessity, more cautious.

Perhaps Sam was right, she told herself. Perhaps she did need to spread her wings further. But it was hard, when she was always on her guard lest she say or do something to betray her true identity. Was loneliness something she'd have to learn to live with? Or would she, in time, feel comfortable enough with Carly Quinn to be able to open up?

There was more, though. It wasn't just loneliness or distrust that caused her to put distance between herself and friends and acquaintances. There was fear. Raw, recurrent fear. Memories of an inferno, a gun, a look of sheer hatred, a threat ground out by a violent soul. Though cloaked at times, the past was ever present.

Sam had asked if she'd explored the Boston area. Yes, she'd done her share of cursory sight-seeing. And she'd gone on occasional jaunts with friends from school. But most often she went out only when necessary, such as to go to the market, the cleaner, the drug store, the library. At other times it was simply safer staying home.

Hearing Sam's disagreement as though he were there, she shook her head sadly. No one could understand why she felt the constant need to glance over her shoulder. No one could understand why she stood far enough back from the trolley tracks to prevent someone's coming from behind and shoving her in front of an oncoming train. No one could understand that tiny flicker of doubt each time she turned her key in the ignition of her yellow Chevette, or why, when sitting in the midst of downtown traffic, she would check twice, three times within minutes to be sure the doors were locked. No one could possibly understand why she would pay more to park in an open-air lot rather than parking for less in a dark, enclosed garage.

No one could possibly understand these things, or feel the mindless terror that prompted them. The gun, the threat, the sudden conviction that death was imminent—even Sam could only begin to sympathize. After all, *he* wasn't the one being hunted!

Take Ryan Cornell. In other circumstances, she might have thought it exciting to have such an attractive man living nearby. Now she could only wonder whether his gentle facade hid another kind of man. What if he *had* been hired to find her? What if he'd taken the apartment below her with the purpose of penetrating the wall she'd built? What if . . . what if Gary Culbert had conjured a far more subtle, far slower, more painful means of revenge?

In his downtown office, Sam cradled the phone against his ear. "Sid? Sam Loomis calling. Sorry to bother you so late but I need information." Sid Aronski was one of the court officers with whom Sam had a working relationship—a lunch now and then, a bottle of whiskey at Christmas, in exchange for information.

"Who you after?"

"Ryan Cornell."

"Cornell?" There was a note of surprise. "What's he done?"

"That's what I want to know. What *has* he done?"

"Beats me," the court officer returned with a shrug, pushing the cat off the worn hassock to make room for his feet. "Besides win maybe nine cases out of the last ten he's tried."

"That good?"

"That good."

"Any monkey business with juries?"

"Cornell? Are you kidding? He's straight."

"Know anything about him personally?"

"Naw. He's a private guy. Doesn't open up like some of them.'

"No lady friends sitting in the back rows drooling?"

"Not that guy. He's got this lady lawyer who assists him sometimes. And the she-reporters love him. Funny, though, but I can't remember him ever showing any interest. In the courtroom, he's got one thing in mind. Getting his client off. He's good at it. Too good. Many more goddamn felons back walking the streets, and we'd do better to lock *ourselves* up for protection."

Sam had spent more than his share of time listening to Sid Aronski's philosophy. He didn't have the patience for it tonight. "Is the guy married?"

"Maybe . . . no . . . hell, I dunno."

"Okay, Sid. Thanks. You've been a help. We'll have lunch sometime soon, yeah?"

"You know where to find me."

Sam had no sooner hung up when he punched out another number. As it rang, he glanced at his watch. It was getting late. He'd really feel bad about disturbing her.

"Hello?" came a groggy voice.

He'd done it. "You were sleeping."

Jennifer Blayne stretched, then blinked and looked around her in surprise. "Sam? Is that you?"

"It's me. Hey, Jen, I'm sorry. I thought maybe I'd catch you just before—"

"God, I'm glad you called." She sat up quickly and thrust a thick mane of hair back from her eyes. "I fell asleep out here on the sofa, fully dressed, every light on in the place."

"You must be exhausted."

"It's been one hell of a week. Between the chemical spill and the Chelmsford murders and that little kid who was pinned under the truck, the station's had me running all over creation."

"That's success." Jennifer Blayne was one of the most visible and popular members of the Channel 4 Eyewitness Team.

"Hah! That's insanity." She yawned. "And you too. What are *you* doing working at an hour like this?"

"Trying to learn what I can about Ryan Cornell."

"Ryan Cornell?" Sam imagined that her voice warmed just a bit. "What about him?"

"What do you know?"

"I wish I could tell you all kinds of spicy little tidbits like the kind of shaving cream he uses or the color of his briefs. Unfortunately, I can't."

Sam cleared his throat and drawled, "No problem, Jen. I really don't care what color his briefs are."

"What *do* you care about?" she returned more quietly, letting the reporter take an edge over the woman.

"That depends. How well do you know him?"

"I've interviewed him. I've seen him at receptions now and again."

"Is he married?"

"Not now."

"But he was?"

"Yes."

"Recently?"

"A year or two ago."

"Is he strapped for alimony?"

"Ryan?" She laughed softly. "Ryan's doing fantastically well. And besides, his wife *is* money. She doesn't need his. Oh, I assume he's giving her something, but it can't be anything hefty."

"Child support?"

"Uh-uh. No kids."

"Does he date?"

"So I'm told," she replied.

"What do you mean? You've never seen him with a date?"

"Nope."

"Think he might be gay?"

The laughter that met his ears this time was a helpless outburst. "Ryan Cornell? Oh, Sam, you're barking up the wrong tree. Ryan Cornell is quite a lover. *That* I got from a colleague of mine who went out with him once. *Just once*. No, there's nothing wrong with him in the lust department."

"Then what is wrong with him?"

"He's a private person. He's very self-contained." Her voice grew more pensive. "He's just come off a bad marriage and seems to want to avoid any kind of commitment to a woman. I honestly think that he's happy enough being a good lawyer. You know," she argued, only half in jest, "sex isn't everything. There are those of us, Sam Loomis—"

"Uh-huh," he cut her off with a smile, unable to resist teasing her for a minute. "You don't have to rationalize, Jennifer. I'm not about to pass judgment on you. If you're tired of being a sex object, that's your problem. If you're swearing off men—"

"Now, did I say that? I know that it's against the rules for you to tell me why you're asking all these questions, but I'll tell you this. If you're planning on taking Ryan Cornell into custody and need a playmate for him, I'll volunteer."

"He turns you on?"

"In many ways. He's a real nice guy."

Sam smiled, feeling more relieved by the minute. "And that's your final word?"

"It is."

"Go back to sleep."

"You bet. Take care."

His smile lingered as he hung up the phone. Jennifer Blayne was a sweetheart; Ryan Cornell could do much worse. But the issue wasn't Ryan and Jennifer, was it? It was Ryan and Carly. Grabbing the receiver once more, he stabbed at the buttons.

"Greg?"

"Yeah. Good timing. I just got through talking with Mertz."

"State committee?"

"Yeah."

"What've you got?"

Greg Reilly proceeded to give him a skeletal dossier on Ryan MacKenzie Cornell. By the time he'd finished, Sam was satisfied. "Thanks, Greg." The genuine warmth in his tone said far more.

"No problem," Greg said, feeling eminently pleased. "Anything else?"

"Yeah. Have a good weekend."

"You mean you're calling it quits?" he teased gently. "Hell, Sam, it's only ten-thirty. I know you've been working since eight this morning, but—"

"Aw, shut up." Sam chuckled, deciding that the kid had his moments. "See ya." He pushed the disconnect button, then punched out a final call.

The jangle of the phone beside her gave Carly a jolt. Accidentally stabbing herself, she swore softly and whipped the injured finger to her mouth. Then she looked at her watch. She had no more idea who would be calling her at this hour than she'd earlier known who was at the door.

She took a deep breath before reaching for the phone. "Hello?" she asked, sounding miraculously, deceptively calm.

"It's me, Carly."

"Sam?" She exhaled. "You frightened me!" In truth, she'd frightened herself. It happened every time she let her thoughts run along the line they had.

"Nothing to be frightened of. That's why I'm calling."

"You're not home already, are you?" She knew that he lived on the North Shore, a good forty minutes' drive from her place.

"I'm in town."

"In town? Poor Ellen! In town?"

"At the office. I wanted to make another call or two about your neighbor."

Carly sat straighter. Strange how she'd been thinking of him too. "You were worried?"

"Not worried," Sam lied, knowing it was for the best. "Curious. From what I've been told though, he's clear."

"What were you told?"

"That the guy's straight as an arrow. Graduated Harvard Law and has been practising here ever since. He's in his own firm—Miller and Cornell—with three other partners and some six or seven associates. He started out handling most anything that could take him into court, but he's been able to grow more selective. Does a lot of white-collar-crime work. Won't touch the mob with a ten-foot pole. And he's doing very well. Not much cause to suspect he'd resort to shady dealings in smoking out Robyn Hart."

A wave of relief swept over her, leaving her feeling strangely light-headed. "No, I don't suppose so. Well, then, if he comes up asking to use the phone again, I should let him in?"

"Would you let another of your neighbors in?"

"Yes."

"Then I don't see any problem. The guys here will do a more thorough check, and I'll let you know if I come up with anything. But the references were good from three sources just now. I doubt there'll be anything more."

"I can relax," she stated, having already begun.

"Yes." He chose not to enlighten her on the man's personal situation. As it was, he'd said enough on the matter of Carly's social life earlier that night. "Thanks, Sam."

"No sweat, Carly. I'll be in touch at the first of the week. You'll remember to call me if there's any problem between now and then?"

"Sure. Take care."

She hung up the phone with a smile on her face, feeling buoyant despite the hour. There was, then, nothing to worry about. She'd needlessly gotten herself in a stew.

Setting her needlepoint aside, she ran a hot bath, which she proceeded to lace with a double dose of scented oil. Her clothes fell quickly to the floor. She piled her hair atop her head. Then she stepped in, sank down and stretched out in the luxurious liquid heat, breathing a long, lingering sigh of delight as she laid her head back and closed her eyes.

Security. Relaxation. What precious things they were. She'd been her own worst enemy today. She owed herself a treat tomorrow. A movie? She could take in a matinee. Or she could drive down to the waterfront and take a cruise around the harbor. Would it be too cold? The museum. That was it! If she did everything she had to by noon, she would take her life in her hands and go to the museum.

FOUR

S ATURDAY MORNING DAWNED clear and seasonally warm, the kind of rich autumn day when anyone old enough to remember pined for the smell of burning leaves. Ryan Cornell remembered. He'd been raised in the verdant Berkshires and knew well the joy of the leaf pile on the lawn, the delight of running and jumping and vanishing in its midst, then sitting back to breathe in that incomparable smell when the pile had been raked to the curb and lit.

At times like these, he missed that simple life, so pure, so straightforward, so filled with love. Sighing, he opened the window farther and leaned out, inhaling the fresh air; its scent was a poignant reminder of all he'd lost. Before long would come winter, with its snow and slush and mess. How he hated that time, coming in tired and cold at the end of the day to a dark and empty house. It was just as well Tom was back. It had been a year, about time he got a place of his own. Perhaps he'd enjoy city life. More action, more diversion, less time to brood on all he couldn't change.

A movement beneath him caught his eye, the bob of a thick auburn ponytail as a slender figure in a sweat shirt, shorts and running shoes moved down the front walk to the street then looked to either side before breaking into an easy jog and crossing to the river path.

Ryan whipped his head in, remembering to duck only after he'd hit the window with a thud. Blindly rubbing the injured spot, he ran to the bedroom and began to rummage madly through an open suitcase. Several knit shirts were tossed aside, as was a hapless pair of jeans. Fishing out his running shorts at last, he tugged them on, hopping precariously first on one foot then the other, then grabbed for his sneakers and laced them in record time. The sweat shirt he'd discarded the night before hung on the doorknob. He swept it up as he ran past and was halfway down the stairs before he'd managed to wriggle into it.

By the time he hit the fresh air he was well warmed up. Breaking into a run, he bolted down the walk, dodged his way across Memorial Drive, and lit into the river path with an enthusiasm he hadn't felt in months. He looked ahead, scanning the path in vain. He glanced down at his watch, only to remember that it was back on the bedside table. At a guess, she had no more than two or three minutes on him.

He quickened his pace, grateful that he'd managed to stay in good shape. But then, running had kept him sane. It was his outlet. Aggression, frustration, helplessness—he regularly battered them into the ground only to find, with each new day, a rerun. Perhaps today would be different.

His eyes studied the path ahead as it gently rounded the river. To either side the Saturday-morning traffic had begun to pick up. Where was she? Had she possibly turned off and headed toward Harvard Square? But why would someone in her right mind do that, when the river run was straight and clear and, with its own path, far less hazardous than the side streets?

Then he saw her, a small figure ahead on the bridge crossing to the other side of the Charles. He ran faster, wondering whether he would collapse when he finally caught her, but pushing himself nonetheless. Her pace was steady. She seemed to be enjoying the day as much as he would have had he not been engaged in this absurd chase. He didn't know what had gotten into him. He'd stopped chasing women years ago. This one was his neighbor. That could be good news, or bad. C. J. Quinn, said her mailbox. Carly, said one of their neighbors, who had come up the front path the evening before as Ryan had stood staring after her.

"Uh, excuse me?" he'd called out as the older gentleman passed, a briefcase in his hand, the evening edition under his arm. "Could you tell me . . . uh, I wondered . . . the woman who just ran inside . . . does she live here?" The outburst had been impulsive, devoid of pride or pretense.

The gentleman stopped on the single stone step before the door. He looked once at the fast-disappearing figure within, then back at Ryan. "Is there a special reason you ask?" he countered tactfully.

It was enough of a positive response for Ryan—in fact, he admired the man's protectiveness. Casting an explanatory glance toward the carton by the door, he approached. "I'm just moving in myself. She, uh, she seemed frightened by something. I just wondered if she'll be all right."

"Just moving in? The Amidons's place?"

"That's right."

A firm hand was extended his way. "I'm Ted Arbuckle. My wife and I live in 103."

He met the clasp. "Ryan Cornell. And. . . ?" He cocked his head toward the lobby.

"Carly Quinn. She's in 304. Nice girl. Quiet."

"Will she be all right? I mean, is there someone up there waiting for her?"

"For Carly?" He shook his head. "Nope. She's alone. But she'll be all right. Seems pretty self-sufficient."

Self-sufficient, perhaps. Spry, without a doubt. He admired her stride as he slowly closed in. She ran lightly, with an athletic kind of grace. Not quite deerlike, since she was more petite than long legged, but then there had been sheer terror on her face last night, as though she were indeed facing the hunter with the bow.

Carly heard the rhythmic slap of his step as he approached and shot a wide-eyed glance over her shoulder. He felt a moment's remorse that he'd been the one to frighten her again. Then he moved forward, passed her, glanced back and slowed.

"Hi," he offered, relieved to be able to match her saner pace.

She stared at him for a minute, as though trying to control some inner urge to race onto Storrow Drive, arms waving wildly, to stop the nearest driver and seek help. He hadn't quite decided whether she was afraid of him, or of men in general when, with the faintest tilt of her head, she slowly smiled.

His day was made. "You do well," he said, dropping his gaze momentarily to the slender legs that hadn't broken pace.

Her smile lingered to soften her gibe. "For a woman?"

"Now, now, I didn't say that," he chided with the gentleness she seemed to inspire. "There's many a man who would have been sitting back there on the edge of the bridge trying to catch his breath after having come half the distance you have." He paused, then took the plunge. "I've been trying to catch you for a mile."

Her smile faded slowly as wariness returned. "You have? Do you run often?"

"Every day. But never here before. And never with someone else. Two firsts," he declared on a triumphant note.

She couldn't resist looking up at him again. His grin, a generous slash of white through his beard, was so hopelessly boyish that, quite against her will, her wariness seemed to lessen. Tearing her eyes away, she sought the path once more.

"You must run often yourself," he speculated.

"When I can." It was evasive enough, she mused, yet not far from the truth. She'd been running since Matthew's death, when she'd wanted nothing more than to exhaust herself into oblivion. It had worked at first, until she'd built up her strength and discovered the sheer exhilaration of the sport. Now she ran as often as possible. Since fall had come, though, the opportunity had grown progressively more elusive. She didn't dare run in the dark, thus precluding most school days. Which left the weekends.

Ryan was silent for a time, wondering how much he dared push. Arbuckle had said she was quiet. Ryan might use the words private, or aloof, even distrustful, or skittish, from the looks of the tightly clenched fists that moved back and forth with her steady stride. Somehow he didn't want to think she was simply disinterested. "You always run by the river?" he asked.

Carly looked up and around. The sky was a pale shade of blue, even paler where the sun skipped over the skyline of Boston, seeming to jump from building to building as her own perspective changed. "It's open here. And peaceful. I leave the cars to battle one another."

Ryan smiled his satisfaction. "I was counting on that. For a while I thought you'd turned off on a side street." At her look of puzzlement, then alarm, he quickly explained. "I saw you leave the building just as I was getting dressed." A slight fabrication, he reasoned, but harmless. "When I got outside, you'd disappeared. I thought that if I could catch up with you, you'd show me the best place to run."

"You found it yourself then, even before you saw me again. Your instinct was good."

He wouldn't tell her about the more lascivious instinct that had set him running double time. His thighs and calves would be telling enough later. For now, he simply wanted to get her talking.

"Do you ever race?" he asked.

"Running?" She crinkled up her nose and he felt a corresponding tickle inside him. "No. I'm not that good. I just do it for fun. You know, exercise, fresh air, 'sweeping out the cobwebs' kind of thing."

"How far do you go?"

She cocked her head toward the buildings rising ahead. "Boston University. I'm almost there."

"What is it . . . four miles round trip?"

Her ponytail slapped her neck with each stride, mirroring the gentle bob of her breasts. "I think so."

He focused on the ponytail. "You can do more, you know."

"Oh?" A smile played at the corners of her mouth.

"Sure. You're barely winded. Why not try for another mile?"

"There's still the return trip to make."

"You can do it. Come on."

She looked up at him. His good-natured smile egged her on. "What if my legs give out on me three-quarters of the way back?"

"I'll carry you."

"You're that strong?"

"You're that light."

When she would have asked him how he knew, she blushed and looked down. Not much was hidden by her running shorts, certainly not the slim, bare lengths of her legs. And she was indeed far shorter then he was. Oh, yes, he could easily carry her. Without the slightest effort, he could toss her over his shoulder and cart her to a van waiting somewhere ahead. Her blush washed out and disappeared.

Ryan instantly sensed the change. "Are you all right?" he asked, with the same soft concern in which he'd intoned those very words the day before.

Struggling against the silent demons that seemed to have struck again, Carly reminded herself of Sam's phone call. Ryan was honest. Safe. "Straight as an arrow," were Sam's precise words. It was time she stood up to her insidious suspicions.

"I'm fine," she murmured, forcing a smile.

"Suddenly tired?" he teased lightly. "Givin' up the race so soon? Tell you what. If you can keep up with me all the way back, I'll spring for breakfast."

"Don't eat breakfast." She returned his banter more easily, steadied by the cadence of her pace.

"Then lunch."

"Can't. Too much to do." If she hoped to get to the museum, she'd have to hustle through other chores as it was.

"You've got to eat sometime."

"I'll grab something on the run."

"That's not healthy."

She shrugged and dashed him a sheepish smile that made his insides tingle. "I'll live." Then she tossed her head back. "This is it for me." She made a wide circle around the lamp post she'd earmarked as her turning point, but was caught by the wrist and gently stopped.

"Dinner at Locke-Ober's?" His eyes gleamed. "How does that strike you?"

"Very extravagantly."

"It's yours for another mile in and then the return."

They stood facing each other, breathing deeply from the first leg of the run. "Why?" she asked softly, tipping her head up to eye him skeptically. "Why would you want to run with me? I'm sure you normally go much faster."

He shot her a mischievous grin. "Only when I'm trying to catch someone." Then the grin faded and he grew startlingly earnest. "I'd like the company," he said simply.

The cars whizzed by them on Storrow Drive, much as life did to two people marking time. Carly felt it then, a kind of kinship with Ryan. In his eyes was a warmth, a sincerity, a loneliness she would never have detected had she not been so thoroughly familiar with it herself.

"Locke-Ober's?" she asked with a hesitant smile.

"Ever been there?"

She shook her head.

"Lobster Savannah . . . shrimp mornay. . . ."

Her smile grew coy. "I'm listening."

"Caviar. Hearts of palm. Chateaubriand."

"Uh-huh?"

"A '79 Châteauneuf-du-Pape Blanc."

"Blanc?" She whistled. "You don't fool around."

"Nope."

She hesitated for a final minute, then cautioned, "I couldn't make it tonight."

"That's okay." He smiled, feeling suddenly victorious. "We could make it next week, the week after, any time that's good for you." Strange, he half wanted to put it off. The anticipation would be thoroughly enjoyable. It had been too long since he'd had something to look forward to. And, after all, there was no cause to rush. He wanted her to be comfortable, confident. Perhaps it was better to wait.

Carly's decision had nothing to do with caviar, lobster, or wine. It was based simply on that strange flicker of kinship she felt for Ryan Cornell. "You're on," she said quietly. Then, cocking her head toward Boston, she raised her brows questioningly. When he gave a smug nod, she broke into stride. He was right beside her. It was a surprisingly reassuring thought.

For the most part they ran in silence. Carly's thoughts were on the pleasure of the day and how secure she felt just then. Ryan's thoughts were on Carly and the world of questions he wanted to ask. But she seemed reticent even now to say too much. He couldn't help but wonder what made her so.

The extra mile he had suggested brought them in view of the first of the Saturday sailboats. "Look. Pretty, isn't it?"

She nodded and gave a smile that dimpled her cheeks becomingly. "You mean to say I've been missing this all along?"

"You bet. Actually, it's kind of late in the season. There won't be too many boats out. Most of them are already dry-docked." They ran on for a bit, enjoying the view, before he ventured to speak again. "You ought to see it at the height of the season. On a clear day, especially at sunset, it's a beautiful sight."

"You've seen it at sunset?"

"My office overlooks the river."

She directed her bobbing gaze toward the downtown skyline. "Which one is yours?"

"You can't see it from this angle. We're too low. It's on the other side of the State House." He took a breath between strides. "If you'd care to run a little farther—"

Her sharp sidelong glance shut him up. The sight of an office building was obviously less enticing than Locke-Ober's. But then, he didn't really blame her. Though relatively new and elegantly decorated, it was . . . an office. Wasn't one law office the same as the next? It was, after all, what went on within its walls that set it apart. And Miss Carly Quinn certainly had no call to see that.

Miss? Or Mrs.? Ryan cast a fleeting glance toward her left hand, waiting for it to come forward in alternate rhythm with its mate. No. There was no band. But there . . . on the right . . . that wide gold band he'd seen last night. She'd obviously been married. A European arrangement? But she lived alone. Separated? Divorced? He found it hard to believe she'd failed at marriage. She seemed quiet and agreeable, far different from so many of the strident women with whom he worked each day. Could it have been her marriage that had instilled such wariness in her? It didn't seem possible. What man in his right mind would harm, even threaten, as gentle a creature as she? Unless her husband had not been all there. Lord only knew he'd seen enough of them!

On reflex, he raised a hand to rub his bearded jaw. Oh, he knew firsthand about crazy husbands. One had nearly put an end to his career, not to mention his life. As if he'd ever have considered bedding a client . . . and *that* woman? Never!

"Hello? Hello? Are you there?"

The breathy voice by his side brought him back to reality. He looked down and smiled in relief. "Sure, I'm here."

"Could've fooled me for a minute there." She crinkled up her nose. Again it made him melt. "Can we turn yet?"

He looked around in surprise to find that they'd just about reached the spot he'd had in mind. "Uh, sure. This is far enough."

"Getting tired?" she teased in an effort to erase what had appeared to be anger from his face. It disconcerted her. She liked it better when he smiled, which he proceeded to do with devastating appeal.

"Tired? Me?" Taking her elbow, he propelled her around, dropping his hold when she matched his gait, heading home. "I'll have you know that you're running with none other than the star of varsity track and field."

"Harvard?" she asked as her eyes spanned his chest. Faint rivulets of sweat marked a charcoal path down its center.

Looking down, he ran his palm across the faded letters. "This thing has seen better days." He chuckled. "So have I, for that matter. There was a time when I used to marathon. No more."

"Are you sorry?"

He pondered the question for a minute, thinking how much more pleasant it was to run like this, totally relaxed, than to run with one eye on the clock. "Sorry? Not really. Anything like that involves a kind of obsession. It can be all-consuming if you do it right. But I had other interests that made their demands. I couldn't do it all."

She assumed he spoke of the law, an obsession in itself. Almost against her will, she felt herself stiffen. It seemed impossible that this man, as surprisingly companionable as he was, should be grouped with those others she'd had the displeasure of meeting during the trial. But of course he might be different. John Meade had been different. As the prosecutor assigned to the Culbert-Barber case, he'd been kind and fair to her. His assistant, Brozniak, was something else. He'd wanted nothing more than to get her into his bed. Some obsession!

"Hello, hello?"

At his miming call to attention, she dashed a glance up at Ryan, whose grin brought her quickly from her trance. "Oops, I left you for a minute there, didn't I?"

"Just so long as it's not *me* you're angry at."

"I may be furious at you later. I'm not used to running this far. I'm apt to be crippled when my calves stiffen up."

"Then we can share my Ben-Gay," he returned, undaunted. "Just stamp on the floor three times and I'll bring it up."

"Is that a promise?"

"You bet."

With a soft chuckle, he looked forward again. They were back in familiar territory now; it wouldn't be long before they reached the apartment and went their separate ways. It might be his last chance for a while to find out more about her. Then he looked to his side and saw the serenity of her expression and he didn't have the heart to disturb it. It beckoned to him, that light and billowy cloud of contentment that hovered above them, between them, large enough to envelop them both. Unable to resist, he yielded. For now, it was enough.

He didn't talk further, nor did she. Rather, they ran in time with each other, comfortably and easily, finding strength in silent partnership. Ryan touched her elbow once to guide her across the street, then dropped his hand as they entered the courtyard and slowed to a breathless walk.

"Good show!" he panted through a grin, leaning down to brace his hands on his knees. His hair hung wet on his brow, giving him an eminently masculine look.

Carly flexed her legs, walking in small, idle circles. "Not bad yourself," she gasped, then splayed her fingers over the muscles of her lower back in support. "Why is it . . . that it's easier to . . . talk when you're . . . running, than when you stop?"

Straightening, he mopped his forehead with a long, muscled arm. "I'm not sure . . . but you're right. I think it must be a . . . kind of illusion. You know, we assume . . . that the words will be broken when we run, so the mind and body make . . . their own connections. We can talk even though our breathing is choppy. But when we stop, our breathing by . . . comparison seems that much rougher."

Carly nodded. She stood taking deep, long drags of air in an effort to ease her laboring lungs. After a minute, when she seemed even shorter of breath, it occurred to her that something else was at work deep within. Apprehension . . . anticipation . . . she had no intention of sticking around to find out.

"Well," she breathed, with feigned nonchalance. Her voice seemed unusually high; she was grateful to be able to blame it on the run. "I'll be going."

Ryan reached out, pausing just short of touching her. "Look, Carly—"

Her sharp stare cut him short. "You know my name," she whispered, appalled. She hadn't told him; she was sure of that.

Unable to comprehend her sudden shift from calm to coiled, Ryan eyed her in puzzlement. He kept his voice gentle. "Of course, I know your name. It's on your mailbox."

"Not my first name."

"Ted Arbuckle filled me in on that. Listen, it's no big thing. You would have told me your name, wouldn't you have? I mean, I hope you weren't going to have me call you Ms. Quinn," he drawled in soft mockery, "through an evening at Locke-Ober's." His lips twitched coaxingly at the corners.

He was right, of course. She was being oversensitive and suspicious. Always suspicious. She hated herself for it. Suitably chastised by Ryan's teasing, she looked away in self-reproach. "Of course not," she murmured. "It's just that I didn't expect you'd ask around."

"It was really only a fluke," he explained. "Arbuckle came up the walk yesterday right after we collided. I pointed after you, wanting to make sure you were all right. As a matter of fact, he wouldn't even admit that you lived here until I'd introduced myself. It was then that he called you by name.

It was all so perfectly logical. She grinned sheepishly. "If I didn't know better, I might suspect you'd hit him with a few of those leading questions you lawyers are known for."

"We lawyers?" As the tables turned, Ryan looked at her skeptically. "And how did you know I was a lawyer?"

Too late, Carly realized her error. She looked up at him, swallowing hard. "My, uh, my friend last night recognized you from some case a few months ago. You were on television a lot?"

"The Duncan case." He nodded. "And your friend? Who was he?" It was one of the questions he'd been aching to ask. Now she'd inadvertently given him the opportunity. He had to admit that he felt slightly guilty. His interest in her friend had nothing to do with the Duncan case or the fact that her friend had recognized him. It was pure jealousy.

Fortunately Carly had spent enough time with Sam, particularly when she'd first arrived, to know precisely how to introduce him. They'd been over it many times. It was nothing more than a version of the truth.

"His name is Sam Loomis. He's a good friend of mine."

"Do you date him?"

"Date? Not in the sense you mean."

"Then in what sense?"

"In the sense of friends. Period."

"And he doesn't want it differently?" Ryan couldn't believe it wasn't so. Even now, amid the compulsion that kept him questioning her when he knew he should let up, he wanted only to reach out and smooth a stray curl from her cheek. With her hair caught loosely up in a ponytail and her face damp and makeup free, she looked no more than twenty, until one looked into her eyes. They were older, more knowing. It was one of the things he found so intriguing. That fleeting look of sadness, of pain and fear and understanding. Once again he wondered what she'd been through in life to have been so thoroughly seasoned.

"What is this?" she teased uneasily. "An interrogation?"

The edge in her voice, underscoring the flicker of apprehension in her eyes, brought him to his senses. He dropped his head in an outward show of contrition, then sighed, looked up and smiled more gently. "No. We lawyer types get carried away every so often." When her lips remained taut, he went on. "Actually, it had nothing to do with lawyer types. That was *me* wanting to know about *you.*"

"About Sam," she corrected softly.

"About Sam as he relates to you. What I *really* want to know," he murmured hastily, helplessly, "is why you wear a wedding band, and whether you're involved with Sam or anyone else. I want to know if you're free."

"Free?" Her voice was weak, seeming to come from far away. Her eyes grew sad beneath the weight of memories. As she looked away, her gaze fell to the leaves beneath the trees, leaves that had been alive and aflame with color mere days before, yet now lay drab and dried, like cold ashes in the hearth. "No," she whispered without looking up, "I don't think I am." Lost in a trance, she headed for the door.

She was through the lobby and on the stairs before Ryan went after her.

FIVE

❀ ❀ ❀

"CARLY, WAIT!" Catching the door just before it closed, he ran through, crossing the lobby in two strides, taking the first three steps in another. Reaching up, he grabbed her hand. He spoke more softly then. "Carly, please. Don't just run off like that."

She kept her head tucked low. "I've got to go," she whispered, but didn't remove her hand from his.

"Not yet," he murmured, climbing another step just until they were at eye level. "We haven't set a date."

She raised her head slowly. "A date?"

"For dinner. Locke-Ober's?"

Her gaze dropped to the railing where her free hand had tightly anchored itself. "Maybe that's not such a good idea."

"Why not? It'd be fun. Don't you need that sometimes?"

"I do. And I have it sometimes. It's just that. . . ." How could she explain her sudden fear, when she didn't understand it herself? Ryan was no threat to her in the usual sense of the word. She accepted that, as Sam had told her to do, as her own instinct had told her to do. But there was something new now, something related to the rapid beat of her pulse, to the warming feel of his hand on hers, to the fact that when she looked into his eyes she didn't want to look away. "It's just that I'm really _not_ free."

Sensing her weakness, since it was his own as well, he offered a soft challenge. "Can you look me in the eye and tell me that?"

She hesitated, then her eyes slowly met his. Her expression was an amalgam of emotions, not the least of which was regret. "I'm not," she whispered in anguish.

Glancing down at her hand, he passed his thumb over her ring. "You don't live with your husband."

"No. And I'm not attached to anyone else," she added, anxious to head off the question she was sure would come. "But I have other things, other responsibilities. I really can't let myself get involved."

"It's just a dinner, Carly. What harm can come of that?"

But he knew. He felt it himself, lured and captured by something far deeper in her wide gray eyes than the promise of companionship, of easy conversation, of a smile. He'd never had quite this reaction to a woman before, this sense of glimpsing a true treasure worth seeking. He felt suddenly stunned and frightened in his way, though he couldn't turn his back as she had done. Very slowly, he climbed another step until he gazed down at her.

Carly tipped her head up as he rose, helpless to either look away or escape. Her mouth felt dry; she swallowed hard. She felt the warmth of his gaze as it seared her eyes and cheeks before sliding to her lips in a vibrant caress. Catching in a sharp breath, she silently pleaded for him to stop. She couldn't handle this kind of attraction, simply couldn't handle it.

But he didn't let go. His hand turned once on hers to cradle it protectively. His thumb moved lightly on her palm. "I won't hurt you," he murmured. "I couldn't hurt you. I don't want you to be frightened."

"But I am!" she countered in a frantic whisper, all too aware of his long, lean body mere inches from her own. "Please, Ryan. Please let me go."

He dropped her hand, but only to gently touch her face. "I can't do that. I'd never forgive myself."

"But I can't be who you need! You don't know me. You don't know me at all! Leave me be, Ryan. Please?"

He stared at her then for what seemed an eternity before slowly shaking his head. The backs of his fingers caressed her cheek; he ran a trembling thumb across her lips. He hesitated, entranced by the unadorned softness of her mouth. Then, yielding to a need as strong as any he'd ever known, he lowered his head.

But Carly's fingers were against his lips, holding him back at that last moment. "No!" she cried on the edge of panic, then forced her voice to a whisper when she felt his compliance. "I can't handle this now. I'm sorry, but I can't." She was aware of her fingers on his mouth and lingered for that briefest instant to savor his maleness, the soft bristle of his mustache and beard, the strength of his lips, before letting her hand drop to her side.

"Can you tell me why?" When she shook her head, he went quickly on. "How can I fight something if I don't know what it is?"

"I'm sorry," she whispered, finally managing to avert her gaze. Fearing that if she lingered she might never have the chance again, she turned and ran up the stairs.

Ryan's voice carried clearly upward. "I'll fight anyway, y'know!" He watched her round the second-floor railing and start toward the third, and raised his voice accordingly. "I don't give up easily!" Then he leaned over the railing with his head tipped way back, reluctant to lose sight of her. His voice echoed in the silence. "I can play dirty. . . . !"

If he'd hoped to appeal to her sense of humor, he failed. The quiet opening and shutting of her door was the only response he got. Long after he knew she was once again entombed in her private world, he stood looking up.

Finally, accepting temporary defeat, he dropped his head forward and began the slow climb. Whereas when he'd bounded in after her, he'd had all the energy in the world, now he felt drained, discouraged, impotent. That was it.

Impotent. It was a chilling feeling, one he'd experienced only once before in his life. That had been the night Alyssa had miscarried. He recalled every agonizing moment, from the instant he'd come home to find her doubled over in pain to that later one, when the doctor had sadly shaken his head. He'd felt so helpless then, as he did now. And he barely knew Carly Quinn!

Eyes dark and puzzled, he let himself into his apartment, closed the door, then passed distractedly to the bedroom. It was nice enough, he mused. The whole place was nice enough. Clean. Comfortable. But it wasn't home.

Home was. . . . Where was it? It wasn't Tom's place, which he'd used only for the year. It wasn't the old house in the Berkshires where he'd grown up. And it certainly wasn't the house he'd shared with Alyssa. Not anymore, at least. He hadn't set foot there in a year. Nor did he miss it. With its four massive columns in front and its twelve silent rooms within and its three acres of land to keep mowed and limed and landscaped, it had been far too pretentious for him from the start. But Alyssa had wanted something befitting la crème de la crème of society. She had it now, for better or worse. Perversely, he wondered whether the termites had made headway on the gardener's shed. Then, feeling minor remorse, he headed for the shower.

An hour later he was buried in work in his downtown office, as he'd been every Saturday for years. It wasn't that the work couldn't wait. While that might have been true when he'd first started out, when he'd had to bust his tail to ensure the success of the firm, things had changed. His reputation was established. His practice thrived. He had reliable lawyers under him, hand picked, personally trained. Oh, yes, his work could wait. But there was nothing he'd rather do. He loved the law. Perhaps Alyssa had been right when she'd accused him of making his work his mistress.

It was late when he returned to Cambridge, later than he'd expected. He'd spent the afternoon in the law library plotting his arguments for an upcoming fraud case and lost track of the hour. Now, rounding the block a second time in search of a parking space, he cursed the impulse on which he'd accepted the Crowley's invitation. A dinner party. Black tie and tails, no less. It was the last thing he needed! No, he caught himself, the last thing he needed was the eligible female they would inevitably pair him with.

Thin lipped, he started around the block again, only to slam on his brakes when the taillight of a car by the curb lit up, telling of its imminent departure. Shifting deftly into reverse, he backed up and waited, watching with growing dismay as the driver proceeded to comb her hair and apply lipstick, then fiddle in her purse for an elusive candy before finally pulling out. Muttering snide remarks under his breath, Ryan quickly took the space, then slid from his silver BMW and headed down the block.

Halfway to the courtyard he stopped and looked up. That was his apartment on the second floor, hers on the third. It was at the windows of the latter that his eyes held.

Carly Quinn. The thought of her was like a gentle breeze, easing his tension instantly. She was different, refreshing, in spite of the mystery that seemed to haunt her. He'd have given up work today for _her_, had she agreed to let him take her to lunch.

Her living-room light was on, shining warmly through the woven drapes. As he watched, a shadow passed before them. His gaze sharpened, but there was nothing more. Lowering his eyes at last, he resumed his walk. In the courtyard, his pace quickened. By the time he reached the stairs, he was filled with resolve.

Bypassing the second-floor landing, he was on the third in no time. He rapped lightly on her door. Then he waited, staring down at the leather of his loafers, listening for any sound that might come from within.

From her comfortable perch in a deep corner of the sofa, Carly stared at the door. She wasn't expecting anyone. She wasn't dressed for company. Her eye fell to the long terry robe that covered her legs curled beneath her. Then the knock came again, and she slowly put aside the needlepoint she'd picked up moments before.

Padding barefoot to the door, she laid a timorous hand on the jamb and put her eye to the viewer. Her heart began to hammer. It was Ryan. Resting her forehead against the wood, she sighed in frustration. If she were in her right mind, she would return to the sofa and let him knock until his knuckles grew sore. But he wouldn't give up, and she would only have more explaining to do when she finally opened the door.

Slowly, she released the bolts. Then she inched the door open, using her body as a shield to her apartment. It would be a none-too-subtle hint that he wasn't invited in, a hint in keeping with the hours of contemplation she'd put in that afternoon. To her dismay, she'd thought of little else but him as she'd wandered from room to room in the museum. None of the American painters or the French or the Dutch had distracted her for long.

Her conclusion? Ryan Cornell was a dangerous man.

She was never more sure of that than when she gazed out at him now. Standing as tall as ever at her door, he wore a shirt, tie and slacks. One side of his blazer was pushed back to allow his hand burial in his pants' pocket. He looked calm and relaxed, and unconscionably handsome.

"Ryan?" She greeted him warily.

"Hi, Carly." He grinned, as though unaware that there had ever been an iota of tension between them. "Listen, I hate to do this to you again . . . but I wonder . . . I've got to make this quick call. Would it be too much of an imposition if I used your phone again? I mean, I won't be long. I know you've got plans."

The first of her deceptions had come back to haunt her. She'd been vague enough, if misleading. The plans she had were for a safe, quiet evening at home. Ryan must have assumed she'd put on her robe as a prelude to dressing up. Even now, she didn't have the courage to correct his misconception. Yet she felt contrite.

"It's all right," she murmured, standing back for him to enter. It was the least she could do to make up for the deception. "Help yourself."

He tossed a light "Thanks" back over his shoulder as he made for the kitchen. In a moment's indulgence, she watched him go, admiring the way his blazer fit his broad shoulders to perfection, the way his slacks moved with his stride, falling to just the right spot at his heel. She wondered if he'd been working. No natty three-piece suit? Then she tore her gaze away and retreated to the sofa to pretend nonchalance to match his calm.

In the kitchen, Ryan lifted the phone and punched out the number of his office. The connection clicked, then rang. As a matter of show, he held the phone to his ear, while his eye closely studied his surroundings. Everything was new and clean, from the round butcher-block table with its white director's chairs and the Plexiglas napkin holder with its mated salt and pepper shakers, to the shining copper-bottomed pots and pans suspended from a pegboard panel. It was a bright and airy kitchen, fresh out of *Metropolitan Home*, very beautiful, very proper. Something was lacking, though. He couldn't quite put his finger on it. It didn't look . . . lived in. It lacked the small personal touches he would have expected from a woman as intriguing as Carly. It lacked . . . history.

Puzzled, he turned his gaze toward the living room. She sat on the sofa with her back to him, occupied with whatever—was it sewing—she'd apparently been doing when he'd knocked on her door. His eyes wandered, taking in the room at a glance. Again, everything was perfect. Modular sofa, marble tables, wall prints, plush carpet. Too perfect. Where was *she* in all of it? If he'd hoped to learn about her through her home, it seemed he'd been thwarted again. Other than that she could afford to live in style, he knew nothing more now than he had before. And he grew all the more curious.

Replacing the receiver on its hook, he entered the living room just as Carly looked up from her work.

"No luck?"

He shook his head. But then, he hadn't expected luck. The office would have been dark and locked up hours ago. "I guess I've missed them. What's that you're doing?"

"Needlepoint."

He took a step closer, coming up behind the sofa to lean over her shoulder. "It's very pretty."

Not trusting the tremor in her hands, she spread the canvas flat on her lap to examine her progress. "I'm working with silk. It's a challenge. The threads separate and the stitch can come out lumpy if you don't pull the strands evenly." She ran a slender finger over the field of gold. "It's rewarding, though."

Ryan was as intrigued by the piece as he was by the finger that caressed it. "What will you do with it when you're done?"

"Have it framed. It's a gift for my father."

"He lives nearby?"

"No." Willing her hands to steadiness, she picked up her needle once more. Though she'd probably have to rework each stitch when he left, it suddenly seemed safer to have her hands and eyes occupied.

"Then you don't see him often?"

She shook her head, but didn't look up. She heard Ryan's sigh, knew that he'd straightened and was looking around the room. There was nothing here to betray her. There was nothing *anywhere* in the apartment to betray her.

"Well," he breathed softly, "I'd better be going."

"On your way out?"

"Actually, in. I've been working all day."

She looked up then and caught a glimpse of fatigue in the depth of his gaze. "Do you always work on Saturdays?" she heard herself ask, knowing she should let him go, yet reluctant.

"It's a good time to get things done. The courts aren't open. The office is quiet. Clients are too busy doing other things to keep me on the phone for hours. I rely on my weekends to clean up the mess of the week."

"I know the feeling. You work Sundays too?"

"At home. I've got a pile of papers that I've got to get to tomorrow. But first I've got to make some headway unpacking the boxes of clothes and other things I moved in yesterday." He rubbed the taut muscles at the back of his neck. "Your place looks a damned sight better than mine at this point."

She grinned. "I have this terrific vacuum cleaner with a self-drive feature. You turn it on, sit back on the sofa with your feet up—" she added a lower aside "—it tends to munch on toes—" then returned her tone to its normal pitch "—and watch it do all the work."

"Does it pick up clothes from the floor?"

"None you'd want to wear again."

He waved his arm in disinterest. "Then you can keep it. I need something that will *really* clean."

"It sounds like you need a personal maid. Used to the fine life, are you?"

He saw the teasing in her eyes, heard the warmth in her tone and found infinite pleasure in having been able to make her relax. "The fine life?" he asked, his lips twitching. "The fine life makes for idle minds, double chins and very boring dinner conversation. As far as I'm concerned, you can take the fine life and shove it. And with that bit of opinionated drivel, I'll take my leave." He paused. "Will you be running tomorrow morning?"

"Yes." It slipped out before she realized what she'd done.

His brows rose in question. "Would you like to . . . ?" He cocked his head toward the door, his invitation obvious.

"Uh, I'm not sure. I don't know just when I'll be going."

Reluctant to push his luck, Ryan nodded. Then he opened the door. "I'm planning to head out at eight, then pick up the newspaper on my way back. I know it's kind of early for a Sunday morning, but if you feel like the company. . . ." His voice trailed off. The invitation could stand by itself. With a wave and a prayer, he shut the door behind him.

Carly gave it much thought. Ryan appealed to her. He intrigued her. He amused her. He also frightened her. Since Matthew's death, she had never been as naturally drawn to any person. Her relationship with Peter had been different—deep and meaningful, if devoid of heat. But heat was an early sign of fire. At the thought, she shuddered.

With the struggle she was waging to adapt to her new life, involvement with Ryan was the last thing she needed. She'd had Matthew and the all-abiding love they'd shared. She'd had Peter and the warmth of an affection based on similarity of interest. She'd had more in the past ten years than many a woman had in a lifetime. More love. More grief. It always seemed to end badly. She couldn't let Ryan in for that.

What the mind resolved, however, the heart could overturn in no time. It was actually several minutes after eight the next morning when Carly found herself on the front walk approaching Ryan, who was very diligently occupied tying the laces of his sneakers for the third time.

He looked up, straightened and offered her a self-conscious smile. "I wasn't sure you'd come."

"Neither was I." Having spent half the night debating the wisdom of joining him, of fostering *any* kind of relationship with him, she looked mildly tired.

"Late night?" he asked cautiously. Her light had been on when he'd returned at one. He couldn't help but wonder if she'd been alone.

"Uh-huh." It wasn't wholly a lie.

He glanced toward the river, shaking off that glimmer of jealousy, then returned a more placid gaze. "Shall we?" When she nodded, they took off slowly, reaching pace only when they turned onto the river path. They went for several minutes in silence, before Carly felt herself begin to relax. There seemed no point in rehashing the pros and cons of her decision. She knew that she was far too susceptible to Ryan's charm. She also knew the danger entailed. But damn it, she *wanted* to run with him. She felt safe and happy. She deserved a splurge now and then. After all, they were only running.

With several successive deep breaths, she shifted her awareness from the tall, lithe man by her side to the fresh, clear world all about. "Another beautiful one, isn't it?"

"Yup. Won't be too many more."

"I wonder whether this path will be cleared in the winter."

"You've never run in the winter?"

"I've never run *here* in the winter."

"You mean along the river?"

"I mean in Boston."

"Then you're new to the area?"

"Uh-huh."

"From . . . ?"

For the briefest minute she felt a pang of guilt. But she'd been given a past, an authenticated one at that, and it behooved her to use it. "San Diego."

"You grew up there?"

"No. I worked there."

"Doing what?"

"Teaching." It came out more easily than she'd expected, the staccato exchange facilitated by the rhythm of the run. Had they been sitting over coffee, looking at each other, she might have had more trouble.

"Is that what you do now?"

"Uh-huh."

"Where?"

"Rand Academy."

"Rand?" He shot her a sidelong glance underscored with a grin. "No kidding? Several of my partners' kids go there. It's supposed to be top ranking."

"We do well in college admissions."

"How long have you been there?"

"Since September."

"And in Cambridge?"

"Since July."

They ran on, reaching the bridge, crossing over to hook onto the river path by Storrow Drive. The traffic was even lighter than it had been the day before. It was as though they had the world to themselves.

"How about you?" she asked between breaths.

"Yeeeeesssss?" he drawled.

"Where did you live before yesterday?"

"In Winchester. About half an hour thataway." He flicked his head northward.

"An apartment?"

"A house."

"All by yourself? I mean," she hastened to add, "you're not married or anything, are you?" She'd just assumed him to be single. Now, posing the question, she wasn't sure whether to be disappointed or mortified.

The punishing glance he gave her precluded both. "If I were married," he stated firmly, "I'd never have come on to you the way I did yesterday. As for 'or anything,' the answer is no."

"Strange," she mused, thinking aloud as, side by side, they followed the curve of the path.

"What is?"

"That you're not attached. I would have thought—"

"—that a dynamic, witty, handsome devil like me would certainly have been caught by now?"

She saw the dark brow he arched in self-mockery and couldn't help but smile. "Not exactly the way I would have put it, but the end result is the same."

"The end result. Ahh. I have to confess that I have had my experience with that end result."

"You've *been* married?"

"That's right. Like you."

At first she said nothing in response to his bait. Then, feeling particularly bold, she took it. "I'm not divorced."

He frowned. "But you live alone. Separated?" When she shook her head, he felt something freeze up inside. The European connection. A right-hand wedding band. "Then your husband is away?"

Carly looked out across the water. Its surface mirrored the few, still clouds, peaceful until the silent rush of a lone racing shell cut an even slash through its plane. "He's dead."

Ryan's pace faltered. A *widow?* At her age? Of all the possibilities, it hadn't entered his mind. "I'm sorry," he murmured, readjusting his stride. "Was it recent?"

Her eyes were distant. "Four years ago."

"Four years?" From mind to tongue, the words spilled out. "You were so young."

"I was twenty-five."

"What happened? Uh—" he shook his head, appalled at himself "—strike that. I shouldn't have asked."

"It's all right." For some reason that she didn't stop to analyze, she wanted him to know. It was the one part of the fabrication that wasn't fabrication at all. "He was in a hotel." Her phrases were clipped by her bobbing pace and that something else that seemed to grip her each time she allowed a return of those thoughts. "There was a fire. He was on the fortieth floor. He couldn't get out."

She was barely aware of the hand on her arm until it tightened to slow her up. Startled back from images of hell, she came to a stunned stop facing Ryan.

"I'm sorry, Carly. That must have been very painful for you." It certainly accounted for the anguish he'd seen in her eyes. Even now, they bore a tortured look.

"Painful for me?" she gasped in a whisper. "Painful for him! The smoke . . . and flame. He tried to reach the stairs, they said. He nearly made it. . . ."

Ryan wasn't sure whether she was on the verge of tears or whether the raggedness of her breathing was due to exertion. But he knew that over the past four years she must have tortured herself many times. It was the torment of the survivor to imagine the terror of life's last moments. He'd been eyewitness to that torment once before, in the grief of a mother whose young daughter had drowned in an improperly attended municipal pool. Then his case had been for negligence. Now, beyond the law and the courtroom, he had no case save compassion.

Bidden by the overwhelming need to comfort, he put his hands on either side of her neck and gently massaged the tight muscles. She seemed far away still. It frightened him. "It's all right, Carly," he began softly. "Things like that just happen sometimes."

"But to Matthew?" Her husband's name was supposed to be Malcolm. Lost in the world of memory, she was oblivious to the slip. "He was so kind and good."

"Tragedy doesn't discriminate. Kind, unkind, good, bad, we don't have any control over it."

Her eyes grew misty, yet there were no tears. "I know. But there are still all those What ifs. What if he'd been out drinking with the rest of the guys? What if he'd been on the third floor? What if the department had never authorized the trip in the first place?"

"But it did," he countered gently, able only to guess that her husband had been on a business trip, perhaps at a convention. "He wasn't on the third floor. And he wasn't out drinking. Don't you see, you can't agonize over what might have been. What's done can't be changed. You can only go on living. You can only look ahead."

Above and beyond his words, it was the glimmer of hope in his eye that captured Carly's senses. Very slowly, she returned from that charred hotel room to the present, to the comfort of this man, to the long fingers that moved gently on her neck. With the sound of approaching footsteps, another runner passed them with a salute. Occasional cars sped by on Storrow Drive. A flock of geese winged southward. Ryan's head shaded her from the rising sun, whose vibrant rays shimmered around the richness of his hair.

"I know you're right," she whispered, lost in his gaze. "And I do try." It was hard to look ahead at times, when so much of the past was a consuming flame. Reason dictated she look ahead, echoing not only Ryan's, Sam's and her father's advice but her own common sense. And though her heart didn't always cooperate, she tried. She did.

Ryan smiled then, feeling pride in the spunk that had raised her chin a fraction of an inch. "It'll work, Carly. You'll see. You're strong and bright."

His eyes held hers, melting her to the core. Then, struck by a sudden wave of self-consciousness, she tore her gaze from his and focused on the drying grass by the side of the path. "I'm sorry."

"For what?"

"Blurting all this out. I usually have better control."

"Maybe that's why it came out. Maybe it needed to come out."

"But to you?" She raised her eyes, perplexed. "We're strangers," she argued in stark reminder to herself.

"Not really," he said gently. "There are times when I look into your eyes and feel I've known you all my life."

"But you haven't."

"Not yet." He smiled again. "Speaking of which —" he tipped her face up with his thumbs "— you never did tell me what you teach."

For a final moment they stood there, looking at each other in silent awareness of something very special that had passed between them. For Carly, it was the sharing of her grief, something she hadn't done in quite that way to any other human being. She had offered Ryan a bit of Robyn. And in that instant, rather than feeling duplicitous, she felt strangely whole.

For Ryan, it was something else. For a few moments at least, he'd penetrated Carly's shell, glimpsed a part of her that he sensed few people saw. She'd kissed him back . . . that was it . . . their lips had never touched . . . yet she had kissed him back.

His thumb moved from her jaw to the softness of her mouth. Entranced, he slowly outlined its sensuous curve, feeling her lips part beneath his touch. His eye sought hers then, and he knew that she was, at that moment, as open to him as she'd ever been. His heartbeat sped; the pulse at her neck kept time. If it was the present he advocated, he had a point to make.

SIX

W HEN HE LOWERED HIS HEAD this time, there was no hand to block his lips from hers. He kissed her in a whisper, barely touching her lips at first, then very slowly, very carefully deepening the touch. Her warmth was intoxicating, every bit as sweet as he'd imagined it to be when he'd lain in bed last night, frustrated and taut. He took his time; there was no rush. In a rare instance in his life, he simply closed his eyes and enjoyed the sensation with total satisfaction. There seemed no goal more precious than this simple tasting of lips, this simple act of acquaintance.

Carly felt it too. Time seemed suspended. Yielding all thought of consequence, she ventured into a world of pleasure. She felt Ryan's lips against hers, firm and manly yet gentle and undemanding. There was a drugging effect to their movement. They were enticing, irresistible. As she opened her lips, she was aware of the tickle of his beard. It was nearly as heady a sensation as the deepening of his kiss.

And she surged with it, surrendering to its lure, feeling lazy and lavish and light. Then his tongue joined the play and she felt something far deeper. It was an awareness, an awakening. She was a woman. For the first time in months and months, she felt her femininity.

With a gasp, she tremblingly pulled back. Her eyes held longer though, clinging to the firm lips that had brought her to such a floating state, then, with a tight swallow, meeting his gaze.

Words were unnecessary. He saw her stunned surprise, felt a bit of it himself. Those brief moments of contact had been more forceful than anything he'd ever felt. Even now his body was a tight coil, not so much in anticipation of what might have come next as in shock at what had just gone by.

Carly caught her breath. "Ryan?" she whispered.

"Shh." He pressed a finger to her lips and gently shook his head. It seemed all wrong to try to analyze what had happened, just as it would have been a travesty to apologize for it. It was one bright moment, over now but leaving in its wake a vibrant memory. Slowly he dropped his hand, then cocked his head toward Boston. With one last steadying breath, she nodded and they resumed the run.

If anything, their pace was faster. When they reached the point where Carly normally turned, Ryan shot her a glance.

"How're ya doin'?" he ventured.

"I'm okay."

So they ran on, turning by unspoken consent at the point to which Ryan had urged her the morning before, then making the round trip with nothing more than an occasional exchange.

"What *do* you teach?"

"English."

He took that in, then cast her a glance. "Speciality?"

"Creative writing."

When a pair of cyclists came toward them, Ryan dropped back a step to fall into single file behind Carly until they passed. "Do much yourself?"

"What?"

"Creative writing."

She released a terse, "Some."

He left it at that, wondering if she was one of those teachers who could teach but not do. He recalled his highschool diving coach. The man was brilliant in explaining technique, in analyzing strength and spotting weakness. Yet he could barely do a simple jackknife, let alone a half gainer with a double back twist. With a fond smile, he refiled the memory in its bank and glanced down at Carly.

"You're happy at Rand?"

"Uh-huh. The kids are great."

"Grades. . . ?"

"That I teach?" She returned his gaze, helpless to ignore the swath of sweat that dampened the front of his sweat shirt. When he nodded, his hair clung to his brow. He looked disturbingly masculine. "Sophomores and juniors," she supplied abruptly, then poured herself into the run.

Ryan quickened his step accordingly. Though warm, he was far from tired. There was a release in pounding the pavement this way, a relief from the urge to ponder the "what now" of things. He'd kissed Carly; she'd kissed him back. They'd shared something he felt was unique enough to pursue. Yet he sensed he was on shaky ground. He had to tread carefully.

As they ran on, Carly wondered what he was thinking. Captured in a surreptitious glance, his expression was intense and calculating. She assumed his mind had turned to his work. Didn't she often use her running time to mentally outline lectures or plan upcoming assignments? If only she could do that now! But her lips still burned from Ryan's kiss and the trail of fire lingered lower. In a bid for diversion, she turned her thoughts to New York.

It had been several years since she'd been back, and even aside from the excitement of seeing her father, she was looking forward to it. The years she and Matthew had spent there had been delightfully irresponsible. He had been an assistant professor of economics, she his student. They had married in the middle of her sophomore year, before she'd reached the age of nineteen. Very much in love, they had been convinced that their fourteen-year difference was irrelevant. And so it had been. They went to school together and studied together. When she graduated, they moved to Chicago, where he was offered a full professorship. There had been more pressure after that — greater responsibility for Matthew, hard-won assignments for Carly — all of which made her memories of New York that much sweeter.

And now she would return. She and her father would eat in style, stroll the avenues together, perhaps take in a show or two. Was it safe? A spasm flicked across her brow. Sam said it was. He had been the one to promote New York from the start. Anonymity in crowds, he'd said. She supposed he had a point. At least, she was determined to believe it. She needed this trip. She needed to see her father's familiar face. For those few days, she would be Robyn again. It would be odd. . . .

When they reached the small incline to the bridge, Ryan took her elbow. They slowed until the roadway cleared, then jogged across and resumed their trek on the other side of the river.

Well after he released it, Carly felt his touch on her arm. How would he take to a deception of the sort she practiced? He was a lawyer; perhaps he would understand. But when his eyes took on that smoldering gleam, he was first and foremost a man. He would expect honesty from her — which was precisely why he was dangerous. Of the men she had met since she'd begun her new life, it seemed that only Ryan had the potential to reach her. That much had been obvious from the very first when he'd caught her in the courtyard and spoken so gently. With Ryan she felt guilt at the dual nature of her life. Guilt. She neither wanted it nor needed it. But she'd made a decision long months ago; now she intended to abide by the consequences.

Feeling suddenly tired, she fell back a bit. Ryan slowed immediately. He watched her closely for several paces, noting the faint drop of her shoulders.

"Are you okay?" he asked softly.

Startled, she looked up. "Hmm? Sure."

"You looked a little sad there."

She shook her head in denial and made a concerted effort to maintain a steady pace.

"Game for trying the Square?" he asked when they neared the side street he wanted to take. At her questioning glance, he explained. "The newspaper. I wanted to pick one up."

The sensible thing, given the train her thoughts had just taken, would have been to go on straight while he made his detour. She could return to her apartment, shower and make breakfast, then sit down with her own paper, which would have been delivered by then. But the air was so fresh and home was so lonely. For just a little longer she would indulge herself.

"Lead on," she said, and he did, guiding her across Memorial Drive to the narrow side streets that zigzagged into the Square. Signs of life were scarce, as was usual on a Sunday morning. But Harvard was everywhere — in the brick buildings that lined the streets, in the Beat Yale decal that graced more than one bumper, in the bevy of deserted sandwich shops that by afternoon would be crowded with students.

At the kiosk in the center of the Square, they stopped. "Want one?" Ryan asked, eyeing the papers stacked into a miniature skyline of newsprint.

She shook her head with a smile. "No, thanks."

"You're sure?" He extracted money from his sock.

"I've got one waiting at home."

Nodding, he paid for the paper, passing a glance at its headline before tucking the thick wad under his arm.

"How about a doughnut?" he asked, spotting a sign at the corner coffee shop.

"Nope."

"Some coffee?"

"Uh-uh."

"A cold drink?"

She shook her head.

"The afternoon?" What the hell. He had nothing to lose.

She sent him a good-humored frown. "What do you mean, the afternoon? It's for sale?"

"I could be bargained down to a very reasonable price."

She chuckled. "You're impossible."

"No. Just lonely. I was planning to work, but. . . ." Tipping back his head, he looked at the sky. "It's such a beautiful day. It's a shame not to take advantage of it. Given New England weather, we'll have snow within the week."

"Go on! It's got to be in the midsixties by now." Her skin felt damp; her pale blue running shirt clung to her chest. As they turned and began to walk in the general direction of home, she savored the stirring of air against her face. "You really think it'll change that quickly?"

"It usually does. Something about the sea breeze, I think." He paused, then sprang. "So, how about it? We could take a ride to Gloucester and spend the afternoon walking the beach."

But she shook her head. "I can't. I've got to work."

"Work? You do that all week. Don't you owe yourself one afternoon of relaxation?"

"I *had* one afternoon of relaxation. Yesterday."

"What did you do?" He remembered going to her apartment when he'd gotten back from work and finding her sitting curled on the sofa in her long white robe. He assumed she'd just showered and was waiting to dress for the evening. Again, he wondered with whom she'd been. But his feelings of jealousy were minor in comparison to those other feelings she evoked. She'd looked so innocent, so appealing, so thoroughly sensuous—even now he fought the urge to reach out and touch her.

"I went to the museum."

"You did?" he asked, diverting ardor into enthusiasm. "The Museum of Fine Arts?"

"Uh-huh. You approve?"

"I suppose."

"What do you mean, you suppose?"

"It depends who you were *with* at the museum."

With a coy smile, she ticked off her companions. "Let's see, George Washington was there, John Hancock, Ben Franklin, Auguste Renoir, Vincent van Gogh—"

"Any *live* males?"

"Several. I didn't know their names. None of them were alone."

"But you were?"

With a sigh, she reluctantly left the banter behind. "In the way you mean, yes." Passing Ferdinand's and The Blue Parrot, they continued on at a comfortable walk.

"Does that bother you?"

She looked at him in surprise. "To go places alone?" It was a loaded question. On the one hand, she had never been one to shy from striking out on her own. On the other, she had indeed been gun-shy since the run-in with Gary Culbert's thug that had resulted in her acceptance into the Witness Protection Program. "No," she began, careful to choose words that weren't a total lie, "I'm used to being alone. Not that it isn't nice to have company sometimes." Fearing that Ryan would hear an invitation she hadn't intended, she rushed on in a higher voice. "So that was for relaxation's sake. Today I work."

"What do you have to do?"

"Grade a stack of essays, make up an exam."

"You have exams coming up already?"

"We're on the trimester system. By Thanksgiving the first term will be over. Exams begin in a week and a half. I have to get my rough copy in to the office by Wednesday so the secretary can get to work. Fortunately I've only got one left to do."

They walked on. In the absence of conversation, Carly realized how much she seemed to have told Ryan, rather than the other way around. But then, the less she knew about him the better. They had no future together.

She was unaware how somber her expression had grown until Ryan caught her on it. "There you go again. Tuning out on me."

Looking quickly up, she forced a smile. "I'm sorry. I was just thinking about exams and all."

He suspected the "all" had nothing to do with exams, but couldn't force the issue. Rather, he concentrated on how best to worm his way into her life. When inspiration hit, his eyes lit up. "Listen, I've got work to do today too. We could work together. I mean, we could work on our own things together—in the same room."

She conjured up an image of them at her kitchen table, knees touching beneath the butcher block, and knew in the instant that she, for one, would never be able to concentrate. "I *really* need to work."

He followed her thinking, but was far from defeated. "Then the library. Harvard Law is as quiet as they come. We wouldn't dare talk there."

But it wasn't the talking that frightened her as much as the looking, the sensing, the savoring of companionship. One such working date could lead to another, then coffee during, then dinner after. It would be all too easy to get used to that kind of thing.

"Thanks, Ryan, but I'd better stay home."

He eyed her askance. "You're sure?" With her nod, he dropped it. For now. There had to be a reason for her reticence. He couldn't believe that she still mourned a husband who had been four years dead. Nor had he found an explanation for that look of abject fear he'd seen in her eyes more than once. He wished he had the courage to ask outright. But he doubted she'd answer, and he feared he'd only jeopardize the frail bond between them.

When the courtyard came into sight, Carly took a deep breath. "This was nice. Thank you."

"I didn't do anything."

"Well, it was fun running anyway." It would have to last her all week.

They walked up the path to the front door. "It *was* fun," he said quietly, then drew the door open and let her pass. Looking down at her, he felt drawn once again. She barely reached his chin, even to the top of the loose ponytail into which she'd gathered her hair. Stray tendrils had freed themselves as she'd run and now clung damply to her neck. In her running shorts and sneakers she seemed small, vulnerable and . . . brave. Brave. The word popped unexpectedly into his mind. He was pondering it distractedly when she stopped at the foot of the stairs and turned to regard him in question.

"Aren't you going to get it?"

"Get what?"

"That note sticking out of your mailbox."

He looked back toward the foyer. Sure enough, a piece of paper had been folded and worked into the narrow slit of the box, with just enough showing to attract his attention.

Carly watched him unfold it and read a brief scrawled message. When he frowned, she momentarily forgot her need for distance.

"Is something wrong?" she asked, coming closer to where he stood staring at the slip of paper.

"I don't know." His eyes were troubled. "It's from Howard Miller, my partner. He wants me to call him right away."

"Does that mean trouble?"

"I'm not sure." He looked again at the note in a futile attempt to uncover some hidden meaning. "If he made the effort to drive all the way in from Wellesley, there must be *something* on his mind." His dark brows knit in the struggle to guess what it was.

"You can use my phone," Carly heard herself offer. Turning, she headed up the stairs, knelt at her door to gather up her newspaper, and let herself in without looking back. Ryan materialized in her foyer moments later.

"I really apologize for this," he said, going straight toward the kitchen, pausing only to drop his paper on the table before lifting the receiver. "I'm giving your phone quite a workout."

She smiled. "It'll survive." Then she set her own paper in the living room and headed down the hall. When she returned, she carried two clean towels, one of which she offered to Ryan before settling on the sofa to mop the sweat from her forehead and neck as she eyed the Sunday headlines. From where she sat, she couldn't help but hear Ryan's half of the conversation.

"Sandy?" He ran the towel across his brow. "Is Howard around?" There was a pause; Ryan worked the towel around his neck. "Yeah, Howard. What's up?" The silence was prolonged and ominous. "*What?*" His voice held disbelief, then shock. "My God."

Twisting in her seat, Carly looked back to find his face a study in pain. Her heart began to thud as she listened to his terse questions. "When?" then, "Where?" and finally, "How?" Then he came alive. "What do you mean, they won't say? We have a right to that information!" His partner tried to calm him, but his anger raged. "Damn it, Howard, the bastard got to him! Suicide, my foot! I'm calling the D.A.—"

Unable to politely ignore what she'd heard, she slowly came to stand at the kitchen door. Ryan was too embroiled in his fury to notice. His brows knit low over his eyes, which were dark and threatening. One hand savagely gripped the phone, the other pressed hard against the wall. His lips were taut. Even his jaw, buffered by the thickness of its beard, seemed set in steel.

"That's a crock of bull! I want an autopsy! They'll rush him through the morgue and get him buried before anyone's the wiser. I'm telling you—"

He was loudly interrupted. Even Carly heard it, though Howard Miller's specific words were indistinct. But Ryan listened, very slowly calming down. When he spoke again, there was an element of defeat in his voice.

"Okay, okay." He sighed, his voice lowering to a murmur. "I'll call you back in ten minutes. Fifteen, then." Replacing the receiver on its hook, he closed his eyes. He looked distraught.

Carly took a step closer. "Ryan?" she said softly. "What is it?"

He looked up in surprise, having momentarily forgotten her presence. At her concern, he was doubly distressed. She didn't need to hear this; Lord knew she'd lived with death too closely already.

Thrusting his fingers through his hair, he scooped it back from his brow. "Nothing you should be bothered with."

"You'd rather not talk about it?"

"I'd rather not burden *you* with it."

She chided him gently. "I'm not fragile. Sometimes it helps to share things. Besides, after the way I dumped it all on you a little while ago. . . ."

He held her gaze then, seeing something he hadn't seen before. She wanted him to talk; it was no empty offer. And it was the first such open invitation she'd made.

He straightened and dropped his head back, then slowly raised it and looked down at her again. His eyes were clouded. "I've been defending a fellow on charges of dealing."

"Drugs?"

"Heroin." His taut-knuckled hands gripped the ends of the towel. "He was a nineteen-year-old kid who's been on the wrong side of the law for years. Very bright. Has run the cops around in circles time and again. But stupid enough to think that a little more money, always a little more money, would get him over the hump."

"But it didn't."

"Not this time. They found him dead in his cell last night. His mother was notified. When she couldn't reach me, she fished Howard's number from the book." He lowered his eyes and scowled at the floor. "It's criminal. Prison is criminal. Totally lawless as we know the law. A guy like Luis needed help. He was lost and desperate. His childhood alternated between running away from home and protecting his mother from beatings by a drunkard of a husband. The kid had nothing going for him but misguided intelligence and a mother who loved him. There's the shame. It was his mother who first called me. I swear, she would have sold herself into bondage if it would have meant raising the money for Luis's defense."

"How *did* she raise it?"

"She didn't. I'm not—I wasn't charging her."

"You do that then?" Not all lawyers did. Another something to respect.

"If I think the case merits it." He paused to rub the end of the towel along the line of his beard beneath his chin. "Sometimes a lawyer takes a case *pro bono* as a favor to someone else. Sometimes he takes it because he believes the client deserves representation. Then there're cases that offer an opportunity to break ground on a legal issue. And there are those cases that are simply interesting or exciting enough for a lawyer to want to handle, whether he's paid or not."

"And Luis's?" Carly prompted, absorbed in Ryan's philosophy.

"Luis," he sighed, "was just someone who needed a helping hand. One helping hand. Life had been tough on him; it didn't seem fair. Not that I felt I could 'save' him. He was what he was, shaped by nineteen years of hell." He raised his eyes, his voice deep and hard. "He was an addict. Do you have any idea what happens to addicts in there?" Carly had read her share on the subject, but he went quickly on. "It's a fate worse than death. Especially where Luis was, in that limbo between the cops and the guys on the inside who could either make or break him." With a muttered "Damn," he looked away in anguish. "I can't believe he killed himself."

"That's what they're saying?"

"That was what they told his mother. Howard's trying to contact someone in the prison." He looked at his watch. "I've got to try him in another ten minutes." He hesitated, cocking his head toward the phone. "Would you mind—"

"Of course not," she said, with a dismissing wave. Her thoughts had already moved on, the investigator in her at work. "But the alternative is murder, isn't it?"

"That's right."

"Do you really think it could be that?"

"He'd been getting his stuff from someone pretty powerful. It's been known to happen," he gritted.

"Committed by an inmate hired by the supplier?"

"Or the cops."

His words hung in the air like sulfur fumes around a rubber plant. Carly couldn't help but stare. Though the police she'd come to know through her own ordeal had been relatively innocuous, she knew well enough of those who weren't. Still, murder? Oh, it had happened. Just the year before, there had been an incident in Chicago. Then the cop had been convicted of manslaughter, a lesser degree, on the grounds that in a scuffle the cop had used undue force that had resulted in the man's banging his head against the back of a truck. The cop had lost his job, but hadn't served a day in jail. The case had pitted the community against the department; its disposition had been a no-win compromise.

"I'm sorry, Ryan," she whispered, returning to the present and his somber expression. "Will you be able to find out?"

"That's what I don't know. That's why Howard is getting onto it." He sent her a wry smile. "He figured that I'd go off the handle with accusations."

"Would you?"

"If I smelled a cover-up, you bet. It *could* have been another inmate, with a guard in the system protecting him. Hell, it *could* have been suicide." His voice dropped. "I just don't know." He looked at his watch again, then grew silent.

"How about some coffee?" she offered, wishing she could ease his wait.

"Hmm? Oh, no, don't go to any trouble for me."

"I was going to make a pot anyway. Would you like some?"

He shrugged, then nodded but said nothing, content to watch her remove a can of coffee from the cabinet, measure the prescribed amount into a filter, and set it into the coffee maker. She moved with a steadiness that was comforting. Strangely so. As though she'd always be there to lend an ear, to offer support. Alyssa would have never thought to ask about his legal life. She had wanted it left in the office, appropriately filed and forgotten after business hours. And he'd done just that, though "business hours" had grown longer and longer. She had refused to accept his love for the law; he had refused to accept her refusal. It had been a standoff, one of the many irreconcilable differences that had led to their divorce.

And now there was Carly. Quiet and alone. Interesting and interested, though fiercely protective of her privacy. He could easily open up to her, as if *she'd* been the one who had vowed to take him for better or for worse, when in fact he'd known her less than two days. She seemed to have so much to give.

"How do you take it?" Her voice broke into his thoughts, and he realized he'd been staring. With a start, he shifted his gaze from her face to the coffee, which had already begun to drip.

He cleared his throat, needing the minute to refocus. "Black is fine." Then he leaned back against the counter, not far from her, and looked around the room. Immaculate, as always. Neat, sparkling. His gaze wandered into the living room to encounter the same. What *was* it that bothered him?

Leaving the kitchen, he idly approached the sofa, rounded it and side-stepped the pair of sculpted tables. His feet took him to the white-lacquered wall system, where he studied the bouquet of silk flowers in their elegant vase, the silent face of the television, the fine collection of books—literary works as well as volumes on art and drama and photography.

Something was missing. Puzzled, he reviewed what he'd seen, then returned pensively to the kitchen in time to see Carly remove two mugs from the cabinet. She was lovely. Lovely and intriguing. But her home? It lacked . . . it lacked . . . fingerprints. That was it. There was nothing in her home to brand it hers, to mark it as unique in the very way she was. It was strange.

Carly offered a gentle smile along with the mug of coffee. He took the brew with a murmured, "Thanks," and leaned back against the counter again. He was eminently aware of Carly, and she of him. When the phone jangled, they were both startled.

On reflex, Ryan reached for it as though it were his own. Carly held her hand suspended. "Hello?" she heard him say, then saw him frown and eye her questioningly. "Robyn?" Stifling a gasp, she managed to shrug. "There's no Robyn here," he responded offhandedly. "You must have the wrong number."

Replacing the receiver, he darted a sheepish gaze Carly's way. "Sorry about that. I guess I'm a little preoccupied. Kinda forgot this wasn't my phone."

Had Carly not been slightly preoccupied herself, she would have been susceptible to the half smile that gave his lips a roguish twist. But her mind was on the call itself, on the name that had passed through those lips moments earlier.

She tossed her head jerkily in an attempt at nonchalance. "No problem. A wrong number's a wrong number." But it hadn't been. Someone had called for Robyn, yet no one who would normally do that had her number. Apprehension sent a chill through her. She had to call Sam. But with Ryan here? Not wise.

But then, Ryan's presence offered a certain solace: protection at its most innocent. The blank look on his face when he'd repeated the name Robyn had seemed authentic enough—unless it was all part of a skillfully slow regimen of psychological torture.

"Hey, I've upset you," he said softly, intruding on this most gruesome of thoughts. "You look like you've seen a ghost."

The ghost of Robyn Hart—close, she thought. "Of course not. Must have been the running. Six miles two mornings in a row. I guess I'm not used to it."

He brushed his fingers against her cheek while his gaze seared her heart with an irresistible tenderness. "You're sure I haven't upset you with talk of my case?"

For an instant, she nearly forgot her own. The thudding of her heart could as easily have been caused by Ryan's touch. In defiance of the worst of her fears, she allowed herself to feel warm and safe and very much cared for. But she mustn't forget, she told herself. A phone call for Robyn was real and serious; Ryan Cornell's appeal was a passing thing, in all likelihood a fabrication of her own emotional need. Rationally, though, what she needed was to contact Sam, but she was hamstrung until Ryan made his call and left.

Tearing her eyes from his, she glanced at the phone. "I'd have to be made of stone not to be affected by your case. Who is your partner calling now?"

"He's seeing what he can get from the warden."

"Then what? If you want an autopsy performed, won't you have to go through a medical examiner?"

Ryan arched a brow at the extent of her knowledge. "If we're in luck, the warden will request the autopsy himself. Most likely we'll have to do the demanding. And yes, the medical examiner will be the one to contact."

"What about the district attorney?" she asked nervously. "You mentioned him before. If you suspect murder, will you go to him?"

"I'll go to him if I suspect *any* foul play." He paused to take a drink of coffee, then took a deep breath and looked at the ceiling. "I don't know. Maybe it was suicide. The guy had a raw deal in life. Who could blame him if he wanted to escape once and for all?" He gave his watch an impatient glance, then snatched up the phone and punched out his partner's number. Taking a seat at the table, Carly watched and waited. When he replaced the receiver a few minutes later, he wore a weary expression.

"What did he say?" she asked, curious enough about Luis's fate to ignore the fact that any conversation would prolong Ryan's stay and delay her call to Sam.

"The warden is convinced it was suicide. He claims there were no suspicious marks on the body."

"Do you believe him?"

Ryan frowned. "Luis had so many marks on him anyway—who knows? Howard's calling in for the autopsy, though. That should tell us something." He stared pensively at the last of his coffee before downing it in a gulp and putting the cup in the sink. Then he turned to Carly.

"Thanks," he said simply.

She stood as he retrieved his newspaper from the counter and headed for the door. She understood that his appreciation was for the phone, the coffee, the sympathetic ear, but she wanted no further sweet words. His compellingly masculine presence was far too potent as it was. Against her will she recalled the kiss they'd shared earlier that morning. Then she thrust it from her mind. She had a phone call to make. And the reason behind that phone call was precisely the reason why it behooved her to keep Ryan Cornell at a distance.

At the open door he eyed her with resignation. "Sure you won't change your mind? I'd much rather spend the afternoon with you than have to see Luis's mother or stop by the prison."

"You'll do that anyway," Carly declared softly, with more admiration than criticism. "I know your type. Work before play. True?"

He hesitated a minute, wishing it weren't so but finally offering a "True" as softly, before giving her a sad smile and starting down the stairs.

Pulse racing, Carly closed the door quietly before bolting for the phone and punching out Sam's number. It was Ellen who answered.

"Hello?"

"Ellen? It's Carly Quinn. I'm really sorry to bother you on a Sunday morning, but is Sam around?"

"Oh, Carly, he's gone to pick up some milk for me at the store. I expect him back any minute. You sound upset. Is something wrong?" Though Ellen knew nothing of Carly's real name or the case that had brought her to Boston, she was well aware that Carly was part of the program and knew enough to be concerned.

"I don't know," Carly murmured. "I got a strange phone call a little while ago. I just wanted to run it past Sam."

"You're at home now?"

"Uh-huh."

"Got the door locked?"

"Oh, damn. Hold on a minute." She started to put the phone down, then raised it again. "Do you want to just have Sam call me back?"

"No, no, Carly. Go bolt the door. I'll hold on."

When Carly returned she was slightly breathless. "There. Thanks, Ellen. God, how could I have done that? I must be going soft!" She paused. "Any sign of him yet?"

"Not yet. I'm at the window watching. He'll be right along. In the meantime you can tell me about school. How's it going?"

"Not bad. Busy right about now." And the last thing on her mind at the moment. Better to shift the conversation back to Ellen, who might be feeling a bit more talkative than she was. "But how about you? How are you feeling?"

"Pretty well. A little tired. The first time round I didn't have a toddler to watch. Sara's into the terrible twos three months before her time. She can't quite understand my being under the weather now and again."

"Jealousy before its time?" Carly ventured sympathetically.

Ellen chuckled. "Could be. Sam tells me you've got a load of nieces and nephews. This must be old hat for you."

"I've never had one of my own. It's always pretty exciting when someone's having a baby."

"Did you want to—have one of your own, that is?"

Carly sighed. It was something she'd asked herself more than once in the past four years. "I don't know. I was so young when I first got married and we were each busy with our careers. If Malcolm—" her voice broke slightly, only in part due to the use of a name so strange to her tongue "—had lived, I'm sure I would have wanted a child by now. I often wonder what would have happened if I'd had one. This relocation would have been that much harder with another person involved, I suppose. On the other hand, it would have been nice to have had someone with me, particularly with my husband gone. Then again, if I'd had a child I might have been more cautious about things to begin with. All this might never have happened." She gave a snort of disgust. "Am I rambling! See what happens when you ask a creative writer a simple question? They say that a born writer is one who is never satisfied with a single side of a story but keeps looking to the far end of the issue. I think they're right."

"Have you had a chance to do much writing?"

"No. School's been too demanding so far. Maybe when things settle down some I'll try."

"It'd be a great outlet, Carly."

"But far too revealing. In the wrong hands. . . ." Her words trailed off, their implication obvious.

"You shouldn't think that way," Ellen scolded gently.

"That's what Sam says."

"Well, he's right. Your cover is so tight nothing can possibly leak out. I'm always amazed when Sam talks about—hey, speak of the devil, there he is. Hold on, Carly. I'll go yell for him before he starts dallying with Sara."

The phone hit the counter with a clatter. Carly heard the fading patter of footsteps, then a muffled, "Sam! It's Carly," then, after a pause, louder, more solid steps returning.

"Carly—" Sam's voice came with reassuring calm over the line "—what happened?"

"Somebody called, Sam. Somebody asking for Robyn."

"Did you recognize the voice?"

"That's the worst part! I didn't hear it! Ryan was here waiting to make a call and when the phone rang he picked it up without thinking."

"Carly—"

"He told whoever it was that there was no Robyn here. I didn't even want to ask whether it was a man or a woman for fear of arousing suspicion. And I couldn't call you until he'd gone. Who could it have been, Sam?"

"Car—"

"Anybody who calls me here knows me as Carly! Anybody who would use the other name doesn't call me here! *Who could it have been?*"

"Sheila."

The babble of chatter gave way to complete silence.

"Sheila?" Carly half whispered.

"Yeah," Sam said with a sigh. "And, boy, am I sorry. I knew at first glance she'd be trouble."

"Sheila who?"

"Sheila Montgomery."

"*Sheila?*" Carly's face lit instantly. "Sheila's here?"

"I'm afraid so."

"Sam, that's great! Sheila's terrific!"

"That was what her transfer papers from the marshal's office in Chicago said, and that was what I believed when I gave her your number. She already knew your name and that you were under my jurisdiction. Did you tell her before you left?"

"She was in on the planning back there."

"Hoffmeister may have been right when he suggested it'd be good for you to have someone to talk to, especially a woman, but now I'm not so sure. She seemed scatterbrained to me. To have called you and asked for Robyn, *particularly* when someone other than you answered the phone, only proves it."

But Carly was full of forgiveness. Sheila had been with her during the entire stint in protective custody. They'd begun as allies and ended fast friends. "She'll be working here?"

"Looks that way," Sam grumbled. He'd have to pair her up with Greg. Let old bedroom eyes tame her.

"When did she get in?"

"She stopped by the office early last week on her way to visit a cousin or someone on the Cape and wasn't due to begin work until a week from Monday. I had no idea she'd contact you so soon or I would have warned you. She must have gotten tired of her cousin." He gave a snort. "Most likely the other way around."

"Sam, Sam, where's your sense of humor? Here I was scared to death that the *wrong* someone had my name, and it's only Sheila. She's not scatterbrained. That's just her personality. Bubbly and enthusiastic. Believe me. I've seen her in action. She's smart as a whip and thorough. And she can be one tough cookie when the going gets rough." Her thoughts slipped back. Her voice grew softer. "I don't know what I would have done without her through those months."

Sam sighed. "Well, it looks like you're going to have her again. At least the friend part of it. She'll be working on other things for us, though you can be damn sure I plan to give her a lecture about watching her tongue."

"I'm sure she was just excited. Go easy on her, Sam. She's been through a lot in life. She's earned her stripes."

"That's a recommendation?"

"Very definitely."

"Then I guess it'll have to do. At any rate, see if she calls again. If she doesn't—" his tone grew momentarily somber "—let me know. She's the only one I can think of who might have—"

"Wait, Sam. There's the intercom. Hold on." Setting the phone on the counter, Carly ran to the panel by the door and pressed the button. "Yes?" she asked, her customary caution softened only by a definite suspicion.

"Carly Quinn?" came a voice made tinny by the mechanism. "This is Sheila Montgomery. Now I know you've got a guy up there with you because I called and completely forgot who I was calling when I heard his sexy voice, but I've just driven up from Provincetown and wanted to say hello. Hello? Are you there?"

Carly grinned. It was Sheila, all right. "I'm here, Sheila. Come on up." Holding the front door release long enough to allow Sheila entry, she returned to the phone. "Sam? It's Sheila. She's on her way up. Hey, I'm sorry to have bothered you. Seems I jumped the gun and got scared. If I'd been a little more patient I guess the mystery would have solved itself."

"No problem, Carly." And well there wasn't, since Carly seemed pleased and no apparent harm had been done by Sheila's carelessness. Sam still vowed to take Sheila down a peg, but another time. "Go greet your friend. Maybe *she* can coax you out on the town. Hey, that's not a bad idea. Why don't you show her the sights? Explore together. As long as she's there, make good use of her."

"Oh, I will," Carly said with a smile. "I will."

SEVEN

[S]HEILA MONTGOMERY TUGGED at the buzzing door and entered
the atrium duly impressed with the surroundings of Robyn Hart's new home.
Carly Quinn. Carly Quinn. Damn it, she'd have to remember. One slipup was
bad enough. But it was hard. The woman she'd known, a frightened woman
caught between two lives, had been Robyn Hart. Carly Quinn was someone
new—new career, new apartment, new boyfriend.

At the thought of the last, Sheila felt a twinge of remorse. Perhaps she
should have waited. But she only wanted to say hi. The Cape had been lonely
all by herself. And Boston was as new to her as it had been to Rob—to Carly.

Pushing her windblown mop of raven hair back from her face, she started
up the stairs. Not bad, she mused again, noting the fine carpeting on the stairs,
the brass railings, the lush plants hanging hither and yon. Not bad at all.
Certainly a sight nicer than the studio she'd rented on Beacon Hill. Though
she'd definitely bought the location, the apartment itself left something to be
desired. But, she reasoned morosely, she was used to it. *This* place, though,
was something else.

Rounding the second-floor landing she headed for the third, then tipped her
head back and caught sight of the face grinning down at her.

Carly leaned on the railing, forearms propped on the brass, and watched
with pleasure as her friend met her gaze. "Sheila Montgomery, you haven't
changed a bit."

Sheila returned the grin and spoke with the faintly nasal twang that was
uniquely hers. "You, Carly Quinn, have." Running quickly up the remaining
flight, she slowed as she approached Carly. "Wow, have you!" She ran an eye
over the smart running suit Carly still wore, then took in the mass of curly hair
that had escaped its ponytail, the flushed cheeks, the light gray eyes. For an
instant she held back. There was something about this woman, something
richer, something more sophisticated that put her in a class above. In that

instant Sheila felt every bit the bodyguard, the woman who'd crossed from the wrong side of the tracks to make it in the world of law enforcement. In Chicago, with a very vulnerable Robyn, it had all seemed irrelevant. Here, though, with this elegant backdrop, with the knowledge that Carly Quinn was an established person, she felt distinctly inferior.

It was Carly who took the final steps and embraced Sheila warmly. "It's great to see you, Sheila! I had no idea you'd be in town!"

"Hey," Sheila began apologetically, "I know this is a bad time." She cast a skittering glance toward Carly's open door. "Maybe I should come back later."

"Don't be silly! I'm alone." Looping her arm around Sheila's waist, she guided the woman toward her apartment and spoke in a softer, more conspiratorial whisper. "He left. Sexy voice and all. You missed him."

Sheila managed a chuckle as she retrieved her bravado. "Damn. And here I thought I'd finally get a look at your type of man. Hey, this is gorgeous!" Inside the apartment, she slowly scanned the room. "My word, you really did it right, didn't you?"

Closing the door, Carly followed Sheila's gaze. "They suggested I change my image. I guess I did. I've never quite lived this way before. I mean, when I was growing up the house was beautiful in an old and elegant kind of way. This is more—"

"Chic. Modern. Perfect." Sheila's eyes took in the stylish decor before returning to Carly. "It's lovely," she said quietly. "You're very lucky."

Feeling suddenly awkward, Carly glanced away. Her home was a luxury, something she doubted Sheila could afford. "Listen, can I get you some coffee? I've got a fresh pot brewed."

"Sure. That'd be great."

Heading for the kitchen, Carly called over her shoulder, "Sam tells me you've been transferred to the Boston office."

"Sam Loomis? He told you I'd seen him?"

"Only when I called him a few minutes ago." She pulled a fresh mug from the cabinet for Sheila and filled it, adding hot coffee to her own, the one she'd used when Ryan had been there earlier. His stood cold and lonely in the sink, a stark reminder that he'd been and gone. "You really gave me a scare. When the phone rang and you asked for Robyn—"

"Listen, I'm sorry about that. I guess I wasn't thinking."

"Don't tell Sam that," Carly advised, arching a brow as she handed Sheila the coffee. "Tell him you thought you recognized *his* voice at the other end of the line or something."

"He was ticked?"

Carly shrugged, then led the way back to the living room. "Only because I was frightened. I was sure that someone had penetrated my cover and I couldn't call Sam until Ryan left—"

"Who *is* Ryan?"

"My neighbor," she said as she sank onto the sofa.

Sheila settled in the armchair across from Carly. "Is he as good-looking as he sounds?"

"He's good-looking."

"Boy, you didn't waste any time! Tell me about him."

"There's not much to tell." At least not much she wanted to tell. "I just met him. He moved in last weekend. His phone isn't going in until tomorrow, so he's been using mine. He was standing right next to it when you called. That was why he answered."

Feeling more bold now that they'd begun to talk, Sheila's eyes narrowed. "I hope you're going after him."

"No, I am not *going after him*. You know my situation. It's shaky, to say the least."

Sheila gave another envious glance at her surroundings. "Doesn't look shaky to me. You've got a new town, a new career. How's the teaching going, by the way?"

"Great. Busy. I enjoy it."

"Then you've got it made. What's to be shaky about?" It sounded like a perfect life to Sheila. What with a husband's life insurance, a job that paid well, plus money from Uncle Sam to work with, Carly had it easy.

Carly didn't see it quite that way. For a minute she was surprised at Sheila's lack of understanding. For a minute too she had forgotten Sheila's lot in life, compared to hers.

"Things aren't that simple," she said quietly. She sipped her coffee and gazed toward the window. "There's still the fact of where I've been, who I've been. If you think *you* had trouble remembering to call me Carly, just think about what it must be like for me. Twenty-nine years as Robyn, four months a Carly—it's an adjustment."

"But it's a fact," Sheila countered. "It's done. Robyn Hart has been wiped off the map. Carly Quinn has been put on it—and in style, I might add." Dryly, at that.

"Mechanically, yes. Emotionally, only maybe. It's been a lonely four months."

"Which is where sexy-voiced gentlemen come into play. You mean that you haven't begun to sow those wild oats of yours?"

"Wild oats?" Carly laughed. "Not quite. I've turned conservative, or hadn't you noticed?"

"You were always conservative—at least while I knew you. But not before. I got the impression you were a spitfire back then."

Carly nodded, smiling. "A spitfire . . . I suppose that's a good way to put it." Then she sobered and her eyes grew distant. "But that's changed. When Peter died, I guess. Or maybe later, when Culbert's thug came after me with a gun." She shivered. "In many ways I'm back where I was as a teenager. Quiet. Private."

"Then you'll just have to bloom all over again."

Carly studied her friend, taking in at a glance the light wool tunic, tights and calf-high boots. She'd always thought of Sheila as a character, a free spirit straitjacketed into an oddly controlled job. More than once she'd wondered if Sheila wouldn't have been happier as an aerobics instructor or a salesgirl at a specialty boutique. Her clothes were usually startling in either color or combination—exotic verging on the garish. It was as though she wanted to shock people into seeing her, then pull out her ID and put them in their place. Though Carly didn't agree with the philosophy, knowing Sheila's background made it no great surprise.

"How about if I let you do the blooming for me?" she teased. "Tell me about this transfer. How did it come about?"

"I requested it."

Carly frowned. "You wanted to leave Chicago? I thought you liked it there."

Sheila made an impish face. "I'd been there for seven years. Time to move on."

"What about Lee? And Harmon? And Mickey?" Sheila's social life had been a constant source of amazement to Carly. It seemed she never had an evening off without a date. The phone calls coming in to the house had been endless.

"Nothing special."

"With *none* of them?"

"Nah. It was going nowhere. I needed a change of scenery."

"Why Boston?"

Sheila eyed her sheepishly. "Because you made it sound so good. Remember those days we spent poring over maps and brochures and real-estate magazines when you were trying to decide where you wanted to go?" Carly remembered and felt a return of the camaraderie revealed in Sheila's smile. "Boston was perfect for you. Not too big, not too small. Lots of schools and universities around." She lowered her voice to a deep drawl. "Lots of up-and-coming businessmen and professionals."

"Wait a minute," Carly reminded her, with a chiding grin. "I never said that. You were the one with the eye out for social possibilities. All *I* wanted was an interesting place to live and teach. Where are you living, anyway?"

"I've taken an apartment on Beacon Hill."

"Not bad."

Sheila gave a comical scowl. "Not great. It's a studio. Subbasement. Kinda small and dark."

"But a good location."

"Hmmph. That's what I'm paying for."

"And lots of interesting guys living nearby?" Carly interjected with a sly smile.

"Damn it, I hope so." Sheila sat back in her chair and took a pose of idle indulgence. "What I'm looking for," she said airily, "is a tall blond with a great physique and a bulging wallet who'll fall madly in love with me and devote the rest of his days to showering me with lavish gifts and his undivided attention."

"Sounds good."

"But it's a dream." She sighed.

"Maybe not."

"Do you dream?"

"Sure. About fires. And guns. And people chasing me."

"Still? Oh, Robyn—"

"Carly."

Feeling a touch of impatience, Sheila ignored the correction. "Don't you know how safe you are?"

"It's one thing to say it, something else to believe it."

"Are you in touch with . . . anyone?"

"From Chicago?" Carly shook her head. "No. That was part of the deal, remember?"

"I know. But you had so many friends. I can remember the calls you used to get. They were all very concerned."

A flicker of pain crossed Carly's brow. "I know. It helped. But I made a choice when I decided to testify for the state. My life—a new life—for that one."

"Are you sorry?"

"Sometimes." She shrugged. "But I can't change things. And I've been lucky."

"You must have new friends—"

Carly's smile was a weary one. "Now you're starting to sound like Sam. And my father. Sure I have friends. But friends do nothing for the dreams, the fear. It's always there, Sheila. What can I say?"

Sheila wished she could feel more sympathy. In her heart, she supposed she did. In her mind, well, looking around and at Carly, the woman had a lot going for her. Good background. A loving family. Memories of a husband who adored her. And financial stability. Bingo.

As though attuned to Sheila's thoughts, Carly threw a hand into the air. "Listen to me. I sound positively morbid. It must be because with you I can air those things I can't with another friend. I'm glad you've come, Sheila," she said more softly. "It'll be nice to keep in touch."

"Speaking of which," Sheila bubbled, leaning forward in her seat, "why don't we celebrate and go out for brunch. I hear there are some terrific places near Faneuil Hall."

Carly grimaced. "I'd love to, but I have to work."

"Today? It's Sunday!"

"What else is new?"

"Come on, Carly. You've got to take some time off."

Where had she heard that before? Thank you, Ryan Cornell. "I took yesterday off. Today I have to work." She was beginning to sound like a broken record.

"But it'd only be for an hour or two."

"I've already *taken* an hour or two," Carly overrode Sheila's coaxing with her own gently teasing tone. "And I've got a good six or seven hours of work to do before tomorrow. Really, Sheila. We'll make it another time, okay?" She put her mug down and stood with Sheila.

"Promise? After all, you've got to show me around. You must know all the ins and outs of Boston by now."

Carly had no intention of getting into *that* particular discussion. The go-round with Sam on Friday night had been enough. "Knowing you, there will be a slew of men to show you the town by the end of the week." Then she thought of something Sam had said. "Hey, weren't you supposed to be staying on the Cape for a while? With a cousin?"

That was what she'd told Sam, Sheila mused. But there wasn't any cousin she'd been visiting on the Cape. They were all back in L.A. getting into one sort of trouble or another, and even if they weren't, they'd have to steal the money to fly east. "I came back early. Just wanted to get settled." She moved to the door. "You're sure I can't change your mind? It'd be fun. Like old times."

Fun? Another discrepancy in perception, Carly mused. True, she and Sheila had done any number of things while Carly had been in protective custody. After all, she hadn't been a prisoner. Well, not in the criminal sense, at least. The Marshal's Service had been most solicitous, planning dinners out, movies, yachting adventures on the lake. To Sheila, it must have seemed a pleasant turn in a job that had to be monotonous at times. To Carly, it was a consolation prize. Not that she hadn't enjoyed Sheila's company. Far from it. But regardless of how lavish the dinner, how engrossing the movie, how exciting the yachting adventure, she could never quite forget why she was where she was. Even in hindsight, her stomach knotted up.

"Maybe another time," she said, accompanying Sheila to the hall.

Sheila swung her large leather bag lithely to her shoulder. "I'll hold you to it, Carly Quinn." She grinned mischievously on her way down the stairs. "While you're doing your work, think of me breezing through the marketplace spending madly, fending off the most handsome of men—" Abruptly she stopped speaking, her attention caught by a most handsome man on the flight below her.

Curious, Carly stepped to the railing and followed her gaze. A tall, blond-haired man with the broadest of shoulders and a cocksure gait had approached the second landing as Sheila reached it. Even from where she stood Carly could see the smile he cast toward Sheila as he made his way down the hall. Eyebrows raised suggestively, Sheila looked up at Carly, tossed her head toward the bold figure as a quiet knock echoed through the atrium, shook one hand in mime of something hot, beamed at Carly again and was on her way.

Shaking her head with a helpless smile, Carly returned to her apartment to shower, then dressed in jeans and a sweater and headed for the kitchen. It was nearly noon and she hadn't eaten a thing. Making a cheese omelet and toast, she let her mind wander to the events of the morning. Sheila. Sam. Ryan.

Ryan. Her gaze fell once more to the cup he'd used. Lifting it, she held it to her, wondering what it was about the man that affected her so. Then, with a burst of determination she thrust the cup under the faucet, rinsed it and upended it in the dishwasher.

For four hours she worked without a break, finding solace in the intense concentration demanded by the papers before her. It was only a faint stiffness in her legs that brought her from her place on the living-room floor. Papers were strewn atop both of the low tables. The Sunday *Globe* lay unread at the end of the sofa.

Walking idly through the apartment, she paused in front of the window and gazed out at the Charles. It looked cold. Strange, when the air had been so warm that morning. But it was nearly dusk now, and morning was long gone. Then she'd been with Ryan. Now she was alone.

She was in very much the same circumstance the following evening, reading through a new batch of papers, when the phone rang. She had been expecting a call from Bryna Moore, an art teacher at Rand and a friend with whom she'd spent an hour that afternoon discussing a possible collaboration in an art-and-writing course. It wasn't Bryna, though. She instantly recognized the deep male voice by the involuntary flutter it sent through her.

"Carly? It's Ryan. How are you?"

"I'm fine," she answered softly, fearing she was better than that now that he'd called. She'd thought of him that morning when she'd left for school, and again when she'd paused in the downstairs foyer to get her mail on her way home. "Are you home?"

"Yup. My phone's in." He chuckled in self-derision. "Obviously." He paused for a minute. "I thought I'd test it out. You're the first person I've called."

She smiled, feeling suddenly warm. "Thank you. I'm honored. But how, uh, how did you know my number?" It was unlisted.

"It was printed on your phone. I have a good memory." He'd made a point to have, where Carly was concerned. He remembered every detail of the precious short time they'd spent together since Friday night, had relived those minutes repeatedly. And repeatedly he'd asked himself what it was about her that had instantly struck such a chord. He'd known his share of women over the years, both before and after his wife, yet none had seemed to have the need, or the reluctance, that Carly Quinn did. Among the many feelings she inspired, curiosity remained high on his list.

Aware now of the silence on her end, he cleared his throat. "I thought you might want to know that we got the autopsy done."

"What did they find?"

"I won't know for sure until the final report comes through in another couple of days. At least it was done. It's a start."

"Were you able to learn *anything*?"

"Just that he did have some signs of recent injury. How recent remains to be seen."

"Is the warden doing any checking on his end? You know, questioning guards and other inmates."

Ryan sighed. "He says he is. But he'll hear what he wants to hear, if you know what I mean."

Indeed she did. "He'll be hesitant to admit that any wrongdoing took place in his facility."

"Which was why the autopsy was so critical. All we can do is wait now for that report."

She nodded, but was silent. When Ryan spoke again, his tone held that something that tugged at her heart.

"I missed you this morning."

"This morning?"

"When I ran. I thought you might be out."

"My God, you must have been up early."

"I was out at six-thirty."

At six-thirty that morning she'd been in the shower, wishing she could have run even as she nursed tired hamstrings. "It's pretty dark then."

"All the more reason why it might have been nice to have you with me. Did you run after school?"

"Actually, no. The traffic was so heavy and it was pretty cold and I was tired." And it was dark then too. "I usually stick to the weekends."

"The mornings are nice. Other than being lonely, that is. But if you came with me it wouldn't be lonely. How about it?"

She twisted the telephone cord around her finger. "I don't know, Ryan—"

"Come on," he coaxed, and the thought of running tempted her nearly as much as the softness of his tone. "It'd be good for you. Fresh air. Exhilaration. It's a great way to start the day, particularly when you have to be cooped up in school."

"But I'm not cooped up," she argued. "I'm forever walking from one classroom to the other. Even outside." She hesitated. "Have you ever seen the school?"

"No."

"It's really beautiful, on the grounds of an estate with four separate buildings. My office is in one, the classrooms in another, the cafeteria in a third. So I do get exercise. Besides, I have to leave here every morning by seven-thirty. And if I've got to shower and dress and dry my hair and put makeup on. . . ." She realized she was babbling and caught herself. "Well, I'd really have to run at six. That'd be pretty early."

"Not for me. I'd be game."

"Thanks, Ryan," she murmured softly, reluctantly. "But I think I'll pass."

"For now. I'll give you that. But I'll keep after you, Carly. You won't know what you're missing until you've tried."

Oh, she knew what she was missing, all right. More than anything she'd like to run each morning with Ryan. But it wasn't wise. It just wasn't wise.

At least, that was what she told herself all week. By the time Saturday morning rolled around, however, she was up early and eager to go. Unfortunately, it was raining. More disappointed than she might have wished, she returned to bed, wondering whether Ryan was in bed just below her, imagining him all warm and mussed from sleep, deciding that he'd most probably taken one look at the swelling puddles, turned over and gone back to sleep.

In fact, he was up at seven, staring gloomily at the rainsodden street. Wearing a pair of blue briefs and a look of disgust, he cursed his luck. He wandered to the living room, as though that window might reveal a ray of sun, then, thwarted there too, returned to the bedroom and thrust a hand through his hair in frustration. Pivoting on his heel, he backtracked to the kitchen, poured a tall glass of orange juice from the carton that looked as lonely in the otherwise empty refrigerator as he felt in his strangely empty life, and faced the window as he drank.

He hadn't planned to run until eight. That was the time he'd met Carly last Sunday. There was always the chance it would clear up. Leaning forward, he looked at the sky. It was dark gray and ominous, heavy, thick. Still, there was always that hope. . . .

Dragging the newspaper in from the hall with one arm and mental thanks that his home delivery had finally begun, he returned to bed to read. But he was restless. Headlines were about all he took in before he put the paper down atop the scattered sheets with an impatient rustle. Lying back on the pillow, he eyed the ceiling. He wondered what she was doing, whether she was awake, whether she'd planned on running, whether she was as frustrated as he. Most likely, he decided, she was sound asleep.

Bounding up, he looked outside again. It was pouring harder than ever. "Hell," he muttered, looked at his watch and sank back down on the edge of the bed. Pulling the paper closer, he extracted the editorial page, spread it with an agitated crackle of newsprint, and focused in on a column written by a colleague of his. Creative sentencing in the courts. An idealistic practice at best, at worst a mandate for discrimination. The piece was well conceived, if written with the verbosity that plagued so much of legal writing. When it was his turn to write an editorial, he'd make certain he consulted an English teacher.

Closing the paper impatiently, he went into the bathroom, quickly showered and put on his running suit, then returned to the window. He could try. Hell, he could always position himself downstairs on the pretense of debating whether to run or not, and wait for her. If she didn't show by eight-fifteen or so, he'd know.

Just then, a blur of yellow caught his eye and, squinting, he leaned forward. Some madman was actually running, if that was what could be called the dodging act he was doing round and about the obstacle course of puddles on the river path. Man, it was teeming! But maybe, just maybe, she'd be as crazy. After all, she hadn't run since last weekend.

He was about to head downstairs when a car approached, speeding eastward along Memorial Drive. Standing at the window in anticipation, he watched the car whisk by the runner, splattering him mercilessly, causing him to lose his stride. With that, Ryan Cornell unzipped his jacket and threw it onto the bed.

A floor above, Carly did the same. It was insane. She didn't know why she'd even bothered to dress. The rain hadn't let up for a minute since she'd awoken. No one in his right mind would be running. The muddy yellow jogger she'd seen could have the path to himself. Much as she wanted the exercise, she wasn't *that* mad. Perhaps there was a message somewhere here. She looked heavenward. The weather was only another of the reasons she shouldn't see Ryan.

With a sigh of defeat, she returned to the bathroom to dress properly. Rain or no rain, she would have to go out later. Her refrigerator was nearly empty. There were clothes to be left and retrieved at the dry cleaners'. She had to pick up a few last skeins of silk thread to finish the needlepoint for her father. Not to mention a luncheon date with Sheila and a hair appointment at three. It was a lousy day for all that, but she would manage.

When Ryan knocked on her door, it was late afternoon. He'd spent the day working. Strike that. *Trying* to work. Something had to give. Patience was one thing, masochism another.

Hearing a faint sound from within, he stood straight, knowing that Carly would be looking out to see who was there. When the door slowly opened, he relaxed.

"Hi," he said with a smile, the simple sight of Carly Quinn melting his heart.

"Hello," she answered shyly. Her own heart beat double time.

"Just wanted to return this." He held out the towel she'd tossed him after they'd run on Sunday. "I finally did my laundry. It's clean."

She put a hesitant hand out to take the towel. "I'd forgotten all about it." Not quite the truth. In the back of her mind there had been the subtle awareness that Ryan had something of hers. It had been reassuring. "Thanks."

"My thanks." Not knowing what else to do with them, he stuck his hands in the pockets of his jeans. "Crummy day."

Hugging the towel to her chest, she chuckled. "Tell me. I've been dodging the raindrops all day, what with a million things to do. I feel a little like a drowned rat." Her newly trimmed hair was damp. Her stocking feet hadn't quite dried out.

"You don't look it," Ryan said softly. She was the image of femininity, wearing a pale pink sweater and a plaid skirt of a matching pink and gray. She seemed small and fragile. Once again he felt a surge of protectiveness. And more. With her hair spilling in damp curls to her shoulders and her expression shy, verging on the self-conscious, she was as desirable as she'd ever been. "You look pretty," he whispered.

He didn't look bad himself in his jeans and dark sweater, she decided, before she looked away in sheer self-defense. "Anything inside and reasonably dry looks pretty on a day like this," she murmured. Then, helpless to resist, she looked back up at him. His hair, too, was damp, looking all the more vibrant. "You were out?"

"Uh-huh."

"Working?"

"This morning."

She nodded and swallowed hard. Her insides were astir with something she begrudged but couldn't shake. Ryan was too intense a man to take lightly, too quietly sensual to ignore. Against her will she responded to the heat of his gaze, the headiness of his presence. She swallowed again.

"Ah, hell," he murmured, stepping quickly into her apartment, closing the door behind him and reaching for her before she could think to flee. He whispered her name as his lips opened on hers. Drawing her body against his, he kissed her deeply.

Carly reeled. Given the caution with which he'd approached her in the past, she hadn't expected this suddenness. Yet it was phenomenally exciting, for the need was there in them both. Minutes, hours, days of denial couldn't alter the fact of the raw biological attraction existing between them. And where more rational thoughts might have intervened had there been time, Ryan's aggression took the choice from her hands.

His lips were warm and moist, his tongue a welcome interloper. He was as thirsty as she, drinking of everything she gave, and she gave mindlessly. Her mouth opened to him, her tongue mated eagerly with his. She'd never known such gentle fire, and it seared her with startling force.

"Ah, Carly," Ryan moaned against her cheek when he finally released her to allow for the air both badly needed. "This is what I've wanted all week." His voice was hoarse, the arms strong that circled her and held her, trembling within bounds of steel. He buried his face in her hair and ran splayed hands up and down her back as though to reassure himself that she was there. "I've wanted to talk with you and hold you and kiss you. I've thought about you so much."

Carly's own arms were around his neck, her face tucked against the warmth of his throat, her brow cushioned by the thickness of his beard. She felt light and secure, at home for the first time in years. But she couldn't find the words to echo his. With the ending of his kiss, the choice was hers once more. And she knew for a fact that sensasions of happiness, of security, of homecoming, were cruel and taunting luxuries.

Clinging to the illusion for just a minute longer, she breathed deeply of his cleanly masculine scent. Then, slowly, she lowered her arms to his shoulders and levered herself away.

"You shouldn't," she whispered, eyeing him timidly.

"Shouldn't think of you? Shouldn't want you?" He locked his hands at the small of her back and kept her lower body pressed to his. "Why not?"

"Because I'm not right for you. You're not right for me."

"Are you kidding? After that kiss?"

Pain welled in her eyes. "It's physical, Ryan. That's all."

He was shaking his head before the last word was out. "No, it's not. Well, maybe it is. But the force behind it—that's far from physical. Physical is only the outlet. If you'd spend time with me, work with me, run with me, go out with me, you'd see."

Sadness mixed with pain in her soulful gaze. Looking up at Ryan, she believed what he said. Which made it all so much harder, so much harder. He didn't know who she was. He *couldn't* know who she was. And in that sense she would be forever deceiving him.

Lowering her eyes, she slowly shook her head. When she pushed against his arms, he released her. Turning her back, she silently walked to the window where, staring out at nothingness, she wrapped her arms around her middle. She felt cold and alone, that much worse for the warmth she'd known in Ryan's arms moments before.

"Carly?" His voice came from across the room, then again, more intimately, when he approached. "Carly? What is it?" he asked, directly behind her now. She could feel the heat of him, though he didn't touch her. And she wanted nothing more than to lean back against him, to be enveloped in the safe harbor of his arms once again. When he kissed her, he made her forget. For a split second she wished he would kiss her and never stop.

"Nothing," she said quietly.

"I know better than that." He slid his hand beneath the fall of her waves and lightly worked at the tautness of her neck. "I've seen it, Carly."

She cast a frightened glance over her shoulder. "Seen what?"

"That haunted look in your eyes. And desire." When she jerked her eyes forward again, he simply continued to stroke her neck. She didn't pull away, a fact that gave proof to his words. "You feel it, too. I know you do. But something's holding you back. I saw it on the stairs that day. You wanted me to kiss you, but you were afraid. Then, when we were running and I did kiss you, you opened to me with the same desire you felt just now. Then, too, something came between us as soon as you could think again. What is it?" he asked with such need that she nearly crumbled.

Which was precisely what she feared the most. Surrender. Confession. Discovery. Not that she doubted Ryan's integrity any longer. She trusted him fully. There was no way he could be faking the emotion she saw in his face. But her cover was something for which she'd given up her job, her friends and, in many respects, her family. To spill all to Ryan would be to poke a hole in that cover. She simply couldn't.

Which left her with the pain of deception.

"Tell me, Carly," he pleaded, his voice low and gravelly. Slipping his hand down her back and around her waist, he came to her side and looked down at her. "Is it your husband? Was your love for him such that you feel guilty experiencing something you might have shared with him?"

"No," she said quickly, then hastily qualified herself. "I did love him. Very deeply. Our marriage was something special. But, no, I don't feel guilty."

Ryan pondered her words and the urgent expression she wore. "It's been four years, you said. Has there been someone else since?"

She hugged herself more tightly, as though to ward off the heartrending concern that even now threatened to make her cave in against him. "There was," she said softly, unable to lie.

"Did you love him?"

"Not in the way I loved Ma—Malcolm."

"Then in what way?"

"Peter was a friend. A co-worker."

"A lover?"

She caught in her breath, then released it with a quiet, "No." What she'd felt for Peter hadn't ever approached the romantic, yet given what he'd sacrificed—in large part at her instigation—she felt nearly as attached to his memory as she did to Matthew's.

"Is he still back in San Diego?"

Involuntarily she winced. "No."

"Then he's here?"

"No."

"Are you in touch with him?"

She paused. To tell Ryan the truth, that Peter had died, would make her sound like a walking jinx. Which perhaps she was. But she didn't want to go into that. "No," she said simply, the finality in her voice conveying itself to Ryan, who took a deep breath and hugged her more tightly to his side.

"What about Sam?"

She was taken by surprise, jolted from one arena to another. Her heart pounded. "Sam? What about him?"

"Are you sure he doesn't have a hold on you?"

"Sam's a friend. I told you that. A very good one, but just a friend."

Ryan studied her intently. "So there's no one else. Then why not me?" he asked. "There are so many things I'd like to do with you, things that are awful to do alone. There are plays and new restaurants opening all the time—you still owe me an evening at Locke-Ober's—and there's the North Shore and the Berkshires and the White Mountains—do you ski?" When she shook her head he went quickly on. "I could teach you." He paused on an up note, the look of pain on her face reminding him of what she'd once said about not being free. He couldn't figure it out. "You're human. You have needs and desires just like the rest of us." His mind continued to labor. "Is it . . . a family problem?"

"No."

"Something physical?" He studied her with sudden alarm, the arm at her waist drawing her around to face him. Perhaps she was trying to spare *him* some sort of pain. "Are you sick?"

She looked up blankly. "Sick?"

He completed the circle with his free arm. "You can tell me, Carly," he urged, though torn apart by the thought. "Maybe I can help. If it's a question of limited time—"

"A fatal disease?" For the first time, she laughed aloud, taken with his flair for drama. "Oh God, Ryan, no. I'm fine. It's nothing like that."

"Then what?" he came back instantly, relieved yet as curious as ever. "What could possibly have such a strong hold on you that it would keep you from feeling, from experiencing and enjoying?"

Her humor vanished as quickly as it had come. With her hands resting on Ryan's forearms, she was aware of their strength, as she was of that of his thighs bracing hers, of his chest, his jaw, his personality. He'd kindled a flame and refused to let it die, and her body was in complete accord.

For a minute she simply looked at him, her eyes brimming with an anguished regret. Her voice was little more than a shaky whisper when she finally spoke. "Please, Ryan. Please don't push."

He held her gaze, his deep brown eyes mirroring her anguish. He half wished she would yell at him, demand he mind his own business, bodily kick him out. At least then he might be able to fight. But looking up at him the way she was, that lost doe, cornered and helpless yet wanting so desperately to survive, he couldn't fight her. He couldn't risk hurting her.

Instead, he gave a low moan and brought her against him. His head lowered protectively over hers. His encompassing arms formed a shield against the world. Eyes closed, he held her tightly, wondering whether she would ever take all he wanted to give. No, he couldn't fight her. Not with force at least.

But he was far from defeated. And she was far from immune. Even now he could feel her arms creeping around his waist.

"Okay," he whispered into her hair. "Okay." He kissed her brow, nudging her head back. "It's okay." His lips brushed her eyes, her cheeks, her jaw. "Come sit with me," he breathed against her ear. "Just for a little while. I won't ask for anything you don't want to give."

She slowly shook her head. "It won't work, Ryan. It won't work."

"Why don't we see?" he asked, pressing slow kisses along the line of her jaw. His hands slid forward along her waist, lightly scoring her sides.

"No," she murmured, but her eyes were closed and she had unknowingly tipped her head to the side to allow him access to her neck. When his fingers skimmed the side swells of her breasts, she sucked in her breath. Then the fingers were gone, returned to her waist, leaving her with nothing to fear but frustration.

Framing her face with both of his hands, Ryan tipped it up. "A last kiss, then," he whispered, and took it before she could think. No, he wouldn't force her. He wouldn't ask anything more than she was willing to give. But he'd found the key to that willingness, and he had every intention of using it.

EIGHT

❀❀❀

"YOU NEVER DID TELL ME about that autopsy report," Carly said as they ran the next morning.

"No point," Ryan responded. "It was worthless."

"Didn't show *anything?*"

His teeth gritted, giving his voice an edge. "Nothing conclusive. The warden claims there had been a scuffle in the prison yard two days before Luis died. The medical examiner claims that the bruises on his body could have come from that."

She cast a glance up at his face. "What do you think?"

Only after several pensive strides did he answer. "I think we'll never know."

"And it ends there?"

"It's ended. Oh, hell!" His sneaker hit a puddle, spattering them both. "Maybe this wasn't such a hot idea. It's damn wet underfoot."

"You're just upset," she said softly, dodging a puddle of her own. "Isn't there anything else that can be done?"

"Luis is dead. The prime witness gone. Nothing came from the inmates. Or the guards. It's not surprising."

"But you still suspect foul play?"

"I don't know. If someone feared Luis would spill his gut when his case came to trial, there'd be good reason to have him dead. He may have committed suicide. Then again, he may have been forced into it by a strong enough threat. His mother was the only person he had in the world. If he had to choose between his life and hers. . . ."

Carly tugged her wool hat lower over her ears. It was cold. It had been so warm last weekend, yet today the wind was cutting and the sky was leaden. "I'm sorry," she said at last.

"So am I."

They ran in silence for a while. Carly wondered what she would have done if she'd been a reporter investigating the possibility of foul play. She would have gone to the warden, then to the files. She would have tried to interview convicts and ex-cons and guards and defense attorneys and the commissioner of corrections. Somehow she doubted she would have learned much more than that foul play was not unknown in correctional institutions. But would anything have come of it? Probably not.

Prison was hell. Ryan's Luis had found that out.

After waiting for a week for his lawyer to show, Gary Culbert was impatient. The guard escorted him to a small windowless conference room, then shut the door, leaving him to pace the floor much as he'd done in his cell for what had seemed fifty hours a day since he'd been incarcerated one hundred and thirty-three days before. He took a cigarette from the pack in the pocket of his regulation blue work shirt and hastily lit it.

In the middle of the room stood a weathered wooden table around which three straight-backed chairs were set at odd angles, left carelessly by whomever had been there last. Completing the stark decor was a scratched metal bookshelf, bare of books, as depressing as the rest of the place, he decided with a snort. At least it was quiet here, a break from the incessant echoes of clanking metal doors and bars and voices raised in barely leashed anger.

The door opened and Philip Mancusi entered. A tall, thin man with a receding hairline and wire-rimmed glasses, wearing his usual three-piece suit, he carried himself well, looking the part of the cocksure lawyer to the hilt.

"Gary." He nodded in greeting, then deposited his briefcase on the table along with an overstuffed brown envelope.

"Where the hell have you been? I've been trying to call you all week! In case you haven't noticed, I don't exactly have a princess phone in my cell!"

Mancusi cast a quelling stare over the rims of his glasses, clearly not intimidated by the outburst. "I've been in court," he said casually, seating himself in one of the chairs. "You're not my only client."

"But I'm sure paying you one hell of a lot!"

"And we both know where the money came from." In the silence that hovered, Culbert scowled, but had no further retort. His lawyer proceeded. "Have a seat, Gary."

Angrily flicking his cigarette in the direction of the tin ashtray, Culbert sat. "What's happening? Are you getting me out of here or not?"

"You were convicted of murder," Mancusi reminded him with a steady gaze. "All I can do is take the appeals step by step. You know that. You're a lawyer."

"Was. Was. That's the operative word. My license was revoked—or had you forgotten?"

"No, I haven't forgotten. But all that can be reversed. You can't give up hope."

"I haven't!" Culbert growled, taking a long drag on his cigarette. "It's the only thing I've got left, which is why I sit here wondering what's going on."

"We were denied the formal motion to stay execution of sentence."

No bail. No freedom. There was a silence, then an explosive "Damn it! Why didn't you tell me?"

"The written decision came down from the appellate court the day before yesterday. I thought it better to tell you in person. I've already begun preparing papers to file a motion for a new trial."

"On what grounds?" Culbert shot back.

Mancusi's shrug belied the pinched look around his mouth. "That's what I'm trying to decide. We could always claim that the prosecutor never fully revealed the extent of the promises made to his witness. The argument could be made for excessive temptation."

Culbert was as dubious as his lawyer. "Flimsy. What would our chances be?" It was a rhetorical question. He knew the score. Standing, he paced to the corner, then turned. "I want that new trial, Phil. This place is driving me insane."

"What did you expect?"

Storming the few feet to the table, Culbert put both hands down flat. His eyes were hard. "I expected you to get me off in the first place. That was what you said you could do. That was what I paid you for."

"That was before the state came up with Robyn Hart. She was a good witness."

"She was an ambitious bitch who latched on to a cause and was determined to use it as a stepping stone in her career."

"She's relocated now."

"Yeah." Culbert straightened. "Probably sniffing around in someone else's dirty laundry."

"If there's a new trial, she'll be back," Mancusi warned.

"And you'll just have to try again to show that she was too emotionally involved to be objective. Hell, the woman lost a husband in a fire. Of course she'd want to nail someone." He raised one hand. "Sure, sure, different fire, different city. But she was far from impartial."

"The jury didn't think so."

"Well, we'll have a different jury this time."

"But the same witness. I'm telling you, Gary, it may be tough." His gaze flicked to his papers, then back to Culbert. "There's one possibility we might explore. The guy who died in that last fire—Bradley? If we can show some involvement between him and Hart—"

"Involvement as in sex?" When the other gave an acquiescent shrug, he scowled. "Come on, Phil. How're you gonna do that?"

"There are ways. Vengeance can be a powerful motive in a woman's mind."

"But you said it yourself. She was a good witness. If you couldn't break her regarding her husband, how in the hell are you gonna do it regarding some two-bit photographer?" Breaking into a spasm of coughing, Culbert stubbed out his cigarette.

Mancusi watched his client, one brow raised. "You should give those things up. They're lousy for your health."

"It's this place that's lousy for my health. I'm getting high blood pressure climbing the walls." Calming himself, he sat back. "Without her the state hasn't got much of a case. Any chance she won't testify?"

Mancusi shrugged. "I don't know. If they've relocated her, she's given up a lot. So has the government. I doubt they'd *let* her renege. That was probably part of the deal."

"But if something happened to her, if she couldn't testify for some reason?"

"We'd probably get the case dismissed. Even with the notes she kept, I could make a case against her character. *If* something happened to her. But it depends what that was." He eyed his client cautiously. "Gary, Gary, I wouldn't even think it, if I were you. You're in enough trouble as it is."

"So what have I got to lose?"

"Exams beginning today?" Ryan asked as he and Carly set out on the river path. Though it was cold, the ground had completely dried. The weekend's rain had stripped the trees of the last of their leaves. Winter was on its way.

"Uh-huh. We had review days Monday and yesterday. I think the kids are ready."

"Will they study?"

A facetious laugh slithered from the back of her throat. "I hope so. Most of them will. I'm worried about a couple, though. One of the girls I counsel is rebelling against everything."

"You counsel?"

She nodded. "All of us do."

"Where do you get the time?"

"It's built into the day. I have four counselees. It's not bad."

"What do you do for them?"

"Get to know them. Keep in close touch. Watch for problems. Be on top of them when they occur."

"Hmmph. Sounds different from the guidance counselors I remember as a kid. Seemed like all they did was give summary approval to the courses I wanted to take, write recommendations, shuffle papers."

"Oh, I do my share of that too. But the theory at this kind of school is that the counselor is a friend."

"That was what they said then."

"But it's true. At least here it is, though come to think of it I didn't get a lot from my guidance counselors either. And they were working full-time at it."

"Maybe that was why they failed. You know, the typical middle-level bureaucrat who creates things to fill his time?"

She ran a bit, then smiled up at him and nodded. "Maybe you're right." She sighed. "Anyway, it's different at Rand. I think it works. The teachers are different. They're very dedicated. They genuinely like kids. And care about what happens."

"You do?" he asked, warmly meeting her gaze. He knew there was a reason he'd run at six since Monday. For every bit of time he spent with Carly, he learned—and liked—more about her.

"Yes. I do," she said conclusively.

"I'm glad." His voice lowered. "I'm also glad you decided to run during the week. Any regrets?"

She tossed him a single shy glance. "Sure. Sore muscles."

"You're doing fine, babe. Just fine."

Given the grin he sent her, she had no regrets at all.

On Thursday morning he had something else on his mind. They'd run in the dark to their usual turning point and were headed back as the sky began to pale.

"Just a week till Thanksgiving. It's hard to believe."

Carly didn't find it so hard to believe. Though the past ten days had zipped by, it seemed forever since she'd seen a family face.

"What are your plans?" Ryan asked.

She smiled. "I'll be with my father." She hesitated, on the verge of returning the question. As the days had gone by, as she'd run each morning with Ryan, she'd wondered more about him. She knew so little of his past. One part of her told her she didn't want to know. The less she knew, the less involved she'd be. It was the other part that goaded her on. "How about you? Will you be turkeying?"

"Of course. My brother and I are driving home for the day." Strange, he mused, how the phrase had slipped out. For Thanksgiving's sake, home *was* that grand old house in which he'd grown up. When he'd been married to Alyssa before things had turned sour, when a brood of kids had filled his mind, Thanksgivings had been in Milton.

"Where's home?"

His lips curved wryly. "Funny you should ask."

"I didn't mean—"

He squeezed her arm and chuckled. "No. It's all right. I was just pondering the same question. Home with a capital H."

It was a poignant issue for Carly, yet she hadn't expected such a quandary in Ryan. "Did you find an answer?" she asked softly.

He raised his eyes to the far horizon. "Ultimately I guess it's where family is. Wherever that is. I used to think it was with my wife. Obviously, that's changed. For the holiday, it's back with my parents."

"Where's that?"

"In the Berkshires. The same old house where I grew up."

"Your parents are still there."

"Yup."

"That's nice."

Something in her tone brought his gaze around. "It is. I'd like you to come with me sometime. They're great, my parents."

"And your brother?"

"Well—" he let out a white huff of breath "—Tom is something else. A little wild. But he'll get there. It was his house I lived in before I moved into your building."

"He's not married?"

"Tom? Hell, no. He's a confirmed bachelor. What he *needs* is a woman to calm him down. But at the rate he's going, he'll never find the right one."

"Why not?"

"His taste is lousy."

"Oh." She smirked. "Must have been interesting living there with him."

"He wasn't there, thank God. He spent the year on the west coast."

"What does he do?"

"Do?" He cast a playful glance her way. For whatever differences he had with his brother, an obvious affection existed. "Tom dabbles here and there. He was into stocks and bonds when he, uh, ran into a little trouble."

"What kind of trouble?"

"A minor hassle about some misappropriated funds. Nothing a good criminal lawyer couldn't handle."

"He stole money from clients?"

"No. Just used what he thought to be investment genius to earn his clients a little more. It backfired."

"What happened?"

"There was an out-of-court settlement. He had to pay them back with interest. Nothing he couldn't swing. Actually, the guy *is* a genius. He could probably be successful at any number of things. Maybe I was his problem. He's spent most of his life being unconventional to my conventional."

"But you're close."

"Closer as the years have gone by."

"What's he doing now?"

"He's writing computer software programs. Sitting at home. Working whenever the mood hits. Making a bundle. Like I said, he's a genius."

Amid his pride, Carly heard a total lack of jealousy in his tone. "You wouldn't be happy doing that."

"No." He met her gaze. "Like I said, I'm more conventional. I don't mind the hours I work. I love my job."

They ran together Friday morning, again silently most of the way. It was comfortable and, as Ryan had suggested, invigorating to start the workday this way. Carly felt fresher when she got to school than she had before, though whether the extra energy she felt was due to running or the company she kept she couldn't say.

"You're awfully quiet," she observed when their building came into sight once more.

"Just thinking."

"About?"

"Work. I've got a sticky trial coming up. A libel case."

"Interesting?"

"Very. My client is one of yours. Actually a college professor. He's being denied tenure because of personal differences between himself and one of the most powerful members of the board of trustees."

"Have you got a case?"

"You bet. The trustee was stupid enough to put it all in writing, then pass it around."

"Sounds pat. What's the problem?"

Ryan frowned. "My man isn't the most diplomatic, which is probably what got him in trouble to start with. I'd give anything to keep him off the stand. He's apt to blow it under cross-examination."

"Can you keep him off?"

"I'm gonna try. But the guy insists he wants to speak for himself." He eyed her askance as they ran up the steps. "You know these professorial types. They like to lecture."

Carly nudged him in the ribs and ran ahead to the door, only to be caught in the foyer in a playful embrace.

"What was that for?" Ryan asked. His grin was only half concealed.

"*That* was for taking a swipe at my profession."

She had time to say no more, for Ryan dipped his head and captured her open lips. His kisses were playful at first, warm jabs in deference to the panting bequeathed by their run. As their bodies quieted, though, the kisses grew slower, deeper, stimulating other senses, causing a breathlessness of their own.

When he finally released her lips, he pressed her ear to his heart. Carly's own was thudding at the pleasure of his touch.

"Dinner tomorrow night?" he murmured softly.

Eyes closed, she reveled in his scent, sweaty but all male and terribly arousing. "Umm."

"Eight o'clock?"

"Mmm."

"Great." He set her back, took her hand and led her into the atrium just as she was realizing what she'd done. When she would have drawn back, he only held her hand tighter. She had to scramble to keep up. Passing his own floor, he continued straight up to hers. At her door, he turned to her, placed a fast peck on her cheek and was off.

"Ryan!" she called, leaning over the railing.

He put one long finger against his lips. "Shh. It's a godawful hour. Everyone's sleeping."

"That wasn't fair!" she whispered loudly. "You took advantage of me!"

Directly beneath her, he craned backward against his own railing, grinning broadly. "I warned you."

"You're impossible!"

He shrugged, then disappeared. She leaned farther forward, saw nothing, heard his door open, then close, and knew she was trapped.

* * *

As Saturday evening approached, Carly grew nervous. She hadn't wanted to be involved with a man, at least not on a romantic level, not yet. With Dennis Sharpe or Roger Hailey or any of the other men who'd asked her out, a date might have been a simple evening spent together. Intuitively she knew it would be more than that with Ryan. Ryan turned her on, emotionally and, yes, physically. Just thinking about him sent tremors of excitement through her body, leaving her with a knot of desire deep down low. When she was in his arms she seemed to forget everything. Therein lay the danger.

Bucking the tide of reason that told her to call him or leave a note, to plead a sudden rush of work or even illness, she indulged in a long bath, took special care with her makeup and hair, then spent forever choosing a dress. By seven-thirty she was ready. Ignoring sweaty palms, she sat down at the kitchen table with a pile of half-corrected exams and tried in vain to apply herself. At seven-forty she returned to the bedroom to comb her hair again. At seven-fifty she ran to the living room to make sure she'd laid out the right bag and coat. Back at the kitchen table she cursed herself for having left so much time. When the doorbell rang at seven fifty-five, though, she took it back.

He looked breathtakingly handsome in a suit and tie, his dark hair neatly combed, his brown eyes sparkling. "Hi," he said, his own breath taken by the vision of beauty he beheld. "You look fantastic."

Hand on the doorknob for support, she smiled shyly. "A change from running gear and six-in-the-morning muzzies, eh?"

"You look great then too. This is just different." His eyes glowed their appreciation. In the mornings she'd been fresh and unadorned, sexy in the way women are when they've just rolled out of bed. Now she was sexy in another way. Her makeup was perfect, accenting her high cheekbones and deep-set eyes. Spilling around her shoulders, her hair looked rich and thick, gloriously tempting. Her dress, a subtle plaid of hunter green and plum with a high neck, long cuffs, wide belt and an array of tiny covered buttons from throat to waist, gave an air of regality. The sheerest of stockings, high-heeled pumps. . . . He caught his breath. She stood straight, almost awkwardly, before him and was dressed as conservatively as possible, yet she couldn't have been more alluring if she'd been preening in a slinky off-the-shoulder gown of red silk with a slit up the thigh.

He began to speak, then cleared his throat when his voice emerged hoarse. "Do you have a coat?" His own, a double-breasted navy topcoat, was slung over his arm. He shifted it when she returned to the sofa for her things, helped her on with her coat, let his hands linger on her shoulders for an instant. "You smell good too." His fingers tightened. "What are you trying to do to me, Carly?"

She cast him a half-fearful glance, then was relieved to see his broad white smile. "You were the one who hoodwinked me into this. You can still get out—"

"No, no." He released her shoulders and held up a hand. "I'll gladly suffer." Shrugging into his coat, he found some solace in the admiring nature of her gaze. He offered her an elbow. "Shall we?"

Sliding her arm through his, she wondered just who would be doing the suffering.

As he had promised that first morning, Ryan took her to Locke-Ober's. Standing at the door of the downstairs grill, the men's only room that had been one of the last bastions in Boston to yield to women's liberation, he cast a despairing eye at the crowd. "I made reservations for us here. The atmosphere is more interesting. But it looks as though every politician in town had the same idea. Locke-Ober's is infamous for its gatherings."

The maître d' approached with a broad smile and an outstretched hand. "Mr. Cornell! Good to see you!"

Ryan warmly met his clasp. "Same here, John. But things are pretty busy down here." Even as he spoke, he raised his free hand to acknowledge several acquaintances who sought his eye. "I was hoping for something a little quieter."

"Shall I give a call upstairs?"

"It's more touristy there."

"There may be something in the back room. It's smaller and quieter."

At Ryan's nod of interest, John picked up the phone on his desk. Within minutes they'd climbed the stairs to the upper enclave and were seated at an intimate table for two in a room that was indeed smaller and quieter. Even then they'd had to pass through a larger dining area. Twice Ryan had nodded to familiar faces.

It occurred then to Carly that she was with a person well-known in Boston circles. Previously she'd been with Ryan only in isolation—her apartment, the foyer and atrium, the paths along the river, at bizarre hours, no less. While on the one hand it was flattering to be with a handsome man who obviously had so many friends, on the other it was downright intimidating. Since she'd come to Boston she'd maintained the lowest possible profile. She didn't want that to change.

Eyes downcast, she took a seat as the upstairs maître d' held her chair. Tucking her purse on her lap, she focused on the single rose in its bud vase in the middle of the table. Ryan settled on her right.

"Enjoy your meal, Mr. Cornell, ma'am."

Ryan smiled. "Thank you, Henry." The maître d' moved off, and Ryan turned his gaze to Carly. "Is this okay?" he asked, puzzled by her sudden unease.

Stifling her qualms, she turned to him with a gentle smile. "This is lovely, Ryan." Her eye skimmed the room. "It's a beautiful place."

He nodded, following her gaze. "Old Boston at its best. Locke-Ober's has been a favorite of mine since my parents brought me here when I was sixteen."

"You must come a lot. They all know you." Even then, the wine steward was approaching, wearing a smile of recognition.

"Good evening, Mr. Cornell. How are you tonight, sir?"

"Fine, Gray. Just fine."

"Would you like anything from the bar?"

Ryan sent Carly an assessing glance, "I think we'll order a bottle of wine. A Montrachet will be fine."

Carly noted that he refrained from pronouncing either of the *t*'s in his extravagant choice of wines.

Where she felt awkward, though, the wine steward did not. "An excellent choice, sir," he said with a broad smile, and left.

Ryan's eyes were on Carly. Strangely though, he seemed content just to look. Or maybe it was that for the life of him he couldn't think of anything he wanted to say.

Carly was no better. She returned his gaze, then looked down, then across the room at the other diners. They were a well-dressed lot, exhibiting proper decorum to match their attire. Conversation was kept at a low hum.

"So you've never—"

"So you often—"

They looked at each other and laughed. "You first," Ryan said.

Carly blushed. "It wasn't important. What were you going to say?"

"I was going to say that I'm pleased to be the first one to bring you here. Have you been around much since you arrived in Boston?"

"I've seen more of Cambridge—the restaurants, that is. Closer to school and all."

He wondered whom she'd been with but refrained from asking. Instead he just nodded.

She fingered the edge of the thick linen tablecloth. "You came into Boston often as a boy?"

"My parents believed in culture. They took us all over, wanted us to know everything about the city, even though we were always very happy to go home again."

"Yet you decided to settle in the city."

"The opportunities for a law practice were better here than they would have been in the Berkshires. And then when I married . . . well, it all made sense."

She wondered about his marriage, but refrained from asking. "Have you ever regretted it—settling in the city?"

"No. I like the city. And Boston is more manageable than some. Not too big, not too small, lots going on." When she chuckled, he tipped his head in an endearing gesture of uncertainty. "No?"

"Oh, yes. I was just thinking that those were some of the same reasons I chose Boston." Instantly she regretted her choice of words. To her relief Ryan took them at surface value.

"Why did you? I mean, why did you decide to leave San Diego?" He'd wondered about it more than once. She'd said that her husband—Matthew, or was it Malcolm, he frowned, confused—had died four years before. And her family was from the mid-West—Des Moines, she'd told him in a breezy reference during one of their morning runs. "Was it because of Peter?"

It took Carly a minute to get her bearings. It was so hard vacillating between Carly and Robyn. When she was with Ryan, she wished Robyn had never existed.

"No." She met his gaze as levelly as she could. "I just wanted a change. When the opening at Rand came up, it seemed perfect."

"But you'd looked into various areas?"

"To settle? Yes."

"I'm glad you chose Boston."

"So am I," she conceded softly.

The effect of their eyes locking was warm — too warm — yet Carly couldn't look away. The steward's arrival with their wine was some diversion, as was the subsequent arrival of their waiter with menus. It was only after they'd ordered that the silence set in again.

Ryan sipped his wine. Carly did the same. She felt his presence through every fiber of her being. Even as she cursed herself for being conned into this dinner, she knew that she hadn't put up much of a fight. What she *really* wanted was to be even closer to Ryan.

As though attuned to her thoughts, Ryan took her hand from the fork she was nervously fingering and held it in his. He ran his thumb over her knuckles, caressing her fingers, polishing the gold of her wedding band in a way that should have been sacrilegious but seemed all the more intimate.

"You're not sorry you've come, are you? You seem uncomfortable."

She could feel her heart thudding. "No. I'm. . . ." But she didn't know what to say. Uncomfortable seemed wrong, yet awkward or confused or excited or frightened seemed no better.

He brought her hand to his mouth. The soft bristle of his beard was as stimulating as the light brush of his lips. "Don't be, Carly. Please. I want you to enjoy yourself."

"I am."

"You're shaking."

She gave a half smile. "You're kissing me." That said it all.

Ryan laughed softly, a deep, rolling sound from his throat. "Not the way I'd like to," he said, then lowered her hand to the table, keeping it tucked in his. He took a deep breath. "Tell me about your childhood," he began, determined to put her at ease. "I can picture a little girl with curls all over her head, wearing pink tights and ruffles up to her chin."

It was Carly's turn to laugh, indeed more easily. "Not quite. I was a tomboy."

"You're kidding."

"No. I had three older brothers. It was a matter of survival."

"Were they close to you in age?"

"Pretty much so. We were each two years apart. I was the last." She smiled. "After me, I think my parents gave up on sweet little quiet things."

"Must have been some household."

"It was." Her smile warmed with memory. "We had a lot of fun. My brothers decided early that I was just another one of the guys. They led me into more than my share of mischief." Her eye fell on Ryan's hand holding hers and she recalled one brother holding her hand, inching her up the old elm tree from which she'd been able to descend only with the help of the firemen, another brother holding her hand, tugging her through a maze of gravestones at dusk, a third brother holding her hand, pulling her to their hideout in the crawlspace beneath the house. Ryan's hand was different, though. His fingers were long, strong but gentle. Soft dark hairs were sprinkled on richly bronzed skin, peering from the crisp white cuff that edged beyond his navy jacket. His hand was that of a man, and she was mesmerized by it as she never had been by her brothers'.

"But your parents held up fine."

She shook off her thoughts. "They loved it. Not that there wasn't a load of yelling and screaming. It seemed that my mother had no sooner washed the kitchen floor than one of us needed drinks for the bunch. Do you know what it's like for a five-year-old to try to juggle four glasses of grape juice? Or what it's like when even one of those glasses spills?"

Ryan chuckled. "Grape juice? I can imagine. Your mother must have had her work cut out for her."

"She did," Carly said more softly. "Poor woman. It wasn't until after she died that we got a housekeeper."

His hand tightened. She had never spoken of her mother before. She had only mentioned her father when she'd talked of Thanksgiving. Though there had always been the possibility of divorce, Ryan had more or less assumed her mother had died. "How old were you when it happened?"

"I was twelve."

He winced. "It must have been very hard."

"Yes. We'd all been pretty happy-go-lucky children. Our parents had provided a warm, loving home. Nothing could go wrong—until it did. It was a shock."

"Very sudden."

"Uh-huh." She gave a sad laugh. "Quieted me down some, I can tell you that."

He ached for her as he had when she'd told him about her husband. "No more tomboy?"

"No. I suppose it was about time anyway. I was—" she made a gesture with her free hand and blushed "—growing up."

He admired the blush, his suggestive gaze fueling it. "I bet you had a line of suitors to keep your brothers jealous."

"Not quite. I started to study and spent hours reading in my room. I suppose that was the beginning of my interest in literature. And writing. I kept a journal. It was an outlet."

Imagining the pain she must have felt with her mother gone and in a household of men at such a critical point in her development as a woman, Ryan wanted to take her in his arms and comfort her. Something in her expression, though, defied pity. She was proud. And self-sufficient—from the start he'd been aware of her self-containment. Now he could begin to understand its roots.

He was about to speak when a couple that had entered the room moments before detoured to their table. The man was tall, bespectacled and distinguished looking. The woman was striking. As a pair they had an intensity that struck an immediate chord in Carly.

When Ryan stood to make the introductions, she felt an irrational discomfort. It was one thing to have him merely nod at acquaintances as they passed, another to hear her name on his lips, spoken softly but clearly, announcing to the world who she was. Swallowing her deepest of fears, she managed to smile and return the warm greeting she was offered. Even as the couple had moved off she was chiding herself for her sensitivity. There was no possible way that anyone could recognize her. Surely she had only imagined that the woman had eyed her particularly closely.

Ryan's soft elaboration on their identities did nothing to ease her mind. "Mark is the executive producer of the evening news on Channel 4. Jennifer is his star attraction."

"She's a reporter," Carly stated, her voice miraculously warm, given the ice suddenly flowing through her veins.

"A good one. And a nice person at that. Some of them are impossible. Pushy and totally egocentric. Jennifer is different. I like her."

Quite unexpectedly, it was Ryan's praise that gave Carly a viable reason for the woman's interest in her. Jealousy, curiosity—either would do. "She likes you too," she said, much relieved. "Have you ever dated her?"

Ryan leaned closer, his voice low, if animated. "Dated Jennifer Blayne? Are you kidding?"

"I thought you said you liked her."

"I do. But liking her is one thing, wanting a relationship with her another. She's not my type at all."

"What is your type?" Carly asked on impulse.

His gaze didn't waver. "A woman who has time for me, for one thing. Jennifer has a career to attend to."

"Don't we all?"

He arched a dark brow. "There are careers . . . and there are careers. For women like Jennifer, a career is the be-all and end-all. Oh, they're fun to be with, I suppose. But I, for one, could never compete with a career that demands that kind of commitment."

"Do I detect a trace of chauvinism?" she couldn't help but tease.

"You bet you do," he countered, undaunted. "And I'm not ashamed of it. At least I recognize what I need. It may not be right, but it's a fact. I respect women like Jennifer. But my type—the type that really turns me on—is softer, more private, more home-oriented. She's interesting and may have a successful career of her own, but there's room for more. She needs me." He held her gaze with a force that nearly stole her breath. "She needs me more than she needs any other person on earth."

Once again Carly's heart was drumming. This time it was the arrival of their meal that softened the edge, steering conversation to a lighter track. Startled by his own intensity, Ryan shook himself out of it by making small talk about the food and the restaurant, relating anecdotes of times he'd been there before. Then he asked Carly about her exams. In turn she pumped him for information on his libel case. With the earlier discussion temporarily shelved, each seemed to take as much interest in hearing the other speak as in speaking.

Drawn into the web of Ryan's congeniality, Carly enjoyed herself. The food was delicious, the wine superb, and Ryan was as attentive a companion as she might have dreamed.

As they ate and talked, though, she had the uncanny sensation of being watched. She ignored it at first. But when she dared cast a glance to the side of the room where Jennifer Blayne was seated, she imagined the woman looked quickly away. It was in a second such glance that Carly's eye caught at another table, another woman. This one didn't look away. Another admirer of Ryan's, Carly wondered? But this one was different. Darker, more serious looking, attractive, but in an ultrapolished kind of way. . . .

"Is something wrong?" Ryan asked, turning his head to follow Carly's gaze. When he turned back, his expression was placid.

"She's staring. Even now. Do you know her?"

"Uh-huh," he said calmly. "She's my ex-wife."

NINE

❀❀❀

C ARLY'S GAZE SWUNG TO RYAN. "Your ex-wife?"

"Uh-huh."

"Oh." She clamped her jaw shut.

Ryan grinned mischievously. "Is that all you have to say?"

She shrugged. "What else should I say?" Her gaze slid back to the woman. "She's stunning."

"Uh-huh."

"So's the man she's with."

"I hadn't noticed."

"Then you don't care?"

Ryan's good humor ran deep. With Carly by his side, he felt perfect. "We're divorced. Alyssa can do whatever she wants with whoever she wants. If you're looking for jealousy, you're in for a disappointment."

"How about curiosity? Aren't you that teeny bit curious about who she's with?"

"I'm sure I'll find out. She'll be over here in a minute."

"She will?"

At Carly's sudden look of dismay, Ryan grinned. "Alyssa is the one who's curious. That's why she's been staring at you. Social climbing is her speciality, gossip an integral part of that. Right about now she's wondering who you are, where you come from, whether you've got a pedigree and who she'll call first when she gets home."

She sounded precisely like the kind of person Carly could do without. "Doesn't that bother you?" she asked, put out that she seemed to be the only one to feel annoyed. "I'd think you'd resent it."

"I might have at one time." Since he'd met Carly—was it only two weeks ago?—he realized all he'd been missing. With Carly he could talk about anything and everything, knowing she cared. He felt closer to her than he had to anyone in years. Remarkable, given the questions that still lurked in his mind.

"You're right," Carly muttered, straightening. "Here she comes."

Ryan squeezed her hand. "Relax. She won't bite. She's all talk."

That was what bothered Carly. Nonetheless, she gathered her composure and produced a smile when the other woman and her companion arrived at their table. Again Ryan stood to make the introductions. Again Carly felt a sense of unease when the couple left. It wasn't that she was ashamed to be with Ryan. On the contrary. Even with Alyssa Cornell standing not three feet from her, Carly felt proud and confident. No, embarrassment was nowhere in the picture. What bothered her was her own visibility. It was good for her, she could hear Sam Loomis saying. There was nothing to fear, nothing to fear. Why, then, did she half expect the evening to be topped off with a photographer popping up to take pictures to splash all over the local rag?

"There, that wasn't so bad," Ryan said when they were alone once again. His eyes toasted her, boosting her spirits some.

"She seems nice enough."

"She is."

"Then what happened?" Instantly she blushed. "I'm sorry. That was inexcusable. It's none of my business."

"I don't mind," he replied softly. "I'd be disappointed if you didn't ask. Alyssa and I just went in different directions. That's all."

"You must have loved her once." She couldn't imagine his having married without that—not Ryan, who seemed to have so much to give.

"I did. When we were first married I thought she was the next best thing to a hard-fought first-degree murder conviction."

Something in the crooked tilt to his mouth spurred Carly on. "And?"

"That was just it. She was the next best thing. Only the next best thing. My work came first. She couldn't accept that. And I don't blame her," he added with a sigh. For the first time that evening he seemed troubled. He lifted his wineglass, drained its remaining drops, put the glass down and studied its slender stem. "I guess I'm no better than a Jennifer Blayne."

"In what sense?"

"My work has always been my life. My career really is the be-all and end-all."

"I don't believe that for a minute, Ryan," Carly chided with a conviction that astonished even her. "I've heard you talk of too many other things, and with feeling. If the law came between you and Alyssa, there had to be something amiss in your relationship from the start."

Ryan raised his eyes to hers. "I suppose there was. When I first met Alyssa, she was quiet and agreeable. Her father was a very wealthy man, as well as an autocrat. She'd been pretty much dominated through life, but she had definite ideas of what she wanted."

"Which was?"

His words flowed. He hadn't shared his feelings so honestly before, and there was a strange relief in it. "A husband who, with the help of her money, would sit back, work part-time, spend every free minute with her. She desperately wanted love." He took a breath. "Unfortunately, when the honeymoon was over and she realized that I intended to work, she felt cheated."

"Didn't she go off on her own — I mean, find things to keep herself busy?"

"If only. No, her solution was to try harder. She was constantly in the office expecting a three-hour lunch. Or she was picking me up from work, taking me to one engagement or another. Or she made plans for the two of us to join a bunch of others for the weekend in New York or a week in the Bahamas.

"It became impossible. I was trying to build my practice, needing to work every free minute, and she fought me every step of the way." His lips thinned. "I tried to give her everything she wanted. Bought her a huge house in Milton. A Mercedes. A fur coat. And since I refused to take the money her father offered, I had an excuse to work all the harder. Then she wanted to have children."

"Didn't you?"

"Oh, yes. Very much." His eyes lit at that particular dream, then dimmed. "But for different reasons than Alyssa's." At Carly's questioning gaze, he explained. "I've always loved kids. Often when we went to friends' houses, I found the kids more interesting than their parents. Alyssa wasn't dumb. She sensed it. She hoped a child would keep me home more. So we tried. And things went from bad to worse. When she didn't become pregnant, she compensated by clinging all the more. Finally she conceived. In her fourth month she miscarried." He stopped talking then and stared darkly at the table.

Carly put her hand on his. "I'm sorry, Ryan."

He turned his palm up to twine her fingers in his, studied them, then shrugged. "Maybe it was for the best. We had so many differences. Her possessiveness was doing to me what my work was doing to her. It was mutual overkill. Things went downhill from there. I started working all the harder. Gradually she withdrew. From me, at least. Alyssa is, above all else, a very social being."

"And you're not?"

"Not in the same sense. Alyssa's life is a show. It's her place in society that gives her pleasure. I don't care about that. I like being with people purely for the enjoyment of it. If the company I keep is boring, I want out."

"There's nothing wrong with that."

"If you're married to Alyssa, there is. Toward the end it was a constant struggle. Our final parting was remarkably amicable, a relief on both sides. I think she's much happier now."

"And you?"

He looked her in the eye. "Right now? Without a doubt."

"In general," she prompted.

His gaze grew melancholy. "Yes, I'm happier. Which isn't to say that I don't want a wife and family. I want those more than anything. It's just that now I've got my eyes wide open. There's more to happiness than the mere fact of family life. It's the quality of that family life that's important. Come to think of it, marriage is almost inconsequential. It's who you're with that counts." He quirked a sudden smile. "Wanna come live with me and have my kids?"

"Ryan," she chided, "you're awful. If you go around asking women questions like that, you're apt to find yourself in a worse mess than you were in before."

"But I'm serious."

"You're not. You barely know me."

"I like what I see."

"You don't know the half."

"Which is why we should live together for a while. Hey—" his eyes sparkled "—I've got a great idea. We could cut through my apartment's ceiling, put in a spiral staircase and have a big place for ourselves."

Carly smiled. "You don't even own your place yet."

"But I will. The Amidons are sure to find something in Florida. It's just a matter of time."

"Then why don't we wait," she teased with a goodnatured crinkle of her nose. "There's no rush."

"No rush? Hell, I'm pushing forty. You may have time. I don't." As though to make his point, he signaled for the waiter. Within seconds he'd ordered dessert to go. Then he turned back to Carly. "Let's get out of here. I think I've about had it with the public eye for one night. Besides, I have to show you what a mean cup of coffee I make. Maybe that'll convince you."

"Don't hold your breath," she scoffed. But it was her breath being held when they entered his apartment half an hour later. Ryan disappeared into the kitchen to dispense their dessert while she looked around his home. "This is nice," she commented when he returned to place two plates on the coffee table.

"It's okay," he shrugged. "A little staid."

"No, it's fine."

He stood straight and looked around. "Maybe it's that it's not mine. I don't feel at home."

She knew what he meant. The furnishings were pleasant and in good condition, but more befitting the Amidons than Ryan.

"Anyway," he went on, "it serves my purpose. Everything's here, if a little bland."

Carly was intrigued. "What would you do if it were yours?"

"Get rid of pea green, for one thing," he stated with his hands on his hips. "It needs character. I'd start with something vivid on the walls. Maybe burgundy . . . or navy."

"Paint the walls navy?" she asked.

"No, no. Art. Something bold and contemporary. I'd throw a rya rug on the floor, chuck those curtains for Levolors to pick up one of the other colors, replace the sofa and chairs with endless sectionals, put a tree over here—"

"A tree?"

"Sure. It'd add life, no?"

She couldn't suppress a chuckle. "That it would."

"Well?" He turned to her expectantly. "What do you think? How would it all look?"

"Interesting."

"You don't like it."

"I do. I do."

"Say that again," he said more quietly, thoughts of decorating fast fleeing from his mind. He came to stand before her.

"I do," she murmured, the softest expression on her face as she was caught up in his web of enchantment.

Wrapping his arms around her waist, he drew her into his kiss. His lips were warm and inviting, pleading for an acceptance she didn't have the strength to deny. It seemed the entire evening had led to this moment; she'd been lost from the instant he'd shown up at her door. Aloof and reserved? Poised and in control? No longer. Carly felt that she was a tree in springtime, coming alive, blossoming in his arms.

When he suddenly bent over and swept her off her feet, she felt a vague inkling of fear. "Ryan," she whispered, clinging helplessly to his neck, "what are you doing?"

"Carrying you off," he murmured, setting her half reclining on the sofa, resuming his kiss before she could protest. Her inkling of fear dissolved into pleasure. There seemed no finer dessert than Ryan's warm lips, his moist tongue, the hands that firmly held her face, the strong body hovering very, very near.

She returned his kiss with a taste of the excitement that shot through her body. Long-dormant desire flared. She basked in the luxury of it. When he pulled back and sat up, she moaned in soft protest. Eyes holding hers, he shrugged out of his coat and unknotted his tie. In fascination she watched him release the first few buttons of his shirt. Then he lifted her, shifted her, until she sat sideways on his lap.

"You're lovely," he murmured as his head lowered, and then he was drugging her further, honing her senses, heating her blood.

Her breath came in short gasps. She felt his hands on her back, caressing her. Her own grew more bold, slipping forward to his chest, charting its manly contours. From the first, Ryan had inspired her curiosity. And she'd fought it. To some extent she still did. But the lure of his body, magnificent as far as she'd seen it, was too much. She wanted, she needed, to know his virile shape.

When his hands touched her breasts she cried out. Her body responded; it seemed she'd been waiting forever for his touch. It had been so long since . . . since. But she hadn't missed a thing until she'd met Ryan. He alone had the power to ignite her senses and stir her to action.

Leaning forward, she put her lips to his throat and placed small, seeking kisses against its racing pulse. He tasted fresh and clean. Swept up in a realm of glorious sensation, she inched lower. Fine hairs began where his shirt parted. Her mouth explored their texture, sampling him with barely leashed hunger. His skin bore a faintly musky smell, very healthy, very male. Eyes closed, she savored it, breathing deeply, losing herself. After everything she'd lived with—and without—for too many years, this sensual delirium was heaven.

"Oh, babe," Ryan groaned thickly, burying his face in her hair. It seemed he'd been waiting forever to touch her this way. His hands roamed in ardent progression, leaving her breasts to trace the curve of her hips and thighs, returning to learn more of her womanly grace. He found her nipples hard even through the material shielding them. Encouraged by her small whimpers, he rubbed them with his thumbs. "God, I need you," he rasped. "You're so special, so special. . . ."

Consumed by the pleasure of the moment, Carly barely heard his words. Never in her life had she known this kind of fire. She'd been a virgin when she'd come to Matthew, and he'd been her teacher, her mentor in every sense. He'd acquainted her with her body and its capabilities, yet he'd always seemed older, more knowing than she was. As lovely as it was, there had been something one-sided about their lovemaking; Matthew had been the masterful leader, Robyn the delighted follower.

It was Ryan who sought her as a partner, an equal. His intense need fueled the flame that drove her on.

Pressing kisses to his chest, she released first one button, then another and another, until his shirt was open to his waist. Tugging his shirttail from his pants, he watched, entranced, as she slid the last button from its hole and gave her fingers access to his flesh. They wandered restlessly, delighting in discovery. She spread her palms over an expanse of firm muscle, moving them in erotic circles while her mind spun dizzily. His ribs expanded with each labored breath; his stomach was lean and hard. The pelt of hair, broader, then tapering, lured her senses again and again in agonizing temptation.

Ryan needed her; her touch set him afire, sending live currents to a gathering point in his groin. In a bid to ease the ache, he shifted her to her back and moved down over her. When her arms encircled him, he held himself on an elbow and impatiently tackled the small buttons at her throat with his free hand.

Hot and constricted, tormented by desire, Carly welcomed the air that met her flesh. She arched closer to Ryan, seeking the feel of his hard length against her, simultaneously shocked and exhilarated by his throbbing, his outer show of all she felt inside.

Breathlessly she cried his name, only vaguely aware that her dress lay half open, though she was acutely conscious of the hands that forayed within its soft wool folds. His strong fingers were electric, sizzling her breasts, her ribs, her waist. Then he lowered his mouth and nibbled hungrily at her flesh, whispering her name, lifting her higher.

Greed surfaced; he couldn't get enough of her. His lips savaged the silk of her bra, the lace at its top, finally the turgid bud at the center of her breast. In unison they moaned, Carly as wild with need as he. His fingers fumbled with her bra's front catch, released it, peeled the fabric to either side. He buried his head between her breasts, turning it this way and that as though to devour all of her at once.

The brush of his beard against her flesh was new and infinitely arousing to Carly. Thrusting her fingers into his hair, she urged him on, seeking to ease her ache. But there was only fire, and it raged hotter. When his mouth closed over her nipple she cried out, then sobbed softly as the tip of his tongue pebbled it and his teeth took it ever so devastatingly in fever-provoking love play. Her hips began to move, undulating in instinctive response to his tentative thrusts.

"Ryan! My, God!" she whimpered, each shuddering breath feeding the flame.

His rasping response fanned it all the more. "Oh, babe!"

Displaced by gentle writhings, Carly's skirt was wrapped high around her thighs. Angling himself just enough, Ryan slid a hand beneath it, along the silken expanse leading home. Arriving with precision, he shaped his palm to her, groaning his desire when she bent her knee in welcome.

His vibrant caress, though, provided only brief solace. Aroused to a state of near oblivion, she strained against him, needing far more than even the thinnest silk bonds allowed. When he sought the waistband of her panty hose, she sucked in her stomach to show him the way. He needed little guidance. Her heat was a potent beacon. His fingers drew tiny circles on her skin, working downward, probing deeper.

Carly squeezed her eyes shut and gasped. Then, while her pulse raced out of control, he opened her, found her moisture and began to stroke it.

Suddenly she was scorched. Flames surrounded her. She could barely breathe.

Reacting as one being burned alive, she stiffened. Images from the past arose with a raging vengeance, a red-hot conflagration threatening to engulf her. In a panic, she grabbed fistfuls of his hair to pull him away, then screamed in utter terror.

"No! No! My God, don't!"

Ryan went rigid. His breath came in great gasps. His head brought painfully up by the force of Carly's hands, he stared down at her, uncomprehending at first, then disbelieving, then with a stark terror of his own. Her eyes were wide, panic filled, unfocused and sightless. She was in another world, another time, experiencing an abject horror that stabbed his gut with ice.

"Carly?" he whispered hoarsely. "Carly! It's me. It's Ryan. *Carly!*" Frantic at the sight of such raw pain, he only knew he had to get her back. His hand trembled as he lifted it to stroke her cheek. "It's all right, Carly," he murmured shakily. "It's all right."

Her eyes shifted to his then, and she blinked. Tiny creases puckered her brow. Her fingers slowly released his hair. Her hands fell to his shoulders. She swallowed hard.

Yes, there'd been fire. First from Ryan's heat, then, in a flashback so startlingly intense that her skin felt blistered. But there was more. There had to be. A deepseated fear of closeness, of commitment. A subconscious realization that, after months of hiding, years of avoiding intimacy, she *just wasn't ready.*

Helplessly she began to shiver. Her eyes filled with tears and Ryan thought he'd die. Sitting up, he took her into his arms and held her tightly, burying her face against his chest, absorbing the silent sobs that shook her. She felt chilled to the bone now, a far cry from the heat of moments before. Heartsick, Ryan could only hope to share his warmth.

"It's all right, sweetheart," he murmured, the ache of unfulfillment quickly forgotten. He rocked her ever so slowly and pressed his cheek to her hair. He didn't try to caress her, simply offered his best shot at comfort.

It worked. Her tears slowed, then stopped. She sniffled and eased herself back from him, chin tucked low, fists clutched knuckle to knuckle holding her dress closed.

"I'm sorry," she whispered raggedly. "So sorry. . . ." She shook her head in dismay, but a strong finger tipped it up.

"Don't be," Ryan said, holding her moist gaze with the gentleness echoed in his voice. "It's all right. You were frightened. That's all. Maybe it happened too fast." Even as he said the words, he knew they were simplistic. She wasn't a virgin, and nothing she'd ever said had led him to suspect that her husband had mistreated her in any way. But he'd seen that distant look in her eyes— and not for the first time. He wondered if she'd been raped, perhaps recently. Yet he couldn't make himself ask.

She lowered her eyes. "Too fast. It was. I wasn't prepared." But that, too, was false. He had felt her body's most intimate response. Still he didn't argue. "I didn't expect. . . ."

Her words trailed off, and she shuddered with the aftershock of terror that shot through her. No, she hadn't expected it. She wouldn't have believed it possible for the past to intrude that way. Well, she'd told Ryan that he didn't know half of it. Maybe now he'd think twice before pursuing her.

It didn't quite work that way. Later that night, lying sprawled in his bed, his arms pillowing his head, Ryan ran through the events of the evening. With the exception of that final debacle, it had all been wonderful. He'd been proud to be with Carly at the restaurant. He'd enjoyed her company from the first. She was warm and receptive, interesting and interested, poised, playful and very, very pretty.

And she had a past. But he'd known that. She'd warned him at the start when she'd said she wasn't free. He hadn't been discouraged then; he wasn't discouraged now.

With a smile he recalled how gallantly she'd pulled herself together after what had happened on the couch. Her struggle had been obvious. But she'd done it. She'd adjusted her clothing as he'd watched, had finger-combed her hair and, blushing, swiped at the last of the tears on her cheeks. She hadn't moved far from him, as though she truly wanted to stay. Miraculously they'd even eaten the dessert that had been witness to their sensual disaster. Disaster? Hell, no. Right up to that last heart-wrenching moment, she'd been his ideal. She still was. If there were hang-ups to overcome, they'd do it together. For the battle, their relationship would be that much more precious.

For a moment he frowned. Was he a starry-eyed idealist, recklessly dreaming dreams destined never to come true? Perhaps, he admitted with a hard swallow. But he couldn't deny the dreams any more than he could deny his feelings. Carly Quinn had a place in his future. He'd find that place, or be damned.

One floor above, Carly lay pondering many of the very same issues. She flipped restlessly from side to side, finally switching on the light and going into the bathroom for a drink of water. Above the sink, the mirror reflected her image. She stood and stared, amazed at how different she looked without the contacts that turned her blue eyes gray. She rarely removed them; they were long-wearing lenses. But the evening's tears had irritated her eyes and she hoped to give them a rest.

Smoothing her hair back from her cheeks with a hand at either side, she studied those vivid blue eyes with which she'd faced the world for more than twenty-nine years. Strange sensations stirred within. She felt momentarily suspended, caught between two worlds. In the mirror was Robyn, so familiar yet distant. She let her hair fall back into waves. Here was Carly, newer, yet with definite merit.

With a frown, she turned from the mirror, padded back to bed and switched off the light. Her problem, she decided, was in trying to cling to Robyn. As usual, Sam was right. She couldn't be both. She had to release the past. But it was easier said than done.

Realizing she hadn't taken her drink, she bobbed up and flicked the light back on, grabbed a pair of oversize tortoiseshell glasses from the nightstand and put them on, then headed for the kitchen this time and warmed a cup of milk in hopes that it would help her relax. Her mind and her body were too keyed up to sleep. Perversely she put the blame on Ryan's coffee, which, as he'd promised, had been good enough for seconds.

She returned to bed with the cup of milk in hand, propped herself against the pillows and sipped the warm liquid. But her thoughts remained jumbled and, try as she might, she couldn't chase the furrows from her brow.

Sensing that sleep was a long way off, she reached for her needlepoint, a new canvas she'd bought just that morning, and spread it flat on the bed. It was a simple scene, an abstraction of whites and browns, blues and grays, a modern depiction of what she imagined to be a typical New England winter. She wasn't quite sure why she'd fallen for the scene. In the past she'd preferred warmer ones, such as the wheat field of gold she'd just finished for her father, or more vivid tones, such as those splashing from the multitude of pillows in her bedroom, or canvases with elaborate detail, such as those with the intertwining of family members' names that she'd given in past years to each of her brothers.

Her glasses slid down her nose. Absently pushing them up, she studied the new piece. It was more calm, more peaceful. It appealed to her need for serenity, perhaps represented a certain acclimatization. What little she'd seen of New England she liked; perhaps it would truly be home one day.

Threading her needle with a strand of steel gray Persian wool, she began working on the roof of the free-form cabin in the woods and imagined it done up inside with bold burgundys or navys, with sectionals from wall to wall, with rya rugs on the floors, and, yes, a tall fig tree at the window facing south.

Sighing in exasperation at the direction of her thoughts, she put the canvas down in her lap and looked up. Ryan's face was foremost in her mind, and with it a world of conflicting emotions. Biting her lip, she raised canvas and needle and applied another diagonal row of stitches, tore half of them out when she realized the tension of the wool was uneven, then dropped the work again and stared at the far wall in frustration. Rolling the canvas loosely, she leaned over to toss it into its basket. Her glasses clattered to the nightstand. She flipped the light off.

Forty minutes later, it was on again and Carly was sitting in the middle of her bed, emotionally exhausted but unable to sleep. Her mind was in a state of turmoil—*I want him, I want him not, I need him, I need him not. How can I, how can I, especially after what happened tonight?* One minute she rued the day she'd met him, the next she saw him as the bright light of her life.

With a small cry of confusion, she abandoned bed once more, to seek a measure of peace beneath the pulsating spray of a warm shower. It was, without doubt, relaxing. She stretched, rolled her head around, hoping to ease tension's grip, and felt generally better when she turned the water off.

Sleep came quickly after that, but it was shallow and troubled. Twice she awoke to squint at the clock. The third time, it was nearly dawn and she found herself tangled in the bedsheets in a cold sweat, with the tail end of an all-too-familiar nightmare horrifyingly fresh in her mind.

Sitting bolt upright, she switched on the light and tried to catch her breath. Fire. So often fire. In one dream she was in its midst; in another, the victim was someone she loved and she stood helplessly outside the flames, screaming, straining at hands that held her, fearing that it had all been her fault, her fault. She didn't need a psychiatrist to find hidden meanings. It was all very obvious.

Eyes wide, pulse racing, she gave a groan of defeat and got out of bed. She doubted she'd sleep now; it was starting to get light. To lie in bed would only mean further annoyance. Far better to wash up and *do* something, she decided. After all, it was Sunday. She'd nap later.

With her contacts in place once more and a fresh cup of decaffeinated coffee—the last thing her overactive nerves needed was stimulation—she sat on the livingroom couch with a stack of exams to correct. She soon put them down, though, for concentration eluded her. Fetching the needlepoint from the bedroom, she began to work.

Yes, it was Sunday. She wondered if she should run, if Ryan would be expecting her. Probably not, after last night, though he'd been ever so kind with a kiss to her brow when he'd finally returned her to her apartment. She wasn't sure if she could face him again.

It was nearly eight-thirty when the soft knock came at her door. Curled in the corner of her sofa with the needlepoint crushed beneath one limp arm, she barely stirred. Exhaustion had taken its toll. When the knock came again, she slowly emerged from the deep sleep that had eluded her through the night. Stretching, she opened one eye, then both. She raised her head, tried to place what it was that had disturbed her, shot a guarded glance at the door. Heart pounding, she jumped up, then paused, hoping she wasn't right in her assumption. Perhaps he'd simply go away if she didn't answer.

Tiptoeing to the door, she peered through the tiny viewer, then closed her eyes and rested her forehead against the cold white metal. True, she could play the coward now, but sooner or later she'd have to face him.

Slowly she opened the door to look up at him. Dressed for running, he wore a long-sleeved all-weather suit. He held a wool cap and gloves in his hand.

He smiled cautiously. His voice was soft. "Hi." Then he took in her rumpled hair, the redness on her cheeks, the hint of grogginess in her eyes, and his smile faded. "I woke you. God, I'm sorry."

When she would have denied his charge, she couldn't. "It's all right." Nervously she tucked a handful of wayward curls behind her ear. "I should have gotten up to run. You, uh, you weren't waiting, were you?"

"I was late myself. I thought I might have missed you." He studied her too closely for comfort. "You look tired. Didn't sleep well?"

Three hours? Maybe four? She averted her gaze. "No."

"Listen, I'm running into the Square to get fresh doughnuts. Make us some coffee, okay?" He was at the stairs before she could stop him. "Be right back."

She opened her mouth to protest, closed it when she realized her protest would be in vain. What Ryan wanted, it appeared, Ryan got. A running mate, a dinner at Locke-Ober's, a kiss, far more. Doughnuts and coffee were the least of it.

Closing her door, she realized that he'd not been at all put off by what had happened last night. Albeit reluctantly, she was glad.

"Are you all set to go?" Sam asked as they strolled side by side through the Public Garden. It was Tuesday. Carly's exams had been given and corrected. After faculty meetings Wednesday morning, she'd be on her way to New York.

"I think so," she said, wrapping her scarf more tightly around her neck. It was sunny but cold. The wind raced in from the harbor, choreographing a lively dance of dried leaves by their feet. "I'm looking forward to it."

"Any worries?"

"Always worries."

He waited for her to go on. When she didn't, he prodded. "Well, what did you decide? Will it be Robyn or Carly?" They'd discussed the issue at length. The woman who would meet John Lyons at LaGuardia could be straight-haired and blue-eyed under the premise that Carly should be kept hidden from her family. Or she could have gray eyes and curly hair, in keeping with Robyn's demise. In the end, Sam had left the choice to the one who struggled with them both.

"It'll be Carly," was the quiet response.

He smiled his approval. "I'm glad. What made you decide?"

She looked up at him then. "I'm tired, I guess. And you're right in everything you've said. I've got to make the break. I've got to forget about Robyn. She's gone. Erased. A nonperson. I can't straddle two identities when one of them is no longer viable. Maybe if I share the new me with my father, it'll make it all easier to accept."

"You'll tell him your name?"

"Yes. I have this need to. And besides, if anyone does follow us—"

"No one will."

"But if anyone does, it'd all be blown if he called me Robyn. Anyway, he'll see that my plane's come from Boston. He still won't know my address. For his own safety, the less information he has the better." She gave a sarcastic laugh. "Maybe we'll pretend that he's taken up with a younger woman. He's booked a suite at the hotel. The clerks will never know the difference."

"Sounds cagey."

"I'm learning."

Lapsing into silence, they crossed the footbridge over the duck pond. Had it been summer they might have leaned on its rail to follow the swan boats with their contingent of riders. They might have tossed peanuts to the mallards, might have bought balloons from a vendor and let them sail from their wrists. But it was near winter, and the only movement on the pond was that inspired by the wind.

"Sam?"

"Uh-huh?"

"I went out with Ryan Cornell last weekend."

"Good girl."

"You didn't . . . you haven't come up with anything on him, have you?"

At her slight stammer, he eyed her intently. "No. Why?"

"Just wondering."

"You like him?"

"He's nice."

"Will you be seeing him again?"

"I suppose." She took a breath. "We run together every morning."

"Sounds serious."

Only when she cast him a defensive glance did she see he was teasing. Somehow she couldn't laugh. "I don't know. It could be. And it scares me to death."

"Why should it? You've got nothing to hide."

"But I do," she argued, eyes wide. "I've got a whole past. It's fine and dandy to want to live in the present, and I do, to an extent, when I'm with Ryan. But what do I do if he sees me without my contacts? What do I do if I have a nightmare and wake up screaming?"

Man that he was, Sam heard Carly clearly. "It *is* serious, isn't it?" If she was thinking of sleeping with the guy, it had to be. Sam knew her well enough to know that.

Awkward, she looked away, wishing for an instant that she hadn't said anything. But she had to talk to someone, and Sam's advice was always sound. "Let's talk hypothetically. What do I do if I *do* get involved with someone?"

"You give him answers."

"But my cover—"

"It doesn't have to be sacrificed."

"But my eyes—"

"You're near-sighted, and you also want to tone down your blues."

"And the dreams?"

"Your husband died in a fire. That's part of the story. It'd be very natural for you to have nightmares. You loved him."

"And my family—what about them?" She had got to thinking after Ryan mentioned meeting his folks sometime. "I mean, if I ever was really serious about someone, I couldn't very well hide my family away. They're a vital part of me. And they call me Robyn."

"After this weekend your father won't."

She regarded him skeptically. "But my brothers will. And the kids. I've always been Aunt Robyn to them. How do you tell a child that his aunt just . . . decided to change her name? Can you actually expect him to remember to call her by something new?"

"Maybe. Maybe not. Anyway, there's always the chance, if you're that deeply involved with a man, that you'll decide to tell him everything. If that man is someone like Ryan Cornell, I believe he could be trusted. And if it was a situation where you'd be forever worried that he'd find out anyway. . . ."

"Damned if I do and damned if I don't, eh?" she muttered.

Sam threw an arm about her shoulder. "It's not that bad, Carly. Take it one step at a time. Time does amazing things. If the time is ever right to reveal everything to a special someone, you'll know it. Hasn't the decision about your father come fairly easily?"

"I suppose."

"Then let it ride. See what happens."

Another thought popped into mind. While they were discussing the matter, Carly rushed to air it. "What about Sheila?"

Sam drew a blank. "What about her?"

"What do I tell Ryan? He knows your name and that we're good friends. And your occupation is no secret; sooner or later he'll know you're a federal marshal. But how do I introduce Sheila? I mean, she's dropped in on me twice now, and Ryan lives right downstairs. He's bound to bump into her at some point. What do I tell him? And won't he think there's something strange about both of you doing what you do?"

"Tell him she's a friend of mine, that you met her through me."

"By the way, how did I meet you?"

"I went to school with one of your brothers. You and I met way back and renewed the friendship when you moved here."

"God, you're good at this," Carly said, admiration mixing with dismay. "You've got all the answers."

"I've been at it a while longer than you have. Speaking of which, I'd better be heading back. *Our* friend Sheila is spending the afternoon with me."

"You're a busy man."

"Yeah. This one's apt to drive me to my grave."

"How could that be? She only started work yesterday."

He shook his head slowly, his sandy hair blown by the wind. "I don't know, Carly. You may like the woman, but I still think she's a flake."

"You just got off on the wrong foot with her."

"Maybe," he grumbled, not at all looking forward to the afternoon. Sheila Montgomery had already made it clear that there were certain cases she'd handle and certain ones she wouldn't. Had hers not been a civil-service position, he'd have canned her on the spot. For the umpteenth time, he reminded himself of the recommendations she had. "What about you?" he asked Carly. "Have you enjoyed seeing her?"

It was only for an instant that Carly hesitated, but it was long enough. "Yes."

"You don't sound convinced."

She tried to put into words what had been nagging at the back of her mind. "I am, I guess. It's just strange. When I'm with Sheila, I feel torn. She's such a blatant reminder of my past. I mean, it's nice not having to hide anything, and she's great fun to be with. It's just. . . ."

"You're ready to move on."

For his faultless insight, Carly sent him a look of gratitude. "I think so."

Not far away, in a Newbury Street café, Sheila Montgomery drained the last of her coffee and turned her full attention to her date. She'd met him the Wednesday before in a bar at the foot of Beacon Hill. Originally from Virginia, he'd said, he was with one of the larger banks in town and was the newest on a long roster of vice-presidents. He was good-looking, smartly dressed and sexy. They'd met at her apartment for a brief but intimate interlude late Friday afternoon, then again on Monday. She liked him. "Thanks, Jordan. This has been lovely."

"My pleasure," he said, eyes gleaming. "It's the least I could do. You've been good to me." His expression elaborated.

She blushed becomingly and spoke more softly. "Will I see you later?"

He glanced at his watch as though it held his appointment calendar. It didn't, but it might have for his response. "I can't make it today. I've got a meeting at five. How about tomorrow?"

"Same time, same place?" she drawled seductively.

Leaning forward as though to whisper, he nipped her earlobe. "You got it."

"Jordan?"

He was still by her ear, lingering at the shot of Shalimar she'd applied in the ladies' room moments before he'd come. "Mmm?"

"How about Thursday? I've got a turkey just right for two, with stuffing and sweet-potato casserole and cranberry sauce — the works. It'd be pretty lonely to eat all that by myself. Join me?"

He took a deep breath. Sheila sensed it had nothing to do with the Shalimar. "Oh, darlin'. I'm sorry. I can't." Straightening in his seat, he waved for the waiter.

"You've got other plans? Hey, listen, if it's a question of time, I could make it earlier or later."

He smiled less comfortably. "I really can't. Another time, huh?"

"I'll even throw in the TV. You can watch the damn games — "

"Sheila, I can't," he said firmly. Pulling out his wallet, he studied the bill set down by the waiter, placed three crisp tens on the tray and stood.

Sheila lingered for a minute, studying his set features, then joined him. They said nothing until they got to the street, where he caught her hand and gave it a squeeze. "Tomorrow . . . your place?"

When she nodded, he flashed her a lascivious grin, winked, turned and headed east down Newbury Street. Walking stiffly, Sheila headed west.

TEN

CHEEKS RED, RYAN AND CARLY sat at the bottom of the atrium stairs. In deference to the cold, they hadn't run as far as usual. Each seemed abundantly aware, though, that it was the last run they'd have together for several days. They lingered.

"That was good," Ryan said. He leaned back on his elbows and flexed one leg.

"Mmm." Sitting with him, looking over at his dark head, his solid frame, Carly knew she'd miss him.

"What time is your flight to Des Moines?"

"I'm not going to Des Moines," she said softly.

"No?" Beneath the random fall of his hair, his brow creased. "I thought you were spending Thanksgiving with your dad."

"I am. I'm meeting him in New York."

"Oh." He thought on, still puzzled. "Then you won't be seeing your brothers and their families?"

"They can't make it."

"I'm sorry, Carly. You'll miss them."

Her eyes acknowledged this, though she tried to make light of it. "I'll see them another time. Dad hasn't been to New York for a while. We thought it would be fun."

"It should be. New York's a fun place."

She nodded.

"What time's your plane?"

"Four o'clock."

"I'll come by for you at three. That should allow plenty—"

"Ryan, you can't do that!"

"Why not?"

"Because you've got work to do. It'd screw up your whole afternoon!"

"It's my afternoon, isn't it?" he asked, eyes twinkling. "And I choose to take you to the airport."

"But the traffic will be awful."

"I don't care."

"Really. I can take a cab."

"Over my dead body." Standing, he grabbed her hand and pulled her up; she fell gently against his muscled length. "Besides," he murmured, his gaze sliding from one to another of her features, "I want to see you safely on that plane. Airports can be decadent places, and a beautiful woman alone is a likely target. All I need is for some guy to pick you up. . . ."

Prickles of fear raised the hair on Carly's neck. Ryan was thinking of something relatively innocent; she was not. For the first time, she wished she weren't going anywhere. Cambridge, this building, Ryan himself seemed suddenly safe and comforting. "No one will pick me up," she asserted mechanically, her focus on Ryan's warm, firm lips.

"I'll see to that." He kissed her boldly, released her reluctantly. "Three o'clock?"

Just then, Carly wanted to throw her arms around his neck, to kiss him madly, to cling to him until she missed her plane. Instead she simply nodded.

Ryan drove her to the airport, insisted on parking and walking her to the gate, then waited with her until her flight was called. They sat quietly, each with so much to say, neither speaking. When it was time, they stood and waited until most of the other passengers had moved through the gate. Knowing she couldn't postpone the inevitable, Carly turned to him.

"I'll see you when I get back?"

"What time . . ." he asked, then cleared his throat of its hoarseness. "What time does your flight get in?"

She saw the direction of his thoughts and began to slowly shake her head.

"What time, Carly?" he demanded more forcefully.

"Same time Monday. Four o'clock. Ryan. . . ." She drew his name out in subtle protest. School didn't reopen until Tuesday; she knew Ryan didn't have the extra day's grace.

"I'll be here."

"But—" Her words were dammed at her lips by his finger, which was as gently obstinate as his expression.

"Till four Monday." He leaned down and, putting his lips where his finger had been, gave her a last, soft kiss, then straightened. "Have a happy Thanksgiving."

She fought the tightness in her throat. "You too, Ryan." She forced a smile. "See you then."

"So, who is she?"

Ryan took his eyes from the road only long enough to shoot his brother a sharp look. "What?"

"Who is she?"

"Who?"

"Whoever it is that's put that expression on your face."

With a glance at the side mirror, Ryan pulled into the left lane to pass a minivan. He wanted nothing to obscure his view of the open road, wanted nothing to distract him from his thoughts. "What expression?" he asked innocently.

"The one you've been wearing for the past half hour. God, it's benevolent. Tender, if you care to be romantic. And don't tell me you're thinking about work. I know you love the law, but not like that."

Ryan waited to speak until he'd returned to the middle lane. Traffic was light, but then, it was barely nine. They'd gotten an early start. He had wanted to make the most of the day. And since he had nothing better to do in Cambridge. . . .

"Am I that transparent?"

"Who is she?"

"One of my neighbors."

His brother eyed him with sharpened interest. "The pretty one with long black hair and sexy legs?"

A smile played at the corner of Ryan's mouth. "She's got sexy legs, all right, but black hair? No way. It's auburn."

"Is the rest of her sexy?"

"What d'you think?" It was a turnaround, Ryan having the upper hand on his brother in the love-life department.

Tom rubbed the back of his neck and grimaced. "I dunno. Alyssa was beautiful enough, but sexy?"

"Carly's nothing like Alyssa."

"Carly it is then. Carly what?"

"Quinn. She's a teacher."

"A *teacher?* Geez, Ryan, a *schoolteacher?*" His voice dropped an octave. "Forget I mentioned sexy. Anyone who has to control thirty wailing banshees six hours a day, five days a week, hasn't got the energy left to be sexy." As though on cue they crept up on a station wagon filled with five such banshees and their parents. The kids were lined up at the back window as far away as possible from the adults. Their mouths were going, all in different directions. When one flashed a peace sign, Tom gave him a grin and returned the gesture, at which point Ryan pulled to the left again and passed them.

"Are you down on kids, or sex?" he teased.

Failing to see humor in the question, Tom scowled in disgust. "I met this great woman. Super lady. Real potential."

"But?"

"I had dinner at her place last weekend." He grunted. "Have you ever tried making love to a woman with three kids running in and out?"

"She didn't put them to bed?"

"Oh, yeah. She did. One came down for a drink of water. The second complained that the first one woke him up. Then the third threw up all over his bed and I had to keep all three of them occupied while she cleaned it up. Talk about a bucket of cold water. . . ."

Ryan laughed. "Where's your compassion? Sounds like the poor woman's got her hands full."

"That was what I told myself when I crossed her name out of my little black book. Anyway—" he drummed his fingers against his thigh "—there's a world of other women out there." The drumming stopped. "Just wish I could find a good one."

"Know what your problem is?"

Tom sent him a droll glance. "What?"

"You've got too much upstairs to be fixated downstairs, if you know what I mean."

"Ahh, hell." Lecture time. His gaze flipped to the window with imminent boredom. Then, in a burst of annoyance, he looked back at Ryan. "No, I don't. Spell it out."

"You're a bright guy. You need someone just as bright. But you're so hung up on sex that you walk right by some of the best women out there." He held up a hand. "Hey, so you don't get them to bed the first night. Maybe it'd be worth it for a woman you could talk to."

"Like a schoolteacher?" Tom drawled.

Ryan was about to correct his brother's misconception of Carly's job, then thought better of it. "Like a schoolteacher," he echoed and let the subject drop. He was in no mood for sermonizing, particularly when, at the moment, it would have been a case of the pot calling the kettle black. He wasn't sure how he was going to get Carly to bed; he just knew they both needed it badly.

Carly's plane landed on schedule Monday at four. Hoisting her bag to her shoulder, she waited behind the other passengers for what seemed an eternity until at last the line began to move down the narrow aisle. She was nearly as excited now as she'd been when she'd landed in New York. It had been a wonderful five days, filled with everything she'd expected and more. But she was glad to be home.

Her eye began to pick through faces the instant she stepped into the terminal. Many of the passengers were students who hurried through to catch the public transit or businessmen heading for cabs. Others were met by friends or relatives. Heart pounding, she stood still, searching the crowd for the one face she'd missed over the holiday. Passengers from behind circled her; she took several slow steps forward and moved to the side and let her bag slide to the floor.

He wasn't there.

She checked her watch. It was nearly four-ten. Once again she scanned the room, its crowd thinning fast. Braced against a wall, she watched the crew filter out and disappear. Five more minutes passed. No Ryan.

Disappointment came in a crushing wave, offset only by a glimmer of fear. Airports were decadent places, he'd said, where a woman alone was a likely target. Not only, it seemed, was Carly alone, but she very definitely was also a likely target.

Shouldering her bag, she left the arrival gate and started down the long corridor. The sooner she got a cab, the sooner she'd be locked back in her safe cocoon. Safe, if alone. She sighed. She'd done it before, she'd do it again. If only she hadn't been so looking forward to. . . .

A tall, dark figure came into sight, running toward her, his topcoat flaring open. She stopped walking. Three weeks before she might have been terrified had such a ravenlike creature homed in. But much had happened in three weeks. Her hopes soared. This man had the steady gait of a runner. No way could that bearded countenance be mistaken for anyone but Ryan. Again her bag slipped to the floor. This time she didn't care whose path she blocked.

"Oh, hell!" Ryan gasped, skidding to a halt before her. Though his hair was blown every which way, he was dressed to kill . . . or to try a case. In either event, he looked thoroughly perturbed. "There was a breakdown in the tunnel. I sat honking my horn for twenty minutes, then was in such a rush that I took a wrong turn and drove in circles around the damn airport, trying to get into the parking lot." He raked his hair back from his brow with tense fingers, then held them at his neck, as though seeing her for the first time. "I'm sorry, babe," he whispered. "I wanted to be here."

A deep, deep affection stirred within Carly and she broke into a smile. "You are here," she breathed, reaching out as though to verify it. With exquisite tenderness, given his most recent state of agitation, Ryan took her into a close embrace.

"I am," he whispered against her hair, then held her back to look at her. "It's good to see you, Carly. I missed you."

"Me too."

His kiss was as urgently tender as his embrace had been. Strange, he'd spent so much time in the past few days thinking about getting Carly into bed, yet the only thing that mattered now was having her here by his side.

"Come on," he said softly, lifting her bag without once taking his eyes from her face, "let's go." He put his arm around her shoulder and they started forward. "I want to hear all about New York. Think you can put up with me for the next couple of hours?"

Her hand found a perfect niche at his waist; her steps matched his comfortably. "I think so." It was the understatement of the year.

The next few weeks flew. Carly would never have believed she could have been so happy, given the circumstances in which she lived. Sam saw the difference, as did her friend Bryna Moore.

"You look pleased with yourself," the other woman observed as the two sat in the school cafeteria one blustery mid-December day.

"Why not?" Carly mused. "We're doing *Pride and Prejudice* in my Lit II class. It's a favorite of mine."

Bryna waved aside the pat offering. "Besides that. You look more confident. Happier. Maybe you're finally feeling more at home?"

Carly knew it was true. Not only was she more relaxed, but also there was Ryan, always Ryan.

Sheila Montgomery, too, noticed Carly's glow. She pondered it as she paced her tiny apartment after returning from Cambridge one chilly Sunday afternoon. It wasn't fair. The woman had everything. And what did Sheila have?

She thrust back the simple cotton drapes on her single small window and scowled out at the street. Two pairs of denim-clad legs passed by, one masculine, one feminine, and she felt worse.

A little luck was all she asked. Where was it? New city, new assignment

. . . and nothing. Jordan was married. She'd suspected as much when he'd brusquely refused her Thanksgiving invitation; she'd confirmed it the follow-ing day when he'd appeared at her door and she'd confronted him. So much for one up-and-coming bank executive.

Even her job grated strangely. Maybe it was Sam Loomis, always guarded, abundantly skeptical of her abilities. Oh, she was good. She didn't doubt it for a minute. She knew just how to handle her wards. Hadn't she proved it last week when the family of one of her charges had staged a near riot outside the courtroom? She'd been firm and in charge, and the clamor had died. But had Sam appreciated her efforts? No, sir.

Then again, maybe she was tired of the whole job. Maybe the real reason she'd requested a transfer from Chicago had been in hope of retrieving the spice that seemed to have vanished somewhere along the line. She was going nowhere. Turning, she made a despairing perusal of her apartment. Oh, she'd done it up well enough, with reds to brighten things. But aside from splurging on her bed—double job covered with ruffles and lace—it was bargain base-ment all the way. Not that there was much of a way to go. Perhaps she was lucky the place was so small. Less to furnish. Less to heat.

But she wasn't a pragmatist by choice. She wanted something better, damn it. Something better!

"I saw her again," Tom called, stretching his long legs over Ryan's coffee table.

Ryan came to the door of his bedroom. A thick towel was knotted low on his hips. He was drying his hair with another. "Saw who?"

"The black-haired lady with the sexy legs."

"Uh, yeah? Where?"

"Here. Downstairs. She was leaving as I was coming in. You're sure she's not your favorite neighbor in disguise?"

Ryan stopped his rubbing and draped the towel around his neck with a half laugh. "Carly? Fat chance. She's as straightforward as the day is long." As soon as he'd said it, he wondered why he'd felt so compelled. He should have left it at the half laugh. The fact was that there was a lot more to Carly than she let on. He'd seen that distant look in her eyes too often.

"Wonder who it could be," Tom said with deceptive nonchalance. For that matter, now that Ryan thought about it, his brother had been different lately. Since he'd returned from the coast? Since Ryan had taken his own place? There was this intense interest in a black-haired lady with sexy legs. . . .

"Beats me," Ryan said, as he made a note to ask Carly about that one. He raised the towel and rubbed his bearded jaw. "Listen, let me get dressed. I'm picking Carly up at two. Why don't you come meet her? Then you can scram." His pointed look elaborated.

"Goin' someplace nice?"

"I thought we'd go up to Rockport."

"On a day like this?"

"Sure. Tom, Tom, where's your sense of adventure?"

Tom grunted. "I think I've passed it on to you."

* * *

Carly was delighted to meet Ryan's brother, whom she instantly recognized as the blond-haired man Sheila had so expressively admired on the stairs several weeks before. Though she'd never seen herself as a matchmaker, she made a mental note of the definite possibilities. Later, alone with Ryan driving northbound on Route 128, she gently explored them.

"Tom is nice."

"Uh-huh."

"A real ladies' man?"

"He's lookin'. His latest fixation is some lady in our building. Black hair. Sexy legs. Do you know of anyone like that?"

"In our building?" Carly frowned. Unless there'd been another fast move, in which case Sam would have her head, there wasn't anyone fitting that description living in the building. "Not that I know of."

"How about visiting?"

The light dawned. "Sheila?"

"Hmm?"

"It might be Sheila." Propitious. "My friend. She drops in to visit at odd times. They passed on the stairs once."

Ryan suspected he'd hit on gold. Nothing would please him more than to do something for Tom. "Think you could arrange an introduction for me?"

"For *you*?" Carly arched a delicate brow.

"Sure," Ryan countered, a sly smile forming. "Got to check her out before I sic her on my little brother. He's at a sensitive time in his life."

"So's she." Carly had been well aware of the subtle restlessness in Sheila. "Maybe we can work something out."

Their afternoon in Rockport was wonderful. Though most of the small shops were closed for the winter, Carly and Ryan ambled down the narrow streets, admiring window displays, browsing through those craft shops that were open. They had steaming clam chowder in a restaurant overlooking the harbor and, arm in arm, admired Motif #1, the shed on the water that had become an art form extraordinaire. Then, driving farther up the coast, Ryan pulled the car to the side of the road, and they walked along the beach.

There was something breathtaking about the winter waves sloshing relentlessly against the shore. They were timeless, ever changing, never changing, their rhythmic force echoing the pulse of eternity. Robyn Hart . . . Carly Quinn . . . the tide was immune to such petty distinctions. The world went on, as it always would.

Mesmerized and slightly awed, Carly stood with Ryan in silent appreciation. When he put his arm around her shoulder and drew her close, she wondered if he felt it too, this sense of being something infinitely small in the face of perpetuity. They were a couple at that moment, finding strength in each other. Illusion, perhaps, but she liked the feeling.

Only when she spotted a piece of driftwood did she break away. "Look!" Running the short distance to where it lay, she knelt down, turned it, lifted it.

Ryan hunkered down beside her. "It's beautiful."

She fingered the damp, ridged forks of gnarled wood. "I'm bringing it home. It'll look great in my living room."

He smiled at her. It *would* look great in her living room. Had she not claimed it first, he might have done so. There was something terribly genuine about it, genuine as the wave of feeling that washed over him then. Taking the driftwood from her, he rose and tucked her by his side to walk the beach a final few minutes before heading home.

Only two things marred her total happiness during those weeks between holidays. The first was the physical frustration that had begun to haunt her. When she was with Ryan, she ached to be in his arms. His lean physique was a constant source of temptation. When she was away from him, the need was, if anything, greater. She found herself lying in bed at night thinking of him in the bedroom below, picturing his long limbs under the sheets, his muscled torso gleaming in the sliver of light coming in from the street.

She recalled every vivid moment of that night on his sofa, and wondered what it would have been like if they'd made love. She imagined his body all bare and hard and hair-spattered, imagined her slighter, paler body entwined with his. If she was tormented, she couldn't help herself. And if Ryan was tormented, he took no step forward. Oh, he was infinitely warm, touching her at every excuse—an arm around her shoulder, a hand in hers, a well-placed thigh, frequent kisses—but he made no attempt to go further. Much as she told herself to be grateful, the ache only grew.

She knew that he was waiting for a sign from her, yet she couldn't quite get herself to give it. Along with those fevered memories of the evening in his apartment went the stark reminder of what had torn them apart. She was frightened. She'd been totally out of control for those few moments when her mind had betrayed her. It could easily happen again. Moreover, lovemaking implied, at least on her part, a commitment that she wasn't yet sure she could make.

For there was still that other side of her that she couldn't ignore. Therein lay the second source of her turmoil as the days passed. Sam kept her up to date on the progress of things in Chicago. Gary Culbert had been denied bail pending appeal of his sentence, which meant that at least she wouldn't have to worry about his walking the streets in search of her. Now rumor had it that his lawyer was about to file a motion for a new trial, and if there was a new trial she would have to return to Chicago to relive her ordeal on the witness stand.

How could she explain it to Ryan? She saw him nearly every day. And what about the danger factor? It was always there, a new trial or no. And it was particularly frightening when she realized that it had been neither Gary Culbert nor Nick Barber who had come after her that dark night in Chicago. It had been a man with a gun and he'd never been caught. She didn't even know his name.

His name was Horace Theakos, better known in the trade as Ham, and he was admitted to the visitors' room after a cursory search by the prison guard. He sat down at one of the several tables and was satisfied to see that he had the room to himself. Culbert had promised that. A little palm money went a long way.

Culbert entered from a door on the opposite side of the room and quietly took a seat. They wouldn't have much time. He'd get right to the point.

"We're filing for a new trial," he said in a very low, very even voice. "And I want something done about that witness." He might have been ordering a bologna sandwich.

Theakos was a large man with angular features. His full shock of black hair was slicked back. His business suit belied his pastime. His eyes were small, black and hard. Gary Culbert would have been the first to run from him in a dark alley.

"That's a tall order, Culbert," he replied under his breath. "I risked a lot las' time."

"That was your fault," Culbert murmured, his lips barely moving. "And you owe me. You let her get away."

"She's a fighter. I din't expect that in such a puny one."

"Such a puny one put me in this place. I want her taken care of."

Theakos didn't budge. "Don' know where she is. Don' know *who* she is. They got her hidden away. Ya' heard what they said at the trial."

"Yeah. I was the one sitting way up in front while you sat hidden in the back." Culbert stared across the table. "You know what she looks like. You know where she's come from. Find her. Just keep it quiet."

"Now you're really dreamin'," Theakos droned softly. "There's no way I can get close to her after las' time. I have to keep my distance. Y'll need someone else."

"*We'll* need someone else, you mean. You're in this over your head, Ham. Don't forget. I know who held the gun last time."

Theakos smiled and whispered through gritted teeth, "Y're a bastard."

"I'm in good company," Culbert retorted as softly. "I want it done right this time. Make it look like an accident. Self-inflicted, if possible. That'll muddy up the state's case but good."

"It'll muddy ya up, if anything leaks."

Culbert's eyes narrowed. "Then we'll go down together. Got that?"

"Guess what?" came the nasal voice over the phone. Carly instantly recognized it as Sheila's.

"What?"

"Harmon called."

"The Chicago Harmon? That's great!" she exclaimed, then caught herself. "Or is it? I thought you were done with him."

Sheila's grin was almost audible. "I was. But that was before he called last night. He wants to see me."

"No kidding? Is he coming to Boston?"

"Uh-uh. I'm flying out there."

"To Chicago? But when will you have time? With the holidays and all. . . ."

"That's when I'm going. Over Christmas. For the long weekend. Isn't it exciting, Carly?"

Carly hadn't heard quite as much enthusiasm in Sheila's voice since she'd first arrived in Boston. "I'm happy for you, Sheila." So much for matchmaking. "Listen, if I don't talk with you before you go, have a wonderful time. Okay?"

Two days before Christmas, Carly was off to the Bahamas to meet her brother and his family. As he'd done at Thanksgiving time, Ryan drove her to the airport.

"I wish you weren't going," he said, as once more they stood at the boarding gate. "It'll be lonely here without you."

"I wish you were going to see your parents."

He shook his head. "Too much to do here. I'll call them, though." He paused. "Can I call you?"

"I'd like that," she said softly, pleased to have that to look forward to. Then she remembered. Jim was certain to have made reservations under his name, or, God forbid, under that of Robyn Hart. "But, uh, I'd better call you. I'm not sure exactly when we'll be at the hotel or out. You know how it is with three young kids to please?"

"Will you?"

"Please them? I'll try."

"Call. Will you call?"

"Yes," she whispered, feeling her insides knot. She hated goodbyes, particularly when it was Ryan she was leaving. Stretching up, she kissed him. Then, fighting the tears that might betray the depth of her feeling for the man, she turned and ran through the gate.

She called twice during the week she was away, both times at night, both times when she was lying in bed thinking positively indecent thoughts.

The first call came on Christmas Eve. Ryan was stretched out on his bed feeling sorry for himself. The loneliness was worse knowing that Carly was within his reach, yet not. When the phone rang, his heart thumped wildly.

"Hello?"

"Ryan?"

So soft, barely a whisper. Self-pity was forgotten amid the torrent of pleasure he derived from hearing her voice and knowing she was thinking of him.

"How are you, Carly?"

"Fine." She drew the phone closer and curled up around it. "The sun's great."

"Getting a tan?"

"Uh-huh. And a rest."

He angled himself up against his headboard. "Even with those kids?"

She chuckled. "Yup. They're more interested in the pool than the beach, which means that Sharon and I bask in peace."

"Sharon?"

"My sister-in-law."

He nodded, but his thoughts weren't of Sharon. He was picturing Carly on the sand. "What's your bathing suit like?"

"My bathing suit?" She blushed. "What kind of a question is that?"

"Indulge me, babe. It's cold and raw here. They're predicting snow for tomorrow."

"For Christmas? That's lovely!"

"It's a pain in the neck. Do you have any idea what a mess it'll be? The streets around here are narrow to begin with. If it snows, they'll be impossible."

"Playing Scrooge, are we?" she teased.

"Just missing you. It's Christmas Eve and I'm lonely."

"I thought you had a cocktail party to go to?"

"I did. I went."

She waited for the punch line. "Well?"

"It was boring. I didn't last an hour." He hesitated, then spoke again, this time more huskily. "Tell me about your bathing suit." If he was to die of frustration, he'd go out in style.

She lowered her eyes. "It's royal blue. . . ."

"Go on."

"With diagonal mauve-and-white stripes."

"Mmm. Sounds nice. Two-piece?" He pictured a long slice of golden silk at her middle and shifted position to ease his burgeoning tautness.

"One."

"Ahh. You're saving it for me."

"Saving what?"

"Your middle."

"Ryan!" she whispered hoarsely. "What if this line is bugged?"

His eyes twinkled. "Then someone's getting horny. I know I am." Getting. That was a laugh.

"Ryan. . . ."

Suddenly he was sober. "We have to talk when you get back, babe. You know that, don't you?"

Her hand was suspended, holding the phone. Tremors of excitement blended with those of apprehension. Oh, yes, they did have to talk. She'd known it was coming, just hadn't been sure when. Since that night when she'd nearly flipped out in his arms, Ryan had been the essence of propriety. But he wasn't a monk . . . thank God. And they could only avoid things so long.

"Yes," she whispered.

"When you get back?"

"Yes."

"Well, then—" he sucked in his lower lip, let it slip slowly from beneath his teeth "—you have fun. You'll call again?"

"Uh-huh."

"And Carly?"

"Yes?"

"Merry Christmas."

Slow tears gathered at her lids. "To you too, Ryan." Her voice cracked. "Talk to ya later."

It wasn't visions of sugar plums that danced in Carly's head that night.

That was on Thursday. Knowing she'd be returning to Boston the following Tuesday, she called again on Sunday. Ryan was full of news.

"This place is mine! Isn't that great? The Amidons called this morning. They've bought something down there and want their stuff shipped as soon as possible."

"No kidding? That *is* great! But what are you going to do when everything's gone? You haven't got any furniture."

"Not yet. We'll go looking when you get back."

"We?"

"You'll help me do the place up right, won't you? I mean, your place is gorgeous. What do I know about decorating?"

"Seems to me you had some pretty solid opinions on that score."

"Yeah. Well. I was just talking. I don't know if any of that will look good." In fact, the one thing he *really* wanted for his new home would take some doing. He'd seen the finished needlepoint Carly had been about to send to her father. It was beautiful, from the subtle blending of reds and oranges to the tiny robin she'd set in the corner. Her mascot, she'd called it, passing it off as a personal quirk unworthy of notice. He'd noticed, and he wanted something with a robin in its corner, too. He wondered if she'd mind working in navy. "I need your help, Carly. And your company. Won't you like going shopping with me?"

More than she would have thought possible. "Of course. It'd be fun. Sure, I'll help you."

"Good. You get back on Tuesday. Maybe I'll take Wednesday off and we can spend the day together."

She couldn't resist teasing him. "And this is the man who had so much to do that he couldn't get home for Christmas?"

Ryan took it all in good humor. "Heeeeey, there are priorities and there are priorities. I need a bed. I mean, hell, I'll be good for nothing in the office if I have to spend my nights on the floor." His voice lowered. "Unless, of course, my upstairs neighbor offered to share her—"

"Ryan." Tingles shot through her. Her whispered, "Please," was muffled into the phone.

Ryan stared down at the coiled black wire he clutched. He'd said they had to talk and precisely about this topic. In the face of Carly's reticence, he grew more determined than ever. But he didn't want to upset her. Not now. Not when she was so far away. If he had a case to argue, he wanted to do it face to face. "Okay." He took a breath. There was something else he wanted to tell her. "Anyway, I think I have an interesting new case."

She was more than willing to go for the diversion. Besides which, contrary to what she might have expected such a short time ago, she found Ryan's practice intriguing. "You think?"

"I have to do some preliminary work to find out if it's feasible."

"It's a good one?"

"Could be. I got a call from the president of a construction firm in Revere. He wants to take on the *Globe* and one of its reporters."

"The *Globe*? Really?" She sounded puzzled, as though she couldn't understand someone wanting to do a thing like that. Ryan found her puzzlement, and its suggestive naiveté, amusing.

"Uh-huh. The reporter did an in-depth story on my client's company. The article led to an investigation by the attorney general's office, indictments against the president and several of his top people and a trial. This week an acquittal came in. If I decide to take the case, we'll be suing for damages."

"Did you represent the company before?"

"No. The guy who did was a cousin of one of the vice presidents. He did okay; he got the acquittal. But the president doesn't think the fellow is aggressive enough to successfully argue for the plaintiff." Left unsaid was that Ryan's reputation for aggressiveness in the courtroom had preceded him. "In the most general sense, forgetting sides, it'd be a fascinating exploration of the issues of freedom of the press and editorial responsibility."

"I'll say," Carly murmured. She pulled her blanket tighter around suddenly chilled feet. "Do you have much of a case?"

"That," he sighed, "is what I have to find out. According to the president, his company has suffered significant losses as a result of both the original publicity and that surrounding the trial. With the acquittal, the law states that he's not guilty."

"*Was* he innocent of whatever he was accused of?"

"Negligence and fraud. The jury said he was."

"The jury just wasn't convinced beyond a reasonable doubt of his guilt," she corrected, working to keep her voice light. "I don't know, Ryan. If that reporter came up with substantiated evidence, the paper may have been justified in printing its article."

"And," Ryan pointed out, playing the devil's advocate, "the grand jury did see cause to return indictments."

"Isn't it possible that the company's gone sanctimonious on the rebound? You know, the indignant rogue?"

Another time and with another person, Ryan would surely have argued, for the sake of argument if nothing else. Now, though, he was filled with generosity. "Mmm. It's possible. But I hope not. It'd be a fun case to try. The mood lately has been in favor of the press; we'd be the definite underdog, which makes it more challenging in a way. I'll have to go over the trial transcript in detail before I make any final decision." It suddenly occurred to him that he was talking on Carly's dime. "Listen, we can talk more when you get back." He gave a sheepish grin. "You're good to run things past. You think. For a layman," he drawled, "you seem to know the score. Are you sure you haven't got a law degree stuffed up your sleeve somewhere?"

Not quite a law degree, but certain other qualifications that would enable her to carry on quite a discussion. She would have to be careful. He was hitting close to home.

"I'm sure," she murmured. Wanting to change the subject yet not quite ready to let him go, she tried a different tack. "Did you get that snow?"

"Oh, yeah. Three inches worth. Not enough to ski on, just enough to snarl traffic."

"Poor baby."

"Don't 'poor baby' me. You'll have to deal with it in a couple of days." Two, to be exact. He was counting them closely.

"Maybe it'll be warm when I get back. After what you said about New England weather. . . ."

"Don't count on it, babe," he said softly. "Winter's here. It'll be a while before we're free and clear."

Those words would haunt Carly long after she hung up the phone.

Tuesday evening found Ryan sitting in a coffee shop at the airport sporting a frown. Carly's plane was late. It would be another thirty minutes at least. That much more time for him to brood.

Elbows propped on the table, he distractedly stroked the bristle of his mustache with his thumb. It had to have been a mix-up. That was all. He must have mistaken the name of her hotel. All he'd wanted to do last night was to hear her voice. It had seemed like an eternity since he'd spoken with her Sunday.

Sitting back, he raised his coffee cup, drained the last of its tepid contents, then shot a glance at his watch. Stretching his leg, he dug some change from the pocket of his pants, tossed it on the table and stood. Head down, he walked slowly toward the arrival gate, wondering how he could feel so very close to a person yet so distant. It was irrational, he knew, and thoroughly emotional. But then, Carly meant a hell of a lot to him.

The sight of her coming into the terminal, though, was enough to chase all brooding from his mind. Her skin a golden tan, she looked well rested and positively beautiful. She was here. And she was looking for him.

He waved once, then quickly wove through the incoming crowd. No less impatient, she did the same toward him. Then they were in each others' arms and Ryan was lifting her clear off her feet.

"Ahh, Carly," he moaned, "it's good to see you."

At that moment, Carly wondered if the whole purpose of her trip hadn't been to come home to Ryan this way. She held on for dear life, reacquainting herself with the feel of him, the smell of him, the wonderful warmth that had no rival in the sun she'd known all week. When he finally set her back down, the eyes that looked up at him were misted with happiness.

"You look great," she breathed.

"Not as good as you," he teased back. "Health personified. I'm jealous."

Her cheek dimpled becomingly. "No need. It'll fade in no time."

They stood there then, grinning at each other, happy to neither move nor speak. Later, in his apartment, when Ryan was to think back on that moment, he would be all the more perplexed. She'd been his then, fully his. Heart and soul. He was sure of it.

Until that phone call had come through.

ELEVEN

A FTER LEAVING THE AIRPORT, they'd stopped for a bite to eat downtown, then picked up fresh eggs and juice at the supermarket before returning to her apartment. Ryan had wanted to hear about her trip; Carly had wanted to hear about all he'd done while she'd been gone. They sat on the sofa facing each other, knees touching, arms and hands astir in tune with the discussion. Ryan felt as alive as Carly looked, their mutual animation reflecting the excitement of being together again.

Then the phone rang, and Ryan had watched the bubble pop. He could remember every word of that half conversation, as well as the slow crumble of Carly's features as she spoke.

"Hello?" she'd answered with a smile. "Sam! How are you?" Eyes on Ryan, she set her hand on her hip. "It was great! The weather was gorgeous!" Then she glanced at the wall clock and looked slightly puzzled. "Is everything okay?" As she listened to Sam's response, her brows knit, her hand fell to her side. When she spoke again, there was an incipient tension in her tone. "Oh." She slowly revolved until her back was to Ryan. Though she lowered her voice, he heard every word. "Oh, God. When? I know, I know. What? Tomorrow?" She shook her head and seemed to shrivel into herself. "I'm spending the day with Ryan." Ever so softly, the slightest bit apologetic. "No. Mmm. Are you sure? Okay." Barely a whisper. "Yes." Then, head down, she put the phone back on its hook, leaving her hand clinging there for several long moments before she turned back to him.

She'd refused to discuss the phone call, other than to acknowledge that it had indeed been her friend, Sam Loomis, that he had a personal problem, that she'd connect with him later. Though she made a valiant attempt to recover from whatever it was Sam had said, the moments of unblemished pleasure she and Ryan had shared were gone.

Thinking back now, Ryan paced to the window and planted both fists on its sill. He'd half hoped to be spending the night with Carly, but she hadn't been in a mood to discuss lovemaking, much less do it. Oh, she'd forced several smiles and had clung tightly to his hand when he'd finally walked to the door, but she'd been so obviously preoccupied that he hadn't had it in himself to push the issue. Instead, he'd simply kissed her good-night and left, trying to curb his own mounting frustration, which was precisely the state he was in now, and in which he remained for a good part of the night.

Come sunup, in defiance of the slush outside, he stubbornly laced his sneakers and headed for the street. To his surprise, Carly materialized behind him on the stairs.

"It's pretty messy," he warned.

"That's all right," was her quiet response. "I need it."

And well she did. Jaws clamped tight, fists clenched, she ran hard. It had been a horrendous night. She needed the outlet. Ryan's unquestioning if somber company was some solace. From time to time, when she felt his eyes on her and met his gaze, she consciously relaxed her facial muscles and gave a semblance of a smile. But inevitably, eyes back on the path, the tension returned.

By the time they returned home, sneakers wet, running suits filthy, they looked as though they'd been through a war. Panting, they walked idly around the front steps for a while before entering.

"Feeling better?" Ryan asked.

She nodded and shot him a look of gratitude. He was so good, she mused. And she'd hurt him last night. He was no fool; he had to know she was being more secretive than usual. Guilt consumed her. She and Ryan had come to share so many things. Having to shut him out now was an agony in itself.

"Are you still game to go shopping?"

"I'm looking forward to it."

He bit his upper lip for a moment as he studied her. "I wasn't sure. If you'd rather—"

"No, Ryan. I'd like to go with you."

"Then I'll come up for you at, say, ten?"

"That's fine." With a tentative smile, she headed into the building.

It was well after nine when Sam arrived. Having showered and dressed as soon as she'd come in from running, Carly was trying unsuccessfully to pass the time reading the morning paper when his quiet knock came. Running to the door, she peered through the viewer, then quickly released the bolts. Her barrage began the instant Sam was over the threshold.

"How did you get in downstairs?"

"Someone was leaving."

She made a face. "So much for security."

"It was only me," Sam offered gently.

"But it could have been *anyone*—"

"Which is why you've got a viewer and all these bolts. Listen, Carly, just relax. It was only a matter of time before they filed the motion for a new trial. We knew they were going to."

"But it's different, somehow, knowing it's done. What did John Meade have to say? He was the one who called, wasn't he?"

They sat on the sofa, facing each other as Carly had done last night with Ryan. Then the air had been charged with excitement; now it was filled with apprehension.

"Actually, my counterpart in Chicago called first. You remember Bill, don't you?"

"Of course I remember Bill," she countered with uncharacteristic gruffness. "He called the shots while I was in protective custody."

"Bill's got an ear to the ground, not to mention well-placed sources. He called me as soon as he heard. That was Monday morning. Meade called soon after that."

"Monday? But why didn't you call me? You knew where I was staying!"

"And ruin your vacation?" He tossed her a quelling glance. "Come on, Carly. What good would that have done? There's nothing for you to do just because they've filed for a new trial."

Her fear-filled eyes held his. "Then why are you here now?"

"To tell you what's happening before someone else does."

"Who else?" she shot back guardedly, at which point he leaned forward and patted her knee.

"Take it easy. Your father will have seen it in the paper. Your brothers—"

"It was all over the press? Damn it, I thought these things usually happened without a mess of fanfare."

"Remember, Culbert used to be a state legislator. And he still maintains his innocence. You can bet that his lawyer will try to soak the public sympathy for everything it's worth—which isn't much. But that means press conferences whenever possible, media leaks—"

Carly held her breath. "Will it work? I mean, I know the *Tribune* would never print anything even vaguely sympathetic about him after everything, but the *Tribune* isn't the only paper in Chicago." Her eyes widened. "Public opinion can be so fickle. Do you think there's a chance that the mood will sway in his favor?"

"Not a chance." Sam's firmness didn't waver. "If anything it'll go the other way. He was a legislator, Carly, a man whose salary came out of the taxpayers' pockets. As a legislator, he was given the public trust, and he violated it. Not only was he getting insurance kickbacks on the buildings he burned, but he was responsible for four deaths. *Four deaths.*" He shook his head. "People don't forget that kind of stuff quickly.

"Besides, in the end it doesn't matter what the public thinks. Culbert was convicted on the evidence before a judge and jury. Even if there *is* a new trial, and I can't imagine that happening, the evidence won't have changed. He'd be convicted a second time."

"Was that Meade's opinion too?"

"For starters, Meade can't envision a new trial being granted. He's been over the transcript from start to finish, and he doesn't see any possible error on which to base a new trial."

It suddenly occurred to Carly that a piece of information was missing. And in that instant she realized the true reason for Sam's visit. Pressing damp palms to the wool of her skirt, she fought to calm her stomach's slow churn. "What *have* they based their motion on? Mancusi would have had to cite something. What was it, Sam?"

Sam spoke more softly then, his eyes filled with a kind of apologetic haze. "They claim they have new evidence."

"What new evidence?"

"About you. They *claim*—" he emphasized the word "—that you were emotionally involved with Peter Bradley, and that that involvement warped your thinking."

"Of course I was emotionally involved with Peter Bradley! We were good friends. We worked together. He was the one person who was willing to work on the investigation with me."

"Romantically. That's the kind of involvement they imply."

"It's not true," Carly stated slowly. "There was never anything like that between us." There couldn't have been, though only she knew that. Her fingers clutched her skirt now for warmth. "What . . . evidence . . . have they got?"

Sam gave his head a quick shake. "I don't know yet. Neither does Meade. That's what we've got to find out. I just wondered—" he seemed to hesitate "—if you knew of any evidence they might have."

Those cold fingers suddenly clenched into fists. "If someone's given evidence of a romantic relationship between Peter Bradley and myself, that person is either mistaken or lying. Peter and I spent a lot of time together. We had to. If there were late nights at one or the other of our apartments, it was in his darkroom or in front of my typewriter. Never once did I wake up in his place; never once did he wake up in mine. I swear it, Sam."

Sam reached forward and, taking her hand, spoke gently. "I believe you, Carly. No need to get defensive. You're a free woman. You can do whatever you want with whoever you want to do it. No one's trying to pass judgment."

"Mancusi will!"

"Maybe, but that's beside the point. Meade just wants to be sure he's got the whole story so he can plan his offense if, and I do mean *if*, the motion for a new trial is granted. Besides, if he knows the facts, he'll better be able to ward off that possibility."

"Well, he knows the facts! There was nothing romantic between Peter and me! We were very dear friends. We thought the same way. I would be less than human if I didn't mourn his death, if I didn't feel guilty at having involved him in the arson investigation."

"Don't blame yourself. He knew the risks."

She sank against the cushions, her energy spent. "Oh, yes, he knew the risks. So did I, for that matter. But we were committed to getting that story. I wish—"

"Don't say it, Carly. What's done is done. There is no way you can bring Peter back. But you can help ensure that the men responsible remain in prison."

"What does that mean?" she asked.

Sam sighed, wondering if he was handling this all wrong. He'd come to see Carly in hopes of keeping her calm. His presence seemed to be having the opposite effect. "All it means is that you should be aware of what's happening. The more you can tell us about your relationship with Bradley, the better it'll be."

"But I've told you everything! There just isn't any more." Her face contorted in sarcasm. "I mean, I wish I had it in writing. But Peter and I just didn't think to document the fact that we weren't lovers. It had nothing to do with our investigation. It was—it is—totally irrelevant!" Just then there was a knock at the door. Sitting forward stiffly, Carly lowered her voice. Her hands fidgeted in her lap. "That'll be Ryan. We're going shopping for furniture. The Amidons bought a place in Florida and want all theirs shipped down."

Sam stood and brought Carly up with him. "Good. Go with him, and enjoy yourself. Maybe he can take your mind off all this."

She raised timid eyes. "You'll let me know if you hear anything, anything at all?"

"Sure I will. You know that, Carly." He squeezed her hand and nudged her toward the door. "Go on. He's waiting."

Ryan was indeed waiting. He was about to ring the doorbell in the suspicion that Carly might not have heard his knock when she opened the door. The thought that she might still be finishing dressing was instantly dispelled by the sight of Sam at her side.

"I'm . . . early." His eyes held Carly's for a minute before sliding to Sam, who held up a hand on cue.

"I'm just leaving." Then, almost as an afterthought, he extended that hand. "Sam Loomis."

"Ryan Cornell." They shook hands. It was a formality. Each knew the other's name, though the benignancy in Sam's gaze contrasted with Ryan's more intense scrutiny.

Then Sam tossed Carly a gentle smile. "Have a good time. I'll talk to you later." Nodding toward Ryan, who took a step into the foyer, he left, at which point Ryan turned that intense scrutiny on Carly. Though she was outwardly calm, he knew her too well to miss the tension in her eyes.

"Is everything all right?" he asked cautiously.

"Just fine." Her response was a little too quick, too pat.

"Sam worked out his problem?"

She nodded. "For now."

"Are you all set to go?"

"Yes." Feeling terribly awkward and well aware of keen brown eyes following her every step, she got her coat and bag. They walked downstairs in silence and were at the front door when Ryan spoke. His head was down, one hand jammed in the pocket of his fleece-lined jacket.

"Listen, maybe we ought to forget this."

"Why?"

He looked up then. "It's obvious you're not in the mood."

"But I am—" she began, only to be interrupted by a deep growl.

"You're not! You're as coiled as a whip! What is it that happened, anyway? Is Loomis in some kind of trouble?"

She winced at the sound of his voice, in part because she felt responsible for his anger. Of course he would wonder. Seeing Sam this morning would only add to his curiosity. And since she had to be so tight-lipped about it all. . . .

"He's not in trouble," she began, drawing into herself. "I told you. It was a personal matter."

"Then there *is* something between you two? Hell, I've asked you that before and you said there wasn't. I thought we had something good going, Carly." The sudden softening of his voice cut through her.

"We do," she whispered. "There's nothing between Sam and me. We're just good friends. Don't you ever share your problems with friends?"

"Not usually. Not until I met you. I thought *we* were friends. What happened to *that* sharing?"

Sagging back against the wall in defeat, she put her hands in her pockets and pressed her arms to her sides. Head down, she studied the tile underfoot. "I'm sorry, Ryan. I'm not . . . free . . . to talk."

"You're not free. Not free. It all comes down to that, doesn't it?" When she didn't answer, but simply stared at the floor, he took a step closer and went on. "I'm still trying to figure it out. What is it, Carly? Why *aren't* you free? All right—" he raised a hand "—I know about your husband. His death must have been a trauma, and I fully sympathize. But that doesn't mean that you have to shut yourself off from the rest of the world."

"I'm not."

"From *me*, then." He took a breath. He hadn't meant to broach it quite this way, but he was helpless to stop himself. Sam's presence this morning, Carly's tension—it was as though a hole had been poked in the dam of his self-restraint and now the words spilled with gathering force. "Monday night I tried to call you in the Bahamas, but I couldn't get through. The hotel had no record of a Carly Quinn registered. Or of anyone by the name of Johnson. I *assumed* that was your brother's name, since it's your maiden name."

Her chest constricted. Things seemed to be closing in on her. Even as she tried to improvise, she fought a wave of growing panic. Damn it, Sam was so good at this type of thing. Where was he now and what would *he* have said?

She ran the tip of her tongue over suddenly dry lips. "I had no idea you'd called."

"Obviously."

Goaded by his sarcasm, she met his gaze. "And I have no idea why you couldn't get through. My room was registered in my own name." So far, no lie. Robyn Hart was her own, if no longer her legal, name. She didn't want to lie. Perhaps stretch the truth a little, but not lie. True, she'd had to show proof of citizenship at customs, but the hotel clerk had not thought to question— if he'd known of it at all—any discrepancy in names. "If the Emerald Beach—"

"Emerald Beach?" Ryan eyed her quizzically. "Weren't you staying at the Balmoral?" When she grimaced, he squeezed his eyes shut. "Damn," he murmured, "I can't believe I did that." There was distinct sheepishness in his eyes when he reopened them. "I was calling the wrong place. That was really dumb."

Carly felt doubly guilty. "No. It was an innocent mistake and may have been my fault at that. I may have mentioned different hotels. I was looking through so many brochures. . . ."

One more step brought his body flush to hers. He put his hands on the wall on either side of her shoulders even as crimson stained his cheeks. "I must be going crazy," he murmured hoarsely. "I'm such a fool. When I couldn't get through I thought I'd go out of my mind. And I've been stewing about it since then. If I didn't want you so much. . . ."

Needing to touch him, Carly put her hands on his waist, then slid them inside his jacket to his back. The tension in his muscles seemed to ease on contact. "I'm sorry," she whispered.

"No. I'm sorry," he said softly. "I've never been the suspicious type, or jealous, for that matter. Until I met you. What with not being able to reach you, then having Sam dominate your mind since you've been back—"

"Sam's not dominating my mind. And it was you I thought of the whole time I was away. You were the one I looked forward to seeing."

He settled more snugly against her, holding just enough of his weight to keep from hurting her, not enough to keep from exciting her. "You mean that?"

She nodded, unable to tear her eyes from the compelling heat of his gaze. Only when his head lowered did her lids flicker shut, and then it was to more fully concentrate on the healing warmth of his lips.

He kissed her slowly at first, taking long, moist sips of her mouth. His senses, too, were centered there, his full concentration devoted to renewing the bond that, earlier, had seemed endangered. He found her mouth soft and sweet, trembling as he moved the tip of his tongue over its curves. When her own tongue emerged to touch his, his body quaked.

Bidden in small part by guilt at the pain she'd caused him, in large part by the wealth of erotic feeling he inspired, Carly met his kiss with a fervor to express all she couldn't say in words. She gave her hands play over the firm muscles of his back, drawing him closer as her lips parted widely in welcome. Her reward was the intense pleasure that spiraled through her limbs.

It was only the click of the front door as it opened that drew them apart. Ryan stayed where he was, gasping softly against her forehead, unable to step back for fear of embarrassing them both.

Eyes shut tight, Carly took short, shallow breaths. She heard the sound of a key in the lock then the pull of the inner door, and wondered which of her neighbors was witness to their impromptu surge of passion. But the door slid shut well before Ryan released her, so she was never to know. Not that it mattered. She'd paid for her place in this building, as had Ryan. If they wanted to neck in the lobby. . . .

Her muffled laugh was echoed by Ryan's.

"Hmm," he murmured, "got kind of carried away there. Wanna go back upstairs?"

"Now? But we're going shopping."

His hoarseness was telling. "The shopping can wait. Let's go to my place. You can get ideas in my bedroom."

"No way." She staved him off good-naturedly, a fast cover for her lingering hesitance. "You've taken the day off, so we'll go shopping. Who was the one who railed about not having any furniture?"

Slowly he pushed from the wall and levered himself straight. He took a deep, if unsteady, breath. "Why do I get the strange feeling you're putting me off?" When she put a hand against his chest and opened her mouth to argue, he raced on. He wanted nothing that hinted of tension to mar a day that had already had its share. "No harm. There'll be a better time." He held the door open. "Ma'am?"

Carly passed through with a demure smile, then took great gulps of the fresh, cold air. Though snow lay in random mounds on the grass, the walkway was dry. Yet she was walking on thin ice. She knew it and wondered fearfully when it would crack.

Sam propped his boot on the open lower drawer of his desk. "John? Sam Loomis calling. I spoke with Carly Quinn this morning."

John Meade cocked his head toward the door of his office, sending his assistant on his way. Then he swiveled in his chair until he faced the window. "How'd she take it?"

"She's upset. It'll be tough on her if that new trial is ordered. She doesn't relish the thought of facing it all again."

"If it's a question of facing it or letting the bastard go free, she doesn't have much of a choice."

The matter-of-fact way it was put rankled Sam. Carly had spoken well of Meade, expressing faith in his ability, an ability that would, of course, place prime concern on the legal issues involved. But Carly was a person, and it was Sam's job to understand her.

"She knows that. She won't fight you."

"What about her relationship with Bradley? She never said a word about it when she was here."

Sam scraped his thumbnail against the worn leather arm of his chair. "There was nothing to say. They were close friends and co-workers. That's it."

"You're sure?"

"I'm a pretty good judge of people. She wasn't lying."

Meade sighed. "Well, we may have to get her back here to go over her story anyway."

Sam wasn't thrilled with that idea. He could just begin to imagine what Carly's reaction would be. "Is that necessary?"

"I'm not sure yet. It depends what we can find out about this 'new evidence' Mancusi claims he's got. If it's anything, and I decide to run through the story with Robyn, we can fly her in for a couple of days."

"She works."

"So do I. Listen, I don't want to have to do it either. Hell, I didn't ask for new evidence; I thought we'd covered it all last time. Do you have any idea what it'll mean in terms of sheer man-hours if we have to go through the whole damn trial again? This isn't a joy ride for me, and I know it'll be tough on her, but it's all part of the deal."

Sam just grunted. It wasn't worth arguing. He was caught in the middle, feeling for Carly even as he knew that what John Meade said was true. All he could do was to hope that it would never come to a trip to Chicago, much less a new trial.

It was after he'd finished with Meade that a niggling thought bade him pick up the phone and punch out another number. Though he didn't know Bill Hoffmeister well, the little they'd dealt with each other had set the groundwork for a mutual respect. Sam wanted input on this one.

Having identified himself to the switchboard operator, he was in the process of mutilating a paper clip when Bill's hello came over the line.

"Bill? Sam Loomis. Got a minute?"

"Sure. What can I do for you, Sam?"

"It's about Carly Quinn. I have this uncomfortable feeling, maybe because she's so damned vulnerable. But with characters like Culbert and Barber, and considering what they tried to do before, do you think I should give her extra cover?"

"Assign someone to guard her? I don't know. I'm not sure we can justify that. There haven't been any threats."

"We won't be the ones to hear them. We have to anticipate them. I think what's got me nervous is the fact that Mancusi chose Carly as the focal point of the appeal."

"She was the star witness."

"Yeah. But they could have tried to find fault with the way the evidence was presented or looked for some technicality involving something the judge or prosecutor did or said. They chose Carly and they're trying to discredit her. If they think she's that crucial to the state's case, isn't there always the possibility that they'll try to find her?"

"There's always that possibility. But they won't be able to find her. We've made sure of that."

"Then you think I should hold off?"

"I don't think there's any cause to worry, not yet at least. Let me put someone on it here. We can monitor Culbert to a certain extent, find out if he has any suspicious visitors, if any sudden withdrawals are made from his bank account, that type of thing."

That was just what Sam wanted. "I'd appreciate it. Carly's tense enough about all this. The more reassuring we can be, the better."

"All the more reason not to put a guard on her. Speaking of which, Sheila Montgomery was in the other day. How's it working out?"

"Okay." Bill was one of those who had recommended her so highly. And though the woman had proved to be capable, there was still something about her that bothered Sam. "She was supposed to be back here Monday. I wasn't too thrilled when I got her call."

"She'll settle down," was the pacifying reply. "Give her time. As a matter of fact, if it ever comes to guarding Robyn, you've got the perfect one in Sheila. They're friends anyway."

"I'll keep it in mind," Sam said, and he did. He sat slouched in his seat with his fist pressed to his cheek for long minutes after Bill Hoffmeister had hung up. Then Greg barreled in, arms piled high with a conglomeration of papers and notebooks and files, and Sam's attention turned his way.

Greg hadn't been bad lately. He'd worked over the holidays without a murmur, had worked *hard*. He'd been more low key, less smart mouthed. He'd been a help.

"Greg," Sam began pensively, "how well have you gotten to know Sheila?" To his knowledge, and mild astonishment, there seemed to be absolutely nothing romantic going on between the two.

Greg eased his multilayered burden onto his desk, caught the stack when an avalanche threatened and looked up in surprise at Sam's question. "Sheila?" he managed a one-shouldered shrug. "Not well."

Sam recalled Greg's choice comments about Carly. Sheila was every bit as attractive in her way. "Any special reason?"

Greg darted Sam an oblique glance as he worked to distribute his goods into two more stable piles. "Any special reason you ask?" he countered cautiously.

"Just wondering. I thought you were into good-looking women—no pun intended."

"None taken. Sure, I appreciate them. And Sheila is good-looking—I have to say that for her." He settled into his chair and eyed Sam through the corridor he'd shaped. "But there's something about her." He frowned. "I'm not sure I can put my finger on it."

"Try."

The quiet command puzzled Greg. He half wondered if he was being baited and wasn't sure he liked the thought. "Why?" he asked with due respect. "I mean, she's a colleague. It's not my place to be analyzing—"

Sam cut him off with a wave of his hand. "Off the record, Greg. Strictly between you and me. Gut feelings. Nothing written. Nothing beyond that door."

"Gut feelings?" Greg echoed, pleased by the request only until he turned his thoughts back to Sheila. He let out a snicker. "Doesn't make it any easier. It's this vague feeling. I mean, she's friendly and all. She's bright. She's got a sense of humor."

"But. . . ."

"You're gonna think I'm nuts."

"We both may be. Go on."

Greg winced. "It's something in her eyes. A sharpness. She's looking at you, but she's looking past you. And the whole time she's bubbling. It's like she's constantly . . . on. Maybe that's it. Nervous energy. It's unsettling." He paused. "What do you think?"

"I think," Sam mused in a slow, quiet voice, "that I agree with you. Unsettling. That's it. Listen, do me a favor?"

"Sure."

"Get closer to her?"

"How . . . closer?"

Sam appreciated his assistant's caution. "Nothing compromising. Just friend-wise. Get her talking. Find out what she does in her spare time, who her friends are, what she wants out of life. It may be that she's just different. Or—" he passed off a self-effacing smile "—that we're being chauvanistic. I mean, hell—" he sobered "—she does her job all right. I can't fault her on that. But I want to know more about her. Think you can oblige?"

"I'll try," Greg said. "When's she coming back, anyway?"

"Monday. Seems she wanted to spend more time with old friends. And since she's accumulated vacation time over the past few years, I couldn't exactly deny her. Didn't tell her I was thrilled, but then, I think she knew that." He was thinking aloud, feeling strangely free to ramble. "Come to think of it, maybe what bothers me about her is that she doesn't like me." He grinned and raised his brows in self-mocking speculation. "There's always that possibility, isn't there? Hey, maybe she'll decide to transfer back to Chicago. Now, that *would* thrill me."

By the time Carly and Ryan returned home, they were exhausted.

"I don't believe it," Carly moaned, bending to unzip her boots the instant they reached the atrium's carpeted stairs. "My feet are killing me." She pulled off first one, then the other. "That's better."

Ryan, leaning against the railing, made no move to help her. "If you think your feet ache, you should feel my head." He turned and headed up the stairs, mumbling, "I need aspirin."

Making her slow way after him, Carly reached the second floor and glanced despairingly toward the third before deciding that the temptation of Ryan's open door was too great. With her feet finally free of the high-heeled demons she'd been walking on since morning, her legs themselves had begun to protest. Feeling like something of a zombie, she dropped her coat, boots and bag on a chair and went straight for the sofa, where she collapsed and gave a helpless moan as she gingerly stretched her legs onto the coffee table. Her head fell back and, eyes closed, she was in the process of massaging her throbbing temples when Ryan returned from the bedroom.

"Aspirin?" he offered.

She shook her head. "I'll be all right."

"How about a Scotch? My aspirin's not working."

Carly turned her head, opened her eyes and snickered. "You just took it." Then she winced and returned her fingers to her head. "Make mine heavy on the water and I'll take it."

He nodded and disappeared into the kitchen, then was back with two glasses, one of which he handed to Carly moments before he sank into the chair opposite her.

"I never thought it would be like this." He took a slow drink. "I feel like I've been through a wringer. When I close my eyes I see endless arrangements of sofas and chairs."

"Uh-huh." Carly moved her head in slow motion against the cushions. "Bedroom sets. If I see one more platform bed with built-in drawers and attached shelves, I'll scream."

"It was supposed to be fun. What happened? I feel dizzy."

"Burnout. In one day. Maybe we just did too much. Six stores in as many hours. . . ." With a grimace, she dragged her legs from the table and folded them by her side. "And we were supposed to be in such good shape." She sighed. "Well, at least you've got something to show for our pains."

"Yeah," he managed to chuckle. "Sales slips totaling half my life's savings."

"*You* were the one who chose those stores. Most people can't get into them. Where did you get those decorator's cards, anyway?"

"A decorator," he stated. "I represented her in a small matter two years ago. Nice lady. When I called her this week to ask where to go, she was more than willing to help. She wanted to come along." His eyes took on a mischievous twinkle. He was feeling better by the minute. Carly's presence had a way . . . or was it the aspirin . . . or the Scotch . . . ? "I told her that I was taking a very special lady with me and that she was somewhat shy and that I wanted to snow her with my quiet expertise."

" 'Somewhat shy'?"

"You are in a way. Anyhow, it worked. The cards were on my desk the next morning."

"Not bad. Are you sorry?"

"Sorry about what?"

"That you didn't let her take you around. You might have gotten it all a lot easier. She would have known just what to suggest. You probably would have gone to half the number of stores."

"Oh, sure. And the finished product would have had the stamp of a designer all over it. No, I'd rather have your stamp. I love what we bought."

"We did get it all, didn't we," she observed in self-satisfaction, stretching more comfortably. "Every major piece of furniture is on order. All that's left now is to pick up accessories."

"Accessories?" Ryan forced the word out as though it had a vile taste. His expression reflected that opinion.

"You know, art and area rugs and window treatments—all the stuff you've got such great ideas about. Since you've ordered the sectional and wall units in slate, you could use either navy *or* burgundy." She pondered the choice. "Burgundy, I think. Very rich, very masculine."

"How can you even *think* about that, after today? God, I need a while to recuperate. I don't think I want to set foot in—"

"Come on, Ryan," she coaxed, amused. "The hard stuff is done. What's left is the fun part."

"Fun? Hah!" he grumbled and took a drink. "I think I'll leave that up to you."

"No way. It's your place. You're the one who's got to live with it."

"But I want you to like it too." He paused, then dared a test. Despite its inauspicious beginnings, the day had been one of closeness and warmth. Even their exhaustion was shared. They'd been a couple shopping together. More than once a salesman had referred to Carly as Ryan's wife. One part of Ryan very definitely liked the way it sounded. "There's still the issue of the spiral staircase. . . ."

Carly sucked in a breath and gripped her drink more tightly. "Ryan. . . ." She slowly shook her head.

"I own the place now. I can do whatever I want."

"You don't own my place."

Though her voice was very soft, her meaning was clear. She wasn't ready yet. But after the day they'd spent together, one more in evidence of their true compatibility, one more cementing them together, Ryan felt positive. It was only a matter of time until she understood that their relationship was meant to be.

"Then how about tomorrow night?" he ventured, thinking how odd it was that he hadn't asked earlier. But then, he and Carly had for the most part taken things one day at a time. He'd been wary of scaring her off. Of course, there was always the chance that he feared rejection. Living together was one thing; he could appreciate her hesitance to commit herself to something as conclusive. But a date was simpler; he didn't want her to refuse.

"New Year's Eve?"

"Do you have plans?"

She paused. "A fellow from Rand is throwing a party. I told him I didn't think I could make it."

"But you don't have a date."

"No."

"Let *me* take you. I've got a party too—a bash being thrown by one of my partners. She's a swell person. You'd like her."

"I don't know, Ryan. I'm not big on parties."

"Neither am I. That's just it. If we were together, we could make an appearance, stick it out as long as we want, then leave. What do you say? It'd be perfect."

Carly drew herself up as though she were in pain. In fact the pain was there, but it was psychological. Ryan's urgent gaze told her how much he wanted to spend the evening with her. One part of her wanted it no less. But there was the part of her that shied from all unnecessary exposure. And there was that other part that feared what would happen after appearances had been made . . . and they left, together, alone.

A sliver of warmth stirred inside her. Oh, yes, there was the fear of what she knew would be inevitable. But for the first time there was a need that surpassed that fear, a desire that seemed to make the fear worth risking. New Year's Eve was a time for hope and joy, for kisses, for love. Damn it, she deserved to splurge.

A shy smile slowly curved her lips. "Okay," she whispered.

Having fully expected to be shot down, given that her expression revealed the war going on inside her, Ryan was momentarily stunned. "You will?" he asked in such surprise that Carly's smile widened.

"Yes."

"That's great!"

His reaction was ample justification for her decision, and, for the first time in four years, Carly found herself looking very much forward to New Year's Eve.

She might have been more wary had she known the scheme that even then Ryan was beginning to hatch.

TWELVE

CARLY SPENT MOST of New Year's Eve day thinking, planning, dreaming. Running with Ryan in the early morning, she was attuned to the air of expectancy shimmering between them. His excitement was obvious. He dropped her at her door with a soulful kiss, the gleam in his eye speaking of his anticipation of the evening to come. Only later, alone, did she wonder if she'd made the right decision.

For the first time she would be introducing Ryan to her friends, to the people she worked with, to those who would know that Carly Quinn was coming out of her shell. For the first time she would be introduced to *his* friends, to the people *he* worked with, to those who would know the reason he hadn't lived and died the law, for a change, for the past month and a half. On all the mornings they'd run, they'd been alone. True, they had bumped into people when they'd gone to Locke-Ober's or, having spent more and more time together since Thanksgiving, caught a movie or strolled down Newbury Street. But New Year's Eve was something else.

At least it had always been so for Carly. She could remember when she'd been a teenager and her brothers had fixed her up. She'd felt awkward then, knowing exactly what she was missing when, on the stroke of midnight, bursts of glee had exploded, throwing people into one anothers' arms. Her dates had kissed her. She'd kissed them back. But the absence of genuine feeling had always grated. After several years, she'd taken to escorting her father to a grand dinner from which they returned well before the witching hour.

Then had come Matthew. They'd seen eye to eye on that particular night and its festivities, and had always chosen to entertain a few close friends at home. It had been warm and lovely ringing in the New Year that way. After Matthew died, she might have preferred to spend the night alone, but her friends wouldn't hear of it. There had always been some quiet get-together to which she was, not wholly against her will, shanghaied.

And now there was Ryan. She had no doubt the evening would be wonderful, even if—perhaps precisely if—it ended as she suspected it would. There was no better night to look toward the future. If she was ever to know whether she could be Ryan's lover, the time was right.

Yet even if things worked out well, she couldn't help but fear that she'd be leading Ryan on. They might well prove to be as wonderful lovers as they were friends, but what then? The spiral staircase Ryan had in mind? A commitment for something even more?

That was what frightened her. Ryan still didn't know. She wasn't free, she wondered if she'd *ever* be free of the dark cloud that hovered. Her life, as she'd chosen it, involved a danger she simply couldn't impose on anyone else, least of all him.

Sam's call brightened her.

"How're you doin'?" he asked gently.

"Fine. Have you heard anything?"

"Only that you're not to worry. I'm in close touch with both Meade and Hoffmeister. They're on top of everything."

"Good." She hadn't really wanted to talk about that, preferring to push it from her mind for the day, at least. "I hope you're planning something smashing with Ellen for tonight."

"Actually, we've hired a sitter. We're spending the night at the Ritz."

"Good for you! You deserve it!"

"Ellen deserves it," Sam corrected with a chuckle. "How about you? Any plans?"

"I'm going out with Ryan."

"Ahh. That does my heart good. Anywhere special?"

"To a party. Actually two."

"Sounds busy. And fun. Enjoy yourself, you hear? Live it up and don't worry about a thing. *You* deserve it!"

She laughed. "That's what I'm telling myself. That's what I'm telling myself."

Late in the afternoon, her father echoed Sam's sentiment. "He sounds like quite a man, this Ryan of yours. Go on out and have a good time. If anyone's earned the right, it's you."

That was the thought that kept a smile on her face. In a way it was defiance that gave backbone to her bravado. She *did* deserve it, damn it. She *had* earned the right to a good time. And a good time she was determined to have. She lingered in a bath, painted her fingernails and toenails a pale mauve to match her dress, took special pains with her makeup and hair, then dressed in silk. When Ryan appeared at her door looking debonair in a dark suit, crisp white shirt and boldly striped tie, she sensed she was in for a New Year's Eve not to be forgotten.

Whatever fears she'd once had of exposure were pushed aside by the sheer pleasure of being with Ryan. He was the consummate escort, mixing easily with her friends, drawing her into an easy mix with his. It wasn't boredom that moved them from one party to the next with speed; contrary to expectation, the company was relaxed and pleasant. Rather, their momentum was spurred by anticipation. When they hit the air after leaving the second party, that anticipation was enough to leave them breathless.

Wordlessly Ryan helped Carly into the car, circled to his side and joined her. Leaning over the center console, he kissed her once. His ardor was barely leashed; she could sense the tension in his body. Then he held back to look at her, giving her one last chance to demur. When she lifted a hand to stroke his neck, he had his answer.

He started the car and they were on their way. Reaching over, he took her hand and held it tightly. Carly's insides quivered. She clutched his fingers as though they were the only real things in existence and didn't take her gaze from his face until they'd left the lights of Boston behind and were headed down Memorial Drive. Then she closed her eyes and tried to contain the excitement that set each of her nerve ends on fire. She tried to blame her condition on the potent punch she'd drunk, but knew she couldn't. She tried to blame it on the fact of seeing Ryan with her friends, but struck out there too. There was one cause for the shimmering current of heat in her veins, and one cause alone. She was with Ryan now, for the night.

It was only when she assumed they were nearing home that she dared open her eyes again. To her surprise, they'd passed their building and were heading north on Route 2.

"Where are we going, Ryan?" she asked cautiously. He must have made reservations for a late supper. But she was stuffed. Between the two parties, there had been hors d'oeuvres to feed an army.

"You'll see," was his quiet reply. And he drove on, holding her hand, eyes glued to the road.

Carly's were too. They passed through Fresh Pond, ruling out two restaurants there that she knew, then sped through Arlington and Belmont to the northbound ramp onto Route 128.

"Ryan?" Looking at him, she thought his features were tense. In turn she was puzzled. But he simply lifted her hand to his lips and pressed a firm kiss to her fingers.

"Shh. Just relax."

"Where are we going?"

"Farther north."

"To a restaurant?"

"In good time."

If he'd meant to reassure her, his words did anything but. For an instant, Carly felt a surge of raw fear. Then, dismissing it as irrational, she concentrated on watching the highway. But when Ryan turned onto Route 3, still heading north, she couldn't contain her apprehension.

"Where are we going?" she demanded, tearing her hand from his as she sat straighter. She recalled the first time she had ever run with Ryan, when she'd been well aware of how easily he might hoist her over his shoulder and carry her off. Over the weeks, she'd come to trust him completely. Suddenly she wondered if she'd been wrong, if she'd misinterpreted every clue, if she'd seen and heard only what she'd wanted to see and hear. Heart thudding, she watched as he shot her a fast glance. Between her own terror and the dark, she couldn't see his perplexity. Only the tautness of his profile was clear, and that upset her further.

"I wanted to surprise you," he said evenly, gripping the wheel with both hands.

"You have. Where are we going?" She clutched the handle of her door, whether in support or poised for flight she didn't know. The latter was an absurd notion, since the car was traveling at the speed limit.

Suddenly that speed diminished and Ryan pulled up on the shoulder of the road. Everything around them was dark as pitch. Though he couldn't see her fear, he could feel it in the vibrations that came his way.

"I rented a place in Vermont for the night. There's a beautiful—"

"You *what?*"

"Rented a place. What's the matter, Carly?" he asked, bewildered and slightly frightened by her reaction. She had to have known what the evening would bring, and he'd only hoped to make it more idyllic. "I thought you'd be pleased." Mixed with the greatest gentleness was a note of hurt in his voice. "There's a beautiful inn in the middle of the woods with cottages strewn all around. I rented one of them. You'll like it. The inn has a terrific restaurant, and if we don't feel like going outside, they'll bring food to us. I stayed there once before. Right after my divorce, when I needed to get away. It was lonely then. I've been looking forward to being there with you."

"A . . . cottage?" she whispered, beginning to feel foolish. If he was planning on doing her harm, he could as easily have done it right here in the dark without having to fabricate a story about an inn in the woods, a cottage and room service. Moreover, if he was lying, he had to have been an actor of Oscar caliber to exude such sincerity. "You rented a cottage?"

"Yes. The thought came to me while you were in the Bahamas, when I had nothing to do but daydream. I'd been wondering when I could get you up there. Yesterday, when you agreed to go out with me tonight, when you seemed as . . . eager as me . . . I called and booked the place."

"You did?" She didn't know whether to laugh or cry, unbelievably relieved and at the same time incredibly excited.

"Like I said—" he reached out to stroke her cheek with the back of his fingers "—I wanted it to be a surprise. Instead, I seem to have scared the hell out of you. Why, Carly? You don't have any cause to be scared with me."

The hurt was in his voice again, and Carly hated herself for putting it there. She tipped her cheek toward his hand, covered that larger, stronger one with her own. "I know," she murmured, then turned her face and kissed his palm. "I know, Ryan." She inhaled the musky scent of his skin and gained strength. "But I can't help myself sometimes. And tonight, well. . . ." Her eyes met his over their hands; even the darkness couldn't dim their gleam of longing. In a final gesture of apology for all she'd thought but not expressed, she leaned forward with an invitation that Ryan accepted instantly.

With both hands he framed her face, kissed her deeply, then pulled back. "You'll come with me?"

"Yes."

He kissed her once more before letting her relax back in her seat and starting the car. Again he held her hand, this time more gently and with reassuring warmth. They'd driven for another half hour before either spoke, and then it was Carly whose eagerness got the best of her.

"How far is it?"

"Another hour and a half."

"And you didn't think I'd ask questions?" she teased.

"I half thought you might have fallen asleep, what with all that booze. Actually I should have gagged and blindfolded you." At her helpless shudder, he squeezed her hand. "Just joking, just joking. Don't like surprises?"

"Not much." Particularly regarding gags and blindfolds. But she couldn't dwell on that when her thoughts were on a mysterious cottage and the fact that she'd be spending the night there with Ryan, waking in his arms. "Ryan! I don't have any clothes!"

"I do," was his smug reply.

"That's fine. So while you're dressed freshly in jeans and a sweater, I'll be wearing a wrinkled silk dress?"

His laughter shimmered through the car. "I've got clothes for you too."

"Clothes for me?"

"I went shopping this morning." He raised one brow and darted her a glance. "Hope I guessed right on sizes."

She laughed. "I hope you did, too." Regardless, she was pleased as punch that he'd shopped for her, that he'd taken the time, that he'd thought everything out. Abduction schemes took great planning, whether evil minded or not. And since this one was so very clearly benevolent, verging on the divine, she fully appreciated it.

Tucking Ryan's hand between both of hers, she laid her head back against the seat and closed her eyes, clearing her mind of all but the most exciting of thoughts. Ryan naked . . . how would he look? *Her* naked . . . would he be pleased? She turned her head to the side and peered at him. His profile was every bit as strong as she already knew his body to be. When he cast her a quick smile, she felt her insides quiver.

And quiver. The ride seemed endless. They paused at one toll booth, then a second. She was grateful to be sitting. Her legs felt like rubber, as if she'd just completed a twenty-mile run. In a sense, she had. The decision she'd reached was a momentous one. She prayed she was doing the right thing.

Leaving the highway at last, Ryan turned onto a local road that took them more deeply into the heart of Vermont. The way was dark. Only the occasional car crossed their path. Had Carly been alone, she might have been terrified. A breakdown here, and a person was truly helpless. But she wasn't alone. Ryan was with her. As though reading her thoughts, he gave her hand a quick shake.

"Hungry?" he asked quietly. "We could stop for something."

"No. I'm fine," she whispered, heart pounding.

Several minutes later they turned in at a private lane. An elegant country home loomed before them, strategically lit by a rash of spotlights and seasonal bulbs. "The inn," Ryan said and carefully directed the car around the main building and onto a narrow path. "The cottages are around this way."

"Don't we have to check in?"

"I did by phone this afternoon. They're expecting us. They've left a key at the door."

As he spoke, the headlights of the car fell on a small cabin, its front light as welcoming as the golden glow from within. Braking, he killed the engine. Then he was out of the car and at her side to help her out. His arms lightly circled her. He studied her face, lit by the warm porch beacon, his gaze shifting rapidly over her in excitement, apprehension and a bit of disbelief that she was actually with him.

"Carly, are you sure?" he asked. The faint tremor in his limbs was telling. She realized that she hadn't been alone in the frustration of the drive. He touched her face tentatively, tracing her features with an unsteady hand, nervously smoothing her hair back from her cheek. "I know I'm probably rushing you, but I want you so badly." He hesitated. "Frightened?"

"A little," she whispered.

"That makes two of us." He took a broken breath. "You know that you don't have to do anything you don't want."

Her breath came in short gasps. Not even the cold night air could check the flow of heat suffusing her limbs. Her body was hot and alive, aching for Ryan's. The height of her own arousal was as frightening as anything—and they'd barely begun! She never dreamed she could feel this way. "I know."

"We'll take it slow, okay?"

When she swallowed and nodded, he brought her to his side and led her to the door, where he left her for an instant to lean toward an old oak swing suspended from the porch overhang. "They said they'd put the key on a nail." His hand searched the back of the swing. "Here it is." Then the door was open and he led her inside, where she saw that the glow that had beckoned came from a warm fire blazing in the hearth.

"Oh, Ryan," she exclaimed softly, "this *is* beautiful." They were in a small living room. A cushiony sofa and two equally soft chairs stood on either side of the fireplace. Before it lay a thick area rug.

Placing the most promising whisper of a kiss on her neck, Ryan slid her coat from her shoulders. "Let me go out for the bags," he breathed against her skin. "I'll be right back."

Not daring to look behind, Carly stepped toward the fire. Its warmth filled the void where Ryan had been, yet without him by her side, she couldn't help but have a moment's unease. Although she'd sworn she wouldn't get emotionally involved with any man, she'd done it. She was here, in an isolated cabin in the woods, with Ryan, and despite everything that told her she was courting trouble, she couldn't help herself. It was almost as though the loneliness she'd suffered over the past months had been nothing more than a preliminary to needing Ryan. Almost. . . .

She heard the trunk of the car slam shut, then Ryan's footsteps on the stairs, the porch. The cabin door closed, a bolt clicked. She wrapped her arms around herself, terrified in that instant of what she was about to do, half wishing she was back alone in her apartment where everything was safe and secure and predictable.

Then Ryan came up from behind and slid his arms around her, and she knew she didn't want to be alone. She wanted to be with him more than anything in the world. His body was her safety, his arms her security, his warm breath by her ear as predictable as his gentle words.

"Don't be frightened, babe. We'll do it right this time. Eyes open. No dark shadows." Slowly he turned her, speaking with infinite tenderness. "I don't know what it is that haunts you, but tonight is ours. I won't let anything come between us."

Carly felt herself captured and held. "Oh, Ryan," she whispered, "You're so good. So patient. I don't want anything to come between us either."

"It won't. You'll see. It'll be as beautiful as anything you've ever known." His deep voice quavered under the same restraint that held his body taut. Lowering his head, he sought her lips, kissing them slowly, then with greater urgency as her response to him burgeoned. He devoured every inch of her mouth, his tongue stroking hers, plumbing deeper for her essence. When he finally drew back, they were both short of breath.

He cleared his throat and cast a reluctant glance to the side. "They left us champagne, I think. Would you like some?"

She shook her head. She was high on Ryan alone, and the ache deep inside her demanded something headier than even the finest of bubblies.

"Carly," he whispered, adoration obvious in his face, "Carly." His hands caressed her back, bringing her even closer. He kissed her softly, lingeringly, once, then again. "What would you like?" he asked, seeming strangely to gain patience, knowing she was his at last.

At first Carly didn't know what to say. The last time things had just . . . happened.

"Tell me, sweetheart," he urged in a whisper. "I want to know what you like."

She'd never been one to verbalize her feelings when it came to making love. But everything with Ryan was so different. And her need was so great.

"I like it when you touch me," she responded in a shy voice.

"Like this?" he asked, moving his hands on her back.

"Mmm." But she wanted more; the quickening of her breath told him so. His hands roved farther, caressing her shoulders, sliding down her sides to her hips and her thighs, inching upward and inward.

"Like this?"

Her answer was a soft moan. He watched the pleasure on her face, felt the way her body arched into his, and though her hands gave no caress but simply clutched his shoulders for support, he felt more aroused by the minute. Not that he'd started out cold; the heat had been building for hours, no, *days*. The evening's festivities with Carly by his side had been a potent aphrodisiac, the two-hour drive further intoxicating. Knowing what was coming, wanting it, needing it, yet being forced to sit and suffer simply thinking about it mile after mile, had been a sweet torment on which he now took revenge.

"Let me take your dress off," he whispered.

Her pulse leaped, and she nodded, her gaze held steadily by his as he put several inches between them and worked slowly at the buttons, then the belt of her silk dress. His eyes dropped as he slid the fabric from her shoulders and let it slither to the floor. She was wearing a lacy slip that outlined her curves, clinging to her pert breasts, her slim waist, her gently flaring hips.

"So lovely." His voice was a thick murmur as he took in all before him, and it was Carly's turn to be aroused by her lover's pleasure. His fingers slid over the silken fabric, moving upward from her thighs to span her waist, then cup her breasts. His thumbs rolled over their crests until her nipples strained outward. Shaken by a jolt of raw desire, Carly bit her lip and moaned, letting her head fall back and her eyes close as she sagged forward against him, her legs suddenly useless.

But Ryan refused to let passion claim her so easily. "Carly," he whispered, "look at me." He had to repeat it before she complied, her eyes dazed and heavy lidded. "You like that?" His thumbs continued their devastating caress.

"Oh, yes," she whispered.

"What else, babe? What else would you like?"

Breathing shallowly, she struggled to concentrate. There was one thing she wanted badly. "I'd like you to undress," she heard herself say, and would have been appalled at her forwardness had it not been for the rasping shudder that shook Ryan's body.

"God, Carly," he cried, wrapping her in his arms, crushing her hips against his hardness, "you're so special!" He'd said it before; he couldn't say it enough. There was an innocent passion about her that nearly drove him mad. Sensing an imminent loss of control, he stepped back and took several deep gulps of air before shrugging out of his jacket and tugging at his tie.

Deprived of his support, Carly sank to her knees on the thick rug, mesmerized by his every movement as though he were a god — more and more with each piece of clothing he removed. Tossing his tie carelessly onto the chair, he attacked the buttons of his shirt and threw that too aside. She had only time enough to begin to marvel at his broad, hair-strewn chest when his hands went to the buckle of his belt, then the fastening of his pants and its zipper. He'd stepped out of his shoes in time to thrust the pants from his legs, taking his socks off with the swoop. Then he stood before her in nothing but a slim pair of briefs that did nothing to hide the turgid rise of his sex.

Carly held out her hands then and he came to her. With a strangled sigh, she buried her face against the lean plane of his stomach and held him tightly, tightly, her breasts cushioning his tumescence. She ran eager hands over the taut muscles of his buttocks and down the backs of his thighs, aware of the throbbing against her and incited by it.

If she'd been worried about unwanted thoughts intruding as they'd done once before, her fears were unfounded. Her mind was filled with Ryan, to the exclusion of all else. His masculine scent filled her nostrils. The feel of his hard muscle delighted her hands. She pressed warm kisses to his waist as her fingertips ventured beneath the band of his briefs. Then, with the boldness of one possessed not by the ash-strewn past but a very fiery present, she slowly drew the fabric down his sinewed legs, discarding it at last and sitting back on her heels to look at him.

He was magnificent, proud in his maleness. Trembling, she tipped her head back to meet his gaze. As she did, she touched him, her fingers encircling his rigidity, stroking his shaft of straining silk.

"Sweet Jesus," he choked, closing his eyes for an instant, then looking down at her again before grasping her arms and tugging her roughly to her feet. "God, Carly, this was supposed to be slow." His fists were bunching up her slip. "But you're unbelievable." She raised her arms and the slip went in the direction his own clothes had gone. "Slow," he gasped. "Slow and easy." His hands were anything but as they fumbled with the catch of her bra and stripped the gossamer fabric from her flesh. Holding her firmly against him, he slid his hands into her panty hose, exploring the texture of her femininity for an instant before peeling the silk from her limbs. When she was naked too, he clutched her to him and buried his face in her neck. Then, muscles trembling in anticipation, he lowered them both to their knees.

His hands framed her face, holding it away from him. "Slow . . . and . . . easy." He repeated the litany once more, though to no avail. He was clearly at the end of a tautly held rope, but no more so than Carly, who was so abundantly aware of his nakedness against her that it was all she could do not to attack him. "Carly. . . ."

"I need you, Ryan," came her whispered plea. Her arms wound around his neck, her body arched into his.

"I can't hold . . . babe . . . I need. . . ." His mouth was inches from hers, his breath catching. He slid his hands down the backs of her thighs and drew them apart, lifting them over his own spread ones. "Lord, I don't . . . think I can wait. . . ."

She felt his hardness and sucked in a tiny cry. "Don't wait! Don't . . . wait!" In one breath-stopping moment as she settled onto him he thrust deeply; her cry of ecstasy merged with his in echo of their bodies, now one.

They stayed very still then, savoring the sense of filling and being filled. Carly whimpered her pleasure; Ryan held her all the more tightly.

"You feel . . . so . . . good." He managed a throaty rasp. Angling her body the slightest bit back, he caught her gaze, then let his own lower to the spot of their mating. Carly's followed and she experienced an overwhelming sense of rightness. Their skin was, oh, so close, his hair-spattered, hers ivory smooth. With his sex buried deep inside her, their fit was snug and perfect.

He pressed her bottom still closer, then slid his hands up her sides until his thumbs grazed the rock-hard tips of her breasts. Sucking in a hard breath, she closed her eyes, felt herself falling backward, landing ever so gently on the rug with Ryan above her, his face reflecting her own dire need. She flexed her muscles and began to move under him. Bowing his back, he withdrew nearly completely, then thrust more deeply than he had before.

"That's it, sweet . . . more . . . yes, ahh, yes. . . ." His urgings brought her to the wild edge of sanity. The flame was lit; the heat burst forth. This time, though, Ryan was at the center of the flame and Carly had nothing to fear. Ever hotter she burned, spurred on by Ryan's impassioned movements. She arched and strained, craving more and more of him. He gave her everything she wanted and then some. When at last her body exploded into brilliant fragments of ecstasy, he gave a hoarse cry and arched a final time into his own mind-shattering climax.

The spasms seemed endless, a timeless sharing of rapture. When, after long moments of suspended delight, Ryan finally collapsed against her, they lay together in the sweet aftermath of heaven. Their hearts pounded, their limbs were drained of the power that had driven them so fiercely moments before.

He moaned, his breathing ragged. She ran her hands over his damp skin, holding him to her, reluctant to release him even when he levered himself up to gaze down at her.

"You're beautiful, babe. Do you know that?"

She shook her head and blushed, still unable to speak. Not so Ryan. Sliding off to her side and gathering her to him, he propped himself on an elbow.

"That was magnificent. A first."

She knew what he meant and said as much through the eloquent fingers she lifted to his face. He caught a wandering one in his mouth and nipped at it. His eyes were the richest of browns, toasting her with their warmth. Then, he slowly mouthed three words. "I . . . love . . . you."

Her own eyes widened, first in joy, then in fear. It was the latter that took momentary control. With her breath lodged in her throat and her expression one of stunned denial, she shook her head, but Ryan was fast to hold it still.

"No, no. Don't fade out on me, Carly. I won't expect anything from you. I just need you to know. That's all."

"But you can't . . ." she breathed feebly "I can't. . . ."

"It's all right," he soothed, his eyes worshipping her with the love he'd professed. A soft smile broke through the darkness of his beard. "Don't say anything. Just know what I feel. Okay?"

It was his expression, so deep and filled with adoration, that stifled her fear. In his arms she felt safe and protected and, yes, loved, as she'd never felt before. For the moment she couldn't think to question that love or to brood on its ramifications. The here and now were far too precious. Very slowly joy spread through her, bringing a soft smile to her lips.

"Okay," she whispered. As Ryan relaxed back on the rug, she closed her eyes and nestled against his chest. Gradually the heartbeat by her ear steadied and her own pulse slowed.

"It wasn't supposed to be like this," he murmured, deep in thought, hypnotized by the low flicker of flame in the hearth and the sacred warmth of the woman in his arms. He shifted her gently to better hold her. "I had it all planned. We were going to sit by the fire and talk, drink a little champagne and usher in the New Year simply enjoying each other's company." He looked down at her. "Because I do. I do enjoy your company." When she propped her chin on his chest and sent him a chiding look that said she'd caught him with his hand in the cookie jar, he had the good grace to blush. "I mean, sure, I wanted to make love to you, but if you hadn't wanted to we could have just lain here all night and I would have been happy."

Given the urgency of his tone, Carly half believed him. "I wouldn't have been, but thank you for saying that," she whispered.

He squeezed her. "What do you mean, you wouldn't have been? Was my body the only reason you came up here with me?"

She rubbed her flushed cheek against his chest. Her laugh was warm and soft against his skin. "Of course not. But I knew what to expect. I knew it was inevitable. I wanted it.'' Facing him again, she was suddenly serious. "I've never been this way with anyone, Ryan. I mean, there haven't been many men, *any* men other than my husband, and even with him I wasn't this way.''

His heart soared. "What way?'' he asked softly, needing to hear it from her.

She averted her eyes, shy in the face of his soul-searching gaze. "Forward. Aggressive. I've never undressed a man.''

A ripple of fire surged through him, and he hugged her. "God, you're amazing!'' he growled. "And there I was thinking you were reticent!''

She had nothing to say to that. The fact was that Ryan brought out things in her she hadn't known existed. Already she was tingling inside again. She slid her foot down his calf, sandwiching her leg between his two. Her hand moved gently across his chest. She savored the sensation of his firm skin, his soft pelt of hair beneath her fingertips. He was everything she could have asked for in a man, and her body sang. She touched him slowly, wonderingly, her fingers shaping his hipbone, slipping over the smooth valley beyond. Opening her eyes, she relished what she saw, a terrain of uncompromising maleness that was even now responding to her touch.

A low sound came from the back of his throat, followed by her name in hoarse question. Spreading her palm flat over his breast, she raised her head to find the light she'd rekindled shining bright in his eyes.

Ryan deftly shifted her body over his, moving it sensuously until she lay comfortably astride him. With a hand beneath each of her arms, he held her higher.

"Kiss me,'' he ordered thickly and met her lips with his open mouth, drinking her sweetness with a thirst that belied his recent quenching. There had been women in the past; he couldn't make claims to the same innocence as Carly. And, for his experience, his appreciation of her was all the greater. Here was one woman he knew he'd never, never tire of.

Stroking her slender length, he deepened the kiss, sucking her tongue, plunging his beyond it to the darkest hollows of her mouth as he couldn't do to her mind. If he'd had his wildest wish, she'd have returned his vow of love. But he knew she wouldn't lie about something like that. And he also knew she wasn't ready. So he meant what he'd told her; for the present, it was enough that she knew what he felt.

"Oh, babe,'' he muttered, his body on fire once more. The touch of her breasts on his chest, her belly on his, her most feminine parts on his most masculine—he suddenly ached as deeply as though he'd been celibate for years. "I want you again. Lord, Carly, I want you again.''

She smiled softly, with a trace of smugness totally new to her, and inched her pelvis in a slow rotation. "I know.'' Then she slid her knees against the rug and, framing his hips, raised herself to take him in.

This time was the slow and easy Ryan had sought before. It was a more leisurely exploration of muscle and flesh, a more conscious mutual seduction, a taunting to the brink, then withholding and rising again, until they scaled a heart-stopping peak together.

Long after, when Ryan could finally muster the strength to move, he hauled himself from her side.

"Where are you going?" she whispered, unable to bear the thought of his warmth leaving her.

He knelt over her and placed a soft kiss on her lips. "Not far, sweet. Just to build up the fire and make us more comfortable."

Curling up on the rug, she watched him add another log to the fire. When he disappeared into an adjacent room, she realized that the only things she knew of the cottage were what she could see from where she lay—the few furnishings nearby, a small desk by the wall, the rug and the fireplace. Her cheeks grew all the more pink at the thought of the rush they'd been in, and she felt a moment's irrational modesty when Ryan returned. His arms were laden with pillows and a quilt, yet he couldn't resist pausing to look down at her delicate form.

Expelling a slow breath, he shook his head in amazement, then was on his knees, punching the pillows into a comfortable mass, spreading the quilt over her legs. If Carly was abundantly aware of her own nakedness, he was not of his. She marveled at his ease of movement, finding pleasure in the fluidity of his leanly solid lines.

The crackling of the fire accompanied a loud pop as he uncorked the champagne. When he came down to sit cross-legged before her, he held two filled glasses. Clasping the quilt to her breasts, she shyly sat up and took the glass he offered.

"What, uh, what time is it?"

His grin was filled with mischief. "Ten after midnight. I'm afraid we missed the moment."

A rich rosy hue glossed her cheeks and she looked down. "Maybe we didn't. . . ."

He chuckled, suspecting as she did that the New Year had arrived as they'd hit that last climactic peak. "What a way to go!" he decided. "I don't believe I've ever done it quite that way."

She laughed softly, self-consciously. "Me either."

Ryan tucked a finger beneath her chin and brought her face up. "I wouldn't have had it any other way. Happy New Year, babe." He held out his glass.

Eyes dewy with tears of happiness, Carly brought her glass up. "Happy New Year, Ryan. May it be a good year."

"A special year," he added, holding her gaze as their glasses touched with a single soft, sweet ring. He held his glass to her lips and she sipped; she held her glass to his lips and he sipped. Then, as though to seal their wishes, each sipped from his own glass, putting his lips where the other's had been.

Tearing his gaze from hers at last, Ryan inhaled deeply. "Not bad." He swirled the bubbly liquid in his glass. "Not bad at all." Then he looked back at Carly. His eyes caressed her every feature, skimming the slender line of her neck, falling to her hand that clutched the quilt. Very gently he reached out and pried her fingers open, letting the quilt fall to her hips. "Your body's beautiful. I don't want you to hide it from me."

Smiling amid another rush of color, she let her gaze drop. "I guess . . . I'm not used to . . . it's been so long."

"I know. But I love everything about you. Please believe that."

Her gaze met his. "I do," she whispered.

Putting first his glass then hers on the rug, he stretched out by her side, drew her into the crook of his shoulder and pulled the quilt over them both. With his free hand, he gathered both of hers to his lips and softly kissed her fingers, then placed them against his heart.

"You took your wedding band off," he murmured. He held his breath as he waited for her response. It came quietly.

"Before you picked me up tonight."

"Was it hard?"

She thought for a minute, frowning slightly. "No. Strangely. I thought it would be, but I just . . . did it. I guess the time was right."

"Does it bother you now?"

"No. I loved Ma—my husband." Somehow she couldn't get herself to say a name that wasn't the right one. Not to Ryan, who deserved so much more than a fabrication. "Nothing can change what we had." She looked up at Ryan. "I think he'd know that."

"I'm sure he would," Ryan answered, proud of her conviction.

"Does it bother you when I talk about him?"

"Of course not. Why should it?"

She tried to find the proper words. "Some men would be jealous."

"Of a man who's dead?" When she flinched, he held her tighter. "How can I be jealous, Carly? He was your husband. I'd feel worse if you said you didn't love him. And you're right. Nothing can change what you had. Nothing *should* change it." He lowered his voice to little more than a whisper. "I don't want to replace him. I want my *own* place in your heart. There's room, I know there is, for him *and* for me. But I can wait," he whispered, taking her face in his palms, threading his fingers into a riot of auburn waves. "As long as I know that you're here for me now, that you'll be with me back in Cambridge, that I can look forward to seeing you at night, waking up beside you in the morning—" When she would have protested, he put a thumb to her lips. "Whenever you can. That's all. Whenever you can." He took a breath. "I love you, Carly. I love you so."

Carly's eyes filled with tears. "Oh, Ryan."

"Shh." His thumbs smoothed the tears away. "Just be with me now, okay?"

Knowing her heart would have it no other way, she forced a tremulous smile and nodded.

THIRTEEN

NEW YEAR'S DAY DAWNED bright and crisp, though Carly and Ryan didn't see much of it. Having made love on and off for most of the night, they slept until well past noon, when Ryan put in a call to the main house for a hearty brunch, which they ate in bed.

"This is positively decadent," Carly commented. Ryan had just removed the large tray from the sheets and was climbing back beneath the covers with her.

"Decadent is fun. Besides, we owe it to ourselves. When was the last time you spent the day in bed?"

"Two years ago. I had the flu. My bones were aching then too." The last was drawled with such meaning that Ryan rose deftly to the occasion.

"Is that a complaint? I'll have you know that it takes two to tango." His eyes took on a lascivious gleam. "I seem to recall *your* waking me a couple of times there."

"Shh." She drew the sheet to her nose. "You're embarrassing me."

"No need to be embarrassed. You enjoyed yourself, didn't you?"

The sheet fell back. "Mmm. And you?"

He grinned. "What do you think?" Tucking her into his arms, he lay back more thoughtfully, speaking again only after a long silence. "Carly?"

"Mmm?"

He paused, debated, then went ahead. It needed to be said. "You hadn't been with a man for a very long time. You couldn't have been protected."

Tipping her head back, she studied the look of concern on his face.

"I didn't do anything, babe. I should have, but—"

She touched a finger to his lips, and left it there to stroke the thickness of his mustache. "It's all right. It's as safe a time for me as it'll ever be." Her period had ended two days before.

"You're sure?"

"Um-hmm."

"Would it upset you if you did become pregnant?"

"Now?" She felt a sudden stab of pain, knowing that to carry Ryan's child would be glorious yet dumb, really dumb. She might have set aside Matthew's wedding band and in that sense released a part of the past, but much as she'd denied its intrusion on her time with Ryan, the past was still a future threat. "I think it would, for now. I'm not ready, Ryan."

"You do want to have children some day, though."

"Oh, yes," she breathed. "Very much."

His features slowly relaxed. "Then we'll talk about it another time."

As he'd done before, he was implying quite a future for them. And as she'd done before, Carly wasn't ready to accede. She knew how much he wanted a family; they had talked about it more than once. Then she'd passed it off more easily; now, though, having shared all they had in the past hours, she found it harder to ignore. Ryan loved her. He wanted her to bear his children. She wondered just how long he was prepared to wait.

"Hey." He squeezed her arm. "Wanna go for a run?"

"A run? Now?"

"Sure. Beats decadence, doesn't it?"

"But we haven't got any running things."

He pondered that for a minute, then smirked. "Hmm. You're right. That was the one thing I forgot when I went shopping." He paused. "Oops."

"What is it?"

"Jackets. I didn't think about jackets either. I bought sweaters and jeans."

She sent him a speculative grin. "And shoes?"

In answer, he offered a slightly sheepish grimace.

"I'll look cute prancing around in freezing temperatures with a sweater and jeans and high heels."

He tossed the problem easily aside. "No sweat. We can buy what we need when the stores reopen tomorrow."

"Tomorrow?" Her grin faded. "Ryan, I wasn't planning on *today*, let alone tomorrow."

"Come on, Carly. What's back there? It's a holiday weekend. No work, no school. Why not spend one more day with me?" His lips thinned and he murmured beneath his breath, "God only knows when I'll get you back here!"

His sudden fierceness made a point that Carly couldn't ignore. When she returned to Cambridge, there would be other things to face. Given her druthers, she'd stay in this lovely dreamworld forever. But since forever was out of the question, she compromised.

"Just till tomorrow," she cautioned.

"If you say."

She sighed and spoke with heartfelt reluctance. "I do. I'll have to spend most of Sunday getting ready for school."

He stared at her long and hard, then gave a single nod. "As long as you won't mind my hanging around while you work."

Once before she had refused him on the grounds that she would never get any work done. Now she yielded. Not that working would be any easier with the constant temptation of his presence, but she had refused him so much and he had been so good about it.

She forced a scowl and feigned annoyance. "As long as you *let* me work. Agreed?"

He grinned. "Agreed. See what a good fellow I am?" Reaching behind him, he dragged out a pillow and batted her over the head before making his escape to the bathroom.

Carly yelped, then sat up, closing one eye as a piece of lint vied for space with her contact lens. Head down, she tried to remove the lint. It was the contact that came out first. She was still working on the lint when Ryan returned.

"Hey, is something wrong?" he asked, sinking back down on the bed. He thought she was crying and was instantly contrite. He'd only been playing; he wouldn't hurt her for the world.

When she looked up he was perplexed. Though there was no sign of tears, her face was decidedly lopsided with one eye squeezed tightly shut.

"It's okay. Just my contact."

Amazed, he looked down at her forefinger, the pale pad of which held a small gray disk. "Your contact! I didn't know you wore them."

"All the time," she murmured, slithering past him off the bed. She wasn't sure if she was more worried about dropping the small lens or opening her bright blue eye. "Give me a minute." She closed the bathroom door behind her.

It took only a minute for her to clear her eye of its irritant and restore a balance of gray. Her taut fingers grasped the edge of the sink while she scrutinized her mirror image. "Close," she whispered, muttered an oath, then recomposed herself to return to Ryan.

Mercifully, it was to be the closest call she would have in Vermont. The rest of the day, and the next, were unqualifiedly wonderful. With Cambridge, and so much of the real world, at a distance, Carly relaxed and enjoyed everything about Ryan. They talked and made love and slept, shared the local paper and its crossword puzzle, dressed up for dinner at the inn and, after buying a few necessities on Saturday morning, took a long walk in the woods.

Even without the snow craved so desperately by every innkeeper in the county, Vermont was beautiful. The forests, shorn of all but their evergreen finery, presented winter at its most striking. Endless clusters of pines and firs undulated across the landscape, stretching their graceful spikes heavenward as though in communion with their creator. Underfoot, dried leaves crackled in reminder of what had been and would be again in time. And through it all wafted the spicy, sprucy scent of fresh air.

Sitting with Ryan on a high boulder not far from the cottage, Carly marveled at the utter serenity of the vista. Its palette was a blend of grays, blues and greens. She had only to squint to soften the lines of the scene, and then she was reminded of the canvas she'd so recently bought. When she told Ryan about it, his response was immediate. It was the opening he'd sought.

"I want it."

"You what?"

"I want it. For my place."

"You're kidding. Surely you want something bolder—"

"No. How big is it?"

It was quite large; she indicated the vague dimensions with her hands.

"See! It'd go perfectly in my bedroom. What do you think?"

"I don't know," she teased. "I've never seen your bedroom."

He threw his arm around her shoulders and gave her a playful hug. "You will, babe. You will."

It was late Saturday afternoon when they finally headed back to Cambridge. The ride home was nearly as quiet as the one up had been, though a kind of peaceful satisfaction replaced the simmering expectation of that first night.

Ryan's thoughts were filled with the wonder of Carly. Driving distractedly, he reviewed everything they'd shared and done during their two-day spree. Casting the occasional glance her way, experiencing the now-familiar tugging at his heart that the simple sight of her brought, he knew that he loved her more than he'd ever loved another being. It had been the best New Year's ever; he felt more positive than he had in years.

Carly, too, felt positive. New year. New woman. Robyn Hart might have had so very much along the way, but Carly Quinn had Ryan. She wondered if she'd known, when she had removed her wedding band Thursday afternoon, just how different she would be without it. At the time she had been cued by propriety; somehow it hadn't seemed right to party with Ryan wearing another man's ring. If there had been deeper motivations, she hadn't recognized them at the time. Now she did. Though she wouldn't allow herself to envision a long-range commitment to Ryan, or any man for that matter, she felt for the first time that she was truly forging a new life. The events of the past two days spoke loud and clear. She had cast a vote for Carly Quinn in the most elemental way possible.

The winter sun had long since sunk below the horizon when they reached Cambridge. Ryan found a space around the corner from their building, shouldered his overnight bag, in which Carly had stowed her dressy things, tossed the hanger bearing his suit over the same shoulder, and threw his free arm around her. Slowly they walked toward home.

Carly wasn't sure when she grew uneasy. At first she thought it was simply her reluctance to see the two-days' idyll come to an end. As sure as she was that Ryan's feelings toward her wouldn't change, she knew that the time they'd shared in Vermont, totally free of work and worry, had been unique.

Then they passed a parked car whose driver, a man, was sitting quietly, staring in his rearview mirror. By habit she looked twice. It was unusual in an area such as this, where people seemed always on the go, to see one as idle. Perhaps he was waiting for someone. Forcing aside suspicion, she concentrated on the security of Ryan's arm around her shoulder.

Then they passed another car, the occupants of which—two men wearing suits and trench coats—lounged against its door.

She looked straight ahead, but the image of the men remained. It was odd; though they didn't look sinister, they seemed distinctly out of place in the neighborhood. There was something about the way they waited, something deliberately casual, deceptively alert. . . .

Uneasy, she looked at Ryan in time to see him shoot a quick look behind as they progressed up the courtyard walk.

"Who do you think they are?" she asked, feigning nonchalance as best she could.

"Beats me." He seemed to ponder the matter for another instant, then dismiss it, for by the time they entered the front foyer his frown was gone.

Not so Carly's. She cast a cautious glance inside while Ryan stopped to pick up his mail, then she raised apprehensive eyes to the third floor as soon as they entered the atrium. If Ryan noticed her hesitation when he gently nudged her on, he interpreted it as an extension of the reluctance he felt himself. His smile was gentle and reassuring.

"Come on, babe. Let's get these things unpacked."

He led the way, passing the second-floor landing to go straight to her place. Several stairs short of the third floor he slowed, then came to a halt. Slightly behind, Carly stopped as well, instinctively reaching for his arm in support.

"Someone broke in!" she cried. The front door of her apartment stood ajar. She stared at it as she tried to deal with the sudden avalanche of possibilities. One seemed worst than the next, and she began to tremble. "Oh, God. . . ."

Ryan took the few remaining steps at a clip, dropping his things by the railing without once taking his eyes from her door and moved forward. In his mind any violation of Carly was a violation of him; while she felt fear, he experienced a surge of raw anger.

Carly, meanwhile, had a split second's mind-flash of a gunman behind that door waiting to blast whoever stepped through. Terrified, she opened her mouth to yell to Ryan when, to her astonishment, the door opened and a very agitated Sam Loomis emerged.

Ryan stopped short. Sam's gaze shifted from Carly to Ryan and back. It took him a minute to speak.

"Are you all right?" he asked, tension evident in his voice.

Carly ran up the stairs. "*I'm* all right, but *what happened?*" Her eyes were wide and filled with fear. "Who . . . ?" She darted an anxious glance at her door. "Did someone break in?"

Sam took a deep breath, let it out in a whoosh. "No one broke in."

"How did *you* get in?" Ryan demanded sharply. Digging into his pocket, Sam held up a single key, which hardly pleased Ryan. "How did you get that?"

Sam and Carly exchanged a glance. It was Carly who spoke, eyes glued to Sam's, heart pounding. "I gave it to him. It's a spare. What happened, Sam?" She imagined a world of things, one more bleak than the next.

"I was worried."

"You were *worried?*" Ryan barked, barely restraining his fury. It was bad enough that when it came to Sam and Carly he felt excluded. It angered him to find that Sam had invaded the space that should have been theirs alone.

Sam lowered his head and spread a hand across his brow to rub both temples with a thumb and finger. When he looked up, he'd schooled his expression to one of deference. He addressed himself to Ryan. "I tried to call Carly yesterday afternoon, then again last night and all day today." He shifted his gaze to Carly. "You said you were planning to spend New Year's Day here." She hadn't quite said that, but he knew she wouldn't disagree. They were in this together. "When I couldn't reach you, I guess I panicked."

"I'll say," Ryan muttered.

Carly put a hand on his arm. "It's all right, Ryan." She sounded far more complacent than she felt. "I'm sorry, Sam. We were in Vermont." There was an urgent question in her eyes as she asked, "There wasn't something special you wanted, was there?"

Sam deftly read between the lines and smiled comfortably. His eyes held gentle apology. "Just to wish you a Happy New Year. That's all. I should have assumed you'd taken off, but you've never done that before." His last words were spoken with meaning.

"I know." She thought of the men outside, realized that they would be from Sam's office *and* that Ryan would realize it too. She moved quickly to avert his suspicion, rationalizing that it was as good a time as any to reveal Sam's position, particularly with Sam there to help her out. "You're just not used to leaving work at work," she scolded, then explained to Ryan, "Sam's with the U.S. marshal's office. He gets carried away at times. Finds it hard to leave his white charger at the stable."

Ryan's eyes were dark and unreadable. "The marshal's office? Then those are your henchmen parked out front?"

Sam glanced at his watch. "Actually, we were supposed to be somewhere half an hour ago. I'd better run." As he sidestepped Carly he gave her arm a squeeze. "Glad you had fun. Talk to you later."

"Sam?" Carly moved to the railing to follow his descending figure. "How about you? How was the Ritz?"

He flashed her a wide grin. "Ritzy." Then, raising a hand in farewell, he was off.

When Carly turned back, Ryan was gone. She went to the door of her apartment to find him standing in her foyer carefully scanning the premises. Stepping forward, she eyed him quizzically.

His slow sweep of the room continued. "Anything look out of place?"

"Of course not. That was *Sam*, Ryan. He wouldn't touch anything."

"Can't be too careful," he muttered, taking off down the hall. As Carly stood stock-still, he perused the bedroom, then, backtracking past her without a word, the kitchen for outward signs of disruption. "Everything looks okay," he said, returning to her at last. "What's with the Ritz?"

With his hands low on his hips and his dark eyes unyielding, he waited. There was an imperiousness about him that she'd never seen before. It might have bothered her had she not been as sensitive to his feelings. But she knew that the jealousy and resentment he felt were largely her fault. If Ryan knew the truth, the *whole* truth, he would easily understand Sam's concern.

"Sam and his wife spent New Year's Eve at the Ritz. It was the first time they've left their daughter overnight. She's barely two."

"Sam's married?"

"Yes, to Ellen."

"Oh." That made him feel slightly better and the tiniest bit foolish. "And he has a daughter?"

"Uh-huh."

He nodded at this, his mind moving on. "How do you know them?"

Carly didn't correct the "them"—in a sense, she knew both Ellen and Sara, too. Feeling uncomfortable, she forced herself to explain. "Sam went to school with one of my brothers. We've known each other for a long time. When I moved here last summer, he jumped right in as an older brother once removed." It sounded very legitimate. She held her breath, releasing it only when Ryan's features slowly began to relax.

"Older brother once removed?"

"Um-hmm."

"That's why you gave him your key?"

"He was the only person I knew when I came here. It was Sam who helped me find this place and get settled. At the time it seemed logical that, of anyone, he should have my spare." That much was very definitely the truth. Not that Sam had ever used the key before. He'd kept it locked in his files, preferring to ring the bell and call up from downstairs as any other visitor would do. The fact that he'd been worried enough about her to take the key from its place, *and* to bring along three of his cohorts, brought home with stark precision the true nature of their relationship. She had to struggle to keep her voice steady. "Just in case . . . you know, just in case I locked myself out or something. . . ."

Ryan stared at her a minute longer. Then, tipping his head to the side, he let out a deep breath. "Damn it, that guy bugs me." He thrust his fingers through his hair, leaving it disheveled, in keeping with his frustration. Turning his back, he stalked several paces, halted with his feet set in a broad stance, tucked his hands in the back pockets of his jeans and eyed the ceiling. "I know you'll say that I'm jealous, and I am." He swiveled around. "He comes between us." He held out a hand when she opened her mouth to argue. "You've told me there's nothing between you two romantically. And it helps to know that he's got a wife and kid at home. You're not the type to fool with married men. I know that. But, hell—" he threw his hand in the air "—he calls and upsets you, he scares the living daylights out of both of us by barging into your apartment—"

"He didn't barge in. He had a key."

"Don't remind me," he murmured, then seemed to lose his momentum, for he shook his head and spoke more quietly, almost to himself. "What is it about him that sets me on edge?"

Drawn as much by his upset as by her own guilt, Carly went to him. "Maybe it's just that he was here before you were," she offered softly. She put both hands up to his shoulders. "It'd be natural for you to distrust him. But you've got to trust me and believe that you've got nothing to fear in Sam. He's been worried about me since I came, getting after me to date and all. He feels a responsibility toward me. Whether it's right or not, it's meant a lot over the months."

Soothed by her tone, Ryan grew more gentle. "Then I should be grateful to him, shouldn't I?"

She nodded, thinking how true that was. And she hated herself for not being able to tell him everything. But Sam's appearance had been a poignant reminder that her future was still precarious. Given the choice between hiding part of herself from Ryan and subjecting him to the fears with which she lived, she still had to opt for the former. Someday, perhaps, she would tell him. . . .

After a late dinner in the Square, they spent the night at Ryan's place. If his passion was particularly intense, Carly welcomed it in reinforcement of all they'd shared in Vermont. Deep down inside she knew that he wouldn't quickly forget Sam, or accept him, for that matter. In compensation, she gave of herself more than she ever had, responding to his fierceness with a high fire of her own.

Sunday morning they ran together. They joked about the variety of activity they'd had in the past few days, wondering if their running time would be better or worse for it, speculating on the long-range effects of lovemaking on hamstrings and quads and other more private bodily spots.

When they came in to shower though, Ryan in his place, she in hers, she was quite serious. Crossing directly to the phone, she called Sam.

"I was wondering when I'd hear from you," he teased.

"I haven't been alone. Listen, Sam, are you sure there wasn't anything more to your worries? Was there any news from Chicago?"

"On a holiday weekend? Are you kidding? No, there was nothing. Hey, I really am sorry about being there like that when you and Ryan came back. Did he calm down?"

"In time. I told him a little about you. You know, about Ellen and Sara and—" she emphasized each word "—how you went to school with my brother."

"Did he buy it?" came the quiet rejoinder.

She sighed. "I think so. I feel awful about lying."

"Do you want to tell him?"

"Not yet."

"Any special reason?" When she didn't answer, he went on. "I'd say you're *very* serious about him. You had a good time in Vermont, didn't you?"

"Oh, yes."

"Are you in love with him?"

"In *love* with him? God, Sam, I haven't known him very long."

"It can happen like that."

"Not to me," she argued forcefully. "There's too much at stake. Love wasn't in the game plan."

"Still—"

"No!" Then she lowered her voice. "No. I can't think about love yet. It's enough that Ryan is patient and good and a wonderful companion." _And lover_, she thought, but couldn't quite say it, though she knew that Sam knew that she and Ryan hadn't gone to Vermont to roast chestnuts.

"Well, I'm glad of that, at least." He caught his breath. "Oh, damn, Sara's screaming and Ellen's across the street. I've got to run."

"Sam?"

"Mmm?"

"Should I . . . do you want . . . I mean, if I take off again. . . ."

"No, Carly." He grinned. "You're a big girl. You don't have to report every little weekend tryst to me. I really jumped to conclusions far too quickly. From now on I'll know to call _Ryan's_ number before I panic."

"He'll love that," she muttered.

"He'll just know I'm concerned." He covered the phone and yelled a muffled, "I'm coming, baby! Daddy's coming!" Then he spoke directly into the receiver again. "Gotta go, Carly. Take it easy."

"Sure, Sam. And thanks."

"For what?"

"For worrying."

He chuckled. "Any time, hon. Anytime."

No, Ryan, I _don't_ agree with you," Carly declared. Wearing her long terry-cloth robe, she sat on the sofa with her legs tucked up beneath her. It was a lazy Saturday morning, and she was thoroughly enjoying a colorful discussion with Ryan. "You can talk until you're blue in the face about the civil rights of your client, and I'd still argue in favor of the first-amendment rights of the press. That reporter saw a story, researched it, wrote it, and the _Globe_ printed it. There's nothing wrong with that."

Ryan's long frame was folded into the chair across from her. In the week since their return from Vermont, he'd spent more time in her place than his own, particularly as of the Monday before when the movers had left him without a stick of furniture. Carly had teased him at the time, accusing him of having planned her seduction to coincide with his needing a place to sleep, but she hadn't minded. She was grateful for an excuse to have him around.

He crossed his ankles on one of her low sculpted tables and scowled at her. "Nothing wrong with that? What about the principle that a man is innocent until proven guilty? What about the danger of trial by the media?" He thumped his chest indignantly. "My client was proved not guilty in a court of law. Which means he's innocent!"

"Watch it, Ryan. You're spilling coffee all over the place." She leaned forward to put her own cup down and hand a napkin across to him, then watched him distractedly blot drips from the navy velour of his robe. "Inno-cent—" she quietly resumed the discussion, settling comfortably back once more "—only in the formal sense that the jury wasn't convinced beyond a reasonable doubt that he was guilty. That doesn't necessarily mean he was entirely without guilt."

Ryan crushed the napkin in his fist. "In the eyes of the law it does."

"But doesn't the public deserve more? I mean, you're a whiz of a lawyer;

you can get people off right and left. Either the jury isn't convinced, or there's a technicality on which the verdict is overturned or you plea-bargain before the whole thing begins. But what about the public's right to know? You've told me the facts of this case, and you agree that your client may have cut corners here and there in the construction of that building. Okay, so a jury wasn't convinced there was malicious intent. Don't you think that the public deserves a warning? Don't you think that a reporter like Mahoney has an obligation to set out the facts as he uncovers them? After all, the A.G.'s office didn't do much of an investigation itself, and it had been receiving complaints for months.''

Ryan sat forward, clutching his coffee cup. "That's not the point. The point is that my client's business has been adversely affected by not only the original series of articles but by slanted press reports of the trial. The press cannot be given the power to make or break. It's not God. It's not judge and jury. And it sure as hell isn't elected by the people!''

"But it is responsible.''

"That's debatable.''

"Come on, Ryan! Do you really think—'' the phone rang but she ignored it "—that Mahoney had a personal motive in ruining Walfleet Construction?''

Ryan thought about that for a minute. "Personal? As in inflated sense of self-importance, maybe.'' Another ring. Ryan's voice softened instantly. "Want me to get that, babe?'' It was as though he'd been playing a part and suddenly reverted to himself. Though Carly was coming to be used to it, at first she'd been stunned by the way he could turn on or off at will. What she realized was that he was strong in his beliefs, and he enjoyed the discussion for discussion's sake. She was finding that she did too.

"No, I'll go.'' She rose from the sofa. "But I still think you're wrong. I've known my share of newspaper people and the ego thing was minimal.'' When the phone rang again, Ryan shooed her with the sweep of his hand. She continued talking as she walked, thankful that given her detachment from this situation she was free to express views so close to her heart. "Investigative reporters work hard. For every one story that pans out, they've hit dead ends on four or five others. It's an ugly job—'' She picked up the phone well after the fourth ring. "Hello?''

"Carly?'' came the cautious voice on the other end of the line. With one word alone, its nasal quality gave it away.

"Sheila! I was beginning to wonder if you'd ever made it back from Chicago. How are you?''

"Great!'' Sheila answered lightly. "But I've been really busy since I got back. How are you? Have a good trip?''

"How did you know about that?''

"Carly, you told me,'' she scolded with playful indignation. "More than once. The Bahamas, Jim and Sharon and the kids, lots of sun. God, was I drooling.''

"Oh, the Bahamas.'' It seemed like an eon ago. She'd been thinking of her more recent trip, that glorious one with Ryan. Standing at the door of the kitchen from where she could see the object of her desire, she grinned. "I had fun. But it was good to get back." Her smile grew more catlike when Ryan pushed himself from the sofa and approached.

"You sound strange. What's happening?"

"Nothing." Carly kept her eyes on Ryan, who moved close up and pressed her slowly back against the wall. His essence, clean, male, and unique, taunted her senses. "Just . . . the usual," she managed in a mildly strangled tone.

"The usual sounds weird. Am I interrupting something."

Ryan was nibbling on her earlobe, marveling at his phenomenal attraction to this woman. He loved every minute he spent with her, intellectual arguments such as the one they'd been having included. She was supremely bright, stimulating both in bed and out. Oh, yes, questions remained; he knew there were things she hadn't told him. Quick to talk of her childhood and even her married years, she seemed to fade out after that. At times when she thought he wasn't looking he still caught that haunted look in her eyes, and he couldn't forget their first few times together and the fear he'd sensed in her. Then, of course, there was Sam. Something about him—a certain air of authority regarding Carly—went beyond simply the "older brother once removed" syndrome. All too often Ryan found himself daydreaming at work, trying to solve the puzzle; yet when he was with Carly, it flew from mind. Even now, as he pressed his lips to the soft pulse beneath her ear, he could think of nothing else.

Carly cleared her throat. "Not really. We were just, uh, just having an argument." Frustrated, she sent Ryan a quelling stare. "You called at an opportune time."

" 'We'? Who's 'we'?"

"Ryan and I." When the man in question ran his tongue down the slender column of her neck, she closed her eyes and tipped her head to ease his access. Her voice was more of a purr. "We were just having coffee."

"Then you're still seeing him?"

"Um-hmm."

"A lot?"

"Um-hmm."

"Does that mean that I can't stop by for a few minutes this afternoon?"

"This afternoon?" Coming to attention, Carly put a hand on Ryan's shoulder to hold him off for a minute. Her eyes held the question, which he answered with an accommodating nod and a whispered explanation. "I've got to stop in at the office for a couple of hours."

She had several things to do herself, particularly now that she seemed to be feeding two mouths more often. Not that she minded; for every time she cooked for Ryan, he took her out another. She hadn't eaten as well in years. "Sure, Sheila. This afternoon's great. But I've got a few errands to run. How about making it after three?"

"After three you got. See you then."

When Ryan took the phone from her and hung it up, she looped her arms around his neck. "That should be nice. Maybe you'll get a chance to meet her. How late will you be?"

"I should be back by four. Think she'll still be here then?"

"Knowing Sheila, yes. She loves to talk."

Arm in arm they walked back to the living room, where they stopped. "This place looks better," Ryan remarked.

"What do you mean?"

"More lived-in. Look, the newspaper's all over the place, there are coffee cups and empty plates. And I like the clay piece on that wall." On the Saturday they'd shopped in Vermont, in addition to buying clothes Ryan had insisted on picking up a small handcrafted plaque that had caught Carly's eye. It was textured, stones intermeshing with clay in a distinctly modern arrangement that was warm and interesting. "Between that and the driftwood you adopted in Rockport—" which had found a fitting resting place on one of the shelves of the wall unit "—your decor has taken on a more personal note."

She poked an elbow into his ribs. "Hah. That's just because you like seeing *your* fingerprints on things. I know your type," she teased. "Has to have a hand in everything."

He turned her into his arms and eyed her more solemnly. "When it comes to you, you're right. I like seeing evidence of the times we've spent together."

"Spoken like a true lawyer," she quipped, but her voice lacked the lightness she'd intended, sounding soft and wispy instead.

"Mmm." He kissed her once. "And if this lawyer doesn't get dressed and to work, he's apt to be out on his ear." He paused, then spoke hesitantly. "Hey, you're sure you don't mind going out with the Walkens tonight?" Cynthia Walken was a partner of Ryan's; it was her party to which they'd gone on New Year's Eve.

"Of course not. We owe them an invitation. They both seemed very nice . . . not that I had much of a chance to talk with either of them that night."

Ryan's grin cut through his beard in a devilish way. "We were in a hurry, weren't we?"

"Um-hmm."

"We'll have to try to be more patient this time."

"I should hope so."

He held her closer. "Know what I could go for?"

"Don't even think it, Ryan Cornell!" Carly exclaimed, pushing herself from his arms and making ceremony of gathering the scattered sections of the newspaper.

Ryan stood with his hands on his hips in a righteous pose. "How did you know what I was going to say?"

"Because I know you," she said, not in the least intimidated by his stance. "And I know that one-track mind of yours. Now, are you going to leave so I can get something done?"

He gave her a wicked grin and strode toward the bedroom. "As soon as I get some clothes on. You weren't thinking of sending me out in the cold like this?"

Eyes glued to his retreating form, Carly knew she didn't want anyone else to see how gorgeous he looked in a rich robe that stopped just short of his knees, broadcasting the longest of muscled calves. "I'll give you five minutes. Then . . . out!"

It was more like ten, for she made the mistake—the very pleasant mistake—of joining him in the bedroom, where he quickly made her forget all those other things she had to do. His kisses were long and lingering, heating her as they always did. She would have thought she'd get used to this, but she never did, so she couldn't help but yield to his fire for those few final minutes before he left. Even then it took a tepid shower to still her ache. The knowledge of Sheila Montgomery's impending visit helped. As always, Sheila was a timely reminder of what her life really was . . . and what it wasn't.

"So, tell me about Chicago. How was Harmon?"

Sheila sat back on the sofa and let her gaze wander around Carly's living room. "Harmon is Harmon."

"What does *that* mean? Are you two on or off?"

"Off."

"You don't sound upset."

She tossed her raven-black hair over her shoulder in a gesture of indifference. "I'm not. He can be a pill some times."

"But you were so excited when he called. You spent Christmas with him, didn't you?"

"Oh, yeah. But he split after that. He wanted to go skiing." She shrugged. "That mattered more to him than me. It's just as well. I found other things to do." She changed the subject, idly fidgeting with a throw pillow. "Tell me about you and Ryan. Thick as thieves, are ya?"

Skipping over the more intimate aspects of their relationship, Carly told Sheila of the days before New Year's, of New Year's Eve itself, of Vermont, of their return. Sheila seemed to want to know everything—whom she'd met at the parties, the name of the inn where they'd stayed, what exploring they'd done there, what they'd ordered for Ryan's place—and she showed enthusiasm even when Carly feared she was rubbing salt on the wound. But Sheila asked, following one question fast with another, so Carly answered, finding a strange kind of satisfaction in giving Sheila, who'd known her in that other world, this proof of her new life.

By the time Ryan arrived, Carly was beginning to feel decidedly guilty about talking so much about herself. She was relieved by the knowledge that Ryan would redirect the discussion. Sure enough, after depositing a large bag and a bouquet of flowers on the kitchen counter, he extracted a dark bottle from the bag, ferreted out three glasses from Carly's cabinet, filled each with mahogany-hued liquid, then joined the women in the living room.

"Sherry, ladies? It's about that hour."

Sheila was about to speak up in favor of a rum and Coke when she caught herself and smiled shyly, suddenly more subdued. "Thank you. This is lovely."

Carly cast her vote of agreement through the smile she gave Ryan. She'd seen the flowers, and though she didn't want to make a big thing of them in front of Sheila, her smile spoke her thanks for that gift as well.

Ryan settled into a free chair. "I'm glad to finally meet you, Sheila. Carly tells me you were away?"

"That's right." She gripped her glass tightly. "I had to take care of some things back in Chicago."

"You haven't been here long, have you?"

"I transferred to the Boston office a little less than two months ago."

"What office is that?" he asked politely, causing Sheila to look in alarm at Carly, not quite sure what to say. It was Carly who spoke, trying to sound as nonchalant as possible.

"I'm sorry. I thought I'd told you. Sheila works with Sam. That's how we met."

It was Ryan's turn to look surprised, and the slightest bit dismayed. At first Carly feared he had suspected something of a strange coincidence in Sheila's occupation. Then she reminded herself of Ryan's displeasure at anything involving Sam Loomis, and she forced herself to relax.

"I didn't know," he stated thoughtfully. Evidently coming to the conclusion that a grudge against Sam shouldn't extend to Sheila, he smiled. "It must be interesting work."

"Sometimes. Sometimes it's pretty boring."

"Isn't any job? Tell me about yours. What kinds of cases are you working on?"

Carly sat back and listened while Sheila recounted several of the assignments she'd had since she'd come to Boston, then, at Ryan's prodding, spoke of some of the more exciting cases she'd handled in Chicago. She had enough sense not to mention Carly's case, taking her cue from Carly's impromptu fabrication of how they'd met. When she asked Ryan about his practice, he obliged with easy conversation. At least Carly thought it was easy, though Sheila seemed less than relaxed. She wondered if there was something about Ryan that made her nervous; Sheila Montgomery was not usually one to shy from men. She didn't have long to speculate though before the downstairs buzzer rang.

Sending a "who in the world could that be" look Ryan's way, she went to the intercom. "Yes?"

"Carly, it's Tom Cornell. Is my brother there?"

Carly paused for a minute, then couldn't quite suppress a grin. She made sure to keep her back to Ryan and Sheila. "He's here. Want to come up?"

"You bet."

She pressed the release, then opened her front door. Only then did she turn back toward the living room. Ryan was wearing a maddeningly innocent expression. Sheila seemed more on edge than ever.

It was to the latter that Carly addressed herself, a mischievous twinkle in her eye. "Relax. You'll like Ryan's brother, Sheila. He's nice."

Within moments, the tall, blond-haired man appeared at the door, greeting Carly with a warm hug—which she hadn't expected but which she supposed she should have, given the strength of Ryan's feelings and the fact that he was sure to have told his brother he was practically living with her—and casting a gaze toward Ryan, whose message on Tom's answering service was simply that he should stop by sometime after four-thirty. He was about to ask what he'd wanted when his gaze fell on Sheila. He stood very still for an instant before daring to dash a pleased, if questioning, glance at Carly.

Taking his arm, Carly led him down into the living room. "Tom, I'd like you to meet a friend of mine, Sheila Montgomery. Sheila, Tom Cornell."

Eyes glued to Sheila, Tom walked around the low tables, took Sheila's hand and raised it to his lips in as courtly a greeting as Carly had seen. She snuck a glance at Ryan to find that he too was amused, then focused back on Sheila, whose eyes were round and more lively than they'd been all afternoon.

"This is a pleasure," Tom said, his voice smooth as velvet and every bit as alluring.

"For me too," Sheila breathed. "I've seen you before."

"Twice."

"You remember?"

"I remember."

Ryan cleared his throat. "I didn't know you'd be by today, Tom," he said with a meaning the other couldn't miss. "Have a seat. Would you like some sherry?"

"Sherry?" Uncomprehending at first, Tom dragged his gaze from Sheila's face to the glass in her hand. "Ah, no. No thanks." Then he shifted his gaze to Carly. "Don't have any beer, by chance?"

With a suspicious look, Carly redirected the question to Ryan, who accommodated her by tossing his head toward the kitchen. "Let me take a look," she said, turning. Sure enough, a six pack sat at the bottom of the bag Ryan had brought. He'd come prepared, she mused, tugging one of the cans free and returning to the living room. "It's not quite as chilled as it should be."

"No problem." Taking the beer from her, Tom smiled. His attention was quickly back on Sheila, whose own had never left him. From where she was sitting Carly could feel the electricity between the two and wondered if it had been the same between her and Ryan. *Had* been? *Continued* to be. She didn't wonder; she knew. Even now, when she met his gaze and he winked, she felt the charge.

Much later, together in bed, Carly and Ryan would laugh at how it had been. Proud of themselves for having brought together two people so very obviously attracted to each other, they hadn't minded that they'd felt utterly superfluous during that time in her apartment. Nor had they minded when they'd had to excuse themselves to dress for a dinner date. Deftly taking the hint, Tom and Sheila had left . . . together. It was perfect.

FOURTEEN

S HEILA SAT AT HER DESK the following Monday feeling strangely disconcerted. She half wished she'd been assigned to the courtroom; at least then she'd have had something to keep her mind busy. As it was, blank report forms lay before her. She took the first, rolled it into the ancient typewriter that had come with her closet of an office—it galled her to think of being on the fifteenth floor without even the tiniest window—struck several keys and promptly chipped a fingernail. Muttering a choice oath, she snatched the paper from the typewriter, crumbled it into a hard ball and slammed it into the wastebasket. Then she sat back in her chair and attempted to file her wounded nail into an acceptable shape.

After a minute she despaired of that and let her hand fall. It came to rest against the purse hanging on the back of her chair. Instinctively her fingers curled around the fine leather, and she pulled the soft pouch onto her lap. It was lovely, as well it should be, she mused, given the amount she'd paid for it. Though a large satchel had always been part of her outfit, she'd never had one quite as nice. A small smile curved her lips. The car was nice, too, a bright, new, shiny Mazda, the sporty model she'd admired from afar for so long. Driving it this weekend, she'd felt elegant, special, important . . . not that she'd had all that much time to drive around.

Her thoughts turned to Tom and her smile grew more poignant. Tom Cornell was something else—very different from the men she'd known, oozing with sexuality yet restrained and respectful. They'd gone to dinner together on Friday night, to the theater on Saturday. Though she'd been awed by the latter, Tom had taken it all in stride, seeming to enjoy her enjoyment as much as the play itself. On Sunday he'd taken her out for brunch, then back to his house where he'd shown her his computer with the enthusiasm of a young boy. Computers had always bored her; she'd never understood their workings and therefore had found them thoroughly intimidating. But Tom's enthusiasm had been catching. Under his patient tutelage, she'd sat at the keyboard responding to prompts, giving commands, making the machine do remarkable things. Together they'd created a game on it, then spent hours playing it. She'd had fun.

And Tom Cornell hadn't even made love to her.

"Sheila?" Her head shot up. Greg Reilly was leaning around her half-open door. "Busy?"

She threw a disparaging gaze at the papers on her desk. "I should be, but I'm not. These things are hard to get into."

He straightened and came in. "Case reports? I know the feeling. Things are pretty slow at my desk too. Must be Monday mornings. Wanna waste a little time with me?"

He didn't need to coax her further. "Sure," she said, pushing the papers back on her desk in a symbolic gesture. "Why not."

He grinned and propped a thigh on the desk corner. "So, how's it going? We missed you while you were away."

"Come on," she chided. "Anyone can do what I do."

"Not the way *you* do it. Sam put Henshaw on the Plymouth County case; she came near to brawling with our witness."

Sheila chuckled. "Theresa Rossi is a handful. One week with her was plenty. I'm glad I was away. Poor Henshaw."

"How was your trip, anyway?"

"Great."

"Do you miss living in Chicago?"

She shrugged indifferently.

"How do you like Boston?"

"I like it. It's cozy."

"Cozy. That's a new one."

"It's an easy city to get around," she explained impassively. "Not overwhelming like New York."

"Have you had a chance to meet people here?"

"A few."

"Anyone special?" He phrased it in the way of an interested suitor feeling out the competition. When she simply shrugged again, he changed the subject. "So." He sighed. "How's your apartment?"

"It's okay."

"Warm enough? Some of those landlords get pretty stingy with the heat."

"It's fine."

He sensed a wariness in her and wondered if he'd lost his touch. Fearing that he was trying too hard, he relaxed and let his gaze fall quite naturally to the soft wool dress she wore. It was loose fitting and simple, with a boat neck and wing sleeves; its red color set off her black hair and pale complexion well. "I like your outfit. Is it new?"

She smoothed the gentle fabric, then tipped her chin up with a hint of defiance. "I went on a shopping spree last week. I felt I deserved something new and bright to carry me through the drab winter months."

"You never look drab, Sheila. I have to say that for you. The office has never been more colorful."

Looking into his eyes, she couldn't help but wonder just what had brought him into her office. Yes, his gaze was warm, but not in the way of typical male appreciation. He'd never been terribly solicitous before. There had never been the slightest spark between them. He was the right age and very definitely good-looking, but he had always been standoffish, Sam's assistant in every sense. His sudden interest made little sense.

Unless, she thought with a jolt, unless he suspected. . . .

"You're kind to say that," she said demurely, then took on an expression of worry. "I only wish Sam felt that way. He distrusts me for some reason. I have no idea why."

"He doesn't distrust you," Greg improvised. "He's just a tough guy to get to know. He plays by every rule. Believe it or not, it was months before I saw him crack a smile." That was the truth.

"Really? But I thought you two were close."

"Not at first. It was political pull that got me in here. He resented that."

Where his studied attempts at flattery had gotten him nowhere, this honest confession seemed to break through Sheila's reserve. Her expression opened and she angled back more comfortably in her seat.

"How did you get him past it?"

"By working my tail off."

"I was afraid you'd say that." She shook her head. "I'm doing the best I can. It doesn't seem to faze him."

"It fazes him. Believe me. He's noticed."

"Hmmph. Could've fooled me. He seems angry every time I come near him." She widened her eyes innocently. "Do you think he's got something against the Chicago office?"

"Nah."

"Then it has to be me." She looked dejected. "I'm doing something wrong."

"You're new. That's all. Give it time."

Give it time. That was what they all said, she mused. Give it time, and you'll meet Mr. Right. Give it time and you'll make it up that ladder. Give it time and you'll have all those things dreams are made of. Well, she'd tired of waiting.

"So there's hope?" she asked, going along with the game.

Before Greg could respond, a knock came at the door, followed seconds later by the appearance of the very man under discussion. "Greg, here you are. Got a minute?"

Greg knew well enough to jump. He'd seen that tense look on Sam's face only once or twice before; it meant trouble.

"Sure."

Sam was gone as quickly as he'd come. At the door, Greg gave Sheila a parting wink, then made a beeline for his office.

Sam stood before the window, head bowed, fingers rubbing his forehead. When he heard Greg's footsteps, then the door closing, he turned.

"What's up?" Greg asked.

"I've just had one hell of a go-round with John Meade in Chicago. He wants

Carly Quinn back there for a couple of days. I tried to get him to come out
here but he won't." He gave a weary sigh. "I'm going to take her."

"You?" Normally such a job would fall to one of the underlings in the
office. As chief deputy, Sam was in demand.

"Yeah. She'll be really upset at having to go at all; the least I can do is to
soften it up some. She likes me and trusts me. It might help." Allowing Greg
no time to comment, he raced on. "Mazur and Stenmar will keep overall track
of things. I want you to cover my desk though. And you'd better watch Judge
Feldstein; if she gets any more threats, we'll have to put someone on her."

"Sure thing."

"Everything else is pretty well set. If all goes well I can be back by Wednesday night."

"Isn't it risky—your going with her? If someone sees you together and
makes the connection. . . ."

Even in as little time as he'd had, Sam had thought it all out. Actually, he'd
thought it all out before, when the trip to Chicago had been no more than a
vague possibility. "We'll be together without being together. She won't have
to know me, but I can keep her in sight all the time. Someone from Hoffmeister's office will meet the plane in Chicago and take over from there. When
I've seen that she's in good hands, I'll find my own way to the state's attorney's
office." He shook his head and raised troubled eyes heavenward in a plea for
strength. "She is not going to like this. Not a bit." Lowering his gaze, he
murmured, "Neither is Ellen, for that matter."

"Ellen will understand."

"Yeah. Unfortunately, Wednesday is our daughter's birthday. It's gonna
take a whole _load_ of understanding!"

There wasn't much Greg could say on that score. He'd met Ellen only once,
just before Christmas. Though he and Sam had grown closer in the past weeks,
he wasn't exactly in a position to offer personal advice. All he could do was
to reassure Sam that he'd be on top of everything crossing his desk, which he
promptly did. He was rewarded with an appreciative nod.

"When will you be leaving?"

Sam had already scooped up his blazer and was tossing it over his shoulders.
"As soon as I can get home to pack a bag and pick up Carly." He grimaced.
"She's not gonna like this. . . ."

"Some great novels are semiautobiographical. Jonathan, tell me what you see
of Hemingway in _A Farewell to Arms._"

Jonathan, a rangy sixteen-year-old at the gawky stage, looked down at his
notes. His deep voice came with deliberation. "I think that the war part is his.
Didn't he fight in World War I?"

Carly sat on the front of her desk with her legs crossed at the ankles.
"Uh-huh." She said nothing more, waiting patiently for an elaboration. It was
Deborah, attractive and poised, who spoke up.

"The love story is fictitious. He didn't get married until after the war, and
that marriage ended in a divorce."

Carly nodded. "That's true."

"But he had been in love," one of the other boys argued. "He remarried before the book came out."

A third, Brendan, joined the fray. "Sure, and his father packed it in the same year."

" 'Packed it in'?" Carly gave each word its due.

Brendan shrugged. "Killed himself. Maybe Hemingway had a fixation on death. To kill Catherine off that way—" The bell rang and there was a moment's hiatus.

Carly rose. "That's it. For tomorrow, think about the tragic quality of that last chapter. A theme. Two pages. And there will be a full test on Friday." At the last there were several sighs and a muffled moan, then all sound of complaint was lost in the gathering of books and papers and the slow dispersal of students.

Carly, too, closed her notebook and set her book atop it before stooping to get her bag. When she stood, she caught her breath. Sam was standing at her door.

"Sam! What a nice surprise!" Then she noted his expression. "Uh-oh, what's wrong?" But she knew; *she knew.*

"Meade called this morning. He wants you in Chicago."

"Oh, no . . ." she whispered.

"Just for a day or two. He wants to go over everything with you in hopes of avoiding that new trial."

"When?"

"Now."

"*Now?* I can't leave now, Sam!" she exclaimed, then looked frantically around. "I teach. I can't just—" she gasped "—just take off!"

He came closer and spoke very gently. "You have to. You haven't any choice."

All color drained from her face. It was bad enough running out on her job. . . . "But what about Ryan?"

"What about him?"

"I . . . he . . . we've been practically living together. If I just disappear, he'll be hurt and angry and suspicious. I can't leave him without an explanation. What'll I say?"

Tucking her books into the crook of his elbow, Sam grasped her arm and guided her toward the door. There wasn't any time to waste; they had little more than an hour to make their plane. "You'll leave a note and say that an emergency's come up at home and that you'll call him. Now, should you speak with the headmaster?"

Carly stared dumbly at him, then looked straight ahead, seeing nothing of the corridor through which he propelled her steadily. "The headmaster. Uh, yes." Forewarned as she'd been, the turn of events was no easier to accept. She couldn't believe what was happening. Her life had been so pleasant. . . .

An hour later she sat on the plane. Beneath the wide brim of her hat, her hair was pulled straight back into a sleek chignon. She wore dark glasses over her colorless contacts. Only after the craft was airborne did she remove the hat and glasses. Her bright blue eyes stunned Sam; even anxiety-clouded, they were brilliant.

"Sorry I couldn't do better for clothes," she whispered, a wry twist to her lips. "I threw out all my Robyn things last summer. Gauzy blouses, floppy blazers—they were too artsy, too whimsical for Carly Quinn."

"You'll do fine," he murmured appreciatively. "I can't believe how different you look. Two things—eyes and hair—it's amazing."

"I feel strange."

His eyes widened in alarm. "Sick?"

Frowning, she tapped her head with her forefinger. "Crazy. Like I'm playing an absurd game. You know, charades or something."

He eyed her sadly. "It's no game, hon. But it'll be okay. Trust me."

She did trust him, and given the upset this trip was bound to be, she needed every bit of help she could get. "Thanks for coming, Sam."

"No problem." He raised a finger to his lips and tossed his head meaningfully toward the rest of the plane.

Nodding her understanding, Carly turned her head toward the window where only the clouds could see her heartache. "RYAN?" Clutching the phone, she spoke timidly.

"Carly! My God, what happened? I couldn't believe it when I found your note! Is it your dad?"

She hated herself for what she was doing but felt, and not for the first time, that she was controlled by others. "Yes."

"His heart?"

She cringed. If all was well, as she assumed it was, John Lyons was playing golf with his brother in Phoenix. She'd called him there a few days earlier, before Ryan had come home from work. "Yes. His heart."

"How is he?"

"He'll be all right. It was just a scare. I think I'll stay with him for another day or two. You found the key, didn't you?"

"Right in my mailbox." He managed a half laugh. "How do you think I got in?"

She'd called her own number, just assuming he'd be there. "Right. That was stupid of me. I guess . . . I guess I'm not myself."

"You sound awful. Damn it, I wish you'd waited. I would have gone with you."

"I couldn't wait, Ryan. The call came early this morning, and I caught the first flight out."

"Want me to come? I can be there in the morning."

"No. No. Really. It's not necessary. It was just a scare. I'll be okay once I get over the shock."

"Then let me have the number so I can reach you. Or the address." If he couldn't be there he wanted to send something—flowers, candy, *anything* to cheer her up. As it was he felt thoroughly helpless.

"Ah . . . no." She tried to think quickly, but it wasn't easy with her heart torn in tiny pieces. "Listen, I'll call you again tomorrow night. Besides, I'll be at the hospital most of the time. I don't know when I'll be back." She swallowed hard, aware of a cold sweat on her palms. "Ryan, I miss you."

"I miss you, too, babe. Are you sure there's nothing I can do?"

"I'm sure. Just take care of things back there, okay?" Her voice cracked, and she knew she had to get off the phone quickly.

"Okay. Carly, I love you."

Hot tears trickled down her cheeks and, in that instant, she knew that she felt the same. "I . . . I'll see you soon," she whispered, then added a choked, "Bye-bye," and hung up the phone.

"Okay, let's go over this one more time."

John Meade stood over her, her inquisitor. Brozniak, his assistant, leaned indolently against the far wall of the office, relentlessly staring, saying nothing. Had it not been for Sam's reassuring presence, Carly would have screamed. If she'd thought a full day of quizzing on Tuesday had been bad, this Wednesday morning was unbearable. She'd barely slept for two nights and was nearly at her limit. Not to mention the fact that her scalp ached. Lacking the patience to blow her hair straight and let it hang long as Robyn Hart used to do, she had pulled it tightly back into a bun for the third day running. Now, for the first time, she could fully appreciate the beauty of letting it curl free and soft in the manner of Carly Quinn.

"I met Peter Bradley when I first came to work at the *Tribune*," she droned. "He was a staff photographer. I was a reporter."

"Had you ever seen him before that?"

"No."

"But you'd heard of him?"

"Yes. He'd won any number of prizes for photojournalism. Nothing like a Pulitzer, but local things. I'd always admired his pictures."

The prosecutor's eyes narrowed. "Admired?"

She scowled back. "Yes. Admired. They were striking, more dramatic than most of the other newspaper stuff."

"Had you ever bought one of his photos?"

"No."

"Had you ever cut one from the paper and framed it?"

"No!"

Meade ran a hand over the few remaining hairs on the top of his head. "Okay. You'd never met him."

She shook her head and spoke slowly, feeling as though she were enunciating for a dimwit. "Not until I started at the *Tribune*."

"How well did you know him then?"

"Not very. I saw him in passing from time to time. It wasn't until I joined the investigative team that we actually worked together." She sighed and raised pleading eyes to the state's attorney. "John, do we have to go over this again? I've already told you as much as I can."

Meade picked up on the slight catch in her voice. "Then there's something else—something you *can't* tell us?"

"No! I've told you! Peter and I were *friends*. That's it!" Annoyed and tired, she looked away. "I just don't see the point in all this. You're looking for something that *isn't there*. If Culbert's lawyer thinks he can prove something, let him try."

"Unfortunately, if it comes to a trial, the burden of proof is on the state. All Mancusi has to do is to plant a seed of doubt in the minds of the jurors. *We're* the ones who have to prove there was no deep emotional involvement between you and Bradley."

Frustrated beyond belief, Carly nearly went wild. "But there was!" she cried. "Nothing romantic, maybe, but we were very good friends. We worked together, sometimes ate together or took in a movie together. You have to understand the kind of camaraderie that develops when you work with someone on something like the arson probe. In a sense you become co-conspirators. You know a story's there and that there may be danger involved, but you believe strongly enough in your cause to go after the story.

"It was a team that did the initial investigation. I was just one member of that team. When things began to get sticky, most of the others bowed out. Our editor felt that we couldn't prove a thing. I disagreed. Most of my investigation was carried out without the formal sanction of the paper. The publisher was scared. One state legislator was involved; no one knew who else might turn up."

She took a breath. "Peter Bradley was the only person willing to go out on a limb to help me. He read my notes and came to believe as strongly as I did. For that I owed him a lot. So maybe Mancusi's got a point. Maybe my testimony *was* jaded by Peter's death."

Meade's eyes were hard and chilling. "Did you ever lie on the stand?"

"No."

"Did you ever so much as stretch the truth?"

"No!" She squeezed her eyes shut and rubbed her forehead.

"Then what we've got to do is to anticipate whatever it is Mancusi's going to produce."

"Manufacture," she corrected angrily, eyes flying open.

"Okay." He sighed. "Let's take it from where you left off. You first worked with Bradley when you joined the investigative team."

"Yes," she gritted. "He was the one we requested when we needed pictures." She had to have said it ten times before.

"Weren't there others?"

"Staff photographers? Of course."

"But you only worked with Bradley."

"I didn't say that. He was the one we *requested*. If he was busy someone else was assigned."

"He was always your first choice."

"Yes." Her head was splitting.

"Why him?"

"Because he was good!"

"He was also very attractive."

She glared and said, "So's Sam," then swiveled in her seat. "Are we making it, Sam?"

Despite the tension of the moment, Sam had trouble suppressing a grin. He admired her grit, always had. "No, Carly, we are not."

Satisfied, she whirled on John defiantly. "Whether or not a man's attractive doesn't mean a thing."

Meade didn't blink. "Sam's married. What was Bradley's excuse?"

"He was gay!" she blurted before she could stop herself, then, realizing what she'd said, she stiffened.

All three men did the same. It was Sam who came forward, kneeling by her chair. "What did you say?"

In mental pain, she frowned, wishing she could take back the words but knowing it was too late. Her voice was a mere whisper. "I said, he was gay."

Understanding the agony she felt at betraying a man so close to her once, he spoke very softly. "It's true?"

Knotting her hands in her lap, she nodded.

Meade exploded. "Well, why in the hell didn't you say something sooner!" he thundered. "Damn it, what was the big secret?"

At that moment Carly positively detested John Meade. She spoke very slowly, with a quiet force that made Sam proud. "It's not your business or anyone else's what Peter Bradley's sexual preference was. He chose not to broadcast it in his lifetime; I wanted to respect his wishes after his death. It doesn't have any bearing on whether or not Gary Culbert or Nick Barber are guilty of arson-related murder. And anyway—" she lowered her voice "—you can't prove it one way or the other."

The state's attorney was not averse to trying. "Did he have a lover?"

"I assume so."

"Who?"

"I don't know."

"You know, but won't tell—"

"John," Sam broke in, standing once again, "take it easy."

Carly put her hand on his arm, but her eyes had never left Meade's. "No, it's okay, Sam. I won't tell because I can't tell. I just don't know. Peter was very sensitive about the whole thing. I didn't learn about it myself until we were working together on the arson investigation. There were long hours and lots of pressure. One day it just slipped out, maybe because he knew I'd keep it in confidence." Her voice grew low and bitter. "Some confidante I turned out to be."

"It needed to be said, Carly," Sam reasoned gently. "For your sake, in more ways than one."

"Sure. I'm off the hook, but Peter's on."

"Don't you think he would have felt it a good enough cause?"

"I don't know," she murmured miserably.

"Aw, come on." Meade scowled. "Times have changed. Gay liberation's brought them out of the closet."

She stared. "Not all of them. Not Peter. He felt frightened and guilty. He said his parents would die if they knew. He didn't want to hurt them that way. Which is just one of the reasons I should never have spoken, one of the reasons you all should forget what I said."

Meade rolled his eyes and mumbled, "My God, you'd think this were a tea party. Listen, Robyn," he stated forcefully, "you seem to be missing the point, which is that Gary Culbert has filed a motion for a new trial based on evidence suggesting that *you* were having an affair with the deceased and therefore may have been less than an objective witness."

"I was *not having an affair* with the deceased."

"Then you were emotionally involved—"

"*Of course I was emotionally involved!*" she cried, clutching at the back of her chair as she turned to face the pacing prosecutor. "I'm a human being! When I witness death first hand it affects me! *But that doesn't make me any less of an objective witness!* When I was on the stand, I told what I did, what I learned, what I saw. That's all!"

Sam touched her shoulder. "It's okay, Carly. Relax."

"I'm sorry, Sam," she murmured brokenly. "This is just so absurd. We're going round and round in circles, getting nowhere. If it's proof that John wants, he'll just have to pay some witness to perjure himself. Evidently that's what Mancusi's done." She turned to glare at Meade. "Your time would be better spent trying to find out who *that* witness is and discrediting *him*." Defeated, she sagged back in her seat. "Beyond that, I don't know what to say."

Sam turned to the prosecutor. "I think she's had enough, John. She just doesn't know any more."

Meade stared long and hard at Carly before relenting, and then only after darting Brozniak a meaningful look. "Okay. That's it then." He looked at his watch. "You folks want to join us for lunch?"

Food was the last thing Carly wanted, the first being to get on a plane and leave Chicago far, far behind. Attuned to her needs and well aware of his own, Sam answered. "Thanks, John, but I think we'll be on our way." He dug a crumpled piece of paper from his jacket pocket and scanned it. "There's an early afternoon flight we can catch. Give me about ten minutes' lead, then send Carly along with Marie." He turned to Carly. "I'll see you on the plane. Okay?"

She forced a wan smile and nodded, then watched him shake hands with the two men and leave. Without him, she felt suddenly more vulnerable, fearing for an instant that Meade might take the opportunity to grill her further. Standing awkwardly, she smoothed her skirt.

"I'm sorry I couldn't help you more."

"You helped us."

Something in his tone sent a shaft of fear through her. "You're going with the homosexuality thing?"

Meade was surprisingly gentle. "Only if I have to. Believe it or not, I understand and admire your feelings. And I'm not inhuman myself. If there's any other possible way—*including* investigating Mancusi's witnesses—I'll do it. But you've got to remember what's at stake here. A new trial will mean a huge expense for the state, not to mention the manpower involved. More important, if there *is* a new trial and Mancusi manages to cast doubt on your credibility as a witness such that a jury is swayed, Culbert may go free. You don't want that any more than I do." He paused. "I'm not really your enemy. Your enemy is up there in the slammer, and I'm just doing my best to try to keep him there."

Carly dropped her chin to her chest, then took a deep breath and raised very weary eyes. "I know, John. It's just that it's difficult for me to have to deal with all of this again. Leaving Chicago last July was one of the hardest things I'd ever done. I felt like I'd been given a life sentence for a noncrime. But I've adjusted. Things are going well for me. I don't want it all spoiled." Seeing Marie at the door, she extended a hand to John. "No offense, but I hope I won't be seeing you."

He grinned. "No offense taken. For the record, I hope the same. Sam'll keep you posted."

"He always does," she said with a rueful sigh, then, with a perfunctory nod toward Brozniak, she took her leave.

When they arrived back at Logan, Sam waited while she repaired to the nearest rest room, switched her contact lenses, loosened her hair, dampened it, and finally, using her blow dryer from her suitcase, let it dry curly. When she emerged, she felt almost normal.

Shaking his head, a grin on his face, he stared at her in amazement. "I can't believe the difference. I mean, you were gorgeous enough the other way, but this way you're . . . you."

"It's funny, but I *feel* like me, too. Now, if I can get over the next hurdle. . . ."

"Which is?"

"Seeing Ryan." She was a bundle of nerves. Not only was she strung taut over all that had happened in Chicago, but, realizing now the depth of her feelings, she was all the more burdened by guilt.

"You spoke with him last night?" Sam asked, steering her toward the parking garage.

"Oh, yes." Her sigh was wistful. "I told him my father was better and I'd probably be flying back on Thursday. I didn't dare say I'd be in today; he would have insisted on meeting the plane. Anyway," she rationalized more lightly, "now I can surprise him." The thought of it caused a thread of excitement to weave slowly through her discouragement. She caught sight of a wall clock. "Hey, you maybe able to make Sara's party after all."

"If the traffic's with us, maybe."

The traffic was with them. Carly was home by four. Dropping her bag on the bed to unpack later, she showered, put on a pair of slacks and a sweater, took a steak from the freezer and made a huge salad. Then she called Ryan at his office. Or tried.

The receptionist answered promptly. "Miller and Cornell."

Heart pounding, Carly made her request. "Mr. Cornell."

"One moment, please."

It was more than one moment—Carly counted every second—before Ryan's secretary finally picked up the phone. "Mr. Cornell's office."

"This is Carly Quinn. Is Mr. Cornell there?"

"I'm sorry, he's not in his office. I expect him back shortly. May I take a message?"

"Uh . . . uh, yes. Would you tell him I called?"

"Certainly. That's Carla—"

"Carly. With a y. Carly Quinn."

"And the number?"

"He knows it."

"Fine. I'll see that he gets the message."

Replacing the receiver, Carly sank into one of the director's chairs by the kitchen table. She felt deflated. Not only had Ryan not been there, but also she'd felt like a stranger when she'd called the place so very dear to his heart. Wondering why she'd never been to his office, she realized with a jolt that it wasn't for lack of invitation. Ryan had suggested it several times; on each occasion she'd declined the offer. In a small way it had to do with her aversion to lawyers, in a larger way with her aversion to exposure. The former was truly absurd, she knew, given her love for Ryan and the respect she'd felt for those of his partners and associates she'd met. And as for the latter, it had dwindled noticeably in the past few weeks.

Pushing herself from the chair, she wandered into the living room and perched on the windowsill overlooking the river. It was dusk. Even as she watched, one, then another, pair of headlights flicked on. Chewing nervously on the inside of her cheek, she glanced at her watch and wondered when Ryan would call. Then, resting her head back against the window frame, she tried to relax.

Indeed she was more confident now about "being seen," and in large part she had Ryan to thank. It was strange; before she'd met him she'd thought of security only in the physical sense. But there was more. She realized now that part of her public reticence had been induced by self-consciousness, by the fear that her disguise was so transparent that anyone and everyone would see through her.

Ryan had changed that. When she was with him, Carly Quinn had a full identity; his love, it seemed, provided the final piece missing from the puzzle of her daily life. He believed in her, so she had to believe in herself.

Her future was something else. Now that she'd admitted to herself that she was in love with the man, things were more complicated. To confess her love and still hold back the truth of her past was unacceptable. Yet she couldn't tell him of that past. Not yet. The Barber-Culbert case was still far too active. And she knew Ryan. If she told him she loved him, he would push for a commitment she was simply unable to make with that other still hanging over her head.

Glancing again at her watch, she crossed the room and sifted through the mail Ryan had brought in during her absence. When she found nothing but meaningless ads and not-so-meaningless bills, she thrust the pile down and paced to the television. Flipping it on, she retreated to the sofa. She rarely watched television. It bored her. But she was unsettled enough to try anything.

It didn't work. Within ten minutes the television screen was black and she had gone in search of her needlepoint. That helped for a time, though more to keep her hands occupied than her mind, which seemed suddenly prone to review the events of the past two days in grand detail. She recalled landing at O'Hare and being driven into the city, passing sights that were heart-wrenchingly familiar, yet different in a "you can't go home again" way.

It had actually been enlightening. She'd felt awkward, a stranger, in the city she'd thought of as home for so long. It was *there* that she'd felt conspicuous and in disguise. And rightfully so, she realized. The woman who had returned to Chicago was only part there. Her heart had remained in Boston.

Her mind skipped around, and for a moment she was in her hotel room again—that cold, lonely place with a bodyguard in the adjoining room. Shivering at the thought, she set down her needlepoint, wrapped her arms around her middle and relived those intense, exhausting hours in the state's attorney's office.

Her stomach knotted, then unknotted, then twisted again. She looked at her watch, leaped up from the sofa and moved aimlessly around the room before checking her watch again.

It was nearly six. Ryan should have called, she reasoned impatiently. Curling into the armchair, she hugged her knees to her chest and tried to define *shortly.* That was when his secretary had said he'd be back, and that had been ninety minutes ago. She swallowed and propped her chin on her knees, realizing that he'd probably been held up in court, or had bumped into a colleague on the way back to the office, or had simply taken a detour along the way.

Another twenty minutes passed. She shifted in her chair, eyeing her front door with trepidation as she began to wonder if something might be wrong. What if he'd been hurt somewhere—if he'd been in an automobile accident or, more bizarre but nonetheless possible, if one of his less reputable clients had attacked him. He wouldn't just *not call.* Would he?

After another thirty minutes of silence, her thoughts took a gruesome turn. She imagined Gary Culbert's henchman making the connection between Ryan and herself and setting out to silence her by injuring him. It would be one of the lowliest forms of emotional blackmail, and it would work in a minute.

She shuddered and moaned, squeezed her eyes shut to exorcise the image and ran her hands up and down her arms to ease her inner chill. The phone didn't ring. The door didn't open. She began to feel as though her world was caving in on her.

FIFTEEN

HEAD DOWN, RYAN CAME UP the courtyard walk, let himself into the building and dispiritedly started up the stairs. It was after eight. The past two nights she had called at nine. He had missed her once today; he prayed she would call again.

If he'd had her number he might have called her back as soon as he'd returned to his office. But he didn't have her number. She hadn't given it to him. He'd thought to call Des Moines for information, but . . . *Johnson?* It had to be one of the most common names in the book.

That first evening after she'd hung up, he'd scoured her apartment for an address book. There had been nothing. No jotted scribbles tacked to a bulletin board. No crumpled listings of friends or relatives. No evidence of her world before Boston. He'd even flipped through her mail in the hopes of finding a handwritten return address, but still he'd struck out. It was like Christmas again. Then he'd simply phoned the wrong place; perhaps, he told himself, he wasn't looking in the right place now. Nonetheless he couldn't quite shake the eerie feeling he had.

Climbing slowly to the third floor, he thought about the power of desperation. This morning, wanting to contact her and having run out of alternatives, he had actually swallowed his pride and called Sam Loomis, who, after all that, was away on business.

Flipping Carly's key from his key case, he fumbled distractedly with her lock. He'd barely pushed the door open an inch when he paused. The light was on, slivering gently into the hall, yet he was sure all the lights had been turned off before he'd left early that morning.

In the instant he conjured three possibilities. The first, that someone had broken in, drew his muscles taut. The second, that Sam Loomis, the only other person with a key, had stopped by, would have set his teeth on edge had he not known Sam was out of town. It was the third that got his heart beating double time. Holding his breath, he pushed the door open, then burst into a broad grin at the sight of Carly curled in a chair across the room.

He slammed the door behind him and tossed his coat on the sofa in passing. "I didn't realize you were home! I thought you'd called from Des Moines!" He was on his haunches in front of her before he realized that the wide-eyed look she wore was not one of delight, but terror. His grin vanished, his pulse rate faltered. "Carly?"

"My God!" she exclaimed in a hoarse whisper, pressing a hand to her chest to still her thudding heart, "I thought you were a thief! It sounded like someone was picking the lock! I've been waiting so long for you to call—I didn't expect you *here!*"

"I didn't expect *you* here," he countered, taking her cold hand in his. "I assumed you were still in Des Moines."

"Didn't you get my message?"

"The message said you'd called. That was all. I was furious when I got it— I couldn't have missed you by more than half an hour. Had my secretary been there, I would have wrung her neck for not forwarding you to the office where I was. But she'd left for a dental appointment, so all I could do was hope that you'd call again at nine. I've been stewing for the past three hours."

"So have I," she whispered, and suddenly something snapped inside her. It had been building from the moment she'd seen Sam at her classroom door on Monday and had been fueled by the extraordinary tension she'd been under since then. That, and missing Ryan and hating herself for having to lie to him and realizing in these past few hours how much she loved him. . . .

As he watched, her composure crumbled. Her eyes filled with tears, her chin began to quiver. Before she had time to do more than fall into his waiting arms, she was crying. Endless sobs shook her body. She clutched at the lapels of his coat. "Oh, God, Ryan . . ."

"Shh. . . ." He pressed her head to his chest and rocked her gently. "It's okay, babe. It's okay. Shh. . . ."

It was a while longer before she could catch her breath enough to talk. "I'm sorry," she gasped, blotting her cheeks. "I didn't mean to break down like this."

He held her away and saw the dark smudges under her eyes. "You look exhausted. You couldn't have slept the whole time you were gone. How is he, Carly? There wasn't a—"

Setback. Her father. "Oh, no. He's fine." She grew self-conscious. "I guess everything just built and built till I couldn't hold it in anymore." She sniffled. "I wanted to surprise you today, and when you didn't call back I began to imagine all kinds of awful things."

Ryan caught her face between his hands with sudden vehemence. "I've missed you." Then his lips were on hers and something burst within them both. He couldn't kiss her hard enough or deep enough; she couldn't take enough of him or give enough of herself. Hands were everywhere, clutching, stroking, reassuring with a fervor not to be denied.

Shifting her to the floor and moving down over her, Ryan kissed her neck, then shoved up her sweater, tore aside her bra and took her ripe nipple in his mouth, sucking strongly and drawing it to a peak before moving hungrily on to its mate.

No less feverish, Carly blindly grappled with the buttons of his vest, then his shirt, spreading the material, running her hands over his warm flesh in wordless stake of her claim.

The air was rent with moans and hoarse urgings. Carly tugged at Ryan's belt and attacked the zipper of his trousers, while he ravaged the fastenings of her slacks. Parting only long enough to strip off their lower garb, they returned to each other in a fluid motion that joined their bodies fully.

With a growl of possession, Ryan surged against her. He was without gentleness, for Carly's writhing body demanded force, and he wasn't sure if he could have taken her any other way, so desperately did he need to put his mark on her, to weld her to him, to make up for the loneliness of their time apart and clear every thought from her mind but the fury of his love. If he was punishing her for having flown so suddenly, so be it. He was out of control, mastered by his own rampant desire.

Carly took it all and then some with unabashed greed. Her body held his, tightened around him to keep him, rebelled each time he withdrew by capturing him all the more deeply at the next thrust. She had never felt such a powerful need to be bound to another person — or to blot every thought from her mind but the frenzy of Ryan's formidable strength.

The climax they reached was simultaneous, hard and mind-shattering, punctuated by loud cries of exultation. Bodies slick, they collapsed on each other, gasping for breath, moaning at the sweet pain each bore.

When finally he rolled to her side, he gathered her to him in an embrace every bit as fierce as their coupling had been. There were no apologies. The stinging spots on his back where she'd dug her nails told Ryan that she'd taken him as forcefully as he'd taken her. He found great satisfaction in that.

It took Carly longer to get her bearings. Raising her head at last, she blinked. Held snug against Ryan's chest, she lay on the rug at the foot of the chair in which she'd been sitting. Her sweater and bra were bunched somewhere just above her breasts. Ryan's shirt and vest flared from his shoulders.

"I can't believe we did this," she whispered.

He grinned down at her, his breathing still heavy. "Decadent again. But I love it." He placed a kiss on the tip of her nose, then, when she raised her lips, on her mouth. "I did miss you. If you ever, so help me, *ever* take off on me that way again, I'll make you sorry you did."

She saw the teasing in his eyes and hoped it would last, for she knew that there well *might* be other times when she would have to take off. Unable to think of that now, she sat up, tugged her sweater to her waist, then looked at her naked lower torso indignantly. "Look what you've done to me, Ryan Cornell. I'm a mess!"

"You're not a mess. You're gorgeous."

She glanced at his own naked body and smiled. "So are you." Then, reaching for her clothes, she began to dress. "Ryan?"

"Hmm?"

"I'd like to see your office sometime."

He lay on his back, arms pillowing his head, unfazed by his nakedness as he watched her reach beneath her sweater and ease herself into her bra. "You would?" His voice was higher than usual; something pleased him. She wasn't quite sure whether it was what she said or what she did. Before she'd decided, he sat up with a grin, reached behind her and fastened the bra's catch. Then he relaxed back once again.

"I want to be able to picture where you are when you're working." Balancing first on one foot then the other, she slipped on her panties and straightened. "And I want that secretary of yours to be able to picture *me* when I call."

Ryan savored the flashing of her eyes, so different from the gut-wrenching look he'd seen there when he'd first come home. "She'll feel awful about the mix-up," he murmured distractedly, watching her step into her slacks, zip the zipper and fasten the tab. "She's really very good." Sitting up again, he caught her hand. "Where're you rushing to? I want to hear about your father."

"My father's fine and I'm rushing to the kitchen. Aren't you hungry?"

"Sure. But we could go out. You just got back."

"I've been back since four. I took a steak out and made a salad before I called you." She slanted him a knowing look. "Don't tell me you've been eating at home all week." Her teasing hit its mark. If she'd learned one thing about Ryan it was that he had no inclination to cook. Oh, he did make coffee, and a mean cup at that, and he was more than willing to work beside her in the kitchen following her directions. On his own, though, he was a lost cause.

He reached for his briefs and pulled them on. "Eat at home? Uh, no. Not exactly."

"I didn't think so. Well, neither have I, so I thought we'd have a quiet dinner here." She hesitated. "Is that okay?"

Ryan shook his head, but in amazement that she could think otherwise. "It's more than okay. I'd like that, babe."

Carly was mesmerized as much by the velvet warmth in Ryan's tone as by the adoration in his eyes. She'd heard it before, seen it before, but never like this, knowing what she felt in return, knowing that it was nearly, nearly within her grasp.

Raising tremulous fingertips to his lips, she traced their firm contour, so smooth within the soft bristle of his beard. Then, eyes round and teary, she dropped her hand and offered a broken, "I'll get dinner. It won't take long," before fleeing to the kitchen.

Ryan stared after her for a minute. She loved him. She *had* to love him. There was no other explanation for the way she looked at him, the way she spoke to him, the way she responded to him, the way she demanded from him—and yes, she did demand. In her quiet, gentle way she demanded strength and comfort, companionship, understanding and appreciation and passion. She seemed attuned to his every need, satisfying him as he satisfied her. *She had to love him.* But she hadn't said so. Not once.

Retreating to the bedroom, he put on the jeans he'd left in her closet. Hanging up his suit and shirt, he grabbed his sweat shirt, went into the bathroom to wash up, emerged after several minutes in the process of tugging the sweat shirt over his head and caught sight of her suitcase lying on the bed where she'd left it when she'd first come home.

He smiled, pleased to know that her thoughts of him had taken precedence over all else. Even now he could hear her in the kitchen opening and closing the refrigerator, rattling silverware and china. Thrusting his arm through the second sleeve, he straightened the sweat shirt and approached the bed. He rubbed one long forefinger over the leather of her case, admiring it even as he dreamed of the matching set they'd buy for their travels together.

Then something caught his eye. Frowning, he reached toward the baggage-claim tag attached to the metal fastening of the shoulder strap that stretched from one end to the other of the case. CHI. Chicago? Had she returned from Des Moines via Chicago? But no. Tags were marked with destinations.

Affixed to the traditional handle at the top of the bag was the tag he sought. He turned it over. BOS, indeed. The return-trip tag. Located where it was in a corner, the first must have been missed by the airport employee who would normally have torn it off before putting a new one on.

Ryan dropped the tag and looked up. Boston to Chicago, then back to Boston. And Des Moines? He had no idea how she'd gotten *there*; he only knew that something was odd.

Enveloped in flames, she was suffocating. Through the inferno's roar, she heard Peter's voice, "It was your idea, all yours!" then Matthew's, "I yelled for you but you didn't hear!" She turned first to the left, then the right, then completely around in search of escape, but there was none. There never was. Paralyzed by terror, she stared at the snakes of fire coiling menacingly at her feet.

Carly bolted upright in bed. The flames were gone. The night was black and silent. Only Ryan lay unknowing witness to her suffering, and he stirred slowly by her side, reaching for her in his sleep, coming more fully awake when he felt her trembling. Groggy, he lifted his head. "Carly? What's wrong?"

"Just a nightmare," she managed to whisper, then forced herself to lie down, curl in a ball facing away from him and pull the covers over her bare shoulders.

As Ryan drew her back against him, his grogginess vanished. "You're all sweaty. It must have been some nightmare."

"Mmm."

"What was it about?"

"Oh, the same thing it always is. Fire."

"Your husband's." He still couldn't remember if it was Matthew or Malcolm and was too embarrassed to ask.

"Mmm."

"Must have been your trip that brought it back," he murmured into her hair. "Being with family, and all."

Carly felt like a rat. Though she didn't lie, she didn't tell the whole truth. It occurred to her that come the day Ryan did find out, he would have a right to be positively furious.

"Hey," he said softly, "maybe you should put something on. You're really shaking."

"I'll be okay. It was just the fright. Give me a minute."

He had to give her several before she finally began to relax. Holding her, gently caressing her shoulder, his arm crossing up between her breasts, he couldn't help but think back on the puzzle of the tags. He hadn't asked Carly about them; one part of him was frightened of what her answer might be. Rather, he talked with her over dinner as though nothing was wrong. But something *was* wrong. In himself. Along with confusion and hurt, there was anger. He managed to push it to the back of his mind when he was with her and she seemed so loving and sincere, but it was there, emerging at times like tonight when she'd fallen asleep in his arms after they'd made love and he'd lain awake brooding long after.

Aside from the fact of the luggage tags, there wasn't much to put his finger on. It was weird—the lack of as common an item as an address book, the absence of details of four years of her life, a haunted look, nightmares. Taken alone, no one thing would have aroused his suspicion. But together, with new things all too often joining the list, something didn't add up. And it irked him. He was angry at her for not trusting him enough to confide in him, and angry at himself for not having the courage to confront her.

But she meant so much to him, and he was so afraid of losing her, that he didn't dare jeopardize the status quo. And so the anger built inside him, having nowhere to go but deeper into his gut. As he lay in the dark with her, holding her quiet now, her cuddling body close to his, he wondered how long he would be able to keep it buried.

Sheila hung up the phone, shivered more in aftermath of the call than the weather, pulled her collar higher around her, then looked cautiously around. Shrinking into her coat, she opened the phone-booth door and quickly began to walk up Chestnut Street toward her car parked about half a block from her apartment.

"Bastard," she muttered to herself. "In such a rush." Absently she kicked at the slush underfoot, leaving a path of elongated footsteps behind. It had stormed all Wednesday night and half of Thursday, giving the metropolitan area its heaviest snowfall of the season. With more than a foot of new white stuff on the ground, everything had been closed on Thursday. It had been beautiful; she'd walked through the Common that afternoon, admiring the crisp cleanness of the scene, the muted silence, the brisk fresh air. By Friday the comings and goings of the city had resumed. Now it was Saturday. The streets were wet, the snow dirty, the sidewalks spattered with mud. Thursday's winter wonderland was nothing but a pleasant memory, now tarnished, as was she.

With a determined thrust of her chin, she quickened her step. Reaching the car, she climbed in, started the motor and took off. Fifteen minutes, two near-skids and numerous oaths later she pulled up at Carly's place.

Carly was waiting just inside the front door. When she saw Sheila wave, she trotted down the front path, slowing only to negotiate the snow-glazed steps with care before climbing into the passenger seat.

"Nice car, Sheila!" She looked around, admiring the elaborate dashboard, the racy floor shift, the fine leather appointments. "I'm surprised you want to take it anywhere in this weather."

"Cars are like people. If they sit around all day, they get fat and rusty."

"People don't get rusty," Carly teased.

"Well, fat then. But cars get rusty. Their batteries die. They get scratched by trucks trying to squeeze down streets that are too narrow. Besides, life's too short. You've got to enjoy it while you can." She plastered a bright smile on her face. "So, where are we going? Chestnut Hill?"

"If you don't mind."

Sheila gave a throaty laugh as she pulled away from the curb and executed a neat, if illegal, U-turn. "I think you've got that backward. You're the one who's doing me a favor by taking me shopping."

"You're taking me; I won't *touch* my car."

"Did it always bother you to drive in the snow?"

"It's not the driving that bothers me," Carly said, turning her head to follow the progress of a child in the playground trying to maneuver down the snow-covered slide in a rubber tube. "It's the thought of losing my parking space." The child fell sideways into the snow. "I wasn't sure how the walking would be for school yesterday, so I drove. Let me tell you, I spent half an hour trying to find a space when I got home. Ryan warned me. He was right."

"How is school?"

"Okay. Of course, I missed more than half the week, between Chicago and the snow. The storm was actually a blessing. I don't think I would have been much good for teaching Thursday morning—"

"Chicago?" Sheila was racking her brain, wondering how she could have missed it. "I didn't realize you'd gone to Chicago." So *that* was where Sam had been. She'd wondered. Greg had simply said he'd had to take off. They really *didn't* trust her.

Carly looked at her in surprise. "You didn't know?"

"How would *I* know? They don't tell me anything." Her bitterness came through in her tone and was further emphasized by her pout. "Sam and Greg play their little games. I think they get a kick out of keeping secrets. It makes them feel important." She stepped on the gas at a traffic light turned green. "Hey, am I going the right way?"

"I think so," Carly said, "but this may be a case of the blind leading the blind. We could end up in Chelsea." The road looked right, according to Ryan's directions, but Carly's thoughts were on what Sheila had said and she felt impelled to respond. "I think you're too sensitive. Some secrets are necessary. And believe me, the last thing they do is to make the keeper feel important."

Sheila cast a quick glance toward Carly. "You haven't told him yet." Carly shook her head. "Feeling guilty?"

"Guilty is putting it mildly. I feel like a heel in the first degree. When I had to take off like that—"

"Whoa. Stop there. I want to hear all about Chicago." And rightly she did. She listened carefully to everything Carly told her, asking more detailed questions when Carly was prone to rush.

"What kind of time are they talking about, anyway?"

Carly frowned. "What do you mean? Wait." She peered out the window, looked at a road sign to the left. "I think we have to go up that hill and follow the road to Newton Corner."

Sheila did it, then got right back on the track of the conversation. "When will you know about a new trial?"

"I don't know. The motion has to be heard before the original trial judge. According to John it could take anywhere from two to six months."

"That long?" Sheila asked thoughtfully.

"Maybe I should be grateful. It gives me plenty of time to decide what to do about Ryan."

"What do you *want* to do?"

Carly made a frustrated sound. "There's one part of me that would like to throw myself into the guy's arms, tell him how much I love him, agree to marry him and have his kids and live happily ever after. Is that Center Street? Make a right there. We follow it for a few minutes."

"Why *don't* you throw yourself into his arms, et cetera?"

"How can I, Sheila? He doesn't know about who I was and what I did. How can I agree to marry him and then subject him to the anguish of all this?"

"If he loves you enough he'll accept it. Does he?"

"I think so. Yes. But that's the problem. He would accept it all right; whether I can live with the knowledge of what I'd be putting him through is something else." Her voice grew more strained. "Of course, that's taking for granted that I do tell him everything."

"Don't you want to?"

"I think I have to. I don't see how we can have a trusting relationship without it."

They lapsed into a silence then, each lost in her own thoughts. The car made its way through the streets of Newton, tree lined and brilliant with its blanket of snow. It was Sheila who spoke first, with caution.

"Maybe you shouldn't tell him." When Carly sent her a disbelieving stare, Sheila said. "At least, not right away. I mean, if you think he's going to be sensitive about it—"

"It's *me* who'll be sensitive."

"Same difference. Why ruin things?"

Carly shook her head. "Oh, Sheila, I don't know."

"What have you got to lose by keeping it to yourself a little longer? If the guy loves you for who you are, it doesn't really matter who you've been." She gained momentum. "And then there's the issue of breaking your cover. Are you sure you want to do that?"

"I trust Ryan," Carly said.

"I know. But things slip out. If you tell Ryan, there's always the chance he would say something to someone else."

"He wouldn't."

"Not intentionally. But by mistake? All it sometimes takes is a drink or two."

"He's not a drinker."

"Well, I'd still think twice." She shrugged. "But it's your affair."

The silence that filled the car this time was riddled with tension. Unable to believe the cynical twist in Sheila's attitude, Carly stared at her for a minute before shifting her gaze to the window. She tried to tell herself that Sheila might be jealous of what she had going with Ryan, but it didn't do much to ease the hurt.

"Hey, Carly." Sheila reached over and squeezed her arm. "I'm sorry. I didn't mean to come on so strong. I'm sure Ryan is trustworthy. Go ahead and tell him, if that's what you want to do."

What Carly wanted to do was not to think about it anymore just then. "Well, I'll see." She sighed, then pointed. "Make a left here. It'll take us to Beacon Street."

"Are we almost there?"

"Another couple of minutes, I think. I've only been here once before, and that was with a friend from school who didn't stop talking the entire way. She was driving; I'm not sure if I was paying attention to where we were going." She frowned, then nodded. "This is right. At the next set of lights make a right. What'll it be—Bloomingdale's or one of the smaller specialty shops at the mall?"

"Smaller specialty shops?"

"They're a little more expensive. Maybe we should stick with—"

"Let's try them," Sheila declared, smiling smugly.

Carly wasn't as positive. "Are you sure? You're talking about a formal gown. It's bound to cost—"

"No problem. I plan to splurge. Tom Cornell might just be worth it."

Two hours later, after having shelled out a frightening sum for a bright red silk and chiffon off-the-shoulder number at Charles Sumner, Sheila was as exuberant as ever, full of smiles as they wandered through Filene's. "I do like that dress. Didn't it look great?"

"It's perfect on you, Sheila—the color, the style. You'll look smashing at the party. Too bad you've got to drive all the way back here to pick it up when the alterations are done, though."

"I don't mind. I wasn't about to pay someone to alter it after what I paid for the dress!"

Carly threw her a glance, amazed that after paying what she had Sheila would think twice about a negligible alteration fee. Actually, Carly was stunned she'd been able to afford the dress at all. "What the hell," were Sheila's exact words when, after no more than a cursory glance at the price tag, she'd given the saleswoman the nod.

Carly regarded her speculatively. "Tell me you've come into an inheritance or something."

"No inheritance," was the terse reply, but Sheila's attention was on the nail-polish counter. She picked up one bottle, assessed its color next to her skin, shook her head and put it back. "I've just decided that it's my turn to enjoy life for a change."

"Does that mean you enjoy Tom?"

"You bet." She picked up two more bottles, discarded one quickly, studied the other.

"You saw him last night?"

"Um-hmm." The final bottle met the same fate as its predecessors. "Hey, I'm hungry." She swung around and narrowed a gaze toward the interior of the mall. "How about some lunch? My feet are about to resign and my throat's gonna close up in a minute if I don't get something wet past it. I don't know how all these people do it. They must have been trained to shop. I guess I missed out on that particular class. But I am starved. There has to be something good around here for—" she straightened her shoulders and lowered her voice to a drawl "—patrons of elegant specialty shops."

Carly couldn't help but laugh. Here was the Sheila she knew and liked, the Sheila who was lighthearted and irreverent. "There's a Charlie's Wildflower on the upper level."

"Say no more." Sheila linked her elbow with Carly's. "Let's go."

Tom Cornell carried the two snifters—one with brandy, one with rum and Coke, back to the sofa, handed the latter to Sheila, then eased his long frame down next to her. "That was a super dinner, Sheila. You're a great cook."

"Comes from living a life without maid service," she quipped. "Actually, I learned to cook from my Uncle Amos."

"*Famous* Amos? I *thought* he was from the West Coast—"

"Not Famous Amos," she chided playfully. "*Uncle* Amos. He was as much of a nanny as I ever had. He took care of us while my mother worked."

"Didn't *he* work?"

"Uh-huh. At keeping sober. He didn't always make it, mind you, but when he did, he was wonderful." She laid her head back against the sofa. "I can remember one time—it was Paulie's birthday."

"Paulie's the third—"

"The fourth," she corrected with a grin. "You're getting there, Tom. Anyway, it was Paulie's birthday and, so help me, there wasn't an ounce of nourishment in the house. My mother wasn't one to worry about little things like food."

"What did she worry about?"

"Men. And clothes."

"And her kids?"

Sheila tossed that one around in her mind. "I guess she did. But you're getting me away from my story. It was Paulie's birthday and we didn't have any food. So Uncle Amos went to the store and brought back six bags of stuff." A sly smile played at the corners of her lips. "To this day I don't know where he got the money. Well, maybe I do, but his intention was good. He cooked the most delicious beef something-or-other—"

"Beef what?"

"I don't know. When I asked him, he said to call it Uncle Amos's Beef."

"Sounds better than beef something-or-other. Why didn't you?"

"Because I'd already had experiences with Uncle Amos's Chicken and Uncle Amos's Fish. Anything 'Uncle Amos' consisted of whatever he felt like adding to the pot at a given time. He was a natural. I stopped worrying about names and started watching him work. I think I learned more from him than from any other person."

"Is he still back there with your brothers?"

She took a gulp of her drink and looked wistfully toward the fire. "We've all split up."

"What are they doing?"

She shifted her gaze to Tom's face. "My brothers? You don't really want to know."

"I do. Maybe if you talked about them more I'd be able to keep them straight."

She studied her glass. "There's not much to keep straight. Jay is the star; he's working an oil rig in Prudhoe Bay. It goes downhill from there. Billy is washing dishes somewhere. Sean is serving one to three for auto theft. And Paulie, well, Paulie has been a senior in high school for several years now."

"And through it all you came out smelling like a rose?"

Her expression was somber, her voice low. "I don't know if I'd say that."

"Well, I would. Look at you. You've got an apartment in one of the greatest areas in town, a new car, a successful career." When he saw the pain in her eyes, he was touched. "You're really something, Sheila, do you know that?"

Snapping from her darker thoughts, she blushed. "I'm not. You keep saying that, but I think it's because you've never dated a policewoman before."

"You're not a policewoman." He slid closer. "You're a deputy U.S. marshal."

"And if I were a policewoman? What would you think then?"

"I'd still think," he murmured against her lips, "that you were the smartest, the prettiest, the funniest sexy lady to enter my house in years." He kissed her slowly, savoring the taste of rum on her tongue.

Sheila relished every minute of it, then couldn't resist a barb. "If I'm so sexy, how come I've never seen your bedroom?"

"Has that been bothering you?"

"Not bothering me. Puzzling me."

He slipped his arm around her shoulder and gathered her closer. "Would you like to see my bedroom?"

She tipped her head to the side and answered on a sing-song note. "Some day."

Tom couldn't believe it. He had paced himself so carefully, had waited for her opening, and she was turning him down? "Not now?"

"I can't."

"Why not?"

"Because I have to get back to Boston. I'm on duty at six tomorrow morning."

"You've got to be kidding." When she shook her head decisively, he let out a breath. "I don't believe it. I fall for a woman who has to go to work at six o'clock on a Sunday morning?"

"Not *every* Sunday morning," she said apologetically. "I'm really only doing my boss a favor tomorrow. He called just before you picked me up to ask if I could fill in for one of the others who has the flu. I couldn't really say no. He's been down on me enough lately."

"Is this the Loomis guy you mentioned?"

"Uh-huh."

"He must be a slave driver."

She shrugged. "A witness in custody needs protection twenty-four hours a day. So does a judge whose life has been threatened. For that matter, a federal fugitive doesn't only run from nine to five. *Someone*'s got to do the work. And *that*—" she broke into slapstick to cover for a world of bitterness "—is what's awful about dating an agent of the U.S. marshal's services. Now, if you'd been sensible enough to fall for a secretary or a bank teller or a teacher like your brother did. . . ."

Tom grinned. "Ryan's fallen, all right." He sat back and spread his arms across the sofa back. "He's hooked."

"Really likes her, does he?"

"Really *loves* her. I haven't seen him this crazy since—no, I take that back—I've *never* seen him this crazy about a woman."

"He was married before, wasn't he?"

"To a sweetheart from the suburbs."

"What happened?"

"Things just didn't work out. They called it quits over a year ago."

Sheila considered this. "Is he heavily into alimony payments?"

"Not really. He got a good settlement. Alyssa's family is loaded. Ryan may be doing well, but she has more than he has any day."

"He is doing well?"

"You bet, and he has himself to thank. He's worked hard." Tom snickered. "I'm getting the impression those days are over, though. He used to spend every waking hour in the office. Now he spends them with Carly." His voice dropped. "Not only the waking ones at that."

"They're living together?" Sheila asked, growing even more alert. Carly hadn't mentioned anything about *living together*.

"Welllll—" he stretched out the word and made a wavering gesture with his hand "—maybe not formally. Ryan's still got his place downstairs. Of course, there's no furniture in it."

"So he sleeps upstairs. Very clever." She downed the last of her drink and gazed into the fire with studied nonchalance. "Tell me about his practice."

Tom eyed her curiously. "What about his practice?"

"What kinds of cases does he handle?"

"Oh, white-collar, blue-collar, ring-around-the—"

"I'm serious, Tom."

"You're thinking of needing a lawyer?"

She swung her head sharply around. "Of course not!"

"The best of us do sometimes," he rejoined in a calm voice that held a certain bait.

Sheila took it. "You have?"

Holding her eyes, he told her of his collision with the law, then grew momentarily tense. "Does it bother you?"

She laughed aloud, feeling an even greater affinity with him for what he'd just told her. "How can you even ask that after hearing the rundown on my family? And my brothers are only the tip of the iceberg. There are cousins doing God knows what."

"But you got your clearance and escaped all that. You're in law enforcement."

"So's your brother. Does he love you any the less for what you did?"

"He was pretty damned mad when it happened."

"But he still loves you," she stated with abrupt force.

"Yes."

Her ferocity died as quickly as it had arisen, replaced by an even smile. "Then who am I to criticize?" She paused. "Lucky for you Ryan's in the profession he is. What are some of the other cases he's handled?"

Tom scowled. "If I didn't know better, I'd wonder whether you were more interested in Ryan than me."

Instantly she relented, leaning forward to press a kiss to his chin. "That's what *you* have that Ryan doesn't have." At Tom's blank look, she laughed. "A chin. His is hidden under a beard. Why does he wear it anyway?"

She'd been only trying to make conversation and was startled when Tom provided a pat response. "To cover a scar, I believe. A souvenir of one of his earliest cases."

"Really? Tell me."

"No way. It's Ryan's business."

"Was he in a fight?" she asked excitedly.

"Uh-uh."

"Someone attacked him? Oh, Lord, Tom, this is getting juicy. Was it his own client?"

"Sheila, it was years ago. The beard's been on so long I don't even remember what the guy looks like with a skin face."

"Does he hold a grudge?" She stroked her lower lip with the tip of one finger. "*Is* he the vengeful type?"

Without a trace of warning, Tom pounced, sliding her sideways on the sofa, pinning her shoulders to the cushion. "If we have enough time to talk about Ryan, we sure as hell have enough time for ourselves." Lowering his head, he kissed her deeply.

At first Sheila responded. Everything about Tom appealed to her, except the fact that she'd met him too late. It was this thought that made her gently lever him away.

"Tom," she gasped, "we can't."

His hands were on her breasts, kneading their fullness, playing electrifying games with her senses. "Why not? I'm quick." In demonstration of his readiness, he inched his body upward on hers.

Holding him off was the hardest thing Sheila had ever done. The feel of his arousal fueled her own. But something nagged at her. A strange kind of guilt. She liked Tom Cornell, really liked him. Of all the men she'd met in recent years, he held the most potential.

Unfortunately, as of this afternoon, she had other plans for her body.

SIXTEEN

❧❧❧

RETURNING FROM THE COURTHOUSE, Sam had just swung through the door of the U.S. marshal's office when his secretary waved him in. The phone was in her hand, the hold button blinking. He quickened his step. "For me?"

"Bill Hoffmeister on your line."

Turning into his own office, he shrugged out of his coat and picked up the phone. "Bill?"

"How're ya doin', Sam?"

"Not bad." The coat landed on a chair to the side; Sam took the one behind his desk. "What's up?" He'd had a strange feeling that something would be. And it wasn't unusual. Witnesses were placed in his care because of active threats. In most cases, he simply took new developments as they came. But the link between Bill Hoffmeister and himself was Carly, and she wasn't the run-of-the-mill criminal-turned-stoolie. It had been over a week since he'd returned with her from Chicago. He had been uneasy wondering if he would get a call.

"I'm not sure. It may be nothing, but I thought you should know. Barber's been talking."

Sam sat forward. "Barber? I thought our threat was from Culbert?"

"It is. Barber's a nobody in the chain of command. He doesn't have money or pull. As a torch, he blew it. But he's pretty confident about getting that new trial. And he's pretty confident about beating the rap."

"Maybe it's the macho in him talking."

"Could be. Could be that he's got to tell himself that or he'll go crazy. Could be, though, that he heard something from Culbert."

"I thought they were separated."

"They are. But you know the internal communication network in prison. Word passes."

"Where did you get yours?"

"From another inmate. He was shipped out to stand trial in Alabama and one of my men made the trip with him. He was feeling his oats, spieling about the guys he left behind. For obvious reasons, my man let him talk."

"Was there anything specific?"

"No. A guy like Barber follows directions. If he's told to do something, he does it. If he's told to believe something, he does. Well, he believes that he's going to be walking the streets before long. *Someone* must have told him that." He hesitated. "I thought you should know."

"I should." Sam rubbed the tense muscles at the back of his neck. "The question is what do I do. I hate to put someone on her. It'd really mess up her life."

"If someone gets through to her, her life will be messed up worse. But maybe we're both jumping to conclusions. So far there's been no sign of anything fishy from Culbert. He hasn't sold anything—his house or his car—to come up with money, and there haven't been any withdrawals from his bank account other than what his family usually draws. Of course, there may be an unlisted account somewhere. And if Mancusi's got power of attorney. . . ."

"Mancusi wouldn't dare. He's a lawyer."

"So was Culbert, and a sleazy one at that. Which means that he may have some tricks up his sleeve we don't know about."

Sam sat back in his chair. "Okay. Listen, I think I'll run all this past Carly. I know it'll make her nervous, but maybe if it does she'll agree to have someone watch her. At least she'll be on the lookout herself for anything strange." As if she wasn't already. She had told him about Ryan's homecoming on the day they returned from Chicago. For those few instants, when a key had jiggled in her lock, she'd been terrified. She was *always* on the lookout.

"Sounds fair. If I hear anything more, I'll let you know."

"Thanks, Bill."

He pressed the button to disconnect the line, then buzzed for his secretary. "Angie, is Greg around?"

"He left a little while ago to get some records at City Hall. He said he wouldn't be long."

"Thanks." Pressing the button for an outside line, he called Rand Academy and left a message for Carly to call him back. Then he sat back in his chair, analyzing his options. When Greg returned forty minutes later, he immediately broached the topic. "How's it going with Sheila?"

Greg set his files down on his desk. "Not bad. She's pretty closed about herself, but I'm working on it." He perched on the front of his desk, facing Sam. "She's really not bad once you get her talking. She's as wary of us as we are of her. Scared as hell of you. It may be a simple case of transplant adjustment."

"Transplant adjustment." Sam chuckled dryly. "That's a novel term. But it could fit, I suppose. Is she happy in Boston?"

"She says she likes it well enough. She's been dating a guy. According to the receptionist, he's been calling her a lot lately. She always brightens when she gets his messages."

"Name?"

Greg hesitated for only an instant. "Thomas Cornell."

"Cornell? Any relation to Ryan?"

"Brother."

Sam sighed. "At least she's in good hands."

"I hope so," Greg replied cautiously. "He was in some kind of scrape involving embezzlement a while ago. His brother managed to settle the thing quietly. There's been nothing since."

"How deeply is Sheila involved with him?"

"I don't know. Couldn't be all *that* deeply. She invited me to her place for dinner tomorrow night."

"She did?" Sam arched a brow. "You *are* making inroads." Then he sobered again. "So what do you think—is she trustworthy?"

He gave a throaty laugh. "I'll let you know Saturday."

When Sam's phone buzzed, he waved Greg back to work. "Yes, Angie?"

"Carly Quinn's on the line."

"I'll take it." He pushed the blinking button. "Carly?"

"Sam? I just got your message. How are you?"

"Fine. Listen, I wonder if I could pick you up at school and we could go somewhere to talk." Once they would have gone back to her place. With Ryan coming and going so much, though, more neutral ground was preferable.

"Is something wrong?" she asked, tensing instantly.

"Not really. I just wanted to discuss something."

"What is it?"

"We'll talk later."

"Sam. . . ."

"Four-thirty?"

She sighed. "Four-thirty."

Sam was waiting in his car when Carly left the administration building. Trotting down the walk, she slid quickly into the passenger seat and he took off.

"What's wrong?" she asked, eyes glued to his face.

"Let's go get a drink."

"Sam! Tell me!"

He managed to put her off until they sat in the quiet booth of a small bar on the outskirts of the Square. Then, over beers, he related the conversation he'd had that morning with Bill Hoffmeister.

"Oh, hell!" she whispered. "I knew he'd try something!"

"We don't know that he has. But forewarned is forearmed."

"Which means?"

"I may want to give you a tail."

She slammed her palm to the thick wooden table. "No!" With a fast glance around, she lowered her voice. "I can't, Sam. Not now. Things are going too well with Ryan. It would ruin everything."

Sam sighed wearily. "I thought you'd feel that way, which is why I haven't put anyone on it yet."

"Do you think there's a real danger?"

"No. But I'd hate to overlook something."

"I'll be careful. I always am. And besides, Ryan is with me practically all the time I'm not in school."

"That's one plus." He leaned back in the booth and eyed her more thoughtfully. "Three months ago you would have reacted very differently to what I just told you." His words were gentle, devoid of criticism. They spurred Carly on to express her own thoughts.

"You're right. You were also right about my needing to be involved with someone. Before I met Ryan, I was afraid of my own shadow."

Sam was shaking his head. "Don't underrate yourself. You were never afraid of your own shadow. More nervous, perhaps. And very definitely more isolated."

"Still," she argued, "he's given me something. More fight, maybe? Then again—" her brows knit "—maybe he's just complicated things. Sometimes I want to tell him everything, sometimes I don't want to tell him a thing. As long as he's in the dark, I can't possibly have a bodyguard. There's no way I could explain one. But if I do tell him and there's someone around all the time, he'll be frustrated and it'll be that much harder on me. He's only human." Her voice softened. "So am I."

"I'm glad, Carly. What you're saying is that other emotions have surpassed fear in your life. And that's important. You *are* human. You do have a life to lead. It's not right that you should be a prisoner of your fears."

"I'm not saying they're not there. I'm scared to death."

"I know." He smiled gently. "But there's more."

She nodded. "I love Ryan." Her voice began to waver. "Problem is there are times when I'm torn apart. Reconciling what I feel for him with . . . with all this other stuff. . . ."

"You're doing a fine job so far. Listen, how's this. Why don't we sit on the guard for a while. Hoffmeister will let us know if he learns anything more. I'll have my people keep a lookout for strangers. I can also have someone ride through the streets near your place and the school from time to time. The police would be glad to send a patrol around."

"I don't want that."

"I don't have to give them details. It's enough if I tell them that the marshal's office is working on something sensitive. They'll keep an eye on the general area without ever knowing your name or address."

She took a deep breath. "I guess that sounds okay." Then she smiled apologetically. "I do appreciate all this, Sam."

He winked. "What are friends for?" He took a last swig of his beer and licked the froth from his lips. "Hey, why don't we go out sometime. The four of us. You and Ryan and Ellen and me. She'd love meeting you. She feels she knows you so well."

"I'd love that too," Carly said. She frowned when a thought came to mind, but in a minute it was gone. "No, it'd do him good."

"Do whom good?"

"Ryan." Her eyes sparkled mischievously, a welcome change from her earlier worry. "He doesn't trust you."

"Doesn't trust *me?* Mr. Clean? Your local Boy Scout in long pants? The Lone Ranger without a mask?"

Through a grin, she said, "He's convinced we have something going on the side."

Sam arched a brow. "Does he know about Ellen?"

She nodded. "And Sara. But you have to understand that the man's law firm does its share of divorce work. He's seen cheating like you and I have never dreamed of."

"I think," Sam observed, his eyes narrowing, "that he's jealous."

"He is. He admits it." There was a certain pride in her tone that caught at Sam's heart.

"He must love you very much."

Her smile was private and exquisitely gentle, her soft-spoken "He does" totally superfluous.

As fate would have it, Ryan was in the foyer tugging his mail from its slot when Sam walked Carly to the door. Sam saw him first and stopped, but Carly urged him on. She badly wanted to smooth things between these two men who, each in his own way, meant so much to her.

She pushed open the door. "Ryan! Hi!"

His head came up from the pile of letters he'd been skimming and a broad smile broke out on his face, only to be tempered seconds later when he caught sight of Sam in tow. "Hi, babe," he said more quietly than he might otherwise have. His wary gaze slid to Sam.

"Sam and I just went for a drink." Honesty seemed the best approach— that, and taking the bull by the horns. "He suggested we all go out for dinner sometime. How about it?"

"Sounds fine," Ryan said evenly.

Sam spoke from behind. "I'll check with Ellen to see when we can get a sitter, and I'll give you a call."

Carly turned back to him for a minute. "Great. I'll wait to hear from you."

Only Sam saw the deeper message in her gaze and knew that despite the brightness of her manner she hadn't forgotten the reason he'd sought her out today. He nodded and, with quiet goodbyes, left. When Carly faced Ryan once more her expression was wiped clean of tension.

"Have a good day?" she asked, getting her own mail before passing through the door he held.

"Busy," he answered succinctly, not quite sure what to make of Sam's taking her for drinks, much less his dinner invitation. "How about you?"

"Busy."

They started up the stairs in silence. When Ryan finally spoke, his tone was vague. "Listen, I think I'll go to my place to change. Do you want to go out for something to eat?"

She stopped, looking up at him. "You're angry."

"No." He, too, stopped. Discouraged, he took a deep breath, then let it out slowly. "It always bothers me when I see him. I know it's wrong, but I can't help it."

"That's why we should go out with Ellen and him." Hooking her arm through his, she resumed the climb. "I know how you feel, but this may be the best thing. If you get to know Sam you'll see that he's really a nice guy."

"I'm sure he's a nice guy. It's his motives I'm not sure about."

"Ryan," she scolded gently, "we'll be with his wife. He loves her very much. You'll see that."

On the second-floor landing they stopped again. Ryan's scowl took on shades of self-reproach. His voice was gruff. "Ach, I'm a beast. Of course we'll have dinner with them." His gaze grew more direct. "Anyway, I'd rather you see him when I'm there than when I'm not."

"It was only for a drink," she said very softly.

"I know. I know." He shifted his briefcase to his left hand and threw his right arm around her shoulder. "Kiss me. That's the problem. You haven't kissed me yet."

She shook her head firmly. "I'm not kissing a bear."

"But if you kiss the bear, he turns into a prince."

"That's a frog."

"You wouldn't want me to croak, would you?"

She closed her eyes for an instant. "You're impossible. Have I told you that before?"

"Many times," he said without a shred of remorse.

She sent him a chiding glance. Standing on tiptoe, she kissed him lightly before breaking away. "Go change and then come up. I'm broiling swordfish."

"You smell like beer," he called after her, but the anger was gone from his voice and she relaxed.

An hour later, she was still relaxed, sitting back in her chair drinking the coffee Ryan had brewed. The table was strewn with dirty plates, which neither of them had the desire to clear.

"Tell you what," Ryan began, turning sideways and propping his stockinged feet on the lower rung of her chair. "If I go out to dinner with Sam and his wife, will you come to a dinner with me?"

"What dinner?"

"There's a convention here next week of the National Criminal Defense Attorneys' Association."

"My God, that's a mouthful."

"Wait'll you hear the rest. There's a banquet on Friday night."

She screwed up her face. "A banquet? As in dressy?"

"Nah. Trial lawyers don't know how to dress. "You know that." They'd already been through Carly's aversion to lawyers, though she'd made a joke of it and had never elaborated on its cause.

"I thought I did, until I met you."

"Is that a compliment?"

"Yes."

"Then, I thank you. But we're skirting the issue. Will you go?"

"To the banquet? I don't know, Ryan. All those lawyers in one room." She was teasing him, but only half so. Ryan excepted, lawyers still gave her the creeps.

"It'll be boring. I can't argue with you about that. But think of how awful it'll be for me if I have to go alone."

"Do you *have* to go?"

The cord in his neck jumped when he grimaced. "I'm speaking."

Eyes widening, Carly sat forward. *"You're speaking?* How can you *do* this to me, Ryan?" She knew she could never refuse him, given the circumstances. He knew it too.

"I agreed to go out with Sam and Ellen," he reminded her.

It was the clincher. She was lost. "All right. But on one condition."

"What's that?"

"That except for the time you're on the podium you stay with me. I won't be left alone to fend for myself in that crowd."

Taking her hand, Ryan swung it gently between their chairs. "What did you ever do before I came along?" he teased.

"I didn't go partying with hordes of shifty lawyers, that's for sure!" she retorted, but her gruffness was mostly for show. "What are you talking on, anyway?"

His eyes danced. "What every lawyer longs to know — how to make friends and influence people."

"You are not," she scolded, squeezing his hand.

"Actually, I was planning to speak about ethics and the image of the criminal lawyer."

"That I do approve of. A much needed topic of discussion."

He tipped his dark head and spied her through half-closed eyes. "Anything else good to say about my profession?"

"You're in it."

A chuckle reverberated in his throat as he leaned forward and smacked a rewarding kiss on her lips. "All the right answers. Smart lady. . . ."

With her Creative Writing class over and the mid-morning break under way, Carly returned to her office to change notebooks and found a message on her desk. The sight of the pink slip sent an involuntary chill through her, bringing thought of yesterday and Sam's call. But this call wasn't from Sam. It was from Ryan. Lifting the phone, she quickly called him back. This time, when she identified herself to his secretary, she was instantly recognized.

"Oh, Mrs. Quinn, I'm sorry about what happened last week. I should have put you through. I had no idea—"

"It's all right." Carly smiled, her voice kind. "You had no way of knowing. I just assumed Ryan would realize I was home."

"Well, you have my apology anyway. Here, let me put you through to him now. Hold on."

Within seconds Ryan was on the line. "Carly! That was quick. I wasn't sure how soon you'd be able to get back to me."

"I'll have you know that I'm forfeiting coffee and doughnuts to make this call," she teased.

"No problem. I'll stuff you with them all weekend. Listen, since it's Friday, I thought maybe you could get away a little early and take the subway in to meet me. You can see the office, we can do something fun around here, maybe get some dinner and then drive home together.''

The thought of riding the T sent a ripple of apprehension through her. It always did, though she knew that with so many people around she was probably safer than ever. But the thought of meeting Ryan, at his office no less, was enough to quell her fears. ''Oh, Ryan, that sounds great! Wait a minute.'' Balancing the phone on her shoulder, she studied her calendar. ''I have an appointment with a student at three. I could come in right after that. Say, around four?''

''Perfect. Do you know how to get here?''

''Uh, no.''

He gave her directions, which she jotted down.

''Sounds easy enough.''

''It is. We're on the thirty-fourth floor. The receptionist will be on the lookout for you.''

A wave of warmth washed over her. ''I'm sure I'll have no problem. See you then?''

''You bet.'' He threw two quick kisses over the line. ''Bye-bye.'' Then he hung up the phone and sat back in his chair, eminently satisfied.

He'd been tough on Carly this morning, waking in a mood reminiscent of the bear she'd called him yesterday. They'd run as usual, though the paths were messy and the pace slower and less rhythmic. He'd come into the office brooding, feeling torn and frustrated, realizing that the thing he wanted most in the world was for Carly to be his, totally and forever. There was still one part of her that mystified him, but he was helpless to do anything about it or about the fact that he needed her more with each passing day. Knowing that she would be coming to him this afternoon cheered him immeasurably.

Carly, too, hung up the phone with a smile on her face. Belatedly she blew an answering kiss toward the phone, then took a deep, satisfied breath. She'd been aware of Ryan's mood that morning, and hadn't asked about it simply because she hadn't wanted to buy trouble. There were some answers she couldn't give him, and she was torn apart by guilt. She wanted to meet him this afternoon, she *had* to meet him this afternoon, if for no other reason than to show him how much she cared. Short of confessing her love, it was the best she could do.

Her student left by three-thirty. Stuffing her bag with books and papers, Carly was into her coat and boots and out the door by three-thirty-five. Intending to take a cab into the Square, she had the good fortune to bump into one of the other teachers, who offered her a ride.

The T wasn't as crowded as it would have been an hour later. Slipping into a seat, she hugged her bag to her and looked around at her fellow riders. Most of the faces were benign; a few unsettled her. It was to these few that her gaze returned from time to time as her imagination went to work. She was beginning to wish she'd taken a cab after all, when she caught herself and recalled what Sam had said the evening before. It *wasn't* right that she should be a prisoner of her fears. She did have a life to lead, and she had every right to lead it in peace. At the moment she was on her way to see Ryan, and it galled her that anything should dampen the excitement she felt.

Lifting her chin in defiance, she stared at the faces in the transit car. To her surprise, not a one stared back. Most were blank, impassive, enduring the trip as a limbo between here and there. As comfortable as she'd been alone in public for ages, she relaxed.

By the time the car disgorged itself at Government Center, she was feeling strong, even gutsy. One part of her dared anyone approach her with intent to harm; that part was tired of waiting and had thrown off the shackles of intimidation. The other part was, very simply, looking forward to seeing Ryan.

"I am not wearing tights!" Ryan's voice rang out loud and clear through the cluster of customers at the photographer's shop. Several heads turned his way in amusement before returning to face similar difficulties.

Trying to suppress her own grin, Carly coaxed him gently. "You'd look great in tights." Then she lowered her voice to a near whisper. "I've seen you in less."

"Yeah," he whispered gruffly, casting a fast glance at the other customers before dragging Carly into a corner, where she alone could see the flush high on his cheeks, "but this is a public place. A picture is something tangible, with a negative and everything. Think of the possibilities for blackmail."

"Come on, Ryan. Romeo and Juliet would be terrific!"

"That's fine and dandy for *you* to say, since *you'd* be all covered up in some—" he gestured vaguely "—some kind of flowing gown. No. *Not* Romeo and Juliet."

With a sigh, Carly turned her sights on the bevy of other samples that plastered the walls. She could afford to be flexible; her mood was incredibly light.

From the moment she'd set foot in the hallowed halls of Miller and Cornell, she'd been treated like royalty. Not only had the receptionist indeed known her, but everyone else, from Ryan's secretary to the copyists and word processors, had greeted her with warm smiles. Ryan had shown her from office to office, introducing her to other lawyers, reacquainting her with people she'd first met on New Year's Eve. And through it all he was so obviously proud. It endeared him to her all the more.

From the office, they had walked to a nearby art gallery where Ryan had seen a painting he wanted her opinion on for his apartment. She had loved it. He bought it, plus a small bronze statue of a pair of lovers, which Carly had thought to be nearly obscene. But she hadn't argued then, any more than she was about to argue now.

The photographer's shop specializing in novelty portraits was in the lower level of the Quincy Market. It was Carly who had peered down through its door and then had been drawn back after browsing through several other shops. She didn't have a picture of Ryan. She couldn't think of one she would rather have more than of the two of them dressed in period costume as lovers from another time.

"How about Henry VIII and Anne Boleyn," Ryan suggested. "I'd do fine with the beard."

"But you'd need too much stuffing and you'd *still* have to wear tights. Besides—" she grimaced "—he had Anne beheaded. Ahh." The grimace yielded to a romantic smile. "Rhett and Scarlett."

Ryan shook his head. "He didn't give a damn. I do. Look. Tarzan and Jane. Now *there's* a costume."

"It's nothing!"

He grinned. "I know."

"Ryan, don't be crude. I won't be Jane. Tarzan was always taking off on vines, leaving her behind to fend for herself in the jungle." Her gaze shifted. "That's a cute one." She pointed, a bright smile on her face. "You'd make a great Raggedy Andy."

"To your Ann? Come on, babe. Those two are made of rags. They couldn't make it—"

"Shh. Okay. Forget Raggedy Ann and Andy." Her arm was linked with his, their hands clasped in his pocket. Carly tugged him farther down the row of sample photos. "George and Martha Washington?"

"D-u-l-l. How about Antony and Cleopatra?"

"I hate asps."

"Ling Ling and Hsing Hsing?" The glance they exchanged was mutually dismissive. "Whoa, who's that?" Ryan asked. "Ma Barker and her boys?"

"That's for families. Besides, we have only one boy here and I *refuse* to play his mother. *Ever*."

They looked further, suggesting and rejecting several more in turn. Then, simultaneously, they saw the one they wanted. Carly looked at it, tipped her head, leaned closer. Ryan stared in fascination, growing more reckless by the minute.

"That's it," he murmured in her ear, never once taking his eyes from the photograph. "Us against the world. I love it!"

So did Carly. Outrageous. Infamous. Dramatic and daring. What did it matter that they had died so violently? Lovers under fire, they died together.

She nodded and grinned, feeling reckless as Ryan. "Bonnie and Clyde. Let's do it!"

"What a treat!" Sheila exclaimed. "I usually have to walk home. Not that I mind it; the exercise is great. It can be awful in lousy weather, though. Come to think of it—" she frowned, forgetting for the moment that she was supposed to be bright and appealing, which implied uncomplaining "—the weather's been progressively lousy since I got here."

Greg negotiated a left from Park to Beacon with ease. "You picked the wrong season to arrive."

"I'll say. I think it's been rainy or cold from day one, not to mention this latest. I don't understand it. We had much more snow in Chicago, but things didn't seem to stay so messy so long."

"Bostonians don't handle snow very well. It used to be worse, though. A real political issue."

"Oh?"

"Certain neighborhoods were up in arms, claiming that others received preferential treatment when it came to plowing."

"Was it true?"

"Yup."

"But it isn't anymore?"

"Oh, it is. It's just that the uproar has died down." With a crooked grin, he said, "You're new. One of the first things to learn about Massachusetts politics is that it's totally political. A little pull goes a long way."

"As in getting jobs?" she teased.

"Right. Mind you—" he held up a hand "—I took the civil-service exam and was more than qualified for the position. But a few well-placed phone calls didn't hurt. Had strings not been pulled for me, they would have been pulled for someone else." He cleared his throat. "Anyway, *you* happen to live in the right area. Any number of pols live on Beacon Hill. Your streets may be narrow, but they're usually well plowed." At her pointing finger, he made a right. "Did you have any trouble getting your car out?"

"Oh, no. A good shovel, scraper and brush did wonders." She laughed, a high nasal chuckle that sounded good-natured enough. "Not to mention elbow grease. Oops. Hold on a minute. There's the market. Would you mind pulling over for a second so I can run in and get same shallots?"

Braking at the corner, he raised both brows. "Shallots? Sounds complex."

"Complex? *Me?*" She sent him her most captivating smile and slid out of the car. Several moments later she returned with a large brown bag in the crook of her arm.

"All that is shallots?" he asked. She laughed again, and he decided that the sound of mischief and allure made her nasal voice not all that bad.

"I guess I needed a couple of other things too," she explained sheepishly. "And while we're on the subject, I'd better warn you that my apartment is nothing fancy. I mean, I contemplated renting a suite for the evening at the Meriden just for the sheer luxury of the surroundings, but I wanted to cook and they wouldn't let me near their kitchen. Somehow I don't think they would have appreciated my checking in with Tupperware for luggage."

Greg couldn't help but laugh. For whatever her faults, the woman was entertaining. "No, I don't think they would." Starting the car again, he drove on. Two blocks later, Sheila pointed to a parking space.

"Why don't you take that one. My place is only six doors up. We won't find anything nearer."

Greg neatly maneuvered into the space, then came around to take the bag from Sheila and help her out. He was pleased that she waited for him; many of the women he knew were more aggressive in their liberation, making a point of helping *themselves* from the seat of a car. Not that there appeared to be anything old-fashioned about Sheila. But the touch was nice. It made him feel masculine.

Gently holding her arm to guide her over occasional patches of ice on the sidewalk, Greg looked down at her. "Where *do* you park your car? Around here?"

She tossed her chin forward. "Over there."

"Which one?"

"The burgundy one. In front of the white Rabbits?"

"The Mazda?" His eyes widened and he quickened his pace for a better look. "Not bad, Montgomery. Not bad at all." Dropping her arm, he leaned low to peer inside the darkened window. Then he straightened and ran his free hand along the sleek front curve of the car. "It looks new."

"It is."

He shot her a glance. "Did you drive it east?"

"Uh-uh. I bought it here."

His gaze returned to the car for a final covetous once-over. "Ve-ry clas-sy."

She dipped her head, a pleased smile on her lips. "Thank you, sir." Then she slipped her arm through his. "But if you stand and stare at my car much longer those shallots are going to freeze. Where will our Shrimp á la Turque—" the words were given a distinctly foreign treatment by her tongue "—be then?" With a gentle tug on his arm, they were on their way once more.

Moments later, Sheila pushed open the door of her apartment, flipped on the lights and turned to ease the bag from Greg's arms. "Please. Make yourself comfortable." She ran down the few stairs, leaving him alone on the landing overlooking her all-inclusive single room. "I'll put these away and then get us a drink. What'll it be?" she called over her shoulder. "Scotch? Bourbon?"

"Scotch is fine." Draping his coat on the rack just inside the door, he propped his elbows on the wrought-iron railing and studied the apartment. Though small, it wasn't bad, he mused. Vaguely U-shaped, it had the open kitchen in which Sheila now puttered as its principal area. In the right arm of the U stood a simple wood table and chairs. At the U's base were a wicker love seat and two matching chairs. In its left arm, quite surprisingly, given the usual choice of a sofa bed for a studio apartment, was a double bed, tucked against the wall but very much a part of the room.

As Sheila had said, there was nothing fancy about the apartment. Its style was eclectic, the furniture secondhand. What held the whole together, though, was the predominance of cherry red. It stood out in a cloth draped over the table and in similar fabric gathered on a rod across the single high window. It lay on the floor in the form of a throw rug beneath the wicker works, whose cushions matched. It was broadcast from the two framed rock posters above the nonworking fireplace, which held a slightly withered poinsettia. And most obviously, it covered the bed in sheets, quilt, lacy pillow covers and dust ruffles.

"Like red, do you?" he called, straightening and starting down the steps with one hand in the pocket of his slacks.

"Love it!" Her back was to him; only as he came closer did he see that she was arranging a small bunch of red and white carnations in a simple glass carafe. "It's bright and daring. It demands notice." Turning, she whisked around him and put the carafe on the center of the table. "Sometimes the shades clash, but this place is so dark and drab that it needed *something* to give it pep."

Greg looked around and shrugged. "Funny. It didn't even occur to me to think of dark or drab."

"Are you kidding? Maybe the dark covers the drab. I've got lights plugged into nearly every outlet and I still feel like it's constantly midnight."

"That's because you're below street level."

"I suppose. Still, gray brick on every wall? If I were ambitious I'd paint it all white. God only knows why anyone would go with yuck gray."

"Your red does a lot. I like it."

Hands propped on her hips, Sheila took a deep breath as she perused the room. "Well, this is only the beginning. From here I'll take a one-bedroom above ground, then a three-bedroom several stories up, then the penthouse, then a mansion in the country, then . . . who knows!" Her grin had broadened with each step.

Greg wondered how she was going to manage it on an agent's salary. "Are those dreams, or plans?"

Her grin vanished, her head shot around and, for the first time in a while, he saw the sharpness in her eyes he'd once commented on to Sam. She was really a stunning woman, with her flowing black hair, her slender curves, and, yes, those snapping eyes that spoke of mystery and fire. Of its own accord, and taking him slightly by surprise, his body tautened.

Simultaneously hers relaxed and she broke into a gentle smile. "Dream or plan? A little of each, I guess." She opened a cabinet and extracted bottles of Scotch and rum, and two glasses.

Greg lounged against the counter by her side. "What do you want from life, Sheila?"

She turned to the refrigerator for Coke, the freezer for ice. "In what sense?"

"Work, for one thing. What are your long-range plans?"

"I just got here. How can I think that far ahead?"

"Tell me dreams, then. What do you want to do?"

She made a face and struggled to separate the ice cubes from their bin. When the cold chips resisted her fingers, she turned to Greg for help. "Can you give these a try? This freezer stinks. The temperature is so uneven that the ice all sticks together."

Greg reached in and fumbled unsuccessfully for a minute. "Got an ice pick or a knife or something?"

She took a knife from the drawer and handed it to him. After several hacks, he had freed enough cubes to fill their glasses. Standing back, Sheila let Greg fix their drinks and hand her hers. Then she led him to the wicker love seat, kicked off her heels and, tucking one leg under her, sat down.

"Tell me about you, Greg," she coaxed. "What do *you* want from life?"

He hadn't exactly planned to talk about himself, but since she seemed interested, he said, "I'd like to work my way up the ladder in the marshal's service. When and if I decide to leave, the experience I'll have had here will stand me in good stead to do other things in law enforcement. At some point I'd love to go to Washington."

They talked about that for a while, with Sheila asking question after question, seeming intrigued by the thought of a career in the nation's capital. When she got up to fix dinner, Greg followed her into the kitchen and talked with her as she worked. He felt surprisingly relaxed, more so than he had expected, given the supposed "unsettling" effect that he was to be investigating. Strangely, as the minutes passed, he felt less and less the investigator and more and more the man. She had a way of doing that, a subtle way, a seemingly innocent way.

It was in her eyes, those eyes that could be so sharp, yet seemed now direct and latently sensual, eyes that lingered on his or fell to focus on the warm pulse beat at his neck or studied his fingers as they curled around his glass. It was in her voice, sometimes bubbly, sometimes serious but strangely sultry in its nasal kind of way.

As they talked through a dinner of shrimp, steamed rice and artichokes in butter sauce, Greg began to wonder what it was that had originally bothered him about Sheila. Nervous energy? If there was nervous energy now, he couldn't see it. Rather, he saw a woman who was composed and poised, mature and apparently unaware of how truly attractive she was. Her sense of humor erupted often, but it was finely tuned to his own. She listened, questioned, spoke as little about herself as possible. By the time they'd polished off dinner and a bottle of wine, he was unbelievably titillated.

Conversation waned. Sheila sipped kahlua-laced coffee, her eyes holding his over the rim of her mug. Then her gaze fell to his throat, and she was captivated by the curling tufts of hair that had escaped once he'd loosened his tie and unbuttoned his shirt collar.

Greg Reilly was a very attractive man, she decided. Tall and well built, he claimed to have been something of a jock at Boston College. She believed him. Though he'd also said that his involvement with sports was now limited to membership in a weekend basketball league, he had easily retained his lean physique and fluidity of movement. With dark wavy hair, deep blue eyes and a faintly ruddy complexion, he was an Irishman to do Boston proud.

"Sheila?" His voice held a sudden warning that brought her eyes instantly up from their intent study of him. "Do you know what you're doing?"

She neither pled innocence nor smiled, but spoke in a soft, sure voice, her eyes steady on his as she lowered the cup to her lap. "Yes."

"It's not very smart."

"Why not?" she asked gently. "We're adults."

"Adults who work together."

"Um-hmm."

"It can complicate things."

"I don't see how," she said in the same quiet voice. Its very guilelessness was a potent stimulant to Greg's growing awareness of her warm body, so near and apparently willing. "You're an attractive man. If you find *me* attractive. . . ." Her voice trailed off, her eyes asking the question.

Greg set his mug on the floor. Then he propped one knee by Sheila's hip and, with his other leg stretched to the floor, he half knelt over her. When she tipped her head up, he spread his fingers under her thick fall of hair and supported her head while his gaze caressed her features.

"I find you attractive," he conceded tightly. "Too attractive. Believe it or not, this wasn't what I had in mind when I came over here tonight."

"Does it matter?" she asked, "Some of the best things just . . . happen. There's nothing complicated about our finding pleasure in each other. You know what you're getting; so do I. One night. No strings attached." Her breath had begun to come faster as she'd spoken. She waited a minute for Greg to say something. When he didn't, but continued to drink her in with his eyes, she knew the battle was ninety-nine percent won. "Greg," she whispered, looking up at him beseechingly, "don't make me beg."

He didn't need to hear more. The lure was too great, and he was far too hungry. He was no saint, had never claimed to be one. Nor had Sam Loomis made sainthood a prerequisite for this particular assignment.

Taking her head between his hands, he captured her lips in a deep, heated kiss. When he finally dragged his mouth from hers and held her back, he saw that her eyes were closed, her lips still parted. He took them again, and again, finding her essence as intoxicating as the artful promise of her body.

Arms circling his back, she moaned softly when he released her lips, and opened her eyes to his. "Take me to bed, Greg," she breathed on a whisper. "Please . . . now. . . ."

She didn't have to ask again. He was aroused, bewitched and more than willing to take his satisfaction from her warm, eager body.

Only later, much later, did he realize that the name she cried at the moment of her climax wasn't his.

SEVENTEEN

❀ ❀ ❀

CARLY COULD HAVE SWORN she was being followed; the prickles at the back of her neck told her so. With a sharp glance behind, she quickened her step, she recalled the last time she'd felt this way, nearly three months before, when she'd run into Ryan. Tonight he wouldn't be there; he had a late meeting and would be out until ten.

After all these weeks of feeling so secure, she wondered why she should have the willies now. But, of course, it had everything to do with her talk with Sam last week, and the fact that, through the weekend, she'd had to suppress it all. Her every thought then had been of Ryan. He was tense about something, and when she'd asked him what it was, he had shrugged and mumbled something about a preoccupation with one of his cases.

She didn't believe him. There were those random times—she would be sitting on the sofa doing needlepoint, or standing at her dresser combing her hair, or waiting in the kitchen for the coffee to drip—when she would look up to find him studying her enigmatically. She wondered whether he suspected something of her past or whether he was growing impatient about the future.

The present wasn't in doubt. When they were together doing things, they were totally compatible. But he never mentioned marriage, and now that she thought of it, he hadn't said he loved her in days.

Running up the steps to the courtyard walk, she cast another look behind. She saw no one. Perhaps it was her imagination again. Then again, perhaps it wasn't. With each passing week, the judge's decision on a new trial grew closer. If someone wanted to permanently prevent her testimony, the time was right.

Fumbling with the lock, she finally let herself in, grabbed her mail and ran up the stairs. Once inside her own apartment, with the bolts safely thrown and the alarm system on, she stood listening to a silence broken only by her thudding heart. Instantly the emptiness of the place closed in on her, and she realized how much she'd come to depend on Ryan's presence.

Dropping her things on a chair, she went to the kitchen and picked up the phone. If she called Sam and told him of her fears, he would insist on assigning her a guard. But she desperately needed to talk, and there was only one other person who knew enough to allow her full freedom on that score. The phone rang eight times. She was ready to hang up when it was finally answered breathlessly.

"Hello?"

"Sheila? I'm sorry. Did I get you from somewhere?"

"Oh, Carly! No! I just this minute walked in!"

"Listen, I really need to talk to someone. Can you come over?"

"Ah. . . ."

"You have plans?"

Sheila thought quickly. Tom had asked to meet her for a light supper, and much as she'd been looking forward to it, instinct told her this was more important.

"Nothing I can't change."

"Are you sure? Hey, I'm really sorry—"

"Don't be silly! Give me half an hour, okay?"

Carly breathed a sigh of relief. "Thanks."

True to her word, Sheila arrived thirty minutes later. Carly buzzed her in, then waited at the front door as she ran up the stairs.

"Thanks for coming," she said as soon as the other was inside.

"Is something wrong?" Sheila asked, dropping her leather pouch on the chair and her coat over its arm.

Carly ran a hand through her hair, lifting the bangs from her brow. "Not really. I'm just nervous. I had to talk with someone. Come on. Let's sit down. How about a rum and Coke?"

Sheila grinned. "I'd never turn down one of those." She walked with Carly toward the kitchen. "What are the nerves about?"

"My imagination, most likely. I sometimes think I'm going out of my mind. When I was walking home from school today, I was sure someone was following me. I mean, no one was. It was barely dusk. But there I was, one eye over my shoulder, scurrying through the slush like a zombie."

"You could *never* look like a zombie," Sheila said, chuckling. "And I'm sure you were imagining the whole thing. Has anything else happened?''

"Sam's been in touch with Bill, and they're trying to keep on top of anything Culbert might try. If I'm not around for that new trial, the outcome might be very different for him. And for Barber. Actually *he* was the one Sam was talking about last week.'' She handed the drink to Sheila, who was regarding her intently.

"Barber? Barber's a nothing.''

"That's what they all say.'' She poured herself a glass of wine. "But I guess he's the one who's been talking about the new trial and the possibility of getting off.''

"You're kidding!''

"Don't I wish!''

"What's he saying?''

Carly headed for the living room. "Nothing specific. Just that he plans to be walking the streets before long.'' She sank onto the sofa. Sheila followed closely.

"He doesn't say how?''

"If only. Then we might have more to go on.''

"So what does Sam say?'' she asked more cautiously.

Carly sighed. "Sam says that if I want he could assign someone to cover me. But that's the *last* thing I want. Ryan would know everything. As it is, he doesn't like Sam. I can just imagine what would happen if either Sam or someone else from the office were to squire me around town. It would be so disruptive.'' She hung her head. "When I let my mind wander, I go mad. Can you imagine if my cover is breached and they decide to give me a new one?'' She looked up then, torment etched in each fine feature. "I don't think I could go through it again, Sheila. New name. New place. New occupation. New friends. No Ryan.''

Sheila reached over and gently patted her knee. "Don't think about that now. There's no cause for alarm yet. Your cover is really solid. Just because some bozo in prison is talking big doesn't mean he's got anything to back it up.''

But Carly wasn't easily mollified. Her voice quavered. "I really love Ryan. There's no way I could leave him. It was different in Chicago. Sure, I had a home and a career and friends. But there was never anyone special like him. He was exactly what was missing in my life. I can't conceive of a future without him. So help me, even if there *is* some awful danger, I think I'd almost rather live with it than give up everything!'' Her voice dropped, weighed down by an element of defeat. "A person can only run so far.''

Sheila sat back quietly for a time, watching her. She sipped her drink thoughtfully. "You're a very lucky woman, to have found someone like Ryan.''

There was a note of wistfulness—no, harder—in her voice that, even amid her own turmoil, Carly couldn't ignore. "I'm sorry. I've been going on and on feeling sorry for myself. You're right. I am lucky.'' She paused, then ventured on. "How about you? Are things looking up?''

"Oh yes,'' Sheila answered quickly. She thought back to the Friday night before and felt a ripple of satisfaction. Things had gone just as she had so carefully planned. Greg was on her side; she had an ally in the office. She had pleased him, and he hadn't been that bad himself. Through the night he'd taken her repeatedly. He was forceful and imaginative in bed. If she'd had to sell herself to someone, she could have done much worse.

"How about Tom?" Carly asked, and Sheila's satisfaction was dimmed by a wave of regret. "You're seeing a lot of him?"

"Uh-huh. He's quite a man." She meant it. While, for the time being at least, her body might be Greg's, Tom was the one who captivated her thoughts. "Very different from Ryan, but every bit as charming. He has a fantastic house. Did you know that?"

"Ryan told me a little about it." Ryan hadn't found it quite that "fantastic," but the time he'd spent there hadn't been under the best of circumstances. "I understand Tom's got a good business going now."

Sheila nodded. "Computers. He's taught me a lot about them. They're not really so bad. Oh, they don't pick up the dirty laundry or do boring case reports or—" she glanced down "—fix rum and Cokes, but they're pretty clever when it comes to things intellectual." She drawled the last for every syllable it was worth.

"Do you think there's any future in it?"

"In computers? Sure—"

"In Tom. You and Tom."

Sheila's flippancy vanished. She grew serious, almost troubled. "I don't know. I hope so. But there's so much. . . ." When her voice trailed off, Carly's picked up.

"He's free, and he's clever and good-looking, and he has those muscles and a wallet."

She'd been teasing, but Sheila didn't crack a smile. "But will he love me? I mean, really love me. Will he be able to accept me for what I am and what I do?"

"He doesn't mind your work, does he?"

Sheila's half laugh was dry. "Only the times I have to be home early for a six o'clock assignment the next morning."

"But his work hours are flexible. You could work around that."

"I know." Work hours were the least of her worries. "Well—" she gave an exaggerated sigh "—we're doin' all right, anyway. But back to you. Do you feel any better?"

"Yes. Talking about it helps."

"Want my professional opinion?"

"Sure."

"I think that you ought to relax and forget about all this. No one's chasing you. No one knows who you are. No one's going to come after you. Hell, if either Barber or Culbert tried anything, they'd only be in worse trouble afterward."

"They haven't got much to lose," Carly reminded her pointedly. "Barber had a record. He's no stranger to prison. But I can't imagine Culbert cares much for it."

"Look. He's not stupid. He knows what would happen if he tried to harm you. He'd have to cover his tracks pretty well. How can he do that? He's in jail."

"He can hire someone—the same thug who came after me last time. I wouldn't be so worried if that hadn't happened." She snorted. "I wouldn't be *here* if that hadn't happened."

"But you are here. And you're safe. Take my word for it." She hesitated, but only for an instant. "You do trust me, Carly, don't you?"

"Yes."

"Then, please. Relax. Enjoy Ryan. Enjoy life. You never can tell," she ventured brashly. "Someone could get to Barber or Culbert before they get to you."

It was a thought that made both of them smile. Only Carly felt guilt at her reaction.

Early the next morning, Sheila strode into Sam and Greg's office. Greg looked up from his work and smiled.

"I wanted to talk with him," she whispered, cocking her head toward Sam, who was on the phone. "Do you think he'll be long?"

Sam looked up, shook his head and motioned her forward. She idled slowly toward Greg's desk. "Hi."

"Hi, yourself," Greg answered softly.

"I missed you yesterday." She'd come looking, only to find that he was out of the office for the day.

"We're trying to arrange security for a trial that's coming up next month. I spent most of the day in Bristol county."

"Ah." She nodded, and looked shyly at her fingers gripping the edge of his desk. "I was hoping you'd come over last night."

Though her voice was little more than a whisper, Greg sent a cautious glance toward his boss before looking back. "I didn't get in until late."

Again she nodded. "I enjoyed myself."

He knew what she was referring to and wasn't sure how to respond. Since leaving her apartment early Saturday morning, he'd been bothered. It wasn't his style to stand in for another man, and one part of him was livid that he had. The other part, the same part that had prompted him to slake his hunger for her over and over again that night, looked at her now and saw her as she'd been then—naked, warm, and willing to do whatever he asked of her.

"So did I," he murmured at last.

"Sheila?" Sam's voice broke into their conversation. When her head spun around, Greg felt strangely relieved. She immediately crossed the room.

Guardedly, Sam nodded toward the free chair by his desk. Sheila had never sought him out before, simply taking her assignments and completing them with little ado and, apparently, more than adequate competency. "What's the problem?"

"Carly. I got a call from her last night. She was terrified. I spent several hours with her."

"Why was she terrified?"

"She imagined someone was following her on her way home from school."

"Why didn't she call me?" He felt a slight hurt, but schooled it carefully, along with a mild sense of guilt.

"She felt that you'd insist on putting someone on her, and she didn't want that. She needed to talk, and since we're close and I'm one of the few people. . . ." Awkward, she cast a glance at Greg, who appeared to be listening to every word. She assumed he was aware of the situation, though she had never mentioned it to him herself.

"It's okay," Sam assured her, appreciating her caution. "Greg knows what's going on." He had taken him into his confidence about Carly even before he'd gone off with her to Chicago.

Sheila smiled a crooked apology toward Greg. "I wasn't sure how much to say. . . ."

"It's okay," Sam said again. "Was she really upset?"

"Yes. She knows it's her imagination, but she's been on edge since she spoke with you last week. "She's adamant about not having a guard because she feels that it would interfere with her life. It occurred to me that, since we're friends anyway and all, I could help. I mean, I know there are other things you've got for me to do, but if you decide to put someone on her, I might be the best one for the job."

Sam studied the woman standing before him. He had thought of the possibility many times and, as yet, had held off. He wasn't sure why, though she was right. She *was* the perfect one for the job, given her friendship with Carly and the fact that she could easily blend into Carly's daily life. As it was, he had already assigned a man to the case, an agent who, as of Monday morning, had silently kept watch over Carly as she'd gone to and from school. It appeared from what Sheila had said that he hadn't been quite that invisible.

He picked up a pencil and absently tapped its eraser against the desk. "You've got a point. She wouldn't have half as much explaining to do with a friend by her side. Of course, there's still Ryan."

Sheila was about to comment on her own relationship with Tom and the fact that that, too, might work out well, when she recalled that Greg was hearing everything she said. "Ryan already knows me and knows that Carly and I are friends. Assuming I fade into the background when the two of them are together, it wouldn't be much of a problem."

Sam shrugged. She had thought it all out. "Well—" he sighed, giving the pencil an idle move "—let me think about it. Maybe I'll give her a call and feel her out about the whole thing."

"She'll fight you," Sheila argued in a last-ditch effort to plead her case. "She went so far as to say that even if her cover is blown she won't budge. I think she's nearing her limit, and her involvement with Ryan isn't helping matters. He may be putting pressure on her for some kind of commitment." It sounded good. "The poor woman's being torn apart."

That Sam could believe. "I know. It's tough on her."

When Sheila would have jumped in to say that she could make things easier, she caught herself. She'd already made her point. Subtlety was in order. The decision had to be Sam's.

"Okay," he said. "I'll let you know what I decide." His tone reeked of finality. With a nod, Sheila turned, sent a gentle smile Greg's way and left.

In the wake of her departure, silence filled the room. It was Sam who broke it, though Greg was right on his wavelength. "How did it go Friday night?"

"Okay. She's nice."

"Is that an endorsement?" He had to admit that she had seemed more subdued, more serious than usual. Perhaps she was settling down. If something about her still bothered him—an unspoken intensity, a strange if subtle urgency—maybe that was *his* problem.

"I . . . think so."

"But you're not sure."

Greg had grown suspicious when Sheila had spoken of Ryan's acceptance of her. It would certainly be convenient—Ryan and Carly and Sheila and Tom. But that was his own ego speaking, and it had little to do with the facts of Sheila's ability on the job.

"I guess I'm sure," he said at last. "She's serious when it comes to work. She was the one who came up with the lead that netted Phillinski while you were in Chicago. She's good with informants, handles them well. Phillinski had been running the feds in circles for two years." He frowned. "No, any doubts I might have are personal."

"She's a lousy cook," Sam speculated, but Greg was quick on the rebound.

"She's a *great* cook. Claims she learned everything she knows from her old Uncle Amos. He recalled the amusing dissertation that had been delivered along with a midnight snack. "Sheila's a character. She lives in a subbasement apartment, which she hates, but she drives a brand new Mazda, which she loves. She serves me Chivas Regal, then helps herself to a rum and Coke. She talks as freely about having come from poverty as about the mansion in the country she plans to have one day." He took a deep breath, then, perplexed, let it out. "She *is* a character."

"Do you think she'd be okay guarding Carly?"

Greg shrugged. "I don't see why not. If they spent all that time together in Chicago and are still friends, Carly must be aware of her eccentricities. Sheila's good company once you get used to her."

Sam thought back to Sheila's arrival in Boston. "That's what Carly's been telling me from the start. Maybe she's right. Maybe I'm too conservative for my own good."

Greg wondered the same about himself. No strings attached, Sheila had assured him, and he wanted it that way. She might have been great in bed, but it didn't change the fact that she stirred nothing else in him. So why did it bother him that she had used his body as she dreamed of Thomas Cornell? It bothered him because of the weird feeling he had that, though he'd been in the dominant position, she had been calling the shots.

Carly sat in class feeling worse by the minute. She'd had it again this morning—that awful sense of being followed. Neither Sheila's pep talk nor a night in Ryan's arms seemed to have made a dent in her paranoia. Her stomach was in knots. She felt decidedly drained.

By lunchtime she discovered one source of her problem. She had gotten her period.

By early afternoon she had the answer to the other. Sam had called. She phoned him back as soon as she returned to her office.

"How could you have done that, Sam?" she cried when he told her about the man he'd had following her.

"I thought about it all weekend and decided that I'd feel better knowing you were covered, at least during those times you were most exposed."

"But I was terrified! I felt your man on my tail from the start!"

"I know, Carly, and I'm sorry. He tried to be discreet, but I think you have fine-tuned antennas in that lovely head of yours. Anyway, I've pretty much decided to let Sheila cover you. She wouldn't be on it full-time. We don't have sufficient evidence of a problem to justify that. But she could walk back and forth from school with you, or drive you if you want, then go with you if you have things to do after—"

"What'll I tell Ryan? He knows Sheila and I are friends, but he's apt to suspect something strange."

"Do you leave with Ryan in the mornings?"

"Sometimes. Sometimes he gives me a lift."

"Then I could have Sheila waiting, watching from her car. If you're alone, she'd be there to join you. If you've got Ryan, you won't need her. And there's no problem in the afternoons. Ryan works."

"I suppose."

"See? An easy solution to a problem that probably isn't any problem at all. I'll keep up the patrols around your place. You weren't aware of those, were you?"

"No."

"Good. I'm sure Ryan wasn't either. Sheila will start tomorrow morning. For tonight, I'll let the same agent—"

"No, Sam. He doesn't need to follow me. I don't care who he is, but he makes me nervous. I'll be all right. It's just one night."

"You're sure? I mean, the whole purpose of this is for your peace of mind."

"And yours," she reminded him tartly.

"Right. Well, that's an idiosyncrasy of mine you'll just have to put up with. But I will pull Ben now if you'd rather."

"I'd rather."

"Then it's done. Give me a call if Sheila gets on your nerves."

"Sam, Sam, Sam. You're still down on her?"

"She may be a damn good deputy, but I don't care what you say, she'll always be a flake to me."

Carly sighed and closed her eyes, feeling lighter of mind but very tired of body. "Well, if I have to have a bodyguard, I'd rather Sheila than anyone else."

"You've got her." His voice grew mischievous. "Have fun."

She smiled wanly. "Thanks."

She should have felt better, but she didn't. The afternoon dragged on. She moved gingerly through two classes, then several student conferences, then a department meeting. By five, when she would have started home, she felt terrible.

Lifting the phone, she called Ryan. He was in conference, but she was quickly dispatched through.

"Carly?" His voice was low and accompanied by the hum of others in the background. "Is everything okay?" She rarely called him at work. He couldn't help but worry.

"Everything's fine," she said quietly. "I, uh, I just thought I'd stick around here for a while and clean up some work. Do you think you could swing by for me on your way home?"

"You sound tired."

"I am."

"I can get away in an hour. Is that too late?"

"No. That's fine."

"You stay in your office. I'll come for you."

"I can wait at the—"

"I won't have you waiting anywhere. If I'm held up in traffic, at least I'll know that you'll be getting something done. Okay?"

"Okay."

"See you then."

"Bye-bye."

The extreme softness of her voice conjured up an image of the vulnerability Ryan had seen in her so often at the start of their relationship. He hadn't seen it as much lately; she seemed more confident, more content. Now, though, he was as affected as ever by it. Replacing the receiver in its cradle, he realized that regardless of how frustrated he might be about whatever it was she hid from him, he would never, ever be immune to her pain.

By the time an hour had passed, Carly had mixed feelings about Ryan's good intent. True, she was in her office, sitting, off her feet. And true, she had gotten some work done, albeit not as much as she might have wished. But she had also discovered that the rest of the school had grown very quiet. And while she doubted she had the strength to walk home, more than anything she wished she were there now, tucked in bed with a heating pad, safe and sound.

By six-twenty she'd begun to fear that he had been tied up longer than expected. The switchboard was off; he couldn't get through if he tried. She was about to try him, when she heard footsteps in the hall. They were steady, confident. She wanted to believe they were Ryan's, though with carpeted rooms at home, she couldn't be sure she recognized the sound. They came quickly closer, with neither hesitancy nor stealth. Sitting very still, eyes on the door, she waited. When Ryan poked his head in, she let out her breath.

He kissed her gently and helped her gather her things. "You do look beat," he said with concern, as he shut the door of her office and guided her down the hall.

When she was finally in the car, she put her head back and closed her eyes, trying to concentrate on anything but the cramps that were painfully constant.

"Want to go out for something?"

"I think I'd just like to lie down for a while."

He turned to study her face, which looked all the more pale in the dim streetlight. "Don't feel well?"

"Just cramps. I got my period this morning."

He reached out to caress her cheek with the back of his hand and felt utterly helpless. "I'm sorry, babe. Is it bad?"

She managed a noncommital reply, but nothing more. Taking his cue, Ryan started the car. Within five minutes they were home. Carly headed straight for the bedroom, kicked off her shoes and curled in a tight ball atop the quilt, coat and all. She was only vaguely aware of a shift in the mattress when Ryan sat down.

He reached for her coat, working at the buttons, finally easing it off and laying it aside. "Want to get undressed?"

She shook her head. "Not yet."

He spread an extra blanket over her feet. "Can I get you anything? Aspirin? Warm milk? A hot-water bottle?"

"Don't have a hot-water bottle," she mumbled against the quilt. "There's a heating pad though. Under the bed."

Without rising, he groped for it, plugged it in and watched her unfold herself enough to place it on her thigh. "Why there? Isn't it your stomach?"

"When I get cramps, my thigh aches."

"Is it always like this?"

"For years it was, then it got better." She moaned softly and shifted position. "This is the worst it's been in months."

"Should you call a doctor?"

"No. He warned me. I'll be okay."

"Warned you?" There was mild panic in Ryan's voice. He felt very male and very out of it. "What do you mean, warned you? What did he warn you about?"

"The IUD. When I got it a few weeks ago. He said there was a chance my period would be worse."

Ryan breathed a pithy oath. "Get rid of the damn thing. I don't care about birth control."

"Well, I do." She smiled gently up at him and put a hand on the tensed muscles of his arm. "Ryan, it's okay. Really." She started to get up. "If it'd make you feel better, I'll go sit with you in the living room."

He pushed her down again, leaving a protective hand to rub her back. "It'd make me feel better to see *you* better. Isn't there anything that helps?"

"Peace." She eyed him in gentle chiding. "And quiet."

"That's a hint."

Closing her eyes, she burrowed deeper into the quilt. "Mmm." It was as much a groan as anything else. When she felt him begin to rise, she reached out to stop him. "No. Don't go. Just lie with me a little."

He leaned low and placed a kiss on her cheek. "Let me change. Then I'll be back."

She nodded and, trying to tune out the pain, focused on the quiet sounds of his undressing. First he slipped his suit jacket from his shoulders and let it fall to the bed. There was near silence as he tugged at his tie and worked at the buttons of his vest, then a swish as it separated from his shirt. She heard the rattle of his belt buckle, the dull click of a button, the rasp of his zipper, the rustle of his trousers. Moments later there was the clatter of wood hangers in the closet, one of which he removed and on which he began, piece by piece, to hang his suit. She pictured him standing by the bed in his shirt, his tie draped down either side of the fabric that tauntingly bared his chest.

She moaned again, louder this time, and Ryan was instantly on a knee, leaning close. "Is it worse?" he asked in alarm.

The sound she made was a poor imitation of a laugh. "I don't believe it," she whispered hoarsely. "I'm lying here listening to you strip and it's totally erotic, but I hurt so much I can't feel a thing."

Ryan stretched out on the bed and took her ever so gently in his arms. "I wish there was *something* I could do."

"This is fine," she murmured against his chest. The faintly musky scent of his warm skin momentarily numbed her brain against that other, more visceral discomfort. In a gesture totally devoid of sexual intent, she ran her hand up his chest and hooked it around his neck. Her thumb fell to caress the point beneath his jaw where beard ended and skin began. After a minute, she tipped her head back and studied the spot. "It's soft here. I never noticed before."

"We all have our weak points." He cleared his throat of its thickness.

"Not weak. Very nice." Her thumb ventured into his beard, her eye following its gentle exploration. "What's this? A scar?" She felt the faint ridge and, on closer examination, saw the slightest line where no hair grew. When he was upright it was invisible. Only now, with his head back against the pillow, could she see it.

He quickly looked down at her, obscuring the breach. "A little one. It's nothing."

"Where'd you get it?"

"An accident when I was younger." He wasn't sure why he didn't tell her the truth, but suspected it had something to do with the frustration he felt inside. If she wasn't opening completely, he didn't have to either. Juvenile perhaps, but he couldn't help himself. Another time, he might have feared she would prod deeper. Already, though, she was shifting position, trying to get more comfortable. "Here—" he eased her out of his arms "—why don't you rest. I'll go see what I can scrounge up in the kitchen."

"Just give me a couple of minutes and I'll get you something."

"You will not." He was tugging on his jeans. "I lived alone for over a year. I'm not completely helpless. Besides, I don't think you'll be good for much for a while. Maybe I can get you some soup or something."

"Uh-uh," she groaned, shaking her head. "I'll just lie here. That'll help."

It didn't help much. She moved restlessly on the bed in an attempt to find a comfortable position. In essence the only relief she got was from the movement itself, which, for those brief instants, masked the pain. Finally she pushed herself up from the bed and, no longer able to bear anything binding around her body, changed into a long-sleeved nightshirt.

Ryan appeared at the bedroom door just as she was attempting to pull the bedcovers back. "Let me help you!" When she slid between the sheets, dragging her heating pad along, he tucked her in. "Why didn't you call?" He glanced at the clothes she'd strewn on the chair. "I could have given you a hand."

"A woman has to do some things alone," Carly murmured, attempting a joke that fell flat.

"Not in my book. A relationship's for sharing. Both the good *and* the bad."

"Ryan. . . ." Her moaned protest stemmed not only from the need she'd had for privacy but also from her own sense of guilt. But she wasn't in the mood for a lecture. Not tonight. Not now. Eyes closed, she burrowed more deeply into the covers.

His voice was soft in concern by her ear. "How about some aspirin?"

She shook her head. "It doesn't help."

"Then something stronger? Maybe if I call your doctor—"

"No. I have my usual prescription, but I hate to take it. It knocks me out."

He tucked an auburn wave behind her ear. "That might be the best thing."

"No," she answered with a vehemence that was instantly spent. She went on more weakly. "I'll be all right. I mean, it's not like I'm unique. Women have been going through this since the beginning of time."

His lips brushed her brow. "But if there's something that can make it easier. . . ." His voice trailed off with the shifting of his thoughts. Slipping an arm under the covers, he searched for her hand and gently took it in his. "I suppose it's all for a good cause," he said quietly. "Your body's working. Some day it'll work a little differently." She opened her eyes in time to see his ardor. "That'll be when you have my baby."

He said it with such quiet conviction that, for an instant, she couldn't think, couldn't breathe, couldn't so much as blink or swallow. It was a beautiful thought but staggering in its implications.

"Ryan, I can't—"

"Don't say a thing," he whispered. His gaze touched her features one by one, pausing at her brow to follow the progress of his fingers as they smoothed her bangs from her damp skin. "I have to believe that some day you'll be mine, Carly."

"I am yours."

He shook his head, his eyes profoundly sad. "Not yet. Not completely. And I promised I wouldn't push." He spoke with quiet urgency. "But there are times when I can't help myself. When I have to say what I feel. Because I do believe it, babe. The two of us—we were meant to be. I don't care what else might have happened in your life. It has no bearing on *us*."

But it does, Carly screamed silently, then lowered her lids in anguish. Curling more tightly into herself, she moaned. "Maybe I should take something after all. I feel like I could crawl into the nearest hole and die." What she wanted to do was to crawl into the nearest hole with Ryan, pull it in after them, and escape together to another dimension. In lieu of that, she would take a pill.

"Where?" he asked.

"The medicine chest. The small prescription bottle on the top shelf. It may be behind something. I haven't taken anything in so long." Lapsing into silence, she thought of how, since she'd first come to Boston, she had avoided taking anything that might leave her less alert. But she had Ryan now to be her eyes and ears, and she desperately needed to sleep.

Ryan was a long time in the bathroom. He stared at the bottle in his hand, looked back to the shelf and, seeing no other prescription, studied the label again. "Percodan?" he called out.

"That's it," she managed. "One."

He rolled a yellow pill into his palm, snapped the top back on the bottle, then, frowning, stared at the label again. "Percodan. One every four hours for pain. P. Demery, M.D." So the directions read, and Ryan had no problem with them. What he did have a problem with was the fact that the prescription was made out to an R. Hart and came from a pharmacy in Chicago.

Very slowly he replaced the bottle in the medicine chest, filled a glass with water from the sink, and returned to Carly. Eyes closed, she didn't see the way he stood looking at her for long, long moments. She barely moved when he sat down on the side of the bed, and opened her eyes only when he lifted her and urged the pill into her mouth. She seemed distracted, far away, which was a very good thing. He needed time to decide what to do.

EIGHTEEN

WEDNESDAY NIGHT RYAN worked late. He did the same on Thursday. Had Carly not had Sheila with her, she might have had more time to worry. But Sheila *was* with her, and, beyond that, there was school and plenty of paperwork, what with the third marking period nearly over.

If Ryan was more tense than usual, she attributed it to fatigue. Both Wednesday and Thursday nights, when he came home late, he seemed content just to stretch out on the living-room sofa and close his eyes. On both occasions she had to wake him to get him into bed, and then he was too groggy to talk.

By Friday morning, though, she was beginning to sense something else. He wasn't looking at her. Not directly at least. It was as though he was the one with something to hide.

They ran. They showered. They dressed, talking from time to time about one inconsequential thing or another. Then he made a point of reminding her about the dinner they were to attend that evening.

"I haven't forgotten," she said softly. They were standing in the kitchen, leaning against the counter drinking coffee. "What time do we have to be there?"

He scrutinized his shoes as if debating whether to have them shined on the way to work. "Cocktails are at six. If we get there at six-thirty, we'll be fine."

"Are you sure? If you need to be there earlier—"

"Six-thirty's plenty." He took a deep breath, stared at the window and absently sipped the dark brew. "Listen, if you'd rather not go, it's no problem."

Hurt and puzzled, she answered slowly. "You're speaking. I wouldn't miss it."

"I know how you hate lawyers. It's bound to be boring."

"Would *you* rather I not go?"

Closing his eyes, he dropped his chin to his chest. "Don't be foolish," he muttered. "*I'm* the one who'll be bored stiff. I hate these things. Your being there is apt to be the only thing that gets me through."

"Funny. You don't sound thrilled about it. What's wrong, Ryan? What is it?"

For the first time that morning, he met her gaze. His eyes were expressionless, his voice steady. "Nothing."

"I don't believe that. You've been walking around here like you have the weight of the world on your shoulders." She put a hand on his arm. "Please, Ryan. I can't stand the tension."

"Maybe I should move out."

She caught her breath. "That's not what I want."

"What do you want?"

"I want you to talk, to tell me what's bothering you. What's that you were saying the other night about sharing—both the good *and* the bad?"

His eyes suddenly sharpened and Carly knew she'd hit a nerve. "Is that what *you* do? Talk? Discuss? Open up freely, with no reservations at all?"

"I . . . I. . . ."

He put his mug down on the counter with a thud. "It goes both ways, Carly. I won't pressure you. Don't pressure me." Turning, he stalked from the kitchen, grabbed his overcoat and briefcase from the living room and was gone.

Carly placed a trembling hand on her stomach. She felt as though she'd been kicked, left with neither breath nor the strength to move. She didn't know how long she stood, rooted to the same spot in the kitchen, when the downstairs buzzer rang. For an instant, her eyes brightened. She wondered if it would be Ryan wanting to apologize, to say he was simply tired or had a troublesome case or was coming down with a cold. When she heard Sheila's nasal twang, she was disappointed.

"Hey, buzz me up!"

Carly did it, then began to put her things together for school. By the time Sheila arrived, Carly had her coat on. Her forced smile of greeting was as much of a tip-off as her otherwise stricken expression.

"Uh-oh," Sheila said, taking several books to relieve some of Carly's load. "You guys had a fight. I sat in my car and watched Ryan storm out of here a minute ago and, man, was he boiling."

"Sheila. Please. I don't need this now." They started down the stairs, walking in silence for a while. When they got to the bottom, Sheila spoke more gently.

"What happened?"

Carly took a deep breath and shrugged. "I guess I got caught at my own game."

"What do you mean?"

"I mean," she said, pushing the front door open, "that Ryan's been brooding about something for days now. It's been worse lately and was horrible this morning. When I asked him about it, he said that if I don't share with him, he doesn't have to share with me." She swallowed hard. "I hadn't realized he'd been that bothered . . . or maybe I've realized it and just chosen to look the other way."

Sheila said very little as they walked down the path. When they got to her car, she propped her elbows on the roof and eyed Carly across the burgundy gleam. "So what are you going to do about it?"

Carly was no less direct. "I'm going to tell him."

"Everything?"

"Yes."

"You're sure?"

Nodding, Carly opened the door and slid in, speaking again when Sheila was in the driver's seat. "I have to." She reasoned aloud. "It was one thing keeping my secrets when our relationship was super. I didn't want to rock the boat then. Now it turns out that the boat's being rocked by the very fact of my keeping those secrets." She took a long, tortured breath and let it out as an evanescent mist against the window. "I don't see where I have any other choice."

Sheila started the car and headed for Rand. "You could stall. See if it'll pass. Make it up to him in other ways."

Carly's head turned quickly. "What ways?"

"Oh, you know," she hedged, vaguely intimidated by Carly's sharp look, "doing little things that he likes." She wrinkled her nose and managed a one-shouldered shrug. "Food. Sex. That kind of thing."

Carly looked away muttering, "I couldn't do that. I'd feel like even more of a crumb than I do now. Besides, that'd be avoiding the issue." She pressed two fingers to her forehead and squeezed her eyes shut. "I knew I'd have to tell him one day. It was only a matter of time. Sam said it once; when the time was right, I'd know it. Well—" she sighed, opening her eyes and looking straight ahead "—the time is right now. We have Ryan's speech and that dinner tonight, but after that I'll tell him."

Though firmly made, the decision weighed heavily on her mind all morning. Ryan phoned during her lunch break, timing his call perfectly to catch her in her office. Her heart skipped a beat at the sound of his voice, but she wasn't sure quite how to respond. "Hi, Ryan," she said softly, cautiously.

"Babe, I'm sorry. I was a bastard this morning. I've been furious at myself since I got in here." His voice lowered to a husky whisper. "I love you. I just wanted you to know that."

Slow tears gathered at Carly's lower lids. She gave a convulsive swallow. "I know. I love you too."

The silence on the line was profound, with Carly as startled by her confession as Ryan. "You what?"

It seemed the most natural thing in the world to say. "I love you."

"So you finally decided to tell me." His voice was lower, almost gruff, but there was a thread of humor in it that Carly recognized instantly.

A smile came to her lips and slowly grew. "Uh-huh." It wasn't even worth denying his implication that she'd known for a long time, or asking how *he'd* known.

"Damn it, Carly, this has to be the cruelest thing you've done to me yet! I have an afternoon of appointments lined up starting in five minutes. There's no way I can get out there now!"

"I didn't expect you to come out," she said. "I only have a few minutes myself. I just wanted you to know how I felt." Her voice softened all the more. "It's a start."

Suddenly his tone matched hers. "It is, babe. And we'll make it work. You'll see."

"I hope so." Even as she said it, an unbidden shiver coursed through her. In her mind, if nothing else, she was committed to telling Ryan everything about her past. If only telling him would make it all go away.

Shortly after Sheila saw Carly safely into her apartment, Ryan came home bearing a bouquet of roses and a smile warm enough to melt even the coldest of hearts. But Carly's heart needed no melting. Accepting the roses with a smile to match his, she flowed into his outstretched arms and murmured the precious words against his lips.

"Tell me again," he ordered after a kiss that left her short of breath.

"I love you," she breathed. "I love you."

He searched her eyes, found that they echoed her words, and let out a long breath. "I was worried you wouldn't say it to my face, that you'd lose your nerve or have second thoughts in the course of the afternoon."

"Come now, Ryan," she teased. "Where's your faith?"

"My faith has been raked over pretty rocky ground lately," he said. His sober expression wiped the grin from her face.

"I know. But I do love you. You've known that for a while."

"Yes." He kissed her again, this time slowly and with a thoroughness that reached to her soul and back. Carly arched closer, loving the feel of his tall, lean body, loving the strength of him, loving the way his arms circled her back in total possession. No longer did she fear the fire he created. Together like this, they *were* the fire, prepared to consume anything and everything that came across their path.

When he released her, it was with a reluctance she shared. "I wish we didn't have to go tonight."

"I know," she whispered, "but we do."

"I could always call in sick."

"You could not. You're the *speaker*, Ryan. You can't let all those wonderful people down. Besides—" her grin wasn't to be contained "—those wonderful people need to hear what you have to say."

He gave her a squeeze. "You're full of it."

"No. I'm serious. Just think. They've come from all over the country. Your talk may be the most important one they'll have heard all week."

"You *are* full of it."

"We won't know that unless we go."

He cleared his throat. "We'd better get dressed then?"

She nodded. "Society can only arrive so late."

The evening started out well enough. Armed with drinks and each other, she and Ryan circulated through the predinner crowd. More accurately, she observed in a moment's grace, the crowd circulated around them. It seemed that Ryan was indeed well-known in the legal community—and sought after, if the number of people who approached them was any indication.

Several members of Ryan's firm were in attendance. Carly was pleased to see these familiar faces in what was to her an otherwise anonymous and potentially threatening group. At several points she was amazed that she was there at all; three months before, she would never have dreamed of appearing like this, so open to speculating eyes. But with Ryan beside her, sometimes with an arm lightly around her waist, other times simply rubbing shoulders with her, she managed to control the urge to hide her face and run.

He held to his promise of keeping her by his side, except for those moments when he was on the podium. What she hadn't expected was that he would be seated at the long rectangular head table, and that she would be seated right beside him. It was heaven; it was hell. His presence was a constant comfort, even as her insides churned at the thought of being in the public eye.

Through dinner, he kept a close watch on her, talking softly with her during those times when the judge on her other side felt obliged to eat. As for herself, she barely tasted the filet mignon before her.

"You're not eating," Ryan whispered at one point. "Don't like the fare?"

"The fare's fine," she replied as softly. "It's the table I don't like. Why is it that the head table is always long and straight, and on a *stage*, no less. Everyone else has a lovely round table. I feel like we're on display."

"We're important people," he teased, feeling incredibly buoyed by the events of the day.

She plucked at a minuscule piece of lint on his sleeve. "I'd rather be less important. You didn't tell me we'd be stuck up here."

"I didn't know. Smile. They're all looking."

She plastered a smile on her face. "When do you speak?"

"Right after this course, I think. Relax, babe. It's not that bad."

"Aren't you nervous?"

"Nah. I've spoken before groups larger and more important than this one."

She passed an eye over the crowd, then ran her gaze down the length of the head table. "This kind of thing always reminds me of The Last Supper."

Stifling a shiver, she looked out at the throng. "Wonder who'll play the part of Judas?"

"No Judas. They're friends, Carly." Beneath the table, he ran his hand along her thigh and leaned closer. "I doubt any of the Apostles were thinking what I am now."

A more natural grin softened the lines of her lips, and she met Ryan's gaze with the warmth he would always inspire. "You have a dirty mind, Ryan Cornell. What do you think they—" she tossed her head toward the crowd "—would think of *that?*"

"They'd be jealous. They are jealous. You may not have noticed, but a number of my illustrious colleagues have been staring at you covetously," he drawled, squeezing her hand when a nearby gavel rapped.

Swept up in the excitement of Ryan's imminent speech, Carly thrust his words into the recesses of her mind. Meanwhile, in a far corner of the room, one of those colleagues was indeed staring at Carly, not with covetousness but the intense curiosity of one trying to place a face. Again and again, as Ryan spoke, the man's gaze returned to her. When recognition finally dawned, it was followed by puzzlement. Not until the address was over, several other speeches and awards given, dessert downed and the dinner adjourned, did he make his move.

The crowd milled in large groups. He wound his way through them to the front of the room where, off the stage now, Ryan stood with Carly by his side. They were surrounded by people. He waited, studying Carly intently, biding his time until the crowd thinned.

Glowing with pride both in Ryan's speech and in his audience's enthusiastic reception of it, Carly didn't see the onlooker at first. Her smile was more relaxed than it had been all evening as she listened to Ryan graciously accept congratulations and thanks and comments on the points he had made. Only when two lawyers moved aside to make way for several others did her gaze bounce off the man waiting several yards away. With Ryan, she turned her attention to the newcomers. But something had jarred her. Her smile faded. For an instant her mind flashed the image of another place, another city, and she felt a sense of unease.

Puzzled, she let her eye wander. Within minutes it settled on the face of the man who stood watchfully to the side, and her pulse lurched. For as long as she lived, she would remember that face along with every detail of the Chicago trial. It was that of Mancusi's assistant, the young associate who had sat at the defense table on the far side of one Gary Culbert.

"Uh, Ryan?" she whispered, tugging at his sleeve, heedless of what she might be interrupting. "I'm going to run to the ladies' room. I'll be back, okay?"

A flicker of concern crossed his face at the sight of hers drained of color. But she managed a smile, and he accepted the fact that she might simply be fatigued. "Sure, babe. We won't stay much longer. Why don't I meet you at the door?"

So much the better. "Okay."

Without another glance at the man whose presence terrified her, she turned and wound her way through the crowd, finding relief for her shaky legs on a cushioned stool in the powder room. She took several deep breaths, raised a trembling hand to her forehead, propped her elbow on the counter and closed her eyes.

Back in the ornate dining room, Ryan had neatly wound up the conversation and was about to make his escape when a man approached and extended his hand.

"Frank Pritzak, Mr. Cornell. That was a very impressive talk."

Ryan nodded, noting that this man seemed more somber faced than the others who'd come by. "Thank you." He frowned. "Pritzak. That's an unusual name. I'm sure I would have remembered it if I'd heard it before. You don't practice locally, do you?"

"Chicago."

A tiny alarm went off in Ryan's mind, but he schooled his expression to one of calm. "Chicago." He nodded. "Are you with a firm?"

"Mancusi and Wolff. We handle mostly criminal work, just as you do." He went quickly on. "I was curious about the woman you're with. She looks very familiar."

"Oh?"

"Has she spent time in Chicago?"

"She's from San Diego."

"Has she been here long?"

"Long enough."

He stared off in the direction Carly had gone. "She looks very much like a woman who testified in one of our cases last summer. She was on the other side. State's witness. I believe she was relocated by the government after the trial. But—" he straightened "—if your woman's been here, I must be wrong."

Ryan stood, heart pounding, waiting for the man to go on. When he did it was on a note of perplexity.

"Funny. I was sure it was her. I suppose the hair's different. The woman I knew had long straight hair. And the eyes. She had blue ones." He chuckled. "Never could mistake those. They stood out across that courtroom like nothing else." He shook his head in admiration. "She was one tough lady, Robyn Hart. It was an arson trial. She'd been a reporter investigating the story for the local paper. Before that, she'd lost her own husband in a fire." As though realizing he was rambling, he cast an apologetic smile Ryan's way. "She was a beautiful woman, even if she *did* screw up our case. Your woman's just as beautiful." He clicked his tongue against the roof of his mouth and narrowed one eye for a moment longer. "Same face. Hmph. I guess I'm just a sucker for the pretty ones." Then, with a philosophical shrug, he relaxed his features and stuck out his hand. "Anyway, enjoy her."

It took every bit of self-control Ryan possessed to shake the other man's hand with a semblance of composure. His limbs felt stiff, his insides frozen. Even his "Thanks" sounded wooden.

Turning, he headed for the door, where he scanned the lobby until at last Carly appeared. He wasn't sure what to say or do; his hands felt like ice. He retrieved their coats and silently led her to the car.

Unaware of the conversation that had taken place in her absence, Carly breathed a sigh of relief as Ryan drove off. "You did well," she said. "They loved you."

"Good crowd, for lawyers."

There was an edge to his voice that she might have easily attributed to sarcasm had she been listening. But she wasn't. Her thoughts were dominated by her own attempt to recover from what had to be the closest call she'd had with true and utter exposure since she had assumed the identity of Carly Quinn. Hands clasped tightly around her purse, she turned her thoughts to what she had to say to Ryan as soon as they got home. After what had happened tonight, it was all the more imperative that she tell him. As each revolution of the wheels brought them closer to Cambridge, the terror she had felt at seeing a face from her past slowly turned to apprehension.

Amid her own tension, she was oblivious to Ryan's. They drove, then arrived home, in silence. Only at Carly's open door did Ryan speak, his tone one of well-modulated nonchalance.

"Listen, I'm going down to my place to make one or two calls. I'll be up a little later."

Simultaneously disappointed and relieved, she nodded and watched him retreat down the stairs. Her gaze clung to his dark head, bowed in concentration, and she wondered, fleetingly, what calls would be so important at an hour like this.

Closing herself into her apartment, she glanced at her watch. Ten o'clock. Not that late at all. The better part of the night was ahead.

Stomach knotting, she changed into a pair of jeans and one of the sweatshirts Ryan had left in her closet, then sank into a chair in the living room to await him. Fifteen minutes later he hadn't come. Heading for the kitchen for some tea to settle her stomach, she wondered what the outcome of the night would be. He would be angry and hurt. But if he loved her. . . .

Another fifteen minutes passed and she grew restless. It was the waiting that was so bad. She half wished she had blurted it all out in the car on the way home, but Ryan had been as quiet as she. She assumed he'd been preoccupied thinking of the dinner. Perhaps he'd been thinking about something one of those people had said. What *had* they said? She tried to remember, but realized that she'd been concentrating solely on Ryan.

Sipping her tea, she shifted in her chair, then stood and wandered around the apartment, waiting, wondering. Who *was* he calling? Another glance at her watch told her it had been forty-five minutes since he had left her at her door. It wasn't like him to stay away for long. For that matter, it wasn't like him to need to use his own phone. Hers had been more than adequate from the start.

A small smile curved her lips as she thought back on those first encounters. She had been intrigued by him then, if a little frightened. But he had quickly put her at ease, taking things ever so slowly and gently, as was his style. This morning, ah, this morning she had seen a side of him she would rather forget. He had been cold and angry, but it had been her fault. She shouldn't have kept things from him for so long. He was too intelligent, too perceptive not to sense that there were some things she never discussed, some things she kept hidden from him.

She sighed. As soon as he arrived, she would tell him.

But he didn't arrive. The slim gold hands of her watch rotated slowly. Eleven. Eleven-ten. Eleven-fifteen. Eleven-twenty-five. She told herself to be patient, but her nerves didn't listen. They jumped and jangled, jolting at any tiny sound. There was no sound, though, of a key in the lock. Finally, unable to bear the suspense any longer, she hurried to the kitchen and dialed his number.

The phone rang. And rang. Nine. Ten. Eleven times. She hung up. Maybe he was in the bathroom. Maybe he was, at that moment, on his way up. Crossing to the door, she put her eye to the viewer and watched in anticipation, heart pounding, palms pressed flat to the cold metal expanse.

When enough time had elapsed to eliminate the possibility of his having been en route when she'd called, she raced back to the phone and tried again. By the eighth ring she wondered if something was wrong. Heedless of the safety factor that three months before would have kept her cowering behind her locks, she left the front door wide open and, barefoot, dashed down the stairs. She knocked on the door, then pounded more loudly, then pressed a finger to the bell in a nonvocal cry for help.

After what seemed an eternity, she dropped her hand and, turning, slowly made her way back upstairs. She locked the door, set the alarm, then slumped in utter disbelief against the wall.

She didn't understand. Ryan would never run out without telling her. He knew she was waiting. He'd said he would be up. After his delight when she'd said she loved him, the flowers, embraces filled with such promise, it didn't make sense.

All she could do was to wait, which she did, huddled in a corner of the sofa as midnight passed and one o'clock became two, then three and four. By dawn she was frantic. It had been one thing when she'd been able to tell herself that a legal emergency had called him out, though she had no idea what kind of legal emergency would do that at such an hour, and she had even less idea why he wouldn't have let her know. But with the passage of more than eight long hours and still no word, she had to assume that something was wrong. It was then, with the first rays of light spilling onto the rug, that her imagination went to work.

Her first thought was that there had been some family emergency that had taken him out so suddenly. Perhaps one of his parents was ill. Perhaps Tom was in trouble again. In either case, he would surely have called. He would never have left her alone and expecting him momentarily. Especially now, when he knew that she loved him.

Her second thought, one that filled her with sudden dread, was that he knew more about her than that she loved him. She recalled the something that had been bothering him, the something he had passed off as a vague "nothing." What if he'd little by little put the pieces together, what if he'd purposely left her, what if, what if he'd finally given up. What if—her blood froze—the man at the dinner had said something.

Trembling, she pressed a fist to her mouth to stifle a cry, for there was a third possibility, coming fast on the second. If, indeed, Ryan had somehow learned the truth about her, he might be in danger. If one of Culbert's men had been following her, Ryan might have been snatched up as a hostage, or a source of information. She imagined him suffering unspeakable tortures and ground her head against her knees to force the thought from her mind.

Instinctively she had known that to tell Ryan the truth would be to risk his safety. There had been good reason why neither her father nor her brothers had been told where she lived; the less they knew, the less they would have to offer an evil-minded hunter. But Ryan knew just about everything to do with her present life, and if he also now knew about her past. . . .

For a moment she thrust aside that possibility and focused on his returning to her with a viable excuse for his absence. Perhaps her secrets *were* better kept, for his safety if nothing else. But that was self-delusion, she knew. Ryan was endangered by simple association with her, whether he knew the truth or not.

With a helpless shudder, she conjured up all kinds of terrifying thoughts. In one, they would be trapped inside her bedroom while deadly gas poured in through the heating vent. In another, their car would be rigged to malfunction when it reached a certain speed on the highway. It would easily pass as an accident. She could see the headline now: "Prominent lawyer and girlfriend killed in freak accident on the Massachusetts Turnpike."

A car bomb would be very effective, as would an ambush on a deserted country road some peaceful Sunday afternoon. They wouldn't have a chance.

Then her eye caught the flicker of sunlight on the frame of the picture that stood on the lacquered shelf against the living-room wall. If they were armed with machine guns of their own, they could protect themselves, or try, as Bonnie and Clyde had done. But Bonnie and Clyde had died.

With a cry of despair, she jumped from the sofa and slammed the picture face down. Shaking all over, she thrust her fingers into her hair, closed her fist and tugged, as though trying to pull from her mind every ugly possibility that lurked there. But it was no use. Ryan was gone, and she didn't know what to do.

She knew what she *wanted* to do, but she waited. To call Sam and dump her tale of woe on him, given the distinct possibility that Ryan had simply left on his own, seemed premature. Unsteady, she brewed a pot of coffee and waited. And waited. And waited, until even that particular humiliation seemed nothing compared to the possible danger Ryan might be in.

Sam was home, as she had prayed. "Hello?"

"Sam?" Her voice was tremulous.

"Carly? Is that you?"

Tears suddenly filled her eyes. "Yes. Sam. . . ."

"What is it, hon? A problem about tonight?" He had been frankly surprised that Ryan had agreed to their dinner date so readily. "Listen, we could make it another—"

"No. It's not that. Well, it is, I guess—" Her voice cracked and she broke. "Oh, God, Sam! I don't know where Ryan is! We went to a dinner last night and got back here and he went downstairs to change and said he'd be up after he made a couple of calls and he never came." Her soft sobs filled the line. Sam had to wait until she'd quieted to speak.

"Did you argue about something?" he asked gently.

"No. Well . . . in a way . . . yesterday morning. But we patched that up. And he brought me flowers. And it was going to be all right because I was going to tell him everything." She began to cry again.

Sam tightened his grip on the phone. "Take it easy, hon. I'm sure there's some explanation. Want me to come out?"

She sniffled. "I hate to ask you. I know it's Saturday. But I'm so worried. I keep imagining all kinds of terrible things. I don't know what to do."

"I'll be there, Carly," he said firmly. "Just stay put. And, please, hon, don't worry. We'll find out where he is. There's got to be some explanation."

That was what she kept telling herself for the forever it seemed to take Sam to arrive. By the time he did, she had composed herself enough to tell him everything, from the events of the day before and the startling presence of that face from Chicago, back to smaller things, things of a more personal nature that might help him help her. She spared nothing, from Ryan's growing frustration, to his wanting her to have his children, to her fear that he had simply dumped her.

"I won't believe that until I hear it from the horse's mouth," was Sam's forceful response. "I saw the way he looked at you the other day. The man's in love. A love like that doesn't just go away."

Carly crossed the room and picked up the photograph she'd turned over earlier. Looking at Ryan's image, so manly, so strong and protective, she felt the deep pain of yearning. "I hope you're right."

"I am. There has to be some explanation for all this. We'll try to get something on the guy from Chicago, but you say Ryan didn't talk with him."

"Not that I know of."

"And the guy didn't speak to you, so I doubt he made the connection."

"I don't care about him! It's *Ryan* I'm worried about!"

"Okay, hon. Okay. Now. Where might he be?"

"I don't know!"

"Think, Carly. Any lead you can give me might help."

Clutching the photograph to her breast, she turned. "I've gone over and over it in my mind. I've been through everything. If he went on his own, he might be just wandering somewhere. If he was forcibly taken away—" she couldn't help but shudder "—he could be anywhere." Her voice broke and Sam stood quickly. "Where are you going?"

"Downstairs. Where did you say he parked his car?"

Relieved at the thought of doing something concrete, she ran for a pair of sneakers and a coat. "I'll show you."

The BMW was gone.

As Sam led her back inside, he tried to bolster her spirits. "If he was abducted, his car would probably still be there, so that's one vote against violence. Let's check his place."

"But I don't have a key."

Extracting a small case from his back pocket, Sam winked. It took him no more than a minute to pick the lock. "Why don't you have a key? He has yours, doesn't he?" He pushed the door open and went in, Carly following closely.

"There was never any need. There's nothing here."

Looking around the bare living room, Sam straightened. "So I see. I thought he ordered furniture."

"He did, but, aside from the bed, it was all custom-made. It won't be ready for another two or three weeks."

With a nod, Sam proceeded to go over the entire apartment in search of a clue as to Ryan's whereabouts. "Nothing," he announced, then sighed. "Well, at least there's no sign of violence here either."

Back in Carly's apartment, he contemplated the options. "Okay. Assuming he was upset and went somewhere just to think things out, where might that be? Would he have gone to his parents' house?"

She shook her head. "I don't think so."

"Or his brother's?"

"Maybe, but I doubt it. He'd want to be alone."

"Were there places the two of you went together?"

She shrugged, eyes glued to the floor, hand closed tight in her pocket around the spare key she'd taken from Ryan's kitchen cabinet. "We used to take drives—up toward Rockport and Gloucester, out along the old Boston Post Road." She paused for an instant, then spoke her agony. "If it were me and I wanted to go somewhere, I'd go back to the place we stayed in Vermont." She looked up, daring to hope. "That might be where he went. He said he'd been there right after his divorce when he needed time to get away and think."

Sam was scribbling in the small notebook he'd taken from his pocket. "Okay. Give me the name and address." As soon as she'd done so, he put in a call to Greg. From where Carly stood staring glumly out the living room window, she caught snatches of the conversation. She jumped when Sam materialized behind her.

"We'll check out Vermont. And his parents' and Tom's and his office. I've also got someone going to the airport, train station, bus depot." He took a breath. "I'll head into town to coordinate everything. Where's Sheila?"

"I think she's with Tom."

"Good. That'd answer one question. Can you call her? I don't think you should be alone." At the widening of her eyes, he spoke very gently. "Not for safety's sake, hon. I just think you could use the company."

"I hate to bother her. She's been busy enough following me around all week."

"That's her job. This she'll do out of friendship." He tossed his head toward the phone. "Go call her. I'll wait until I know she's on her way."

With lingering reluctance, Carly put through the call. Sheila was indeed at Tom's house—with no sign of Ryan—and promised to be over as quickly as she could. Knowing that, Sam left.

When Sheila arrived, Tom was right on her heels. "He insisted," she explained by way of apology when Carly's worried gaze flew back and forth between the two.

"Damn right I insisted," Tom announced, but kindly. At the sight of a forlorn Carly, he went to her. "He's my brother," he said softly, then very gently put his arms around her in offer of comfort. She was stiff at first, yielding only gradually to his warmth. "I'm worried too. There has to be some explanation for his disappearance. I can't believe he'd knowingly put you through this pain. He loves you very much."

Whether bidden by his heartfelt words or by the strong arms that offered a support she badly needed, tears formed in her eyes, gathered in large pools, then began a slow trickle down her cheeks. She tried to check them, and bit her lip to stifle the sobs threatening to erupt, but Tom wouldn't allow it.

His arms tightened. "Cry, Carly. It's all right. You can't keep it bottled up. It'll only hurt more."

She wept softly, hands clinging to the light wool of his sweater. "It hurts."

"I know. But it'll be okay. Sam will find him, and until then, we'll be with you." Over her head, he cast a glance at Sheila. Tears were in her eyes too. He had no way of knowing that her thoughts were of his tenderness, his goodness, and her own awful lack of those qualities. She returned his sad smile before going to stand, deep in thought, before the window.

"I love him," Carly whispered.

"I know."

"What if he doesn't come back?"

"He'll be back." Very gently he began to rub her back, coaxing warmth into her chilled body. "You'll see. He'll be back."

Sam had the same conviction, but his reasoning ran along different lines, as he sat brooding at his desk. Ryan Cornell had flown to Chicago that morning. Chicago. Strange coincidence. Though he had a head start on them, he would be found and followed; Bill Hoffmeister had already put his best men on the case. If by some chance Ryan wasn't on the up-and-up, they would soon know it and obtain whatever evidence they needed to pursue the case.

He had been on an early flight and would have already landed. No doubt Hoffmeister's men were checking on car rentals and calling every hotel in the area. If things went well, they would locate him before he made his contact, *if* that was what he'd gone to Chicago to do. In any case, Sam would be there to meet his plane when he returned to Logan.

Brows furrowed, he closed his eyes and thought of Carly. How could he live with *himself*, knowing how he'd encouraged her from the start! But he was jumping to conclusions. He had no proof that Ryan had gone to Chicago with evil intent. Not yet. Hell, he'd cleared him himself. It just didn't make sense. The man had no motive whatsoever—unless, having discovered Carly's secret, he'd been so enraged at her deception that he'd lost his marbles. But Ryan Cornell? Cool, levelheaded, straight-as-an-arrow Ryan Cornell?

Lifting the phone, he dialed Carly's number. When a man answered, he was taken aback. Then he put two and two together.

"Tom?"

"Yes."

"Sam Loomis. I'm Carly's friend."

"Sure, Sam. Any word?"

"Yeah. We've got a lead on him."

"Where is he?"

"I'd rather not say yet." He wasn't sure how fully Carly had filled Tom in on the scenario, and, on the chance that she'd simply told him Ryan was missing, was reluctant to spill anything else. Not to mention the fact that if Ryan was into something, there was always a chance Tom might be somehow involved. "We're working on it." He paused. "Is Sheila there?"

"Right here."

That was a relief at least. "How's Carly?"

"Pretty unhappy."

"Can you reassure her at all?"

"I've been trying."

"Well, tell her that he seems to be well." The airline had reported that he had checked in alone, that yes, he had looked tired and rumpled, but that there was no sign of anyone coercing him to make the flight. "And that as soon as I know anything more, I'll call."

"I'll tell her."

"Thanks. Hey, and tell her that if *she* gets a call or anything, she's to let me know immediately."

"Where are you?"

"At my office. She knows the number."

"Okay. And Sam, thanks. We really appreciate all you're doing." He sounded genuine enough to Sam, whose gut instinct was to trust him. Particularly with Sheila there.

"Carly's pretty special," Sam said in closing. "I only wish I could do more."

Tom hung up the phone. Carly was at his elbow, eyes round, face ashen. "What did he say?"

"They have a lead." Urging her to the sofa, he sat down with her. Taking both of her hands in his, and he spoke gently. "He couldn't say anything more, except that he thinks Ryan's fine."

Carly's relief was short-lived. "If he's fine, why would he run off like that? Where is he? What's wrong?"

"We don't know that yet. It may be nothing but a misunderstanding."

"There wasn't any misunderstanding! Ryan clearly told me that he'd be back up after he made his calls." Shoulders slumped, she looked away. "I don't understand, Tom. I just don't understand."

He pushed a lock of hair back from her face. "You look exhausted. Did you sleep at all last night?" She shook her head. "Maybe you should lie down."

"I can't sleep."

"Then rest. Here on the sofa."

She looked up at him, taking solace in his concern. "I'll be all right." She gave his hand a feeble squeeze. "I'm glad you're here, Tom. I felt so alone."

He quirked a boyish grin. "Hey, what's family for?"

"I'm not exactly family."

"You will be. Take my word for it."

Leaving her curled in a corner of the sofa, he returned to the kitchen where Sheila stood, head down, leaning against the counter. "What else did Sam say?" she whispered, lifting her gaze at his approach.

He shook his head, his own discouragement showing. "Nothing." Then, in need of comfort himself, he put his arms around her and drew her to him. "Ah, Sheila. Sometimes we think we understand someone so well, and then. . . ." He hugged her tighter. "I never would have dreamed Ryan would go off like this. Carly means more to him than anyone in the world."

Eyes closed against his shoulder, arms firm around his back, Sheila struggled with her own warring devils. Tom was so good, as Ryan had seemed to be. But he was right; people weren't always what they seemed. Even the smallest thing—a moment's greed or anger or frustration—could chart an irrevocable course.

It appeared that Ryan had embarked on such a course. For her own sake, even more than for Carly's, she had to know which one it was. For that reason among others, Sam's assigning her to stay close to Carly was propitious indeed.

NINETEEN

❀ ❀ ❀

RYAN SAT ON THE PLANE on Sunday afternoon, a fist pressed to his jaw, his eyes fixed on the blanket of clouds below. It all fit. He should have put the pieces together sooner. Had it not been for Pritzak, though, it might have gone on forever. It appeared that Carly wasn't going to tell him.

He thought back to all the signs. The fear in her eyes that first night when, frightened in the dark, she must have thought she was being followed. The slip of her husband's name. Her reticence to speak about those years since Matthew had died. The nightmares. Her quickness on legal issues, her aversion to lawyers, her vehemence when they had discussed the case he considered taking against the *Globe*. Her sudden disappearance, then the tag on her luggage. The absence of an address book that might identify her. Even the stone wall he'd run into trying to call her in the Bahamas.

The newspapers he'd read in the library yesterday had told him as much as he needed to know. Even the pictures had been revealing. No, Pritzak hadn't been imagining the similarity. True, Robyn Hart's hair had been long and straight, while Carly's curled naturally. And her eyes—Robyn Hart's eyes had apparently been blue according to Pritzak. But then, so were Carly's. Contact lenses could do wonders. It had never occurred to him to question why he'd never seen her without them.

He understood now why her pills had been made out to R. Hart, why that phone call had come for Robyn so long ago, why the needlepoint pillows and wall hangings all bore tiny robins in their corners. And he understood now her relationship with Sam Loomis.

Squeezing his eyes shut, he rubbed his throbbing temple. Having spent Friday night driving around Boston and Saturday night walking the streets of Chicago, he hadn't slept more than a couple of hours in the past sixty. But all the driving and walking in the world hadn't eased his agony. He might now know exactly what Carly had to hide, but the future of their relationship was as shaky as ever.

He had wanted her to come to him. But she hadn't. And he wasn't sure if he could continue to live with her, knowing she didn't trust him enough. But could he bear to live without her? That was the crux of his worry. He cursed the fate that had sentenced him to such pain.

In the end, the anger and hurt he felt were nothing compared to his love for Carly. His time in Chicago had given him a glimpse of all she had suffered before she met him. At least now he knew what enemy he fought. And he loved her. If he could make her life easier, that was what he had to do. He could only pray that one day she would love him enough, trust him enough to confide in him and make his life complete.

The plane landed in an early evening mist. Hauling his small bag from the overhead compartment, Ryan waited with the rest of the passengers until the deplaning began. He walked slowly, head down, into the terminal. When a hand clamped onto his arm, he stiffened.

"Let's go," Sam commanded softly enough not to attract attention.

He tried to shake the hand loose, but it cut into his arm with a strength he would never have guessed the other man possessed. "What's this about?" he barked.

"A few questions."

"What for?" Again he tried to pry loose, but Sam's grip only tightened.

"Let's not make a scene. I just want to talk with you."

"You should have done that a hell of a long time ago!"

Ignoring the outburst, Sam walked quickly down the corridor, then tossed his head to the side and guided Ryan into a small room where they were joined by Greg Reilly and another, more burly-looking, man. With the door closed firmly and his arm suddenly released, Ryan glared at the threesome, finally homing in on Sam.

"What's going on?"

"You were in Chicago."

"Obviously."

"What for?"

"Use your imagination."

"I am. And I don't like what it's saying. So I want to hear it from you. What were you doing in Chicago?"

"Walking."

"Tell us something we don't know. We've had a tail on you since last night."

"Haven't your men got better things to do—like protecting Carly?"

"That's what we are trying to do. What else did you do in Chicago?"

Ryan simmered. "I learned things I should have known weeks ago."

"Like what?"

"Hell! You know it all! You're the one who set it up!"

"What did you learn in Chicago?"

Hands on his hips in a stance of disgust, Ryan looked around the room. There was a desk, a phone, a few chairs. Far nicer than the usual interrogation room. But the men hovering around him were every bit as hostile as the local jailer. He'd seen plenty of them in the past, though as lawyer to clients in trouble, he'd been spared the worst of the guards' ire. Now he felt on the hot seat, and he was livid.

"What is this, Loomis?" he asked, eyes narrowing. "What do *you* think I did in Chicago?"

Sam didn't bat an eyelash. "I think you might have made contact with someone working for Culbert."

Of all the things Ryan had expected him to say, this wasn't one. Stunned, he tried to understand. "Made contact . . . Culbert? You think *I* might try to harm her?"

"You ran out awful quick Friday night right after you saw that guy at the dinner."

Incredulous, Ryan stared. "Goddammit, I'm in love with the woman! I wouldn't do anything to harm her!"

"You already have," Sam said with deadly force, heedless of the surfacing of his personal feelings. "She was crushed when you didn't show."

With the knifelike thrust of pain into his gut, Ryan closed his eyes. "God, I didn't want to do that," he whispered hoarsely.

"Why did you? You knew you couldn't get a flight out till morning."

"I knew," he said. Feeling suddenly weary, he sank into the nearest chair. "But I couldn't face her. Not with what I'd learned. Not with all those mysterious pieces finally falling into place. Not with the hurt I felt."

Head down, he didn't see Sam motion for the other two to leave. Only when the door closed quietly did he glance to the side and find that they were alone.

Taking a seat opposite him, Sam spoke more quietly. "Tell me everything you did, Ryan. Everything from the time you left her Friday night to the time you boarded that plane in Chicago this afternoon." He lowered his voice even more. "I love her too, y'know. Not in the way you do, but she's a very special person."

Ironically, though Ryan might have been wildly jealous at such a confession a week before, it was now the thing that most effectively broke his resistance. It was a show of trust, something he needed desperately.

Marginally encouraged, he began to speak. "I went down to my place and paced the floor for a while. I felt sick. Absolutely sick. It occurred to me to hire an investigator and send *him* to Chicago, but if what I'd been thinking was right and she was in the Witness Protection Program, I didn't want to do anything to risk her cover. Even the best investigator can be bought."

Sam sat, silent and patient, watching intently as Ryan's lower lip covered the upper then slid slowly down. "I knew what I had to do—what I had to find out for myself. And I didn't want to wait. I thought about leaving Carly a note, about concocting some story about an emergency trip, but I didn't want to lie." His gaze sharpened. "There'd already been enough of that. I was furious at her. Maybe subconsciously I wanted to hurt her back by making her sit up there waiting. It was stupid. But I didn't know what else to do. Anyway, I drove around for a while, stopping every so often just to think. By dawn I was at the airport. I was on the first flight out to Chicago." He looked up. "Is she all right?"

Sam nodded. "Tom's been with her. And Sheila."

"Sheila." Ryan gave a coarse laugh. "I bought that story too—about their meeting through you. I should have realized there was more to it. But I was blinded by everything I felt for Carly."

"Not too blind to begin to question."

Ryan's lips thinned. "No. Not after a while, at least." Then his tone grew urgent. "You have to understand. I want to marry her. I want to have children with her. But she held back, and I couldn't understand it. There were so many things I didn't understand—little things, little contradictions. Once I got to Chicago, I went to the library and pored over old newspaper articles. Pritzak— that guy at the dinner Friday night—mentioned her name and the gist of the case. It wasn't hard to find. Everything jelled."

"And then?"

"Then I walked around, just as your men said. I've been trying to decide what to do ever since."

"Have you?"

In that instant, as Ryan's gaze met Sam's head-on, any hostility that might have existed between them in the past vanished. They were suddenly allies, on the same side of the fence, each wanting the best for Carly.

"I'm going back to her. I'll just have to be patient, I guess. Maybe someday she'll tell me on her own."

"She was going to Friday night."

"What?"

"She'd already decided. She was going to tell you everything."

"She told you that?"

"Uh-huh."

"And I ran out."

"Uh-huh."

Ryan wore a look of self-disgust. "What an idiot I am."

"No. I probably would have done the same thing, given similar circum-stances. Maybe we're both idiots."

Feeling strangely calm now and at ease with the man he'd distrusted for so long, Ryan lapsed into a moment's thought. "That night after New Year's, when we came back from Vermont and found you there—"

"I thought she was in trouble. Until she met you, she hadn't dared stray from her place, let alone go somewhere for the night. I thought someone had gotten to her."

"And that mysterious trip a few weeks ago. Her father wasn't sick, was he?"

The light dawned. "I tried to reach you, but you were out of town too. I didn't even make the connection."

"I took her to Chicago to meet with the state's attorney. We only had a few hours' notice. She wasn't happy about going. It wasn't pleasant for her."

"The papers said that Culbert's lawyer filed for a new trial. Will there be one?"

"I don't know. The judge is considering the motion. But Carly can tell you all about that. Maybe you ought to get home. I doubt she's had any more sleep than you have."

A look of anguish crossed Ryan's face. "She may not want to see me after I ran off the way I did."

"She'll want to see you. She was frantic that one of Culbert's men did you harm."

"Does she know where I was?" he asked more cautiously.

Sam shook his head. "I didn't say anything. When I thought you might have been . . . well, let's just say that I've been putting her off all weekend. She'll be very glad to see you."

Ryan stood. "I hope so." Then he extended his hand. "Thanks, Sam. I appreciate everything you've done for her."

Sam met his grasp firmly. "She's an easy one to do things for. She asks for so little."

"Do you think there's any danger?"

"I don't know. Culbert and Barber are both restless. They've got great hopes for this new trial. We'll have to wait and see what the judge decides. Obviously, if something should happen to Carly in the meantime, their chances for a new trial will be that much better." He frowned his frustration. "All we can do is to keep an ear out and investigate anything that looks fishy."

"Like guys who fly out to Chicago for kicks?"

"Like those."

With a weary smile, Ryan opened the door. Instantly Greg and his sidekick came to attention, but Sam was quick to hold them back with an upraised palm. Passing them, he walked Ryan to the garage.

"Want me to come?"

"Thanks. But no. Carly and I have a lot of talking to do. It's enough that you and I understand each other. I'll take care of her. You keep your eyes peeled."

"Roger," Sam said and, turning, rejoined his men.

Ryan didn't go straight home. He needed a few extra minutes to digest his discussion with Sam and think through things one more time. When he arrived in Cambridge it was dark. After parking, he walked toward the building, his sharp eyes on the third floor windows that were Carly's.

They were dark.

Heart pounding, he took the stairs two at a time, knocked on her door, then rang the bell. Unable to wait, he fished in his pocket for his key and let himself in, only to find the place deserted. Puzzled, he tried to think. Tom might have taken her out for something to eat. Or she might have gone to Sheila's. Neither thought pleased him. He wanted to see her *now*. Having thought everything out, he was as ready as he'd ever be. And after two long days, he needed her.

Dejected, he retraced his steps to the second floor and let himself into his apartment, determined to unpack and clean up, then go back and wait for her.

Flipping on the lights, he saw nothing but loneliness—wall-to-wall carpet as stark without furniture as he felt without Carly. She was his color, his comfort, his joy. Without her, his life was empty.

He didn't turn on the bedroom light, choosing not to be reminded of that void in his life, but dropped his bag on the bed and began to undress. Then he heard a tiny cry and froze. There in the darkness, lit only by the palest hint of moonlight, was a small bundle of arms and legs and long hair that curled over hunched shoulders.

"My God . . . Carly?" He was across the room on his knees in an instant, prying her rigid hands from her mouth.

She cried his name then and threw herself into his arms, clinging to him with a strength that belied two days with little food or sleep. "Ryan," she sobbed. "I thought you weren't coming back."

"Oh, baby," he moaned, "I'd come back. I love you. Don't you know that?"

"There's so much I have to tell you," she managed in a broken rush. "I'm not who you think. I was somebody else before . . . in Chicago . . . a reporter. Robyn Hart. I testified for the state on an arson case and when someone tried to kill me they put me in the Witness Protection Program."

"I know. I know."

For an instant she was still, only intermittent gasps breaking the silence. Then she drew her face from his neck and stared up at him. His cheeks were wet. Bewildered, she raised a finger to touch his tears.

"You know?"

He pressed her hand to his bearded jaw. "I spent the weekend in Chicago."

"Ch-Chicago?"

Shifting her onto his lap, he settled back into her corner. Holding her tightly but gently, he told her everything. "I'm sorry to have left you that way Friday night. I was hurt and confused. I didn't know what to do. Sam met me at the airport today. He half thought I'd made contact with Culbert in Chicago."

"With Culbert? How could he think that?"

"It's his job. He's protecting you. I must have looked pretty strange when I disappeared, to go to Chicago, no less. But we got everything straightened out. He said Tom and Sheila were with you."

"I sent them home."

Thoughts of her safety were foremost in his mind. "You shouldn't have."

"I couldn't take it anymore. I needed to be alone."

Ryan frowned, as though just then realizing where she was. "How did you get in?"

The night couldn't hide her sheepish expression. "Sam picked the lock when we first went looking for you." Her voice dropped. "I stole the key from your key board. Do you mind?"

"Of course not. I should have given you one sooner." He glanced off into the darkness. "Your Sam. He's not such a bad guy after all."

For the first time since he'd returned, Carly felt the horror of the past begin to recede. Tension very slowly seeped from her limbs. The ice that had encased her senses grew moist. "I missed you so, Ryan. I can imagine what you must have felt when I raced off to Chicago with Sam."

"Thank God I didn't know then that you were with him. I didn't figure that out till a little while ago. I think I would have gone mad if I'd known."

"I half wish you had. Maybe this would have all come out sooner."

He held her back and gazed into her eyes. "But you were going to tell me? Before I left?"

Reaching up, she kissed him softly. "Friday night. I waited and waited, but you didn't come."

"Will you ever forgive me?"

"Will *you* ever forgive *me?*"

"There's nothing to forgive," he whispered. "You were frightened. I can now understand why. I only wish I'd been able to share some of that fear with you."

"But I didn't want that. Don't you see? It's bad enough that I have to live with it, but to impose it on someone else makes it even worse."

"I love you, Carly. That gives me the right to know, the right to share *everything* with you."

She wasn't sure she totally agreed, but couldn't think about it with his lips suddenly sipping hers. The knowledge that he was here with her, safe and loving, made her mind whirl. A soft moan slid from far back in her throat and she opened her mouth, craving more than his gentleness offered.

He needed little encouragement. Her invitation touched off a spark, igniting his passion like a match to dried leaves. With a shudder, he kissed her more deeply. Their lips meshed, their tongues dueled. He sought from her every bit of her sweetness, and, brimming with it, she gave eagerly.

He groaned, shifting her to face him, easing her legs around his hips. "Do you know how much I need you? Do you know how much I love you?" Pressing his hands against her buttocks, he showed her how his body ached, and she thrilled to the fact even as her own body matched his yearning.

Sliding his hands beneath the band of her sweat shirt, he touched the slender span of her back and, finding no barrier, sought her breasts. He held their fullness and kneaded them, aware of their swelling at his touch. Deftly whipping the sweat shirt over her head, he feasted his eyes on what he'd felt.

"Your breasts are beautiful," he said thickly. "See how the moon catches them?"

Carly looked down. Her breasts were high and full, gleaming softly in the silver light, their tips waiting for his touch. She would never have believed she could be further aroused by the sight of her own body, but at that moment her body gloried in Ryan's searing gaze. Dear God, how she'd missed him. Even aside from his passion, she had missed their conversations, his quiet companionship, his caring. Two days—and she'd had a glimpse of what life would be like without him. She prayed it would never come to be.

Excitement shot through her when he lifted his hands. With thumbs and forefingers alone he touched her nipples, rolling them slowly, tugging them taut. Closing her eyes against the sweet torment, she cried his name and arched closer.

"You're mine," he whispered. "These are mine. When I touch them they respond as though they were made for me."

"I think they were," she managed in a strangled gasp. "No one's ever made me feel the way you do." Needing to touch him, she ran her hands over the fabric of his shirt, lauding the swell of his chest, its firm muscle, the symmetrically ridged contour of his rib cage. They fell past his belt to graze the hardness beneath his zipper. There she caressed him, spreading her palm over his strength, closing her fingers around his tumescence as much as the straining fabric would allow.

Ryan's hands fell to the delta of her womanhood. Slowly, devastatingly, he massaged her there. "So warm," he murmured against her lips moments before his tongue plunged into her mouth. One kiss followed another, and the intimate petting went on. Releasing him only long enough to unfasten his belt and lower his zipper, she slid her hands under his shorts to his hot flesh. He convulsed helplessly, urging her into a tighter, more erotic grasp, his breath coming in tortured gasps as, increasingly, was hers. When he could bear no more, he made a low sound.

Slipping his arms under her to hold her to him as he stood, he carried her from the dark of the bedroom into the brighter living room. She eyed him warily.

"But the bed. . . ."

"This room's too empty," he explained. "I want to fill it with you."

His words thrilled her, his very presence still new and imbuing her with untold relief. That he was safe seemed a dear gift; that he was back loving her was incredible.

Her feet slid to the floor when he stopped in the middle of the room, and she saw the same hunger in his eyes that she felt in his body. Only then letting him go, and never once taking her eyes from his, she stripped off her jeans and panties in one quick move, then finished the work she'd begun on his pants.

Fumbling in his haste, he had his shirt barely unbuttoned when she finished. Swallowing hard, he watched her slip to her knees and press her head to his stomach. She turned her face from side to side, driven wild by his scent and the firmness of his skin. Her lips traced a fiery path over his hard muscles, her tongue a tool of rampant heat. When her mouth ventured lower, he felt his knees tremble. Ripping the shirt open, he thrust it aside, then collapsed onto his knees and took her to the rug with him.

But Carly had begun something she couldn't stop. Never in her life had she felt as uninhibited. She'd been blessed with Ryan's return; her gratitude knew no bounds. Every inch of his body was precious and desirable; she showed him this in no uncertain terms. The past days' agony had left her starving for him, and now her soul was bared and she was proclaiming it his.

Her lips sampled the haired plane of his thighs, moving from one to the other and ever upward. The swath of skin at his groin was smooth at the side. She nibbled her way in until once more her lips approached the core of his maleness. Hands never idle, she explored and fondled, cupping, gently squeezing, only realizing that he'd shifted her when she felt his breath between her thighs.

Arousal and excitement and passion took new meaning then. Holding him still with one hand while the other caressed him lower, she used her tongue in an exploration of silk. Intoxicated by the eroticism of the act, she instinctively sought more.

She barely felt the hands that bent her knee up. Somewhere in the background of her own heady daze, she was aware of encroaching kisses at the top of her thigh. She moaned her delight when his fingers slid against the source of her heat, forging deeper with each glide, slowly, tenderly opening her wide. Then, as his lips found her moistness and sucked gently, his hands shifted to cup the curve of her buttocks, caressing her intimately closer. She had to struggle to maintain her own gentle touch against the urgency that was building, filling her with nearly unbearable need.

She stroked him as he stroked her, matching the deep plunge of his tongue with searing swirls of her own. She attempted to devour him as she was being devoured, and rather than becoming less for losing part of herself in him, she was more.

Every muscle straining against the limits of the flesh, Ryan suddenly twisted, rising over her, coming down to take her lips in the kiss of a heavenly soulmate. At that moment he entered her. His hips surged forward, grinding her against the rug, his hardness a fiery prod electrifying the pathway to her womb.

Then, feeling the quick gathering in both their bodies, he held himself above her. "Look at me," he gasped in a hoarse whisper. She opened her eyes to the wealth of love he offered. "I love you," he mouthed, withdrawing nearly completely, then slowly, ever so slowly filling her again.

She caught in a breath, her eyes wide at the exquisitely gentle motion, but she knew that the excitement she felt went far beyond the simple mating of flesh. Her heart was Ryan's, her soul was Ryan's. She was naked before him, exposed and adored. As she mouthed his words in return, she felt a graceful crescendo begin in her body, rise higher, flame hotter, gain a force that finally exploded with a cry from her lips.

Ryan held himself on a wire-taut thread of control in a bid to savor the glorious sensation of her contracting around him. Eyes bright and passion fired, he marveled at her beauty as she arched in the throes of her climax. Head thrown back, her neck glistened. Her pulse throbbed. Her breasts shimmered. She gave him everything she possessed, making his life in that instant as rich and full as anything he'd ever known.

Then, slowly, she opened her eyes and smiled. It was his undoing. The very innocence she exuded stimulated him as much as her womanly intricacies. On trembling arms he bowed his back, withdrew one last time, then drove forward into a climax that stole every thought from mind but one, and that one was on his tongue at the supreme moment. "Carly!"

His body pulsed wildly, blindly, for what seemed an eternity of indescribable pleasure. Finally collapsing, he gasped for breath. "Ahh, Carly. . . ." It was a hoarse moan muffled against her hair. "You can't believe what that . . . was. . . ."

Her smile grew less innocent and more smug. She had a head start on him for composure. "I think I can."

Very slowly, his limbs heavy and languorous, he slid to the side, drawing Carly with him. Nose to nose they lay in quiet enjoyment of the sounds and feel of each other's life's breath.

"You're wonderful," he murmured at last.

"So are you," she whispered. "I do love you."

There was a slight tremor in the hand he raised to brush loose wisps of hair from her face. His fingers returned to trace her features, which relaxed and glowed with happiness. "When I first saw you that night in the courtyard, you looked so frightened. I wanted to protect you then. I wanted to see you smile the way you did just now." He sucked in a breath of remembrance. "That really turned me on."

She halted his hand in its wanderings and pressed it to her lips. "You mean that all I have to do is smile and . . . wham?"

"Well," he drawled, "I'm not saying that the rest of you didn't help. You're quite a lover."

"When one is stimulated by another who is just a little better, one always rises to the occasion."

"Tell me you teach that to your students."

She grinned. "Not in the same context, that's for sure. But I do believe it. Playing tennis, skiing, bicycling, writing, it's the challenge that works."

"Tell me about your writing, Carly. I read as many of your articles as I could find while I was in the library in Chicago. You were good. Do you miss it?"

Taking a deep breath, she rested her head back on his outstretched arm. "I haven't had a chance to miss it. When I was in protective custody all those months, I was too nervous and upset to think about anything much. Then, after the trial, when I moved here, I was too busy trying to get ready for school. When I wasn't working, I was preoccupied with sheer survival."

"I wish I could have spared you some of that."

"It wasn't your job to. I had to learn to live with Carly Quinn myself. A crutch would have done as much harm as good."

"But still, I hurt when I think of what you went through."

"I was the lucky one," she said quietly. "I lived."

"You're thinking of Peter."

"He was a wonderful person—talented and dedicated. We were just about ready to wrap up our story. We had gotten this last tip and felt that if we could *be* there, if we could get pictures, we would have irrefutable proof."

"Of Culbert's involvement?"

"More of Barber's. We'd already tied the two of them together pretty conclusively. We never expected Culbert to be there at the scene of the crime."

"You testified that he was."

"And he was. Peter had pictures. It was a deserted old apartment building that would have cost untold millions to renovate without the insurance money Culbert was counting on. Barber set up the fire the way he always did—using a cigarette attached to a matchbook, which was in turn attached to a fuse and then something highly flammable like a plastic bag filled with cleaning solvent.

It was perfect. The evidence self-destructed during the fire. There was never anything left afterward. Which was why Peter wanted to get pictures inside before we called the police.

"Culbert and Barber were outside in a dark corner talking. We thought we had time. We knew that between Barber's technique and Culbert's connections neither the police nor the fire department would find evidence of arson. So we wanted proof." She frowned, still disbelieving. "We were sure we had time. What we hadn't counted on was Barber lighting the cigarette when he did—or the entire building seeming to explode. By the time I could get to an alarm, Peter was trapped." She shivered and whispered, "It was awful. There wasn't anything I could do. By the time the firemen pulled him out, he had third-degree burns over ninety percent of his body. He lay in critical condition for a week before he died."

Ryan's arms tightened. "I'm sorry, babe. So sorry."

She took a shuddering breath, closed her eyes and reminded herself that it was over. Ryan's solid presence beside her helped. "The film was lost in the fire. That was one of the reasons why my testimony was so critical."

"Did you ever have second thoughts? In light of everything that's happened since, it would be only natural to have some regrets—"

"About Peter, yes. About the investigation itself, no. I felt too strongly about the issue of arson."

"Because of Matthew?"

"Uh-huh. Now that I think of it, I'm sure that much of the strength in my writing came from anger. I felt so helpless when he died. Writing was my vent." She spread a palm down the solid span of Ryan's chest. It wasn't a sensual gesture so much as a touchstone to the present. "The anger's gone now. Maybe testifying did that for me." She lowered her eyes. "But I suppose if I want to be completely honest I'd have to admit that there have been times when I've had second thoughts about testifying and being relocated. I had to leave my family and friends. It was scary coming to a new city alone, even with Sam to help me." She looked up and dared a smile. "But I've found you, so that made the whole thing worthwhile."

Ryan took her in his arms and rolled on the carpet until she lay atop him. "You're incredible. I can't say that enough. Since I met you I've been a human being. Before that I was nothing more than an automaton of a lawyer."

"That's not what Sam told me. He said you were brilliant."

"He did?"

"He trusted you from the start, regardless of what he might have thought for a while this weekend."

"This weekend." It's every detail contrasted sharply with the warmth of the moment. "Let's forget this weekend."

Resting her cheek on his chest, she nuzzled the soft skin by his nipple. "No. Let's not forget." Her head came up in a flash. "I want you to know who I am and where I've come from. I want you to love Robyn Hart too."

He lifted his head and caught her lips in a long, moist kiss. "I do. Because she's here." His hand came to rest on her breast. "She's in you. And I love you." His hand lingered to caress her, and where she had thought herself spent new fires blazed. "Carly?"

"Yes?"

"Take your contacts out. Let me see your eyes."

Her breath caught. It was the last thing she had expected him to say. She wore her contacts so constantly that she gave them little thought. When she looked up to protest, she saw the urgency in his eyes and understood that with the revelations of the weekend there was one more to be made.

"I want to see you as you were born." He ran his hands down the ivory warmth of her slender torso. "I want to see you as no one else does."

Her gaze lingered on his for a minute. Then, slowly, she pushed herself up until she sat astride him. Carefully she removed first one lens then the other, long lashes shading the eyes that studied the gray disks in her palm.

"Look at me, babe," he murmured huskily.

Strangely shy, she hesitated. Then, closing her hand loosely, she slowly raised her lids, to be rewarded by Ryan's soft gasp when her bright blue eyes met his. In a gesture of awe, he framed her face with his large palms.

"They're beautiful," he breathed. "Very beautiful. Will you do this for me each time we make love?" When she shook her head, he frowned. "Why not? You have nothing to hide from me now."

"I can't see you," she mumbled, chin tucked low again.

"What?"

When she tipped up her face, she spoke with greater determination. "I can't see you. Not the way I want." Her boldness gained momentum. "When we make love, I want to be able to see everything about you. Clearly." Her free hand swept slowly over his chest. "I can feel you, how warm and hairy you are. I can feel this." She rubbed the tip of her finger over his nipple and felt it harden. "But it's a blur. I want to see it. I want to see the way your eyes crinkle at the corners when you smile at me. Your smile turns me on too. Did I ever tell you that?"

"No," he rasped, suddenly and acutely aware of where she sat. "Oh, babe." Grasping her under her arms, he brought her forward until her breasts teased his chest and her lips met his. "Make me yours."

It took little effort. Already Carly's body clamored for his. Her kiss transmitted the message of her slowly undulating hips, and it was amplified all the more by the brush of their bellies against each other's.

Very carefully, her breath coming faster, she placed her contacts on his chest. "Lie still," she commanded in a purr, then propped her hands on the rug by his shoulder and bent her head again. She kissed his eyes and his nose, wove her way along his bearded jaw, then finally took his open mouth with one that matched it in heat and hunger. Drawing away at last, she spread her hands over his torso and told him how much she loved his leanness, his strength. When she felt him grow beneath her, she fell forward again and raised herself to taunt him there.

But if she had planned to arouse him to a state of subjugation, her scheme backfired. Before he would ever reach the begging stage, she would take him of her own free will. As lovers they were equals, with desires as wild and needs as great.

When Ryan lifted her hips, she welcomed him eagerly, arching her back, sighing at the pleasure of his hardness deep inside her.

"That's it," he urged in a moan when she began to move. His fingers grasped the soft flesh of her bottom and guided her, while her hands claimed the sinewed brace of his shoulders. She rode him well; he was a joy of a beast. Together they raced across a plain of rapture and scaled a multitude of passionate peaks, arriving at last on the highest, reaching out for its ultimate glory. At that moment they were one as fate had decreed. At that moment a forever together seemed the greatest promise of all.

But the moment passed. Pulse rates slowed, breathing eased. Damp bodies lay limp in the aftermath of the exertion. When Carly finally slid to Ryan's side, it was with a reluctance that went beyond physical lassitude.

Ryan let out an unsteady breath. Hooking an arm around her shoulder, he hugged her. He felt particularly blessed. Carly Quinn, Robyn Hart—both were his.

"Marry me," he whispered. "Marry me, Carly."

Her heart contracted. For a minute she couldn't breathe. It had all been so wonderful up to that point. Stricken, she managed to push herself up and grope for the lenses that nestled in the hair on his chest.

"I'd better get these back in," she murmured unsteadily, but the sudden rise and fall of his chest impeded her search.

He grabbed her wrist and held it firm. A tenseness ran through him but it was more urgent than angry. "I asked you something. Something important. The contacts can wait. I can't. Will you marry me?"

She swallowed hard and moistened her lips. "Let's, let's talk about it later—"

"No!" He bolted up, heedless of the tiny disks that fell to the rug. "We have to talk about it now," he insisted, but gently once more. "I want you to marry me. As soon as possible."

Needing a diversion, she felt for and located first one, then the other, of the lenses. But she was aware of Ryan's alertness, could feel it in the powerful vibrations seeming to emanate from his pores.

"Carly?"

"I can't."

Something snapped inside him, letting loose the anguish that seemed to have been gathering for weeks. "Why in the hell not?"

"Because it's too soon."

"For what?"

"For us to know."

"That's absurd. You say you love me."

Her head shot up, eyes searching blindly. "I do."

"And I love you," he barked. Then, realizing the contradiction of his tone, he gentled it. "There are no more secrets between us. So there's no reason why we shouldn't get married."

Tucking her chin low, she huddled into herself. "I can't. Not yet."

"Explain."

"Too much can still happen."

Ryan shook his head as if to clear it of nonsense. "What could possibly happen? We could have a fight? We could suddenly decide that we're incompatible? That's insane. I'm not saying that our marriage would be one endless bed of roses. No marriage is like that. We'll have our small differences; every couple does. But what we've shared in the past three months, what we had just now on this rug—that has to account for something!''

"You don't understand," she whispered, slowly raising her head. Her gaze held a mix of defeat, of fear, of anguish. "I'm still a witness for the state of Illinois. I'm not my own person. If they call, I have to go. Look at what happened a few weeks ago. Meade called Sam, and within hours I had to drop everything to run off to Chicago."

"What's that got to do with marriage?"

"There's the danger."

"_What_ danger?"

"Culbert. Barber. Whoever out there thinks that he'd be better off with me out of the way."

Ryan stormed to his feet. "That's crazy! No one's taking potshots at you!" He paced halfway across the room, then turned and, mindless of his naked-ness, cocked his hands on his hips. "You're one innocent woman! You couldn't harm a flea! You've already given your testimony. It's over. Done."

"No, it's not," she cried. "If there's a new trial, it could be just beginning."

"Baloney," he fumed, needing to quash that possibility. "There won't be any new trial. I've heard of Meade. He's known to be one of the most careful prosecutors in the country. Even Sam said he tried a solid case. Besides, there's no way either one of those bastards would go to the effort of seeking you out. It'd be suicide!"

In an attempt to minimize Ryan's sheer physical dominance, Carly rose. Her own frustration was seeking outlet. She wasn't any happier refusing Ryan's proposal than he was. "Come on, Ryan. Since when did thoughts of suicide deter a convicted killer? Let's not be naive. Barber and Culbert were both given stiff sentences. If they have to serve them, they'll be losing the best years of their lives. On the other hand, if they can wangle a new trial and somehow throw in a glitch, they'll be home free. What have they got to lose?"

He threw up his hands. "Damn it, Carly, you can't live your life thinking that someone's on your trail."

"Someone was once." Turning away, she hugged her arms around her. With the dredging up of a nightmare, she felt chilled to the bone. "I was walking home after work," she began in a tiny voice. "It wasn't long after the indictments had come down. I'd walked the same route for years. I knew every nook and cranny along the way. But I wasn't watching. I thought of myself as an innocent witness to a crime. I felt _impelled_ to testify—because of Matthew and whatever—but I also knew it was the right thing to do. I never dreamed someone would try to hurt me. Things like that only happened in B movies. I didn't imagine. . . ." Her words trailed off as her voice cracked. Only when she felt Ryan's gentle hands on her shoulders did she realize he'd approached.

"What happened, babe?" He sensed her need to tell him and, though his own insides knotted, he needed to know as well. If he was ever to convince her to marry him, he had to know what had happened.

She took a steadying breath. "It was an alley. Dark and narrow with a big dumpster in the middle and garbage strewn all about. I never saw him. Suddenly there was this arm around my neck and something hard sticking into my ribs." She gasped for air. "He dragged me back, back where no one could see us. I struggled, but he was very big and his arm tightened around my throat. I could barely breathe." She was panting softly. Ryan moved his hands in slow circles to remind her that he was there, that it was all in the past. But it didn't do much good. The memories were too vivid.

"He didn't say much and when he did it was in this low snarl to mask his normal voice." She was shaking. "I'll never forget those words. 'Think you're pretty smart, do ya?' he said. 'Din't no one ever teach ya not to play with fire?' Then he gave this horrid-sounding kind of laugh. 'Little girls get burned. They end up in an alley with a bullet in their brain.' "

"Oh, God," Ryan whispered into her hair as he brought her trembling body against his for support. He wrapped his arms around hers. "How did you ever get away?"

"I was so scared. So scared." She spoke quickly and in short bursts as though fearing that any minute she would run out of breath. "I knew it was the end. But I didn't want to die! So I started struggling again. I was desperate. I must have taken him by surprise. I surprised myself. Then I began to run."

"But he had a gun. Why didn't he use it?"

Her laugh, verging on the hysterical, held a none-too-pleasant ring. "He tried. But my legs were so wobbly that I was weaving around, running in this jagged pattern. And I started to scream. And scream. I didn't realize I was out of the alley until I heard the screech of brakes. Then I passed out."

Ryan's own legs were shaky. "Sweet Lord. Did the *car* hit you?"

"No. It stopped in time. But by the time the police got there and I'd come to enough to tell what had happened, whoever had attacked me in the alley was long gone."

"He was never identified?"

"No." Enervated, she sagged back against Ryan's strong body. As though only then realizing the point of her dissertation, she managed to turn in his arms. "But it happened. And I'll never forget it. That's why I was put into the program. That's why I don't think I'll feel really safe until these appeals and motions are settled. And until then—" her gaze held great sorrow "—I can't marry you. It's bad enough that I fear something might happen to you in the course of the battle if there ever was one. This weekend, I was so frightened. . . ."

He kissed her brow and pressed her head to his chest. "Nothing's going to happen to me. Or to you. I won't let it. Sam won't let it. Everything's going to be all right."

She had to look at him again to convey her urgency. "I want to marry you, Ryan. I want to have our babies. But I don't want either you or them to be hurt by the decisions I've made in my life. Can you understand that?"

"I hear you. I'm not sure I agree. If you want to put our marriage off for a couple of months, just until something gives regarding this new trial, I won't be happy, but I could live with it. As far as children go, though, you're talking of time, Carly. Even if we *were* to marry now, it'd take nine months before a baby arrived. By then a new trial would either have taken place or be ruled out. Are you telling me that even after that you're going to be nervous?"

"I don't know," she said honestly.

"But it could go on forever! You can't live that way!"

"I don't know how else to live," she whispered in defeat.

"Then you're a fool," Ryan muttered, releasing her, stepping back. "All of life has danger. Hell, one or the other of us could be killed in a car, an airplane, walking across the street—" When she gasped and reached out to erase those thoughts, he refused to be silenced. "Do you think you're the only one to ever be threatened?" he asked, eyes ablaze. "Well, you're not." He thrust out his jaw, tipped his head back and pointed. "See that scar? It didn't come from some little childhood accident. I was slashed!" He whipped the word at her, and it struck with deadly force. Her eyes widened. The muscles of her throat constricted. But Ryan was so intent on countering her self-pity that he ignored her pain.

"I was doing my father-in-law a favor by representing one of his friends in a divorce. Personally, I couldn't stand the woman. But she did have a right to representation. We were in the midst of messy negotiations when I happened to bump into her husband at a party. We were all in the same social circle— the one I divorced right along with my wife." When Carly simply stared, he went on. "This guy was drunk and angry and jealous of every other man in the room. And since I was visible evidence of his humiliation, he took it out on me. He accused me of having a personal interest in his wife," Ryan sputtered, then suddenly grew more calm. "I never did figure out if it was a steak knife or a grapefruit knife." Sighing, he turned away and stared blindly out at the night. "The plastic surgeon did wonders. But I was self-conscious. So I grew a beard. After a while I began to see it as a symbolic change. I haven't handled a divorce case since. That was ten years ago." He sighed heavily. "I never pressed charges. Same social circle and all. The fellow was obviously disturbed. He was contrite afterward." He snorted. "I got a great settlement for his wife."

When no sound came from behind him, he turned to Carly, who stood with a hand over her mouth. "Don't you see, babe? Nothing in life is a given. If you'd ever told me that I'd be physically attacked in a divorce case, I'd have thought you were crazy. But it happened. Two inches lower and I might have died. I gave up divorce work because I didn't want to have to deal with that pettiness, those irrational emotions. But the rest of my practice grew. Hell—" he chuckled dryly "—any number of my criminal clients have been far more dangerous than that man; they would have hit the jugular instantly."

Carly stood frozen, trying to absorb it all. "I didn't know," she murmured at last.

"Of course you didn't." He took a step closer. "Because it's behind me. Because I don't put that fear on a pedestal and worship it."

"I'm not—" she began in self-defense, only to have Ryan interrupt her with a conciliatory wave.

"I know. I didn't mean that. All I mean," he said slowly, "is that I live with whatever life brings. That's what you have to learn how to do."

Silence filled the room while Carly pondered what he'd said. "It's so hard."

"I know." He closed the space between them and took her face in his hands. "I know. But I can help. Please let me try."

"Will you be patient?" she whispered timidly.

"How patient?"

"Patient as in holding off on marriage for just a little while?" Despite his argument, there was an unease deep inside her that she knew she had to deal with before she could agree to marry him.

"That's asking a lot," he stated soberly.

"I know."

"Does it mean that in time you'll say yes?"

"If nothing happens—"

"None of that talk."

"Just a couple of months, until I know more."

He gave pretense of considering her proposal, though in fact there was no consideration to be made. He had already decided to take whatever she would give. Marriage in a couple of months . . . he could have done worse. "You're a tough negotiator, Carly Quinn."

But his eyes were warm and she knew she had won. Feeling abruptly light-headed, she threw her arms around his neck and clung fiercely. "I love you, Ryan. Oh, my God!" Stepping back, she stared from one to the other of her open palms.

Ryan looked at her in alarm. "What's wrong?"

"My contacts." She dropped to her knees and began to gingerly pat the rug. "I dropped them. I don't know when. Was I here . . . or there. . . ." Sitting back on her haunches, she squinted across the floor. Then she looked up in dismay. "If I don't find them, I won't be able to leave this apartment!"

Ryan's grin was one of pure masculine pleasure. "I think I'd like that, babe. Mmm. I think I'd like that very much."

TWENTY

❀❀❀

CARLY'S RELIEF WAS IMMEASURABLE now that Ryan knew everything. She spent hours talking of her life after Matthew's death, those four years that she had previously avoided, and Ryan wanted to hear it all. Regarding the trial, they discussed what had been and what might yet be. She was able to share her fears and was all the more relaxed for it. More than once she told him so. On each occasion, Ryan simply gave her that smug "I told you so" smile and hugged her tightly. They grew closer by the day.

Sheila continued to cover Carly, making sure she was never alone, but, as the weeks passed, given Ryan's full awareness of the situation, there was less and less need. Ryan timed himself to drop Carly at school on his way to work, and though Sheila always picked her up afterward and saw her safely home, often coming in for a drink, Ryan was with her the rest of the time.

It was a late February day, cold but mercifully dry, when Carly mentioned her to Ryan. They were running along the river path, keeping a rapid pace to ward off the chill.

"I'm worried about Sheila."

"What about?"

"She seems tense."

"More so than usual?" he quipped with a smirk. Strangely, Ryan had come to share Sam's view of Sheila. He sensed the intensity in her and couldn't quite shake the feeling that, while controlled on the outside, she sizzled inside.

"Mmm. I thought things were going well between Tom and her."

"They are. As far as I know. They see each other often enough."

Sheila had told her that. But there were a lot of things Sheila hadn't told her. "Do you think they're sleeping together?"

Ryan slanted her a look of amusement. "That's none of your business."

"You're right," she countered, undaunted. "But what do you think? When we were in Chicago, she used to drop little hints. It sounded like she slept with every guy she dated. But something's different with Tom. She's quieter."

"Maybe she really likes him."

"He seems to like her." They'd been out as a foursome more than once. The attraction between Sheila and Tom was highly visible.

"He does. I know Tom. Funny, though, he doesn't talk about her much to me either. Like he's saving her for himself."

They ran on a bit before Carly spoke again. "Then that can't be what's bothering her. I wonder if she's bored with her work."

"She likes being assigned to you."

"I haven't needed her much lately. I think she's offended."

"Nah. Sheila's beyond that. Besides, Sam has her on other things. It's not like she's sitting around waiting for you to call."

"I wonder, though. When I see her, she's so full of questions. She wants to know *everything*. As if she's starved for conversation. It's weird."

"Maybe that's just her. Haven't you always said that?"

"Mmm," she agreed, "but still. . . ."

For the few days after that, Carly made a point of trying to coax Sheila to talk more about herself, but in vain. Sheila was as skilled in evasion as she was in handling courtroom security. For each question she had an answer, albeit a flippant or a humorous or a diversionary one, such that it took Carly a while to realize she'd learned nothing at all.

In the end, she decided that Sheila was simply drawing the line between deputy and witness, and in the final analysis Carly was relieved. Her own greatest source of strength and support now was Ryan; Sheila's role in her life was fast fading.

* * *

Or so she thought. Early in March Sam learned that the decision on a new trial was imminent. Within hours he received a phone call from Bill Hoffmeister saying that Gary Culbert had sold extensive interests in real-estate ventures in California and Hawaii. Sam promptly instructed Sheila to stick to Carly like glue.

Carly took the news with remarkable calm, but then, in her presence, Sam downplayed the worst of his fears. Her tension emerged during quiet times, when she would find herself chewing on her lip or shredding a napkin in her lap or staring out a window. When Ryan caught her at it, she confessed. Much as she regretted it, her fears had become his. Though she didn't know it, he was in constant touch with Sam.

As a bodyguard, Sheila was as diligent as any of them might have wished. She was always there when Carly was alone, whether at school or at home, but she kept a low profile, waiting to the side, ever watchful. Carly had begun to wonder whether she'd simply grown more sedate when, one afternoon, shades of the old Sheila surfaced.

Classes had just finished. As arranged, Sheila was there to walk Carly back to her office. Tipping her face up to a pale sun, she took a deep breath. "Hey, Carl, it's early yet. Feel like taking a ride?"

The March wind whipped through Carly's hair as they crossed the campus. The air held a promise of mildness conducive to spring fever. "A ride?"

"Into town. It's so nice out. We could drive around the North End and along the waterfront."

"Oh, Sheila, I don't know," Carly waffled, drawing open the door of the administration building. "I have a whole stack of papers to read through for tomorrow. If I get them done now, I won't have to worry about doing them tonight when Ryan's home." More than anything, she enjoyed sitting with Ryan in the evenings. Often he brought work home to do, and then she would relax on the sofa with him, sometimes grading papers, sometimes needlepointing, sometimes just watching him and counting her lucky stars.

But Sheila was at her most persuasive. "It won't take long. My car's never seen Boston in the spring." At Carly's scowl of skepticism, she backtracked. "All right, so it's not quite spring yet. But at least the roads are clear and dry for a change. And the air is fresh. And I do have a quick errand to do. Besides, we've been stuffed up here all day. We could use a break."

Carly laughed. "In case you haven't noticed, I work here. I don't feel 'stuffed up.' I like it."

"Well, I don't," Sheila announced, then softened. "Humor me, Carly? You haven't got any appointments. Let's take off—just for an hour?"

"Really antsy?" Carly teased.

"Yeah."

With a wistful glance at the papers piled high on her desk, Carly relented. "Okay. But just for an hour."

"No more," Sheila vowed, as she grabbed her coat and bag, then Carly's arm, and led her at a clip toward the car.

Moments later they were on Memorial Drive, headed toward Boston. "This is nice," Carly said, breathing the air off the ocean through her open window. "Ryan says it'll get cold again."

"Ryan's a killjoy."

"He's lived here a lot longer than we have." She sighed. "At least the worst of it's behind us."

Sheila nodded and sent her a guarded glance before taking the Massachusetts Avenue bridge to the other side of the river. Then they hooked onto Commonwealth Avenue and followed it in.

"I love this street," Sheila said. "So pretty with grass and trees in the middle. I can't wait till everything blooms in another couple of months. And look there." She pointed to the four- and five-story buildings they passed. "I bet one of those town houses is more impressive than the next. You know — high ceilings, elaborate wood moldings, beautiful oak floors, a fireplace in every room." Her eyes grew momentarily distant. "Someday. . . ."

Carly's own dreams centered around one spiral staircase. She smiled. "You'll have it someday, Sheila. Just wait and see. You'll have it."

Sheila snapped. "If one more person tells me to wait. . . ." When Carly looked at her in surprise, she grinned instantly. "Good things come to those who wait," she said, but in a mocking tone this time. "I'm waiting, I'm waiting." Moments later, she pulled to the side of the road. "Now it's your turn. See that bakery just around the corner? I'm going to run in and get some pastry for tonight."

"You're seeing Tom?"

"Umm. This place has strawberry cream tarts like you've never tasted in your life. Stay put. I'll keep an eye on you through the window. I won't be long." Before Carly could utter a word, she was gone, returning less than five minutes later with two small boxes.

"For you," she said, handing one to Carly.

Touched, Carly eyed her in bewilderment. "What's this for?"

"Dessert. And for putting up with my whims to take afternoon drives."

Carly smiled. "Your whims aren't all that bad. You were right. The break feels good."

"See? What did I tell ya?" Sheila started the car, tossed a quick glance over her shoulder, and pulled out. The shiny Mazda sped along Arlington Street, around the Public Garden, down Charles Street and up Beacon before veering off onto streets new to Carly.

"How do you find your way around here?" she asked.

"This is my home turf. I walk these streets all the time." As if to prove it, she made a sharp left, then a sharp right, then several more turns in succession. Before Carly knew what had happened, Sheila had maneuvered through the Government Center traffic and into the North End. There she drove more slowly, the better for them to appreciate the flavor of Italy in the clusters of small shops and homes fronting the narrow streets.

"Flavorful," Carly observed, eyes warm in survey of the vibrant window displays. "It's supposed to be great in the summer when the festivals start." They passed a bakery whose tempting aroma seeped into the car.

"You didn't see it last year?"

"Had no one to go with. Maybe this year with Ryan. . . ." Her voice trailed off, her thoughts daring to advance that far.

Sheila drove through to Commercial Street and on along the waterfront.

"Speaking of Ryan, where's his office? Isn't it somewhere nearby? I've never seen it."

Carly looked from one street sign to the other. "Uh, State Street? I think — you make a right here."

Sheila followed while Carly directed haltingly. By a miracle Carly couldn't explain, given the fact that they approached from a direction totally new to her, they arrived at the new high rise that housed, among others, Ryan's firm. Pulling over to the curb, Sheila bent her head low to admire the structure.

"Nice place," she drawled. "How high up is he?"

Carly's gaze joined hers in scaling the earthen-hued walls. "Thirty-fourth floor. He has a gorgeous view. Hey, want to go inside? Ryan would love to —"

"Oh, no. We shouldn't disturb him."

"I'm sure he wouldn't mind." She grinned, eyes glued to the upper stories of the building. "Besides, I feel like a jimmy fanatic in an ice-cream parlor. I'm drooling at the thought that he's so close —"

Sheila's low whisper cut her off. "Oh, hell."

With a frown, Carly focused on the woman in the driver's seat. "What is it?"

When Sheila said nothing but simply stared toward the building's huge bank of doors, Carly shifted her gaze. It took her but a minute to see what Sheila saw. She stiffened instantly, her voice as tight a whisper as Sheila's had been. "My God. . . ."

"Do you recognize him?"

"Yes!"

"Then it's not me?"

"Oh, no," Carly wailed softly, raising a trembling hand to her mouth. "He's there. He used to lounge like that at the back of the courtroom. When I was testifying, I'd look back. There was always something sinister about him." Then, suddenly hit by the import of that single man's presence against the ocher stone of Ryan's building, she caught her breath. "Sheila?" she managed to gasp at last.

Sheila already had the car in motion. "You bet. We're getting out of here."

"But Ryan! Someone has to warn Ryan!"

"Once we've gone a little way, I'll call Sam."

"What if he's done something to Ryan? He was standing there so idly. Maybe he's done something already! Maybe Ryan's hurt!" She grabbed Sheila's arm. "We have to go back."

"No," Sheila said calmly. "Not back. We go ahead. Trust me."

Her tone held a ring of authority that Carly couldn't ignore. For the first time since they'd been together in Chicago, Sheila was in charge.

Slumping in her seat, Carly stared blindly at the floor. "How could he have known?" she whispered. "Everyone assured me my cover was tight. But he broke it. *How?*"

"Let's not worry about that yet. The most important thing is to get you away and let Sam pick him up."

"Who is he?" Carly asked, her voice high-pitched, directed more to herself than to Sheila. "The courtroom was always so crowded, but there were those people who stood out. Culbert's family glared. The press, too, though I knew most of the reporters. There was a little old lady in the back row, a kid who looked like a college student on the far right, two gray-haired men in the center . . . and him. *Who is he?*"

"Beats me," Sheila answered tersely. Pulling over to the curb by a pay phone on Cambridge Street, she grabbed for her purse. Carly knew there was a gun inside. "Wait here. I'll call Sam."

Clutching the door handle for dear life, Carly sat ramrod straight, looking out at the people who passed. She imagined the man at Ryan's building having communicated by walkie-talkie with someone who was even now on their trail. Glancing in the side mirror, she was horrified to see two young men eyeing the car. She held her breath when they passed, still admiring the sleek lines of the hood.

Then Sheila opened the door and slid in. "Okay. Sam's on his way to Ryan's office."

"What does he want us to do?"

Gunning the engine, Sheila pulled away from the curb. "We're taking off. You're going to be stashed away for a little while, at least until we find out who that man is and why he was there outside Ryan's building."

"And Ryan?"

"After Sam makes sure he's all right, he'll join us."

"Where?" She pictured the small house on the shore of Lake Michigan where she'd been squirreled away for four months. It had been quaint and cozy, as so-called safe houses went.

"Sam suggested a certain place in Vermont?"

"In Vermont! The inn?"

"Where you stayed over New Year's. You said you loved the place. Sam thought you'd be comfortable there."

Carly grimaced. "Slightly different circumstances. I hate to taint it with this."

"Everything will be all right," Sheila soothed again. "Once Ryan's there with you, it'll be New Year's Eve revisited."

Carly doubted that. "But we can't just show up there."

"Sam's calling to make the arrangements. They'll have something. And if they don't, they'll make something."

Carly closed her eyes. "I can't believe this is happening. After so many false alarms, I really thought I was home free." She raised a hand to her forehead, only to snap her eyes open on a new thought. "I have to stop at home. I'll need some things."

Sheila took her eyes from the road long enough to glance at her watch. "Uh, I don't know. . . ."

"If I have to be holed up somewhere, at least I can feel like a human being. How long will we be staying in Vermont?"

"Not long."

"But you can't be sure. If Sam can't find that guy, it may be a while longer. The apartment's right on the way. It'll only take a minute." It seemed imperative that she stop. She needed the boost of a familiar place.

"What if someone's there?"

"Someone?"

"As in dark and dangerous?"

Carly sucked in a breath and shook her head to deny the thought. "Oh, God," she murmured, shaking. Pressing a fist to her mouth, she chewed on it. Her words were muffled. "I can't believe this is happening."

On Memorial Drive now, Sheila halted at a traffic light. One look Carly's way told her of the woman's distress. As she watched, Carly grabbed the door handle and looked around as though contemplating escape. It was then that Sheila yielded. Anything to keep Carly from getting hysterical.

"I suppose we can stop at your apartment. If we stick close together, there won't be any problem. Sam may have already sent someone by the place. But we can't stay long. Just long enough for you to stick a couple of things into a bag."

Carly nodded, feeling numb. "What about you?"

"Me?"

"Your things. You're coming to Vermont with me, aren't you?"

She dismissed the problem with a wave of her hand. "I'll be all right. If we have to stay there for any length of time, Sam will have someone pick up my things. Come to think of it, that's what he could do for you. We really shouldn't stop—"

"I *have* to." Carly needed things of her own. What with everything she'd given up—and rebuilt—in the past year, she wasn't about to go anywhere without some familiar trappings of her identity.

Sheila concentrated on driving. When they arrived at Carly's building, Carly jumped out and ran ahead. She didn't think of the possible peril; one part of her actually wanted to be a decoy to draw danger away from Ryan.

The apartment was undisturbed, as neat as she'd left it that morning. While Sheila scouted around for anything suspicious, Carly stood in the middle of the living room trying to calm herself, to think clearly.

"Why can't we just stay here?" she asked when Sheila joined her.

"Because Sam says no."

"Then I'll call him," she suggested, starting for the phone.

But Sheila beat her to it, holding the receiver firmly in place. "Be sensible, Carly. Sam has his hands full trying to get that man."

"Let me call Ryan—"

"And tip someone off that you're here? If your cover's been blown, this line might be tapped."

"I don't want to go to Vermont."

"You have to. And the longer we spend here, the greater the danger will be." It took every resource Sheila had to project a semblance of composure. She was as nervous as Carly. "Now, go put some things in a bag. But be quick. We have to move." She watched Carly move slowly off. "Quick!" She glanced at her watch, then back at the retreating figure. Needing a shot of strength, she quickly poured herself a drink, downed it in record time, and was by the door when Carly emerged from the bedroom. "All set?"

"I don't want to do this." Dropping the bag on a chair, she wandered to the wall unit and lifted the clay plaque from its hook. "Ryan bought this for me in Vermont. It's always held special meaning." Hugging the plaque, she turned, eyes filled with anguish. "I can't believe all this is in danger."

"Not if we hurry. Let's go." Crossing the room, Sheila grabbed Carly's bag.

If Carly heard the impatience in her voice, she was too lost in emotion to heed it. She turned around again. "We picked up the driftwood in Rockport. The picture was done at the—"

"Carly! We're wasting time!" She forced a softness into her tone and spoke more slowly. "We have to leave. Now." She took Carly's elbow.

Understanding Sheila's plight and knowing that her urgings were for the best, Carly didn't resist. She slid the plaque to the cushion of the chair as she passed and gave a final glance around the place she truly felt was home, before turning her back and leaving with Sheila.

Arriving home shortly after six, Ryan took the steps at a quickened pace. He was uneasy. As he'd walked from his car and glanced up, he hadn't seen any lights. True, it was barely dark outside, still. . . .

His key turned easily in the lock. He pushed the door open. "Carly?" He flipped on the light. "Carly?"

There was no answer.

He searched the apartment. She wasn't there. He tried to think of where she might be. She hadn't said anything to him about having late appointments or meetings, and she was always careful to let him know, especially now that she knew he would panic at any misunderstanding.

For a minute he wondered if he was simply uneasy about the strange meeting he'd had that afternoon. A potential client. An arsonist. Of course, given Carly's experiences and the emotions that now were his, he wouldn't accept the case. But somehow he sensed that his visitor had expected that all along. And it wasn't the arsonist himself who lingered in his mind as much as the man who had brought him in. Something about the way he talked. . . .

Lifting the phone, he dialed Sam's number. When the phone rang for an inordinately long time, he feared Sam had left. Then a man answered breathlessly.

"Is Sam Loomis there?"

"I think he just left. This is Greg Reilly, his assistant."

"I have to talk to him. It's Ryan Cornell."

Greg was instantly alert. "Hold on," he said. "Let me see if I can catch him."

Ryan held on for what seemed forever. Finally Sam came on the line. "Ryan. Any problem?"

"I don't know. I just walked in and Carly's not here. She's usually so good about telling me if she's going to be late. Do you know if she's with Sheila?"

Sam muffled the phone against his chest as he spoke to Greg. "Do you know where Sheila is?"

Greg shrugged. "With Carly, I assume. Or she may be done for the day."

"Try her number," Sam ordered, then returned to Ryan. "Greg's trying Sheila. Hold on."

There was no answer at Sheila's. Greg shook his head and put down his receiver.

"Sheila's not answering either," Sam told Ryan. "Maybe the two of them went somewhere?"

"It's not like Carly. She's almost always here to meet me. Besides, I had a weird meeting this afternoon."

"What meeting—wait. Let me come over. In the meantime you call the school and anyone else who might know where she is."

Ryan's hand was tense on the phone. "Bring your key. If the switchboard at Rand is closed I may drive over there. If I'm not here, let yourself in. I'll be back."

The switchboard was indeed closed. He called Bryna Moore, who hadn't seen Carly since that morning. He called Dennis Sharpe, who hadn't seen her since lunch. He paced the floor, wondering if he was making something out of nothing. Throat parched, he went to the kitchen for a glass of water, then was reaching for his car keys when the phone rang.

"Ryan? This is Sheila."

"Sheila! I've been worried. Is Carly with you?"

"No. That's why I'm calling. I went to pick her up at school and she wasn't there. She left a note saying that she had to get away. I've been driving around trying to spot her car, but I don't know where to look."

"Oh, my God." At least there was a note. But why would she have to get away? "Christ, Sheila. Where have you looked?"

"I've been all over the school and in and out of Boston. She talked about Rockport, but I've been driving around here for an hour and I don't see any sign of her."

"You're in Rockport now?"

"I'm at a pay phone on the highway. I'm wondering, she talked so much about that place in Vermont. Do you think she might have gone there?"

"Maybe. I'll call there. I can't believe she'd take off. . . ."

There was a click. "My three minutes are up. Listen, I'll keep looking. I'm sure nothing's wrong. The tension may have just gotten to her. She may be mortified if you follow her."

"Damn it, I don't care." The phone clicked again. "Okay, Sheila. Call back if you hear anything." At least Sam would be there.

But Sheila didn't know that. She diligently wiped the smug expression from her face before she returned to the car where Carly waited.

"Ryan's on his way," she announced. "And Sam has an APB out for that fellow we saw."

"Then Ryan's all right?" Carly asked, needing that one bit of reassurance to counter her fears.

"Fine. He'll meet us at the inn."

Five minutes later, they crossed the border into Vermont.

* * *

Sam arrived at Carly's apartment to find it deserted. He and Greg waited five minutes, ten, fifteen. When Ryan didn't reappear, Sam called Tom.

"You haven't by chance seen Sheila Montgomery, have you?" he asked with more nonchalance than he felt.

"Sheila?" Tom echoed cautiously. "No. She said she had to work tonight."

Sam darted a glance at Greg, who had checked the assignment schedule just before they left the office. Sheila was not working. "Then Ryan?"

"Is something wrong?"

"I don't know. Ryan called me a little while ago saying that Carly hadn't come home. I'm at their place now. And Ryan's nowhere either."

Ryan, Carly, and Sheila. Three people who meant a lot to Tom. "I'm coming over," he said, promptly hung up the phone and was on his way.

Neither Sam nor Greg had learned anything more by the time he arrived. Ryan still hadn't shown.

"Okay," Sam said, walking slowly around the living room as he tried to organize his thoughts. "Ryan said that Carly hadn't come home. He thought she might be with Sheila. But she's not. And we can't locate Sheila either." He faced Tom. "You two didn't have plans?"

"For tomorrow. Not tonight."

Sam turned to Greg. "When was the last time you saw her?"

Abundantly aware of Tom, Greg was uncomfortable. "Uh, this morning. She stopped in at the office before meeting Carly at Rand." With fresh sweet rolls and coffee, no less. Sheila had been at her most enchanting.

"And she was to have stuck around there until Carly was done for the day," Sam said, stroking his jaw, deep in thought. "Damn it, I had a feeling. . . ."

"What feeling?" Tom asked, suddenly aware that there was more to Sam's concern for Sheila than might have appeared at first.

But Sam only shook his head. "And Carly. Where in the hell could she be?" He paused, trying to recall every word Ryan had said. "He said something about a meeting this afternoon. 'Weird' was the word he used. Know anything about it, Tom?"

"Hell, no. I don't keep track of Ryan's clients."

Sam turned to Greg. "See if you can get someone in his office. Find out who that meeting was with."

As Greg headed for the kitchen, Tom lifted the small clay plaque and sank into the chair, studying the piece. "This is crazy. Carly wouldn't up and run off. She and Ryan were closer than ever since he returned from Chicago."

"Then you know everything?"

"They both told me. I thought they had things straightened out. Even if Carly was terrified by something, she would have gone to Ryan first." He rubbed a small stone on the plaque, then stood and, as though he'd done it any number of times, returned the piece to its hook on the wall. "They bought this when they were in Vermont. They're collectors." He gestured toward the shelf. "Mementos of their life together." He eyed Sam. "This whole thing is weird. Do you think someone got to Carly?"

Before he could answer, Greg returned, the page of his small notebook filled with jottings. "Ryan had a whole *afternoon* of meetings. Smythe and Reading at twelve-thirty, Frazier at one-fifteen, Dunn at two, Walsh and Thiess at two-thirty—''

"Walsh and Thiess?"

Greg checked his notes. "The guy who gave me this stuff said that the last was scribbled in. The names may be off. A last-minute thing, I guess."

"Thiess," Sam repeated, reaching for something he couldn't quite grasp. "That name sounds famil—uh-oh. . . ."

Tom was on his feet in an instant. "What is it?"

But Sam held up a hand and took his turn at the phone. When he returned, his expression was grim. "That was Meade in Chicago. Thiess is an alias used by a guy named Theakos. Horace Theakos. He's served time more than once. A reputed arson expert."

"Geeeeez," Tom breathed, running a hand through his blond hair, disheveling it all the more. "What does that mean?"

"That means that either your brother is on the take—"

"No way! He wouldn't harm Carly for the world."

"And he did call that meeting weird," Sam said, then raised his eyes and spoke with deadly gravity. "I think he's being set up. He may be in as much danger as Carly." On his way back to the kitchen, he shot a glance at Greg. "I'm calling out the troops."

He made one call, then a second and a third. Tom and Greg stared at one another. Finally Tom spoke.

"Where does Sheila fit into all this?"

Greg shrugged and avoided his gaze. "Beats me. She may just be shopping somewhere. Likes to buy new things lately. . . ." His voice trailed off, his thoughts taking a twist. The eyes he raised to Tom were more wary. "She does like to buy things. Where's she getting the money?"

"*I'm* not bankrolling her." Not that he wouldn't, given the chance.

"So where does she get it?"

"She saves," Tom replied defensively.

"On an agent's salary? I know what *I* make and there's precious little left over after taxes and the rent and food and gas. That new car of hers. . . ."

Tom's features were rigid. "What are you getting at?"

"She's come into a hell of a lot of money all of a sudden."

"Now wait a minute. You're suggesting—"

"That *she* was the one who was bought off."

"That's a goddamn lousy accusation."

The two men stood eye to eye. Fully understanding the enormity of his accusation—and its ramifications, should it prove true—Greg didn't flinch. "But it'd explain a lot. New car, new clothes, new bag, lofty dreams, but a dump of an apartment."

"Her apartment? You've seen her apartment?"

"Many times." His gaze narrowed, and though he knew he was inflicting pain, he needed to speak. "It'd also explain why she came on to me the way she did. A bosom buddy in the office—"

"Came on to you?" Tom clenched his fists by his sides. "What are you talking about?"

For the first time, Greg's tone softened. "She seduced me, Tom. While she wanted you. And if you think *you're* hurt, think of how I felt when she cried out your name when we made love."

"You're crazy!" Tom exploded. "Sheila's no easy lay. Hell, she's in love with me and still she—"

"Wouldn't go to bed with you?" Greg paused, finding no satisfaction in the other's stunned silence. "She didn't, did she?" The answer that never came was answer enough. "Then she did have some sense of morals, at least. If she knew what she was planning, and that she was trading her body for my loyalty, that's something. And loving you—which I'm sure she does—and feeling guilt—"

"What's going on here?" Sam growled, walking a tight wire himself.

Dragging his gaze from Tom's, Greg sighed. "I think we have a problem."

"What problem?" Sam asked, only to have the phone ring before Greg could answer. Retracing his steps on the run, Sam picked it up.

"Yes," he barked.

It was Ryan, sounding nearly desperate. "Thank God you're off the phone. This is the third time—"

"I know. I have everything working. Where in the hell are you?"

"I'm on the highway. Eighty-nine. Carly's in Vermont."

Sam's gaze flew to the far living-room wall and the plaque Tom had replaced. "Vermont? What's she doing there? What are *you* doing there?"

"Lord, Sam, I think it's bad. Right after I spoke with you, I got a call from Sheila."

"Sheila! Where is she?"

"She said she was calling from a pay phone near Rockport. She said that Carly hadn't been there when she'd arrived at school to pick her up. It didn't occur to me then that Sheila was supposed to be there all day. She said that Carly left a note for her saying that she needed to get away. She said she hadn't seen her and that she'd been looking all over, going to the places Carly had mentioned she and I had been. Vermont—you know, that cottage we rented at New Year's—seemed the obvious place. Sheila suggested it herself." He took a breath and raced on. "But I've been driving along and little things keep coming to me. That meeting I had this afternoon. A rush job. Two fellows, one of whom is accused of arson. But neither of them seemed particularly committed to retaining me. And one of them—not the one in trouble, but a guy with him—talked this funny way. Instead of 'didn't' he said 'din't.' I couldn't figure out why it bothered me—until I remembered Carly telling me about that guy who tried to kill her in that alley back in Chicago. I told myself that maybe it was a coincidence. But there's something else."

"What?"

Greg and Tom had come to stand in the kitchen, but Sam's every sense focused on what Ryan was saying.

"Right before I left I took a drink of water. I put the glass in the sink. It didn't occur to me till a couple of minutes ago that there was another glass there. One with the remains of a dark liquid in the bottom. Carly is meticulous. She'd never walk out in the morning leaving anything in the sink. And

Sheila claimed she hadn't seen her." He paused, almost afraid to ask. "Check it, Sam. What's in that glass?"

Sam had already turned and was lifting the glass. He sniffed, then tipped it to his mouth to taste its tepid contents. "Rum and Coke." His eye caught Greg's, then Tom's as, with quiet urgency, he addressed Ryan. "How far are you from that inn?"

"About forty minutes." He'd been pushing seventy most of the way, praying the police wouldn't stop him.

"Okay. Keep going. I'll make some more calls, then move. Greg and Tom are with me. We'll take a helicopter. It shouldn't take long."

"For God's sake, hurry!" Ryan begged, then slammed down the phone and, leaving the phone-booth door rattling in his wake, bolted for his car.

"I still can't believe this is happening," Carly said, dazed as the lights of the inn appeared at the end of the drive.

Sheila said nothing, simply steered down the dark side road, heading straight for the small cottage that held such beautiful memories for Carly.

"Don't we need a key?" Reminders of that other trip. Then the key had been hooked behind the swing.

"I told Sam what you'd said about last time. He was going to instruct the inn to leave it in the same place. The fewer people who see you, the better."

But as the dim cottage light came into sight, Carly forgot to ask how Sam had ever thought to get the same one. "That's . . . my car. . . ." she stammered, perplexed. The yellow Chevette stood out in the night, a beacon of its own. "What. . . ."

Sheila pulled to an abrupt halt in front of the door. Without a word, she reached for her bag.

"Sheila, what's going on?"

It was only after she'd spoken that, in a haze of horror, she caught the glint of the small service revolver that emerged from the bag.

"Come on," Sheila grated. "Let's go see who's there."

"Someone stole my car!" Carly sucked in a breath. "That man, the one from Chicago, the one we saw before. He knows about Ryan. He knows about me. He must have!" She grabbed the other woman's arm. "Oh, no, Sheila! We can't go in! He'll be waiting! But how did he get my car?" she murmured half to herself, withdrawing her hand, raising it to her forehead.

Sheila spoke calmly and clearly. "I gave him the keys."

"You?"

Slowly and with deliberation, the gun turned on her.

Sheila's face was shrouded in darkness, her characteristically nasal voice nearly unrecognizable for its sudden venom. "Get out. Now. And don't try anything or I'll use this."

"I don't understand. . . ."

The sharp poke to her ribs made the first point, Sheila's grating tone the next. "You will. Now get out."

By the time Carly had managed to force her wobbly legs into action, Sheila was by her side of the car, clamping a firm hand on her arm, hauling her forward.

The door of the cottage opened and Carly instinctively drew back. There, silhouetted but unmistakable, was the same man who hours earlier had been at Ryan's building.

"Took you long enough," he growled.

"She wanted to stop by her place for some things," Sheila explained with a snort. "As if she'll need them. . . ." Pressing the gun to Carly's ribs, she pushed her on. The man stood aside, then closed the door firmly when the women were inside.

"That was dumb, stopping," he snarled.

Sheila's retort was cold. "She was getting hysterical. I had to do something."

"Wasted good time."

"We're all right."

"What's going on, Sheila?" Carly cried, unwilling to believe that Sheila, *Sheila*, had betrayed her.

It was the man who spoke. "Nothing that should not have happened a long time ago. You caused me a load of trouble."

"Who are you?" Carly whispered fearfully, eyeing the man whose ominous advance brought him directly before her. It was all she could do not to cower.

"Name's Ham Theakos," he announced with a kind of perverted pride. "Don' remember me?"

"From the courtroom—"

"From the alley."

If Carly had had any hopes for salvation, they were dashed with his curt statement. "You?" she breathed, stunned.

His smile was ugly. "Me. You got away from me then. Won't happen now."

Carly looked wide-eyed from his harsh features to Sheila's. "This has to be a joke."

"No joke," Sheila stated bluntly.

"But *why*? What have I ever done—"

"You opened your mouth when you should not have," Theakos grated. "You stuck your nose in where it din't belong."

But Carly's eyes were glued to Sheila's. "*Why*, Sheila? You were supposed to be protecting me."

"I'm always protecting someone. This time I'm protecting myself."

"But we were friends."

"Hah! We were only friends because back in Chicago you had no one else. In other circumstances, you wouldn't have looked at me twice. But we were stuck in that house together, day after day, week after week, and it was only natural. *Real* friends? Never."

Shock raised Carly's voice an octave. "Then you had this in mind *from the start*? You *asked* for that transfer just so that—"

"Not exactly," Sheila interrupted, chin tipped up defensively. "Actually, it was much the way I told you. I was bored in Chicago. Nothing was working out there. I decided I needed a change and Boston seemed as good a place to go as any."

Try as she might to understand it, Carly couldn't. "Then you made this little deal—" she dared a glance at Theakos "—after you got here?"

"Remember when I went back to Chicago?" Sheila asked smugly.

"You went *looking* to do me harm?"

"Wellllll, that's pushing it a little. While I was there, seeing Harmon and visiting old friends at Hoffmeister's office, Ham, here, was snooping around looking for an in."

"And you gave it to him," Carly stated, crushed beyond belief.

"Why not? The price was right and there was cash up front. I'd had a good look at the way you were living. Pretty clothes. Fancy home. Super guy. You had everything. Now it's my turn."

"*At my expense?*"

"The way I see it," Sheila went on baldly, "we all have to compromise a little in life." Her eyes hardened. "I've done my share of compromising. Now I want a little of that luxury I've been looking at from the wrong side of the fence all my life."

"This isn't the way," Carly whispered, even as she sensed that Sheila was past remorse. "And what about Tom—"

Sheila stiffened. "What about him?" She didn't want his name brought into this. It had no bearing.

"He loves you."

"I love him."

"And you think that he'll really be able to live with you after this?" She couldn't suppress a shudder. Where she found the strength to think clearly, she didn't know. But something drove her on, perhaps the need for a temporary diversion from her very real terror.

"He'll never know."

"Do you believe that? Ryan won't take anything happening to me sitting down. Neither will Sam." A new thought bloomed. "That call you made—"

"Was never made. Not to Sam, at least."

Carly glanced again at Theakos. "Then you knew he'd be at Ryan's office."

"I called Ham from the bakery. He was waiting for my call at a phone booth near Ryan's building. He'd just come from a meeting with Ryan."

"*With Ryan?*"

The smile Sheila gave her then was enough to freeze her blood. "It's all pretty brilliant, if I do say so myself. Took a lot of planning, especially when you began to clam up on me after Ryan returned from Chicago." She cast a conspiratorial glance at Theakos. "But I think we covered everything. Ryan will be under suspicion simply for having met with Ham and his buddy. You will have been overcome at the thought that he might have been planning to betray you. It'd be perfectly natural that you'd commit suicide."

"*Commit suicide?* I'd never commit suicide!"

"Maybe not on your own," Sheila purred, "but with a little push and no one around to say differently, which reminds me." She turned to Theakos. "We'd better get moving. I called Ryan. He should get here just in time to find her hanging. He'll be the one to call the police. The distraught lover."

For an instant, Carly was utterly paralyzed. Remembrance of Ryan's Luis— whose death was still listed as a suicide despite Ryan's doubts—flashed through her brain. Sheila was right. They would never know. She had to move.

With a burst of energy born of desperation, she broke for the door, only to have Theakos haul her right off her feet and back. "Not so fast, li'l lady. First we need a note."

Carly struggled wildly against the arms that held her. "Let . . . me . . . go!"

"First the note," he gritted. "Every suicide needs a note."

She kicked back with her legs, but her captor was that much stronger than she was. She'd taken him by surprise in the Chicago alley; this time he was prepared. Her flailing arms hit air. "I'm . . . not writing . . . any. . . ."

He lowered his head until his thin lips were by her ear. "If you don't write it, we'll wait and murder your lover when he arrives. Then it'll look like a double suicide."

The fight left Carly instantly. "You wouldn't," she gasped, looking at Sheila, pleading for any last remnants of sanity. There were none.

"We would. Very easily." Extracting a piece of paper and a pen from the small desk against the wall, Sheila slapped them down flat.

Theakos shoved Carly forward, forcing her onto the hard wood chair. "Write what she tells you."

"This won't work, Sheila," Carly began, only to be stopped, then filled with dread, by Sheila's whimsical look.

"My beloved Ryan," she began to dictate. When Carly stared at her in horror, Ham pressed a gun to her neck.

"Write," he ordered. "If your boyfriend gets here before we're done, he's a goner. You wan' him shot?"

Carly tried to catch her breath. When Sheila rapped a long fingernail against the stationery, she tried to focus, but her eyes were flooded with tears. Shaking, she lifted the pen.

"My beloved Ryan," Sheila repeated, then waited until the words were written. "I never thought it would come to this. But I know what you're planning—"

When Carly dropped the pen, Theakos prodded her again with the gun. Mustering shreds of strength, she retrieved the pen and wrote falteringly.

"I know what you're planning," Sheila continued, speaking slowly, pausing for Carly to catch up, "and I can't bear to live. I've never loved another human being as I love you."

"Sheila—" Carly sobbed.

"Write!" There was not the slightest hint of feeling in Sheila's voice. "I've never loved another human being as I love you. I'm so sorry. For both of us." She paused. "Just sign it, Carly."

The script was indistinguishable at points and blurred where Carly's tears had fallen. When she was done writing, Sheila lifted the paper and read it over.

"Not bad. Even those smudges. Shows how upset she was. Perfect."

Theakos snaked his hand into the drawer, heedless of Carly's recoiling when his arm grazed her breast, and drew out an envelope. "Put it in," he commanded. When, fumbling badly, Carly finally managed that, he directed her to put Ryan's name on the envelope. Then, propping the note in a visible spot on the desk, he grabbed her arm and pulled her from the chair. "Let's get on with it," he growled. "I got a plane to catch."

TWENTY-ONE

B EFORE CARLY COULD utter the smallest cry, she was gagged with one of the scarves Theakos had pulled from his pocket. She jerked in pain when the knot caught her hair but Theakos only tugged it tighter. When her tongue fought against the stifling intrusion, her mouth went dry. She felt as though she was suffocating. Nausea welled up from the pit of her stomach. She swallowed convulsively, breathing fast and hard through her nose.

Driven by primal instinct, she struggled against the arms that pinned hers back, against a second scarf being bound around her wrists. She twisted and turned against Sheila, who tried to hold her still.

"Better hurry," Sheila managed to grunt. "She'll fight us all the way."

Theakos's answer was a snarl. "I've handled worse."

They were the words of a coldhearted killer. In that instant of stark realization Carly panicked. She whirled around. She reared back. Then she bucked against Sheila, toppling them both to the floor, but Theakos grabbed her before she could do more than roll to her knees. When she tried to pull away, he shook her hard.

"Goddammit!" Sheila yelled and raised a hand to hit her, only to be stopped by Theakos's meaty grip.

"No marks," he growled, glaring at Sheila as though she were a dimwit. "Can' be any outward sign of a fight. Why d'ya think I'm usin' scarves?"

Sheila scrambled to her feet. "I thought you liked the color," she grumbled, brushing herself off.

"Dumb broad." Theakos's quelling look applied the epithet first to Sheila then to a fast-breathing Carly, whom he tugged up.

Carly made frantic sounds, but, muffled by the gag, they remained deep in her throat. A cold sweat bathed her brow. Her body was a mass of tremors. But she continued to thrash against Theakos's hulking form, her legs scissoring and stabbing, landing with no apparent effect.

Theakos tightened his grip. "You tie," he gritted toward Sheila, then squeezed Carly with such sharpness that she grew faint.

Seizing the moment, Sheila quickly retrieved the scarf from the floor and, grasping first one, then the other of Carly's ankles, secured them fast.

Carly regained awareness as she was being carried toward the bedroom. At first she thought she was having another of her nightmares, but the bite of her shackles was too real, as was the bulk and bodily smell of Ham Theakos. She tried to scream, but couldn't. She thought she might vomit, but didn't. She writhed in his grip, thrashing her head from side to side, wearing herself out with her efforts but knowing that it was now or never.

When she hit the bed, she brought her knees up in an attempt to kick out at her captor, but he was too fast. Sprawling half across her, he pinned her down so that her knees banged uselessly against his back.

"Get the cord," he ordered.

Panting in terror, Carly saw Sheila approach holding a thin nylon cord. She moaned and tried to roll away, eyes bulging, ever pleading. But the cord slipped over her head and, trussed as she was, she was helpless to stop its tightening.

Theakos hauled her up over his shoulder. "Now the chair."

When Sheila disappeared for an instant, Carly rammed her chin against his back. Defying the dizzying rush of blood to her head, she squirmed madly, but Theakos was unfazed.

Sheila returned with the wood chair Carly had sat on moments before.

He tossed his head. "Middle of the room."

She put it there, and Carly was set standing on it, held still by Theakos, who tossed the end of the nylon cord to Sheila.

"Over the rafter," was his gruff command.

Carly could barely breathe. Her gaze dimmed. She didn't want to die. Not now. Not when the future was so bright.

In her daze she was aware of Theakos's grumblings, of his low curse when Sheila repeatedly missed her goal. She wanted to laugh hysterically at the farce of it all. Such a well-planned murder to be thwarted by bad aim.

Then all thought of laughter died, replaced by the most soulful dread Carly had ever known when the cord successfully cleared the rafter and tumbled down the other side. She writhed in hideous desperation, thinking, in vivid flashes, of her parents, her brothers, of Matthew and, mostly, mostly Ryan. Ryan, who was her soulmate. Ryan, whom she loved more than life itself. Ryan, who would now be alone. A low cry of agony burst from her throat, but had nowhere to go. The cord tightened. She whimpered futilely.

Then a loud crash shook the cottage and before Carly could begin to understand, a blur of darkness barreled through from the other room. With the advantage of both speed and surprise, Ryan hurled himself at Theakos, knocking the burly man away from Carly.

Had Carly not been in a state of shock, her legs would have crumbled. But she stood rigid, trembling inside, eyes fixed on Ryan as he grappled with his husky opponent. Only when Sheila made a dive for the bed did she try to cry out, but it was too late.

Grabbing the gun that lay there, Sheila lunged back for Carly just as three uniformed policemen burst into the room.

"Drop it!" one yelled. All held large rifles cocked to fire.

"No, *you* drop it," Sheila cried, dragging Carly stumbling down from the chair with the gun pressed to her head. "Guns down, or she gets it."

All movement in the room ceased. The air was still, thick, the silence broken only by random gasps from Ryan and the man who lay half beneath him.

For an instant it was a standoff. But only for an instant. En route to the cottage, the troopers had been alerted to the identities and skills of Carly's abductors. Each of them knew that she would be dead if any one of them fired. And then there was Ryan who, ignoring their commands to stop, had raced ahead and broken into the cabin. His life, too, was now on the line. Slowly they lowered their rifles.

"Now back out," Sheila ordered, inching forward with Carly as a shield.

Theakos was on his feet, training his own gun on Ryan. Ryan's eyes never left Carly. When the police were in the other room and Sheila was watching each step from the door, she raised her voice. "Get out. And shut that door."

One by one the men left, closing the door behind them. Only then did Sheila release Carly with a shove that sent her toppling to the floor. Ryan was by her side in a flash, tearing at the noose, then the scarves that bound her hands and feet. Together they worked at the gag. When it was free and she could breathe, she collapsed against him, panting loudly, trembling uncontrollably. Face buried against his chest, she could think of nothing but the fact that he was there with her, that she was still alive. His hands moved convulsively, hugging her, then stroking her hair, shifting to rub her back, touching her face. For an instant he forgot the two with their guns. When Theakos spoke, he looked up in abrupt alarm, his arms crushing Carly to him as though he feared she would be taken away again.

But Theakos was looking at Sheila, his face distorted with rage. "You really done it." His gun jabbed the air with each word. "How in hell did the cops get here?"

"How would I know?" Sheila countered breathlessly. "I didn't expect this any more than you did."

"You were the brains," he roared angrily. "You had it all worked out."

"Something goofed."

"No kiddin'." He moved to the lamp and turned it off. The dim spill of light from the living room lent an even more sinister aura to the room. "I ought to shoot *you* and say I was set up too."

Sheila eyed Ryan and Carly. "But they'd know better. Are you going to shoot both of them and say I did it?"

"Not a bad idea."

"But dumb."

"She's right," Ryan said, trying to think clearly even though he felt as though he'd been to hell and back. Well . . . partway back.

"Shut up," Theakos growled, his attention still on Sheila.

But Ryan wasn't about to give up. "There are cops all over the place. You haven't got a chance. Attempted murder is better than murder—"

His words were cut off by the well-aimed kick Theakos sent his way. It caught him in the ribs, knocking him off balance. When Carly winced, Ryan regained his hold of her, pressing his mouth to her ear. "It's okay, babe. It's okay. Everything's going to be all right." But her trembling continued, and it was all he could do to control his fury at the two who had made her this way.

"So, brains," Theakos started in on Sheila again, "got any bright ideas?"

She scowled. "I'm thinking."

Her thought was disrupted by the blare of a bullhorn from outside, its words slow and distinct. *"Theakos and Montgomery. You are surrounded. Drop your weapons and come out with your hands up."*

"No . . . way . . . Jose," Sheila stated slowly and distinctly.

"Come on, Sheila," Ryan coaxed. "You can't win."

She gritted her teeth. "I can and I will. I haven't come this far only to spend the rest of my life in jail." She held up her free hand. "Let me think."

"Do it fast," Theakos grumbled.

"Theakos and Montgomery. You are surrounded. Repeat. You are surrounded. There is no means of escape."

Theakos shifted from one leg to the next. Sheila tapped a finger to her mouth.

"We have hostages," she murmured, thinking her plan aloud. "We'll have to demand free passage somewhere." Her eyes lit. "Zaire. The United States has no extradition treaty with Zaire. And I've always wanted to see Africa."

Theakos cursed, his beady eyes darkening in disgust. Africa was the last place *he* wanted to see. Though the brunt of his anger was directed at Sheila, who had somehow bungled what should have been a simple murder, his wrath also spread to Gary Culbert, who'd been responsible for all this from the start.

"We'll ask for money," Sheila said. "Five hundred thousand, a plane and a pilot in exchange for two hostages."

Carly pressed closer to Ryan. She couldn't think, could barely comprehend Sheila's words. Her entire being felt numb. She wanted to sleep, to escape it all.

But suddenly Sheila was tugging at her, forcing her from Ryan's arms while Theakos placed his gun by Ryan's head. "Up, Carly," she ordered. "We have some dealing to do."

When Carly clung to Ryan, Sheila lowered her voice to a menacing whisper. "If you'd rather, we can kill you both now."

Carly managed to climb to her feet. She moaned when Sheila twisted one arm up painfully behind her. Ryan's reflex rush forward was halted by Theakos.

"If I have to kill you," he rasped, taking his cue from Sheila's psychological play, "I'll have nothing to lose in killing her too."

Ryan fell back to his seat on the floor. Aching, he watched Sheila nudge Carly forward. When Carly stumbled, Sheila hauled her roughly up. "I don't have to worry about marks, now," she warned, her tone more ruthless than ever. "Watch your step, Carly. If I go, you go."

Making her cautious way into the living room, she switched off the lamp as

Theakos had done. The last thing they needed was to be in a fish bowl. As it was, there was plenty of light spilling in from outside, the flicker of red and blue lights heralding what was beyond. Holding Carly carefully before her, Sheila parted the light drapes. Though night reigned, it couldn't hide the line of bumper-to-bumper cruisers that obstructed the narrow drive. Sneering an oath, she tugged Carly to the door, then slowly opened it just far enough to call out.

"We have hostages here. They'll die if you try something."

"*You are surrounded,*" the megaphone replied. "*You haven't got a chance.*" Helmeted heads lurked behind every car, rifles pointed, primed and aimed.

"Then neither have they," she yelled back, tightening her hold on Carly, careful to stay covered herself. "If you want them alive, you'll do what I tell you."

"*Send them out. Make it easier on yourselves.*"

Carly flinched when Sheila's shout battered her eardrum. "We want five hundred thousand in cash, free passage to the nearest airport, a plane and a pilot. And we want them by midnight. That gives you a little more than three hours."

Without awaiting a reply, she slammed the door, retraced her steps to the bedroom and threw Carly toward Ryan, who still sat on the floor, his back now braced against the foot of the bed. He caught her easily and enclosed her chilled form in his arms.

Sheila joined Theakos, who stood some distance from the bed, his gun pointed at the couple on the floor. "There," she said. "Now we wait."

"That was stupid, too," Theakos snorted.

"What was?"

"Midnight. Where they gonna get that kind of money at this hour of the night? The banks are closed."

Sheila tossed her head in a gesture of indifference. "Banks can be opened. The right call here or there can do wonders. Don't worry, they'll manage."

"And if they don't?"

"They can beg us for a time extension," she blurted crossly. Then, as though she'd exhausted her store of bravado, she stumbled through the darkness to a nearby easy chair and, for the first time, realized what had happened. Everything had gone wrong. Had things run as planned, Carly would have already been dead, and she'd be on her way back to Boston to fall into Tom's arms in despair at having failed to find Carly.

Tom. It was over. He would never love her now. She would never be free to love *him* now.

She looked over at Ryan to find him studying her closely, and her dismay turned to anger. If she correctly read the somber expression that even the darkness couldn't hide, he pitied her. "Have you got a problem?" she barked.

"Obviously I do," Ryan stated quietly. He rubbed his jaw along Carly's brow, pressed his hand against her head, holding her face to his throat. "I haven't got any five hundred thousand dollars."

She made a face. "Come on. You have a lucrative law practice, an expensive condo, a gorgeous car—"

"But no five hundred thou."

"Then your law firm can dig it up. The rent in that building must be hefty. I'm sure that Miller and Cornell has ample resources."

"The firm wouldn't yield to a ransom demand."

"Then your wife will. She's loaded." She smirked at the last. "I understand she's got a terrific house. That should be worth something."

"She's my *ex*-wife. And her money is hers, as is the house. You won't get anything from her." He paused, calculating. "I guess you'll have to hope Tom can come up with something."

"Tom's got nothing to do with this," she snapped.

"He's my brother. And he should be arriving here shortly."

Sheila blanched. "Here? But I only called you, and you must have left immediately. How would Tom know anything about this?"

"Tom was with Sam."

"With Sam? How would *Sam* know anything about this?"

"Sam was the first one I called when I got home and found that Carly wasn't there. I was already on my way when he and Greg—"

"*Greg?*" Sheila's eyes were wide with horror. She was oblivious to Theakos's slow simmering nearby.

Goaded by her obvious discomfort, Ryan went calmly on. "He and Greg went to Carly's place. Tom joined them there."

"Sam, Greg *and* Tom?" Sheila asked, then turned her eyes away and murmured, "I never dreamed they'd all get together. I never dreamed you'd go to Sam in the first place!" She looked back angrily. "I thought you distrusted him. That was what Carly said."

Carly tipped her head up to respond, but Ryan held her quiet. "She didn't tell you everything."

"I'll say," Sheila grumbled, eyeing Carly with an irrational hatred. When she raised her gun, Theakos uncoiled to stop her.

"Kill her now, and they'll be all over us in no time. Wait. You gave 'em a deadline. Just wait."

Sheila's lips gave an ugly twist. "She ruined everything. Don't you see? She ruined everything!"

"Not her," Ryan injected. "You. You weren't quite smart enough, Sheila. That's all there is to it."

Sheila leaped to her feet. "You . . . shut . . . up," she gritted, holding the gun, now aimed at Ryan, with both hands.

He was undaunted. "You know, Sheila. Some day, when Carly and I are happily married, I might be able to forgive you for what you've done to her." His voice grew sharper. "Tom's something else. You might as well aim that gun at *him* and pull the trigger. He loved you."

Nearing his limit, Theakos threw his hands in the air. "Goddammit, I'm sick of hearin' that. Who in the hell cares if he loved her or if she loved him. You—" he pointed a finger at Ryan "—screwed that up by bustin' in here." The finger moved toward Sheila, though the eyes stayed on Ryan. "She can't go back. Whoever he is, the guy's history for her." Finally, Theakos shifted his narrow gaze to Sheila. "If you know what's good for you, you'll sit down and shut up yourself. He's trying to get you ruffled, or din't that occur to you?"

It hadn't. She'd been too busy trying to sort things out, trying to absorb what was happening. Suitably chastised, she slumped back into her chair and stared glumly at the couple by the foot of the bed. It wasn't fair—he in his business suit that was barely wrinkled despite the tussle he'd had with Theakos, she in her skirt and sweater, seeming fragile and all the more feminine for it. And the two of them, in an absurdly tense situation, looking like lovers at ease in a room glowing with vague flickers of red and blue. . . .

"How're ya doin'?" Ryan whispered, tucking Carly more securely in the crook of his shoulder.

She tipped her head back. "Okay." It was the first word she'd said since Ryan had saved her from what had seemed to be certain death. Her whisper was slightly hoarse, her throat was dry. "How did you get here so fast?"

He grinned. "I sped."

"You could have been killed that way."

"Uh-uh," he murmured in the same hushed tones she was using. "My mission was a good one. God watches out for his own."

"Is He still watching? I think we need help."

"It's coming. Have faith."

As though in answer, a faint hum arose outside the cottage. As it neared, it took on a choppy tone.

Crossing to the window, but being sure to stand carefully to the side, Theakos peered out. He saw nothing. But the sound couldn't be mistaken. "Helicopter," he grunted. "Maybe the banker."

It wasn't the banker. Within minutes, the bullhorn blared again. "*Sheila. It's Sam. Come to the door.*"

Sheila sat in her chair, nostrils flaring, jaw tense.

"*Sheila. Come to the door.*"

Still she made no move.

"*Something can be worked out, Sheila. You've been under stress. We can make a case for leniency.*"

"Hah," Sheila snorted, talking to no one in particular. "That's a pipe dream if I ever heard one. He's been out to get me since I arrived in Boston. Now he's suddenly on my side?"

"He's right, though," Carly said softly. "There's always a chance—"

"Oh, keep still," Sheila grumbled, and for a while, everyone did.

Ryan held Carly tightly, biding his time. He knew that to make a break for it now would be suicide, for himself and Carly. There were two guns and they were in the wrong hands. All he could do was to put his faith in the troops outside.

"*Sheila. It's Tom.*"

"Oh, God," she said, but her tone was beseeching.

"*I have to speak to you.*"

She clenched her hand in her lap, propping the gun on her knee.

"*Sheila. Please.*"

Had he sounded angry or commanding, she might have resisted him. But even the bullhorn couldn't hide his anguish. And it cut through her as nothing else could.

Bolting from the chair, she reached for Carly's arm.

"Whadya think you're doing?" Theakos demanded in a vicious growl.

"I'm going to talk to him," she replied shakily, as she pulled Carly up and headed for the living room.

Nudging Ryan up, Theakos quickly followed. "Don' do it. It's dumb."

"I have to."

"It's a trap."

They were in the living room now, with Sheila fast approaching the front door. "Tom wouldn't hurt me," she half-whispered, unable to think clearly.

Holding the gun to Ryan's back and pushing him forward, Theakos caught up. "You're crazy if you think that. He's lost you and he knows it. Hell, it was his brother's girl you were gonna kill."

"Sheila. I have to talk to you."

"And I have to talk to you," she whispered, barely aware that Theakos had taken up position at the side window. With Carly as her plate of armor, she inched the door open. "Tom?" Her voice quavered on the single name.

"I'm coming," was the quick reply and Sheila scanned the glare of headlights and flashers for sign of him.

"Get him away," Theakos growled from the window, his own eye trained toward the mass of lights.

"It's okay," Sheila soothed.

"Get him away!"

A figure separated from the maze of cars, approaching slowly, arms spread wide to show that he was unarmed.

"Get rid of him!" Theakos yelled. His fear came from the sure knowledge that the man who approached was Sheila's Achilles heel.

"I want to talk—" Sheila began, only to be interrupted by Theakos's coarse threat.

"I'll kill him. You want that?"

Sheila cast a quick glance to the side and saw that while Theakos had his gun pressed to Ryan's neck, he could as easily shift it and shoot. Then she looked forward again to see Tom continuing his slow, steady approach.

Her hand trembled on Carly's arm. Somehow there seemed nothing more important than to talk with Tom, to try to explain.

"I'm going," she whispered.

"Don't . . . you . . . dare." Theakos paused. Everything was out of control. He didn't understand it. He'd killed before and gotten away free and clear. But he'd always been dealing with the low life. That was it. These people were different and they were going to kill *him*. "He takes one more step and I shoot," he warned a final time. The cold steel in his voice said he meant every word.

Again Sheila looked at Theakos, and suddenly she was frightened. She knew his type. There was a madness in him. There was a madness in *her*. She couldn't let Tom suffer because she'd been weak.

"Don't, Tom!" she yelled. "He'll shoot!"

But Tom kept walking.

"Stop him," Theakos growled.

"Tom! Please! No farther!"

Tom was on the front path and walking.

"Tom!" A hint of panic tinged her nasal cry. Then she heard Theakos's gun cock. Thrusting Carly to the side, she raced from the cottage.

The shot was deflected by Ryan, who batted at Theakos's arm split seconds before twisting and diving in Carly's direction. In the same instant, the night air was rent by a barrage of gunfire and splintering glass. Scrambling across the floor on his belly, Ryan covered Carly's quivering body with his own and pressed them both flat.

As quickly as it had erupted, all sound died. The silence lingered for an awesome eternity. Then there were the sounds of running feet, on the path, on the front steps, into the cottage.

"Carly?" It was Sam's voice.

Ryan raised his head. "We're here," he mumbled, half afraid to move farther. "What happened?"

Joined now by half a dozen troopers, Sam moved to examine the body that lay in a tumbled heap in the middle of the room where the force of bullets had blown it. Moments later, he was back, kneeling by Ryan and Carly. "Is she all right?"

Carly lifted her head and Ryan pulled her to a sitting position. "She's fine," he said, turning her to him and holding her convulsively. "She's fine." Without releasing his hold, he stood and glanced to the side. "Is he . . . ?"

"Dead."

"How's Tom?"

"Unhurt."

"And Sheila?" Carly whispered.

When Sam didn't answer, she tried to break from Ryan. But he wouldn't let her go. "It's okay, babe. It had to be. It's better this way."

"My God," she breathed. "Oh, my God." Again she tried to escape Ryan's protective hold. Though he refused to allow it, he began to move her toward the door.

The scene outside was gut-wrenchingly still. Police seemed to be all around, but Tom was alone, kneeling over Sheila's lifeless form.

An anguished cry broke from Carly's throat. This time, when she pulled away, Ryan released her. On trembling legs she ran forward, falling to her knees beside Tom, staring down at Sheila's bullet-riddled body.

"She was crazy and unconventional," Tom murmured brokenly. "There was always that mystery about her. But she was exciting and warm. I loved her."

"I know," Carly whispered. She put her arms around him, and in that instant, yielding to grief and terror, she began to cry. Slowly, Tom's trembling arms circled her and held her with the force of his own emotions.

Throat tight, Ryan watched and waited until at last they stood. Only then did he approach, slip his arm around Carly's waist and, with a firm hand on his brother's shoulder, lead them away from the place which, for all three, was best put behind.

When they left, Greg approached to gaze a final time at the woman who had, in her way, bewitched him, too.

The night was far from over. There were long hours spent at the local police station, then a weary drive home. It was dawn when at last Ryan and Carly returned to Cambridge.

"Want to sleep?" he asked as they entered her place.

"I don't think I can," she said tremulously.

Ryan smoothed a wave behind her ear. "Maybe you should try."

She shook her head. "I'd only have nightmares."

"But I'll be there to hold you."

"Oh, Ryan," she whispered, sagging into his arms, "it was so awful. I keep thinking of that cord and the guns. If you hadn't come just then—"

"I did come. That's all that matters."

She rubbed her face against his neck, trying to dispel other images. "I still can't believe Sheila planned it all." The hurt lingered, a raw wound festering with sadness. "All that time we were together she was so friendly. I guess Sam was right in distrusting her." She faltered, her voice dropping to a whisper. "I wish they hadn't had to kill her."

"She came out with a gun," Ryan reasoned gently. "They didn't know she would never have used it on Tom."

"Poor Tom . . . to see her die like that right in front of him. Will he be okay?" Tom had stayed with them during the questioning at the police station, then had returned to Boston with Sam and Greg.

"He'll be fine. It may take a while, but he'll be fine." Ryan paused. "He really came through for us, didn't he? He had to know the risk he was taking, coming forward like that."

Hearing the note of deep affection and admiration in Ryan's tone, Carly looked up. "He's a good man. You should be proud of him."

"I am," he said hoarsely, then buried his face in her hair until he'd regained his composure. "We'll have to keep him close. He may need it for a while."

Lapsing into silence, he led Carly toward the bedroom. "Come on. Let's lie down. I just want to hold you."

Fully dressed, they stretched out on the bed. Ryan's body was as tense as Carly's. With their minds viewing and reviewing all that had happened, relaxation remained elusive.

"Ryan?"

"Mmm?"

"Will it be all over the papers? I don't want the publicity. Everyone will know who I am—"

"Shh," he soothed. "I spoke with Sam about that. There's bound to be something in the Vermont press, but it'll be minimal. With both of them dead, the case is over." He tucked in his chin and looked down at her. "Anyway, you're safe now. You know that, don't you?"

"I keep telling myself, but it's hard to believe."

"Believe it. Culbert will get his new trial all right, but it'll be for conspiracy to murder. And the sentence will be for a term after the one he's already serving."

"He could hire someone else."

"For what purpose?"

"Vengeance?"

Ryan shook his head with a conviction that gave his words extra force. "It was one thing when he thought he could wipe you out as a witness. But there'd be no point in it now. Even if he wanted to do something out of pure malice, you can be sure that he'll be severely restricted as to visitors and calls. He won't be *able* to do anything. Besides, chances are Theakos didn't have a chance to tell him your new name. He's probably being interrogated right now. We'll know more in time."

"Then I won't need another identity?"

"Hell, no." He grinned. "And if you did, I'd take it right along with you." His arms closed around her and brought her close. "We're in this together, whether you like it or not." His tone sobered. "I nearly lost you last night. I'm not planning on doing that ever again."

Slow tears formed in Carly's eyes. "Running into you on the walk that night was the best thing that ever happened to me."

"Me too, babe. Me too."

It was days before Carly could sleep through the night without waking in the throes of a nightmare. But, as he had promised, Ryan was always there to hold her tightly and gently talk her out of her terror.

To her relief, there was no mention of the events in Vermont in the Boston papers. When she felt sufficiently strong, Carly phoned her father and, censoring the most gory details, told him what had happened. He took it well, though he insisted on speaking with Ryan, who assured him that Carly was fine. Sensing that with Ryan his daughter was in good hands, John Lyons relaxed.

Carly took the rest of the week off from school, knowing that she would be unable to concentrate. Ryan worked for the most part in the apartment, spending hours on the phone, taking Carly with him when he needed to go into the office for an hour or two. They talked with Tom every day, convinced him to spend the weekend with them in a beachfront cottage on Cape Cod. It was a quiet, restorative time for them all, a time for healing, for counting blessings, for looking toward the future.

Returning to Cambridge on Sunday night, Carly was busy making dinner when she suddenly realized that Ryan had been out of sight for too long. Curious, she wandered through the living room and into the bedroom. At the bathroom door she came to an abrupt halt.

He stood before the sink, the remnants of white lather on his jaw.

Stepping slowly forward, she reached to touch his newly shaved face. Only a mustache remained. At first glance it looked lonesome.

"Well," he said, eyeing himself critically in the mirror, "what do you think?"

Astounded, Carly took the ends of the towel and gently dabbed at the last of the lather. "I think . . . you look . . . as handsome as you did before."

"Then you like it?" he asked more tentatively, stroking the mustache, then his jaw before he closed his hand over hers.

"I love it." With every second she looked at him, he seemed to grow more dashing. "But why?"

He turned to her then, taking both of her hands in his and holding them to his chest. His deep brown eyes melted warmly into hers. "Because I have nothing to hide anymore. I want to see my scar." Only then did her eyes go to the pale ridge that underscored his jaw from ear to chin. "I want *you* to see my scar. It should be a reminder to us that life is never without its risks. Nothing is a given, Carly. We've both lived through ordeals, separately and together, and there may be others in the future. But we can't dwell on them. We'll learn to live with them, just as I'm going to learn to live with this scar."

"You look . . . so different," she murmured.

"You will too," he said confidently.

"What do you mean?"

Releasing her hands, he went to the bedroom closet, dug into the pocket of a jacket and returned carrying a small box. "For you."

Carly stared at the box.

"Go on. Open it."

Trembling, she carefully lifted the lid, then caught her breath. On a bed of black velvet lay the most exquisite marquis diamond she had ever seen. "Ryan," she breathed at last and looked up at him again.

"I've been carrying it around for days. Had Tom not been with us this weekend, I might have given it to you sooner. Will you wear it, babe? Will you marry me?" Removing the ring from its box, he held it out.

Very slowly, Carly moved her left hand forward until the ring found a perfect niche on her third finger. Then, she threw her arms around Ryan's neck and in that instant knew that nothing in the world could keep her from this man she loved. Nothing at all.

EPILOGUE

W ITHIN A WEEK AFTER, and independent of, the attempt on Carly's life, motions for a new trial were denied Gary Culbert and Nick Barber. Gary Culbert was subsequently tried and convicted on charges of conspiracy to murder and given a lengthy sentence to be served from and after the original. He served out neither. After three years' incarceration, he suffered a stroke and was transferred to a state hospital, where he died four months later. It was on that day that the United States Supreme Court denied his last appeal.

Sam Loomis continued to thrive as chief deputy to the U.S. marshal in Boston. Eventually when the United States' presidency changed hands and political parties, he retired from public service and took a prestigious position as head of security for a large electronics firm in the area. With Carly Quinn's file going inactive, he and his wife, Ellen, became close friends of the Cornells.

It took some time for Greg Reilly to recover from what he considered a major error in judgment on his part. Only with Sam's steady encouragement did he continue at his job, and then it was in a sober and dedicated manner. His hard work paid off. After two years and with Sam's glowing recommendation, he landed a Secret Service post in Washington.

Tom Cornell, badly shaken by Sheila's death, floundered for several months, keeping the latest of hours with the fastest of women in the hopes of burying his hurt. Realizing at last that he was getting nowhere, he rented out his Winchester home and took a traveling job with an international computer concern. In London some time later, he met a woman who, while not as unconventional as Sheila, was caring enough to restore his faith in the happily ever after.

Three weeks after Ryan proposed, he and Carly were married. It was a simple ceremony witnessed by both the bride's and groom's families, as well as by the numerous friends they had quickly come to share. They honeymooned in the Caribbean and returned, gloriously happy, to see to the installation of a large, open spiral staircase connecting upstairs and downstairs.

Though Carly continued to teach, she also began to write. Her earliest works were therapeutic pieces on fear and self-identity, pieces that went no further than Ryan's eyes and ears. As she regained confidence, though, she broadened her outlook to focus on articles of local interest, which found enthusiastic reception in regional publications. In time she was solicited to do an in-depth biographical study of a prominent member of the Boston community.

It was the start of a new career, and the timing couldn't have been better. For, after three years of marriage, and with the horrors of the past finally fading, Carly and Ryan had a son. He was a healthy boy, with his father's thick dark hair and his mother's bright blue eyes. And he was a joy to them both. Ryan was as attentive a father as he was a husband, loving his law practice but loving coming home more. As for Carly, she was in seventh heaven. What used to be the kitchen of Ryan's old apartment was converted into a large study for her. She quite happily arranged her writing hours to fit the baby's schedule, then those of the two other children who came in subsequent years. By that time, the Cornell family was firmly ensconced in a spacious home in Lincoln, with acres of fields, a profusion of maples, oaks and willows, the most beautiful pine grove, and a large golden retriever named Red. The house was modern and sprawling, with a master suite, twin sky-lit studies for Carly and Ryan, and for all the children separate bedrooms, each boasting a large needle-point hanging with a tiny robin in the corner.

Over the years, many framed photographs joined that of Bonnie and Clyde. There were pictures of Ryan's family and of Carly's, many, many of their children, and the largest a portrait of Carly and Ryan on their wedding day. She would pick it up often and study it, mindful of the miracle that had made it possible.

But of the many, many fingerprints that Carly Quinn Cornell was to leave over the years, none were more gentle, more loving, more indelible than those on her husband.

"We have to stop meeting this way," Ryan would tease in his deep, sexy baritone when, on a spring afternoon, they savored a moment's privacy in an overgrown corner of their woods.

"Who chased who?" she countered, slipping her arms around his neck as his hands pressed her hips to his.

"*Whom*. And I only wanted to make sure you didn't get lost."

She cleared her throat, even then feeling the quickening of her pulse that his body never failed to inspire. "I am getting lost," she murmured more breathlessly, as she raised her lips to meet his kiss.

It had been that way from the first; it would always be that way. Some things, like fingerprints, never changed.

ABOUT THE AUTHOR

Barbara Delinsky is the *New York Times* bestselling and award-winning author of more than fifty novels, including the highly acclaimed *The Passions of Chelsea Kane* and *More Than Friends*. Ms. Delinsky has been awarded the Romance Writers of America Golden Leaf Award and the RWA Golden Medallion Award. Published worldwide in fourteen foreign languages, she has over fifteen million copies of her books in print.